The Complete Works of Robert Burns

ROBERT BURNS

Boston 1855

TABLE OF CONTENTS

DEDICATION

TO THE NOBLEMEN AND GENTLEMEN OF THE CALEDONIAN HUNT

[On the title-page of the second or Edinburgh edition, were these words: "Poems, chiefly in the Scottish Dialect, by Robert Burns, printed for the Author, and sold by William Creech, 1787." The motto of the Kilmarnock edition was omitted; a very numerous list of subscribers followed: the volume was printed by the celebrated Smellie.]

My Lords and Gentlemen:

A Scottish Bard, proud of the name, and whose highest ambition is to sing in his country's service, where shall he so properly look for patronage as to the illustrious names of his native land: those who bear the honours and inherit the virtues of their ancestors? The poetic genius of my country found me, as the prophetic bard Elijah did Elisha-at the plough, and threw her inspiring mantle over me. She bade me sing the loves, the joys, the rural scenes and rural pleasures of my native soil, in my native tongue; I tuned my wild, artless notes as she inspired. She whispered me to come to this ancient metropolis of Caledonia, and lay my songs under your honoured protection: I now obey her dictates.

Though much indebted to your goodness, I do not approach you, my Lords and Gentlemen, in the usual style of dedication, to thank you for past favours: that path is so hackneyed by prostituted learning that honest rusticity is ashamed of it. Nor do I present this address with the venal soul of a servile author, looking for a continuation of those favours: I was bred to the plough, and am independent. I come to claim the common Scottish name with you, my illustrious countrymen; and to tell the world that I glory in the title. I come to congratulate my country that the blood of her ancient heroes still runs uncontaminated, and that from your courage, knowledge, and public spirit, she may expect protection, wealth, and liberty. In the last place, I come to proffer my warmest wishes to the great fountain of honour, the Monarch of the universe, for your welfare and happiness.

When you go forth to waken the echoes, in the ancient and favourite amusement of your forefathers, may Pleasure ever be of your party: and may social joy await your return! When harassed in courts or camps with the jostlings of bad men and bad measures, may the honest consciousness of injured worth attend your return to your native seats; and may domestic happiness, with a smiling welcome, meet you at your gates! May corruption shrink at your kindling indignant glance; and may tyranny in the ruler, and licentiousness in the people, equally find you an inexorable foe!

I have the honour to be,

With the sincerest gratitude and highest respect,

My Lords and Gentlemen,

Your most devoted humble servant,

ROBERT BURNS.

Edinburgh, April 4, 1787.

PREFACE

I cannot give to my country this edition of one of its favourite poets, without stating that I have deliberately omitted several pieces of verse ascribed to Burns by other editors, who too hastily, and I think on insufficient testimony, admitted them among his works. If I am unable to share in the hesitation expressed by one of them on the authorship of the stanzas on "Pastoral Poetry," I can as little share in the feelings with which they have intruded into the charmed circle of his poetry such compositions as "Lines on the Ruins of Lincluden College," "Verses on the Destruction of the Woods of Drumlanrig," "Verses written on a Marble Slab in the Woods of Aberfeldy," and those entitled "The Tree of Liberty." These productions, with the exception of the last, were never seen by any one even in the handwriting of Burns, and are one and all wanting in that original vigour of language and manliness of sentiment which distinguish his poetry. With respect to "The Tree of Liberty" in particular, a subject dear to the heart of the Bard, can any one conversant with his genius imagine that he welcomed its growth or celebrated its fruit with such "capon craws" as these?

"Upo' this tree there grows sic fruit, Its virtues a' can tell, man; It raises man aboon the brute, It mak's him ken himsel', man. Gif ance the peasant taste a bit, He's greater than a lord, man, An' wi' a beggar shares a mite O' a' he can afford, man."

There are eleven stanzas, of which the best, compared with the "A man's a man for a' that" of Burns, sounds like a cracked pipkin against the "heroic clang" of a Damascus blade. That it is extant in the handwriting of the poet cannot be taken as a proof that it is his own composition, against the internal testimony of utter want of all the marks by which we know him-the Burns-stamp, so to speak, which is visible on all that ever came from his pen. Misled by his handwriting, I inserted in my former edition of his works an epitaph, beginning

"Here lies a rose, a budding rose,"

the composition of Shenstone, and which is to be found in the church-yard of Hales-Owen: as it is not included in every edition of that poet's acknowledged works, Burns, who was an admirer of his genius, had, it seems, copied it with his own hand, and hence my error. If I hesitated about the exclusion of "The Tree of Liberty," and its three false brethren, I could have no scruples regarding the fine song of "Evan Banks," claimed and justly for Miss Williams by Sir Walter Scott, or the humorous song called "Shelah O'Neal," composed by the late Sir Alexander Boswell. When I have stated that I have arranged the Poems, the Songs, and the Letters of Burns, as nearly as possible in the order in which they were written; that I have omitted no piece of either verse or prose which bore the impress of his hand, nor included any by which his high reputation would likely be impaired, I have said all that seems necessary to be said, save that the following letter came too late for insertion in its proper place: it is characteristic and worth a place anywhere.

ALLAN CUNNINGHAM TO DR ARCHIBALD LAURIE

Mossgiel, 13th Nov. 1786.

Dear Sir,
I have along with this sent the two volumes of Ossian, with the remaining volume of the Songs. Ossian I am not in such a hurry about; but I wish the Songs, with the volume of the Scotch Poets, returned as soon as they can conveniently be dispatched. If they are left at Mr. Wilson, the bookseller's shop, Kilmarnock, they will easily reach me.
My most respectful compliments to Mr. and Mrs. Laurie; and a Poet's warmest wishes for their happiness to the young ladies; particularly the fair musician, whom I think much better qualified than ever David was, or could be, to charm an evil spirit out of a Saul.
Indeed, it needs not the Feelings of a poet to be interested in the welfare of one of the sweetest scenes of domestic peace and kindred love that ever I saw; as I think the peaceful unity of St. Margaret's Hill can only be excelled by the harmonious concord of the Apocalyptic Zion.
I am, dear Sir, yours sincerely,
Robert Burns.

LIFE OF ROBERT BURNS

Robert Burns, the chief of the peasant poets of Scotland, was born in a little mud-walled cottage on the banks of Doon, near "Alloway's auld haunted kirk," in the shire of Ayr, on the 25th day of January, 1759. As a natural mark of the event, a sudden storm at the same moment swept the land: the gabel-wall of the frail dwelling gave way, and the babe-bard was hurried through a tempest of wind and sleet to the shelter of a securer hovel. He was the eldest born of three sons and three daughters; his father, William, who in his native Kincardineshire wrote his name Burness, was bred a gardener, and sought for work in the West; but coming from the lands of the noble family of the Keiths, a suspicion accompanied him that he had been out-as rebellion was softly called-in the forty-five: a suspicion fatal to his hopes of rest and bread, in so loyal a district; and it was only when the clergyman of his native parish certified his loyalty that he was permitted to toil. This suspicion of Jacobitism, revived by Burns himself, when he rose into fame, seems not to have influenced either the feelings, or the tastes of Agnes Brown, a young woman on the Doon, whom he wooed and married in December, 1757, when he was thirty-six years old. To support her, he leased a small piece of ground, which he converted into a nursery and garden, and to shelter her, he raised with his own hands that humble abode where she gave birth to her eldest son.

The elder Burns was a well-informed, silent, austere man, who endured no idle gaiety, nor indecorous language: while he relaxed somewhat the hard, stern creed of the Covenanting times, he enforced all the work-day, as well as sabbath-day observances, which the Calvinistic kirk requires, and scrupled at promiscuous dancing, as the staid of our own day scruple at the waltz. His wife was of a milder mood: she was blest with a singular fortitude of temper; was as devout of heart, as she was calm of mind; and loved, while busied in her household concerns, to sweeten the bitterer moments of life, by chanting the songs and ballads of her country, of which her store was great. The garden and nursery prospered so much, that he was induced to widen his views, and by the help of his kind landlord, the laird of Doonholm, and the more questionable aid of borrowed money, he entered upon a neighbouring farm, named Mount Oliphant, extending to an hundred acres. This was in 1765; but the land was hungry and sterile; the seasons proved rainy and rough; the toil was certain, the reward unsure; when to his sorrow, the laird of Doonholm-a generous Ferguson,-died: the strict terms of the lease, as well as the rent, were exacted by a harsh factor, and with his wife and children, he was obliged, after a losing struggle of six years, to relinquish the farm, and seek shelter on the grounds of Lochlea, some ten miles off, in the parish of Tarbolton. When, in after-days, men's characters were in the hands of his eldest son, the scoundrel factor sat for that lasting portrait of insolence and wrong, in the "Twa Dogs."

In this new farm William Burns seemed to strike root, and thrive. He was strong of body and ardent of mind: every day brought increase of vigour to his three sons, who, though very young, already put their hands to the plough, the reap-hook, and the flail. But it seemed that nothing which he undertook was decreed in the end to prosper: after four seasons of prosperity a change ensued: the farm was far from cheap; the gains under any lease were then so little, that the loss of a few pounds was ruinous to a farmer: bad seed and wet seasons had their usual influence: "The gloom of hermits and the moil of galley-slaves," as the poet, alluding to those days, said, were endured to no purpose; when, to crown all, a difference arose between the landlord and the tenant, as to the terms of the lease; and the early days of the poet, and the declining years of his father, were harassed by disputes, in which sensitive minds are sure to suffer.

Amid these labours and disputes, the poet's father remembered the worth of religious and moral instruction: he took part of this upon himself. A week-day in Lochlea wore the sober looks of a Sunday: he read the Bible and explained, as intelligent peasants are accustomed to do, the sense, when dark or difficult; he loved to discuss the spiritual meanings, and gaze on the mystical splendours of the Revelations. He was aided in these labours, first, by the schoolmaster of Alloway-mill, near the Doon; secondly, by John Murdoch, student of divinity, who undertook to teach arithmetic, grammar, French, and Latin, to the boys of Lochlea, and the sons of five neighboring farmers. Murdoch, who was an enthusiast in learning, much of a pedant, and such a judge of genius that he thought wit should always be laughing, and poetry wear an eternal smile, performed his task well: he found Robert to be quick in apprehension, and not afraid to study when knowledge was the reward. He taught him to turn verse into its natural prose order; to supply all the ellipses, and not to desist till the sense was clear and plain: he also, in their walks, told him the names of different objects both in Latin and French; and though his knowledge of these languages never amounted to much, he approached the grammar of the English tongue, through the former, which was of material use to him, in his poetic compositions. Burns was, even in those early days, a sort of enthusiast in all that concerned the glory of Scotland; he used to fancy himself a soldier of the days of the Wallace and the Bruce: loved to strut after the bag-pipe and the drum, and read of the bloody struggles of his country for freedom and existence, till "a Scottish prejudice," he says, "was poured into my veins, which will boil there till the flood-gates of life are shut in eternal rest."

In this mood of mind Burns was unconsciously approaching the land of poesie. In addition to the histories of the Wallace and the Bruce, he found, on the shelves of his neighbours, not only whole bodies of divinity, and sermons without limit, but the works of some of the best English, as well as Scottish poets, together with songs and ballads innumerable. On these he loved to pore whenever a moment of leisure came; nor was verse his sole favourite; he desired to drink knowledge at any fountain, and Guthrie's Grammar, Dickson on Agriculture, Addison's Spectator, Locke on the Human Understanding, and Taylor's Scripture Doctrine of Original Sin, were as welcome to his heart as Shakspeare, Milton, Pope, Thomson, and Young. There is a mystery in the workings of genius: with these poets in his head and hand, we see not that he has advanced one step in the way in which he was soon to walk, "Highland Mary" and "Tam O' Shanter" sprang from other inspirations.

Burns lifts up the veil himself, from the studies which made him a poet. "In my boyish days," he says to Moore, "I owed much to an old woman (Jenny Wilson) who resided in the family, remarkable for her credulity and superstition. She had, I suppose, the largest collection in the country of tales and songs, concerning devils, ghosts, fairies, brownies, witches, warlocks, spunkies, kelpies, elf-candles, dead-lights, wraiths, apparitions, cantraips, giants, enchanted towers, dragons, and other trumpery. This cultivated the latent seeds of poesie; but had so strong an effect upon my imagination that to this hour, in my nocturnal rambles, I sometimes keep a look-out on suspicious places." Here we have the young poet taking lessons in the classic lore of his native land: in the school of Janet Wilson he profited largely; her tales gave a hue, all their own, to many noble effusions. But her teaching was at the hearth-stone: when he was in the fields, either driving a cart or walking to labour, he had ever in his hand a collection of songs, such as any stall in the land could supply him with; and over these he pored, ballad by ballad, and verse by verse, noting the true, tender, and the natural sublime from affectation and fustian. "To this," he said, "I am convinced that I owe much of my critic craft, such as it is."His mother, too, unconsciously led him in the ways of the muse: she loved to recite or sing to him a strange, but clever ballad, called "the Life and Age of Man:" this strain of piety and imagination was in his mind when he wrote "Man was made to Mourn."

He found other teachers-of a tenderer nature and softer influence. "You know," he says to Moore, "our country custom of coupling a man and woman together as partners in the labours of harvest. In my fifteenth autumn my partner was a bewitching creature, a year younger than myself: she was in truth a bonnie, sweet, sonsie lass, and unwittingly to herself, initiated me in that delicious passion, which, in spite of acid disappointment, gin-horse prudence, and bookworm philosophy, I hold to be the first of human joys. How she caught the contagion I cannot tell; I never expressly said I loved her: indeed I did not know myself why I liked so much to loiter behind with her, when returning in the evenings from our labours; why the tones of her voice made my heart strings thrill like an Æolian harp, and particularly why my pulse beat such a furious ratan, when I looked and fingered over her little hand, to pick out the cruel nettle-stings and thistles. Among other love-inspiring qualities, she sang sweetly, and it was her favourite reel to which I attempted to give an embodied vehicle in rhyme; thus with me began love and verse." This intercourse with the fair part of the creation, was to his slumbering emotions, a voice from heaven to call them into life and poetry.

From the school of traditionary lore and love, Burns now went to a rougher academy. Lochlea, though not producing fine crops of corn, was considered excellent for flax; and while the cultivation of this commodity was committed to his father and his brother Gilbert, he was sent to Irvine at Midsummer, 1781, to learn the trade of a flax-dresser, under one Peacock, kinsman to his mother. Some time before, he had spent a portion of a summer at a school in Kirkoswald, learning mensuration and land-surveying, where he had mingled in scenes of sociality with smugglers, and enjoyed the pleasure of a silent walk, under the moon, with the young and the beautiful. At Irvine he laboured by day to acquire a knowledge of his business, and at night he associated with the gay and the thoughtless, with whom he learnt to empty his glass, and indulge in free discourse on topics forbidden at Lochlea. He had one small room for a lodging, for which he gave a shilling a week: meat he seldom tasted, and his food consisted chiefly of oatmeal and potatoes sent from his father's house. In a letter to his father, written with great purity and simplicity of style, he thus gives a picture of himself, mental and bodily: "Honoured Sir, I have purposely delayed writing, in the hope that I should have the pleasure of seeing you on new years' day, but work comes so hard upon us that I do not choose to be absent on that account. My health is nearly the same as when you were here, only my sleep is a little sounder, and on the whole, I am rather better than otherwise, though I mend by very slow degrees: the weakness of my nerves had so debilitated my mind that I dare neither review past wants nor look forward into futurity, for the least anxiety or perturbation in my breast produces most unhappy effects on my whole frame. Sometimes indeed, when for an hour or two my spirits are a little lightened, I glimmer a little into futurity; but my principal and indeed my only pleasurable employment is looking backwards and forwards in a moral and religious way. I am quite transported at the thought that ere long, perhaps very soon, I shall bid an eternal adieu to all the pains and uneasinesses, and disquietudes of this weary life. As for the world, I despair of ever making a figure in it: I am not formed for the bustle of the busy, nor the flutter of the gay. I foresee that poverty and obscurity probably await me, and I am in some measure prepared and daily preparing to meet them. I have but just time and paper to return you my grateful thanks for the lessons of virtue and piety you have given me, which were but too much neglected at the time of giving them, but which, I hope, have been remembered ere it is yet too late." This remarkable letter was written in the twenty-second year of his age; it alludes to the illness which seems to have been the companion of his youth, a nervous headache, brought on by constant toil and anxiety; and it speaks of the melancholy which is the common attendant of genius, and its sensibilities, aggravated by despair of distinction. The catastrophe which happened ere this letter was well in his father's hand, accords ill with quotations from the Bible, and hopes fixed in heaven:-"As we gave," he says, "a welcome carousal to the new year, the shop took fire, and burnt to ashes, and I was left, like a true poet, not worth a sixpence."

This disaster was followed by one more grievous: his father was well in years when he was married, and age and a constitution injured by toil and disappointment, began to press him down, ere his sons had grown up to man's estate. On all sides the clouds began to darken: the farm was unprosperous: the speculations in flax failed; and the landlord of Lochlea, raising a question upon the meaning of the lease, concerning rotation of crop, pushed the matter to a lawsuit, alike ruinous to a poor man either in its success or its failure. "After three years tossing and whirling," says Burns, "in the vortex of litigation, my father was just saved from the horrors of a jail by a consumption, which, after two years' promises, kindly slept in and carried him away to where the 'wicked cease from troubling and the weary are at rest.' His all went among the hell-hounds that prowl in the kennel of justice. The finishing evil which brought up the rear of this infernal file, was my constitutional melancholy being increased to such a degree, that for three months I was in a state of mind scarcely to be envied by the hopeless wretches who have got their mittimus, 'Depart from me, ye cursed.'"

Robert Burns was now the head of his father's house. He gathered together the little that law and misfortune had spared, and took the farm of

Mossgiel, near Mauchline, containing one hundred and eighteen acres, at a rent of ninety pounds a year: his mother and sisters took the domestic superintendence of home, barn, and byre; and he associated his brother Gilbert in the labours of the land. It was made a joint affair: the poet was young, willing, and vigorous, and excelled in ploughing, sowing, reaping, mowing, and thrashing. His wages were fixed at seven pounds per annum, and such for a time was his care and frugality, that he never exceeded this small allowance. He purchased books on farming, held conversations with the old and the knowing; and said unto himself, "I shall be prudent and wise, and my shadow shall increase in the land." But it was not decreed that these resolutions were to endure, and that he was to become a mighty agriculturist in the west. Farmer Attention, as the proverb says, is a good farmer, all the world over, and Burns was such by fits and by starts. But he who writes an ode on the sheep he is about to shear, a poem on the flower that he covers with the furrow, who sees visions on his way to market, who makes rhymes on the horse he is about to yoke, and a song on the girl who shows the whitest hands among his reapers, has small chance of leading a market, or of being laird of the fields he rents. The dreams of Burns were of the muses, and not of rising markets, of golden locks rather than of yellow corn: he had other faults. It is not known that William Burns was aware before his death that his eldest son had sinned in rhyme; but we have Gilbert's assurance, that his father went to the grave in ignorance of his son's errors of a less venial kind-unwitting that he was soon to give a two-fold proof of both in "Rob the Rhymer's Address to his Bastard Child"-a poem less decorous than witty.

The dress and condition of Burns when he became a poet were not at all poetical, in the minstrel meaning of the word. His clothes, coarse and homely, were made from home-grown wool, shorn off his own sheeps' backs, carded and spun at his own fireside, woven by the village weaver, and, when not of natural hodden-gray, dyed a half-blue in the village vat. They were shaped and sewed by the district tailor, who usually wrought at the rate of a groat a day and his food; and as the wool was coarse, so also was the workmanship. The linen which he wore was home-grown, home-hackled, home-spun, home-woven, and home-bleached, and, unless designed for Sunday use, was of coarse, strong harn, to suit the tear and wear of barn and field. His shoes came from rustic tanpits, for most farmers then prepared their own leather; were armed, sole and heel, with heavy, broad-headed nails, to endure the clod and the road: as hats were then little in use, save among small lairds or country gentry, westland heads were commonly covered with a coarse, broad, blue bonnet, with a stopple on its flat crown, made in thousands at Kilmarnock, and known in all lands by the name of scone bonnets. His plaid was a handsome red and white check-for pride in poets, he said, was no sin-prepared of fine wool with more than common care by the hands of his mother and sisters, and woven with more skill than the village weaver was usually required to exert. His dwelling was in keeping with his dress, a low, thatched house, with a kitchen, a bedroom and closet, with floors of kneaded clay, and ceilings of moorland turf: a few books on a shelf, thumbed by many a thumb; a few hams drying above head in the smoke, which was in no haste to get out at the roof-a wooden settle, some oak chairs, chaff beds well covered with blankets, with a fire of peat and wood burning at a distance from the gable wall, on the middle of the floor. His food was as homely as his habitation, and consisted chiefly of oatmeal-porridge, barley-broth, and potatoes, and milk. How the muse happened to visit him in this clay biggin, take a fancy to a clouterly peasant, and teach him strains of consummate beauty and elegance, must ever be a matter of wonder to all those, and they are not few, who hold that noble sentiments and heroic deeds are the exclusive portion of the gently nursed and the far descended.

Of the earlier verses of Burns few are preserved: when composed, he put them on paper, but the kept them to himself: though a poet at sixteen, he seems not to have made even his brother his confidante till he became a man, and his judgment had ripened. He, however, made a little clasped paper book his treasurer, and under the head of "Observations, Hints, Songs, and Scraps of Poetry," we find many a wayward and impassioned verse, songs rising little above the humblest country strain, or bursting into an elegance and a beauty worthy of the highest of minstrels. The first words noted down are the stanzas which he composed on his fair companion of the harvest-field, out of whose hands he loved to remove the nettle-stings and the thistles: the prettier song, beginning "Now westlin win's and slaughtering guns," written on the lass of Kirkoswald, with whom, instead of learning mensuration, he chose to wander under the light of the moon: a strain better still, inspired by the charms of a neighbouring maiden, of the name of Annie Ronald; another, of equal merit, arising out of his nocturnal adventures among the lasses of the west; and, finally, that crowning glory of all his lyric compositions, "Green grow the rashes." This little clasped book, however, seems not to have been made his confidante till his twenty-third or twenty-fourth year: he probably admitted to its pages only the strains which he loved most, or such as had taken a place in his memory: at whatever age it was commenced, he had then begun to estimate his own character, and intimate his fortunes, for he calls himself in its pages "a man who had little art in making money, and still less in keeping it."

We have not been told how welcome the incense of his songs rendered him to the rustic maidens of Kyle: women are not apt to be won by the charms of verse; they have little sympathy with dreamers on Parnassus, and allow themselves to be influenced by something more substantial than the roses and lilies of the muse. Burns had other claims to their regard then those arising from poetic skill: he was tall, young, good-looking, with dark, bright eyes, and words and wit at will: he had a sarcastic sally for all lads who presumed to cross his path, and a soft, persuasive word for all lasses on whom he fixed his fancy: nor was this all-he was adventurous and bold in love trystes and love excursions: long, rough roads, stormy nights, flooded rivers, and lonesome places, were no letts to him; and when the dangers or labours of the way were braved, he was alike skilful in eluding vigilant aunts, wakerife mothers, and envious or suspicions sisters: for rivals he had a blow as ready us he had a word, and was familiar with snug stack-yards, broomy glens, and nooks of hawthorn and honeysuckle, where maidens love to be wooed. This rendered him dearer to woman's heart than all the lyric effusions of his fancy; and when we add to such allurements, a warm, flowing, and persuasive eloquence, we need not wonder that woman listened and was won; that one of the most charming damsels of the West said, an hour with him in the dark was worth a lifetime of light with any other body; or that the accomplished and beautiful Duchess of Gordon declared, in a latter day, that no man ever carried her so completely off her feet as Robert Burns.

It is one of the delusions of the poet's critics and biographers, that the sources of his inspiration are to be found in the great classic poets of the land, with some of whom he had from his youth been familiar: there is little or no trace of them in any of his compositions. He read and wondered-he warmed his fancy at their flame, he corrected his own natural taste by theirs, but he neither copied nor imitated, and there are but two or three allusions to Young and Shakspeare in all the range of his verse. He could not but feel that he was the scholar of a different school, and that his thirst was to be slaked at other fountains. The language in which those great bards embodied their thoughts was unapproachable to an Ayrshire peasant; it was to him as an almost foreign tongue: he had to think and feel in the not ungraceful or inharmonious language of his own vale, and then, in a manner, translate it into that of Pope or of Thomson, with the additional difficulty of finding English words to express the exact meaning of those of Scotland, which had chiefly been retained because equivalents could not be found in the more elegant and grammatical tongue. Such strains as those of the polished Pope or the sublimer Milton were beyond his power, less from deficiency of genius than from lack of language: he could, indeed, write English with ease and fluency; but when he desired to be tender or impassioned, to persuade or subdue, he had recourse to the Scottish, and he found it sufficient.

The goddesses or the Dalilahs of the young poet's song were, like the language in which he celebrated them, the produce of the district; not dames high and exalted, but lasses of the barn and of the byre, who had never been in higher company than that of shepherds or ploughmen, or danced in a politer assembly than that of their fellow-peasants, on a barn-floor, to the sound of the district fiddle. Nor even of these did he choose the loveliest to lay out the wealth of his verse upon: he has been accused, by his brother among others, of lavishing the colours of his fancy on very ordinary faces. "He had always," says Gilbert, "a jealousy of people who were richer than himself; his love, therefore, seldom settled on persons of this description. When he selected any one, out of the sovereignty of his good pleasure, to whom he should pay his particular attention, she was instantly invested with a sufficient stock of charms out of the plentiful stores of his own imagination: and there was often a great dissimilitude between his fair captivator, as she appeared to others and as she seemed when invested with the attributes he gave her." "My heart," he himself, speaking of those days, observes, "was completely tinder, and was eternally lighted up by some goddess or other." Yet, it must be acknowledged that sufficient room exists for believing that Burns and his brethren of the West had very different notions of the captivating and the beautiful; while they were moved by rosy checks and looks of rustic health, he was moved, like a sculptor, by beauty of form or by harmony of motion, and by expression, which lightened up ordinary features and rendered them captivating. Such, I have been told, were several of the lasses of the West, to whom, if he did not surrender his heart, he rendered homage: and both elegance of form and beauty of face were visible to all in those of whom he afterwards sang-the Hamiltons and the Burnets of Edinburgh, and the Millers and M'Murdos of the Nith.

The mind of Burns took now a wider range: he had sung of the maidens of Kyle in strains not likely soon to die, and though not weary of the softnesses of love, he desired to try his genius on matters of a sterner kind-what those subjects were he tells us; they were homely and at hand, of a native nature and of Scottish growth: places celebrated in Roman story, vales made famous in Grecian song-hills of vines and groves of myrtle had few charms for him. "I am hurt," thus he writes in August, 1785, "to see other towns, rivers, woods, and haughs of Scotland immortalized in song, while my dear native county, the ancient Baillieries of Carrick, Kyle, and Cunningham, famous in both ancient and modern times for a gallant and warlike race of inhabitants-a county where civil and religious liberty have ever found their first support and their asylum-a county, the birth-place of many famous philosophers, soldiers, and statesmen, and the scene of many great events recorded in history, particularly the actions of the glorious Wallace-yet we have never had one Scotch poet of any eminence to make the fertile banks of Irvine, the romantic woodlands and sequestered scenes of Ayr. and the mountainous source and winding sweep of the Doon, emulate Tay, Forth, Ettrick, and Tweed. This is a complaint I would gladly remedy, but, alas! I am far unequal to the task, both in genius and education." To fill up with glowing verse the outline which this sketch indicates, was to raise the long-laid spirit of national song-to waken a strain to which the whole land would yield response-a miracle unattempted-certainly unperformed-since the days of the Gentle Shepherd. It is true that the tongue of the muse had at no time been wholly silent; that now and then a burst of sublime woe, like the song of "Mary, weep no more for me," and of lasting merriment and humour, like that of "Tibbie Fowler," proved that the fire of natural poesie smouldered, if it did not blaze; while the social strains of the unfortunate Fergusson revived in the city, if not in the field, the memory of him who sang the "Monk and the Miller's wife." But notwithstanding these and other productions of equal merit, Scottish poesie, it must be owned, had lost much of its original ecstasy and fervour, and that the boldest efforts of the muse no more equalled the songs of Dunbar, of Douglas, of Lyndsay, and of James the Fifth, than the sound of an artificial cascade resembles the undying thunders of Corra.

To accomplish this required an acquaintance with man beyond what the forge, the change-house, and the market-place of the village supplied; a look further than the barn-yard and the furrowed field, and a livelier knowledge and deeper feeling of history than, probably, Burns ever possessed. To all ready and accessible sources of knowledge he appears to have had recourse; he sought matter for his muse in the meetings, religious as well as social, of the district-consorted with staid matrons, grave plodding farmers-with those who preached as well as those who listened-with sharp-tongued attorneys, who laid down the law over a Mauchline gill-with country squires, whose wisdom was great in the game-laws, and in contested elections-and with roving smugglers, who at that time hung, as a cloud, on all the western coast of Scotland. In the company of farmers and fellow-peasants, he witnessed scenes which he loved to embody in verse, saw pictures of peace and joy, now woven into the web of his song, and had a poetic impulse given to him both by cottage devotion and cottage merriment. If he was familiar with love and all its outgoings and incomings-had met his lass in the midnight shade, or walked with her under the moon, or braved a stormy night and a haunted road for her sake-he was as well acquainted with the joys which belong to social intercourse, when instruments of music speak to the feet, when the reek of punchbowls gives a tongue to the staid and demure, and bridal festivity, and harvest-homes, bid a whole valley lift up its voice and be glad. It is more difficult to decide what poetic use he could make of his intercourse with that loose and lawless class of men, who, from love of gain, broke the laws and braved the police of their country: that he found among smugglers, as he says, "men of noble virtues, magnanimity, generosity, disinterested friendship, and modesty," is easier to believe than that he escaped the contamination of their sensual manners and prodigality. The people of Kyle regarded this conduct with suspicion: they were not to be expected to know that when Burns ranted and housed with smugglers, conversed with tinkers huddled in a kiln, or listened to the riotous mirth of a batch of "randie gangrel bodies" as they "toomed their powks and pawned their duds," for liquor in Poosie Nansie's, he was taking sketches for the future entertainment and instruction of the world; they could not foresee that from all this moral strength and poetic beauty would arise.

While meditating something better than a ballad to his mistress's eyebrow, he did not neglect to lay out the little skill he had in cultivating the grounds of Mossgiel. The prosperity in which he found himself in the first and second seasons, induced him to hope that good fortune had not yet forsaken him: a genial summer and a good market seldom come together to the farmer, but at first they came to Burns; and to show that he was worthy of them, he bought books on agriculture, calculated rotation of crops, attended sales, held the plough with diligence, used the scythe, the reap-hook, and the flail, with skill, and the malicious even began to say that there was something more in him than wild sallies of wit and foolish rhymes. But the farm lay high, the bottom was wet, and in a third season, indifferent seed and a wet harvest robbed him at once of half his crop: he seems to have regarded this as an intimation from above, that nothing which he undertook would prosper: and consoled himself with joyous friends and with the society of the muse. The judgment cannot be praised which selected a farm with a wet cold bottom, and sowed it with unsound seed; but that man who despairs because a wet season robs him of the fruits of the field, is unfit for the warfare of life, where fortitude is as much required as by a general on a field of battle, when the tide of success threatens to flow against him. The poet seems to have believed, very early in life, that he was none of the elect of Mammon; that he was too much of a genius ever to acquire wealth by steady labour, or by, as he loved to call it, gin-horse prudence, or grubbing industry.

And yet there were hours and days in which Burns, even when the rain fell on his unhoused sheaves, did not wholly despair of himself: he laboured, nay sometimes he slaved on his farm; and at intervals of toil, sought to embellish his mind with such knowledge as might be useful, should chance, the goddess who ruled his lot, drop him upon some of the higher places of the land. He had, while he lived at Tarbolton, united with some half-dozen young men, all sons of farmers in that neighbourhood, in forming a club, of which the object was to charm away a few evening hours in the week with agreeable chit-chat, and the discussion of topics of economy or love. Of this little society the poet was president, and the first question they were called on to settle was this, "Suppose a young man bred a farmer, but without any fortune, has it in his power to marry either of two women; the one a girl of large fortune, but neither handsome in person, nor agreeable in conversation, but who can manage the household affairs of a farm well enough; the other of them, a girl every way agreeable in person, conversation, and behaviour, but without any fortune, which of them shall he choose?" This question was started by the poet, and once every week the club were called to the consideration of matters connected with rural life and industry: their expenses were limited to threepence a week; and till the departure of Burns to the distant Mossgiel, the club continued to live and thrive; on his removal it lost the spirit which gave it birth, and was heard of no more; but its aims and its usefulness were revived in Mauchline, where the poet was induced to establish a society which only differed from the other in spending the moderate fines arising from non-attendance, on books, instead of liquor. Here, too, Burns was the president, and the members were chiefly the sons of husbandmen, whom he found, he said, more natural in their manners, and more agreeable than the self-sufficient mechanics of villages and towns, who were ready to dispute on all topics, and inclined to be convinced on none. This club had the pleasure of subscribing for the first edition of the works of its great associate. It has been questioned by his first biographer, whether the refinement of mind, which follows the reading of books of eloquence and delicacy,-the mental improvement resulting from such calm discussions as the Tarbolton and Mauchline clubs indulged in, was not injurious to men engaged in the barn and at the plough. A well-ordered mind will be strengthened, as well as embellished, by elegant knowledge, while over those naturally barren and ungenial all that is refined or noble will pass as a sunny shower scuds over lumps of granite, bringing neither warmth nor life.

In the account which the poet gives to Moore of his early poems, he says little about his exquisite lyrics, and less about "The Death and dying Words of Poor Mailie," or her "Elegy," the first of his poems where the inspiration of the muse is visible; but he speaks with exultation of the fame which those indecorous sallies, "Holy Willie's Prayer" and "The Holy Tulzie" brought from some of the clergy, and the people of Ayrshire. The west of Scotland is ever in the van, when mutters either political or religious are agitated. Calvinism was shaken, at this time, with a controversy among its professors, of which it is enough to say, that while one party rigidly adhered to the word and letter of the Confession of Faith, and preached up the palmy and wholesome days of the Covenant, the other sought to soften the harsher rules and observances of the kirk, and to bring moderation and charity into its discipline as well as its councils. Both believed themselves right, both were loud and hot, and personal,-bitter with a bitterness only known in religious controversy. The poet sided with the professors of the New Light, as the more tolerant were called, and handled the professors of the Old Light, as the other party were named, with the most unsparing severity. For this he had sufficient cause:-he had experienced the mercilessness of kirk-discipline, when his frailties caused him to visit the stool of repentance; and moreover his friend Gavin Hamilton, a writer in Mauchline, had been sharply censured by the same authorities, for daring to gallop on Sundays. Moodie, of Riccarton, and Russel, of Kilmarnock, were the first who tasted of the poet's wrath. They, though professors of the Old Light, had quarrelled, and, it is added, fought: "The Holy Tulzie," which recorded, gave at the same time wings to the scandal; while for "Holy Willie," an elder of Mauchline, and an austere and hollow pretender to righteousness, he reserved the fiercest of all his lampoons. In "Holy Willie's Prayer," he lays a burning hand on the terrible doctrine of predestination: this is a satire, daring, personal, and profane. Willie claims praise in the singular, acknowledges folly in the plural, and makes heaven accountable for his sins! in a similar strain of undevout satire, he congratulates Goudie, of Kilmarnock, on his Essays on Revealed Religion. These poems, particularly the two latter, are the sharpest lampoons in the language.

While drudging in the cause of the New Light controversialists, Burns was not unconsciously strengthening his hands for worthier toils: the applause which selfish divines bestowed on his witty, but graceless effusions, could not be enough for one who knew how fleeting the fame was which came from the heat of party disputes; nor was he insensible that songs of a beauty unknown for a century to national poesy, had been unregarded in the hue and cry which arose on account of "Holy Willie's Prayer" and "The Holy Tulzie." He hesitated to drink longer out of the agitated puddle of Calvinistic controversy, he resolved to slake his thirst at the pure well-springs of patriot feeling and domestic love; and accordingly, in the last and best of his controversial compositions, he rose out of the lower regions of lampoon into the upper air of true poetry. "The Holy Fair," though stained in one or two verses with personalities, exhibits a scene glowing with character and incident and life: the aim of the poem is not so much to satirize one or two Old Light divines, as to expose and rebuke those almost indecent festivities, which in too many of the western parishes accompanied the administration of the sacrament. In the earlier days of the church, when men were staid and sincere, it was, no doubt, an impressive sight to see rank succeeding rank, of the old and the young, all calm and all devout, seated before the tent of the preacher, in the sunny hours of June, listening to his eloquence, or partaking of the mystic bread and wine; but in these our latter days, when discipline is relaxed, along with the sedate and the pious come swarms of the idle and the profligate, whom no eloquence can edify and no solemn rite affect. On these, and such as these, the poet has poured his satire; and since this desirable reprehension the Holy Fairs, east as well as west, have become more decorous, if not more devout.

His controversial sallies were accompanied, or followed, by a series of poems which showed that national character and manners, as Lockhart has truly and happily said, were once more in the hands of a national poet. These compositions are both numerous and various: they record the poet's own experience and emotions; they exhibit the highest moral feeling, the purest patriotic sentiments, and a deep sympathy with the fortunes, both here and hereafter of his fellow-men; they delineate domestic manners, man's stern as well as social hours, and mingle the serious with the joyous, the sarcastic with the solemn, the mournful with the pathetic, the amiable with the gay, and all with an ease and unaffected force and freedom known only to the genius of Shakspeare. In "The Twa Dogs" he seeks to reconcile the labourer to his lot, and intimates, by examples drawn from the hall as well as the cottage, that happiness resides in the humblest abodes, and is even partial to the clouted shoe. In "Scotch Drink" he excites man to love his country, by precepts both heroic and social; and proves that while wine and brandy are the tipple of slaves, whiskey and ale are the drink of the free: sentiments of a similar kind distinguish his "Earnest Cry and Prayer to the Scotch Representatives in the House of Commons," each of whom he exhorts by name to defend the remaining liberties and immunities of his country. A higher tone distinguishes the "Address to the Deil:" he records all the names, and some of them are strange ones; and all the acts, and some of them are as whimsical as they are terrible, of this far kenned and noted personage; to these he adds some of the fiend's doings as they stand in Scripture, together with his own experiences; and concludes by a hope, as unexpected as merciful and relenting, that Satan may not be exposed to an eternity of torments. "The Dream" is a humorous sally, and may be almost regarded as prophetic. The poet feigns himself present, in slumber, at the Royal birth-day; and supposes that he addresses his majesty, on his household matters as well as the affairs of the nation. Some of the princes, it has been satirically hinted, behaved afterwards in such a way as if they wished that the scripture of the Burns should be fulfilled: in this strain, he has imitated the license and equalled the wit of some of the elder Scottish Poets.

"The Vision" is wholly serious; it exhibits the poet in one of those fits of despondency which the dull, who have no misgivings, never know: he dwells with sarcastic bitterness on the opportunities which, for the sake of song, he has neglected of becoming wealthy, and is drawing a sad parallel between rags and riches, when the muse steps in and cheer his despondency, by assuring him of undying fame. "Halloween" is a strain of a more homely kind, recording the superstitious beliefs, and no less superstitious doings of Old Scotland, on that night, when witches and elves and evil spirits are let loose among the children of men: it reaches far back into manners and customs, and is a picture, curious and valuable. The tastes and feelings of husbandmen inspired "The old Farmer's Address to his old mare Maggie," which exhibits some pleasing recollections of his days of courtship and hours of sociality. The calm, tranquil picture of household happiness and devotion in "the Cotter's Saturday Night," has induced Hogg, among others, to believe that it has less than usual of the spirit of the poet, but it has all the spirit that was required; the toil of the week has ceased, the labourer has returned to his well-ordered home-his "cozie ingle and his clean hearth-stane,"-and with his wife and children beside him, turns his thoughts to the praise of that God to whom he owes all: this he performs with a reverence and an awe, at once natural, national, and poetic. "The Mouse" is a brief and happy and very moving poem: happy, for it delineates, with wonderful truth and life, the agitation of the mouse when the coulter broke into its abode; and moving, for the poet takes the lesson of ruin to himself, and feels the present and dreads the future. "The Mountain Daisy," once, more properly, called by Burns "The Gowan," resembles "The Mouse" in incident and in moral, and is equally happy, in language and conception. "The Lament" is a dark, and all but tragic page, from the poet's own life. "Man was made to Mourn'" takes the part of the humble and the homeless, against the coldness and selfishness of the wealthy and the powerful, a favourite topic of meditation with Burns. He refrained, for awhile, from making "Death and Doctor Hernbook" public; a poem which deviates from the offensiveness of personal satire, into a strain of humour, at once airy and original.

His epistles in verse may be reckoned amongst his happiest productions: they are written in all moods of mind, and are, by turns, lively and sad; careless and serious;-now giving advice, then taking it; laughing at learning, and lamenting its want; scoffing at propriety and wealth, yet admitting, that without the one he cannot be wise, nor wanting the other, independent. The Epistle to David Sillar is the first of these compositions: the poet has no news to tell, and no serious question to ask: he has only to communicate his own emotions of joy, or of sorrow, and these he relates and discusses with singular elegance as well as ease, twining, at the same time, into the fabric of his composition, agreeable allusions to the taste and affections of his correspondent. He seems to have rated the intellect of Sillar as the highest among his rustic friends: he pays him more deference, and addresses him in a higher vein than he observes to others. The Epistles to Lapraik, to Smith, and to Rankine, are in a more familiar, or social mood, and lift the veil from the darkness of the poet's condition, and exhibit a mind of first-rate power, groping, and that surely, its way to distinction, in spite of humility of birth, obscurity of condition, and the coldness of the wealthy or the titled. The epistles of other poets owe some of their fame to the rank or the reputation of those to whom they are addressed; those of Burns are written, one and all, to nameless and undistinguished men. Sillar was a country schoolmaster, Lapraik a moorland laird, Smith a small shop-keeper, and Rankine a farmer, who loved a gill and a joke. Yet these men

were the chief friends, the only literary associates of the poet, during those early years, in which, with some exceptions, his finest works were written.
Burns, while he was writing the poems, the chief of which we have named, was a labouring husbandman on the little farm of Mossgiel, a pursuit which affords but few leisure hours for either reading or pondering; but to him the stubble-field was musing-ground, and the walk behind the plough, a twilight saunter on Parnassus. As, with a careful hand and a steady eye, he guided his horses, and saw an evenly furrow turned up by the share, his thoughts were on other themes; he was straying in haunted glens, when spirits have power-looking in fancy on the lasses "skelping barefoot," in silks and in scarlets, to a field-preaching-walking in imagination with the rosy widow, who on Halloween ventured to dip her left sleeve in the burn, where three lairds' lands met-making the "bottle clunk," with joyous smugglers, on a lucky run of gin or brandy-or if his thoughts at all approached his acts-he was moralizing on the daisy oppressed by the furrow which his own ploughshare had turned. That his thoughts were thus wandering we have his own testimony, with that of his brother Gilbert; and were both wanting, the certainty that he composed the greater part of his immortal poems in two years, from the summer of 1784 to the summer of 1786, would be evidence sufficient. The muse must have been strong within him, when, in spite of the rains and sleets of the "ever-dropping west"-when in defiance of the hot and sweaty brows occasioned by reaping and thrashing-declining markets, and showery harvests-the clamour of his laird for his rent, and the tradesman for his account, he persevered in song, and sought solace in verse, when all other solace was denied him.

The circumstances under which his principal poems were composed, have been related: the "Lament of Mailie" found its origin in the catastrophe of a pet ewe; the "Epistle to Sillar" was confided by the poet to his brother while they were engaged in weeding the kale-yard; the "Address to the Deil" was suggested by the many strange portraits which belief or fear had drawn of Satan, and was repeated by the one brother to the other, on the way with their carts to the kiln, for lime; the "Cotter's Saturday Night" originated in the reverence with which the worship of God was conducted in the family of the poet's father, and in the solemn tone with which he desired his children to compose themselves for praise and prayer; "the Mouse," and its moral companion "the Daisy," were the offspring of the incidents which they relate; and "Death and Doctor Hornbook" was conceived at a freemason-meeting, where the hero of the piece had shown too much of the pedant, and composed on his way home, after midnight, by the poet, while his head was somewhat dizzy with drink. One of the most remarkable of his compositions, the "Jolly Beggars," a drama, to which nothing in the language of either the North or South can be compared, and which was unknown till after the death of the author, was suggested by a scene which he saw in a low ale-house, into which, on a Saturday night, most of the sturdy beggars of the district had met to sell their meal, pledge their superfluous rags, and drink their gains. It may be added, that he loved to walk in solitary spots; that his chief musing-ground was the banks of the Ayr; the season most congenial to his fancy that of winter, when the winds were heard in the leafless woods, and the voice of the swollen streams came from vale and hill; and that he seldom composed a whole poem at once, but satisfied with a few fervent verses, laid the subject aside, till the muse summoned him to another exertion of fancy. In a little back closet, still existing in the farm-house of Mossgiel, he committed most of his poems to paper.

But while the poet rose, the farmer sank. It was not the cold clayey bottom of his ground, nor the purchase of unsound seed-corn, not the fluctuation in the markets alone, which injured him; neither was it the taste for freemason socialities, nor a desire to join the mirth of comrades, either of the sea or the shore: neither could it be wholly imputed to his passionate following of the softer sex-indulgence in the "illicit rove," or giving way to his eloquence at the feet of one whom he loved and honoured; other farmers indulged in the one, or suffered from the other, yet were prosperous. His want of success arose from other causes; his heart was not with his task, save by fits and starts: he felt he was designed for higher purposes than ploughing, and harrowing, and sowing, and reaping: when the sun called on him, after a shower, to come to the plough, or when the ripe corn invited the sickle, or the ready market called for the measured grain, the poet was under other spells, and was slow to avail himself of those golden moments which come but once in the season. To this may be added, a too superficial knowledge of the art of farming, and a want of intimacy with the nature of the soil he was called to cultivate. He could speak fluently of leas, and faughs, and fallows, of change of seed and rotation of crops, but practical knowledge and application were required, and in these Burns was deficient. The moderate gain which those dark days of agriculture brought to the economical farmer, was not obtained: the close, the all but niggardly care by which he could win and keep his crown-piece,-gold was seldom in the farmer's hand,-was either above or below the mind of the poet, and Mossgiel, which, in the hands of an assiduous farmer, might have made a reasonable return for labour, was unproductive, under one who had little skill, less economy, and no taste for the task.

Other reasons for his failure have been assigned. It is to the credit of the moral sentiments of the husbandmen of Scotland, that when one of their class forgets what virtue requires, and dishonours, without reparation, even the humblest of the maidens, he is not allowed to go unpunished. No proceedings take place, perhaps one hard word is not spoken; but he is regarded with loathing by the old and the devout; he is looked on by all with cold and reproachful eyes-sorrow is foretold as his lot, sure disaster as his fortune; and is these chance to arrive, the only sympathy expressed is, "What better could he expect?" Something of this sort befel Burns: he had already satisfied the kirk in the matter of "Sonsie, smirking, dear-bought Bess," his daughter, by one of his mother's maids; and now, to use his own words, he was brought within point-blank of the heaviest metal of the kirk by a similar folly. The fair transgressor, both for her fathers and her own youth, had a large share of public sympathy. Jean Armour, for it is of her I speak, was in her eighteenth year; with dark eyes, a handsome foot, and a melodious tongue, she made her way to the poet's heart-and, as their stations in life were equal, it seemed that they had only to be satisfied themselves to render their union easy. But her father, in addition to being a very devout man, was a zealot of the Old Light; and Jean, dreading his resentment, was willing, while she loved its unforgiven satirist, to love him in secret, in the hope that the time would come when she might safely avow it: she admitted the poet, therefore, to her company in lonesome places, and walks beneath the moon, where they both forgot themselves, and were at last obliged to own a private marriage as a protection from kirk censure. The professors of the Old Light rejoiced, since it brought a scoffing rhymer within reach of their hand; but her father felt a twofold sorrow, because of the shame of a favourite daughter, and for having committed the folly with one both loose in conduct and profane of speech. He had cause to be angry, but his anger, through his zeal, became tyrannous: in the exercise of what he called a father's power, he compelled his child to renounce the poet as her husband and burn the marriage-lines; for he regarded her marriage, without the kirk's permission, with a man so utterly cast away, as a worse crime than her folly. So blind is anger! She could renounce neither her husband nor his offspring in a lawful way, and in spite of the destruction of the marriage lines, and renouncing the name of wife, she was as much Mrs. Burns as marriage could make her. No one concerned seemed to think so. Burns, who loved her tenderly, went all but mad when she renounced him: he gave up his share of Mossgiel to his brother, and roamed, moody and idle, about the land, with no better aim in life than a situation in one of our western sugar-isles, and a vague hope of distinction as a poet.

How the distinction which he desired as a poet was to be obtained, was, to a poor bard in a provincial place, a sore puzzle: there were no enterprising booksellers in the western land, and it was not to be expected that the printers of either Kilmarnock or Paisley had money to expend on a speculation in rhyme: it is much to the honour of his native county that the publication which he wished for was at last made easy. The best of his poems, in his own handwriting, had found their way into the hands of the Ballantynes, Hamiltons, Parkers, and Mackenzies, and were much admired. Mrs. Stewart, of Stair and Afton, a lady of distinction and taste, had made, accidentally, the acquaintance both of Burns and some of his songs, and was ready to befriend him; and so favourable was the impression on all hands, that a subscription, sufficient to defray the outlay of paper and print, was soon filled up-one hundred copies being subscribed for by the Parkers alone. He soon arranged materials for a volume, and put them into the hands of a printer in Kilmarnock, the Wee Johnnie of one of his biting epigrams. Johnnie was startled at the unceremonious freedom of most of the pieces, and asked the poet to compose one of modest language and moral aim, to stand at the beginning, and excuse some of those free ones which followed: Burns, whose "Twa Dogs" was then incomplete, finished the poem at a sitting, and put it in the van, much to his printer's satisfaction. If the "Jolly Beggars" was omitted for any other cause than its freedom of sentiment and language, or "Death and Doctor Hornbook" from any other feeling than that of being too personal, the causes of their exclusion have remained a secret. It is less easy to account for the emission of many songs of high merit which he had among his papers: perhaps he thought those which he selected were sufficient to test the taste of the public. Before he printed the whole, he, with the consent of his brother, altered his name from Burness to Burns, a change which, I am told, he in after years regretted.

In the summer of the year 1786, the little volume, big with the hopes and fortunes of the bard made its appearance: it was entitled simply, "Poems, chiefly in the Scottish Dialect; by Robert Burns;" and accompanied by a modest preface, saying, that he submitted his book to his country with fear and with trembling, since it contained little of the art of poesie, and at the best was but a voice given, rude, he feared, and uncouth, to the loves, the hopes, and the fears of his own bosom. Had a summer sun risen on a winter morning, it could not have surprised the Lowlands of Scotland more than this Kilmarnock volume surprised and delighted the people, one and all. The milkmaid sang his songs, the ploughman repeated his poems; the old quoted both, and ever the devout rejoiced that idle verse had at last mixed a tone of morality with its mirth. The volume penetrated even into Nithsdale. "Keep it out of the way of your children," said a Cameronian divine, when he lent it to my father, "lest ye find them, as I found mine, reading it on the Sabbath." No wonder that such a volume made its way to the hearts of a peasantry whose taste in poetry had been the marvel of many writers: the poems were mostly on topics with which they were familiar: the language was that of the fireside, raised above the vulgarities of common life, by a purifying spirit of expression and the exalting fervour of inspiration: and there was such a brilliant and graceful mixture of the elegant and the homely, the lofty and the low, the familiar and the elevated-such a rapid succession of scenes which moved to tenderness or tears; or to subdued mirth or open laughter-unlooked for allusions to scripture, or touches of sarcasm and scandal-of superstitions to scare, and of humour to delight-while through the whole was diffused, as the scent of flowers through summer air, a moral meaning-a sentimental beauty, which sweetened and sanctified all. The poet's expectations from this little venture were humble: he hoped as much money from it as would pay for his passage to the West Indies, where he proposed to enter into the service of some of the Scottish settlers, and help to manage the double mystery of sugar-making and slavery.

The hearty applause which I have recorded came chiefly from the husbandman, the shepherd, and the mechanic: the approbation of the magnates of the west, though not less-warm, was longer in coming. Mrs. Stewart of Stair, indeed, commended the poems and cheered their author: Dugald Stewart received his visits with pleasure, and wondered at his vigour of conversation as much as at his muse: the door of the house of Hamilton was open to him, where the table was ever spread, and the hand ever ready to help: while the purses of the Ballantynes and the Parkers were always as open to him as were the doors of their houses. Those persons must be regarded as the real patrons of the poet: the high names of the district are not to be found among those who helped him with purse and patronage in 1786, that year of deep distress and high distinction. The Montgomerys came with their praise when his fame was up; the Kennedys and the Boswells were silent: and though the Cunninghams gave effectual aid, it was when the muse was crying with a loud voice before him, "Come all and see the man whom I delight to honour." It would be unjust as well as ungenerous not to mention the name of Mrs. Dunlop among the poet's best and early patrons: the distance at which she lived from Mossgiel had kept his name from her till his poems appeared: but his works induced her to desire his acquaintance, and she became his warmest and surest friend.

To say the truth, Burns endeavoured in every honourable way to obtain the notice of those who had influence in the land: he copied out the best of his unpublished poems in a fair hand, and inserting them in his printed volume, presented it to those who seemed slow to buy: he rewarded the notice of this one with a song-the attentions of that one with a sally of encomiastic verse: he left psalms of his own composing in the manse when he feasted with a divine: he enclosed "Holy Willie's Prayer," with an injunction to be grave, to one who loved mirth: he sent the "Holy Fair" to one whom he invited to drink a gill out of a mutchkin stoup, at Mauchline market; and on accidentally meeting with Lord Daer, he immediately commemorated the event in a sally of verse, of a strain more free and yet as flattering as ever flowed from the lips of a court bard. While musing over the names of those on whom fortune had smiled, yet who had neglected to smile on him, he remembered that he had met Miss Alexander, a young beauty of the west, in the walks of Ballochmyle; and he recorded the impression which this fair vision made on him in a song of unequalled elegance and melody. He had met her in the woods in July, on the 18th of November he sent her the song, and reminded her of the circumstance from which it arose, in a letter which it is evident he had laboured to render polished and complimentary. The young lady took no notice of either the song or the poet, though willing, it is said, to hear of both now:-this seems to have been the last attempt he made on the taste or the sympathies of the gentry of his native district: for on the very day following we find him busy in making arrangements for his departure to Jamaica.

For this step Burns had more than sufficient reasons: the profits of his volume amounted to little more than enough to waft him across the Atlantic: Wee Johnnie, though the edition was all sold, refused to risk another on speculation: his friends, both Ballantynes and Parkers, volunteered to relieve the printer's anxieties, but the poet declined their bounty, and gloomily indented himself in a ship about to sail from Greenock, and called on his muse to take farewell of Caledonia, in the last song he ever expected to measure in his native land. That fine lyric, beginning "The gloomy night is gathering fast," was the offspring of these moments of regret and sorrow. His feelings were not expressed in song alone: he remembered his mother and his natural daughter, and made an assignment of all that pertained to him at Mossgiel-and that was but little-and of all the advantage which a cruel, unjust, and insulting law allowed in the proceeds of his poems, for their support and behoof. This document was publicly read in the presence of the poet, at the market-cross of Ayr, by his friend William Chalmers, a notary public. Even this step was to Burns one of danger: some ill-advised person had uncoupled the merciless pack of the law at his heels, and he was obliged to shelter himself as he best could, in woods, it is said, by day and in barns by night, till the final hour of his departure came. That hour arrived, and his chest was on the way to the ship, when a letter was put into his hand which seemed to light him to brighter prospects.

Among the friends whom his merits had procured him was Dr. Laurie, a district clergyman, who had taste enough to admire the deep sensibilities as well as the humour of the poet, and the generosity to make known both his works and his worth to the warm-hearted and amiable Blacklock, who boldly proclaimed him a poet of the first rank, and lamented that he was not in Edinburgh to publish another edition of his poems. Burns was ever a man of impulse: he recalled his chest from Greenock; he relinquished the situation he had accepted on the estate of one Douglas; took a secret leave of his mother, and, without an introduction to any one, and unknown personally to all, save to Dugald Stewart, away he walked, through Glenap, to Edinburgh, full of new hope and confiding in his genius. When he arrived, he scarcely knew what to do: he hesitated to call on the professor;

he refrained from making himself known, as it has been supposed he did, to the enthusiastic Blacklock; but, sitting down in an obscure lodging, he sought out an obscure printer, recommended by a humble comrade from Kyle, and began to negotiate for a new edition of the Poems of the Ayrshire Ploughman. This was not the way to go about it: his barge had well nigh been shipwrecked in the launch; and he might have lived to regret the letter which hindered his voyage to Jamaica, had he not met by chance in the street a gentleman of the west, of the name of Dalzell, who introduced him to the Earl of Glencairn, a nobleman whose classic education did not hurt his taste for Scottish poetry, and who was not too proud to lend his helping hand to a rustic stranger of such merit as Burns. Cunningham carried him to Creech, then the Murray of Edinburgh, a shrewd man of business, who opened the poet's eyes to his true interests: the first proposals, then all but issued, were put in the fire, and new ones printed and diffused over the island. The subscription was headed by half the noblemen of the north: the Caledonian Hunt, through the interest of Glencairn, took six hundred copies: duchesses and countesses swelled the list, and such a crowding to write down names had not been witnessed since the signing of the solemn league and covenant.

While the subscription-papers were filling and the new volume printing on a paper and in a type worthy of such high patronage, Burns remained in Edinburgh, where, for the winter season, he was a lion, and one of an unwonted kind. Philosophers, historians, and scholars had shaken the elegant coteries of the city with their wit, or enlightened them with their learning, but they were all men who had been polished by polite letters or by intercourse with high life, and there was a sameness in their very dress as well as address, of which peers and peeresses had become weary. They therefore welcomed this rustic candidate for the honour of giving wings to their hours of lassitude and weariness, with a welcome more than common; and when his approach was announced, the polished circle looked for the advent of a lout from the plough, in whose uncouth manners and embarrassed address they might find matter both for mirth and wonder. But they met with a barbarian who was not at all barbarous: as the poet met in Lord Daer feelings and sentiments as natural as those of a ploughman, so they met in a ploughman manners worthy of a lord: his air was easy and unperplexed: his address was perfectly well-bred, and elegant in its simplicity: he felt neither eclipsed by the titled nor struck dumb before the learned and the eloquent, but took his station with the ease and grace of one born to it. In the society of men alone he spoke out: he spared neither his wit, his humour, nor his sarcasm-he seemed to say to all-"I am a man, and you are no more; and why should I not act and speak like one?"-it was remarked, however, that he had not learnt, or did not desire, to conceal his emotions-that he commended with more rapture than was courteous, and contradicted with more bluntness than was accounted polite. It was thus with him in the company of men: when woman approached, his look altered, his eye beamed milder; all that was stern in his nature underwent a change, and he received them with deference, but with a consciousness that he could win their attention as he had won that of others, who differed, indeed, from them only in the texture of their kirtles. This natural power of rendering himself acceptable to women had been observed and envied by Sillar, one of the dearest of his early comrades; and it stood him in good stead now, when he was the object to whom the Duchess of Gordon, the loveliest as well as the wittiest of women-directed her discourse. Burns, she afterwards said, won the attention of the Edinburgh ladies by a deferential way of address-by an ease and natural grace of manners, as new as it was unexpected-that he told them the stories of some of his tenderest songs or liveliest poems in a style quite magical-enriching his little narratives, which had one and all the merit of being short, with personal incidents of humour or of pathos.

In a party, when Dr. Blair and Professor Walker were present, Burns related the circumstances under which he had composed his melancholy song, "The gloomy night is gathering fast," in a way even more touching than the verses: and in the company of the ruling beauties of the time, he hesitated not to lift the veil from some of the tenderer parts of his own history, and give them glimpses of the romance of rustic life. A lady of birth-one of his must willing listeners-used, I am told, to say, that she should never forget the tale which he related of his affection for Mary Campbell, his Highland Mary, as he loved to call her. She was fair, he said, and affectionate, and as guileless as she was beautiful; and beautiful he thought her in a very high degree. The first time he saw her was during one of his musing walks in the woods of Montgomery Castle; and the first time he spoke to her was during the merriment of a harvest-kirn. There were others there who admired her, but he addressed her, and had the luck to win her regard from them all. He soon found that she was the lass whom he had long sought, but never before found-that her good looks were surpassed by her good sense; and her good sense was equalled by her discretion and modesty. He met her frequently: she saw by his looks that he was sincere; she put full trust in his love, and used to wander with him among the green knowes and stream-banks till the sun went down and the moon rose, talking, dreaming of love and the golden days which awaited them. He was poor, and she had only her half-year's fee, for she was in the condition of a servant; but thoughts of gear never darkened their dream: they resolved to wed, and exchanged vows of constancy and love. They plighted their vows on the Sabbath to render them more sacred-they made them by a burn, where they had courted, that open nature might be a witness-they made them over an open Bible, to show that they thought of God in this mutual act-and when they had done they both took water in their hands, and scattered it in the air, to intimate that as the stream was pure so were their intentions. They parted when they did this, but they parted never to meet more: she died in a burning fever, during a visit to her relations to prepare for her marriage; and all that he had of her was a lock of her long bright hair, and her Bible, which she exchanged for his.

Even with the tales which he related of rustic love and adventure his own story mingled; and ladies of rank heard, for the first time, that in all that was romantic in the passion of love, and in all that was chivalrous in sentiment, men of distinction, both by education and birth, were at least equalled by the peasantry of the land. They listened with interest, and inclined their feathers beside the bard, to hear how love went on in the west, and in no case it ran quite smooth. Sometimes young hearts were kept asunder by the sordid feelings of parents, who could not be persuaded to bestow their daughter, perhaps an only one, on a wooer who could not count penny for penny, and number cow for cow: sometimes a mother desired her daughter to look higher than to one of her station: for her beauty and her education entitled her to match among the lairds, rather than the tenants; and sometimes, the devotional tastes of both father and mother, approving of personal looks and connexions, were averse to see a daughter bestow her hand on one, whose language in religion was indiscreet, and whose morals were suspected. Yet, neither the vigilance of fathers, nor the suspicious care of aunts and mothers, could succeed in keeping those asunder whose hearts were together; but in these meetings circumspection and invention were necessary: all fears were to be lulled by the seeming carelessness of the lass,-all perils were to be met and braved by the spirit of the lad. His home, perhaps, was at a distance, and he had wild woods to come through, and deep streams to pass, before he could see the signal-light, now shown and now withdrawn, at her window; he had to approach with a quick eye and a wary foot, lest a father or a brother should see, and deter him: he had sometimes to wish for a cloud upon the moon, whose light, welcome to him on his way in the distance, was likely to betray him when near; and he not unfrequently reckoned a wild night of wind and rain as a blessing, since it helped to conceal his coming, and proved to his mistress that he was ready to brave all for her sake. Of rivals met and baffled; of half-willing and half-unconsenting maidens, persuaded and won; of the light-hearted and the careless becoming affectionate and tender; and the coy, the proud, and the satiric being gained by "persuasive words, and more persuasive sighs," as dames had been gained of old, he had tales enow. The ladies listened, and smiled at the tender narratives of the poet.

Of his appearance among the sons as well as the daughters of men, we have the account of Dugald Stewart. "Burns," says the philosopher, "came to Edinburgh early in the winter: the attentions which he received from all ranks and descriptions of persons, were such as would have turned any head but his own. He retained the same simplicity of manners and appearance which had struck me so forcibly when I first saw him in the country: his dress was suited to his station; plain and unpretending, with sufficient attention to neatness: he always wore boots, and, when on more than usual ceremony, buckskin breeches. His manners were manly, simple, and independent; strongly expressive of conscious genius and worth, but without any indication of forwardness, arrogance, or vanity. He took his share in conversation, but not more than belonged to him, and listened with apparent deference on subjects where his want of education deprived him of the means of information. If there had been a little more of gentleness and accommodation in his temper, he would have been still more interesting; but he had been accustomed to give law in the circle of his ordinary acquaintance, and his dread of anything approaching to meanness or servility, rendered his manner somewhat decided and hard. Nothing perhaps was more remarkable among his various attainments, than the fluency and precision and originality of language, when he spoke in company; more particularly as he aimed at purity in his turn of expression, and avoided more successfully than most Scotsmen, the peculiarities of Scottish phraseology. From his conversation I should have pronounced him to have been fitted to excel in whatever walk of ambition he had chosen to exert his abilities. He was passionately fond of the beauties of nature, and I recollect he once told me, when I was admiring a distant prospect in one of our morning walks, that the sight of so many smoking cottages gave a pleasure to his mind, which none could understand who had not witnessed, like himself, the happiness and worth which cottages contained."

Such was the impression which Burns made at first on the fair, the titled, and the learned of Edinburgh; an impression which, though lessened by intimacy and closer examination on the part of the men, remained unimpaired, on that of the softer sex, till his dying-day. His company, during the season of balls and festivities, continued to be courted by all who desired to be reckoned gay or polite. Cards of invitation fell thick on him; he was not more welcome to the plumed and jewelled groups, whom her fascinating Grace of Gordon gathered about her, than he was to the grave divines and polished scholars, who assembled in the rooms of Stewart, or Blair, or Robertson. The classic socialities of Tytler, afterwards Lord Woodhouslee, or the elaborate supper-tables of the whimsical Monboddo, whose guests imagined they were entertained in the manner of Lucullus or of Cicero, were not complete without the presence of the ploughman of Kyle; and the feelings of the rustic poet, facing such companies, though of surprise and delight at first, gradually subsided, he said, as he discerned, that man differed from man only in the polish, and not in the grain. But Edinburgh offered tables and entertainers of a less orderly and staid character than those I have named-where the glass circulated with greater rapidity; where the wit flowed more freely; and where there were neither highbred ladies to charm conversation within the bounds of modesty, nor serious philosophers, nor grave divines, to set a limit to the license of speech, or the hours of enjoyment. To these companions-and these were all of the better classes, the levities of the rustic poet's wit and humour were as welcome us were the tenderest of his narratives to the accomplished Duchess of Gordon and the beautiful Miss Burnet of Monboddo; they raised a social roar not at all classic, and demanded and provoked his sallies of wild humour, or indecorous mirth, with as much delight as he had witnessed among the lads of Kyle, when, at mill or forge, his humorous sallies abounded as the ale flowed. In these enjoyments the rough, but learned William Nicol, and the young and amiable Robert Ainslie shared: the name of the poet was coupled with those of profane wits, free livers, and that class of half-idle gentlemen who hang about the courts of law, or for a season or two wear the livery of Mars, and handle cold iron.

Edinburgh had still another class of genteel convivialists, to whom the poet was attracted by principles as well as by pleasure; these were the relics of that once numerous body, the Jacobites, who still loved to cherish the feelings of birth or education rather than of judgment, and toasted the name of Stuart, when the last of the race had renounced his pretensions to a throne, for the sake of peace and the cross. Young men then, and high names were among them, annually met on the pretender's birth-day, and sang songs in which the white rose of Jacobitism flourished; toasted toasts announcing adherence to the male line of the Bruce and the Stuart, and listened to the strains of the laureate of the day, who prophesied, in drink, the dismissal of the intrusive Hanoverian, by the right and might of the righteous and disinherited line. Burns, who was descended from a northern race, whoso father was suspected of having drawn the claymore in 1745, and who loved the blood of the Keith-Marishalls, under whose banners his ancestors had marched, readily united himself to a band in whose sentiments, political and social, he was a sharer. He was received with acclamation: the dignity of laureate was conferred upon him, and his inauguration ode, in which he recalled the names and the deeds of the Grahams, the Erskines, the Boyds, and the Gordons, was applauded for its fire, as well as for its sentiments. Yet, though he ate and drank and sang with Jacobites, he was only as far as sympathy and poesie went, of their number: his reason renounced the principles and the religion of the Stuart line; and though he shed a tear over their fallen fortunes-though he sympathized with the brave and honourable names that perished in their cause-though he cursed "the butcher, Cumberland," and the bloody spirit which commanded the heads of the good and the heroic to be stuck where they would affright the passer-by, and pollute the air-he had no desire to see the splendid fabric of constitutional freedom, which the united genius of all parties had raised, thrown wantonly down. His Jacobitism influenced, not his head, but his heart, and gave a mournful hue to many of his lyric compositions.

Meanwhile his poems were passing through the press. Burns made a few emendations of those published in the Kilmarnock edition, and he added others which, as he expressed it, he had carded and spun, since he passed Glenbuck. Some rather coarse lines were softened or omitted in the "Twa Dogs;" others, from a change of his personal feelings, were made in the "Vision:" "Death and Doctor Hornbook," excluded before, was admitted now: the "Dream" was retained, in spite of the remonstrances of Mrs. Stewart, of Stair, and Mrs. Dunlop; and the "Brigs of Ayr," in compliment to his patrons in his native district, and the "Address to Edinburgh," in honour of his titled and distinguished friends in that metropolis, were printed for the first time. He was unwilling to alter what he had once printed: his friends, classic, titled, and rustic, found him stubborn and unpliable, in matters of criticism; yet he was generally of a complimental mood: he loaded the robe of Coila in the "Vision," with more scenes than it could well contain, that he might include in the landscape, all the country-seats of his friends, and he gave more than their share of commendation to the Wallaces, out of respect to his friend Mrs. Dunlop. Of the critics of Edinburgh he said, they spun the thread of their criticisms so fine that it was unfit for either warp or weft; and of its scholars, he said, they were never satisfied with any Scottish poet, unless they could trace him in Horace. One morning at Dr. Blair's breakfast-table, when the "Holy Fair" was the subject of conversation, the reverend critic said, "Why should

'Moody speel the holy door With tidings of salvation?'

if you had said, with tidings of damnation, the satire would have been the better and the bitterer." "Excellent!" exclaimed the poet, "the alteration is capital, and I hope you will honour me by allowing me to say in a note at whose suggestion it was made." Professor Walker, who tells the anecdote, adds that Blair evaded, with equal good humour and decision, this not very polite request; nor was this the only slip which the poet made on this occasion: some one asked him in which of the churches of Edinburgh he had received the highest gratification: he named the High-church, but gave the preference over all preachers to Robert Walker, the colleague and rival in eloquence of Dr. Blair himself, and that in a tone so pointed and decisive as to make all at the table stare and look embarrassed. The poet confessed afterwards that he never reflected on his blunder without pain and mortification. Blair probably had this in his mind, when, on reading the poem beginning "When Guildford good our pilot stood," he exclaimed, "Ah! the politics of Burns always smell of the smithy," meaning, that they were vulgar and common.

In April, the second or Edinburgh, edition was published: it was widely purchased, and as warmly commended. The country had been prepared for it by the generous and discriminating criticisms of Henry Mackenzie, published in that popular periodical, "The Lounger," where he says, "Burns possesses the spirit as well as the fancy of a poet; that honest pride and independence of soul, which are sometimes the muse's only dower, break forth on every occasion, in his works." The praise of the author of the "Man of Feeling" was not more felt by Burns, than it was by the whole island: the harp of the north had not been swept for centuries by a hand so forcible, and at the same time so varied, that it awakened every tone, whether of joy or woe: the language was that of rustic life; the scenes of the poems were the dusty barn, the clay-floored reeky cottage, and the furrowed field; and the characters were cowherds, ploughmen, and mechanics. The volume was embellished by a head of the poet from the hand of the now venerable Alexander Nasmith; and introduced by a dedication to the noblemen and gentlemen of the Caledonian Hunt, in a style of vehement independence, unknown hitherto in the history of subscriptions. The whole work, verse, prose, and portrait, won public attention, and kept it: and though some critics signified their displeasure at expressions which bordered on profanity, and at a license of language which they pronounced impure, by far the greater number united their praise to the all but general voice; nay, some scrupled not to call him, from his perfect ease and nature and variety, the Scottish Shakspeare. No one rejoiced more in his success and his fame, than the matron of Mossgiel.

Other matters than his poems and socialities claimed the attention of Burns in Edinburgh. He had a hearty relish for the joyous genius of Allan Ramsay; he traced out his residences, and rejoiced to think that while he stood in the shop of his own bookseller, Creech, the same floor had been trod by the feet of his great forerunner. He visited, too, the lowly grave of the unfortunate Robert Fergusson; and it must be recorded to the shame of the magistrates of Edinburgh, that they allowed him to erect a headstone to his memory, and to the scandal of Scotland, that in such a memorial he had not been anticipated. He seems not to have regarded the graves of scholars or philosophers; and he trod the pavements where the warlike princes and nobles had walked without any emotion. He loved, however, to see places celebrated in Scottish song, and fields where battles for the independence of his country had been stricken; and, with money in his pocket which his poems had produced, and with a letter from a witty but weak man, Lord Buchan, instructing him to pull birks on the Yarrow, broom on the Cowden-knowes, and not to neglect to admire the ruins of Drybrugh Abbey, Burns set out on a border tour, accompanied by Robert Ainslie, of Berrywell. As the poet had talked of returning to the plough, Dr. Blair imagined that he was on his way back to the furrowed field, and wrote him a handsome farewell, saying he was leaving Edinburgh with a character which had survived many temptations; with a name which would be placed with the Ramsays and the Fergussons, and with the hopes of all, that, in a second volume, on which his fate as a poet would very much depend, he might rise yet higher in merit and in fame. Burns, who received this communication when laying his leg over the saddle to be gone, is said to have muttered, “Ay, but a man’s first book is sometimes like his first babe, healthier and stronger than those which follow.”

On the 6th of May, 1787, Burns reached Berrywell: he recorded of the laird, that he was clear-headed, and of Miss Ainslie, that she was amiable and handsome-of Dudgeon, the author of “The Maid that tends the Goats,” that he had penetration and modesty, and of the preacher, Bowmaker, that he was a man of strong lungs and vigorous remark. On crossing the Tweed at Coldstream he took off his hat, and kneeling down, repeated aloud the two last verses of the “Cotter’s Saturday Night:” on returning, he drunk tea with Brydone, the traveller, a man, he said, kind and benevolent: he cursed one Cole as an English Hottentot, for having rooted out an ancient garden belonging to a Romish ruin; and he wrote of Macdowal, of Caverton-mill, that by his skill in rearing sheep, he sold his flocks, ewe and lamb, for a couple of guineas each: that he washed his sheep before shearing-and by his turnips improved sheep-husbandry; he added, that lands were generally let at sixteen shillings the Scottish acre; the farmers rich, and, compared to Ayrshire, their houses magnificent. On his way to Jedburgh he visited an old gentleman in whose house was an arm-chair, once the property of the author of “The Seasons;” he reverently examined the relic, and could scarcely be persuaded to sit in it: he was a warm admirer of Thomson.

In Jedburgh, Burns found much to interest him: the ruins of a splendid cathedral, and of a strong castle-and, what was still more attractive, an amiable young lady, very handsome, with “beautiful hazel eyes, full of spirit, sparkling with delicious moisture,” and looks which betokened a high order of female mind. He gave her his portrait, and entered this remembrance of her attractions among his memoranda:-“My heart is thawed into melting pleasure, after being so long frozen up in the Greenland bay of indifference, amid the noise and nonsense of Edinburgh. I am afraid my bosom has nearly as much tinder as ever. Jed, pure be thy streams, and hallowed thy sylvan banks: sweet Isabella Lindsay, may peace dwell in thy bosom uninterrupted, except by the tumultuous throbbings of rapturous love!” With the freedom of Jedburgh, handsomely bestowed by the magistrates, in his pocket, Burns made his way to Wauchope, the residence of Mrs. Scott, who had welcomed him into the world as a poet in verses lively and graceful: he found her, he said, “a lady of sense and taste, and of a decision peculiar to female authors.” After dining with Sir Alexander Don, who, he said, was a clever man, but far from a match for his divine lady, a sister of his patron Glencairn, he spent an hour among the beautiful ruins of Dryburgh Abbey; glanced on the splendid remains of Melrose; passed, unconscious of the future, over that ground on which have arisen the romantic towers of Abbotsford; dined with certain of the Souters of Selkirk; and visited the old keep of Thomas the Rhymer, and a dozen of the hills and streams celebrated in song. Nor did he fail to pay his respects, after returning through Dunse, to Sir James Hall, of Dunglass, and his lady, and was much pleased with the scenery of their romantic place. He was now joined by a gentleman of the name of Kerr, and crossing the Tweed a second time, penetrated into England, as far as the ancient town of Newcastle, where he smiled at a facetious Northumbrian, who at dinner caused the beef to be eaten before the broth was served, in obedience to an ancient injunction, lest the hungry Scotch should come and snatch it. On his way back he saw, what proved to be prophetic of his own fortune-the roup of an unfortunate farmer's stock: he took out his journal, and wrote with a troubled brow, "Rigid economy, and decent industry, do you preserve me from being the principal dramatis personæ, in such a scene of horror." He extended his tour to Carlisle, and from thence to the banks of the Nith, where he looked at the farm of Ellisland, with the intention of trying once more his fortune at the plough, should poetry and patronage fail him.

On his way through the West, Burns spent a few days with his mother at Mossgiel: he had left her an unknown and an almost banished man: he returned in fame and in sunshine, admired by all who aspired to be thought tasteful or refined. He felt offended alike with the patrician stateliness of Edinburgh and the plebeian servility of the husbandmen of Ayrshire; and dreading the influence of the unlucky star which had hitherto ruled his lot, he bought a pocket Milton, he said, for the purpose of studying the intrepid independence and daring magnanimity, and noble defiance of hardships, exhibited by Satan! In this mood he reached Edinburgh-only to leave it again on three hurried excursions into the Highlands. The route which he took and the sentiments which the scenes awakened, are but faintly intimated in the memoranda which he made. His first journey seems to have been performed in ill-humour; at Stirling, his Jacobitism, provoked at seeing the ruined palace of the Stuarts, broke out in some unloyal lines which he had the indiscretion to write with a diamond on the window of a public inn. At Carron, where he was refused a sight of the magnificent foundry, he avenged himself in epigram. At Inverary he resented some real or imaginary neglect on the part of his Grace of Argyll, by a stinging lampoon; nor can he be said to have fairly regained his serenity of temper, till he danced his wrath away with some Highland ladies at Dumbarton.

His second excursion was made in the company of Dr. Adair, of Harrowgate: the reluctant doors of Carron foundry were opened to him, and he expressed his wonder at the blazing furnaces and broiling labours of the place; he removed the disloyal lines from the window of the inn at Stirling, and he paid a two days' visit to Ramsay of Ochtertyre, a distinguished scholar, and discussed with him future topics for the muse. "I have been in the company of many men of genius," said Ramsay afterwards to Currie, "some of them poets, but never witnessed such flashes of intellectual brightness as from him-the impulse of the moment, sparks of celestial fire." From the Forth he went to the Devon, in the county of Clackmannan, where, for the first time, he saw the beautiful Charlotte Hamilton, the sister of his friend Gavin Hamilton, of Mauchline. "She is not only beautiful," he thus writes to her brother, "but lovely: her form is elegant, her features not regular, but they have the smile of sweetness, and the settled complacency of good nature in the highest degree. Her eyes are fascinating; at once expressive of good sense, tenderness and a noble mind. After the exercise of our riding to the Falls, Charlotte was exactly Dr. Donne's mistress:-

"Her pure and eloquent blood Spoke in her cheeks, and so distinctly wrought, That one would almost say her body thought."

Accompanied by this charming dame, he visited an old lady, Mrs. Bruce, of Clackmannan, who, in the belief that she had the blood of the royal Bruce in her veins, received the poet with something of princely state, and, half in jest, conferred the honour of knighthood upon him, with her ancestor's sword, saying, in true Jacobitical mood, that she had a better right to do that than some folk had! In the same pleasing company he visited the famous cataract on the Devon, called the Cauldron Lian, and the Rumbling bridge, a single arch thrown, it is said by the devil, over the Devon, at the height of a hundred feet in the air. It was the complaint of his companions that Burns exhibited no raptures, and poured out no unpremeditated verses at such magnificent scenes. But he did not like to be tutored or prompted: "Look, look!" exclaimed some one, as Carron foundry belched forth flames-"look, Burns, look! good heavens, what a grand sight!-look!" "I would not look-look, sir, at your bidding," said the bard, turning away, "were it into the mouth of hell!" When he visited, at a future time, the romantic Linn of Creehope, in Nithsdale, he looked silently at its wonders, and showed none of the hoped-for rapture. "You do not admire it, I fear," said a gentleman who accompanied him; "I could not admire it more, sir," replied Burns, "if He who made it were to desire me to do it." There are other reasons for the silence of Burns amid the scenes of the Devon: he was charmed into love by the sense and the beauty of Charlotte Hamilton, and rendered her homage in that sweet song, "The Banks of the Devon," and in a dozen letters written with more than his usual care, elegance, and tenderness. But the lady was neither to be won by verse nor by prose: she afterwards gave her hand to Adair, the poet's companion, and, what was less meritorious, threw his letters into the fire.

The third and last tour into the North was in company of Nicol of the High-School of Edinburgh: on the fields of Bannockburn and Falkirk-places of triumph and of woe to Scotland, he gave way to patriotic impulses, and in these words he recorded them:-"Stirling, August 20, 1787: this morning I knelt at the tomb of Sir John the Graham, the gallant friend of the immortal Wallace; and two hours ago I said a fervent prayer for old Caledonia, over the hole in a whinstone where Robert the Bruce fixed his royal standard on the banks of Bannockburn." He then proceeded northward by Ochtertyre, the water of Earn, the vale of Glen Almond, and the traditionary grave of Ossian. He looked in at princely Taymouth; mused an hour or two among the Birks of Aberfeldy; gazed from Birnam top; paused amid the wild grandeur of the pass of Killiecrankie, at the stone which marks the spot where a second patriot Graham fell, and spent a day at Blair, where he experienced the graceful kindness of the Duke of Athol, and in a strain truly elegant, petitioned him, in the name of Bruar Water, to hide the utter nakedness of its otherwise picturesque banks, with plantations of birch and oak. Quitting Blair he followed the course of the Spey, and passing, as he told his brother, through a wild country, among cliffs gray with eternal snows, and glens gloomy and savage, reached Findhorn in mist and darkness; visited Castle Cawdor, where Macbeth murdered Duncan; hastened through Inverness to Urquhart Castle, and the Falls of Fyers, and turned southward to Kilravock, over the fatal moor of Culloden. He admired the ladies of that classic region for their snooded ringlets, simple elegance of dress, and expressive eyes: in Mrs. Rose, of Kilravock Castle, he found that matronly grace and dignity which he owned he loved; and in the Duke and Duchess of Gordon a renewal of that more than kindness with which they had welcomed him in Edinburgh. But while he admired the palace of Fochabers, and was charmed by the condescensions of the noble proprietors, he forgot that he had left a companion at the inn, too proud and captious to be pleased at favours showered on others: he hastened back to the inn with an invitation and an apology: he found the fiery pedant in a foaming rage, striding up and down the street, cursing in Scotch and Latin the loitering postilions for not yoking the horses, and hurrying him away. All apology and explanation was in vain, and Burns, with a vexation which he sought not to conceal, took his seat silently beside the irascible pedagogue, and returned to the South by Broughty Castle, the banks of Endermay and Queensferry. He parted with the Highlands in a kindly mood, and loved to recal the scenes and the people, both in conversation and in song.

On his return to Edinburgh he had to bide the time of his bookseller and the public: the impression of his poems, extending to two thousand eight hundred copies, was sold widely: much of the money had to come from a distance, and Burns lingered about the northern metropolis, expecting a settlement with Creech, and with the hope that those who dispensed his country's patronage might remember one who then, as now, was reckoned an ornament to the land. But Creech, a parsimonious man, was slow in his payments; the patronage of the country was swallowed up in the sink of politics, and though noblemen smiled, and ladies of rank nodded their jewelled heads in approbation of every new song he sung and every witty sally he uttered, they reckoned any further notice or care superfluous: the poet, an observant man, saw all this; but hope was the cordial of his heart, he said, and he hoped and lingered on. Too active a genius to remain idle, he addressed himself to the twofold business of love and verse. Repulsed by the stately Beauty of the Devon, he sought consolation in the society of one, as fair, and infinitely more witty; and as an accident had for a time deprived him of the use of one of his legs, he gave wings to hours of pain, by writing a series of letters to this Edinburgh enchantress, in which he signed himself Sylvander, and addressed her under the name of Clarinda. In these compositions, which no one can regard as serious, and which James Grahame the poet called "a romance of real Platonic affection," amid much affectation both of language and sentiment, and a desire to say fine and startling things, we can see the proud heart of the poet throbbing in the dread of being neglected or forgotten by his country. The love which he offers up at the altar of wit and beauty, seems assumed and put on, for its rapture is artificial, and its brilliancy that of an icicle: no woman was ever wooed and won in that Malvolio way; and there is no doubt that Mrs. M'Lehose felt as much offence as pleasure at this boisterous display of regard. In aftertimes he loved to remember her:-when wine circulated, Mrs. Mac was his favourite toast.

During this season he began his lyric contributions to the Musical Museum of Johnson, a work which, amid many imperfections of taste and arrangement, contains more of the true old music and genuine old songs of Scotland, than any other collection with which I am acquainted. Burns gathered oral airs, and fitted them with words of mirth or of woe, of tenderness or of humour, with unexampled readiness and felicity; he eked out old fragments and sobered down licentious strains so much in the olden spirit and feeling, that the new cannot be distinguished from the ancient; nay, he inserted lines and half lines, with such skill and nicety, that antiquarians are perplexed to settle which is genuine or which is simulated. Yet with all this he abated not of the natural mirth or the racy humour of the lyric muse of Scotland: he did not like her the less because she walked like some of the maidens of her strains, high-kilted at times, and spoke with the freedom of innocence. In these communications we observe how little his border-jaunt among the fountains of ancient song contributed either of sentiment or allusion, to his lyrics; and how deeply his strains, whether of pity or of merriment, were coloured by what he had seen, and heard, and felt in the Highlands. In truth, all that lay beyond the Forth was an undiscovered land to him; while the lowland districts were not only familiar to his mind and eye, but all their more romantic vales and hills and streams were already musical in songs of such excellence as induced him to dread failure rather than hope triumph. Moreover, the Highlands teemed with jacobitical feelings, and scenes hallowed by the blood or the sufferings of men heroic, and perhaps misguided; and the poet, willingly yielding to an impulse which was truly romantic, and believed by thousands to be loyal, penned his songs on Drumossie, and Killiecrankie, as the spirit of sorrow or of bitterness prevailed. Though accompanied, during his northern excursions, by friends whose socialities and conversation forbade deep thought, or even serious remark, it will be seen by those who read his lyrics with care, that his wreath is indebted for some of its fairest flowers to the Highlands.

The second winter of the poet's abode in Edinburgh had now arrived: it opened, as might have been expected, with less rapturous welcomes and with more of frosty civility than the first. It must be confessed, that indulgence in prolonged socialities, and in company which, though clever, could not be called select, contributed to this; nor must it be forgotten that his love for the sweeter part of creation was now and then carried beyond the limits of poetic respect, and the delicacies of courtesy; tending to estrange the austere and to lessen the admiration at first common to all. Other causes may be assigned for this wane of popularity: he took no care to conceal his contempt for all who depended on mere scholarship for eminence, and he had a perilous knack in sketching with a sarcastic hand the characters of the learned and the grave. Some indeed of the high literati of the north-Home, the author of Douglas, was one of them-spoke of the poet as a chance or an accident: and though they admitted that he was a poet, yet he was not one of settled grandeur of soul, brightened by study. Burns was probably aware of this; he takes occasion in some of his letters to suggest, that the hour may be at hand when he shall be accounted by scholars as a meteor, rather than a fixed light, and to suspect that the praise bestowed on his genius was partly owing to the humility of his condition. From his lingering so long about Edinburgh, the nobility began to dread a second volume by subscription, the learned to regard him as a fierce Theban, who resolved to carry all the outworks to the temple of Fame without the labour of making regular approaches; while a third party, and not the least numerous, looked on him with distrust, as one who hovered between Jacobite and Jacobin; who disliked the loyal-minded, and loved to lampoon the reigning family. Besides, the marvel of the inspired ploughman had begun to subside; the bright gloss of novelty was worn off, and his fault lay in his unwillingness to see that he had made all the sport which the

Philistines expected, and was required to make room for some "salvage" of the season, to paw, and roar, and shake the mane. The doors of the titled, which at first opened spontaneous, like those in Milton's heaven, were now unclosed for him with a tardy courtesy: he was received with measured stateliness, and seldom requested to repeat his visit. Of this changed aspect of things he complained to a friend: but his real sorrows were mixed with those of the fancy:-he told Mrs. Dunlop with what pangs of heart he was compelled to take shelter in a corner, lest the rattling equipage of some gaping blockhead should mangle him in the mire. In this land of titles and wealth such querulous sensibilities must have been frequently offended.

Burns, who had talked lightly hitherto of resuming the plough, began now to think seriously about it, for he saw it must come to that at last. Miller, of Dalswinton, a gentleman of scientific acquirements, and who has the merit of applying the impulse of steam to navigation, had offered the poet the choice of his farms, on a fair estate which he had purchased on the Nith: aided by a westland farmer, he selected Ellisland, a beautiful spot, fit alike for the steps of ploughman or poet. On intimating this to the magnates of Edinburgh, no one lamented that a genius so bright and original should be driven to win his bread with the sweat of his brow: no one, with an indignant eye, ventured to tell those to whom the patronage of this magnificent empire was confided, that they were misusing the sacred trust, and that posterity would curse them for their coldness or neglect: neither did any of the rich nobles, whose tables he had adorned by his wit, offer to enable him to toil free of rent, in a land of which he was to be a permanent ornament;-all were silent-all were cold-the Earl of Glencairn alone, aided by Alexander Wood, a gentleman who merits praise oftener than he is named, did the little that was done or attempted to be done for him: nor was that little done on the peer's part without solicitation:-"I wish to go into the excise;" thus he wrote to Glencairn; "and I am told your lordship's interest will easily procure me the grant from the commissioners: and your lordship's patronage and goodness, which have already rescued me from obscurity, wretchedness, and exile, emboldens me to ask that interest. You have likewise put it in my power to save the little tie of home that sheltered an aged mother, two brothers, and three sisters from destruction. I am ill qualified to dog the heels of greatness with the impertinence of solicitation, and tremble nearly as much at the thought of the cold promise as the cold denial." The farm and the excise exhibit the poet's humble scheme of life: the money of the one, he thought, would support the toil of the other, and in the fortunate management of both, he looked for the rough abundance, if not the elegancies suitable to a poet's condition.

While Scotland was disgraced by sordidly allowing her brightest genius to descend to the plough and the excise, the poet hastened his departure from a city which had witnessed both his triumph and his shame: he bade farewell in a few well-chosen words to such of the classic literati-the Blairs, the Stewarts, the Mackenzies, and the Tytlers-as had welcomed the rustic bard and continued to countenance him; while in softer accents he bade adieu to the Clarindas and Chlorises of whose charms he had sung, and, having wrung a settlement from Creech, he turned his steps towards Mossgiel and Mauchline. He had several reasons, and all serious ones, for taking Ayrshire in his way to the Nith: he desired to see his mother, his brothers and sisters, who had partaken of his success, and were now raised from pining penury to comparative affluence: he desired to see those who had aided him in his early struggles into the upper air-perhaps those, too, who had looked coldly on, and smiled at his outward aspirations after fame or distinction; but more than all, he desired to see one whom he once and still dearly loved, who had been a sufferer for his sake, and whom he proposed to make mistress of his fireside and the sharer of his fortunes. Even while whispering of love to Charlotte Hamilton, on the banks of the Devon, or sighing out the affected sentimentalities of platonic or pastoral love in the ear of Clarinda, his thoughts wandered to her whom he had left bleaching her webs among the daisies on Mauchline braes-she had still his heart, and in spite of her own and her father's disclamation, she was his wife. It was one of the delusions of this great poet, as well as of those good people, the Armours, that the marriage had been dissolved by the destruction of the marriage-lines, and that Robert Burns and Jean Armour were as single as though they had neither vowed nor written themselves man and wife. Be that as it may, the time was come when all scruples and obstacles were to be removed which stood in the way of their union: their hands were united by Gavin Hamilton, according to law, in April, 1788: and even the Reverend Mr. Auld, so mercilessly lampooned, smiled forgivingly as the poet satisfied a church wisely scrupulous regarding the sacred ceremony of marriage.

Though Jean Armour was but a country lass of humble degree, she had sense and intelligence, and personal charms sufficient not only to win and fix the attentions of the poet, but to sanction the praise which he showered on her in song. In a letter to Mrs. Dunlop, he thus describes her: "The most placid good nature and sweetness of disposition, a warm heart, gratefully devoted with all its powers to love me; vigorous health and sprightly cheerfulness, set off to the best advantage by a more than commonly handsome figure: these I think in a woman may make a good wife, though she should never have read a page but the Scriptures, nor have danced in a brighter assembly than a penny-pay wedding." To the accomplished Margaret Chalmers, of Edinburgh, he adds, to complete the picture, "I have got the handsomest figure, the sweetest temper, the soundest constitution, and kindest heart in the country: a certain late publication of Scots' poems she has perused very devoutly, and all the ballads in the land, as she has the finest wood-note wild you ever heard." With his young wife, a punch bowl of Scottish marble, and an eight-day clock, both presents from Mr. Armour, now reconciled to his eminent son-in-law, with a new plough, and a beautiful heifer, given by Mrs. Dunlop, with about four hundred pounds in his pocket, a resolution to toil, and a hope of success, Burns made his appearance on the banks of the Nith, and set up his staff at Ellisland. This farm, now a classic spot, is about six miles up the river from Dumfries; it extends to upwards of a hundred acres: the soil is kindly; the holmland portion of it loamy and rich, and it has at command fine walks on the river side, and views of the Friar's Carse, Cowehill, and Dalswinton. For a while the poet had to hide his head in a smoky hovel; till a house to his fancy, and offices for his cattle and his crops were built, his accommodation was sufficiently humble; and his mind taking its hue from his situation, infused a bitterness into the letters in which he first made known to his western friends that he had fixed his abode in Nithsdale. "I am here," said he, "at the very elbow of existence: the only things to be found in perfection in this country are stupidity and canting; prose they only know in graces and prayers, and the value of these they estimate as they do their plaiden-webs, by the ell: as for the muses, they have as much an idea of a rhinoceros as of a poet." "This is an undiscovered clime," he at another period exclaims, "it is unknown to poetry, and prose never looked on it save in drink. I sit by the fire, and listen to the hum of the spinning-wheel: I hear, but cannot see it, for it is hidden in the smoke which eddies round and round me before it seeks to escape by window and door. I have no converse but with the ignorance which encloses me: No kenned face but that of my old mare, Jenny Geddes-my life is dwindled down to mere existence."

When the poet's new house was built and plenished, and the atmosphere of his mind began to clear, he found the land to be fruitful, and its people intelligent and wise. In Riddel, of Friar's Carse, he found a scholar and antiquarian; in Miller, of Dalswinton, a man conversant with science as well as with the world; in M'Murdo, of Drumlanrig, a generous and accomplished gentleman; and in John Syme, of Ryedale, a man much after his own heart, and a lover of the wit and socialities of polished life. Of these gentlemen Riddel, who was his neighbour, was the favourite: a door was made in the march-fence which separated Ellisland from Friar's Carse, that the poet might indulge in the retirement of the Carse hermitage, a little lodge in the wood, as romantic as it was beautiful, while a pathway was cut through the dwarf oaks and birches which fringed the river bank, to enable the poet to saunter and muse without lot or interruption. This attention was rewarded by an inscription for the hermitage, written with elegance as well as feeling, and which was the first fruits of his fancy in this unpoetic land. In a happier strain he remembered Matthew Henderson: this is one of the sweetest as well as happiest of his poetic compositions. He heard of his friend's death, and called on nature animate and inanimate, to lament the loss of one who held the patent of his honours from God alone, and who loved all that was pure and lovely and good. "The Whistle" is another of his Ellisland compositions: the contest which he has recorded with such spirit and humour took place almost at his door: the heroes were Fergusson, of Craigdarroch, Sir Robert Laurie, of Maxwelltown, and Riddel, of the Friar's Carse: the poet was present, and drank bottle and bottle about with the best, and when all was done he seemed much disposed, as an old servant at Friar's Carse remembered, to take up the victor.

Burns had become fully reconciled to Nithsdale, and was on the most intimate terms with the muse when he produced Tam O' Shanter, the crowning glory of all his poems. For this marvellous tale we are indebted to something like accident: Francis Grose, the antiquary, happened to visit Friar's Carse, and as he loved wine and wit, the total want of imagination was no hinderance to his friendly intercourse with the poet: "Alloway's auld haunted kirk" was mentioned, and Grose said he would include it in his illustrations of the antiquities of Scotland, if the bard of the Doon would write a poem to accompany it. Burns consented, and before he left the table, the various traditions which belonged to the ruin were passing through his mind. One of these was of a farmer, who, on a night wild with wind and rain, on passing the old kirk was startled by a light glimmering inside the walls; on drawing near he saw a caldron hung over a fire, in which the heads and limbs of children were simmering: there was neither witch nor fiend to guard it, so he unhooked the caldron, turned out the contents, and carried it home as a trophy. A second tradition was of a man of Kyle, who, having been on a market night detained late in Ayr, on crossing the old bridge of Doon, on his way home, saw a light streaming through the gothic window of Alloway kirk, and on riding near, beheld a batch of the district witches dancing merrily round their master, the devil, who kept them "louping and flinging" to the sound of a bagpipe. He knew several of the old crones, and smiled at their gambols, for they were dancing in their smocks: but one of them, and she happened to be young and rosy, had on a smock shorter than those of her companions by two spans at least, which so moved the farmer that he exclaimed, "Weel luppan, Maggie wi' the short sark!" Satan stopped his music, the light was extinguished, and out rushed the hags after the farmer, who made at the gallop for the bridge of Doon, knowing that they could not cross a stream: he escaped; but Maggie, who was foremost, seized his horse's tail at the middle of the bridge, and pulled it off in her efforts to stay him.

This poem was the work of a single day: Burns walked out to his favourite musing path, which runs towards the old tower of the Isle, along Nithside, and was observed to walk hastily and mutter as he went. His wife knew by these signs that he was engaged in composition, and watched him from the window; at last wearying, and moreover wondering at the unusual length of his meditations, she took her children with her and went to meet him; but as he seemed not to see her, she stept aside among the broom to allow him to pass, which he did with a flushed brow and dropping eyes, reciting these lines aloud:-

"Now Tam! O, Tum! had thae been queans, A' plump and strapping in their teens, Their sacks, instead o' creeshie flannen, Been snaw-white seventeen hunder linen! Thir breeks o' mine, my only pair, That ance were plush, o' gude blue hair, I wad hae gien them off my hurdies, For ae blink o' the bonnie burdies!"

He embellished this wild tradition from fact as well as from fancy: along the road which Tam came on that eventful night his memory supplied circumstances which prepared him for the strange sight at the kirk of Alloway. A poor chapman had perished, some winters before, in the snow; a murdered child had been found by some early hunters; a tippling farmer had fallen from his horse at the expense of his neck, beside a "meikle stane"; and a melancholy old woman had hanged herself at the bush aboon the well, as the poem relates: all these matters the poet pressed into the service of the muse, and used them with a skill which adorns rather than oppresses the legend. A pert lawyer from Dumfries objected to the language as obscure: "Obscure, sir!" said Burns; "you know not the language of that great master of your own art-the devil. If you had a witch for your client you would not be able to manage her defence!"

He wrote few poems after his marriage, but he composed many songs: the sweet voice of Mrs. Burns and the craving of Johnson's Museum will in some measure account for the number, but not for their variety, which is truly wonderful. In the history of that mournful strain, "Mary in Heaven," we read the story of many of his lyrics, for they generally sprang from his personal feelings: no poet has put more of himself into his poetry than Burns, "Robert, though ill of a cold," said his wife, "had been busy all day-a day of September, 1789, with the shearers in the field, and as he had got most of the corn into the stack-yard, was in good spirits; but when twilight came he grew sad about something, and could not rest: he wandered first up the waterside, and then went into the stack-yard: I followed, and begged him to come into the house, as he was ill, and the air was sharp and cold. He said, 'Ay, ay,' but did not come: he threw himself down on some loose sheaves, and lay looking at the sky, and particularly at a large, bright star, which shone like another moon. At last, but that was long after I had left him, he came home-the song was already composed." To the memory of Mary Campbell he dedicated that touching ode; and he thus intimates the continuance of his early affection for "The fair haired lass of the west," in a letter of that time to Mrs. Dunlop. "If there is another life, it must be only for the just, the benevolent, the amiable, and the humane. What a flattering idea, then, is a world to come! There shall I, with speechless agony of rapture, again recognise my lost, my ever dear Mary, whose bosom was fraught with truth, honour, constancy, and love." These melancholy words gave way in their turn to others of a nature lively and humorous: "Tam Glen," in which the thoughts flow as freely as the waters of the Nith, on whose banks he wrote it; "Findlay," with its quiet vein of sly simplicity; "Willie brewed a peck o' maut," the first of social, and "She's fair and fause," the first of sarcastic songs, with "The deil's awa wi' the Exciseman," are all productions of this period-a period which had besides its own fears and its own forebodings.

For a while Burns seemed to prosper in his farm: he held the plough with his own hand, he guided the harrows, he distributed the seed-corn equally among the furrows, and he reaped the crop in its season, and saw it safely covered in from the storms of winter with "thack and rape;" his wife, too, superintended the dairy with a skill which she had brought from Kyle, and as the harvest, for a season or two, was abundant, and the dairy yielded butter and cheese for the market, it seemed that "the luckless star" which ruled his lot had relented, and now shone unboding and benignly. But much more is required than toil of hand to make a successful farmer, nor will the attention bestowed only by fits and starts, compensate for carelessness or oversight: frugality, not in one thing but in all, is demanded, in small matters as well as in great, while a careful mind and a vigilant eye must superintend the labours of servants, and the whole system of in-door and out-door economy. Now, during the three years which Burns stayed in Ellisland, he neither wrought with that constant diligence which farming demands, nor did he bestow upon it the unremitting attention of eye and mind which such a farm required: besides his skill in husbandry was but moderate-the rent, though of his own fixing, was too high for him and for the times; the ground, though good, was not so excellent as he might have had on the same estate-he employed more servants than the number of acres demanded, and spread for them a richer board than common: when we have said this we need not add the expensive tastes induced by poetry, to keep readers from starting, when they are told that Burns, at the close of the third year of occupation, resigned his lease to the landlord, and bade farewell for ever to the plough. He was not, however, quite desolate; he had for a year or more been appointed on the excise, and had superintended a district extending to ten large parishes, with applause; indeed, it has been assigned as the chief reason for failure in his farm, that when the plough or the sickle summoned him to the field, he was to be found, either pursuing the defaulters of the revenue, among the valleys of Dumfrieshire, or measuring out pastoral verse to the beauties of the land. He retired to a house in the Bank-vennel of Dumfries, and commenced a town-life: he commenced it with an empty pocket, for Ellisland had swallowed up all the profits of his poems: he had now neither a barn to produce meal nor barley, a barn-yard to yield a fat hen, a field to which he could go at Martinmas for a mart, nor a dairy to supply milk and cheese and butter to the table-he had, in short, all to buy and little to buy with. He regarded it as a compensation that he had no farm-rent to provide, no bankruptcies to dread, no horse to keep, for his excise duties were now confined to Dumfries, and that the burthen of a barren farm was removed from his mind, and his muse at liberty to renew her unsolicited strains.

But from the day of his departure from "the barren" Ellisland, the downward course of Burns may be dated. The cold neglect of his country had driven him back indignantly to the plough, and he hoped to gain from the furrowed field that independence which it was the duty of Scotland to have provided: but he did not resume the plough with all the advantages he possessed when he first forsook it: he had revelled in the luxuries of polished life-his tastes had been rendered expensive as well as pure: he had witnessed, and he hoped for the pleasures of literary retirement, while the hands which had led jewelled dames over scented carpets to supper tables leaded with silver took hold of the hilts of the plough with more of reluctance than good-will. Edinburgh, with its lords and its ladies, its delights and its hopes, spoiled him for farming. Nor were his new labours more acceptable to his haughty spirit than those of the plough: the excise for a century had been a word of opprobrium or of hatred in the north: the duties which it imposed were regarded, not by peasants alone, as a serious encroachment upon the ancient rights of the nation, and to mislead a gauger, or resist him, even to blood, was considered by few as a fault. That the brightest genius of the nation-one whose tastes and sensibilities were so peculiarly its own-should be, as a reward, set to look after run-rum and smuggled tobacco, and to gauge ale-wife's barrels, was a regret and a marvel to many, and a source of bitter merriment to Burns himself.

The duties of his situation were however performed punctually, if not with pleasure: he was a vigilant officer; he was also a merciful and considerate one: though loving a joke, and not at all averse to a dram, he walked among suspicious brewers, captious ale-wives, and frowning shop-keepers as uprightly as courteously: he smoothed the ruggedest natures into acquiescence by his gayety and humour, and yet never gave cause for a malicious remark, by allowing his vigilance to slumber. He was brave, too, and in the capture of an armed smuggler, in which he led the attack, showed that he neither feared water nor fire: he loved, also, to counsel the more forward of the smugglers to abandon their dangerous calling; his sympathy for the helpless poor induced him to give them now and then notice of his approach; he has been known to interpret the severe laws of the excise into tenderness and mercy in behalf of the widow and the fatherless. In all this he did but his duty to his country and his kind: and his conduct was so regarded by a very competent and candid judge. "Let me look at the books of Burns," said Maxwell, of Terraughty, at the meeting of the district magistrates, "for they show that an upright officer may be a merciful one." With a salary of some seventy pounds a year, the chance of a few guineas annually from the future editions of his poems, and the hope of rising at some distant day to the more lucrative situation of supervisor, Burns continued to live in Dumfries; first in the Bank-vennel, and next in a small house in a humble street, since called by his name.

In his earlier years the poet seems to have scattered songs as thick as a summer eve scatters its dews; nor did he scatter them less carelessly: he appears, indeed, to have thought much less of them than of his poems: the sweet song of Mary Morison, and others not at all inferior, lay unregarded among his papers till accident called them out to shine and be admired. Many of these brief but happy compositions, sometimes with his name, and oftener without, he threw in dozens at a time into Johnson, where they were noticed only by the captious Ritson: but now a work of higher pretence claimed a share in his skill: in September, 1792, he was requested by George Thomson to render, for his national collection, the poetry worthy of the muses of the north, and to take compassion on many choice airs, which had waited for a poet like the author of the Cotter's Saturday Night, to wed them to immortal verse. To engage in such an undertaking, Burns required small persuasion, and while Thomson asked for strains delicate and polished, the poet characteristically stipulated that his contributions were to be without remuneration, and the language seasoned with a sprinkling of the Scottish dialect. As his heart was much in the matter, he began to pour out verse with a readiness and talent unknown in the history of song: his engagement with Thomson, and his esteem for Johnson, gave birth to a series of songs as brilliant as varied, and as naturally easy as they were gracefully original. In looking over those very dissimilar collections it is not difficult to discover that the songs which he wrote for the more stately work, while they are more polished and elegant than those which he contributed to the less pretending one, are at the same time less happy in their humour and less simple in their pathos. "What pleases me as simple and naive," says Burns to Thomson, "disgusts you as ludicrous and low. For this reason 'Fye, gie me my coggie, sirs,' 'Fye, let us a' to the bridal,' with several others of that cast, are to me highly pleasing, while 'Saw ye my Father' delights me with its descriptive simple pathos:" we read in these words the reasons of the difference between the lyrics of the two collections.

The land where the poet lived furnished ready materials for song: hills with fine woods, vales with clear waters, and dames as lovely as any recorded in verse, were to be had in his walks and his visits; while, for the purposes of mirth or of humour, characters, in whose faces originality was legibly written, were as numerous in Nithsdale as he had found them in the west. He had been reproached, while in Kyle, with seeing charms in very ordinary looks, and hanging the garlands of the muse on unlovely altars; he was liable to no such censure in Nithsdale; he poured out the incense of poetry only on the fair and captivating: his Jeans, his Lucys, his Phillises, and his Jessies were ladies of such mental or personal charms as the Reynolds's and the Lawrences of the time would have rejoiced to lay out their choicest colours on. But he did not limit himself to the charms of those whom he could step out to the walks and admire: his lyrics give evidence of the wandering of his thoughts to the distant or the dead-he loves to remember Charlotte Hamilton and Mary Campbell, and think of the sighs and vows on the Devon and the Doon, while his harpstrings were still quivering to the names of the Millers and the M'Murdos-to the charms of the lasses with golden or with flaxen locks, in the valley where he dwelt. Of Jean M'Murdo and her sister Phillis he loved to sing; and their beauty merited his strains: to one who died in her bloom, Lucy Johnston, he addressed a song of great sweetness; to Jessie Lewars, two or three songs of gratitude and praise: nor did he forget other beauties, for the accomplished Mrs. Riddel is remembered, and the absence of fair Clarinda is lamented in strains both impassioned and pathetic.

But the main inspirer of the latter songs of Burns was a young woman of humble birth: of a form equal to the most exquisite proportions of sculpture, with bloom on her cheeks, and merriment in her large bright eyes, enough to drive an amatory poet crazy. Her name was Jean Lorimer; she was not more than seventeen when the poet made her acquaintance, and though she had got a sort of brevet-right from an officer of the army, to use his southron name of Whelpdale, she loved best to be addressed by her maiden designation, while the poet chose to veil her in the numerous lyrics, to which she gave life, under the names of "Chloris," "The lass of Craigie-burnwood," and "The lassie wi' the lintwhite locks." Though of a temper not much inclined to conceal anything, Burns complied so tastefully with the growing demand of the age for the exterior decencies of life, that when the scrupling dames of Caledonia sung a new song in her praise, they were as unconscious whence its beauties came, as is the lover of art, that the shape and gracefulness of the marble nymph which he admires, are derived from a creature who sells the use of her charms indifferently to sculpture or to love. Fine poetry, like other arts called fine, springs from "strange places," as the flower in the fable said, when it bloomed on the dunghill; nor is Burns more to be blamed than was Raphael, who painted Madonnas, and Magdalens with dishevelled hair and lifted eyes, from a loose lady, whom the pope, "Holy at Rome-here Antichrist," charitably prescribed to the artist, while he laboured in the cause of the church. Of the poetic use which he made of Jean Lorimer's charms, Burns gives this account to

Thomson. "The lady of whom the song of Craigie-burnwood was made is one of the finest women in Scotland, and in fact is to me in a manner what Sterne's Eliza was to him-a mistress, or friend, or what you will, in the guileless simplicity of platonic love. I assure you that to my lovely friend you are indebted for many of my best songs. Do you think that the sober gin-horse routine of my existence could inspire a man with life and love and joy-could fire him with enthusiasm, or melt him with pathos, equal to the genius of your book? No! no! Whenever I want to be more than ordinary in song-to be in some degree equal to your diviner airs-do you imagine I fast and pray for the celestial emanation? Quite the contrary. I have a glorious recipe; the very one that for his own use was invented by the divinity of healing and poesy, when erst he piped to the flocks of Admetus. I put myself in a regimen of admiring a fine woman; and in proportion to the adorability of her charms, in proportion are you delighted with my verses. The lightning of her eye is the godhead of Parnassus, and the witchery of her smile, the divinity of Helicon."

Most of the songs which he composed under the influences to which I have alluded are of the first order: "Bonnie Lesley," "Highland Mary," "Auld Rob Morris," "Duncan Gray," "Wandering Willie," "Meg o' the Mill," "The poor and honest sodger," "Bonnie Jean," "Phillis the fair," "John Anderson my Jo," "Had I a cave on some wild distant shore," "Whistle and I'll come to you, my lad," "Bruce's Address to his men at Bannockburn," "Auld Lang Syne," "Thine am I, my faithful fair," "Wilt thou be my dearie," "O Chloris, mark how green the groves," "Contented wi' little, and cantie wi' mair," "Their groves of sweet myrtle," "Last May a braw wooer came down the long glen," "O Mally's meek, Mally's sweet," "Hey for a lass wi' a tocher," "Here's a health to ane I loe dear," and the "Fairest maid on Devon banks." Many of the latter lyrics of Burns were more or less altered, to put them into better harmony with the airs, and I am not the only one who has wondered that a bard so impetuous and intractable in most matters, should have become so soft and pliable, as to make changes which too often sacrificed the poetry for the sake of a fuller and more swelling sound. It is true that the emphatic notes of the music must find their echo in the emphatic words of the verse, and that words soft and liquid are fitter for ladies' lips, than words hissing and rough; but it is also true that in changing a harsher word for one more harmonious the sense often suffers, and that happiness of expression, and that dance of words which lyric verse requires, lose much of their life and vigour. The poet's favourite walk in composing his songs was on a beautiful green sward on the northern side of the Nith, opposite Lincluden: and his favourite posture for composition at home was balancing himself on the hind legs of his arm-chair.

While indulging in these lyrical nights, politics penetrated into Nithsdale, and disturbed the tranquillity of that secluded region. First, there came a contest far the representation of the Dumfries district of boroughs, between Patrick Miller, younger, of Dalswinton, and Sir James Johnstone, of Westerhall, and some two years afterwards, a struggle for the representation of the county of Kirkcudbright, between the interest of the Stewarts, of Galloway, and Patrick Heron, of Kerroughtree. In the first of these the poet mingled discretion with his mirth, and raised a hearty laugh, in which both parties joined; for this sobriety of temper, good reasons may be assigned: Miller, the elder, of Dalswinton, had desired to oblige him in the affair of Ellisland, and his firm and considerate friend, M'Murdo, of Drumlanrig, was chamberlain to his Grace of Queensbury, on whoso interest Miller stood. On the other hand, his old Jacobitical affections made him the secret well-wisher to Westerhall, for up to this time, at least till acid disappointment and the democratic doctrine of the natural equality of man influenced him, Burns, or as a western rhymer of his day and district worded the reproach-Rob was a Tory. His situation, it will therefore be observed, disposed him to moderation, and accounts for the milkiness of his Epistle to Fintray, in which he marshals the chiefs of the contending factions, and foretells the fierceness of the strife, without pretending to foresee the event. Neither is he more explicit, though infinitely more humorous, in his ballad of "The Five Carlins," in which he impersonates the five boroughs-Dumfries, Kirkcudbright, Lochmaben, Sanquhar, and Annan, and draws their characters as shrewd and calculating dames, met in much wrath and drink to choose a representative.

But the two or three years which elapsed between the election for the boroughs, and that for the county adjoining, wrought a serious change in the temper as well as the opinions of the poet. His Jacobitism, as has been said was of a poetic kind, and put on but in obedience to old feelings, and made no part of the man: he was in his heart as democratic as the kirk of Scotland, which educated him-he acknowledged no other superiority but the mental: "he was disposed, too," said Professor Walker, "from constitutional temper, from education and the accidents of life, to a jealousy of power, and a keen hostility against every system which enabled birth and opulence to anticipate those rewards which he conceived to belong to genius and virtue." When we add to this, a resentment of the injurious treatment of the dispensers of public patronage, who had neglected his claims, and showered pensions and places on men unworthy of being named with him, we have assigned causes for the change of side and the tone of asperity and bitterness infused into "The Heron Ballads." Formerly honey was mixed with his gall: a little praise sweetened his censure: in these election lampoons he is fierce and even venomous:-no man has a head but what is empty, nor a heart that is not black: men descended without reproach from lines of heroes are stigmatized as cowards, and the honest and conscientious are reproached as miserly, mean, and dishonourable.

Such is the spirit of party. "I have privately," thus writes the poet to Heron, "printed a good many copies of the ballads, and have sent them among friends about the country. You have already, as your auxiliary, the sober detestation of mankind on the heads of your opponents; find I swear by the lyre of Thalia, to muster on your side all the votaries of honest laughter and fair, candid ridicule." The ridicule was uncandid, and the laughter dishonest. The poet was unfortunate in his political attachments: Miller gained the boroughs which Burns wished he might lose, and Heron lost the county which he foretold he would gain. It must also be recorded against the good taste of the poet, that he loved to recite "The Heron Ballads," and reckon them among his happiest compositions.

From attacking others, the poet was-in the interval between penning these election lampoons-called on to defend himself: for this he seems to have been quite unprepared, though in those yeasty times he might have expected it. "I have been surprised, confounded, and distracted," he thus writes to Graham, of Fintray, "by Mr. Mitchell, the collector, telling me that he has received an order from your board to inquire into my political conduct, and blaming me as a person disaffected to government. Sir, you are a husband and a father: you know what you would feel, to see the much-loved wife of your bosom, and your helpless prattling little ones, turned adrift into the world, degraded and disgraced, from a situation in which they had been respectable and respected. I would not tell a deliberate falsehood, no, not though even worse horrors, if worse can be than those I have mentioned, hung over my head, and I say that the allegation, whatever villain has made it, is a lie! To the British constitution, on Revolution principles, next after my God, I am devotedly attached. To your patronage as a man of some genius, you have allowed me a claim; and your esteem as an honest man I know is my due. To these, sir, permit me to appeal: by these I adjure you to save me from that misery which threatens to overwhelm me, and which with my latest breath I will say I have not deserved." In this letter, another, intended for the eye of the Commissioners of the Board of Excise, was enclosed, in which he disclaimed entertaining the idea of a British republic-a wild dream of the day-but stood by the principles of the constitution of 1688, with the wish to see such corruptions as had crept in, amended. This last remark, it appears, by a letter from the poet to Captain Erskine, afterwards Earl of Mar, gave great offence, for Corbet, one of the superiors, was desired to inform him, "that his business was to act, and not to think; and that whatever might be men or measures, it was his duty to be silent and obedient." The intercession of Fintray, and the explanations of Burns, were so far effectual, that his political offense was forgiven, "only I understand," said he, "that all hopes of my getting officially forward are blasted." The records of the Excise Office exhibit no trace of this memorable matter, and two noblemen, who were then in the government, have assured me that this harsh proceeding received no countenance at head-quarters, and must have originated with some ungenerous or malicious person, on whom the poet had spilt a little of the nitric acid of his wrath.

That Burns was numbered among the republicans of Dumfries I well remember: but then those who held different sentiments from the men in power, were all, in that loyal town, stigmatized as democrats: that he either desired to see the constitution changed, or his country invaded by the liberal French, who proposed to set us free with the bayonet, and then admit us to the "fraternal embrace," no one ever believed. It is true that he spoke of premiers and peers with contempt; that he hesitated to take off his hat in the theatre, to the air of "God save the king;" that he refused to drink the health of Pitt, saying he preferred that of Washington-a far greater man; that he wrote bitter words against that combination of princes, who desired to put down freedom in France; that he said the titled spurred and the wealthy switched England and Scotland like two hack-horses; and that all the high places of the land, instead of being filled by genius and talent, were occupied, as were the high-places of Israel, with idols of wood or of stone. But all this and more had been done and said before by thousands in this land, whose love of their country was never questioned. That it was bad taste to refuse to remove his hat when other heads were bared, and little better to refuse to pledge in company the name of Pitt, because he preferred Washington, cannot admit of a doubt; but that he deserved to be written down traitor, for mere matters of whim or caprice, or to be turned out of the unenvied situation of "gauging auld wives' barrels," because he thought there were some stains on the white robe of the constitution, seems a sort of tyranny new in the history of oppression. His love of country is recorded in too many undying lines to admit of a doubt now: nor is it that chivalrous love alone which men call romantic; it is a love which may be laid up in every man's heart and practised in every man's life; the words are homely, but the words of Burns are always expressive:-

"The kettle of the kirk and state Perhaps a clout may fail in't, But deil a foreign tinkler loon Shall ever ca' a nail in't. Be Britons still to Britons true, Amang ourselves united; For never but by British hands Shall British wrongs be righted."

But while verses, deserving as these do to become the national motto, and sentiments loyal and generous, were overlooked and forgotten, all his rash words about freedom, and his sarcastic sallies about thrones and kings, were treasured up to his injury, by the mean and the malicious. His steps were watched and his words weighed; when he talked with a friend in the street, he was supposed to utter sedition; and when ladies retired from the table, and the wine circulated with closed doors, he was suspected of treason rather than of toasting, which he often did with much humour, the charms of woman; even when he gave as a sentiment, "May our success be equal to the justice of our cause," he was liable to be challenged by some gunpowder captain, who thought that we deserved success in war, whether right or wrong. It is true that he hated with a most cordial hatred all who presumed on their own consequence, whether arising from wealth, titles, or commissions in the army; officers he usually called "the epauletted puppies," and lords he generally spoke of as "feather-headed fools," who could but strut and stare and be no answer in kind to retort his satiric flings, his unfriends reported that it was unsafe for young men to associate with one whose principles were democratic, and scarcely either modest or safe for young women to listen to a poet whose notions of female virtue were so loose and his songs so free. These sentiments prevailed so far that a gentleman on a visit from London, told me he was dissuaded from inviting Burns to a dinner, given by way of welcome back to his native place, because he was the associate of democrats and loose people; and when a modest dame of Dumfries expressed, through a friend, a wish to have but the honour of speaking to one of whose genius she was an admirer, the poet declined the interview, with a half-serious smile, saying, "Alas! she is handsome, and you know the character publicly assigned to me." She escaped the danger of being numbered, it is likely, with the Annas and the Chlorises of his freer strains.

The neglect of his country, the tyranny of the Excise, and the downfall of his hopes and fortunes, were now to bring forth their fruits-the poet's health began to decline. His drooping looks, his neglect of his person, his solitary saunterings, his escape from the stings of reflection into socialities, and his distempered joy in the company of beauty, all spoke, as plainly as with a tongue, of a sinking heart and a declining body. Yet though he was sensible of sinking health, hope did not at once desert him: he continued to pour out such tender strains, and to show such flashes of wit and humour at the call of Thomson, as are recorded of no other lyrist: neither did he, when in company after his own mind, hang the head, and speak mournfully, but talked and smiled and still charmed all listeners by his witty vivacities.

On the 20th of June, 1795, he writes thus of his fortunes and condition to his friend Clarke, "Still, still the victim of affliction; were you to see the emaciated figure who now holds the pen to you, you would not know your old friend. Whether I shall ever get about again is only known to HIM, the Great Unknown, whoso creature I am. Alas, Clarke, I begin to fear the worst! As to my individual self I am tranquil, and would despise myself if I were not: but Burns's poor widow and half-a-dozen of his dear little ones, helpless orphans! Here I am as weak as a woman's tear. Enough of this! 'tis half my disease. I duly received your last, enclosing the note: it came extremely in time, and I am much obliged to your punctuality. Again I must request you to do me the same kindness. Be so very good as by return of post to enclose me another note: I trust you can do so without inconvenience, and it will seriously oblige me. If I must go, I leave a few friends behind me, whom I shall regret while consciousness remains. I know I shall live in their remembrance. O, dear, dear Clarke! that I shall ever see you again is I am afraid highly improbable." This remarkable letter proves both the declining health, and the poverty of the poet: his digestion was so bad that he could taste neither flesh nor fish: porridge and milk he could alone swallow, and that but in small quantities. When it is recollected that he had no more than thirty shillings a week to keep house, and live like a gentleman, no one need wonder that his wife had to be obliged to a generous neighbour for some of the chief necessaries for her coming confinement, and that the poet had to beg, in extreme need, two guinea notes from a distant friend.

His sinking state was not unobserved by his friends, and Syme and M'Murdo united with Dr. Maxwell in persuading him, at the beginning of the summer, to seek health at the Brow-well, a few miles east of Dumfries, where there were pleasant walks on the Solway-side, and salubrious breezes from the sea, which it was expected would bring the health to the poet they had brought to many. For a while, his looks brightened up, and health seemed inclined to return: his friend, the witty and accomplished Mrs. Riddel, who was herself ailing, paid him a visit. "I was struck," she said, "with his appearance on entering the room: the stamp of death was impressed on his features. His first words were, 'Well, Madam, have you any commands for the other world?' I replied that it seemed a doubtful case which of us should be there soonest; he looked in my face with an air of great kindness, and expressed his concern at seeing me so ill, with his usual sensibility. At table he ate little or nothing: we had a long conversation about his present state, and the approaching termination of all his earthly prospects. He showed great concern about his literary fame, and particularly the publication of his posthumous works; he said he was well aware that his death would occasion some noise, and that every scrap of his writing would be revived against him, to the injury of his future reputation; that letters and verses, written with unguarded freedom, would be handed about by vanity or malevolence when no dread of his resentment would restrain them, or prevent malice or envy from pouring forth their venom on his name. I had seldom seen his mind greater, or more collected. There was frequently a considerable degree of vivacity in his sallies; but the concern and dejection I could not disguise, damped the spirit of pleasantry he seemed willing to indulge." This was on the evening of the 5th of July; another lady who called to see him, found him seated at a window, gazing on the sun, then setting brightly on the summits of the green hills of Nithsdale. "Look how lovely the sun is," said the poet, "but he will soon have done with shining for me."

He now longed for home: his wife, whom he ever tenderly loved, was about to be confined in child-bed: his papers were in sad confusion, and required arrangement; and he felt that desire to die, at least, among familiar things and friendly faces, so common to our nature. He had not long before, though much reduced in pocket, refused with scorn an offer of fifty pounds, which a speculating bookseller made, for leave to publish his looser compositions; he had refused an offer of the like sum yearly, from Perry of the Morning Chronicle, for poetic contributions to his paper, lest it might embroil him with the ruling powers, and he had resented the remittance of five pounds from Thomson, on account of his lyric contributions, and desired him to do so no more, unless he wished to quarrel with him; but his necessities now, and they had at no time been so great, induced him to solicit five pounds from Thomson, and ten pounds from his cousin, James Burness, of Montrose, and to beg his friend Alexander Cunningham to intercede with the Commissioners of Excise, to depart from their usual practice, and grant him his full salary; "for without that," he added, "if I die not of disease, I must perish with hunger." Thomson sent the five pounds, James Burness sent the ten, but the Commissioners of Excise refused to be either merciful or generous. Stobie, a young expectant in the customs, was both;-he performed the duties of the dying poet, and refused to touch the salary. The mind of Burns was haunted with the fears of want and the terrors of a jail; nor were those fears without foundation; one Williamson, to whom he was indebted for the cloth to make his volunteer regimentals, threatened the one; and a feeling that he was without money for either his own illness or the confinement of his wife, threatened the other.

Burns returned from the Brow-well, on the 18th of July: as he walked from the little carriage which brought him up the Mill hole-brae to his own door, he trembled much, and stooped with weakness and pain, and kept his feet with difficulty: his looks were woe-worn and ghastly, and no one who saw him, and there were several, expected to see him again in life. It was soon circulated through Dumfries, that Burns had returned worse from the Brow-well; that Maxwell thought ill of him, and that, in truth, he was dying. The anxiety of all classes was great; differences of opinion were forgotten, in sympathy for his early fate: wherever two or three were met together their talk was of Burns, of his rare wit, matchless humour, the vivacity of his conversation, and the kindness of his heart. To the poet himself, death, which he now knew was at hand, brought with it no fear; his good-humour, which small matters alone ruffled, did not forsake him, and his wit was ever ready. He was poor-he gave his pistols, which he had used against the smugglers on the Solway, to his physician, adding with a smile, that he had tried them and found them an honour to their maker, which was more than he could say of the bulk of mankind! He was proud-he remembered the indifferent practice of the corps to which he belonged, and turning to

Gibson, one of his fellow-soldiers, who stood at his bedside with wet eyes, "John," said he, and a gleam of humour passed over his face, "pray don't let the awkward-squad fire over me." It was almost the last act of his life to copy into his Common-place Book, the letters which contained the charge against him of the Commissioners of Excise, and his own eloquent refutation, leaving judgment to be pronounced by the candour of posterity.

It has been injuriously said of Burns, by Coleridge, that the man sunk, but the poet was bright to the last: he did not sink in the sense that these words imply: the man was manly to the latest draught of breath. That he was a poet to the last, can be proved by facts, as well as by the word of the author of Christabel. As he lay silently growing weaker and weaker, he observed Jessie Lewars, a modest and beautiful young creature, and sister to one of his brethren of the Excise, watching over him with moist eyes, and tending him with the care of a daughter; he rewarded her with one of those songs which are an insurance against forgetfulness. The lyrics of the north have nothing finer than this exquisite stanza:-

"Altho' thou maun never be mine, Altho' even hope is denied, 'Tis sweeter for thee despairing, Than aught in the world beside."

His thoughts as he lay wandered to Charlotte Hamilton, and he dedicated some beautiful stanzas to her beauty and her coldness, beginning, "Fairest maid on Devon banks."

It was a sad sight to see the poet gradually sinking; his wife in hourly expectation of her sixth confinement, and his four helpless children-a daughter, a sweet child, had died the year before-with no one of their lineage to soothe them with kind words or minister to their wants. Jessie Lewars, with equal prudence and attention, watched over them all: she could not help seeing that the thoughts of the desolation which his death would bring, pressed sorely on him, for he loved his children, and hoped much from his boys. He wrote to his father-in-law, James Armour, at Mauchline, that he was dying, his wife nigh her confinement, and begged that his mother-in-law would hasten to them and speak comfort. He wrote to Mrs. Dunlop, saying, "I have written to you so often without receiving any answer that I would not trouble you again, but for the circumstances in which I am. An illness which has long hung about me in all probability will speedily send me beyond that bourne whence no traveller returns. Your friendship, with which for many years you honoured me, was a friendship dearest to my soul: your conversation and your correspondence were at once highly entertaining and instructive-with what pleasure did I use to break up the seal! The remembrance yet adds one pulse more to my poor palpitating heart. Farewell!" A tremor pervaded his frame; his tongue grew parched, and he was at times delirious: on the fourth day after his return, when his attendant, James Maclure, held his medicine to his lips, he swallowed it eagerly, rose almost wholly up, spread out his hands, sprang forward nigh the whole length of the bed, fell on his face, and expired. He died on the 21st of July, when nearly thirty-seven years and seven months old.

The burial of Burns, on the 25th of July, was an impressive and mournful scene: half the people of Nithsdale and the neighbouring parts of Galloway had crowded into Dumfries, to see their poet "mingled with the earth," and not a few had been permitted to look at his body, laid out for interment. It was a calm and beautiful day, and as the body was borne along the street towards the old kirk-yard, by his brethren of the volunteers, not a sound was heard but the measured step and the solemn music: there was no impatient crushing, no fierce elbowing-the crowd which filled the street seemed conscious of what they were now losing for ever. Even while this pageant was passing, the widow of the poet was taken in labour; but the infant born in that unhappy hour soon shared his father's grave. On reaching the northern nook of the kirk-yard, where the grave was made, the mourners halted; the coffin was divested of the mort-cloth, and silently lowered to its resting-place, and as the first shovel-full of earth fell on the lid, the volunteers, too agitated to be steady, justified the fears of the poet, by three ragged volleys. He who now writes this very brief and imperfect account, was present: he thought then, as he thinks now, that all the military array of foot and horse did not harmonize with either the genius or the fortunes of the poet, and that the tears which he saw on many cheeks around, as the earth was replaced, were worth all the splendour of a show which mocked with unintended mockery the burial of the poor and neglected Burns. The body of the poet was, on the 5th of June, 1815, removed to a more commodious spot in the same burial-ground-his dark, and waving locks looked then fresh and glossy-to afford room for a marble monument, which embodies, with neither skill nor grace, that well-known passage in the dedication to the gentlemen of the Caledonian Hunt:-"The poetic genius of my country found me, as the prophetic bard, Elijah, did Elisha, at the plough, and threw her inspiring mantle over me." The dust of the bard was again disturbed, when the body of Mrs. Burns was laid, in April, 1834, beside the remains of her husband: his skull was dug up by the district craniologists, to satisfy their minds by measurement that he was equal to the composition of "Tam o' Shanter," or "Mary in Heaven." This done, they placed the skull in a leaden box, "carefully lined with the softest materials," and returned it, we hope for ever, to the hallowed ground.

Thus lived and died Robert Burns, the chief of Scottish poets: in his person he was tall and sinewy, and of such strength and activity, that Scott alone, of all the poets I have seen, seemed his equal: his forehead was broad, his hair black, with an inclination to curl, his visage uncommonly swarthy, his eyes large, dark and lustrous, and his voice deep and manly. His sensibility was strong, his passions full to overflowing, and he loved, nay, adored, whatever was gentle and beautiful. He had, when a lad at the plough, an eloquent word and an inspired song for every fair face that smiled on him, and a sharp sarcasm or a fierce lampoon for every rustic who thwarted or contradicted him. As his first inspiration came from love, he continued through life to love on, and was as ready with the lasting incense of the muse for the ladies of Nithsdale as for the lasses of Kyle: his earliest song was in praise of a young girl who reaped by his side, when he was seventeen-his latest in honour of a lady by whose side he had wandered and dreamed on the banks of the Devon. He was of a nature proud and suspicious, and towards the close of his life seemed disposed to regard all above him in rank as men who unworthily possessed the patrimony of genius: he desired to see the order of nature restored, and worth and talent in precedence of the base or the dull. He had no medium in his hatred or his love; he never spared the stupid, as if they were not to be endured because he was bright; and on the heads of the innocent possessors of titles or wealth he was ever ready to shower his lampoons. He loved to start doubts in religion which he knew inspiration only could solve, and he spoke of Calvinism with a latitude of language that grieved pious listeners. He was warm-hearted and generous to a degree, above all men, and scorned all that was selfish and mean with a scorn quite romantic. He was a steadfast friend and a good neighbour: while he lived at Ellisland few passed his door without being entertained at his table; and even when in poverty, on the Millhole-brae, the poor seldom left his door but with blessings on their lips. Of his modes of study he has himself informed us, as well as of the seasons and the places in which he loved to muse. He composed while he strolled along the secluded banks of the Doon, the Ayr, or the Nith: as the images crowded on his fancy his pace became quickened, and in his highest moods he was excited even to tears. He loved the winter for its leafless trees, its swelling floods, and its winds which swept along the gloomy sky, with frost and snow on their wings: but he loved the autumn more-he has neglected to say why-the muse was then more liberal of her favours, and he composed with a happy alacrity unfelt in all other seasons. He filled his mind and heart with the materials of song-and retired from gazing on woman's beauty, and from the excitement of her charms, to record his impressions in verse, as a painter delineates oil his canvas the looks of those who sit to his pencil. His chief place of study at Ellisland is still remembered: it extends along the river-bank towards the Isle: there the neighbouring gentry love to walk and peasants to gather, and hold it sacred, as the place where he composed Tam O' Shanter. His favourite place of study when residing in Dumfries, was the ruins of Lincluden College, made classic by that sublime ode, "The Vision," and that level and clovery sward contiguous to the College, on the northern side of the Nith: the latter place was his favourite resort; it is known now by the name of Burns's musing ground, and there he conceived many of his latter lyrics. In case of interruption he completed the verses at the fireside, where he swung to and fro in his arm-chair till the task was done: he then submitted the song to the ordeal of his wife's voice, which was both sweet and clear, and while she sung he listened attentively, and altered or amended till the whole was in harmony, music and words.

The genius of Burns is of a high order: in brightness of expression and unsolicited ease and natural vehemence of language, he stands in the first rank of poets: in choice of subjects, in happiness of conception, and loftiness of imagination, he recedes into the second. He owes little of his fame to his objects, for, saving the beauty of a few ladies, they were all of an ordinary kind: he sought neither in romance nor in history for themes to the muse; he took up topics from life around which were familiar to all, and endowed them with character, with passion, with tenderness, with humour-elevating all that he touched into the regions of poetry and morals. He went to no far lands for the purpose of surprising us with wonders, neither did he go to crowns or coronets to attract the stare of the peasantry around him, by things which to them were as a book shut and sealed: "The Daisy" grew on the lands which he ploughed; "The Mouse" built her frail nest on his own stubble-field; "The Haggis" reeked on his own table; "The Scotch Drink" of which he sang was the produce of a neighbouring still; "The Twa Dogs," which conversed so wisely and wittily, were, one of them at least, his own collies; "The Vision" is but a picture, and a brilliant one, of his own hopes and fears; "Tam Samson" was a friend whom he loved; "Doctor Hornbook" a neighbouring pedant; "Matthew Henderson" a social captain on half-pay; "The Scotch Bard" who had gone to the West Indies was Burns himself; the heroine of "The Lament," was Jean Armour; and "Tam O' Shanter" a facetious farmer of Kyle, who rode late and loved pleasant company, nay, even "The Deil" himself, whom he had the hardihood to address, was a being whose eldrich croon bad alarmed the devout matrons of Kyle, and had wandered, not unseen by the bard himself, among the lonely glens of the Doon. Burns was one of the first to teach the world that high moral poetry resided in the humblest subjects: whatever he touched became elevated; his spirit possessed and inspired the commonest topics, and endowed them with life and beauty.

His songs have all the beauties and but few of them the faults of his poems: they flow to the music as readily as if both air and words came into the world together. The sentiments are from nature, they are rarely strained or forced, and the words dance in their places and echo the music in its pastoral sweetness, social glee, or in the tender and the moving. He seems always to write with woman's eye upon him: he is gentle, persuasive and impassioned: he appears to watch her looks, and pours out his praise or his complaint according to the changeful moods of her mind. He looks on her, too, with a sculptor's as well as a poet's eye: to him who works in marble, the diamonds, emeralds, pearls, and elaborate ornaments of gold, but load and injure the harmony of proportion, the grace of form, and divinity of sentiment of his nymph or his goddess-so with Burns the fashion of a lady's boddice, the lustre of her satins, or the sparkle of her diamonds, or other finery with which wealth or taste has loaded her, are neglected us idle frippery; while her beauty, her form, or her mind, matters which are of nature and not of fashion, are remembered and praised. He is none of the millinery bards, who deal in scented silks, spider-net laces, rare gems, set in rarer workmanship, and who shower diamonds and pearls by the bushel on a lady's locks: he makes bright eyes, flushing cheeks, the magic of the tongue, and the "pulses' maddening play" perform all. His songs are, in general, pastoral pictures: he seldom finishes a portrait of female beauty without enclosing it in a natural frame-work of waving woods, running streams, the melody of birds, and the lights of heaven. Those who desire to feel Burns in all his force, must seek some summer glen, when a country girl searches among his many songs for one which sympathizes with her own heart, and gives it full utterance, till wood and vale is filled with the melody. It is remarkable that the most naturally elegant and truly impassioned songs in our literature were written by a ploughman in honour of the rustic lasses around him.

His poetry is all life and energy, and bears the impress of a warm heart and a clear understanding: it abounds with passions and opinions-vivid pictures of rural happiness and the raptures of successful love, all fresh from nature and observation, and not as they are seen through the spectacles of books. The wit of the clouted shoe is there without its coarseness: there is a prodigality of humour without licentiousness, a pathos ever natural and manly, a social joy akin sometimes to sadness, a melancholy not unallied to mirth, and a sublime morality which seeks to elevate and soothe. To a love of man he added an affection for the flowers of the valley, the fowls of the air, and the beasts of the field: he perceived the tie of social sympathy which united animated with unanimated nature, and in many of his finest poems most beautifully he has enforced it. His thoughts are original and his style new and unborrowed: all that he has written is distinguished by a happy carelessness, a bounding elasticity of spirit, and a singular felicity of expression, simple yet inimitable; he is familiar yet dignified, careless, yet correct, and concise, yet clear and full. All this and much more is embodied in the language of humble life-a dialect reckoned barbarous by scholars, but which, coming from the lips of inspiration, becomes classic and elevated.

The prose of this great poet has much of the original merit of his verse, but it is seldom so natural and so sustained: it abounds with fine outflashings and with a genial warmth and vigour, but it is defaced by false ornament and by a constant anxiety to say fine and forcible things. He seems not to know that simplicity was as rare and as needful a beauty in prose as in verse; he covets the pauses of Sterne and the point and antithesis of Junius, like one who believes that to write prose well he must be ever lively, ever pointed, and ever smart. Yet the account which he wrote of himself to Dr. Moore is one of the most spirited and natural narratives in the language, and composed in a style remote from the strained and groped-for witticisms and put-on sensibilities of many of his letters:-"Simple," as John Wilson says, "we may well call it; rich in fancy, overflowing in feeling, and dashed off in every other paragraph with the easy boldness of a great master."

PREFACE

[The first edition, printed at Kilmarnock, July, 1786, by John Wilson, bore on the title-page these simple words:-"Poems, chiefly in the Scottish Dialect, by Robert Burns;" the following motto, marked "Anonymous," but evidently the poet's own composition, was more ambitious:-
"The simple Bard, unbroke by rules of art, He pours the wild effusions of the heart: And if inspired, 'tis nature's pow'rs inspire- Hers all the melting thrill, and hers the kindling fire."]
The following trifles are not the production of the Poet, who, with all the advantages of learned art, and perhaps amid the elegancies and idlenesses of upper life, looks down for a rural theme with an eye to Theocritus or Virgil. To the author of this, these, and other celebrated names their countrymen, are, at least in their original language, a fountain shut up, and a book sealed. Unacquainted with the necessary requisites for commencing poet by rule, he sings the sentiments and manners he felt and saw in himself and his rustic compeers around him in his and their native language. Though a rhymer from his earliest years, at least from the earliest impulse of the softer passions, it was not till very lately that the applause, perhaps the partiality, of friendship awakened his vanity so for as to make him think anything of his worth showing: and none of the following works were composed with a view to the press. To amuse himself with the little creations of his own fancy, amid the toil and fatigue of a laborious life; to transcribe the various feelings-the loves, the griefs, the hopes, the fears-in his own breast; to find some kind of counterpoise to the struggles of a world, always an alien scene, a task uncouth to the poetical mind-these were his motives for courting the Muses, and in these he found poetry to be its own reward.
Now that he appears in the public character of an author, he does it with

fear and trembling. So dear is fame to the rhyming tribe, that even he, an obscure, nameless Bard, shrinks aghast at the thought of being branded as-an impertinent blockhead, obtruding his nonsense on the world; and, because he can make a shift to jingle a few doggerel Scotch rhymes together, looking upon himself as a poet of no small consequence, forsooth!

It is an observation of that celebrated poet, Shenstone, whose divine elegies do honour to our language, our nation, and our species, that "Humility has depressed many a genius to a hermit, but never raised one to fame!" If any critic catches at the word genius the author tells him, once for all, that he certainly looks upon himself as possessed of some poetic abilities, otherwise his publishing in the manner he has done would be a manœuvre below the worst character, which, he hopes, his worst enemy will ever give him. But to the genius of a Ramsay, or the glorious dawnings of the poor, unfortunate Fergusson, he, with equal unaffected sincerity, declares, that even in his highest pulse of vanity, he has not the most distant pretensions. These two justly admired Scotch poets he has often had in his eye in the following pieces, but rather with a view to kindle at their flame, than for servile imitation.

To his Subscriber, the Author returns his most sincere thanks. Not the mercenary bow over a counter, but the heart-throbbing gratitude of the Bard, conscious how much he owes to benevolence and friendship for gratifying him, if he deserves it, in that dearest wish of every poetic bosom-to be distinguished. He begs his readers, particularly the learned and the polite, who may honour him with a perusal, that they will make every allowance for education and circumstances of life; but if, after a fair, candid, and impartial criticism, he shall stand convicted of dulness and nonsense, let him be done by as he would in that case do by others-let him be condemned, without mercy, in contempt and oblivion.

PART I. THE POETICAL WORKS OF ROBERT BURNS

CHAPTER I.
WINTER.

A DIRGE.
[This is one of the earliest of the poet's recorded compositions: it was written before the death of his father, and is called by Gilbert Burns, 'a juvenile production.' To walk by a river while flooded, or through a wood on a rough winter day, and hear the storm howling among the leafless trees, exalted the poet's thoughts. "In such a season," he said, "just after a train of misfortunes, I composed Winter, a Dirge."]
The wintry west extends his blast, And hail and rain does blaw; Or the stormy north sends driving forth The blinding sleet and snaw; While tumbling brown, the burn comes down, And roars frae bank to brae; And bird and beast in covert rest, And pass the heartless day.
"The sweeping blast, the sky o'ercast,"[1] The joyless winter day Let others fear, to me more dear Than all the pride of May: The tempest's howl, it soothes my soul, My griefs it seems to join; The leafless trees my fancy please, Their fate resembles mine!
Thou Power Supreme, whose mighty scheme These woes of mine fulfil, Here, firm, I rest, they must be best, Because they are Thy will! Then all I want (O, do thou grant This one request of mine!) Since to enjoy Thou dost deny, Assist me to resign!
FOOTNOTES:
[1] Dr. Young.
CHAPTER II.

THE DEATH AND DYING WORDS OF POOR MAILIE, THE AUTHOR'S ONLY PET YOWE. AN UNCO MOURNFU' TALE.

[This tale is partly true; the poet's pet ewe got entangled in her tether, and tumbled into a ditch; the face of ludicrous and awkward sorrow with which this was related by Hughoc, the herd-boy, amused Burns so much, who was on his way to the plough, that he immediately composed the poem, and repeated it to his brother Gilbert when they met in the evening; the field where the poet held the plough, and the ditch into which poor Mailie fell, are still pointed out.]

As Mailie, an' her lambs thegither, Were ae day nibbling on the tether, Upon her cloot she coost a hitch, An' owre she warsl'd in the ditch: There, groaning, dying, she did lie, When Hughoc[2] he cam doytin by. Wi' glowing e'en an' lifted han's, Poor Hughoc like a statue stan's; He saw her days were near-hand ended, But, waes my heart! he could na mend it! He gaped wide but naething spak- At length poor Mailie silence brak.

"O thou, whose lamentable face Appears to mourn my woefu' case! My dying words attentive hear, An' bear them to my master dear.

"Tell him, if e'er again he keep As muckle gear as buy a sheep, O bid him never tie them mair Wi' wicked strings o' hemp or hair! But ca' them out to park or hill, An' let them wander at their will; So may his flock increase, and grow To scores o' lambs, an' packs of woo'!

"Tell him he was a master kin' An' ay was gude to me an' mine; An' now my dying charge I gie him, My helpless lambs, I trust them wi' him.

"O, bid him save their harmless lives Frae dogs, and tods, an' butchers' knives! But gie them guid cow-milk their fill, Till they be fit to fend themsel; An' tent them duly, e'en an' morn, Wi' teats o' hay, an' ripps o' corn.

"An' may they never learn the gaets Of ither vile, wanrestfu' pets! To sink thro' slaps, an' reave an' steal At stacks o' pease, or stocks o' kail. So may they, like their great forbears, For monie a year come thro' the sheers; So wives will gie them bits o' bread, An' bairns greet for them when they're dead.

"My poor toop-lamb, my son an' heir, O, bid him breed him up wi' care; An' if he live to be a beast, To pit some havins in his breast! An' warn him what I winna name, To stay content wi' yowes at hame An' no to rin an' wear his cloots, Like ither menseless, graceless brutes.

"An' niest my yowie, silly thing, Gude keep thee frae a tether string! O, may thou ne'er forgather up Wi' ony blastit, moorland toop, But ay keep mind to moop an' mell Wi' sheep o' credit like thysel!

"And now, my bairns, wi' my last breath I lea'e my blessin wi' you baith: An' when you think upo' your mither, Mind to be kind to ane anither.

"Now, honest Hughoc, dinna fail To tell my master a' my tale; An' bid him

burn this cursed tether, An', for thy pains, thou'se get my blather."
This said, poor Mailie turn'd her head, And clos'd her een amang the dead.
FOOTNOTES:
[2] A neibor herd-callan.

CHAPTER III.

POOR MAILIE'S ELEGY.

[Burns, when he calls on the bards of Ayr and Doon to join in the lament for Mailie, intimates that he regards himself as a poet. Hogg calls it a very elegant morsel: but says that it resembles too closely "The Ewie and the Crooked Horn," to be admired as original: the shepherd might have remembered that they both resemble Sempill's "Life and death of the Piper of Kilbarchan."]

Lament in rhyme, lament in prose, Wi' saut tears trickling down your nose; Our bardie's fate is at a close, Past a' remead; The last sad cape-stane of his woes; Poor Mailie's dead.

It's no the loss o' warl's gear, That could sae bitter draw the tear, Or mak our bardie, dowie, wear The mourning weed; He's lost a friend and neebor dear, In Mailie dead.

Thro' a' the toun she trotted by him; A long half-mile she could descry him; Wi' kindly bleat, when she did spy him, She run wi' speed: A friend mair faithfu' ne'er cam nigh him, Than Mailie dead.

I wat she was a sheep o' sense, An' could behave hersel wi' mense: I'll say't, she never brak a fence, Thro' thievish greed. Our bardie, tamely, keeps the spence Sin' Mailie's dead.

Or, if he wonders up the howe, Her living image in her yowe Comes bleating to him, owre the knowe, For bits o' bread; An' down the briny pearls rowe For Mailie dead.

She was nae get o' moorland tips,[3] Wi' tawted ket, an hairy hips; For her forbears were brought in ships Frae yont the Tweed: A bonnier fleesh ne'er cross'd the clips Than Mailie dead.

Wae worth the man wha first did shape That vile, wanchancie thing-a rape! It maks guid fellows girn an' gape, Wi' chokin dread; An' Robin's bonnet wave wi' crape, For Mailie dead.

O, a' ye bards on bonnie Doon! An' wha on Ayr your chanters tune! Come, join the melancholious croon O' Robin's reed! His heart will never get aboon! His Mailie's dead!

FOOTNOTES:
[3] VARIATION.
'She was nae get o' runted rams, Wi' woo' like goats an' legs like trams; She was the flower o' Farlie lambs, A famous breed! Now Robin, greetin, chews the hams O' Mailie dead.'

CHAPTER IV.

FIRST EPISTLE TO DAVIE, A BROTHER POET

[In the summer of 1781, Burns, while at work in the garden, repeated this Epistle to his brother Gilbert, who was much pleased with the performance, which he considered equal if not superior to some of Allan Ramsay's Epistles, and said if it were printed he had no doubt that it would be well received by people of taste.]

-January, [1784.]

I.

While winds frae aff Ben-Lomond blaw, And bar the doors wi' driving snaw, And hing us owre the ingle, I set me down to pass the time, And spin a verse or twa o' rhyme, In hamely westlin jingle. While frosty winds blaw in the drift, Ben to the chimla lug, I grudge a wee the great folks' gift, That live sae bien an' snug: I tent less and want less Their roomy fire-side; But hanker and canker To see their cursed pride.

II.

It's hardly in a body's power To keep, at times, frae being sour, To see how things are shar'd; How best o' chiels are whiles in want. While coofs on countless thousands rant, And ken na how to wair't; But Davie, lad, ne'er fash your head, Tho' we hae little gear, We're fit to win our daily bread, As lang's we're hale and fier: "Muir spier na, nor fear na,"[4] Auld age ne'er mind a feg, The last o't, the warst o't, Is only but to beg.

III.

To lie in kilns and barns at e'en When banes are craz'd, and bluid is thin, Is, doubtless, great distress! Yet then content could make us blest; Ev'n then, sometimes we'd snatch a taste O' truest happiness. The honest heart that's free frae a' Intended fraud or guile, However Fortune kick the ba', Has ay some cause to smile: And mind still, you'll find still, A comfort this nae sma'; Nae mair then, we'll care then, Nae farther we can fa'.

IV.

What tho', like commoners of air, We wander out we know not where, But either house or hall? Yet nature's charms, the hills and woods, The sweeping vales, and foaming floods, Are free alike to all. In days when daisies deck the ground, And blackbirds whistle clear, With honest joy our hearts will bound To see the coming year: On braes when we please, then, We'll sit and sowth a tune; Syne rhyme till't we'll time till't, And sing't when we hae done.

V.

It's no in titles nor in rank; It's no in wealth like Lon'on bank, To purchase peace and rest; It's no in makin muckle mair; It's no in books, it's no in lear, To make us truly blest; If happiness hae not her seat And centre in the breast, We may be wise, or rich, or great, But never can be blest: Nae treasures, nor pleasures, Could make us happy lang; The heart ay's the part ay That makes us right or wrang.

VI.

Think ye, that sic as you and I, Wha drudge and drive thro' wet an' dry, Wi' never-ceasing toil; Think ye, are we less blest than they, Wha scarcely tent us in their way, As hardly worth their while? Alas! how aft, in haughty mood God's creatures they oppress! Or else, neglecting a' that's guid, They riot in excess! Baith careless and fearless Of either heaven or hell! Esteeming and deeming It's a' an idle tale!

VII.

Then let us cheerfu' acquiesce; Nor make one scanty pleasures less, By pining at our state; And, even should misfortunes come, I, here wha sit, hae met wi' some, An's thankfu' for them yet. They gie the wit of age to youth; They let us ken oursel'; They make us see the naked truth, The real guid and ill. Tho' losses, and crosses, Be lessons right severe, There's wit there, ye'll get there, Ye'll find nae other where.

VIII.

But tent me, Davie, ace o' hearts! (To say aught less wad wrang the cartes, And flatt'ry I detest,) This life has joys for you and I; And joys that riches ne'er could buy: And joys the very best. There's a' the pleasures o' the heart, The lover an' the frien'; Ye hae your Meg your dearest part, And I my darling Jean! It warms me, it charms me, To mention but her name: It heats me, it beets me, And sets me a' on flame!

IX.

O, all ye pow'rs who rule above! O, Thou, whose very self art love! Thou know'st my words sincere! The life-blood streaming thro' my heart, Or my more dear immortal part, Is not more fondly dear! When heart-corroding care and grief Deprive my soul of rest, Her dear idea brings relief And solace to my breast. Thou Being, All-seeing, O hear my fervent pray'r! Still take her, and make her Thy most peculiar care!

X.

All hail, ye tender feelings dear! The smile of love, the friendly tear, The sympathetic glow! Long since, this world's thorny ways Had number'd out my weary days, Had it not been for you! Fate still has blest me with a friend, In every care and ill; And oft a more endearing hand, A tie more tender still. It lightens, it brightens The tenebrific scene, To meet with, and greet with My Davie or my Jean!

XI.

O, how that name inspires my style The words come skelpin, rank and file, Amaist before I ken! The ready measure rins as fine, As Phœbus and the famous Nine Were glowrin owre my pen. My spaviet Pegasus will limp, 'Till ance he's fairly het; And then he'll hilch, and stilt, and jimp, An' rin an unco fit: But least then, the beast then Should rue this hasty ride, I'll light now, and dight now His sweaty, wizen'd hide.

FOOTNOTES:

[4] Ramsay.

CHAPTER V.

SECOND EPISTLE TO DAVIE, A BROTHER POET.

[David Sillar, to whom these epistles are addressed, was at that time master of a country school, and was welcome to Burns both as a scholar and a writer of verse. This epistle he prefixed to his poems printed at Kilmarnock in the year 1789: he loved to speak of his early comrade, and supplied Walker with some very valuable anecdotes: he died one of the magistrates of Irvine, on the 2d of May, 1830, at the age of seventy.]

AULD NIBOR, I'm three times doubly o'er your debtor, For your auld-farrent, frien'ly letter; Tho' I maun say't, I doubt ye flatter, Ye speak sae fair. For my puir, silly, rhymin clatter Some less maun sair.

Hale be your heart, hale be your fiddle; Lang may your elbuck jink and diddle, To cheer you thro' the weary widdle O' war'ly cares, Till bairn's bairns kindly cuddle Your auld, gray hairs.

But Davie, lad, I'm red ye're glaikit; I'm tauld the Muse ye hae negleckit; An' gif it's sae, ye sud be licket Until yo fyke; Sic hauns as you sud ne'er be faiket, Be hain't who like.

For me, I'm on Parnassus' brink, Rivin' the words to gar them clink; Whyles daez't wi' love, whyles daez't wi' drink, Wi' jads or masons; An' whyles, but ay owre late, I think Braw sober lessons.

Of a' the thoughtless sons o' man, Commen' me to the Bardie clan; Except it be some idle plan O' rhymin' clink, The devil-haet, that I sud ban, They ever think.

Nae thought, nae view, nae scheme o' livin', Nae cares to gie us joy or grievin'; But just the pouchie put the nieve in, An' while ought's there, Then hiltie skiltie, we gae scrievin', An' fash nae mair.

Leeze me on rhyme! it's aye a treasure, My chief, amaist my only pleasure, At hame, a-fiel', at work, or leisure, The Muse, poor hizzie! Tho' rough an' raploch be her measure, She's seldom lazy.

Haud to the Muse, my dainty Davie: The warl' may play you monie a shavie; But for the Muse she'll never leave ye, Tho' e'er so puir, Na, even tho' limpin' wi' the spavie Frae door to door.

CHAPTER VI.

ADDRESS TO THE DEIL

"O Prince! O Chief of many throned Pow'rs, That led th' embattled Seraphim to war."

Milton

[The beautiful and relenting spirit in which this fine poem finishes moved the heart on one of the coldest of our critics. "It was, I think," says Gilbert Burns, "in the winter of 1784, as we were going with carts for coals to the family fire, and I could yet point out the particular spot, that Robert first repeated to me the 'Address to the Deil.' The idea of the address was suggested to him by running over in his mind the many ludicrous accounts we have of that august personage."]

O thou! whatever title suit thee, Auld Hornie, Satan, Kick, or Clootie, Wha in yon cavern grim an' sootie, Closed under hatches, Spairges about the brunstane cootie, To scaud poor wretches!

Hear me, auld Hangie, for a wee, An' let poor damned bodies be; I'm sure sma' pleasure it can gie, E'en to a deil, To skelp an' scaud poor dogs like me, An' hear us squeel!

Great is thy pow'r, an' great thy fame; Far kend an' noted is thy name; An' tho' yon lowin heugh's thy hame, Thou travels far; An', faith! thou's neither lag nor lame, Nor blate nor scaur.

Whyles, ranging like a roaring lion, For prey, a' holes an' corners tryin; Whyles, on the strong-winged tempest flyin, Tirlin the kirks; [66]Whiles, in the human bosom pryin, Unseen thou lurks.

I've heard my reverend Graunie say, In lanely glens ye like to stray; Or where auld-ruin'd castles, gray, Nod to the moon, Ye fright the nightly wand'rer's way Wi' eldricht croon.

When twilight did my Graunie summon, To say her prayers, douce, honest woman! Aft yont the dyke she's heard you bummin, Wi' eerie drone; Or, rustlin, thro' the boortries comin, Wi' heavy groan.

Ae dreary, windy, winter night, The stars shot down wi' sklentin light, Wi' you, mysel, I gat a fright Ayont the lough; Ye, like a rash-buss, stood in sight, Wi' waving sough.

The cudgel in my nieve did shake. Each bristl'd hair stood like a stake, When wi' an eldritch, stoor quaick-quaick- Amang the springs, Awa ye squatter'd, like a drake, On whistling wings.

Let warlocks grim, an' wither'd hags, Tell how wi' you, on rag weed nags, They skim the muirs an' dizzy crags Wi' wicked speed; And in kirk-yards renew their leagues Owre howkit dead.

Thence countra wives, wi' toil an' pain, May plunge an' plunge the kirn in vain: For, oh! the yellow treasure's taen By witching skill; An' dawtit, twal-pint hawkie's gaen As yell's the bill.

Thence mystic knots mak great abuse On young guidmen, fond, keen, an' crouse; When the best wark-lume i' the house By cantrip wit, Is instant made no worth a louse, Just at the bit,

When thowes dissolve the snawy hoord, An' float the jinglin icy-boord, Then water-kelpies haunt the foord, By your direction; An' nighted trav'llers are allur'd To their destruction.

An' aft your moss-traversing spunkies Decoy the wight that late an' drunk is, The bleezin, curst, mischievous monkeys Delude his eyes, Till in some miry slough he sunk is, Ne'er mair to rise.

When masons' mystic word an' grip In storms an' tempests raise you up, Some cock or cat your rage maun stop, Or, strange to tell! The youngest brother ye wad whip Aff straught to hell!

Lang syne, in Eden's bonie yard, When youthfu' lovers first were pair'd, An' all the soul of love they shar'd, The raptur'd hour, Sweet on the fragrant, flow'ry sward, In shady bow'r:

Then you, ye auld, snick-drawing dog! Ye came to Paradise incog. An' play'd on man a cursed brogue, (Black be your fa'!) An' gied the infant world a shog, 'Maist ruin'd a'.

D'ye mind that day, when in a bizz, Wi' reekit duds, an' reestit gizz, Ye did present your smoutie phiz 'Mang better folk, An' sklented on the man of Uzz Your spitefu' joke?

An' how ye gat him i' your thrall, An' brak him out o' house an' hall, While scabs an' botches did him gall, Wi' bitter claw, An' lows'd his ill tongu'd, wicked scawl, Was warst ava?

But a' your doings to rehearse, Your wily snares an' fechtin fierce, Sin' that day Michael did you pierce, Down to this time, Wad ding a' Lallan tongue, or Erse, In prose or rhyme.

An' now, auld Cloots, I ken ye're thinkin, A certain Bardie's rantin, drinkin, [67]Some luckless hour will send him linkin To your black pit; But, faith! he'll turn a corner jinkin, An' cheat you yet.

But fare ye well, auld Nickie-ben! O wad ye tak a thought an' men'! Ye aiblins might-I dinna ken- Still hae a stake- I'm wae to think upo' yon den Ev'n for your sake!

"AULD MARE MAGGIE."

"AULD MARE MAGGIE."

CHAPTER VII.

THE AULD FARMER'S NEW-YEAR MORNING SALUTATION TO HIS AULD MARE MAGGIE,

ON GIVING HER THE ACCUSTOMED RIPP OF CORN TO HANSEL IN THE NEW YEAR

["Whenever Burns has occasion," says Hogg, "to address or mention any subordinate being, however mean, even a mouse or a flower, then there is a gentle pathos in it that awakens the finest feelings of the heart." The Auld Farmer of Kyle has the spirit of knight-errant, and loves his mare according to the rules of chivalry; and well he might: she carried him safely home from markets, triumphantly from wedding-brooses; she ploughed the stiffest land; faced the steepest brae, and, moreover, bore home his bonnie bride with a consciousness of the loveliness of the load.]

A guid New-year I wish thee, Maggie! Hae, there's a rip to thy auld baggie: Tho' thou's howe-backit, now, an' knaggie, I've seen the day Thou could hae gaen like onie staggie Out-owre the lay.

Tho' now thou's dowie, stiff, an' crazy, An' thy auld hide as white's a daisy, I've seen thee dappl't, sleek, and glaizie, A bonny gray: He should been tight that daur't to raize thee, Ance in a day.

Thou ance was i' the foremost rank, A filly, buirdly, steeve, an' swank, An set weel down a shapely shank, As e'er tread yird; An' could hae flown out-owre a stank, Like ony bird.

It's now some nine-an'-twenty year, Sin' thou was my guid-father's Meere; He gied me thee, o' tocher clear, An' fifty mark; Tho' it was sma', 'twas weel-won gear, An' thou was stark.

When first I gaed to woo my Jenny, Ye then was trottin wi' your minnie: Tho' ye was trickle, slee, an' funny, Ye ne'er was donsie: But hamely, tawie, quiet an' cannie, An' unco sonsie.

That day ye pranc'd wi' muckle pride, When ye bure hame my bonnie bride: An' sweet an' gracefu' she did ride, Wi' maiden air! Kyle-Stewart I could bragged wide, For sic a pair.

Tho' now ye dow but hoyte and hoble, An' wintle like a saumont-coble, That day, ye was a jinker noble, For heels an' win'! An' ran them till they a' did wauble, Far, far, behin'!

When thou an' I were young an' skeigh, An' stable-meals at fairs were dreigh, How thou wad prance, an' snore, an' skreigh, An' tak the road! Town's bodies ran, an' stood abeigh, An' ca't thee mad.

When thou was corn't, an' I was mellow, We took the road ay like a swallow: At Brooses thou had ne'er a fellow, For pith an' speed; But every tail thou pay't them hollow, Where'er thou gaed.

The sma', droop-rumpl't, hunter cattle, Might aiblins waur't thee for a brattle; But sax Scotch miles thou try't their mettle, An' gar't them whaizle: Nae whip nor spur, but just a whattle O' saugh or hazle.

Thou was a noble fittie-lan', As e'er in tug or tow was drawn: Aft thee an' I, in aught hours gaun, In guid March-weather, Hae turn'd sax rood beside our han' For days thegither.

Thou never braindg't, an' fetch't, an' fliskit, But thy auld tail thou wad hae whiskit, An' spread abreed thy weel-fill'd brisket, Wi' pith an' pow'r, 'Till spiritty knowes wad rair't and risket, An' slypet owre.

When frosts lay lang, an' snaws were deep, An' threaten'd labour back to keep, I gied thy cog a wee-bit heap Aboon the timmer; I ken'd my Maggie wad na sleep For that, or simmer.

In cart or car thou never reestit; The steyest brae thou wad hae fac't it; Thou never lap, an' sten't, an' breastit, Then stood to blaw; But just thy step a wee thing hastit, Thou snoov't awa.

My pleugh is now thy bairntime a'; Four gallant brutes as e'er did draw; Forbye sax mae, I've sell't awa, That thou hast nurst: They drew me thretteen pund an' twa, The vera worst.

Monie a sair daurk we twa hae wrought, An, wi' the weary warl' fought! An' monie an anxious day, I thought We wad be beat! Yet here to crazy age we're brought, Wi' something yet.

And think na, my auld, trusty servan', That now perhaps thou's less deservin, An' thy auld days may end in starvin, For my last fow, A heapit stimpart, I'll reserve ane Laid by for you.

We've worn to crazy years thegither; We'll toyte about wi' ane anither; Wi' tentie care I'll flit thy tether, To some hain'd rig, Whare ye may nobly rax your leather, Wi' sma' fatigue.

CHAPTER VIII.

TO A HAGGIS.

[The vehement nationality of this poem is but a small part of its merit. The haggis of the north is the minced pie of the south; both are characteristic of the people: the ingredients which compose the former are all of Scottish growth, including the bag which contains them; the ingredients of the latter are gathered chiefly from the four quarters of the globe: the haggis is the triumph of poverty, the minced pie the triumph of wealth.]

Fair fa' your honest, sonsie face, Great chieftain o' the pudding-race! Aboon them a' ye tak your place, Painch, tripe, or thairm: Weel are ye wordy o' a grace As lang's my arm.

The groaning trencher there ye fill, Your hurdies like a distant hill, Your pin wad help to mend a mill In time o' need, While thro' your pores the dews distil Like amber bead.

His knife see rustic-labour dight, An' cut you up wi' ready slight, Trenching your gushing entrails bright Like onie ditch; And then, O what a glorious sight, Warm-reekin, rich!

Then horn for horn they stretch an' strive, Deil tak the hindmost, on they drive, 'Till a' their weel-swall'd kytes belyve Are bent like drums; Then auld Guidman, maist like to rive, Bethankit hums.

Is there that o'er his French ragout, Or olio that wad staw a sow, Or fricassee wad mak her spew Wi' perfect sconner, Looks down wi' sneering, scornfu' view On sic a dinner?

Poor devil! see him owre his trash, As feckless as a wither'd rash, His spindle shank a guid whip-lash, His nieve a nit; Thro' bloody flood or field to dash, O how unfit!

But mark the rustic, haggis-fed, The trembling earth resounds his tread, Clap in his walie nieve a blade, He'll mak it whissle; An' legs, an' arms, an' heads will sned, Like taps o' thrissle.

Ye pow'rs wha mak mankind your care, And dish them out their bill o' fare, Auld Scotland wants nae stinking ware That jaups in luggies; But, if ye wish her gratefu' pray'r, Gie her a Haggis!

CHAPTER IX.

A PRAYER, UNDER THE PRESSURE OF VIOLENT ANGUISH.

["There was a certain period of my life," says Burns, "that my spirit was broke by repeated losses and disasters, which threatened and indeed effected the ruin of my fortune. My body, too, was attacked by the most dreadful distemper, a hypochondria or confirmed melancholy. In this wretched state, the recollection of which makes me yet shudder, I hung my harp on the willow-trees, except in some lucid intervals, in one of which I composed the following."]

O Thou Great Being! what Thou art Surpasses me to know; Yet sure I am, that known to Thee Are all Thy works below.

Thy creature here before Thee stands, All wretched and distrest; Yet sure those ills that wring my soul Obey Thy high behest.

Sure Thou, Almighty, canst not act From cruelty or wrath! O, free my weary eyes from tears, Or close them fast in death!

But if I must afflicted be, To suit some wise design; Then, man my soul with firm resolves To bear and not repine!

CHAPTER X.

A PRAYER IN THE PROSPECT OF DEATH.

[I have heard the third verse of this very moving Prayer quoted by scrupulous men as a proof that the poet imputed his errors to the Being who had endowed him with wild and unruly passions. The meaning is very different: Burns felt the torrent-strength of passion overpowering his resolution, and trusted that God would be merciful to the errors of one on whom he had bestowed such o'ermastering gifts.]

O Thou unknown, Almighty Cause Of all my hope and fear? In whose dread presence, ere an hour Perhaps I must appear!

If I have wander'd in those paths Of life I ought to shun; As something, loudly, in my breast, Remonstrates I have done;

Thou know'st that Thou hast formed me, With passions wild and strong; And list'ning to their witching voice Has often led me wrong.

Where human weakness has come short, Or frailty stept aside, Do Thou, All-Good! for such thou art, In shades of darkness hide.

Where with intention I have err'd, No other plea I have, But, Thou art good; and goodness still Delighteth to forgive.

CHAPTER XI.

STANZAS ON THE SAME OCCASION.

[These verses the poet, in his common-place book, calls "Misgivings in the Hour of Despondency and Prospect of Death." He elsewhere says they were composed when fainting-fits and other alarming symptoms of a pleurisy, or some other dangerous disorder, first put nature on the alarm.]

Why am I loth to leave this earthly scene? How I so found it full of pleasing charms? Some drops of joy with draughts of ill between: Some gleams of sunshine 'mid renewing storms: Is it departing pangs my soul alarms? Or Death's unlovely, dreary, dark abode? For guilt, for guilt, my terrors are in arms; I tremble to approach an angry God, And justly smart beneath his sin-avenging rod.

Fain would I say, "Forgive my foul offence!" Fain promise never more to disobey; But, should my Author health again dispense, Again I might desert fair virtue's way: Again in folly's path might go astray; Again exalt the brute and sink the man; Then how should I for heavenly mercy pray, Who act so counter heavenly mercy's plan? Who sin so oft have mourn'd, yet to temptation ran?

O Thou, great Governor of all below! If I may dare a lifted eye to Thee, Thy nod can make the tempest cease to blow, Or still the tumult of the raging sea: With that controlling pow'r assist ev'n me Those headlong furious passions to confine; For all unfit I feel my pow'rs to be, To rule their torrent in th' allowed line; O, aid me with Thy help, Omnipotence Divine!

CHAPTER XII.

A WINTER NIGHT.

"Poor naked wretches, wheresoe'er you are That bide the pelting of the pitiless storm! How shall your houseless heads and unfed sides, Your looped and widow'd raggedness defend you From seasons such as these?" Shakspeare.

["This poem," says my friend Thomas Carlyle, "is worth several homilies on mercy, for it is the voice of Mercy herself. Burns, indeed, lives in sympathy: his soul rushes forth into all the realms of being: nothing that has existence can be indifferent to him."]

When biting Boreas, fell and doure, Sharp shivers thro' the leafless bow'r; When Phœbus gies a short-liv'd glow'r Far south the lift, Dim-darkening through the flaky show'r, Or whirling drift:

Ae night the storm the steeples rocked, Poor labour sweet in sleep was locked, While burns, wi' snawy wreeths up-choked, Wild-eddying swirl. Or through the mining outlet bocked, Down headlong hurl.

Listening, the doors an' winnocks rattle, I thought me on the ourie cattle, Or silly sheep, wha bide this brattle O' winter war, And through the drift, deep-lairing sprattle Beneath a scar.

Ilk happing bird, wee, helpless thing, That, in the merry months o' spring, Delighted me to hear thee sing, What comes o' thee? Whare wilt thou cower thy chittering wing, An' close thy e'e?

Ev'n you on murd'ring errands toil'd, Lone from your savage homes exiled, The blood-stained roost, and sheep-cote spoiled My heart forgets, While pitiless the tempest wild Sore on you beats.

Now Phoebe, in her midnight reign, Dark muffled, viewed the dreary plain; Still crowding thoughts, a pensive train, Rose in my soul, When on my ear this plaintive strain Slow, solemn, stole:-

"Blow, blow, ye winds, with heavier gust! And freeze, thou bitter-biting frost: Descend, ye chilly, smothering snows! Not all your rage, as now united, shows More hard unkindness, unrelenting, Vengeful malice unrepenting, Than heaven-illumined man on brother man bestows; See stern oppression's iron grip, Or mad ambition's gory hand, Sending, like blood-hounds from the slip, Woe, want, and murder o'er a land! Even in the peaceful rural vale, Truth, weeping, tells the mournful tale, How pamper'd luxury, flattery by her side, The parasite empoisoning her ear. With all the servile wretches in the rear, Looks o'er proud property, extended wide; And eyes the simple rustic hind, Whose toil upholds the glittering show, A creature of another kind, Some coarser substance, unrefin'd, Placed for her lordly use thus far, thus vile, below. Where, where is love's fond, tender throe, With lordly honour's lofty brow, The powers you proudly own? Is there, beneath love's noble name, Can harbour, dark, the selfish aim, To bless himself alone! Mark maiden innocence a prey To love-pretending snares, This boasted honour turns away, Shunning soft pity's rising sway, Regardless of the tears and unavailing prayers! Perhaps this hour, in misery's squalid nest, She strains your infant to her joyless breast, And with a mother's fears shrinks at the rocking blast! Oh ye! who, sunk in beds of down, Feel not a want but what yourselves create, Think, for a moment, on his wretched fate, Whom friends and fortune quite disown! Ill satisfied keen nature's clamorous call, Stretched on his straw he lays himself to sleep, While through the ragged roof and chinky wall, Chill o'er his slumbers piles the drifty heap! Think on the dungeon's grim confine, Where guilt and poor misfortune pine! Guilt, erring man, relenting view! But shall thy legal rage pursue The wretch, already crushed low By cruel fortune's undeserved blow? Affliction's sons are brothers in distress, A brother to relieve, how exquisite the bliss!"

I heard nae mair, for Chanticleer Shook off the pouthery snaw, And hailed the morning with a cheer- A cottage-rousing craw!

But deep this truth impressed my mind- Through all his works abroad, The heart benevolent and kind The most resembles God.

CHAPTER XIII.

REMORSE. A FRAGMENT.

["I entirely agree," says Burns, "with the author of the Theory of Moral Sentiments, that Remorse is the most painful sentiment that can embitter the human bosom; an ordinary pitch of fortitude may bear up admirably well, under those calamities, in the procurement of which we ourselves have had no hand; but when our follies or crimes have made us wretched, to bear all with manly firmness, and at the same time have a proper penitential sense of our misconduct, is a glorious effort of self-command."]

Of all the numerous ills that hurt our peace, That press the soul, or wring the mind with anguish, Beyond comparison the worst are those That to our folly or our guilt we owe. In every other circumstance, the mind Has this to say, 'It was no deed of mine;' But when to all the evil of misfortune This sting is added-'Blame thy foolish self!' Or worser far, the pangs of keen remorse; The torturing, gnawing consciousness of guilt,- Of guilt, perhaps, where we've involved others; The young, the innocent, who fondly lov'd us,

Nay, more, that very love their cause of ruin! O burning hell! in all thy store of torments, There's not a keener lash! Lives there a man so firm, who, while his heart Feels all the bitter horrors of his crime, Can reason down its agonizing throbs; And, after proper purpose of amendment, Can firmly force his jarring thoughts to peace? O, happy! happy! enviable man! O glorious magnanimity of soul!

CHAPTER XIV.

THE JOLLY BEGGARS.

A CANTATA.

[This inimitable poem, unknown to Currie and unheardof while the poet lived, was first given to the world, with other characteristic pieces, by Mr. Stewart of Glasgow, in the year 1801. Some have surmised that it is not the work of Burns; but the parentage is certain: the original manuscript at the time of its composition, in 1785, was put into the hands of Mr. Richmond of Mauchline, and afterwards given by Burns himself to Mr. Woodburn, factor of the laird of Craigen-gillan; the song of "For a' that, and a' that" was inserted by the poet, with his name, in the Musical Museum of February, 1790. Cromek admired, yet did not, from overruling advice, print it in the Reliques, for which he was sharply censured by Sir Walter Scott, in the Quarterly Review. The scene of the poem is in Mauchline, where Poosie Nancy had her change-house. Only one copy in the handwriting of Burns is supposed to exist; and of it a very accurate fac-simile has been given.]

RECITATIVO.

When lyart leaves bestrow the yird, Or wavering like the bauckie-bird, Bedim cauld Boreas' blast; When hailstanes drive wi' bitter skyte And infant frosts begin to bite, In hoary cranreuch drest; Ae night at e'en a merry core O' randie, gangrel bodies, In Poosie-Nansie's held the splore, To drink their orra duddies: Wi' quaffing and laughing, They ranted an' they sang; Wi' jumping and thumping, The vera girdle rang.

First, neist the fire, in auld red rags, Ane sat, weel brac'd wi' mealy bags, And knapsack a' in order; His doxy lay within his arm, Wi' usquebae an' blankets warm- She blinket on her sodger: An' ay he gies the tozie drab The tither skelpin' kiss, While she held up her greedy gab Just like an aumous dish. Ilk smack still, did crack still, Just like a cadger's whip, Then staggering and swaggering He roar'd this ditty up-

AIR.

Tune-"Soldiers' Joy."

I am a son of Mars, Who have been in many wars, And show my cuts and scars Wherever I come; This here was for a wench, And that other in a trench, When welcoming the French At the sound of the drum. Lal de daudle, andc.

My 'prenticeship I past Where my leader breath'd his last, When the bloody die was cast On the heights of Abram; I served out my trade When the

gallant game was play'd, And the Moro low was laid At the sound of the drum. Lal de daudle, andc.
I lastly was with Curtis, Among the floating batt'ries, And there I left for witness An arm and a limb; Yet let my country need me, With Elliot to head me, I'd clatter on my stumps At the sound of a drum. Lal de dandle, andc.
And now tho' I must beg, With a wooden arm and leg, And many a tatter'd rag Hanging over my bum I'm as happy with my wallet, My bottle and my callet, As when I used in scarlet To follow a drum. Lal de daudle, andc.
What tho' with hoary locks I must stand the winter shocks, Beneath the woods and rocks Oftentimes for a home, When the tother bag I sell, And the tother bottle tell, I could meet a troop of hell, At the sound of a drum. Lal de daudle, andc.
RECITATIVO.
He ended; and kebars sheuk Aboon the chorus roar; While frighted rattons backward leuk, And seek the benmost bore; A fairy fiddler frae the neuk, He skirl'd out-encore! But up arose the martial Chuck, And laid the loud uproar.
AIR.
Tune-"Soldier laddie."
I once was a maid, tho' I cannot tell when, And still my delight is in proper young men; Some one of a troop of dragoons was my daddie, No wonder I'm fond of a sodger laddie. Sing, Lal de dal, andc.
The first of my loves was a swaggering blade, To rattle the thundering drum was his trade; His leg was so tight, and his cheek was so ruddy, Transported I was with my sodger laddie. Sing, Lal de dal, andc.
But the godly old chaplain left him in the lurch, The sword I forsook for the sake of the church; He ventur'd the soul, and I risk'd the body, 'Twas then I prov'd false to my sodger laddie. Sing, Lal de dal, andc.
Full soon I grew sick of my sanctified sot, The regiment at large for a husband I got; From the gilded spontoon to the fife I was ready, I asked no more but a sodger laddie. Sing, Lal de dal, andc.
But the peace it reduc'd me to beg in despair, Till I met my old boy in a Cunningham fair; His rags regimental they flutter'd so gaudy, My heart is rejoic'd at my sodger laddie. Sing, Lal de dal, andc.
And now I have liv'd-I know not how long, And still I can join in a cup or a song; But whilst with both hands I can hold the glass steady, Here's to thee, my hero, my sodger laddie. Sing, Lal de dal, andc.
RECITATIVO.
Poor Merry Andrew in the neuk, Sat guzzling wi' a tinkler hizzie; They mind't na wha the chorus teuk, Between themselves they were sae busy: At length wi' drink and courting dizzy He stoitered up an' made a face; Then turn'd, an' laid a smack on Grizzie, Syne tun'd his pipes wi' grave grimace.

AIR.

Tune-"Auld Sir Symon."

Sir Wisdom's a fool when he's fou, Sir Knave is a fool in a session; He's there but a 'prentice I trow, But I am a fool by profession.

My grannie she bought me a beuk, And I held awa to the school; I fear I my talent misteuk, But what will ye hae of a fool?

For drink I would venture my neck, A hizzie's the half o' my craft, But what could ye other expect, Of ane that's avowedly daft?

I ance was ty'd up like a stirk, For civilly swearing and quaffing; I ance was abused in the kirk, Fer touzling a lass i' my daffin.

Poor Andrew that tumbles for sport, Let naebody name wi' a jeer; There's ev'n I'm tauld i' the court A tumbler ca'd the premier.

Observ'd ye, yon reverend lad Maks faces to tickle the mob; He rails at our mountebank squad, Its rivalship just i' the job.

And now my conclusion I'll tell, For faith I'm confoundedly dry; The chiel that's a fool for himsel', Gude L-d! he's far dafter than I.

RECITATIVO.

Then neist outspak a raucle carlin, Wha kent fu' weel to cleek the sterling, For monie a pursie she had hooked, And had in mony a well been ducked. Her dove had been a Highland laddie, But weary fa' the waefu' woodie! Wi' sighs and sobs she thus began To wail her braw John Highlandman.

AIR.

Tune-"O an ye were dead, guidman."

A Highland lad my love was born, The Lalland laws he held in scorn; But he still was faithfu' to his clan, My gallant braw John Highlandman.

CHORUS.

Sing, hey my braw John Highlandman! Sing, ho my braw John Highlandman! There's not a lad in a' the lan' Was match for my John Highlandman.

With his philibeg an' tartan plaid, An' gude claymore down by his side, The ladies' hearts he did trepan, My gallant braw John Highlandman. Sing, hey, andc.

We ranged a' from Tweed to Spey, An' liv'd like lords and ladies gay; For a Lalland face he feared none, My gallant braw John Highlandman. Sing, hey, andc.

They banished him beyond the sea, But ere the bud was on the tree, Adown my cheeks the pearls ran, Embracing my John Highlandman. Sing, hey, andc.

But, och! they catch'd him at the last, And bound him in a dungeon fast; My curse upon them every one, They've hang'd my braw John Highlandman. Sing, hey, andc.

And now a widow, I must mourn, The pleasures that will ne'er return: No comfort but a hearty can, When I think on John Highlandman. Sing, hey, andc.

RECITATIVO.

A pigmy scraper, wi' his fiddle, Wha us'd at trysts and fairs to driddle, Her strappan limb and gausy middle He reach'd na higher, Had hol'd his heartie like a riddle, An' blawn't on fire.

Wi' hand on hainch, an' upward e'e, He croon'd his gamut, one, two, three, Then in an Arioso key, The wee Apollo Set off wi' Allegretto glee His giga solo.

AIR.

Tune-"Whistle o'er the lave o't."

Let me ryke up to dight that tear, And go wi' me and be my dear, And then your every care and fear May whistle owre the lave o't.

CHORUS.

I am a fiddler to my trade, An' a' the tunes that e'er I play'd, The sweetest still to wife or maid, Was whistle owre the lave o't.

At kirns and weddings we'se be there, And O! sae nicely's we will fare; We'll house about till Daddie Care Sings whistle owre the lave o't I am, andc.

Sae merrily the banes we'll byke, And sun oursells about the dyke, And at our leisure, when ye like, We'll whistle owre the lave o't. I am, andc.

But bless me wi' your heav'n o' charms, And while I kittle hair on thairms, Hunger, cauld, and a' sic harms, May whistle owre the lave o't. I am, andc.

RECITATIVO.

Her charms had struck a sturdy caird, As weel as poor gut-scraper; He taks the fiddler by the beard, And draws a roosty rapier- He swoor by a' was swearing worth, To speet him like a pliver, Unless he wad from that time forth Relinquish her for ever.

Wi' ghastly e'e, poor tweedle-dee Upon his hunkers bended, And pray'd for grace wi' ruefu' face, And sae the quarrel ended. But tho' his little heart did grieve When round the tinkler prest her, He feign'd to snirtle in his sleeve, When thus the caird address'd her:

AIR.

Tune-"Clout the Caudron."

My bonny lass, I work in brass, A tinkler is my station: I've travell'd round all Christian ground In this my occupation: I've taen the gold, an' been enrolled In many a noble sqadron: But vain they search'd, when off I march'd To go and clout the caudron. I've taen the gold, andc.

Despise that shrimp, that wither'd imp, Wi' a' his noise and caprin, And tak a share wi' those that bear The budget and the apron. And by that stoup, my faith and houp, An' by that dear Kilbaigie, If e'er ye want, or meet wi' scant, May I ne'er weet my craigie. An' by that stoup, andc.

RECITATIVO.

The caird prevail'd-th' unblushing fair In his embraces sunk, Partly wi' love o'ercome sae sair, An' partly she was drunk. Sir Violino, with an air That show'd a man of spunk, Wish'd unison between the pair, An' made the bottle clunk To their health that night.

But urchin Cupid shot a shaft, That play'd a dame a shavie, A sailor rak'd her fore and aft, Behint the chicken cavie. Her lord, a wight o' Homer's craft, Tho' limping wi' the spavie, He hirpl'd up and lap like daft, And shor'd them Dainty Davie O boot that night.

He was a care-defying blade As ever Bacchus listed, Tho' Fortune sair upon him laid, His heart she ever miss'd it. He had nae wish but-to be glad, Nor want but-when he thirsted; He hated nought but-to be sad, And thus the Muse suggested His sang that night.

AIR

Tune-"For a' that, an' a' that."

I am a bard of no regard Wi' gentle folks, an' a' that: But Homer-like, the glowran byke, Frae town to town I draw that.

CHORUS

For a' that, an' a' that, An' twice as muckle's a' that; I've lost but ane, I've twa behin', I've wife enough for a' that.

I never drank the Muses' stank, Castalia's burn, an' a' that; But there it streams, and richly reams, My Helicon I ca' that. For a' that, andc.

Great love I bear to a' the fair, Their humble slave, an' a' that; But lordly will, I hold it still A mortal sin to thraw that. For a' that, andc.

In raptures sweet, this hour we meet, Wi' mutual love, an a' that: But for how lang the flie may stang, Let inclination law that. For a' that, andc.

Their tricks and craft have put me daft. They've ta'en me in, and a' that; But clear your decks, and here's the sex! I like the jads for a' that

CHORUS

For a' that, an' a' that, An' twice as muckle's a' that; My dearest bluid, to do them guid, They're welcome till't for a' that

RECITATIVO

So sung the bard-and Nansie's wa's Shook with a thunder of applause, Re-echo'd from each mouth: They toom'd their pocks, an' pawn'd their duds, They scarcely left to co'er their fuds, To quench their lowan drouth. Then owre again, the jovial thrang, The poet did request, To loose his pack an' wale a sang, A ballad o' the best; He rising, rejoicing, Between his twa Deborahs Looks round him, an' found them Impatient for the chorus.

AIR

Tune-"Jolly Mortals, fill your Glasses."

See! the smoking bowl before us, Mark our jovial ragged ring! Round and round take up the chorus, And in raptures let us sing.

CHORUS.

A fig for those by law protected! Liberty's a glorious feast! Courts for cowards were erected, Churches built to please the priest.

What is title? what is treasure? What is reputation's care? If we lead a life of pleasure, 'Tis no matter how or where! A fig, andc.

With the ready trick and fable, Round we wander all the day; And at night, in barn or stable, Hug our doxies on the hay. A fig, andc.

Does the train-attended carriage Through the country lighter rove? Does the sober bed of marriage Witness brighter scenes of love? A fig, andc.

Life is all a variorum, We regard not how it goes; Let them cant about decorum Who have characters to lose. A fig, andc.

Here's to budgets, bags, and wallets! Here's to all the wandering train! Here's our ragged brats and wallets! One and all cry out-Amen!

A fig for those by law protected! Liberty's a glorious feast! Courts for cowards were erected, Churches built to please the priest.

FOOTNOTES:

[5] A peculiar sort of whiskey.

CHAPTER XV.

DEATH AND DR. HORNBOOK.

A TRUE STORY.

[John Wilson, raised to the unwelcome elevation of hero to this poem, was, at the time of its composition, schoolmaster in Tarbolton: he as, it is said, a fair scholar, and a very worthy man, but vain of his knowledge in medicine-so vain, that he advertised his merits, and offered advice gratis. It was his misfortune to encounter Burns at a mason meeting, who, provoked by a long and pedantic speech, from the Dominie, exclaimed, the future lampoon dawning upon him, "Sit down, Dr. Hornbook." On his way home, the poet seated himself on the ledge of a bridge, composed the poem, and, overcome with poesie and drink, fell asleep, and did not awaken till the sun was shining over Galston Moors. Wilson went afterwards to Glasgow, embarked in mercantile and matrimonial speculations, and prospered, and is still prospering.]

Some books are lies frae end to end, And some great lies were never penn'd: Ev'n ministers, they ha'e been kenn'd, In holy rapture, A rousing whid, at times, to vend, And nail't wi' Scripture.

But this that I am gaun to tell, Which lately on a night befel, Is just as true's the Deil's in h-ll Or Dublin-city; That e'er he nearer comes oursel 'S a muckle pity.

The Clachan yill had made me canty, I was na fou, but just had plenty; I stacher'd whyles, but yet took tent ay To free the ditches; An' hillocks, stanes, and bushes, kenn'd ay Frae ghaists an' witches.

The rising moon began to glow'r The distant Cumnock hills out-owre: To count her horns with a' my pow'r, I set mysel; But whether she had three or four, I could na tell.

I was come round about the hill, And todlin down on Willie's mill, Setting my staff with a' my skill, To keep me sicker; Tho' leeward whyles, against my will, I took a bicker.

I there wi' something did forgather, That put me in an eerie swither; An awfu' scythe, out-owre ae shouther, Clear-dangling, hang; A three-taed leister on the ither Lay, large an' lang.

Its stature seem'd lang Scotch ells twa, The queerest shape that e'er I saw, For fient a wame it had ava: And then, its shanks, They were as thin, as sharp an' sma' As cheeks o' branks.

"Guid-een," quo' I; "Friend, hae ye been mawin, When ither folk are busy sawin?" It seem'd to mak a kind o' stan', But naething spak; At length, says I, "Friend, where ye gaun, Will ye go back?"

It spak right howe,-"My name is Death, But be na fley'd."-Quoth I, "Guid faith, Ye're may be come to stap my breath; But tent me, billie; I red ye weel, take care o' skaith, See, there's a gully!"

"Guidman," quo' he, "put up your whittle, I'm no design'd to try its mettle; But if I did, I wad be kittle To be mislear'd, I wad nae mind it, no that spittle Out-owre my beard."

"Weel, weel!" says I, "a bargain be't; Come, gies your hand, an' sae we're gree't; We'll ease our shanks an' tak a seat, Come, gies your news! This while ye hae been mony a gate At mony a house.

"Ay, ay!" quo' he, an' shook his head, "It's e'en a lang, lang time indeed Sin' I began to nick the thread, An' choke the breath: Folk maun do something for their bread, An' sae maun Death.

"Sax thousand years are near hand fled Sin' I was to the butching bred, An' mony a scheme in vain's been laid, To stap or scar me; Till ane Hornbook's ta'en up the trade, An' faith, he'll waur me.

"Ye ken Jock Hornbook i' the Clachan, Deil mak his kings-hood in a spleuchan! He's grown sae weel acquaint wi' Buchan[6] An' ither chaps, The weans haud out their fingers laughin And pouk my hips.

"See, here's a scythe, and there's a dart, They hae pierc'd mony a gallant heart; But Doctor Hornbook, wi' his art And cursed skill, Has made them baith no worth a ft, Damn'd haet they'll kill.

"'Twas but yestreen, nae farther gaen, I threw a noble throw at ane; Wi' less, I'm sure, I've hundreds slain; But-deil-ma-care, It just play'd dirl on the bane, But did nae mair.

"Hornbook was by, wi' ready art, And had sae fortified the part, That when I looked to my dart, It was sae blunt, Fient haet o't wad hae pierc'd the heart Of a kail-runt.

"I drew my scythe in sic a fury, I near-hand cowpit wi' my hurry, But yet the bauld Apothecary, Withstood the shock; I might as weel hae tried a quarry O' hard whin rock.

"Ev'n them he canna get attended, Although their face he ne'er had kend it, Just sh in a kail-blade, and send it, As soon's he smells't, Baith their disease, and what will mend it, At once he tells't.

"And then a' doctor's saws and whittles, Of a' dimensions, shapes, an' mettles, A' kinds o' boxes, mugs, an' bottles, He's sure to hae; Their Latin names as fast he rattles As A B C.

"Calces o' fossils, earths, and trees; True sal-marinum o' the seas; The farina of beans and pease, He has't in plenty; Aqua-fortis, what you please, He can content ye.

"Forbye some new, uncommon weapons, Urinus spiritus of capons; Or mite-horn shavings, filings, scrapings, Distill'd per se; Sal-alkali o' midge-tail clippings, And mony mae."

"Waes me for Johnny Ged's-Hole[7] now," Quo' I, "If that thae news be true! His braw calf-ward whare gowans grew, Sae white and bonie, Nae doubt they'll rive it wi' the plew; They'll ruin Johnie!"

The creature grain'd an eldritch laugh, And says, "Ye need na yoke the plough, Kirkyards will soon be till'd eneugh, Tak ye nae fear; They'll a' be trench'd wi' mony a sheugh In twa-three year.

"Whare I kill'd ane a fair strae death, By loss o' blood or want of breath, This night I'm free to tak my aith, That Hornbook's skill Has clad a score i' their last claith, By drap an' pill.

"An honest wabster to his trade, Whase wife's twa nieves were scarce weel bred, Gat tippence-worth to mend her head, When it was sair; The wife slade cannie to her bed, But ne'er spak mair

"A countra laird had ta'en the batts, Or some curmurring in his guts, His only son for Hornbook sets, An' pays him well. The lad, for twa guid gimmer-pets, Was laird himsel.

"A bonnie lass, ye kend her name, Some ill-brewn drink had hov'd her wame; She trusts hersel, to hide the shame, In Hornbook's care; Horn sent her aff to her lang hame, To hide it there.

"That's just a swatch o' Hornbook's way; Thus goes he on from day to day, Thus does he poison, kill, an' slay, An's weel paid for't; Yet stops me o' my lawfu' prey, Wi' his d-mn'd dirt:

"But, hark! I'll tell you of a plot, Though dinna ye be speaking o't; I'll nail the self-conceited sot, As dead's a herrin': Niest time we meet, I'll wad a groat, He gets his fairin'!"

But just as he began to tell, The auld kirk-hammer strak' the bell Some wee short hour ayont the twal, Which rais'd us baith: I took the way that pleas'd mysel', And sae did Death.

FOOTNOTES:

[6] Buchan's Domestic Medicine.

[7] The grave-digger.

CHAPTER XVI.

THE TWA HERDS:

OR,

THE HOLY TULZIE.

[The actors in this indecent drama were Moodie, minister of Ricartoun, and

Russell, helper to the minister of Kilmarnock: though apostles of the "Old Light," they forgot their brotherhood in the vehemence of controversy, and went, it is said, to blows. "This poem," says Burns, "with a certain description of the clergy as well as laity, met with a roar of applause."]

O a' ye pious godly flocks, Weel fed on pastures orthodox, Wha now will keep you frae the fox, Or worrying tykes, Or wha will tent the waifs and crocks, About the dykes?

The twa best herds in a' the wast, That e'er ga'e gospel horn a blast, These five and twenty simmers past, O! dool to tell, Ha'e had a bitter black out-cast Atween themsel.

O, Moodie, man, and wordy Russell, How could you raise so vile a bustle, Ye'll see how New-Light herds will whistle And think it fine: The Lord's cause ne'er got sic a twistle Sin' I ha'e min'.

O, sirs! whae'er wad ha'e expeckit Your duty ye wad sae negleckit, Ye wha were ne'er by lairds respeckit, To wear the plaid, But by the brutes themselves eleckit, To be their guide.

What flock wi' Moodie's flock could rank, Sae hale and hearty every shank, Nae poison'd sour Arminian stank, He let them taste, Frae Calvin's well, ay clear they drank,- O sic a feast!

The thummart, wil'-cat, brock, and tod, Weel kend his voice thro' a' the wood, He smelt their ilka hole and road, Baith out and in, And weel he lik'd to shed their bluid, And sell their skin.

What herd like Russell tell'd his tale, His voice was heard thro' muir and dale, He kend the Lord's sheep, ilka tail, O'er a' the height, And saw gin they were sick or hale, At the first sight.

He fine a mangy sheep could scrub, Or nobly fling the gospel club, And New-Light herds could nicely drub, Or pay their skin; Could shake them o'er the burning dub, Or heave them in.

Sic twa-O! do I live to see't, Sic famous twa should disagreet, An' names, like villain, hypocrite, Ilk ither gi'en, While New-Light herds, wi' laughin' spite, Say neither's liein'!

An' ye wha tent the gospel fauld, There's Duncan, deep, and Peebles, shaul, But chiefly thou, apostle Auld, We trust in thee, That thou wilt work them, hot and cauld, Till they agree.

Consider, Sirs, how we're beset; There's scarce a new herd that we get But comes frae mang that cursed set I winna name; I hope frae heav'n to see them yet In fiery flame.

Dalrymple has been lang our fae, M'Gill has wrought us meikle wae, And that curs'd rascal call'd M'Quhae, And baith the Shaws, That aft ha'e made us black and blae, Wi' vengefu' paws.

Auld Wodrow lang has hatch'd mischief, We thought ay death wad bring relief, But he has gotten, to our grief, Ane to succeed him, A chield wha'll soundly buff our beef; I meikle dread him.

And mony a ane that I could tell, Wha fain would openly rebel, Forbye turn-coats amang oursel, There's Smith for ane, I doubt he's but a grey-nick quill, An' that ye'll fin'.

O! a' ye flocks o'er a' the hills, By mosses, meadows, moors, and fells, Come, join your counsel and your skills To cow the lairds, And get the brutes the powers themsels To choose their herds;

Then Orthodoxy yet may prance, And Learning in a woody dance, And that fell cur ca'd Common Sense, That bites sae sair, Be banish'd o'er the sea to France: Let him bark there.

Then Shaw's and Dalrymple's eloquence, M'Gill's close nervous excellence, M'Quhae's pathetic manly sense, And guid M'Math, Wi' Smith, wha thro' the heart can glance, May a' pack aff.

CHAPTER XVII.

HOLY WILLIE'S PRAYER.

"And send the godly in a pet to pray."

Pope.

[Of this sarcastic and too daring poem many copies in manuscript were circulated while the poet lived, but though not unknown or unfelt by Currie, it continued unpublished till printed by Stewart with the Jolly Beggars, in 1801. Holy Willie was a small farmer, leading elder to Auld, a name well known to all lovers of Burns; austere in speech, scrupulous in all outward observances, and, what is known by the name of a "professing Christian." He experienced, however, a "sore fall;" he permitted himself to be "filled fou," and in a moment when "self got in" made free, it is said, with the money of the poor of the parish. His name was William Fisher.]

O thou, wha in the heavens dost dwell, Wha, as it pleases best thysel', Sends ane to heaven, and ten to hell, A' for thy glory, And no for ony gude or ill They've done afore thee!

I bless and praise thy matchless might, Whan thousands thou hast left in night, That I am here afore thy sight, For gifts and grace, A burnin' and a shinin' light To a' this place.

What was I, or my generation, That I should get sic exaltation, I wha deserve sic just damnation, For broken laws, Five thousand years 'fore my creation, Thro' Adam's cause.

When frae my mither's womb I fell, Thou might hae plunged me in hell, To gnash my gums, to weep and wail, In burnin' lake, Whar damned devils roar and yell, Chain'd to a stake.

Yet I am here a chosen sample; To show thy grace is great and ample; I'm here a pillar in thy temple, Strong as a rock, A guide, a buckler, an example, To a' thy flock.

But yet, O Lord! confess I must, At times I'm fash'd wi' fleshly lust; And sometimes, too, wi' warldly trust, Vile self gets in; But thou remembers we are dust, Defil'd in sin.

O Lord! yestreen thou kens, wi' Meg- Thy pardon I sincerely beg, O! may't ne'er be a livin' plague To my dishonour, An' I'll ne'er lift a lawless leg Again upon her.

Besides, I farther maun allow, Wi' Lizzie's lass, three times I trow- But Lord, that Friday I was fou, When I came near her, Or else, thou kens, thy servant true Wad ne'er hae steer'd her.

Maybe thou lets this fleshly thorn, Beset thy servant e'en and morn, Lest he owre high and proud should turn, 'Cause he's sae gifted; If sae, thy han' maun e'en be borne Until thou lift it.

Lord, bless thy chosen in this place, For here thou hast a chosen race: But God confound their stubborn face, And blast their name, Wha bring thy elders to disgrace And public shame.

Lord, mind Gawn Hamilton's deserts, He drinks, and swears, and plays at carts, Yet has sae mony takin' arts, Wi' grit and sma', Frae God's ain priests the people's hearts He steals awa.

An' whan we chasten'd him therefore, Thou kens how he bred sic a splore, As set the warld in a roar O' laughin' at us;- Curse thou his basket and his store, Kail and potatoes.

Lord, hear my earnest cry and pray'r, Against the presbyt'ry of Ayr; Thy strong right hand, Lord, mak it bare Upo' their heads, Lord weigh it down, and dinna spare, For their misdeeds.

O Lord my God, that glib-tongu'd Aiken, My very heart and saul are quakin', To think how we stood groanin', shakin', And swat wi' dread, While Auld wi' hingin lips gaed sneakin' And hung his head.

Lord, in the day of vengeance try him, Lord, visit them wha did employ him, And pass not in thy mercy by 'em, Nor hear their pray'r; But for thy people's sake destroy 'em, And dinna spare.

But, Lord, remember me an mine, Wi' mercies temp'ral and divine, That I for gear and grace may shine, Excell'd by nane, And a' the glory shall be thine, Amen, Amen!

CHAPTER XVIII.

EPITAPH ON HOLY WILLIE.

[We are informed by Richmond of Mauchline, that when he was clerk in Gavin Hamilton's office, Burns came in one morning and said, "I have just composed a poem, John, and if you will write it, I will repeat it." He repeated Holy Willie's Prayer and Epitaph; Hamilton came in at the moment, and having read them with delight, ran laughing with them in his hand to Robert Aiken. The end of Holy Willie was other than godly; in one of his visits to Mauchline, he drank more than was needful, fell into a ditch on his way home, and was found dead in the morning.]

Here Holy Willie's sair worn clay Takes up its last abode; His saul has ta'en some other way, I fear the left-hand road.

Stop! there he is, as sure's a gun, Poor, silly body, see him; Nae wonder he's as black's the grun, Observe wha's standing wi' him.

Your brunstane devilship I see, Has got him there before ye; But hand your nine-tail cat a wee, Till ance you've heard my story.

Your pity I will not implore, For pity ye hae nane; Justice, alas! has gi'en him o'er, And mercy's day is gaen.

But hear me, sir, deil as ye are, Look something to your credit; A coof like him wad stain your name, If it were kent ye did it.

CHAPTER XIX.

THE INVENTORY;

IN ANSWER TO A MANDATE BY THE SURVEYOR OF THE TAXES.

[We have heard of a poor play-actor who, by a humorous inventory of his effects, so moved the commissioners of the income tax, that they remitted all claim on him then and forever; we know not that this very humorous inventory of Burns had any such effect on Mr. Aiken, the surveyor of the taxes. It is dated "Mossgiel, February 22d, 1786," and is remarkable for wit and sprightliness, and for the information which it gives us of the poet's habits, household, and agricultural implements.]

Sir, as your mandate did request, I send you here a faithfu' list, O' gudes, an' gear, an' a' my graith, To which I'm clear to gi'e my aith.

Imprimis, then, for carriage cattle, I have four brutes o' gallant mettle, As ever drew afore a pettle. My lan' afore's[8] a gude auld has been, An' wight, an' wilfu' a' his days been. My lan ahin's[9] a weel gaun fillie, That aft has borne me hame frae Killie,[10] An' your auld burro' mony a time, In days when riding was nae crime- But ance, whan in my wooing pride, I like a blockhead boost to ride, The wilfu' creature sae I pat to, (L-d pardon a' my sins an' that too!) I play'd my fillie sic a shavie, She's a' bedevil'd with the spavie. My fur ahin's[11] a wordy beast, As e'er in tug or tow was trac'd. The fourth's a Highland Donald hastie, A d-n'd red wud Kilburnie blastie! Forbye a cowt o' cowt's the wale, As ever ran afore a tail. If he be spar'd to be a beast, He'll draw me fifteen pun' at least.- Wheel carriages I ha'e but few, Three carts, an' twa are feckly new; Ae auld wheelbarrow, mair for token, Ae leg an' baith the trams are broken; I made a poker o' the spin'le, An' my auld mither brunt the trin'le.

For men I've three mischievous boys, Run de'ils for rantin' an' for noise; A gaudsman ane, a thrasher t'other. Wee Davock hauds the nowt in fother. I rule them as I ought, discreetly, An' aften labour them completely; An' ay on Sundays, duly, nightly, I on the Questions targe them tightly; Till, faith, wee Davock's turn'd sae gleg, Tho' scarcely langer than your leg, He'll screed you aff Effectual calling, As fast as ony in the dwalling. I've nane in female servan' station, (Lord keep me ay frae a' temptation!) I ha'e nae wife- and that my bliss is, An' ye have laid nae tax on misses; An' then, if kirk folks dinna clutch me, I ken the devils darena touch me. Wi' weans I'm mair than weel contented, Heav'n sent me ane mae than I wanted. My sonsie smirking dear-bought Bess, She stares the daddy in her face, Enough of ought ye like but grace; But her, my bonnie sweet wee lady, I've paid enough for her already, An' gin ye tax her or her mither, B' the L-d! ye'se get them a'thegither.

And now, remember, Mr. Aiken, Nae kind of license out I'm takin'; Frae this time forth, I do declare I'se ne'er ride horse nor hizzie mair; Thro' dirt and dub for life I'll paidle, Ere I sae dear pay for a saddle; My travel a' on foot I'll shank it, I've sturdy bearers, Gude be thankit. The kirk and you may tak' you that, It puts but little in your pat; Sae dinna put me in your buke. Nor for my ten white shillings luke.

This list wi' my ain hand I wrote it, the day and date as under noted; Then know all ye whom it concerns,

Subscripsi huic

Robert Burns.

FOOTNOTES:

[8] The fore-horse on the left-hand in the plough.

[9] The hindmost on the left-hand in the plough.

[10] Kilmarnock.

[11] The hindmost horse on the right-hand in the plough.

CHAPTER XX.

THE HOLY FAIR.

A robe of seeming truth and trust Did crafty observation; And secret hung, with poison'd crust, The dirk of Defamation: A mask that like the gorget show'd, Dye-varying on the pigeon; And for a mantle large and broad, He wrapt him in Religion.

Hypocrisy a-la-mode.

[The scene of this fine poem is the church-yard of Mauchline, and the subject handled so cleverly and sharply is the laxity of manners visible in matters so solemn and terrible as the administration of the sacrament. "This was indeed," says Lockhart, "an extraordinary performance: no partisan of any sect could whisper that malice had formed its principal inspiration, or that its chief attraction lay in the boldness with which individuals, entitled and accustomed to respect, were held up to ridicule: it was acknowledged, amidst the sternest mutterings of wrath, that national manners were once more in the hands of a national poet." "It is no doubt," says Hogg, "a reckless piece of satire, but it is a clever one, and must have cut to the bone. But much as I admire the poem I must regret that it is partly borrowed from Ferguson."]

Upon a simmer Sunday morn, When Nature's face is fair, I walked forth to view the corn, An' snuff the caller air. The rising sun owre Galston muirs, Wi' glorious light was glintin'; The hares were hirplin down the furs, The lav'rocks they were chantin' Fu' sweet that day.

As lightsomely I glowr'd abroad, To see a scene sae gay, Three hizzies, early at the road, Cam skelpin up the way; Twa had manteeles o' dolefu' black, But ane wi' lyart lining; The third, that gaed a-wee a-back, Was in the fashion shining Fu' gay that day.

The twa appear'd like sisters twin, In feature, form, an' claes; Their visage, wither'd, lang, an' thin, An' sour as ony slaes: The third cam up, hap-step-an'-lowp, As light as ony lambie, An' wi' a curchie low did stoop, As soon as e'er she saw me, Fu' kind that day.

Wi' bonnet aff, quoth I, "Sweet lass, I think ye seem to ken me; I'm sure I've seen that bonnie face, But yet I canna name ye." Quo' she, an' laughin' as she spak, An' taks me by the hands, "Ye, for my sake, hae gi'en the feck, Of a' the ten commands A screed some day.

"My name is Fun-your cronie dear, The nearest friend ye hae; An' this is Superstition here, An' that's Hypocrisy. I'm gaun to Mauchline holy fair, To spend an hour in daffin: Gin ye'll go there, yon runkl'd pair, We will get famous laughin' At them this day."

Quoth I, "With a' my heart I'll do't; I'll get my Sunday's sark on, An' meet you on the holy spot; Faith, we'se hae fine remarkin'!" Then I gaed hame at crowdie-time An' soon I made me ready; For roads were clad, frae side to side, Wi' monie a wearie body, In droves that day.

Here farmers gash, in ridin' graith Gaed hoddin by their cottars; There, swankies young, in braw braid-claith, Are springin' o'er the gutters. The lasses, skelpin barefit, thrang, In silks an' scarlets glitter; Wi' sweet-milk cheese, in monie a whang, An' farls bak'd wi' butter, Fu' crump that day.

When by the plate we set our nose, Weel heaped up wi' ha'pence, A greedy glowr Black Bonnet throws, An' we maun draw our tippence. Then in we go to see the show, On ev'ry side they're gath'rin', Some carrying dails, some chairs an' stools, An' some are busy blethrin' Right loud that day.

Here stands a shed to fend the show'rs, An' screen our countra gentry, There, racer Jess, and twa-three wh-res, Are blinkin' at the entry. [83]Here sits a raw of titlin' jades, Wi' heaving breast and bare neck, An' there's a batch o' wabster lads, Blackguarding frae Kilmarnock For fun this day.

Here some are thinkin' on their sins, An' some upo' their claes; Ane curses feet that fyl'd his shins, Anither sighs an' prays: On this hand sits a chosen swatch, Wi' screw'd up grace-proud faces; On that a set o' chaps at watch, Thrang winkin' on the lasses To chairs that day.

O happy is that man an' blest! Nae wonder that it pride him! Wha's ain dear lass that he likes best, Comes clinkin' down beside him; Wi' arm repos'd on the chair back, He sweetly does compose him; Which, by degrees, slips round her neck, An's loof upon her bosom, Unkenn'd that day.

Now a' the congregation o'er Is silent expectation; For Moodie speeds the holy door, Wi' tidings o' damnation. Should Hornie, as in ancient days, 'Mang sons o' God present him, The vera sight o' Moodie's face, To's ain het hame had sent him Wi' fright that day.

Hear how he clears the points o' faith Wi' ratlin' an' wi' thumpin'! Now meekly calm, now wild in wrath, He's stampin an' he's jumpin'! His lengthen'd chin, his turn'd-up snout, His eldritch squeel and gestures, Oh, how they fire the heart devout, Like cantharidian plasters, On sic a day.

But hark! the tent has chang'd its voice: There's peace an' rest nae langer: For a' the real judges rise, They canna sit for anger. Smith opens out his cauld harangues, On practice and on morals; An' aff the godly pour in thrangs, To gie the jars an' barrels A lift that day.

What signifies his barren shine, Of moral pow'rs and reason? His English style, an' gestures fine, Are a' clean out o' season. Like Socrates or Antonine, Or some auld pagan heathen, The moral man he does define, But ne'er a word o' faith in That's right that day.

In guid time comes an antidote Against sic poison'd nostrum; For Peebles, frae the water-fit, Ascends the holy rostrum: See, up he's got the word o' God, An' meek an' mim has view'd it, While Common-Sense has ta'en the road, An' aff, an' up the Cowgate,[12] Fast, fast, that day.

Wee Miller, neist the guard relieves, An' orthodoxy raibles, Tho' in his heart he weel believes, An' thinks it auld wives' fables: But faith! the birkie wants a manse, So, cannily he hums them; Altho' his carnal wit an' sense Like hafflins-ways o'ercomes him At times that day.

Now but an' ben, the Change-house fills, Wi' yill-caup commentators: Here's crying out for bakes and gills, An' there the pint-stowp clatters; While thick an' thrang, an' loud an' lang, Wi' logic, an' wi' scripture, They raise a din, that, in the end, Is like to breed a rupture O' wrath that day.

Leeze me on drink! it gies us mair Than either school or college: It kindles wit, it waukens lair, It pangs us fou' o' knowledge, Be't whisky gill, or penny wheep, Or any stronger potion, It never fails, on drinking deep, To kittle up our notion By night or day.

The lads an' lasses, blythely bent To mind baith saul an' body, Sit round the table, weel content, An' steer about the toddy. On this ane's dress, an' that ane's leuk, They're making observations; While some are cozie i' the neuk, An' formin' assignations To meet some day.

But now the Lord's ain trumpet touts, Till a' the hills are rairin', An' echoes back return the shouts: Black Russell is na' sparin': His piercing words, like Highlan' swords, Divide the joints and marrow; His talk o' Hell, where devils dwell, Our vera sauls does harrow[13] Wi' fright that day.

A vast, unbottom'd boundless pit, Fill'd fou o' lowin' brunstane, Wha's ragin' flame, an' scorchin' heat, Wad melt the hardest whunstane! The half asleep start up wi' fear, An' think they hear it roarin', When presently it does appear, 'Twas but some neibor snorin' Asleep that day.

'Twad be owre lang a tale to tell How monie stories past, An' how they crowded to the yill, When they were a' dismist: How drink gaed round, in cogs an' caups, Amang the furms an' benches: An' cheese an' bread, frae women's laps, Was dealt about in lunches, An' dawds that day.

In comes a gaucie, gash guidwife, An' sits down by the fire, Syne draws her kebbuck an' her knife; The lasses they are shyer. The auld guidmen, about the grace, Frae side to side they bother, Till some ane by his bonnet lays, An' gi'es them't like a tether, Fu' lang that day.

Waesucks! for him that gets nae lass, Or lasses that hae naething; Sma' need has he to say a grace, Or melvie his braw claithing! O wives, be mindfu' ance yoursel How bonnie lads ye wanted, An' dinna, for a kebbuck-heel, Let lasses be affronted On sic a day!

Now Clinkumbell, wi' ratlin tow, Begins to jow an' croon; Some swagger hame, the best they dow, Some wait the afternoon. At slaps the billies halt a blink, Till lasses strip their shoon: Wi' faith an' hope, an' love an' drink, They're a' in famous tune For crack that day.

How monie hearts this day converts O' sinners and o' lasses! Their hearts o' stane, gin night, are gane, As saft as ony flesh is. There's some are fou o' love divine; There's some are fou o' brandy; An' monie jobs that day begin May end in houghmagandie Some ither day.

FOOTNOTES:

[12] A street so called, which faces the tent in Mauchline.

[13] Shakespeare's Hamlet.

CHAPTER XXI.

THE ORDINATION.

"For sense they little owe to frugal heav'n- To please the mob they hide the little giv'n."

[This sarcastic sally was written on the admission of Mr. Mackinlay, as one of the ministers to the Laigh, or parochial Kirk of Kilmarnock, on the 6th of April, 1786. That reverend person was an Auld Light professor, and his ordination incensed all the New Lights, hence the bitter levity of the poem. These dissensions have long since past away: Mackinlay, a pious and kind-hearted sincere man, lived down all the personalities of the satire, and though unwelcome at first, he soon learned to regard them only as a proof of the powers of the poet.]

Kilmarnock wabsters fidge an' claw, An' pour your creeshie nations; An' ye wha leather rax an' draw, Of a' denominations, Swith to the Laigh Kirk, ane an' a', An' there tak up your stations; Then aff to Begbie's in a raw, An' pour divine libations For joy this day.

Curst Common-Sense, that imp o' hell, Cam in wi' Maggie Lauder;[14] But Oliphant aft made her yell, An' Russell sair misca'd her; This day Mackinlay taks the flail, And he's the boy will blaud her! He'll clap a shangan on her tail, An' set the bairns to daud her Wi' dirt this day.

Mak haste an' turn King David owre, An' lilt wi' holy clangor; O' double verse come gie us four, An' skirl up the Bangor: This day the Kirk kicks up

a stoure, Nae mair the knaves shall wrang her, For Heresy is in her pow'r, And gloriously she'll whang her Wi' pith this day.
Come, let a proper text be read, An' touch it aff wi' vigour, How graceless Ham[15] leugh at his dad, Which made Canaan a niger; Or Phineas[16] drove the murdering blade, Wi' wh-re-abhorring rigour; Or Zipporah,[17] the scauldin' jad, Was like a bluidy tiger I' th' inn that day.
There, try his mettle on the creed, And bind him down wi' caution, That stipend is a carnal weed He taks but for the fashion; And gie him o'er the flock, to feed, And punish each transgression; Especial, rams that cross the breed, Gie them sufficient threshin', Spare them nae day.
Now, auld Kilmarnock, cock thy tail, And toss thy horns fu' canty; Nae mair thou'lt rowte out-owre the dale, Because thy pasture's scanty; For lapfu's large o' gospel kail Shall fill thy crib in plenty, An' runts o' grace the pick and wale, No gi'en by way o' dainty, But ilka day.
Nae mair by Babel's streams we'll weep, To think upon our Zion; And hing our fiddles up to sleep, Like baby-clouts a-dryin': Come, screw the pegs, wi' tunefu' cheep, And o'er the thairms be tryin'; Oh, rare! to see our elbucks wheep, An' a' like lamb-tails flyin' Fu' fast this day!
Lang Patronage, wi' rod o' airn, Has shor'd the Kirk's undoin', As lately Fenwick, sair forfairn, Has proven to its ruin: Our patron, honest man! Glencairn, He saw mischief was brewin'; And like a godly elect bairn He's wal'd us out a true ane, And sound this day.
Now, Robinson, harangue nae mair, But steek your gab for ever. Or try the wicked town of Ayr, For there they'll think you clever; Or, nae reflection on your lear, Ye may commence a shaver; Or to the Netherton repair, And turn a carpet-weaver Aff-hand this day.
Mutrie and you were just a match We never had sic twa drones: Auld Hornie did the Laigh Kirk watch, Just like a winkin' baudrons: And ay' he catch'd the tither wretch, To fry them in his caudrons; But now his honour maun detach, Wi' a' his brimstane squadrons, Fast, fast this day.
See, see auld Orthodoxy's faes She's swingein' through the city; Hark, how the nine-tail'd cat she plays! I vow it's unco pretty: There, Learning, with his Greekish face, Grunts out some Latin ditty; And Common Sense is gaun, she says, To mak to Jamie Beattie Her plaint this day.
But there's Morality himsel', Embracing all opinions; Hear, how he gies the tither yell, Between his twa companions; See, how she peels the skin an' fell. As ane were peelin' onions! Now there-they're packed aff to hell, And banished our dominions, Henceforth this day.
O, happy day! rejoice, rejoice! Come bouse about the porter! Morality's demure decoys Shall here nae mair find quarter: Mackinlay, Russell, are the boys, That Heresy can torture: They'll gie her on a rape a hoyse, And cowe her measure shorter By th' head some day.
Come, bring the tither mutchkin in, And here's for a conclusion, To every

New Light[18] mother's son, From this time forth Confusion: If mair they deave us wi' their din, Or Patronage intrusion, We'll light a spunk, and ev'ry skin, We'll rin them aff in fusion Like oil, some day.

FOOTNOTES:

[14] Alluding to a scoffing ballad which was made on the admission of the late reverend and worthy Mr. Lindsay to the Laigh Kirk.

[15] Genesis, ix. 22.

[16] Numbers, xxv. 8.

[17] Exodus, iv. 25.

[18] "New Light" is a cant phrase in the West of Scotland, for those religions opinions which Dr. Taylor of Norwich has defended.

CHAPTER XXII.

THE CALF.

TO THE REV. MR. JAMES STEVEN.

On his text, Malachi, iv. 2-"And ye shall go forth, and grow up as Calves of the stall."

[The laugh which this little poem raised against Steven was a loud one. Burns composed it during the sermon to which it relates and repeated it to Gavin Hamilton, with whom he happened on that day to dine. The Calf-for the name it seems stuck-came to London, where the younger brother of Burns heard him preach in Covent Garden Chapel, in 1796.]

Right, Sir! your text I'll prove it true, Though Heretics may laugh; For instance; there's yoursel' just now, God knows, an unco Calf!

And should some patron be so kind, As bless you wi' a kirk, I doubt na, Sir, but then we'll find, Ye're still as great a Stirk.

But, if the lover's raptur'd hour Shall ever be your lot, Forbid it, ev'ry heavenly power, You e'er should be a stot!

Tho', when some kind, connubial dear, Your but-and-ben adorns, The like has been that you may wear A noble head of horns.

And in your lug, most reverend James, To hear you roar and rowte, Few men o' sense will doubt your claims To rank among the nowte.

And when ye're number'd wi' the dead, Below a grassy hillock, Wi' justice they may mark your head- "Here lies a famous Bullock!"

CHAPTER XXIII.

TO JAMES SMITH.

"Friendship! mysterious cement of the soul! Sweet'ner of life and solder of society! I owe thee much!-"

Blair.

[The James Smith, to whom this epistle is addressed, was at that time a small shop-keeper in Mauchline, and the comrade or rather follower of the poet in all his merry expeditions with "Yill-caup commentators." He was present in Poosie Nansie's when the Jolly Beggars first dawned on the fancy of Burns: the comrades of the poet's heart were not generally very successful in life: Smith left Mauchline, and established a calico-printing manufactory at Avon near Linlithgow, where his friend found him in all appearance prosperous in 1788; but this was not to last; he failed in his speculations and went to the West Indies, and died early. His wit was ready, and his manners lively and unaffected.]

Dear Smith, the sleest, paukie thief, That e'er attempted stealth or rief, Ye surely hae some warlock-breef Owre human hearts; For ne'er a bosom yet was prief Against your arts.

For me, I swear by sun an' moon, And ev'ry star that blinks aboon, Ye've cost me twenty pair o' shoon Just gaun to see you; And ev'ry ither pair that's done, Mair ta'en I'm wi' you.

That auld capricious carlin, Nature, To mak amends for scrimpit stature, She's turn'd you aff, a human creature On her first plan; And in her freaks, on every feature She's wrote, the Man.

Just now I've ta'en the fit o' rhyme, My barmie noddle's working prime, My fancy yerkit it up sublime Wi' hasty summon: Hae ye a leisure-moment's time To hear what's comin'?

Some rhyme a neighbour's name to lash; Some rhyme (vain thought!) for needfu' cash: Some rhyme to court the countra clash, An' raise a din; For me, an aim I never fash; I rhyme for fun.

The star that rules my luckless lot, Has fated me the russet coat, An' damn'd my fortune to the groat; But in requit, Has blest me with a random shot O' countra wit.

This while my notion's ta'en a sklent, To try my fate in guid black prent; But still the mair I'm that way bent, Something cries "Hoolie! I red you, honest man, tak tent! Ye'll shaw your folly.

"There's ither poets much your betters, Far seen in Greek, deep men o' letters, Hae thought they had ensur'd their debtors, A' future ages: Now moths deform in shapeless tatters, Their unknown pages."

Then farewell hopes o' laurel-boughs, To garland my poetic brows! Henceforth I'll rove where busy ploughs Are whistling thrang, An' teach the lanely heights an' howes My rustic sang.

I'll wander on, with tentless heed How never-halting moments speed, Till fate shall snap the brittle thread; Then, all unknown, I'll lay me with th' inglorious dead, Forgot and gone!

But why o' death begin a tale? Just now we're living sound and hale, Then top and maintop crowd the sail, Heave care o'er side! And large, before enjoyment's gale, Let's tak the tide.

This life, sae far's I understand, Is a' enchanted fairy land, Where pleasure is the magic wand, That, wielded right, Maks hours like minutes, hand in hand, Dance by fu' light.

The magic wand then let us wield; For, ance that five-an'-forty's speel'd, See crazy, weary, joyless eild, Wi' wrinkl'd face, Comes hostin', hirplin', owre the field, Wi' creepin' pace.

When ance life's day draws near the gloamin', Then fareweel vacant careless roamin'; An' fareweel cheerfu' tankards foamin', An' social noise; An' fareweel dear, deluding woman! The joy of joys!

O Life! how pleasant in thy morning, Young Fancy's rays the hills adorning! Cold-pausing Caution's lesson scorning, We frisk away, Like school-boys, at th' expected warning, To joy and play.

We wander there, we wander here, We eye the rose upon the brier, Unmindful that the thorn is near, Among the leaves; And tho' the puny wound appear, Short while it grieves.

Some, lucky, find a flow'ry spot, For which they never toil'd nor swat; They drink the sweet and eat the fat, But care or pain; And, haply, eye the barren hut With high disdain.

With steady aim some Fortune chase; Keen hope does ev'ry sinew brace; Thro' fair, thro' foul, they urge the race, And seize the prey; Then cannie, in some cozie place, They close the day.

And others, like your humble servan', Poor wights! nae rules nor roads observin'; To right or left, eternal swervin', They zig-zag on; 'Till curst with age, obscure an' starvin', They aften groan.

Alas! what bitter toil an' straining- But truce with peevish, poor complaining! Is fortune's fickle Luna waning? E'en let her gang! Beneath what light she has remaining, Let's sing our sang.

My pen I here fling to the door, And kneel, "Ye Pow'rs," and warm implore, "Tho' I should wander terra e'er, In all her climes, Grant me but this, I ask no more, Ay rowth o' rhymes.

"Gie dreeping roasts to countra lairds, Till icicles hing frae their beards; Gie fine braw claes to fine life-guards, And maids of honour! And yill an' whisky gie to cairds, Until they sconner.

"A title, Dempster merits it; A garter gie to Willie Pitt; Gie wealth to some be-ledger'd cit, In cent. per cent. But give me real, sterling wit, And I'm content.

"While ye are pleas'd to keep me hale, I'll sit down o'er my scanty meal, Be't water-brose, or muslin-kail, Wi' cheerfu' face, As lang's the muses dinna fail To say the grace."

An anxious e'e I never throws Behint my lug, or by my nose; I jouk beneath misfortune's blows As weel's I may; Sworn foe to sorrow, care, and prose, I rhyme away.

O ye douce folk, that live by rule, Grave, tideless-blooded, calm and cool, Compar'd wi' you-O fool! fool! fool! How much unlike! Your hearts are just a standing pool, Your lives a dyke!

Nae hair-brain'd, sentimental traces, In your unletter'd nameless faces! In arioso trills and graces Ye never stray, But gravissimo, solemn basses Ye hum away.

Ye are sae grave, nae doubt ye're wise; Nae ferly tho' ye do despise The hairum-scarum, ram-stam boys, The rattling squad: I see you upward cast your eyes- Ye ken the road-

Whilst I-but I shall haud me there- Wi' you I'll scarce gang ony where- Then, Jamie, I shall say nae mair, But quat my sang, Content wi' you to mak a pair, Whare'er I gang.

CHAPTER XXIV.

THE VISION.

DUAN FIRST.[19]

[The Vision and the Briggs of Ayr, are said by Jeffrey to be "the only pieces by Burns which can be classed under the head of pure fiction:" but Tam O' Shanter and twenty other of his compositions have an equal right to be classed with works of fiction. The edition of this poem published at Kilmarnock, differs in some particulars from the edition which followed in Edinburgh. The maiden whose foot was so handsome as to match that of Coila, was a Bess at first, but old affection triumphed, and Jean, for whom the honour was from the first designed, regained her place. The robe of Coila, too, was expanded, so far indeed that she got more cloth than she could well carry.]

The sun had clos'd the winter day, The curlers quat their roaring play, An' hunger'd maukin ta'en her way To kail-yards green, While faithless snaws ilk step betray Whare she has been.

The thresher's weary flingin'-tree The lee-lang day had tired me; And when the day had closed his e'e Far i' the west, Ben i' the spence, right pensivelie, I gaed to rest.

There, lanely, by the ingle-cheek, I sat and ey'd the spewing reek, That fill'd, wi' hoast-provoking smeek, The auld clay biggin'; An' heard the restless rattons squeak About the riggin'.

All in this mottie, misty clime, I backward mused on wastet time, How I had spent my youthfu' prime, An' done nae thing, But stringin' blethers up in rhyme, For fools to sing.

Had I to guid advice but harkit, I might, by this hae led a market, Or strutted in a bank an' clarkit My cash-account: While here, half-mad, half-fed, half-sarkit, Is a' th' amount.

I started, mutt'ring, blockhead! coof! And heav'd on high my waukit loof, To swear by a' yon starry roof, Or some rash aith, That I, henceforth, would be rhyme-proof Till my last breath-

When, click! the string the snick did draw: And, jee! the door gaed to the wa'; An' by my ingle-lowe I saw, Now bleezin' bright, A tight outlandish hizzie, braw Come full in sight.

Ye need na doubt, I held my wisht; The infant aith, half-form'd, was crusht; I glowr'd as eerie's I'd been dusht In some wild glen; When sweet, like modest worth, she blusht, And stepped ben.

Green, slender, leaf-clad holly-boughs Were twisted, gracefu', round her brows, I took her for some Scottish Muse, By that same token; An' come to stop those reckless vows, Wou'd soon be broken.

A "hair-brain'd, sentimental trace" Was strongly marked in her face; A wildly-witty, rustic grace Shone full upon her: Her eye, ev'n turn'd on empty space, Beam'd keen with honour.

Down flow'd her robe, a tartan sheen, 'Till half a leg was scrimply seen: And such a leg! my bonnie Jean Could only peer it; Sae straught, sae taper, tight, and clean, Nane else came near it.

Her mantle large, of greenish hue, My gazing wonder chiefly drew; Deep lights and shades, bold-mingling, threw A lustre grand; And seem'd to my astonish'd view, A well-known land.

Here, rivers in the sea were lost; There, mountains to the skies were tost: Here, tumbling billows mark'd the coast, With surging foam; There, distant shone Art's lofty boast, The lordly dome.

Here, Doon pour'd down his far-fetch'd floods; There, well-fed Irwine stately thuds: Auld hermit Ayr staw thro' his woods, On to the shore; And many a lesser torrent scuds, With seeming roar.

Low, in a sandy valley spread, An ancient borough rear'd her head; Still, as in Scottish story read, She boasts a race, To ev'ry nobler virtue bred, And polish'd grace.

By stately tow'r, or palace fair, Or ruins pendent in the air, Bold stems of heroes, here and there, I could discern; Some seem'd to muse, some seem'd to dare, With feature stern.

My heart did glowing transport feel, To see a race[20] heroic wheel, And brandish round the deep-dy'd steel In sturdy blows; While back-recoiling seem'd to reel Their southron foes.

His Country's Saviour,[21] mark him well! Bold Richardton's[22] heroic swell; The chief on Sark[23] who glorious fell, In high command; And He whom ruthless fates expel His native land.

There, where a sceptr'd Pictish shade[24] Stalk'd round his ashes lowly laid, I mark'd a martial race portray'd In colours strong; Bold, soldier-featur'd, undismay'd They strode along.

Thro' many a wild romantic grove,[25] Near many a hermit-fancy'd cove, (Fit haunts for friendship or for love,) In musing mood, An aged judge, I saw him rove, Dispensing good.

With deep-struck, reverential awe,[26] The learned sire and son I saw, To Nature's God and Nature's law, They gave their lore, This, all its source and end to draw; That, to adore.

Brydone's brave ward[27] I well could spy, Beneath old Scotia's smiling eye; Who call'd on Fame, low standing by, To hand him on, Where many a Patriot-name on high And hero shone.

DUAN SECOND

With musing-deep, astonish'd stare, I view'd the heavenly-seeming fair; A whisp'ring throb did witness bear Of kindred sweet, When with an elder sister's air She did me greet.

"All hail! My own inspired bard! In me thy native Muse regard! Nor longer mourn thy fate is hard, Thus poorly low! I come to give thee such reward As we bestow.

"Know, the great genius of this land, Has many a light aërial band, Who, all beneath his high command, Harmoniously, As arts or arms they understand, Their labours ply.

"They Scotia's race among them share; Some fire the soldier on to dare; Some rouse the patriot up to bare Corruption's heart. Some teach the bard, a darling care, The tuneful art.

"'Mong swelling floods of reeking gore, They, ardent, kindling spirits, pour; Or 'mid the venal senate's roar, They, sightless, stand, To mend the honest patriot-lore, And grace the hand.

"And when the bard, or hoary sage, Charm or instruct the future age, They bind the wild, poetic rage In energy, Or point the inconclusive page Full on the eye.

"Hence Fullarton, the brave and young; Hence Dempster's zeal-inspired tongue; Hence sweet harmonious Beattie sung His 'Minstrel' lays; Or tore, with noble ardour stung, The sceptic's bays.

"To lower orders are assign'd The humbler ranks of human-kind, The rustic bard, the lab'ring hind, The artisan; All choose, as various they're inclin'd The various man.

"When yellow waves the heavy grain, The threat'ning storm some, strongly, rein; Some teach to meliorate the plain, With tillage-skill; And some instruct the shepherd-train, Blythe o'er the hill.

"Some hint the lover's harmless wile; Some grace the maiden's artless smile; Some soothe the lab'rer's weary toil, For humble gains, And make his cottage-scenes beguile His cares and pains.

"Some, bounded to a district-space, Explore at large man's infant race, To mark the embryotic trace Of rustic bard: And careful note each op'ning grace, A guide and guard.

"Of these am I-Coila my name; And this district as mine I claim, Where once the Campbells, chiefs of fame, Held ruling pow'r: I mark'd thy embryo-tuneful flame, Thy natal hour.

"With future hope, I oft would gaze, Fond, on thy little early ways, Thy rudely carroll'd, chiming phrase, In uncouth rhymes, Fir'd at the simple, artless lays Of other times.

"I saw thee seek the sounding shore, Delighted with the dashing roar; Or when the north his fleecy store Drove through the sky, I saw grim Nature's visage hoar Struck thy young eye.

"Or when the deep green-mantled earth Warm cherish'd ev'ry flow'ret's birth, And joy and music pouring forth In ev'ry grove, I saw thee eye the general mirth With boundless love.

"When ripen'd fields, and azure skies, Called forth the reaper's rustling noise, I saw thee leave their evening joys, And lonely stalk, To vent thy bosom's swelling rise In pensive walk.

"When youthful love, warm-blushing, strong, Keen-shivering shot thy nerves along, Those accents, grateful to thy tongue, Th' adored Name I taught thee how to pour in song, To soothe thy flame.

"I saw thy pulse's maddening play, Wild send thee pleasure's devious way, Misled by Fancy's meteor-ray, By passion driven; But yet the light that led astray Was light from Heaven.

"I taught thy manners-painting strains, The loves, the ways of simple swains, Till now, o'er all my wide domains Thy fame extends; And some, the pride of Coila's plains, Become thy friends.

"Thou canst not learn, nor can I show, To paint with Thomson's landscape glow; Or wake the bosom-melting throe, With Shenstone's art; Or pour, with Gray, the moving flow, Warm on the heart.

"Yet, all beneath the unrivall'd rose, The lowly daisy sweetly blows; Tho' large the forest's monarch throws His army shade, Yet green the juicy hawthorn grows, Adown the glade.

"Then never murmur nor repine; Strive in thy humble sphere to shine; And, trust me, not Potosi's mine, Nor king's regard, Can give a bliss o'ermatching thine, A rustic bard.

"To give my counsels all in one, Thy tuneful flame still careful fan; Preserve the dignity of man, With soul erect; And trust, the universal plan Will all protect.

"And wear thou this,"-she solemn said, And bound the holly round my head: The polish'd leaves and berries red Did rustling play; And like a passing thought, she fled In light away.

FOOTNOTES:

[19] Duan, a term of Ossian's for the different divisions of a digressive poem. See his "Cath-Loda," vol. ii. of Macpherson's translation.

[20] The Wallaces.

[21] Sir William Wallace.

[22] Adam Wallace, of Richardton, cousin to the immortal preserver of Scottish independence.

[23] Wallace, Laird of Craigie, who was second in command under Douglas, Earl of Ormond, at the famous battle on the banks of Sark, fought anno 1448. That glorious victory was principally owing to the judicious conduct and intrepid valour of the gallant laird of Craigie, who died of his wounds after the action.

[24] Coilus, king of the Picts, from whom the district of Kyle is said to take its name, lies buried, as tradition says, near the family seat of the

Montgomeries of Coilsfield, where his burial-place is still shown.
[25] Barskimming, the seat of the late Lord Justice-Clerk (Sir Thomas Miller of Glenlee, afterwards President of the Court of Session.)
[26] Catrine, the seat of Professor Dugald Steward.
[27] Colonel Fullarton.

CHAPTER XXV.

HALLOWEEN.[28]

"Yes! let the rich deride, the proud disdain, The simple pleasures of the lowly train; To me more dear, congenial to my heart, One native charm, than all the gloss of art."
Goldsmith.

[This Poem contains a lively and striking picture of some of the superstitious observances of old Scotland: on Halloween the desire to look into futurity was once all but universal in the north; and the charms and spells which Burns describes, form but a portion of those employed to enable the peasantry to have a peep up the dark vista of the future. The scene is laid on the romantic shores of Ayr, at a farmer's fireside, and the actors in the rustic drama are the whole household, including supernumerary reapers and bandsmen about to be discharged from the engagements of harvest. "I never can help regarding this," says James Hogg, "as rather a trivial poem!"]

Upon that night, when fairies light On Cassilis Downans[29] dance, Or owre the lays, in splendid blaze, On sprightly coursers prance; Or for Colean the rout is ta'en, Beneath the moon's pale beams; There, up the Cove,[30] to stray an' rove Amang the rocks an' streams To sport that night.

Amang the bonnie winding banks Where Doon rins, wimplin', clear, Where Bruce[31] ance rul'd the martial ranks, An' shook his Carrick spear, Some merry, friendly, countra folks, Together did convene, To burn their nits, an' pou their stocks, An' haud their Halloween Fu' blythe that night.

The lasses feat, an' cleanly neat, Mair braw than when they're fine; Their faces blythe, fu' sweetly kythe, Hearts leal, an' warm, an' kin'; The lads sae trig, wi' wooer babs, Weel knotted on their garten, Some unco blate, an' some wi' gabs, Gar lasses' hearts gang startin' Whiles fast at night.

Then, first and foremost, thro' the kail, Their stocks[32] maun a' be sought ance; They steek their een, an' graip an' wale, For muckle anes an' straught anes. Poor hav'rel Will fell aff the drift, An' wander'd through the bow-kail, An' pou't, for want o' better shift, A runt was like a sow-tail, Sae bow't that night.

Then, straught or crooked, yird or nane, They roar an' cry a' throu'ther; The vera wee-things, todlin', rin Wi' stocks out-owre their shouther; An' gif the custoc's sweet or sour, Wi' joctelegs they taste them; Syne coziely, aboon the door, Wi' cannie care, they've placed them To lie that night.

The lasses staw frae mang them a' To pou their stalks o' corn;[33] But Rab slips out, an' jinks about, Behint the muckle thorn: He grippet Nelly hard an' fast; Loud skirl'd a' the lasses; But her tap-pickle maist was lost, When kiuttlin' in the fause-house[34] Wi' him that night.

The auld guidwife's weel hoordet nits[35] Are round an' round divided; An' monie lads' an' lasses' fates Are there that night decided: Some kindle, couthie, side by side, An' burn thegither trimly; Some start awa' wi' saucy pride, And jump out-owre the chimlie Fu' high that night.

Jean slips in twa wi' tentie e'e; Wha 'twas, she wadna tell; But this is Jock, an' this is me, She says in to hersel': He bleez'd owre her, an' she owre him, As they wad never mair part; 'Till, fuff! he started up the lum, An' Jean had e'en a sair heart To see't that night.

Poor Willie, wi' his bow-kail runt, Was brunt wi' primsie Mallie; An' Mallie, nae doubt, took the drunt, To be compar'd to Willie; Mall's nit lap out wi' pridefu' fling, An' her ain fit it brunt it; While Willie lap, and swoor, by jing, 'Twas just the way he wanted To be that night.

Nell had the fause-house in her min', She pits hersel an' Rob in; In loving bleeze they sweetly join, 'Till white in ase they're sobbin'; Nell's heart, was dancin' at the view, She whisper'd Rob to leuk for't: Rob, stowlins, prie'd her bonie mou', Fu' cozie in the neuk for't, Unseen that night.

But Merran sat behint their backs, Her thoughts on Andrew Bell; She lea'es them gashin' at their cracks, And slips out by hersel': She through the yard the nearest taks, An' to the kiln she goes then, An' darklins graipit for the bauks, And in the blue-clue[36] throws then, Right fear't that night.

An' ay she win't, an' ay she swat, I wat she made nae jaukin'; 'Till something held within the pat, Guid L-d! but she was quaukin'! But whether 'twas the Deil himsel', Or whether 'twas a bauk-en', Or whether it was Andrew Bell, She did na wait on talkin' To spier that night.

Wee Jenny to her graunie says, "Will ye go wi' me, graunie? I'll eat the apple[37] at the glass, I gat frae uncle Johnnie:" She fuff't her pipe wi' sic a lunt, In wrath she was sae vap'rin', She notic't na, an aizle brunt Her braw new worset apron Out thro' that night.

"Ye little skelpie-limmer's face! I daur you try sic sportin', As seek the foul Thief onie place, For him to spae your fortune: Nae doubt but ye may get a sight! Great cause ye hae to fear it; For monie a ane has gotten a fright, An' liv'd an' died deleeret On sic a night.

"Ae hairst afore the Sherra-moor, I mind't as weel's yestreen, I was a gilpey then, I'm sure I was na past fifteen: The simmer had been cauld an' wat, An' stuff was unco green; An' ay a rantin' kirn we gat, An' just on Halloween It fell that night.

"Our stibble-rig was Rab M'Graen, A clever, sturdy fellow: He's sin gat Eppie Sim wi' wean, That liv'd in Achmacalla: He gat hemp-seed,[38] I mind it weel, And he made unco light o't; But monie a day was by himsel',

He was sae sairly frighted That vera night."

Then up gat fechtin' Jamie Fleck, An' he swoor by his conscience, That he could saw hemp-seed a peck; For it was a' but nonsense; The auld guidman raught down the pock, An' out a' handfu' gied him; Syne bad him slip frae 'mang the folk, Sometime when nae ane see'd him, An' try't that night.

He marches thro' amang the stacks, Tho' he was something sturtin; The graip he for a harrow taks, An' haurls at his curpin; An' ev'ry now an' then he says, "Hemp-seed, I saw thee, An' her that is to be my lass, Come after me, an' draw thee As fast that night."

He whistl'd up Lord Lennox' march, To keep his courage cheery; Altho' his hair began to arch, He was sae fley'd an' eerie; 'Till presently he hears a squeak, An' then a grane an' gruntle; He by his shouther gae a keek, An' tumbl'd wi' a wintle Out-owre that night.

He roar'd a horrid murder-shout, In dreadfu' desperation! An' young an' auld cam rinnin' out, An' hear the sad narration; He swoor 'twas hilchin Jean M'Craw, Or crouchie Merran Humphie, 'Till, stop! she trotted thro' them a'; An' wha was it but Grumphie Asteer that night!

Meg fain wad to the barn hae gaen, To win three wechts o' naething;[39] But for to meet the deil her lane, She pat but little faith in: She gies the herd a pickle nits, An' twa red cheekit apples, To watch, while for the barn she sets, In hopes to see Tam Kipples That vera night.

She turns the key wi' cannie thraw, An' owre the threshold ventures; But first on Sawnie gies a ca', Syne bauldly in she enters: A ratton rattled up the wa', An' she cried, L-d preserve her! An' ran thro' midden-hole an' a', An' pray'd wi' zeal and fervour, Fu' fast that night.

They hoy't out Will, wi sair advice; They hecht him some fine braw ane; It chanc'd the stack he faddom't thrice,[40] Was timmer-propt for thrawin'; He taks a swirlie auld moss-oak, For some black, grousome carlin; An' loot a winze, an' drew a stroke, 'Till skin in blypes cam haurlin' Aff's nieves that night.

A wanton widow Leezie was, As canty as a kittlin; But, och! that night, amang the shaws, She got a fearfu' settlin'! She thro' the whins, an' by the cairn, An' owre the hill gaed scrievin, Whare three lairds' lands met at a burn,[41] To dip her left sark-sleeve in, Was bent that night.

Whyles owre a linn the burnie plays, As through the glen it wimpl't; Whyles round a rocky scaur it strays, Whyles in a wiel it dimpl't; Whyles glitter'd to the nightly rays, Wi' bickering, dancing dazzle; Whyles cookit underneath the braes, Below the spreading hazel, Unseen that night.

Amang the brackens on the brae, Between her an' the moon, The deil, or else an outler quey, Gat up an' gae a croon: Poor Leezie's heart maist lap the hool! Near lav'rock-height she jumpit, But mist a fit, an' in the pool Out-owre the lugs she plumpit, Wi' a plunge that night.

In order, on the clean hearth-stane, The luggies three[42] are ranged, And ev'ry time great care is ta'en, To see them duly changed: Auld uncle John, wha wedlock's joys Sin Mar's-year did desire, Because he gat the toom-dish thrice, He heav'd them on the fire In wrath that night.

Wi' merry sangs, and friendly cracks, I wat they did na weary; An' unco tales, an' funnie jokes, Their sports were cheap an' cheery; Till butter'd so'ns[43] wi' fragrant lunt, Set a' their gabs a-steerin'; Syne, wi' a social glass o' strunt, They parted aff careerin' Fu' blythe that night.

FOOTNOTES:

[28] Is thought to be a night when witches, devils, and other mischief-making beings are all abroad on their baneful midnight errands: particularly those aërial people, the Fairies, are said on that night to hold a grand anniversary.

[29] Certain little, romantic, rocky green hills, in the neighbourhood of the ancient seat of the Earls of Cassilis.

[30] A noted cavern near Colean-house, called the Cove of Colean which, as well as Cassilis Downans, is famed in country story for being a favourite haunt of fairies.

[31] The famous family of that name, the ancestors of Robert, the great deliverer of his country, were Earls of Carrick.

[32] The first ceremony of Halloween is pulling each a stock, or plant of kail. They must go out, hand-in-hand, with eyes shut, and pull the first they meet with: its being big or little, straight or crooked, is prophetic of the size and shape of the grand object of all their spells-the husband or wife. If any yird, or earth, stick to the root, that is tocher, or fortune; and the taste of the custoc, that is, the heart of the stem, is indicative of the natural temper and disposition. Lastly, the stems, or, to give them their ordinary appellation, the runts, are placed somewhere above the head of the door; and the Christian names of the people whom chance brings into the house are, according to the priority of placing the runts, the names in question.

[33] They go to the barn-yard, and pull each at three several times, a stalk of oats. If the third stalk wants the top-pickle, that is, the grain at the top of the stalk, the party in question will come to the marriage-bed anything but a maid.

[34] When the corn is in a doubtful state, by being too green or wet, the stack-builder, by means of old timber, andc., makes a large apartment in his stack, with an opening in the side which is fairest exposed to the wind: this he calls a fause-house.

[35] Burning the nuts is a famous charm. They name the lad and lass to each particular nut, as they lay them in the fire, and according as they burn quietly together, or start from beside one another, the course and issue of the courtship will be.

[36] Whoever would, with success, try this spell, must strictly observe these directions: Steal out, all alone, to the kiln, and, darkling, throw into the pot a

clue of blue yarn; wind it in a clue off the old one; and towards the latter end, something will hold the thread; demand "wha hauds?" i.e. who holds? an answer will be returned from the kiln-pot, naming the Christian and surname of your future spouse.

[37] Take a candle, and go alone to a looking-glass; eat an apple before it, and some traditions say, you should comb your hair all the time; the face of your conjugal companion, to be, will be seen in the glass, as if peeping over your shoulder.

[38] Steal out unperceived, and sow a handful of hemp-seed, harrowing it with anything you can conveniently draw after you. Repeat, now and then, "Hemp-seed, I saw thee; hemp-seed, I saw thee; and him (or her) that is to be my true love, come after me and pou thee." Look over your left shoulder, and you will see the appearance of the person invoked, in the attitude of pulling hemp. Some traditions say, "Come after me, and shaw thee," that is, show thyself; in which case it simply appears. Others omit the harrowing, and say, "Come after me, and harrow thee."

[39] This charm must likewise be performed, unperceived, and alone. You go to the barn, and open both doors, taking them off the hinges, if possible; for there is danger that the being about to appear may shut the doors and do you some mischief. Then take that instrument used in winnowing the corn, which, in our country dialect, we call a wecht; and go through all the attitudes of letting down corn against the wind. Repeat it three times; and the third time, an apparition will pass through the barn, in at the windy door, and out at the other, having both the figure in question, and the appearance or retinue marking the employment or station in life.

[40] Take an opportunity of going unnoticed, to a bean stack, and fathom it three times round. The last fathom of the last time, you will catch in your arms the appearance of your future conjugal yoke-fellow.

[41] You go out, one or more, for this is a social spell, to a south running spring or rivulet, where "three lairds' lands meet," and dip your left shirt-sleeve. Go to bed in sight of a fire, and hang your wet sleeve before it to dry. Lie awake: and, some time near midnight, an apparition having the exact figure of the grand object in question, will come and turn the sleeve, as if to dry the other side of it.

[42] Take three dishes: put clean water in one, foul water in another, and leave the third empty; blindfold a person and lead him to the hearth where the dishes are ranged; he (or she) dips the left hand: if by chance in the clean water, the future husband or wife will come to the bar of matrimony a maid; if in the foul, a widow; if in the empty dish, it foretells, with equal certainty, no marriage at all. It is repeated three times, and every time the arrangement of the dishes is altered.

[43] Sowens, with butter instead of milk to them, is always the Halloween supper.

CHAPTER XXVI.

MAN WAS MADE TO MOURN.

A DIRGE.

[The origin of this fine poem is alluded to by Burns in one of his letters to Mrs. Dunlop: "I had an old grand-uncle with whom my mother lived in her girlish years: the good old man was long blind ere he died, during which time his highest enjoyment was to sit and cry, while my mother would sing the simple old song of 'The Life and Age of Man.'" From that truly venerable woman, long after the death of her distinguished son, Cromek, in collecting the Reliques, obtained a copy by recitation of the older strain. Though the tone and sentiment coincide closely with "Man was made to Mourn," I agree with Lockhart, that Burns wrote it in obedience to his own habitual feelings.]

When chill November's surly blast Made fields and forests bare, One ev'ning as I wandered forth Along the banks of Ayr, I spy'd a man whose aged step Seem'd weary, worn with care; His face was furrow'd o'er with years, And hoary was his hair.

"Young stranger, whither wand'rest thou?" Began the rev'rend sage; "Does thirst of wealth thy step constrain, Or youthful pleasure's rage? Or haply, prest with cares and woes, Too soon thou hast began To wander forth, with me to mourn The miseries of man.

"The sun that overhangs yon moors, Out-spreading far and wide, Where hundreds labour to support A haughty lordling's pride: I've seen yon weary winter-sun Twice forty times return, And ev'ry time had added proofs That man was made to mourn.

"O man! while in thy early years, [96]How prodigal of time! Misspending all thy precious hours, Thy glorious youthful prime! Alternate follies take the sway; Licentious passions burn; Which tenfold force gives nature's law, That man was made to mourn.

"Look not alone on youthful prime, Or manhood's active might; Man then is useful to his kind, Supported in his right: But see him on the edge of life, With cares and sorrows worn; Then age and want-oh! ill-match'd pair!- Show man was made to mourn.

"A few seem favorites of fate, In pleasure's lap carest: Yet, think not all the rich and great Are likewise truly blest. But, oh! what crowds in every land, All wretched and forlorn! Thro' weary life this lesson learn- That man was made to mourn.

"Many and sharp the num'rous ills Inwoven with our frame! More pointed still we make ourselves, Regret, remorse, and shame! And man, whose heaven-erected face The smiles of love adorn, Man's inhumanity to man Makes countless thousands mourn!

"See yonder poor, o'erlabour'd wight, So abject, mean, and vile, Who begs a brother of the earth To give him leave to toil; And see his lordly fellow-worm The poor petition spurn, Unmindful, though a weeping wife And helpless offspring mourn.

"If I'm design'd yon lordling's slave- By Nature's law design'd- Why was an independent wish E'er planted in my mind? If not, why am I subject to His cruelty or scorn? Or why has man the will and power To make his fellow mourn?

"Yet, let not this too much, my son, Disturb thy youthful breast; This partial view of human-kind Is surely not the best! The poor, oppressed, honest man Had never, sure, been born, Had there not been some recompense To comfort those that mourn!

"O Death! the poor man's dearest friend- The kindest and the best! Welcome the hour, my aged limbs Are laid with thee at rest! The great, the wealthy, fear thy blow, From pomp and pleasure torn! But, oh! a blest relief to those That weary-laden mourn."

CHAPTER XXVII.

TO RUIN.

["I have been," says Burns, in his common-place book, "taking a peep through, as Young finely says, 'The dark postern of time long elapsed.' 'Twas a rueful prospect! What a tissue of thoughtlessness, weakness, and folly! my life reminded me of a ruined temple. What strength, what proportion in some parts, what unsightly gaps, what prostrate ruins in others!" The fragment, To Ruin, seems to have had its origin in moments such as these.]

I.

All hail! inexorable lord! At whose destruction-breathing word, The mightiest empires fall! Thy cruel, woe-delighted train, The ministers of grief and pain, A sullen welcome, all! With stern-resolv'd, despairing eye, I see each aimed dart; For one has cut my dearest tie, And quivers in my heart. Then low'ring and pouring, The storm no more I dread; Though thick'ning and black'ning, Round my devoted head.

II.

And thou grim pow'r, by life abhorr'd, While life a pleasure can afford, Oh! hear a wretch's prayer! No more I shrink appall'd, afraid; I court, I beg thy friendly aid, To close this scene of care! [97]When shall my soul, in silent peace, Resign life's joyless day; My weary heart its throbbings cease, Cold mould'ring in the clay? No fear more, no tear more, To stain my lifeless face; Enclasped, and grasped Within thy cold embrace!

CHAPTER XXVIII.

TO

JOHN GOUDIE OF KILMARNOCK.

ON THE PUBLICATION OF HIS ESSAYS

[This burning commentary, by Burns, on the Essays of Goudie in the Macgill controversy, was first published by Stewart, with the Jolly Beggars, in 1801; it is akin in life and spirit to Holy Willie's Prayer; and may be cited as a sample of the wit and the force which the poet brought to the great, but now forgotten, controversy of the West.]

O Goudie! terror of the Whigs, Dread of black coats and rev'rend wigs, Sour Bigotry, on her last legs, Girnin', looks back, Wishin' the ten Egyptian plagues Wad seize you quick.

Poor gapin', glowrin' Superstition, Waes me! she's in a sad condition: Fie! bring Black Jock, her state physician, To see her water: Alas! there's ground o' great suspicion She'll ne'er get better.

Auld Orthodoxy lang did grapple, But now she's got an unco ripple; Haste, gie her name up i' the chapel, Nigh unto death; See, how she fetches at the thrapple, An' gasps for breath.

Enthusiasm's past redemption, Gaen in a gallopin' consumption, Not a' the quacks, wi' a' their gumption, Will ever mend her. Her feeble pulse gies strong presumption Death soon will end her.

'Tis you and Taylor[44] are the chief, Wha are to blame for this mischief, But gin the Lord's ain focks gat leave, A toom tar-barrel, An' twa red peats wad send relief, An' end the quarrel.

FOOTNOTES:

[44] Dr. Taylor, of Norwich.

CHAPTER XXIX.

TO

J. LAPRAIK.

AN OLD SCOTTISH BARD.

April 1st, 1785.

(FIRST EPISTLE.)

["The epistle to John Lapraik," says Gilbert Burns, "was produced exactly on the occasion described by the author. Rocking is a term derived from primitive times, when our country-women employed their spare hours in spinning on the roke or distaff. This simple instrument is a very portable one; and well fitted to the social inclination of meeting in a neighbour's house; hence the phrase of going a rocking, or with the roke. As the connexion the phrase had with the implement was forgotten when the roke gave place to the spinning-wheel, the phrase came to be used by both sexes on social occasions, and men talk of going with their rokes as well as women."]

While briers an' woodbines budding green, An' paitricks scraichin' loud at e'en, An' morning poussie whidden seen, Inspire my muse, This freedom in an unknown frien' I pray excuse.

On Fasten-een we had a rockin', To ca' the crack and weave our stockin', And there was muckle fun an' jokin', Ye need na doubt; At length we had a hearty yokin' At sang about.

There was ae sang, amang the rest, Aboon them a' it pleas'd me best, That some kind husband had addrest To some sweet wife; It thirl'd the heart-strings thro' the breast, A' to the life.

I've scarce heard aught describ'd sae weel, What gen'rous manly bosoms feel, Thought I, "Can this be Pope or Steele, Or Beattie's wark?" They told me 'twas an odd kind chiel About Muirkirk. [98]

It pat me fidgin-fain to hear't, And sae about him there I spier't, Then a' that ken't him round declar'd He had injine, That, nane excell'd it, few cam near't, It was sae fine.

That, set him to a pint of ale, An' either douce or merry tale, Or rhymes an' sangs he'd made himsel', Or witty catches, 'Tween Inverness and Tiviotdale, He had few matches.

Then up I gat, an' swoor an aith, Tho' I should pawn my pleugh and graith, Or die a cadger pownie's death At some dyke-back, A pint an' gill I'd gie them baith To hear your crack.

But, first an' foremost, I should tell, Amaist as soon as I could spell, I to the crambo-jingle fell, Tho' rude an' rough, Yet crooning to a body's sel', Does weel eneugh.

I am nae poet in a sense, But just a rhymer, like, by chance, An' hae to learning nae pretence, Yet what the matter? Whene'er my Muse does on me glance, I jingle at her.

Your critic-folk may cock their nose, And say, "How can you e'er propose, You, wha ken hardly verse frae prose, To mak a sang?" But, by your leaves, my learned foes, Ye're may-be wrang.

What's a' your jargon o' your schools, Your Latin names for horns an' stools; If honest nature made you fools, What sairs your grammars? Ye'd better taen up spades and shools, Or knappin-hammers.

A set o' dull, conceited hashes, Confuse their brains in college classes! They gang in stirks and come out asses, Plain truth to speak; An' syne they think to climb Parnassus By dint o' Greek!

Gie me ae spark o' Nature's fire! That's a' the learning I desire; Then though I drudge thro' dub an' mire At pleugh or cart, My muse, though hamely in attire, May touch the heart.

O for a spunk o' Allan's glee, Or Fergusson's, the bauld and slee, Or bright Lapraik's, my friend to be, If I can hit it! That would be lear eneugh for me, If I could get it.

Now, sir, if ye hae friends enow, Tho' real friends, I b'lieve, are few, Yet, if your catalogue be fou, I'se no insist, But gif ye want ae friend that's true-I'm on your list.

I winna blaw about mysel; As ill I like my fauts to tell; But friends an' folk that wish me well, They sometimes roose me; Tho' I maun own, as monie still As far abuse me.

There's ae wee faut they whiles lay to me, I like the lasses-Gude forgie me! For monie a plack they wheedle frae me, At dance or fair; May be some ither thing they gie me They weel can spare.

But Mauchline race, or Mauchline fair; I should be proud to meet you there! We'se gie ae night's discharge to care, If we forgather, An' hae a swap o' rhymin'-ware Wi' ane anither.

The four-gill chap, we'se gar him clatter, An' kirsen him wi' reekin' water; Syne we'll sit down an' tak our whitter, To cheer our heart; An' faith, we'se be acquainted better, Before we part.

Awa, ye selfish, warly race, Wha think that havins, sense, an' grace, Ev'n love an' friendship, should give place To catch-the-plack! I dinna like to see your face, Nor hear your crack.

But ye whom social pleasure charms, Whose hearts the tide of kindness warms, Who hold your being on the terms, "Each aid the others," Come to my bowl, come to my arms, My friends, my brothers!

But, to conclude my lang epistle, As my auld pen's worn to the grissle; Twa lines frae you wad gar me fissle, Who am, most fervent, While I can either sing or whissle, Your friend and servant.

CHAPTER XXX.

To

J. LAPRAIK.

(SECOND EPISTLE.)

[The John Lapraik to whom these epistles are addressed lived at Dalfram in the neighbourhood of Muirkirk, and was a rustic worshipper of the Muse: he unluckily, however, involved himself in that Western bubble, the Ayr Bank, and consoled himself by composing in his distress that song which moved the heart of Burns, beginning

"When I upon thy bosom lean."

He afterwards published a volume of verse, of a quality which proved that the inspiration in his song of domestic sorrow was no settled power of soul.]

April 21st, 1785.

While new-ca'd ky, rowte at the stake, An' pownies reek in pleugh or braik, This hour on e'enin's edge I take To own I'm debtor, To honest-hearted, auld Lapraik, For his kind letter.

Forjesket sair, wi' weary legs, Rattlin' the corn out-owre the rigs, Or dealing thro' amang the naigs Their ten hours' bite, My awkart muse sair pleads and begs, I would na write.

The tapetless ramfeezl'd hizzie, She's saft at best, and something lazy, Quo' she, "Ye ken, we've been sae busy, This month' an' mair, That trouth, my head is grown right dizzie, An' something sair."

Her dowff excuses pat me mad: "Conscience," says I, "ye thowless jad! I'll write, an' that a hearty blaud, This vera night; So dinna ye affront your trade, But rhyme it right.

"Shall bauld Lapraik, the king o' hearts, Tho' mankind were a pack o' cartes,

Roose you sae weel for your deserts, In terms sae friendly, Yet ye'll neglect to show your parts, An' thank him kindly?"

Sae I gat paper in a blink An' down gaed stumpie in the ink: Quoth I, "Before I sleep a wink, I vow I'll close it; An' if ye winna mak it clink, By Jove I'll prose it!"

Sae I've begun to scrawl, but whether In rhyme or prose, or baith thegither, Or some hotch-potch that's rightly neither, Let time mak proof; But I shall scribble down some blether Just clean aff-loof.

My worthy friend, ne'er grudge an' carp, Tho' fortune use you hard an' sharp; Come, kittle up your moorland-harp Wi' gleesome touch! Ne'er mind how fortune waft an' warp; She's but a b-tch.

She's gien me monie a jirt an' fleg, Sin' I could striddle owre a rig; But, by the L-d, tho' I should beg Wi' lyart pow, I'll laugh, an' sing, an' shake my leg, As lang's I dow!

Now comes the sax an' twentieth simmer, I've seen the bud upo' the timmer, Still persecuted by the limmer Frae year to year; But yet despite the kittle kimmer, I, Rob, am here.

Do ye envy the city gent, Behint a kist to lie and sklent, Or purse-proud, big wi' cent. per cent. And muckle wame, In some bit brugh to represent A bailie's name?

Or is't the paughty, feudal Thane, Wi' ruffl'd sark an' glancing cane, Wha thinks himsel nae sheep-shank bane, But lordly stalks, While caps and bonnets aff are taen, As by he walks!

"O Thou wha gies us each guid gift! Gie me o' wit an' sense a lift, Then turn me, if Thou please, adrift, Thro' Scotland wide; Wi' cits nor lairds I wadna shift, In a' their pride!"

Were this the charter of our state, "On pain' o' hell be rich an' great," Damnation then would be our fate, Beyond remead; But, thanks to Heav'n, that's no the gate We learn our creed.

For thus the royal mandate ran, When first the human race began, "The social, friendly, honest man, Whate'er he be, 'Tis he fulfils great Nature's plan, An' none but he!"

O mandate, glorious and divine! The followers o' the ragged Nine, Poor thoughtless devils! yet may shine In glorious light, While sordid sons o' Mammon's line Are dark as night.

Tho' here they scrape, an' squeeze, an' growl, Their worthless nievfu' of a soul May in some future carcase howl The forest's fright; Or in some day-detesting owl May shun the light.

Then may Lapraik and Burns arise, To reach their native kindred skies, And sing their pleasures, hopes, an' joys, In some mild sphere, Still closer knit in friendship's ties Each passing year!

CHAPTER XXXI.

TO

J. LAPRAIK.
(THIRD EPISTLE.)

[I have heard one of our most distinguished English poets recite with a sort of ecstasy some of the verses of these epistles, and praise the ease of the language and the happiness of the thoughts. He averred, however, that the poet, when pinched for a word, hesitated not to coin one, and instanced, "tapetless," "ramfeezled," and "forjesket," as intrusions in our dialect. These words seem indeed, to some Scotchmen, strange and uncouth, but they are true words of the west.]

Sept. 13th, 1785.

Guid speed an' furder to you, Johnny, Guid health, hale han's, an' weather bonny; Now when ye're nickan down fu' canny The staff o' bread, May ye ne'er want a stoup o' bran'y To clear your head.

May Boreas never thresh your rigs, Nor kick your rickles aff their legs, Sendin' the stuff o'er muirs an' haggs Like drivin' wrack; But may the tapmast grain that wags Come to the sack.

I'm bizzie too, an' skelpin' at it, But bitter, daudin' showers hae wat it, Sae my auld stumpie pen I gat it Wi' muckle wark, An' took my jocteleg an' whatt it, Like ony clark.

It's now twa month that I'm your debtor For your braw, nameless, dateless letter, Abusin' me for harsh ill nature On holy men, While deil a hair yoursel' ye're better, But mair profane.

But let the kirk-folk ring their bells, Let's sing about our noble sel's; We'll cry nae jads frae heathen hills To help, or roose us, But browster wives an' whiskey stills, They are the muses.

Your friendship, Sir, I winna quat it An' if ye mak' objections at it, Then han' in nieve some day we'll knot it, An' witness take, An' when wi' Usquabae we've wat it It winna break.

But if the beast and branks be spar'd Till kye be gaun without the herd, An' a' the vittel in the yard, An' theekit right, I mean your ingle-side to guard Ae winter night.

Then muse-inspirin' aqua-vitæ Shall make us baith sae blythe an' witty, Till ye forget ye're auld an' gatty, An' be as canty, As ye were nine year less than thretty, Sweet ane an' twenty!

But stooks are cowpet wi' the blast, An' now the sin keeks in the west, Then I maun rin amang the rest An' quat my chanter; Sae I subscribe myself in haste, Yours, Rab the Ranter.

CHAPTER XXXII.

TO
WILLIAM SIMPSON,
OCHILTREE.

[The person to whom this epistle is addressed, was schoolmaster of Ochiltree, and afterwards of New Lanark: he was a writer of verses too, like many more of the poet's comrades;-of verses which rose not above the barren level of mediocrity: "one of his poems," says Chambers, "was a laughable elegy on the death of the Emperor Paul." In his verses to Burns, under the name of a Tailor, there is nothing to laugh at, though they are intended to be laughable as well as monitory.]

May, 1785.

I gat your letter, winsome Willie; Wi' gratefu' heart I thank you brawlie; Tho' I maun say't, I wad be silly, An' unco vain, Should I believe, my coaxin' billie, Your flatterin' strain.

But I'se believe ye kindly meant it, I sud be laith to think ye hinted Ironic satire, sidelins sklented On my poor Musie; Tho' in sic phraisin' terms ye've penn'd it, I scarce excuse ye.

My senses wad be in a creel, Should I but dare a hope to speel, Wi' Allan, or wi' Gilbertfield, The braes o' fame; Or Fergusson, the writer chiel, A deathless name.

(O Fergusson! thy glorious parts Ill suited law's dry, musty arts! My curse upon your whunstane hearts, Ye Enbrugh gentry! The tythe o' what ye waste at cartes Wad stow'd his pantry!)

Yet when a tale comes i' my head, Or lasses gie my heart a screed, As whiles they're like to be my dead (O sad disease!) I kittle up my rustic reed, It gies me ease.

Auld Coila, now, may fidge fu' fain, She's gotten poets o' her ain, Chiels wha their chanters winna hain, But tune their lays, Till echoes a' resound again Her weel-sung praise.

Nae poet thought her worth his while, To set her name in measur'd stile; She lay like some unkenn'd-of isle Beside New-Holland, Or whare wild-meeting oceans boil Besouth Magellan.

Ramsay an' famous Fergusson Gied Forth and Tay a lift aboon; Yarrow an' Tweed, to monie a tune, Owre Scotland rings, While Irwin, Lugar, Ayr, an' Doon, Nae body sings.

Th' Ilissus, Tiber, Thames, an' Seine, Glide sweet in monie a tunefu' line! But, Willie, set your fit to mine, An' cock your crest, We'll gar our streams an' burnies shine Up wi' the best.

We'll sing auld Coila's plains an' fells, Her moor's red-brown wi' heather bells, Her banks an' braes, her dens an' dells, Where glorious Wallace Aft bure the gree, as story tells, Frae southron billies. [102]

At Wallace' name, what Scottish blood But boils up in a spring-tide flood! Oft have our fearless fathers strode By Wallace' side, Still pressing onward, red-wat shod, Or glorious dy'd.

O sweet are Coila's haughs an' woods, When lintwhites chant amang the buds, And jinkin' hares, in amorous whids Their loves enjoy, While thro' the braes the cushat croods With wailfu' cry!

Ev'n winter bleak has charms to me When winds rave thro' the naked tree;

Or frosts on hills of Ochiltree Are hoary gray: Or blinding drifts wild-furious flee, Dark'ning the day.

O Nature! a' thy shews an' forms To feeling, pensive hearts hae charms! Whether the summer kindly warms, Wi' life an' light, Or winter howls, in gusty storms, The lang, dark night!

The muse, nae Poet ever fand her, 'Till by himsel' he learn'd to wander, Adown some trotting burn's meander, An' no think lang; O sweet, to stray an' pensive ponder A heart-felt sang!

The warly race may drudge an' drive, Hog-shouther, jundie, stretch an' strive, Let me fair Nature's face descrive, And I, wi' pleasure, Shall let the busy, grumbling hive Bum owre their treasure.

Fareweel, my "rhyme-composing brither!" We've been owre lang unkenn'd to ither: Now let us lay our heads thegither, In love fraternal; May envy wallop in a tether, Black fiend, infernal!

While Highlandmen hate tolls an' taxes; While moorlan' herds like guid fat braxies; While terra firma, on her axes Diurnal turns, Count on a friend, in faith an' practice, In Robert Burns.

POSTSCRIPT

My memory's no worth a preen: I had amaist forgotten clean, Ye bade me write you what they mean, By this New Light, 'Bout which our herds sae aft hae been, Maist like to fight.

In days when mankind were but callans, At grammar, logic, an' sic talents, They took nae pains their speech to balance, Or rules to gie, But spak their thoughts in plain, braid Lallans, Like you or me.

In thae auld times, they thought the moon, Just like a sark, or pair o' shoon, Wore by degrees, 'till her last roon, Gaed past their viewing, An' shortly after she was done, They gat a new one.

This past for certain-undisputed; It ne'er cam i' their heads to doubt it, 'Till chiels gat up an' wad confute it, An' ca'd it wrang; An' muckle din there was about it, Baith loud an' lang.

Some herds, weel learn'd upo' the beuk, Wad threap auld folk the thing misteuk; For 'twas the auld moon turned a neuk, An' out o' sight, An' backlins-comin', to the leuk, She grew mair bright.

This was deny'd, it was affirm'd; The herds an' hissels were alarm'd: The rev'rend gray-beards rav'd and storm'd That beardless laddies Should think they better were inform'd Than their auld daddies.

Frae less to mair it gaed to sticks; Frae words an' aiths to clours an' nicks, An' monie a fallow gat his licks, Wi' hearty crunt; An' some, to learn them for their tricks, Were hang'd an' brunt.

This game was play'd in monie lands, An' Auld Light caddies bure sic hands, That, faith, the youngsters took the sands Wi' nimble shanks, 'Till lairds forbade, by strict commands, Sic bluidy pranks.

But New Light herds gat sic a cowe, Folk thought them ruin'd stick-an'-

stowe, Till now amaist on every knowe, Ye'll find ane plac'd; An' some their New Light fair avow, Just quite barefac'd.

Nae doubt the Auld Light flocks are bleatin'; Their zealous herds are vex'd an' sweatin': Mysel', I've even seen them greetin' Wi' girnin' spite, To hear the moon sae sadly lie'd on By word an' write.

But shortly they will cowe the loons; Some Auld Light herds in neibor towns Are mind't in things they ca' balloons, To tak a flight, An' stay ae month amang the moons And see them right.

Guid observation they will gie them: An' when the auld moon's gaun to lea'e them, The hindmost shaird, they'll fetch it wi' them, Just i' their pouch, An' when the New Light billies see them, I think they'll crouch!

Sae, ye observe that a' this clatter Is naething but a "moonshine matter;" But tho' dull prose-folk Latin splatter In logic tulzie, I hope we bardies ken some better Than mind sic brulzie.

CHAPTER XXXIII.

ADDRESS

TO AN

ILLEGITIMATE CHILD.

[This hasty and not very decorous effusion, was originally entitled "The Poet's Welcome; or, Rab the Rhymer's Address to his Bastard Child." A copy, with the more softened, but less expressive title, was published by Stewart, in 1801, and is alluded to by Burns himself, in his biographical letter to Moore. "Bonnie Betty," the mother of the "sonsie-smirking, dear-bought Bess," of the Inventory, lived in Largieside: to support this daughter the poet made over the copyright of his works when he proposed to go to the West Indies. She lived to be a woman, and to marry one John Bishop, overseer at Polkemmet, where she died in 1817. It is said she resembled Burns quite as much as any of the rest of his children.]

Thou's welcome, wean, mischanter fa' me, If ought of thee, or of thy mammy, Shall ever daunton me, or awe me, My sweet wee lady, Or if I blush when thou shalt ca' me Tit-ta or daddy.

Wee image of my bonny Betty, I, fatherly, will kiss and daut thee, As dear and near my heart I set thee Wi' as gude will As a' the priests had seen me get thee That's out o' hell.

What tho' they ca' me fornicator, An' tease my name in kintry clatter: The mair they talk I'm kent the better, E'en let them clash; An auld wife's tongue's a feckless matter To gie ane fash.

Sweet fruit o' mony a merry dint, My funny toil is now a' tint, Sin' thou came to the warl asklent, Which fools may scoff at; In my last plack thy part's be in't The better ha'f o't.

An' if thou be what I wad hae thee, An' tak the counsel I sall gie thee, A lovin' father I'll be to thee, If thou be spar'd; Thro' a' thy childish years I'll e'e thee, An' think't weel war'd.

Gude grant that thou may ay inherit Thy mither's person, grace, an' merit, An' thy poor worthless daddy's spirit, Without his failins; 'Twill please me mair to hear an' see it Than stocket mailens.

CHAPTER XXXIV.

NATURE'S LAW.

A POEM HUMBLY INSCRIBED TO G. H. ESQ.

"Great nature spoke, observant man obey'd."

Pope.

[This Poem was written by Burns at Mossgiel, and "humbly inscribed to Gavin Hamilton, Esq." It is supposed to allude to his intercourse with Jean Armour, with the circumstances of which he seems to have made many of his comrades acquainted. These verses were well known to many of the admirers of the poet, but they remained in manuscript till given to the world by Sir Harris Nicolas, in Pickering's Aldine Edition of the British Poets.]

Let other heroes boast their scars, The marks of sturt and strife; And other poets sing of wars, The plagues of human life; Shame fa' the fun; wi' sword and gun To slap mankind like lumber! I sing his name, and nobler fame, Wha multiplies our number.

Great Nature spoke with air benign, "Go on, ye human race! This lower world I you resign; Be fruitful and increase. The liquid fire of strong desire I've pour'd it in each bosom; Here, in this hand, does mankind stand, And there, is beauty's blossom."

The hero of these artless strains, A lowly bard was he, Who sung his rhymes in Coila's plains With meikle mirth an' glee; Kind Nature's care had given his share, Large, of the flaming current; And all devout, he never sought To stem the sacred torrent.

He felt the powerful, high behest, Thrill vital through and through; And sought a correspondent breast, To give obedience due: Propitious Powers screen'd the young flowers, From mildews of abortion; And lo! the bard, a great reward, Has got a double portion!

Auld cantie Coil may count the day, As annual it returns, The third of Libra's equal sway, That gave another B, With future rhymes, an' other times, To emulate his sire; To sing auld Coil in nobler style, With more poetic fire.

Ye Powers of peace, and peaceful song, Look down with gracious eyes; And bless auld Coila, large and long, With multiplying joys: Lang may she stand to prop the land, The flow'r of ancient nations; And B[urns's] spring, her fame to sing, Thro' endless generations!

CHAPTER XXXV.

TO THE REV. JOHN M'MATH.

[Poor M'Math was at the period of this epistle assistant to Wodrow, minister of Tarbolton: he was a good preacher, a moderate man in matters of discipline, and an intimate of the Coilsfield Montgomerys. His dependent condition depressed his spirits: he grew dissipated; and finally, it is said, enlisted as a common soldier, and died in a foreign land.]

Sept. 17th, 1785.

While at the stook the shearers cow'r To shun the bitter blaudin' show'r, Or in gulravage rinnin' scow'r To pass the time, To you I dedicate the hour In idle rhyme.

My musie, tir'd wi' mony a sonnet On gown, an' ban', and douse black bonnet, Is grown right eerie now she's done it, Lest they should blame her, An' rouse their holy thunder on it And anathem her.

I own 'twas rash, an' rather hardy, That I, a simple countra bardie, Shou'd meddle wi' a pack sae sturdy, Wha, if they ken me, Can easy, wi' a single wordie, Lowse hell upon me.

But I gae mad at their grimaces, Their sighin' cantin' grace-proud faces, Their three-mile prayers, and hauf-mile graces, Their raxin' conscience, Whase greed, revenge, an' pride disgraces, Waur nor their nonsense.

There's Gaun,[45] miska't waur than a beast, Wha has mair honour in his breast Than mony scores as guid's the priest Wha sae abus't him. An' may a bard no crack his jest What way they've use't him.

See him, the poor man's friend in need, The gentleman in word an' deed, An' shall his fame an' honour bleed By worthless skellums, An' not a muse erect her head To cowe the blellums?

O Pope, had I thy satire's darts To gie the rascals their deserts, I'd rip their rotten, hollow hearts, An' tell aloud Their jugglin' hocus-pocus arts To cheat the crowd.

God knows, I'm no the thing I shou'd be, Nor am I even the thing I cou'd be, But twenty times, I rather wou'd be An atheist clean, Than under gospel colours hid be Just for a screen.

An honest man may like a glass, An honest man may like a lass, But mean revenge, an' malice fause He'll still disdain, An' then cry zeal for gospel laws, Like some we ken.

They take religion in their mouth; They talk o' mercy, grace, an' truth, For what?-to gie their malice skouth On some puir wight, An' hunt him down, o'er right, an' ruth, To ruin straight.

All hail, Religion! maid divine! Pardon a muse sae mean as mine, Who in her rough imperfect line, Thus daurs to name thee; To stigmatize false friends of thine Can ne'er defame thee.

Tho' blotch'd an' foul wi' mony a stain, An' far unworthy of thy train, With trembling voice I tune my strain To join with those, Who boldly daur thy cause maintain In spite o' foes:

In spite o' crowds, in spite o' mobs, In spite of undermining jobs, In spite o' dark banditti stabs At worth an' merit, By scoundrels, even wi' holy robes, But hellish spirit.

O Ayr! my dear, my native ground, Within thy presbyterial bound A candid lib'ral band is found Of public teachers, As men, as Christians too, renown'd, An' manly preachers.

Sir, in that circle you are nam'd; Sir, in that circle you are fam'd; An' some, by whom your doctrine's blam'd, (Which gies you honour,) Even Sir, by them your heart's esteem'd, An' winning manner.

Pardon this freedom I have ta'en, An' if impertinent I've been, Impute it not, good Sir, in ane Whase heart ne'er wrang'd ye, But to his utmost would befriend Ought that belang'd ye.

FOOTNOTES:

[45] Gavin Hamilton, Esq.

CHAPTER XXXVI.

TO A MOUSE,

ON TURNING HER UP IN HER NEST WITH THE PLOUGH, NOVEMBER, 1785.

[This beautiful poem was imagined while the poet was holding the plough, on the farm of Mossgiel: the field is still pointed out: and a man called Blane is still living, who says he was gaudsman to the bard at the time, and chased the mouse with the plough-pettle, for which he was rebuked by his young master, who inquired what harm the poor mouse had done him. In the night that followed, Burns awoke his gaudsman, who was in the same bed with him, recited the poem as it now stands, and said, "What think you of our mouse now?"]

Wee, sleekit, cow'rin', tim'rous beastie, O, what a panic's in thy breastie! Thou need na start awa sae hasty, Wi' bickering brattle! I wad be laith to rin an' chase thee, Wi' murd'ring pattle!

I'm truly sorry man's dominion Has broken nature's social union, An' justifies that ill opinion, Which makes thee startle At me, thy poor earth-born companion, An' fellow-mortal!

I doubt na, whyles, but thou may thieve; What then? poor beastie, thou maun live! A daimen icker in a thrave 'S a sma' request: I'll get a blessin' wi' the lave, And never miss't!

Thy wee bit housie, too, in ruin; Its silly wa's the win's are strewin'! An' naething, now, to big a new ane, O' foggage green! An' bleak December's winds ensuin', Baith snell and keen!

Thou saw the fields laid bare an' waste, An' weary winter comin' fast, An' cozie here, beneath the blast, Thou thought to dwell, 'Till, crash! the cruel coulter past Out thro' thy cell.

That wee bit heap o' leaves an' stibble, Has cost thee mony a weary nibble! Now thou's turn'd out, for a' thy trouble, But house or hald, To thole the winter's sleety dribble, An' cranreuch cauld!

But, Mousie, thou art no thy lane, In proving foresight may be vain: The best laid schemes o' mice an' men, Gang aft a-gley, An' lea'e us nought but grief and pain, For promis'd joy.

Still thou art blest, compar'd wi' me! The present only toucheth thee: But, Och! I backward cast my e'e, On prospects drear! An' forward, tho' I canna see, I guess an' fear.

CHAPTER XXXVII.

SCOTCH DRINK.

"Gie him strong drink, until he wink, That's sinking in despair; An' liquor guid to fire his bluid, That's prest wi' grief an' care; There let him bouse, an' deep carouse, Wi' bumpers flowing o'er, Till he forgets his loves or debts, An' minds his griefs no more."

Solomon's Proverb, xxxi. 6, 7.

["I here enclose you," said Burns, 20 March, 1786, to his friend Kennedy, "my Scotch Drink; I hope some time before we hear the gowk, to have the pleasure of seeing you at Kilmarnock: when I intend we shall have a gill between us, in a mutchkin stoup."]

Let other poets raise a fracas 'Bout vines, an' wines, an' dru'ken Bacchus, An' crabbit names and stories wrack us, An' grate our lug, I sing the juice Scotch bear can mak us, In glass or jug.

O, thou, my Muse! guid auld Scotch drink; Whether thro' wimplin' worms thou jink, Or, richly brown, ream o'er the brink, In glorious faem, Inspire me, till I lisp an' wink, To sing thy name!

Let husky wheat the haughs adorn, An' aits set up their awnie horn, An' pease an' beans, at e'en or morn, Perfume the plain, Leeze me on thee, John Barleycorn, Thou king o' grain!

On thee aft Scotland chows her cood, In souple scones, the wale o' food! Or tumblin' in the boilin' flood Wi' kail an' beef; But when thou pours thy strong heart's blood, There thou shines chief.

Food fills the wame an' keeps us livin'; Tho' life's a gift no worth receivin' When heavy dragg'd wi' pine an' grievin'; But, oil'd by thee, The wheels o' life gae down-hill, scrievin,' Wi' rattlin' glee.

Thou clears the head o' doited Lear; Thou cheers the heart o' drooping Care; Thou strings the nerves o' Labour sair, At's weary toil; Thou even brightens dark Despair Wi' gloomy smile.

Aft, clad in massy, siller weed, Wi' gentles thou erects thy head; Yet humbly kind in time o' need, The poor man's wine, His wee drap parritch, or his bread, Thou kitchens fine.

Thou art the life o' public haunts; But thee, what were our fairs an' rants? Ev'n godly meetings o' the saunts, By thee inspir'd, When gaping they besiege the tents, Are doubly fir'd.

That merry night we get the corn in, O sweetly then thou reams the horn in! Or reekin' on a new-year morning In cog or dicker, An' just a wee drap sp'ritual burn in, An' gusty sucker!

When Vulcan gies his bellows breath, An' ploughmen gather wi' their graith, O rare! to see thee fizz an' freath I' th' lugget caup! Then Burnewin comes on like Death At ev'ry chap.

Nae mercy, then, for airn or steel; The brawnie, bainie, ploughman chiel, Brings hard owrehip, wi' sturdy wheel, The strong forehammer, Till block an' studdie ring an' reel Wi' dinsome clamour.

When skirlin' weanies see the light, Thou maks the gossips clatter bright, How fumblin' cuifs their dearies slight; Wae worth the name! Nae howdie gets a social night, Or plack frae them.

When neibors anger at a plea, An' just as wud as wud can be, How easy can the barley-bree Cement the quarrel! It's aye the cheapest lawyer's fee, To taste the barrel.

Alake! that e'er my muse has reason To wyte her countrymen wi' treason! But monie daily weet their weason Wi' liquors nice, An' hardly, in a winter's season, E'er spier her price.

Wae worth that brandy, burning trash! Fell source o' monie a pain an' brash! Twins monie a poor, doylt, druken hash, O' half his days; An' sends, beside, auld Scotland's cash To her warst faes.

Ye Scots, wha wish auld Scotland well, Ye chief, to you my tale I tell, Poor plackless devils like mysel', It sets you ill, Wi' bitter, dearthfu' wines to mell, Or foreign gill.

May gravels round his blather wrench, An' gouts torment him inch by inch, Wha twists his gruntle wi' a glunch O' sour disdain, Out owre a glass o' whiskey punch Wi' honest men;

O whiskey! soul o' plays an' pranks! Accept a Bardie's gratefu' thanks! When wanting thee, what tuneless cranks Are my poor verses! Thou comes-they rattle i' their ranks At ither's as!

Thee, Ferintosh! O sadly lost! Scotland lament frae coast to coast! Now colic grips, an' barkin' hoast, May kill us a'; For loyal Forbes' charter'd boast, Is ta'en awa.

Thae curst horse-leeches o' th' Excise, Wha mak the whiskey stells their prize! Haud up thy han', Deil! ance, twice, thrice! There, seize the blinkers! An' bake them up in brunstane pies For poor d-n'd drinkers.

Fortune! if thou'll but gie me still Hale breeks, a scone, an' whiskey gill, An' rowth o' rhyme to rave at will, Tak' a' the rest, An' deal't about as thy blind skill Directs thee best.

CHAPTER XXXVIII.

THE AUTHOR'S EARNEST CRY AND PRAYER TO THE SCOTCH REPRESENTATIVES IN THE HOUSE OF COMMONS.

'Dearest of distillation! last and best! -How art thou lost!'

Parody on Milton

["This Poem was written," says Burns, "before the act anent the Scottish distilleries, of session 1786, for which Scotland and the author return their most grateful thanks." Before the passing of this lenient act, so sharp was the law in the North, that some distillers[108] relinquished their trade; the price of barley was affected, and Scotland, already exasperated at the refusal of a militia, for which she was a petitioner, began to handle her claymore, and was perhaps only hindered from drawing it by the act mentioned by the poet. In an early copy of the poem, he thus alludes to Colonel Hugh Montgomery, afterwards Earl of Eglinton:-

"Thee, sodger Hugh, my watchman stented, If bardies e'er are represented, I ken if that yere sword were wanted Ye'd lend yere hand; But when there's aught to say anent it Yere at a stand."

The poet was not sure that Montgomery would think the compliment to his ready hand an excuse in full for the allusion to his unready tongue, and omitted the stanza.]

Ye Irish lords, ye knights an' squires, Wha represent our brughs an' shires, An' doucely manage our affairs In Parliament, To you a simple Bardie's prayers Are humbly sent.

Alas! my roupet Muse is hearse! Your honours' hearts wi' grief 'twad pierce, To see her sittin' on her a-e Low i' the dust, An' scriechin' out prosaic verse, An' like to brust!

Tell them wha hae the chief direction, Scotland an' me's in great affliction, E'er sin' they laid that curst restriction On aqua-vitæ; An' rouse them up to strong conviction, An' move their pity.

Stand forth, an' tell yon Premier youth, The honest, open, naked truth: Tell him o' mine an' Scotland's drouth, His servants humble: The muckie devil blaw ye south, If ye dissemble!

Does ony great man glunch an' gloom? Speak out, an' never fash your thumb! Let posts an' pensions sink or soom Wi' them wha grant 'em: If honestly they canna come, Far better want 'em.

In gath'rin votes you were na slack; Now stand as tightly by your tack; Ne'er claw your lug, an' fidge your back, An' hum an' haw; But raise your arm, an' tell your crack Before them a'.

Paint Scotland greetin' owre her thrizzle, Her mutchkin stoup as toom's a whissle: An' damn'd excisemen in a bussle, Seizin' a stell, Triumphant crushin't like a mussel Or lampit shell.

Then on the tither hand present her, A blackguard smuggler, right behint her, An' cheek-for-chow, a chuffie vintner, Colleaguing join, Picking her pouch as bare as winter Of a' kind coin.

Is there, that bears the name o' Scot, But feels his heart's bluid rising hot, To see his poor auld mither's pot Thus dung in staves, An' plunder'd o' her hindmost groat By gallows knaves?

Alas! I'm but a nameless wight, Trode i' the mire out o' sight! But could I like Montgomeries fight, Or gab like Boswell, There's some sark-necks I wad draw tight, An' tie some hose well.

God bless your honours, can ye see't, The kind, auld, canty carlin greet, An' no get warmly on your feet, An' gar them hear it! An' tell them with a patriot heat, Ye winna bear it?

Some o' you nicely ken the laws, To round the period an' pause, An' wi' rhetorie clause on clause To mak harangues: Then echo thro' Saint Stephen's wa's Auld Scotland's wrangs.

Dempster, a true blue Scot I'se warran'; Thee, aith-detesting, chaste Kilkerran;[46] An' that glib-gabbet Highland baron, The Laird o' Graham;[47] An' ane, a chap that's damn'd auldfarren, Dundas his name.

Erskine, a spunkie Norland billie; True Campbells, Frederick an' Hay; An' Livingstone, the bauld Sir Willie: An' monie ithers, Whom auld Demosthenes or Tully Might own for brithers.

Arouse, my boys! exert your mettle, To get auld Scotland back her kettle: Or faith! I'll wad my new pleugh-pettle, Ye'll see't or lang, She'll teach you, wi' a reekin' whittle, Anither sang.

This while she's been in crankous mood, Her lost militia fir'd her bluid; (Deil na they never mair do guid, Play'd her that pliskie!) An' now she's like to rin red-wud About her whiskey.

An' L-d, if once they pit her till't, Her tartan petticoat she'll kilt, An' durk an' pistol at her belt, She'll tak the streets, An' rin her whittle to the hilt, I' th' first she meets!

For God sake, sirs, then speak her fair, An' straik her cannie wi' the hair, An' to the muckle house repair, Wi' instant speed, An' strive, wi' a' your wit and lear, To get remead.

Yon ill-tongu'd tinkler, Charlie Fox, May taunt you wi' his jeers an' mocks; But gie him't het, my hearty cocks! E'en cowe the cadie! An' send him to his dicing box, An' sportin' lady.

Tell yon guid bluid o' auld Boconnock's I'll be his debt twa mashlum bonnocks, An' drink his health in auld Nanse Tinnock's[48] Nine times a-week, If he some scheme, like tea an' winnocks, Wad kindly seek.

Could he some commutation broach, I'll pledge my aith in guid braid Scotch, He need na fear their foul reproach Nor erudition, Yon mixtie-maxtie queer hotch-potch, The Coalition.

Auld Scotland has a raucle tongue; She's just a devil wi' a rung; An' if she promise auld or young To tak their part, Tho' by the neck she should be strung, She'll no desert.

An' now, ye chosen Five-and-Forty, May still your mither's heart support ye, Then, though a minister grow dorty, An' kick your place, Ye'll snap your fingers, poor an' hearty, Before his face.

God bless your honours a' your days, Wi' sowps o' kail and brats o' claise,

In spite o' a' the thievish kaes, That haunt St. Jamie's: Your humble Poet signs an' prays While Rab his name is.

POSTSCRIPT.

Let half-starv'd slaves in warmer skies See future wines, rich clust'ring, rise; Their lot auld Scotland ne'er envies, But blythe and frisky, She eyes her freeborn, martial boys, Tak aff their whiskey.

What tho' their Phœbus kinder warms, While fragrance blooms and beauty charms! When wretches range, in famish'd swarms, The scented groves, Or hounded forth, dishonour arms In hungry droves.

Their gun's a burden on their shouther; They downa bide the stink o' powther; Their bauldest thought's a' hank'ring swither To stan' or rin, Till skelp-a shot-they're aff, a' throther To save their skin.

But bring a Scotsman frae his hill, Clap in his check a Highland gill, Say, such is royal George's will, An' there's the foe, He has nae thought but how to kill Twa at a blow. [110]

Nae could faint-hearted doubtings tease him; Death comes, wi' fearless eye he sees him; Wi' bluidy han' a welcome gies him; An' when he fa's, His latest draught o' breathin' lea'es him In faint huzzas!

Sages their solemn een may steek, An' raise a philosophic reek, An' physically causes seek, In clime an' season; But tell me whiskey's name in Greek, I'll tell the reason.

Scotland, my auld, respected mither! Tho' whiles ye moistify your leather, Till whare ye sit, on craps o' heather Ye tine your dam; Freedom and whiskey gang thegither!- Tak aff your dram!

FOOTNOTES:

[46] Sir Adam Ferguson.

[47] The Duke of Montrose.

[48] A worthy old hostess of the author's in Mauchline, where he sometimes studies politics over a glass of guid auld Scotch drink.

CHAPTER XXXIX.

ADDRESS TO THE UNCO GUID,

OR THE

RIGIDLY RIGHTEOUS.

"My son, these maxims make a rule, And lump them ay thegither; The Rigid Righteous is a fool, The Rigid Wise anither: The cleanest corn that e'er was dight May hae some pyles o' caff in; So ne'er a fellow-creature slight For random fits o' daffin."

Solomon.-Eccles. ch. vii. ver. 16.

["Burns," says Hogg, in a note on this Poem, "has written more from his own heart and his own feelings than any other poet. External nature had few charms for him; the sublime shades and hues of heaven and earth never excited his enthusiasm: but with the secret fountains of passion in the human soul he was well acquainted." Burns, indeed, was not what is called a descriptive poet: yet with what exquisite snatches of description are some of his poems adorned, and in what fragrant and romantic scenes he enshrines the heroes and heroines of many of his finest songs! Who the high, exalted, virtuous dames were, to whom the Poem refers, we are not told. How much men stand indebted to want of opportunity to sin, and how much of their good name they owe to the ignorance of the world, were inquiries in which the poet found pleasure.]

I.

O ye wha are sae guid yoursel', Sae pious and sae holy, Ye've nought to do but mark and tell Your neibor's fauts and folly! Whase life is like a weel-gaun mill, Supply'd wi' store o' water, The heaped happer's ebbing still, And still the clap plays clatter.

II.

Hear me, ye venerable core, As counsel for poor mortals, That frequent pass douce Wisdom's door For glaikit Folly's portals; I, for their thoughtless, careless sakes, Would here propone defences, Their donsie tricks, their black mistakes, Their failings and mischances.

III.

Ye see your state wi' theirs compar'd, And shudder at the niffer, But cast a moment's fair regard, What maks the mighty differ? Discount what scant occasion gave, That purity ye pride in, And (what's aft mair than a' the lave) Your better art o' hiding.

IV.

Think, when your castigated pulse Gies now and then a wallop, What ragings must his veins convulse, That still eternal gallop: Wi' wind and tide fair i' your tail, Right on ye scud your sea-way; But in the teeth o' baith to sail, It makes an unco lee-way.

V.

See social life and glee sit down, All joyous and unthinking, 'Till, quite transmugrify'd, they're grown Debauchery and drinking; O would they stay to calculate Th' eternal consequences; Or your more dreaded hell to state, D-mnation of expenses!

VI.

Ye high, exalted, virtuous dames, Ty'd up in godly laces, Before ye gie poor frailty names, Suppose a change o' cases; A dear lov'd lad, convenience snug, A treacherous inclination- [111]But, let me whisper, i' your lug, Ye're aiblins nae temptation.

VII.

Then gently scan your brother man, Still gentler sister woman; Though they may gang a kennin' wrang, To step aside is human: One point must still be greatly dark, The moving why they do it: And just as lamely can ye mark, How far perhaps they rue it.

VIII.

Who made the heart, 'tis He alone Decidedly can try us, He knows each chord-its various tone, Each spring-its various bias: Then at the balance let's be mute, We never can adjust it; What's done we partly may compute, But know not what's resisted.

CHAPTER XL.

TAM SAMSON'S ELEGY.[49]

"An honest man's the noblest work of God."

Pope.

[Tam Samson was a west country seedsman and sportsman, who loved a good song, a social glass, and relished a shot so well that he expressed a wish to die and be buried in the moors. On this hint Burns wrote the Elegy: when Tam heard o' this he waited on the poet, caused him to recite it, and expressed displeasure at being numbered with the dead: the author, whose wit was as ready as his rhymes, added the Per Contra in a moment, much to the delight of his friend. At his death the four lines of Epitaph were cut on his gravestone. "This poem has always," says Hogg, "been a great country favourite: it abounds with happy expressions.

'In vain the burns cam' down like waters, An acre braid.'

What a picture of a flooded burn! any other poet would have given us a long description: Burns dashes it down at once in a style so graphic no one can mistake it.

'Perhaps upon his mouldering breast Some spitefu' moorfowl bigs her nest.' Match that sentence who can."]

Has auld Kilmarnock seen the deil? Or great M'Kinlay[50] thrawn his heel? Or Robinson[51] again grown weel, To preach an' read? "Na, waur than a'!" cries ilka chiel, Tam Samson's dead!

Kilmarnock lang may grunt an' grane, An' sigh, an' sob, an' greet her lane, An' cleed her bairns, man, wife, an wean, In mourning weed; To death, she's dearly paid the kane, Tam Samson's dead!

The brethren o' the mystic level May hing their head in woefu' bevel, While by their nose the tears will revel, Like ony bead; Death's gien the lodge an unco devel, Tam Samson's dead!

When Winter muffles up his cloak, And binds the mire like a rock; When to the lochs the curlers flock, Wi' gleesome speed, Wha will they station at the cock? Tam Samson's dead!

He was the king o' a' the core, To guard or draw, or wick a bore, Or up the rink like Jehu roar In time o' need; But now he lags on death's hog-score, Tam Samson's dead!

Now safe the stately sawmont sail, And trouts be-dropp'd wi' crimson hail, And eels weel ken'd for souple tail, And geds for greed, Since dark in death's fish-creel we wail Tam Samson dead.

Rejoice, ye birring patricks a'; Ye cootie moor-cocks, crousely craw; Ye maukins, cock your fud fu' braw, Withouten dread; Your mortal fae is now awa'- Tam Samson's dead!

That woefu' morn be ever mourn'd Saw him in shootin' graith adorn'd, While pointers round impatient burn'd, Frae couples freed; But, Och! he gaed and ne'er return'd! Tam Samson's dead!

In vain auld age his body batters; In vain the gout his ancles fetters; In vain the burns cam' down like waters, An acre braid! Now ev'ry auld wife, greetin', clatters, Tam Samson's dead!

Owre many a weary hag he limpit, An' ay the tither shot he thumpit, Till coward death behind him jumpit, Wi' deadly feide; Now he proclaims, wi' tout o' trumpet, Tam Samson's dead!

When at his heart he felt the dagger, He reel'd his wonted bottle swagger, But yet he drew the mortal trigger Wi' weel-aim'd heed; "L-d, five!" he cry'd, an' owre did stagger; Tam Samson's dead!

Ilk hoary hunter mourn'd a brither; Ilk sportsman youth bemoan'd a father; Yon auld grey stane, amang the heather, Marks out his head, Whare Burns has wrote in rhyming blether Tam Samson's dead!

There low he lies, in lasting rest; Perhaps upon his mould'ring breast Some spitefu' muirfowl bigs her nest, To hatch an' breed; Alas! nae mair he'll them molest! Tam Samson's dead!

When August winds the heather wave, And sportsmen wander by yon grave, Three volleys let his mem'ry crave O' pouther an' lead, 'Till echo answer frae her cave Tam Samson's dead!

Heav'n rest his soul, whare'er he be! Is th' wish o' mony mae than me; He had twa fauts, or may be three, Yet what remead? Ae social, honest man want we: Tam Samson's dead!

EPITAPH.

Tam Samson's weel-worn clay here lies, Ye canting zealots spare him! If honest worth in heaven rise, Ye'll mend or ye win near him.

PER CONTRA.

Go, Fame, an' canter like a filly Thro' a' the streets an' neuks o' Killie, Tell ev'ry social honest billie To cease his grievin', For yet, unskaith'd by death's gleg gullie, Tam Samson's livin'.

FOOTNOTES:

[49] When this worthy old sportsman went out last muirfowl season, he supposed it was to be, in Ossian's phrase, "the last of his fields."

[50] A preacher, a great favourite with the million. Vide the Ordination, stanza II

[51] Another preacher, an equal favourite with the few, who was at that time ailing. For him see also the Ordination, stanza IX.

CHAPTER XLI.

LAMENT,

OCCASIONED BY THE UNFORTUNATE ISSUE

OF A

FRIEND'S AMOUR.

"Alas! how oft does goodness wound itself! And sweet affection prove the spring of woe."

Home.

[The hero and heroine of this little mournful poem, were Robert Burns and Jean Armour. "This was a most melancholy affair," says the poet in his letter to Moore, "which I cannot yet bear to reflect on, and had very nearly given me one or two of the principal qualifications for a place among those who have lost the chart and mistaken the reckoning of rationality." Hogg and Motherwell, with an ignorance which is easier to laugh at than account for, say this Poem was "written on the occasion of Alexander Cunningham's darling sweetheart alighting him and marrying another:-she acted a wise part." With what care they had read the great poet whom they jointly edited in is needless to say: and how they could read the last two lines of the third verse and commend the lady's wisdom for slighting her lover, seems a problem which defies definition. This mistake was pointed out by a friend, and corrected in a second issue of the volume.]

I.

O thou pale orb, that silent shines, While care-untroubled mortals sleep! Thou seest a wretch who inly pines, And wanders here to wail and weep! With woe I nightly vigils keep, Beneath thy wan, unwarming beam, And mourn, in lamentation deep, How life and love are all a dream.

II.

A joyless view thy rays adorn The faintly marked distant hill: I joyless view thy trembling horn, Reflected in the gurgling rill: My fondly-fluttering heart, be still: Thou busy pow'r, Remembrance, cease! Ah! must the agonizing thrill For ever bar returning peace!

III.

No idly-feign'd poetic pains, My sad, love-lorn lamentings claim; No shepherd's pipe-Arcadian strains; No fabled tortures, quaint and tame: The plighted faith; the mutual flame; The oft-attested Pow'rs above; The promis'd father's tender name; These were the pledges of my love!

IV.

Encircled in her clasping arms, How have the raptur'd moments flown! How have I wish'd for fortune's charms, For her dear sake, and hers alone! And must I think it!-is she gone, My secret heart's exulting boast? And does she heedless hear my groan? And is she ever, ever lost?

V.

Oh! can she bear so base a heart, So lost to honour, lost to truth, As from the fondest lover part, The plighted husband of her youth! Alas! life's path may be unsmooth! Her way may lie thro' rough distress! Then, who her pangs and pains will soothe, Her sorrows share, and make them less?

VI.

Ye winged hours that o'er us past, Enraptur'd more, the more enjoy'd, Your dear remembrance in my breast, My fondly-treasur'd thoughts employ'd, That breast, how dreary now, and void, For her too scanty once of room! Ev'n ev'ry ray of hope destroy'd, And not a wish to gild the gloom!

VII.

The morn that warns th' approaching day, Awakes me up to toil and woe: I see the hours in long array, That I must suffer, lingering slow. Full many a pang, and many a throe, Keen recollection's direful train, Must wring my soul, ere Phœbus, low, Shall kiss the distant, western main.

VIII.

And when my nightly couch I try, Sore-harass'd out with care and grief, My toil-beat nerves, and tear-worn eye, Keep watchings with the nightly thief: Or if I slumber, fancy, chief, Reigns haggard-wild, in sore affright: Ev'n day, all-bitter, brings relief, From such a horror-breathing night.

IX.

O! thou bright queen, who o'er th' expanse Now highest reign'st, with boundless sway! Oft has thy silent-marking glance Observ'd us, fondly-wand'ring, stray! The time, unheeded, sped away, While love's luxurious pulse beat high, Beneath thy silver-gleaming ray, To mark the mutual kindling eye.

X.

Oh! scenes in strong remembrance set! Scenes never, never to return! Scenes, if in stupor I forget, Again I feel, again I burn! From ev'ry joy and pleasure torn, Life's weary vale I'll wander thro'; And hopeless, comfortless, I'll mourn A faithless woman's broken vow.

CHAPTER XLII.

DESPONDENCY.

AN ODE.

["I think," said Burns, "it is one of the greatest pleasures attending a poetic genius, that we can give our woes, cares, joys, and loves an embodied form in verse, which to me is ever immediate ease." He elsewhere says, "My passions raged like so many devils till they got vent in rhyme." That eminent painter, Fuseli, on seeing his wife in a passion, said composedly, "Swear my love, swear heartily: you know not how much it will ease you!" This poem was printed in the Kilmarnock edition, and gives a true picture of those bitter moments experienced by the bard, when love and fortune alike deceived him.]

I.

Oppress'd with grief, oppress'd with care, A burden more than I can bear, [114]I set me down and sigh: O life! thou art a galling load, Along a rough, a weary road, To wretches such as I! Dim-backward as I cast my view, What sick'ning scenes appear! What sorrows yet may pierce me thro' Too justly I may fear! Still caring, despairing, Must be my bitter doom; My woes here shall close ne'er But with the closing tomb!

II.

Happy, ye sons of busy life, Who, equal to the bustling strife, No other view regard! Ev'n when the wished end's deny'd, Yet while the busy means are ply'd, They bring their own reward: Whilst I, a hope-abandon'd wight, Unfitted with an aim, Meet ev'ry sad returning night And joyless morn the same; You, bustling, and justling, Forget each grief and pain; I, listless, yet restless, Find every prospect vain.

III.

How blest the solitary's lot, Who, all-forgetting, all forgot, Within his humble cell, The cavern wild with tangling roots, Sits o'er his newly-gather'd fruits, Beside his crystal well! Or, haply, to his ev'ning thought, By unfrequented stream, The ways of men are distant brought, A faint collected dream; While praising, and raising His thoughts to heav'n on high, As wand'ring, meand'ring, He views the solemn sky.

IV.

Than I, no lonely hermit plac'd Where never human footstep trac'd, Less fit to play the part; The lucky moment to improve, And just to stop, and just to move, With self-respecting art: But, ah! those pleasures, loves, and joys, Which I too keenly taste, The solitary can despise, Can want, and yet be blest! He needs not, he heeds not, Or human love or hate, Whilst I here, must cry here At perfidy ingrate!

V.

Oh! enviable, early days, When dancing thoughtless pleasure's maze, To care, to guilt unknown! How ill exchang'd for riper times, To feel the follies, or the crimes, Of others, or my own! Ye tiny elves that guiltless sport, Like linnets in the bush, Ye little know the ills ye court, When manhood is your wish! The losses, the crosses, That active man engage! The fears all, the tears all, Of dim declining age!

CHAPTER XLIII.

THE

COTTER'S SATURDAY NIGHT.

INSCRIBED TO ROBERT AIKEN, ESQ.

"Let not ambition mock their useful toil, Their homely joys, and destiny obscure: Nor grandeur hear, with a disdainful smile, The short and simple annals of the poor."

Gray

[The house of William Burns was the scene of this fine, devout, and tranquil drama, and William himself was the saint, the father, and the husband, who gives life and sentiment to the whole. "Robert had frequently remarked to me," says Gilbert Burns, "that he thought there was something peculiarly venerable in the phrase, 'Let us worship God!' used by a decent sober head of a family, introducing family worship." To this sentiment of the author the world is indebted for the "Cotter's Saturday Night." He owed some little, however, of the inspiration to Fergusson's "Farmer's Ingle," a poem of great merit. The calm tone and holy composure of the Cotter's Saturday Night have been mistaken by Hogg for want of nerve and life. "It is a dull, heavy, lifeless poem," he says, "and the only beauty it possesses, in my estimation, is, that it is a sort of family picture of the poet's family. The worst thing of all, it is not original, but is a decided imitation of Fergusson's beautiful pastoral, 'The Farmer's Ingle:' I have a perfect contempt for all plagiarisms and imitations." Motherwell tries to qualify the censure of his brother editor, by quoting Lockhart's opinion-at once lofty and just, of this fine picture of domestic happiness and devotion.]

I.

My lov'd, my honour'd, much respected friend! No mercenary bard his homage pays; With honest pride, I scorn each selfish end: My dearest meed, a friend's esteem and praise: To you I sing, in simple Scottish lays, The lowly train in life's sequester'd scene; The native feelings strong, the guileless ways; What Aiken in a cottage would have been; Ah! tho' his work unknown, far happier there, I ween!

II.

November chill blaws loud wi' angry sugh; The short'ning winter-day is near a close; The miry beasts retreating frae the pleugh: The black'ning trains o' craws to their repose: The toil-worn Cotter frae his labour goes, This night his weekly moil is at an end, Collects his spades, his mattocks, and his hoes, Hoping the morn in ease and rest to spend, And weary, o'er the moor, his course does homeward bend.

III.

At length his lonely cot appears in view, Beneath the shelter of an aged tree; Th' expectant wee-things, toddlin', stacher thro' To meet their Dad, wi' flichterin' noise an' glee. His wee bit ingle, blinkin' bonnily. His clean hearth-stane, his thriftie Wifie's smile, The lisping infant prattling on his knee, Does a' his weary kiaugh and care beguile, An' makes him quite forget his labour and his toil.

IV.

Belyve, the elder bairns come drapping in, At service out amang the farmers roun': Some ca' the pleugh, some herd, some tentie rin A cannie errand to a neebor town: Their eldest hope, their Jenny, woman grown, In youthfu' bloom, love sparkling in her e'e, Comes hame, perhaps to shew a braw new gown, Or deposite her sair won penny-fee, To help her parents dear, if they in hardship be.

V.

With joy unfeign'd, brothers and sisters meet, An' each for other's welfare kindly spiers: The social hours, swift-wing'd, unnotic'd, fleet; Each tells the unco's that he sees or hears; The parents, partial, eye their hopeful years;

Anticipation forward points the view. The Mother, wi' her needle an' her shears, Gars auld claes look amaist as weel's the new; The Father mixes a' wi' admonition due.

VI.

Their master's an' their mistress's command, The younkers a' are warned to obey; And mind their labours wi' an eydent hand, An' ne'er, tho' out of sight, to jauk or play: "And O! be sure to fear the Lord alway! And mind your duty, duly, morn and night! Lest in temptation's path ye gang astray, Implore His counsel and assisting might: They never sought in vain, that sought the Lord aright!"

VII.

But, hark! a rap comes gently to the door; Jenny, wha kens the meaning o' the same, Tells how a neebor lad cam o'er the moor, To do some errands, and convoy her hame. The wily Mother sees the conscious flame Sparkle in Jenny's e'e, and flush her cheek, With heart-struck anxious care, inquires his name, While Jenny hafflins is afraid to speak; Weel pleas'd the Mother hears it's nae wild, worthless rake.

VIII.

Wi' kindly welcome, Jenny brings him ben; A strappan youth; he taks the Mother's eye; Blythe Jenny sees the visit's no ill ta'en; The Father cracks of horses, pleughs, and kye. The youngster's artless heart o'erflows wi' joy, But blate, an laithfu', scarce can weel behave; The Mother, wi' a woman's wiles, can spy What makes the youth sae bashfu' and sae grave; Weel pleas'd to think her bairn's respected like the lave.

IX.

O happy love! Where love like this is found! O heart-felt raptures!-bliss beyond compare! I've paced much this weary, mortal round, And sage experience bids me this declare- "If heaven a draught of heavenly pleasure spare, One cordial in this melancholy vale, 'Tis when a youthful, loving, modest pair, In other's arms, breathe out the tender tale, Beneath the milk-white thorn that scents the ev'ning gale."

X.

Is there, in human form, that bears a heart- A wretch! a villain! lost to love and truth! That can, with studied, sly, ensnaring art, Betray sweet Jenny's unsuspecting youth? Curse on his perjur'd arts! dissembling smooth! Are honour, virtue, conscience, all exil'd? Is there no pity, no relenting ruth, Points to the parents fondling o'er their child? Then paints the ruin'd maid, and their distraction wild?

XI.

But now the supper crowns their simple board, The halesome parritch, chief of Scotia's food: The soupe their only hawkie does afford, That 'yont the hallan snugly chows her cood: The dame brings forth in complimental mood, To grace the lad, her weel-hain'd kebbuck, fell, An' aft he's prest, an' aft he ca's it guid; The frugal wifie, garrulous, will tell, How 'twas a towmond auld, sin' lint was i' the bell.

XII.

The cheerfu' supper done, wi' serious face, They, round the ingle, form a circle wide; The Sire turns o'er, with patriarchal grace, The big ha'-Bible, ance his father's pride; His bonnet rev'rently is laid aside, His lyart haffets wearing thin an' bare; Those strains that once did sweet in Zion glide, He wales a portion with judicious care; And 'Let us worship God!' he says, with solemn air.

XIII.

They chant their artless notes in simple guise; They tune their hearts, by far the noblest aim: Perhaps Dundee's wild-warbling measures rise, Or plaintive Martyrs, worthy of the name; Or noble Elgin beets the heaven-ward flame, The sweetest far of Scotia's holy lays: Compar'd with these, Italian trills are tame; The tickl'd ear no heart-felt raptures raise; Nae unison hae they with our Creator's praise.

XIV.

The priest-like Father reads the sacred page, How Abram was the friend of God on high; Or, Moses bade eternal warfare wage With Amalek's ungracious progeny; Or how the royal bard did groaning lie Beneath the stroke of Heaven's avenging ire; Or Job's pathetic plaint, and wailing cry; Or rapt Isaiah's wild, seraphic fire; Or other holy seers that tune the sacred lyre.

XV.

Perhaps the Christian volume is the theme, How guiltless blood for guilty man was shed; How He, who bore in Heaven the second name, Had not on earth whereon to lay his head: How His first followers and servants sped, The precepts sage they wrote to many a land: How he who lone in Patmos banished, Saw in the sun a mighty angel stand; And heard great Bab'lon's doom pronounc'd by Heaven's command.

XVI.

Then kneeling down, to Heaven's eternal King, The Saint, the Father, and the Husband prays: Hope 'springs exulting on triumphant wing,'[52] That thus they all shall meet in future days: There ever bask in uncreated rays, No more to sigh, or shed the bitter tear, Together hymning their Creator's praise, In such society, yet still more dear: While circling Time moves round in an eternal sphere.

XVII.

Compar'd with this, how poor Religion's pride, In all the pomp of method and of art, When men display to congregations wide, Devotion's ev'ry grace, except the heart! The Pow'r, incens'd, the pageant will desert, The pompous strain, the sacerdotal stole; But haply, in some cottage far apart, May hear, well pleas'd, the language of the soul; And in His book of life the inmates poor enrol.

XVIII.

Then homeward all take off their sev'ral way; The youngling cottagers retire to rest: Their Parent-pair their secret homage pay, And proffer up to Heaven the warm request, That He, who stills the raven's clam'rous nest, And decks the lily fair in flow'ry pride, Would, in the way His wisdom sees the best, For them and for their little ones provide; But, chiefly, in their hearts with grace divine preside.

XIX.

From scenes like these, old Scotia's grandeur springs, That makes her lov'd at home, rever'd abroad: Princes and lords are but the breath of kings, "An honest man's the noblest work of God;"[53] And certes, in fair virtue's heav'nly road, The cottage leaves the palace far behind; What is a lordship's pomp? a cumbrous load, Disguising oft the wretch of human kind, Studied in arts of Hell, in wickedness refin'd!

XX.

O Scotia! my dear, my native soil! For whom my warmest wish to Heaven is sent! Long may thy hardy sons of rustic toil Be blest with health, and peace, and sweet content! And, O! may heaven their simple lives prevent From luxury's contagion, weak and vile! Then, howe'er crowns and coronets be rent, A virtuous populace may rise the while, And stand a wall of fire around their much-lov'd Isle.

XXI.

O Thou! who pour'd the patriotic tide That stream'd through Wallace's undaunted heart: Who dar'd to nobly stem tyrannic pride, Or nobly die, the second glorious part, (The patriot's God, peculiarly Thou art, His friend, inspirer, guardian, and reward!) O never, never, Scotia's realm desert; But still the patriot, and the patriot bard, In bright succession raise, her ornament and guard!

FOOTNOTES:

[52] Pope.

[53] Pope.

CHAPTER XLIV.

THE FIRST PSALM.

[This version was first printed in the second edition of the poet's work. It cannot be regarded as one of his happiest compositions: it is inferior, not indeed in ease, but in simplicity and antique rigour of language, to the common version used in the Kirk of Scotland. Burns had admitted "Death and Dr. Hornbook" into Creech's edition, and probably desired to balance it with something at which the devout could not cavil.]

The man, in life wherever plac'd, Hath happiness in store, Who walks not in the wicked's way, Nor learns their guilty lore!

Nor from the seat of scornful pride Casts forth his eyes abroad, But with humility and awe Still walks before his God.

That man shall flourish like the trees Which by the streamlets grow; The fruitful top is spread on high, And firm the root below.

But he whose blossom buds in guilt Shall to the ground be cast, And, like the rootless stubble, tost Before the sweeping blast.

For why? that God the good adore Hath giv'n them peace and rest, But hath decreed that wicked men Shall ne'er be truly blest.

CHAPTER XLV.

THE FIRST SIX VERSES OF THE NINETIETH PSALM.

[The ninetieth Psalm is said to have been a favourite in the household of William Burns: the version used by the Kirk, though unequal, contains beautiful verses, and possesses the same strain of sentiment and moral reasoning as the poem of "Man was made to Mourn." These verses first appeared in the Edinburgh edition; and they might have been spared; for in the hands of a poet ignorant of the original language of the Psalmist, how could they be so correct in sense and expression as in a sacred strain is not only desirable but necessary?]

O Thou, the first, the greatest friend Of all the human race! Whose strong right hand has ever been Their stay and dwelling place!

Before the mountains heav'd their heads Beneath Thy forming hand, Before this ponderous globe itself Arose at Thy command;

That Pow'r which rais'd and still upholds This universal frame, From countless, unbeginning time Was ever still the same.

Those mighty periods of years Which seem to us so vast, Appear no more before Thy sight Than yesterday that's past.

Thou giv'st the word: Thy creature, man, Is to existence brought; Again thou say'st, "Ye sons of men, Return ye into nought!"

Thou layest them, with all their cares, In everlasting sleep; As with a flood Thou tak'st them off With overwhelming sweep.

They flourish like the morning flow'r, In beauty's pride array'd; But long ere night, cut down, it lies All wither'd and decay'd.

CHAPTER XLVI.

TO A MOUNTAIN DAISY, ON TURNING ONE DOWN WITH THE PLOUGH IN APRIL, 1786.

[This was not the original title of this sweet poem: I have a copy in the handwriting of Burns entitled "The Gowan." This more natural name he changed as he did his own, without reasonable cause; and he changed it about the same time, for he ceased to call himself Burness and his poem "The Gowan," in the first edition of his works. The field at Mossgiel where he turned down the Daisy is said to be the same field where some five months before he turned up the Mouse; but this seems likely only to those who are little acquainted with tillage-who think that in time and place reside the chief charms of verse; and who feel not the beauty of "The Daisy," till they seek and find the spot on which it grew. Sublime morality and the deepest emotions of the soul pass for little with those who remember only what the genius loves to forget.]

Wee, modest, crimson-tipped flow'r, Thou's met me in an evil hour; For I maun crush amang the stoure Thy slender stem: To spare thee now is past my pow'r, Thou bonnie gem.

Alas! it's no thy neebor sweet, The bonnie lark, companion meet! Bending thee 'mang the dewy weet, Wi' spreckl'd breast, When upward-springing, blythe, to greet The purpling east.

Cauld blew the bitter-biting north Upon thy early, humble birth; Yet cheerfully thou glinted forth Amid the storm, Scarce rear'd above the parent earth Thy tender form.

The flaunting flowers our gardens yield, High shelt'ring woods and wa's maun shield But thou, beneath the random bield O' clod or stane, Adorns the histie stibble-field, Unseen, alane.

There, in thy scanty mantle clad, Thy snawie bosom sunward spread, Thou lifts thy unassuming head In humble guise; But now the share uptears thy bed, And low thou lies!

Such is the fate of artless maid, Sweet flow'ret of the rural shade! By love's simplicity betray'd, And guileless trust, 'Till she, like thee, all soil'd, is laid Low i' the dust.

Such is the fate of simple bard, On life's rough ocean luckless starr'd! Unskilful he to note the card Of prudent lore, 'Till billows rage, and gales blow hard, And whelm him o'er!

Such fate to suffering worth is giv'n, Who long with wants and woes has striv'n, By human pride or cunning driv'n To mis'ry's brink, 'Till wrenched of every stay but Heav'n, He, ruin'd, sink!

Ev'n thou who mourn'st the Daisy's fate, That fate is thine-no distant date; Stern Ruin's ploughshare drives, elate, Full on thy bloom, 'Till crush'd beneath the furrow's weight, Shall be thy doom!

CHAPTER XLVII.

EPISTLE TO A YOUNG FRIEND.

MAY, 1786.

[Andrew Aikin, to whom this poem of good counsel is addressed, was one of the sons of Robert Aiken, writer in Ayr, to whom the Cotter's Saturday Night is inscribed. He became a merchant in Liverpool, with what success we are not informed, and died at St. Petersburgh. The poet has been charged with a desire to teach hypocrisy rather than truth to his "Andrew dear;" but surely to conceal one's own thoughts and discover those of others, can scarcely be called hypocritical: it is, in fact, a version of the celebrated precept of prudence, "Thoughts close and looks loose." Whether he profited by all the counsel showered upon him by the muse we know not: he was much respected-his name embalmed, like that of his father, in the poetry of his friend, is not likely soon to perish.]

I.

I lang hae thought, my youthfu' friend, A something to have sent you, Though it should serve nae ither end Than just a kind memento; But how the subject-theme may gang, Let time and chance determine; Perhaps it may turn out a sang, Perhaps, turn out a sermon.

II.

Ye'll try the world soon, my lad, And, Andrew dear, believe me, Ye'll find mankind an unco squad, And muckle they may grieve ye: For care and trouble set your thought, Ev'n when your end's attain'd; And a' your views may come to nought, Where ev'ry nerve is strained.

III.

I'll no say men are villains a'; The real, harden'd wicked, Wha hae nae check but human law, Are to a few restricked; But, och! mankind are unco weak, An' little to be trusted; If self the wavering balance shake, It's rarely right adjusted!

IV.

Yet they wha fa' in Fortune's strife, Their fate we should na censure, For still th' important end of life They equally may answer; A man may hae an honest heart, Tho' poortith hourly stare him; A man may tak a neebor's part, Yet hae nae cash to spare him.

V.

Ay free, aff han' your story tell, When wi' a bosom crony; But still keep something to yoursel' Ye scarcely tell to ony. Conceal yoursel' as weel's ye can Frae critical dissection; But keek thro' ev'ry other man, Wi' sharpen'd, sly inspection.

VI.

The sacred lowe o' weel-plac'd love, Luxuriantly indulge it; But never tempt th' illicit rove, Tho' naething should divulge it: I waive the quantum o' the sin, The hazard of concealing; But, och! it hardens a' within, And petrifies the feeling!

VII.

To catch dame Fortune's golden smile, Assiduous wait upon her; And gather gear by ev'ry wile That's justified by honour; Not for to hide it in a hedge, Nor for a train-attendant; But for the glorious privilege Of being independent.

VIII.

The fear o' Hell's a hangman's whip, To haud the wretch in order; But where ye feel your honour grip, Let that ay be your border: Its slightest touches, instant pause- Debar a' side pretences; And resolutely keep its laws, Uncaring consequences.

IX.

The great Creator to revere Must sure become the creature; But still the preaching cant forbear, And ev'n the rigid feature: Yet ne'er with wits profane to range, Be complaisance extended; An Atheist laugh's a poor exchange For Deity offended!

X.

When ranting round in pleasure's ring, Religion may be blinded; Or if she gie a random sting, It may be little minded; But when on life we're tempest-driv'n, A conscience but a canker- A correspondence fix'd wi' Heav'n Is sure a noble anchor!

XI.

Adieu, dear, amiable youth! Your heart can ne'er be wanting! May prudence, fortitude, and truth Erect your brow undaunting! In ploughman phrase, 'God send you speed,' Still daily to grow wiser: And may you better reck the rede Than ever did th' adviser!

CHAPTER XLVIII.

TO A LOUSE,

ON SEEING ONE IN A LADY'S BONNET, AT CHURCH

[A Mauchline incident of a Mauchline lady is related in this poem, which to many of the softer friends of the bard was anything but welcome: it appeared in the Kilmarnock copy of his Poems, and remonstrance and persuasion were alike tried in vain to keep it out of the Edinburgh edition. Instead of regarding it as a seasonable rebuke to pride and vanity, some of his learned commentators called it course and vulgar-those classic persons might have remembered that Julian, no vulgar person, but an emperor and a scholar, wore a populous beard, and was proud of it.]

Ha! whare ye gaun, ye crowlin ferlie! Your impudence protects you sairly: I canna say by ye strunt rarely, Owre gauze and lace; Tho' faith, I fear, ye dine but sparely On sic a place.

Ye ugly, creepin', blastit wonner, Detested, shunn'd, by saunt an' sinner, How dare you set your fit upon her, Sae fine a lady! Gae somewhere else, and seek your dinner On some poor body.

Swith, in some beggar's haffet squattle; There ye may creep, and sprawl, and sprattle Wi' ither kindred, jumping cattle, In shoals and nations; Whare horn nor bane ne'er daur unsettle Your thick plantations.

Now haud you there, ye're out o' sight, Below the fatt'rells, snug an' tight; Na, faith ye yet! ye'll no be right 'Till ye've got on it, The vera topmost, tow'ring height O' Miss's bonnet.

My sooth! right bauld ye set your nose out, As plump an' gray as onie grozet; O for some rank, mercurial rozet, Or fell, red smeddum, I'd gie you sic a hearty doze o't, Wad dross your droddum!

I wad na been surpris'd to spy You on an auld wife's flainen toy; Or aiblins some bit duddie boy, On's wyliecoat; But Miss's fine Lunardi! fie! How daur ye do't? [121]

O, Jenny, dinna toss your head, An' set your beauties a' abread! Ye little ken what cursed speed The blastie's makin'! Thae winks and finger-ends, I dread, Are notice takin'!

O wad some Power the giftie gie us To see oursels as others see us! It wad frae monie a blunder free us An' foolish notion; What airs in dress an' gait wad lea'e us, And ev'n devotion!

CHAPTER XLIX.

EPISTLE TO J. RANKINE,

ENCLOSING SOME POEMS.

[The person to whom these verses are addressed lived at Adamhill in Ayrshire, and merited the praise of rough and ready-witted, which the poem bestows. The humorous dream alluded to, was related by way of rebuke to a west country earl, who was in the habit of calling all people of low degree "Brutes!-damned brutes." "I dreamed that I was dead," said the rustic satirist to his superior, "and condemned for the company I kept. When I came to hell-door, where mony of your lordship's friends gang, I chappit, and 'Wha are ye, and where d'ye come frae?' Satan exclaimed. I just said, that my name was Rankine, and I came frae yere lordship's land. 'Awa wi' you,' cried Satan, ye canna come here: hell's fou o' his lordship's damned brutes already.'"]

O rough, rude, ready-witted Rankine, The wale o' cocks for fun an' drinkin'! There's monie godly folks are thinkin', Your dreams[54] an' tricks Will send you, Korah-like, a-sinkin' Straught to auld Nick's.

Ye hae sae monie cracks an' cants, And in your wicked, dru'ken rants, Ye mak a devil o' the saunts, An' fill them fou; And then their failings, flaws, an' wants, Are a' seen through.

Hypocrisy, in mercy spare it! That holy robe, O dinna tear it! Spare't for their sakes wha aften wear it, The lads in black! But your curst wit, when it comes near it, Rives't aff their back.

Think, wicked sinner, wha ye're skaithing, It's just the blue-gown badge and claithing O' saunts; tak that, ye lea'e them naething To ken them by, Frae ony unregenerate heathen, Like you or I.

I've sent you here some rhyming ware, A' that I bargain'd for, an' mair; Sae, when you hae an hour to spare, I will expect Yon sang,[55] ye'll sen't wi cannie care, And no neglect.

Tho' faith, sma' heart hae I to sing! My muse dow scarcely spread her wing! I've play'd mysel' a bonnie spring, An' danc'd my fill! I'd better gaen an' sair't the king, At Bunker's Hill.

'Twas ae night lately, in my fun, I gaed a roving wi' the gun, An' brought a paitrick to the grun', A bonnie hen, And, as the twilight was begun, Thought nane wad ken.

The poor wee thing was little hurt; I straikit it a wee for sport, Ne'er thinkin' they wad fash me for't; But, deil-ma-care! Somebody tells the poacher-court The hale affair.

Some auld us'd hands had taen a note, That sic a hen had got a shot; I was suspected for the plot; I scorn'd to lie; So gat the whissle o' my groat, An' pay't the fee.

But, by my gun, o' guns the wale, An' by my pouther an' my hail, An' by my hen, an' by her tail, I vow an' swear! The game shall pay o'er moor an' dale, For this niest year.

As soon's the clockin-time is by, An' the wee pouts begun to cry, L-d, I'se hae sportin' by an' by, For my gowd guinea; Tho' I should herd the buckskin kye For't, in Virginia.

Trowth, they had muckle for to blame! 'Twas neither broken wing nor limb, But twa-three draps about the wame Scarce thro' the feathers; An' baith a yellow George to claim, An' thole their blethers!

It pits me ay as mad's a hare; So I can rhyme nor write nae mair; But pennyworths again is fair, When time's expedient: Meanwhile I am, respected Sir, Your most obedient.

FOOTNOTES:

[54] A certain humorous dream of his was then making a noise in the country-side.

[55] A song he had promised the author.

CHAPTER L.

ON A SCOTCH BARD, GONE TO THE WEST INDIES.

[Burns in this Poem, as well as in others, speaks openly of his tastes and passions: his own fortunes are dwelt on with painful minuteness, and his errors are recorded with the accuracy, but not the seriousness of the confessional. He seems to have been fond of taking himself to task. It was written when "Hungry ruin had him in the wind," and emigration to the West Indies was the only refuge which he could think of, or his friends suggest, from the persecutions of fortune.]

A' ye wha live by sowps o' drink, A' ye wha live by crambo-clink, A' ye wha live and never think, Come, mourn wi' me! Our billie's gien us a' a jink, An' owre the sea.

Lament him a' ye rantin' core, Wha dearly like a random-splore, Nae mair he'll join the merry roar In social key; For now he's taen anither shore, An' owre the sea!

The bonnie lasses weel may wiss him, And in their dear petitions place him; The widows, wives, an' a' may bless him, Wi' tearfu' e'e; For weel I wat they'll sairly miss him That's owre the sea!

O Fortune, they hae room to grumble! Hadst thou taen' aff some drowsy bummle Wha can do nought but fyke and fumble, 'Twad been nae plea, But he was gleg as onie wumble, That's owre the sea!

Auld, cantie Kyle may weepers wear, An' stain them wi' the saut, saut tear; 'Twill mak her poor auld heart, I fear, In flinders flee; He was her laureate monie a year, That's owre the sea!

He saw Misfortune's cauld nor-west Lang mustering up a bitter blast; A jillet brak his heart at last, Ill may she be! So, took a birth afore the mast, An' owre the sea.

To tremble under fortune's cummock, On scarce a bellyfu' o' drummock, Wi' his proud, independent stomach, Could ill agree; So, row't his hurdies in a hammock, An' owre the sea.

He ne'er was gien to great misguiding, Yet coin his pouches wad na bide in; Wi' him it ne'er was under hiding: He dealt it free; The muse was a' that he took pride in, That's owre the sea.

Jamaica bodies, use him weel, An' hap him in a cozie biel; Ye'll find him ay a dainty chiel, And fou o' glee; He wad na wrang'd the vera deil, That's owre the sea.

Fareweel, my rhyme-composing billie! Your native soil was right ill-willie; But may ye flourish like a lily, Now bonnilie! I'll toast ye in my hindmost gillie, Tho' owre the sea!

CHAPTER LI.

THE FAREWELL.

"The valiant, in himself, what can he suffer? Or what does he regard his single woes? But when, alas! he multiplies himself, To dearer selves, to the lov'd tender fair, The those whose bliss, whose beings hang upon him, To helpless children! then, O then! he feels The point of misery fest'ring in his heart, And weakly weeps his fortune like a coward. Such, such am I! undone."

Thomson.

[In these serious stanzas, where the comic, as in the lines to the Scottish bard, are not permitted to mingle, Burns bids farewell to all on whom his heart had any claim. He seems to have looked on the sea as only a place of peril, and on the West Indies as a charnel-house.]

I.

Farewell, old Scotia's bleak domains, Far dearer than the torrid plains Where rich ananas blow! Farewell, a mother's blessing dear! A brother's sigh! a sister's tear! My Jean's heart-rending throe! Farewell, my Bess! tho' thou'rt bereft Of my parental care, A faithful brother I have left, My part in him thou'lt share! Adieu too, to you too, My Smith, my bosom frien'; When kindly you mind me, O then befriend my Jean!

II.

What bursting anguish tears my heart! From thee, my Jeany, must I part! Thou weeping answ'rest-"No!" Alas! misfortune stares my face, And points to ruin and disgrace, I for thy sake must go! Thee, Hamilton, and Aiken dear, A grateful, warm adieu; I, with a much-indebted tear, Shall still remember you! All-hail then, the gale then, Wafts me from thee, dear shore! It rustles, and whistles I'll never see thee more!

CHAPTER LII.

WRITTEN

ON THE BLANK LEAF OF A COPY OF MY POEMS, PRESENTED TO AN OLD SWEETHEART, THEN MARRIED.

[This is another of the poet's lamentations, at the prospect of "torrid climes" and the roars of the Atlantic. To Burns, Scotland was the land of promise, the west of Scotland his paradise; and the land of dread, Jamaica! I found these lines copied by the poet into a volume which he presented to Dr. Geddes: they were addressed, it is thought, to the "Dear E." of his earliest correspondence.]

Once fondly lov'd and still remember'd dear; Sweet early object of my youthful vows! Accept this mark of friendship, warm, sincere,- Friendship! 'tis all cold duty now allows.

And when you read the simple artless rhymes, One friendly sigh for him-he asks no more,- Who distant burns in flaming torrid climes, Or haply lies beneath th' Atlantic roar.

CHAPTER LIII.

A DEDICATION

TO

GAVIN HAMILTON, ESQ.

[The gentleman to whom these manly lines are addressed, was of good birth, and of an open and generous nature: he was one of the first of the gentry of the west to encourage the muse of Coila to stretch her wings at full length. His free life, and free speech, exposed him to the censures of that stern divine, Daddie Auld, who charged him with the sin of absenting himself from church for three successive days; for having, without the fear of God's servant before him, profanely said damn it, in his presence, and far having gallopped on Sunday. These charges were contemptuously dismissed by the presbyterial court. Hamilton was the brother of the Charlotte to whose charms, on the banks of Devon, Burns, it is said, paid the homage of a lover, as well as of a poet. The poem had a place in the Kilmarnock edition, but not as an express dedication.]

Expect na, Sir, in this narration, A fleechin', fleth'rin dedication, To roose you up, an' ca' you guid, An' sprung o' great an' noble bluid, Because ye're surnam'd like his Grace; Perhaps related to the race; Then when I'm tir'd-and sae are ye, Wi' monie a fulsome, sinfu' lie, [124]Set up a face, how I stop short, For fear your modesty be hurt.

This may do-maun do, Sir, wi' them wha Maun please the great folk for a wamefou; For me! sae laigh I needna bow, For, Lord be thankit, I can plough; And when I downa yoke a naig, Then, Lord be thankit, I can beg;

Sae I shall say, an' that's nae flatt'rin', It's just sic poet, an' sic patron.
The Poet, some guid angel help him, Or else, I fear some ill ane skelp him, He may do weel for a' he's done yet, But only-he's no just begun yet.
The Patron, (Sir, ye maun forgie me, I winna lie, come what will o' me,) On ev'ry hand it will allow'd be, He's just-nae better than he should be.
I readily and freely grant, He downa see a poor man want; What's no his ain, he winna tak it; What ance he says, he winna break it; Ought he can lend he'll no refus't, 'Till aft his guidness is abus'd; And rascals whyles that do him wrang, E'en that, he does na mind it lang: As master, landlord, husband, father, He does na fail his part in either.
But then, nae thanks to him for a' that; Nae godly symptom ye can ca' that; It's naething but a milder feature, Of our poor sinfu', corrupt nature: Ye'll get the best o' moral works, 'Mang black Gentoos and pagan Turks, Or hunters wild on Ponotaxi, Wha never heard of orthodoxy.
That he's the poor man's friend in need, The gentleman in word and deed, It's no thro' terror of damnation; It's just a carnal inclination.
Morality, thou deadly bane, Thy tens o' thousands thou hast slain! Vain is his hope, whose stay and trust is In moral mercy, truth and justice!
No-stretch a point to catch a plack; Abuse a brother to his back; Steal thro' a winnock frae a whore, But point the rake that taks the door; Be to the poor like onie whunstane, And haud their noses to the grunstane, Ply ev'ry art o' legal thieving; No matter-stick to sound believing.
Learn three-mile pray'rs an' half-mile graces, Wi' weel-spread looves, and lang wry faces; Grunt up a solemn, lengthen'd groan, And damn a' parties but your own; I'll warrant then, ye're nae deceiver, A steady, sturdy, staunch believer.
O ye wha leave the springs o' Calvin, For gumlie dubs of your ain delvin'! Ye sons of heresy and error, Ye'll some day squeal in quaking terror! When Vengeance draws the sword in wrath, And in the fire throws the sheath; When Ruin, with his sweeping besom, Just frets 'till Heav'n commission gies him: While o'er the harp pale Mis'ry moans, And strikes the ever-deep'ning tones, Still louder shrieks, and heavier groans!
Your pardon, Sir, for this digression. I maist forgat my dedication; But when divinity comes cross me My readers still are sure to lose me.
So, Sir, ye see 'twas nae daft vapour, But I maturely thought it proper, When a' my works I did review, To dedicate them, Sir, to you: Because (ye need na tak it ill) I thought them something like yoursel'.
Then patronize them wi' your favour, And your petitioner shall ever- I had amaist said, ever pray, But that's a word I need na say: For prayin' I hae little skill o't; I'm baith dead sweer, an' wretched ill o't; But I'se repeat each poor man's pray'r, That kens or hears about you, Sir-
"May ne'er misfortune's gowling bark, Howl thro' the dwelling o' the Clerk! May ne'er his gen'rous, honest heart, For that same gen'rous spirit smart!

May Kennedy's far-honour'd name Lang beet his hymeneal flame, Till Hamiltons, at least a dizen, Are frae their nuptial labours risen: [125] Five bonnie lasses round their table, And seven braw fellows, stout an' able To serve their king and country weel, By word, or pen, or pointed steel! May health and peace, with mutual rays, Shine on the ev'ning o' his days; 'Till his wee curlie John's-ier-oe, When ebbing life nae mair shall flow, The last, sad, mournful rites bestow."

I will not wind a lang conclusion, With complimentary effusion: But whilst your wishes and endeavours Are blest with Fortune's smiles and favours, I am, dear Sir, with zeal most fervent, Your much indebted, humble servant.

But if (which pow'rs above prevent) That iron-hearted carl, Want, Attended in his grim advances By sad mistakes and black mischances, While hopes, and joys, and pleasures fly him, Make you as poor a dog as I am, Your humble servant then no more; For who would humbly serve the poor! But by a poor man's hope in Heav'n! While recollection's pow'r is given, If, in the vale of humble life, The victim sad of fortune's strife, I, thro' the tender gushing tear, Should recognise my Master dear, If friendless, low, we meet together, Then Sir, your hand-my friend and brother.

CHAPTER LIV.

ELEGY

ON

THE DEATH OF ROBERT RUISSEAUX.

[Cromek found these verses among the loose papers of Burns, and printed them in the Reliques. They contain a portion of the character of the poet, record his habitual carelessness in worldly affairs, and his desire to be distinguished.]

Now Robin lies in his last lair, He'll gabble rhyme, nor sing nae mair, Cauld poverty, wi' hungry stare, Nae mair shall fear him; Nor anxious fear, nor cankert care, E'er mair come near him.

To tell the truth, they seldom fash't him, Except the moment that they crush't him; For sune as chance or fate had hush't 'em, Tho' e'er sae short, Then wi' a rhyme or song he lash't 'em, And thought it sport.

Tho' he was bred to kintra wark, And counted was baith wight and stark. Yet that was never Robin's mark To mak a man; But tell him he was learned and clark, Ye roos'd him than!

CHAPTER LV.

LETTER TO JAMES TENNANT,

OF GLENCONNER.

[The west country farmer to whom this letter was sent was a social man. The poet depended on his judgment in the choice of a farm, when he resolved to quit the harp for the plough: but as Ellisland was his choice, his skill may be questioned.]

Auld comrade dear, and brither sinner, How's a' the folk about

Glenconner? How do you this blae eastlin wind, That's like to blaw a body blind? For me, my faculties are frozen, My dearest member nearly dozen'd, I've sent you here, by Johnie Simson, Twa sage philosophers to glimpse on; Smith, wi' his sympathetic feeling, An' Reid, to common sense appealing. Philosophers have fought and wrangled, An' meikle Greek and Latin mangled, Till wi' their logic-jargon tir'd, An' in the depth of science mir'd, To common sense they now appeal, What wives and wabsters see and feel. But, hark ye, friend! I charge you strictly Peruse them, an' return them quickly, For now I'm grown sae cursed douce I pray and ponder butt the house, My shins, my lane, I there sit roastin', Perusing Bunyan, Brown, an' Boston; Till by an' by, if I haud on, I'll grunt a real gospel groan: Already I begin to try it, To cast my e'en up like a pyet, When by the gun she tumbles o'er, Flutt'ring an' gasping in her gore: [126]Sae shortly you shall see me bright, A burning and a shining light.

My heart-warm love to guid auld Glen, The ace an' wale of honest men: When bending down wi' auld gray hairs, Beneath the load of years and cares, May He who made him still support him, An' views beyond the grave comfort him, His worthy fam'ly far and near, God bless them a' wi' grace and gear!

My auld schoolfellow, preacher Willie, The manly tar, my mason Billie, An' Auchenbay, I wish him joy; If he's a parent, lass or boy, May he be dad, and Meg the mither, Just five-and-forty years thegither! An' no forgetting wabster Charlie, I'm tauld he offers very fairly. An' Lord, remember singing Sannock, Wi' hale breeks, saxpence, an' a bannock, An' next my auld acquaintance, Nancy, Since she is fitted to her fancy; An' her kind stars hae airted till her A good chiel wi' a pickle siller. My kindest, best respects I sen' it, To cousin Kate, an' sister Janet; Tell them, frae me, wi' chiels be cautious, For, faith, they'll aiblins fin' them fashious; To grant a heart is fairly civil, But to grant the maidenhead's the devil An' lastly, Jamie, for yoursel', May guardian angels tak a spell, An' steer you seven miles south o' hell: But first, before you see heaven's glory, May ye get monie a merry story, Monie a laugh, and monie a drink, And aye eneugh, o' needfu' clink.

Now fare ye weel, an' joy be wi' you, For my sake this I beg it o' you. Assist poor Simson a' ye can, Ye'll fin' him just an honest man; Sae I conclude, and quat my chanter, Your's, saint or sinner,

Rob the Ranter.

CHAPTER LVI.

ON THE

BIRTH OF A POSTHUMOUS CHILD.

[From letters addressed by Burns to Mrs. Dunlop, it would appear that this "Sweet Flow'ret, pledge o' meikle love," was the only son of her daughter, Mrs. Henri, who had married a French gentleman. The mother soon followed the father to the grave: she died in the south of France, whither she had gone in search of health.]

Sweet flow'ret, pledge o' meikle love, And ward o' mony a pray'r, What heart o' stane wad thou na move, Sae helpless, sweet, and fair!

November hirples o'er the lea, Chill on thy lovely form; And gane, alas! the shelt'ring tree, Should shield thee frae the storm.

May He who gives the rain to pour, And wings the blast to blaw, Protect thee frae the driving show'r, The bitter frost and snaw!

May He, the friend of woe and want, Who heals life's various stounds, Protect and guard the mother-plant, And heal her cruel wounds!

But late she flourish'd, rooted fast, Fair on the summer-morn: Now feebly bends she in the blast, Unshelter'd and forlorn.

Blest be thy bloom, thou lovely gem, Unscath'd by ruffian hand! And from thee many a parent stem Arise to deck our land!

CHAPTER LVII.

TO MISS CRUIKSHANK,

A VERY YOUNG LADY.

WRITTEN ON THE BLANK LEAF OF A BOOK, PRESENTED TO HER BY THE AUTHOR.

[The beauteous rose-bud of this poem was one of the daughters of Mr. Cruikshank, a master in the High School of Edinburgh, at whose table Burns was a frequent guest during the year of hope which he spent in the northern metropolis.][127]

Beauteous rose-bud, young and gay, Blooming in thy early May, Never may'st thou, lovely flow'r, Chilly shrink in sleety show'r! Never Boreas' hoary path, Never Eurus' poisonous breath, Never baleful stellar lights, Taint thee with untimely blights! Never, never reptile thief Riot on thy virgin leaf! Nor even Sol too fiercely view Thy bosom blushing still with dew!

May'st thou long, sweet crimson gem, Richly deck thy native stem: 'Till some evening, sober, calm, Dropping dews and breathing balm, While all around the woodland rings, And ev'ry bird thy requiem sings; Thou, amid the dirgeful sound, Shed thy dying honours round, And resign to parent earth The loveliest form she e'er gave birth.

CHAPTER LVIII.

WILLIE CHALMERS.

[Lockhart first gave this poetic curiosity to the world: he copied it from a small manuscript volume of Poems given by Burns to Lady Harriet Don, with an explanation in these words: "W. Chalmers, a gentleman in Ayrshire, a particular friend of mine, asked me to write a poetic epistle to a young lady, his Dulcinea. I had seen her, but was scarcely acquainted with her, and wrote as follows." Chalmers was a writer in Ayr. I have not heard that the lady was influenced by this volunteer effusion: ladies are seldom rhymed into the matrimonial snare.]

I.

Wi' braw new branks in mickle pride, And eke a braw new brechan, My Pegasus I'm got astride, And up Parnassus pechin; Whiles owre a bush wi' downward crush The doitie beastie stammers; Then up he gets and off he sets For sake o' Willie Chalmers.

II.

I doubt na, lass, that weel kenn'd name May cost a pair o' blushes; I am nae stranger to your fame, Nor his warm urged wishes. Your bonnie face sae mild and sweet His honest heart enamours, And faith ye'll no be lost a whit, Tho' waired on Willie Chalmers.

III.

Auld Truth hersel' might swear ye're fair, And Honour safely back her, And Modesty assume your air, And ne'er a ane mistak' her: And sic twa love-inspiring een Might fire even holy Palmers; Nae wonder then they've fatal been To honest Willie Chalmers.

IV.

I doubt na fortune may you shore Some mim-mou'd pouthered priestie, Fu' lifted up wi' Hebrew lore, And band upon his breastie: But Oh! what signifies to you His lexicons and grammars; The feeling heart's the royal blue, And that's wi' Willie Chalmers.

V.

Some gapin' glowrin' countra laird, May warstle for your favour; May claw his lug, and straik his beard, And hoast up some palaver. My bonnie maid, before ye wed Sic clumsy-witted hammers, Seek Heaven for help, and barefit skelp Awa' wi' Willie Chalmers.

VI.

Forgive the Bard! my fond regard For ane that shares my bosom, Inspires my muse to gie 'm his dues, For de'il a hair I roose him. May powers aboon unite you soon, And fructify your amours,- And every year come in mair dear To you and Willie Chalmers.

CHAPTER LIX.

LYING AT A REVEREND FRIEND'S HOUSE ON NIGHT, THE AUTHOR LEFT THE FOLLOWING VERSES IN THE ROOM WHERE HE SLEPT.

[Of the origin of those verses Gilbert Burns gives the following account. "The first time Robert heard the spinet played was at the house of Dr. Lawrie, then minister of Loudon, now in Glasgow. Dr. Lawrie has several daughters; one of them played; the father and the mother led down the dance; the rest of the sisters, the brother, the poet and the other guests mixed in it. It was a delightful family scene for our poet, then lately introduced to the world; his mind was roused to a poetic enthusiasm, and the stanzas were left in the room where he slept."]

I.

O thou dread Power, who reign'st above! I know thou wilt me hear, When for this scene of peace and love I make my prayer sincere.

II.

The hoary sire-the mortal stroke, Long, long, be pleased to spare; To bless his filial little flock And show what good men are.

III.

She who her lovely offspring eyes With tender hopes and fears, O, bless her with a mother's joys, But spare a mother's tears!

IV.

Their hope-their stay-their darling youth, In manhood's dawning blush-Bless him, thou God of love and truth, Up to a parent's wish!

V.

The beauteous, seraph sister-band, With earnest tears I pray, Thous know'st the snares on ev'ry hand- Guide Thou their steps alway.

VI.

When soon or late they reach that coast, O'er life's rough ocean driven, May they rejoice, no wanderer lost, A family in Heaven!

CHAPTER LX.

TO GAVIN HAMILTON, ESQ.,

MAUCHLINE.

(RECOMMENDING A BOY.)

[Verse seems to have been the natural language of Burns. The Master Tootie whose skill he records, lived in Mauchline, and dealt in cows: he was an artful and contriving person, great in bargaining and intimate with all the professional tricks by which old cows are made to look young, and six-pint hawkies pass for those of twelve.]

Mossgiel, May 3, 1786.

I.

I hold it, Sir, my bounden duty, To warn you how that Master Tootie, Alias, Laird M'Gaun, Was here to hire yon lad away 'Bout whom ye spak the tither day, An' wad ha'e done't aff han': But lest he learn the callan tricks, As, faith, I muckle doubt him, Like scrapin' out auld Crummie's nicks, An' tellin' lies about them; As lieve then, I'd have then, Your clerkship he should sair, If sae be, ye may be Not fitted otherwhere.

II.

Altho' I say't, he's gleg enough, An' bout a house that's rude an' rough The boy might learn to swear; But then, wi' you, he'll be sae taught, An' get sic fair example straught, I havena ony fear. Ye'll catechize him every quirk, An' shore him weel wi' Hell; An' gar him follow to the kirk- -Ay when ye gang yoursel'. If ye then, maun be then Frae hame this comin' Friday; Then please Sir, to lea'e Sir, The orders wi' your lady.

III.

My word of honour I hae gien, In Paisley John's, that night at e'n, To meet the Warld's worm; To try to get the twa to gree, An' name the airles[56] an' the fee, In legal mode an' form: I ken he weel a snick can draw, When simple bodies let him; An' if a Devil be at a', In faith he's sure to get him. To phrase you, an' praise you, Ye ken your Laureat scorns: The pray'r still, you share still, Of grateful Minstrel Burns.

FOOTNOTES:

[56] The airles-earnest money.

CHAPTER LXI.

TO MR. M'ADAM,

OF CRAIGEN-GILLAN.

[It seems that Burns, delighted with the praise which the Laird of Craigen-Gillan bestowed on his verses,-probably the Jolly Beggars, then in the hands of Woodburn, his steward,-poured out this little unpremeditated natural acknowledgment.]

Sir, o'er a gill I gat your card, I trow it made me proud; See wha tak's notice o' the bard I lap and cry'd fu' loud.

Now deil-ma-care about their jaw, The senseless, gawky million: I'll cock my nose aboon them a'- I'm roos'd by Craigen-Gillan!

'Twas noble, Sir; 'twas like yoursel', To grant your high protection: A great man's smile, ye ken fu' well, Is ay a blest infection.

Tho' by his[57] banes who in a tub Match'd Macedonian Sandy! On my ain legs thro' dirt and dub, I independent stand ay.-

And when those legs to gude, warm kail, Wi' welcome canna bear me; A lee dyke-side, a sybow-tail, And barley-scone shall cheer me.

Heaven spare you lang to kiss the breath O' many flow'ry simmers! And bless your bonnie lasses baith, I'm tauld they're loosome kimmers!

And God bless young Dunaskin's laird, The blossom of our gentry! And may he wear an auld man's beard, A credit to his country.

FOOTNOTES:

[57] Diogenes.

CHAPTER LXII.

ANSWER TO A POETICAL EPISTLE

SENT TO THE AUTHOR BY A TAILOR.

[The person who in the name of a Tailor took the liberty of admonishing Burns about his errors, is generally believed to have been William Simpson, the schoolmaster of Ochiltree: the verses seem about the measure of his capacity, and were attributed at the time to his hand. The natural poet took advantage of the mask in which the made poet concealed himself, and rained such a merciless storm upon him, as would have extinguished half the Tailors in Ayrshire, and made the amazed dominie

"Strangely fidge and fyke."

It was first printed in 1801, by Stewart.]

What ails ye now, ye lousie bh, To thresh my back at sic a pitch? Losh, man! hae mercy wi' your natch, Your bodkin's bauld, I didna suffer ha'f sae much Frae Daddie Auld.

What tho' at times when I grow crouse, I gie their wames a random pouse, Is that enough for you to souse Your servant sae? Gae mind your seam, ye prick-the-louse, An' jag-the-flae.

King David o' poetic brief, Wrought 'mang the lasses sic mischief, As fill'd his after life wi' grief, An' bluidy rants, An' yet he's rank'd amang the chief O' lang-syne saunts.

And maybe, Tam, for a' my cants, My wicked rhymes, an' druken rants, I'll gie auld cloven Clootie's haunts An unco' slip yet, An' snugly sit among the saunts At Davie's hip get.

But fegs, the Session says I maun Gae fa' upo' anither plan, Than garrin lasses cowp the cran Clean heels owre body, And sairly thole their mither's ban Afore the howdy.

This leads me on, to tell for sport, How I did wi' the Session sort, Auld Clinkum at the inner port Cried three times-"Robin! Come hither, lad, an' answer for't, Ye're blamed for jobbin'."

Wi' pinch I pat a Sunday's face on, An' snoov'd away before the Session; I made an open fair confession- I scorn'd to lee; An' syne Mess John, beyond expression, Fell foul o' me.

CHAPTER LXIII.

TO J. RANKINE.

[With the Laird of Adamhill's personal character the reader is already acquainted: the lady about whose frailties the rumour alluded to was about to rise, has not been named, and it would neither be delicate nor polite to guess.]

I am a keeper of the law In some sma' points, altho' not a'; Some people tell me gin I fa' Ae way or ither. The breaking of ae point, though sma', Breaks a' thegither

I hae been in for't once or twice, And winna say o'er far for thrice, Yet never met with that surprise That broke my rest, But now a rumour's like to rise, A whaup's i' the nest.

CHAPTER LXIV.

LINES

WRITTEN ON A BANK-NOTE.

[The bank-note on which these characteristic lines were endorsed, came into the hands of the late James Gracie, banker in Dumfries: he knew the handwriting of Burns, and kept it as a curiosity. The concluding lines point to the year 1786, as the date of the composition.]

Wae worth thy power, thou cursed leaf, Fell source o' a' my woe an' grief; For lack o' thee I've lost my lass, For lack o' thee I scrimp my glass. I see the children of affliction Unaided, through thy cursed restriction I've seen the oppressor's cruel smile Amid his hapless victim's spoil: And for thy potence vainly wished, To crush the villain in the dust. For lack o' thee, I leave this much-lov'd shore, Never, perhaps, to greet old Scotland more.

R. B.

CHAPTER LXV.

A DREAM.

"Thoughts, words, and deeds, the statute blames with reason; But surely dreams were ne'er indicted treason."

On reading, in the public papers, the "Laureate's Ode," with the other parade of June 4th, 1786, the author was no sooner dropt asleep, than he imagined himself transported to the birth-day levee; and, in his dreaming fancy, made the following "Address."

[The prudent friends of the poet remonstrated with him about this Poem, which they appeared to think would injure his fortunes and stop the royal bounty to which he was thought entitled. Mrs. Dunlop, and Mrs. Stewart, of Stair, solicited him in vain to omit it in the Edinburgh edition of his poems. I know of no poem for which a claim of being prophetic would be so successfully set up: it is full of point as well as of the future. The allusions require no comment.]

Guid-mornin' to your Majesty! May Heaven augment your blisses, On ev'ry new birth-day ye see, A humble poet wishes! My bardship here, at your levee, On sic a day as this is, Is sure an uncouth sight to see, Amang thae birth-day dresses Sae fine this day.

I see ye're complimented thrang, By many a lord an' lady; "God save the King!" 's a cuckoo sang That's unco easy said ay; The poets, too, a venal gang, Wi' rhymes weel-turn'd and ready, Wad gar you trow ye ne'er do wrang, But ay unerring steady, On sic a day.

For me, before a monarch's face, Ev'n there I winna flatter; For neither pension, post, nor place, Am I your humble debtor: So, nae reflection on your grace, Your kingship to bespatter; There's monie waur been o' the race, And aiblins ane been better Than you this day.

'Tis very true, my sov'reign king, My skill may weel be doubted: But facts are chiels that winna ding, An' downa be disputed: Your royal nest beneath your wing, Is e'en right reft an' clouted, And now the third part of the string, An' less, will gang about it Than did ae day.

Far be't frae me that I aspire To blame your legislation, Or say, ye wisdom want, or fire, To rule this mighty nation. But faith! I muckle doubt, my sire, Ye've trusted ministration To chaps, wha, in a barn or byre, Wad better fill'd their station Than courts yon day.

And now ye've gien auld Britain peace, Her broken shins to plaister; Your sair taxation does her fleece, Till she has scarce a tester; For me, thank God, my life's a lease, Nae bargain wearing faster, Or, faith! I fear, that, wi' the geese, I shortly boost to pasture I' the craft some day.

I'm no mistrusting Willie Pitt, When taxes he enlarges, (An' Will's a true guid fallow's get, A name not envy spairges,) That he intends to pay your debt, An' lessen a' your charges; But, G-d-sake! let nae saving-fit Abridge your bonnie barges An' boats this day.

Adieu, my Liege! may freedom geck Beneath your high protection; An' may ye rax corruption's neck, And gie her for dissection! But since I'm here, I'll no neglect, In loyal, true affection, To pay your Queen, with due respect, My fealty an' subjection This great birth-day

Hail, Majesty Most Excellent! While nobles strive to please ye, Will ye accept a compliment A simple poet gi'es ye? Thae bonnie bairntime, Heav'n has lent, Still higher may they heeze ye In bliss, till fate some day is sent, For ever to release ye Frae care that day.

For you, young potentate o' Wales, I tell your Highness fairly, Down pleasure's stream, wi' swelling sails, I'm tauld ye're driving rarely; But some day ye may gnaw your nails, An' curse your folly sairly, That e'er ye brak Diana's pales, Or rattl'd dice wi' Charlie, By night or day.

Yet aft a ragged cowte's been known To mak a noble aiver; So, ye may doucely fill a throne, For a' their clish-ma-claver: There, him at Agincourt wha shone, Few better were or braver; And yet, wi' funny, queer Sir John, He was an unco shaver For monie a day.

For you, right rev'rend Osnaburg, Nane sets the lawn-sleeve sweeter, Altho' a ribbon at your lug, Wad been a dress completer: As ye disown yon paughty dog That bears the keys of Peter, Then, swith! an' get a wife to hug, Or, trouth! ye'll stain the mitre Some luckless day.

Young, royal Tarry Breeks, I learn, Ye've lately come athwart her; A glorious galley,[58] stem an' stern, Weel rigg'd for Venus' barter; But first hang out, that she'll discern Your hymeneal charter, [132]Then heave aboard your grapple airn, An', large upon her quarter, Come full that day.

Ye, lastly, bonnie blossoms a', Ye royal lasses dainty, Heav'n mak you guid as weel as braw, An' gie you lads a-plenty: But sneer na British Boys awa', For kings are unco scant ay; An' German gentles are but sma', They're better just than want ay On onie day.

God bless you a'! consider now, Ye're unco muckle dautet; But ere the course o' life be thro', It may be bitter sautet: An' I hae seen their coggie fou, That yet hae tarrow't at it; But or the day was done, I trow, The laggen they hae clautet Fu' clean that day.

FOOTNOTES:

[58] Alluding to the newspaper account of a certain royal sailor's amour

CHAPTER LXVI.

A BARD'S EPITAPH.

[This beautiful and affecting poem was printed in the Kilmarnock edition: Wordsworth writes with his usual taste and feeling about it: "Whom did the poet intend should be thought of, as occupying that grave, over which, after modestly setting forth the moral discernment and warm affections of the 'poor inhabitant' it is supposed to be inscribed that

'Thoughtless follies laid him low, And stained his name!'

Who but himself-himself anticipating the but too probable termination of his own course? Here is a sincere and solemn avowal-a confession at once devout, poetical, and human-a history in the shape of a prophecy! What more was required of the biographer, than to have put his seal to the writing, testifying that the foreboding had been realized and that the record was authentic?"]

Is there a whim-inspired fool, Owre fast for thought, owre hot for rule, Owre blate to seek, owre proud to snool, Let him draw near; And owre this grassy heap sing dool, And drap a tear.

Is there a bard of rustic song, Who, noteless, steals the crowds among, That weekly this area throng, O, pass not by! But with a frater-feeling strong, Here heave a sigh.

Is there a man, whose judgment clear, Can others teach the course to steer, Yet runs, himself, life's mad career, Wild as the wave; Here pause-and, through the starting tear, Survey this grave.

The poor inhabitant below Was quick to learn and wise to know, And keenly felt the friendly glow, And softer flame, But thoughtless follies laid him low, And stain'd his name!

Reader, attend-whether thy soul Soars fancy's flights beyond the pole, Or darkling grubs this earthly hole, In low pursuit; Know, prudent, cautious self-control, Is wisdom's root.

CHAPTER LXVII.

THE TWA DOGS.

A TALE.

[Cromek, an anxious and curious inquirer, informed me, that the Twa Dogs was in a half-finished state, when the poet consulted John Wilson, the printer, about the Kilmarnock edition. On looking over the manuscripts, the printer, with a sagacity common to his profession, said, "The Address to the Deil" and "The Holy Fair" were grand things, but it would be as well to have a calmer and sedater strain, to put at the front of the volume. Burns was struck with the remark, and on his way home to Mossgiel, completed the Poem, and took it next day to Kilmarnock, much to the satisfaction of "Wee Johnnie." On the 17th February Burns says to John Richmond, of Mauchline, "I have completed my Poem of the Twa Dogs, but have not shown it to the world." It is difficult to fix the dates with anything like accuracy, to compositions which are not struck off at one heat of the fancy. "Luath was one of the poet's dogs, which some person had wantonly killed," says Gilbert Burns; "but Cæsar was merely the creature of the imagination." The Ettrick Shepherd, a judge of collies, says that Luath is true to the life, and that many a hundred times he has seen the dogs bark for very joy, when the cottage children were merry.]

Twas in that place o' Scotland's isle That bears the name o' Auld King Coil, [133]Upon a bonnie day in June, When wearing through the afternoon, Twa dogs that were na thrang at hame, Forgather'd ance upon a time. The first I'll name, they ca'd him Cæsar, Was keepit for his honour's pleasure; His hair, his size, his mouth, his lugs, Show'd he was nane o' Scotland's dogs; But whalpit some place far abroad, Where sailors gang to fish for cod.

His locked, letter'd, braw brass collar Show'd him the gentleman and scholar; But though he was o' high degree, The fient a pride-nae pride had he; But wad hae spent an hour caressin', Ev'n wi' a tinkler-gypsey's messin'. At kirk or market, mill or smiddie, Nae tawted tyke, though e'er sae duddie, But he wad stan't, as glad to see him, And stroan't on stanes and hillocks wi' him.

The tither was a ploughman's collie, A rhyming, ranting, raving billie, Wha for his friend an' comrade had him, And in his freaks had Luath ca'd him, After some dog in Highland sang,[59] Was made lang syne-Lord know how lang.

He was a gash an' faithful tyke, As ever lap a sheugh or dyke. His honest, sonsie, baws'nt face, Ay gat him friends in ilka place. His breast was white, his touzie back Weel clad wi' coat o' glossy black; His gaucie tail, wi' upward curl, Hung o'er his hurdies wi' a swirl.

Nae doubt but they were fain o' ither, An' unco pack an' thick thegither; Wi' social nose whyles snuff'd and snowkit, Whyles mice and moudiewarts they howkit; Whyles scour'd awa in lang excursion, An' worry'd ither in diversion; Until wi' daffin weary grown, Upon a knowe they sat them down, And there began a lang digression About the lords o' the creation.

CÆSAR.

I've aften wonder'd, honest Luath, What sort o' life poor dogs like you have; An' when the gentry's life I saw, What way poor bodies liv'd ava.

Our laird gets in his racked rents, His coals, his kain, and a' his stents; He rises when he likes himsel'; His flunkies answer at the bell; He ca's his coach, he ca's his horse; He draws a bonnie silken purse As lang's my tail, whare, through the steeks, The yellow letter'd Geordie keeks.

Frae morn to e'en its nought but toiling, At baking, roasting, frying, boiling; An' though the gentry first are stechin, Yet even the ha' folk fill their pechan Wi' sauce, ragouts, and sic like trashtrie, That's little short o' downright wastrie. Our whipper-in, wee, blastit wonner, Poor worthless elf, eats a dinner, Better than ony tenant man His honour has in a' the lan'; An' what poor cot-folk pit their painch in, I own it's past my comprehension.

LUATH.

Trowth, Cæsar, whyles they're fash't eneugh A cotter howkin in a sheugh, Wi' dirty stanes biggin' a dyke, Baring a quarry, and sic like; Himself, a wife, he thus sustains, A smytrie o' wee duddie weans, An' nought but his han' darg, to keep Them right and tight in thack an' rape.

An' when they meet wi' sair disasters, Like loss o' health, or want o' masters, Ye maist wad think a wee touch langer An' they maun starve o' cauld and hunger; But, how it comes, I never kenn'd yet, They're maistly wonderfu' contented: An' buirdly chiels, an' clever hizzies, Are bred in sic a way as this is.

CÆSAR.

But then to see how ye're negleckit, How huff'd, and cuff'd, and disrespeckit! L-d, man, our gentry care as little For delvers, ditchers, an' sic cattle; They gang as saucy by poor folk, As I wad by a stinking brock.

I've notic'd, on our Laird's court-day, An' mony a time my heart's been wae, Poor tenant bodies, scant o' cash, How they maun thole a factor's snash: He'll stamp an' threaten, curse an' swear, He'll apprehend them, poind their gear; While they maun stan', wi' aspect humble, An' hear it a', an' fear an' tremble!

I see how folk live that hae riches; But surely poor folk maun be wretches!

LUATH.

They're no sae wretched's ane wad think; Tho' constantly on poortith's brink: They're sae accustom'd wi' the sight, The view o't gies them little fright. Then chance an' fortune are sae guided, They're ay in less or mair provided; An' tho' fatigu'd wi' close employment, A blink o' rest's a sweet enjoyment.

The dearest comfort o' their lives, Their grushie weans, an' faithfu' wives; The prattling things are just their pride, That sweetens a' their fire-side; An' whyles twalpennie worth o' nappy Can mak' the bodies unco happy; They lay aside their private cares, To mind the Kirk and State affairs: They'll talk o' patronage and priests; Wi' kindling fury in their breasts; Or tell what new taxation's comin', And ferlie at the folk in Lon'on.

As bleak-fac'd Hallowmass returns, They get the jovial, ranting kirns, When rural life, o' ev'ry station, Unite in common recreation; Love blinks, Wit slaps, an' social Mirth Forgets there's Care upo' the earth.

That merry day the year begins, They bar the door on frosty win's; The nappy reeks wi' mantling ream, An' sheds a heart-inspiring steam; The luntin pipe, an sneeshin mill, Are handed round wi' right guid will; The cantie auld folks crackin' crouse, The young anes rantin' thro' the house,- My heart has been sae fain to see them, That I for joy hae barkit wi' them.

Still it's owre true that ye hae said, Sic game is now owre aften play'd. There's monie a creditable stock O' decent, honest, fawsont folk, Are riven out baith root and branch, Some rascal's pridefu' greed to quench, Wha thinks to knit himsel' the faster In favour wi' some gentle master, Wha aiblins, thrang a parliamentin', For Britain's guid his saul indentin'-

CÆSAR.

Haith, lad, ye little ken about it! For Britain's guid! guid faith, I doubt it! Say rather, gaun as Premiers lead him, An' saying, aye or no's they bid him, At operas an' plays parading, Mortgaging, gambling, masquerading; Or may be, in a frolic daft, To Hague or Calais takes a waft, To mak a tour, an' tak' a whirl, To learn bon ton, an' see the worl'.

There, at Vienna or Versailles, He rives his father's auld entails; Or by Madrid he takes the rout, To thrum guitars, an' fecht wi' nowt; Or down Italian vista startles, Wh-re-hunting amang groves o' myrtles Then bouses drumly German water, To mak' himsel' look fair and fatter, An' clear the consequential sorrows, Love-gifts of carnival signoras. For Britain's guid!- for her destruction Wi' dissipation, feud, an' faction.

LUATH.

Hech, man! dear sirs! is that the gate They waste sae mony a braw estate! Are we sae foughten an' harass'd For gear to gang that gate at last!

O, would they stay aback frae courts, An' please themsels wi' countra sports, It wad for ev'ry ane be better, The Laird, the Tenant, an' the Cotter! For thae frank, rantin', ramblin' billies, Fient haet o' them's ill-hearted fellows; Except for breakin' o' their timmer, Or speakin' lightly o' their limmer, Or shootin' o' a hare or moor-cock, The ne'er a bit they're ill to poor folk.

But will ye tell me, Master Cæsar, Sure great folk's life's a life o' pleasure? Nae cauld or hunger e'er can steer them, The vera thought o't need na fear them.

CÆSAR.

L-d, man, were ye but whyles whare I am, The gentles ye wad ne'er envy 'em.

It's true, they needna starve or sweat, Thro' winters cauld, or simmer's heat; They've nae sair wark to craze their banes, An' fill auld age wi' grips an' granes: But human bodies are sic fools, For a' their colleges and schools, That when nae real ills perplex them, They mak enow themsels to vex them; An' ay the less they hae to sturt them, In like proportion, less will hurt them.

A country fellow at the pleugh, His acres till'd, he's right eneugh; A country girl at her wheel, Her dizzen's done, she's unco weel: But Gentlemen, an' Ladies warst, Wi' ev'n down want o' wark are curst. They loiter, lounging, lank, an' lazy; Tho' deil haet ails them, yet uneasy; Their days insipid, dull, an' tasteless; Their nights unquiet, lang an' restless; An' even their sports, their balls an' races, Their galloping thro' public places, There's sic parade, sic pomp, an' art, The joy can scarcely reach the heart. The men cast out in party matches, Then sowther a' in deep debauches; Ae night they're mad wi' drink and wh-ring, Niest day their life is past enduring. The Ladies arm-in-arm in clusters, As great and gracious a' as sisters; But hear their absent thoughts o' ither, They're a' run deils an' jads thegither. Whyles, o'er the wee bit cup an' platie, They sip the scandal potion pretty; Or lee-lang nights, wi' crabbit leuks Pore owre the devil's pictur'd beuks; Stake on a chance a farmer's stack-yard, An' cheat like onie unhang'd blackguard.

There's some exception, man an' woman; But this is Gentry's life in common.

By this, the sun was out o' sight, An' darker gloaming brought the night: The bum-clock humm'd wi' lazy drone; The kye stood rowtin i' the loan; When up they gat, and shook their lugs, Rejoic'd they were na men, but dogs; An' each took aff his several way, Resolv'd to meet some ither day.

FOOTNOTES:

[59] Cuchullin's dog in Ossian's Fingal.

CHAPTER LXVIII.

LINES

ON

MEETING WITH LORD DAER.

["The first time I saw Robert Burns," says Dugald Stewart, "was on the 23rd of October, 1786, when he dined at my house in Ayrshire, together with our common friend, John Mackenzie, surgeon in Mauchline, to whom I am indebted for the pleasure of his acquaintance. My excellent and much-lamented friend, the late Basil, Lord Daer, happened to arrive at Catrine the same day, and, by the kindness and frankness of his manners, left an impression on the mind of the poet which was never effaced. The verses which the poet wrote on the occasion are among the most imperfect of his pieces, but a few stanzas may perhaps be a matter of curiosity, both on account of the character to which they relate and the light which they throw on the situation and the feelings of the writer before his work was known to the public." Basil, Lord Daer, the uncle of the present Earl of Selkirk, was born in the year 1769, at the family seat of St. Mary's Isle: he distinguished himself early at school, and at college excelled in literature and science; he had a greater regard for democracy than was then reckoned consistent with his birth and rank. He was, when Burns met him, in his twenty-third year; was very tall, something careless in his dress, and had the taste and talent common to his distinguished family. He died in his thirty-third year.]

This wot ye all whom it concerns, I, Rhymer Robin, alias Burns, October twenty-third, A ne'er-to-be-forgotten day, Sae far I sprachled up the brae, I dinner'd wi' a Lord.

I've been at druken writers' feasts, Nay, been bitch-fou' 'mang godly priests, Wi' rev'rence be it spoken: I've even join'd the honour'd jorum, When mighty squireships of the quorum Their hydra drouth did sloken.

But wi' a Lord-stand out, my shin! A Lord-a Peer-an Earl's son!- Up higher yet, my bonnet! And sic a Lord!-lang Scotch ells twa, Our Peerage he o'erlooks them a', As I look o'er my sonnet.

But, oh! for Hogarth's magic pow'r! To show Sir Bardie's willyart glow'r, And how he star'd and stammer'd, When goavan, as if led wi' branks, An'

stumpan on his ploughman shanks, He in the parlour hammer'd.
I sidling shelter'd in a nook, An' at his lordship steal't a look, Like some portentous omen; Except good sense and social glee, An' (what surpris'd me) modesty, I marked nought uncommon.
I watch'd the symptoms o' the great, The gentle pride, the lordly state, The arrogant assuming; The fient a pride, nae pride had he, Nor sauce, nor state, that I could see, Mair than an honest ploughman.
Then from his lordship I shall learn, Henceforth to meet with unconcern One rank as weel's another; Nae honest worthy man need care To meet with noble youthful Daer, For he but meets a brother.
CHAPTER LXIX.
ADDRESS TO EDINBURGH.
["I enclose you two poems," said Burns to his friend Chalmers, "which I have carded and spun since I passed Glenbuck. One blank in the Address to Edinburgh, 'Fair B,' is the heavenly Miss Burnet, daughter to Lord Monboddo, at whose house I have had the honour to be more than once. There has not been anything nearly like her, in all the combinations of beauty, grace, and goodness the great Creator has formed, since Milton's Eve, on the first day of her existence." Lord Monboddo made himself ridiculous by his speculations on human nature, and acceptable by his kindly manners and suppers in the manner of the ancients, where his viands were spread under ambrosial lights, and his Falernian was wreathed with flowers. At these suppers Burns sometimes made his appearance. The "Address" was first printed in the Edinburgh edition: the poet's hopes were then high, and his compliments, both to town and people, were elegant and happy.]
I.
Edina! Scotia's darling seat! All hail thy palaces and tow'rs, Where once beneath a monarch's feet Sat Legislation's sov'reign pow'rs! From marking wildly-scatter'd flow'rs, As on the banks of Ayr I stray'd, And singing, lone, the ling'ring hours, I shelter in thy honour'd shade.
II.
Here wealth still swells the golden tide, As busy Trade his labour plies; There Architecture's noble pride Bids elegance and splendour rise; Here Justice, from her native skies, High wields her balance and her rod; There Learning, with his eagle eyes, Seeks Science in her coy abode.
III.
Thy sons, Edina! social, kind, With open arms the stranger hail; Their views enlarg'd, their liberal mind, Above the narrow, rural vale; Attentive still to sorrow's wail, Or modest merit's silent claim; And never may their sources fail! And never envy blot their name!
IV.
Thy daughters bright thy walks adorn, Gay as the gilded summer sky, Sweet

as the dewy milk-white thorn, Dear as the raptur'd thrill of joy! Fair Burnet strikes th' adoring eye, Heav'n's beauties on my fancy shine; I see the Sire of Love on high, And own his work indeed divine!

V.

There, watching high the least alarms, Thy rough, rude fortress gleams afar, Like some bold vet'ran, gray in arms, And mark'd with many a seamy scar: The pond'rous wall and massy bar, Grim-rising o'er the rugged rock, Have oft withstood assailing war, And oft repell'd th' invader's shock.

VI.

With awe-struck thought, and pitying tears, I view that noble, stately dome, Where Scotia's kings of other years, Fam'd heroes! had their royal home: Alas, how chang'd the times to come! Their royal name low in the dust! Their hapless race wild-wand'ring roam, Tho' rigid law cries out, 'twas just!

VII.

Wild beats my heart to trace your steps, Whose ancestors, in days of yore, [137]Thro' hostile ranks and ruin'd gaps Old Scotia's bloody lion bore: Ev'n I who sing in rustic lore, Haply, my sires have left their shed, And fac'd grim danger's loudest roar, Bold-following where your fathers led!

VIII.

Edina! Scotia's darling seat! All hail thy palaces and tow'rs, Where once beneath a monarch's feet Sat Legislation's sov'reign pow'rs! From marking wildly-scatter'd flow'rs, As on the hanks of Ayr I stray'd, And singing, lone, the ling'ring hours, I shelter in thy honour'd shade.

CHAPTER LXX.

EPISTLE TO MAJOR LOGAN.

[Major Logan, of Camlarg, lived, when this hasty Poem was written, with his mother and sister at Parkhouse, near Ayr. He was a good musician, a joyous companion, and something of a wit. The Epistle was printed, for the first time, in my edition of Burns, in 1834, and since then no other edition has wanted it.]

Hail, thairm-inspirin', rattlin' Willie! Though fortune's road be rough an' hilly To every fiddling, rhyming billie, We never heed, But tak' it like the unback'd filly, Proud o' her speed.

When idly goavan whyles we saunter Yirr, fancy barks, awa' we canter Uphill, down brae, till some mishanter, Some black bog-hole, Arrests us, then the scathe an' banter We're forced to thole.

Hale be your heart! Hale be your fiddle! Lang may your elbuck jink and diddle, To cheer you through the weary widdle O' this wild warl', Until you on a crummock driddle A gray-hair'd carl.

Come wealth, come poortith, late or soon, Heaven send your heart-strings ay in tune, And screw your temper pins aboon A fifth or mair, The melancholious, lazy croon O' cankrie care.

May still your life from day to day Nae "lente largo" in the play, But "allegretto forte" gay Harmonious flow: A sweeping, kindling, bauld strathspey- Encore! Bravo!

A blessing on the cheery gang Wha dearly like a jig or sang, An' never think o' right an' wrang By square an' rule, But as the clegs o' feeling stang Are wise or fool.

My hand-waled curse keep hard in chase The harpy, hoodock, purse-proud race, Wha count on poortith as disgrace- Their tuneless hearts! May fireside discords jar a base To a' their parts!

But come, your hand, my careless brither, I' th' ither warl', if there's anither, An' that there is I've little swither About the matter; We check for chow shall jog thegither, I'se ne'er bid better.

We've faults and failings-granted clearly, We're frail backsliding mortals merely, Eve's bonny squad, priests wyte them sheerly For our grand fa'; But stilt, but still, I like them dearly- God bless them a'!

Ochon! for poor Castalian drinkers, When they fa' foul o' earthly jinkers, The witching curs'd delicious blinkers Hae put me hyte, And gart me weet my waukrife winkers, Wi' girnan spite.

But by yon moon!-and that's high swearin'- An' every star within my hearin'! An' by her een wha was a dear ane! I'll ne'er forget; I hope to gie the jads a clearin' In fair play yet.

My loss I mourn, but not repent it, I'll seek my pursie whare I tint it, Ance to the Indies I were wonted, Some cantraip hour, By some sweet elf I'll yet be dinted, Then, vive l'amour!

Faites mes baisemains respectueuse, To sentimental sister Susie, An' honest Lucky; no to roose you, Ye may be proud, That sic a couple fate allows ye To grace your blood.

Nae mair at present can I measure, An' trowth my rhymin' ware's nae treasure; But when in Ayr, some half-hour's leisure, Be't light, be't dark, Sir Bard will do himself the pleasure To call at Park.

Robert Burns.

Mossgiel, 30th October, 1786.

CHAPTER LXXI.

THE BRIGS OF AYR,

A POEM,

INSCRIBED TO J. BALLANTYNE, ESQ., AYR.

[Burns took the hint of this Poem from the Planestanes and Causeway of Fergusson, but all that lends it life and feeling belongs to his own heart and his native Ayr: he wrote it for the second edition of his poems, and in compliment to the patrons of his genius in the west. Ballantyne, to whom the Poem is inscribed, was generous when the distresses of his farming speculations pressed upon him: others of his friends figure in the scene: Montgomery's courage, the learning of Dugald Stewart, and condescension and kindness of Mrs. General Stewart, of Stair, are gratefully recorded.]

The simple Bard, rough at the rustic plough, Learning his tuneful trade from ev'ry bough; The chanting linnet, or the mellow thrush, Hailing the setting sun, sweet, in the green thorn bush: The soaring lark, the perching red-breast shrill, Or deep-ton'd plovers, gray, wild-whistling o'er the hill; Shall he, nurst in the peasant's lowly shed, To hardy independence bravely bred, By early poverty to hardship steel'd, And train'd to arms in stern misfortune's field- Shall he be guilty of their hireling crimes, The servile, mercenary Swiss of rhymes? Or labour hard the panegyric close, With all the venal soul of dedicating prose? No! though his artless strains he rudely sings, And throws his hand uncouthly o'er the strings, He glows with all the spirit of the Bard, Fame, honest fame, his great, his dear reward! Still, if some patron's gen'rous care he trace, Skill'd in the secret to bestow with grace; When Ballantyne befriends his humble name, And hands the rustic stranger up to fame, With heart-felt throes his grateful bosom swells, The godlike bliss, to give, alone excels.

'Twas when the stacks get on their winter hap, And thack and rape secure the toil-won crap; Potato-bings are snugged up frae skaith Of coming Winter's biting, frosty breath; The bees, rejoicing o'er their summer toils, Unnumber'd buds, an' flow'rs delicious spoils, Seal'd up with frugal care in massive waxen piles, Are doom'd by man, that tyrant o'er the weak, The death o' devils smoor'd wi' brimstone reek The thundering guns are heard on ev'ry side, The wounded coveys, reeling, scatter wide; The feather'd field-mates, bound by Nature's tie, Sires, mothers, children, in one carnage lie: (What warm, poetic heart, but inly bleeds, And execrates man's savage, ruthless deeds!) Nae mair the flow'r in field or meadow springs; Nae mair the grove with airy concert rings, Except, perhaps, the robin's whistling glee, Proud o' the height o' some bit half-lang tree: The hoary morns precede the sunny days, Mild, calm, serene, wide spreads the noontide blaze, While thick the gossamer waves wanton in the rays. 'Twas in that season, when a simple bard, Unknown and poor, simplicity's reward, Ae night, within the ancient brugh of Ayr, By whim inspired, or haply prest wi' care, He left his bed, and took his wayward rout, And down by Simpson's[60] wheel'd the left about: (Whether impell'd by all-directing Fate, To witness what I after shall narrate; Or whether, rapt in meditation high, He wander'd out he knew not where nor why) The drowsy Dungeon-clock,[61] had number'd two, And Wallace Tow'r[61] had sworn the fact was true: The tide-swol'n Firth, with sullen sounding roar, Through the still night dash'd hoarse along the shore. All else was hush'd as Nature's closed e'e: The silent moon shone high o'er tow'r and tree: The chilly frost, beneath the silver beam, Crept, gently-crusting, o'er the glittering stream.-

When, lo! on either hand the list'ning Bard, The clanging sugh of whistling wings is heard; Two dusky forms dart thro' the midnight air, Swift as the gos[62] drives on the wheeling hare; Ane on th' Auld Brig his airy shape uprears, The ither flutters o'er the rising piers: Our warlock Rhymer instantly descry'd The Sprites that owre the brigs of Ayr preside. (That Bards are second-sighted is nae joke, And ken the lingo of the sp'ritual folk; Fays, Spunkies, Kelpies, a', they can explain them, And ev'n the vera deils they brawly ken them.) Auld Brig appear'd of ancient Pictish race, The very wrinkles gothic in his face: He seem'd as he wi' Time had warstl'd lang, Yet, teughly doure, he bade an unco bang. New Brig was buskit in a braw new coat, That he at Lon'on, frae ane Adams got; In's hand five taper staves as smooth's a bead, Wi' virls and whirlygigums at the head. The Goth was stalking round with anxious search, Spying the time-worn flaws in ev'ry arch;- It chanc'd his new-come neebor took his e'e, And e'en a vex'd and angry heart had he! Wi' thieveless sneer to see his modish mien, He, down the water, gies him this guid-e'en:-

AULD BRIG.

I doubt na', frien', ye'll think ye're nae sheep-shank, Ance ye were streekit o'er frae bank to bank! But gin ye be a brig as auld as me, Tho' faith, that day I doubt ye'll never see; There'll be, if that date come, I'll wad a boddle, Some fewer whigmeleeries in your noddle.

NEW BRIG.

Auld Vandal, ye but show your little mense, Just much about it wi' your scanty sense; Will your poor, narrow foot-path of a street, Where twa wheel-barrows tremble when they meet- Your ruin'd formless bulk o' stane en' lime, Compare wi' bonnie Brigs o' modern time? There's men o' taste wou'd tak the Ducat-stream,[63] Tho' they should cast the vera sark and swim, Ere they would grate their feelings wi' the view Of sic an ugly, Gothic hulk as you.

AULD BRIG.

Conceited gowk! puff'd up wi' windy pride!- This mony a year I've stood the flood an' tide; And tho' wi' crazy eild I'm sair forfairn, I'll be a Brig, when ye're a shapeless cairn! As yet ye little ken about the matter, But twa-three winters will inform ye better. When heavy, dark, continued a'-day rains, Wi' deepening deluges o'erflow the plains; When from the hills where springs the brawling Coil, Or stately Lugar's mossy fountains boil, Or where the Greenock winds his moorland course, Or haunted Garpal[64] draws his feeble source, Arous'd by blust'ring winds an' spotting thowes, In mony a torrent down the snaw-broo rowes; While crashing ice born on the roaring speat, Sweeps dams, an' mills, an' brigs, a' to the gate; And from Glenbuck,[65] down to the Ratton-key,[66] Auld Ayr is just one lengthen'd tumbling sea- Then down ye'll hurl, deil nor ye never rise! And dash the gumlie jaups up to the pouring skies. A lesson sadly teaching, to your cost, That Architecture's noble art is lost!

NEW BRIG.

Fine Architecture, trowth, I needs must say't o't! The L-d be thankit that we've tint the gate o't! Gaunt, ghastly, ghaist-alluring edifices, Hanging with threat'ning jut like precipices; O'er-arching, mouldy, gloom-inspiring coves, Supporting roofs fantastic, stony groves; Windows and doors, in nameless sculpture drest, With order, symmetry, or taste unblest; Forms like some bedlam Statuary's dream, The craz'd creations of misguided whim; Forms might be worshipp'd on the bended knee, And still the second dread command be free, Their likeness is not found on earth, in air, or sea. Mansions that would disgrace the building taste Of any mason reptile, bird or beast; Fit only for a doited monkish race, Or frosty maids forsworn the dear embrace; Or cuifs of later times wha held the notion That sullen gloom was sterling true devotion; Fancies that our guid Brugh denies protection! And soon may they expire, unblest with resurrection!

AULD BRIG.

O ye, my dear-remember'd ancient yealings, Were ye but here to share my wounded feelings! Ye worthy Proveses, an' mony a Bailie, Wha in the paths o' righteousness did toil ay; Ye dainty Deacons and ye douce Conveeners, To whom our moderns are but causey-cleaners: Ye godly Councils wha hae blest this town; Ye godly Brethren o' the sacred gown, Wha meekly gie your hurdies to the smiters; And (what would now be strange) ye godly writers; A' ye douce folk I've borne aboon the broo, Were ye but here, what would ye say or do! How would your spirits groan in deep vexation, To see each melancholy alteration; And, agonizing, curse the time and place When ye begat the base, degen'rate race! Nae langer rev'rend men, their country's glory, In plain braid Scots hold forth a plain braid story! Nae langer thrifty citizens an' douce, Meet owre a pint, or in the council-house; But staumrel, corky-headed, graceless gentry, The herryment and ruin of the country; Men, three parts made by tailors and by barbers, Wha waste your weel-hain'd gear on d-d new Brigs and Harbours!

NEW BRIG.

Now haud you there! for faith ye've said enough, And muckle mair than ye can mak to through; As for your Priesthood, I shall say but little, Corbies and Clergy, are a shot right kittle: But under favour o' your langer beard, Abuse o' Magistrates might weel be spar'd: To liken them to your auld-warld squad, I must needs say, comparisons are odd. In Ayr, wag-wits nae mair can have a handle To mouth 'a citizen,' a term o' scandal; Nae mair the Council waddles down the street, In all the pomp of ignorant conceit; Men wha grew wise priggin' owre hops an' raisins, Or gather'd lib'ral views in bonds and seisins, If haply Knowledge, on a random tramp, Had shor'd them with a glimmer of his lamp, And would to Common-sense for once betray'd them, Plain, dull Stupidity stept kindly in to aid them

What farther clishmaclaver might been said, What bloody wars, if Spirites had blood to shed, No man can tell; but all before their sight, A fairy train appear'd in order bright: Adown the glitt'ring stream they featly danc'd;

Bright to the moon their various dresses glanc'd: They footed owre the wat'ry glass so neat, The infant ice scarce bent beneath their feet: While arts of minstrelsy among them rung, And soul-ennobling bards heroic ditties sung.- O had M'Lauchlan,[67] thairm-inspiring Sage, Been there to hear this heavenly band engage, When thro' his dear strathspeys they bore with highland rage; Or when they struck old Scotia's melting airs, The lover's raptur'd joys or bleeding cares; How would his highland lug been nobler fir'd, And ev'n his matchless hand with finer touch inspir'd! No guess could tell what instrument appear'd, But all the soul of Music's self was heard, Harmonious concert rung in every part, While simple melody pour'd moving on the heart.

The Genius of the stream in front appears, A venerable Chief advanc'd in years; His hoary head with water-lilies crown'd, His manly leg with garter tangle bound. Next came the loveliest pair in all the ring, Sweet Female Beauty hand in hand with Spring; Then, crown'd with flow'ry hay, came Rural Joy, And Summer, with his fervid-beaming eye: [141]All-cheering Plenty, with her flowing horn, Led yellow Autumn, wreath'd with nodding corn; Then Winter's time-bleach'd looks did hoary show, By Hospitality with cloudless brow. Next follow'd Courage, with his martial stride, From where the Feal wild woody coverts hide; Benevolence, with mild, benignant air, A female form, came from the tow'rs of Stair: Learning and Worth in equal measures trode From simple Catrine, their long-lov'd abode: Last, white-rob'd Peace, crown'd with a hazel wreath, To rustic Agriculture did bequeath The broken iron instruments of death; At sight of whom our Sprites forgat their kindling wrath.

FOOTNOTES:

[60] A noted tavern at the auld Brig end.

[61] The two steeples.

[62] The gos-hawk or falcon.

[63] A noted ford, just above the Auld Brig.

[64] The banks of Garpal Water is one of the few places in the West of Scotland, where those fancy-scaring beings, known by the name of Ghaists, still continue pertinaciously to inhabit.

[65] The source of the river Ayr.

[66] A small landing-place above the large key.

[67] A well known performer of Scottish music on the violin.

CHAPTER LXXII.

ON

THE DEATH OF ROBERT DUNDAS, ESQ.,

OF ARNISTON,

LATE LORD PRESIDENT OF THE COURT OF SESSION.

[At the request of Advocate Hay, Burns composed this Poem, in the hope that it might interest the powerful family of Dundas in his fortunes. I found it inserted in the handwriting of the poet, in an interleaved copy of his Poems, which he presented to Dr. Geddes, accompanied by the following surly note:-"The foregoing Poem has some tolerable lines in it, but the incurable wound of my pride will not suffer me to correct, or even peruse it. I sent a copy of it with my best prose letter to the son of the great man, the theme of the piece, by the hands of one of the noblest men in God's world, Alexander Wood, surgeon: when, behold! his solicitorship took no more notice of my Poem, or of me, than I had been a strolling fiddler who had made free with his lady's name, for a silly new reel. Did the fellow imagine that I looked for any dirty gratuity?" This Robert Dundas was the elder brother of that Lord Melville to whose hands, soon after these lines were written, all the government patronage in Scotland was confided, and who, when the name of Burns was mentioned, pushed the wine to Pitt, and said nothing. The poem was first printed by me, in 1834.]

Lone on the bleaky hills the straying flocks Shun the fierce storms among the sheltering rocks; Down from the rivulets, red with dashing rains, The gathering floods burst o'er the distant plains; Beneath the blasts the leafless forests groan; The hollow caves return a sullen moan.

Ye hills, ye plains, ye forests and ye caves, Ye howling winds, and wintry swelling waves! Unheard, unseen, by human ear or eye, Sad to your sympathetic scenes I fly; Where to the whistling blast and waters' roar Pale Scotia's recent wound I may deplore.

O heavy loss, thy country ill could bear! A loss these evil days can ne'er repair! Justice, the high vicegerent of her God, Her doubtful balance ey'd, and sway'd her rod; Hearing the tidings of the fatal blow She sunk, abandon'd to the wildest woe.

Wrongs, injuries, from many a darksome den, Now gay in hope explore the paths of men: See from this cavern grim Oppression rise, And throw on poverty his cruel eyes; Keen on the helpless victim see him fly, And stifle, dark, the feebly-bursting cry:

Mark ruffian Violence, distain'd with crimes, Rousing elate in these degenerate times; View unsuspecting Innocence a prey, As guileful Fraud points out the erring way: While subtile Litigation's pliant tongue The life-blood equal sucks of Right and Wrong: Hark, injur'd Want recounts th' unlisten'd tale, And much-wrong'd Mis'ry pours th' unpitied wail!

Ye dark waste hills, and brown unsightly plains, To you I sing my grief-inspired strains: Ye tempests, rage! ye turbid torrents, roll! Ye suit the joyless tenor of my soul. Life's social haunts and pleasures I resign, Be nameless wilds and lonely wanderings mine, To mourn the woes my country must endure, That wound degenerate ages cannot cure.

CHAPTER LXXIII.

ON READING IN A NEWSPAPER THE DEATH OF JOHN M'LEOD, ESQ.

BROTHER TO A YOUNG LADY, A PARTICULAR FRIEND OF THE AUTHOR'S.

[John M'Leod was of the ancient family of Raza, and brother to that Isabella M'Leod, for whom Burns, in his correspondence, expressed great regard. The little [142]Poem, when first printed, consisted of six verses: I found a seventh in M'Murdo Manuscripts, the fifth in this edition, along with an intimation in prose, that the M'Leod family had endured many unmerited misfortunes. I observe that Sir Harris Nicolas has rejected this new verse, because, he says, it repeats the same sentiment as the one which precedes it. I think differently, and have retained it.]

Sad thy tale, thou idle page, And rueful thy alarms: Death tears the brother of her love From Isabella's arms.

Sweetly deck'd with pearly dew The morning rose may blow; But cold successive noontide blasts May lay its beauties low.

Fair on Isabella's morn The sun propitious smil'd; But, long ere noon, succeeding clouds Succeeding hopes beguil'd.

Fate oft tears the bosom chords That nature finest strung: So Isabella's heart was form'd, And so that heart was wrung.

Were it in the poet's power, Strong as he shares the grief That pierces Isabella's heart, To give that heart relief!

Dread Omnipotence, alone, Can heal the wound He gave; Can point the brimful grief-worn eyes To scenes beyond the grave.

Virtue's blossoms there shall blow, And fear no withering blast; There Isabella's spotless worth Shall happy be at last.

CHAPTER LXXIV.

TO MISS LOGAN,

WITH BEATTIE'S POEMS FOR A NEW YEAR'S GIFT.

JAN. 1, 1787.

[Burns was fond of writing compliments in books, and giving them in presents among his fair friends. Miss Logan, of Park house, was sister to Major Logan, of Camlarg, and the "sentimental sister Susie," of the Epistle to her brother. Both these names were early dropped out of the poet's correspondence.]

Again the silent wheels of time Their annual round have driv'n, And you, tho' scarce in maiden prime, Are so much nearer Heav'n.

No gifts have I from Indian coasts The infant year to hail: I send you more than India boasts In Edwin's simple tale.

Our sex with guile and faithless love Is charg'd, perhaps, too true; But may, dear maid, each lover prove An Edwin still to you!

CHAPTER LXXV.

THE AMERICAN WAR.

A FRAGMENT.

[Dr. Blair said that the politics of Burns smelt of the smithy, which, interpreted, means, that they were unstatesman-like, and worthy of a country ale-house, and an audience of peasants. The Poem gives us a striking picture of the humorous and familiar way in which the hinds and husbandmen of Scotland handle national topics: the smithy is a favourite resort, during the winter evenings, of rustic politicians; and national affairs and parish scandal are alike discussed. Burns was in those days, and some time after, a vehement Tory: his admiration of "Chatham's Boy," called down on him the dusty indignation of the republican Ritson.]

I.

When Guildford good our pilot stood, And did our hellim thraw, man, Ae night, at tea, began a plea, Within America, man: Then up they gat the maskin-pat, And in the sea did jaw, man; An' did nae less in full Congress, Than quite refuse our law, man.

II.

Then thro' the lakes Montgomery takes, I wat he was na slaw, man; Down Lowrie's burn he took a turn, And Carleton did ca', man; But yet, what-reck, he, at Quebec, Montgomery-like did fa', man, Wi' sword in hand, before his band, Amang his en'mies a', man. [143]

III.

Poor Tammy Gage, within a cage, Was kept at Boston ha', man; Till Willie Howe took o'er the knowe For Philadelphia, man; Wi' sword an' gun he thought a sin Guid Christian blood to draw, man: But at New York, wi' knife an' fork, Sir-loin he hacked sma', man.

IV.

Burgoyne gaed up, like spur an' whip, Till Fraser brave did fa', man, Then lost his way, ae misty day, In Saratoga shaw, man. Cornwallis fought as lang's he dought, An' did the buckskins claw, man; But Clinton's glaive frae rust to save, He hung it to the wa', man.

V.

Then Montague, an' Guilford, too, Began to fear a fa', man; And Sackville dour, wha stood the stoure, The German Chief to thraw, man; For Paddy Burke, like ony Turk, Nae mercy had at a', man; An' Charlie Fox threw by the box, An' lows'd his tinkler jaw, man.

VI.

Then Rockingham took up the game, Till death did on him ca', man; When Shelburne meek held up his cheek, Conform to gospel law, man; Saint Stephen's boys, wi' jarring noise, They did his measures thraw, man, For North an' Fox united stocks, An' bore him to the wa', man.

VII.

Then clubs an' hearts were Charlie's cartes, He swept the stakes awa', man, Till the diamond's ace, of Indian race, Led him a sair faux pas, man; The Saxon lads, wi' loud placads, On Chatham's boy did ca', man; An' Scotland drew her pipe, an' blew, "Up, Willie, waur them a', man!"

VIII.

Behind the throne then Grenville's gone, A secret word or twa, man; While slee Dundas arous'd the class, Be-north the Roman wa', man: An' Chatham's wraith, in heavenly graith, (Inspired Bardies saw, man) Wi' kindling eyes cry'd "Willie, rise! Would I hae fear'd them a', man?"

IX.

But, word an' blow, North, Fox, and Co., Gowff'd Willie like a ba', man, Till Suthron raise, and coost their claise Behind him in a raw, man; An' Caledon threw by the drone, An' did her whittle draw, man; An' swoor fu' rude, thro' dirt an' blood To make it guid in law, man.

CHAPTER LXXVI.

THE DEAN OF FACULTY.

A NEW BALLAD.

[The Hal and Bob of these satiric lines were Henry Erskine, and Robert Dundas: and their contention was, as the verses intimate, for the place of Dean of the Faculty of Advocates: Erskine was successful. It is supposed that in characterizing Dundas, the poet remembered "the incurable wound which his pride had got" in the affair of the elegiac verses on the death of the elder Dundas. The poem first appeared in the Reliques of Burns.]

I.

Dire was the hate at old Harlaw, That Scot to Scot did carry; And dire the discord Langside saw, For beauteous, hapless Mary: But Scot with Scot ne'er met so hot, Or were more in fury seen, Sir, Than 'twixt Hal and Bob for the famous job- Who should be Faculty's Dean, Sir.-

II.

This Hal for genius, wit, and lore, Among the first was number'd; But pious Bob, 'mid learning's store, Commandment tenth remember'd.- Yet simple Bob the victory got, And won his heart's desire; Which shows that heaven can boil the pot, Though the devil p-s in the fire.-

III.

Squire Hal besides had in this case Pretensions rather brassy, For talents to deserve a place Are qualifications saucy; So, their worships of the Faculty, Quite sick of merit's rudeness, Chose one who should owe it all, d'ye see, To their gratis grace and goodness.-

IV.

As once on Pisgah purg'd was the sight Of a son of Circumcision, So may be, on this Pisgah height, Bob's purblind, mental vision: Nay, Bobby's mouth may be open'd yet Till for eloquence you hail him, And swear he has the angel met That met the Ass of Balaam.

CHAPTER LXXVII.

TO A LADY,

WITH A PRESENT OF A PAIR OF DRINKING-GLASSES.

[To Mrs. M'Lehose, of Edinburgh, the poet presented the drinking-glasses alluded to in the verses: they are, it seems, still preserved, and the lady on occasions of high festival, indulges, it is said, favourite visiters with a draught from them of "The blood of Shiraz' scorched vine."]

Fair Empress of the Poet's soul, And Queen of Poetesses; Clarinda, take this little boon, This humble pair of glasses.

And fill them high with generous juice, As generous as your mind; And pledge me in the generous toast- "The whole of human kind!"

"To those who love us!"-second fill; But not to those whom we love; Lest we love those who love not us!- A third-"to thee and me, love!"

CHAPTER LXXVIII.

TO CLARINDA.

[This is the lady of the drinking-glasses; the Mrs. Mac of many a toast among the poet's acquaintances. She was, in those days, young and beautiful, and we fear a little giddy, since she indulged in that sentimental and platonic flirtation with the poet, contained in the well-known letters to Clarinda. The letters, after the poet's death, appeared in print without her permission: she obtained an injunction against the publication, which still remains in force, but her anger seems to have been less a matter of taste than of whim, for the injunction has been allowed to slumber in the case of some editors, though it has been enforced against others.]

Clarinda, mistress of my soul, The measur'd time is run! The wretch beneath the dreary pole So marks his latest sun.

To what dark cave of frozen night Shall poor Sylvander hie; Depriv'd of thee, his life and light, The sun of all his joy.

We part-but, by these precious drops That fill thy lovely eyes! No other light shall guide my steps Till thy bright beams arise.

She, the fair sun of all her sex, Has blest my glorious day; And shall a glimmering planet fix My worship to its ray?

CHAPTER LXXIX.

VERSES

WRITTEN UNDER THE PORTRAIT OF FERGUSSON, THE POET, IN A COPY OF THAT AUTHOR'S WORKS PRESENTED TO A YOUNG LADY.

[Who the young lady was to whom the poet presented the portrait and Poems of the ill-fated Fergusson, we have not been told. The verses are dated Edinburgh, March 19th, 1787.]

Curse on ungrateful man, that can be pleas'd, And yet can starve the author of the pleasure! O thou my elder brother in misfortune, By far my elder brother in the muses, With tears I pity thy unhappy fate! Why is the bard unpitied by the world, Yet has so keen a relish of its pleasures?

CHAPTER LXXX.

PROLOGUE

SPOKEN BY MR. WOODS ON HIS BENEFIT NIGHT,

MONDAY, 16 April, 1787.

[The Woods for whom this Prologue was written, was in those days a popular actor in Edinburgh. He had other claims on Burns: he had been the friend as well as comrade of poor Fergusson, and possessed some poetical talent. He died in Edinburgh, December 14th, 1802.]

When by a generous Public's kind acclaim, That dearest meed is granted- honest fame; When here your favour is the actor's lot, Nor even the man in private life forgot; What breast so dead to heavenly virtue's glow, But heaves impassion'd with the grateful throe?

Poor is the task to please a barbarous throng, It needs no Siddons' powers in Southerne's song; But here an ancient nation fam'd afar, For genius, learning high, as great in war- Hail, Caledonia, name for ever dear! Before whose sons I'm honoured to appear! Where every science-every nobler art- That can inform the mind, or mend the heart, Is known; as grateful nations oft have found Far as the rude barbarian marks the bound. Philosophy, no idle pedant dream, Here holds her search by heaven-taught Reason's beam; Here History paints, with elegance and force, The tide of Empires' fluctuating course; Here Douglas forms wild Shakspeare into plan, And Harley[68] rouses all the god in man. When well-form'd taste and sparkling wit unite, With manly lore, or female beauty bright, (Beauty, where faultless symmetry and grace, Can only charm as in the second place,) Witness my heart, how oft with panting fear, As on this night, I've met these judges here! But still the hope Experience taught to live, Equal to judge-you're candid to forgive. Nor hundred-headed Riot here we meet, With decency and law beneath his feet: Nor Insolence assumes fair Freedom's name; Like Caledonians, you applaud or blame.

O Thou dread Power! whose Empire-giving hand Has oft been stretch'd to shield the honour'd land! Strong may she glow with all her ancient fire: May every son be worthy of his sire; Firm may she rise with generous disdain At Tyranny's, or direr Pleasure's chain; Still self-dependent in her native shore, Bold may she brave grim Danger's loudest roar, Till Fate the curtain drop on worlds to be no more.

FOOTNOTES:

[68] The Man of Feeling, by Mackenzie.

CHAPTER LXXXI.

SKETCH.

[This Sketch is a portion of a long Poem which Burns proposed to call "The Poet's Progress." He communicated the little he had done, for he was a courter of opinions, to Dugald Stewart. "The Fragment forms," said he, "the postulata, the axioms, the definition of a character, which, if it appear at all, shall be placed in a variety of lights. This particular part I send you, merely as a sample of my hand at portrait-sketching." It is probable that the professor's response was not favourable for we hear no more of the Poem.]

A little, upright, pert, tart, tripping wight, And still his precious self his dear delight; Who loves his own smart shadow in the streets Better than e'er the fairest she he meets: A man of fashion, too, he made his tour, Learn'd vive la bagatelle, et vive l'amour: So travell'd monkeys their grimace improve, Polish their grin, nay, sigh for ladies' love. Much specious lore, but little understood; Veneering oft outshines the solid wood: His solid sense-by inches you must tell. But mete his cunning by the old Scots ell; His meddling vanity, a busy fiend, Still making work his selfish craft must mend.

CHAPTER LXXXII.

TO MRS. SCOTT,

OF WAUCHOPE.

[The lady to whom this epistle is addressed was a painter and a poetess: her pencil sketches are said to have been beautiful; and she had a ready skill in rhyme, as the verses addressed to Burns fully testify. Taste and poetry belonged to her family; she was the niece of Mrs. Cockburn, authoress of a beautiful variation of The Flowers of the Forest.]

I mind it weel in early date, When I was beardless, young and blate, An' first could thresh the barn; [146]Or hand a yokin at the pleugh; An' tho' forfoughten sair enough, Yet unco proud to learn: When first amang the yellow corn A man I reckon'd was, An' wi' the lave ilk merry morn Could rank my rig and lass, Still shearing, and clearing, The tither stooked raw, Wi' claivers, an' haivers, Wearing the day awa.

E'en then, a wish, I mind its pow'r, A wish that to my latest hour Shall strongly heave my breast, That I for poor auld Scotland's sake Some usefu' plan or beuk could make, Or sing a sang at least. The rough burr-thistle, spreading wide Amang the bearded bear, I turn'd the weeder-clips aside, An' spar'd the symbol dear: No nation, no station, My envy e'er could raise, A Scot still, but blot still, I knew nae higher praise.

But still the elements o' sang In formless jumble, right an' wrang, Wild floated in my brain; 'Till on that har'st I said before, My partner in the merry core, She rous'd the forming strain: I see her yet, the sonsie quean, That lighted up her jingle, Her witching smile, her pauky een That gart my heart-strings tingle: I fired, inspired, At every kindling keek, But bashing and dashing I feared aye to speak.

Health to the sex, ilk guid chiel says, Wi' merry dance in winter days, An' we to share in common: The gust o' joy, the balm of woe, The saul o' life, the heaven below, Is rapture-giving woman. Ye surly sumphs, who hate the name, Be mindfu' o' your mither: She, honest woman, may think shame That ye're connected with her. Ye're wae men, ye're nae men That slight the lovely dears; To shame ye, disclaim ye, Ilk honest birkie swears.

For you, no bred to barn and byre, Wha sweetly tune the Scottish lyre, Thanks to you for your line: The marled plaid ye kindly spare, By me should gratefully be ware; 'Twad please me to the nine. I'd be mair vauntie o' my hap, Douce hingin' owre my curple Than ony ermine ever lap, Or proud imperial purple. Fareweel then, lang heel then, An' plenty be your fa'; May losses and crosses Ne'er at your hallan ca'.

CHAPTER LXXXIII.

EPISTLE TO WILLIAM CREECH.

[A storm of rain detained Burns one day, during his border tour, at Selkirk, and he employed his time in writing this characteristic epistle to Creech, his bookseller. Creech was a person of education and taste; he was not only the most popular publisher in the north, but he was intimate with almost all the distinguished men who, in those days, adorned Scottish literature. But though a joyous man, a lover of sociality, and the keeper of a good table, he was close and parsimonious, and loved to hold money to the last moment that the law allowed.]

Selkirk, 13 May, 1787.

Auld chukie Reekie's[69] sair distrest, Down droops her ance weel-burnisht crest, Nae joy her bonnie buskit nest Can yield ava, Her darling bird that she lo'es best, Willie's awa!

O Willie was a witty wight, And had o' things an unco slight; Auld Reekie ay he keepit tight, An' trig an' braw: But now they'll busk her like a fright, Willie's awa!

The stiffest o' them a' he bow'd; The bauldest o' them a' he cow'd; [147]They durst nae mair than he allow'd, That was a law; We've lost a birkie weel worth gowd, Willie's awa!

Now gawkies, tawpies, gowks, and fools, Frae colleges and boarding-schools, May sprout like simmer puddock stools In glen or shaw; He wha could brush them down to mools, Willie's awa!

The brethren o' the Commerce-Chaumer[70] May mourn their loss wi' doofu' clamour; He was a dictionar and grammar Amang them a'; I fear they'll now mak mony a stammer, Willie's awa!

Nae mair we see his levee door Philosophers and poets pour,[71] And toothy critics by the score In bloody raw! The adjutant o' a' the core, Willie's awa!

Now worthy Gregory's Latin face, Tytler's and Greenfield's modest grace; Mackenzie, Stewart, sic a brace As Rome n'er saw; They a' maun meet some ither place, Willie's awa!

Poor Burns-e'en Scotch drink canna quicken, He cheeps like some bewilder'd chicken, Scar'd frae its minnie and the cleckin By hoodie-craw; Grief's gien his heart an unco kickin', Willie's awa!

Now ev'ry sour-mou'd girnin' blellum, And Calvin's fock are fit to fell him; And self-conceited critic skellum His quill may draw; He wha could brawlie ward their bellum, Willie's awa!

Up wimpling stately Tweed I've sped, And Eden scenes on crystal Jed, And Ettrick banks now roaring red, While tempests blaw; But every joy and pleasure's fled, Willie's awa!

May I be slander's common speech; A text for infamy to preach; And lastly, streekit out to bleach In winter snaw; When I forget thee! Willie Creech, Tho' far awa!

May never wicked fortune touzle him! May never wicked man bamboozle him! Until a pow as auld's Methusalem He canty claw! Then to the blessed New Jerusalem, Fleet wing awa!

FOOTNOTES:

[69] Edinburgh.

[70] The Chamber of Commerce in Edinburgh, of which Creech was Secretary.

[71] Many literary gentlemen were accustomed to meet at Mr. Creech's house at breakfast.

CHAPTER LXXXIV.

THE HUMBLE PETITION OF BRUAR WATER TO THE NOBLE DUKE OF ATHOLE.

[The Falls of Bruar in Athole are exceedingly beautiful and picturesque; and their effect, when Burns visited them, was much impaired by want of shrubs and trees. This was in 1787: the poet, accompanied by his future biographer, Professor Walker, went, when close on twilight, to this romantic scene: "he threw himself," said the Professor, "on a heathy seat, and gave himself up to a tender, abstracted, and voluptuous enthusiasm of imagination. In a few days I received a letter from Inverness, for the poet had gone on his way, with the Petition enclosed." His Grace of Athole obeyed the injunction: the picturesque points are now crowned with thriving woods, and the beauty of the Falls is much increased.]

I.

My Lord, I know your noble ear Woe ne'er assails in vain; Embolden'd thus, I beg you'll hear Your humble slave complain, How saucy Phœbus' scorching beams In flaming summer-pride, Dry-withering, waste my foamy streams, And drink my crystal tide.

II.

The lightly-jumpin' glowrin' trouts, That thro' my waters play, If, in their random, wanton spouts, They near the margin stray; [148]If, hapless chance! they linger lang, I'm scorching up so shallow, They're left the whitening stanes amang, In gasping death to wallow.

III.

Last day I grat wi' spite and teen, As Poet Burns came by, That to a bard I should be seen Wi' half my channel dry: A panegyric rhyme, I ween, Even as I was he shor'd me; But had I in my glory been, He, kneeling, wad ador'd me.

IV.

Here, foaming down the shelvy rocks, In twisting strength I rin; There, high my boiling torrent smokes, Wild-roaring o'er a linn: Enjoying large each spring and well, As Nature gave them me, I am, altho' I say't mysel', Worth gaun a mile to see.

V.

Would then my noble master please To grant my highest wishes, He'll shade my banks wi' tow'ring trees, And bonnie spreading bushes. Delighted doubly then, my Lord, You'll wander on my banks, And listen mony a grateful bird Return you tuneful thanks.

VI.

The sober laverock, warbling wild, Shall to the skies aspire; The gowdspink, music's gayest child, Shall sweetly join the choir: The blackbird strong, the lintwhite clear, The mavis mild and mellow; The robin pensive autumn cheer, In all her locks of yellow.

VII.

This, too, a covert shall insure To shield them from the storm; And coward maukin sleep secure, Low in her grassy form: Here shall the shepherd make his seat, To weave his crown of flow'rs; Or find a shelt'ring safe retreat From prone-descending show'rs.

VIII.

And here, by sweet, endearing stealth, Shall meet the loving pair, Despising worlds with all their wealth As empty idle care. The flow'rs shall vie in all their charms The hour of heav'n to grace, And birks extend their fragrant arms To screen the dear embrace.

IX.

Here haply too, at vernal dawn, Some musing bard may stray, And eye the smoking, dewy lawn, And misty mountain gray; Or, by the reaper's nightly beam, Mild-chequering thro' the trees, Rave to my darkly-dashing stream, Hoarse-swelling on the breeze.

X.

Let lofty firs, and ashes cool, My lowly banks o'erspread, And view, deep-bending in the pool, Their shadows' wat'ry bed! Let fragrant birks in woodbines drest My craggy cliffs adorn; And, for the little songster's nest, The close embow'ring thorn.

XI.

So may old Scotia's darling hope, Your little angel band, Spring, like their fathers, up to prop Their honour'd native land! So may thro' Albion's farthest ken, To social-flowing glasses, The grace be-"Athole's honest men, And Athole's bonnie lasses?"

CHAPTER LXXXV.

ON SCARING SOME WATER-FOWL IN LOCH-TURIT.

[When Burns wrote these touching lines, he was staying with Sir William Murray, of Ochtertyre, during one of his Highland tours. Loch-Turit is a wild lake among the recesses of the hills, and was welcome from its loneliness to the heart of the poet.]

Why, ye tenants of the lake, For me your wat'ry haunt forsake? Tell me, fellow-creatures, why At my presence thus you fly?

Why disturb your social joys, Parent, filial, kindred ties?- Common friend to you and me, Nature's gifts to all are free: Peaceful keep your dimpling wave, Busy feed, or wanton lave: Or, beneath the sheltering rock, Bide the surging billow's shock.

Conscious, blushing for our race, Soon, too soon, your fears I trace. Man, your proud usurping foe, Would be lord of all below: Plumes himself in Freedom's pride, Tyrant stern to all beside.

The eagle, from the cliffy brow, Marking you his prey below, In his breast no pity dwells, Strong necessity compels: But man, to whom alone is giv'n A ray direct from pitying heav'n, Glories in his heart humane- And creatures for his pleasure slain.

In these savage, liquid plains, Only known to wand'ring swains, Where the mossy riv'let strays, Far from human haunts and ways; All on Nature you depend, And life's poor season peaceful spend.

Or, if man's superior might Dare invade your native right, On the lofty ether borne, Man with all his pow'rs you scorn; Swiftly seek, on clanging wings, Other lakes and other springs; And the foe you cannot brave, Scorn at least to be his slave.

CHAPTER LXXXVI.

WRITTEN WITH A PENCIL,

OVER THE CHIMNEY-PIECE, IN THE PARLOUR OF THE INN AT KENMORE, TAYMOUTH.

[The castle of Taymouth is the residence of the Earl of Breadalbane: it is a magnificent structure, contains many fine paintings: has some splendid old trees and romantic scenery.]

Admiring Nature in her wildest grace, These northern scenes with weary feet I trace; O'er many a winding dale and painful steep, Th' abodes of covey'd grouse and timid sheep, My savage journey, curious I pursue, 'Till fam'd Breadalbane opens to my view.- The meeting cliffs each deep-sunk glen divides, The woods, wild scatter'd, clothe their ample sides; Th' outstretching lake, embosom'd 'mong the hills, The eye with wonder and amazement fills; The Tay, meand'ring sweet in infant pride, The palace, rising on its verdant side; The lawns, wood-fring'd in Nature's native taste; The hillocks, dropt in Nature's careless haste; The arches, striding o'er the new-born stream; The village, glittering in the noontide beam-

Poetic ardours in my bosom swell, Lone wand'ring by the hermit's mossy cell: The sweeping theatre of hanging woods; Th' incessant roar of headlong tumbling floods-

Here Poesy might wake her heav'n-taught lyre, And look through Nature with creative fire; Here, to the wrongs of fate half reconcil'd, Misfortune's lighten'd steps might wander wild; And Disappointment, in these lonely bounds, Find balm to soothe her bitter-rankling wounds: Here heart-struck Grief might heav'nward stretch her scan, And injur'd Worth forget and pardon man.

CHAPTER LXXXVII.

WRITTEN WITH A PENCIL,

STANDING BY THE FALL OF FYERS,

NEAR LOCH-NESS

[This is one of the many fine scenes, in the Celtic Parnassus of Ossian: but when Burns saw it, the Highland passion of the stream was abated, for there had been no rain for some time to swell and send it pouring down its precipices in a way worthy of the scene. The descent of the water is about two hundred feet. There is another fall further up the stream, very wild and[150] savage, on which the Fyers makes three prodigious leaps into a deep gulf where nothing can be seen for the whirling foam and agitated mist.]

Among the heathy hills and ragged woods The roaring Fyers pours his mossy floods; Till full he dashes on the rocky mounds, Where, thro' a shapeless breach, his stream resounds, As high in air the bursting torrents flow, As deep-recoiling surges foam below, Prone down the rock the whitening sheet descends, And viewless Echo's ear, astonish'd, rends. Dim seen, through rising mists and ceaseless show'rs, The hoary cavern, wide surrounding, low'rs. Still thro' the gap the struggling river toils, And still below, the horrid cauldron boils-

CHAPTER LXXXVIII.

POETICAL ADDRESS

TO MR. W. TYTLER,

WITH THE PRESENT OF THE BARD'S PICTURE.

[When these verses were written there was much stately Jacobitism about Edinburgh, and it is likely that Tytler, who laboured to dispel the cloud of calumny which hung over the memory of Queen Mary, had a bearing that way. Taste and talent have now descended in the Tytlers through three generations: an uncommon event in families. The present edition of the Poem has been completed from the original in the poet's handwriting.]

Revered defender of beauteous Stuart, Of Stuart, a name once respected, A name, which to love, was once mark of a true heart, But now 'tis despis'd and neglected.

Tho' something like moisture conglobes in my eye, Let no one misdeem me disloyal; A poor friendless wand'rer may well claim a sigh, Still more, if that wand'rer were royal.

My fathers that name have rever'd on a throne, My fathers have fallen to right it; Those fathers would spurn their degenerate son, That name should he scoffingly slight it.

Still in prayers for King George I most heartily join, The Queen and the rest of the gentry, Be they wise, be they foolish, is nothing of mine; Their title's avow'd by my country.
But why of that epocha make such a fuss, That gave us th' Electoral stem? If bringing them over was lucky for us, I'm sure 'twas as lucky for them.
But loyalty truce! we're on dangerous ground, Who knows how the fashions may alter? The doctrine, to-day, that is loyalty sound, To-morrow may bring us a halter.
I send you a trifle, the head of a bard, A trifle scarce worthy your care; But accept it, good Sir, as a mark of regard, Sincere as a saint's dying prayer.
Now life's chilly evening dim shades on your eye, And ushers the long dreary night; But you, like the star that athwart gilds the sky, Your course to the latest is bright.

CHAPTER LXXXIX.

WRITTEN IN
FRIARS-CARSE HERMITAGE,
ON THE BANKS OF NITH.
JUNE. 1788.
[FIRST COPY.]

[The interleaved volume presented by Burns to Dr. Geddes, has enabled me to present the reader with the rough draught of this truly beautiful Poem, the first-fruits perhaps of his intercourse with the muses of Nithside.]
Thou whom chance may hither lead, Be thou clad in russet weed, Be thou deck'd in silken stole, Grave these maxims on thy soul. Life is but a day at most, Sprung from night, in darkness lost; Day, how rapid in its flight- Day, how few must see the night; Hope not sunshine every hour, Fear not clouds will always lower. Happiness is but a name, Make content and ease thy aim. Ambition is a meteor gleam; Fame, a restless idle dream: Pleasures, insects on the wing Round Peace, the tenderest flower of Spring; Those that sip the dew alone, Make the butterflies thy own; Those that would the bloom devour, Crush the locusts-save the flower. For the future be prepar'd, Guard wherever thou canst guard; But, thy utmost duly done, Welcome what thou canst not shun. Follies past, give thou to air, Make their consequence thy care: Keep the name of man in mind, And dishonour not thy kind. Reverence with lowly heart Him whose wondrous work thou art; Keep His goodness still in view, Thy trust-and thy example, too.
Stranger, go! Heaven be thy guide! Quod the Beadsman on Nithside.

CHAPTER XC.

WRITTEN IN
FRIARS-CARSE HERMITAGE,
ON NITHSIDE.
DECEMBER, 1788.

[Of this Poem Burns thought so well that he gave away many copies in his own handwriting: I have seen three. When corrected to his mind, and the manuscripts showed many changes and corrections, he published it in the new edition of his Poems as it stands in this second copy. The little Hermitage where these lines were written, stood in a lonely plantation belonging to the estate of Friars-Carse, and close to the march-dyke of Ellisland; a small door in the fence, of which the poet had the key, admitted him at pleasure, and there he found seclusion such as he liked, with flowers and shrubs all around him. The first twelve lines of the Poem were engraved neatly on one of the window-panes, by the diamond pencil of the Bard. On Riddel's death, the Hermitage was allowed to go quietly to decay: I remember in 1803 turning two outlyer stots out of the interior.]

Thou whom chance may hither lead, Be thou clad in russet weed, Be thou deck'd in silken stole, Grave these counsels on thy soul.

Life is but a day at most, Sprung from night, in darkness lost; Hope not sunshine ev'ry hour. Fear not clouds will always lour. As Youth and Love with sprightly dance Beneath thy morning star advance, Pleasure with her siren air May delude the thoughtless pair: Let Prudence bless enjoyment's cup, Then raptur'd sip, and sip it up.

As thy day grows warm and high, Life's meridian flaming nigh, Dost thou spurn the humble vale? Life's proud summits would'st thou scale? Check thy climbing step, elate, Evils lurk in felon wait: Dangers, eagle-pinion'd, bold, Soar around each cliffy hold, While cheerful peace, with linnet song, Chants the lowly dells among.

As the shades of ev'ning close, Beck'ning thee to long repose; As life itself becomes disease, Seek the chimney-nook of ease. There ruminate, with sober thought, On all thou'st seen, and heard, and wrought; And teach the sportive younkers round, Saws of experience, sage and sound. Say, man's true genuine estimate, The grand criterion of his fate, Is not-Art thou high or low? Did thy fortune ebb or flow? Wast thou cottager or king? Peer or peasant?-no such thing! Did many talents gild thy span? Or frugal nature grudge thee one? Tell them, and press it on their mind, As thou thyself must shortly find, The smile or frown of awful Heav'n, To virtue or to vice is giv'n. Say, to be just, and kind, and wise, There solid self-enjoyment lies; That foolish, selfish, faithless ways Lead to the wretched, vile, and base.

Thus, resign'd and quiet, creep To the bed of lasting sleep; Sleep, whence thou shalt ne'er awake, Night, where dawn shall never break, Till future life, future no more, To light and joy the good restore, To light and joy unknown before.

Stranger, go! Hea'vn be thy guide! Quod the beadsman of Nithside.

CHAPTER XCI.

TO CAPTAIN RIDDEL,

OF GLENRIDDEL.

EXTEMPORE LINES ON RETURNING A NEWSPAPER.

[Captain Riddel, the Laird of Friars-Carse, was Burns's neighbour, at Ellisland: he was a kind, hospitable man, and a good antiquary. The "News and Review" which he sent to the poet contained, I have heard, some sharp strictures on his works: Burns, with his usual strong sense, set the proper value upon all contemporary criticism; genius, he knew, had nothing to fear from the folly or the malice of all such nameless "chippers and hewers." He demanded trial by his peers, and where were such to be found?]

Ellisland, Monday Evening.

Your news and review, Sir, I've read through and through, Sir, With little admiring or blaming; The papers are barren of home-news or foreign, No murders or rapes worth the naming.

Our friends, the reviewers, those chippers and hewers, Are judges of mortar and stone, Sir, But of meet or unmeet in a fabric complete, I'll boldly pronounce they are none, Sir.

My goose-quill too rude is to tell all your goodness Bestow'd on your servant, the Poet; Would to God I had one like a beam of the sun, And then all the world, Sir, should know it!

CHAPTER XCII.

A MOTHER'S LAMENT

FOR THE DEATH OF HER SON.

["The Mother's Lament," says the poet, in a copy of the verses now before me, "was composed partly with a view to Mrs. Fergusson of Craigdarroch, and partly to the worthy patroness of my early unknown muse, Mrs. Stewart, of Afton."]

Fate gave the word, the arrow sped, And pierc'd my darling's heart; And with him all the joys are fled Life can to me impart. By cruel hands the sapling drops, In dust dishonour'd laid: So fell the pride of all my hopes, My age's future shade.

The mother-linnet in the brake Bewails her ravish'd young; So I, for my lost darling's sake, Lament the live day long. Death, oft I've fear'd thy fatal blow, Now, fond I bare my breast, O, do thou kindly lay me low With him I love, at rest!

CHAPTER XCIII.

FIRST EPISTLE

TO ROBERT GRAHAM, ESQ.

OF FINTRAY.

[In his manuscript copy of this Epistle the poet says "accompanying a request." What the request was the letter which enclosed it relates. Graham was one of the leading men of the Excise in Scotland, and had promised Burns a situation as exciseman: for this the poet had qualified himself; and as he began to dread that farming would be unprofitable, he wrote to remind his patron of his promise, and requested to be appointed to a division in his own neighbourhood. He was appointed in due time: his division was extensive, and included ten parishes.]

When Nature her great master-piece designed, And fram'd her last, best work, the human mind, Her eye intent on all the mazy plan, She form'd of various parts the various man.

Then first she calls the useful many forth; Plain plodding industry, and sober worth: Thence peasants, farmers, native sons of earth, And merchandise' whole genus take their birth: Each prudent cit a warm existence finds, And all mechanics' many-apron'd kinds. Some other rarer sorts are wanted yet, The lead and buoy are needful to the net; The caput mortuum of gross desires Makes a material for mere knights and squires; The martial phosphorus is taught to flow, She kneads the lumpish philosophic dough, Then marks th' unyielding mass with grave designs, Law, physic, politics, and deep divines: Last, she sublimes th' Aurora of the poles, The flashing elements of female souls.

The order'd system fair before her stood, Nature, well pleas'd, pronounc'd it very good; But ere she gave creating labour o'er, Half-jest, she tried one curious labour more. [153]Some spumy, fiery, ignis fatuus matter, Such as the slightest breath of air might scatter; With arch alacrity and conscious glee (Nature may have her whim as well as we, Her Hogarth-art perhaps she meant to show it) She forms the thing, and christens it-a Poet. Creature, tho' oft the prey of care and sorrow, When blest to-day, unmindful of to-morrow. A being form'd t'amuse his graver friends, Admir'd and prais'd-and there the homage ends: A mortal quite unfit for fortune's strife, Yet oft the sport of all the ills of life; Prone to enjoy each pleasure riches give, Yet haply wanting wherewithal to live; Longing to wipe each tear, to heal each groan, Yet frequent all unheeded in his own.

But honest Nature is not quite a Turk, She laugh'd at first, then felt for her poor work. Pitying the propless climber of mankind, She cast about a standard tree to find; And, to support his helpless woodbine state, Attach'd him to the generous truly great, A title, and the only one I claim, To lay strong hold for help on bounteous Graham.

Pity the tuneful muses' hapless train, Weak, timid landsmen on life's stormy main! Their hearts no selfish stern absorbent stuff, That never gives-tho' humbly takes enough; The little fate allows, they share as soon, Unlike sage proverb'd wisdom's hard-wrung boon. The world were blest did bliss on them depend, Ah, that "the friendly e'er should want a friend!" Let prudence number o'er each sturdy son Who life and wisdom at one race begun, Who feel by reason and who give by rule, (Instinct's a brute, and sentiment a fool!) Who make poor will do wait upon I should- We own they're prudent, but who feels they're good? Ye wise ones, hence! ye hurt the social eye! God's image rudely etch'd on base alloy! But come ye who the godlike pleasure know, Heaven's attribute distinguished-to bestow! Whose arms of love would grasp the human race: Come thou who giv'st with all a courtier's grace; Friend of my life, true patron of my rhymes! Prop of my dearest hopes for future times.

Why shrinks my soul half blushing, half afraid, Backward, abash'd to ask thy friendly aid? I know my need, I know thy giving hand, I crave thy friendship at thy kind command; But there are such who court the tuneful nine- Heavens! should the branded character be mine! Whose verse in manhood's pride sublimely flows, Yet vilest reptiles in their begging prose. Mark, how their lofty independent spirit Soars on the spurning wing of injur'd merit! Seek not the proofs in private life to find; Pity the best of words should be but wind! So to heaven's gates the lark's shrill song ascends, But grovelling on the earth the carol ends. In all the clam'rous cry of starving want, They dun benevolence with shameless front; Oblige them, patronize their tinsel lays, They persecute you all your future days! Ere my poor soul such deep damnation stain, My horny fist assume the plough again; The pie-bald jacket let me patch once more; On eighteen-pence a week I've liv'd before. Tho', thanks to Heaven, I dare even that last shift! I trust, meantime, my boon is in thy gift: That, plac'd by thee upon the wish'd-for height, Where, man and nature fairer in her sight, My muse may imp her wing for some sublimer flight.

CHAPTER XCIV.

ON THE DEATH OF SIR JAMES HUNTER BLAIR.

[I found these lines written with a pencil in one of Burns's memorandum-books: he said he had just composed them, and pencilled them down lest they should escape from his memory. They differed in nothing from the printed copy of the first Liverpool edition. That they are by Burns there cannot be a doubt, though they were, I know not for what reason, excluded from several editions of the Posthumous Works of the poet.]

The lamp of day, with ill-presaging glare, Dim, cloudy, sunk beneath the western wave; Th' inconstant blast howl'd thro' the darkening air, And hollow whistled in the rocky cave.

Lone as I wander'd by each cliff and dell, Once the lov'd haunts of Scotia's royal train;[72] Or mus'd where limpid streams once hallow'd well,[73] Or mould'ring ruins mark the sacred fane.[74]

Th' increasing blast roared round the beetling rocks, The clouds, swift-wing'd, flew o'er the starry sky, The groaning trees untimely shed their locks, And shooting meteors caught the startled eye.

The paly moon rose in the livid east, And 'mong the cliffs disclos'd a stately form, In weeds of woe that frantic beat her breast, And mix'd her wailings with the raving storm.

Wild to my heart the filial pulses glow, 'Twas Caledonia's trophied shield I view'd: Her form majestic droop'd in pensive woe, The lightning of her eye in tears imbued.

Revers'd that spear, redoubtable in war, Reclined that banner, erst in fields unfurl'd, That like a deathful meteor gleam'd afar, And brav'd the mighty monarchs of the world.-

"My patriot son fills an untimely grave!" With accents wild and lifted arms-she cried; "Low lies the hand that oft was stretch'd to save, Low lies the heart that swell'd with honest pride.

"A weeping country joins a widow's tear, The helpless poor mix with the orphan's cry; The drooping arts surround their patron's bier, And grateful science heaves the heart-felt sigh!

"I saw my sons resume their ancient fire; I saw fair freedom's blossoms richly blow: But ah! how hope is born but to expire! Relentless fate has laid their guardian low.

"My patriot falls, but shall he lie unsung, While empty greatness saves a worthless name! No; every muse shall join her tuneful tongue, And future ages hear his growing fame.

"And I will join a mother's tender cares, Thro' future times to make his virtues last; That distant years may boast of other Blairs!"- She said, and vanish'd with the sweeping blast.

FOOTNOTES:

[72] The King's Park, at Holyrood-house.

[73] St. Anthony's Well.

[74] St. Anthony's Chapel.

CHAPTER XCV.

EPISTLE TO HUGH PARKER.

[This little lively, biting epistle was addressed to one of the poet's Kilmarnock companions. Hugh Parker was the brother of William Parker, one of the subscribers to the Edinburgh edition of Burns's Poems: he has been dead many years: the Epistle was recovered, luckily, from his papers, and printed for the first time in 1834.]

In this strange land, this uncouth clime, A land unknown to prose or rhyme; Where words ne'er crost the muse's heckles, Nor limpet in poetic shackles: A land that prose did never view it, Except when drunk he stacher't thro' it, Here, ambush'd by the chimla cheek, Hid in an atmosphere of reek, I hear a wheel thrum i' the neuk, I hear it-for in vain I leuk.- The red peat gleams, a fiery kernel, Enhusked by a fog infernal: Here, for my wonted rhyming raptures, I sit and count my sins by chapters; For life and spunk like ither Christians, I'm dwindled down to mere existence, Wi' nae converse but Gallowa' bodies, Wi' nae kend face but Jenny Geddes.[75] Jenny, my Pegasean pride! Dowie she saunters down Nithside, And ay a westlin leuk she throws, While tears hap o'er her auld brown nose! Was it for this, wi' canny care, Thou bure the bard through many a shire? At howes or hillocks never stumbled, And late or early never grumbled?- O had I power like inclination, I'd heeze thee up a constellation, To canter with the Sagitarre, Or loup the ecliptic like a bar; Or turn the pole like any arrow; Or, when auld Phœbus bids good-morrow, Down the zodiac urge the race, And cast dirt on his godship's face; For I could lay my bread and kail He'd ne'er cast saut upo' thy tail.- Wi' a' this care and a' this grief, And sma,' sma' prospect of relief, And nought but peat reek i' my head, How can I write what ye can read?- Tarbolton, twenty-fourth o' June, Ye'll find me in a better tune; [155]But till we meet and weet our whistle, Tak this excuse for nae epistle.

Robert Burns.

FOOTNOTES:

[75] His mare.

CHAPTER XCVI.

LINES

INTENDED TO BE WRITTEN UNDER

A NOBLE EARL'S PICTURE.

[Burns placed the portraits of Dr. Blacklock and the Earl of Glencairn, over his parlour chimney-piece at Ellisland: beneath the head of the latter he wrote some verses, which he sent to the Earl, and requested leave to make public. This seems to have been refused; and, as the verses were lost for years, it was believed they were destroyed: a rough copy, however, is preserved, and is now in the safe keeping of the Earl's name-son, Major James Glencairn Burns. James Cunningham, Earl of Glencairn, died 20th January, 1791, aged 42 years; he was succeeded by his only and childless brother, with whom this ancient race was closed.]

Whose is that noble dauntless brow? And whose that eye of fire? And whose that generous princely mien, E'en rooted foes admire? Stranger! to justly show that brow, And mark that eye of fire, Would take His hand, whose vernal tints His other works inspire.

Bright as a cloudless summer sun, With stately port he moves; His guardian seraph eyes with awe The noble ward he loves- Among th' illustrious Scottish sons That chief thou may'st discern; Mark Scotia's fond returning eye- It dwells upon Glencairn.

CHAPTER XCVII.

ELEGY

ON THE YEAR 1788

A SKETCH.

[This Poem was first printed by Stewart, in 1801. The poet loved to indulge in such sarcastic sallies: it is full of character, and reflects a distinct image of those yeasty times.]

For Lords or Kings I dinna mourn, E'en let them die-for that they're born, But oh! prodigious to reflec'! A Towmont, Sirs, is gane to wreck! O Eighty-eight, in thy sma' space What dire events ha'e taken place! Of what enjoyments thou hast reft us! In what a pickle thou hast left us!

The Spanish empire's tint a-head, An' my auld toothless Bawtie's dead; The tulzie's sair 'tween Pitt and Fox, And our guid wife's wee birdie cocks; The tane is game, a bluidie devil, But to the hen-birds unco civil: The tither's something dour o' treadin', But better stuff ne'er claw'd a midden- Ye ministers, come mount the pu'pit, An' cry till ye be hearse an' roupet, For Eighty-eight he wish'd you weel, An' gied you a' baith gear an' meal; E'en mony a plack, and mony a peck, Ye ken yoursels, for little feck!

Ye bonnie lasses, dight your e'en, For some o' you ha'e tint a frien'; In Eighty-eight, ye ken, was ta'en, What ye'll ne'er ha'e to gie again.

Observe the very nowt an' sheep, How dowf and dowie now they creep; Nay, even the yirth itsel' does cry, For Embro' wells are grutten dry. O Eighty-nine, thou's but a bairn, An' no owre auld, I hope, to learn! Thou beardless boy, I pray tak' care, Thou now has got thy daddy's chair, Nae hand-cuff'd, mizl'd, hap-shackl'd Regent, But, like himsel' a full free agent. Be sure ye follow out the plan Nae waur than he did, honest man! As muckle better as ye can.

January 1, 1789.

CHAPTER XCVIII.

ADDRESS TO THE TOOTHACHE.

["I had intended," says Burns to Creech, 30th May, 1789, "to have troubled you with a long letter, but at present the delightful sensation of an omnipotent toothache so engrosses all my inner man, as to put it out of my power even to write nonsense." The poetic Address to the Toothache seems to belong to this period.]

My curse upon thy venom'd stang, That shoots my tortur'd gums alang; [156]And thro' my lugs gies mony a twang, Wi' gnawing vengeance; Tearing my nerves wi' bitter pang, Like racking engines!

When fevers burn, or ague freezes, Rheumatics gnaw, or cholic squeezes; Our neighbours' sympathy may ease us, Wi' pitying moan; But thee-thou hell o' a' diseases, Ay mocks our groan!

Adown my beard the slavers trickle! I kick the wee stools o'er the mickle, As round the fire the giglets keckle, To see me loup; While, raving mad, I wish a heckle Were in their doup.

O' a' the num'rous human dools, Ill har'sts, daft bargains, cutty-stools, Or worthy friends rak'd i' the mools, Sad sight to see! The tricks o' knaves, or fash o' fools, Thou bears't the gree.

Where'er that place be priests ca' hell, Whence a' the tones o' mis'ry yell, And ranked plagues their numbers tell, In dreadfu' raw, Thou, Toothache, surely bear'st the bell Amang them a'!

O thou grim mischief-making chiel, That gars the notes of discord squeel, 'Till daft mankind aft dance a reel In gore a shoe-thick!- Gie' a' the faes o' Scotland's weal A towmond's Toothache.

CHAPTER XCIX.

ODE
SACRED TO THE MEMORY OF
MRS. OSWALD,
OF AUCHENCRUIVE.

[The origin of this harsh effusion shows under what feelings Burns sometimes wrote. He was, he says, on his way to Ayrshire, one stormy day in January, and had made himself comfortable, in spite of the snow-drift, over a smoking bowl, at an inn at the Sanquhar, when in wheeled the whole funeral pageantry of Mrs. Oswald. He was obliged to mount his horse and ride for quarters to New Cumnock, where, over a good fire, he penned, in his very ungallant indignation, the Ode to the lady's memory. He lived to think better of the name.]

Dweller in yon dungeon dark, Hangman of creation, mark! Who in widow-weeds appears, Laden with unhonoured years, Noosing with care a bursting purse, Baited with many a deadly curse?

STROPHE.

View the wither'd beldam's face- Can thy keen inspection trace Aught of Humanity's sweet melting grace? Note that eye, 'tis rheum o'erflows, Pity's flood there never rose. See these hands, ne'er stretch'd to save, Hands that took-but never gave. Keeper of Mammon's iron chest, Lo, there she goes, unpitied and unblest She goes, but not to realms of everlasting rest!

ANTISTROPHE.

Plunderer of armies, lift thine eyes, (Awhile forbear, ye tort'ring fiends;) Seest thou whose step, unwilling hither bends? No fallen angel, hurl'd from upper skies; 'Tis thy trusty quondam mate, Doom'd to share thy fiery fate, She, tardy, hell-ward plies.

EPODE.

And are they of no more avail, Ten thousand glitt'ring pounds a-year? In other worlds can Mammon fail, Omnipotent as he is here? O, bitter mock'ry of the pompous bier, While down the wretched vital part is driv'n! The cave-lodg'd beggar, with a conscience clear, Expires in rags, unknown, and goes to Heav'n.

CHAPTER C.

FRAGMENT INSCRIBED
TO THE RIGHT HON. C.J. FOX.

[It was late in life before Burns began to think very highly of Fox: he had hitherto spoken of him rather as a rattler of dice, and a frequenter of soft company, than as a statesman. As his hopes from the Tories vanished,[157] he began to think of the Whigs: the first did nothing, and the latter held out hopes; and as hope, he said was the cordial of the human heart, he continued to hope on.]

How wisdom and folly meet, mix, and unite; How virtue and vice blend their black and their white; How genius, th' illustrious father of fiction,

Confounds rule and law, reconciles contradiction- I sing: if these mortals, the critics, should bustle, I care not, not I-let the critics go whistle!
But now for a patron, whose name and whose glory At once may illustrate and honour my story.
Thou first of our orators, first of our wits; Yet whose parts and acquirements seem mere lucky hits; With knowledge so vast, and with judgment so strong, No man with the half of 'em e'er went far wrong; With passions so potent, and fancies so bright, No man with the half of 'em e'er went quite right;- A sorry, poor misbegot son of the muses, For using thy name offers fifty excuses.
Good L-d, what is man? for as simple he looks, Do but try to develope his hooks and his crooks; With his depths and his shallows, his good and his evil, All in all he's a problem must puzzle the devil.
On his one ruling passion Sir Pope hugely labours, That, like th' old Hebrew walking-switch, eats up its neighbours; Mankind are his show-box-a friend, would you know him? Pull the string, ruling passion the picture will show him. What pity, in rearing so beauteous a system, One trifling particular, truth, should have miss'd him; For spite of his fine theoretic positions, Mankind is a science defies definitions.
Some sort all our qualities each to its tribe, And think human nature they truly describe; Have you found this, or t'other? there's more in the wind, As by one drunken fellow his comrades you'll find.
But such is the flaw, or the depth of the plan, In the make of that wonderful creature, call'd man, No two virtues, whatever relation they claim, Nor even two different shades of the same, Though like as was ever twin brother to brother, Possessing the one shall imply you've the other.
But truce with abstraction, and truce with a muse, Whose rhymes you'll perhaps, Sir, ne'er deign to peruse: Will you leave your justings, your jars, and your quarrels, Contending with Billy for proud-nodding laurels. My much-honour'd Patron, believe your poor poet, Your courage much more than your prudence you show it; In vain with Squire Billy, for laurels you struggle, He'll have them by fair trade, if not, he will smuggle; Not cabinets even of kings would conceal 'em, He'd up the back-stairs, and by G-he would steal 'em. Then feats like Squire Billy's you ne'er can achieve 'em; It is not, outdo him, the task is, out-thieve him.

CHAPTER CI.

ON SEEING
A WOUNDED HARE
LIMP BY ME,
WHICH A FELLOW HAD JUST SHOT.

[This Poem is founded on fact. A young man of the name of Thomson told me-quite unconscious of the existence of the Poem-that while Burns lived at Ellisland-he shot at and hurt a hare, which in the twilight was feeding on his father's wheat-bread. The poet, on observing the hare come bleeding past him, "was in great wrath," said Thomson, "and cursed me, and said little hindered him from throwing me into the Nith; and he was able enough to do it, though I was both young and strong." The boor of Nithside did not use the hare worse than the critical Dr. Gregory, of Edinburgh, used the Poem: when Burns read his remarks he said, "Gregory is a good man, but he crucifies me!"]

Inhuman man! curse on thy barb'rous art, And blasted be thy murder-aiming eye; May never pity soothe thee with a sigh, Nor ever pleasure glad thy cruel heart. [158]

Go live, poor wanderer of the wood and field! The bitter little that of life remains: No more the thickening brakes and verdant plains To thee shall home, or food, or pastime yield.

Seek, mangled wretch, some place of wonted rest, No more of rest, but now thy dying bed! The sheltering rushes whistling o'er thy head, The cold earth with thy bloody bosom prest.

Oft as by winding Nith, I, musing, wait The sober eve, or hail the cheerful dawn; I'll miss thee sporting o'er the dewy lawn, And curse the ruffian's aim, and mourn thy hapless fate.

CHAPTER CII.

TO DR. BLACKLOCK,

IN ANSWER TO A LETTER.

[This blind scholar, though an indifferent Poet, was an excellent and generous man: he was foremost of the Edinburgh literati to admire the Poems of Burns, promote their fame, and advise that the author, instead of shipping himself for Jamaica, should come to Edinburgh and publish a new edition. The poet reverenced the name of Thomas Blacklock to the last hour of his life.-Henry Mackenzie, the Earl of Glencairn, and the Blind Bard, were his three favourites.]

Ellisland, 21st Oct. 1789.

Wow, but your letter made me vauntie! And are ye hale, and weel, and cantie? I kenn'd it still your wee bit jauntie Wad bring ye to: Lord send you ay as weel's I want ye, And then ye'll do.

The ill-thief blaw the heron south! And never drink be near his drouth! He tauld mysel' by word o' mouth, He'd tak my letter: I lippen'd to the chief in trouth, And bade nae better.

But aiblins honest Master Heron, Had at the time some dainty fair one, To ware his theologic care on, And holy study; And tir'd o' sauls to waste his lear on E'en tried the body.

But what dy'e think, my trusty fier, I'm turn'd a gauger-Peace be here! Parnassian queans, I fear, I fear, Ye'll now disdain me! And then my fifty pounds a year Will little gain me.

Ye glaiket, gleesome, dainty damies, Wha, by Castalia's wimplin' streamies,

Lowp, sing, and lave your pretty limbies, Ye ken, ye ken, That strang necessity supreme is 'Mang sons o' men.

I hae a wife and twa wee laddies, They maun hae brose and brats o' duddies; Ye ken yoursels my heart right proud is- I need na vaunt, But I'll sned besoms-thraw saugh woodies, Before they want.

Lord help me thro' this warld o' care! I'm weary sick o't late and air! Not but I hae a richer share Than mony ithers: But why should ae man better fare, And a' men brithers?

Come, firm Resolve, take then the van, Thou stalk o' carl-hemp in man! And let us mind, faint-heart ne'er wan A lady fair: Wha does the utmost that he can, Will whyles do mair.

But to conclude my silly rhyme, (I'm scant o' verse, and scant o' time,) To make a happy fire-side clime To weans and wife, That's the true pathos and sublime Of human life.

My compliments to sister Beckie; And eke the same to honest Lucky, I wat she is a dainty chuckie, As e'er tread clay! And gratefully, my guid auld cockie, I'm yours for ay,

Robert Burns.

CHAPTER CIII.

DELIA.

AN ODE.

[These verses were first printed in the Star newspaper, in May, 1789. It is said that one day a friend read to the poet some verses from the Star, composed on the pattern of Pope's song, by a Person of Quality. "These lines are beyond you," he added: "the muse of Kyle cannot match the muse of London." Burns mused a moment, then recited "Delia, an Ode."]

Fair the face of orient day, Fair the tints of op'ning rose, But fairer still my Delia dawns, More lovely far her beauty blows.

Sweet the lark's wild-warbled lay, Sweet the tinkling rill to hear; But, Delia, more delightful still Steal thine accents on mine ear.

The flow'r-enamoured busy bee The rosy banquet loves to sip; Sweet the streamlet's limpid lapse To the sun-brown'd Arab's lip;-

But, Delia, on thy balmy lips Let me, no vagrant insect, rove! O, let me steal one liquid kiss! For, oh! my soul is parch'd with love.

CHAPTER CIV.

TO JOHN M'MURDO, ESQ.

[John M'Murdo, Esq., one of the chamberlains of the Duke of Queensberry, lived at Drumlanrig: he was a high-minded, warm-hearted man, and much the friend of the poet. These lines accompanied a present of books: others were added soon afterwards on a pane of glass in Drumlanrig castle.

"Blest be M'Murdo to his latest day! No envious cloud o'ercast his evening ray; No wrinkle furrowed by the hand of care, Nor ever sorrow add one silver hair! O may no son the father's honour stain, Nor ever daughter give the mother pain."

How fully the poet's wishes were fulfilled need not be told to any one acquainted with the family.]

O, could I give thee India's wealth, As I this trifle send! Because thy joy in both would be To share them with a friend.

But golden sands did never grace The Heliconian stream; Then take what gold could never buy- An honest Bard's esteem.

CHAPTER CV.

PROLOGUE,

SPOKEN AT THE THEATRE, DUMFRIES,

1 JAN. 1790.

[This prologue was written in December, 1789, for Mr. Sutherland, who recited it with applause in the little theatre of Dumfries, on new-year's night. Sir Harris Nicolas, however, has given to Ellisland the benefit of a theatre! and to Burns the whole barony of Dalswinton for a farm!]

No song nor dance I bring from yon great city That queens it o'er our taste-the more's the pity: Tho', by-the-by, abroad why will you roam? Good sense and taste are natives here at home: But not for panegyric I appear, I come to wish you all a good new year! Old Father Time deputes me here before ye, Not for to preach, but tell his simple story: The sage grave ancient cough'd, and bade me say, "You're one year older this important day." If wiser too-he hinted some suggestion, But 'twould be rude, you know, to ask the question; And with a would-be roguish leer and wink, He bade me on you press this one word-"think!"

Ye sprightly youths, quite flushed with hope and spirit, Who think to storm the world by dint of merit, To you the dotard has a deal to say, In his sly, dry, sententious, proverb way; He bids you mind, amid your thoughtless rattle, That the first blow is ever half the battle: That tho' some by the skirt may try to snatch him, Yet by the forelock is the hold to catch him; That whether doing, suffering, or forbearing, You may do miracles by persevering.

Last, tho' not least in love, ye youthful fair, Angelic forms, high Heaven's peculiar care! [160]To yon old Bald-pate smooths his wrinkled brow, And humbly begs you'll mind the important now! To crown your happiness he asks your leave, And offers bliss to give and to receive.

For our sincere, tho' haply weak endeavours, With grateful pride we own your many favours, And howsoe'er our tongues may ill reveal it, Believe our glowing bosoms truly feel it.

CHAPTER CVI.

SCOTS PROLOGUE,

FOR MR. SUTHERLAND'S BENEFIT NIGHT,

DUMFRIES.

[Burns did not shine in prologues: he produced some vigorous lines, but they did not come in harmony from his tongue, like the songs in which he recorded the loveliness of the dames of Caledonia. Sutherland was manager of the theatre, and a writer of rhymes.-Burns said his players were a very decent set: he had seen them an evening or two.]

What needs this din about the town o' Lon'on, How this new play an' that new sang is comin'? Why is outlandish stuff sae meikle courted? Does nonsense mend like whiskey, when imported? Is there nae poet, burning keen for fame, Will try to gie us songs and plays at hame? For comedy abroad he need nae toil, A fool and knave are plants of every soil; Nor need he hunt as far as Rome and Greece To gather matter for a serious piece; There's themes enough in Caledonian story, Would show the tragic muse in a' her glory.

Is there no daring bard will rise, and tell How glorious Wallace stood, how hapless fell? Where are the muses fled that could produce A drama worthy o' the name o' Bruce; How here, even here, he first unsheath'd the sword, 'Gainst mighty England and her guilty lord, And after mony a bloody, deathless doing, Wrench'd his dear country from the jaws of ruin? O for a Shakspeare or an Otway scene, To draw the lovely, hapless Scottish Queen! Vain all th' omnipotence of female charms 'Gainst headlong, ruthless, mad Rebellion's arms.

She fell, but fell with spirit truly Roman, To glut the vengeance of a rival woman; A woman-tho' the phrase may seem uncivil- As able and as cruel as the Devil! One Douglas lives in Home's immortal page, But Douglases were heroes every age: And tho' your fathers, prodigal of life, A Douglas follow'd to the martial strife, Perhaps if bowls row right, and right succeeds, Ye yet may follow where a Douglas leads!

As ye hae generous done, if a' the land Would take the muses' servants by the hand; Not only hear, but patronize, befriend them, And where ye justly can commend, commend them; And aiblins when they winna stand the test, Wink hard, and say the folks hae done their best! Would a' the land do this, then I'll be caution Ye'll soon hae poets o' the Scottish nation, Will gar fame blaw until her trumpet crack, And warsle time, on' lay him on his back! For us and for our stage should ony spier, "Whose aught thae chiels maks a' this bustle here!" My best leg foremost, I'll set up my brow, We have the honour to belong to you! We're your ain bairns, e'en guide us as ye like, But like good withers, shore before ye strike.- And gratefu' still I hope ye'll ever find us, For a' the patronage and meikle kindness We've got frae a' professions, sets, and ranks: God help us! we're but poor-ye'se get but thanks.

CHAPTER CVII.

SKETCH.

NEW YEAR'S DAY.

TO MRS. DUNLOP.

[This is a picture of the Dunlop family: it was printed from a hasty sketch, which the poet called extempore. The major whom it mentions, was General Andrew Dunlop, who died in 1804: Rachel Dunlop was afterwards married to Robert Glasgow, Esq. Another of the Dunlops served with distinction in India, where he rose to the rank of General. They were a gallant race, and all distinguished.]

This day, Time winds th' exhausted chain, To run the twelvemonth's length again: [161]I see the old, bald-pated follow, With ardent eyes, complexion sallow, Adjust the unimpair'd machine, To wheel the equal, dull routine.

The absent lover, minor heir, In vain assail him with their prayer; Deaf as my friend, he sees them press, Nor makes the hour one moment less. Will you (the Major's with the hounds, The happy tenants share his rounds; Coila's fair Rachel's care to-day, And blooming Keith's engaged with Gray) From housewife cares a minute borrow- That grandchild's cap will do to-morrow- And join with me a moralizing, This day's propitious to be wise in. First, what did yesternight deliver? "Another year is gone for ever." And what is this day's strong suggestion? "The passing moment's all we rest on!" Rest on-for what? what do we here? Or why regard the passing year? Will time, amus'd with proverb'd lore, Add to our date one minute more? A few days more-a few years must- Repose us in the silent dust. Then is it wise to damp our bliss? Yes-all such reasonings are amiss! The voice of nature loudly cries, And many a message from the skies, That something in us never dies: That on this frail, uncertain state, Hang matters of eternal weight: That future life in worlds unknown Must take its hue from this alone; Whether as heavenly glory bright, Or dark as misery's woeful night.-

Since then, my honour'd, first of friends, On this poor being all depends, Let us th' important now employ, And live as those who never die.-

Tho' you, with days and honours crown'd, Witness that filial circle round, (A sight, life's sorrows to repulse, A sight, pale envy to convulse,) Others now claim your chief regard; Yourself, you wait your bright reward.

CHAPTER CVIII.

TO A GENTLEMAN

WHO HAD SENT HIM A NEWSPAPER, AND OFFERED TO CONTINUE IT FREE OF EXPENSE.

[These sarcastic lines contain a too true picture of the times in which they were written. Though great changes have taken place in court and camp, yet Austria, Russia, and Prussia keep the tack of Poland: nobody says a word of Denmark: emasculated Italy is still singing; opera girls are still dancing; but Chatham Will, glaikit Charlie, Daddie Burke, Royal George, and Geordie Wales, have all passed to their account.]

Kind Sir, I've read your paper through, And, faith, to me 'twas really new! How guess'd ye, Sir, what maist I wanted? This mony a day I've grain'd and gaunted, To ken what French mischief was brewin'; Or what the drumlie Dutch were doin'; That vile doup-skelper, Emperor Joseph, If Venus yet had got his nose off; Or how the collieshangie works Atween the Russians and the Turks: Or if the Swede, before he halt, Would play anither Charles the Twalt: If Denmark, any body spak o't; Or Poland, wha had now the tack o't; How cut-throat Prussian blades were hingin'; How libbet Italy was singin'; If Spaniard, Portuguese, or Swiss Were sayin' or takin' aught amiss: Or how our merry lads at hame, In Britain's court kept up the game: How royal George, the Lord leuk o'er him! Was managing St. Stephen's quorum; If sleekit Chatham Will was livin'; Or glaikit Charlie got his nieve in: How daddie Burke the plea was cookin', If Warren Hastings' neck was yeukin; How cesses, stents, and fees were rax'd, Or if bare a-s yet were tax'd; The news o' princes, dukes, and earls, Pimps, sharpers, bawds, and opera girls; If that daft buckie, Geordie Wales, Was threshin' still at hizzies' tails; Or if he was grown oughtlins douser, And no a perfect kintra cooser.- A' this and mair I never heard of; And but for you I might despair'd of. So, gratefu', back your news I send you, And pray, a' guid things may attend you!

Ellisland, Monday morning, 1790.

[162]

CHAPTER CIX.

THE KIRK'S ALARM;[76]

A SATIRE.

[FIRST VERSION.]

[The history of this Poem is curious. M'Gill, one of the ministers of Ayr, long suspected of entertaining heterodox opinions concerning original sin and the Trinity, published "A Practical Essay on the Death of Jesus Christ," which, in the opinion of the more rigid portion of his brethren, inclined both to Arianism and Socinianism. This essay was denounced as heretical, by a minister of the name Peebles, in a sermon preached November 5th, 1788, and all the west country was in a flame. The subject was brought before the Synod, and was warmly debated till M'Gill expressed his regret for the disquiet he had occasioned, explained away or apologized for the challenged passages in his Essay, and declared his adherence to the Standard doctrines of his mother church. Burns was prevailed upon to bring his satire to the aid of M'Gill, but he appears to have done so with reluctance.]

Orthodox, orthodox, Wha believe in John Knox, Let me sound an alarm to your conscience: There's a heretic blast Has been blawn in the wast, That what is no sense must be nonsense.

Dr. Mac,[77] Dr. Mac, You should stretch on a rack, To strike evil doers wi' terror; To join faith and sense Upon ony pretence, Is heretic, damnable error.

Town of Ayr, town of Ayr, It was mad, I declare, To meddle wi' mischief a-brewing; Provost John[78] is still deaf To the church's relief, And orator Bob[79] is its ruin.

D'rymple mild,[80] D'rymple mild, Thro' your heart's like a child, And your life like the new driven snaw, Yet that winna save ye, Auld Satan must hav ye, For preaching that three's ane an' twa.

Rumble John,[81] Rumble John, Mount the steps wi' a groan, Cry the book is wi' heresy cramm'd; Then lug out your ladle, Deal brimstone like adle, And roar every note of the danm'd.

Simper James,[82] Simper James, Leave the fair Killie dames, There's a holier chase in your view; I'll lay on your head That the pack ye'll soon lead. For puppies like you there's but few.

Singet Sawney,[83] Singet Sawney, Are ye herding the penny, Unconscious what evil await? Wi' a jump, yell, and howl, Alarm every soul, For the foul thief is just at your gate.

Daddy Auld,[84] Daddy Auld, There's a tod in the fauld, A tod meikle waur than the clerk; Though yo can do little skaith, Ye'll be in at the death, And gif ye canna bite, ye may bark.

Davie Bluster,[85] Davie Bluster, If for a saint ye do muster, The corps is no nice of recruits; Yet to worth let's be just, Royal blood ye might boast, If the ass was the king of the brutes.

Jamy Goose,[86] Jamy Goose, Ye ha'e made but toom roose, In hunting the wicked lieutenant; But the Doctor's your mark, For the L-d's haly ark; He has cooper'd and cawd a wrang pin in't.

Poet Willie,[87] Poet Willie, Fie the Doctor a volley, Wi' your liberty's chain and your wit; O'er Pegasus' side Ye ne'er laid astride, Ye but smelt, man, the place where he .

[163]

Andro Gouk,[88], Andro Gouk, Ye may slander the book, And the book not the waur, let me tell ye; Ye are rich and look big, But lay by hat and wig, And ye'll ha'e a calf's head o' sma' value.

Barr Steenie,[89] Barr Steenie, What mean ye, what mean ye? If ye'll meddle nae mair wi' the matter, Ye may ha'e some pretence To havins and sense, Wi' people wha ken ye nae better.

Irvine side,[90] Irvine side, Wi' your turkey-cock pride, Of manhood but sum' is your share, Ye've the figure 'tis true, Even your faes will allow, And your friends they dae grunt you nae mair.

Muirland Jock,[91] Muirland Jock, When the L-d makes a rock To crush Common sense for her sins, If ill manners were wit, There's no mortal so fit To confound the poor Doctor at ance.

Holy Will,[92] Holy Will, There was wit i' your skull, When ye pilfer'd the alms o' the poor; The timmer is scant, When ye're ta'en for a saunt, Wha should swing in a rape for an hour.

Calvin's sons, Calvin's sons, Seize your spir'tual guns, Ammunition you never can need; Your hearts are the stuff, Will be powther enough, And your skulls are storehouses o' lead.

Poet Burns, Poet Burns, Wi' your priest-skelping turns, Why desert ye your auld native shire? Your muse is a gipsie, E'en tho' she were tipsie, She could ca' us nae waur than we are.

FOOTNOTES:

[76] This Poem was written a short time after the publication of M'Gill's Essay.

[77] Dr. M'Gill.

[78] John Ballantyne.

[79] Robert Aiken.

[80] Dr. Dalrymple.

[81] Mr. Russell.

[82] Mr. M'Kinlay.

[83] Mr. Moody, of Riccarton.

[84] Mr. Auld of Mauchline.

[85] Mr. Grant, of Ochiltree.

[86] Mr. Young, of Cumnock.

[87] Mr. Peebles, Ayr.

[88] Dr. Andrew Mitchell, of Monkton.

[89] Mr. Stephen Young, of Barr.

[90] Mr. George Smith, of Galston.

[91] Mr. John Shepherd, Muirkirk.

[92] Holy Willie, alias William Fisher, Elder in Mauchline.

CHAPTER CX.

THE KIRK'S ALARM.

A BALLAD.

[SECOND VERSION.]

[This version is from the papers of Miss Logan, of Afton. The origin of the Poem is thus related to Graham of Fintry by the poet himself: "Though I dare say you have none of the solemn League and Covenant fire Which shone so conspicuous in Lord George Gordon, and the Kilmarnock weavers, yet I think you must have heard of Dr. M'Gill, one of the clergymen of Ayr, and his heretical book, God help him, poor man! Though one of the worthiest, as well as one of the ablest of the whole priesthood of the Kirk of Scotland, in every sense of that ambiguous term, yet the poor doctor and his numerous family are in imminent danger of being thrown out (9th December, 1790) to the mercy of the winter winds. The enclosed ballad on that business, is, I confess too local: but I laughed myself at some conceits in it, though I am convinced in my conscience there are a good many heavy stanzas in it too." The Kirk's Alarm was first printed by Stewart, in 1801. Cromek calls it, "A silly satire, on some worthy ministers of the gospel, in Ayrshire."]

I.

Orthodox, orthodox, Who believe in John Knox, Let me sound an alarm to your conscience- There's a heretic blast, Has been blawn i' the wast, That what is not sense must be nonsense, Orthodox, That what is not sense must be nonsense.

II.

Doctor Mac, Doctor Mac, Ye should stretch on a rack, And strike evil doers wi' terror; To join faith and sense, Upon any pretence, Was heretic damnable error, Doctor Mac, Was heretic damnable error.

III.

Town of Ayr, town of Ayr, It was rash I declare, To meddle wi' mischief a-brewing; Provost John is still deaf, To the church's relief, And orator Bob is its ruin, Town Of Ayr, And orator Bob is its ruin. [164]

IV.

D'rymple mild, D'rymple mild, Tho' your heart's like a child, And your life like the new-driven snaw, Yet that winna save ye, Old Satan must have ye For preaching that three's are an' twa, D'rymple mild, For preaching that three's are an' twa.

V.

Calvin's sons, Calvin's sons, Seize your spiritual guns, Ammunition ye never can need; Your hearts are the stuff, Will be powder enough, And your skulls are a storehouse of lead, Calvin's sons, And your skulls are a storehouse of lead.

VI.

Rumble John, Rumble John, Mount the steps with a groan, Cry the book is with heresy cramm'd; Then lug out your ladle, Deal brimstone like aidle, And roar every note o' the damn'd, Rumble John, And roar every note o' the damn'd.

VII.

Simper James, Simper James, Leave the fair Killie dames, There's a holier chase in your view; I'll lay on your head, That the pack ye'll soon lead, For puppies like you there's but few, Simper James, For puppies like you there's but few.

VIII.

Singet Sawnie, Singet Sawnie, Are ye herding the penny, Unconscious what danger awaits? With a jump, yell, and howl, Alarm every soul, For Hannibal's just at your gates, Singet Sawnie, For Hannibal's just at your gates.

IX.

Andrew Gowk, Andrew Gowk, Ye may slander the book, And the book nought the waur-let me tell you; Tho' ye're rich and look big, Yet lay by hat and wig, And ye'll hae a calf's-head o' sma' value, Andrew Gowk, And ye'll hae a calf's-head o' sma' value.

X.

Poet Willie, Poet Willie, Gie the doctor a volley, Wi' your "liberty's chain" and your wit; O'er Pegasus' side, Ye ne'er laid a stride Ye only stood by when he , Poet Willie, Ye only stood by when he .

XI.

Barr Steenie, Barr Steenie, What mean ye? what mean ye? If ye'll meddle nae mair wi' the matter, Ye may hae some pretence, man, To havins and sense, man, Wi' people that ken ye nae better, Barr Steenie, Wi' people that ken ye nae better.

XII.

Jamie Goose, Jamie Goose, Ye hae made but toom roose, O' hunting the wicked lieutenant; But the doctor's your mark, For the L-d's holy ark, He has cooper'd and ca'd a wrong pin in't, Jamie Goose, He has cooper'd and ca'd a wrong pin in't.

XIII.

Davie Bluster, Davie Bluster, For a saunt if ye muster, It's a sign they're no nice o' recruits, Yet to worth let's be just, Royal blood ye might boast, If the ass were the king o' the brutes, Davie Bluster, If the ass were the king o' the brutes.

XIV.

Muirland George, Muirland George, Whom the Lord made a scourge, To claw common sense for her sins; If ill manners were wit, There's no mortal so fit, [165]To confound the poor doctor at ance, Muirland George, To confound the poor doctor at ance.

XV.

Cessnockside, Cessnockside, Wi' your turkey-cock pride, O' manhood but sma' is your share; Ye've the figure, it's true, Even our faes maun allow, And your friends daurna say ye hae mair, Cessnockside, And your friends daurna say ye hae mair.

XVI.

Daddie Auld, Daddie Auld, There's a tod i' the fauld A tod meikle waur than the clerk;[93] Tho' ye downa do skaith, Ye'll be in at the death, And if ye canna bite ye can bark, Daddie Auld, And if ye canna bite ye can bark.

XVII.

Poet Burns, Poet Burns, Wi' your priest-skelping turns, Why desert ye your auld native shire? Tho' your Muse is a gipsy, Yet were she even tipsy, She could ca' us nae waur than we are, Poet Burns, She could ca' us nae waur than we are.

POSTSCRIPT.

Afton's Laird, Afton's Laird, When your pen can be spar'd, A copy o' this I bequeath, On the same sicker score I mentioned before, To that trusty auld worthy Clackleith, Afton's Laird, To that trusty auld worthy Clackleith.

FOOTNOTES:

[93] Gavin Hamilton.

CHAPTER CXI.

PEG NICHOLSON.

[These hasty verses are to be found in a letter addressed to Nicol, of the High School of Edinburgh, by the poet, giving him on account of the unlooked-for death of his mare, Peg Nicholson, the successor of Jenny Geddes. She had suffered both in the employ of the joyous priest and the thoughtless poet. She acquired her name from that frantic virago who attempted to murder George the Third.]

Peg Nicholson was a good bay mare, As ever trode on airn; But now she's floating down the Nith, And past the mouth o' Cairn.

Peg Nicholson was a good bay mare, And rode thro' thick an' thin; But now she's floating down the Nith, And wanting even the skin.

Peg Nicholson was a good bay mare, And ance she bore a priest; But now she's flouting down the Nith, For Solway fish a feast.

Peg Nicholson was a good bay mare, And the priest he rode her sair; And much oppress'd and bruis'd she was; As priest-rid cattle are, andc. andc.

CHAPTER CXII.

ON

CAPTAIN MATTHEW HENDERSON,

A GENTLEMAN WHO HELD THE PATENT FOR HIS HONOURS IMMEDIATELY FROM ALMIGHTY GOD.

"Should the poor be flattered?"

Shakspeare.

But now his radiant course is run, For Matthew's course was bright; His soul was like the glorious sun, A matchless heav'nly light!

[Captain Matthew Henderson, a gentleman of very agreeable manners and great propriety of character, usually lived in Edinburgh, dined constantly at Fortune's Tavern, and was a member of the Capillaire Club, which was composed of all who desired to be thought witty or joyous: he died in 1789: Burns, in a note to the Poem, says, "I loved the man much, and have not flattered his memory." Henderson seems indeed to have been universally liked. "In our travelling party," says Sir James Campbell, of Ardkinglass, "was Matthew Henderson, then (1759) and afterwards well known and much esteemed in the town of Edinburgh; at that time an officer in the twenty-fifth regiment of foot, and like myself on his way to join the army; and I may say with truth, that in the course of a long life I have never known a more estimable character, than Matthew Henderson." Memoirs of Campbell, of Ardkinglass, p. 17.]

O death! thou tyrant fell and bloody! The meikle devil wi' a woodie [166]Haurl thee hame to his black smiddie, O'er hurcheon hides, And like stock-fish come o'er his studdie Wi' thy auld sides!

He's gane! he's gane! he's frae us torn, The ae best fellow e'er was born!

Thee, Matthew, Nature's sel' shall mourn By wood and wild, Where, haply, pity strays forlorn, Frae man exil'd!

Ye hills! near neebors o' the starns, That proudly cock your cresting cairns! Ye cliffs, the haunts of sailing yearns, Where echo slumbers! Come join, ye Nature's sturdiest bairns, My wailing numbers!

Mourn, ilka grove the cushat kens! Ye haz'lly shaws and briery dens! Ye burnies, wimplin' down your glens, Wi' toddlin' din, Or foaming strang, wi' hasty stens, Frae lin to lin!

Mourn, little harebells o'er the lea; Ye stately foxgloves fair to see; Ye woodbines, hanging bonnilie, In scented bow'rs; Ye roses on your thorny tree, The first o' flow'rs.

At dawn, when ev'ry grassy blade Droops with a diamond at its head, At ev'n, when beans their fragrance shed I' th' rustling gale, Ye maukins whiddin thro' the glade, Come join my wail.

Mourn, ye wee songsters o' the wood; Ye grouse that crap the heather bud; Ye curlews calling thro' a clud; Ye whistling plover; An' mourn, ye whirring paitrick brood!- He's gane for ever!

Mourn, sooty coots, and speckled teals; Ye fisher herons, watching eels: Ye duck and drake, wi' airy wheels Circling the lake; Ye bitterns, till the quagmire reels, Rair for his sake.

Mourn, clam'ring craiks, at close o' day, 'Mang fields o' flowering clover gay; And when ye wing your annual way Frae our cauld shore, Tell thae far warlds, wha lies in clay, Wham we deplore.

Ye houlets, frae your ivy bow'r, In some auld tree, or eldritch tow'r, What time the moon, wi' silent glow'r, Sets up her horn, Wail thro' the dreary midnight hour 'Till waukrife morn!

O rivers, forests, hills, and plains! Oft have ye heard my canty strains: But now, what else for me remains But tales of woe? And frae my een the drapping rains Maun ever flow.

Mourn, spring, thou darling of the year! Ilk cowslip cup shall kep a tear: Thou, simmer, while each corny spear Shoots up its head, The gay, green, flow'ry tresses shear For him that's dead!

Thou, autumn, wi' thy yellow hair, In grief thy sallow mantle tear: Thou, winter, hurling thro' the air The roaring blast, Wide, o'er the naked world declare The worth we've lost!

Mourn him, thou sun, great source of light! Mourn, empress of the silent night! And you, ye twinkling starnies bright, My Matthew mourn! For through your orbs he's ta'en his flight, Ne'er to return.

O, Henderson! the man-the brother! And art thou gone, and gone for ever? And hast thou crost that unknown river Life's dreary bound? Like thee, where shall I find another, The world around?

Go to your sculptur'd tombs, ye great, In a' the tinsel trash o' state! But by thy honest turf I'll wait, Thou man of worth! And weep the ae best fellow's fate E'er lay in earth.

[167]

THE EPITAPH.

Stop, passenger!-my story's brief, And truth I shall relate, man; I tell nae common tale o' grief- For Matthew was a great man.

If thou uncommon merit hast, Yet spurn'd at fortune's door, man, A look of pity hither cast- For Matthew was a poor man.

If thou a noble sodger art, That passest by this grave, man, There moulders here a gallant heart- For Matthew was a brave man.

If thou on men, their works and ways, Canst throw uncommon light, man, Here lies wha weel had won thy praise- For Matthew was a bright man.

If thou at friendship's sacred ca' Wad life itself resign, man, Thy sympathetic tear maun fa'- For Matthew was a kind man!

If thou art staunch without a stain, Like the unchanging blue, man, This was a kinsman o' thy ain- For Matthew was a true man.

If thou hast wit, and fun, and fire, And ne'er guid wine did fear, man, This was thy billie, dam and sire- For Matthew was a queer man.

If ony whiggish whingin sot, To blame poor Matthew dare, man, May dool and sorrow be his lot! For Matthew was a rare man.

CHAPTER CXIII.

THE FIVE CARLINS.

A SCOTS BALLAD.

Tune-Chevy Chase.

[This is a local and political Poem composed on the contest between Miller, the younger, of Dalswinton, and Johnstone, of Westerhall, for the representation of the Dumfries and Galloway district of Boroughs. Each town or borough speaks and acts in character: Maggy personates Dumfries; Marjory, Lochmaben; Bess of Solway-side, Annan; Whiskey Jean, Kirkcudbright; and Black Joan, Sanquhar. On the part of Miller, all the Whig interest of the Duke of Queensberry was exerted, and all the Tory interest on the side of the Johnstone: the poet's heart was with the latter. Annan and Lochmaben stood staunch by old names and old affections: after a contest, bitterer than anything of the kind remembered, the Whig interest prevailed.]

There were five carlins in the south, They fell upon a scheme, To send a lad to London town, To bring them tidings hame.

Not only bring them tidings hame, But do their errands there; And aiblins gowd and honour baith Might be that laddie's share.

There was Maggy by the banks o' Nith, A dame wi' pride eneugh; And Marjory o' the mony lochs, A carlin auld and teugh.

And blinkin' Bess of Annandale, That dwelt near Solway-side; And whiskey Jean, that took her gill In Galloway sae wide.

And black Joan, frae Crighton-peel, O' gipsey kith an' kin;- Five wighter

carlins were na found The south countrie within.
To send a lad to London town, They met upon a day; And mony a knight, and mony a laird, This errand fain wad gae.
O mony a knight, and mony a laird, This errand fain wad gae; But nae ane could their fancy please, O ne'er a ane but twae.
The first ane was a belted knight, Bred of a border band; And he wad gae to London town, Might nae man him withstand.
And he wad do their errands weel, And meikle he wad say; And ilka ane about the court Wad bid to him gude-day.
The neist cam in a sodger youth, And spak wi' modest grace, And he wad gae to London town, If sae their pleasure was. [168]
He wad na hecht them courtly gifts, Nor meikle speech pretend; But he wad hecht an honest heart, Wad ne'er desert his friend.
Then wham to chuse, and wham refuse, At strife thir carlins fell; For some had gentlefolks to please, And some wad please themsel'.
Then out spak mim-mou'd Meg o' Nith, And she spak up wi' pride, And she wad send the sodger youth, Whatever might betide.
For the auld gudeman o' London court She didna care a pin; But she wad send the sodger youth To greet his eldest son.
Then slow raise Marjory o' the Lochs And wrinkled was her brow; Her ancient weed was russet gray, Her auld Scotch heart was true.
"The London court set light by me- I set as light by them; And I wilt send the sodger lad To shaw that court the same."
Then up sprang Bess of Annandale, And swore a deadly aith, Says, "I will send the border-knight Spite o' you carlins baith.
"For far-off fowls hae feathers fair, And fools o' change are fain; But I hae try'd this border-knight, I'll try him yet again."
Then whiskey Jean spak o'er her drink, "Ye weel ken, kimmersa', The auld gudeman o' London court, His back's been at the wa'.
"And mony a friend that kiss'd his caup, Is now a fremit wight; But it's ne'er be sae wi' whiskey Jean,- We'll send the border-knight."
Says black Joan o' Crighton-peel, A carlin stoor and grim,- "The auld gudeman, or the young gudeman, For me may sink or swim.
"For fools will prate o' right and wrang, While knaves laugh in their sleeve; But wha blaws best the horn shall win, I'll spier nae courtier's leave."
So how this mighty plea may end There's naebody can tell: God grant the king, and ilka man, May look weel to himsel'!

CHAPTER CXIV.

THE LADDIES BY THE BANKS O' NITH.

[This short Poem was first published by Robert Chambers. It intimates pretty strongly, how much the poet disapproved of the change which came over the Duke of Queensberry's opinions, when he supported the right of the Prince of Wales to assume the government, without consent of

Parliament, during the king's alarming illness, in 1788.]

The laddies by the banks o' Nith, Wad trust his Grace wi' a', Jamie, But he'll sair them, as he sair'd the King, Turn tail and rin awa', Jamie.

Up and waur them a', Jamie, Up and waur them a'; The Johnstones hae the guidin' o't, Ye turncoat Whigs awa'.

The day he stude his country's friend, Or gied her faes a claw, Jamie: Or frae puir man a blessin' wan, That day the Duke ne'er saw, Jamie.

But wha is he, his country's boast? Like him there is na twa, Jamie, There's no a callant tents the kye, But kens o' Westerha', Jamie.

To end the wark here's Whistlebirk,[94] Lang may his whistle blaw, Jamie; And Maxwell true o' sterling blue: And we'll be Johnstones a', Jamie.

FOOTNOTES:

[94] Birkwhistle: a Galloway laird, and elector.

[169]

CHAPTER CXV.

EPISTLE TO ROBERT GRAHAM, ESQ.

OF FINTRAY:

ON THE CLOSE OF THE DISPUTED ELECTION BETWEEN SIR JAMES JOHNSTONE AND CAPTAIN MILLER, FOR THE DUMFRIES DISTRICT OF BOROUGHS.

["I am too little a man," said Burns, in the note to Fintray, which accompanied this poem, "to have any political attachment: I am deeply indebted to, and have the warmest veneration for individuals of both parties: but a man who has it in his power to be the father of a country, and who acts like his Grace of Queensberry, is a character that one cannot speak of with patience." This Epistle was first printed in my edition of Burns in 1834: I had the use of the Macmurdo and the Afton manuscripts for that purpose: to both families the poet was much indebted for many acts of courtesy and kindness.]

Fintray, my stay in worldly strife, Friend o' my muse, friend o' my life, Are ye as idle's I am? Come then, wi' uncouth, kintra fleg, O'er Pegasus I'll fling my leg, And ye shall see me try him.

I'll sing the zeal Drumlanrig bears, Who left the all-important cares Of princes and their darlings; And, bent on winning borough towns, Came shaking hands wi' wabster lowns, And kissing barefit carlins.

Combustion thro' our boroughs rode, Whistling his roaring pack abroad Of mad unmuzzled lions; As Queensberry buff and blue unfurl'd, And Westerha' and Hopeton hurl'd To every Whig defiance.

But cautious Queensberry left the war, Th' unmanner'd dust might soil his star; Besides, he hated bleeding: But left behind him heroes bright, Heroes in Cæsarean fight, Or Ciceronian pleading.

O! for a throat like huge Mons-meg, To muster o'er each ardent Whig Beneath Drumlanrig's banner; Heroes and heroines commix, All in the field of politics, To win immortal honour.

M'Murdo[95] and his lovely spouse, (Th' enamour'd laurels kiss her brows!) Led on the loves and graces: She won each gaping burgess' heart, While he, all-conquering, play'd his part Among their wives and lasses.

Craigdarroch[96] led a light-arm'd corps, Tropes, metaphors and figures pour, Like Hecla streaming thunder: Glenriddel,[97] skill'd in rusty coins, Blew up each Tory's dark designs, And bar'd the treason under.

In either wing two champions fought, Redoubted Staig[98] who set at nought The wildest savage Tory: And Welsh,[99] who ne'er yet flinch'd his ground, High-wav'd his magnum-bonum round With Cyclopeian fury.

Miller brought up th' artillery ranks, The many-pounders of the Banks, Resistless desolation! While Maxwelton, that baron bold, 'Mid Lawson's[100] port intrench'd his hold, And threaten'd worse damnation.

To these what Tory hosts oppos'd, With these what Tory warriors clos'd. Surpasses my descriving: Squadrons extended long and large, With furious speed rush to the charge, Like raging devils driving.

What verse can sing, what prose narrate, The butcher deeds of bloody fate Amid this mighty tulzie! Grim Horror grinn'd-pale Terror roar'd, As Murther at his thrapple shor'd, And hell mix'd in the brulzie.

As highland craigs by thunder cleft, When lightnings fire the stormy lift, Hurl down with crashing rattle: As flames among a hundred woods; As headlong foam a hundred floods; Such is the rage of battle!

The stubborn Tories dare to die; As soon the rooted oaks would fly Before the approaching fellers: The Whigs come on like Ocean's roar, When all his wintry billows pour Against the Buchan Bullers.

[170]

Lo, from the shades of Death's deep night, Departed Whigs enjoy the fight, And think on former daring: The muffled murtherer[101] of Charles The Magna Charter flag unfurls, All deadly gules it's bearing.

Nor wanting ghosts of Tory fame. Bold Scrimgeour[102] follows gallant Graham,[103] Auld Covenanters shiver. (Forgive, forgive, much-wrong'd Montrose! Now death and hell engulph thy foes, Thou liv'st on high for ever!)

Still o'er the field the combat burns, The Tories, Whigs, give way by turns; But fate the word has spoken: For woman's wit and strength o' man, Alas! can do but what they can! The Tory ranks are broken.

O that my een were flowing burns, My voice a lioness that mourns Her darling cubs' undoing! That I might greet, that I might cry, While Tories fall, while Tories fly, And furious Whigs pursuing!

What Whig but melts for good Sir James! Dear to his country by the names Friend, patron, benefactor! Not Pulteney's wealth can Pulteney save! And Hopeton falls, the generous brave! And Stewart,[104] bold as Hector.

Thou, Pitt, shalt rue this overthrow; And Thurlow growl a curse of woe;

And Melville melt in wailing! How Fox and Sheridan rejoice! And Burke shall sing, O Prince, arise, Thy power is all prevailing!

For your poor friend, the Bard, afar He only hears and sees the war, A cool spectator purely; So, when the storm the forests rends, The robin in the hedge descends, And sober chirps securely.

FOOTNOTES:

[95] John M'Murdo, Esq., of Drumlanrig.

[96] Fergusson of Craigdarroch.

[97] Riddel of Friars-Carse.

[98] Provost Staig of Dumfries.

[99] Sheriff Welsh.

[100] A wine merchant in Dumfries.

[101] The executioner of Charles I. was masked.

[102] Scrimgeour, Lord Dundee.

[103] Graham, Marquis of Montrose.

[104] Stewart of Hillside.

CHAPTER CXVI.

ON
CAPTAIN GROSE'S
PEREGRINATIONS THROUGH SCOTLAND,
COLLECTING THE
ANTIQUITIES OF THAT KINGDOM.

[This "fine, fat, fodgel wight" was a clever man, a skilful antiquary, and fond of wit and wine. He was well acquainted with heraldry, and was conversant with the weapons and the armor of his own and other countries. He found his way to Friars-Carse, in the Vale of Nith, and there, at the social "board of Glenriddel," for the first time saw Burns. The Englishman heard, it is said, with wonder, the sarcastic sallies and eloquent bursts of the inspired Scot, who, in his turn, surveyed with wonder the remarkable corpulence, and listened with pleasure to the independent sentiments and humourous turns of conversation in the joyous Englishman. This Poem was the fruit of the interview, and it is said that Grose regarded some passages as rather personal.]

Hear, Land o' Cakes and brither Scots, Frae Maidenkirk to Johnny Groat's; If there's a hole in a' your coats, I rede you tent it: A chiel's amang you taking notes, And, faith, he'll prent it!

If in your bounds ye chance to light Upon a fine, fat, fodgel wight, O' stature short, but genius bright, That's he, mark weel- And wow! he has an unco slight O' cauk and keel.

By some auld, houlet-haunted biggin, Or kirk deserted by its riggin, It's ten to one ye'll find him snug in Some eldritch part, Wi' deils, they say, L-d save's! colleaguin' At some black art.

Ilk ghaist that haunts auld ha' or chaumer, Ye gipsey-gang that deal in glamour, And you deep read in hell's black grammar, Warlocks and witches; Ye'll quake at his conjuring hammer, Ye midnight bs!

It's tauld he was a sodger bred, And ane wad rather fa'n than fled; [171]But now he's quat the spurtle-blade, And dog-skin wallet, And ta'en the-Antiquarian trade, I think they call it.

He has a fouth o' auld nick-nackets: Rusty airn caps and jinglin' jackets, Wad haud the Lothians three in tackets, A towmont guid; And parritch-pats, and auld saut-backets, Afore the flood.

Of Eve's first fire he has a cinder; Auld Tubal-Cain's fire-shool and fender; That which distinguished the gender O' Balaam's ass; A broom-stick o' the witch o' Endor, Weel shod wi' brass.

Forbye, he'll shape you aff, fu' gleg, The cut of Adam's philibeg: The knife that nicket Abel's craig He'll prove you fully, It was a faulding jocteleg, Or lang-kail gully.-

But wad ye see him in his glee, For meikle glee and fun has he, Then set him down, and twa or three Guid fellows wi' him; And port, O port! shine thou a wee, And then ye'll see him!

Now, by the pow'rs o' verse and prose! Thou art a dainty chiel, O Grose!-Whae'er o' thee shall ill suppose, They sair misca' thee; I'd take the rascal by the nose, Wad say, Shame fa' thee!

CHAPTER CXVII.

WRITTEN IN A WRAPPER,

ENCLOSING

A LETTER TO CAPTAIN GROSE.

[Burns wrote out some antiquarian and legendary memoranda, respecting certain ruins in Kyle, and enclosed them in a sheet of a paper to Cardonnel, a northern antiquary. As his mind teemed with poetry he could not, as he afterwards said, let the opportunity, pass of sending a rhyming inquiry after his fat friend, and Cardonnel spread the condoling inquiry over the North-

"Is he slain by Highlan' bodies? And eaten like a wether-haggis?"]

Ken ye ought o' Captain Grose? Igo and ago, If he's amang his friends or foes? Iram, coram, dago.

Is he south or is he north? Igo and ago, Or drowned in the river Forth? Iram, coram, dago.

Is he slain by Highlan' bodies? Igo and ago, And eaten like a wether-haggis? Iram, coram, dago.

Is he to Abram's bosom gane? Igo and ago, Or haudin' Sarah by the wame? Iram, coram, dago.

Where'er he be, the L-d be near him! Igo and ago, As for the deil, he daur na steer him! Iram, coram, dago.

But please transmit the enclosed letter, Igo and ago, Which will oblige your humble debtor, Iram, coram, dago.

So may he hae auld stanes in store, Igo and ago, The very stanes that Adam bore, Iram, coram, dago.

So may ye get in glad possession, Igo and ago, The coins o' Satan's coronation! Iram, coram, dago.

CHAPTER CXVIII.

TAM O' SHANTER.

A TALE.

"Of brownys and of bogilis full is this buke."

Gawin Douglas

[This is a West-country legend, embellished by genius. No other Poem in our language displays such variety of power, in the same number of lines. It was[172] written as an inducement to Grose to admit Alloway-Kirk into his work on the Antiquities of Scotland; and written with such ecstasy, that the poet shed tears in the moments of composition. The walk in which it was conceived, on the braes of Ellisland, is held in remembrance in the vale, and pointed out to poetic inquirers: while the scene where the poem is laid-the crumbling ruins-the place where the chapman perished in the snow-the tree on which the poor mother of Mungo ended her sorrows-the cairn where the murdered child was found by the hunters-and the old bridge over which Maggie bore her astonished master when all hell was in pursuit, are first-rate objects of inspection and inquiry in the "Land of Burns." "In the inimitable tale of Tam o' Shanter," says Scott "Burns has left us sufficient evidence of his ability to combine the ludicrous with the awful, and even the horrible. No poet, with the exception of Shakspeare, ever possessed the power of exciting the most varied and discordant emotions with such rapid transitions."]

When chapman billies leave the street, And drouthy neebors neebors meet, As market-days are wearing late, An' folk begin to tak' the gate; While we sit bousing at the nappy, An' gettin' fou and unco happy, We think na on the lang Scots miles, The mosses, waters, slaps, and stiles, That lie between us and our hame, Where sits our sulky sullen dame, Gathering her brows like gathering storm, Nursing her wrath to keep it warm.

This truth fand honest Tam O' Shanter, As he frae Ayr ae night did canter, (Auld Ayr, wham ne'er a town surpasses, For honest men and bonny lasses.) O Tam! hadst thou but been sae wise, As ta'en thy ain wife Kate's advice! She tauld thee weel thou was a skellum, A blethering, blustering, drunken blellum; That frae November till October, Ae market-day thou wasna sober; That ilka melder, wi' the miller, Thou sat as lang as thou had siller; That ev'ry naig was ca'd a shoe on, The smith and thee gat roaring fou on; That at the Lord's house, ev'n on Sunday, Thou drank wi' Kirton Jean till Monday. She prophesy'd, that late or soon, Thou would be found deep drown'd in Doon; Or catch'd wi' warlocks in the mirk, By Alloway's auld haunted kirk.

Ah, gentle dames! it gars me greet, To think how mony counsels sweet,

How mony lengthen'd sage advices, The husband frae the wife despises! But to our tale:-Ae market night, Tam had got planted unco right; Fast by an ingle bleezing finely, Wi' reaming swats, that drank divinely; And at his elbow, Souter Johnny, His ancient, trusty, drouthy crony; Tam lo'ed him like a vera brither; They had been fou' for weeks thegither! The night drave on wi' sangs an' clatter; And ay the ale was growing better: The landlady and Tam grew gracious; Wi' favors secret, sweet, and precious; The Souter tauld his queerest stories; The landlord's laugh was ready chorus:[105] The storm without might rair and rustle- Tam did na mind the storm a whistle.

Care, mad to see a man sae happy, E'en drown'd himself amang the nappy! As bees flee hame wi' lades o' treasure, The minutes wing'd their way wi' pleasure: Kings may be blest, but Tam was glorious, O'er a' the ills o' life victorious.

But pleasures are like poppies spread, You seize the flow'r, its bloom is shed; Or like the snow falls in the river, A moment white-then melts for ever; Or like the borealis race, That flit ere you can point their place; Or like the rainbow's lovely form Evanishing amid the storm. Nae man can tether time or tide; The hour approaches Tam maun ride; That hour, o' night's black arch the key-stane, That dreary hour he mounts his beast in; And sic a night he taks the road in As ne'er poor sinner was abroad in.

The wind blew as 'twad blawn its last; The rattling show'rs rose on the blast; The speedy gleams the darkness swallow'd; Loud, deep, and lang the thunder bellow'd: That night, a child might understand, The de'il had business on his hand.

Weel mounted on his gray mare, Meg, A better never lifted leg, Tam skelpit on thro' dub and mire, Despising wind, and rain, and fire; Whiles holding fast his guid blue bonnet; Whiles crooning o'er some auld Scots sonnet; Whiles glow'ring round wi' prudent cares, Lest bogles catch him unawares; Kirk-Alloway was drawing nigh, Whare ghaists and houlets nightly cry.-

[173]

By this time he was cross the foord, Whare in the snaw the chapman smoor'd; And past the birks and meikle stane, Where drunken Charlie brak's neck-bane; And thro' the whins, and by the cairn, Where hunters fand the murder'd bairn; And near the thorn, aboon the well, Where Mungo's mither hang'd hersel'. Before him Doon pours all his floods; The doubling storm roars thro' the woods; The lightnings flash from pole to pole; Near and more the thunders roll; When, glimmering thro' the groaning trees, Kirk-Alloway seem'd in a bleeze; Thro' ilka bore the beams were glancing; And loud resounded mirth and dancing.

Inspiring, bold John Barleycorn! What dangers thou canst make us scorn! Wi' tippenny, we fear nae evil; Wi' usquabae we'll face the devil! The swats sae ream'd in Tammie's noddle, Fair play, he car'd nae deils a boddle. But Maggie stood right sair astonish'd, 'Till, by the heel and hand admonish'd,

She ventur'd forward on the light; And wow! Tam saw an unco sight! Warlocks and witches in a dance; Nae cotillion brent new frae France, But hornpipes, jigs, strathspeys, and reels, Put life and mettle in their heels: A winnock-bunker in the east, There sat auld Nick, in shape o' beast; A towzie tyke, black, grim, and large, To gie them music was his charge; He screw'd the pipes and gart them skirl, Till roof and rafters a' did dirl.- Coffins stood round, like open presses; That shaw'd the dead in their last dresses; And by some devilish cantrip slight Each in its cauld hand held a light- By which heroic Tam was able To note upon the haly table, A murderer's banes in gibbet airns; Twa span-lang, wee, unchristen'd bairns; A thief, new-cutted frae a rape, Wi' his last gasp his gab did gape; Five tomahawks, wi' bluid red-rusted; Five scimitars, wi' murder crusted; A garter, which a babe had strangled; A knife, a father's throat had mangled, Whom his ain son o' life bereft, The gray hairs yet stack to the heft:[106] Wi' mair o' horrible and awfu', Which ev'n to name would be unlawfu'.

As Tammie glowr'd, amaz'd, and curious, The mirth and fun grew fast and furious: The piper loud and louder blew; The dancers quick and quicker flew; They reel'd, they set, they cross'd, they cleekit, 'Till ilka carlin swat and reekit, And coost her duddies to the wark, And linket at it in her sark!

Now Tam, O Tam! had thae been queans A' plump and strapping, in their teens; Their sarks, instead o' creeshie flannen, Been snaw-white seventeen hunder linen, Thir breeks o' mine, my only pair, That ance were plush, o' guid blue hair, I wad hae gi'en them off my hurdies, For ae blink o' the bonnie burdies!

But wither'd beldams, auld and droll, Rigwoodie hags, wad spean a foal, Lowping an' flinging on a cummock, I wonder didna turn thy stomach.

But Tam kenn'd what was what fu' brawlie, There was a winsome wench and walie, That night enlisted in the core, (Lang after kenn'd on Carrick shore; For mony a beast to dead she shot, And perish'd mony a bonnie boat, And shook baith meikle corn and bear, And kept the country-side in fear.) Her cutty sark, o' Paisley harn, That, while a lassie, she had worn, In longitude tho' sorely scanty, It was her best, and she was vauntie-

[174]

Ah! little kenn'd the reverend grannie, That sark she coft for her wee Nannie, Wi' twa pund Scots ('twas a' her riches), Wad ever grac'd a dance of witches! But here my muse her wing maun cour; Sic flights are far beyond her pow'r; To sing how Nannie lap and flang, (A souple jade she was and strung,) And how Tam stood, like ane bewitch'd; And thought his very een enrich'd; Even Satan glowr'd, and fidg'd fu' fain, And hotch'd and blew wi' might and main: 'Till first ae caper, syne anither, Tam tint his reason a' thegither, And roars out, "Weel done, Cutty-sark!" And in an instant all was dark: And scarcely had he Maggie rallied, When out the hellish legion sallied.

As bees bizz out wi' angry fyke, When plundering herds assail their byke; As open pussie's mortal foes, When, pop! she starts before their nose; As eager runs the market-crowd, When "Catch the thief!" resounds aloud; So Maggie runs, the witches follow, Wi' mony an eldritch screech and hollow.

Ah, Tam! Ah, Tam! thou'll get thy fairin'! In hell they'll roast thee like a herrin'! In vain thy Kate awaits thy comin'! Kate soon will be a woefu' woman! Now do thy speedy utmost, Meg, And win the key-stane[107] of the brig; There at them thou thy tail may toss, A running stream they darena cross! But ere the key-stane she could make, The fient a tail she had to shake! For Nannie, far before the rest, Hard upon noble Maggie prest, And flew at Tam wi' furious ettle; But little wist she Maggie's mettle- Ae spring brought off her master hale, But left behind her ain gray tail: The carlin claught her by the rump, And left poor Maggie scarce a stump.

Now, wha this tale o' truth shall read, Ilk man and mother's son, take heed: Whene'er to drink you are inclin'd, Or cutty-sarks run in your mind, Think! ye may buy the joys o'er dear- Remember Tam O' Shanter's mare.

FOOTNOTES:

[105] VARIATION.

The cricket raised its cheering cry, The kitten chas'd its tail in joy.

[106] VARIATION.

Three lawyers' tongues turn'd inside out, Wi' lies seem'd like a beggar's clout; And priests' hearts rotten black as muck, Lay stinking vile, in every neuk.

[107] It is a well-known fact that witches, or any evil spirits, have no power to follow a poor wight any further than the middle of the next running stream. It may be proper likewise to mention to the benighted traveller, that when he falls in with bogles, whatever danger there may be in his going forward, there is much more hazard in turning back.

CHAPTER CXIX.

ADDRESS OF BEELZEBUB

TO THE

PRESIDENT OF THE HIGHLAND SOCIETY.

[This Poem made its first appearance, as I was assured by my friend the late Thomas Pringle, in the Scots Magazine, for February, 1818, and was printed from the original in the handwriting of Burns. It was headed thus, "To the Right honorable the Earl of Brendalbyne, President of the Right Honourable and Honourable the Highland Society, which met on the 23d of May last, at the Shakspeare, Covent Garden, to concert ways and means to frustrate the designs of four hundred Highlanders, who, as the Society were informed by Mr. M. , of As, were so audacious as to attempt an escape from their lawful lairds and masters, whose property they were, by emigrating from the lands of Mr. Macdonald, of Glengarry, to the wilds of Canada, in search of that fantastic thing-Liberty." The Poem was

communicated by Burns to his friend Rankine of Adam Hill, in Ayrshire.]
Long life, my Lord, an' health be yours, Unskaith'd by hunger'd Highland boors; Lord grant mae duddie desperate beggar, Wi' dirk, claymore, or rusty trigger, May twin auld Scotland o' a life She likes-as lambkins like a knife. Faith, you and As were right To keep the Highland hounds in sight; I doubt na! they wad bid nae better Than let them ance out owre the water; Then up among the lakes and seas They'll mak' what rules and laws they please; Some daring Hancock, or a Franklin'; May set their Highland bluid a ranklin'; Some Washington again may head them, Or some Montgomery fearless lead them, Till God knows what may be effected When by such heads and hearts directed- Poor dunghill sons of dirt and mire May to Patrician rights aspire! Nae sage North, now, nor sager Sackville, To watch and premier o'er the pack vile, An' whare will ye get Howes and Clintons To bring them to a right repentance, To cowe the rebel generation, An' save the honour o' the nation? They an' be dd! what right hae they To meat or sleep, or light o' day? Far less to riches, pow'r, or freedom, But what your lordship likes to gie them? [175]
But hear, my lord! Glengarry, hear! Your hand's owre light on them, I fear; Your factors, grieves, trustees, and bailies, I canna' say but they do gaylies; They lay aside a' tender mercies, An' tirl the hallions to the birses; Yet while they're only poind't and herriet, They'll keep their stubborn Highland spirit; But smash them! crash them a' to spails! An' rot the dyvors i' the jails! The young dogs, swinge them to the labour; Let wark an' hunger mak' them sober! The hizzies, if they're aughtlins fawsont, Let them in Drury-lane be lesson'd! An' if the wives an' dirty brats E'en thigger at your doors an' yetts, Flaffan wi' duds an' grey wi' beas', Frightin' awa your deuks an' geese, Get out a horsewhip or a jowler, The langest thong, the fiercest growler, An' gar the tattered gypsies pack Wi' a' their bastards on their back! Go on, my Lord! I lang to meet you, An' in my house at hame to greet you; Wi' common lords ye shanna mingle, The benmost neuk beside the ingle, At my right han' assigned your seat 'Tween Herod's hip an Polycrate,- Or if you on your station tarrow, Between Almagro and Pizarro, A seat I'm sure ye're weel deservin't; An' till ye come-Your humble rervant,
Beelzebub.
June 1st, Anno Mundi 5790.
CHAPTER CXX.
TO
JOHN TAYLOR.
[Burns, it appears, was, in one of his excursions in revenue matters, likely to be detained at Wanlockhead: the roads were slippery with ice, his mare kept her feet with difficulty, and all the blacksmiths of the village were pre-engaged. To Mr. Taylor, a person of influence in the place, the poet, in despair, addressed this little Poem, begging his interference: Taylor spoke to

a smith; the smith flew to his tools, sharpened or frosted the shoes, and it is said lived for thirty years to boast that he had "never been well paid but ance, and that was by a poet, who paid him in money, paid him in drink, and paid him in verse."]

With Pegasus upon a day, Apollo weary flying, Through frosty hills the journey lay, On foot the way was plying,

Poor slip-shod giddy Pegasus Was but a sorry walker; To Vulcan then Apollo goes, To get a frosty calker.

Obliging Vulcan fell to work, Threw by his coat and bonnet, And did Sol's business in a crack; Sol paid him with a sonnet.

Ye Vulcan's sons of Wanlockhead, Pity my sad disaster; My Pegasus is poorly shod- I'll pay you like my master.

Robert Burns.

Ramages, 3 o'clock, (no date.)

CHAPTER CXXI.

LAMENT

OF

MARY, QUEEN OF SCOTS,

ON THE APPROACH OF SPRING.

[The poet communicated this "Lament" to his friend, Dr. Moore, in February, 1791, but it was composed about the close of the preceding year, at the request of Lady Winifred Maxwell Constable, of Terreagles, the last in direct descent of the noble and ancient house of Maxwell, of Nithsdale. Burns expressed himself more than commonly pleased with this composition; nor was he unrewarded, for Lady Winifred gave him a valuable snuff-box, with the portrait of the unfortunate Mary on the lid. The bed still keeps its place in Terreagles, on which the queen slept as she was on her way to take refuge with her cruel and treacherous cousin, Elizabeth; and a letter from her no less unfortunate grandson, Charles the First, calling the Maxwells to arm in his cause, is preserved in the family archives.]

I.

Now Nature hangs her mantle green On every blooming tree, And spreads her sheets o' daisies white Out o'er the grassy lea: Now Phœbus cheers the crystal streams, And glads the azure skies; But nought can glad the weary wight That fast in durance lies.

II.

Now lav'rocks wake the merry morn, Aloft on dewy wing; [176]The merle, in his noontide bow'r, Makes woodland echoes ring; The mavis wild wi' mony a note, Sings drowsy day to rest: In love and freedom they rejoice, Wi' care nor thrall opprest.

III.

Now blooms the lily by the bank, The primrose down the brae; The hawthorn's budding in the glen, And milk-white is the slae; The meanest hind in fair Scotland May rove their sweets amang; But I, the Queen of a' Scotland, Maun lie in prison strang!

IV.

I was the Queen o' bonnie France, Where happy I hae been; Fu' lightly rase I in the morn, As blythe lay down at e'en: And I'm the sov'reign o' Scotland, And mony a traitor there; Yet here I lie in foreign bands And never-ending care.

V.

But as for thee, thou false woman! My sister and my fae, Grim vengeance yet shall whet a sword That thro' thy soul shall gae! The weeping blood in woman's breast Was never known to thee; Nor th' balm that draps on wounds of woe Frae woman's pitying e'e.

VI.

My son! my son! may kinder stars Upon thy fortune shine; And may those pleasures gild thy reign, That ne'er wad blink on mine! God keep thee frae thy mother's faes, Or turn their hearts to thee: And where thou meet'st thy mother's friend Remember him for me!

VII.

O! soon, to me, may summer suns Nae mair light up the morn! Nae mair, to me, the autumn winds Wave o'er the yellow corn! And in the narrow house o' death Let winter round me rave; And the next flow'rs that deck the spring Bloom on my peaceful grave!

CHAPTER CXXII.

THE WHISTLE.

["As the authentic prose history," says Burns, "of the 'Whistle' is curious, I shall here give it. In the train of Anne of Denmark, when she came to Scotland with our James the Sixth, there came over also a Danish gentleman of gigantic stature and great prowess, and a matchless champion of Bacchus. He had a little ebony whistle, which at the commencement of the orgies, he laid on the table, and whoever was the last able to blow it, everybody else being disabled by the potency of the bottle, was to carry off the whistle as a trophy of victory. The Dane produced credentials of his victories, without a single defeat, at the courts of Copenhagen, Stockholm, Moscow, Warsaw, and several of the petty courts in Germany; and challenged the Scotch Bacchanalians to the alternative of trying his prowess, or else of acknowledging their inferiority. After man overthrows on the part of the Scots, the Dane was encountered by Sir Robert Lawrie, of Maxwelton, ancestor of the present worthy baronet of that name; who, after three days and three nights' hard contest, left the Scandinavian under the table,

'And blew on the whistle his requiem shrill.'

"Sir Walter, son to Sir Robert before mentioned, afterwards lost the whistle to Walter Riddel, of Glenriddel, who had married a sister of Sir Walter's.- On Friday, the 16th of October, 1790, at Friars-Carse, the whistle was once more contended for, as related in the ballad, by the present Sir Robert of Maxwelton; Robert Riddel, Esq., of Glenriddel, lineal descendant and representative of Walter Riddel, who won the whistle, and in whose family it had continued; and Alexander Fergusson, Esq., of Craigdarroch, likewise descended of the great Sir Robert; which last gentleman carried off the hard-won honours of the field."

The jovial contest took place in the dining-room of Friars-Carse, in the presence of the Bard, who drank bottle and bottle about with them, and seemed quite disposed to take up the conqueror when the day dawned.]

I sing of a whistle, a whistle of worth, I sing of a whistle, the pride of the North, Was brought to the court of our good Scottish king, And long with this whistle all Scotland shall ring.

Old Loda,[108] still rueing the arm of Fingal, The god of the bottle sends down from his hall- "This whistle's your challenge-to Scotland get o'er, And drink them to hell, Sir! or ne'er see me more!"

[177]

Old poets have sung, and old chronicles tell, What champions ventur'd, what champions fell; The son of great Loda was conqueror still, And blew on his whistle his requiem shrill.

Till Robert, the Lord of the Cairn and the Scaur, Unmatch'd at the bottle, unconquer'd in war, He drank his poor godship as deep as the sea, No tide of the Baltic e'er drunker than he.

Thus Robert, victorious, the trophy has gain'd; Which now in his house has for ages remain'd; Till three noble chieftains, and all of his blood, The jovial contest again have renew'd.

Three joyous good fellows, with hearts clear of flaw; Craigdarroch, so famous for wit, worth, and law; And trusty Glenriddel, so skill'd in old coins; And gallant Sir Robert, deep-read in old wines.

Craigdarroch began, with a tongue smooth as oil, Desiring Glenriddel to yield up the spoil; Or else he would muster the heads of the clan, And once more, in claret, try which was the man.

"By the gods of the ancients!" Glenriddel replies, "Before I surrender so glorious a prize, I'll conjure the ghost of the great Rorie More,[109] And bumper his horn with him twenty times o'er."

Sir Robert, a soldier, no speech would pretend, But he ne'er turn'd his back on his foe-or his friend, Said, toss down the whistle, the prize of the field, And, knee-deep in claret, he'd die or he'd yield.

To the board of Glenriddel our heroes repair, So noted for drowning of sorrow and care; Bur for wine and for welcome not more known to fame Than the sense, wit, and taste of a sweet lovely dame.

A bard was selected to witness the fray, And tell future ages the feats of the day; A bard who detested all sadness and spleen, And wish'd that Parnassus a vineyard had been.

The dinner being over, the claret they ply, And ev'ry new cork is a new spring of joy; In the bands of old friendship and kindred so set, And the bands grew the tighter the more they were wet.

Gay Pleasure ran riot as bumpers ran o'er; Bright Phœbus ne'er witness'd so joyous a core, And vow'd that to leave them he was quite forlorn, Till Cynthia hinted he'd find them next morn.

Six bottles a-piece had well wore out the night, When gallant Sir Robert, to finish the fight, Turn'd o'er in one bumper a bottle of red, And swore 'twas the way that their ancestor did.

Then worthy Glenriddel, so cautions and sage, No longer the warfare, ungodly, would wage; A high-ruling Elder to wallow in wine! He left the foul business to folks less divine.

The gallant Sir Robert fought hard to the end; But who can with fate and quart-bumpers contend? Though fate said-a hero shall perish in light; So up rose bright Phœbus-and down fell the knight.

Next up rose our bard, like a prophet in drink;- "Craigdarroch, thou'lt soar when creation shall sink; But if thou would flourish immortal in rhyme, Come-one bottle more-and have at the sublime!

"Thy line, that have struggled for freedom with Bruce, Shall heroes and patriots ever produce: So thine be the laurel, and mine be the bay; The field thou hast won, by yon bright god of day!"

FOOTNOTES:

[108] See Ossian's Carie-thura.

[109] See Johnson's Tour to the Hebrides

[178]

CHAPTER CXXIII.

ELEGY ON MISS BURNET, OF MONBODDO.

[This beautiful and accomplished lady, the heavenly Burnet, as Burns loved to call her, was daughter to the odd and the elegant, the clever and the whimsical Lord Monboddo. "In domestic circumstances," says Robert Chambers, "Monboddo was particularly unfortunate. His wife, a very beautiful woman, died in child-bed. His son, a promising boy, in whose education he took great delight, was likewise snatched from his affections by a premature death; and his second daughter, in personal loveliness one of the first women of the age, was cut off by consumption, when only twenty-five years old." Her name was Elizabeth.]

Life ne'er exulted in so rich a prize As Burnet, lovely from her native skies; Nor envious death so triumph'd in a blow, As that which laid th' accomplish'd Burnet low.

Thy form and mind, sweet maid, can I forget? In richest ore the brightest jewel set! In thee, high Heaven above was truest shown, As by his noblest work, the Godhead best is known.

In vain ye flaunt in summer's pride, ye groves; Thou crystal streamlet with thy flowery shore, Ye woodland choir that chant your idle loves, Ye cease to charm-Eliza is no more!

Ye heathy wastes, immix'd with reedy fens; Ye mossy streams, with sedge and rushes stor'd; Ye rugged cliffs, o'erhanging dreary glens, To you I fly, ye with my soul accord.

Princes, whose cumb'rous pride was all their worth, Shall venal lays their pompous exit hail? And thou, sweet excellence! forsake our earth, And not a muse in honest grief bewail?

We saw thee shine in youth and beauty's pride, And virtue's light, that beams beyond the spheres; But like the sun eclips'd at morning tide, Thou left'st us darkling in a world of tears.

The parent's heart that nestled fond in thee, That heart how sunk, a prey to grief and care; So leck'd the woodbine sweet yon aged tree; So from it ravish'd, leaves it bleak and bare.

CHAPTER CXXIV.

LAMENT FOR JAMES, EARL OF GLENCAIRN.

[Burns lamented the death of this kind and accomplished nobleman with melancholy sincerity: he moreover named one of his sons for him: he went into mourning when he heard of his death, and he sung of his merits in a strain not destined soon to lose the place it has taken among the verses which record the names of the noble and the generous. He died January 30, 1791, in the forty-second year of his age. James Cunningham was succeeded in his title by his brother, and with him expired, in 1796, the last of a race, whose name is intimately connected with the History of Scotland, from the days of Malcolm Canmore.]

I.

The wind blew hollow frae the hills, By fits the sun's departing beam Look'd on the fading yellow woods That wav'd o'er Lugar's winding stream: Beneath a craggy steep, a bard, Laden with years and meikle pain, In loud lament bewail'd his lord, Whom death had all untimely ta'en.

II.

He lean'd him to an ancient aik, Whose trunk was mould'ring down with years; His locks were bleached white with time, His hoary cheek was wet wi' tears; And as he touch'd his trembling harp, And as he tun'd his doleful sang, The winds, lamenting thro' their caves, To echo bore the notes alang.

III.

"Ye scattered birds that faintly sing, The reliques of the vernal quire! Ye woods that shed on a' the winds The honours of the aged year! A few short months, and glad and gay, Again ye'll charm the ear and e'e; But nocht in all revolving time Can gladness bring again to me.

IV.

"I am a bending aged tree, That long has stood the wind and rain; But now has come a cruel blast, And my last hold of earth is gane: Nae leaf o' mine shall greet the spring, Nae simmer sun exalt my bloom; But I maun lie before the storm, And ithers plant them in my room.

[179]

V.

"I've seen sae mony changefu' years, On earth I am a stranger grown; I wander in the ways of men, Alike unknowing and unknown: Unheard, unpitied, unrelieved, I bear alane my lade o' care, For silent, low, on beds of dust, Lie a' that would my sorrows share.

VI.

"And last (the sum of a' my griefs!) My noble master lies in clay; The flow'r amang our barons bold, His country's pride! his country's stay- In weary being now I pine, For a' the life of life is dead, And hope has left my aged ken, On forward wing for ever fled.

VII.

"Awake thy last sad voice, my harp! The voice of woe and wild despair; Awake! resound thy latest lay- Then sleep in silence evermair! And thou, my last, best, only friend, That fillest an untimely tomb, Accept this tribute from the bard Though brought from fortune's mirkest gloom.

VIII.

"In poverty's low barren vale Thick mists, obscure, involve me round; Though oft I turn'd the wistful eye, Nae ray of fame was to be found: Thou found'st me, like the morning sun, That melts the fogs in limpid air, The friendless bard and rustic song Became alike thy fostering care.

IX.

"O! why has worth so short a date? While villains ripen fray with time; Must thou, the noble, gen'rous, great, Fall in bold manhood's hardy prime! Why did I live to see that day? A day to me so full of woe!- O had I met the mortal shaft Which laid my benefactor low.

X.

"The bridegroom may forget the bride Was made his wedded wife yestreen; The monarch may forget the crown That on his head an hour has been; The mother may forget the child That smiles sae sweetly on her knee; But I'll remember thee, Glencairn, And a' that thou hast done for me!"

CHAPTER CXXV.

LINES SENT TO SIR JOHN WHITEFOORD, BART. OF WHITEFOORD WITH THE FOREGOING POEM.

[Sir John Whitefoord, a name of old standing in Ayrshire, inherited the love of his family for literature, and interested himself early in the fame and fortunes of Burns.]

Thou, who thy honour as thy God rever'st, Who, save thy mind's reproach, nought earthly fear'st, To thee this votive offering I impart, The tearful tribute of a broken heart. The friend thou valuedst, I, the patron, lov'd; His worth, his honour, all the world approv'd, We'll mourn till we too go as he has gone, And tread the dreary path to that dark world unknown.

CHAPTER CXXVI.

ADDRESS TO THE SHADE OF THOMSON, ON CROWNING HIS BUST AT EDNAM WITH BAYS.

["Lord Buchan has the pleasure to invite Mr. Burns to make one at the coronation of the bust of Thomson, on Ednam Hill, on the 22d of September: for which day perhaps his muse may inspire an ode suited to the occasion. Suppose Mr. Burns should, leaving the Nith, go across the country, and meet the Tweed at the nearest point from his farm, and, wandering along the pastoral banks of Thomson's pure parent stream, catch inspiration in the devious walk, till he finds Lord Buchan sitting on the ruins of Dryburgh. There the Commendator will give him a hearty welcome, and try to light his lamp at the pure flame of native genius, upon the altar of Caledonian virtue." Such was the invitation of the Earl of Buchan to Burns. To request the poet to lay down his sickle when his harvest was half reaped, and traverse[180] one of the wildest and most untrodden ways in Scotland, for the purpose of looking at the fantastic coronation of the bad bust of on excellent poet, was worthy of Lord Buchan. The poor bard made answer, that a week's absence in the middle of his harvest was a step he durst not venture upon-but he sent this Poem. The poet's manuscript affords the following interesting variations:-

"While cold-eyed Spring, a virgin coy, Unfolds her verdant mantle sweet, Or pranks the sod in frolic joy, A carpet for her youthful feet:

"While Summer, with a matron's grace, Walks stately in the cooling shade, And oft delighted loves to trace The progress of the spiky blade:

"While Autumn, benefactor kind, With age's hoary honours clad, Surveys, with self-approving mind, Each creature on his bounty fed."]

While virgin Spring, by Eden's flood, Unfolds her tender mantle green, Or pranks the sod in frolic mood, Or tunes Æolian strains between:

While Summer, with a matron grace, Retreats to Dryburgh's cooling shade, Yet oft, delighted, stops to trace The progress of the spiky blade:

While Autumn, benefactor kind, By Tweed erects his aged head, And sees, with self-approving mind, Each creature on his bounty fed:

While maniac Winter rages o'er The hills whence classic Yarrow flows, Rousing the turbid torrent's roar, Or sweeping, wild, a waste of snows:

So long, sweet Poet of the year! Shall bloom that wreath thou well hast won; While Scotia, with exulting tear, Proclaims that Thomson was her son.

CHAPTER CXXVII.

TO ROBERT GRAHAM, ESQ., OF FINTRAY.

[By this Poem Burns prepared the way for his humble request to be removed to a district more moderate in its bounds than one which extended over ten country parishes, and exposed him both to fatigue and expense. This wish was expressed in prose, and was in due time attended to, for Fintray was a gentleman at once kind and considerate.]

Late crippl'd of an arm, and now a leg, About to beg a pass for leave to beg: Dull, listless, teas'd, dejected, and deprest, (Nature is adverse to a cripple's rest;) Will generous Graham list to his Poet's wail? (It soothes poor misery, hearkening to her tale,) And hear him curse the light he first survey'd, And doubly curse the luckless rhyming trade?

Thou, Nature, partial Nature! I arraign; Of thy caprice maternal I complain: The lion and the bull thy care have found, One shakes the forests, and one spurns the ground: Thou giv'st the ass his hide, the snail his shell, Th' envenom'd wasp, victorious, guards his cell; Thy minions, kings, defend, control, devour, In all th' omnipotence of rule and power; Foxes and statesmen, subtile wiles insure; The cit and polecat stink, and are secure; Toads with their poison, doctors with their drug, The priest and hedgehog in their robes are snug; Ev'n silly woman has her warlike arts, Her tongue and eyes, her dreaded spear and darts;- But, oh! thou bitter stepmother and hard, To thy poor fenceless, naked child-the Bard! A thing unteachable in world's skill, And half an idiot too, more helpless still; No heels to bear him from the op'ning dun; No claws to dig, his hated sight to shun; No horns, but those by luckless Hymen worn, And those, alas! not Amalthea's horn: No nerves olfact'ry, Mammon's trusty cur, Clad in rich dullness' comfortable fur;- In naked feeling, and in aching pride, He bears the unbroken blast from every side. Vampyre booksellers drain him to the heart, And scorpion critics cureless venom dart.

Critics!-appall'd I venture on the name, Those cut-throat bandits in the paths of fame. Bloody dissectors, worse than ten Monroes! He hacks to teach, they mangle to expose.

His heart by causeless wanton malice wrung, By blockheads' daring into madness stung; His well-won bays, than life itself more dear, By miscreants torn, who ne'er one sprig must wear: [181]Foil'd, bleeding, tortur'd, in the unequal strife, The hapless poet flounders on through life; Till, fled each hope that once his bosom fir'd, And fled each muse that glorious once inspir'd, Low sunk in squalid, unprotected age, Dead, even resentment, for his injur'd page, He heeds or feels no more the ruthless critic's rage!

So, by some hedge, the gen'rous steed deceas'd, For half-starv'd snarling curs a dainty feast: By toil and famine wore to skin and bone, Lies senseless of each tugging bitch's son.

O dullness! portion of the truly blest! Calm sheltered haven of eternal rest! Thy sons ne'er madden in the fierce extremes Of fortune's polar frost, or torrid beams. If mantling high she fills the golden cup, With sober selfish ease they sip it up; Conscious the bounteous meed they well deserve, They only wonder "some folks" do not starve. The grave sage hern thus easy picks his frog, And thinks the mallard a sad worthless dog. When disappointment snaps the clue of hope, And thro' disastrous night they darkling grope, With deaf endurance sluggishly they bear, And just conclude that "fools are fortune's care." So, heavy, passive to the tempest's shocks, Strong on the sign-post stands the stupid ox.

Not so the idle muses' mad-cap train, Not such the workings of their moon-struck brain; In equanimity they never dwell, By turns in soaring heav'n or vaulted hell I dread thee, fate, relentless and severe, With all a poet's, husband's, father's fear! Already one strong hold of hope is lost, Glencairn, the truly noble, lies in dust; (Fled, like the sun eclips'd as noon appears, And left us darkling in a world of tears:) O! hear my ardent, grateful, selfish pray'r!- Fintray, my other stay, long bless and spare! Thro' a long life his hopes and wishes crown; And bright in cloudless skies his sun go down! May bliss domestic smooth his private path; Give energy to life; and soothe his latest breath, With many a filial tear circling the bed of death!

CHAPTER CXXVIII.

TO ROBERT GRAHAM, ESQ., OF FINTRAY.

ON RECEIVING A FAVOUR.

[Graham of Fintray not only obtained for the poet the appointment in Excise, which, while he lived in Edinburgh, he desired, but he also removed him, as he wished, to a better district; and when imputations were thrown out against his loyalty, he defended him with obstinate and successful eloquence. Fintray did all that was done to raise Burns out of the toiling humility of his condition, and enable him to serve the muse without fear of want.]

I call no goddess to inspire my strains, A fabled muse may suit a bard that feigns; Friend of my life! my ardent spirit burns, And all the tribute of my heart returns, For boons accorded, goodness ever new, The gift still dearer, as the giver, you.

Thou orb of day! thou other paler light! And all ye many sparkling stars of night; If aught that giver from my mind efface; If I that giver's bounty e'er disgrace; Then roll to me, along your wandering spheres, Only to number out a villain's years!

CHAPTER CXXIX.

A VISION.

[This Vision of Liberty descended on Burns among the magnificent ruins of the College of Lincluden, which stand on the junction of the Cluden and the Nith, a short mile above Dumfries. He gave us the Vision; perhaps, he dared not in those yeasty times venture on the song, which his secret visitant poured from her lips. The scene is chiefly copied from nature: the swellings of the Nith, the howling of the fox on the hill, and the cry of the owl, unite at times with the natural beauty of the spot, and give it life and voice. These ruins were a favourite haunt of the poet.]

As I stood by yon roofless tower, Where the wa'-flower scents the dewy air, Where th' howlet mourns in her ivy bower And tells the midnight moon her care;

The winds were laid, the air was still, The Stars they shot along the sky; The fox was howling on the hill, And the distant echoing glens reply. [182]

The stream, adown its hazelly path, Was rushing by the ruin'd wa's, Hasting to join the sweeping Nith,[109A] Whose distant roaring swells and fa's.

The cauld blue north was streaming forth Her lights, wi' hissing eerie din; Athort the lift they start and shift, Like fortune's favours, tint as win.

By heedless chance I turn'd mine eyes, And, by the moon-beam, shook to see A stern and stalwart ghaist arise, Attir'd as minstrels wont to be.[109B]

Had I a statue been o' stane, His darin' look had daunted me; And on his bonnet grav'd was plain, The sacred posy-'Libertie!'

And frae his harp sic strains did flow, Might rous'd the slumb'ring dead to hear; But, oh! it was a tale of woe, As ever met a Briton's ear.

He sang wi' joy the former day, He weeping wail'd his latter times; But what he said it was nae play,- I winna ventur't in my rhymes.

FOOTNOTES:

[109A]VARIATIONS

To join yon river on the Strath.

[109B]VARIATIONS

Now looking over firth and fauld, Her horn the pale-fac'd Cynthia rear'd; When, lo, in form of minstrel auld, A storm and stalwart ghaist appear'd.

CHAPTER CXXX.

TO JOHN MAXWELL OF TERRAUGHTY, ON HIS BIRTHDAY.

[John Maxwell of Terraughty and Munshes, to whom these verses are addressed, though descended from the Earls of Nithsdale, cared little about lineage, and claimed merit only from a judgment sound and clear-a knowledge of business which penetrated into all the concerns of life, and a skill in handling the most difficult subjects, which was considered unrivalled. Under an austere manner, he hid much kindness of heart, and was in a fair way of doing an act of gentleness when giving a refusal. He loved to meet Burns: not that he either cared for or comprehended poetry; but he was pleased with his knowledge of human nature, and with the keen and piercing remarks in which he indulged. He was seventy-one years old when these verses were written, and survived the poet twenty years.]

Health to the Maxwell's vet'ran chief! Health, ay unsour'd by care or grief: Inspir'd, I turn'd Fate's sybil leaf This natal morn; I see thy life is stuff o' prief, Scarce quite half worn.

This day thou metes three score eleven, And I can tell that bounteous Heaven (The second sight, ye ken, is given To ilka Poet) On thee a tack o' seven times seven Will yet bestow it.

If envious buckies view wi' sorrow Thy lengthen'd days on this blest morrow, May desolation's lang teeth'd harrow, Nine miles an hour, Rake them like Sodom and Gomorrah, In brunstane stoure-

But for thy friends, and they are mony, Baith honest men and lasses bonnie, May couthie fortune, kind and cannie, In social glee, Wi' mornings blythe and e'enings funny Bless them and thee!

Fareweel, auld birkie! Lord be near ye, And then the Deil he daur na steer ye; Your friends ay love, your faes ay fear ye; For me, shame fa' me, If neist my heart I dinna wear ye While Burns they ca' me!

Dumfries, 18 Feb. 1792.

CHAPTER CXXXI.

THE RIGHTS OF WOMAN.

AN OCCASIONAL ADDRESS SPOKEN BY MISS FONTENELLE ON HER BENEFIT NIGHT,

Nov. 26, 1792.

[Miss Fontenelle was one of the actresses whom Williamson, the manager, brought for several seasons to Dumfries: she was young and pretty, indulged in little levities of speech, and rumour added, perhaps maliciously, levities of action. The Rights of Man had been advocated by Paine, the Rights of Woman by Mary Wol[183]stonecroft, and nought was talked of, but the moral and political regeneration of the world. The line

"But truce with kings and truce with constitutions,"

got an uncivil twist in recitation, from some of the audience. The words were eagerly caught up, and had some hisses bestowed on them.]

While Europe's eye is fix'd on mighty things, The fate of empires and the fall of kings; While quacks of state must each produce his plan, And even children lisp the Rights of Man; Amid this mighty fuss just let me mention, The Rights of Woman merit some attention.

First on the sexes' intermix'd connexion, One sacred Right of Woman is protection. The tender flower that lifts its head, elate, Helpless, must fall before the blasts of fate, Sunk on the earth, defac'd its lovely form, Unless your shelter ward th' impending storm.

Our second Right-but needless here is caution, To keep that right inviolate's the fashion, Each man of sense has it so full before him, He'd die before he'd wrong it-'tis decorum.- There was, indeed, in far less polish'd days, A time, when rough, rude man had haughty ways; Would swagger, swear, get drunk, kick up a riot, Nay, even thus invade a lady's quiet.

Now, thank our stars! these Gothic times are fled; Now, well-bred men-and you are all well-bred- Most justly think (and we are much the gainers) Such conduct neither spirit, wit, nor manners.

For Right the third, our last, our best, our dearest, That right to fluttering female hearts the nearest, Which even the Rights of Kings in low prostration Most humbly own-'tis dear, dear admiration! In that blest sphere alone we live and move; There taste that life of life-immortal love.- Smiles, glances, sighs, tears, fits, flirtations, airs, 'Gainst such an host what flinty savage dares- When awful Beauty joins with all her charms, Who is so rash as rise in rebel arms?

But truce with kings and truce with constitutions, With bloody armaments and revolutions, Let majesty your first attention summon, Ah! ça ira! the majesty of woman!

CHAPTER CXXXII.

MONODY, ON A LADY FAMED FOR HER CAPRICE.

[The heroine Of this rough lampoon was Mrs. Riddel of Woodleigh Park: a lady young and gay, much of a wit, and something of a poetess, and till the hour of his death the friend of Burns himself. She pulled his displeasure on her, it is said, by smiling more sweetly than he liked on some "epauletted coxcombs," for so he sometimes designated commissioned officers: the lady soon laughed him out of his mood. We owe to her pen an account of her last interview with the poet, written with great beauty and feeling.]

How cold is that bosom which folly once fired, How pale is that cheek where the rouge lately glisten'd! How silent that tongue which the echoes oft tired, How dull is that ear which to flattery so listen'd!

If sorrow and anguish their exit await, From friendship and dearest affection remov'd; How doubly severer, Maria, thy fate, Thou diest unwept as thou livedst unlov'd.

Loves, Graces, and Virtues, I call not on you; So shy, grave, and distant, ye shed not a tear: But come, all ye offspring of Folly so true, And flowers let us cull for Maria's cold bier.

We'll search through the garden for each silly flower, We'll roam through the forest for each idle weed; But chiefly the nettle, so typical, shower, For none e'er approach'd her but rued the rash deed.

We'll sculpture the marble, we'll measure the lay; Here Vanity strums on her idiot lyre; There keen indignation shall dart on her prey, Which spurning Contempt shall redeem from his ire.

THE EPITAPH.

Here lies, now a prey to insulting neglect, What once was a butterfly, gay in life's beam: Want only of wisdom denied her respect, Want only of goodness denied her esteem

CHAPTER CXXXIII.

EPISTLE FROM ESOPUS TO MARIA.

[Williamson, the actor, Colonel Macdouall, Captain Gillespie, and Mrs. Riddel, are the characters which pass over the stage in this strange composition: it is printed from the Poet's own manuscript, and seems a sort of outpouring of wrath and contempt, on persons who, in his eyes, gave themselves airs beyond their condition, or their merits. The verse of the

lady is held up to contempt and laughter: the satirist celebrates her
"Motley foundling fancies, stolen or strayed;"
and has a passing hit at her
"Still matchless tongue that conquers all reply."]

From those drear solitudes and frowsy cells, Where infamy with sad repentance dwells; Where turnkeys make the jealous portal fast, And deal from iron hands the spare repast; Where truant 'prentices, yet young in sin, Blush at the curious stranger peeping in; Where strumpets, relics of the drunken roar, Resolve to drink, nay, half to whore, no more; Where tiny thieves not destin'd yet to swing, Beat hemp for others, riper for the string: From these dire scenes my wretched lines I date, To tell Maria her Esopus' fate.

"Alas! I feel I am no actor here!" 'Tis real hangmen, real scourges bear! Prepare, Maria, for a horrid tale Will turn thy very rouge to deadly pale; Will make they hair, tho' erst from gipsy polled, By barber woven, and by barber sold, Though twisted smooth with Harry's nicest care, Like hoary bristles to erect and stare. The hero of the mimic scene, no more I start in Hamlet, in Othello roar; Or haughty Chieftain, 'mid the din of arms, In Highland bonnet woo Malvina's charms; While sans culottes stoop up the mountain high, And steal from me Maria's prying eye. Blest Highland bonnet! Once my proudest dress, Now prouder still, Maria's temples press. I see her wave thy towering plumes afar, And call each coxcomb to the wordy war. I see her face the first of Ireland's sons,[110] And even out-Irish his Hibernian bronze; The crafty colonel[111] leaves the tartan'd lines, For other wars, where he a hero shines; The hopeful youth, in Scottish senate bred, Who owns a Bushby's heart without the head; Comes, 'mid a string of coxcombs to display That veni, vidi, vici, is his way; The shrinking bard adown the alley skulks, And dreads a meeting worse than Woolwich hulks; Though there, his heresies in church and state Might well award him Muir and Palmer's fate: Still she undaunted reels and rattles on, And dares the public like a noontide sun. (What scandal call'd Maria's janty stagger The ricket reeling of a crooked swagger, Whose spleen e'en worse than Burns' venom when He dips in gall unmix'd his eager pen,- And pours his vengeance in the burning line, Who christen'd thus Maria's lyre divine; The idiot strum of vanity bemused, And even th' abuse of poesy abused! Who call'd her verse, a parish workhouse made For motley foundling fancies, stolen or stray'd?)

A workhouse! ah, that sound awakes my woes, And pillows on the thorn my rack'd repose! In durance vile here must I wake and weep, And all my frowsy couch in sorrow steep; That straw where many a rogue has lain of yore, And vermin'd gipsies litter'd heretofore.

Why, Lonsdale, thus thy wrath on vagrants pour? Must earth no rascal save thyself endure? Must thou alone in guilt immortal swell, And make a vast monopoly of hell? Thou know'st, the virtues cannot hate thee worse, The vices also, must they club their curse? Or must no tiny sin to others fall, Because thy guilt's supreme enough for all?

Maria, send me too thy griefs and cares; In all of thee sure thy Esopus shares. As thou at all mankind the flag unfurls, Who on my fair one satire's vengeance hurls? Who calls thee, pert, affected, vain coquette, A wit in folly, and a fool in wit? Who says, that fool alone is not thy due, And quotes thy treacheries to prove it true? Our force united on thy foes we'll turn, And dare the war with all of woman born: For who can write and speak as thou and I? My periods that deciphering defy, And thy still matchless tongue that conquers all reply.

FOOTNOTES:

[110] Captain Gillespie.

[111] Col. Macdouall.

CHAPTER CXXXIV.

POEM ON PASTORAL POETRY.

[Though Gilbert Burns says there is some doubt of this Poem being by his brother, and though Robert Chambers declares that he "has scarcely a doubt that it is not by the Ayrshire Bard," I must print it as his, for I have no doubt on the subject. It was found among the papers of the poet, in his own handwriting: the second, the fourth, and the concluding verses bear the Burns' stamp, which no one has been successful in counterfeiting: they resemble the verses of Beattie, to which Chambers has compared them, as little as the cry of the eagle resembles the chirp of the wren.]

Hail Poesie! thou Nymph reserv'd! In chase o' thee, what crowds hae swerv'd Frae common sense, or sunk enerv'd 'Mang heaps o' clavers; And och! o'er aft thy joes hae starv'd Mid a' thy favours!

Say, Lassie, why thy train amang, While loud the trump's heroic clang, And sock or buskin skelp alang, To death or marriage; Scarce ane has tried the shepherd-sang But wi' miscarriage?

In Homer's craft Jock Milton thrives; Eschylus' pen Will Shakspeare drives; Wee Pope, the knurlin, 'till him rives Horatian fame; In thy sweet sang, Barbauld, survives Even Sappho's flame.

But thee, Theocritus, wha matches? They're no herd's ballats, Maro's catches; Squire Pope but busks his skinklin patches O' heathen tatters; I pass by hunders, nameless wretches, That ape their betters.

In this braw age o' wit and lear, Will nane the Shepherd's whistle mair Blaw sweetly in its native air And rural grace; And wi' the far-fam'd Grecian share A rival place?

Yes! there is ane; a Scottish callan- There's ane; come forrit, honest Allan! Thou need na jouk behint the hallan, A chiel sae clever; The teeth o' time may gnaw Tantallan, But thou's for ever!

Thou paints auld nature to the nines, In thy sweet Caledonian lines; Nae gowden stream thro' myrtles twines, Where Philomel, While nightly breezes sweep the vines, Her griefs will tell!

In gowany glens thy burnie strays, Where bonnie lasses bleach their claes; Or trots by hazelly shaws and braes, Wi' hawthorns gray, Where blackbirds join the shepherd's lays At close o' day.

Thy rural loves are nature's sel'; Nae bombast spates o' nonsense swell; Nae snap conceits, but that sweet spell O' witchin' love; That charm that can the strongest quell, The sternest move.

CHAPTER CXXXV.

SONNET,

WRITTEN ON THE TWENTY-FIFTH OF JANUARY, 1793,

THE BIRTHDAY OF THE AUTHOR, ON HEARING A

THRUSH SING IN A MORNING WALK.

[Burns was fond of a saunter in a leafless wood, when the winter storm howled among the branches. These characteristic lines were composed on the morning of his birthday, with the Nith at his feet, and the ruins of Lincluden at his side: he is willing to accept the unlooked-for song of the thrush as a fortunate omen.]

Sing on, sweet thrush, upon the leafless bough, Sing on, sweet bird, I listen to thy strain: See, aged Winter, 'mid his surly reign, At thy blythe carol clears his furrow'd brow.

So, in lone Poverty's dominion drear, Sits meek Content with light unanxious heart, Welcomes the rapid moments, bids them part, Nor asks if they bring aught to hope or fear.

I thank Thee, Author of this opening day! Thou whose bright sun now gilds yon orient skies! Riches denied, Thy boon was purer joys, What wealth could never give nor take away.

Yet come, thou child of poverty and care, The mite high Heaven bestow'd, that mite with thee I'll share.

CHAPTER CXXXVI.

SONNET, ON THE DEATH OF ROBERT RIDDEL, ESQ. OF GLENRIDDEL, April, 1794.

[The death of Glencairn, who was his patron, and the death of Glenriddel, who was his friend, and had, while he lived at Ellisland, been his neighbor, weighed hard on the mind of Burns, who, about this time, began to regard his own future fortune with more of dismay than of hope. Riddel united antiquarian pursuits with those of literature, and experienced all the vulgar prejudices entertained by the peasantry against those who indulge in such researches. His collection of what the rustics of the vale called "queer quairns and swine-troughs," is now scattered or neglected: I have heard a competent judge say, that they threw light on both the public and domestic history of Scotland.]

No more, ye warblers of the wood-no more! Nor pour your descant, grating, on my soul; Thou young-eyed Spring, gay in thy verdant stole,

More welcome were to me grim Winter's wildest roar.
How can ye charm, ye flow'rs, with all your dyes? Ye blow upon the sod that wraps my friend: How can I to the tuneful strain attend? That strain flows round th' untimely tomb where Riddel lies.
Yes, pour, ye warblers, pour the notes of woe! And soothe the Virtues weeping on this bier: The Man of Worth, who has not left his peer, Is in his "narrow house" for ever darkly low.
Thee, Spring, again with joy shall others greet, Me, mem'ry of my loss will only meet.

CHAPTER CXXXVII.

IMPROMPTU, ON MRS. R'S BIRTHDAY.

[By compliments such as these lines contain, Burns soothed the smart which his verses "On a lady famed for her caprice" inflicted on the accomplished Mrs. Riddel.]
Old Winter, with his frosty beard, Thus once to Jove his prayer preferr'd,- What have I done of all the year, To bear this hated doom severe? My cheerless suns no pleasure know; Night's horrid car drags, dreary, slow: My dismal months no joys are crowning, But spleeny English, hanging, drowning.
Now, Jove, for once be mighty civil, To counterbalance all this evil; Give me, and I've no more to say, Give me Maria's natal day! That brilliant gift shall so enrich me, Spring, Summer, Autumn, cannot match me; 'Tis done! says Jove; so ends my story, And Winter once rejoiced in glory.

CHAPTER CXXXVIII.

LIBERTY. A FRAGMENT.

[Fragment of verse were numerous, Dr. Currie said, among the loose papers of the poet. These lines formed the commencement of an ode commemorating the achievement of liberty for America under the directing genius of Washington and Franklin.]
Thee, Caledonia, thy wild heaths among, Thee, fam'd for martial deed and sacred song, To thee I turn with swimming eyes; Where is that soul of freedom fled? Immingled with the mighty dead! Beneath the hallow'd turf where Wallace lies! Hear it not, Wallace, in thy bed of death! Ye babbling winds, in silence sweep; Disturb not ye the hero's sleep, Nor give the coward secret breath. Is this the power in freedom's war, That wont to bid the battle rage? Behold that eye which shot immortal hate, Crushing the despot's proudest bearing!

CHAPTER CXXXIX.

VERSES TO A YOUNG LADY.

[This young lady was the daughter of the poet's friend, Graham of Fintray; and the gift alluded to was a copy of George Thomson's Select Scottish Songs: a work which owes many attractions to the lyric genius of Burns.]
Here, where the Scottish muse immortal lives, In sacred strains and tuneful

numbers join'd, Accept the gift;-tho' humble he who gives, Rich is the tribute of the grateful mind.

So may no ruffian feeling in thy breast, Discordant jar thy bosom-chords among; But peace attune thy gentle soul to rest, Or love ecstatic wake his seraph song.

Or pity's notes in luxury of tears, As modest want the tale of woe reveals; While conscious virtue all the strain endears, And heaven-born piety her sanction seals.

CHAPTER CXL.

THE VOWELS.

A TALE.

[Burns admired genius adorned by learning; but mere learning without genius he always regarded as pedantry. Those critics who scrupled too much about words he called eunuchs of literature, and to one, who taxed him with writing obscure language in questionable grammar, he said, "Thou art but a Gretna-green match-maker between vowels and consonants!"]

'Twas where the birch and sounding thong are ply'd, The noisy domicile of pedant pride; Where ignorance her darkening vapour throws, And cruelty directs the thickening blows; upon a time, Sir Abece the great, In all his pedagogic powers elate, His awful chair of state resolves to mount, And call the trembling vowels to account.-

First enter'd A, a grave, broad, solemn wight, But, ah! deform'd, dishonest to the sight! His twisted head look'd backward on the way, And flagrant from the scourge he grunted, ai!

Reluctant, E stalk'd in; with piteous race The justling tears ran down his honest face! That name! that well-worn name, and all his own, Pale he surrenders at the tyrant's throne! The pedant stifles keen the Roman sound Not all his mongrel diphthongs can compound; And next the title following close behind, He to the nameless, ghastly wretch assign'd.

The cobweb'd gothic dome resounded Y! In sullen vengeance, I, disdain'd reply: The pedant swung his felon cudgel round, And knock'd the groaning vowel to the ground!

In rueful apprehension enter'd O, The wailing minstrel of despairing woe; Th' Inquisitor of Spain the most expert Might there have learnt new mysteries of his art; So grim, deform'd, with horrors entering U, His dearest friend and brother scarcely knew!

As trembling U stood staring all aghast, The pedant in his left hand clutched him fast, In helpless infants' tears he dipp'd his right, Baptiz'd him eu, and kick'd him from his sight.

CHAPTER CXLI.

VERSES TO JOHN RANKINE.

[With the "rough, rude, ready-witted Rankine," of Adamhill, in Ayrshire, Burns kept up a will o'-wispish sort of a correspondence in rhyme, till the day of his death: these communications, of which this is one, were sometimes graceless, but always witty. It is supposed, that those lines were suggested by Falstaff's account of his ragged recruits:-

"I'll not march through Coventry with them, that's flat!"]

Ae day, as Death, that grusome carl, Was driving to the tither warl' A mixtie-maxtie motley squad, And mony a guilt-bespotted lad; Black gowns of each denomination, And thieves of every rank and station, From him that wears the star and garter, To him that wintles in a halter: Asham'd himsel' to see the wretches, He mutters, glowrin' at the bitches, "By G-d, I'll not be seen behint them, Nor 'mang the sp'ritual core present them, Without, at least, ae honest man, To grace this d-d infernal clan." By Adamhill a glance he threw, "L-d G-d!" quoth he, "I have it now, There's just the man I want, i' faith!" And quickly stoppit Rankine's breath.

CHAPTER CXLII.

ON SENSIBILITY.

TO MY DEAR AND MUCH HONOURED FRIEND, MRS. DUNLOP, OF DUNLOP.

[These verses were occasioned, it is said, by some sentiments contained in a communication from Mrs. Dunlop. That excellent lady was sorely tried with domestic afflictions for a time, and to these he appears to allude; but he deadened the effect of his sympathy, when he printed the stanzas in the Museum, changing the fourth line to,

"Dearest Nancy, thou canst tell!"

and so transferring the whole to another heroine.]

Sensibility how charming, Thou, my friend, canst truly tell: But distress with horrors arming, Thou host also known too well.

Fairest flower, behold the lily, Blooming in the sunny ray: Let the blast sweep o'er the valley, See it prostrate on the clay.

Hear the woodlark charm the forest, Telling o'er his little joys: Hapless bird! a prey the surest, To each pirate of the skies.

Dearly bought, the hidden treasure, Finer feeling can bestow; Chords that vibrate sweetest pleasure, Thrill the deepest notes of woe.

CHAPTER CXLIII.

LINES, SENT TO A GENTLEMAN WHOM HE HAD OFFENDED.

[The too hospitable board of Mrs. Riddel occasioned these repentant strains: they were accepted as they were meant by the party. The poet had, it seems, not only spoken of mere titles and rank with disrespect, but had allowed his tongue unbridled license of speech, on the claim of political importance, and domestic equality, which Mary Wolstonecroft and her followers patronized, at which Mrs. Riddel affected to be grievously offended.]

The friend whom wild from wisdom's way, The fumes of wine infuriate send; (Not moony madness more astray;) Who but deplores that hapless

friend?
Mine was th' insensate frenzied part, Ah, why should I such scenes outlive Scenes so abhorrent to my heart! 'Tis thine to pity and forgive.

CHAPTER CXLIV.

ADDRESS, SPOKEN BY MISS FONTENELLE ON HER BENEFIT NIGHT.

[This address was spoken by Miss Fontenelle, at the Dumfries theatre, on the 4th of December, 1795.]

Still anxious to secure your partial favour, And not less anxious, sure, this night than ever, A Prologue, Epilogue, or some such matter, 'Twould vamp my bill, said I, if nothing better; So sought a Poet, roosted near the skies, Told him I came to feast my curious eyes; Said nothing like his works was ever printed; And last, my Prologue-business slyly hinted! "Ma'am, let me tell you," quoth my man of rhymes, "I know your bent-these are no laughing times: Can you-but, Miss, I own I have my fears, Dissolve in pause-and sentimental tears; With laden sighs, and solemn-rounded sentence, Rouse from his sluggish slumbers, fell Repentance; Paint Vengeance as he takes his horrid stand, Waving on high the desolating brand, Calling the storms to bear him o'er a guilty land?"

I could no more-askance the creature eyeing, D'ye think, said I, this face was made for crying? I'll laugh, that's poz-nay more, the world shall know it; And so your servant: gloomy Master Poet! Firm as my creed, Sirs, 'tis my fix'd belief, That Misery's another word for Grief; I also think-so may I be a bride! That so much laughter, so much life enjoy'd.

Thou man of crazy care and ceaseless sigh, Still under bleak Misfortune's blasting eye; Doom'd to that sorest task of man alive- To make three guineas do the work of five: [189]Laugh in Misfortune's face-the beldam witch! Say, you'll be merry, tho' you can't be rich.

Thou other man of care, the wretch in love, Who long with jiltish arts and airs hast strove; Who, us the boughs all temptingly project, Measur'st in desperate thought-a rope-thy neck- Or, where the beetling cliff o'erhangs the deep, Peerest to meditate the healing leap: Would'st thou be cur'd, thou silly, moping elf? Laugh at their follies-laugh e'en at thyself: Learn to despise those frowns now so terrific, And love a kinder-that's your grand specific.

To sum up all, be merry, I advise; And as we're merry, may we still be wise.

CHAPTER CXLV.

ON SEEING MISS FONTENELLE IN A FAVOURITE CHARACTER.

[The good looks and the natural acting of Miss Fontenelle pleased others as well as Burns. I know not to what character in the range of her personations he alludes: she was a favourite on the Dumfries boards.]

Sweet naiveté of feature, Simple, wild, enchanting elf, Not to thee, but thanks to nature, Thou art acting but thyself.

Wert thou awkward, stiff, affected, Spurning nature, torturing art; Loves and graces all rejected, Then indeed thou'dst act a part.

R. B.

CHAPTER CXLVI.

TO CHLORIS.

[Chloris was a Nithsdale beauty. Love and sorrow were strongly mingled in her early history: that she did not look so lovely in other eyes as she did in those of Burns is well known: but he had much of the taste of an artist, and admired the elegance of her form, and the harmony of her motion, as much as he did her blooming face and sweet voice.]

'Tis Friendship's pledge, my young, fair friend, Nor thou the gift refuse, Nor with unwilling ear attend The moralizing muse.

Since thou in all thy youth and charms, Must bid the world adieu, (A world 'gainst peace in constant arms) To join the friendly few.

Since, thy gay morn of life o'ercast, Chill came the tempest's lower; (And ne'er misfortune's eastern blast Did nip a fairer flower.)

Since life's gay scenes must charm no more, Still much is left behind; Still nobler wealth hast thou in store- The comforts of the mind!

Thine is the self-approving glow, On conscious honour's part; And, dearest gift of heaven below, Thine friendship's truest heart.

The joys refin'd of sense and taste, With every muse to rove: And doubly were the poet blest, These joys could he improve.

CHAPTERCXLVII.

POETICAL INSCRIPTION FOR AN ALTAR TO INDEPENDENCE.

[It was the fashion of the feverish times of the French Revolution to plant trees of Liberty, and raise altars to Independence. Heron of Kerroughtree, a gentleman widely esteemed in Galloway, was about to engage in an election contest, and these noble lines served the purpose of announcing the candidate's sentiments on freedom.]

Thou of an independent mind, With soul resolv'd, with soul resign'd; Prepar'd Power's proudest frown to brave, Who wilt not be, nor have a slave; Virtue alone who dost revere, Thy own reproach alone dost fear, Approach this shrine, and worship here.

CHAPTER CXLVIII.

THE HERON BALLADS.

[BALLAD FIRST.]

[This is the first of several party ballads which Burns wrote to serve Patrick Heron, of Kerroughtree, in two elections for the Stewartry of Kirkcudbright, in which he was opposed, first, by Gordon of Balmaghie, and secondly, by the Hon. Montgomery Stewart. There is a personal bitterness in these lampoons, which did not mingle with the strains in which the poet recorded the contest between Miller and Johnstone. They are printed here as matters of poetry, and I feel sure that none will be displeased, and some will smile.]

I.

Whom will you send to London town, To Parliament and a' that? Or wha in a' the country round The best deserves to fa' that? For a' that, and a' that; Thro Galloway and a' that; Where is the laird or belted knight That best deserves to fa' that?

II.

Wha sees Kerroughtree's open yett, And wha is't never saw that? Wha ever wi' Kerroughtree meets And has a doubt of a' that? For a' that, and a' that, Here's Heron yet for a' that, The independent patriot, The honest man, an' a' that.

III.

Tho' wit and worth in either sex, St. Mary's Isle can shaw that; Wi' dukes and lords let Selkirk mix, And weel does Selkirk fa' that. For a' that, and a' that, Here's Heron yet for a' that! The independent commoner Shall be the man for a' that.

IV.

But why should we to nobles jouk, And it's against the law that; For why, a lord may be a gouk, Wi' ribbon, star, an' a' that. For a' that, an' a' that, Here's Heron yet for a' that! A lord may be a lousy loun, Wi' ribbon, star, an' a' that.

V.

A beardless boy comes o'er the hills, Wi' uncle's purse an' a' that; But we'll hae ane frae 'mang oursels, A man we ken, an' a' that. For a' that, an' a' that, Here's Heron yet for a' that! For we're not to be bought an' sold Like naigs, an' nowt, an' a' that.

VI.

Then let us drink the Stewartry, Kerroughtree's laird, an' a' that, Our representative to be, For weel he's worthy a' that. For a' that, an' a' that, Here's Heron yet for a' that, A House of Commons such as he, They would be blest that saw that.

CHAPTERCXLIX.

THE HERON BALLADS.

[BALLAD SECOND.]

[In this ballad the poet gathers together, after the manner of "Fy! let us a' to the bridal," all the leading electors of the Stewartry, who befriended Heron, or opposed him; and draws their portraits in the colours of light or darkness, according to the complexion of their politics. He is too severe in most instances, and in some he is venomous. On the Earl of Galloway's family, and on the Murrays of Broughton and Caillie, as well as on Bushby of Tinwaldowns, he pours his hottest satire. But words which are unjust, or undeserved, fall off their victims like rain-drops from a wild-duck's wing. The Murrays of Broughton and Caillie have long borne, from the vulgar, the stigma of treachery to the cause of Prince Charles Stewart: from such infamy the family is wholly free: the traitor, Murray, was of a race now extinct; and while he was betraying the cause in which so much noble and gallant blood was shed, Murray of Broughton and Caillie was performing the duties of an honourable and loyal man: he was, like his great-grandson now, representing his native district in parliament.]

THE ELECTION.

I.

Fy, let us a' to Kirkcudbright, For there will be bickerin' there; For Murray's[112] light horse are to muster, And O, how the heroes will swear! [191]An' there will be Murray commander, And Gordon[113] the battle to win; Like brothers they'll stand by each other, Sae knit in alliance an' kin.

II.

An' there will be black-lippit Johnnie,[114] The tongue o' the trump to them a'; And he get na hell for his haddin' The deil gets na justice ava'; And there will Kempleton's birkie, A boy no sae black at the bane, But, as for his fine nabob fortune, We'll e'en let the subject alane.

III.

An' there will be Wigton's new sheriff, Dame Justice fu' brawlie has sped, She's gotten the heart of a Bushby, But, Lord, what's become o' the head? An' there will be Cardoness,[115] Esquire, Sae mighty in Cardoness' eyes; A wight that will weather damnation, For the devil the prey will despise.

IV.

An' there will be Douglasses[116] doughty, New christ'ning towns far and near; Abjuring their democrat doings, By kissing theo' a peer; An' there will be Kenmure[117] sae gen'rous, Whose honour is proof to the storm, To save them from stark reprobation, He lent them his name to the firm.

V.

But we winna mention Redcastle,[118] The body, e'en let him escape! He'd venture the gallows for siller, An' 'twere na the cost o' the rape. An' where is our king's lord lieutenant, Sae fam'd for his gratefu' return? The billie is gettin' his questions, To say in St. Stephen's the morn.

VI.

An' there will be lads o' the gospel, Muirhead,[119] wha's as gude as he's true; An' there will be Buittle's[120] apostle, Wha's more o' the black than the blue; An' there will be folk from St. Mary's,[121] A house o' great merit and note, The deil ane but honours them highly,- The deil ane will gie them his vote!

VII.

An' there will be wealthy young Richard,[122] Dame Fortune should hing by the neck; For prodigal, thriftless, bestowing, His merit had won him respect: An' there will be rich brother nabobs, Tho' nabobs, yet men of the first, An' there will be Collieston's[123] whiskers, An' Quintin, o' lads not the worst.

VIII.

An' there will be stamp-office Johnnie,[124] Tak' tent how ye purchase a dram; An' there will be gay Cassencarrie, An' there will be gleg Colonel Tam; An' there will be trusty Kerroughtree,[125] Whose honour was ever his law, If the virtues were pack'd in a parcel, His worth might be sample for a'.

IX.

An' can we forget the auld major, Wha'll ne'er be forgot in the Greys, Our flatt'ry we'll keep for some other, Him only 'tis justice to praise. An' there will be maiden Kilkerran, And also Barskimming's gude knight, An' there will be roarin' Birtwhistle, Wha luckily roars in the right.

X.

An' there, frae the Niddisdale borders, Will mingle the Maxwells in droves; Teugh Johnnie, staunch Geordie, an' Walie, That griens for the fishes an' loaves; An' there will be Logan Mac Douall,[126] Sculdudd'ry an' he will be there, An' also the wild Scot of Galloway, Sodgerin', gunpowder Blair.

XI.

Then hey the chaste interest o' Broughton, An' hey for the blessings 'twill bring? It may send Balmaghie to the Commons, In Sodom 'twould make him a king; An' hey for the sanctified My, Our land who wi' chapels has stor'd; He founder'd his horse among harlots, But gied the auld naig to the Lord.

FOOTNOTES:

[112] Murray, of Broughton and Caillie.

[113] Gordon of Balmaghie.

[114] Bushby, of Tinwald-Downs.

[115] Maxwell, of Cardoness.

[116] The Douglasses, of Orchardtown and Castle-Douglas.

[117] Gordon, afterwards Viscount Kenmore.

[118] Laurie, of Redcastle.

[119] Morehead, Minister of Urr.

[120] The Minister of Buittle.

[121] Earl of Selkirk's family.

[122] Oswald, of Auchuncruive.

[123] Copland, of Collieston and Blackwood.

[124] John Syme, of the Stamp-office.

[125] Heron, of Kerroughtree.

[126] Colonel Macdouall, of Logan.

CHAPTERCL.

THE HERON BALLADS.

[BALLAD THIRD.]

[This third and last ballad was written on the contest between Heron and

Stewart, which followed close on that with Gordon. Heron carried the election, but was unseated by the decision of a Committee of the House of Commons: a decision which it is said he took so much to heart that it affected his health, and shortened his life.]

AN EXCELLENT NEW SONG.

Tune.-"Buy broom besoms."

Wha will buy my troggin, Fine election ware; Broken trade o' Broughton, A' in high repair. Buy braw troggin, Frae the banks o' Dee; Wha wants troggin Let him come to me.

There's a noble Earl's[127] Fame and high renown For an auld sang- It's thought the gudes were stown. Buy braw troggin, andc.

Here's the worth o' Broughton[128] In a needle's ee; Here's a reputation Tint by Balmaghie. Buy braw troggin, andc.

Here's an honest conscience Might a prince adorn; Frae the downs o' Tinwald-[129] So was never worn. Buy braw troggin, andc.

Here's its stuff and lining, Cardoness'[130] head; Fine for a sodger A' the wale o' lead. Buy braw troggin, andc.

Here's a little wadset Buittle's[131] scrap o' truth, Pawn'd in a gin-shop Quenching holy drouth. Buy braw troggin, andc.

Here's armorial bearings Frae the manse o' Urr;[132] The crest, an auld crab-apple Rotten at the core. Buy braw troggin, andc.

Here is Satan's picture, Like a bizzard gled, Pouncing poor Redcastle,[133] Sprawlin' as a taed. Buy braw troggin, andc.

Here's the worth and wisdom Collieston[134] can boast; By a thievish midge They had been nearly lost. Buy braw troggin, andc.

Here is Murray's fragments O' the ten commands; Gifted by black Jock[135] To get them aff his hands. Buy braw troggin, andc.

Saw ye e'er sic troggin? If to buy ye're slack, Hornie's turnin' chapman, He'll buy a' the pack. Buy braw troggin, Frae the banks o' Dee; Wha wants troggin Let him come to me.

FOOTNOTES:

[127] The Earl of Galloway.

[128] Murray, of Broughton and Caillie.

[129] Bushby, of Tinwald-downs.

[130] Maxwell, of Cardoness.

[131] The Minister of Buittle.

[132] Morehead, of Urr.

[133] Laurie, of Redcastle.

[134] Copland, of Collieston and Blackwood.

[135] John Bushby, of Tinwald-downs.

CHAPTER CLI.

POEM, ADDRESSED TO MR. MITCHELL, COLLECTOR OF EXCISE.

DUMFRIES, 1796.

[The gentlemen to whom this very modest, and, under the circumstances, most affecting application for his salary was made, filled the office of Collector of Excise for the district, and was of a kind and generous nature: but few were aware that the poet was suffering both from ill-health and poverty.]

Friend of the Poet, tried and leal, Wha, wanting thee, might beg or steal; Alake, alake, the meikle deil Wi' a' his witches Are at it, skelpin' jig and reel, In my poor pouches!

I modestly fu' fain wad hint it, That one pound one, I sairly want it, If wi' the hizzie down ye sent it, It would be kind; And while my heart wi' life-blood dunted I'd bear't in mind.

So may the auld year gang out moaning To see the new come laden, groaning, Wi' double plenty o'er the loanin To thee and thine; Domestic peace and comforts crowning The hale design.

POSTSCRIPT.

Ye've heard this while how I've been licket, And by felt death was nearly nicket; Grim loon! he got me by the fecket, And sair me sheuk; But by guid luck I lap a wicket, And turn'd a neuk.

But by that health, I've got a share o't, And by that life, I'm promised mair o't, My hale and weel I'll tak a care o't, A tentier way: Then farewell folly, hide and hair o't, For ance and aye!

CHAPTER CLII.

TO MISS JESSY LEWARS, DUMFRIES.

WITH JOHNSON'S 'MUSICAL MUSEUM.'

[Miss Jessy Lewars watched over the declining days of the poet, with the affectionate reverence of a daughter: for this she has the silent gratitude of all who admire the genius of Burns; she has received more, the thanks of the poet himself, expressed in verses not destined soon to die.]

Thine be the volumes, Jessy fair, And with them take the Poet's prayer; That fate may in her fairest page, With every kindliest, best presage Of future bliss, enrol thy name: With native worth and spotless fame, And wakeful caution still aware Of ill-but chief, man's felon snare; All blameless joys on earth we find, And all the treasures of the mind- These be thy guardian and reward; So prays thy faithful friend, The Bard.

June 26, 1796.

CHAPTER CLIII.

POEM ON LIFE, ADDRESSED TO COLONEL DE PEYSTER.

DUMFRIES, 1796.

[This is supposed to be the last Poem written by the hand, or conceived by the muse of Burns. The person to whom it is addressed was Colonel of the gentlemen Volunteers of Dumfries, in whose ranks Burns was a private: he was a Canadian by birth, and prided himself on having defended Detroit, against the united efforts of the French and Americans. He was rough and austere, and thought the science of war the noblest of all sciences: he affected a taste for literature, and wrote verses.]

My honoured colonel, deep I feel Your interest in the Poet's weal; Ah! now sma' heart hae I to speel The steep Parnassus, Surrounded thus by bolus, pill, And potion glasses.

O what a canty warld were it, Would pain and care and sickness spare it; And fortune favour worth and merit, As they deserve! (And aye a rowth, roast beef and claret; Syne, wha wad starve?) [194]

Dame Life, tho' fiction out may trick her, And in paste gems and frippery deck her; Oh! flickering, feeble, and unsicker I've found her still, Ay wavering like the willow-wicker, 'Tween good and ill.

Then that curst carmagnole, auld Satan, Watches, like baudrons by a rattan, Our sinfu' saul to get a claut on Wi' felon ire; Syne, whip! his tail ye'll ne'er cast saut on- He's aff like fire.

Ah Nick! ah Nick! it is na fair, First shewing us the tempting ware, Bright wines and bonnie lasses rare, To put us daft; Syne, weave, unseen, thy spider snare O' hell's damn'd waft.

Poor man, the flie, aft bizzes bye, And aft as chance he comes thee nigh, Thy auld danm'd elbow yeuks wi' joy, And hellish pleasure; Already in thy fancy's eye, Thy sicker treasure!

Soon heels-o'er gowdie! in he gangs, And like a sheep head on a tangs, Thy girning laugh enjoys his pangs And murd'ring wrestle, As, dangling in the wind, he hangs A gibbet's tassel.

But lest you think I am uncivil, To plague you with this draunting drivel, Abjuring a' intentions evil, I quat my pen: The Lord preserve us frae the devil, Amen! amen!

PART II. EPITAPHS EPIGRAMS FRAGMENTS ETC

CHAPTER I. ON THE AUTHOR'S FATHER.

[William Burness merited his son's eulogiums: he was an example of piety, patience, and fortitude.]

O ye whose cheek the tear of pity stains, Draw near with pious rev'rence and attend! Here lie the loving husband's dear remains, The tender father and the gen'rous friend. The pitying heart that felt for human woe; The dauntless heart that feared no human pride; The friend of man, to vice alone a foe; "For ev'n his failings lean'd to virtue's side."

CHAPTER II. ON R.A., ESQ.

[Robert Aiken, Esq., to whom "The Cotter's Saturday Night" is addressed: a kind and generous man.]

Know thou, O stranger to the fame Of this much lov'd, much honour'd name! (For none that knew him need be told) A warmer heart death ne'er made cold.

CHAPTER III. ON A FRIEND.

[The name of this friend is neither mentioned nor alluded to in any of the poet's productions.]

An honest man here lies at rest As e'er God with his image blest! The friend of man, the friend of truth; The friend of age, and guide of youth; Few hearts like his, with virtue warm'd, Few heads with knowledge so inform'd: If there's another world, he lives in bliss; If there is none, he made the best of this.

CHAPTER IV.
FOR GAVIN HAMILTON.

[These lines allude to the persecution which Hamilton endured for presuming to ride on Sunday, and say, "damn it," in the presence of the minister of Mauchline.]
The poor man weeps-here Gavin sleeps, Whom canting wretches blam'd: But with such as he, where'er he be, May I be sav'd or damn'd!

CHAPTER V.
ON WEE JOHNNY.

HIC JACET WEE JOHNNY.
[Wee Johnny was John Wilson, printer of the Kilmarnock edition of Burns's Poems: he doubted the success of the speculation, and the poet punished him in these lines, which he printed unaware of their meaning.]
Whoe'er thou art, O reader, know, That death has murder'd Johnny! An' here his body lies fu' low- For saul he ne'er had ony.

CHAPTER VI.
ON JOHN DOVE,
INNKEEPER, MAUCHLINE.

[John Dove kept the Whitefoord Arms in Mauchline: his religion is made to consist of a comparative appreciation of the liquors he kept.]
Here lies Johnny Pidgeon; What was his religion? Wha e'er desires to ken, To some other warl' Maun follow the carl, For here Johnny Pidgeon had nane!
Strong ale was ablution- Small beer, persecution, A dram was memento mori; But a full flowing bowl Was the saving his soul, And port was celestial glory.

CHAPTER VII.
ON A WAG IN MAUCHLINE.

[This laborious and useful wag was the "Dear Smith, thou sleest pawkie thief," of one of the poet's finest epistles: he died in the West Indies.]
Lament him, Mauchline husbands a', He aften did assist ye; For had ye staid

whole weeks awa, Your wives they ne'er had missed ye. Ye Mauchline bairns, as on ye press To school in bands thegither, O tread ye lightly on his grass,- Perhaps he was your father.

CHAPTER VIII.
ON A CELEBRATED RULING ELDER.

[Souter Hood obtained the distinction of this Epigram by his impertinent inquiries into what he called the moral delinquencies of Burns.]
Here souter Hood in death does sleep;- To h-ll, if he's gane thither, Satan, gie him thy gear to keep, He'll haud it weel thegither.

CHAPTER IX.
ON A NOISY POLEMIC.

[This noisy polemic was a mason of the name of James Humphrey: he astonished Cromek by an eloquent dissertation on free grace, effectual-calling, and predestination.]
Below thir stanes lie Jamie's banes: O Death, it's my opinion, Thou ne'er took such a blethrin' b-ch Into thy dark dominion!

CHAPTER X.
ON MISS JEAN SCOTT.

[The heroine of these complimentary lines lived in Ayr, and cheered the poet with her sweet voice, as well as her sweet looks.]
Oh! had each Scot of ancient times, Been Jeany Scott, as thou art, The bravest heart on English ground Had yielded like a coward!

CHAPTER XI.
ON A HENPECKED COUNTRY SQUIRE.

[Though satisfied with the severe satire of these lines, the poet made a second attempt.]
As father Adam first was fool'd, A case that's still too common, Here lies a man a woman rul'd, The devil rul'd the woman.

CHAPTER XII.
ON THE SAME.

[The second attempt did not in Burns's fancy exhaust this fruitful subject: he tried his hand again.]
O Death, hadst thou but spared his life, Whom we this day lament, We

freely wad exchang'd the wife, And a' been weel content!
Ev'n as he is, cauld in his graff, The swap we yet will do't; Take thou the carlin's carcase aff, Thou'se get the soul to boot.

CHAPTER XIII.
ON THE SAME.

[In these lines he bade farewell to the sordid dame, who lived, it is said, in Netherplace, near Mauchline.]
One Queen Artemisia, as old stories tell, When depriv'd of her husband she loved so well, In respect for the love and affection he'd show'd her, She reduc'd him to dust and she drank up the powder. But Queen Netherplace, of a diff'rent complexion, When call'd on to order the fun'ral direction, Would have eat her dear lord, on a slender pretence, Not to show her respect, but to save the expense.

CHAPTER XIV.
THE HIGHLAND WELCOME.

[Burns took farewell of the hospitalities of the Scottish Highlands in these happy lines.]
When Death's dark stream I ferry o'er, A time that surely shall come; In Heaven itself I'll ask no more Than just a Highland welcome.

CHAPTER XV.
ON WILLIAM SMELLIE.

[Smellie, author of the Philosophy of History; a singular person, of ready wit, and negligent in nothing save his dress.]
Shrewd Willie Smellie to Crochallan came, The old cock'd hat, the gray surtout, the same; His bristling beard just rising in its might, 'Twas four long nights and days to shaving night:
His uncomb'd grizzly locks wild staring, thatch'd A head for thought profound and clear, unmatch'd: Yet tho' his caustic wit was biting, rude, His heart was warm, benevolent, and good.

CHAPTER XVI.
VERSES
WRITTEN ON A WINDOW OF THE INN AT CARRON.

[These lines were written on receiving what the poet considered an uncivil refusal to look at the works of the celebrated Carron foundry.]
We came na here to view your warks In hopes to be mair wise, But only,

lest we gang to hell, It may be nae surprise:
For whan we tirl'd at your door, Your porter dought na hear us; Sae may, shou'd we to hell's yetts come Your billy Satan sair us!

CHAPTER XVII.
THE BOOK-WORMS.

[Burns wrote this reproof in a Shakspeare, which he found splendidly bound and gilt, but unread and worm-eaten, in a noble person's library.]
Through and through the inspir'd leaves, Ye maggots, make your windings; But oh! respect his lordship's taste, And spare his golden bindings.

CHAPTER XVIII.
LINES ON STIRLING.

[On visiting Stirling, Burns was stung at beholding nothing but desolation in the palaces of our princes and our halls of legislation, and vented his indignation in those unloyal lines: some one has said that they were written by his companion, Nicol, but this wants confirmation.]
Here Stuarts once in glory reign'd, And laws for Scotland's weal ordain'd; But now unroof'd their palace stands, Their sceptre's sway'd by other hands; The injured Stuart line is gone, A race outlandish fills their throne; An idiot race, to honour lost; Who know them best despise them most.

CHAPTER XIX.
THE REPROOF.

[The imprudence of making the lines written at Stirling public was hinted to Burns by a friend; he said, "Oh, but I mean to reprove myself for it," which he did in these words.]
Rash mortal, and slanderous Poet, thy name Shall no longer appear in the records of fame; Dost not know that old Mansfield, who writes like the Bible, Says the more 'tis a truth, Sir, the more 'tis a libel?

CHAPTER XX.
THE REPLY.

[The minister of Gladsmuir wrote a censure on the Stirling lines, intimating, as a priest, that Burns's race was nigh run, and as a prophet, that oblivion awaited his muse. The poet replied to the expostulation.]
Like Esop's lion, Burns says, sore I feel All others' scorn-but damn that ass's heel.

CHAPTER XXI.
LINES WRITTEN UNDER THE PICTURE OF THE CELEBRATED MISS BURNS.

[The Miss Burns of these lines was well known in those days to the bucks of the Scottish metropolis: there is still a letter by the poet, claiming from the magistrates of Edinburgh a liberal interpretation of the laws of social morality, in belief of his fair namesake.]
Cease, ye prudes, your envious railings, Lovely Burns has charms-confess: True it is, she had one failing- Had a woman ever less?

CHAPTER XXII.
EXTEMPORE IN THE COURT OF SESSION.

[These portraits are strongly coloured with the partialities of the poet: Dundas had offended his pride, Erskine had pleased his vanity; and as he felt he spoke.]
LORD ADVOCATE.
He clench'd his pamphlets in his fist, He quoted and he hinted, 'Till in a declamation-mist His argument he tint it: He gaped for't, he grap'd for't, He fand it was awa, man; But what his common sense came short He eked out wi' law, man.
MR. ERSKINE.
Collected Harry stood awee, Then open'd out his arm, man: His lordship sat wi' rueful e'e, And ey'd the gathering storm, man; Like wind-driv'n hail it did assail, Or torrents owre a linn, man; The Bench sae wise lift up their eyes, Half-wauken'd wi' the din, man.

CHAPTER XXIII.
THE HENPECKED HUSBAND.

[A lady who expressed herself with incivility about her husband's potations with Burns, was rewarded by these sharp lines.]
Curs'd be the man, the poorest wretch in life, The crouching vassal to the tyrant wife! Who has no will but by her high permission; Who has not sixpence but in her possession; Who must to her his dear friend's secret tell; Who dreads a curtain lecture worse than hell! Were such the wife had fallen to my part, I'd break her spirit, or I'd break her heart; I'd charm her with the magic of a switch, I'd kiss her maids, and kick the perverse bh.

CHAPTER XXIV.
WRITTEN AT INVERARY.

[Neglected at the inn of Inverary, on account of the presence of some northern chiefs, and overlooked by his Grace of Argyll, the poet let loose his wrath and his rhyme: tradition speaks of a pursuit which took place on the part of the Campbell, when he was told of his mistake, and of a resolution not to be soothed on the part of the bard.]
Whoe'er he be that sojourns here, I pity much his case, Unless he's come to wait upon The Lord their God, his Grace.
There's naething here but Highland pride And Highland cauld and hunger; If Providence has sent me here, T'was surely in his anger.

CHAPTER XXV.
ON ELPHINSTON'S TRANSLATIONS.
OF MARTIAL'S EPIGRAMS.

[Burns thus relates the origin of this sally:-"Stopping at a merchant's shop in Edinburgh, a friend of mine one day put Elphinston's Translation of Martial into my hand, and desired my opinion of it. I asked permission to write my opinion on a blank leaf of the book; which being granted, I wrote this epigram."]
O thou, whom poesy abhors, Whom prose has turned out of doors, Heard'st thou that groan? proceed no further; 'Twas laurell'd Martial roaring murther!

CHAPTER XXVI.
INSCRIPTION.
ON THE HEADSTONE OF FERGUSSON.

[Some social friends, whose good feelings were better than their taste, have ornamented with supplemental iron work the headstone which Burns erected, with this inscription to the memory of his brother bard, Fergusson.]
Here lies
Robert Fergusson, Poet.
Born, September 5, 1751;
Died, Oct. 15, 1774.
No sculptured marble here, nor pompous lay, "No storied urn nor animated bust;" This simple stone directs pale Scotia's way To pour her sorrows o'er her poet's dust.

CHAPTER XXVII.
ON A SCHOOLMASTER.

[The Willie Michie of this epigram was, it is said, schoolmaster of the parish of Cleish, in Fifeshire: he met Burns during his first visit to Edinburgh.] Here lie Willie Michie's banes; O, Satan! when ye tak' him, Gi' him the schoolin' o' your weans, For clever de'ils he'll mak' them.

CHAPTER XXVIII.
A GRACE BEFORE DINNER.

[This was an extempore grace, pronounced by the poet at a dinner-table, in Dumfries: he was ever ready to contribute the small change of rhyme, for either the use or amusement of a company.]
O thou, who kindly dost provide For every creature's want! We bless thee, God of Nature wide, For all thy goodness lent: And if it please thee, Heavenly Guide, May never worse be sent; But, whether granted or denied, Lord bless us with content! Amen.

CHAPTER XXIX.
A GRACE BEFORE MEAT.

[Pronounced, tradition says, at the table of Mrs. Riddel, of Woodleigh-Park.]
O thou in whom we live and move, Who mad'st the sea and shore, Thy goodness constantly we prove, And grateful would adore. And if it please thee, Power above, Still grant us with such store, The friend we trust, the fair we love, And we desire no more.

CHAPTER XXX.
ON WAT.

[The name of the object of this fierce epigram might be found, but in gratifying curiosity, some pain would be inflicted.]
Sic a reptile was Wat, Sic a miscreant slave, [199]That the very worms damn'd him When laid in his grave. "In his flesh there's a famine," A starv'd reptile cries; "An' his heart is rank poison," Another replies.

CHAPTER XXXI.
ON CAPTAIN FRANCIS GROSE.

[This was a festive sally: it is said that Grose, who was very fat, though he joined in the laugh, did not relish it.]
The devil got notice that Grose was a-dying, So whip! at the summons, old Satan came flying; But when he approach'd where poor Francis lay moaning, And saw each bed-post with its burden a-groaning, Astonish'd! confounded! cry'd Satan, "By , I'll want him, ere I take such a damnable

load!"

CHAPTER XXXII.
IMPROMPTU, TO MISS AINSLIE.

[These lines were occasioned by a sermon on sin, to which the poet and Miss Ainslie of Berrywell had listened, during his visit to the border.]
Fair maid, you need not take the hint, Nor idle texts pursue:- 'Twas guilty sinners that he meant, Not angels such as you!

CHAPTER XXXIII.
THE KIRK OF LAMINGTON.

[One rough, cold day, Burns listened to a sermon, so little to his liking, in the kirk of Lamington, in Clydesdale, that he left this protest on the seat where he sat.]
As cauld a wind as ever blew, As caulder kirk, and in't but few; As cauld a minister's e'er spak, Ye'se a' be het ere I come back.

CHAPTER XXXIV.
THE LEAGUE AND COVENANT.

[In answer to a gentleman, who called the solemn League and Covenant ridiculous and fanatical.]
The solemn League and Covenant Cost Scotland blood-cost Scotland tears; But it sealed freedom's sacred cause- If thou'rt a slave, indulge thy sneers.

CHAPTER XXXV.
WRITTEN ON A PANE OF GLASS,

IN THE INN AT MOFFAT.
[A friend asked the poet why God made Miss Davies so little, and a lady who was with her, so large: before the ladies, who had just passed the window, were out of sight, the following answer was recorded on a pane of glass.]
Ask why God made the gem so small, And why so huge the granite? Because God meant mankind should set The higher value on it.

CHAPTER XXXVI.
SPOKEN,ON BEING APPOINTED TO THE EXCISE.

[Burns took no pleasure in the name of gauger: the situation was unworthy of him, and he seldom hesitated to say so.]

Searching auld wives' barrels, Och-hon! the day! That clarty barm should stain my laurels; But-what'll ye say! These movin' things ca'd wives and weans Wad move the very hearts o' stanes!

CHAPTER XXXVII.
LINES ON MRS. KEMBLE.

[The poet wrote these lines in Mrs. Riddel's box in the Dumfries Theatre, in the winter of 1794: he was much moved by Mrs. Kemble's noble and pathetic acting.]
Kemble, thou cur'st my unbelief Of Moses and his rod; At Yarico's sweet notes of grief The rock with tears had flow'd.

CHAPTER XXXVIII.
TO MR. SYME.

[John Syme, of Ryedale, a rhymer, a wit, and a gentleman of education and intelligence, was, while Burns resided in Dumfries, his chief companion: he was bred to the law.]
No more of your guests, be they titled or not, And cook'ry the first in the nation; Who is proof to thy personal converse and wit, Is proof to all other temptation.

CHAPTER XXXIX.
TO MR. SYME.
WITH A PRESENT OF A DOZEN OF PORTER.

[The tavern where these lines were written was kept by a wandering mortal of the name of Smith; who, having visited in some capacity or other the Holy Land, put on his sign, "John Smith, from Jerusalem." He was commonly known by the name of Jerusalem John.]
O, had the malt thy strength of mind, Or hops the flavour of thy wit, 'Twere drink for first of human kind, A gift that e'en for Syme were fit.
Jerusalem Tavern, Dumfries.

CHAPTER XL.
A GRACE.

[This Grace was spoken at the table of Ryedale, where to the best cookery was added the richest wine, as well as the rarest wit: Hyslop was a distiller.]
Lord, we thank and thee adore, For temp'ral gifts we little merit; At present we will ask no more, Let William Hyslop give the spirit.

CHAPTER XLI.
INSCRIPTION ON A GOBLET.

[Written on a dinner-goblet by the hand of Burns. Syme, exasperated at having his set of crystal defaced, threw the goblet under the grate: it was taken up by his clerk, and it is still preserved as a curiosity.]
There's death in the cup-sae beware! Nay, more-there is danger in touching; But wha can avoid the fell snare? The man and his wine's sae bewitching!

CHAPTER XLII.
THE INVITATION.

[Burns had a happy knack in acknowledging civilities. These lines were written with a pencil on the paper in which Mrs. Hyslop, of Lochrutton, enclosed an invitation to dinner.]
The King's most humble servant I, Can scarcely spare a minute; But I am yours at dinner-time, Or else the devil's in it.

CHAPTER XLIII.
THE CREED OF POVERTY.

[When the commissioners of Excise told Burns that he was to act, and not to think; he took out his pencil and wrote "The Creed of Poverty."]
In politics if thou would'st mix, And mean thy fortunes be; Bear this in mind-be deaf and blind; Let great folks hear and see.

CHAPTER XLIV.
WRITTEN IN A LADY'S POCKET-BOOK.

[That Burns loved liberty and sympathized with those who were warring in its cause, these lines, and hundreds more, sufficiently testify.]
Grant me, indulgent Heav'n, that I may live To see the miscreants feel the pains they give, Deal Freedom's sacred treasures free as air, Till slave and despot be but things which were.

CHAPTER XLV.
THE PARSON'S LOOKS.

[Some sarcastic person said, in Burns's hearing, that there was falsehood in the Reverend Dr. Burnside's looks: the poet mused for a moment, and replied in lines which have less of truth than point.]
That there is falsehood in his looks I must and will deny; They say their master is a knave- And sure they do not lie.

CHAPTER XLVI.
THE TOAD-EATER.

[This reproof was administered extempore to one of the guests at the table of Maxwell, of Terraughty, whose whole talk was of Dukes with whom he had dined, and of earls with whom he had supped.]
What of earls with whom you have supt, And of dukes that you dined with yestreen? Lord! a louse, Sir, is still but a louse, Though it crawl on the curl of a queen.

CHAPTER XLVII.
ON ROBERT RIDDEL.

[I copied these lines from a pane of glass in the Friars-Carse Hermitage, on which they had been traced with the diamond of Burns.]
To Riddel, much-lamented man, This ivied cot was dear; Reader, dost value matchless worth? This ivied cot revere.

CHAPTER XLVIII.
THE TOAST.

[Burns being called on for a song, by his brother volunteers, on a festive occasion, gave the following Toast.]
Instead of a song, boys, I'll give you a toast- Here's the memory of those on the twelfth that we lost!- That we lost, did I say? nay, by Heav'n, that we found; For their fame it shall last while the world goes round. The next in succession, I'll give you-the King! Whoe'er would betray him, on high may he swing; And here's the grand fabric, our free Constitution, As built on the base of the great Revolution; And longer with politics not to be cramm'd, Be Anarchy curs'd, and be Tyranny damn'd; And who would to Liberty e'er prove disloyal, May his son be a hangman, and he his first trial.

CHAPTER XLIX.
ON A PERSON NICKNAMED
THE MARQUIS.

[In a moment when vanity prevailed against prudence, this person, who kept a respectable public-house in Dumfries, desired Burns, to write his epitaph.]
Here lies a mock Marquis, whose titles were shamm'd; If ever he rise, it will be to be damn'd.

CHAPTER L.
LINES WRITTEN ON A WINDOW.

[Burns traced these words with a diamond, on the window of the King's Arms Tavern, Dumfries, as a reply, or reproof, to one who had been witty on excisemen.]
Ye men of wit and wealth, why all this sneering 'Gainst poor Excisemen? give the cause a hearing; What are you, landlords' rent-rolls? teasing ledgers: What premiers-what? even monarchs' mighty gaugers: Nay, what are priests, those seeming godly wise men? What are they, pray, but spiritual Excisemen?

CHAPTER LI.
LINESW RITTEN ON A WINDOW OF THE GLOBE TAVERN, DUMFRIES.

[The Globe Tavern was Burne's favourite "Howff," as he called it. It had other attractions than good liquor; there lived "Anna, with the golden locks."]
The greybeard, old Wisdom, may boast of his treasures, Give me with gay Folly to live; I grant him his calm-blooded, time-settled pleasures, But Folly has raptures to give.

CHAPTER LII.
THE SELKIRK GRACE.

[On a visit to St. Mary's Isle, Burns was requested by the noble owner to say grace to dinner; he obeyed in these lines, now known in Galloway by the name of "The Selkirk Grace."]
Some hae meat and canna eat, And some wad eat that want it; But we hae meat and we can eat, And sae the Lord be thanket.

CHAPTER LIII.
TO DR. MAXWELL,
ON JESSIE STAIG'S RECOVERY.

[Maxwell was a skilful physician; and Jessie Staig, the Provost's oldest daughter, was a young lady of great beauty: she died early.]
Maxwell, if merit here you crave That merit I deny, You save fair Jessie from the grave- An angel could not die.

CHAPTER LIV.
EPITAPH.

[These lines were traced by the hand of Burns on a goblet belonging to Gabriel Richardson, brewer, in Dumfries: it is carefully preserved in the family.]
Here brewer Gabriel's fire's extinct, And empty all his barrels: He's blest-if, as he brew'd, he drink- In upright virtuous morals.

CHAPTER LV.
EPITAPH
ON WILLIAM NICOL.

[Nicol was a scholar, of ready and rough wit, who loved a joke and a gill.]
Ye maggots, feast on Nicol's brain, For few sic feasts ye've gotten; And fix your claws in Nicol's heart, For deil a bit o't's rotten.

CHAPTER LVI.
ON THE DEATH OF A LAP-DOG,
NAMED ECHO.

[When visiting with Syme at Kenmore Castle, Burns wrote this Epitaph, rather reluctantly, it is said, at the request of the lady of the house, in honour of her lap dog.]
In wood and wild, ye warbling throng, Your heavy loss deplore; Now half extinct your powers of song, Sweet Echo is no more.
Ye jarring, screeching things around, Scream your discordant joys; Now half your din of tuneless sound With Echo silent lies.

CHAPTER LVII.
ON A NOTED COXCOMB.

[Neither Ayr, Edinburgh, nor Dumfries have contested the honour of producing the person on whom these lines were written:-coxcombs are the growth of all districts.]
Light lay the earth on Willy's breast, His chicken-heart so tender; But build a castle on his head, His skull will prop it under.

CHAPTER LVIII.
ON SEEING THE BEAUTIFUL SEAT OF
LORD GALLOWAY.

[This, and the three succeeding Epigrams, are hasty squibs thrown amid the tumult of a contested election, and must not be taken as the fixed and deliberate sentiments of the poet, regarding an ancient and noble house.]

What dost thou in that mansion fair?- Flit, Galloway, and find Some narrow, dirty, dungeon cave, The picture of thy mind!

CHAPTER LIX.
ON THE SAME.

No Stewart art thou, Galloway, The Stewarts all were brave; Besides, the Stewarts were but fools, Not one of them a knave.

CHAPTER LX.
ON THE SAME.

Bright ran thy line, O Galloway, Thro' many a far-fam'd sire! So ran the far-fam'd Roman way, So ended in a mire.

CHAPTER LXI.
TO THE SAME,
ON THE AUTHOR BEING THREATENED WITH HIS RESENTMENT.

Spare me thy vengeance, Galloway, In quiet let me live: I ask no kindness at thy hand, For thou hast none to give.

CHAPTER LXII.
ON A COUNTRY LAIRD.

[Mr. Maxwell, of Cardoness, afterwards Sir David, exposed himself to the rhyming wrath of Burns, by his activity in the contested elections of Heron.]
Bless Jesus Christ, O Cardoness, With grateful lifted eyes, Who said that not the soul alone But body too, must rise: For had he said, "the soul alone From death I will deliver;" Alas! alas! O Cardoness, Then thou hadst slept for ever.

CHAPTER LXIII.
ON JOHN BUSHBY.

[Burns, in his harshest lampoons, always admitted the talents of Bushby: the peasantry, who hate all clever attorneys, loved to handle his character with unsparing severity.]
Here lies John Bushby, honest man! Cheat him, Devil, gin ye can.

CHAPTER LXIV.

THE TRUE LOYAL NATIVES.

[At a dinner-party, where politics ran high, lines signed by men who called themselves the true loyal natives of Dumfries, were handed to Burns: he took a pencil, and at once wrote this reply.]
Ye true "Loyal Natives," attend to my song, In uproar and riot rejoice the night long; From envy or hatred your corps is exempt, But where is your shield from the darts of contempt?

CHAPTER LXV.
ON A SUICIDE.

[Burns was observed by my friend, Dr. Copland Hutchinson, to fix, one morning, a bit of paper on the grave of a person who had committed suicide: on the paper these lines were pencilled.]
Earth'd up here lies an imp o' hell, Planted by Satan's dibble- Poor silly wretch, he's damn'd himsel' To save the Lord the trouble.

CHAPTER LXVI.
EXTEMPORE
PINNED ON A LADY'S COUCH.

["Printed," says Sir Harris Nicolas, "from a copy in Burns's handwriting," a slight alteration in the last line is made from an oral version.]
If you rattle along like your mistress's tongue, Your speed will outrival the dart: But, a fly for your load, you'll break down on the road If your stuff has the rot, like her heart.

CHAPTER LXVII.
LINES
TO JOHN RANKINE.

[These lines were said to have been written by the poet to Rankine, of Adamhill, with orders to forward them when he died.]
He who of Rankine sang lies stiff and dead, And a green grassy hillock hides his head; Alas! alas! a devilish change indeed.

CHAPTER LXVIII.
JESSY LEWARS.

[Written on the blank side of a list of wild beasts, exhibiting in Dumfries. "Now," said the poet, who was then very ill, "it is fit to be presented to a lady."]

Talk not to me of savages From Afric's burning sun, No savage e'er could rend my heart As, Jessy, thou hast done. But Jessy's lovely hand in mine, A mutual faith to plight, Not even to view the heavenly choir Would be so blest a sight.

CHAPTER LXIX.
THE TOAST.

[One day, when Burns was ill and seemed in slumber, he observed Jessy Lewars moving about the house with a light step lest she should disturb him. He took a crystal goblet containing wine-and-water for moistening his lips, wrote these words upon it with a diamond, and presented it to her.]
Fill me with the rosy-wine, Call a toast-a toast divine; Give the Poet's darling flame, Lovely Jessy be the name; Then thou mayest freely boast, Thou hast given a peerless toast.

CHAPTER LXX.
ON MISS JESSY LEWARS.

[The constancy of her attendance on the poet's sick-bed and anxiety of mind brought a slight illness upon Jessy Lewars. "You must not die yet," said the poet: "give me that goblet, and I shall prepare you for the worst." He traced these lines with his diamond, and said, "That will be a companion to 'The Toast.'"]
Say, sages, what's the charm on earth Can turn Death's dart aside? It is not purity and worth, Else Jessy had not died.
R. B.

CHAPTER LXXI.
ON THE RECOVERY OF JESSY LEWARS.

[A little repose brought health to the young lady. "I knew you would not die," observed the poet, with a smile: "there is a poetic reason for your recovery;" he wrote, and with a feeble hand, the following lines.]
But rarely seen since Nature's birth, The natives of the sky; Yet still one seraph's left on earth, For Jessy did not die.
R. B.

CHAPTER LXXII.
TAM, THE CHAPMAN.

[Tam, the chapman, is said by the late William Cobbett, who knew him, to have been a Thomas Kennedy, a native of Ayrshire, agent to a mercantile

house in the west of Scotland. Sir Harris Nicolas confounds him with the Kennedy to whom Burns addressed several letters and verses, which I printed in my edition of the poet in 1834: it is perhaps enough to say that the name of the one was Thomas and the name of the other John.]
As Tam the Chapman on a day, Wi' Death forgather'd by the way, Weel pleas'd he greets a wight so famous, And Death was nae less pleas'd wi' Thomas, Wha cheerfully lays down the pack, And there blaws up a hearty crack; His social, friendly, honest heart, Sae tickled Death they could na part: Sac after viewing knives and garters, Death takes him hame to gie him quarters.

CHAPTER LXXIII.

[These lines seem to owe their origin to the precept of Mickle.
"The present moment is our ain, The next we never saw."]
Here's a bottle and an honest friend! What wad you wish for mair, man? Wha kens before his life may end, What his share may be o' care, man? Then catch the moments as they fly, And use them as ye ought, man? Believe me, happiness is shy, And comes not ay when sought, man.

CHAPTER LXXIV.

[The sentiment which these lines express, was one familiar to Burns, in the early, as well as concluding days of his life.]
Though fickle Fortune has deceived me, She promis'd fair and perform'd but ill; Of mistress, friends, and wealth bereav'd me, Yet I bear a heart shall support me still.-
I'll act with prudence as far's I'm able, But if success I must never find, Then come misfortune, I bid thee welcome, I'll meet thee with an undaunted mind.

CHAPTER LXXV.
TO JOHN KENNEDY.

[The John Kennedy to whom these verses and the succeeding lines were addressed, lived, in 1796, at Dumfries-house, and his taste was so much esteemed by the poet, that he submitted his "Cotter's Saturday Night" and the "Mountain Daisy" to his judgment: he seems to have been of a social disposition.]
Now, Kennedy, if foot or horse E'er bring you in by Mauchline Cross, L-d, man, there's lasses there wad force A hermit's fancy. And down the gate in faith they're worse And mair unchancy.
But as I'm sayin', please step to Dow's, And taste sic gear as Johnnie brews,

Till some bit callan bring me news That ye are there, And if we dinna hae a bouze I'se ne'er drink mair.
It's no I like to sit an' swallow, Then like a swine to puke and wallow, But gie me just a true good fellow, Wi' right ingine, And spunkie ance to make us mellow, And then we'll shine.
Now if ye're ane o' warl's folk, Wha rate the wearer by the cloak, An' sklent on poverty their joke Wi' bitter sneer, Wi' you nae friendship I will troke, Nor cheap nor dear.
But if, as I'm informed weel, Ye hate as ill's the very deil The flinty heart that canna feel- Come, Sir, here's tae you! Hae, there's my haun, I wiss you weel, And gude be wi' you.
Robert Burness.
Mossgiel, 3 March, 1786.

CHAPTER LXXVI.
TO JOHN KENNEDY.

Farewell, dear friend! may guid luck hit you, And 'mang her favourites admit you! If e'er Detraction shore to smit you, May nane believe him! And ony deil that thinks to get you, Good Lord deceive him!
R. B.
Kilmarnock, August, 1786

CHAPTER LXXVII.

[Cromek found these characteristic lines among the poet's papers.]
There's naethin like the honest nappy! Whaur'll ye e'er see men sae happy, Or women, sonsie, saft an' sappy, 'Tween morn an' morn As them wha like to taste the drappie In glass or horn?
I've seen me daezt upon a time; I scarce could wink or see a styme; [206]Just ae hauf muchkin does me prime, Ought less is little, Then back I rattle on the rhyme, As gleg's a whittle.

CHAPTER LXXVIII.
ON THE BLANK LEAF OF A WORK BY HANNAH MORE.
PRESENTED BY MRS C.

Thou flattering work of friendship kind, Still may thy pages call to mind The dear, the beauteous donor; Though sweetly female every part, Yet such a head, and more the heart, Does both the sexes honour. She showed her taste refined and just, When she selected thee, Yet deviating, own I must, For so approving me! But kind still, I'll mind still The giver in the gift; I'll

bless her, and wiss her A Friend above the Lift.
Mossgiel, April, 1786.

CHAPTER LXXIX.
TO THE MEN AND BRETHREN OF THE MASONIC LODGE AT TARBOLTON.

Within your dear mansion may wayward contention Or withering envy ne'er enter: May secrecy round be the mystical bound, And brotherly love be the centre.
Edinburgh, 23 August, 1787.

CHAPTER LXXX.
IMPROMPTU.

[The tumbler on which these verses are inscribed by the diamond of Burns, found its way to the hands of Sir Walter Scott, and is now among the treasures of Abbotsford.]
You're welcome, Willie Stewart, You're welcome, Willie Stewart; There's ne'er a flower that blooms in May, That's half sae welcome's thou art.
Come bumpers high, express your joy, The bowl we maun renew it; The tappit-hen, gae bring her ben, To welcome Willie Stewart.
My foes be strang, and friends be slack, Ilk action may he rue it, May woman on him turn her back, That wrongs thee, Willie Stewart.

CHAPTER LXXXI.
PRAYER FOR ADAM ARMOUR.

[The origin of this prayer is curious. In 1785, the maid-servant of an innkeeper at Mauchline, having been caught in what old ballad-makers delicately call "the deed of shame," Adam Armour, the brother of the poet's bonnie Jean, with one or two more of his comrades, executed a rustic act of justice upon her, by parading her perforce through the village, placed on a rough, unpruned piece of wood: an unpleasant ceremony, vulgarly called "Riding the Stang." This was resented by Geordie and Nanse, the girl's master and mistress; law was restored to, and as Adam had to hide till the matter was settled, he durst not venture home till late on the Saturday nights. In one of these home-comings he met Burns who laughed when he heard the story, and said, "You have need of some one to pray for you." "No one can do that better than yourself," was the reply, and this humorous intercession was made on the instant, and, as it is said, "clean off loof." From Adam Armour I obtained the verses, and when he wrote them out, he told the story in which the prayer originated.]

Lord, pity me, for I am little, An elf of mischief and of mettle, That can like ony wabster's shuttle, Jink there or here, Though scarce as lang's a gude kale-whittle, I'm unco queer.

Lord pity now our waefu' case, For Geordie's Jurr we're in disgrace, Because we stang'd her through the place, 'Mang hundreds laughin', For which we daurna show our face Within the clachan.

And now we're dern'd in glens and hallows, And hunted as was William Wallace, By constables, those blackguard fellows, And bailies baith, O Lord, preserve us frae the gallows! That cursed death.

Auld, grim, black-bearded Geordie's sel', O shake him ewre the mouth o' hell, And let him hing and roar and yell, Wi' hideous din, And if he offers to rebel Just heave him in.

When Death comes in wi' glimmering blink, And tips auld drunken Nanse the wink' Gaur Satan gie her a-e a clink Behint his yett, And fill her up wi' brimstone drink, Red reeking het!

There's Jockie and the hav'rel Jenny, Some devil seize them in a hurry, And waft them in th' infernal wherry, Straught through the lake, And gie their hides a noble curry, Wi' oil of aik.

As for the lass, lascivious body, She's had mischief enough already, Weel stang'd by market, mill, and smiddie, She's suffer'd sair; But may she wintle in a widdie, If she wh-re mair.

PART III. SONGS AND BALLADS

I. HANDSOME NELL.

Tune.-"I am a man unmarried."

["This composition," says Burns in his "Common-place Book," "was the first of my performances, and done at an early period in life, when my heart glowed with honest, warm simplicity; unacquainted and uncorrupted with the ways of a wicked world. The subject of it was a young girl who really deserved all the praises I have bestowed on her."]

I.

O once I lov'd a bonnie lass, Ay, and I love her still; And whilst that honour warms my breast, I'll love my handsome Nell.

II.

As bonnie lasses I hae seen, And mony full as braw; But for a modest gracefu' mien The like I never saw.

III.

A bonnie lass, I will confess, Is pleasant to the e'e, But without some better qualities She's no a lass for me.

IV.

But Nelly's looks are blithe and sweet, And what is best of a', Her reputation is complete, And fair without a flaw.

V.

She dresses ay sae clean and neat, Both decent and genteel: And then there's something in her gait Gars ony dress look weel.

VI.

A gaudy dress and gentle air May slightly touch the heart; But it's innocence and modesty That polishes the dart.

VII.

'Tis this in Nelly pleases me, 'Tis this enchants my soul; For absolutely in my breast She reigns without control

II. LUCKLESS FORTUNE.

[Those lines, as Burns informs us, were written to a tune of his own composing, consisting of three parts, and the words were the echo of the air.]
O raging fortune's withering blast Has laid my leaf full low, O! O raging fortune's withering blast Has laid my leaf full low, O! My stem was fair, my bud was green, My blossom sweet did blow, O; The dew fell fresh, the sun rose mild, And made my branches grow, O. But luckless fortune's northern storms Laid a' my blossoms low, O; But luckless fortune's northern storms Laid a' my blossoms low, O.

III. I DREAM'D I LAY.

[These melancholy verses were written when the poet was some seventeen years old: his early days were typical of his latter.]
I.
I dream'd I lay where flowers were springing Gaily in the sunny beam; List'ning to the wild birds singing, By a falling crystal stream: Straight the sky grew black and daring; Thro' the woods the whirlwinds rave; Trees with aged arms were warring. O'er the swelling drumlie wave.
II.
Such was my life's deceitful morning, Such the pleasure I enjoy'd: But lang or noon, loud tempests storming, A' my flowery bliss destroy'd. Tho' fickle fortune has deceiv'd me, She promis'd fair, and perform'd but ill; Of mony a joy and hope bereav'd me, I bear a heart shall support me still.

IV. TIBBIE, I HAE SEEN THE DAY.

Tune-"Invercald's Reel."
[The Tibbie who "spak na, but gaed by like stoure," was, it is said, the daughter of a man who was laird of three acres of peatmoss, and thought it became her to put on airs in consequence.]
CHORUS.
O Tibbie, I hae seen the day, Ye wad na been sae shy; For lack o' gear ye lightly me, But, trowth, I care na by.
I.
Yestreen I met you on the moor, Ye spak na, but gaed by like stoure; Ye geck at me because I'm poor, But fient a hair care I.
II.

I doubt na, lass, but ye may think, Because ye hae the name o' clink, That ye can please me at a wink, Whene'er ye like to try.

III.

But sorrow tak him that's sae mean, Altho' his pouch o' coin were clean, Wha follows ony saucy quean, That looks sae proud and high.

IV.

Altho' a lad were e'er sae smart, If that he want the yellow dirt, Ye'll cast your head anither airt, And answer him fu' dry.

V.

But if he hae the name o' gear, Ye'll fasten to him like a brier, Tho' hardly he, for sense or lear, Be better than the kye.

VI.

But, Tibbie, lass, tak my advice, Your daddie's gear maks you sae nice; The deil a ane wad spier your price, Were ye as poor as I.

VII.

There lives a lass in yonder park, I would nae gie her in her sark, For thee, wi' a' thy thousan' mark; Ye need na look sae high.

V. MY FATHER WAS A FARMER.

Tune-"The Weaver and his Shuttle, O."

["The following song," says the poet, "is a wild rhapsody, miserably deficient in versification, but as the sentiments are the genuine feelings of my heart, for that reason I have a particular pleasure in conning it over."]

I.

My father was a farmer Upon the Carrick border, O, And carefully he bred me, In decency and order, O; He bade me act a manly part, Though I had ne'er a farthing, O; For without an honest manly heart, No man was worth regarding, O.

II.

Then out into the world My course I did determine, O; Tho' to be rich was not my wish, yet to be great was charming, O: My talents they were not the worst, Nor yet my education, O; Resolv'd was I, at least to try, To mend my situation, O.

III.

In many a way, and vain essay, I courted fortune's favour, O; Some cause unseen still stept between, To frustrate each endeavour, O: Sometimes by foes I was o'erpower'd, Sometimes by friends forsaken, O, And when my hope was at the top, I still was worst mistaken, O.

IV.

Then sore harass'd, and tir'd at last, With fortune's vain delusion, O, I dropt my schemes, like idle dreams, And came to this conclusion, O: The past was bad, and the future hid; Its good or ill untried, O; But the present hour,

was in my pow'r And so I would enjoy it, O.
V.
No help, nor hope, nor view had I, Nor person to befriend me, O; So I must toil, and sweat and broil, And labour to sustain me, O: To plough and sow, to reap and mow, My father bred me early, O; For one, he said, to labour bred, Was a match for fortune fairly, O.
VI.
Thus all obscure, unknown, and poor, Thro' life I'm doom'd to wander, O, Till down my weary bones I lay, In everlasting slumber, O. No view nor care, but shun whate'er Might breed me pain or sorrow, O: I live to-day as well's I may, Regardless of to-morrow, O.
VII.
But cheerful still, I am as well, As a monarch in a palace, O, Tho' Fortune's frown still hunts me down, With all her wonted malice, O: I make indeed my daily bread, But ne'er can make it farther, O; But, as daily bread is all I need, I do not much regard her, O.
VIII.
When sometimes by my labour I earn a little money, O, Some unforeseen misfortune Comes gen'rally upon me, O: Mischance, mistake, or by neglect, Or my goodnatur'd folly, O; But come what will, I've sworn it still, I'll ne'er be melancholy, O.
IX.
All you who follow wealth and power, With unremitting ardour, O, The more in this you look for bliss, You leave your view the farther, O: Had you the wealth Potosi boasts, Or nations to adorn you, O, A cheerful honest-hearted clown I will prefer before you, O.

VI. JOHN BARLEYCORN:
A BALLAD.

[Composed on the plan of an old song, of which David Laing has given an authentic version in his very curious volume of Metrical Tales.]
I.
There were three kings into the east, Three kings both great and high; And they hae sworn a solemn oath John Barleycorn should die.
II.
They took a plough and plough'd him down, Put clods upon his head; And they ha'e sworn a solemn oath John Barleycorn was dead.
III.
But the cheerful spring came kindly on, And show'rs began to fall; John Barleycorn got up again, And sore surpris'd them all.
IV.
The sultry suns of summer came, And he grew thick and strong; His head

weel arm'd wi' pointed spears That no one should him wrong.
V.
The sober autumn enter'd mild, When he grew wan and pale; His beading joints and drooping head Show'd he began to fail.
VI.
His colour sicken'd more and more, He faded into age; And then his enemies began To show their deadly rage.
VII.
They've ta'en a weapon, long and sharp, And cut him by the knee; Then ty'd him fast upon a cart, Like a rogue for forgerie.
VIII.
They laid him down upon his back, And cudgell'd him full sore; They hung him up before the storm. And turn'd him o'er and o'er.
IX.
They filled up a darksome pit With water to the brim; They heaved in John Barleycorn, There let him sink or swim.
X.
They laid him out upon the floor, To work him farther woe; And still, as signs of life appear'd, They toss'd him to and fro.
XI.
They wasted o'er a scorching flame The marrow of his bones; But a miller us'd him worst of all- He crush'd him 'tween the stones.
XII.
And they ha'e ta'en his very heart's blood, And drank it round and round; And still the more and more they drank, Their joy did more abound.
XIII.
John Barleycorn was a hero bold, Of noble enterprise; For if you do but taste his blood, 'Twill make your courage rise.
XIV.
'Twill make a man forget his woe; 'Twill heighten all his joy: 'Twill make the widow's heart to sing, Tho' the tear were in her eye.
XV.
Then let us toast John Barleycorn, Each man a glass in hand; And may his great posterity Ne'er fail in old Scotland!

VII. THE RIGS O' BARLEY.

Tune-"Corn rigs are bonnie."
[Two young women of the west, Anne Ronald and Anne Blair, have each, by the district traditions, been claimed as the heroine of this early song.]
I.
It was upon a Lammas night, When corn rigs are bonnie, [211]Beneath the moon's unclouded light, I held awa to Annie: The time flew by wi' tentless

heed, 'Till 'tween the late and early, Wi' sma' persuasion she agreed, To see me through the barley.

II.

The sky was blue, the wind was still, The moon was shining clearly; I set her down wi' right good will, Amang the rigs o' barley: I ken't her heart was a' my ain; I lov'd her most sincerely; I kiss'd her owre and owre again, Amang the rigs o' barley.

III.

I lock'd her in my fond embrace! Her heart was beating rarely: My blessings on that happy place. Amang the rigs o' barley! But by the moon and stars so bright. That shone that hour so clearly? She ay shall bless that happy night, Amang the rigs o' barley!

IV.

I hae been blithe wi' comrades dear; I hae been merry drinkin'; I hae been joyfu' gath'rin' gear; I hae been happy thinkin': But a' the pleasures e'er I saw, Tho' three times doubled fairly, That happy night was worth them a', Amang the rigs o' barley.

CHORUS.

Corn rigs, an' barley rigs, An' corn rigs are bonnie: I'll ne'er forget that happy night, Amang the rigs wi' Annie.

VIII. MONTGOMERY'S PEGGY.

Tune-"Galla-Water."

["My Montgomery's Peggy," says Burns, "was my deity for six or eight months: she had been bred in a style of life rather elegant: it cost me some heart-aches to get rid of the affair." The young lady listened to the eloquence of the poet, poured out in many an interview, and then quietly told him that she stood unalterably engaged to another.]

I.

Altho' my bed were in yon muir, Amang the heather, in my plaidie, Yet happy, happy would I be, Had I my

dear Montgomery's Peggy.

II.

When o'er the hill beat surly storms, And winter nights were dark and rainy; I'd seek some dell, and in my arms I'd shelter dear Montgomery's Peggy.

III.

Were I a baron proud and high, And horse and servants waiting ready, Then a' 'twad gie o' joy to me, The sharin't with Montgomery's Peggy.

IX. THE MAUCHLINE LADY.

Tune-"I had a horse, I had nae mair."

[The Mauchline lady who won the poet's heart was Jean Armour: she loved to relate how the bard made her acquaintance: his dog run across some linen webs which she was bleaching among Mauchline gowans, and he apologized so handsomely that she took another look at him. To this interview the world owes some of our most impassioned strains.]
When first I came to Stewart Kyle, My mind it was nae steady; Where'er I gaed, where'er I rade, A mistress still I had ay: But when I came roun' by Mauchline town, Not dreadin' any body, My heart was caught before I thought, And by a Mauchline lady.

X. THE HIGHLAND LASSIE.

Tune-"The deuks dang o'er my daddy!"
["The Highland Lassie" was Mary Campbell, whose too early death the poet sung in strains that will endure[212] while the language lasts. "She was," says Burns, "a warm-hearted, charming young creature as ever blessed a man with generous love."]
I.
Nae gentle dames, tho' e'er sae fair, Shall ever be my muse's care: Their titles a' are empty show; Gie me my Highland lassie, O. Within the glen sae bushy, O, Aboon the plains sae rushy, O, I set me down wi' right good-will, To sing my Highland lassie, O.
II.
Oh, were yon hills and valleys mine, Yon palace and yon gardens fine, The world then the love should know I bear my Highland lassie, O.
III.
But fickle fortune frowns on me, And I maun cross the raging sea; But while my crimson currents flow, I'll love my Highland lassie, O.
IV.
Altho' thro' foreign climes I range, I know her heart will never change, For her bosom burns with honour's glow, My faithful Highland lassie, O.
V.
For her I'll dare the billows' roar, For her I'll trace a distant shore, That Indian wealth may lustre throw Around my Highland lassie, O.
VI.
She has my heart, she has my hand, by sacred truth and honour's band! 'Till the mortal stroke shall lay me low, I'm thine, my Highland lassie, O. Farewell the glen sae bushy, O! Farewell the plain sae rushy, O! To other lands I now must go, To sing my Highland lassie, O.

XI. PEGGY.

[The heroine of this song is said to have been "Montgomery's Peggy."]

Tune-"I had a horse, I had nae mair."

I.

Now westlin winds and slaughtering guns Bring autumn's pleasant weather; The moor-cock springs, on whirring wings, Amang the blooming heather: Now waving grain, wide o'er the plain, Delights the weary farmer; And the moon shines bright, when I rove at night To muse upon my charmer.

II.

The partridge loves the fruitful fells; The plover loves the mountains; The woodcock haunts the lonely dells; The soaring hern the fountains; Thro' lofty groves the cushat roves The path of man to shun it; The hazel bush o'erhangs the thrush, The spreading thorn the linnet.

III.

Thus ev'ry kind their pleasure find, The savage and the tender; Some social join, and leagues combine; Some solitary wander: Avaunt, away! the cruel sway, Tyrannic man's dominion; The sportsman's joy, the murd'ring cry, The flutt'ring, gory pinion.

IV.

But Peggy, dear, the ev'ning's clear, Thick flies the skimming swallow; The sky is blue, the fields in view, All fading-green and yellow: Come, let us stray our gladsome way, And view the charms of nature; The rustling corn, the fruited thorn, And every happy creature.

V.

We'll gently walk, and sweetly talk, Till the silent moon shine clearly; I'll grasp thy waist, and, fondly prest, Swear how I love thee dearly: [213]Not vernal show'rs to budding flow'rs, Not autumn to the farmer, So dear can be as thou to me, My fair, my lovely charmer!

XII. THE RANTIN' DOG, THE DADDIE O'T.

Tune-"East nook o' Fife."

[The heroine of this humorous ditty was the mother of "Sonsie, smirking, dear-bought Bess," a person whom the poet regarded, as he says, both for her form and her grace.]

I.

O wha my babie-clouts will buy? O wha will tent me when I cry? Wha will kiss me where I lie?- The rantin' dog, the daddie o't.

II.

O wha will own he did the fau't? O wha will buy the groanin' maut? O wha will tell me how to ca't? The rantin' dog, the daddie o't.

III.

When I mount the creepie chair, Wha will sit beside me there? Gie me Rob, I'll seek nae mair, The rantin' dog, the daddie o't.

IV.

Wha will crack to me my lane? Wha will make me fidgin' fain? Wha will kiss me o'er again?- The rantin' dog, the daddie o't.

XIII. MY HEART WAS ANCE.

Tune-"To the weavers gin ye go."
["The chorus of this song," says Burns, in his note to the Museum, "is old, the rest is mine." The "bonnie, westlin weaver lad" is said to have been one of the rivals of the poet in the affection of a west landlady.]
I.
My heart was ance as blythe and free As simmer days were lang, But a bonnie, westlin weaver lad Has gart me change my sang. To the weavers gin ye go, fair maids, To the weavers gin ye go; I rede you right gang ne'er at night, To the weavers gin ye go.
II.
My mither sent me to the town, To warp a plaiden wab; But the weary, weary warpin o't Has gart me sigh and sab.
III.
A bonnie westlin weaver lad, Sat working at his loom; He took my heart as wi' a net, In every knot and thrum.
IV.
I sat beside my warpin-wheel, And ay I ca'd it roun'; But every shot and every knock, My heart it gae a stoun.
V.
The moon was sinking in the west Wi' visage pale and wan, As my bonnie westlin weaver lad Convoy'd me thro' the glen.
VI.
But what was said, or what was done, Shame fa' me gin I tell; But, oh! I fear the kintra soon Will ken as weel's mysel. To the weavers gin ye go, fair maids, To the weavers gin ye go; I rede you right gang ne'er at night, To the weavers gin ye go.

XIV. NANNIE.

Tune-"My Nannie, O."
[Agnes Fleming, servant at Calcothill, inspired this fine song: she died at an advanced age, and was more remarkable for the beauty of her form than face. When questioned about the love of Burns, she smiled and said, "Aye, atweel he made a great wark about me."]
I.
Behind yon hills, where Lugar flows, 'Mang moors an' mosses many, O, [214]The wintry sun the day has closed, And I'll awa to Nannie, O.
II.

The westlin wind blaws loud an' shrill; The night's baith mirk and rainy, O; But I'll get my plaid, an' out I'll steal, An' owre the hills to Nannie, O.
III.
My Nannie's charming, sweet, an' young; Nae artfu' wiles to win ye, O: May ill befa' the flattering tongue That wad beguile my Nannie, O.
IV.
Her face is fair, her heart is true, As spotless as she's bonnie, O: The op'ning gowan, wat wi' dew, Nae purer is than Nannie, O.
V.
A country lad is my degree, An' few there be that ken me, O; But what care I how few they be? I'm welcome ay to Nannie, O.
VI.
My riches a's my penny-fee, An' I maun guide it cannie, O; But warl's gear ne'er troubles me, My thoughts are a' my Nannie, O.
VII.
Our auld guidman delights to view His sheep an' kye thrive bonnie, O; But I'm as blythe that hauds his pleugh, An' has nae care but Nannie, O.
VIII.
Come weel, come woe, I care na by, I'll tak what Heav'n will sen' me, O: Nae ither care in life have I, But live, an' love my Nannie, O.

XV. A FRAGMENT.

Tune-"John Anderson my jo."
[This verse, written early, and probably intended for the starting verse of a song, was found among the papers of the poet.]
One night as I did wander, When corn begins to shoot, I sat me down to ponder, Upon an auld tree root: Auld Ayr ran by before me, And bicker'd to the seas; A cushat crooded o'er me, That echoed thro' the braes.

XVI. BONNIE PEGGY ALISON.

Tune-"Braes o' Balquihidder."
[On those whom Burns loved, he poured out songs without limit. Peggy Alison is said, by a western tradition, to be Montgomery's Peggy, but this seems doubtful.]
CHORUS.
I'll kiss thee yet, yet, An' I'll kiss thee o'er again; An' I'll kiss thee yet, yet, My bonnie Peggy Alison!
I.
Ilk care and fear, when thou art near, I ever mair defy them, O; Young kings upon their hansel throne Are no sae blest as I am, O!
II.

When in my arms, wi' a' thy charms, I clasp my countless treasure, O, I seek nae mair o' Heaven to share Than sic a moment's pleasure, O!
III.
And by thy een, sae bonnie blue, I swear, I'm thine for ever, O!- And on thy lips I seal my vow, And break it shall I never, O! I'll kiss thee yet, yet, An' I'll kiss thee o'er again; An' I'll kiss thee yet, yet, My bonnie Peggy Alison!

XVII. THERE'S NOUGHT BUT CARE.

Tune-"Green grow the rashes."
["Man was made when nature was but an apprentice; but woman is the last and most perfect work of nature," says an old writer, in a rare old book: a passage [215]which expresses the sentiment of Burns; yet it is all but certain, that the Ploughman Bard was unacquainted with "Cupid's Whirlygig," where these words are to be found.]
CHORUS.
Green grow the rashes, O! Green grow the rashes, O! The sweetest hours that e'er I spend Are spent amang the lasses, O.
I.
There's nought but care on ev'ry han', In every hour that passes, O: What signifies the life o' man, An' 'twere na for the lasses, O.
II.
The warly race may riches chase, An' riches still may fly them, O; An' tho' at last they catch them fast, Their hearts can ne'er enjoy them, O.
III.
But gie me a canny hour at e'en, My arms about my dearie, O; An' warly cares, an' warly men, May a' gae tapsalteerie, O.
IV.
For you sae douce, ye sneer at this, Ye're nought but senseless asses, O: The wisest man the warl' e'er saw, He dearly lov'd the lasses, O.
V.
Auld Nature swears the lovely dears Her noblest work she classes, O: Her 'prentice han' she try'd on man, An' then she made the lasses, O. Green grow the rashes, O! Green grow the rashes, O! The sweetest hours that e'er I spend Are spent amang the lasses, O.

XVIII. MY JEAN!

Tune-"The Northern Lass."
[The lady on whom this passionate verse was written was Jean Armour.]
Though cruel fate should bid us part, Far as the pole and line, Her dear idea round my heart, Should tenderly entwine. Though mountains rise, and deserts howl, And oceans roar between; Yet, dearer than my deathless soul,

I still would love my Jean

XIX. ROBIN.

Tune-"Daintie Davie."

[Stothard painted a clever little picture from this characteristic ditty: the cannie wife, it was evident, saw in Robin's palm something which tickled her, and a curious intelligence sparkled in the eyes of her gossips.]

I.

There was a lad was born in Kyle, But whatna day o' whatna style I doubt it's hardly worth the while To be sae nice wi' Robin. Robin was a rovin' boy, Rantin' rovin', rantin' rovin'; Robin was a rovin' boy, Rantin' rovin' Robin!

II.

Our monarch's hindmost year but ane Was five-and-twenty days begun, Twas then a blast o' Janwar win' Blew hansel in on Robin.

III.

The gossip keekit in his loof, Quo' she, wha lives will see the proof. This waly boy will be nae coof, I think we'll ca' him Robin

IV.

He'll hae misfortunes great and sma', But ay a heart aboon them a'; He'll be a credit to us a', We'll a' be proud o' Robin.

V.

But sure as three times three mak nine, I see by ilka score and line, This chap will dearly like our kin', So leeze me on thee, Robin.

VI.

Guid faith, quo' she, I doubt you gar, The bonnie lasses lie aspar, [216]But twenty fauts ye may hae waur, So blessin's on thee, Robin! Robin was a rovin' boy, Rantin' rovin', rantin' rovin'; Robin was a rovin' boy, Rantin' rovin' Robin!

XX. HER FLOWING LOCKS.

Tune-(unknown.)

[One day-it is tradition that speaks-Burns had his foot in the stirrup to return from Ayr to Mauchline, when a young lady of great beauty rode up to the inn, and ordered refreshments for her servants; he made these lines at the moment, to keep, he said, so much beauty in his memory.]

Her flowing locks, the raven's wing, Adown her neck and bosom hing; How sweet unto that breast to cling, And round that neck entwine her! Her lips are roses wat wi' dew, O, what a feast her bonnie mou'! Her cheeks a mair celestial hue, A crimson still diviner.

XXI. O LEAVE NOVELS.

Tune-" Mauchline belles."
[Who these Mauchline belles were the bard in other verse informs us:-
"Miss Miller is fine, Miss Markland's divine, Miss Smith, she has wit, and Miss Betty is braw; There's beauty and fortune to get with Miss Morton, But Armour's the jewel for me o' them a'."]
I.
O leave novels, ye Mauchline belles, Ye're safer at your spinning-wheel; Such witching books are baited hooks For rakish rooks, like Rob Mossgiel.
II.
Your fine Tom Jones and Grandisons, They make your youthful fancies reel; They heat your brains, and fire your veins, And then you're prey for Rob Mossgiel.
III.
Beware a tongue that's smoothly hung, A heart that warmly seems to feel; That feeling heart but acts a part- 'Tis rakish art in Rob Mossgiel.
IV.
The frank address, the soft caress, Are worse than poison'd darts of steel; The frank address and politesse Are all finesse in Rob Mossgiel.

XXII. YOUNG PEGGY.

Tune-"Last time I cam o'er the muir."
[In these verses Burns, it is said, bade farewell to one on whom he had, according to his own account, wasted eights months of courtship. We hear no more of Montgomery's Peggy.]
I.
Young Peggy blooms our bonniest lass, Her blush is like the morning, The rosy dawn, the springing grass, With early gems adorning: Her eyes outshone the radiant beams That gild the passing shower, And glitter o'er the crystal streams, And cheer each fresh'ning flower.
II.
Her lips, more than the cherries bright, A richer dye has graced them; They charm th' admiring gazer's sight, And sweetly tempt to taste them: Her smile is, as the evening mild, When feather'd tribes are courting, And little lambkins wanton wild, In playful bands disporting.
III.
Were fortune lovely Peggy's foe, Such sweetness would relent her, As blooming spring unbends the brow Of surly, savage winter. Detraction's eye no aim can gain, Her winning powers to lessen; And fretful envy grins in vain The poison'd tooth to fasten.
IV.

Ye powers of honour, love, and truth, From every ill defend her; Inspire the highly-favour'd youth, The destinies intend her: [217]Still fan the sweet connubial flame Responsive in each bosom, And bless the dear parental name With many a filial blossom.

XXIII. THE CURE FOR ALL CARE.

Tune-"Prepare, my dear brethren, to the tavern let's fly."
[Tarbolton Lodge, of which the poet was a member, was noted for its socialities. Masonic lyrics are all of a dark and mystic order; and those of Burns are scarcely an exception.]
I.
No churchman am I for to rail and to write, No statesman nor soldier to plot or to fight, No sly man of business, contriving to snare- For a big-bellied bottle's the whole of my care.
II.
The peer I don't envy, I give him his bow; I scorn not the peasant, tho' ever so low; But a club of good fellows, like those that are here, And a bottle like this, are my glory and care.
III.
Here passes the squire on his brother-his horse; There centum per centum, the cit with his purse; But see you The Crown, how it waves in the air! There a big-bellied bottle still eases my care.
IV.
The wife of my bosom, alas! she did die; For sweet consolation to church I did fly; I found that old Solomon proved it fair, That a big-bellied bottle's a cure for all care.
V.
I once was persuaded a venture to make; A letter inform'd me that all was to wreck;- But the pursy old landlord just waddled up stairs, With a glorious bottle that ended my cares.
VI.
"Life's cares they are comforts,"[136]-a maxim laid down By the bard, what d'ye call him, that wore the black gown; And faith I agree with th' old prig to a hair; For a big-bellied bottle's a heav'n of care.
VII.
ADDED IN A MASON LODGE.
Then fill up a bumper and make it o'erflow. The honours masonic prepare for to throw; May every true brother of the compass and square Have a big-bellied bottle when harass'd with care!

FOOTNOTES:

[136] Young's Night Thoughts.

XXIV. ELIZA.

Tune-"Gilderoy."
[My late excellent friend, John Galt, informed me that the Eliza of this song was his relative, and that her name was Elizabeth Barbour.]
I.
From thee, Eliza, I must go, And from my native shore; The cruel Fates between us throw A boundless ocean's roar: But boundless oceans roaring wide Between my love and me, They never, never can divide My heart and soul from thee!
II.
Farewell, farewell, Eliza dear, The maid that I adore! A boding voice is in mine ear, We part to meet no more! The latest throb that leaves my heart, While death stands victor by, That throb, Eliza, is thy part, And thine that latest sigh!

XXV. THE SONS OF OLD KILLIE.

Tune-"Shawnboy."
["This song, wrote by Mr. Burns, was sung by him in the Kilmarnock-Kilwinning Lodge, in 1786, and given by him to Mr. Parker, who was Master of the Lodge." [218]These interesting words are on the original, in the poet's handwriting, in the possession of Mr. Gabriel Neil, of Glasgow.]
I.
Ye sons of old Killie, assembled by Willie, To follow the noble vocation; Your thrifty old mother has scarce such another To sit in that honoured station. I've little to say, but only to pray, As praying's the ton of your fashion; A prayer from the muse you well may excuse, 'Tis seldom her favourite passion.
II.
Ye powers who preside o'er the wind and the tide, Who marked each element's border; Who formed this frame with beneficent aim, Whose sovereign statute is order; Within this dear mansion, may wayward contention Or withered envy ne'er enter; May secrecy round be the mystical bound, And brotherly love be the centre.

XXVI. MENIE.

Tune.-"Johnny's grey breeks."
[Of the lady who inspired this song no one has given any account: It first appeared in the second edition of the poet's works, and as the chorus was

written by an Edinburgh gentleman, it has been surmised that the song was a matter of friendship rather than of the heart.]

I.

Again rejoicing nature sees Her robe assume its vernal hues, Her leafy locks wave in the breeze, All freshly steep'd in morning dews. And maun I still on Menie doat, And bear the scorn that's in her e'e? For it's jet, jet black, an' it's like a hawk, An' it winna let a body be.

II.

In vain to me the cowslips blaw, In vain to me the vi'lets spring; In vain to me, in glen or shaw, The mavis and the lintwhite sing.

III.

The merry plough-boy cheers his team, Wi' joy the tentie seedsman stalks; But life to me's a weary dream, A dream of ane that never wauks.

IV.

The wanton coot the water skims, Amang the reeds the ducklings cry, The stately swan majestic swims, And every thing is blest but I.

V.

The sheep-herd steeks his faulding slap, And owre the moorland whistles shrill; Wi' wild, unequal, wand'ring step, I meet him on the dewy hill.

VI.

And when the lark, 'tween light and dark, Blythe waukens by the daisy's side, And mounts and sings on flittering wings, A woe-worn ghaist I hameward glide.

VII.

Come, Winter, with thine angry howl, And raging bend the naked tree: Thy gloom will sooth my cheerless soul, When nature all is sad like me! And maun I still on Menie doat, And bear the scorn that's in her e'e? For it's jet, jet black, an' it's like a hawk, An' it winna let a body be.

XXVII. THE FAREWELL TO THE BRETHREN OF ST. JAMES'S LODGE, TARBOLTON.

Tune-"Good-night, and joy be wi' you a'."

[Burns, it is said, sung this song in the St. James's Lodge of Tarbolton, when his chest was on the way to Greenock: men are yet living who had the honour of hearing him-the concluding verse affected the whole lodge.]

I.

Adieu! a heart-warm, fond adieu! Dear brothers of the mystic tie! Ye favour'd, ye enlighten'd few, Companions of my social joy! [219]Tho' I to foreign lands must hie, Pursuing Fortune's slidd'ry ba', With melting heart, and brimful eye, I'll mind you still, tho' far awa'.

II.

Oft have I met your social band, And spent the cheerful, festive night; Oft honour'd with supreme command, Presided o'er the sons of light: And by that hieroglyphic bright, Which none but craftsmen ever saw! Strong mem'ry on my heart shall write Those happy scenes when far awa'.

III.

May freedom, harmony, and love Unite you in the grand design, Beneath th' Omniscient Eye above, The glorious architect divine! That you may keep th' unerring line, Still rising by the plummet's law, Till order bright completely shine, Shall be my pray'r when far awa'.

IV.

And you farewell! whose merits claim, Justly, that highest badge to wear! Heav'n bless your honour'd, noble name, To masonry and Scotia dear! A last request permit me here, When yearly ye assemble a', One round-I ask it with a tear,- To him, the Bard that's far awa'.

XXVIII. ON CESSNOCK BANKS.

Tune-"If he be a butcher neat and trim."

[There are many variations of this song, which was first printed by Cromek from the oral communication of a Glasgow Lady, on whose charms, the poet, in early life, composed it.]

I.

On Cessnock banks a lassie dwells; Could I describe her shape and mien; Our lasses a' she far excels, An she has twa sparkling roguish een.

II.

She's sweeter than the morning dawn When rising Phœbus first is seen, And dew-drops twinkle o'er the lawn; An' she has twa sparkling roguish een

III.

She's stately like yon youthful ash, That grows the cowslip braes between, And drinks the stream with vigour fresh; An' she has twa sparkling roguish een.

IV.

She's spotless like the flow'ring thorn, With flow'rs so white and leaves so green, When purest in the dewy morn; An' she has twa sparkling roguish een.

V.

Her looks are like the vernal May, When evening Phœbus shines serene, While birds rejoice on every spray- An' she has twa sparkling roguish een.

VI.

Her hair is like the curling mist That climbs the mountain-sides at e'en, When flow'r-reviving rains are past; An' she has twa sparkling roguish een.

VII.

Her forehead's like the show'ry bow, When gleaming sunbeams intervene, And gild the distant mountain's brow; An' she has twa sparkling roguish

een.
VIII.
Her cheeks are like yon crimson gem, The pride of all the flow'ry scene, Just opening on its thorny stem; An' she has twa sparkling roguish een.
IX.
Her teeth are like the nightly snow When pale the morning rises keen, While hid the murmuring streamlets flow; An' she has twa sparkling roguish een
X.
Her lips are like yon cherries ripe, That sunny walls from Boreas screen- They tempt the taste and charm the sight; An' she has twa, sparkling roguish een.
XI.
Her teeth are like a flock of sheep, With fleeces newly washen clean, That slowly mount the rising steep; An' she has twa glancin' roguish een.
XII.
Her breath is like the fragrant breeze That gently stirs the blossom'd bean, When Phœbus sinks behind the seas; An' she has twa sparkling roguish een.
XIII.
Her voice is like the ev'ning thrush That sings on Cessnock banks unseen, While his mate sits nestling in the bush; An' she has twa sparkling roguish een.
XIV.
But it's not her air, her form, her face, Tho' matching beauty's fabled queen, 'Tis the mind that shines in ev'ry grace, An' chiefly in her roguish een.

XXIX. MARY!

Tune-"Blue Bonnets."
[In the original manuscript Burns calls this song "A Prayer for Mary;" his Highland Mary is supposed to be the inspirer.]
I.
Powers celestial! whose protection Ever guards the virtuous fair, While in distant climes I wander, Let my Mary be your care: Let her form sae fair and faultless, Fair and faultless as your own, Let my Mary's kindred spirit Draw your choicest influence down.
II.
Make the gales you waft around her Soft and peaceful as her breast; Breathing in the breeze that fans her, Soothe her bosom into rest: Guardian angels! O protect her, When in distant lands I roam; To realms unknown while fate exiles me, Make her bosom still my home.

XXX. THE LASS OF BALLOCHMYLE.

Tune-"Miss Forbes's Farewell to Banff."

[Miss Alexander, of Ballochmyle, as the poet tells her in a letter, dated November, 1786, inspired this popular song. He chanced to meet her in one of his favourite walks on the banks of the Ayr, and the fine scene and the lovely lady set the muse to work. Miss Alexander, perhaps unaccustomed to this forward wooing of the muse, allowed the offering to remain unnoticed for a time: it is now in a costly frame, and hung in her chamber-as it deserves to be.]

I.

'Twas even-the dewy fields were green, On every blade the pearls hang, The zephyr wanton'd round the bean, And bore its fragrant sweets alang: In ev'ry glen the mavis sang, All nature listening seem'd the while, Except where greenwood echoes rang Amang the braes o' Ballochmyle!

II.

With careless step I onward stray'd, My heart rejoic'd in nature's joy, When musing in a lonely glade, A maiden fair I chanc'd to spy; Her look was like the morning's eye, Her air like nature's vernal smile, Perfection whisper'd passing by, Behold the lass o' Ballochmyle!

III.

Fair is the morn in flow'ry May, And sweet is night in autumn mild When roving thro' the garden gay, Or wand'ring in the lonely wild; But woman, nature's darling child! There all her charms she does compile; Even there her other works are foil'd By the bonnie lass o' Ballochmyle.

IV.

O, had she been a country maid, And I the happy country swain, Tho' shelter'd in the lowest shed That ever rose on Scotland's plain, Thro' weary winter's wind and rain, With joy, with rapture, I would toil; And nightly to my bosom strain The bonnie lass of Ballochmyle. [221]

V.

Then pride might climb the slippery steep, Where fame and honours lofty shine: And thirst of gold might tempt the deep Or downward seek the Indian mine; Give me the cot below the pine, To tend the flocks, or till the soil, And ev'ry day have joys divine With the bonnie lass o' Ballochmyle.

XXXI. THE GLOOMY NIGHT.

Tune-"Roslin Castle."

["I had taken," says Burns, "the last farewell of my friends, my chest was on the road to Greenock, and I had composed the last song I should ever measure in Caledonia-

'The gloomy night is gathering fast."']

I.

The gloomy night is gath'ring fast, Loud roars the wild inconstant blast; Yon murky cloud is foul with rain, I see it driving o'er the plain; The hunter now has left the moor, The scatter'd coveys meet secure; While here I wander, prest with care, Along the lonely banks of Ayr.
II.
The Autumn mourns her rip'ning corn, By early Winter's ravage torn; Across her placid, azure sky, She sees the scowling tempest fly: Chill runs my blood to hear it rave- I think upon the stormy wave, Where many a danger I must dare, Far from the bonnie banks of Ayr.
III.
'Tis not the surging billow's roar, 'Tis not that fatal deadly shore; Tho' death in ev'ry shape appear, The wretched have no more to fear! But round my heart the ties are bound, That heart transpierc'd with many a wound; These bleed afresh, those ties I tear, To leave the bonnie banks of Ayr.
IV.
Farewell old Coila's hills and dales, Her heathy moors and winding vales; The scenes where wretched fancy roves, Pursuing past, unhappy loves! Farewell, my friends! farewell, my foes! My peace with these, my love with those- The bursting tears my heart declare; Farewell, the bonnie banks of Ayr!

XXXII. O WHAR DID YE GET

Tune-"Bonnie Dundee."
[This is one of the first songs which Burns communicated to Johnson's Musical Museum: the starting verse is partly old and partly new: the second is wholly by his hand.]
I.
O, whar did ye get that hauver meal bannock? O silly blind body, O dinna ye see? I gat it frae a young brisk sodger laddie, Between Saint Johnston and bonnie Dundee. O gin I saw the laddie that gae me't! Aft has he doudl'd me up on his knee; May Heaven protect my bonnie Scots laddie, And send him safe hame to his babie and me!
II.
My blessin's upon thy sweet wee lippie, My blessin's upon thy bonnie e'e brie! Thy smiles are sae like my blythe sodger laddie, Thou's ay the dearer and dearer to me! But I'll big a bower on yon bonnie banks, Where Tay rins wimplin' by sae clear; And I'll cleed thee in the tartan sae fine, And mak thee a man like thy daddie dear.

XXXIII. THE JOYFUL WIDOWER.

Tune-"Maggy Lauder."

[Most of this song is by Burns: his fancy was fierce with images of matrimonial joy or infelicity, and he had them ever ready at the call of the muse. It was first printed in the Musical Museum.]

I.

I married with a scolding wife The fourteenth of November; She made me weary of my life, By one unruly member. [222]Long did I bear the heavy yoke, And many griefs attended; But to my comfort be it spoke, Now, now her life is ended.

II.

We liv'd full one-and-twenty years A man and wife together; At length from me her course she steer'd, And gone I know not whither: Would I could guess, I do profess, I speak, and do not flatter, Of all the woman in the world, I never could come at her.

III.

Her body is bestowed well, A handsome grave does hide her; But sure her soul is not in hell, The deil would ne'er abide her. I rather think she is aloft, And imitating thunder; For why,-methinks I hear her voice Tearing the clouds asunder.

XXXIV. COME DOWN THE BACK STAIRS.

Tune-"Whistle, and I'll come to you, my lad."

[The air of this song was composed by John Bruce, a Dumfries fiddler. Burns gave another and happier version to the work of Thomson: this was written for the Museum of Johnson, where it was first published.]

CHORUS.

O whistle, and I'll come To you, my lad; O whistle, and I'll come To you, my lad: Tho' father and mither Should baith gae mad, O whistle, and I'll come To you, my lad.

Come down the back stairs When ye come to court me; Come down the back stairs When ye come to court me; Come down the back stairs, And let naebody see, And come as ye were na Coming to me.

XXXV. I AM MY MAMMY'S AE BAIRN.

Tune-"I'm o'er young to marry yet."

[The title, and part of the chorus only of this song, are old; the rest is by Burns, and was written for Johnson.]

I.

I am my mammy's ae bairn, Wi' unco folk I weary, Sir; And lying in a man's bed, I'm fley'd it make me eerie, Sir. I'm o'er young to marry yet; I'm o'er young to marry yet; I'm o'er young-'twad be a sin To tak' me frae my mammy yet.

II.
Hallowmas is come and gane, The nights are lang in winter, Sir; And you an' I in ae bed, In trouth, I dare na venture, Sir.
III.
Fu' loud and shrill the frosty wind, Blaws through the leafless timmer, Sir; But, if ye come this gate again, I'll aulder be gin simmer, Sir. I'm o'er young to marry yet; I'm o'er young to marry yet; I'm o'er young, 'twad be a sin To tak me frae my mammy yet.

XXXVI. BONNIE LASSIE, WILL YE GO.

Tune-"The birks of Aberfeldy."
[An old strain, called "The Birks of Abergeldie," was the forerunner of this sweet song: it was written, the poet says, standing under the Falls of Aberfeldy, near Moness, in Perthshire, during one of the tours which he made to the north, in the year 1787.]
CHORUS.
Bonnie lassie, will ye go, Will ye go, will ye go; Bonnie lassie, will ye go To the birks of Aberfeldy?
I.
Now simmer blinks on flowery braes, And o'er the crystal streamlet plays; [223]Come let us spend the lightsome days In the birks of Aberfeldy.
II.
The little birdies blithely sing, While o'er their heads the hazels hing, Or lightly flit on wanton wing In the birks of Aberfeldy.
III.
The braes ascend, like lofty wa's, The foamy stream deep-roaring fa's, O'erhung wi' fragrant spreading shaws, The birks of Aberfeldy.
IV.
The hoary cliffs are crown'd wi' flowers, White o'er the linns the burnie pours, And rising, weets wi' misty showers The birks of Aberfeldy.
V.
Let Fortune's gifts at random flee, They ne'er shall draw a wish frae me, Supremely blest wi' love and thee, In the birks of Aberfeldy. Bonnie lassie, will ye go, Will ye go, will ye go; Bonnie lassie, will ye go To the birks of Aberfeldy?

XXXVII. MACPHERSON'S FAREWELL.

Tune-"M'Pherson's Rant."
[This vehement and daring song had its origin in an older and inferior strain, recording the feelings of a noted freebooter when brought to "Justify his deeds on the gallows-tree" at Inverness.]

I.
Farewell, ye dungeons dark and strong, The wretch's destinie! Macpherson's time will not be long On yonder gallows-tree. Sae rantingly, sae wantonly, Sae dauntingly gaed he; He play'd a spring, and danc'd it round, Below the gallows-tree.
II.
Oh, what is death but parting breath? On many a bloody plain I've dar'd his face, and in this place I scorn him yet again!
III.
Untie these bands from off my hands, And bring to me my sword; And there's no a man in all Scotland, But I'll brave him at a word.
IV.
I've liv'd a life of sturt and strife; I die by treacherie: It burns my heart I must depart, And not avenged be.
V.
Now farewell light-thou sunshine bright, And all beneath the sky! May coward shame distain his name, The wretch that dares not die! Sae rantingly, sae wantonly, Sae dauntingly gaed he; He play'd a spring, and danc'd it round, Below the gallows-tree.

XXXVIII. BRAW LADS OF GALLA WATER.

Tune-"Galla Water."
[Burns found this song in the collection of Herd; added the first verse, made other but not material emendations, and published it in Johnson: in 1793 he wrote another version for Thomson.]
CHORUS.
Braw, braw lads of Galla Water; O braw lads of Galla Water: I'll kilt my coats aboon my knee, And follow my love thro' the water.
I.
Sae fair her hair, sae brent her brow, Sae bonny blue her een, my dearie; Sae white her teeth, sae sweet her mou', The mair I kiss she's ay my dearie.
II.
O'er yon bank and o'er yon brae, O'er yon moss amang the heather; [224]I'll kilt my coats aboon my knee, And follow my love thro' the water.
III.
Down amang the broom, the broom, Down amang the broom, my dearie, The lassie lost a silken snood, That cost her mony a blirt and bleary. Braw, braw lads of Galla Water; O braw lads of Galla-Water: I'll kilt my coats aboon my knee, And follow my love thro' the water.

XXXIX. STAY, MY CHARMER.

Tune-"An Gille dubh ciar dhubh."

[The air of this song was picked up by the poet in one of his northern tours: his Highland excursions coloured many of his lyric compositions.]

I.

Stay, my charmer, can you leave me? Cruel, cruel, to deceive me! Well you know how much you grieve me; Cruel charmer, can you go? Cruel charmer, can you go?

II.

By my love so ill requited; By the faith you fondly plighted; By the pangs of lovers slighted; Do not, do not leave me so! Do not, do not leave me so!

XL. THICKEST NIGHT, O'ERHANG MY DWELLING.

Tune-"Strathallan's Lament."

[The Viscount Strathallan, whom this song commemorates, was William Drummond: he was slain at the carnage of Culloden. It was long believed that he escaped to France and died in exile.]

I.

Thickest night, surround my dwelling! Howling tempests, o'er me rave! Turbid torrents, wintry swelling, Roaring by my lonely cave!

II.

Crystal streamlets gently flowing, Busy haunts of base mankind, Western breezes softly blowing, Suit not my distracted mind.

III.

In the cause of Right engaged, Wrongs injurious to redress, Honour's war we strongly waged, But the heavens denied success.

IV.

Ruin's wheel has driven o'er us, Not a hope that dare attend, The wild world is all before us- But a world without a friend.

XLI. MY HOGGIE.

Tune-"What will I do gin my Hoggie die?"

[Burns was struck with the pastoral wildness of this Liddesdale air, and wrote these words to it for the Museum: the first line only is old.]

What will I do gin my Hoggie die? My joy, my pride, my Hoggie! My only beast, I had nae mae, And vow but I was vogie! The lee-lang night we watch'd the fauld, Me and my faithfu' doggie; We heard nought but the roaring linn, Amang the braes sae scroggie; But the houlet cry'd frae the castle wa', The blitter frae the boggie, The tod reply'd upon the hill, I trembled for my Hoggie. When day did daw, and cocks did craw, The morning it was foggie; An' unco tyke lap o'er the dyke, And maist has kill'd my Hoggie.

XLII. HER DADDIE FORBAD.

Tune-"Jumpin' John."
[This is one of the old songs which Ritson accuses Burns of amending for the Museum: little of it, how[225]ever, is his, save a touch here and there-but they are Burns's touches.]
I.
Her daddie forbad, her minnie forbad; Forbidden she wadna be: She wadna trow't, the browst she brew'd Wad taste sae bitterlie. The lang lad they ca' jumpin' John Beguiled the bonnie lassie, The lang lad they ca' Jumpin' John Beguiled the bonnie lassie.
II.
A cow and a cauf, a yowe and a hauf, And thretty gude shillin's and three; A vera gude tocher, a cotter-man's dochter, The lass wi' the bonnie black e'e. The lang lad they ca' Jumpin' John Beguiled the bonnie lassie, The lang lad they ca' Jumpin' John Beguiled the bonnie lassie.

XLIII. UP IN THE MORNING EARLY

Tune-"Cold blows the wind."
["The chorus of this song," says the poet, in his notes on the Scottish Lyrics, "is old, the two stanzas are mine." The air is ancient, and was a favourite of Mary Stuart, the queen of William the Third.]
CHORUS.
Up in the morning's no for me, Up in the morning early; When a' the hills are cover'd wi' snaw, I'm sure it's winter fairly.
I.
Cauld blaws the wind frae east to west, The drift is driving sairly; Sae loud and shill I hear the blast, I'm sure it's winter fairly.
II.
The birds sit chittering in the thorn, A' day they fare but sparely; And lang's the night frae e'en to morn- I'm sure it's winter fairly. Up in the morning's no for me, Up in the morning early; When a' the hills are cover'd wi' snaw, I'm sure it's winter fairly.

XLIV. THE YOUNG HIGHLAND ROVER.

Tune-"Morag."
[The Young Highland Rover of this strain is supposed by some to be the Chevalier, and with more probability by others, to be a Gordon, as the song was composed in consequence of the poet's visit to "bonnie Castle-Gordon," in September, 1787.]

I.
Loud blaw the frosty breezes, The snaws the mountains cover; Like winter on me seizes, Since my young Highland rover Far wanders nations over. Where'er he go, where'er he stray. May Heaven be his warden: Return him safe to fair Strathspey, And bonnie Castle-Gordon!
II.
The trees now naked groaning, Shall Soon wi' leaves be hinging. The birdies dowie moaning, Shall a' be blithely singing, And every flower be springing. Sae I'll rejoice the lee-lang day When by his mighty Warden My youth's returned to fair Strathspey, And bonnie Castle-Gordon.

XLV. HEY, THE DUSTY MILLER

Tune-"The Dusty Miller."
[The Dusty Miller is an old strain, modified for the Museum by Burns: it is a happy specimen of his taste and skill in making the new look like the old.]
I.
Hey, the dusty miller, And his dusty coat; He will win a shilling, Or he spend a groat. Dusty was the coat, Dusty was the colour, Dusty was the kiss That I got frae the miller.
II.
Hey, the dusty miller, And his dusty sack; Leeze me on the calling Fills the dusty peck. Fills the dusty peck, Brings the dusty siller; I wad gie my coatie For the dusty miller.

XLVI. THERE WAS A LASS.

Tune-"Duncan Davison."
[There are several other versions of Duncan Davison, which it is more delicate to allude to than to quote: this one is in the Museum.]
I.
There was a lass, they ca'd her Meg, And she held o'er the moors to spin; There was a lad that follow'd her, They ca'd him Duncan Davison. The moor was driegh, and Meg was skiegh, Her favour Duncan could na win; For wi' the roke she wad him knock. And ay she shook the temper-pin.
II.
As o'er the moor they lightly foor, A burn was clear, a glen was green, Upon the banks they eas'd-their shanks, And ay she set the wheel between: But Duncan swore a haly aith, That Meg should be a bride the morn, Then Meg took up her spinnin' graith, And flang them a' out o'er the burn.
III.
We'll big a house,-a wee, wee house, And we will live like king and queen, Sae blythe and merry we will be When ye set by the wheel at e'en. A man

may drink and no be drunk; A man may fight and no be slain; A man may kiss a bonnie lass, And ay be welcome back again.

XLVII. THENIEL MENZIES' BONNIE MARY.

Tune.-"The Ruffian's Rant."
[Burns, it is believed, wrote this song during his first Highland tour, when he danced among the northern dames, to the tune of "Bab at the Bowster," till the morning sun rose and reproved them from the top of Ben Lomond.]
I.
In coming by the brig o' Dye, At Darlet we a blink did tarry; As day was dawin in the sky, We drank a health to bonnie Mary. Theniel Menzies' bonnie Mary; Theniel Menzies' bonnie Mary; Charlie Gregor tint his plaidie, Kissin' Theniel's bonnie Mary.
II.
Her een sae bright, her brow sae white, Her haffet locks as brown's a berry; And ay, they dimpl't wi' a smile, The rosy checks o' bonnie Mary.
III.
We lap and danced the lee lang day, Till piper lads were wae and weary; But Charlie gat the spring to pay, For kissin' Theniel's bonnie Mary. Theniel Menzies' bonnie Mary; Theniel Menzies' bonnie Mary; Charlie
Gregor tint his plaidie, Kissin' Theniel's bonnie Mary.

XLVIII. THE BANKS OF THE DEVON.

Tune.-"Bhannerach dhon na chri."
[These verses were composed on a charming young lady, Charlotte Hamilton, sister to the poet's friend, Gavin Hamilton of Mauchline, residing, when the song was written, at Harvieston, on the banks of the Devon, in the county of Clackmannan.]
I.
How pleasant the banks of the clear winding Devon, With green spreading bushes, and flowers blooming fair! [227]But the bonniest flower on the banks of the Devon Was once a sweet bud on the braes of the Ayr. Mild be the sun on this sweet blushing flower, In the gay rosy morn, as it bathes in the dew; And gentle the fall of the soft vernal shower, That steals on the evening each leaf to renew.
II.
O spare the dear blossom, ye orient breezes, With chill hoary wing, as ye usher the dawn; And far be thou distant, thou reptile that seizes The verdure and pride of the garden and lawn! Let Bourbon exult in his gay gilded Lilies, And England, triumphant, display her proud Rose: A fairer than either adorns the green valleys, Where Devon, sweet Devon,

meandering flows.

XLIX. WEARY FA' YOU, DUNCAN GRAY.

Tune-"Duncan Gray."

[The original Duncan Gray, out of which the present strain was extracted for Johnson, had no right to be called a lad of grace: another version, and in a happier mood, was written for Thomson.]

I.

Weary fa' you, Duncan Gray- Ha, ha, the girdin o't! Wae gae by you, Duncan Gray- Ha, ha, the girdin o't! When a' the lave gae to their play, Then I maun sit the lee lang day, And jog the cradle wi' my tae, And a' for the girdin o't!

II.

Bonnie was the Lammas moon- Ha, ha, the girdin o't! Glowrin' a' the hills aboon- Ha, ha, the girdin o't! The girdin brak, the beast cam down, I tint my curch, and baith my shoon; Ah! Duncan, ye're an unco loon- Wae on the bad girdin o't!

III.

But, Duncan, gin ye'll keep your aith- Ha, ha, the girdin o't! I'se bless you wi' my hindmost breath- Ha, ha, the girdin o't! Duncan, gin ye'll keep your aith, The beast again can bear us baith, And auld Mess John will mend the skaith, And clout the bad girdin o't.

L. THE PLOUGHMAN.

Tune-"Up wi' the ploughman."

[The old words, of which these in the Museum are an altered and amended version, are in the collection of Herd.]

I.

The ploughman he's a bonnie lad, His mind is ever true, jo, His garters knit below his knee, His bonnet it is blue, jo. Then up wi' him my ploughman lad, And hey my merry ploughman! Of a' the trades that I do ken, Commend me to the ploughman.

II.

My ploughman he comes hame at e'en, He's aften wat and weary; Cast off the wat, put on the dry, And gae to bed, my dearie!

III.

I will wash my ploughman's hose, And I will dress his o'erlay; I will mak my ploughman's bed, And cheer him late and early.

IV.

I hae been east, I hae been west, I hae been at Saint Johnston; The bonniest sight that e'er I saw Was the ploughman laddie dancin'.

V.
Snaw-white stockins on his legs, And siller buckles glancin'; A gude blue bonnet on his head- And O, but he was handsome! [228]
VI.
Commend me to the barn-yard, And the corn-mou, man; I never gat my coggie fou, Till I met wi' the ploughman. Up wi' him my ploughman lad, And hey my merry ploughman! Of a' the trades that I do ken,
Commend me to the ploughman.

LI. LANDLADY, COUNT THE LAWIN.

Tune-"Hey tutti, taiti."
[Of this song, the first and second verses are by Burns: the closing verse belongs to a strain threatening Britain with an invasion from the iron-handed Charles XII. of Sweden, to avenge his own wrongs and restore the line of the Stuarts.]
I.
Landlady, count the lawin, The day is near the dawin; Ye're a' blind drunk, boys, And I'm but jolly fou, Hey tutti, taiti, How tutti, taiti- Wha's fou now?
II.
Cog an' ye were ay fou, Cog an' ye were ay fou, I wad sit and sing to you If ye were ay fou.
III.
Weel may ye a' be! Ill may we never see! God bless the king, And the companie! Hey tutti, taiti, How tutti, taiti- Wha's fou now?

LII. RAVING WINDS AROUND HER BLOWING.

Tune-"Macgregor of Rura's Lament."
["I composed these verses," says Burns, "on Miss Isabella M'Leod, of Raza, alluding to her feelings on the death of her sister, and the still more melancholy death of her sister's husband, the late Earl of Loudon, in 1796."]
I.
Raving winds around her blowing, Yellow leaves the woodlands strowing, By a river hoarsely roaring, Isabella stray'd deploring- "Farewell hours that late did measure Sunshine days of joy and pleasure; Hail, thou gloomy night of sorrow, Cheerless night that knows no morrow!
II.
"O'er the past too fondly wandering, On the hopeless future pondering; Chilly grief my life-blood freezes, Fell despair my fancy seizes. Life, thou soul of every blessing, Load to misery most distressing, Gladly how would I resign thee, And to dark oblivion join thee!"

LIII. HOW LONG AND DREARY IS THE NIGHT.

To a Gaelic air.
[Composed for the Museum: the air of this affecting strain is true Highland: Burns, though not a musician, had a fine natural taste in the matter of national melodies.]
I.
How long and dreary is the night When I am frae my dearie! I sleepless lie frae e'en to morn, Tho' I were ne'er sae weary. I sleepless lie frae e'en to morn, Tho' I were ne'er sae weary.
II.
When I think on the happy days I spent wi' you, my dearie, And now what lands between us lie, How can I but be eerie! And now what lands between us lie, How can I be but eerie!
III.
How slow ye move, ye heavy hours, As ye were wae and weary! [229]It was na sae ye glinted by, When I was wi' my dearie. It was na sae ye glinted by, When I was wi' my dearie.

LIV. MUSING ON THE ROARING OCEAN.

Tune-"Druimion dubh."
[The air of this song is from the Highlands: the verses were written in compliment to the feelings of Mrs. M'Lauchlan, whose husband was an officer serving in the East Indies.]
I.
Musing on the roaring ocean, Which divides my love and me; Wearying heaven in warm devotion, For his weal where'er he be.
II.
Hope and fear's alternate billow Yielding late to nature's law, Whisp'ring spirits round my pillow Talk of him that's far awa.
III.
Ye whom sorrow never wounded, Ye who never shed a tear, Care-untroubled, joy-surrounded, Gaudy day to you is dear.
IV.
Gentle night, do thou befriend me; Downy sleep, the curtain draw; Spirits kind, again attend me, Talk of him that's far awa!

LV. BLITHE WAS SHE.

Tune-"Andro and his cutty gun."
[The heroine of this song, Euphemia Murray, of Lintrose was justly called

the "Flower of Strathmore:" she is now widow of Lord Methven, one of the Scottish judges, and mother of a fine family. The song was written at Ochtertyre, in June 1787.]

CHORUS.

Blithe, blithe and merry was she, Blithe was she but and ben: Blithe by the banks of Ern, And blithe in Glenturit glen.

I.

By Auchtertyre grows the aik, On Yarrow banks the birken shaw; But Phemie was a bonnier lass Than braes of Yarrow ever saw.

II.

Her looks were like a flow'r in May, Her smile was like a simmer morn; She tripped by the banks of Ern, As light's a bird upon a thorn.

III.

Her bonnie face it was as meek As any lamb upon a lea; The evening sun was ne'er sae sweet, As was the blink o' Phemie's ee.

IV.

The Highland hills I've wander'd wide, And o'er the Lowlands I hae been; But Phemie was the blithest lass That ever trod the dewy green. Blithe, blithe and merry was she, Blithe was she but and ben: Blithe by the banks of Ern. And blithe in Glenturit glen.

LVI. THE BLUDE RED ROSE AT YULE MAY BLAW.

Tune-"To daunton me."

[The Jacobite strain of "To daunton me," must have been in the mind of the poet when he wrote this pithy lyric for the Museum.]

I.

The blude red rose at Yule may blaw, The simmer lilies bloom in snaw, The frost may freeze the deepest sea; But an auld man shall never daunton me. To daunton me, and me so young, Wi' his fause heart and flatt'ring tongue. That is the thing you ne'er shall see; For an auld man shall never daunton me.

II.

For a' his meal and a' his maut, For a' his fresh beef and his saut, For a' his gold and white monie, An auld man shall never daunton me. [230]

III.

His gear may buy him kye and yowes, His gear may buy him glens and knowes; But me he shall not buy nor fee, For an auld man shall never daunton me.

IV.

He hirples twa fauld as he dow, Wi' his teethless gab and Ma auld beld pow, And the rain rains down frae his red bleer'd ee- That auld man shall never daunton me. To daunton me, and me sae young, Wi' his fause heart and flatt'ring tongue, That is the thing you ne'er shall see; For an auld man shall never daunton me.

LVII. COME BOAT ME O'ER TO CHARLIE.

Tune-"O'er the water to Charlie."

[The second stanza of this song, and nearly all the third, are by Burns. Many songs, some of merit, on the same subject, and to the same air, were in other days current in Scotland.]

I.

Come boat me o'er, come row me o'er, Come boat me o'er to Charlie; I'll gie John Ross another bawbee, To boat me o'er to Charlie. We'll o'er the water and o'er the sea, We'll o'er the water to Charlie; Come weal, come woe, we'll gather and go, And live or die wi' Charlie.

II.

I lo'e weel my Charlie's name, Tho' some there be abhor him: But O, to see auld Nick gaun hame, And Charlie's faes before him!

III.

I swear and vow by moon and stars, And sun that shines so early, If I had twenty thousand lives, I'd die as aft for Charlie. We'll o'er the water and o'er the sea, We'll o'er the water to Charlie; Come weal, come woe, we'll gather and go, And live or die wi' Charlie!

LVIII. A ROSE-BUD BY MY EARLY WALK.

Tune-"The Rose-bud."

[The "Rose-bud" of these sweet verses was Miss Jean Cruikshank, afterwards Mrs. Henderson, daughter of William Cruikshank, of St. James's Square, one of the masters of the High School of Edinburgh: she is also the subject of a poem equally sweet.]

I.

A rose-bud by my early walk, Adown a corn-enclosed bawk, Sae gently bent its thorny stalk, All on a dewy morning. Ere twice the shades o' dawn are fled, In a' its crimson glory spread, And drooping rich the dewy head, It scents the early morning.

II.

Within the bush, her covert nest A little linnet fondly prest, The dew sat chilly on her breast Sae early in the morning. She soon shall see her tender brood, The pride, the pleasure o' the wood, Amang the fresh green leaves bedew'd, Awake the early morning.

III.

So thou, dear bird, young Jeany fair, On trembling string or vocal air, Shall sweetly pay the tender care That tends thy early morning. So thou, sweet rose-bud, young and gay, Shalt beauteous blaze upon the day, And bless the parent's evening ray That watch'd thy early morning.

LIX. RATTLIN', ROARIN' WILLIE.

Tune-"Rattlin', roarin' Willie."
["The hero of this chant," says Burns "was one of the worthiest fellows in the world-William Dunbar, Esq., Write to the Signet, Edinburgh, and Colonel of the Crochallan corps-a club of wits, who took that title at the time of raising the fencible regiments."]
I.
O rattlin', roarin' Willie, O, he held to the fair, An' for to sell his fiddle, An' buy some other ware; [231]But parting wi' his fiddle, The saut tear blint his ee; And rattlin', roarin' Willie, Ye're welcome hame to me!
II.
O Willie, come sell your fiddle, O sell your fiddle sae fine; O Willie, come sell your fiddle, And buy a pint o' wine! If I should sell my fiddle, The warl' would think I was mad; For mony a rantin' day My fiddle and I hae had.
III.
As I cam by Crochallan, I cannily keekit ben- Rattlin', roarin' Willie Was sittin' at yon board en'; Sitting at yon board en', And amang good companie; Rattlin', roarin' Willie, Ye're welcome hame to me I

LX. BRAVING ANGRY WINTER'S STORMS.

Tune-"Neil Gow's Lamentations for Abercairny."
["This song," says the poet, "I composed on one of the most accomplished of women, Miss Peggy Chalmers that was, now Mrs. Lewis Hay, of Forbes and Co.'s bank, Edinburgh." She now lives at Pau, in the south of France.]
I.
Where, braving angry winter's storms, The lofty Ochels rise, Far in their shade my Peggy's charms First blest my wondering eyes; As one who by some savage stream, A lonely gem surveys, Astonish'd, doubly marks its beam, With art's most polish'd blaze.
II.
Blest be the wild, sequester'd shade, And blest the day and hour, Where Peggy's charms I first survey'd, When first I felt their power! The tyrant Death, with grim control, May seize my fleeting breath; But tearing Peggy from my soul Must be a stronger death.

LXI. TIBBIE DUNBAR.

Tune-"Johnny M'Gill."

[We owe the air of this song to one Johnny M'Gill, a fiddler of Girvan, who bestowed his own name on it: and the song itself partly to Burns and partly to some unknown minstrel. They are both in the Museum.]

I.

O, Wilt thou go wi' me, Sweet Tibbie Dunbar? O, wilt thou go wi' me, Sweet Tibbie Dunbar? Wilt thou ride on a horse, Or be drawn in a car, Or walk by my side, O, sweet Tibbie Dunbar?

II.

I care na thy daddie, His lands and his money, I care na thy kindred, Sae high and sae lordly: But say thou wilt hae me For better for waur- And come in thy coatie, Sweet Tibbie Dunbar!

LXII. STREAMS THAT GLIDE IN ORIENT PLAINS.

Tune-"Morag."

[We owe these verses to the too brief visit which the poet, in 1787, made to Gordon Castle: he was hurried away, much against his will, by his moody and obstinate friend William Nicol.]

I.

Streams that glide in orient plains, Never bound by winter's chains; Glowing here on golden sands, There commix'd with foulest stains From tyranny's empurpled bands; These, their richly gleaming waves, I leave to tyrants and their slaves; Give me the stream that sweetly laves The banks by Castle-Gordon.

II.

Spicy forests, ever gay, Shading from the burning ray, Hapless wretches sold to toil, [232]Or the ruthless native's way, Bent on slaughter, blood, and spoil: Woods that ever verdant wave, I leave the tyrant and the slave, Give me the groves that lofty brave The storms by Castle-Gordon.

III.

Wildly here without control, Nature reigns and rules the whole; In that sober pensive mood, Dearest to the feeling soul, She plants the forest, pours the flood; Life's poor day I'll musing rave, And find at night a sheltering cave, Where waters flow and wild woods wave, By bonnie Castle-Gordon.

LXIII. MY HARRY WAS A GALLANT GAY.

Tune-"Highland's Lament."

["The chorus," says Burns, "I picked up from an old woman in Dumblane: the rest of the song is mine." He composed it for Johnson: the tone is Jacobitical.]

I.

My Harry was a gallant gay, Fu' stately strode he on the plain: But now he's banish'd far away, I'll never see him back again, O for him back again! O for him back again! I wad gie a' Knockhaspie's land For Highland Harry back again.

II.

When a' the lave gae to their bed, I wander dowie up the glen; I set me down and greet my fill, And ay I wish him back again.

III.

O were some villains hangit high. And ilka body had their ain! Then I might see the joyfu' sight, My Highland Harry back again. O for him back again! O for him back again! I wad gie a' Knockhaspie's land For Highland Harry back again.

LXIV. THE TAILOR.

Tune-"The Tailor fell thro' the bed, thimbles an' a'."

[The second and fourth verses are by Burns, the rest is very old, the air is also very old, and is played at trade festivals and processions by the Corporation of Tailors.]

I.

The Tailor fell thro' the bed, thimbles an' a', The Tailor fell thro' the bed, thimbles an' a'; The blankets were thin, and the sheets they were sma', The Tailor fell thro' the bed, thimbles an' a'.

II.

The sleepy bit lassie, she dreaded nae ill, The sleepy bit lassie, she dreaded nae ill; The weather was cauld, and the lassie lay still, She thought that a tailor could do her nae ill.

III.

Gie me the groat again, canny young man; Gie me the groat again, canny young man; The day it is short, and the night it is lang, The dearest siller that ever I wan!

IV.

There's somebody weary wi' lying her lane; There's somebody weary wi' lying her lane; There's some that are dowie, I trow would be fain To see the bit tailor come skippin' again.

LXV. SIMMER'S A PLEASANT TIME.

Tune-"Ay waukin o'."

[Tytler and Ritson unite in considering the air of these words as one of our most ancient melodies. The first verse of the song is from the hand of Burns; the rest had the benefit of his emendations: it is to be found in the Museum.]

I.
Simmer's a pleasant time, Flow'rs of ev'ry colour; The water rins o'er the heugh, And I long for my true lover. Ay waukin O, Waukin still and wearie: Sleep I can get nane For thinking on my dearie. [233]
II.
When I sleep I dream, When I wauk I'm eerie; Sleep I can get nane For thinking on my dearie.
III.
Lanely night comes on, A' the lave are sleeping; I think on my bonnie lad And I bleer my een with greetin'. Ay waukin O, Waukin still and wearie: Sleep I can get nane For thinking on my dearie.

LXVI. BEWARE O' BONNIE ANN.

Tune-"Ye gallants bright."
[Burns wrote this song in honour of Ann Masterton, daughter of Allan Masterton, author of the air of Strathallan's Lament: she is now Mrs. Derbishire, and resides in London.]
I.
Ye gallants bright, I red ye right, Beware o' bonnie Ann; Her comely face sae fu' o' grace, Your heart she will trepan. Her een sae bright, like stars by night, Her skin is like the swan; Sae jimply lac'd her genty waist, That sweetly ye might span.
II.
Youth, grace, and love attendant move, And pleasure leads the van: In a' their charms, and conquering arms, They wait on bonnie Ann. The captive bands may chain the hands, But love enclaves the man; Ye Gallants braw, I red you a', Beware of bonnie Ann!

LXVII. WHEN ROSY MAY.

Tune-"The gardener wi' his paidle."
[The air of this song is played annually at the precession of the Gardeners: the title only is old; the rest is the work of Burns. Every trade had, in other days, an air of its own, and songs to correspond; but toil and sweat came in harder measures, and drove melodies out of working-men's heads.]
I.
When rosy May comes in wi' flowers, To deck her gay green-spreading bowers, Then busy, busy are his hours- The gard'ner wi' his paidle The crystal waters gently fa'; The merry birds are lovers a'; The scented breezes round him blaw- The gard'ner wi' his paidle.
II.
When purple morning starts the hare To steal upon her early fare, Then

thro' the dews he maun repair- The gard'ner wi' his paidle. When day, expiring in the west, The curtain draws of nature's rest, He flies to her arms he lo'es best- The gard'ner wi' his paidle.

LXVIII. BLOOMING NELLY.

Tune-"On a bank of flowers."
[One of the lyrics of Allan Ramsay's collection seems to have been in the mind of Burns when he wrote this: the words and air are in the Museum.]
I.
On a bank of flowers, in a summer day, For summer lightly drest, The youthful blooming Nelly lay, With love and sleep opprest; When Willie wand'ring thro' the wood, Who for her favour oft had sued, He gaz'd, he wish'd, he fear'd, he blush'd, And trembled where he stood.
II.
Her closed eyes like weapons sheath'd, Were seal'd in soft repose; Her lips still as she fragrant breath'd, It richer dy'd the rose. The springing lilies sweetly prest, Wild-wanton, kiss'd her rival breast; He gaz'd, he wish'd, he fear'd, he blush'd- His bosom ill at rest. [234]
III.
Her robes light waving in the breeze Her tender limbs embrace; Her lovely form, her native ease, All harmony and grace: Tumultuous tides his pulses roll, A faltering, ardent kiss he stole; He gaz'd, he wish'd, he fear'd, he blush'd, And sigh'd his very soul.
IV.
As flies the partridge from the brake, On fear-inspired wings, So Nelly, starting, half awake, Away affrighted springs: But Willie follow'd, as he should, He overtook her in a wood; He vow'd, he pray'd, he found the maid Forgiving all and good.

LXIX. THE DAY RETURNS.

Tune-"Seventh of November."
[The seventh of November was the anniversary of the marriage of Mr. and Mrs. Riddel, of Friars-Carse, and these verses were composed in compliment to the day.]
I.
The day returns, my bosom burns, The blissful day we twa did meet, Tho' winter wild in tempest toil'd, Ne'er summer-sun was half sae sweet. Than a' the pride that loads the tide, And crosses o'er the sultry line; Than kingly robes, than crowns and globes, Heaven gave me more-it made thee mine!
II.
While day and night can bring delight, Or nature aught of pleasure give,

While joys above my mind can move, For thee, and thee alone I live. When that grim foe of life below, Comes in between to make us part, The iron hand that breaks our band, It breaks my bliss-it breaks my heart.

LXX. MY LOVE SHE'S BUT A LASSIE YET.

Tune-"Lady Bandinscoth's Reel."
[These verses had their origin in an olden strain, equally lively and less delicate: some of the old lines keep their place: the title is old. Both words and all are in the Musical Museum.]
I.
My love she's but a lassie yet, My love she's but a lassie yet, We'll let her stand a year or twa, Shell no be half so saucy yet. I rue the day I sought her, O; I rue the day I sought her, O; Wha gets her needs na say he's woo'd, But he may say he's bought her, O!
II.
Come, draw a drap o' the best o't yet; Come, draw a drap o' the best o't yet; Gae seek for pleasure where ye will, But here I never miss'd it yet. We're a' dry wi' drinking o't; We're a' dry wi' drinking o't; The minister kiss'd the fiddler's wife, An' could na preach for thinkin' o't.

LXXI. JAMIE, COME TRY ME.

Tune-"Jamy, come try me."
[Burns in these verses caught up the starting note of an old song, of which little more than the starting words deserve to be remembered: the word and air are in the Musical Museum.]
CHORUS.
Jamie, come try me, Jamie, come try me; If thou would win my love, Jamie, come try me.
I.
If thou should ask my love, Could I deny thee? If thou would win my love, Jamie, come try me.
II.
If thou should kiss me, love, Wha could espy thee? If thou wad be my love, Jamie, come try me. Jamie, come try me, Jamie, come try me; If thou would win my love, Jamie, come try me.
[235]

LXXII. MY BONNIE MARY.

Tune-"Go fetch to me a pint o' wine."
[Concerning this fine song, Burns in his notes says, "This air is Oswald's:

the first half-stanza of the song is old, the rest is mine." It is believed, however, that the whole of the song is from his hand: in Hogg and Motherwell's edition of Burns, the starting lines are supplied from an olden strain: but some of the old strains in that work are to be regarded with suspicion.]

I.

Go fetch to me a pint o' wine, An' fill it in a silver tassie; That I may drink, before I go, A service to my bonnie lassie; The boat rocks at the pier o' Leith; Fu' loud the wind blaws frae the ferry; The ship rides by the Berwick-law, And I maun leave my bonnie Mary.

II.

The trumpets sound, the banners fly, The glittering spears are ranked ready; The shouts o' war are heard afar, The battle closes thick and bloody; It's not the roar o' sea or shore Wad make me langer wish to tarry; Nor shouts o' war that's heard afar- It's leaving thee, my bonnie Mary.

LXXIII. THE LAZY MIST.

Tune-"The lazy mist."

[All that Burns says about the authorship of The Lazy Mist, is, "This song is mine." The air, which is by Oswald, together with the words, is in the Musical Museum.]

I.

The lazy mist hangs from the brow of the hill, Concealing the course of the dark winding rill; How languid the scenes, late so sprightly, appear! As Autumn to Winter resigns the pale year. The forests are leafless, the meadows are brown, And all the gay foppery of summer is flown: Apart let me wander, apart let me muse, How quick Time is flying, how keen Fate pursues!

II.

How long have I liv'd, but how much liv'd in vain! How little of life's scanty span may remain! What aspects, old Time, in his progress, has worn! What ties cruel Fate in my bosom has torn! How foolish, or worse, till our summit is gain'd! And downward, how weaken'd, how darken'd, how pain'd! Life is not worth having with all it can give- For something beyond it poor man sure must live.

LXXIV. THE CAPTAIN'S LADY.

Tune-"O mount and go."

[Part of this song belongs to an old maritime strain, with the same title: it was communicated, along with many other songs, made or amended by Burns, to the Musical Museum.]

CHORUS.
O mount and go, Mount and make you ready; O mount and go, And be the Captain's Lady.
I.
When the drums do beat, And the cannons rattle, Thou shall sit in state, And see thy love in battle.
II.
When the vanquish'd foe Sues for peace and quiet, To the shades we'll go, And in love enjoy it. O mount and go, Mount and make you ready; O mount and go, And be the Captain's Lady.

LXXV. OF A' THE AIRTS THE WIND CAN BLAW

Tune-"Miss Admiral Gordon's Strathspey."
[Bums wrote this charming song in honour of Joan Armour: he archly says in his notes, "P.S. it was during[236] the honeymoon." Other versions are abroad; this one is from the manuscripts of the poet.]
I.
Of a' the airts the wind can blaw, I dearly like the west, For there the bonnie lassie lives, The lassie I lo'e best: There wild-woods grow, and rivers row, And mony a hill between; But day and night my fancy's flight Is ever wi' my Jean.
II.
I see her in the dewy flowers, I see her sweet and fair: I hear her in the tunefu' birds, I hear her charm the air: There's not a bonnie flower that springs By fountain, shaw, or green, There's not a bonnie bird that sings, But minds me o' my Jean.
III.
O blaw, ye westlin winds, blaw saft Among the leafy trees, Wi' balmy gale, frae hill and dale Bring hame the laden bees; And bring the lassie back to me That's aye sae neat and clean; Ae smile o' her wad banish care, Sae charming is my Jean.
IV.
What sighs and vows amang the knowes Hae passed atween us twa! How fond to meet, how wae to part, That night she gaed awa! The powers aboon can only ken, To whom the heart is seen, That nane can be sae dear to me As my sweet lovely Jean!

LXXVI. FIRST WHEN MAGGY WAS MY CARE.

Tune-"Whistle o'er the lave o't."
[The air of this song was composed by John Bruce, of Dumfries, musician: the words, though originating in an olden strain, are wholly by Burns, and

I.
"John Anderson, my jo, John, When we were first acquent, Your locks were like the raven, Your bonnie brow was brent; But now your brow is beld, John, Your locks are like the snaw; But blessings on your frosty pow, John Anderson, my jo.
[238]
II.
John Anderson, my jo, John, We clamb the hill thegither; And mony a canty day, John, We've had wi' ane anither: Now we maun totter down, John, But hand in hand we'll go; And sleep thegither at the foot, John Anderson, my jo.

LXXXI. OUR THRISSLES FLOURISHED FRESH AND FAIR.

Tune-"Awa Whigs, awa."
[Burns trimmed up this old Jacobite ditty for the Museum, and added some of the bitterest bits: the second and fourth verses are wholly his.]
CHORUS.
Awa Whigs, awa! Awa Whigs, awa! Ye're but a pack o' traitor louns, Ye'll do nae good at a'.
I
Our thrissles flourish'd fresh and fair, And bonnie bloom'd our roses; But Whigs came like a frost in June, And wither'd a' our posies.
II.
Our ancient crown's fa'n in the dust- Deil blin' them wi' the stoure o't; And write their names in his black beuk, Wha gae the Whigs the power o't.
III.
Our sad decay in Church and State Surpasses my descriving: The Whigs came o'er us for a curse, And we hae done wi' thriving.
IV.
Grim vengeance lang ha's taen a nap, But we may see him wauken; Gude help the day when royal heads Are hunted like a maukin. Awa Whigs, awa! Awa Whigs, awa! Ye're but a pack o' traitor louns, Ye'll do nae gude at a'.

LXXXII. CA' THE EWES.

Tune-"Ca' the ewes to the knowes."
[Most of this sweet pastoral is of other days: Burns made several emendations, and added the concluding verse. He afterwards, it will be observed, wrote for Thomson a second version of the subject and the air.]
CHORUS
Ca' the ewes to the knowes, Ca' them whare the heather grows, Ca' them whare the burnie rowes, My bonnie dearie!

I.
As I gaed down the water-side, There I met my shepherd lad, He row'd me sweetly in his plaid, An' he ca'd me his dearie.
II.
Will ye gang down the water-side, And see the waves sae sweetly glide, Beneath the hazels spreading wide? The moon it shines fu' clearly.
III.
I was bred up at nae sic school, My shepherd lad, to play the fool, And a' the day to sit in dool, And naebody to see me.
IV.
Ye sall get gowns and ribbons meet, Cauf-leather shoon upon your feet, And in my arms ye'se lie and sleep, And ye shall be my dearie.
V.
If ye'll but stand to what ye've said, I'se gang wi' you, my shepherd lad, And ye may rowe me in your plaid, And I shall be your dearie.
VI.
While waters wimple to the sea; While day blinks in the lift sae hie; 'Till clay-cauld death sall blin' my e'e, Ye sall be my dearie. Ca' the ewes to the knowes, Ca' them whare the heather grows, Ca' them whare the burnie rowes, My bonnie dearie.
[239]

LXXXIII. MERRY HAE I BEEN TEETHIN' A HECKLE.

Tune-"Lord Breadalbone's March."
[Part of this song is old: Sir Harris Nicolas says it does not appear to be in the Museum: let him look again.]
I.
O merry hae I been teethin' a heckle, And merry hae I been shapin' a spoon; O merry hae I been cloutin a kettle, And kissin' my Katie when a' was done. O a' the lang day I ca' at my hammer, An' a' the lang day I whistle and sing, A' the lang night I cuddle my kimmer, An' a' the lang night as happy's a king.
II.
Bitter in dool I lickit my winnins, O' marrying Bess to gie her a slave: Blest be the hour she cool'd in her linens, And blythe be the bird that sings on her grave. Come to my arms, my Katie, my Katie, An' come to my arms and kiss me again! Drunken or sober, here's to thee, Katie! And blest be the day I did it again.

LXXXIV. THE BRAES O' BALLOCHMYLE.

Tune-"The Braes o' Ballochmyle."

[Mary Whitefoord, eldest daughter of Sir John Whitefoord, was the heroine of this song: it was written when that ancient family left their ancient inheritance. It is in the Museum, with an air by Allan Masterton.]

I.

The Catrine woods were yellow seen, The flowers decay'd on Catrine lea, Nae lav'rock sang on hillock green, But nature sicken'd on the e'e. Thro' faded groves Maria sang, Hersel' in beauty's bloom the while, And ay the wild-wood echoes rang, Fareweel the Braes o' Ballochmyle!

II.

Low in your wintry beds, ye flowers, Again ye'll nourish fresh and fair; Ye birdies dumb, in withering bowers, Again ye'll charm the vocal air. But here, alas! for me nae mair Shall birdie charm, or floweret smile; Fareweel the bonnie banks of Ayr, Fareweel, fareweel! sweet Ballochmyle!

LXXXV. TO MARY IN HEAVEN.

Tune-"Death of Captain Cook."

[This sublime and affecting Ode was composed by Burns in one of his fits of melancholy, on the anniversary of Highland Mary's death. All the day he had been thoughtful, and at evening he went out, threw himself down by the side of one of his corn-ricks, and with his eyes fixed on "a bright, particular star," was found by his wife, who with difficulty brought him in from the chill midnight air. The song was already composed, and he had only to commit it to paper. It first appeared in the Museum.]

I.

Thou lingering star, with less'ning ray, That lov'st to greet the early morn, Again thou usherest in the day My Mary from my soul was torn. O Mary! dear departed shade! Where is thy place of blissful rest? Seest thou thy lover lowly laid? Hear'st thou the groans that rend his breast?

II.

That sacred hour can I forget, Can I forget the hallow'd grove, Where by the winding Ayr we met, To live one day of parting love! Eternity cannot efface Those records dear of transports past; Thy image at our last embrace; Ah! little thought we 'twas our last!

III.

Ayr, gurgling, kiss'd his pebbled shore, O'erhung with wild woods, thick'ning green; The fragrant birch, and hawthorn, hoar, Twin'd am'rous round the raptured scene; The flow'rs sprang wanton to be prest, The birds sang love on every spray- Till too, too soon, the glowing west Proclaim'd the speed of winged day.

IV.

Still o'er these scenes my mem'ry wakes, And fondly broods with miser care! [240]Time but th' impression stronger makes, As streams their channels deeper wear. My Mary, dear departed shade! Where is thy place of blissful rest? Seest thou thy lover lowly laid? Hear'st thou the groans that rend his breast?

LXXXVI. EPPIE ADAIR.

Tune-"My Eppie."
["This song," says Sir Harris Nicolas, "which has been ascribed to Burns by some of his editors, is in the Musical Museum without any name." It is partly an old strain, corrected by Burns: he communicated it to the Museum.]
I.
An' O! my Eppie, My jewel, my Eppie! Wha wadna be happy Wi' Eppie Adair? By love, and by beauty, By law, and by duty, I swear to be true to My Eppie Adair!
II.
An' O! my Eppie, My jewel, my Eppie! Wha wadna be happy Wi' Eppie Adair? A' pleasure exile me, Dishonour defile me, If e'er I beguile thee, My Eppie Adair!

LXXXVII. THE BATTLE OF SHERIFF-MUIR.

Tune-"Cameronian Rant."
[One Barclay, a dissenting clergyman in Edinburgh, wrote a rhyming dialogue between two rustics, on the battle of Sheriff-muir: Burns was in nowise pleased with the way in which the reverend rhymer handled the Highland clans, and wrote this modified and improved version.]
I.
"O cam ye here the fight to shun, Or herd the sheep wi' me, man? Or were ye at the Sherra-muir, And did the battle see, man?" I saw the battle, sair and tough, And reekin' red ran mony a sheugh. My heart, for fear, gaed sough for sough, To hear the thuds, and see the cluds, O' clans frae woods, in tartan duds, Wha glaum'd at kingdoms three, man.
II.
The red-coat lads, wi' black cockades, To meet them were na slaw, man; They rush'd and push'd, and blude outgush'd, And mony a bouk did fa', man: The great Argyll led on his files, I wat they glanc'd for twenty miles: They hough'd the clans like nine-pin kyles, They hack'd and hash'd, while broad-swords clash'd, And thro' they dash'd, and hew'd, and smash'd, 'Till fey men died awa, man.
III.
But had you seen the philibegs, And skyrin tartan trews, man; When in the teeth they dar'd our Whigs And covenant true blues, man; In lines extended

lang and large, When bayonets opposed the targe, And thousands hasten'd to the charge, Wi' Highland wrath they frae the sheath, Drew blades o' death, 'till, out o' breath, They fled like frighted doos, man.
IV.
"O how deil, Tam, can that be true? The chase gaed frae the north, man; I saw myself, they did pursue The horsemen back to Forth, man; And at Dumblane, in my ain sight, They took the brig wi' a' their might, And straught to Stirling winged their flight; But, cursed lot! the gates were shut; And mony a huntit, poor red-coat, For fear amaist did swarf, man!"
V.
My sister Kate cam up the gate Wi' crowdie unto me, man; She swore she saw some rebels run Frae Perth unto Dundee, man: Their left-hand general had nae skill, The Angus lads had nae good-will That day their neebors' blood to spill; For fear, by foes, that they should lose Their cogs o' brose-they scar'd at blows. And so it goes, you see, man. [241]
VI.
They've lost some gallant gentlemen, Amang the Highland clans, man! I fear my Lord Panmure is slain, Or fallen in Whiggish hands, man: Now wad ye sing this double fight, Some fell for wrang, and some for right; And mony bade the world guid-night; Then ye may tell, how pell and mell, By red claymores, and muskets' knell, Wi' dying yell, the Tories fell, And Whigs to hell did flee, man.

LXXXVIII. YOUNG JOCKEY.

Tune-"Young Jockey."
[With the exception of three or four lines, this song, though marked in the Museum as an old song with additions, is the work of Burns. He often seems to have sat down to amend or modify old verses, and found it easier to make verses wholly new.]
I.
Young Jockey was the blythest lad In a' our town or here awa: Fu' blythe he whistled at the gaud, Fu' lightly danced he in the ha'. He roosed my een, sae bonnie blue, He roos'd my waist sae genty sma', And ay my heart came to my mou' When ne'er a body heard or saw.
II.
My Jockey toils upon the plain, Thro' wind and weet, thro' frost and snaw; And o'er the lea I leuk fu' fain, When Jockey's owsen hameward ca'. An' ay the night comes round again, When in his arms he takes me a', An' ay he vows he'll be my ain, As lang's he has a breath to draw.

LXXXIX. O WILLIE BREW'D.

Tune-"Willie brew'd a peck o' maut."
[The scene of this song is Laggan, in Nithsdale, a small estate which Nicol bought by the advice of the poet. It was composed in memory of the house-heating. "We had such a joyous meeting," says Burns, "that Masterton and I agreed, each in our own way, to celebrate the business." The Willie who made the browst was, therefore, William Nicol; the Allan who composed the air, Allan Masterton; and he who wrote this choicest of convivial songs, Robert Burns.]
I.
O, Willie brew'd a peck o' maut, And Rob and Allan came to see: Three blither hearts, that lee-lang night Ye wad na find in Christendie. We are na fou, we're no that fou, But just a drappie in our e'e; The cock may craw, the day may daw, And aye we'll taste the barley bree.
II.
Here are we met, three merry boys, Three merry boys, I trow, are we; And mony a night we've merry been, And mony mae we hope to be!
III.
It is the moon-I ken her horn, That's blinkin in the lift sae hie; She shines sae bright to wyle us hame, But, by my sooth, she'll wait a wee!
IV.
Wha first shall rise to gang awa', A cuckold, coward loon is he! Wha last beside his chair shall fa', He is the king amang us three! We are na fou, we're no that fou, But just a drappie in our e'e; The cock may craw, the day may daw, And aye we'll taste the barley bree.

XC. WHARE HAE YE BEEN.

Tune-"Killiecrankie."
["This song," says Sir Harris Nicolas, "is in the Museum without Burns's name." It was composed by Burns on the battle of Killiecrankie, and sent in his own handwriting to Johnson; he puts it in the mouth of a Whig.]
I.
Whare hae ye been sae braw, lad? Whare hae ye been sae brankie, O? O, whare hae ye been sae braw, lad? Cam ye by Killiecrankie, O? [242]An' ye had been whare I hae been, Ye wad na been so cantie, O; An' ye had seen what I hae seen, On the braes o' Killiecrankie, O.
II.
I fought at land, I fought at sea; At hame I fought my auntie, O; But I met the Devil an' Dundee, On the braes o' Killiecrankie, O. The bauld Pitcur fell in a furr, An' Clavers got a clankie, O; Or I had fed on Athole gled, On the braes o' Killiecrankie, O.

XCI. I GAED A WAEFU' GATE YESTREEN.

Air-"The blue-eyed lass."
[This blue-eyed lass was Jean Jeffry, daughter to the minister of Lochmaben: she was then a rosy girl of seventeen, with winning manners and laughing blue eyes. She is now Mrs. Renwick, and lives in New York.]
I.
I gaed a waefu' gate yestreen, A gate, I fear, I'll dearlie rue; I gat my death frae twa sweet een, Twa lovely een o' bonnie blue. 'Twas not her golden ringlets bright; Her lips, like roses, wat wi' dew, Her heaving bosom, lily-white- It was her een sae bonnie blue.
II.
She talk'd, she smil'd, my heart she wyl'd; She charm'd my soul-I wist na how: And ay the stound, the deadly wound, Cam frae her een sae bonnie blue. But spare to speak, and spare to speed; She'll aiblins listen to my vow: Should she refuse, I'll lay my dead To her twa een sae bonnie blue.

XCII. THE BANKS OF NITH.

Tune-"Robie donna Gorach."
[The command which the Comyns held on the Nith was lost to the Douglasses: the Nithsdale power, on the downfall of that proud name, was divided; part went to the Charteris's and the better portion to the Maxwells: the Johnstones afterwards came in for a share, and now the Scots prevail.]
I.
The Thames flows proudly to the sea, Where royal cities stately stand; But sweeter flows the Nith, to me, Where Comyns ance had high command: When shall I see that honour'd land, That winding stream I love so dear! Must wayward Fortune's adverse hand For ever, ever keep me here?
II.
How lovely, Nith, thy fruitful vales, Where spreading hawthorns gaily bloom! How sweetly wind thy sloping dales, Where lambkins wanton thro' the broom! Tho' wandering now, must be my doom, Far from thy bonnie banks and braes, May there my latest hours consume, Amang the friends of early days!

XCIII. MY HEART IS A-BREAKING, DEAR TITTIE.

Tune-"Tam Glen."
[Tam Glen is the title of an old Scottish song, and older air: of the former all that remains is a portion of the chorus. Burns when he wrote it sent it to the Museum.]
I.
My heart is a-breaking, dear Tittie! Some counsel unto me come len', To

anger them a' is a pity, But what will I do wi' Tam Glen?
II.
I'm thinking wi' sic a braw fellow, In poortith I might make a fen'; What care I in riches to wallow, If I maunna marry Tam Glen?
III.
There's Lowrie the laird o' Dumeller, "Gude day to you, brute!" he comes ben: He brags and he blaws o' his siller, But when will he dance like Tam Glen?
IV.
My minnie does constantly deave me, And bids me beware o' young men; They flatter, she says, to deceive me, But wha can think so o' Tam Glen? [243]
V.
My daddie says, gin I'll forsake him, He'll gie me guid hunder marks ten: But, if it's ordain'd I maun take him, O wha will I get but Tam Glen?
VI.
Yestreen at the Valentine's dealing, My heart to my mou' gied a sten; For thrice I drew ane without failing, And thrice it was written-Tam Glen.
VII.
The last Halloween I was waukin My droukit sark-sleeve, as ye ken; His likeness cam up the house staukin, And the very grey breeks o' Tam Glen!
VIII.
Come counsel, dear Tittie! don't tarry- I'll gie you my bonnie black hen, Gif ye will advise me to marry The lad that I lo'e dearly, Tam Glen.

XCIV. FRAE THE FRIENDS AND LAND I LOVE.

Air-"Carron Side."
[Burns says, "I added the four last lines, by way of giving a turn to the theme of the poem, such as it is." The rest of the song is supposed to be from the same hand: the lines are not to be found in earlier collections.]
I.
Frae the friends and land I love, Driv'n by fortune's felly spite, Frae my best belov'd I rove, Never mair to taste delight; Never mair maun hope to find, Ease frae toil, relief frae care: When remembrance wracks the mind, Pleasures but unveil despair.
II.
Brightest climes shall mirk appear, Desert ilka blooming shore, Till the Fates, nae mair severe, Friendship, love, and peace restore; Till Revenge, wi' laurell'd head, Bring our banish'd hame again; And ilka loyal bonnie lad Cross the seas and win his ain.

XCV. SWEET CLOSES THE EVENING.

Tune-"Craigie-burn-wood."
[This is one of several fine songs in honour of Jean Lorimer, of Kemmis-hall, Kirkmahoe, who for some time lived on the banks of the Craigie-burn, near Moffat. It was composed in aid of the eloquence of a Mr. Gillespie, who was in love with her: but it did not prevail, for she married an officer of the name of Whelpdale, lived with him for a month or so: reasons arose on both sides which rendered separation necessary; she then took up her residence in Dumfries, where she had many opportunities of seeing the poet. She lived till lately.]
CHORUS.
Beyond thee, dearie, beyond thee, dearie, And O, to be lying beyond thee; O sweetly, soundly, weel may he sleep That's laid in the bed beyond thee!
I.
Sweet closes the evening on Craigie-burn-wood, And blithely awaukens the morrow; But the pride of the spring in the Craigie-burn-wood Can yield to me nothing but sorrow.
II.
I see the spreading leaves and flowers, I hear the wild birds singing; But pleasure they hae nane for me, While care my heart is wringing.
III.
I canna tell, I maunna tell, I darena for your anger; But secret love will break my heart, If I conceal it langer.
IV.
I see thee gracefu', straight, and tall, I see thee sweet and bonnie; But oh! what will my torments be, If thou refuse thy Johnnie!
V.
To see thee in anither's arms, In love to lie and languish, 'Twad be my dead, that will be seen, My heart wad burst wi' anguish.
VI.
But, Jeanie, say thou wilt be mine, Say, thou lo'es nane before me; [244]And a' my days o' life to come I'll gratefully adore thee. Beyond thee, dearie, beyond thee, dearie, And O, to be lying beyond thee; O sweetly, soundly, weel may he sleep That's laid in the bed beyond thee!

XCVI. COCK UP YOUR BEAVER.

Tune-"Cock up your beaver."
["Printed," says Sir Harris Nicolas, "in the Musical Museum, but not with Burns's name." It is an old song, eked out and amended by the poet: all the last verse, save the last line, is his; several of the lines too of the first verse, have felt his amending hand: he communicated it to the Museum.]
I.

When first my brave Johnnie lad Came to this town, He had a blue bonnet That wanted the crown; But now he has gotten A hat and a feather,- Hey, brave Johnnie lad, Cock up your beaver!

II.

Cock up your beaver, And cock it fu' sprush, We'll over the border And gie them a brush; There's somebody there We'll teach better behaviour- Hey, brave Johnnie lad, Cock up your beaver!

XCVII. MEIKLE THINKS MY LUVE.

Tune-"My tocher's the jewel."

[These verses were written by Burns for the Museum, to an air by Oswald: but he wished them to be sung to a tune called "Lord Elcho's favourite," of which he was an admirer.]

I.

O Meikle thinks my luve o' my beauty, And meikle thinks my luve o' my kin; But little thinks my luve I ken brawlie My tocher's the jewel has charms for him. It's a' for the apple he'll nourish the tree; It's a' for the hiney he'll cherish the bee; My laddie's sae meikle in luve wi' the siller, He canna hae lure to spare for me.

II.

Your proffer o' luve's an airl-penny, My tocher's the bargain ye wad buy; But an ye be crafty, I am cunnin', Sae ye wi' anither your fortune maun try. Ye're like to the timmer o' yon rotten tree, Ye'll slip frae me like a knotless thread, And ye'll crack your credit wi' mae nor me.

XCVIII. GANE IS THE DAY.

Tune-"Gudewife count the lawin."

[The air as well as words of this song were furnished to the Museum by Burns. "The chorus," he says, "is part of an old song."]

I.

Gane is the day, and mirk's the night, But we'll ne'er stray for fau't o' light, For ale and brandy's stars and moon, And blude-red wine's the rising sun. Then gudewife count the lawin, The lawin, the lawin; Then gudewife count the lawin, And bring a coggie mair!

II.

There's wealth and ease for gentlemen, And simple folk maun fight and fen; But here we're a' in ae accord, For ilka man that's drunk's a lord.

III.

My coggie is a haly pool, That heals the wounds o' care and dool; And pleasure is a wanton trout, An' ye drink but deep ye'll find him out. Then gudewife count the lawin; The lawin, the lawin, Then gudewife count the

lawin, And bring a coggie mair!
[245]

XCIX. THERE'LL NEVER BE PEACE.

Tune-"There art few gude fellows when Willie's awa."
[The bard was in one of his Jacobitical moods when he wrote this song. The air is a well known one, called "There's few gude fellows when Willie's awa." But of the words none, it is supposed, are preserved.]
I.
By yon castle wa', at the close of the day, I heard a man sing, though his head it was gray; And as he was singing the tears down came, There'll never be peace till Jamie comes hame. The church is in ruins, the state is in jars; Delusions, oppressions, and murderous wars: We darena weel say't, though we ken wha's to blame, There'll never be peace till Jamie comes hame!
II.
My seven braw sons for Jamie drew sword, And now I greet round their green beds in the yerd. It brak the sweet heart of my faithfu' auld dame- There'll never be peace till Jamie comes hame. Now life is a burthen that bows me down, Since I tint my bairns, and he tint his crown; But till my last moments my words are the same- There'll never be peace till Jamie comes hame!

C. HOW CAN I BE BLYTHE AND GLAD?

Tune-"The bonnie lad that's far awa."
[This lamentation was written, it is said, in allusion to the sufferings of Jean Armour, when her correspondence with Burns was discovered by her family.]
I.
O how can I be blythe and glad, Or how can I gang brisk and braw, When the bonnie lad that I lo'e best Is o'er the hills and far awa? When the bonnie lad that I lo'e best Is o'er the hills and far awa.
II.
It's no the frosty winter wind, It's no the driving drift and snaw; But ay the tear comes in my e'e, To think on him that's far awa. But ay the tear comes in my e'e, To think on him that's far awa.
III.
My father pat me frae his door, My friends they line disown'd me a', But I hae ane will tak' my part, The bonnie lad that's far awa. But I hae ane will tak' my part, The bonnie lad that's far awa.
IV.
A pair o' gloves he gae to me, And silken snoods he gae me twa; And I will

wear them for his sake, The bonnie lad that's far awa. And I will wear them for his sake, The bonnie lad that's far awa.
V.
O weary Winter soon will pass, And spring will cleed the birken shaw; And my young babie will be born, And he'll be hame that's far awa. And my young babie will be born, And he'll be hame that's far awa.

CI. I DO CONFESS THOU ART SAE FAIR.

Tune-"I do confess thou art sae fair."
["I do think," says Burns, in allusion to this song, "that I have improved the simplicity of the sentiments by giving them a Scottish dress." The original song is of great elegance and beauty: it was written by Sir Robert Aytoun, secretary to Anne of Denmark, Queen of James I.]
I.
I do confess thou art sae fair, I wad been o'er the lugs in love, Had I na found the slightest prayer That lips could speak thy heart could muve. I do confess thee sweet, but find Thou art sae thriftless o' thy sweets, Thy favours are the silly wind, That kisses ilka thing it meets.
II.
See yonder rose-bud, rich in dew, Amang its native briers sae coy; [246]How sune it tines its scent and hue When pou'd and worn a common toy! Sic fate, ere lang, shall thee betide, Tho' thou may gaily bloom awhile; Yet sune thou shalt be thrown aside Like ony common weed and vile.

CII. YON WILD MOSSY MOUNTAINS.

Tune-"Yon wild mossy mountains."
["This song alludes to a part of my private history, which is of no consequence to the world to know." These are the words of Burns: he sent the song to the Musical Museum; the heroine is supposed to be the "Nannie," who dwelt near the Lugar.]
I.
Yon wild mossy mountains sae lofty and wide, That nurse in their bosom the youth o' the Clyde, Where the grouse lead their coveys thro' the heather to feed, And the shepherd tents his flock as he pipes on his reed. Where the grouse lead their coveys thro' the heather to feed, And the shepherd tents his flock as he pipes on his reed.
II.
Not Gowrie's rich valleys, nor Forth's sunny shores, To me hae the charms o' yon wild, mossy moors; For there, by a lanely and sequester'd stream, Resides a sweet lassie, my thought and my dream. For there, by a lanely and sequester'd stream, Resides a sweet lassie, my thought and my dream.

III.
Amang thae wild mountains shall still be my path, Ilk stream foaming down its ain green, narrow strath; For there, wi' my lassie, the day lang I rove, While o'er us unheeded flee the swift hours o' love. For there wi' my lassie, the day lang I rove, While o'er us unheeded flee the swift hours o' love.
IV.
She is not the fairest, altho' she is fair; O' nice education but sma' is her share; Her parentage humble as humble can be; But I lo'e the dear lassie because she lo'es me. Her parentage humble as humble can be; But I lo'e the dear lassie because she lo'es me.
V.
To beauty what man but maun yield him a prize, In her armour of glances, and blushes, and sighs? And when wit and refinement hae polish'd her darts, They dazzle our een as they flee to our hearts. And when wit and refinement hae polish'd her darts, They dazzle our een, as they flee to our hearts.
VI.
But kindness, sweet kindness, in the fond sparkling e'e, Has lustre outshining the diamond to me: And the heart beating love as I'm clasp'd in her arms, O, these are my lassie's all-conquering charms! And the heart beating love as I'm clasp'd in her arms, O, these are my lassie's all-conquering charms!

CIII. IT IS NA, JEAN, THY BONNIE FACE.

Tune-"The Maid's Complaint."
[Burns found this song in English attire, bestowed a Scottish dress upon it, and published it in the Museum, together with the air by Oswald, which is one of his best.]
I.
It is na, Jean, thy bonnie face, Nor shape that I admire, Altho' thy beauty and thy grace Might weel awake desire. Something in ilka part o' thee, To praise, to love, I find; But dear as is thy form to me, Still dearer is thy mind.
[247]
II.
Nae mair ungen'rous wish I hae, Nor stronger in my breast, Than, if I canna mak thee sae, at least to see thee blest. Content am I, if heaven shall give But happiness to thee: And as wi' thee I'd wish to live, For thee I'd bear to die.

CIV. WHEN I THINK ON THE HAPPY DAYS.

[These verses were in latter years expanded by Burns into a song, for the collection of Thomson: the song will be found in its place: the variations are worthy of preservation.]

I.

When I think on the happy days I spent wi' you, my dearie; And now what lands between us lie, How can I be but eerie!

II.

How slow ye move, ye heavy hours, As ye were wae and weary! It was na sae ye glinted by, When I was wi' my dearie.

CV.WHAN I SLEEP I DREAM.

[This presents another version of song LXV. Variations are to a poet what changes are in the thoughts of a painter, and speak of fertility of sentiment in both.]

I.

Whan I sleep I dream, Whan I wauk I'm eerie, Sleep I canna get, For thinkin' o' my dearie.

II.

Lanely night comes on, A' the house are sleeping, I think on the bonnie lad That has my heart a keeping. Ay waukin O, waukin ay and wearie, Sleep I canna get, for thinkin' o' my dearie.

III.

Lanely nights come on, A' the house are sleeping, I think on my bonnie lad, An' I blear my een wi' greetin'! Ay waukin, andc.

CVI. I MURDER HATE.

[These verses are to be found in a volume which may be alluded to without being named, in which many of Burns's strains, some looser than these, are to be found.]

I.

I murder hate by field or flood, Tho' glory's name may screen us: In wars at hame I'll spend my blood, Life-giving wars of Venus.

II.

The deities that I adore Are social Peace and Plenty, I'm better pleas'd to make one more, Than be the death of twenty.

CVII. O GUDE ALE COMES.

[These verses are in the museum; the first two are old, the concluding one is by Burns.]

I.

O gude ale comes, and gude ale goes, Gude ale gars me sell my hose, Sell

my hose, and pawn my shoon, Gude ale keeps my heart aboon.
II.
I had sax owsen in a pleugh, They drew a' weel eneugh, I sell'd them a' just ane by ane; Gude ale keeps my heart aboon.
III.
Gude ale hands me bare and busy, Gars me moop wi' the servant hizzie, Stand i' the stool when I hae done, Gude ale keeps my heart aboon. O gude ale comes, andc.
[248]

CVIII. ROBIN SHURE IN HAIRST.

[This is an old chaunt, out of which Burns brushed some loose expressions, added the third and fourth verses, and sent it to the Museum.]
I.
Robin shure in hairst, I shure wi' him, Fient a heuk had I, Yet I stack by him.
II.
I gaed up to Dunse, To warp a wab o' plaiden, At his daddie's yett, Wha met me but Robin.
III.
Was na Robin bauld, Tho' I was a cotter, Play'd me sic a trick, And me the eller's dochter? Robin share in hairst, andc.
IV.
Robin promis'd me A' my winter vittle; Fient haet he had but three Goose feathers and a whittle. Robin share in hairst, andc.

CIX. BONNIE PEG.

[A fourth verse makes the moon a witness to the endearments of these lovers; but that planet sees more indiscreet matters than it is right to describe.]
I.
As I came in by our gate end, As day was waxin' weary, O wha came tripping down the street, But Bonnie Peg my dearie!
II.
Her air sae sweet, and shape complete, Wi' nae proportion wanting; The Queen of Love did never move Wi' motion mair enchanting.
III.
Wi' linked hands, we took the sands A-down yon winding river; And, oh! that hour and broomy bower, Can I forget it ever?

CX. GUDEEN TO YOU, KIMMER.

[This song in other days was a controversial one, and continued some sarcastic allusions to Mother Rome and her brood of seven sacraments, five of whom were illegitimate. Burns changed the meaning, and published his altered version in the Museum.]

I.

Gudeen to you, Kimmer, And how do ye do? Hiccup, quo' Kimmer, The better that I'm fou. We're a' noddin, nid nid noddin, We're a' noddin, at our house at hame.

II.

Kate sits i' the neuk, Suppin hen broo; Deil tak Kate An' she be na noddin too! We're a' noddin, andc.

III.

How's a' wi' you, Kimmer, And how do ye fare? A pint o' the best o't, And twa pints mair. We're a' noddin, andc.

IV.

How's a' wi' you, Kimmer, And how do ye thrive; How many bairns hae ye? Quo' Kimmer, I hae five. We're a' noddin, andc.

V.

Are they a' Johnie's? Eh! atweel no: Twa o' them were gotten When Johnie was awa. We're a noddin, andc. [249]

VI.

Cats like milk, And dogs like broo; Lads like lasses weel, And lasses lads too. We're a' noddin, andc.

CXI. AH, CHLORIS, SINCE IT MAY NA BE.

Tune-"Major Graham."

[Sir Harris Nicolas found these lines on Chloris among the papers of Burns, and printed them in his late edition of the poet's works.]

I.

Ah, Chloris, since it may na be, That thou of love wilt hear; If from the lover thou maun flee, Yet let the friend be dear.

II.

Altho' I love my Chloris mair Than ever tongue could tell; My passion I will ne'er declare, I'll say, I wish thee well.

III.

Tho' a' my daily care thou art, And a' my nightly dream, I'll hide the struggle in my heart, And say it is esteem.

CXII. O SAW YE MY DEARIE.

Tune-"Eppie Macnab."

["Published in the Museum," says Sir Harris Nicolas, "without any name." Burns corrected some lines in the old song, which had more wit, he said, than decency, and added others, and sent his amended version to Johnson.]
I.
O saw ye my dearie, my Eppie M'Nab? O saw ye my dearie, my Eppie M'Nab? She's down in the yard, she's kissin' the laird, She winna come hame to her ain Jock Rab. O come thy ways to me, my Eppie M'Nab! O come thy ways to me, my Eppie M'Nab! Whate'er thou hast done, be it late, be it soon, Thou's welcome again to thy ain Jock Rab.
II.
What says she, my dearie, my Eppie M'Nab? What says she, my dearie, my Eppie M'Nab? She lets thee to wit, that she has thee forgot, And for ever disowns thee, her ain Jock Rab. O had I ne'er seen thee, my Eppie M'Nab! O had I ne'er seen thee, my Eppie M'Nab! As light as the air, and fause as thou's fair, Thou's broken the heart o' thy ain Jock Rab.

CXIII. WHA IS THAT AT MY BOWER-DOOR.

Tune-"Lass an I come near thee."
[The "Auld man and the Widow," in Ramsay's collection is said, by Gilbert Burns, to have suggested this song to his brother: it first appeared in the Museum.]
I.
Wha is that at my bower door? O, wha is it but Findlay? Then gae your gate, ye'se nae be here!- Indeed, maun I, quo' Findlay. What mak ye sae like a thief? O come and see, quo' Findlay; Before the morn ye'll work mischief; Indeed will I, quo' Findlay.
II.
Gif I rise and let you in? Let me in, quo' Findlay; Ye'll keep me waukin wi' your din; Indeed will I, quo' Findlay. In my bower if you should stay? Let me stay, quo' Findlay; I fear ye'll bide till break o' day; Indeed will I, quo' Findlay.
III.
Here this night if ye remain;- I'll remain, quo' Findlay; I dread ye'll learn the gate again; Indeed will I, quo' Findlay. What may pass within this bower,- Let it pass, quo' Findlay; Ye maun conceal till your last hour; Indeed will I, quo' Findlay!
[250]

CXIV. WHAT CAN A YOUNG LASSIE.

Tune-"What can a young lassie do wi' an auld man."
[In the old strain, which partly suggested this song, the heroine threatens

only to adorn her husband's brows: Burns proposes a system of domestic annoyance to break his heart.]

I.

What can a young lassie, what shall a young lassie, What can a young lassie do wi' an auld man? Bad luck on the pennie that tempted my minnie To sell her poor Jenny for siller an' lan'! Bad luck on the pennie that tempted my minnie To sell her poor Jenny for siller an' lan'!

II.

He's always compleenin' frae mornin' to e'enin', He hosts and he hirples the weary day lang; He's doyl't and he's dozin', his bluid it is frozen, O, dreary's the night wi' a crazy auld man! He's doyl't and he's dozin', his bluid it is frozen, O, dreary's the night wi' a crazy auld man!

III.

He hums and he hankers, he frets and he cankers, I never can please him, do a' that I can; He's peevish and jealous of a' the young fellows: O, dool on the day I met wi' an auld man! He's peevish and jealous of a' the young fellows: O, dool on the day I met wi' an auld man!

IV.

My auld auntie Katie upon me takes pity, I'll do my endeavour to follow her plan; I'll cross him, and wrack him, until I heart-break him, And then his auld brass will buy me a new pan. I'll cross him, and wrack him, until I heart-break him, And then his auld brass will buy me a new pan.

CXV. THE BONNIE WEE THING.

Tune-"Bonnie wee thing."

["Composed," says the poet, "on my little idol, the charming, lovely Davies."]

I.

Bonnie wee thing, cannie wee thing, Lovely wee thing, wert thou mine, I wad wear thee in my bosom, Lest my jewel I should tine. Wishfully I look and languish In that bonnie face o' thine; And my heart it stounds wi' anguish, Lest my wee thing be na mine.

II.

Wit, and grace, and love, and beauty In ae constellation shine; To adore thee is my duty, Goddess o' this soul o' mine! Bonnie wee thing, cannie wee thing. Lovely wee thing, wert thou mine, I wad wear thee in my bosom, Lest my jewel I should tine!

CXVI. THE TITHER MOON.

To a Highland Air.

["The tune of this song," says Burns, "is originally from the Highlands. I have heard a Gaelic song to it, which was not by any means a lady's song." "It occurs," says Sir Harris Nicolas, "in the Museum, without the name of Burns." It was sent in the poet's own handwriting to Johnson, and is believed to be his composition.]

I.

The tither morn, When I forlorn, Aneath an oak sat moaning, I did na trow I'd see my Jo, Beside me, gain the gloaming. But he sae trig, Lap o'er the rig. And dawtingly did cheer me, When I, what reck, Did least expec', To see my lad so near me. [251]

II.

His bonnet he, A thought ajee, Cock'd sprush when first he clasp'd me; And I, I wat, Wi' fainness grat, While in his grips be press'd me. Deil tak' the war! I late and air Hae wish'd since Jock departed; But now as glad I'm wi' my lad, As short syne broken-hearted.

III.

Fu' aft at e'en Wi' dancing keen, When a' were blythe and merry, I car'd na by, Sae sad was I In absence o' my dearie. But praise be blest, My mind's at rest, I'm happy wi' my Johnny: At kirk and fair, I'se ay be there, And be as canty's ony.

CXVII. AE FOND KISS.

Tune-"Rory Dall's Port."

[Believed to relate to the poet's parting with Clarinda. "These exquisitely affecting stanzas," says Scott, "contain the essence of a thousand love-tales." They are in the Museum.]

I.

Ae fond kiss, and then we sever; Ae fareweel, and then for ever! Deep in heart-wrung tears I'll pledge thee, Warring sighs and groans I'll wage thee. Who shall say that fortune grieves him While the star of hope she leaves him? Me, nae cheerfu' twinkle lights me; Dark despair around benights me.

II.

I'll ne'er blame my partial fancy, Naething could resist my Nancy; But to see her, was to love her; Love but her, and love for ever.- Had we never lov'd sae kindly, Had we never lov'd sae blindly, Never met-or never parted, We had ne'er been broken hearted.

III.

Fare thee weel, thou first and fairest! Fare thee weel, thou best and dearest! Thine be ilka joy and treasure, Peace, enjoyment, love, and pleasure! Ae fond kiss, and then we sever; Ae farewell, alas! for ever! Deep in heart-wrung tears I'll pledge thee, Warring sighs and groans I'll wage thee!

CXVIII. LOVELY DAVIES.

Tune-"Miss Muir."
[Written for the Museum, in honour of the witty, the handsome, the lovely, and unfortunate Miss Davies.]
I.
O how shall I, unskilfu', try The poet's occupation, The tunefu' powers, in happy hours, That whispers inspiration? Even they maun dare an effort mair, Than aught they ever gave us, Or they rehearse, in equal verse, The charms o' lovely Davies. Each eye it cheers, when she appears, Like Phœbus in the morning. When past the shower, and ev'ry flower The garden is adorning. As the wretch looks o'er Siberia's shore, When winter-bound the wave is; Sae droops our heart when we maun part Frae charming lovely Davies.
II.
Her smile's a gift, frae 'boon the lift, That maks us mair than princes; A scepter'd hand, a king's command, Is in her darting glances: The man in arms, 'gainst female charms, Even he her willing slave is; He hugs his chain, and owns the reign Of conquering, lovely Davies. My muse to dream of such a theme, Her feeble pow'rs surrender: [252]The eagle's gaze alone surveys The sun's meridian splendour: I wad in vain essay the strain, The deed too daring brave is! I'll drap the lyre, and mute admire The charms o' lovely Davies.

CXIX. THE WEARY PUND O' TOW.

Tune-"The weary Pund o' Tow."
["This song," says Sir Harris Nicolas, "is in the Musical Museum; but it is not attributed to Burns. Mr. Allan Cunningham does not state upon what authority he has assigned it to Burns." The critical knight might have, if he had pleased, stated similar objections to many songs which he took without scruple from my edition, where they were claimed for Burns, for the first time, and on good authority. I, however, as it happens, did not claim the song wholly for the poet: I said "the idea of the song is old, and perhaps some of the words." It was sent by Burns to the Museum, and in his own handwriting.]
I.
The weary pund, the weary pund, The weary pund o' tow: I think my wife will end her life Before she spin her tow. I bought my wife a stane o' lint As gude as e'er did grow; And a' that she has made o' that, Is ae poor pund o' tow.
II.
There sat a bottle in a bole, Beyont the ingle low, And ay she took the tither souk, To drouk the stowrie tow.

III.

Quoth I, for shame, ye dirty dame, Gae spin your tap o' tow! She took the rock, and wi' a knock She brak it o'er my pow.

IV.

At last her feet-I sang to see't- Gaed foremost o'er the knowe; And or I wad anither jad, I'll wallop in a tow. The weary pund, the weary pund, The weary pund o' tow! I think my wife will end her life Before she spin her tow.

CXX. NAEBODY.

Tune-"Naebody."

[Burns had built his house at Ellisland, sowed his first crop, the woman he loved was at his side, and hope was high; no wonder that he indulged in this independent strain.]

I.

I hae a wife o' my ain- I'll partake wi' naebody; I'll tak cuckold frae nane, I'll gie cuckold to naebody. I hae a penny to spend, There-thanks to naebody; I hae naething to lend, I'll borrow frae naebody.

II.

I am naebody's lord- I'll be slave to naebody; I hae a guid braid sword, I'll tak dunts frae naebody. I'll be merry and free, I'll be sad for naebody; Naebody cares for me, I'll care for naebody.

CXXI. O, FOR ANE-AND-TWENTY, TAM!

Tune-"The Moudiewort."

[In his memoranda on this song in the Museum, Burns says simply, "This song is mine." The air for a century before had to bear the burthen of very ordinary words.]

CHORUS.

An O, for ane-and-twenty, Tam, An' hey, sweet ane-and-twenty, Tam, I'll learn my kin a rattlin' sang, An I saw ane-and-twenty, Tam.

I.

They snool me sair, and haud me down, And gar me look like bluntie, Tam! But three short years will soon wheel roun'- And then comes ane-and-twenty, Tam.

II.

A gleib o' lan', a claut o' gear, Was left me by my auntie, Tam, At kith or kin I need na spier, An I saw ane-and-twenty, Tam. [253]

III.

They'll hae me wed a wealthy coof, Tho' I mysel' hae plenty, Tam; But hear'st thou, laddie-there's my loof- I'm thine at ane-and-twenty, Tam. An

O, for ane-and-twenty, Tam! An hey, sweet ane-and-twenty, Tam! I'll learn my kin a rattlin' song, An I saw ane-and-twenty, Tam.

CXXII. O KENMURE'S ON AND AWA.

Tune-"O Kenmure's on and awa, Willie."
[The second and third, and concluding verses of this Jacobite strain, were written by Burns: the whole was sent in his own handwriting to the Museum.]
I.
O Kenmure's on and awa, Willie! O Kenmure's on and awa! And Kenmure's lord's the bravest lord, That ever Galloway saw.
II.
Success to Kenmure's band, Willie! Success to Kenmure's band; There's no a heart that fears a Whig, That rides by Kenmure's hand.
III.
Here's Kenmure's health in wine, Willie! Here's Kenmure's health in wine; There ne'er was a coward o' Kenmure's blude, Nor yet o' Gordon's line.
IV.
O Kenmure's lads are men, Willie! O Kenmure's lads are men; Their hearts and swords are metal true- And that their faes shall ken.
V.
They'll live or die wi' fame, Willie! They'll live or die wi' fame; But soon wi' sounding victorie, May Kenmure's lord come hame.
VI.
Here's him that's far awa, Willie, Here's him that's far awa; And here's the flower that I love best- The rose that's like the snaw!

CXXIII. MY COLLIER LADDIE.

Tune-"The Collier Laddie."
[The Collier Laddie was communicated by Burns, and in his handwriting, to the Museum: it is chiefly his own composition, though coloured by an older strain.]
I.
Where live ye, my bonnie lass? An' tell me what they ca' ye; My name, she says, is Mistress Jean, And I follow the Collier Laddie. My name she says, is Mistress Jean, And I follow the Collier Laddie.
II.
See you not yon hills and dales, The sun shines on sae brawlie! They a' are mine, and they shall be thine, Gin ye'll leave your Collier Laddie. They a' are mine, and they shall be thine, Gin ye'll leave your Collier Laddie.
III.

Ye shall gang in gay attire, Weel buskit up sae gaudy; And ane to wait on every hand, Gin ye'll leave your Collier Laddie. And ane to wait on every hand, Gin ye'll leave your Collier Laddie.

IV.

Tho' ye had a' the sun shines on, And the earth conceals sae lowly; I wad turn my back on you and it a', And embrace my Collier Laddie. I wad turn my back on you and it a', And embrace my Collier Laddie.

V.

I can win my five pennies a day, And spen't at night fu' brawlie; And make my bed in the Collier's neuk, And lie down wi' my Collier Laddie. And make my bed in the Collier's neuk, And lie down wi' my Collier Laddie.

VI.

Luve for luve is the bargain for me, Tho' the wee cot-house should haud me; And the world before me to win my bread, And fair fa' my Collier Laddie. And the world before me to win my bread, And fair fa' my Collier Laddie.

[254]

CXXIV. NITHSDALE'S WELCOME HAME.

[These verses were written by Burns for the Museum: the Maxwells of Terreagles are the lineal descendants of the Earls of Nithsdale.]

I.

The noble Maxwells and their powers Are coming o'er the border, And they'll gae bigg Terreagle's towers, An' set them a' in order. And they declare Terreagles fair, For their abode they chuse it; There's no a heart in a' the land, But's lighter at the news o't.

II.

Tho' stars in skies may disappear, And angry tempests gather; The happy hour may soon be near That brings us pleasant weather: The weary night o' care and grief May hae a joyful morrow; So dawning day has brought relief-Fareweel our night o' sorrow!

CXXV. AS I WAS A-WAND'RING.

Tune-"Rinn Meudial mo Mhealladh."

[The original song in the Gaelic language was translated for Burns by an Inverness-shire lady; he turned it into verse, and sent it to the Museum.]

I.

As I was a-wand'ring ae midsummer e'enin', The pipers and youngsters were making their game; Amang them I spied my faithless fause lover, Which bled a' the wound o' my dolour again. Weel, since he has left me, may pleasure gae wi' him; I may be distress'd, but I winna complain; I

flatter my fancy I may get anither, My heart it shall never be broken for ane.
II.
I could na get sleeping till dawin for greetin', The tears trickled down like the hail and the rain: Had I na got greetin', my heart wad a broken, For, oh! luve forsaken's a tormenting pain.
III.
Although he has left me for greed o' the siller, I dinna envy him the gains he can win; I rather wad bear a' the lade o' my sorrow Than ever hae acted sae faithless to him. Weel, since he has left me, may pleasure gae wi' him, I may be distress'd, but I winna complain; I flatter my fancy I may get anither, My heart it shall never be broken for ane.

CXXVI. BESS AND HER SPINNING-WHEEL.

Tune-"The sweet lass that lo'es me."
[There are several variations of this song, but they neither affect the sentiment, nor afford matter for quotation.]
I.
O leeze me on my spinning-wheel, O leeze me on the rock and reel; Frae tap to tae that cleeds me bien, And haps me fiel and warm at e'en! I'll set me down and sing and spin, While laigh descends the simmer sun, Blest wi' content, and milk and meal- O leeze me on my spinning-wheel!
II.
On ilka hand the burnies trot, And meet below my theekit cot; The scented birk and hawthorn white, Across the pool their arms unite, Alike to screen the birdie's nest, And little fishes' caller rest: The sun blinks kindly in the biel', Where blithe I turn my spinning-wheel.
III.
On lofty aiks the cushats wail, And Echo cons the doolfu' tale; The lintwhites in the hazel braes, Delighted, rival ither's lays: The craik amang the clover hay, The paitrick whirrin o'er the ley, The swallow jinkin round my shiel, Amuse me at my spinning-wheel.
IV.
Wi' sma' to sell, and less to buy, Aboon distress, below envy, [255]O wha wad leave this humble state, For a' the pride of a' the great? Amid their flaring, idle toys, Amid their cumbrous, dinsome joys, Can they the peace and pleasure feel Of Bessy at her spinning-wheel?

CXXVII. O LUVE WILL VENTURE IN.

Tune-"The Posie."
["The Posie is my composition," says Burns, in a letter to Thomson. "The air was taken down from Mrs. Burns's voice." It was first printed in the

Museum.]

I.

O luve will venture in Where it daurna weel be seen; O luve will venture in Where wisdom ance has been. But I will down yon river rove, Among the wood sae green- And a' to pu' a posie To my ain dear May.

II.

The primrose I will pu', The firstling o' the year, And I will pu' the pink, The emblem o' my dear, For she's the pink o' womankind, And blooms without a peer- And a' to be a posie To my ain dear May.

III.

I'll pu' the budding rose, When Phœbus peeps in view, For it's like a baumy kiss O' her sweet bonnie mou'; The hyacinth's for constancy, Wi' its unchanging blue- And a' to be a posie To my ain dear May.

IV.

The lily it is pure, And the lily it is fair, And in her lovely bosom I'll place the lily there; The daisy's for simplicity, And unaffected air- And a' to be a posie To my ain dear May.

V.

The hawthorn I will pu' Wi' its locks o' siller gray, Where, like an aged man, It stands at break of day. But the songster's nest within the bush I winna tak away- And a' to be a posie To my ain dear May.

VI.

The woodbine I will pu' When the e'ening star is near, And the diamond drops o' dew Shall be her e'en sae clear; The violet's for modesty, Which weel she fa's to wear, And a' to be a posie To my ain dear May.

VII.

I'll tie the posie round, Wi' the silken band o' luve, And I'll place it in her breast, And I'll swear by a' above, That to my latest draught of life The band shall ne'er remove, And this will be a posie To my ain dear May.

CXXVIII. COUNTRY LASSIE.

Tune-"The Country Lass."

[A manuscript copy before me, in the poet's handwriting, presents two or three immaterial variations of this dramatic song.]

I.

In simmer, when the hay was mawn, And corn wav'd green in ilka field, While claver blooms white o'er the lea, And roses blaw in ilka bield; Blithe Bessie in the milking shiel, Says-I'll be wed, come o't what will; Out spak a dame in wrinkled eild- O' guid advisement comes nae ill.

II.

It's ye hae wooers mony ane, And, lassie, ye're but young ye ken; Then wait a wee, and cannie wale, A routhie butt, a routhie ben: [256]There's Johnie o'

the Buskie-glen, Fu' is his burn, fu' is his byre; Tak this frae me, my bonnie hen, It's plenty beets the luver's fire.
III.
For Johnie o' the Buskie-glen, I dinna care a single flie; He lo'es sae weel his craps and kye, He has nae luve to spare for me: But blithe's the blink o' Robie's e'e, And weel I wat he lo'es me dear: Ae blink o' him I wad nae gie For Buskie-glen and a' his gear.
IV.
O thoughtless lassie, life's a faught; The canniest gate, the strife is sair; But ay fu' han't is fechtin best, An hungry care's an unco care: But some will spend, and some will spare, An' wilfu' folk maun hae their will; Syne as ye brew, my maiden fair, Keep mind that ye maun drink the yill.
V.
O, gear will buy me rigs o' land, And gear will buy me sheep and kye; But the tender heart o' leesome luve, The gowd and siller canna buy; We may be poor-Robie and I, Light is the burden luve lays on; Content and luve brings peace and joy- What mair hae queens upon a throne?

CXXIX. FAIR ELIZA.

A Gaelic Air.
[The name of the heroine of this song was at first Rabina: but Johnson, the publisher, alarmed at admitting something new into verse, caused Eliza to be substituted; which was a positive fraud; for Rabina was a real lady, and a lovely one, and Eliza one of air.]
I.
Turn again, thou fair Eliza, Ae kind blink before we part, Rue on thy despairing lover! Canst thou break his faithfu' heart? Turn again, thou fair Eliza; If to love thy heart denies, For pity hide the cruel sentence Under friendship's kind disguise!
II.
Thee, dear maid, hae I offended? The offence is loving thee: Canst thou wreck his peace for ever, Wha for time wad gladly die? While the life beats in my bosom, Thou shalt mix in ilka throe; Turn again, thou lovely maiden. Ae sweet smile on me bestow.
III.
Not the bee upon the blossom, In the pride o' sunny noon; Not the little sporting fairy, All beneath the simmer moon; Not the poet, in the moment Fancy lightens in his e'e, Kens the pleasure, feels the rapture, That thy presence gies to me.

CXXX. YE JACOBITES BY NAME.

Tune-"Ye Jacobites by name."

["Ye Jacobites by name," appeared for the first time in the Museum: it was sent in the handwriting of Burns.]

I.

Ye Jacobites by name, give and ear, give an ear; Ye Jacobites by name, give an ear; Ye Jacobites by name, Your fautes I will proclaim, Your doctrines I maun blame- You shall hear.

II.

What is right, and what is wrang, by the law, by the law? What is right and what is wrang, by the law? What is right and what is wrang? A short sword, and a lang, A weak arm, and a strang For to draw.

III.

What makes heroic strife, fam'd afar, fam'd afar? What makes heroic strife, fam'd afar? What makes heroic strife? To whet th' assassin's knife, Or hunt a parent's life Wi' bluidie war.

[257]

IV.

Then let your schemes alone, in the state, in the state; Then let your schemes alone in the state; Then let your schemes alone, Adore the rising sun, And leave a man undone To his fate.

CXXXI. THE BANKS OF DOON.

[FIRST VERSION.]

[An Ayrshire legend says the heroine of this affecting song was Miss Kennedy, of Dalgarrock, a young creature, beautiful and accomplished, who fell a victim to her love for her kinsman, McDoual, of Logan.]

I.

Ye flowery banks o' bonnie Doon, How can ye bloom sae fair; How can ye chant, ye little birds, And I sae fu' o' care!

II.

Thou'll break my heart, thou bonnie bird, That sings upon the bough; Thou minds me o' the happy days When my fause love was true.

III.

Thou'll break my heart, thou bonnie bird, That sings beside thy mate; For sae I sat, and sae I sang, And wist na o' my fate.

IV.

Aft hae I rov'd by bonnie Doon, To see the woodbine twine, And ilka bird sang o' its love; And sae did I o' mine.

V.

Wi' lightsome heart I pu'd a rose, Frae aff its thorny tree: And my fause luver staw the rose, But left the thorn wi' me.

CXXXII. THE BANKS O' DOON.

[SECOND VERSION.]
Tune-"Caledonian Hunt's Delight."
[Burns injured somewhat the simplicity of the song by adapting it to a new air, accidentally composed by an amateur who was directed, if he desired to create a Scottish air, to keep his fingers to the black keys of the harpsichord and preserve rhythm.]
I.
Ye banks and braes o' bonnie Doon, How can ye bloom sae fresh and fair; How can ye chant, ye little birds, And I sae weary, fu' o' care! Thou'lt break my heart, thou warbling bird, That wantons thro' the flowering thorn: Thou minds me o' departed joys, Departed-never to return!
II.
Aft hae I rov'd by bonnie Doon, To see the rose and woodbine twine; And ilka bird sang o' its luve, And fondly sae did I o' mine. Wi' lightsome heart I pu'd a rose, Fu' sweet upon its thorny tree; And my fause luver stole my rose, But, ah! he left the thorn wi' me.

CXXXIII. WILLIE WASTLE.

Tune-"The eight men of Moidart."
[The person who is raised to the disagreeable elevation of heroine of this song, was, it is said, a farmer's wife of the old school of domestic care and uncleanness, who lived nigh the poet, at Ellisland.]
I.
Willie Wastle dwalt on Tweed, The spot they call'd it Linkum-doddie. Willie was a wabster guid, Cou'd stown a clue wi' onie bodie; He had a wife was dour and din, O Tinkler Madgie was her mither; Sic a wife as Willie had, I wad nae gie a button for her.
II.
She has an e'e-she has but ane, The cat has twa the very colour; [258]Five rusty teeth, forbye a stump, A clapper-tongue wad deave a miller: A whiskin' beard about her mou', Her nose and chin they threaten ither- Sic a wife as Willie had, I wad nae gie a button for her.
III.
She's bow hough'd, she's hem shinn'd, A limpin' leg, a hand-breed shorter; She's twisted right, she's twisted left, To balance fair in ilka quarter: She has a hump upon her breast, The twin o' that upon her shouther- Sic a wife as Willie had, I wad nae gie a button for her.
IV.
Auld baudrans by the ingle sits, An' wi' her loof her face a-washin'; But Willie's wife is nae sae trig, She dights her grunzie wi' a hushion. Her walie

nieves like midden-creels, Her face wad fyle the Logan-Water- Sic a wife as Willie had, I wad nae gie a button for her.

CXXXIV. LADY MARY ANN.

Tune-"Craigtown's growing."
[The poet sent this song to the Museum, in his own handwriting: yet part of it is believed to be old; how much cannot be well known, with such skill has he made his interpolations and changes.]
I.
O, Lady Mary Ann Looks o'er the castle wa', She saw three bonnie boys Playing at the ba'; The youngest he was The flower amang them a'- My bonnie laddie's young, But he's growin' yet.
II.
O father! O father! An' ye think it fit, We'll send him a year To the college yet: We'll sew a green ribbon Round about his hat, And that will let them ken He's to marry yet.
III.
Lady Mary Ann Was a flower i' the dew, Sweet was its smell, And bonnie was its hue; And the langer it blossom'd The sweeter it grew; For the lily in the bud Will be bonnier yet.
IV.
Young Charlie Cochran Was the sprout of an aik; Bonnie and bloomin' And straught was its make: The sun took delight To shine for its sake, And it will be the brag O' the forest yet.
V.
The simmer is gane, When the leaves they were green, And the days are awa, That we hae seen; But far better days I trust will come again, For my bonnie laddie's young, But he's growin' yet.

CXXXV. SUCH A PARCEL OF ROGUES IN A NATION.

Tune.-"A parcel of rogues in a nation."
[This song was written by Burns in a moment of honest indignation at the northern scoundrels who sold to those of the south the independence of Scotland, at the time of the Union.]
I.
Fareweel to a' our Scottish fame, Fareweel our ancient glory, Fareweel even to the Scottish name, Sae fam'd in martial story. Now Sark rins o'er the Solway sands, And Tweed rins to the ocean, [259]To mark where England's province stands- Such a parcel of rogues in a nation.
II.
What force or guile could not subdue, Thro' many warlike ages, Is wrought

now by a coward few For hireling traitor's wages. The English steel we could disdain; Secure in valour's station; But English gold has been our bane- Such a parcel of rogues in a nation.
III.
O would, or I had seen the day That treason thus could sell us, My auld gray head had lien in clay, Wi' Bruce and loyal Wallace! But pith and power, till my last hour, I'll mak' this declaration; We've bought and sold for English gold- Such a parcel of rogues in a nation.

CXXXVI. THE CARLE OF KELLYBURN BRAES.

Tune-"Kellyburn Braes."
[Of this song Mrs. Burns said to Cromek, when running her finger over the long list of lyrics which her husband had written or amended for the Museum, "Robert gae this one a terrible brushing." A considerable portion of the old still remains.]
I.
There lived a carle on Kellyburn braes, (Hey, and the rue grows bonnie wi' thyme), And he had a wife was the plague o' his days; And the thyme it is wither'd, and rue is in prime.
II.
Ae day as the carle gaed up the lang glen, (Hey, and the rue grows bonnie wi' thyme), He met wi' the devil; says, "How do yow fen?" And the thyme it is wither'd, and rue is in prime.
III.
"I've got a bad wife, sir; that's a' my complaint; (Hey, and the rue grows bonnie wi' thyme), For, saving your presence, to her ye're a saint; And the thyme it is wither'd, and rue is in prime."
IV.
"It's neither your stot nor your staig I shall crave, (Hey, and the rue grows bonnie wi' thyme), But gie me your wife, man, for her I must have, And the thyme it is wither'd, and rue is in prime."
V.
"O welcome, most kindly," the blythe carle said, (Hey, and the rue grows bonnie wi' thyme), "But if ye can match her, ye're waur nor ye're ca'd, And the thyme it is wither'd, and rue is in prime."
VI.
The devil has got the auld wife on his back; (Hey, and the rue grows bonnie wi' thyme), And, like a poor pedlar, he's carried his pack; And the thyme it is wither'd, and rue is in prime.
VII.
He's carried her hame to his ain hallan-door; (Hey, and the rue grows bonnie wi' thyme). Syne bade her gae in, for a b-h and a w-e, And the

thyme it is wither'd, and rue is in prime.

VIII.

Then straight he makes fifty, the pick o' his band, (Hey, and the rue grows bonnie wi' thyme), Turn out on her guard in the clap of a hand; And the thyme it is wither'd, and rue is in prime.

IX.

The carlin gaed thro' them like ony wud bear, (Hey, and the rue grows bonnie wi' thyme), Whate'er she gat hands on cam near her nae mair; And the thyme it is wither'd, and rue is in prime.

X.

A reekit wee devil looks over the wa'; (Hey, and the rue grows bonnie wi' thyme), "O, help, master, help, or she'll ruin us a', And the thyme it is wither'd, and rue is in prime."

XI.

The devil he swore by the edge o' his knife, (Hey, and the rue grows bonnie wi' thyme), [260]He pitied the man that was tied to a wife; And the thyme it is wither'd, and rue is in prime.

XII.

The devil he swore by the kirk and the bell, (Hey, and the rue grows bonnie wi' thyme), He was not in wedlock, thank heav'n, but in hell; And the thyme it is wither'd, and rue is in prime.

XIII.

Then Satan has travelled again wi' his pack; (Hey, and the rue grows bonnie wi' thyme), And to her auld husband he's carried her back: And the thyme it is wither'd, and rue is in prime.

XIV.

"I hae been a devil the feck o' my life; (Hey, and the rue grows bonnie wi' thyme), But ne'er was in hell, till I met wi' a wife; And the thyme it is wither'd, and rue is in prime."

CXXXVII. JOCKEY'S TA'EN THE PARTING KISS.

Tune-"Jockey's ta'en the parting kiss."

[Burns, when he sent this song to the Museum, said nothing of its origin: and he is silent about it in his memoranda.]

I.

Jockey's ta'en the parting kiss, O'er the mountains he is gane; And with him is a' my bliss, Nought but griefs with me remain. Spare my luve, ye winds that blaw, Plashy sleets and beating rain! Spare my luve, thou feathery snaw, Drifting o'er the frozen plain.

II.

When the shades of evening creep O'er the day's fair, gladsome e'e, Sound and safely may he sleep, Sweetly blithe his waukening be! He will think on her he loves, Fondly he'll repeat her name; For where'er he distant roves, Jockey's heart is still at hame.

CXXXVIII. LADY ONLIE.

Tune-"The Ruffian's Rant."
[Communicated to the Museum in the handwriting of Burns: part, but not much, is believed to be old.]
I.
A' the lads o' Thornie-bank, When they gae to the shore o' Bucky, They'll step in an' tak' a pint Wi' Lady Onlie, honest Lucky! Lady Onlie, honest Lucky! Brews good ale at shore o' Bucky; I wish her sale for her gude ale, The best on a' the shore o' Bucky.
II.
Her house sae bien, her curch sae clean, I wat she is a dainty chucky; And cheerlie blinks the ingle-gleed Of Lady Onlie, honest Lucky! Lady Onlie, honest Lucky, Brews good ale at shore o' Bucky I wish her sale for her gude ale, The best on a' the shore o' Bucky.

CXXXIX. THE CHEVALIER'S LAMENT.

Tune-"Captain O'Kean."
["Composed," says Burns to M'Murdo, "at the desire of a friend who had an equal enthusiasm for the air and subject." The friend alluded to is supposed to be Robert Cleghorn: he loved the air much, and he was much of a Jacobite.]
I.
The small birds rejoice in the green leaves returning, The murmuring streamlet winds clear thro' the vale; The hawthorn trees blow in the dew of the morning, And wild scatter'd cowslips bedeck the green dale: But what can give pleasure, or what can seem fair, While the lingering moments are number'd by care? No flow'rs gaily springing, nor birds sweetly singing, Can soothe the sad bosom of joyless despair.
II.
The deed that I dared, could it merit their malice, A king and a father to place on his throne? His right are these hills, and his right are these valleys, Where the wild beasts find shelter, but I can find none; But 'tis not my sufferings thus wretched, forlorn: My brave gallant friends! 'tis your ruin I mourn; Your deeds proved so loyal in hot-bloody trial- Alas! I can make you no sweeter return!

CXL. SONG OF DEATH.

Air-"Oran an Aoig."
["I have just finished the following song," says Burns to Mrs. Dunlop, "which to a lady, the descendant of Wallace, and herself the mother of several soldiers, needs neither preface nor apology."]
Scene-A field of battle. Time of the day, evening. The wounded and dying of the victorious army are supposed to join in the following song:
I.
Farewell, thou fair day, thou green earth, and ye skies, Now gay with the bright setting sun; Farewell loves and friendships, ye dear tender ties- Our race of existence is run!
II.
Thou grim king of terrors, thou life's gloomy foe! Go frighten the coward and slave; Go, teach them to tremble, fell tyrant! but know, No terrors hast thou to the brave!
III.
Thou strik'st the dull peasant-he sinks in the dark, Nor saves e'en the wreck of a name; Thou strik'st the young hero-a glorious mark! He falls in the blaze of his fame!
IV.
In the field of proud honour-our swords in our hands, Our king and our country to save- While victory shines on life's last ebbing sands, Oh! who would not die with the brave!

CXLI. FLOW GENTLY, SWEET AFTON.

Tune-"Afton Water."
[The scenes on Afton Water are beautiful, and the poet felt them, as well as the generous kindness of his earliest patroness, Mrs. General Stewart, of Afton-lodge, when he wrote this sweet pastoral.]
I.
Flow gently, sweet Afton! among thy green braes, Flow gently, I'll sing thee a song in thy praise; My Mary's asleep by thy murmuring stream- Flow gently, sweet Afton, disturb not her dream.
II.
Thou stock-dove, whose echo resounds thro' the glen; Ye wild whistling blackbirds in yon thorny den; Thou green-crested lapwing, thy screaming forbear- I charge you disturb not my slumbering fair.
III.
How lofty, sweet Afton! thy neighbouring hills, Far mark'd with the courses of clear, winding rills; There daily I wander as noon rises high, My flocks and my Mary's sweet cot in my eye.
IV.
How pleasant thy banks and green valleys below, Where wild in the

woodlands the primroses blow! There, oft as mild evening weeps over the lea, The sweet-scented birk shades my Mary and me.

V.

Thy crystal stream, Afton, how lovely it glides, And winds by the cot where my Mary resides; How wanton thy waters her snowy feet lave, As gathering sweet flow'rets she stems thy clear wave.

VI.

Flow gently, sweet Afton! among thy green braes, Flow gently, sweet river, the theme of my lays! My Mary's asleep by thy murmuring stream- Flow gently, sweet Afton! disturb not her dream.

CXLII. THE SMILING SPRING.

Tune-"The Bonnie Bell."

["Bonnie Bell," was first printed in the Museum: who the heroine was the poet has neglected to tell us, and it is a pity.]

I.

The smiling Spring comes in rejoicing, And surly Winter grimly flies; Now crystal clear are the falling waters, And bonnie blue are the sunny skies; Fresh o'er the mountains breaks forth the morning, The ev'ning gilds the ocean's swell; All creatures joy in the sun's returning, And I rejoice in my bonnie Bell.

II.

The flowery Spring leads sunny Summer, And yellow Autumn presses near, Then in his turn comes gloomy Winter, Till smiling Spring again appear. Thus Seasons dancing, life advancing, Old Time and Nature their changes tell, But never ranging, still unchanging, I adore my bonnie Bell.

CXLIII. THE CARLES OF DYSART.

Tune-"Hey ca' thro'."

[Communicated to the Museum by Burns in his own handwriting: part of it is his composition, and some believe the whole.]

I.

Up wi' the carles o' Dysart, And the lads o' Buckhaven, And the kimmers o' Largo, And the lasses o' Leven. Hey, ca' thro', ca' thro', For we hae mickle ado; Hey, ca' thro', ca' thro', For we hae mickle ado.

II.

We hae tales to tell, And we hae sangs to sing; We hae pennies to spend, And we hae pints to bring.

III.

We'll live a' our days, And them that come behin', Let them do the like, And spend the gear they win. Hey, ca' thro', ca' thro', For we hae mickle ado, Hey, ca' thro', ca' thro', For we hae mickle ado.

CXLIV. THE GALLANT WEAVER.

Tune-"The Weavers' March."
[Sent by the poet to the Museum. Neither tradition nor criticism has noticed it, but the song is popular among the looms, in the west of Scotland.]
I.
Where Cart rins rowin to the sea, By mony a flow'r and spreading tree, There lives a lad, the lad for me, He is a gallant weaver. Oh, I had wooers aught or nine, They gied me rings and ribbons fine; And I was fear'd my heart would tine, And I gied it to the weaver.
II.
My daddie sign'd my tocher-band, To gie the lad that has the land; But to my heart I'll add my hand, And gie it to the weaver. While birds rejoice in leafy bowers; While bees delight in op'ning flowers; While corn grows green in simmer showers, I'll love my gallant weaver.

CXLV. THE BAIRNS GAT OUT.

Tune-"The deuks dang o'er my daddie."
[Burns found some of the sentiments and a few of the words of this song in a strain, rather rough and home-spun, of Scotland's elder day. He communicated it to the Museum.]
I.
The bairns gat out wi' an unco shout, The deuks dang o'er my daddie, O! [263]The fien'-ma-care, quo' the feirrie auld wife, He was but a paidlin body, O! He paidles out, an' he paidles in, An' he paidles late an' early, O! This seven lang years I hae lien by his side, An' he is but a fusionless carlie, O!
II.
O, hand your tongue, my feirrie auld wife, O, haud your tongue, now Nansie, O! I've seen the day, and sae hae ye, Ye wadna been sae donsie, O! I've seen the day ye butter'd my brose, And cuddled me late and early, O! But downa do's come o'er me now, And, oh! I feel it sairly, O!

CXLVI. SHE'S FAIR AND FAUSE.

Tune-"She's fair and fause."
[One of the happiest as well as the most sarcastic of the songs of the North: the air is almost as happy as the words.]
I.

She's fair and fause that causes my smart, I lo'ed her meikle and lang; She's broken her vow, she's broken my heart, And I may e'en gae hang. A coof cam in wi' routh o' gear, And I hae tint my dearest dear; But woman is but warld's gear, Sae let the bonnie lass gang.
II.
Whae'er ye be that woman love, To this be never blind, Nae ferlie 'tis tho' fickle she prove, A woman has't by kind. O woman, lovely woman fair! An angel form's fa'n to thy share, 'Twad been o'er meikle to gien thee mair- I mean an angel mind.

CXLVII. THE EXCISEMAN.

Tune-"The Deil cam' fiddling through the town."
[Composed and sung by the poet at a festive meeting of the excisemen of the Dumfries district.]
I.
The deil cam' fiddling through the town, And danced awa wi' the Exciseman, And ilka wife cries-"Auld Mahoun, I wish you luck o' the prize, man!" The deil's awa, the deil's awa, The deil's awa wi' the Exciseman; He's danc'd awa, he's danc'd awa, He's danc'd awa wi' the Exciseman!
II.
We'll mak our maut, we'll brew our drink, We'll dance, and sing, and rejoice, man; And mony braw thanks to the meikle black deil That danc'd awa wi' the Exciseman.
III.
There's threesome reels, there's foursome reels, There's hornpipes and strathspeys, man; But the ae best dance e'er cam to the land Was-the deil's awa wi' the Exciseman. The deil's awa, the deil's awa, The deil's awa wi' the Exciseman: He's danc'd awa, he's danc'd awa, He's danc'd awa wi' the Exciseman.

CXLVIII. THE LOVELY LASS OF INVERNESS.

Tune-"Lass of Inverness."
[As Burns passed slowly over the moor of Culloden, in one of his Highland tours, the lament of the Lass of Inverness, it is said, rose on his fancy: the first four lines are partly old.]
I.
The lovely lass o' Inverness, Nae joy nor pleasure can she see; For e'en and morn, she cries, alas! And ay the saut tear blin's her e'e: Drumossie moor-Drumossie day- A waefu' day it was to me! For there I lost my father dear, My father dear, and brethren three.
II.

Their winding sheet the bluidy clay, Their graves are growing green to see: And by them lies the dearest lad That ever blest a woman's e'e! Now wae to thee, thou cruel lord, A bluidy man I trow thou be; For mony a heart thou host made sair, That ne'er did wrong to thine or thee.

CXLIX. A RED, RED ROSE.

Tune-"Graham's Strathspey."

[Some editors have pleased themselves with tracing the sentiments of this song in certain street ballads: it resembles them as much as a sour sloe resembles a drop-ripe damson.]

I.

O, my luve's like a red, red rose, That's newly sprung in June: O, my luve's like the melodie, That's sweetly play'd in tune.

II.

As fair art thou, my bonnie lass, So deep in luve am I: And I will luve thee still, my dear, 'Till a' the seas gang dry.

III.

'Till a' the seas gang dry, my dear, And the rocks melt wi' the sun: I will luve thee still, my dear, While the sands o' life shall run.

IV.

And fare thee weel, my only luve! And fare thee weel a-while! And I will come again, my luve, Tho' it were ten thousand mile.

CL. LOUIS, WHAT RECK I BY THEE.

Tune-"Louis, what reck I by thee."

[The Jeannie of this very short, but very clever song, is Mrs. Burns. Her name has no chance of passing from the earth if impassioned verse can preserve it.]

I.

Louis, what reck I by thee, Or Geordie on his ocean? Dyvor, beggar loons to me- I reign in Jeannie's bosom.

II.

Let her crown my love her law, And in her breast enthrone me. Kings and nations-swith, awa! Reif randies, I disown ye!

CLI. HAD I THE WYTE.

Tune-"Had I the wyte she bade me."

[Burns in evoking this song out of the old verses did not cast wholly out the spirit of ancient license in which our minstrels indulged. He sent it to the Museum.]

I.
Had I the wyte, had I the wyte, Had I the wyte she bade me; She watch'd me by the hie-gate side. And up the loan she shaw'd me; And when I wadna venture in, A coward loon she ca'd me; Had kirk and state been in the gate, I lighted when she bade me.
II.
Sae craftilie she took me ben, And bade me make nae clatter; "For our ramgunshoch glum gudeman Is out and owre the water:" Whae'er shall say I wanted grace When I did kiss and dawte her, Let him be planted in my place, Syne say I was the fautor.
III.
Could I for shame, could I for shame, Could I for shame refused her? And wadna manhood been to blame, Had I unkindly used her? He claw'd her wi' the ripplin-kame, And blue and bluidy bruised her; When sic a husband was frae hame, What wife but had excused her?
IV.
I dighted ay her een sae blue, And bann'd the cruel randy; And weel I wat her willing mou', Was e'en like sugar-candy. [265]A gloamin-shot it was I wot, I lighted on the Monday; But I cam through the Tysday's dew, To wanton Willie's brandy.

CLII. COMING THROUGH THE RYE.

Tune-"Coming through the rye."
[The poet in this song removed some of the coarse chaff, from the old chant, and fitted it for the Museum, when it was first printed.]
I.
Coming through the rye, poor body, Coming through the rye, She draiglet a' her petticoatie, Coming through the rye. Jenny's a' wat, poor body, Jenny's seldom dry; She draiglet a' her petticoatie, Coming through the rye.
II.
Gin a body meet a body- Coming through the rye, Gin a body kiss a body- Need a body cry?
III.
Gin a body meet a body Coming through the glen, Gin a body kiss a body- Need the world ken? Jenny's a' wat, poor body; Jenny's seldom dry; She draiglet a' her petticoatie, Coming through the rye.

CLIII. YOUNG JAMIE, PRIDE OF A' THE PLAIN.

Tune-"The carlin o' the glen."
[Sent to the Museum by Burns in his own handwriting: part only is thought to be his]

I.
Young Jamie, pride of a' the plain, Sae gallant and sae gay a swain; Thro' a' our lasses he did rove, And reign'd resistless king of love: But now wi' sighs and starting tears, He strays amang the woods and briers; Or in the glens and rocky caves His sad complaining dowie raves.
II.
I wha sae late did range and rove, And chang'd with every moon my love, I little thought the time was near, Repentance I should buy sae dear: The slighted maids my torment see, And laugh at a' the pangs I dree; While she, my cruel, scornfu' fair, Forbids me e'er to see her mair!

CLIV. OUT OVER THE FORTH.

Tune-"Charlie Gordon's welcome hame."
[In one of his letters to Cunningham, dated 11th March 1791, Burns quoted the four last lines of this tender and gentle lyric, and inquires how he likes them.]
I.
Out over the Forth I look to the north, But what is the north and its Highlands to me? The south nor the east gie ease to my breast, The far foreign land, or the wild rolling sea.
II.
But I look to the west, when I gae to rest, That happy my dreams and my slumbers may be; For far in the west lives he I Io'e best, The lad that is dear to my babie and me.

CLV. THE LASS OF ECCLEFECHAN.

Tune-"Jacky Latin."
[Burns in one of his professional visits to Ecclefechan was amused with a rough old district song, which some one sung: he rendered, at a leisure moment, the language more delicate and the sentiments less warm, and sent it to the Museum.]
I.
Gat ye me, O gat ye me, O gat ye me wi' naething? Rock and reel, and spinnin' wheel, A mickle quarter basin. [266]Bye attour, my gutcher has A hich house and a laigh ane, A' for bye, my bonnie sel', The toss of Ecclefechan.
II.
O haud your tongue now, Luckie Laing, O hand your tongue and jauner; I held the gate till you I met, Syne I began to wander: I tint my whistle and my sang, I tint my peace and pleasure: But your green graff, now, Luckie Laing, Wad airt me to my treasure.

CLVI. THE COOPER O' CUDDIE.

Tune-"Bab at the bowster."

[The wit of this song is better than its delicacy: it is printed in the Museum, with the name of Burns attached.]

I.

The cooper o' Cuddie cam' here awa, And ca'd the girrs out owre us a'- And our gudewife has gotten a ca' That anger'd the silly gude-man, O. We'll hide the cooper behind the door; Behind the door, behind the door; We'll hide the cooper behind the door, And cover him under a mawn, O.

II.

He sought them out, he sought them in, Wi', deil hae her! and, deil hae him! But the body was sae doited and blin', He wist na where he was gaun, O.

III.

They cooper'd at e'en, they cooper'd at morn, 'Till our gude-man has gotten the scorn; On ilka brow she's planted a horn, And swears that they shall stan', O. We'll hide the cooper behind the door, Behind the door, behind the door; We'll hide the cooper behind the door, And cover him under a mawn, O.

CLVII. SOMEBODY.

Tune-"For the sake of somebody."

[Burns seems to have borrowed two or three lines of this lyric from Ramsay: he sent it to the Museum.]

I.

My heart is sair-I dare na tell- My heart is sair for somebody; I could wake a winter night For the sake o' somebody. Oh-hon! for somebody! Oh-hey! for somebody! I could range the world around, For the sake o' somebody!

II.

Ye powers that smile on virtuous love, O, sweetly smile on somebody! Frae ilka danger keep him free, And send me safe my somebody. Oh-hon! for somebody! Oh-hey! for somebody! I wad do-what wad I not? For the sake o' somebody!

CLVIII. THE CARDIN' O'T.

Tune-"Salt-fish and dumplings."

["This song," says Sir Harris Nicolas, "is in the Musical Museum, but not with Burns's name to it." It was given by Burns to Johnson in his own handwriting.]

I.

I coft a stane o' haslock woo', To make a wat to Johnny o't; For Johnny is my only jo, I lo'e him best of ony yet. The cardin' o't, the spinnin' o't, The warpin' o't, the winnin' o't; When ilka ell cost me a groat, The tailor staw the lynin o't.

II.

For though his locks be lyart gray, And tho' his brow be beld aboon; Yet I hae seen him on a day, The pride of a' the parishen. The cardin' o't, the spinnin' o't, The warpin' o't, the winnin' o't; When ilka ell cost me a groat, The tailor staw the lynin o't.

CLIX. WHEN JANUAR' WIND.

Tune-"The lass that made the bed for me."

[Burns found an old, clever, but not very decorous strain, recording an adventure which Charles the Second, while under Presbyterian rule in Scotland, had with a young lady of the house of Port Letham, and exercising his taste and skill upon it, produced the present-still too free song, for the Museum.]

I.

When Januar' wind was blawing cauld, As to the north I took my way, The mirksome night did me enfauld, I knew na where to lodge till day.

II.

By my good luck a maid I met, Just in the middle o' my care; And kindly she did me invite To walk into a chamber fair.

III.

I bow'd fu' low unto this maid, And thank'd her for her courtesie; I bow'd fu' low unto this maid, And bade her mak a bed to me.

IV.

She made the bed baith large and wide, Wi' twa white hands she spread it down; She put the cup to her rosy lips, And drank, "Young man, now sleep ye soun'."

V.

She snatch'd the candle in her hand, And frae my chamber went wi' speed; But I call'd her quickly back again To lay some mair below my head.

VI.

A cod she laid below my head, And served me wi' due respect; And to salute her wi' a kiss, I put my arms about her neck.

VII.

"Haud aff your hands, young man," she says, "And dinna sae uncivil be: If ye hae onto love for me, O wrang na my virginitie!"

VIII.

Her hair was like the links o' gowd, Her teeth were like the ivorie; Her cheeks like lilies dipt in wine, The lass that made the bed to me.

IX.
Her bosom was the driven snaw, Twa drifted heaps sae fair to see; Her limbs the polish'd marble stane, The lass that made the bed to me.
X.
I kiss'd her owre and owre again, And ay she wist na what to say; I laid her between me and the wa'- The lassie thought na lang till day.
XI.
Upon the morrow when we rose, I thank'd her for her courtesie; But aye she blush'd, and aye she sigh'd, And said, "Alas! ye've ruin'd me."
XII.
I clasp'd her waist, and kiss'd her syne, While the tear stood twinklin' in her e'e; I said, "My lassie, dinna cry, For ye ay shall mak the bed to me."
XIII.
She took her mither's Holland sheets, And made them a' in sarks to me: Blythe and merry may she be, The lass that made the bed to me.
XIV.
The bonnie lass made the bed to me, The braw lass made the bed to me: I'll ne'er forget till the day I die, The lass that made the bed to me!

CLX. SAE FAR AWA.

Tune-"Dalkeith Maiden Bridge."
[This song was sent to the Museum by Burns, in his own handwriting.]
I.
O, sad and heavy should I part, But for her sake sae far awa; Unknowing what my way may thwart, My native land sae far awa. [268]Thou that of a' things Maker art, That form'd this fair sae far awa, Gie body strength, then I'll ne'er start At this my way sae far awa.
II.
How true is love to pure desert, So love to her, sae far awa: And nocht can heal my bosom's smart, While, oh! she is sae far awa. Nane other love, nane other dart, I feel but hers, sae far awa; But fairer never touch'd a heart Than hers, the fair sae far awa.

CLXI. I'LL AY CA' IN BY YON TOWN.

Tune-"I'll gae nae mair to yon town."
[Jean Armour inspired this very sweet song. Sir Harris Nicolas says it is printed in Cromek's Reliques: it was first printed in the Museum.]
I.
I'll ay ca' in by yon town, And by yon garden green, again; I'll ay ca' in by yon town, And see my bonnie Jean again. There's nane sall ken, there's nane sall guess, What brings me back the gate again; But she my fairest

faithfu' lass, And stownlins we sall meet again.
II.
She'll wander by the aiken tree, When trystin-time draws near again; And when her lovely form I see, O haith, she's doubly dear again! I'll ay ca' in by yon town, And by yon garden green, again; I'll ay ca' in by yon town, And see my bonnie Jean again.

CLXII. O, WAT YE WHA'S IN YON TOWN.

Tune-"I'll ay ca' in by yon town."
[The beautiful Lucy Johnstone, married to Oswald, of Auchencruive, was the heroine of this song: it was not, however, composed expressly in honour of her charms. "As I was a good deal pleased," he says in a letter to Syme, "with my performance, I, in my first fervour, thought of sending it to Mrs. Oswald." He sent it to the Museum, perhaps also to the lady.]
CHORUS.
O, wat ye wha's in yon town, Ye see the e'enin sun upon? The fairest dame's in yon town, That e'enin sun is shining on.
I.
Now haply down yon gay green shaw, She wanders by yon spreading tree; How blest ye flow'rs that round her blaw, Ye catch the glances o' her e'e!
II.
How blest ye birds that round her sing, And welcome in the blooming year! And doubly welcome be the spring, The season to my Lucy dear.
III.
The sun blinks blithe on yon town, And on yon bonnie braes of Ayr; But my delight in yon town, And dearest bliss, is Lucy fair.
IV.
Without my love, not a' the charms O' Paradise could yield me joy; But gie me Lucy in my arms, And welcome Lapland's dreary sky!
V.
My cave wad be a lover's bower, Tho' raging winter rent the air; And she a lovely little flower, That I wad tent and shelter there.
VI.
O sweet is she in yon town, Yon sinkin sun's gane down upon; A fairer than's in you town His setting beam ne'er shone upon.
VII.
If angry fate is sworn my foe, And suffering I am doom'd to bear; I careless quit aught else below, But spare me-spare me, Lucy dear!
VIII.
For while life's dearest blood is warm, Ae thought frae her shall ne'er depart, [269]And she-as fairest is her form! She has the truest, kindest heart! O, wat ye wha's in yon town, Ye see the e'enin sun upon? The fairest

dame's in yon town That e'enin sun is shining on.

CLXIII. O MAY, THY MORN.

Tune-"May, thy morn."
[Our lyrical legends assign the inspiration of this strain to the accomplished Clarinda. It has been omitted by Chambers in his "People's Edition" of Burns.]
I.
O May, thy morn was ne'er sae sweet As the mirk night o' December; For sparkling was the rosy wine, And private was the chamber: And dear was she I dare na name, But I will ay remember. And dear was she I dare na name, But I will ay remember.
II.
And here's to them, that, like oursel, Can push about the jorum; And here's to them that wish us weel, May a' that's guid watch o'er them, And here's to them we dare na tell, The dearest o' the quorum. Ami here's to them we dare na tell, The dearest o' the quorum!

CLXIV. LOVELY POLLY STEWART.

Tune-"Ye're welcome, Charlie Stewart."
[The poet's eye was on Polly Stewart, but his mind seems to have been with Charlie Stewart, and the Jacobite ballads, when he penned these words;-they are in the Museum.]
I.
O lovely Polly Stewart! O charming Polly Stewart! There's not a flower that blooms in May That's half so fair as thou art. The flower it blaws, it fades and fa's, And art can ne'er renew it; But worth and truth eternal youth Will give to Polly Stewart.
II.
May he whose arms shall fauld thy charms Possess a leal and true heart; To him be given to ken the heaven He grasps in Polly Stewart. O lovely Polly Stewart! O charming Polly Stewart! There's ne'er a flower that blooms in May That's half so sweet as thou art.

CLXV. THE HIGHLAND LADDIE.

Tune-"If thou'lt play me fair play."
[A long and wearisome ditty, called "The Highland Lad and Lowland Lassie," which Burns compressed into these stanzas, for Johnson's Museum.]
I.

The bonniest lad that e'er I saw, Bonnie laddie, Highland laddie, Wore a plaid, and was fu' braw, Bonnie Highland laddie. On his head a bonnet blue, Bonnie laddie, Highland laddie; His royal heart was firm and true, Bonnie Highland laddie.

II.

Trumpets sound, and cannons roar, Bonnie lassie; Lowland lassie; And a' the hills wi' echoes roar, Bonnie Lowland lassie. Glory, honour, now invite, Bonnie lassie, Lowland lassie, For freedom and my king to fight, Bonnie Lowland lassie.

III.

The sun a backward course shall take, Bonnie laddie, Highland laddie, Ere aught thy manly courage shake, Bonnie Highland laddie. Go, for yourself procure renown, Bonnie laddie, Highland laddie; And for your lawful king, his crown, Bonnie Highland laddie.

CLXVI. ANNA, THY CHARMS.

Tune-"Bonnie Mary."

[The heroine of this short, sweet song is unknown: it was inserted in the third edition of his Poems.]

Anna, thy charms my bosom fire, And waste my soul with care; But ah! how bootless to admire, When fated to despair! Yet in thy presence, lovely fair, To hope may be forgiv'n; For sure 'twere impious to despair, So much in sight of Heav'n.

CLXVII. CASSILLIS' BANKS.

Tune-[unknown.]

[It is supposed that "Highland Mary," who lived sometime on Cassillis's banks, is the heroine of these verses.]

I.

Now bank an' brae are claith'd in green, An' scattered cowslips sweetly spring; By Girvan's fairy-haunted stream, The birdies flit on wanton wing. To Cassillis' banks when e'ening fa's, There wi' my Mary let me flee, There catch her ilka glance of love, The bonnie blink o' Mary's e'e!

II.

The chield wha boasts o' warld's walth Is aften laird o' meikle care; But Mary she is a' my ain- Ah! fortune canna gie me mair. Then let me range by Cassillis' banks, Wi' her, the lassie dear to me, And catch her ilka glance o' love, The bonnie blink o' Mary's e'e!

CLXVIII. TO THEE, LOVED NITH.

Tune-[unknown.]
[There are several variations extant of these verses, and among others one which transfers the praise from the Nith to the Dee: but to the Dee, if the poet spoke in his own person, no such influences could belong.]
I.
To thee, lov'd Nith, thy gladsome plains, Where late wi' careless thought I rang'd, Though prest wi' care and sunk in woe, To thee I bring a heart unchang'd.
II.
I love thee, Nith, thy banks and braes, Tho' mem'ry there my bosom tear; For there he rov'd that brake my heart, Yet to that heart, ah! still how dear!

CLXIX. BANNOCKS O' BARLEY.

Tune-"The Killogie."
["This song is in the Museum," says Sir Harris Nicolas, "but without Burns's name." Burns took up an old song, and letting some of the old words stand, infused a Jacobite spirit into it, wrote it out, and sent it to the Museum.]
I.
Bannocks o' bear meal, Bannocks o' barley; Here's to the Highlandman's Bannocks o' barley. Wha in a brulzie Will first cry a parley? Never the lads wi' The bannocks o' barley.
II.
Bannocks o' bear meal, Bannocks o' barley; Here's to the lads wi' The bannocks o' barley. Wha in his wae-days Were loyal to Charlie? Wha but the lads wi' The bannocks o' barley?

CLXX. HEE BALOU.

Tune-"The Highland Balou."
["Published in the Musical Museum," says Sir Harris Nicolas, "but without the name of the author." It is an[271] old strain, eked out and amended by Burns, and sent to the Museum in his own handwriting.]
I.
Hee balou! my sweet wee Donald, Picture o' the great Clanronald; Brawlie kens our wanton chief Wha got my young Highland thief.
II.
Leeze me on thy bonnie craigie, An' thou live, thou'll steal a naigie: Travel the country thro' and thro', And bring hame a Carlisle cow.
III.
Thro' the Lawlands, o'er the border, Weel, my babie, may thou furder: Herry the louns o' the laigh countree, Syne to the Highlands hame to me.

CLXXI. WAE IS MY HEART.

Tune-"Wae is my heart."

[Composed, it is said, at the request of Clarke, the musician, who felt, or imagined he felt, some pangs of heart for one of the loveliest young ladies in Nithsdale, Phillis M'Murdo.]

I.

Wae is my heart, and the tear's in my e'e; Lang, lang, joy's been a stranger to me; Forsaken and friendless, my burden I bear, And the sweet voice of pity ne'er sounds in my ear.

II.

Love, thou hast pleasures, and deep hae I loved; Love, thou hast sorrows, and sair hae I proved; But this bruised heart that now bleeds in my breast, I can feel by its throbbings will soon be at rest.

III.

O, if I were happy, where happy I hae been, Down by yon stream, and yon bonnie castle green; For there he is wand'ring, and musing on me, Wha wad soon dry the tear frae his Phillis's e'e.

CLXXII. HERE'S HIS HEALTH IN WATER.

Tune-"The job of journey-work."

[Burns took the hint of this song from an older and less decorous strain, and wrote these words, it has been said, in humorous allusion to the condition in which Jean Armour found herself before marriage; as if Burns could be capable of anything so insulting. The words are in the Museum.]

Altho' my back be at the wa', An' tho' he be the fautor; Altho' my back be at the wa', Yet here's his health in water! O! wae gae by his wanton sides, Sae brawlie he could flatter; Till for his sake I'm slighted sair, And dree the kintra clatter. But tho' my back be at the wa', And tho' he be the fautor; But tho' my back be at the wa', Yet here's his health in water!

CLXXIII. MY PEGGY'S FACE.

Tune-"My Peggy's Face."

[Composed in honour of Miss Margaret Chalmers, afterwards Mrs. Lewis Hay, one of the wisest, and, it is said, the wittiest of all the poet's lady correspondents. Burns, in the note in which he communicated it to Johnson, said he had a strong private reason for wishing it to appear in the second volume of the Museum.]

I.

My Peggy's face, my Peggy's form, The frost of hermit age might warm; My

Peggy's worth, my Peggy's mind, Might charm the first of human kind. I love my Peggy's angel air, Her face so truly, heav'nly fair, Her native grace so void of art, But I adore my Peggy's heart.

II.

The lily's hue, the rose's dye, The kindling lustre of an eye; Who but owns their magic sway? Who but knows they all decay! The tender thrill, the pitying tear, The gen'rous purpose, nobly dear, The gentle look, that rage disarms- These are all immortal charms.

[272]

CLXXIV. GLOOMY DECEMBER.

Tune-"Wandering Willie."

[These verses were, it is said, inspired by Clarinda, and must be taken as a record of his feelings at parting with one dear to him in the last moment of existence-the Mrs. Mac of many a toast, both in serious and festive hours.]

I.

Ance mair I hail thee, thou gloomy December! Ance mair I hail thee wi' sorrow and care: Sad was the parting thou makes me remember, Parting wi' Nancy, oh! ne'er to meet mair. Fond lovers' parting is sweet painful pleasure, Hope beaming mild on the soft parting hour; But the dire feeling, O farewell for ever! Is anguish unmingled, and agony pure.

II.

Wild as the winter now tearing the forest, 'Till the last leaf o' the summer is flown, Such is the tempest has shaken my bosom, Since my last hope and last comfort is gone! Still as I hail thee, thou gloomy December, Still shall I hail thee wi' sorrow and care; For sad was the parting thou makes me remember, Parting wi' Nancy, oh! ne'er to meet mair.

CLXXV. MY LADY'S GOWN, THERE'S GAIRS UPON'T.

Tune-"Gregg's Pipes."

[Most of this song is from the pen of Burns: he corrected the improprieties, and infused some of his own lyric genius into the old strain, and printed the result in the Museum.]

I.

My lady's gown, there's gairs upon't, And gowden flowers sae rare upon't; But Jenny's jimps and jirkinet, My lord thinks meikle mair upon't. My lord a-hunting he is gane, But hounds or hawks wi' him are nane; By Colin's cottage lies his game, If Colin's Jenny be at hame.

II.

My lady's white, my lady's red, And kith and kin o' Cassillis' blude; But her ten-pund lands o' tocher guid Were a' the charms his lordship lo'ed.

III.
Out o'er yon muir, out o'er yon moss, Whare gor-cocks thro' the heather pass, There wons auld Colin's bonnie lass, A lily in a wilderness.
IV.
Sae sweetly move her genty limbs, Like music notes o' lovers' hymns: The diamond dew is her een sae blue, Where laughing love sae wanton swims.
V.
My lady's dink, my lady's drest, The flower and fancy o' the west; But the lassie that a man lo'es best, O that's the lass to make him blest. My lady's gown, there's gairs upon't, And gowden flowers sae rare upon't; But Jenny's jimps and jirkinet, My lord thinks meikle mair upon't.

CLXXVI. AMANG THE TREES.

Tune-"The King of France, he rade a race."
[Burns wrote these verses in scorn of those, and they are many, who prefer
"The capon craws and queer ha ha's!"
of emasculated Italy to the original and delicious airs, Highland and Lowland, of old Caledonia: the song is a fragment-the more's the pity.]
I.
Amang the trees, where humming bees At buds and flowers were hinging, O, Auld Caledon drew out her drone, And to her pipe was singing, O; 'Twas pibroch, sang, strathspey, or reels, She dirl'd them aff fu' clearly, O, When there cam a yell o' foreign squeels, That dang her tapsalteerie, O.
II.
Their capon craws and queer ha ha's, They made our lugs grow eerie, O; The hungry bike did scrape and pike, 'Till we were wae and weary, O; But a royal ghaist wha ance was cas'd A prisoner aughteen year awa, He fir'd a fiddler in the north That dang them tapsalteerie, O.
[273]

CLXXVII. THE GOWDEN LOCKS OF ANNA.

Tune-"Banks of Banna."
["Anne with the golden locks," one of the attendant maidens in Burns's Howff, in Dumfries, was very fair and very tractable, and, as may be surmised from the song, had other pretty ways to render herself agreeable to the customers than the serving of wine. Burns recommended this song to Thomson; and one of his editors makes him say, "I think this is one of the best love-songs I ever composed," but these are not the words of Burns; this contradiction is made openly, lest it should be thought that the bard had the bad taste to prefer this strain to dozens of others more simple, more impassioned, and more natural.]

I.
Yestreen I had a pint o' wine, A place where body saw na'; Yestreen lay on this breast o' mine The gowden locks of Anna. The hungry Jew in wilderness Rejoicing o'er his manna, Was naething to my hinny bliss Upon the lips of Anna.
II.
Ye monarchs tak the east and west, Frae Indus to Savannah! Gie me within my straining grasp The melting form of Anna. There I'll despise imperial charms, An empress or sultana, While dying raptures in her arms I give and take with Anna!
III.
Awa, thou flaunting god o' day! Awa, thou pale Diana! Ilk star gae hide thy twinkling ray, When I'm to meet my Anna. Come, in thy raven plumage, night! Sun, moon, and stars withdrawn a'; And bring an angel pen to write My transports wi' my Anna!
IV.
The kirk an' state may join and tell- To do sic things I maunna: The kirk and state may gang to hell, And I'll gae to my Anna. She is the sunshine of my e'e, To live but her I canna: Had I on earth but wishes three, The first should be my Anna.

CLXXVIII. MY AIN KIND DEARIE O.

[This is the first song composed by Burns for the national collection of Thomson: it was written in October, 1792. "On reading over the Lea-rig," he says, "I immediately set about trying my hand on it, and, after all, I could make nothing more of it than the following." The first and second verses were only sent: Burns added the third and last verse in December.]
I.
When o'er the hill the eastern star Tells bughtin-time is near, my jo; And owsen frae the furrow'd field Return sae dowf and weary, O! Down by the burn, where scented birks[137] Wi' dew are hanging clear, my jo; I'll meet thee on the lea-rig, My ain kind dearie O!
II.
In mirkest glen, at midnight hour, I'd rove, and ne'er be eerie, O; If thro' that glen I gaed to thee, My ain kind dearie O! Altho' the night were ne'er sae wild, And I were ne'er sae wearie, O, I'd meet thee on the lea-rig, My ain kind dearie O!
III.
The hunter lo'es the morning sun, To rouse the mountain deer, my jo; At noon the fisher seeks the glen, Alang the burn to steer, my jo; Gie me the hour o' gloamin gray, It maks my heart sae cheery, O, To meet thee on the lea-ring, My ain kind dearie O!

FOOTNOTES:

[137] For "scented birks," in some copies, "birken buds."

CLXXIX. TO MARY CAMPBELL.

["In my very early years," says Burns to Thomson "when I was thinking of going to the West Indies, I took the following farewell of a dear girl. You must know that all my earlier love-songs were the breathings of ardent passion, and though it might have been easy in after times to have given them a polish, yet that polish, to me, would have defaced the legend of my heart, so[274] faithfully inscribed on them. Their uncouth simplicity was, as they say of wines, their race." The heroine of this early composition was Highland Mary.]

I.

Will ye go to the Indies, my Mary, And leave old Scotia's shore? Will ye go to the Indies, my Mary, Across th' Atlantic's roar?

II.

O sweet grows the lime and the orange, And the apple on the pine; But a' the charms o' the Indies Can never equal thine.

III.

I hae sworn by the Heavens to my Mary, I hae sworn by the Heavens to be true; And sae may the Heavens forget me When I forget my vow!

IV.

O plight me your faith, my Mary, And plight me your lily white hand; O plight me your faith, my Mary, Before I leave Scotia's strand.

V.

We hae plighted our troth, my Mary, In mutual affection to join; And curst be the cause that shall part us! The hour and the moment o' time!

CLXXX. THE WINSOME WEE THING.

[These words were written for Thomson: or rather made extempore. "I might give you something more profound," says the poet, "yet it might not suit the light-horse gallop of the air, so well as this random clink."]

I.

She is a winsome wee thing, She is a handsome wee thing, She is a bonnie wee thing, This sweet wee wife o' mine.

II.

I never saw a fairer, I never lo'ed a dearer; And niest my heart I'll wear her, For fear my jewel tine.

III.

She is a winsome wee thing, She is a handsome wee thing, She is a bonnie wee thing, This sweet wee wife o' mine.
IV.
The warld's wrack we share o't, The warstle and the care o't; Wi' her I'll blythely bear it, And think my lot divine.

CLXXXI. BONNIE LESLEY.

["I have just," says Burns to Thomson, "been looking over the 'Collier's bonnie Daughter,' and if the following rhapsody, which I composed the other day, on a charming Ayrshire girl, Miss Leslie Baillie, as she passed through this place to England, will suit your taste better than the Collier Lassie, fall on and welcome." This lady was soon afterwards married to Mr. Cuming, of Logie.]
I.
O saw ye bonnie Lesley As she ga'ed o'er the border? She's gane, like Alexander, To spread her conquests farther.
II.
To see her is to love her, And love but her for ever; For Nature made her what she is, And never made anither!
III.
Thou art a queen, fair Lesley, Thy subjects we, before thee: Thou art divine, fair Lesley, The hearts o' men adore thee.
IV.
The deil he could na scaith thee, Or aught that wad belang thee; He'd look into thy bonnie face, And say, "I canna wrang thee."
V.
The powers aboon will tent thee; Misfortune sha' na steer thee: Thou'rt like themselves so lovely, That ill they'll ne'er let near thee.
[275]
VI.
Return again, fair Lesley, Return to Caledonie; That we may brag, we hae a lass There's nane again sae bonnie.

CLXXXII. HIGHLAND MARY.

Tune-"Katherine Ogie."
[Mary Campbell, of whose worth and beauty Burns has sung with such deep feeling, was the daughter of a mariner, who lived in Greenock. She became acquainted with the poet while on service at the castle of Montgomery, and their strolls in the woods and their roaming trysts only served to deepen and settle their affections. Their love had much of the solemn as well as of the romantic: on the day of their separation they

plighted their mutual faith by the exchange of Bibles: they stood with a running-stream between them, and lifting up water in their hands vowed love while woods grew and waters ran. The Bible which the poet gave was elegantly bound: 'Ye shall not swear by my name falsely,' was written in the bold Mauchline hand of Burns, and underneath was his name, and his mark as a freemason. They parted to meet no more: Mary Campbell was carried off suddenly by a burning fever, and the first intimation which the poet had of her fate, was when, it is said, he visited her friends to meet her on her return from Cowal, whither she had gone to make arrangements for her marriage. The Bible is in the keeping of her relations: we have seen a lock of her hair; it was very long and very bright, and of a hue deeper than the flaxen. The song was written for Thomson's work.]

I.

Ye banks, and braes, and streams around The castle o' Montgomery, Green be your woods, and fair your flowers, Your waters never drumlie! There Simmer first unfauld her robes, And there the langest tarry; For there I took the last farewell O' my sweet Highland Mary.

II.

How sweetly bloom'd the gay green birk, How rich the hawthorn's blossom, As underneath their fragrant shade I clasp'd her to my bosom! The golden hours, on angel wings, Flew o'er me and my dearie; For dear to me, as light and life, Was my sweet Highland Mary!

III.

Wi' mony a vow, and lock'd embrace, Our parting was fu' tender; And, pledging aft to meet again, We tore oursels asunder; But oh! fell death's untimely frost, That nipt my flower sae early!- Now green's the sod, and cauld's the clay, That wraps my Highland Mary!

IV.

O pale, pale now, those rosy lips I aft hae kissed sae fondly! And clos'd for ay the sparkling glance That dwelt on me sae kindly! And mouldering now in silent dust, That heart that lo'ed me dearly- But still within my bosom's core Shall live my Highland Mary!

CLXXXIII. AULD ROB MORRIS.

[The starting lines of this song are from one of no little merit in Ramsey's collection: the old strain is sarcastic; the new strain is tender: it was written for Thomson.]

I.

There's auld Rob Morris that wons in yon glen, He's the king o' guid fellows and wale of auld men; He has gowd in his coffers, he has owsen and kine, And ae bonnie lassie, his darling and mine.

II.

She's fresh as the morning, the fairest in May; She's sweet as the ev'ning amang the new hay; As blythe and as artless as the lamb on the lea, And dear to my heart as the light to my e'e.

III.

But oh! she's an heiress,-auld Robin's a laird, And my daddie has nought but a cot-house and yard; A wooer like me mamma hope to come speed; The wounds I must hide that will soon be my dead. [276]

IV.

The day comes to me, but delight brings me nane; The night comes to me, but my rest it is gane: I wander my lane like a night-troubled ghaist, And I sigh as my heart it wad burst in my breast.

V.

O had she but been of a lower degree, I then might hae hop'd she wad smil'd upon me! O, how past descriving had then been my bliss, As now my distraction no words can express!

CLXXXIV. DUNCAN GRAY.

[This Duncan Gray of Burns, has nothing in common with the wild old song of that name, save the first line, and a part of the third, neither has it any share in the sentiments of an earlier strain, with the same title, by the same hand. It was written for the work of Thomson.]

I.

Duncan Gray cam here to woo, Ha, ha, the wooing o't; On blythe yule night when we were fou, Ha, ha, the wooing o't. Maggie coost her head fu' high, Look'd asklent and unco skeigh, Gart poor Duncan stand abeigh; Ha, ha, the wooing o't.

II.

Duncan fleech'd, and Duncan pray'd, Ha, ha, the wooing o't; Meg was deaf as Ailsa Craig, Ha, ha, the wooing o't. Duncan sigh'd baith out and in, Grat his een baith bleer't and blin', Spak o' lowpin o'er a linn; Ha, ha, the wooing o't.

III.

Time and chance are but a tide, Ha, ha, the wooing o't; Slighted love is sair to bide, Ha, ha, the wooing o't. Shall I, like a fool, quoth he, For a haughty hizzie die? She may gae to-France for me! Ha, ha, the wooing o't.

IV.

How it comes let doctors tell, Ha, ha, the wooing o't; Meg grew sick-as he grew heal, Ha, ha, the wooing o't. Something in her bosom wrings, For relief a sigh she brings: And O, her een, they spak sic things! Ha, ha, the wooing o't.

V.

Duncan was a lad o' grace. Ha, ha, the wooing o't; Maggie's was a piteous case, Ha, ha, the wooing o't. Duncan could na be her death, Swelling pity smoor'd his wrath; Now they're crouse and canty baith, Ha, ha, the wooing o't.

CLXXXV. O POORTITH CAULD.

Tune-"I had a horse."
[Jean Lorimer, the Chloris and the "Lassie with the lint-white locks" of Burns, was the heroine of this exquisite lyric: she was at that time very young; her shape was fine, and her "dimpled cheek and cherry mou" will be long remembered in Nithsdale.]
I.
O poortith cauld, and restless love, Ye wreck my peace between ye; Yet poortith a' I could forgive, An' twere na' for my Jeanie. O why should fate sic pleasure have, Life's dearest bands untwining? Or why sae sweet a flower as love Depend on fortune's shining?
II.
This warld's wealth when I think on, It's pride, and a' the lave o't- Fie, fie on silly coward man, That he should be the slave o't!
III.
Her een sae bonnie blue betray How she repays my passion; But prudence is her o'erword ay, She talks of rank and fashion. [277]
IV.
O wha can prudence think upon, And sic a lassie by him? O wha can prudence think upon, And sae in love as I am?
V.
How blest the humble cotter's fate![138] He wooes his simple dearie; The silly bogles, wealth and state, Can never make them eerie. O why should Fate sic pleasure have, Life's dearest bands untwining? Or why sae sweet a flower as love Depend on Fortune's shining?

FOOTNOTES:

[138] "The wild-wood Indian's Fate," in the original MS.

CLXXXVI. GALLA WATER.

["Galla Water" is an improved version of an earlier song by Burns: but both songs owe some of their attractions to an older strain, which the exquisite air has made popular over the world. It was written for Thomson.]
I.
There's braw, braw lads on Yarrow braes, That wander thro' the blooming heather; But Yarrow braes nor Ettrick shaws Can match the lads o' Galla

Water.
II.
But there is ane, a secret ane, Aboon them a' I lo'e him better; And I'll be his, and he'll be mine, The bonnie lad o' Galla Water.
III.
Altho' his daddie was nae laird, And tho' I hae nae meikle tocher; Yet rich in kindest, truest love, We'll tent our flocks by Galla Water.
IV.
It ne'er was wealth, it ne'er was wealth, That coft contentment, peace, or pleasure; The bands and bliss o' mutual love, O that's the chiefest warld's treasure!

CLXXXVII. LORD GREGORY.

[Dr. Wolcot wrote a Lord Gregory for Thomson's collection, in imitation of which Burns wrote his, and the Englishman complained, with an oath, that the Scotchman sought to rob him of the merit of his composition. Wolcot's song was, indeed, written first, but they are both but imitations of that most exquisite old ballad, "Fair Annie of Lochryan," which neither Wolcot nor Burns valued as it deserved: it far surpasses both their songs.]
I.
O mirk, mirk is this midnight hour, And loud the tempest's roar; A waefu' wanderer seeks thy tow'r, Lord Gregory, ope thy door!
II.
An exile frae her father's ha', And a' for loving thee; At least some pity on me shaw, If love it may na be.
III.
Lord Gregory, mind'st thou not the grove By bonnie Irwin-side, Where first I own'd that virgin-love I lang, lang had denied?
IV.
How often didst thou pledge and vow Thou wad for ay be mine; And my fond heart, itsel' sae true, It ne'er mistrusted thine.
V.
Hard is thy heart, Lord Gregory, And flinty is thy breast- Thou dart of heaven that flashest by, O wilt thou give me rest!
VI.
Ye mustering thunders from above, Your willing victim see! But spare and pardon my fause love, His wrangs to heaven and me!

CLXXXVIII. MARY MORISON.

Tune-"Bide ye yet."
["The song prefixed," observes Burns to Thomson, "is one of my juvenile

works. I leave it in your hands.[278] I do not think it very remarkable either for its merits or its demerits." "Of all the productions of Burns," says Hazlitt, "the pathetic and serious love-songs which he has left behind him, in the manner of the old ballads, are, perhaps, those which take the deepest and most lasting hold of the mind. Such are the lines to Mary Morison." The song is supposed to have been written on one of a family of Morisons at Mauchline.]

I.

O Mary, at thy window be, It is the wish'd, the trysted hour! Those smiles and glances let me see That make the miser's treasure poor: How blithely wad I bide the stoure, A weary slave frae sun to sun; Could I the rich reward secure, The lovely Mary Morison!

II.

Yestreen, when to the trembling string The dance gaed thro' the lighted ha', To thee my fancy took its wing, I sat, but neither heard or saw: Tho' this was fair, and that was braw, And yon the toast of a' the town, I sigh'd, and said amang them a', "Ye are na Mary Morison."

III.

O Mary, canst thou wreck his peace, Wha for thy sake wad gladly die? Or canst thou break that heart of his, Whase only faut is loving thee? If love for love thou wilt na gie, At least be pity to me shown; A thought ungentle canna be The thought o' Mary Morison.

CLXXXIX. WANDERING WILLIE.

[FIRST VERSION.]

[The idea of this song is taken from verses of the same name published by Herd: the heroine is supposed to have been the accomplished Mrs. Riddel. Erskine and Thomson sat in judgment upon it, and, like true critics, squeezed much of the natural and original spirit out of it. Burns approved of their alterations; but he approved, no doubt, in bitterness of spirit.]

I.

Here awa, there awa, wandering Willie, Now tired with wandering, haud awa hame; Come to my bosom, my ae only dearie, And tell me thou bring'st me my Willie the same.

II.

Loud blew the cauld winter winds at our parting; It was na the blast brought the tear in my e'e; Now welcome the simmer, and welcome my Willie, The simmer to nature, my Willie to me.

III.

Ye hurricanes, rest in the cave o' your slumbers! O how your wild horrors a lover alarms! Awaken, ye breezes, row gently, ye billows, And waft my dear laddie ance mair to my arms.

IV.
But if he's forgotten his faithfulest Nannie, O still flow between us, thou wide roaring main; May I never see it, may I never trow it, But, dying, believe that my Willie's my ain.

CXC. WANDERING WILLIE.

[LAST VERSION.]
[This is the "Wandering Willie" as altered by Erskine and Thomson, and approved by Burns, after rejecting several of their emendations. The changes were made chiefly with the view of harmonizing the words with the music-an Italian mode of mending the harmony of the human voice.]
I.
Here awa, there awa, wandering Willie, Here awa, there awa, haud awa hame; Come to my bosom, my ain only dearie, Tell me thou bring'st me my Willie the same.
II.
Winter winds blew loud and cauld at our parting, Fears for my Willie brought tears in my e'e; Welcome now simmer, and welcome my Willie, The simmer to nature, my Willie to me. [279]
III.
Rest, ye wild storms, in the cave of your slumbers, How your dread howling a lover alarms! Wauken, ye breezes, row gently, ye billows, And waft my dear laddie ance mair to my arms.
IV.
But oh, if he's faithless, and minds na his Nannie, Flow still between us, thou wide roaring main; May I never see it, may I never trow it, But, dying, believe that my Willie's my ain.

CXCI. OPEN THE DOOR TO ME, OH!

[Written for Thomson's collection: the first version which he wrote was not happy in its harmony: Burns altered and corrected it as it now stands, and then said, "I do not know if this song be really mended."]
I.
Oh, open the door, some pity to show, Oh, open the door to me, Oh![139] Tho' thou has been false, I'll ever prove true, Oh, open the door to me, Oh!
II.
Cauld is the blast upon my pale cheek, But caulder thy love for me, Oh! The frost that freezes the life at my heart, Is nought to my pains frae thee, Oh!
III.
The wan moon is setting behind the white wave, And time is setting with

me, Oh! False friends, false love, farewell! for mair I'll ne'er trouble them, nor thee, Oh!
IV.
She has open'd the door, she has open'd it wide; She sees his pale corse on the plain, Oh! My true love! she cried, and sank down by his side, Never to rise again, Oh!

FOOTNOTES:

[139] This second line was originally-"If love it may na be, Oh!"

CXCII. JESSIE.

Tune-"Bonnie Dundee."
[Jessie Staig, the eldest daughter of the provost of Dumfries, was the heroine of this song. She became a wife and a mother, but died early in life: she is still affectionately remembered in her native place.]
I.
True hearted was he, the sad swain o' the Yarrow, And fair are the maids on the banks o' the Ayr, But by the sweet side o' the Nith's winding river, Are lovers as faithful, and maidens as fair: To equal young Jessie seek Scotland all over; To equal young Jessie you seek it in vain; Grace, beauty, and elegance fetter her lover, And maidenly modesty fixes the chain.
II.
O, fresh is the rose in the gay, dewy morning, And sweet is the lily at evening close; But in the fair presence o' lovely young Jessie Unseen is the lily, unheeded the rose. Love sits in her smile, a wizard ensnaring; Enthron'd in her een he delivers his law: And still to her charms she alone is a stranger- Her modest demeanour's the jewel of a'!

CXCIII. THE POOR AND HONEST SODGER.

Air-"The Mill, Mill, O."
[Burns, it is said, composed this song, once very popular, on hearing a maimed soldier relate his adventures, at Brownhill, in Nithsdale: it was published by Thomson, after suggesting some alterations, which were properly rejected.]
I.
When wild war's deadly blast was blawn And gentle peace returning, Wi' mony a sweet babe fatherless, And mony a widow mourning; I left the lines and tented field, Where lang I'd been a lodger, My humble knapsack a' my wealth, A poor and honest sodger.
II.

A leal, light heart was in my breast, My hand unstain'd wi' plunder; [280] And for fair Scotia, hame again, I cheery on did wander. I thought upon the banks o' Coil, I thought upon my Nancy, I thought upon the witching smile That caught my youthful fancy.

III.

At length I reach'd the bonny glen, Where early life I sported; I pass'd the mill, and trysting thorn, Where Nancy aft I courted: Wha spied I but my ain dear maid, Down by her mother's dwelling! And turn'd me round to hide the flood That in my een was swelling.

IV.

Wi' alter'd voice, quoth I, sweet lass, Sweet as yon hawthorn's blossom, O! happy, happy, may he be That's dearest to thy bosom! My purse is light, I've far to gang, And fain wud be thy lodger; I've serv'd my king and country lang- Take pity on a sodger.

V.

Sae wistfully she gaz'd on me, And lovelier was then ever; Quo' she, a sodger ance I lo'd, Forget him shall I never: Our humble cot, and hamely fare, Ye freely shall partake it, That gallant badge-the dear cockade- Ye're welcome for the sake o't.

VI.

She gaz'd-she redden'd like a rose- Syne pale like onie lily; She sank within my arms, and cried, Art thou my ain dear Willie? By him who made yon sun and sky- By whom true love's regarded, I am the man: and thus may still True lovers be rewarded!

VII.

The wars are o'er, and I'm come hame, And find thee still true-hearted; Tho' poor in gear, we're rich in love, And mair we'se ne'er be parted. Quo' she, my grandsire left me gowd, A mailen plenish'd fairly; And come, my faithful sodger lad, Thou'rt welcome to it dearly!

VIII.

For gold the merchant ploughs the main, The farmer ploughs the manor; But glory is the sodger's prize, The sodger's wealth is honour; The brave poor sodger ne'er despise, Nor count him as a stranger; Remember he's his country's stay, In day and hour of danger.

CXCIV. MEG O' THE MILL.

Air-"Hey! bonnie lass, will you lie in a barrack?"

["Do you know a fine air," Burns asks Thomson, April, 1973, "called 'Jackie Hume's Lament?' I have a song of considerable merit to that air: I'll enclose you both song and tune, as I have them ready to send to the Museum." It is probable that Thomson liked these verses too well to let them go willingly from his hands: Burns touched up the old song with the same starting line, but a less delicate conclusion, and published it in the Museum.]

I.

O ken ye what Meg o' the Mill has gotten? An' ken ye what Meg o' the Mill has gotten? She has gotten a coof wi' a claute o' siller, And broken the heart o' the barley Miller.

II.

The Miller was strappin, the Miller was ruddy; A heart like a lord and a hue like a lady: The Laird was a widdiefu', bleerit knurl; She's left the guid-fellow and ta'en the churl.

III.

The Miller he hecht her a heart leal and loving; The Laird did address her wi' matter mair moving, A fine pacing horse wi' a clear chained bridle, A whip by her side and a bonnie side-saddle.

IV.

O wae on the siller, it is sae prevailing; And wae on the love that is fixed on a mailen' A tocher's nae word in a true lover's parle, But gie me my love, and a fig for the warl!

CXCV. BLYTHE HAE I BEEN.

Tune-"Liggeram Cosh."

[Burns, who seldom praised his own compositions, told Thomson, for whose work he wrote it, that "Blythe hae I been on yon hill," was one of the finest songs he had ever made in his life, and composed on one of the most lovely women in the world. The heroine was Miss Lesley Baillie.]

I.

Blythe hae I been on yon hill As the lambs before me; Careless ilka thought and free As the breeze flew o'er me. Now nae langer sport and play, Mirth or sang can please me; Lesley is sae fair and coy, Care and anguish seize me.

II.

Heavy, heavy is the task, Hopeless love declaring: Trembling, I dow nocht but glow'r, Sighing, dumb, despairing! If she winna ease the thraws In my bosom swelling, Underneath the grass-green sod Soon maun be my dwelling.

CXCVI. LOGAN WATER.

["Have you ever, my dear sir," says Burns to Thomson, 25th June, 1793, "felt your bosom ready to burst with indignation on reading of those mighty villains who divide kingdom against kingdom, desolate provinces, and lay nations waste, out of wantoness of ambition, or often from still more ignoble passions? In a mood of this kind to-day I recollected the air of Logan Water. If I have done anything at all like justice to my feelings, the following song, composed in three-quarters of an hour's meditation in my elbow-chair, ought to have some merit." The poet had in mind, too, during this poetic fit, the beautiful song of Logan-braes, by my friend John Mayne, a Nithsdale poet.]

I.

O Logan, sweetly didst thou glide, That day I was my Willie's bride! And years synsyne hae o'er us run Like Logan to the simmer sun. But now thy flow'ry banks appear Like drumlie winter, dark and drear, While my dear lad maun face his faes, Far, far frae me and Logan braes!

II.

Again the merry month o' May Has made our hills and valleys gay; The birds rejoice in leafy bowers, The bees hum round the breathing flowers; Blythe Morning lifts his rosy eye, And Evening's tears are tears of joy: My soul, delightless, a' surveys, While Willie's far frae Logan braes.

III.

Within yon milk-white hawthorn bush, Amang her nestlings sits the thrush; Her faithfu' mate will share her toil, Or wi' his song her cares beguile: But I, wi' my sweet nurslings here, Nae mate to help, nae mate to cheer, Pass widow'd nights and joyless days, While Willie's far frae Logan braes.

IV.

O wae upon you, men o' state, That brethren rouse to deadly hate! As ye make mony a fond heart mourn, Sae may it on your heads return! How can your flinty hearts enjoy The widow's tears, the orphan's cry?[140] But soon may peace bring happy days And Willie hame to Logan braes!

FOOTNOTES:

[140] Originally-

"Ye mind na, 'mid your cruel joys, The widow's tears, the orphan's cries."

CXCVII. THE RED, RED ROSE.

Air-"Hughie Graham."

[There are snatches of old song so exquisitely fine that, like fractured crystal, they cannot be mended or eked out, without showing where the hand of the restorer has been. This seems the case with the first verse of this song, which the poet found in Witherspoon, and completed by the addition of the second verse, which he felt to be inferior, by desiring Thomson to make his own the first verse, and let the other follow, which would conclude the strain with a thought as beautiful as it was original.]

I.

O were my love yon lilac fair, Wi' purple blossoms to the spring; And I, a bird to shelter there, When wearied on my little wing! [282]How I wad mourn, when it was torn By autumn wild, and winter rude! But I wad sing on wanton wing, When youthfu' May its bloom renewed.

II.

O gin my love were yon red rose, That grows upon the castle wa'; And I mysel' a drap o' dew, Into her bonnie breast to fa'! Oh, there beyond expression blest, I'd feast on beauty a' the night; Seal'd on her silk-saft faulds to rest, Till fley'd awa by Phœbus' light.

CXCVIII. BONNIE JEAN.

[Jean M'Murdo, the heroine of this song, the eldest daughter of John M'Murdo of Drumlanrig, was, both in merit and look, very worthy of so sweet a strain, and justified the poet from the charge made against him in the West, that his beauties were not other men's beauties. In the M'Murdo manuscript, in Burns's handwriting, there is a well-merited compliment which has slipt out of the printed copy in Thomson:-

"Thy handsome foot thou shalt na set In barn or byre to trouble thee."]

I.

There was a lass, and she was fair, At kirk and market to be seen, When a' the fairest maids were met, The fairest maid was bonnie Jean.

II.

And aye she wrought her mammie's wark, And ay she sang so merrilie: The blithest bird upon the bush Had ne'er a lighter heart than she.

III.

But hawks will rob the tender joys That bless the little lintwhite's nest; And frost will blight the fairest flowers, And love will break the soundest rest.

IV.

Young Robie was the brawest lad, The flower and pride of a' the glen; And he had owsen, sheep, and kye, And wanton naigies nine or ten.

V.

He gaed wi' Jeanie to the tryste, He danc'd wi' Jeanie on the down; And, lang ere witless Jeanie wist, Her heart was tint, her peace was stown.

VI.

As in the bosom o' the stream, The moon-beam dwells at dewy e'en; So trembling, pure, was tender love Within the breast o' bonnie Jean.

VII.

And now she works her mammie's wark, And ay she sighs wi' care and pain; Yet wist na what her ail might be, Or what wad mak her weel again.

VIII.

But did na Jeanie's heart loup light, And did na joy blink in her e'e, As Robie tauld a tale of love, Ae e'enin' on the lily lea?

IX.

The sun was sinking in the west, The birds sung sweet in ilka grove; His

cheek to hers he fondly prest, And whisper'd thus his tale o' love:
X.
O Jeanie fair, I lo'e thee dear; O canst thou think to fancy me! Or wilt thou leave thy mammie's cot, And learn to tent the farms wi' me?
XI.
At barn or byre thou shalt na drudge, Or naething else to trouble thee; But stray amang the heather-bells, And tent the waving corn wi' me.
XII.
Now what could artless Jeanie do? She had nae will to say him na: At length she blush'd a sweet consent, And love was ay between them twa.

CXCIX. PHILLIS THE FAIR.

Tune-"Robin Adair."
[The ladies of the M'Murdo family were graceful and beautiful, and lucky in finding a poet capable of recording their charms in lasting strains. The heroine of this song was Phyllis M'Murdo; a favourite of the poet. The verses were composed at the request of Clarke, the musician, who believed himself in love with his "charming pupil." She laughed at the presumptuous fiddler.]
I.
While larks with little wing Fann'd the pure air, Tasting the breathing spring, Forth I did fare: Gay the sun's golden eye Peep'd o'er the mountains high; Such thy morn! did I cry, Phillis the fair.
II.
In each bird's careless song, Glad I did share; While yon wild flowers among, Chance led me there: Sweet to the opening day, Rosebuds bent the dewy spray; Such thy bloom! did I say, Phillis the fair.
III.
Down in a shady walk Doves cooing were, I mark'd the cruel hawk, Caught in a snare: So kind may fortune be, Such make his destiny! He who would injure thee, Phillis the fair.

CC. HAD I A CAVE.

Tune-"Robin Adair."
[Alexander Cunningham, on whose unfortunate love-adventure Burns composed this song for Thomson, was a jeweller in Edinburgh, well connected, and of agreeable and polished manners. The story of his faithless mistress was the talk of Edinburgh, in 1793, when these words were written: the hero of the lay has been long dead; the heroine resides, a widow, in Edinburgh.]
I.

Had I a cave on some wild, distant shore, Where the winds howl to the waves' dashing roar; There would I weep my woes, There seek my lost repose, Till grief my eyes should close, Ne'er to wake more.
II.
Falsest of womankind, canst thou declare, All thy fond plighted vows-fleeting as air! To thy new lover hie, Laugh o'er thy perjury, Then in thy bosom try What peace is there!

CCI. BY ALLAN STREAM.

["Bravo! say I," exclaimed Burns, when he wrote these verses for Thomson. "It is a good song. Should you think so too, not else, you can set the music to it, and let the other follow as English verses. Autumn is my propitious season; I make more verses in it than all the year else." The old song of "O my love Annie's very bonnie," helped the muse of Burns with this lyric.]
I.
By Allan stream I chanced to rove While Phœbus sank beyond Benledi; The winds were whispering through the grove, The yellow corn was waving ready; I listened to a lover's sang, And thought on youthfu' pleasures mony: And aye the wild wood echoes rang- O dearly do I lo'e thee, Annie!
II.
O happy be the woodbine bower, Nae nightly bogle make it eerie; Nor ever sorrow stain the hour, The place and time I met my dearie! Her head upon my throbbing breast, She, sinking, said, "I'm thine for ever?" While mony a kiss the seal impress, The sacred vow,-we ne'er should sever. [284]
III.
The haunt o' Spring's the primrose brae, The Simmer joys the flocks to follow; How cheery, thro' her shortening day, Is Autumn, in her weeds o' yellow! But can they melt the glowing heart, Or chain the soul in speechless pleasure, Or thro' each nerve the rapture dart, Like meeting her, our bosom's treasure?

CCII. O WHISTLE, AND I'LL COME TO YOU.

[In one of the variations of this song the name of the heroine is Jeanie: the song itself owes some of the sentiments as well as words to an old favourite Nithsdale chant of the same name. "Is Whistle, and I'll come to you, my lad," Burns inquires of Thomson, "one of your airs? I admire it much, and yesterday I set the following verses to it." The poet, two years afterwards, altered the fourth line thus:-
"Thy Jeany will venture wi' ye, my lad,"
and assigned this reason: "In fact, a fair dame at whose shrine I, the priest of the Nine, offer up the incense of Parnassus; a dame whom the Graces

have attired in witchcraft, and whom the Loves have armed with lightning; a fair one, herself the heroine of the song, insists on the amendment, and dispute her commands if you dare."]

I.

O whistle, and I'll come to you, my lad, O whistle, and I'll come to you, my lad: Tho' father and mither and a' should gae mad, O whistle, and I'll come to you, my lad. But warily tent, when you come to court me, And come na unless the back-yett be a-jee; Syne up the back-stile and let naebody see, And come as ye were na comin' to me. And come as ye were na comin' to me.

II.

At kirk, or at market, whene'er ye meet me, Gang by me as tho' that ye car'd na a flie; But steal me a blink o' your bonnie black e'e, Yet look as ye were na lookin' at me. Yet look as ye were na lookin' at me.

III.

Ay vow and protest that ye care na for me, And whiles ye may lightly my beauty a wee; But court na anither, tho' jokin' ye be, For fear that she wyle your fancy frae me. For fear that she wyle your fancy frae me.

IV.

O whistle, and I'll come to you, my lad, O whistle, and I'll come to you, my lad: Tho' father and mither and a' should gae mad, O whistle, and I'll come to you, my lad.

CCIII. ADOWN WINDING NITH.

["Mr. Clarke," says Burns to Thompson, "begs you to give Miss Phillis a corner in your book, as she is a particular flame of his. She is a Miss Phillis M'Murdo, sister to 'Bonnie Jean;' they are both pupils of his." This lady afterwards became Mrs. Norman Lockhart, of Carnwath.]

I.

Adown winding Nith I did wander, To mark the sweet flowers as they spring; Adown winding Nith I did wander, Of Phillis to muse and to sing. Awa wi' your belles and your beauties, They never wi' her can compare: Whaever has met wi' my Phillis, Has met wi' the queen o' the fair.

II.

The daisy amus'd my fond fancy, So artless, so simple, so wild; Thou emblem, said I, o' my Phillis, For she is simplicity's child.

III.

The rose-bud's the blush o' my charmer, Her sweet balmy lip when 'tis prest: How fair and how pure is the lily, But fairer and purer her breast.

IV.

Yon knot of gay flowers in the arbour, They ne'er wi' my Phillis can vie: Her breath is the breath o' the woodbine, Its dew-drop o' diamond, her eye.

V.
Her voice is the song of the morning, That wakes thro' the green-spreading grove, When Phœbus peeps over the mountains, On music, and pleasure, and love.
VI.
But beauty how frail and how fleeting, The bloom of a fine summer's day! While worth in the mind o' my Phillis Will flourish without a decay. [285]Awa wi' your belles and your beauties, They never wi' her can compare: Whaever has met wi' my Phillis Has met wi' the queen o' the fair.

CCIV. COME, LET ME TAKE THEE.

Air-"Cauld Kail."
[Burns composed this lyric in August, 1793, and tradition says it was produced by the charms of Jean Lorimer. "That tune, Cauld Kail," he says to Thomson, "is such a favorite of yours, that I once roved out yesterday for a gloaming-shot at the Muses; when the Muse that presides over the shores of Nith, or rather my old inspiring, dearest nymph, Coila, whispered me the following."]
I.
Come, let me take thee to my breast, And pledge we ne'er shall sunder; And I shall spurn as vilest dust The warld's wealth and grandeur: And do I hear my Jeanie own That equal transports move her? I ask for dearest life alone, That I may live to love her.
II.
Thus in my arms, wi' a' thy charms, I clasp my countless treasure; I'll seek nae mair o' heaven to share, Than sic a moment's pleasure: And by thy een, sae bonnie blue, I swear I'm thine for ever! And on thy lips I seal my vow, And break it shall I never.

CCV. DAINTY DAVIE.

[From the old song of "Daintie Davie" Burns has borrowed only the title and the measure. The ancient strain records how the Rev. David Williamson, to escape the pursuit of the dragoons, in the time of the persecution, was hid, by the devout Lady of Cherrytrees, in the same bed with her ailing daughter. The divine lived to have six wives beside the daughter of the Lady of Cherrytrees, and other children besides the one which his hiding from the dragoons produced. When and its upshot, he is said to have exclaimed, "God's fish! that beats me and the oak: the man ought to be made a bishop."]
I.
Now rosy May comes in wi' flowers, To deck her gay, green-spreading

bowers; And now comes in my happy hours, To wander wi' my Davie. Meet me on the warlock knowe, Dainty Davie, dainty Davie, There I'll spend the day wi' you, My ain dear dainty Davie.
II.
The crystal waters round us fa', The merry birds are lovers a', The scented breezes round us blaw, A wandering wi' my Davie.
III.
When purple morning starts the hare, To steal upon her early fare, Then thro' the dews I will repair, To meet my faithfu' Davie
IV.
When day, expiring in the west, The curtain draws o' nature's rest, I flee to his arms I lo'e best, And that's my ain dear Davie. Meet me on the warlock knowe, Bonnie Davie, dainty Davie, There I'll spend the day wi' you, My ain dear dainty Davie.

CCVI. BRUCE TO HIS MEN AT BANNOCKBURN.

[FIRST VERSION.]
Tune-"Hey, tuttie taitie."
[Syme of Ryedale states that this fine ode was composed during a storm of rain and fire, among the wilds of Glenken in Galloway: the poet himself gives an account much less romantic. In speaking of the air to Thomson, he says, "There is a tradition which I have met with in many places in Scotland, that it was Robert Bruce's march at the battle of Bannockburn. This thought, in my solitary wanderings, warmed me to a pitch of enthusiasm on the theme of liberty and independence, which I threw into a kind of Scottish ode, fitted to the air, that[286] one might suppose to be the royal Scot's address to his heroic followers on that eventful morning." It was written in September, 1793.]
I.
Scots, wha hae wi' Wallace bled, Scots, wham Bruce has aften led; Welcome to your gory bed, Or to victorie!
II.
Now's the day, and now's the hour; See the front o' battle lour: See approach proud Edward's pow'r- Chains and slaverie!
III.
Wha will be a traitor-knave? Wha can fill a coward's grave? Wha sae base as be a slave! Let him turn and flee!
IV.
Wha for Scotland's king and law Freedom's sword will strongly draw, Freeman stand, or freeman fa', Let him follow me!
V.
By oppression's woes and pains! By our sons in servile chains! We will drain

our dearest veins, But they shall be free!

VI.

Lay the proud usurpers low! Tyrants fall in every foe! Liberty's in every blow!- Let us do or die!

CCVII. BANNOCKBURN.
ROBERT BRUCE'S ADDRESS TO HIS ARMY.

[SECOND VERSION.]

[Thomson acknowledged the charm which this martial and national ode had for him, but he disliked the air, and proposed to substitute that of Lewis Gordon in its place. But Lewis Gordon required a couple of syllables more in every fourth line, which loaded the verse with expletives, and weakened the simple energy of the original: Burns consented to the proper alterations, after a slight resistance; but when Thomson, having succeeded in this, proposed a change in the expression, no warrior of Bruce's day ever resisted more sternly the march of a Southron over the border. "The only line," says the musician, "which I dislike in the whole song is,

'Welcome to your gory bed:'

gory presents a disagreeable image to the mind, and a prudent general would avoid saying anything to his soldiers which might tend to make death more frightful than it is." "My ode," replied Burns, "pleases me so much that I cannot alter it: your proposed alterations would, in my opinion, make it tame." Thomson cries out, like the timid wife of Coriolanus, "Oh, God, no blood!" while Burns exclaims, like that Roman's heroic mother, "Yes, blood! it becomes a soldier more than gilt his trophy." The ode as originally written was restored afterwards in Thomson's collection.]

I.

Scots, wha hae wi' Wallace bled, Scots, wham Bruce has aften led; Welcome to your gory bed, Or to glorious victorie!

II.

Now's the day, and now's the hour- See the front o' battle lour; See approach proud Edward's power- Edward! chains and slaverie!

III.

Wha will be a traitor-knave? Wha can fill a coward's grave? Wha sae base as be a slave? Traitor! coward! turn and flee!

IV.

Wha for Scotland's king and law Freedom's sword will strongly draw, Freeman stand, or freeman fa', Caledonian! on wi' me!

V.

By oppression's woes and pains! By our sons in servile chains! We will drain our dearest veins, But they shall be-shall be free!

VI.

Lay the proud usurpers low! Tyrants fall in every foe! Liberty's in every blow! Forward! let us do, or die!
[287]

CCVIII. BEHOLD THE HOUR.

Tune-"Oran-gaoil."
["The following song I have composed for the Highland air that you tell me in your last you have resolved to give a place to in your book. I have this moment finished the song, so you have it glowing from the mint." These are the words of Burns to Thomson: he might have added that the song was written on the meditated voyage of Clarinda to the West Indies, to join her husband.]
I.
Behold the hour, the boat arrive; Thou goest, thou darling of my heart! Sever'd from thee can I survive? But fate has will'd, and we must part. I'll often greet this surging swell, Yon distant isle will often hail: "E'en here I took the last farewell; There, latest mark'd her vanish'd sail."
II.
Along the solitary shore While flitting sea-fowl round me cry, Across the rolling, dashing roar, I'll westward turn my wistful eye: Happy, thou Indian grove, I'll say, Where now my Nancy's path may be! While thro' thy sweets she loves to stray, O tell me, does she muse on me?

CCIX. THOU HAST LEFT ME EVER.

Tune-"Fee him, father."
["I do not give these verses," says Burns to Thomson, "for any merit they have. I composed them at the time in which 'Patie Allan's mither died, about the back o' midnight,' and by the lee side of a bowl of punch, which had overset every mortal in company, except the hautbois and the muse." To the poet's intercourse with musicians we owe some fine songs.]
I.
Thou hast left me ever, Jamie! Thou hast left me ever; Thou hast left me ever, Jamie! Thou hast left me ever. Aften hast thou vow'd that death Only should us sever; Now thou's left thy lass for ay- I maun see thee never, Jamie, I'll see thee never!
II.
Thou hast me forsaken, Jamie! Thou hast me forsaken; Thou hast me forsaken, Jamie! Thou hast me forsaken. Thou canst love anither jo, While my heart is breaking: Soon my weary een I'll close, Never mair to waken, Jamie, Ne'er mair to waken!

CCX. AULD LANG SYNE.

["Is not the Scotch phrase," Burns writes to Mrs. Dunlop, "Auld lang syne, exceedingly expressive? There is an old song and tune which has often thrilled through my soul: I shall give you the verses on the other sheet. Light be the turf on the breast of the heaven-inspired poet who composed this glorious fragment." "The following song," says the poet, when he communicated it to George Thomson, "an old song of the olden times, and which has never been in print, nor even in manuscript, until I took it down from an old man's singing, is enough to recommend any air." These are strong words, but there can be no doubt that, save for a line or two, we owe the song to no other minstrel than "minstrel Burns."]

I.

Should auld acquaintance be forgot, And never brought to min'? Should auld acquaintance be forgot, And days o' lang syne? For auld lang syne, my dear, For auld lang syne, We'll tak a cup o' kindness yet, For auld lang syne!

II.

We twa hae run about the braes, And pu't the gowans fine; But we've wander'd mony a weary foot, Sin' auld lang syne.

III.

We twa hae paidl't i' the burn, Frae mornin' sun till dine: But seas between us braid hae roar'd, Sin' auld lang syne.

IV.

And here's a hand, my trusty fiere, And gie's a hand o' thine; And we'll take a right guid willie-waught, For auld lang syne.

[288]

V.

And surely ye'll be your pint-stowp, And surely I'll be mine; And we'll tak a cup o' kindness yet, For auld lang syne. For auld lang syne, my dear, For auld lang syne, We'll tak a cup o' kindness yet, For auld lang syne!

CCXI. FAIR JEANY.

Tune-"Saw ye my father?"

[In September, 1793, this song, as well as several others, was communicated to Thomson by Burns. "Of the poetry," he says, "I speak with confidence: but the music is a business where I hint my ideas with the utmost diffidence."]

I.

Where are the joys I have met in the morning, That danc'd to the lark's early song? Where is the peace that awaited my wand'ring, At evening the wild woods among?

II.

No more a-winding the course of yon river, And marking sweet flow'rets so fair: No more I trace the light footsteps of pleasure, But sorrow and sad sighing care.

III.

Is it that summer's forsaken our valleys, And grim, surly winter is near? No, no, the bees' humming round the gay roses, Proclaim it the pride of the year.

IV.

Fain would I hide, what I fear to discover, Yet long, long too well have I known, All that has caused this wreck in my bosom, Is Jeany, fair Jeany alone.

V.

Time cannot aid me, my griefs are immortal, Nor hope dare a comfort bestow: Come then, enamour'd and fond of my anguish, Enjoyment I'll seek in my woe.

CCXII.DELUDED SWAIN, THE PLEASURE.

[To the air of the "Collier's dochter," Burns bids Thomson add the following old Bacchanal: it is slightly altered from a rather stiff original.]

I.

Deluded swain, the pleasure The fickle fair can give thee, Is but a fairy treasure- Thy hopes will soon deceive thee.

II.

The billows on the ocean, The breezes idly roaming, The clouds uncertain motion- They are but types of woman.

III.

O! art thou not ashamed To doat upon a feature? If man thou wouldst be named, Despise the silly creature.

IV.

Go find an honest fellow; Good claret set before thee: Hold on till thou art mellow, And then to bed in glory.

CCXIII. NANCY.

[This song was inspired by the charms of Clarinda. In one of the poet's manuscripts the song commences thus:

Thine am I, my lovely Kate, Well thou mayest discover Every pulse along my veins Tell the ardent lover.

This change was tried out of compliment, it is believed, to Mrs. Thomson; but Nancy ran more smoothly on the even road of lyrical verse than Kate.]

I.

Thine am I, my faithful fair, Thine, my lovely Nancy; Ev'ry pulse along my

veins, Ev'ry roving fancy.
II.
To thy bosom lay my heart, There to throb and languish: [289]Tho' despair had wrung its core, That would heal its anguish.
III.
Take away those rosy lips, Rich with balmy treasure: Turn away thine eyes of love, Lest I die with pleasure.
IV.
What is life when wanting love? Night without a morning: Love's the cloudless summer sun, Nature gay adorning.

CCXIV. HUSBAND, HUSBAND.

Tune-"Jo Janet."
["My Jo Janet," in the collection of Allan Ramsay, was in the poet's eye when he composed this song, as surely as the matrimonial bickerings recorded by the old minstrels were in his mind. He desires Thomson briefly to tell him how he likes these verses: the response of the musician was, "Inimitable."]
I.
Husband, husband, cease your strife, Nor longer idly rave, sir; Tho' I am your wedded wife, Yet I am not your slave, sir. "One of two must still obey, Nancy, Nancy; Is it man or woman, say, My spouse, Nancy?"
II.
If 'tis still the lordly word, Service and obedience; I'll desert my sov'reign lord, And so, good bye, allegiance! "Sad will I be, so bereft, Nancy, Nancy; Yet I'll try to make a shift, My spouse, Nancy."
III.
My poor heart then break it must, My last hour I'm near it: When you lay me in the dust, Think, think, how you will bear it. "I will hope and trust in heaven, Nancy, Nancy; Strength to bear it will be given, My spouse, Nancy."
IV.
Well, sir, from the silent dead, Still I'll try to daunt you; Ever round your midnight bed Horrid sprites shall haunt you. "I'll wed another, like my dear Nancy, Nancy; Then all hell will fly for fear, My spouse, Nancy."

CCXV. WILT THOU BE MY DEARIE.

Air-"The Sutor's Dochter."
[Composed, it is said, in honour of Janet Miller, of Dalswinton, mother to the present Earl of Marr, and then, and long after, one of the loveliest women in the south of Scotland.]

I.

Wilt thou be my dearie? When sorrow wrings thy gentle heart, Wilt thou let me cheer thee? By the treasure of my soul, That's the love I bear thee! I swear and vow that only thou Shall ever be my dearie. Only thou, I swear and vow, Shall ever be my dearie.

II.

Lassie, say thou lo'es me; Or if thou wilt no be my ain, Say na thou'lt refuse me: If it winna, canna be, Thou, for thine may choose me, Let me, lassie, quickly die, Trusting that thou lo'es me. Lassie, let me quickly die, Trusting that thou lo'es me.

CCXVI. BUT LATELY SEEN.

Tune-"The winter of life."

[This song was written for Johnson's Museum, in 1794: the air is East Indian: it was brought from Hindostan by a particular friend of the poet. Thomson set the words to the air of Gil Morrice: they are elsewhere set to the tune of the Death of the Linnet.]

I.

But lately seen in gladsome green, The woods rejoiced the day; Thro' gentle showers and laughing flowers, In double pride were gay: But now our joys are fled On winter blasts awa! Yet maiden May, in rich array, Again shall bring them a'.

II.

But my white pow, nae kindly thowe Shall melt the snaws of age; My trunk of eild, but buss or bield, Sinks in Time's wintry rage. Oh! age has weary days, And nights o' sleepless pain! Thou golden time o' youthfu' prime, Why comes thou not again?

CCXVII. TO MARY.

Tune-"Could aught of song."

[These verses, inspired partly by Hamilton's very tender and elegant song,

"Ah! the poor shepherd's mournful fate,"

and some unrecorded "Mary" of the poet's heart, is in the latter volumes of Johnson. "It is inserted in Johnson's Museum," says Sir Harris Nicolas, "with the name of Burns attached." He might have added that it was sent by Burns, written with his own hand.]

I.

Could aught of song declare my pains, Could artful numbers move thee, The muse should tell, in labour'd strains, O Mary, how I love thee! They who but feign a wounded heart May teach the lyre to languish; But what avails the pride of art, When wastes the soul with anguish?

II.
Then let the sudden bursting sigh The heart-felt pang discover; And in the keen, yet tender eye, O read th' imploring lover. For well I know thy gentle mind Disdains art's gay disguising; Beyond what Fancy e'er refin'd, The voice of nature prizing.

CCXVIII. HERE'S TO THY HEALTH, MY BONNIE LASS.

Tune-"Laggan Burn."
["This song is in the Musical Museum, with Burns's name to it," says Sir Harris Nicolas. It is a song of the poet's early days, which he trimmed up, and sent to Johnson.]
I.
Here's to thy health, my bonnie lass, Gude night, and joy be wi' thee; I'll come na mair to thy bower-door, To tell thee that I lo'e thee. O dinna think, my pretty pink, But I can live without thee: I vow and swear I dinna care How lang ye look about ye.
II.
Thou'rt ay sae free informing me Thou hast na mind to marry; I'll be as free informing thee Nae time hae I to tarry. I ken thy friends try ilka means, Frae wedlock to delay thee; Depending on some higher chance- But fortune may betray thee.
III.
I ken they scorn my low estate, But that does never grieve me; But I'm as free as any he, Sma' siller will relieve me. I count my health my greatest wealth, Sae long as I'll enjoy it: I'll fear na scant, I'll bode nae want, As lang's I get employment.
IV.
But far off fowls hae feathers fair, And ay until ye try them: [291]Tho' they seem fair, still have a care, They may prove waur than I am. But at twal at night, when the moon shines bright, My dear, I'll come and see thee; For the man that lo'es his mistress weel, Nae travel makes him weary.

CCXIX. THE FAREWELL.

Tune-"It was a' for our rightfu' king."
["It seems very doubtful," says Sir Harris Nicolas, "how much, even if any part of this song was written by Burns: it occurs in the Musical Museum, but not with his name." Burns, it is believed, rather pruned and beautified an old Scottish lyric, than composed this strain entirely. Johnson received it from him in his own handwriting.]
I.
It was a' for our rightfu' king, We left fair Scotland's strand; It was a' for

our rightfu' king We e'er saw Irish land, My dear; We e'er saw Irish land.
II.
Now a' is done that men can do, And a' is done in vain; My love and native land farewell, For I maun cross the main, My dear; For I maun cross the main.
III.
He turn'd him right, and round about Upon the Irish shore; And gae his bridle-reins a shake, With adieu for evermore, My dear; With adieu for evermore.
IV.
The sodger from the wars returns, The sailor frae the main; But I hae parted frae my love, Never to meet again, My dear; Never to meet again
V.
When day is gane, and night is come, And a' folk bound to sleep; I think on him that's far awa', The lee-lang night, and weep, My dear; The lee-lang night, and weep.

CCXX. O STEER HER UP.

Tune-"O steer her up, and haud her gaun."
[Burns, in composing these verses, took the introductory lines of an older lyric, eked them out in his own way, and sent them to the Museum.]
I.
O steer her up and haud her gaun- Her mother's at the mill, jo; And gin she winna take a man, E'en let her take her will, jo: First shore her wi' a kindly kiss, And ca' another gill, jo, And gin she take the thing amiss, E'en let her flyte her fill, jo.
II.
O steer her up, and be na blate, An' gin she take it ill, jo, Then lea'e the lassie till her fate, And time nae longer spill, jo: Ne'er break your heart for ae rebute, But think upon it still, jo, That gin the lassie winna do't, Ye'll fin' anither will, jo.

CCXXI. O AY MY WIFE SHE DANG ME.

Tune-"My wife she dang me."
[Other verses to the same air, belonging to the olden times, are still remembered in Scotland: but they are only sung when the wine is in, and the sense of delicacy out. This song is in the Museum.]
I.
O ay my wife she dang me, And aft my wife did bang me, [292]If ye gie a woman a' her will, Gude faith, she'll soon o'er-gang ye. On peace and rest my mind was bent, And fool I was I married; But never honest man's

intent, As cursedly miscarried.
II.
Some sairie comfort still at last, When a' their days are done, man; My pains o' hell on earth are past, I'm sure o' bliss aboon, man. O ay my wife she dang me, And aft my wife did bang me, If ye gie a woman a' her will, Gude faith, she'll soon o'er-gang ye.

CCXXII. OH, WERT THOU IN THE CAULD BLAST.

Tune-"Lass o' Livistone."
[Tradition says this song was composed in honour of Jessie Lewars, the Jessie of the poet's death-bed strains. It is inserted in Thomson's collection: variations occur in several manuscripts, but they are neither important nor curious.]
I.
Oh, wert thou in the cauld blast, On yonder lea, on yonder lea, My plaidie to the angry airt, I'd shelter thee, I'd shelter thee: Or did misfortune's bitter storms Around thee blaw, around thee blaw, Thy bield should be my bosom, To share it a', to share it a'.
II.
Or were I in the wildest waste, Sae black and bare, sae black and bare, The desert were a paradise, If thou wert there, if thou wert there: Or were I monarch o' the globe, Wi' thee to reign, wi' thee to reign, The brightest jewel in my crown Wad be my queen, wad be my queen.

CCXXIII. HERE IS THE GLEN.

Tune-"Banks of Cree."
[Of the origin of this song the poet gives the following account. "I got an air, pretty enough, composed by Lady Elizabeth Heron, of Heron, which she calls 'The Banks of Cree.' Cree is a beautiful romantic stream: and as her ladyship is a particular friend of mine, I have written the following song to it."]
I.
Here is the glen, and here the bower, All underneath the birchen shade; The village-bell has told the hour- O what can stay my lovely maid?
II.
'Tis not Maria's whispering call; 'Tis but the balmy-breathing gale, Mix'd with some warbler's dying fall, The dewy star of eve to hail.
III.
It is Maria's voice I hear! So calls the woodlark in the grove, His little, faithful mate to cheer, At once 'tis music-and 'tis love.
IV.

And art thou come? and art thou true? O welcome, dear to love and me! And let us all our vows renew Along the flow'ry banks of Cree.

CCXXIV. ON THE SEAS AND FAR AWAY.

Tune-"O'er the hills," andc.
["The last evening," 29th of August, 1794, "as I was straying out," says Burns, "and thinking of 'O'er the hills and far away,' I spun the following stanzas for it. I was pleased with several lines at first, but I own now that it appears rather a flimsy business. I give you leave to abuse this song, but do it in the spirit of Christian meekness."]
I.
How can my poor heart be glad, When absent from my sailor lad? How can I the thought forego, He's on the seas to meet the foe? [293]Let me wander, let me rove, Still my heart is with my love: Nightly dreams, and thoughts by day, Are with him that's far away. On the seas and far away, On stormy seas and far away; Nightly dreams, and thoughts by day, Are ay with him that's far away.
II.
When in summer's noon I faint, As weary flocks around me pant, Haply in this scorching sun My sailor's thund'ring at his gun: Bullets, spare my only joy! Bullets, spare my darling boy! Fate, do with me what you may- Spare but him that's far away!
III.
At the starless midnight hour, When winter rules with boundless power: As the storms the forests tear, And thunders rend the howling air, Listening to the doubling roar, Surging on the rocky shore, All I can-I weep and pray, For his weal that's far away.
IV.
Peace, thy olive wand extend, And bid wild war his ravage end, Man with brother man to meet, And as a brother kindly greet: Then may heaven with prosp'rous gales, Fill my sailor's welcome sails, To my arms their charge convey- My dear lad that's far away. On the seas and far away On stormy seas and far away; Nightly dreams, and thoughts by day, Are ay with him that's far away.

CCXXV. CA' THE YOWES.

[Burns formed this song upon an old lyric, an amended version of which he had previously communicated to the Museum: he was fond of musing in the shadow of Lincluden towers, and on the banks of Cluden Water.]
I.
Ca' the yowes to the knowes, Ca' them whare the heather growes, Ca' them

whare the burnie rowes- My bonnie dearie! Hark the mavis' evening sang Sounding Cluden's woods amang! Then a faulding let us gang, My bonnie dearie.

II.

We'll gae down by Cluden side, Thro' the hazels spreading wide, O'er the waves that sweetly glide To the moon sae clearly.

III.

Yonder Cluden's silent towers, Where at moonshine midnight hours, O'er the dewy bending flowers, Fairies dance so cheery.

IV.

Ghaist nor bogle shalt thou fear; Thou'rt to love and heaven sae dear, Nocht of ill may come thee near, My bonnie dearie.

V.

Fair and lovely as thou art, Thou hast stown my very heart; I can die-but canna part- My bonnie dearie! Ca' the yowes to the knowes, Ca' them whare the heather growes; Ca' them where the burnie rowes- My bonnie dearie!

CCXXVI. SHE SAYS SHE LOVES ME BEST OF A'.

Tune-"Onagh's Waterfall."

[The lady of the flaxen ringlets has already been noticed: she is described in this song with the accuracy of a painter, and more than the usual elegance of one: it is needless to add her name, or to say how fine her form and how resistless her smiles.]

I.

Sae flaxen were her ringlets, Her eyebrows of a darker hue, Bewitchingly o'er-arching Twa laughin' een o' bonnie blue. Her smiling sae wyling, Wad make a wretch forget his woe; What pleasure, what treasure, Unto these rosy lips to grow: [294]Such was my Chloris' bonnie face, When first her bonnie face I saw; And ay my Chloris' dearest charm, She says she lo'es me best of a'.

II.

Like harmony her motion; Her pretty ankle is a spy, Betraying fair proportion, Wad mak a saint forget the sky. Sae warming, sae charming, Her faultless form and gracefu' air; Ilk feature-auld Nature Declar'd that she could do nae mair: Hers are the willing chains o' love, By conquering beauty's sovereign law; And ay my Chloris' dearest charm, She says she lo'es me best of a'.

III.

Let others love the city, And gaudy show at sunny noon; Gie me the lonely valley, The dewy eve, and rising moon; Fair beaming, and streaming, Her silver light the boughs amang; While falling, recalling, The amorous thrush concludes his sang; There, dearest Chloris, wilt thou rove By wimpling burn and leafy shaw, And hear my vows o' truth and love, And say thou lo'es me best of a'?

CCXXVII. SAW YE MY PHELY.

[QUASI DICAT PHILLIS.]
Tune-"When she came ben she bobbit."
[The despairing swain in this song was Stephen Clarke, musician, and the young lady whom he persuaded Burns to accuse of inconstancy and coldness was Phillis M'Murdo.]
I.
O saw ye my dear, my Phely? O saw ye my dear, my Phely? She's down i' the grove, she's wi' a new love! She winna come hame to her Willy.
II.
What says she, my dearest, my Phely? What says she, my dearest, my Phely? She lets thee to wit that she has thee forgot, And for ever disowns thee, her Willy.
III.
O had I ne'er seen thee, my Phely! O had I ne'er seen thee, my Phely! As light as the air, and fause as thou's fair, Thou's broken the heart o' thy Willy.

CCXXVIII. HOW LANG AND DREARY IS THE NIGHT.

Tune-"Cauld Kail in Aberdeen."
[On comparing this lyric, corrected for Thomson, with that in the Museum, it will be seen that the former has more of elegance and order: the latter quite as much nature and truth: but there is less of the new than of the old in both.]
I.
How lang and dreary is the night, When I am frae my dearie; I restless lie frae e'en to morn, Though I were ne'er sae weary. For oh! her lanely nights are lang; And oh! her dreams are eerie; And oh, her widow'd heart is sair, That's absent frae her dearie.
II.
When I think on the lightsome days I spent wi' thee my dearie; And now what seas between us roar- How can I be but eerie?
III.
How slow ye move, ye heavy hours; The joyless day how dreary! It was na sae ye glinted by, When I was wi' my dearie. For oh! her lanely nights are lang; And oh, her dreams are eerie; And oh, her widow'd heart is sair, That's absent frae her dearie.

CCXXIX. LET NOT WOMAN E'ER COMPLAIN.

Tune-"Duncan Gray."

["These English songs," thus complains the poet, in the letter which conveyed this lyric to Thomson, "gravel me to death: I have not that command of the lan[295]guage that I have of my native tongue. I have been at 'Duncan Gray,' to dress it in English, but all I can do is deplorably stupid. For instance:"]

I.

Let not woman e'er complain Of inconstancy in love; Let not woman e'er complain Fickle man is apt to rove: Look abroad through nature's range, Nature's mighty law is change; Ladies, would it not be strange, Man should then a monster prove?

II.

Mark the winds, and mark the skies; Ocean's ebb, and ocean's flow: Sun find moon but set to rise, Round and round the seasons go: Why then ask of silly man To oppose great nature's plan? We'll be constant while we can-You can be no more, you know.

CCXXX. THE LOVER'S MORNING SALUTE TO HIS MISTRESS.

Tune-"Deil tak the Wars."

[Burns has, in one of his letters, partly intimated that this morning salutation to Chloris was occasioned by sitting till the dawn at the punch-bowl, and walking past her window on his way home.]

I.

Sleep'st thou, or wak'st thou, fairest creature? Rosy Morn now lifts his eye, Numbering ilka bud which nature Waters wi' the tears o' joy: Now through the leafy woods, And by the reeking floods, Wild nature's tenants freely, gladly stray; The lintwhite in his bower Chants o'er the breathing flower; The lav'rock to the sky Ascends wi' sangs o' joy, While the sun and thou arise to bless the day.

II.

Phœbus gilding the brow o' morning, Banishes ilk darksome shade, Nature gladdening and adorning; Such to me my lovely maid. When absent frae my fair, The murky shades o' care With starless gloom o'ercast my sullen sky; But when, in beauty's light, She meets my ravish'd sight, When thro' my very heart Her beaming glories dart- 'Tis then I wake to life, to light, and joy.

CCXXXI. CHLORIS.

Air-"My lodging is on the cold ground."

[The origin of this song is thus told by Burns to Thomson. "On my visit the other day to my fair Chloris, that is the poetic name of the lovely goddess of my inspiration, she suggested an idea which I, on my return from the visit, wrought into the following song." The poetic elevation of Chloris is great: she lived, when her charms faded, in want, and died all but destitute.]

I.

My Chloris, mark how green the groves, The primrose banks how fair: The balmy gales awake the flowers, And wave thy flaxen hair.

II.

The lav'rock shuns the palace gay, And o'er the cottage sings; For nature smiles as sweet, I ween, To shepherds as to kings

III.

Let minstrels sweep the skilfu' string In lordly lighted ha': The shepherd stops his simple reed, Blythe, in the birken shaw.

IV.

The princely revel may survey Our rustic dance wi' scorn; But are their hearts as light as ours, Beneath the milk-white thorn?

V.

The shepherd, in the flow'ry glen, In shepherd's phrase will woo: The courtier tells a finer tale- But is his heart as true? [296]

VI.

These wild-wood flowers I've pu'd, to deck That spotless breast o' thine: The courtier's gems may witness love- But 'tis na love like mine.

CCXXXII. CHLOE.

Air-"Daintie Davie."

[Burns, despairing to fit some of the airs with such verses of original manufacture as Thomson required, for the English part of his collection, took the liberty of bestowing a Southron dress on some genuine Caledonian lyrics. The origin of this song may be found in Ramsay's miscellany: the bombast is abated, and the whole much improved.]

I.

It was the charming month of May, When all the flow'rs were fresh and gay, One morning, by the break of day, The youthful charming Chloe From peaceful slumber she arose, Girt on her mantle and her hose, And o'er the flowery mead she goes, The youthful charming Chloe. Lovely was she by the dawn, Youthful Chloe, charming Chloe, Tripping o'er the pearly lawn, The youthful charming Chloe.

II.

The feather'd people you might see, Perch'd all around, on every tree, In notes of sweetest melody They hail the charming Chloe; Till painting gay the eastern skies, The glorious sun began to rise, Out-rivall'd by the radiant eyes Of youthful, charming Chloe. Lovely was she by the dawn, Youthful Chloe, charming Chloe, Tripping o'er the pearly lawn, The youthful, charming Chloe.

CCXXXIII. LASSIE WI' THE LINT-WHITE LOCKS.

Tune-"Rothemurche's Rant."
["Conjugal love," says the poet, "is a passion which I deeply feel and highly venerate: but somehow it does not make such a figure in poesie as that other species of the passion, where love is liberty and nature law. Musically speaking, the first is an instrument of which the gamut is scanty and confined, but the tones inexpressibly sweet, while the last has powers equal to all the intellectual modulations of the human soul." It must be owned that the bard could render very pretty reasons for his rapture about Jean Lorimer.]
I.
Lassie wi' the lint-white locks, Bonnie lassie, artless lassie, Wilt thou wi' me tent the flocks? Wilt thou be my dearie, O? Now nature cleeds the flowery lea, And a' is young and sweet like thee; O wilt thou share its joy wi' me, And say thoul't be my dearie, O?
II.
And when the welcome simmer shower Has cheer'd ilk drooping little flower, We'll to the breathing woodbine bower At sultry noon, my dearie, O.
III.
When Cynthia lights wi' silver ray, The weary shearer's hameward way; Thro' yellow waving fields we'll stray, And talk o' love my dearie, O.
IV.
And when the howling wintry blast Disturbs my lassie's midnight rest; Enclasped to my faithfu' breast, I'll comfort thee, my dearie, O. Lassie wi' the lint-white locks, Bonnie lassie, artless lassie, Wilt thou wi' me tent the flocks? Wilt thou be my dearie, O?

CCXXXIV. FAREWELL, THOU STREAM.

Air-"Nancy's to the greenwood gane."
[This song was written in November, 1794: Thomson pronounced it excellent.]
I.
Farewell, thou stream that winding flows Around Eliza's dwelling! O mem'ry! spare the cruel throes Within my bosom swelling: [297]Condemn'd to drag a hopeless chain, And yet in secret languish, To feel a fire in ev'ry vein, Nor dare disclose my anguish.

II.
Love's veriest wretch, unseen, unknown, I fain my griefs would cover; The bursting sigh, th' unweeting groan, Betray the hapless lover. I know thou doom'st me to despair, Nor wilt, nor canst relieve me; But oh, Eliza, hear one prayer- For pity's sake forgive me!
III.
The music of thy voice I heard, Nor wist while it enslav'd me; I saw thine eyes, yet nothing fear'd, 'Till fears no more had sav'd me: The unwary sailor thus aghast, The wheeling torrent viewing; 'Mid circling horrors sinks at last In overwhelming ruin.

CCXXXV. O PHILLY, HAPPY BE THAT DAY.

Tune-"The Sow's Tail."
["This morning" (19th November, 1794), "though a keen blowing frost," Burns writes to Thomson, "in my walk before breakfast I finished my duet: whether I have uniformly succeeded, I will not say: but here it is for you, though it is not an hour old."]
HE.
O Philly, happy be that day, When roving through the gather'd hay, My youthfu' heart was stown away, And by thy charms, my Philly.
SHE.
O Willy, ay I bless the grove Where first I own'd my maiden love, Whilst thou didst pledge the powers above, To be my ain dear Willy.
HE.
As songsters of the early year Are ilka day mair sweet to hear, So ilka day to me mair dear And charming is my Philly.
SHE.
As on the brier the budding rose Still richer breathes and fairer blows, So in my tender bosom grows The love I bear my Willy.
HE.
The milder sun and bluer sky That crown my harvest cares wi' joy, Were ne'er sae welcome to my eye As is a sight o' Philly.
SHE.
The little swallow's wanton wing, Tho' wafting o'er the flowery spring, Did ne'er to me sic tidings bring, As meeting o' my Willy.
HE.
The bee that thro' the sunny hour Sips nectar in the opening flower, Compar'd wi' my delight is poor, Upon the lips o' Philly.
SHE.
The woodbine in the dewy weet When evening shades in silence meet, Is nocht sae fragrant or sae sweet As is a kiss o' Willy.
HE.

Let Fortune's wheel at random rin, And fools may tyne, and knaves may win My thoughts are a' bound up in ane, And that's my ain dear Philly.
SHE.
What's a' joys that gowd can gie? I care nae wealth a single flie; The lad I love's the lad for me, And that's my ain dear Willy.

CCXXXVI. CONTENTED WI' LITTLE.

Tune-"Lumps o' Pudding."
[Burns was an admirer of many songs which the more critical and fastidious regarded as rude and homely. "Todlin Hame" he called an unequalled composition for wit and humour, and "Andro wi' his cutty Gun," the[298] work of a master. In the same letter, where he records these sentiments, he writes his own inimitable song, "Contented wi' Little."]
I.
Contented wi' little, and cantie wi' mair, Whene'er I forgather wi' sorrow end care, I gie them a skelp, as they're creepin alang, Wi' a cog o' guid swats, and an auld Scottish sang.
II.
I whyles claw the elbow o' troublesome thought; But man is a sodger, and life is a faught: My mirth and guid humour are coin in my pouch, And my freedom's my lairdship nae monarch dare touch.
III.
A towmond o' trouble, should that be my fa', A night o' guid fellowship sowthers it a': When at the blithe end o' our journey at last, Wha the deil ever thinks o' the road he has past?
IV.
Blind chance, let her snapper and stoyte on her way; Be't to me, be't frae me, e'en let the jade gae: Come ease, or come travail; come pleasure or pain; My warst word is-"Welcome, and welcome again!"

CCXXXVII. CANST THOU LEAVE ME THUS.

Tune-"Roy's Wife."
[When Burns transcribed the following song for Thomson, on the 20th of November, 1794, he added, "Well! I think this, to be done in two or three turns across my room, and with two or three pinches of Irish blackguard, is not so far amiss. You see I am resolved to have my quantum of applause from somebody." The poet in this song complains of the coldness of Mrs. Riddel: the lady replied in a strain equally tender and forgiving.]
I.
Canst thou leave me thus, my Katy? Canst thou leave me thus, my Katy? Well thou know'st my aching heart- And canst thou leave me thus for pity?

In this thy plighted, fond regard, Thus cruelly to part, my Katy? Is this thy faithful swain's reward- An aching, broken heart, my Katy!
II.
Farewell! and ne'er such sorrows tear That fickle heart of thine, my Katy! Thou may'st find those will love thee dear- But not a love like mine, my Katy! Canst thou leave me thus, my Katy? Canst thou leave me thus, my Katy? Well thou know'st my aching heart- And canst thou leave me thus for pity?

CCXXXVIII. MY NANNIE'S AWA.

Tune-"There'll never be peace."
[Clarinda, tradition avers, was the inspirer of this song, which the poet composed in December, 1794, for the work of Thomson. His thoughts were often in Edinburgh: on festive occasions, when, as Campbell beautifully says, "The wine-cup shines in light," he seldom forgot to toast Mrs. Mac.]
I.
Now in her green mantle blythe nature arrays, And listens the lambkins that bleat o'er the braes, While birds warble welcome in ilka green shaw; But to me it's delightless-my Nannie's awa!
II.
The snaw-drap and primrose our woodlands adorn, And violets bathe in the weet o' the morn; They pain my sad bosom, sae sweetly they blaw, They mind me o' Nannie-and Nanny's awa!
III.
Thou lav'rock that springs frae the dews of the lawn, The shepherd to warn o' the gray-breaking dawn, And thou mellow mavis that hails the night fa', Give over for pity-my Nannie's awa!
IV.
Come autumn sae pensive, in yellow and gray, And soothe me with tidings o' nature's decay: The dark dreary winter, and wild driving snaw, Alane can delight me-now Nannie's awa!

CCXXXIX. O WHA IS SHE THAT LOVES ME.

Tune-"Morag."
["This song," says Sir Harris Nicolas, "is said, in Thomson's collection, to have been written for that work by Burns: but it is not included in Mr. Cunningham's edition." If sir Harris would be so good as to look at page 245; vol. V., of Cunningham's edition of Burns, he will find the song; and if he will look at page 28, and page 193 of vol. III., of his own edition, he will find that he has not committed the error of which he accuses his fellow-

editor, for he has inserted the same song twice. The same may be said of the song to Chloris, which Sir Harris has printed at page 312, vol. II,. and at page 189, vol. III., and of "Ae day a braw wooer came down the lang glen," which appears both at page 224 of vol. II., and at page 183 of vol, III.]

I.

O wha is she that lo'es me, And has my heart a-keeping? O sweet is she that lo'es me, As dews of simmer weeping, In tears the rosebuds steeping! O that's the lassie of my heart, My lassie ever dearer; O that's the queen of womankind, And ne'er a ane to peer her.

II.

If thou shalt meet a lassie In grace and beauty charming, That e'en thy chosen lassie, Erewhile thy breast sae warming Had ne'er sic powers alarming.

III.

If thou hadst heard her talking, And thy attentions plighted, That ilka body talking, But her by thee is slighted, And thou art all delighted.

IV.

If thou hast met this fair one; When frae her thou hast parted, If every other fair one, But her, thou hast deserted, And thou art broken-hearted; O that's the lassie o' my heart, My lassie ever dearer; O that's the queen o' womankind, And ne'er a ane to peer her.

CCXL. CALEDONIA.

Tune-"Caledonian Hunt's Delight."

[There is both knowledge of history and elegance of allegory in this singular lyric: it was first printed by Currie.]

I.

There was once a day-but old Time then was young- That brave Caledonia, the chief of her line, From some of your northern deities sprung, (Who knows not that brave Caledonia's divine?) From Tweed to the Orcades was her domain, To hunt, or to pasture, or do what she would: Her heav'nly relations there fixed her reign, And pledg'd her their godheads to warrant it good.

II.

A lambkin in peace, but a lion in war, The pride of her kindred the heroine grew; Her grandsire, old Odin, triumphantly swore "Whoe'er shall provoke thee, th' encounter shall rue!" With tillage or pasture at times she would sport, To feed her fair flocks by her green rustling corn; But chiefly the woods were her fav'rite resort, Her darling amusement, the hounds and the horn.

III.

Long quiet she reign'd; till thitherward steers A flight of bold eagles from

Adria's strand: Repeated, successive, for many long years, They darken'd the air, and they plunder'd the land: Their pounces were murder, and terror their cry, They'd conquer'd and ruin'd a world beside; She took to her hills, and her arrows let fly- The daring invaders they fled or they died.
IV.
The fell harpy-raven took wing from the north, The scourge of the seas, and the dread of the shore; The wild Scandinavian boar issu'd forth To wanton in carnage, and wallow in gore; [300]O'er countries and kingdoms their fury prevail'd, No arts could appease them, no arms could repel; But brave Caledonia in vain they assail'd, As Largs well can witness, and Loncartie tell.
V.
The Cameleon-savage disturbed her repose, With tumult, disquiet, rebellion, and strife; Provok'd beyond bearing, at last she arose, And robb'd him at once of his hope and his life: The Anglian lion, the terror of France, Oft prowling, ensanguin'd the Tweed's silver flood: But, taught by the bright Caledonian lance, He learned to fear in his own native wood.
VI.
Thus bold, independent, unconquer'd, and free, Her bright course of glory for ever shall run: For brave Caledonia immortal must be; I'll prove it from Euclid as clear as the sun: Rectangle-triangle, the figure we'll choose, The upright is Chance, and old Time is the base; But brave Caledonia's the hypothenuse; Then ergo, she'll match them, and match them always.

CCXLI. O LAY THY LOOF IN MINE, LASS.

Tune-"Cordwainer's March."
[The air to which these verses were written, is commonly played at the Saturnalia of the shoemakers on King Crispin's day. Burns sent it to the Museum.]
I.
O lay thy loof in mine, lass, In mine, lass, in mine, lass; And swear on thy white hand, lass, That thou wilt be my ain. A slave to love's unbounded sway, He aft has wrought me meikle wae; But now he is my deadly fae, Unless thou be my ain.
II.
There's monie a lass has broke my rest, That for a blink I hae lo'ed best; But thou art queen within my breast, For ever to remain. O lay thy loof in mine, lass, In mine, lass, in mine, lass; And swear on thy white hand, lass, That thou wilt be my ain.

CCXLII. THE FETE CHAMPETRE.

Tune-"Killiecrankie."

[Written to introduce the name of Cunninghame, of Enterkin, to the public. Tents were erected on the banks of Ayr, decorated with shrubs, and strewn with flowers, most of the names of note in the district were invited, and a splendid entertainment took place; but no dissolution of parliament followed as was expected, and the Lord of Enterkin, who was desirous of a seat among the "Commons," poured out his wine in vain.]

I.

O wha will to Saint Stephen's house, To do our errands there, man? O wha will to Saint Stephen's house, O' th' merry lads of Ayr, man? Or will we send a man-o'-law? Or will we send a sodger? Or him wha led o'er Scotland a' The meikle Ursa-Major?

II.

Come, will ye court a noble lord, Or buy a score o' lairds, man? For worth and honour pawn their word, Their vote shall be Glencaird's, man? Ane gies them coin, ane gies them wine, Anither gies them clatter; Anbank, wha guess'd the ladies' taste, He gies a Fête Champêtre.

III.

When Love and Beauty heard the news, The gay green-woods amang, man; Where gathering flowers and busking bowers, They heard the blackbird's sang, man; A vow, they seal'd it with a kiss, Sir Politicks to fetter, As theirs alone, the patent-bliss To hold a Fête Champêtre.

IV.

Then mounted Mirth, on gleesome wing, O'er hill and dale she flew, man; Ilk wimpling burn, ilk crystal spring, Ilk glen and shaw she knew, man: [301]She summon'd every social sprite That sports by wood or water, On th' bonny banks of Ayr to meet, And keep this Fête Champêtre.

V.

Cauld Boreas, wi' his boisterous crew, Were bound to stakes like kye, man; And Cynthia's car, o' silver fu', Clamb up the starry sky, man: Reflected beams dwell in the streams, Or down the current shatter; The western breeze steals thro' the trees, To view this Fête Champêtre.

VI.

How many a robe sae gaily floats! What sparkling jewels glance, man! To Harmony's enchanting notes, As moves the mazy dance, man. The echoing wood, the winding flood, Like Paradise did glitter, When angels met, at Adam's yett, To hold their Fête Champêtre.

VII.

When Politics came there, to mix And make his ether-stane, man! He circled round the magic ground, But entrance found he nane, man: He blush'd for shame, he quat his name, Forswore it, every letter, Wi' humble prayer to join and share This festive Fête Champêtre.

CCXLIII. HERE'S A HEALTH.

Tune-"Here's a health to them that's awa."
[The Charlie of this song was Charles Fox; Tammie was Lord Erskine; and M'Leod, the maiden name of the Countess of Loudon, was then, as now, a name of influence both in the Highlands and Lowlands. The buff and blue of the Whigs had triumphed over the white rose of Jacobitism in the heart of Burns, when he wrote these verses.]
I.
Here's a health to them that's awa, Here's a health to them that's awa; And wha winna wish guid luck to our cause, May never guid luck be their fa'! It's guid to be merry and wise, It's guid to be honest and true, It's good to support Caldonia's cause, And bide by the buff and the blue.
II.
Here's a health to them that's awa, Here's a health to them that's awa, Here's a health to Charlie the chief of the clan, Altho' that his band be sma'. May liberty meet wi' success! May prudence protect her frae evil! May tyrants and tyranny tine in the mist, And wander their way to the devil!
III.
Here's a health to them that's awa, Here's a health to them that's awa; Here's a health to Tammie, the Norland laddie, That lives at the lug o' the law! Here's freedom to him that wad read, Here's freedom to him that wad write! There's nane ever fear'd that the truth should be heard, But they wham the truth wad indite.
IV.
Here's a health to them that's awa, Here's a health to them that's awa, Here's Chieftain M'Leod, a chieftain worth gowd, Tho' bred amang mountains o' snaw! Here's a health to them that's awa, Here's a health to them that's awa; And wha winna wish guid luck to our cause, May never guid luck be their fa'!

CCXLIV. IS THERE, FOR HONEST POVERTY.

Tune-"For a' that, and a' that."
[In this noble lyric Burns has vindicated the natural right of his species. He modestly says to Thomson, "I do not give you this song for your book, but merely by way of vive la bagatelle; for the piece is really not poetry, but will be allowed to be two or three pretty good prose thoughts inverted into rhyme." Thomson took the song, but hazarded no praise.]
I.
Is there, for honest poverty, That hangs his head, and a' that? [302]The coward-slave, we pass him by, We dare be poor for a' that! For a' that, and

a' that, Our toils obscure, and a' that; The rank is but the guinea's stamp, The man's the gowd for a' that!

II.

What tho' on hamely fare we dine, Wear hoddin gray, and a' that; Gie fools their silks, and knaves their wine, A man's a man, for a' that! For a' that, and a' that, Their tinsel show, and a' that; The honest man, though e'er sae poor, Is king o' men for a' that!

III.

Ye see yon birkie, ca'd-a lord, Wha struts, and stares, and a' that; Though hundreds worship at his word, He's but a coof for a' that: For a' that, and a' that, His riband, star, and a' that, The man of independent mind, He looks and laughs at a' that.

IV.

A king can make a belted knight, A marquis, duke, and a' that, But an honest man's aboon his might, Guid faith, he maunna fa' that! For a' that, and a' that, Their dignities, and a' that, The pith o' sense, and pride o' worth, Are higher ranks than a' that.

V.

Then let us pray that come it may- As come it will for a' that- That sense and worth, o'er a' the earth, May bear the gree, and a' that; For a' that, and a' that, It's comin' yet for a' that, That man to man, the warld o'er, Shall brothers be for a' that!

CCXLV. CRAIGIE-BURN WOOD.

[Craigie-burn Wood was written for George Thomson: the heroine was Jean Lorimer. How often the blooming looks and elegant forms of very indifferent characters lend a lasting lustre to painting and poetry.]

I.

Sweet fa's the eve on Craigie-burn, And blithe awakes the morrow; But a' the pride o' spring's return Can yield me nocht but sorrow.

II.

I see the flowers and spreading trees I hear the wild birds singing; But what a weary wight can please, And care his bosom wringing?

III.

Fain, fain would I my griefs impart, Yet dare na for your anger; But secret love will break my heart, If I conceal it langer.

IV.

If thou refuse to pity me, If thou shall love anither, When yon green leaves fade frae the tree, Around my grave they'll wither.

CCXLVI. O LASSIE, ART THOU SLEEPING YET.

Tune-"Let me in this ae night."

[The thoughts of Burns, it is said, wandered to the fair Mrs. Riddel, of Woodleigh Park, while he composed this song for Thomson. The idea is taken from an old lyric, of more spirit than decorum.]

I.

O Lassie, art thou sleeping yet, Or art thou waking, I would wit? For love has bound me hand and foot, And I would fain be in, jo. O let me in this ae night, This ae, ae, ae night; For pity's sake this ae night, O rise and let me in, jo!

II.

Thou hear'st the winter wind and weet! Nae star blinks thro' the driving sleet: Tak pity on my weary feet, And shield me frae the rain, jo. [303]

III.

The bitter blast that round me blaws, Unheeded howls, unheeded fa's; The cauldness o' thy heart's the cause Of a' my grief and pain, jo. O let me in this ae night, This ae, ae, ae night; For pity's sake this ae night, O rise and let me in, jo!

CCXLVII. O TELL NA ME O' WIND AND RAIN.

[The poet's thoughts, as rendered in the lady's answer, are, at all events, not borrowed from the sentiments expressed by Mrs. Riddel, alluded to in song CCXXXVII.; there she is tender and forgiving: here she in stern and cold.]

I.

O tell na me o' wind and rain, Upbraid na me wi' cauld disdain! Gae back the gate ye cam again, I winna let you in, jo. I tell you now this ae night, This ae, ae, ae night, And ance for a' this ae night, I winna let you in, jo!

II.

The snellest blast, at mirkest hours, That round the pathless wand'rer pours, Is nocht to what poor she endures, That's trusted faithless man, jo.

III.

The sweetest flower that deck'd the mead, Now trodden like the vilest weed: Let simple maid the lesson read, The weird may be her ain, jo.

IV.

The bird that charm'd his summer-day, Is now the cruel fowler's prey; Let witless, trusting woman say How aft her fate's the same, jo. I tell you now this ae night, This ae, ae, ae night; And ance for a' this ae night, I winna let you in jo!

CCXLVIII. THE DUMFRIES VOLUNTEERS.

Tune-"Push about the jorum."

[This national song was composed in April, 1795. The poet had been at a public meeting, where he was less joyous than usual: as something had been expected from him, he made these verses, when he went home, and sent them, with his compliments, to Mr. Jackson, editor of the Dumfries Journal. The original, through the kindness of my friend, James Milligan, Esq., is now before me.]

I.

Does haughty Gaul invasion threat, Then let the loons beware, Sir, There's wooden walls upon our seas, And volunteers on shore, Sir. The Nith shall run to Corsincon, And Criffel sink in Solway, Ere we permit a foreign foe On British ground to rally!

II.

O let us not, like snarling tykes, In wrangling be divided; Till slap come in an unco loon And wi' a rung decide it. Be Britain still to Britain true, Amang oursels united; For never but by British hands Maun British wrangs be righted!

III.

The kettle o' the kirk and state, Perhaps a clout may fail in't; But deil a foreign tinkler loon Shall ever ca' a nail in't. Our fathers' bluid the kettle bought, And wha wad dare to spoil it; By heaven! the sacrilegious dog Shall fuel be to boil it.

IV.

The wretch that wad a tyrant own, And the wretch his true-born brother, Who would set the mob aboon the throne, May they be damned together! Who will not sing, "God save the King," Shall hang as high's the steeple; But while we sing, "God save the King," We'll ne'er forget the people.

CCXLIX. ADDRESS TO THE WOOD-LARK.

Tune-"Where'll bonnie Ann lie."

[The old song to the same air is yet remembered: but the humour is richer than the delicacy; the same may be said of many of the fine hearty lyrics of the elder days of Caledonia. These verses were composed in May, 1795, for Thomson.]

I.

O stay, sweet warbling woodlark, stay! Nor quit for me the trembling spray; A hapless lover courts thy lay, Thy soothing fond complaining.

II.

Again, again that tender part, That I may catch thy melting art; For surely that would touch her heart, Wha kills me wi' disdaining.

III.

Say, was thy little mate unkind, And heard thee as the careless wind? Oh, nocht but love and sorrow join'd, Sic notes o' woe could wauken.

IV.

Thou tells o' never-ending care; O' speechless grief and dark despair: For pity's sake, sweet bird, nae mair! Or my poor heart is broken!

CCL. ON CHLORIS BEING ILL.

Tune-"Ay wakin', O."
[An old and once popular lyric suggested this brief and happy song for Thomson: some of the verses deserve to be held in remembrance.
Ay waking, oh, Waking ay and weary; Sleep I canna get For thinking o' my dearie.]
I.
Long, long the night, Heavy comes the morrow, While my soul's delight Is on her bed of sorrow.
Can I cease to care? Can I cease to languish? While my darling fair Is on the couch of anguish?
II.
Every hope is fled, Every fear is terror; Slumber even I dread, Every dream is horror.
III.
Hear me, Pow'rs divine! Oh, in pity hear me! Take aught else of mine, But my Chloris spare me! Long, long the night, Heavy comes the morrow, While my soul's delight Is on her bed of sorrow.

CCLI. CALEDONIA.

Tune-"Humours of Glen."
[Love of country often mingles in the lyric strains of Burns with his personal attachments, and in few more beautifully than in the following, written for Thomson the heroine was Mrs. Burns.]
I.
Their groves o' sweet myrtle let foreign lands reckon, Where bright-beaming summers exalt the perfume; Far dearer to me yon lone glen o' green brockan, Wi' the burn stealing under the lang yellow broom: Far dearer to me are yon humble broom bowers, Where the blue-bell and gowan lurk lowly unseen; For there, lightly tripping amang the wild flowers, A listening the linnet, aft wanders my Jean.
II.
Tho' rich is the breeze in their gay sunny valleys, And cauld Caledonia's blast on the wave; Their sweet-scented woodlands that skirt the proud palace, What are they?-The haunt of the tyrant and slave! [305]The slave's spicy forests, and gold-bubbling fountains, The brave Caledonian views wi' disdain; He wanders as free as the winds of his mountains, Save love's willing fetters, the chains o' his Jean.

CCLII. 'TWAS NA HER BONNIE BLUE EEN.

Tune-"Laddie, lie near me."

[Though the lady who inspired these verses is called Mary by the poet, such, says tradition, was not her name: yet tradition, even in this, wavers, when it avers one while that Mrs. Riddel, and at another time that Jean Lorimer was the heroine.]

I.

'Twas na her bonnie blue een was my ruin; Fair tho' she be, that was ne'er my undoing: 'Twas the dear smile when naebody did mind us, 'Twas the bewitching, sweet stown glance o' kindness.

II.

Sair do I fear that to hope is denied me, Sair do I fear that despair maun abide me! But tho' fell fortune should fate us to sever, Queen shall she be in my bosom for ever.

III.

Mary, I'm thine wi' a passion sincerest, And thou hast plighted me love o' the dearest! And thou'rt the angel that never can alter- Sooner the sun in his motion would falter.

CCLIII. HOW CRUEL ARE THE PARENTS.

Tune-"John Anderson, my jo."

["I am at this moment," says Burns to Thomson, when he sent him this song, "holding high converse with the Muses, and have not a word to throw away on a prosaic dog, such as you are." Yet there is less than the poet's usual inspiration in this lyric, for it is altered from an English one.]

I.

How cruel are the parents Who riches only prize, And, to the wealthy booby, Poor woman sacrifice! Meanwhile the hapless daughter Has but a choice of strife; To shun a tyrant father's hate, Become a wretched wife.

II.

The ravening hawk pursuing, The trembling dove thus flies, To shun impelling ruin Awhile her pinions tries: Till of escape despairing, No shelter or retreat, She trusts the ruthless falconer, And drops beneath his feet!

CCLIV. MARK YONDER POMP.

Tune-"Deil tak the wars."

[Burns tells Thomson, in the letter enclosing this song, that he is in a high fit of poetizing, provided he is not cured by the strait-waistcoat of criticism. "You see," said he, "how I answer your orders; your tailor could not be more punctual." This strain in honour of Chloris is original in conception, but wants the fine lyrical flow of some of his other compositions.]

I.

Mark yonder pomp of costly fashion Round the wealthy, titled bride: But when compar'd with real passion, Poor is all that princely pride. What are the showy treasures? What are the noisy pleasures? The gay gaudy glare of vanity and art: The polish'd jewel's blaze May draw the wond'ring gaze, And courtly grandeur bright The fancy may delight, But never, never can come near the heart.

II.

But did you see my dearest Chloris In simplicity's array; Lovely as yonder sweet opening flower is, Shrinking from the gaze of day; O then the heart alarming, And all resistless charming, [306]In Love's delightful fetters she chains the willing soul! Ambition would disown The world's imperial crown, Even

Avarice would deny His worship'd deity, And feel thro' every vein Love's raptures roll.

CCLV. THIS IS NO MY AIN LASSIE.

Tune-"This is no my ain house."

[Though composed to the order of Thomson, and therefore less likely to be the offspring of unsolicited inspiration, this is one of the happiest modern songs. When the poet wrote it, he seems to have been beside the "fair dame at whose shrine," he said, "I, the priest of the Nine, offer up the incense of Parnassus."]

I.

O this is no my ain lassie, Fair tho' the lassie be; O weel ken I my ain lassie, Kind love is in her e'e. I see a form, I see a face, Ye weel may wi' the fairest place: It wants, to me, the witching grace, The kind love that's in her e'e.

II.

She's bonnie, blooming, straight, and tall, And lang has had my heart in thrall; And ay it charms my very saul, The kind love that's in her e'e.

III.

A thief sae pawkie is my Jean, To steal a blink, by a' unseen; But gleg as light are lovers' een, When kind love is in the e'e.

IV.

It may escape the courtly sparks, It may escape the learned clerks; But weel the watching lover marks The kind love that's in her e'e. O this is no my ain lassie, Fair tho' the lassie be; O weel ken I my ain lassie, Kind love is in her e'e.

CCLVI. NOW SPRING HAS CLAD THE GROVE IN GREEN.

TO MR. CUNNINGHAM.

[Composed in reference to a love disappointment of the poet's friend, Alexander Cunningham, which also occasioned the song beginning,
"Had I a cave on some wild distant shore."]

I.

Now spring has clad the grove in green, And strew'd the lea wi' flowers: The furrow'd waving corn is seen Rejoice in fostering showers; While ilka thing in nature join Their sorrows to forego, O why thus all alone are mine The weary steps of woe?

II.

The trout within yon wimpling burn Glides swift, a silver dart, And safe beneath the shady thorn Defies the angler's art: My life was ance that careless stream, That wanton trout was I; But love, wi' unrelenting beam, Has scorch'd my fountains dry.

III.

The little flow'ret's peaceful lot, In yonder cliff that grows, Which, save the linnet's flight, I wot, Nae ruder visit knows, Was mine; till love has o'er me past, And blighted a' my bloom, And now beneath the with'ring blast My youth and joy consume.

IV.

The waken'd lav'rock warbling springs And climbs the early sky, Winnowing blythe her dewy wings In morning's rosy eye; As little reckt I sorrow's power, Until the flow'ry snare O' witching love, in luckless hour, Made me the thrall o' care.

V.

O had my fate been Greenland snows, Or Afric's burning zone, Wi' man and nature leagu'd my foes, So Peggy ne'er I'd known! [307]The wretch whase doom is, "hope nae mair." What tongue his woes can tell! Within whase bosom, save despair, Nae kinder spirits dwell.

CCLVII. O BONNIE WAS YON ROSY BRIER.

[To Jean Lorimer, the heroine of this song, Burns presented a copy of the last edition of his poems, that of 1793, with a dedicatory inscription, in which he moralizes upon her youth, her beauty, and steadfast friendship, and signs himself Coila.]

I.

O Bonnie was yon rosy brier, That blooms sae far frae haunt o' man, And bonnie she, and ah, how dear! It shaded frae the e'enin sun.

II.

Yon rosebuds in the morning dew How pure, amang the leaves sae green:

But purer was the lover's vow They witness'd in their shade yestreen.
III.
All in its rude and prickly bower, That crimson rose, how sweet and fair! But love is far a sweeter flower Amid life's thorny path o' care.
IV.
The pathless wild, and wimpling burn, Wi' Chloris in my arms, be mine; And I the world, nor wish, nor
scorn, Its joys and griefs alike resign.

CCLVIII. FORLORN, MY LOVE, NO COMFORT NEAR.

Tune-"Let me in this ae night."
["How do you like the foregoing?" Burns asks Thomson, after having copies this song for his collection. "I have written it within this hour: so much for the speed of my Pegasus: but what say you to his bottom?"]
I.
Forlorn, my love, no comfort near, Far, far from thee, I wander here; Far, far from thee, the fate severe At which I most repine, love. O wert thou, love, but near me; But near, near, near me; How kindly thou wouldst cheer me, And mingle sighs with mine, love
II.
Around me scowls a wintry sky, That blasts each bud of hope and joy; And shelter, shade, nor home have I, Save in those arms of thine, love.
III.
Cold, alter'd friendship's cruel part, To poison Fortune's ruthless dart, Let me not break thy faithful heart, And say that fate is mine, love.
IV.
But dreary tho' the moments fleet, O let me think we yet shall meet! That only ray of solace sweet Can on thy Chloris shine, love. O wert thou, love, but near me; But near, near, near me; How kindly thou wouldst cheer me, And mingle sighs with mine, love.

CCLIX. LAST MAY A BRAW WOOER.

Tune-"The Lothian Lassie."
["Gateslack," says Burns to Thomson, "is the name of a particular place, a kind of passage among the Lowther Hills, on the confines of Dumfrieshire: Dalgarnock, is also the name of a romantic spot near the Nith, where are still a ruined church and burial-ground." To this, it may be added that Dalgarnock kirk-yard is the scene where the author of Waverley finds Old Mortality repairing the Cameronian grave-stones.]
I.
Last May a braw wooer cam down the lang glen, And sair wi' his love he

did deave me; I said there was naething I hated like men, The deuce gae wi'm, to believe, believe me, The deuce gae wi'm, to believe me!

II.

He spak o' the darts in my bonnie black een, And vow'd for my love, he was dying; I said he might die when he liked for Jean, The Lord forgie me for lying, for lying, The Lord forgie me for lying!

[308]

III.

A weel-stocked mailen-himsel' for the laird- And marriage aff-hand, were his proffers: I never loot on that I kenn'd it, or car'd, But thought I may hae waur offers, waur offers, But thought I might hae waur offers.

IV.

But what wad ye think? In a fortnight or less- The deil tak his taste to gae near her! He up the Gateslack to my black cousin Bess, Guess ye how, the jad! I could bear her, could bear her, Guess ye how, the jad! I could bear her.

V.

But a' the niest week as I fretted wi' care, I gaed to the tryste o' Dalgarnock, And wha but my fine fickle lover was there! I glowr'd as I'd seen a warlock, a warlock, I glowr'd as I'd seen a warlock.

VI.

But owre my left shouther I gae him a blink, Lest neebors might say I was saucy; My wooer he caper'd as he'd been in drink, And vow'd I was his dear lassie, dear lassie, And vow'd I was his dear lassie.

VII.

I spier'd for my cousin fu' couthy and sweet, Gin she had recovered her hearin', And how my auld shoon suited her shauchled feet, But, heavens! how he fell a swearin', a swearin', But, heavens! how he fell a swearin'.

VIII.

He begged, for Gudesake, I wad be his wife, Or else I wad kill him wi' sorrow; So, e'en to preserve the poor body in life, I think I maun wed him to-morrow, to-morrow, I think I maun wed him to morrow.

CCLX. CHLORIS.

Tune-"Caledonian Hunt's Delight."

["I am at present," says Burns to Thomson, when he communicated these verses, "quite occupied with the charming sensations of the toothache, so have not a word to spare-such is the peculiarity of the rhythm of this air, that I find it impossible to make another stanza to suit it." This is the last of his strains in honour of Chloris.]

I.

Why, why tell thy lover, Bliss he never must enjoy: Why, why undeceive

him, And give all his hopes the lie?
II.
O why, while fancy raptured, slumbers, Chloris, Chloris all the theme, Why, why wouldst thou, cruel, Wake thy lover from his dream?

CCLXI. THE HIGHLAND WIDOW'S LAMENT.

[This song is said to be Burns's version of a Gaelic lament for the ruin which followed the rebellion of the year 1745: he sent it to the Museum.]
I.
Oh! I am come to the low countrie, Och-on, och-on, och-rie! Without a penny in my purse, To buy a meal to me.
II.
It was na sae in the Highland hills, Och-on, och-on, och-rie! Nae woman in the country wide Sae happy was as me.
III.
For then I had a score o' kye, Och-on, och-on, och-rie! Feeding on yon hills so high, And giving milk to me.
IV.
And there I had three score o' yowes, Och-on, och-on, och-rie! Skipping on yon bonnie knowes, And casting woo' to me.
V.
I was the happiest of a' the clan, Sair, sair, may I repine; For Donald was the brawest lad, And Donald he was mine.
VI.
Till Charlie Stewart cam' at last, Sae far to set us free; [309]My Donald's arm was wanted then, For Scotland and for me.
VII.
Their waefu' fate what need I tell, Right to the wrang did yield: My Donald and his country fell Upon Culloden's field.
VIII.
Oh! I am come to the low countrie, Och-on, och-on, och-rie! Nae woman in the world wide Sae wretched now as me.

CCLXII. TO GENERAL DUMOURIER. PARODY ON ROBIN ADAIR.

[Burns wrote this "Welcome" on the unexpected defection of General Dumourier.]
I.
You're welcome to despots, Dumourier; You're welcome to despots, Dumourier; How does Dampiere do? Aye, and Bournonville, too? Why did they not come along with you, Dumourier?

II.
I will fight France with you, Dumourier; I will fight France with you, Dumourier; I will fight France with you, I will take my chance with you; By my soul I'll dance a dance with you, Dumourier.
III.
Then let us fight about, Dumourier; Then let us fight about, Dumourier; Then let us fight about, Till freedom's spark is out, Then we'll be damn'd, no doubt, Dumourier.

CCLXIII. PEG-A-RAMSEY.

Tune-"Cauld is the e'enin blast."
[Most of this song is old: Burns gave it a brushing for the Museum.]
I.
Cauld is the e'enin' blast O' Boreas o'er the pool, And dawin' it is dreary When birks are bare at Yule.
II.
O bitter blaws the e'enin' blast When bitter bites the frost, And in the mirk and dreary drift The hills and glens are lost.
III.
Ne'er sae murky blew the night That drifted o'er the hill, But a bonnie Peg-a-Ramsey Gat grist to her mill.

CCLXIV. THERE WAS A BONNIE LASS.

[A snatch of an old strain, trimmed up a little for the Museum.]
I.
There was a bonnie lass, And a bonnie, bonnie lass, And she lo'ed her bonnie laddie dear; Till war's loud alarms Tore her laddie frae her arms, Wi' mony a sigh and tear.
II.
Over sea, over shore, Where the cannons loudly roar, He still was a stranger to fear; And nocht could him quell, Or his bosom assail, But the bonnie lass he lo'ed sae dear.

CCLXV. O MALLY'S MEEK, MALLY'S SWEET.

[Burns, it is said, composed these verses, on meeting a country girl, with her shoes and stockings in her lap, walking homewards from a Dumfries fair. He was struck with her beauty, and as beautifully has he recorded it. This was his last communication to the Museum.]
I.
O Mally's meek, Mally's sweet, Mally's modest and discreet, Mally's rare,

Mally's fair, Mally's every way complete. [310]As I was walking up the street, A barefit maid I chanc'd to meet; But O the road was very hard For that fair maiden's tender feet.

II.

It were mair meet that those fine feet Were weel lac'd up in silken shoon, And 'twere more fit that she should sit, Within yon chariot gilt aboon.

III.

Her yellow hair, beyond compare, Comes trinkling down her swan-white neck; And her two eyes, like stars in skies, Would keep a sinking ship frae wreck. O Mally's meek, Mally's sweet, Mally's modest and discreet, Mally's rare, Mally's fair, Mally's every way complete.

CCLXVI. HEY FOR A LASS WI' A TOCHER.

Tune-"Balinamona Ora."

[Communicated to Thomson, 17th of February, 1796, to be printed as part of the poet's contribution to the Irish melodies: he calls it "a kind of rhapsody."]

I.

Awa wi' your witchcraft o' beauty's alarms, The slender bit beauty you grasp in your arms: O, gie me the lass that has acres o' charms, O, gie me the lass wi' the weel-stockit farms. Then hey for a lass wi' a tocher, Then hey for a lass wi' a tocher; Then hey for a lass wi' a tocher, The nice yellow guineas for me.

II.

Your beauty's a flower, in the morning that blows, And withers the faster, the faster it grows; But the rapturous charm o' the bonnie green knowes, Ilk spring they're new deckit wi' bonnie white yowes.

III.

And e'en when this beauty your bosom has blest, The brightest o' beauty may cloy when possest; But the sweet yellow darlings wi' Geordie imprest, The langer ye hae them-the mair they're carest. Then hey for a lass wi' a tocher, Then hey for a lass wi' a tocher; Then hey for a lass wi' a tocher, The nice yellow guineas for me.

CCLXVII. JESSY.

Tune-"Here's a health to them that's awa."

[Written in honour of Miss Jessie Lewars, now Mrs. Thomson. Her tender and daughter-like attentions soothed the last hours of the dying poet, and if immortality can be considered a recompense, she has been rewarded.]

I.

Here's a health to ane I lo'e dear; Here's a health to ane I lo'e dear; Thou art sweet as the smile when fond lovers meet, And soft as their parting tear-Jessy!

II.

Altho' thou maun never be mine, Altho' even hope is denied; 'Tis sweeter for thee despairing, Then aught in the world beside-Jessy!

III.

I mourn through the gay, gaudy day, As, hopeless, I muse on thy charms: But welcome the dream o' sweet slumber, For then I am lockt in thy arms-Jessy!

IV.

I guess by the dear angel smile, I guess by the love rolling e'e; But why urge the tender confession 'Gainst fortune's fell cruel decree?-Jessy! Here's a health to ane I lo'e dear; Here's a health to ane I lo'e dear; Thou art sweet as the smile when fond lovers meet, And soft as their parting tear-Jessy!

[311]

CCLXVIII. FAIREST MAID ON DEVON BANKS.

Tune-"Rothemurche."

[On the 12th of July, 1796, as Burns lay dying at Brow, on the Solway, his thoughts wandered to early days, and this song, the last he was to measure in this world, was dedicated to Charlotte Hamilton, the maid of the Devon.]

I.

Fairest maid on Devon banks, Crystal Devon, winding Devon, Wilt thou lay that frown aside, And smile as thou were wont to do? Full well thou know'st I love thee, dear! Could'st thou to malice lend an ear! O! did not love exclaim "Forbear, Nor use a faithful lover so."

II.

Then come, thou fairest of the fair, Those wonted smiles, O let me share; And by thy beauteous self I swear, No love but thine my heart shall know. Fairest maid on Devon banks, Crystal Devon, winding Devon, Wilt thou lay that frown aside, And smile as thou were wont to do?

PART IV. GENERAL CORRESPONDENCE

I.

TO WILLIAM BURNESS.

[This was written by Burns in his twenty-third year, when learning flax-dressing in Irvine, and is the earliest of his letters which has reached us. It has much of the scriptural deference to paternal authority, and more of the Complete Letter Writer than we look for in an original mind.]

Irvine, Dec. 27, 1781.

Honoured Sir,

I have purposely delayed writing in the hope that I should have the pleasure of seeing you on New-Year's day; but work comes so hard upon us, that I do not choose to be absent on that account, as well as for some other little reasons which I shall tell you at meeting. My health is nearly the same as when you were here, only my sleep is a little sounder, and on the whole I am rather better than otherwise, though I mend by very slow degrees. The weakness of my nerves has so debilitated my mind, that I dare neither review past wants, nor look forward into futurity; for the least anxiety or perturbation in my breast produces most unhappy effects on my whole frame. Sometimes, indeed, when for an hour or two my spirits are alightened, I glimmer a little into futurity; but my principal, and indeed my only pleasurable employment is looking backwards and forwards in a moral and religious way; I am quite transported at the thought, that ere long, perhaps very soon, I shall bid an eternal adieu to all the pains, and uneasiness, and disquietudes of this weary life: for I assure you I am heartily tired of it; and if I do not very much deceive myself, I could contentedly and gladly resign it.

"The soul, uneasy, and confined at home, Rests and expatiates in a life to

come."[141]
It is for this reason I am more pleased with the 15th, 16th, and 17th verses of the 7th chapter of Revelations, than with any ten times as many verses in the whole Bible, and would not exchange the noble enthusiasm with which they inspire me for all that this world has to offer. As for this world, I despair of ever making a figure in it. I am not formed for the bustle of the busy, nor the flutter of the gay. I shall never again be capable of entering into such scenes. Indeed I am altogether unconcerned at the thoughts of this life. I foresee that poverty and obscurity probably await me, and I am in some measure prepared, and daily preparing to meet them. I have but just time and paper to return you my grateful thanks for the lessons of virtue and piety you have given me, which were too much neglected at the time of giving them, but which I hope have been remembered ere it is yet too late. Present my dutiful respects to my mother, and my compliments [312]to Mr. and Mrs. Muir; and with wishing you a merry New-Year's day, I shall conclude. I am, honoured sir, your dutiful son,
Robert Burness.
P.S. My meal is nearly out, but I am going to borrow till I get more.

FOOTNOTES:

[141] Pope. Essay on Man

II.

TO MR. JOHN MURDOCH,
SCHOOLMASTER,
STABLES-INN BUILDINGS, LONDON.
[John Murdoch, one of the poet's early teachers, removed from the west of Scotland to London, where he lived to a good old age, and loved to talk of the pious William Burness and his eminent son.]
Lochlea, 15th January, 1783.
Dear Sir,
As I have an opportunity of sending you a letter without putting you to that expense which any production of mine would but ill repay, I embrace it with pleasure, to tell you that I have not forgotten, nor ever will forget, the many obligations I lie under to your kindness and friendship.
I do not doubt, Sir, but you will wish to know what has been the result of all the pains of an indulgent father, and a masterly teacher; and I wish I could gratify your curiosity with such a recital as you would be pleased with; but that is what I am afraid will not be the case. I have, indeed, kept pretty clear of vicious habits; and, in this respect, I hope, my conduct will not disgrace the education I have gotten; but, as a man of the world, I am most

miserably deficient. One would have thought that, bred as I have been, under a father, who has figured pretty well as un homme des affaires, I might have been, what the world calls, a pushing, active fellow; but to tell you the truth, Sir, there is hardly anything more my reverse. I seem to be one sent into the world to see and observe; and I very easily compound with the knave who tricks me of my money, if there be anything original about him, which shows me human nature in a different light from anything I have seen before. In short, the joy of my heart is to "study men, their manners, and their ways;" and for this darling subject, I cheerfully sacrifice every other consideration. I am quite indolent about those great concerns that set the bustling, busy sons of care agog; and if I have to answer for the present hour, I am very easy with regard to anything further. Even the last, worst shift of the unfortunate and the wretched, does not much terrify me: I know that even then, my talent for what country folks call a "sensible crack," when once it is sanctified by a hoary head, would procure me so much esteem, that even then-I would learn to be happy.[142] However, I am under no apprehensions about that; for though indolent, yet so far as an extremely delicate constitution permits, I am not lazy; and in many things, expecially in tavern matters, I am a strict economist; not, indeed, for the sake of the money; but one of the principal parts in my composition is a kind of pride of stomach; and I scorn to fear the face of any man living: above everything, I abhor as hell, the idea of sneaking in a corner to avoid a dun-possibly some pitiful, sordid wretch, who in my heart I despise and detest. 'Tis this, and this alone, that endears economy to me. In the matter of books, indeed, I am very profuse. My favourite authors are of the sentimental kind, such as Shenstone, particularly his "Elegies;" Thomson; "Man of Feeling"-a book I prize next to the Bible; "Man of the World;" Sterne, especially his "Sentimental Journey;" Macpherson's "Ossian," andc.; these are the glorious models after which I endeavour to form my conduct, and 'tis incongruous, 'tis absurd to suppose that the man whose mind glows with sentiments lighted up at their sacred flame-the man whose heart distends with benevolence to all the human race-he "who can soar above this little scene of things"-can he descend to mind the paltry concerns about which the terræfilial race fret, and fume, and vex themselves! O how the glorious triumph swells my heart! I forget that I am a poor, insignificant devil, unnoticed and unknown, stalking up and down fairs and markets, when I happen to be in them, reading a page or two of mankind, and "catching the manners living as they rise," whilst the men of business jostle me on every side, as an idle encumbrance in their way.-But I dare say I have by this time tired your patience; so I shall conclude with begging you to give Mrs. Murdoch-not my compliments, for that is a mere common-place story; but my warmest, kindest [313] wishes for her welfare; and accept of the same for yourself, from,

Dear Sir, yours.-R. B

FOOTNOTES:

[142] The last shift alluded to here must be the condition of an itinerant beggar.-Currie

III.

TO MR. JAMES BURNESS,
WRITER, MONTROSE.[143]

[James Burness, son of the poet's uncle, lives at Montrose, and, as may be surmised, is now very old: fame has come to his house through his eminent cousin Robert, and dearer still through his own grandson, Sir Alexander Burnes, with whose talents and intrepidity the world is well acquainted.]

Lochlea, 21st June, 1783.

Dear Sir,

My father received your favour of the 10th current, and as he has been for some months very poorly in health, and is in his own opinion (and indeed, in almost everybody's else) in a dying condition, he has only, with great difficulty, written a few farewell lines to each of his brothers-in-law. For this melancholy reason, I now hold the pen for him to thank you for your kind letter, and to assure you, Sir, that it shall not be my fault if my father's correspondence in the north die with him. My brother writes to John Caird, and to him I must refer you for the news of our family.

I shall only trouble you with a few particulars relative to the wretched state of this country. Our markets are exceedingly high; oatmeal 17d. and 18d. per peck, and not to be gotten even at that price. We have indeed been pretty well supplied with quantities of white peas from England and elsewhere, but that resource is likely to fail us, and what will become of us then, particularly the very poorest sort, Heaven only knows. This country, till of late, was flourishing incredibly in the manufacture of silk, lawn, and carpet-weaving; and we are still carrying on a good deal in that way, but much reduced from what it was. We had also a fine trade in the shoe way, but now entirely ruined, and hundreds driven to a starving condition on account of it. Farming is also at a very low ebb with us. Our lands, generally speaking, are mountainous and barren; and our landholders, full of ideas of farming gathered from the English and the Lothians, and other rich soils in Scotland, make no allowance for the odds of the quality of land, and consequently stretch us much beyond what in the event we will be found able to pay. We are also much at a loss for want of proper methods in our improvements of farming. Necessity compels us to leave our old schemes, and few of us have opportunities of being well informed in new ones. In short, my dear Sir, since the unfortunate beginning of this American war, and its as unfortunate conclusion, this country has been, and still is, decaying very fast. Even in higher life, a couple of our Ayrshire noblemen, and the major part of our knights and squires, are all insolvent. A miserable job of a Douglas, Heron, and Co.'s bank, which no doubt you heard of, has undone numbers of them; and imitating English and French, and other foreign luxuries and fopperies, has ruined as many more. There is a great trade of smuggling carried on along our coasts, which, however destructive to the interests of the kingdom at large, certainly enriches this corner of it, but too often at the expense of our morals. However, it enables individuals to make, at least for a time, a splendid appearance; but Fortune, as is usual with her when she is uncommonly lavish of her favours, is generally even with them at the last; and happy were it for numbers of them if she would leave them no worse than when she found them.

My mother sends you a small present of a cheese, 'tis but a very little one, as our last year's stock is sold off; but if you could fix on any correspondent in Edinburgh or Glasgow, we would send you a proper one in the season. Mrs. Black promises to take the cheese under her care so far, and then to send it to you by the Stirling carrier.

I shall conclude this long letter with assuring you that I shall be very happy to hear from you, or any of our friends in your country, when opportunity serves.

My father sends you, probably for the last time in this world, his warmest wishes for your welfare and happiness; and my mother and the rest of the family desire to enclose their kind compliments to you, Mrs. Burness, and the rest of your family, along with those of,

Dear Sir,

Your affectionate Cousin,

R. B.

FOOTNOTES:

[143] This gentleman (the son of an elder brother of my father's), when he was very young, lost his father, and having discovered in his father's repositories some of my father's letters, he requested that the correspondence might be renewed. My father continued till the last year of his life to correspond with his nephew, and it was afterwards kept up by my brother. Extracts from some of my brother's letters to his cousin are introduced, for the purpose of exhibiting the poet before he had attracted the notice of the public, and in his domestic family relations afterwards.-Gilbert Burns.

IV.

TO MISS E.

[The name of the lady to whom this and the three succeeding letters were addressed, seems to have been known to Dr. Currie, who introduced them in his first edition, but excluded them from his second. They were restored by Gilbert Burns, without naming the lady.]

Lochlea, 1783.

I verily believe, my dear E., that the pure, genuine feelings of love are as rare in the world as the pure genuine principles of virtue and piety. This I hope will account for the uncommon style of all my letters to you. By uncommon, I mean their being written in such a serious manner, which, to tell you the truth, has made me often afraid lest you should take me for some zealous bigot, who conversed with his mistress as he would converse with his minister. I don't know how it is, my dear, for though, except your company, there is nothing on earth gives me much pleasure as writing to you, yet it never gives me those giddy raptures so much talked of among lovers. I have often thought that if a well-grounded affection be not really a part of virtue, 'tis something extremely akin to it. Whenever the thought of my E. warms my heart, every feeling of humanity, every principle of generosity kindles in my breast. It extinguishes every dirty spark of malice and envy which are but too apt to infest me. I grasp every creature in the arms of universal benevolence, and equally participate in the pleasures of the happy, and sympathize with the miseries of the unfortunate. I assure you, my dear, I often look up to the Divine Disposer of events with an eye of gratitude for the blessing which I hope he intends to bestow on me in bestowing you. I sincerely wish that he may bless my endeavors to make your life as comfortable and happy as possible, both in sweetening the rougher parts of my natural temper, and bettering the unkindly circumstances of my fortune. This, my dear, is a passion, at least in my view, worthy of a man, and I will add worthy of a Christian. The sordid earth-worm may profess love to a woman's person, whilst in reality his affection is centred in her pocket; and the slavish drudge may go a-wooing as he goes to the horse-market to choose one who is stout and firm, and as we may say of an old horse, one who will be a good drudge and draw kindly. I disdain their dirty, puny ideas. I would be heartily out of humour with myself if I thought I were capable of having so poor a notion of the sex, which were designed to crown the pleasures of society. Poor devils! I don't envy them their happiness who have such notions. For my part, I propose quite other pleasures with my dear partner.

R. B.

V.

TO MISS E.
Lochlea, 1783.
My dear E.:
I do not remember, in the course of your acquaintance and mine, ever to have heard your opinion on the ordinary way of falling in love, amongst people of our station of life: I do not mean the persons who proceed in the way of bargain, but those whose affection is really placed on the person.
Though I be, as you know very well, but a very awkward lover myself, yet as I have some opportunities of observing the conduct of others who are much better skilled in the affair of courtship than I am, I often think it is owing to lucky chance more than to good management, that there are not more unhappy marriages than usually are.
It is natural for a young fellow to like the acquaintance of the females, and customary for him to keep them company when occasion serves: some one of them is more agreeable to him than the rest; there is something, he knows not what, pleases him, he knows not how, in her company. This I take to be what is called love with the greater part of us; and I must own, dear E., it is a hard game, such a one as you have to play when you meet with such a lover. You cannot refuse but he is sincere, and yet though you use him ever so favourably, per[315]haps in a few months, or at farthest in a year or two, the same unaccountable fancy may make him as distractedly fond of another, whilst you are quite forgot. I am aware that perhaps the next time I have the pleasure of seeing you, you may bid me take my own lesson home, and tell me that the passion I have professed for you is perhaps one of those transient flashes I have been describing; but I hope, my dear E., you will do me the justice to believe me, when I assure you that the love I have for you is founded on the sacred principles of virtue and honour, and by consequence so long as you continue possessed of those amiable qualities which first inspired my passion for you, so long must I continue to love you. Believe me, my dear, it is love like this alone which can render the marriage state happy. People may talk of flames and raptures as long as they please, and a warm fancy, with a flow of youthful spirits, may make them feel something like what they describe; but sure I am the nobler faculties of the mind, with kindred feelings of the heart, can only be the foundation of friendship, and it has always been my opinion that the married life was only friendship in a more exalted degree. If you will be so good as to grant my wishes, and it should please Providence to spare us to the latest periods of life, I can look forward and see that even then, though bent down with wrinkled age; even then, when all other worldly circumstances will be indifferent to me, I will regard my E. with the tenderest affection, and for this plain reason, because she is still possessed of those noble qualities, improved to a much higher degree, which first inspired my affection for her.

"O! happy state when souls each other draw, When love is liberty and nature law."[144]
I know were I to speak in such a style to many a girl, who thinks herself possessed of no small share of sense, she would think it ridiculous; but the language of the heart is, my dear E., the only courtship I shall ever use to you.
When I look over what I have written, I am sensible it is vastly different from the ordinary style of courtship, but I shall make no apology-I know your good nature will excuse what your goody sense may see amiss.
R. B.

FOOTNOTES:

[144] Pope. Eloisa to Abelard.

VI.

TO MISS E.
Lochlea, 1783.
I have often thought it a peculiarly unlucky circumstance in love, that though in every other situation in life, telling the truth is not only the safest, but actually by far the easiest way of proceeding, a lover is never under greater difficulty in acting, or more puzzled for expression, than when his passion is sincere, and his intentions are honourable. I do not think that it is very difficult for a person of ordinary capacity to talk of love and fondness, which are not felt, and to make vows of constancy and fidelity, which are never intended to be performed, if he be villain enough to practise such detestable conduct: but to a man whose heart glows with the principles of integrity and truth, and who sincerely loves a woman of amiable person, uncommon refinement of sentiment and purity of manners-to such an one, in such circumstances, I can assure you, my dear, from my own feelings at this present moment, courtship is a task indeed. There is such a number of foreboding fears and distrustful anxieties crowd into my mind when I am in your company, or when I sit down to write to you, that what to speak, or what to write, I am altogether at a loss.
There is one rule which I have hitherto practised, and which I shall invariably keep with you, and that is honestly to tell you the plain truth. There is something so mean and unmanly in the arts of dissimulation and falsehood, that I am surprised they can be acted by any one in so noble, so generous a passion, as virtuous love. No, my dear E., I shall never endeavour to gain your favour by such detestable practices. If you will be so good and so generous as to admit me for your partner, your companion, your bosom friend through life, there is nothing on this side of eternity

shall give me greater transport; but I shall never think of purchasing your hand by any arts unworthy of a man, and I will add of a Christian. There is one thing, my dear, which I earnestly request of you, and it is this; that you would soon either put an end to my hopes by a peremptory refusal, or cure me of my fears by a generous consent.

It would oblige me much if you would send me a line or two when convenient. I shall only add further that, if a behaviour regulated (though perhaps but very imperfectly) by the[316] rules of honour and virtue, if a heart devoted to love and esteem you, and an earnest endeavour to promote your happiness; if these are qualities you would wish in a friend, in a husband, I hope you shall ever find them in your real friend, and sincere lover.

R. B.

VII.

TO MISS E.

Lochlea, 1783.

I ought, in good manners, to have acknowledged the receipt of your letter before this time, but my heart was so shocked, with the contents of it, that I can scarcely yet collect my thoughts so as to write you on the subject. I will not attempt to describe what I felt on receiving your letter. I read it over and over, again and again, and though it was in the politest language of refusal, still it was peremptory; "you were sorry you could not make me a return, but you wish me," what without you I never can obtain, "you wish me all kind of happiness." It would be weak and unmanly to say that, without you I never can be happy; but sure I am, that sharing life with you would have given it a relish, that, wanting you, I can never taste.

Your uncommon personal advantages, and your superior good sense, do not so much strike me; these, possibly, in a few instances may be met with in others; but that amiable goodness, that tender feminine softness, that endearing sweetness of disposition, with all the charming offspring of a warm feeling heart-these I never again expect to meet with, in such a degree, in this world. All these charming qualities, heightened by an education much beyond anything I have ever met in any woman I ever dared to approach, have made an impression on my heart that I do not think the world can ever efface. My imagination had fondly flattered myself with a wish, I dare not say it ever reached a hope, that possibly I might one day call you mine. I had formed the most delightful images, and my fancy fondly brooded over them; but now I am wretched for the loss of what I really had no right to expect. I must now think no more of you as a mistress; still I presume to ask to be admitted as a friend. As such I wish to be allowed to wait on you, and as I expect to remove in a few days a little

further off, and you, I suppose, will perhaps soon leave this place, I wish to see or hear from you soon; and if an expression should perhaps escape me, rather too warm for friendship, I hope you will pardon it in, my dear Miss-(pardon me the dear expression for once) * * * *
R. B

VIII.

TO ROBERT RIDDEL, ESQ.
OF GLENRIDDEL
[These memoranda throw much light on the early days of Burns, and on the history of his mind and compositions. Robert Riddel, of the Friars-Carse, to whom these fragments were sent, was a good man as well as a distinguished antiquary.]
My Dear Sir,
On rummaging over some old papers I lighted on a MS. of my early years, in which I had determined to write myself out; as I was placed by fortune among a class of men to whom my ideas would have been nonsense. I had meant that the book should have lain by me, in the fond hope that some time or other, even after I was no more, my thoughts would fall into the hands of somebody capable of appreciating their value. It sets off thus:-
"Observations, Hints, Songs, Scraps of Poetry, andc., by Robert Burness: a man who had little art in making money, and still less in keeping it; but was, however, a man of some sense, a great deal of honesty, and unbounded good-will to every creature, rational and irrational.-As he was but little indebted to scholastic education, and bred at a plough-tail, his performances must be strongly tinctured with his unpolished, rustic way of life; but as I believe they are really his own, it may be some entertainment to a curious observer of human nature to see how a ploughman thinks, and feels, under the pressure of love, ambition, anxiety, grief, with the like cares and passions, which, however diversified by the modes and manners of life, operate pretty much alike, I believe, on all the species."
"There are numbers in the world who do not want sense to make a figure, so much as an opinion of their own abilities to put them upon recording their observations, and allowing them the same importance which they do to those which appear in print."-Shenstone.
[317]
"Pleasing, when youth is long expired, to trace The forms our pencil, or our pen designed! Such was our youthful air, and shape, and face, Such the soft image of our youthful mind."-Ibid.
April, 1783.
Notwithstanding all that has been said against love, respecting the folly and weakness it lends a young inexperienced mind into; still I think it in a great

measure deserves the highest encomiums that have been passed upon it. If anything on earth deserves the name of rapture or transport, it is the feelings of green eighteen in the company of the mistress of his heart, when she repays him with an equal return of affection.

August.

There is certainly some connexion between love and music, and poetry; and therefore, I have always thought it a fine touch of nature, that passage in a modern love-composition:

"As towards her cot she jogged along, Her name was frequent in his song."

For my own part I never had the least thought or inclination of turning poet till I got once heartily in love, and then rhyme and song were in a manner the spontaneous language of my heart. The following composition was the first of my performances, and done at an early period of life, when my heart glowed with honest warm simplicity; unacquainted and uncorrupted with the ways of a wicked world. The performance is indeed, very puerile and silly; but I am always pleased with it, as it recalls to my mind those happy days when my heart was yet honest, and my tongue was sincere. The subject of it was a young girl who really deserved all the praises I have bestowed on her. I not only had this opinion of her then-but I actually think so still, now that the spell is long since broken, and the enchantment at an end.

O once I lov'd a bonnie lass.[145]

Lest my works should be thought below criticism: or meet with a critic, who, perhaps, will not look on them with so candid and favourable an eye, I am determined to criticise them myself.

The first distich of the first stanza is quite too much in the flimsy strain of our ordinary street ballads: and, on the other hand, the second distich is too much in the other extreme. The expression is a little awkward, and the sentiment too serious. Stanza the second I am well pleased with; and I think it conveys a fine idea of that amiable part of the sex-the agreeables; or what in our Scotch dialect we call a sweet sonsie lass. The third stanza has a little of the flimsy turn in it; and the third line has rather too serious a cast. The fourth stanza is a very indifferent one; the first line, is, indeed, all in the strain of the second stanza, but the rest is most expletive. The thoughts in the fifth stanza come finely up to my favourite idea-a sweet sonsie lass: the last line, however, halts a little. The same sentiments are kept up with equal spirit and tenderness in the sixth stanza, but the second and fourth lines ending with short syllables hurt the whole. The seventh stanza has several minute faults; but I remember I composed it in a wild enthusiasm of passion, and to this hour I never recollect it but my heart melts, my blood sallies, at the remembrance.

September.

I entirely agree with that judicious philosopher, Mr. Smith, in his excellent

Theory of Moral Sentiments, that remorse is the most painful sentiment that can embitter the human bosom. Any ordinary pitch of fortitude may bear up tolerably well under those calamities, in the procurement of which we ourselves have had no hand; but when our own follies, or crimes, have made us miserable and wretched, to bear up with manly firmness, and at the same time have a proper penitent sense of our misconduct, is a glorious effort of self-command.

Of all the numerous ills that hurt our peace, That press the soul, or wring the mind with anguish, Beyond comparison the worst are those That to our folly or our guilt we owe. In every other circumstance, the mind Has this to say, 'It was no deed of mine;' But when to all the evil of misfortune This sting is added-'Blame thy foolish self!' Or worser far, the pangs of keen remorse; The torturing, gnawing consciousness of guilt- Of guilt, perhaps, where we've involved others; The young, the innocent, who fondly lov'd us, Nay, more, that very love their cause of ruin! [318]O burning hell; in all thy store of torments, There's not a keener lash! Lives there a man so firm, who, while his heart Feels all the bitter horrors of his crime, Can reason down its agonizing throbs; And, after proper purpose of amendment, Can firmly force his jarring thoughts to peace? O, happy! happy! enviable man! O glorious magnanimity of soul!

March, 1784.

I have often observed, in the course of my experience of human life, that every man, even the worst, has something good about him; though very often nothing else than a happy temperament of constitution inclining him to this or that virtue. For this reason no man can say in what degree any other person, besides himself, can be, with strict justice, called wicked. Let any, of the strictest character for regularity of conduct among us, examine impartially how many vices he has never been guilty of, not from any care or vigilance, but for want of opportunity, or some accidental circumstance intervening; how many of the weaknesses of mankind he has escaped, because he was out of the line of such temptation; and, what often, if not always, weighs more than all the rest, how much he is indebted to the world's good opinion, because the world does not know all: I say, any man who can thus think, will scan the failings, nay, the faults and crimes, of mankind around him, with a brother's eye.

I have often courted the acquaintance of that part of mankind, commonly known by the ordinary phrase of blackguards, sometimes farther than was consistent with the safety of my character; those who by thoughtless prodigality or headstrong passions, have been driven to ruin. Though disgraced by follies, nay sometimes, stained with guilt, I have yet found among them, in not a few instances, some of the noblest virtues, magnanimity, generosity, disinterested friendship, and even modesty.

April.

As I am what the men of the world, if they knew such a man, would call a whimsical mortal, I have various sources of pleasure and enjoyment, which are, in a manner, peculiar to myself, or some here and there such other out-of-the-way person. Such is the peculiar pleasure I take in the season of winter, more than the rest of the year. This, I believe, may be partly owing to my misfortunes giving my mind a melancholy cast: but there is something even in the-

"Mighty tempest, and the hoary waste Abrupt and deep, stretch'd o'er the buried earth,"-

which raises the mind to a serious sublimity, favourable to everything great and noble. There is scarcely any earthly object gives me more-I do not know if I should call it pleasure-but something which exalts me, something which enraptures me-than to walk in the sheltered side of a wood, or high plantation, in a cloudy winter-day, and hear the stormy wind howling among the trees, and raving over the plain. It is my best season for devotion: my mind is wrapt up in a kind of enthusiasm to Him, who, in the pompous language of the Hebrew bard, "walks on the wings of the wind." In one of these seasons, just after a train of misfortunes, I composed the following:-

The wintry west extends his blast.[146]

Shenstone finely observes, that love-verses, writ without any real passion, are the most nauseous of all conceits; and I have often thought that no man can be a proper critic of love-composition, except he himself, in one or more instances, have been a warm votary of this passion. As I have been all along a miserable dupe to love, and have been led into a thousand weaknesses and follies by it, for that reason I put the more confidence in my critical skill, in distinguishing foppery and conceit from real passion and nature. Whether the following song will stand the test, I will not pretend to say, because it is my own; only I can say it was, at the time, genuine from the heart:-

Behind yon hills, where Lugar flows.[147]

March, 1784.

There was a certain period of my life that my spirit was broke by repeated losses and disasters which threatened, and indeed effected, the utter ruin of my fortune. My body, too, was attacked by that most dreadful distemper, a hypochondria, or confirmed melancholy. In this wretched [319]state, the recollection of which makes me shudder, I hung my harp on the willow trees, except in some lucid intervals, in one of which I composed the following:-

O thou Great Being! what Thou art.[148]

April.

The following song is a wild rhapsody, miserably deficient in versification; but as the sentiments are the genuine feelings of my heart, for that reason I have a particular pleasure in conning it over.

My father was a farmer Upon the Carrick border, O.[149]

April.

I think the whole species of young men may be naturally enough divided into two grand classes, which I shall call the grave and the merry; though, by the by, these terms do not with propriety enough express my ideas. The grave I shall cast into the usual division of those who are goaded on by the love of money, and those whose darling wish is to make a figure in the world. The merry are the men of pleasure of all denominations; the jovial lads, who have too much fire and spirit to have any settled rule of action; but, without much deliberation, follow the strong impulses of nature: the thoughtless, the careless, the indolent-in particular he who, with a happy sweetness of natural temper, and a cheerful vacancy of thought, steals through life-generally, indeed, in poverty and obscurity; but poverty and obscurity are only evils to him who can sit gravely down and make a repining comparison between his own situation and that of others; and lastly, to grace the quorum, such are, generally, those whose heads are capable of all the towerings of genius, and whose hearts are warmed with all the delicacy of feeling.

August.

The foregoing was to have been an elaborate dissertation on the various species of men; but as I cannot please myself in the arrangement of my ideas, I must wait till farther experience and nicer observation throw more light on the subject.-In the mean time I shall set down the following fragment, which, as it is the genuine language of my heart, will enable anybody to determine which of the classes I belong to:

There's nought but care on ev'ry han', In ev'ry hour that passes, O.[150]

As the grand end of human life is to cultivate an intercourse with that Being to whom we owe life, with every enjoyment that renders life delightful; and to maintain an integritive conduct towards our fellow-creatures; that so, by forming piety and virtue into habit, we may be fit members for that society of the pious and the good, which reason and revelation teach us to expect beyond the grave, I do not see that the turn of mind, and pursuits of such a one as the above verses describe-one who spends the hours and thoughts which the vocations of the day can spare with Ossian, Shakspeare, Thomson, Shenstone, Sterne, andc.; or, as the maggot takes him, a gun, a fiddle, or a song to make or mend; and at all times some heart's-dear bonnie lass in view-I say I do not see that the turn of mind and pursuits of such an one are in the least more inimical to the sacred interests of piety and virtue, than the even lawful, bustling and straining after the world's riches and honours: and I do not see but he may gain heaven as well-which, by the by, is no mean consideration-who steals through the vale of life, amusing himself with every little flower that fortune throws in his way, as he, who straining straight forward, and perhaps spattering all about him, gains some of life's little eminencies, where, after all, he can only see and be seen a little more conspicuously than what, in the pride of his heart, he is apt to term the poor, indolent devil he has left behind him.

August.

A Prayer, when fainting fits, and other alarming symptoms of a pleurisy or some other dangerous disorder, which indeed still threatens me, first put nature on the alarm:-

O thou unknown, Almighty Cause Of all my hope and fear![151]

August.

Misgivings in the hour of despondency and prospect of death:-

Why am I loth to leave this earthly scene.[152]

EGOTISMS FROM MY OWN SENSATIONS.

May.

I don't well know what is the reason of it, but somehow or other, though I am when I have a mind pretty generally beloved, yet I never could get the art of commanding respect.-I imagine it is owing to my being deficient in what Sterne calls "that understrapping virtue of discretion."-I am so apt to a lapsus linguæ, that I sometimes think the character of a certain great man I have read of somewhere is very much apropos to myself-that he was a compound of great talents and great folly.-N.B. To try if I can discover the causes of this wretched infirmity, and, if possible, to mend it.

August.

However I am pleased with the works of our Scotch poets, particularly the excellent Ramsay, and the still more excellent Fergusson, yet I am hurt to see other places of Scotland, their towns, rivers, woods, haughs, andc., immortalized in such celebrated performances, while my dear native country, the ancient bailieries of Carrick, Kyle, and Cunningham, famous both in ancient and modern times for a gallant and warlike race of inhabitants; a country where civil, and particularly religious liberty have ever found their first support, and their last asylum; a country, the birth-place of many famous philosophers, soldiers, statesman, and the scene of many important events recorded in Scottish history, particularly a great many of the actions of the glorious Wallace, the Saviour of his country; yet, we have never had one Scotch poet of any eminence, to make the fertile banks of Irvine, the romantic woodlands and sequestered scenes on Ayr, and the healthy mountainous source and winding sweep of Doon, emulate Tay, Forth, Ettrick, Tweed, andc. This is a complaint I would gladly remedy, but, alas! I am far unequal to the task, both in native genius and education. Obscure I am, and obscure I must be, though no young poet, nor young soldier's heart, ever beat more fondly for fame than mine-

"And if there is no other scene of being Where my insatiate wish may have its fill,- This something at my heart that heaves for room, My best, my

dearest part, was made in vain."
September.
There is a great irregularity in the old Scotch songs, a redundancy of syllables with respect to that exactness of accent and measure that the English poetry requires, but which glides in, most melodiously, with the respective tunes to which they are set. For instance, the fine old song of "The Mill, Mill, O,"[153] to give it a plain prosaic reading, it halts prodigiously out of measure; on the other hand, the song set to the same tune in Bremner's collection of Scotch songs, which begins "To Fanny fair could I impart," andc., it is most exact measure, and yet, let them both be sung before a real critic, one above the biases of prejudice, but a thorough judge of nature,-how flat and spiritless will the last appear, how trite, and lamely methodical, compared with the wild warbling cadence, the heart-moving melody of the first!-This is particularly the case with all those airs which end with a hypermetrical syllable. There is a degree of wild irregularity in many of the compositions and fragments which are daily sung to them by my compeers, the common people-a certain happy arrangement of old Scotch syllables, and yet, very frequently, nothing, not even like rhyme or sameness of jingle, at the ends of the lines. This has made me sometimes imagine that perhaps it might be possible for a Scotch poet, with a nice judicious ear, to set compositions to many of our most favourite airs, particularly that class of them mentioned above, independent of rhyme altogether.
There is a noble sublimity, a heart-melting tenderness, in some of our ancient ballads, which show them to be the work of a masterly hand: and it has often given me many a heart-ache to reflect that such glorious old bards-bards who very probably owed all their talents to native genius, yet have described the exploits of heroes, the pangs of disappointment, and the meltings of love, with such fine strokes of nature-that their very names (O how mortifying to a bard's vanity!) are now "buried among the wreck of things which were."
O ye illustrious names unknown! who could feel so strongly and describe so well: the last, the meanest of the muses' train-one who, though far inferior to your flights, yet eyes [321]your path, and with trembling wing would sometimes soar after you-a poor rustic bard unknown, pays this sympathetic pang to your memory! Some of you tell us, with all the charms of verse, that you have been unfortunate in the world-unfortunate in love: he, too, has felt the loss of his little fortune, the loss of friends, and, worse than all, the loss of the woman he adored. Like you, all his consolation was his muse: she taught him in rustic measures to complain. Happy could he have done it with your strength of imagination and flow of verse! May the turf lie lightly on your bones! and may you now enjoy that solace and rest which this world rarely gives to the heart tuned to all the feelings of poesy

and love!

September.

The following fragment is done something in imitation of the manner of a noble old Scottish piece, called M'Millan's Peggy, and sings to the tune of Galla Water.-My Montgomery's Peggy was my deity for six or eight months. She had been bred (though, as the world says, without any just pretence for it) in a style of life rather elegant; but, as Vanbrugh says in one of his comedies, my "dd star found me out" there too: for though I began the affair merely in a gaitié de cœur, or, to tell the truth, which will scarcely be believed, a vanity of showing my parts in courtship, particularly my abilities at a billet-doux, which I always piqued myself upon, made me lay siege to her; and when, as I always do in my foolish gallantries, I had fettered myself into a very warm affection for her, she told me one day, in a flag of truce, that her fortress had been for some time before the rightful property of another; but, with the greatest friendship and politeness, she offered me every allegiance except actual possession. I found out afterwards that what she told me of a pre-engagement was really true; but it cost me some heart-aches to get rid of the affair.

I have even tried to imitate in this extempore thing that irregularity in the rhymes, which, when judiciously done, has such a fine effect on the ear.

"Altho' my bed were in yon muir."[154]

September.

There is another fragment in imitation of an old Scotch song, well known among the country ingle-sides.-I cannot tell the name, neither of the song nor the tune, but they are in fine unison with one another.-By the way, these old Scottish airs are so nobly sentimental, that when one would compose to them, to "south the tune," as our Scotch phrase is, over and over, is the readiest way to catch the inspiration, and raise the bard into that glorious enthusiasm so strongly characteristic of our old Scotch poetry. I shall here set down one verse of the piece mentioned above, both to mark the song and tune I mean, and likewise as a debt I owe to the author, as the repeating of that verse has lighted up my flame a thousand times:-

When clouds in skies do come together To hide the brightness of the sun, There will surely be some pleasant weather When a' their storms are past and gone.[155]

Though fickle fortune has deceived me, She promis'd fair and perform'd but ill; Of mistress, friends, and wealth bereav'd me, Yet I bear a heart shall support me still.

I'll act with prudence as far as I'm able, But if success I must never find, Then come misfortune, I bid thee welcome, I'll meet thee with an undaunted mind.

The above was an extempore, under the pressure of a heavy train of misfortunes, which, indeed, threatened to undo me altogether. It was just at the close of that dreadful period mentioned already, and though the weather has brightened up a little with me, yet there has always been since a tempest brewing round me in the grim sky of futurity, which I pretty plainly see will some time or other, perhaps ere long, overwhelm me, and drive me into some doleful dell, to pine in solitary, squalid wretchedness.-However, as I hope my poor country muse, who, all rustic, awkward, and unpolished as she is, has more charms for me than any other of the pleasures of life beside-as I hope she will not then desert me, I may even then learn to be, if not happy, at least easy, and south a sang to soothe my misery.

'Twas at the same time I set about composing an air in the old Scotch style.-I am not musical [322]scholar enough to prick down my tune properly, so it can never see the light, and perhaps 'tis no great matter; but the following were the verses I composed to suit it:-

O raging fortune's withering blast Has laid my leaf full low, O![156]

The tune consisted of three parts, so that the above verses just went through the whole air.

October, 1785.

If ever any young man, in the vestibule of the world, chance to throw his eye over these pages, let him pay a warm attention to the following observations, as I assure him they are the fruit of a poor devil's dear-bought experience.-I have literally, like that great poet and great gallant, and by consequence, that great fool, Solomon, "turned my eyes to behold madness and folly." Nay, I have, with all the ardour of a lively, fanciful, and whimsical imagination, accompanied with a warm, feeling, poetic heart, shaken hands with their intoxicating friendship.

In the first place, let my pupil, as he tenders his own peace, keep up a regular, warm intercourse with the Deity. * * * *

This is all worth quoting in my MSS., and more than all.

R. B.

FOOTNOTES:

[145] See Songs and Ballads, No. I.

[146] See Winter. A Dirge. Poem I.

[147] Song XIV.

[148] Poem IX.

[149] Song V

[150] Song XVII.

[151] Poem X.

[152] Poem XI.

[153] "The Mill, Mill, O," is by Allan Ramsay.

[154] Song VIII.

[155] Alluding to the misfortunes he feelingly laments before this verse.

(This is the author's note.)
[156] Song II.

IX.

TO MR. JAMES BURNESS,
MONTROSE.
[The elder Burns, whose death this letter intimates, lies buried in the kirk-yard of Alloway, with a tombstone recording his worth.]
Lochlea, 17th Feb. 1784.
Dear Cousin,
I would have returned you my thanks for your kind favour of the 13th of December sooner, had it not been that I waited to give you an account of that melancholy event, which, for some time past, we have from day to day expected.
On the 13th current I lost the best of fathers. Though, to be sure, we have had long warning of the impending stroke; still the feelings of nature claim their part, and I cannot recollect the tender endearments and parental lessons of the best of friends and ablest of instructors, without feeling what perhaps the calmer dictates of reason would partly condemn.
I hope my father's friends in your country will not let their connexion in this place die with him. For my part I shall ever with pleasure-with pride, acknowledge my connexion with those who were allied by the ties of blood and friendship to a man whose memory I shall ever honour and revere.
I expect, therefore, my dear Sir, you will not neglect any opportunity of letting me hear from you, which will very much oblige,
My dear Cousin, yours sincerely,
R. B.

X.

TO JAMES BURNESS,
MONTROSE.
[Mrs. Buchan, the forerunner in extravagance and absurdity of Joanna Southcote, after attempting to fix her tent among the hills of the west and the vales of the Nith, finally set up her staff at Auchengibbert-Hill, in Galloway, where she lectured her followers, and held out hopes of their reaching the stars, even in this life. She died early: one or two of her people, as she called them, survived till within these half-dozen years.]
Mossgiel, August, 1784.
We have been surprised with one of the most extraordinary phenomena in the moral world which, I dare say, had happened in the course of this half century. We have had a party of Presbytery relief, as they call themselves,

for some time in this country. A pretty thriving society of them has been in the burgh of Irvine for some years past, till about two years ago, a Mrs. Buchan from Glasgow came among them, and began to spread some fanatical notions of religion among them, and, in a short time, made many converts; and, among others, their preacher, Mr. Whyte, who, upon that account, has been suspended and formally deposed by his brethren. He continued, however, to preach in private to his party, and was supported, both he and their spiritual mother, as they affect to call old Buchan, by the contributions of the rest, several of whom were in good circumstances; till, in spring last, the populace rose and mobbed Mrs. Buchan, and put her out of the town; on which all her followers voluntarily quitted the place likewise, and with such precipitation, that many of them never shut their [323] doors behind them; one left a washing on the green, another a cow bellowing at the crib without food, or anybody to mind her, and after several stages, they are fixed at present in the neighbourhood of Dumfries. Their tenets are a strange jumble of enthusiastic jargon; among others, she pretends to give them the Holy Ghost by breathing on them, which she does with postures and practices that are scandalously indecent; they have likewise disposed of all their effects, and hold a community of goods, and live nearly an idle life, carrying on a great farce of pretended devotion in barns and woods, where they lodge and lie all together, and hold likewise a community of women, as it is another of their tenets that they can commit no mortal sin. I am personally acquainted with most of them, and I can assure you the above mentioned are facts.

This, my dear Sir, is one of the many instances of the folly of leaving the guidance of sound reason and common sense in matters of religion.

Whenever we neglect or despise these sacred monitors, the whimsical notions of a perturbated brain are taken for the immediate influences of the Deity, and the wildest fanaticism, and the most inconstant absurdities, will meet with abettors and converts. Nay, I have often thought, that the more out-of-the-way and ridiculous the fancies are, if once they are sanctified under the sacred name of religion, the unhappy mistaken votaries are the more firmly glued to them.

R. B.

XI.

TO MISS.

[This has generally been printed among the early letters of Burns. Cromek thinks that the person addressed was the "Peggy" of the Common-place Book. This is questioned by Robert Chambers, who, however, leaves both name and date unsettled.]

My dear Countrywoman,

I am so impatient to show you that I am once more at peace with you, that I send you the book I mentioned directly, rather than wait the uncertain time of my seeing you. I am afraid I have mislaid or lost Collins' Poems, which I promised to Miss Irvin. If I can find them, I will forward them by you; if not, you must apologize for me.

I know you will laugh at it when I tell you that your piano and you together have played the deuce somehow about my heart. My breast has been widowed these many months, and I thought myself proof against the fascinating witchcraft; but I am afraid you will "feelingly convince me what I am." I say, I am afraid, because I am not sure what is the matter with me. I have one miserable bad symptom; when you whisper, or look kindly to another, it gives me a draught of damnation. I have a kind of wayward wish to be with you ten minutes by yourself, though what I would say, Heaven above knows, for I am sure I know not. I have no formed design in all this; but just, in the nakedness of my heart, write you down a mere matter-of-fact story. You may perhaps give yourself airs of distance on this, and that will completely cure me; but I wish you would not: just let us meet, if you please, in the old beaten way of friendship.

I will not subscribe myself your humble servant, for that is a phrase, I think at least fifty miles off from the heart; but I will conclude with sincerely wishing that the Great Protector of innocence may shield you from the barbed dart of calumny, and hand you by the covert snare of deceit.

R. B.

XII.

TO MR. JOHN RICHMOND,
OF EDINBURGH.

[John Richmond, writer, one of the poet's Mauchline friends, to whom we are indebted for much valuable information concerning Burns and his productions-Connel was the Mauchline carrier.]

Mossgiel, Feb. 17, 1786.

My dear Sir,

I have not time at present to upbraid you for your silence and neglect; I shall only say I received yours with great pleasure. I have enclosed you a piece of rhyming ware for your perusal. I have been very busy with the muses since I saw you, and have composed, among several others, "The Ordination," a poem on Mr. M'Kinlay's being called to Kilmarnock; "Scotch Drink," a poem; "The Cotter's Saturday Night;" "An Address to the Devil," andc. I have likewise completed my poem on the "Dogs," but have not shown it to the world. My chief patron now is Mr. Aiken, in Ayr, who is pleased to express great approbation of my works. Be so good as send me Fergusson, by[324] Connel, and I will remit you the money. I have no news to acquaint you with about Mauchline, they are just going on in the old way. I have some very important news with respect to myself, not the most agreeable-news that I am sure you cannot guess, but I shall give you the particulars another time. I am extremely happy with Smith; he is the only friend I have now in Mauchline. I can scarcely forgive your long neglect of me, and I beg you will let me hear from you regularly by Connel. If you would act your part as a friend, I am sure neither good nor bad fortune should strange of alter me. Excuse haste, as I got yours but yesterday.

I am, my dear Sir,

Yours,

R. B.

XIII.

TO MR. JOHN KENNEDY,

DUMFRIES HOUSE.

[Who the John Kennedy was to whom Burns addressed this note, enclosing "The Cotter's Saturday night," it is now, perhaps, vain to inquire: the Kennedy to whom Mr. Cobbett introduces us was a Thomas-perhaps a relation.]

Mossgiel, 3d March, 1786.

Sir,

I have done myself the pleasure of complying with your request in sending you my Cottager.-If you have a leisure minute, I should be glad you would copy it, and return me either the original or the transcript, as I have not a copy of it by me, and I have a friend who wishes to see it.

"Now, Kennedy, if foot or horse."[157]

Robt. Burness.

FOOTNOTES:

[157] Poem LXXV.

XIV.

TO MR. ROBERT MUIR,

KILMARNOCK.

[The Muirs-there were two brothers-were kind and generous patrons of the poet. They subscribed for half-a-hundred copies of the Kilmarnock edition of his works, and befriended him when friends were few.]

Mossgiel, 20th March, 1786.

Dear Sir,

I am heartily sorry I had not the pleasure of seeing you as you returned through Mauchline; but as I was engaged, I could not be in town before the evening.

I here enclose you my "Scotch Drink," and "may thefollow with a blessing for your edification." I hope, some time before we hear the gowk, to have the pleasure of seeing you at Kilmarnock, when I intend we shall have a gill between us, in a mutchkin-stoup; which will be a great comfort and consolation to,

Dear Sir,

Your humble servant,

Robt. Burness.

XV.

TO MR. AIKEN.

[Robert Aiken, the gentleman to whom the "Cotter's Saturday Night" is inscribed, is also introduced in the "Brigs of Ayr." This is the last letter to which Burns seems to have subscribed his name in the spelling of his ancestors.]

Mossgiel, 3d April, 1786.

Dear Sir,

I received your kind letter with double pleasure, on account of the second flattering instance of Mrs. C.'s notice and approbation, I assure you I

"Turn out the burnt o' my shin,"

as the famous Ramsay, of jingling memory, says, at such a patroness. Present her my most grateful acknowledgment in your very best manner of telling truth. I have inscribed the following stanza on the blank leaf of Miss More's Work:-[158]

My proposals for publishing I am just going to send to press. I expect to hear from you by the first opportunity.

I am ever, dear Sir,

Yours,

Robt. Burness.

FOOTNOTES:

[158] See Poem LXXVIII.

XVI.

TO MR. M'WHINNIE,

WRITER, AYR.

[Mr. M'Whinnie obtained for Burns several subscriptions for the first

edition of his Poems, of which this note enclosed the proposals.][325]
Mossgiel, 17th April, 1786.

It is injuring some hearts, those hearts that elegantly bear the impression of the good Creator, to say to them you give them the trouble of obliging a friend; for this reason, I only tell you that I gratify my own feelings in requesting your friendly offices with respect to the enclosed, because I know it will gratify yours to assist me in it to the utmost of your power.

I have sent you four copies, as I have no less than eight dozen, which is a great deal more than I shall ever need.

Be sure to remember a poor poet militant in your prayers. He looks forward with fear and trembling to that, to him, important moment which stamps the die with-with-with, perhaps, the eternal disgrace of,

My dear Sir,
Your humble,
afflicted, tormented,
Robert Burns.

XVII.

TO MR. JOHN KENNEDY.

["The small piece," the very last of his productions, which the poet enclosed in this letter, was "The Mountain Daisy," called in the manuscript more properly "The Gowan."]

Mossgiel, 20th April, 1786.

Sir,

By some neglect in Mr. Hamilton, I did not hear of your kind request for a subscription paper 'till this day. I will not attempt any acknowledgment for this, nor the manner in which I see your name in Mr. Hamilton's subscription list. Allow me only to say, Sir, I feel the weight of the debt.

I have here likewise enclosed a small piece, the very latest of my productions. I am a good deal pleased with some sentiments myself, as they are just the native querulous feelings of a heart, which, as the elegantly melting Gray says, "melancholy has marked for her own."

Our race comes on a-pace; that much-expected scene of revelry and mirth; but to me it brings no joy equal to that meeting with which your last flattered the expectation of,

Sir,
Your indebted humble servant,
R. B.

XVIII.

TO MON. JAMES SMITH,

MAUCHLINE.
[James Smith, of whom Burns said he was small of stature, but large of soul, kept at that time a draper's shop in Mauchline, and was comrade to the poet in many a wild adventure.]
Monday Morning, Mossgiel, 1786.
My Dear Sir,
I went to Dr. Douglas yesterday, fully resolved to take the opportunity of Captain Smith: but I found the Doctor with a Mr. and Mrs. White, both Jamaicans, and they have deranged my plans altogether. They assure him that to send me from Savannah la Mar to Port Antonio will cost my master, Charles Douglas, upwards of fifty pounds; besides running the risk of throwing myself into a pleuritic fever, in consequence of hard travelling in the sun. On these accounts, he refuses sending me with Smith, but a vessel sails from Greenock the first of September, right for the place of my destination. The Captain of her is an intimate friend of Mr. Gavin Hamilton's, and as good a fellow as heart could wish: with him I am destined to go. Where I shall shelter, I know not, but I hope to weather the storm. Perish the drop of blood of mine that fears them! I know their worst, and am prepared to meet it;-
"I'll laugh an' sing, an' shake my leg, As lang's I dow."
On Thursday morning, if you can muster as much self-denial as to be out of bed about seven o'clock, I shall see you, as I ride through to Cumnock. After all, Heaven bless the sex! I feel there is still happiness for me among them:
"O woman, lovely woman! Heaven design'd you To temper man!-we had been brutes without you."[159]
R. B.

FOOTNOTES:

[159] Otway. Venice Preserved.

XIX.

TO MR. JOHN KENNEDY.
[Burns was busy in a two-fold sense at present: he was seeking patrons in every quarter for his contemplated volume, and was composing for it some of his most exquisite poetry.]
Mossgiel, 16 May, 1796.
Dear Sir,
I have sent you the above hasty copy as I promised. In about three or four weeks I shall [326]probably set the press a-going. I am much hurried at present, otherwise your diligence, so very friendly in my subscription,

should have a more lengthened acknowledgment from,
Dear Sir,
Your obliged servant,
R. B.

XX.

TO MR. DAVID BRICE.

[David Brice was a shoemaker, and shared with Smith the confidence of the poet in his love affairs. He was working in Glasgow when this letter was written.]

Mossgiel, June 12, 1786.

Dear Brice,

I received your message by G. Patterson, and as I am not very throng at present, I just write to let you know that there is such a worthless, rhyming reprobate, as your humble servant, still in the land of the living, though I can scarcely say, in the place of hope. I have no news to tell you that will give me any pleasure to mention, or you to hear.

Poor ill-advised ungrateful Armour came home on Friday last. You have heard all the particulars of that affair, and a black affair it is. What she thinks of her conduct now, I don't know; one thing I do know-she has made me completely miserable. Never man loved, or rather adored a woman more than I did her; and, to confess a truth between you and me, I do still love her to distraction after all, though I won't tell her so if I were to see her, which I don't want to do. My poor dear unfortunate Jean! how happy have I been in thy arms! It is not the losing her that makes me so unhappy, but for her sake I feel most severely: I foresee she is in the road to, I am afraid, eternal ruin. * * * *

May Almighty God forgive her ingratitude and perjury to me, as I from my very soul forgive her: and may his grace be with her and bless her in all her future life! I can have no nearer idea of the place of eternal punishment than what I have felt in my own breast on her account. I have tried often to forget her; I have run into all kinds of dissipation and riots, mason-meetings, drinking matches, and other mischief, to drive her out of my head, but all in vain. And now for a grand cure; the ship is on her way home that is to take me out to Jamaica; and then, farewell dear old Scotland! and farewell dear ungrateful Jean! for never never will I see you more.

You will have heard that I am going to commence poet in print; and to morrow my works go to the press. I expect it will be a volume of about two hundred pages-it is just the last foolish action I intend to do; and then turn a wise man as fast as possible.

Believe me to be, dear Brice,
Your friend and well-wisher,

R. B.

XXI.

TO MR. ROBERT AIKEN.

[This letter was written under great distress of mind. That separation which Burns records in "The Lament," had, unhappily, taken place between him and Jean Armour, and it would appear, that for a time at least a coldness ensued between the poet and the patron, occasioned, it is conjectured, by that fruitful subject of sorrow and disquiet. The letter, I regret to say, is not wholly here.]

[Ayrshire, 1786.]

Sir,

I was with Wilson, my printer, t'other day, and settled all our by-gone matters between us. After I had paid him all demands, I made him the offer of the second edition, on the hazard of being paid out of the first and readiest, which he declines. By his account, the paper of a thousand copies would cost me about twenty-seven pounds, and the printing about fifteen or sixteen: he offers to agree to this for the printing, if I will advance for the paper, but this, you know, is out of my power; so farewell hopes of a second edition till I grow rich! an epoch which I think will arrive at the payment of the British national debt.

There is scarcely anything hurts me so much in being disappointed of my second edition, as not having it in my power to show my gratitude to Mr. Ballantyne, by publishing my poem of "The Brigs of Ayr." I would detest myself as a wretch, if I thought I were capable in a very long life of forgetting the honest, warm, and tender delicacy with which he enters into my interests. I am sometimes pleased with myself in my greateful sensations; but I believe, on the whole, I have very little merit in it, as my gratitude is not a virtue, the consequence of reflection; but sheerly the instinctive emotion of my heart, too inattentive to allow worldly maxims and views to settle into selfish habits.[327] I have been feeling all the various rotations and movements within, respecting the excise. There are many things plead strongly against it; the uncertainty of getting soon into business; the consequences of my follies, which may perhaps make it impracticable for me to stay at home; and besides I have for some time been pining under secret wretchedness, from causes which you pretty well know-the pang of disappointment, the sting of pride, with some wandering stabs of remorse, which never fail to settle on my vitals like vultures, when attention is not called away by the calls of society, or the vagaries of the muse. Even in the hour of social mirth, my gayety is the madness of an intoxicated criminal under the hands of the executioner. All these reasons urge me to go abroad, and to all these reasons I have only one answer-the feelings of a father. This, in the present mood I am in, overbalances everything that can be laid in the scale against it. * * * *

You may perhaps think it an extravagant fancy, but it is a sentiment which strikes home to my very soul: though sceptical in some points of our current belief, yet, I think, I have every evidence for the reality of a life beyond the stinted bourne of our present existence; if so, then, how should I, in the presence of that tremendous Being, the Author of existence, how should I meet the reproaches of those who stand to me in the dear relation of children, whom I deserted in the smiling innocency of helpless infancy? O, thou great unknown Power!-thou almighty God! who has lighted up reason in my breast, and blessed me with immortality!-I have frequently wandered from that order and regularity necessary for the perfection of thy works, yet thou hast never left me nor forsaken me! * * * *

Since I wrote the foregoing sheet, I have seen something of the storm of mischief thickening over my folly-devoted head. Should you, my friends, my benefactors, be successful in your applications for me, perhaps it may not be in my power, in that way, to reap the fruit of your friendly efforts. What I have written in the preceding pages, is the settled tenor of my present resolution; but should inimical circumstances forbid me closing with your kind offer, or enjoying it only threaten to entail farther misery- * * * *

To tell the truth, I have little reason for complaint; as the world, in general, has been kind to me fully up to my deserts. I was, for some time past, fast getting into the pining, distrustful snarl of the misanthrope. I saw myself alone, unlit for the struggle of life, shrinking at every rising cloud in the chance-directed atmosphere of fortune, while all defenceless I looked about in vain for a cover. It never occurred to me, at least never with the force it deserved, that this world is a busy scene, and man, a creature destined for a progressive struggle; and that, however I might possess a warm heart and inoffensive manners (which last, by the by, was rather more than I could well boast); still, more than these passive qualities, there was something to be done. When all my school-fellows and youthful compeers (those misguided few excepted who joined, to use a Gentoo phrase, the "hallachores" of the human race) were striking off with eager hope and earnest intent, in some one or other of the many paths of busy life, I was "standing idle in the market-place," or only left the chase of the butterfly from flower to flower, to hunt fancy from whim to whim. * * * *

You see, Sir, that if to know one's errors were a probability of mending them, I stand a fair chance; but according to the reverend Westminster divines, though conviction must precede conversion, it is very far from always implying it. * * * *

R. B.

XXII.

TO JOHN RICHMOND,
EDINBURGH.

[The minister who took upon him to pronounce Burns a single man, as he intimates in this letter, was the Rev. Mr. Auld, of Mauchline: that the law of the land and the law of the church were at variance on the subject no one can deny.]

Mossgiel, 9th July, 1786.

My Dear Friend,

With the sincerest grief I read your letter. You are truly a son of misfortune. I shall be extremely anxious to hear from you how your health goes on; if it is in any way re-establishing, or if Leith promises well; in short, how you feel in the inner man.

No news worth anything: only godly Bryan was in the inquisition yesterday, and half the country-side as witness against him. He still stands out steady and denying: but proof was led yesternight of circumstances highly suspi[328]cious: almost de facto one of the servant girls made faith that she upon a time rashly entered the house-to speak in your cant, "in the hour of cause."

I have waited on Armour since her return home; not from any the least view of reconciliation, but merely to ask for her health and-to you I will confess it-from a foolish hankering fondness-very ill placed indeed. The mother forbade me the house, nor did Jean show the penitence that might have been expected. However, the priest, I am informed, will give me a certificate as a single man, if I comply with the rules of the church, which for that very reason I intend to do.

I am going to put on sack-cloth and ashes this day. I am indulged so far as to appear in my own seat. Peccavi, pater, miserere mei. My book will be ready in a fortnight. If you have any subscribers, return them by Connel. The Lord stand with the righteous: amen, amen.

R. B.

XXIII.

TO JOHN BALLANTYNE,
OF AYR.

[There is a plain account in this letter of the destruction of the lines of marriage which united, as far as a civil contract in a manner civil can, the poet and Jean Armour. Aiken was consulted, and in consequence of his advice, the certificate of marriage was destroyed.]

Honoured Sir,

My proposals came to hand last night, and knowing that you would wish to

have it in your power to do me a service as early as anybody, I enclose you half a sheet of them. I must consult you, first opportunity, on the propriety of sending my quondam friend, Mr. Aiken, a copy. If he is now reconciled to my character as an honest man, I would do it with all my soul; but I would not be beholden to the noblest being ever God created, if he imagined me to be a rascal. Apropos, old Mr. Armour prevailed with him to mutilate that unlucky paper yesterday. Would you believe it? though I had not a hope, nor even a wish, to make her mine after her conduct; yet, when he told me the names were all out of the paper, my heart died within me, and he cut my veins with the news. Perdition seize her falsehood!
R. B.

XXIV.

TO MR. DAVID BRICE.
SHOEMAKER, GLASGOW.
[The letters of Burns at the sad period of his life are full of his private sorrows. Had Jean Armour been left to the guidance of her own heart, the story of her early years would have been brighter.]
Mossgiel, 17th July, 1786.
I have been so throng printing my Poems, that I could scarcely find as much time as to write to you. Poor Armour is come back again to Mauchline, and I went to call for her, and her mother forbade me the house, nor did she herself express much sorrow for what she has done. I have already appeared publicly in church, and was indulged in the liberty of standing in my own seat. I do this to get a certificate as a bachelor, which Mr. Auld has promised me. I am now fixed to go for the West Indies in October. Jean and her friends insisted much that she should stand along with me in the kirk, but the minister would not allow it, which bred a great trouble I assure you, and I am blamed as the cause of it, though I am sure I am innocent; but I am very much pleased, for all that, not to have had her company. I have no news to tell you that I remember. I am really happy to hear of your welfare, and that you are so well in Glasgow. I must certainly see you before I leave the country. I shall expect to hear from you soon, and am,
Dear Brice,
Yours,-R. B

XXV.

TO MR. JOHN RICHMOND.
[When this letter was written the poet was skulking from place to place: the merciless pack of the law had been uncoupled at his heels. Mr. Armour did

not wish to imprison, but to drive him from the country.]

Old Rome Forest, 30th July, 1786.

My dear Richmond,

My hour is now come-you and I will never meet in Britain more. I have orders within three weeks at farthest, to repair aboard the Nancy, Captain Smith, from Clyde to Jamaica, and call at Antigua. This, except to our friend Smith, whom God long preserve, is a secret about Mauchline. Would you believe it? Armour[329] has got a warrant to throw me in jail till I find security for an enormous sum. This they keep an entire secret, but I got it by a channel they little dream of; and I am wandering from one friend's house to another, and, like a true son of the gospel, "have nowhere to lay my head." I know you will pour an execration on her head, but spare the poor, ill-advised girl, for my sake; though may all the furies that rend the injured, enraged lover's bosom, await her mother until her latest hour! I write in a moment of rage, reflecting on my miserable situation-exiled, abandoned, forlorn. I can write no more-let me hear from you by the return of coach. I will write you ere I go.

I am dear Sir,

Yours, here and hereafter,

R. B.

XXVI.

TO MR. ROBERT MUIR,

KILMARNOCK.

[Burns never tried to conceal either his joys or his sorrows: he sent copies of his favorite pieces, and intimations of much that befel him to his chief friends and comrades-this brief note was made to carry double.]

Mossgiel, Friday noon.

My Friend, my Brother,

Warm recollection of an absent friend presses so hard upon my heart, that I send him the prefixed bagatelle (the Calf), pleased with the thought that it will greet the man of my bosom, and be a kind of distant language of friendship.

You will have heard that poor Armour has repaid me double. A very fine boy and a girl have awakened a thought and feelings that thrill, some with tender pressure and some with foreboding anguish, through my soul.

The poem was nearly an extemporaneous production, on a wager with Mr. Hamilton, that I would not produce a poem on the subject in a given time.

If you think it worth while, read it to Charles and Mr. W. Parker, and if they choose a copy of it, it is at their service, as they are men whose friendship I shall be proud to claim, both in this world and that which is to come.

I believe all hopes of staying at home will be abortive, but more of this

when, in the latter part of next week, you shall be troubled with a visit from,
My dear Sir,
Your most devoted,
R. B.

XXVII.

TO MRS. DUNLOP,
OF DUNLOP.

[Mrs. Dunlop was a poetess, and had the blood of the Wallaces in her veins: though she disliked the irregularities of the poet, she scorned to got into a fine moral passion about follies which could not be helped, and continued her friendship to the last of his life.]

Ayrshire, 1786.

Madam,

I am truly sorry I was not at home yesterday, when I was so much honoured with your order for my copies, and incomparably more by the handsome compliments you are pleased to pay my poetic abilities. I am fully persuaded that there is not any class of mankind so feelingly alive to the titillations of applause as the sons of Parnassus: nor is it easy to conceive how the heart of the poor bard dances with rapture, when those, whose character in life gives them a right to be polite judges, honour him with their approbation. Had you been thoroughly acquainted with me, Madam, you could not have touched my darling heart-chord more sweetly than by noticing my attempts to celebrate your illustrious ancestor, the Saviour of his Country.

"Great patriot hero! ill-requited chief!"[160]

The first book I met with in my early years, which I perused with pleasure, was, "The Life Of Hannibal;" the next was, "The History of Sir William Wallace:" for several of my earlier years I had few other authors; and many a solitary hour have I stole out, after the laborious vocations of the day, to shed a tear over their glorious, but unfortunate stories. In those boyish days I remember, in particular, being struck with that part of Wallace's story where these lines occur-

"Syne to the Leglen wood, when it was late, To make a silent and safe retreat."

I chose a fine summer Sunday, the only day my line of life allowed, and walked half a dozen [330] of miles to pay my respects to the Leglen wood, with as much devout enthusiasm as ever pilgrim did to Loretto; and, as I explored every den and dell where I could suppose my heroic countryman to have lodged, I recollect (for even then I was a rhymer) that my heart glowed with a wish to be able to make a song on him in some measure equal to his merits.

R. B.

FOOTNOTES:

[160] Thomson.

XXVIII.

TO MR. JOHN KENNEDY.

[It is a curious chapter in the life of Burns to count the number of letters which he wrote, the number of fine poems he composed, and the number of places which he visited in the unhappy summer and autumn of 1786.]

Kilmarnock, August, 1786.

My dear Sir,

Your truly facetious epistle of the 3d inst. gave me much entertainment. I was sorry I had not the pleasure of seeing you as I passed your way, but we shall bring up all our lee way on Wednesday, the 16th current, when I hope to have it in my power to call on you and take a kind, very probably a last adieu, before I go for Jamaica; and I expect orders to repair to Greenock every day.-I have at last made my public appearance, and am solemnly inaugurated into the numerous class.-Could I have got a carrier, you should have had a score of vouchers for my authorship; but now you have them, let them speak for themselves.-

Farewell, my dear friend! may guid luck hit you, And 'mang her favourites admit you! If e'er Detraction shore to smit you, May nane believe him! And ony de'il that thinks to get you, Good Lord deceive him.

R. B.

XXIX.

TO MR. JAMES BURNESS,
MONTROSE.

[The good and generous James Burness, of Montrose, was ever ready to rejoice with his cousin's success or sympathize with his sorrows, but he did not like the change which came over the old northern surname of Burness, when the bard modified it into Burns: the name now a rising one in India, is spelt Burnes.]

Mossgiel, Tuesday noon, Sept. 26, 1786.

My dear Sir,

I this moment receive yours-receive it with the honest hospitable warmth of a friend's welcome. Whatever comes from you wakens always up the better blood about my heart, which your kind little recollections of my parental friends carries as far as it will go. 'Tis there that man is blest! 'Tis there, my friend, man feels a consciousness of something within him above the trodden clod! The grateful reverence to the hoary (earthly) author of his being-the burning glow when he clasps the woman of his soul to his bosom-the tender yearnings of heart for the little angels to whom he has given existence-these nature has poured in milky streams about the human heart; and the man who never rouses them to action, by the inspiring influences of their proper objects, loses by far the most pleasurable part of his existence.

My departure is uncertain, but I do not think it will be till after harvest. I will be on very short allowance of time indeed, if I do not comply with your friendly invitation. When it will be I don't know, but if I can make my wish good, I will endeavour to drop you a line some time before. My best compliments to Mrs. ; I shouldequally mortified should I drop in when she is abroad, but of that I suppose there is little chance.

What I have wrote heaven knows; I have not time to review it; so accept of it in the beaten way of friendship. With the ordinary phrase-perhaps rather more than the ordinary sincerity,

I am, dear Sir,

Ever yours,

R. B.

XXX.

TO MISS ALEXANDER.

[This letter, Robert Chambers says, concluded with requesting Miss Alexander to allow the poet to print the song which it enclosed, in a second edition of his Poems. Her neglect in not replying to this request is a very good poetic reason for his wrath. Many of Burns's letters have been printed, it is right to say, from the rough drafts found among the poet's papers at his death. This is one.][331]

Mossgiel, 18th Nov. 1786.

Madam,

Poets are such outré beings, so much the children of wayward fancy and capricious whim, that I believe the world generally allows them a larger latitude in the laws of propriety, than the sober sons of judgment and prudence. I mention this as an apology for the liberties that a nameless stranger has taken with you in the enclosed poem, which he begs leave to present you with. Whether it has poetical merit any way worthy of the theme, I am not the proper judge; but it is the best my abilities can produce; and what to a good heart will, perhaps, be a superior grace, it is equally sincere as fervent.

The scenery was nearly taken from real life, though I dare say, Madam, you do not recollect it, as I believe you scarcely noticed the poetic reveur as he wandered by you. I had roved out as chance directed, in the favourite haunts of my muse on the banks of the Ayr, to view nature in all the gayety of the vernal year. The evening sun was flaming over the distant western hills; not a breath stirred the crimson opening blossom, or the verdant spreading leaf. It was a golden moment for a poetic heart. I listened to the feathered warblers, pouring their harmony on every hand, with a congenial kindred regard, and frequently turned out of my path, lest I should disturb their little songs, or frighten them to another station. Surely, said I to myself, he must be a wretch indeed, who, regardless of your harmonious endeavour to please him, can eye your elusive flights to discover your secret recesses, and to rob you of all the property nature gives you-your dearest comforts, your helpless nestlings. Even the hoary hawthorn twig that shot across the way, what heart at such a time but must have been interested in its welfare, and wished it preserved from the rudely-browsing cattle, or the withering eastern blast? Such was the scene,-and such the hour, when, in a corner of my prospect, I spied one of the fairest pieces of nature's workmanship that ever crowned a poetic landscape or met a poet's eye, those visionary bards excepted, who hold commerce with aërial beings! Had Calumny and Villany taken my walk, they had at that moment sworn eternal peace with such an object.

What an hour of inspiration for a poet! It would have raised plain dull historic prose into metaphor measure.

The enclosed song was the work of my return home: and perhaps it but poorly answers what might have been expected from such a scene.

I have the honour to be,

Madam,

Your most obedient and very

humble Servant,

R. B.

XXXI.

TO MRS. STEWART,

OF STAIR AND AFTON.

[Mrs. Stewart, of Stair and Afton, was the first person of note in the West who had the taste to see and feel the genius of Burns. He used to relate how his heart fluttered when he first walked into the parlour of the towers of Stair, to hear the lady's opinion of some of his songs.]

Madam,

The hurry of my preparations for going abroad has hindered me from performing my promise so soon as I intended. I have here sent you a parcel of songs, andc., which never made their appearance, except to a friend or two at most. Perhaps some of them may be no great entertainment to you, but of that I am far from being an adequate judge. The song to the tune of "Ettrick Banks" [The bonnie lass of Ballochmyle] you will easily see the impropriety of exposing much, even in manuscript. I think, myself, it has some merit: both as a tolerable description of one of nature's sweetest scenes, a July evening, and one of the finest pieces of nature's workmanship, the finest indeed we know anything of, an amiable, beautiful young woman;[161] but I have no common friend to procure me that permission, without which I would not dare to spread the copy.

I am quite aware, Madam, what task the world would assign me in this letter. The obscure bard, when any of the great condescend to take notice of him, should heap the altar with the incense of flattery. Their high ancestry, their own great and godlike qualities and actions, should be recounted with the most exaggerated description. This, Madam, is a task for which I am altogether unfit. Besides a certain disqualifying pride of heart, I know nothing of your connexions in life, and have no access to where [332] your real character is to be found-the company of your compeers: and more, I am afraid that even the most refined adulation is by no means the road to your good opinion.

One feature of your character I shall ever with grateful pleasure remember;-the reception I got when I had the honour of waiting on you at Stair. I am little acquainted with politeness, but I know a good deal of benevolence of temper and goodness of heart. Surely did those in exalted stations know how happy they could make some classes of their inferiors by condescension and affability, they would never stand so high, measuring out with every look the height of their elevation, but condescend as sweetly as did Mrs. Stewart of Stair.

R. B.

FOOTNOTES:

[161] Miss Alexander.

XXXII.

IN THE NAME OF THE NINE. AMEN.

[The song or ballad which one of the "Deil's yeld Nowte" was commanded to burn, was "Holy Willie's Prayer," it is believed. Currie interprets the "Deil's yeld Nowte," to mean old bachelors, which, if right, points to some other of his compositions, for purgation by fire. Gilbert Burns says it is a scoffing appellation sometimes given to sheriff's officers and other executors of the law.]

We, Robert Burns, by virtue of a warrant from Nature, bearing date the twenty-fifth day of January, Anno Domini one thousand seven hundred and fifty-nine,[162] Poet Laureat, and Bard in Chief, in and over the districts and countries of Kyle, Cunningham, and Carrick, of old extent, To our trusty and well-beloved William Chalmers and John M'Adam, students and practitioners in the ancient and mysterious science of confounding right and wrong.

Right Trusty:

Be it known unto you that whereas in the course of our care and watchings over the order and police of all and sundry the manufacturers, retainers, and venders of poesy; bards, poets, poetasters, rhymers, jinglers, songsters, ballad-singers, andc. andc. andc. andc., male and female-We have discovered a certain nefarious, abominable, and wicked song or ballad, a copy whereof We have here enclosed; Our Will therefore is, that Ye pitch upon and appoint the most execrable individual of that most execrable species, known by the appellation, phrase, and nick-name of The Deil's Yeld Nowte: and after having caused him to kindle a fire at the Cross of Ayr, ye shall, at noontide of the day, put into the said wretch's merciless hands the said copy of the said nefarious and wicked song, to be consumed by fire in the presence of all beholders, in abhorrence of, and terrorem to, all such compositions and composers. And this in nowise leave ye undone, but have it executed in every point as this our mandate bears, before the twenty-fourth current, when in person We hope to applaud your faithfulness and zeal.

Given at Mauchline this twentieth day of November, Anno Domini one thousand seven hundred and eighty-six.

God save the Bard!

FOOTNOTES:

[162] His birth-day.

XXXIII.

TO MR. ROBERT MUIR.

[The expedition to Edinburgh, to which this short letter alludes, was undertaken, it is needless to say, in consequence of a warm and generous commendation of the genius of Burns written by Dr. Blacklock, to the Rev. Mr. Lawrie, and communicated by Gavin Hamilton to the poet, when he was on the wing for the West Indies.]

Mossgiel, 18th Nov., 1786.

My dear Sir,

Enclosed you have "Tam Samson," as I intend to print him. I am thinking for my Edinburgh expedition on Monday or Tuesday, come se'ennight, for pos. I will see you on Tuesday first.

I am ever,
Your much indebted,
R. B.

XXXIV.

TO DR. MACKENZIE,
MAUCHLINE;
ENCLOSING THE VERSES ON DINING WITH LORD DAER.
[To the kind and venerable Dr. Mackenzie, the poet was indebted for some valuable friendships, and his biographers for some valuable information respecting the early days of Burns.]
Wednesday Morning.
Dear Sir,
I never spent an afternoon among great folks with half that pleasure as when, in company with you, I had the honour of paying my devoirs to the plain, honest, worthy man, the[333] professor. [Dugald Stewart.] I would be delighted to see him perform acts of kindness and friendship, though I were not the object; he does it with such a grace. I think his character, divided into ten parts, stands thus-four parts Socrates-four parts Nathaniel-and two parts Shakspeare's Brutus.
The foregoing verses were really extempore, but a little corrected since. They may entertain you a little with the help of that partiality with which you are so good as to favour the performances of,
Dear Sir,
Your very humble servant,
R. B.

XXXV.

TO GAVIN HAMILTON, ESQ.,
MAUCHLINE.
[From Gavin Hamilton Burns and his brother took the farm of Mossgiel: the landlord was not slow in perceiving the genius of Robert: he had him frequently at his table, and the poet repaid this notice by verse not likely soon to die.]
Edinburgh, Dec. 7th, 1786.
Honoured Sir,
I have paid every attention to your commands, but can only say what perhaps you will have heard before this reach you, that Muirkirklands were bought by a John Gordon, W.S., but for whom I know not; Mauchlands, Haugh, Miln, andc., by a Frederick Fotheringham, supposed to be for Ballochmyle Laird, and Adamhill and Shawood were bought for Oswald's

folks.-This is so imperfect an account, and will be so late ere it reach you, that were it not to discharge my conscience I would not trouble you with it; but after all my diligence I could make it no sooner nor better.

For my own affairs, I am in a fair way of becoming as eminent as Thomas à Kempis or John Bunyan; and you may expect henceforth to see my birth-day inserted among the wonderful events, in the Poor Robin's and Aberdeen Almanacks, along with the Black Monday, and the battle of Bothwell bridge.-My Lord Glencairn and the Dean of Faculty, Mr. H. Erskine, have taken me under their wing; and by all probability I shall soon be the tenth worthy, and the eighth wise man in the world. Through my lord's influence it is inserted in the records of the Caledonian Hunt, that they universally, one and all, subscribe for the second edition.-My subscription bills come out to-morrow, and you shall have some of them next post.-I have met, in Mr. Dalrymple, of Orangefield, what Solomon emphatically calls "a friend that sticketh closer than a brother."-The warmth with which he interests himself in my affairs is of the same enthusiastic kind which you, Mr. Aiken, and the few patrons that took notice of my earlier poetic days, showed for the poor unlucky devil of a poet.

I always remember Mrs. Hamilton and Miss Kennedy in my poetic prayers, but you both in prose and verse.

May cauld ne'er catch you but a hap, Nor hunger but in plenty's lap! Amen!

R. B.

XXXVI.

TO JOHN BALLANTYNE, ESQ.,
BANKER, AYR.

[This is the second letter which Burns wrote, after his arrival in Edinburgh, and it is remarkable because it distinctly imputes his introduction to the Earl of Glencairn, to Dalrymple, of Orangefield; though he elsewhere says this was done by Mr. Dalzell;-perhaps both those gentlemen had a hand in this good deed.]

Edinburgh, 13th Dec. 1786.

My Honoured Friend,

I would not write you till I could have it in my power to give you some account of myself and my matters, which, by the by, is often no easy task.-I arrived here on Tuesday was se'ennight, and have suffered ever since I came to town with a miserable headache and stomach complaint, but am now a good deal better.-I have found a worthy warm friend in Mr. Dalrymple, of Orangefield, who introduced me to Lord Glencairn, a man whose worth and brotherly kindness to me, I shall remember when time shall be no more.-By his interest it is passed in the "Caledonian Hunt," and entered in their books, that they are to take each a copy of the second edition, for which they are to pay one guinea.-I have been introduced to a good many of the noblesse, but my avowed patrons and patronesses are the Duchess of Gordon-the Countess of Glencairn, with my Lord, and Lady Betty[163]-the Dean of Faculty-Sir John Whitefoord-I [334] have likewise warm friends among the literati; Professors Stewart, Blair, and Mr. Mackenzie-the Man of Feeling.-An unknown hand left ten guineas for the Ayrshire bard with Mr. Sibbald, which I got.-I since have discovered my generous unknown friend to be Patrick Miller, Esq., brother to the Justice Clerk; and drank a glass of claret with him, by invitation, at his own house, yesternight. I am nearly agreed with Creech to print my book, and I suppose I will begin on Monday. I will send a subscription bill or two, next post; when I intend writing my first kind patron, Mr. Aiken. I saw his son to-day, and he is very well.

Dugald Stewart, and some of my learned friends, put me in the periodical paper, called The Lounger,[164] a copy of which I here enclose you.-I was, Sir, when I was first honoured with your notice, too obscure; now I tremble lest I should be ruined by being dragged too suddenly into the glare of polite and learned observation.

I shall certainly, my ever honoured patron, write you an account of my every step; and better health and more spirits may enable me to make it something better than this stupid matter-of-fact epistle.

I have the honour to be,

Good Sir,

Your ever grateful humble servant,

R. B.

If any of my friends write me, my direction is, care of Mr. Creech, bookseller.

FOOTNOTES:

[163] Lady Betty Cunningham.

[164] The paper here alluded to, was written by Mr. Mackenzie, the celebrated author of "The Man of Feeling."

XXXVII.

TO MR. ROBERT MUIR.

["Muir, thy weaknesses," says Burns, writing of this gentleman to Mrs. Dunlop, "thy weaknesses were the aberrations of human nature; but thy heart glowed with everything generous, manly, and noble: and if ever emanation from the All-good Being animated a human form, it was thine."]

Edinburgh, Dec. 20th, 1786.

My dear Friend,

I have just time for the carrier, to tell you that I received your letter; of which I shall say no more but what a lass of my acquaintance said of her bastard wean; she said she "did na ken wha was the father exactly, but she suspected it was some o' the bonny blackguard smugglers, for it was like them." So I only say your obliging epistle was like you. I enclose you a parcel of subscription bills. Your affair of sixty copies is also like you; but it would not be like me to comply.

Your friend's notion of my life has put a crotchet in my head of sketching it in some future epistle to you. My compliments to Charles and Mr. Parker.

R. B.

XXXVIII.

TO MR. WILLIAM CHALMERS,

WRITER, AYR.

[William Chalmers drew out the assignment of the copyright of Burns's Poems, in favour of his brother Gilbert, and for the maintenance of his natural child, when engaged to go to the West Indies, in the autumn of 1786.]

Edinburgh, Dec. 27, 1786.

My dear Friend,

I confess I have sinned the sin for which there is hardly any forgiveness-ingratitude to friendship-in not writing you sooner; but of all men living, I had intended to have sent you an entertaining letter; and by all the plodding, stupid powers, that in nodding, conceited majesty, preside over the dull routine of business-a heavily solemn oath this!-I am, and have been, ever since I came to Edinburgh, as unfit to write a letter of humour, as to write a commentary on the Revelation of St. John the Divine, who was banished to the Isle of Patmos, by the cruel and bloody Domitian, son to Vespasian and brother to Titus, both emperors of Rome, and who was himself an emperor, and raised the second or third persecution, I forget which, against the Christians, and after throwing the said Apostle John, brother to the Apostle James, commonly called James the Greater, to distinguish him from another James, who was, on some account or other, known by the name of James the Less-after throwing him into a cauldron of boiling oil, from which he was miraculously preserved, he banished the poor son of Zebedee to a desert island in the Archipelago, where he was gifted with the second sight, and saw as many wild beasts as I have seen since I came to Edinburgh; which, a circumstance not[335] very uncommon in story-telling, brings me back to where I set out.

To make you some amends for what, before you reach this paragraph, you will have suffered, I enclose you two poems I have carded and spun since I past Glenbuck.

One blank in the address to Edinburgh-"Fair B," is heavenly Miss Burnet, daughter to Lord Monboddo, at whose house I have had the honour to be more than once. There has not been anything nearly like her in all the combinations of beauty, grace, and goodness the great Creator has formed since Milton's Eve on the first day of her existence.
My direction is-care of Andrew Bruce, merchant, Bridge-street.
R. B.

XXXIX.

TO THE EARL OF EGLINTOUN.
[Archibald Montgomery, eleventh Earl of Eglinton, and Colonel Hugh Montgomery, of Coilsfield, who succeeded his brother in his titles and estates, were patrons, and kind ones, of Burns.]
Edinburgh, January 1787.
My Lord,
As I have but slender pretensions to philosophy, I cannot rise to the exalted ideas of a citizen of the world, but have all those national prejudices, which I believe glow peculiarly strong in the breast of a Scotchman. There is scarcely anything to which I am so feelingly alive as the honour and welfare of my country: and, as a poet, I have no higher enjoyment than singing her sons and daughters. Fate had cast my station in the veriest shades of life; but never did a heart pant more ardently than mine to be distinguished; though, till very lately, I looked in vain on every side for a ray of light. It is easy then to guess how much I was gratified with the countenance and approbation of one of my country's most illustrious sons, when Mr. Wauchope called on me yesterday on the part of your lordship. Your munificence, my lord, certainly deserves my very grateful acknowledgments; but your patronage is a bounty peculiarly suited to my feelings. I am not master enough of the etiquette of life to know, whether there be not some impropriety in troubling your lordship with my thanks, but my heart whispered me to do it. From the emotions of my inmost soul I do it. Selfish ingratitude I hope I am incapable of; and mercenary servility, I trust, I shall ever have so much honest pride as to detest.
R. B.

XL.

TO MR. GAVIN HAMILTON.
[This letter was first published by Hubert Chambers, who considered it as closing the enquiry, "was Burns a married man?" No doubt Burns thought himself unmarried, and the Rev. Mr. Auld was of the same opinion, since he offered him a certificate that he was single: but no opinion of priest or

lawyer, including the disclamation of Jean Armour, and the belief of Burns, could have, in my opinion, barred the claim of the children to full legitimacy, according to the law of Scotland.]

Edinburgh, Jan. 7, 1787.

To tell the truth among friends, I feel a miserable blank in my heart, with the want of her, and I don't think I shall ever meet with so delicious an armful again. She has her faults; and so have you and I; and so has everybody:

Their tricks and craft hae put me daft; They've ta'en me in and a' that; But clear your decks, and here's the sex, I like the jads for a' that. For a' that and a' that, And twice as muckle's a' that.

I have met with a very pretty girl, a Lothian farmer's daughter, whom I have almost persuaded to accompany me to the west country, should I ever return to settle there. By the bye, a Lothian farmer is about an Ayrshire squire of the lower kind; and I had a most delicious ride from Leith to her house yesternight, in a hackney-coach with her brother and two sisters, and brother's wife. We had dined altogether at a common friend's house in Leith, and danced, drank, and sang till late enough. The night was dark, the claret had been good, and I thirsty. * * * * *

R. B.

XLI.

TO JOHN BALLANTYNE, ESQ.

[This letter contains the first intimation that the poet desired to resume the labours of the farmer. The old[336] saw of "Willie Gaw's Skate," he picked up from his mother, who had a vast collection of such sayings.]

Edinburgh, Jan. 14, 1787.

My Honoured Friend,

It gives me a secret comfort to observe in myself that I am not yet so far gone as Willie Gaw's Skate, "past redemption;" for I have still this favourable symptom of grace, that when my conscience, as in the case of this letter, tells me I am leaving something undone that I ought to do, it teases me eternally till I do it.

I am still "dark as was Chaos"[165] in respect to futurity. My generous friend, Mr. Patrick Miller, has been talking with me about a lease of some farm or other in an estate called Dalswinton, which he has lately bought, near Dumfries. Some life-rented embittering recollections whisper me that I will be happier anywhere than in my old neighbourhood, but Mr. Miller is no judge of land; and though I dare say he means to favour me, yet he may give me, in his opinion, an advantageous bargain that may ruin me. I am to take a tour by Dumfries as I return, and have promised to meet Mr. Miller on his lands some time in May.

I went to a mason-lodge yesternight, where the most Worshipful Grand Master Charters, and all the Grand Lodge of Scotland visited. The meeting was numerous and elegant; all the different lodges about town were present, in all their pomp. The Grand Master, who presided with great solemnity and honour to himself as a gentleman and mason, among other general toasts, gave "Caledonia, and Caledonia's Bard, Brother Burns," which rung through the whole assembly with multiplied honours and repeated acclamations. As I had no idea such a thing would happen, I was downright thunderstruck, and, trembling in every nerve, made the best return in my power. Just as I had finished, some of the grand officers said, so loud that I could hear, with a most comforting accent, "Very well indeed!" which set me something to rights again.

I have to-day corrected my 152d page. My best good wishes to Mr. Aiken.

I am ever,

Dear Sir,

Your much indebted humble servant,

R. B.

FOOTNOTES:

[165] See Blair's Grave. This was a favourite quotation with Burns.

XLII.

TO JOHN BALLANTYNE.

[I have not hesitated to insert all letters which show what Burns was musing on as a poet, or planning as a man.]

January , 1787.

While here I sit, sad and solitary by the side of a fire in a little country inn, and drying my wet clothes, in pops a poor fellow of sodger, and tells me he is going to Ayr. By heavens! say I to myself, with a tide of good spirits which the magic of that sound, Auld Toon o' Ayr, conjured up, I will sent my last song to Mr. Ballantyne. Here it is-

Ye flowery banks o' bonnie Doon, How can ye blume sae fair; How can ye chant, ye little birds, And I sae fu' o' care![166]

FOOTNOTES:

[166] Song CXXXI.

XLIII.

TO MRS. DUNLOP.

[The friendship of Mrs. Dunlop purified, while it strengthened the national prejudices of Burns.]
Edinburgh, 15th January, 1787.
Madam,
Yours of the 9th current, which I am this moment honoured with, is a deep reproach to me for ungrateful neglect. I will tell you the real truth, for I am miserably awkward at a fib-I wished to have written to Dr. Moore before I wrote to you; but though every day since I received yours of December 30th, the idea, the wish to write to him has constantly pressed on my thoughts, yet I could not for my soul set about it. I know his fame and character, and I am one of "the sons of little men." To write him a mere matter-of-fact affair, like a merchant's order, would be disgracing the little character I have; and to write the author of "The View of Society and Manners" a letter of sentiment-I declare every artery runs cold at the thought. I shall try, however, to write to him to-morrow or next day. His kind interposition in my behalf I have already experienced, as a gentleman waited on me the other day, on the part of Lord Eglintoun, with ten guineas, by[337] way of subscription for two copies of my next edition.
The word you object to in the mention I have made of my glorious countryman and your immortal ancestor, is indeed borrowed from Thomson; but it does not strike me us an improper epithet. I distrusted my own judgment on your finding fault with it, and applied for the opinion of some of the literati here, who honour me with their critical strictures, and they all allow it to be proper. The song you ask I cannot recollect, and I have not a copy of it. I have not composed anything on the great Wallace, except what you have, seen in print; and the enclosed, which I will print in this edition. You will see I have mentioned some others of the name. When I composed my "Vision" long ago, I had attempted a description of Koyle, of which the additional stanzas are a part, as it originally stood. My heart glows with a wish to be able to do justice to the merits of the "Saviour of his Country," which sooner or later I shall at least attempt.
You are afraid I shall grow intoxicated with my prosperity as a poet; alas! Madam, I know myself and the world too well. I do not mean any airs of affected modesty; I am willing to believe that my abilities deserve some notice; but in a most enlightened, informed age and nation, when poetry is and has been the study of man of the first natural genius, aided with all the powers of polite learning, polite books, and polite company-to be dragged forth to the full glare of learned and polite observation, with all my imperfections of awkward rusticity and crude unpolished ideas on my head-I assure you, Madam, I do not dissemble when I tell you I tremble for the consequences. The novelty of a poet in my obscure situation, without any of those advantages which are reckoned necessary for that character, at least at this time of day, has raised a partial tide of public notice which has borne

me to a height, where I am absolutely, feelingly certain, my abilities are inadequate to support me; and too surely do I see that time when the same tide will leave me, and recede, perhaps, as far below the mark of truth. I do not say this in the ridiculous affectation of self-abasement and modesty. I have studied myself, and know what ground I occupy; and, however a friend or the world may differ from me in that particular, I stand for my own opinion, in silent resolve, with all the tenaciousness of property. I mention this to you once for all to disburthen my mind, and I do not wish to hear or say more about it-But,

"When proud fortune's ebbing tide recedes,"

you will bear me witness, that when my bubble of fame was at the highest, I stood unintoxicated with the inebriating cup in my hand, looking forward with rueful resolve to the hastening time, when the blow of Calumny should dash it to the ground with all the eagerness of vengeful triumph.

Your patronizing me and interesting yourself in my fame and character as a poet, I rejoice in; it exalts me in my own idea; and whether you can or cannot aid me in my subscription is a trifle. Has a paltry subscription-bill any charms to the heart of a bard, compared with the patronage of the descendant of the immortal Wallace?

R. B.

XLIV.

TO DR. MOORE.

[Dr. Moore, the accomplished author of Zeluco and father of Sir John Moore, interested himself in the fame and fortune of Burns, as soon as the publication of his Poems made his name known to the world.]

Edinburgh, Jan. 1787.

Sir,

Mrs. Dunlop has been so kind as to send me extracts of letters she has had from you, where you do the rustic bard the honour of noticing him and his works. Those who have felt the anxieties and solicitudes of authorship, can only know what pleasure it gives to be noticed in such a manner, by judges of the first character. Your criticism, Sir, I receive with reverence; only I am sorry they mostly came too late: a peccant passage or two that I would certainly have altered, were gone to the press.

The hope to be admired for ages, is, in by far the greater part of those even who are authors of repute, an unsubstantial dream. For my part, my first ambition was, and still my strongest wish is, to please my compeers, the rustic inmates of the hamlet, while ever-changing language and manners shall allow me to be relished and understood. I am very willing to admit that I have some poetical abilities; and as few, if any, writers, either moral or poetical, are intimately acquainted with the classes of mankind[338] among

whom I have chiefly mingled, I may have seen men and manners in a different phasis from what is common, which may assist originality of thought. Still I know very well the novelty of my character has by far the greatest share in the learned and polite notice I have lately had; and in a language where Pope and Churchill have raised the laugh, and Shenstone and Gray drawn the tear; where Thomson and Beattie have painted the landscape, and Lyttelton and Collins described the heart, I am not vain enough to hope for distinguished poetic fame.
R. B.

XLV.

TO THE REV. G. LAURIE,
NEWMILLS, NEAR KILMARNOCK.
[It has been said in the Life of Burns, that for some time after he went to Edinburgh, he did not visit Dr. Blacklock, whose high opinion of his genius induced him to try his fortune in that city: it will be seen by this letter that he had neglected also, for a time, at least, to write to Dr. Laurie, who introduced him to the Doctor.]
Edinburgh, Feb. 5th, 1787.
Reverend and Dear Sir,
When I look at the date of your kind letter, my heart reproaches me severely with ingratitude in neglecting so long to answer it. I will not trouble you with any account, by way of apology, of my hurried life and distracted attention: do me the justice to believe that my delay by no means proceeded from want of respect. I feel, and ever shall feel for you the mingled sentiments of esteem for a friend and reverence for a father.
I thank you, Sir, with all my soul for your friendly hints, though I do not need them so much as my friends are apt to imagine. You are dazzled with newspaper accounts and distant reports; but, in reality, I have no great temptation to be intoxicated with the cup of prosperity. Novelty may attract the attention of mankind awhile; to it I owe my present éclat; but I see the time not far distant when the popular tide which has borne me to a height of which I am, perhaps, unworthy, shall recede with silent celerity, and leave me a barren waste of sand, to descend at my leisure to my former station. I do not say this in the affectation of modesty; I see the consequence is unavoidable, and am prepared for it. I had been at a good deal of pains to form a just, impartial estimate of my intellectual powers before I came here; I have not added, since I came to Edinburgh, anything to the account; and I trust I shall take every atom of it back to my shades, the coverts of my unnoticed, early years.
In Dr. Blacklock, whom I see very often, I have found what I would have expected in our friend, a clear head and an excellent heart.

By far the most agreeable hours I spend in Edinburgh must be placed to the account of Miss Laurie and her piano-forte. I cannot help repeating to you and Mrs. Laurie a compliment that Mr. Mackenzie, the celebrated "Man of Feeling," paid to Miss Laurie, the other night, at the concert. I had come in at the interlude, and sat down by him till I saw Miss Laurie in a seat not very distant, and went up to pay my respects to her. On my return to Mr. Mackenzie he asked me who she was; I told him 'twas the daughter of a reverend friend of mine in the west country. He returned, there was something very striking, to his idea, in her appearance. On my desiring to know what it was, he was pleased to say, "She has a great deal of the elegance of a well-bred lady about her, with all the sweet simplicity of a country girl."

My compliments to all the happy inmates of St. Margaret's.

R. B.

XLVI.

TO DR. MOORE.

[In the answer to this letter, Dr. Moore says that the poet was a great favourite in his family, and that his youngest son, at Winchester school, had translated part of "Halloween" into Latin verse, for the benefit of his comrades.]

Edinburgh, 15th February, 1787.

Sir,

Pardon my seeming neglect in delaying so long to acknowledge the honour you have done me, in your kind notice of me, January 23d. Not many months ago I knew no other employment than following the plough, nor could boast anything higher than a distant acquaintance with a country clergyman. Mere greatness never embarrasses me; I have nothing to ask from the great, and I do not fear their judgment: but genius, polished by learning, and at its proper point of elevation in the eye of the world, this of late I frequently meet with, and[339] tremble at its approach. I scorn the affectation of seeming modesty to cover self-conceit. That I have some merit I do not deny; but I see with frequent wringings of heart, that the novelty of my character, and the honest national prejudice of my countrymen, have borne me to a height altogether untenable to my abilities. For the honour Miss Williams has done me, please, Sir, return her in my name my most grateful thanks. I have more than once thought of paying her in kind, but have hitherto quitted the idea in hopeless despondency. I had never before heard of her; but the other day I got her poems, which for several reasons, some belonging to the head, and others the offspring of the heart, give me a great deal of pleasure. I have little pretensions to critic lore; there are, I think, two characteristic features in her poetry-the unfettered wild flight of native genius, and the querulous sombre tenderness of "time-settled sorrow."

I only know what pleases me, often without being able to tell why.

R. B.

XLVII.

TO JOHN BALLANTYNE, ESQ.

[The picture from which Beugo engraved the portrait alluded to in this letter, was painted by the now venerable Alexander Nasmyth-the eldest of living British artists:-it is, with the exception of a profile by Miers, the only portrait for which we are quite sure that the poet sat.]

Edinburgh, Feb. 24th, 1787.

My honoured Friend,

I will soon be with you now, in guid black prent;-in a week or ten days at farthest. I am obliged, against my own wish, to print subscribers' names; so if any of my Ayr friends have subscription bills, they must be sent in to Creech directly. I am getting my phiz done by an eminent engraver, and if it can be ready in time, I will appear in my book, looking like all other fools to my title-page.

R. B.

XLVIII.

TO THE EARL OF GLENCAIRN.

[The Earl of Glencairn seems to have refused, from motives of delicacy, the request of the poet: the verses, long lost, were at last found, and are now, through the kindness of my friend, Major James Glencairn Burns, printed with the rest of his eminent father's works.]

Edinburgh, 1787

My Lord,

I wanted to purchase a profile of your lordship, which I was told was to be got in town; but I am truly sorry to see that a blundering painter has spoiled a "human face divine." The enclosed stanzas I intended to have written below a picture or profile of your lordship, could I have been so happy as to procure one with anything of a likeness.

As I will soon return to my shades, I wanted to have something like a material object for my gratitude; I wanted to have it in my power to say to a friend, there is my noble patron, my generous benefactor. Allow me, my lord, to publish these verses. I conjure your lordship, by the honest throe of gratitude, by the generous wish of benevolence, by all the powers and feelings which compose the magnanimous mind, do not deny me this petition. I owe much to your lordship: and, what has not in some other instances always been the case with me, the weight of the obligation is a pleasing load. I trust I have a heart as independent as your lordship's, than which I can say nothing more; and I would not be beholden to favours that would crucify my feelings. Your dignified character in life, and manner of supporting that character, are flattering to my pride; and I would be jealous of the purity of my grateful attachment, where I was under the patronage of one of the much favoured sons of fortune.

Almost every poet has celebrated his patrons, particularly when they were names dear to fame, and illustrious in their country; allow me, then, my lord, if you think the verses have intrinsic merit, to tell the world how much I have the honour to be,

Your lordship's highly indebted,
And ever grateful humble servant,
R. B.

XLIX.

TO THE EARL OF BUCHAN.

[The Earl of Buchan, a man of talent, but more than tolerably vain, advised Burns to visit the battle-fields and scenes celebrated in song on the Scottish border, with the hope, perhaps, that he would drop a few of his[340] happy verses in Dryburgh Abbey, the residence of his lordship.]

My Lord,

The honour your lordship has done me, by your notice and advice in yours of the 1st instant, I shall ever gratefully remember:-

"Praise from thy lips, 'tis mine with joy to boast, They best can give it who deserve it most."[167]

Your lordship touches the darling chord of my heart when you advise me to fire my muse at Scottish story and Scotch scenes. I wish for nothing more than to make a leisurely pilgrimage through my native country; to sit and muse on those once hard-contended fields, where Caledonia, rejoicing, saw her bloody lion borne through broken ranks to victory and fame; and, catching the inspiration, to pour the deathless names in song. But, my lord, in the midst of these enthusiastic reveries, a long-visaged, dry, moral-looking phantom strides across my imagination, and pronounces these emphatic words:-

"I, Wisdom, dwell with Prudence. Friend, I do not come to open the ill-closed wounds of your follies and misfortunes, merely to give you pain: I wish through these wounds to imprint a lasting lesson on your heart. I will not mention how many of my salutary advices you have despised: I have given you line upon line and precept upon precept; and while I was chalking out to you the straight way to wealth and character, with audacious effrontery you have zigzagged across the path, contemning me to my face:

you know the consequences. It is not yet three months since home was so hot for you that you were on the wing for the western shore of the Atlantic, not to make a fortune, but to hide your misfortune.

"Now that your dear-loved Scotia puts it in your power to return to the situation of your forefathers, will you follow these will-o'-wisp meteors of fancy and whim, till they bring you once more to the brink of ruin? I grant that the utmost ground you can occupy is but half a step from the veriest poverty; but still it is half a step from it. If all that I can urge be ineffectual, let her who seldom calls to you in vain, let the call of pride prevail with you. You know how you feel at the iron gripe of ruthless oppression: you know how you bear the galling sneer of contumelious greatness. I hold you out the conveniences, the comforts of life, independence, and character, on the one hand; I tender you civility, dependence, and wretchedness, on the other. I will not insult your understanding by bidding you make a choice."

This, my lord, is unanswerable. I must return to my humble station, and woo my rustic muse in my wonted way at the plough-tail. Still, my lord, while the drops of life warm my heart, gratitude to that dear-loved country in which I boast my birth, and gratitude to those her distinguished sons who have honoured me so much with their patronage and approbation, shall, while stealing through my humble shades; ever distend my bosom, and at times, as now, draw forth the swelling tear.

R. B.

FOOTNOTES:

[167] Imitated from Pope's Eloisa to Abelard.

L.

TO MR. JAMES CANDLISH.

[James Candlish, a student of medicine, was well acquainted with the poetry of Lowe, author of that sublime lyric, "Mary's Dream," and at the request of Burns sent Lowe's classic song of "Pompey's Ghost," to the Musical Museum.]

Edinburgh, March 21, 1787.

My ever dear old Acquaintance,

I was equally surprised and pleased at your letter, though I dare say you will think by my delaying so long to write to you that I am so drowned in the intoxication of good fortune as to be indifferent to old, and once dear connexions. The truth is, I was determined to write a good letter, full of argument, amplification, erudition, and, as Bayes says, all that. I thought of it, and thought of it, and, by my soul, I could not; and, lest you should mistake the cause of my silence, I just sit down to tell you so. Don't give yourself credit, though, that the strength of your logic scares me: the truth is, I never mean to meet you on that ground at all. You have shown me one thing which was to be demonstrated: that strong pride of reasoning, with a little affectation of singularity, may mislead the best of hearts. I likewise, since you and I were first acquainted, in the pride of despising old woman's stories, ventured in "the daring path Spinosa trod;" but experience of the weakness, not the strength of human powers, made me glad to grasp at revealed religion.

I am still, in the Apostle Paul's phrase, "The old man with his deeds," as when we[341] were sporting about the "Lady Thorn." I shall be four weeks here yet at least; and so I shall expect to hear from you; welcome sense, welcome nonsense.

I am, with the warmest sincerity,

R. B.

LI.

TO .

[The name of the friend to whom this letter was addressed is still unknown, though known to Dr. Currie. The Esculapian Club of Edinburgh have, since the death of Burns, added some iron-work, with an inscription in honour of the Ayrshire poet to the original headstone. The cost to the poet was £5 10s.]

Edinburgh, March, 1787.

My dear Sir,

You may think, and too justly, that I am a selfish, ungrateful fellow, having received so many repeated instances of kindness from you, and yet never putting pen to paper to say thank you; but if you knew what a devil of a life my conscience has led me on that account, your good heart would think yourself too much avenged. By the bye, there is nothing in the whole frame of man which seems to be so unaccountable as that thing called conscience. Had the troublesome yelping cur powers efficient to prevent a mischief, he might be of use; but at the beginning of the business, his feeble efforts are to the workings of passion as the infant frosts of an autumnal morning to the unclouded fervour of the rising sun: and no sooner are the tumultuous doings of the wicked deed over, than, amidst the bitter native consequences of folly, in the very vortex of our horrors, up starts conscience, and harrows us with the feelings of the damned.

I have enclosed you, by way of expiation, some verse and prose, that, if they merit a place in your truly entertaining miscellany, you are welcome to. The prose extract is literally as Mr. Sprott sent it me.

The inscription on the stone is as follows:-

"HERE LIES ROBERT FERGUSSON, POET.

Born, September 5th, 1751-Died, 16th October 1774.
"No scuptur'd marble here, nor pompous lay, 'No storied urn or animated bust;' This simple stone directs pale Scotia's way To pour her sorrows o'er her poet's dust."
On the other side of the stone is as follows:
"By special grant of the managers to Robert Burns, who erected this stone, this burial place is to remain for ever sacred to the memory of Robert Fergusson."
Session-house, within the Kirk of Canongate, the twenty-second day of February, one thousand seven hundred eighty-seven years.
Sederunt of the Managers of the Kirk and Kirk-Yard funds of Canongate.
Which day, the treasurer to the said funds produced a letter from Mr. Robert Burns, of date the 6th current, which was read and appointed to be engrossed in their sederunt book, and of which letter the tenor follows:-
"To the honourable baillies of Canongate, Edinburgh.-Gentlemen, I am sorry to be told that the remains of Robert Fergusson, the so justly celebrated poet, a man whose talents for ages to come will do honour to our Caledonian name, lie in your church-yard among the ignoble dead, unnoticed and unknown.
"Some memorial to direct the steps of the lovers of Scottish song, when they wish to shed a tear over the 'narrow house' of the bard who is no more, is surely a tribute due to Fergusson's memory: a tribute I wish to have the honour of paying.
"I petition you then, gentlemen, to permit me to lay a simple stone over his revered ashes, to remain an unalienable property to his deathless fame. I have the honour to be, gentlemen, your very humble servant (sic subscribitur),
Robert Burns."
Thereafter the said managers, in consideration of the laudable and disinterested motion of Mr. Burns, and the propriety of his request, did, and hereby do, unanimously, grant power and liberty to the said Robert Burns to erect a headstone at the grave of the said Robert Fergusson, and to keep up and preserve the same to his memory in all time coming. Extracted forth of the records of the managers, by
William Sprott, Clerk.

LII.

TO MRS. DUNLOP.
[The poet alludes in this letter to the profits of the Edinburgh edition of his Poems: the exact sum is no[342] where stated, but it could not have been less than seven hundred pounds.]
Edinburgh, March 22d, 1787.

Madam,
I read your letter with watery eyes. A little, very little while ago, I had scarce a friend but the stubborn pride of my own bosom: now I am distinguished, patronized, befriended by you. Your friendly advices, I will not give them the cold name of criticisms, I receive with reverence. I have made some small alterations in what I before had printed. I have the advice of some very judicious friends among the literati here, but with them I sometimes find it necessary to claim the privilege of thinking for myself. The noble Karl of Glencairn, to whom I owe more than to any man, does me the honor of giving me his strictures: his hints, with respect to impropriety or indelicacy, I follow implicitly.
You kindly interest yourself in my future views and prospects; there I can give you no light. It is all
"Dark as was Chaos ere the infant sun Was roll'd together, or had tried his beams Athwart the gloom profound."[168]
The appellation of a Scottish bard, is by far my highest pride; to continue to deserve it is my most exalted ambition. Scottish scenes and Scottish story are the themes I could wish to sing. I have no dearer aim than to have it in my power, unplagued with the routine of business, for which heaven knows I am unfit enough, to make leisurely pilgrimages through Caledonia; to sit on the fields of her battles; to wander on the romantic banks of her rivers; and to muse by the stately towers or venerable ruins, once the honoured abodes of her heroes.
But these are all Utopian thoughts: I have dallied long enough with life; 'tis time to be in earnest. I have a fond, an aged mother to care for: and some other bosom ties perhaps equally tender. Where the individual only suffers by the consequences of his own thoughtlessness, indolence, or folly, he may be excusable; nay, shining abilities, and some of the nobler virtues, may half sanctify a heedless character; but where God and nature have intrusted the welfare of others to his care; where the trust is sacred, and the ties are dear, that man must be far gone in selfishness, or strangely lost to reflection, whom these connexions will not rouse to exertion.
I guess that I shall clear between two and three hundred pounds by my authorship; with that sum I intend, so far as I may be said to have any intention, to return to my old acquaintance, the plough, and if I can meet with a lease by which I can live, to commence farmer. I do not intend to give up poetry; being bred to labour, secures me independence, and the muses are my chief, sometimes have been my only enjoyment. If my practice second my resolution, I shall have principally at heart the serious business of life; but while following my plough, or building up my shocks, I shall cast a leisure glance to that dear, that only feature of my character, which gave me the notice of my country, and the patronage of a Wallace.
Thus, honoured Madam, I have given you the bard, his situation, and his

views, native as they are in his own bosom.
R. B.

FOOTNOTES:

[168] Blair's Grave.

LIII.

TO MRS. DUNLOP.
[This seems to be a letter acknowledging the payment of Mrs. Dunlop's subscription for his poems.]
Edinburgh, 15 April, 1787.
Madam,
There is an affectation of gratitude which I dislike. The periods of Johnson and the pause of Sterne, may hide a selfish heart. For my part, Madam, I trust I have too much pride for servility, and too little prudence for selfishness. I have this moment broken open your letter, but
"Rude am I in speech, And therefore little can I grace my cause In speaking for myself-"[169]
so I shall not trouble you with any fine speeches and hunted figures. I shall just lay my hand on my heart and say, I hope I shall ever have the truest, the warmest sense of your goodness.
I come abroad in print, for certain on Wednesday. Your orders I shall punctually attend to; only, by the way, I must tell you that I was paid before for Dr. Moore's and Miss Williams's copies, through the medium of Commissioner Cochrane in this place, but that we can settle when I have the honour of waiting on you.
[343]
Dr. Smith[170] was just gone to London the morning before I received your letter to him.
R. B.

FOOTNOTES:

[169] From Othello.
[170] Adam Smith.

LIV.

TO MR. SIBBALD,
BOOKSELLER IN EDINBURGH.
[This letter first appeared in that very valuable work, Nicholl's Illustrations

of Literature.]
Lawn Market.
Sir,
So little am I acquainted with the words and manners of the more public and polished walks of life, that I often feel myself much embarrassed how to express the feelings of my heart, particularly gratitude:-
"Rude am I in my speech, And little therefore shall I grace my cause In speaking for myself-"
The warmth with which you have befriended an obscure man and a young author in the last three magazines-I can only say, Sir, I feel the weight of the obligation, I wish I could express my sense of it. In the mean time accept of the conscious acknowledgment from,
Sir,
Your obliged servant,
R. B.

LV.

TO DR. MOORE.
[The book to which the poet alludes, was the well-known View of Society by Dr. Moore, a work of spirit and observation.]
Edinburgh, 23d April, 1787.
I received the books, and sent the one you mentioned to Mrs. Dunlop. I am ill skilled in beating the coverts of imagination for metaphors of gratitude. I thank you, Sir, for the honour you have done me; and to my latest hour will warmly remember it. To be highly pleased with your book is what I have in common with the world; but to regard these volumes as a mark of the author's friendly esteem, is a still more supreme gratification.
I leave Edinburgh in the course of ten days or a fortnight, and after a few pilgrimages over some of the classic ground of Caledonia, Cowden Knowes, Banks of Yarrow, Tweed, andc., I shall return to my rural shades, in all likelihood never more to quit them. I have formed many intimacies and friendships here, but I am afraid they are all of too tender a construction to bear carriage a hundred and fifty miles. To the rich, the great, the fashionable, the polite, I have no equivalent to offer; and I am afraid my meteor appearance will by no means entitle me to a settled correspondence with any of you, who are the permanent lights of genius and literature.
My most respectful compliments to Miss Williams. If once this tangent flight of mine were over, and I were returned to my wonted leisurely motion in my old circle, I may probably endeavour to return her poetic compliment in kind.
R. B.

LVI.

TO MRS. DUNLOP.
[This letter was in answer to one of criticism and remonstrance, from Mrs. Dunlop, respecting "The Dream," which she had begged the poet to omit, lest it should harm his fortunes with the world.]
Edinburgh, 30th April, 1787.
Your criticisms, Madam, I understand very well, and could have wished to have pleased you better. You are right in your guess that I am not very amenable to counsel. Poets, much my superiors, have so flattered those who possessed the adventitious qualities of wealth and power, that I am determined to flatter no created being, either in prose or verse.
I set as little by princes, lords, clergy, critics, andc., as all these respective gentry do by my bardship. I know what I may expect from the word, by and by-illiberal abuse, and perhaps contemptuous neglect.
I am happy, Madam, that some of my own favourite pieces are distinguished by your particular approbation. For my "Dream," which has unfortunately incurred your loyal displeasure, I hope in four weeks, or less, to have the honour of appearing, at Dunlop, in its defence in person.
R. B.

LVII.

TO THE REV. DR. HUGH BLAIR.
[The answer of Dr. Blair to this letter contains the following passage: "Your situation, as you say, was indeed very singular: and in being brought out all at once from the shades of deepest privacy to so great a share of public notice and observation, you had to stand a severe trial. I am happy you have stood it so well, and, as far as I have known or heard, though in the midst of many temptations, without reproach to your character or behaviour."]
Lawn-market, Edinburgh, 3d May, 1787.
Reverend and much-respected Sir,
I leave Edinburgh to-morrow morning, but could not go without troubling you with half a line, sincerely to thank you for the kindness, patronage, and friendship you have shown me. I often felt the embarrassment of my singular situation; drawn forth from the veriest shades of life to the glare of remark; and honoured by the notice of those illustrious names of my country whose works, while they are applauded to the end of time, will ever instruct and mend the heart. However the meteor-like novelty of my appearance in the world might attract notice, and honour me with the acquaintance of the permanent lights of genius and literature, those who are truly benefactors of the immortal nature of man, I knew very well that my

utmost merit was far unequal to the task of preserving that character when once the novelty was over; I have made up my mind that abuse, or almost even neglect, will not surprise me in my quarters.

I have sent you a proof impression of Beugo's work[171] for me, done on Indian paper, as a trifling but sincere testimony with what heart-warm gratitude I am, andc.

R. B.

FOOTNOTES:

[171] The portrait of the poet after Nasmyth.

LVIII.

TO THE EARL OF GLENCAIRN.

[The poet addressed the following letter to the Earl of Glencairn, when he commenced his journey to the Border. It was first printed in the third edition of Lockhart's Life of Burns; an eloquent and manly work.]

My Lord,

I go away to-morrow morning early, and allow me to vent the fulness of my heart, in thanking your lordship for all that patronage, that benevolence and that friendship with which you have honoured me. With brimful eyes, I pray that you may find in that great Being, whose image you so nobly bear, that friend which I have found in you. My gratitude is not selfish design-that I disdain-it is not dodging after the heels of greatness-that is an offering you disdain. It is a feeling of the same kind with my devotion.

R. B.

LIX.

TO MR. WILLIAM DUNBAR.

[William Dunbar, Colonel of the Crochallan Fencibles. The name has a martial sound, but the corps which he commanded was club of wits, whose courage was exercised on "paitricks, teals, moorpowts, and plovers."]

Lawn-market, Monday morning.

Dear Sir,

In justice to Spenser, I must acknowledge that there is scarcely a poet in the language could have been a more agreeable present to me; and in justice to you, allow me to say, Sir, that I have not met with a man in Edinburgh to whom I would so willingly have been indebted for the gift. The tattered rhymes I herewith present you, and the handsome volumes of Spenser for which I am so much indebted to your goodness, may perhaps be not in proportion to one another; but be that as it may, my gift, though far less

valuable, is as sincere a mark of esteem as yours.
The time is approaching when I shall return to my shades; and I am afraid my numerous Edinburgh friendships are of so tender a construction, that they will not bear carriage with me. Yours is one of the few that I could wish of a more robust constitution. It is indeed very probable that when I leave this city, we part never more to meet in this sublunary sphere; but I have a strong fancy that in some future eccentric planet, the comet of happier systems than any with which astronomy is yet acquainted, you and I, among the harum scarum sons of imagination and whim, with a hearty shake of a hand, a metaphor and a laugh, shall recognise old acquaintance:
"Where wit may sparkle all its rays, Uncurs'd with caution's fears; That pleasure, basking in the blaze, Rejoice for endless years." [345]
I have the honour to be, with the warmest sincerity, dear Sir, andc.
R. B.

LX.

TO JAMES JOHNSON.
[James Johnson was an engraver in Edinburgh, and proprietor of the Musical Museum; a truly national work, for which Burns wrote or amended many songs.]
Lawn-market, Friday noon, 3 May, 1787.
Dear Sir,
I have sent you a song never before known, for your collection; the air by M'Gibbon, but I know not the author of the words, as I got it from Dr. Blacklock.
Farewell, my dear Sir! I wished to have seen you, but I have been dreadfully throng, as I march to-morrow. Had my acquaintance with you been a little older, I would have asked the favour of your correspondence, as I have met with few people whose company and conversation gives me so much pleasure, because I have met with few whose sentiments are so congenial to my own.
When Dunbar and you meet, tell him that I left Edinburgh with the idea of him hanging somewhere about my heart.
Keep the original of the song till we meet again, whenever that may be.
R. B.

LXI.

TO WILLIAM CREECH, ESQ.
Edinburgh.
[This characteristic letter was written during the poet's border tour: he narrowly escaped a soaking with whiskey, as well as with water; for

according to the Ettrick Shepherd, "a couple of Yarrow lads, lovers of poesy and punch, awaited his coming to Selkirk, but would not believe that the parson-looking, black-avised man, who rode up to the inn, more like a drouket craw than a poet, could be Burns, and so went disappointed away."]

Selkirk, 13th May, 1787.

My honoured friend,

The enclosed I have just wrote, nearly extempore, in a solitary inn in Selkirk, after a miserable wet day's riding. I have been over most of East Lothian, Berwick, Roxburgh, and Selkirk-shires; and next week I begin a tour through the north of England. Yesterday I dined with Lady Harriet, sister to my noble patron,[172] Quem Deus conservet! I would write till I would tire you as much with dull prose, as I dare say by this time you are with wretched verse, but I am jaded to death; so, with a grateful farewell,

I have the honour to be,

Good Sir, yours sincerely,

R. B.

Auld chuckie Reekie's sair distrest, Down drops her ance weel burnish'd crest, Nae joy her bonnie buskit nest Can yield ava; Her darling bird that she loves best, Willie's awa.[173]

FOOTNOTES:

[172] James, Earl of Glencairn.
[173] See Poem LXXXIII.

LXII.

TO MR. PATISON,

Bookseller, Paisley.

[This letter has a business air about it: the name of Patison is nowhere else to be found in the poet's correspondence.]

Berrywell, near Dunse, May 17th, 1787.

Dear Sir,

I am sorry I was out of Edinburgh, making a slight pilgrimage to the classic scenes of this country, when I was favoured with yours of the 11th instant, enclosing an order of the Paisley banking company on the royal bank, for twenty-two pounds seven shillings sterling, payment in full, after carriage deducted, for ninety copies of my book I sent you. According to your motions, I see you will have left Scotland before this reaches you, otherwise I would send you "Holy Willie" with all my heart. I was so hurried that I absolutely forgot several things I ought to have minded, among the rest sending books to Mr. Cowan; but any order of yours will be answered at

Creech's shop. You will please remember that non-subscribers pay six shillings, this is Creech's profit; but those who have subscribed, though their names have been neglected in the printed list, which is very incorrect, are supplied at subscription price. I was not at Glasgow, nor do I intend for London; and I think Mrs. Fame is very idle to tell[346] so many lies on a poor poet. When you or Mr. Cowan write for copies, if you should want any direct to Mr. Hill, at Mr. Creech's shop, and I write to Mr. Hill by this post, to answer either of your orders. Hill is Mr. Creech's first clerk, and Creech himself is presently in London. I suppose I shall have the pleasure, against your return to Paisley, of assuring you how much I am, dear Sir, your obliged humble servant,

R. B.

LXIII.

TO W. NICOL, ESQ.,

Master of the High School, Edinburgh.

[Jenny Geddes was a zealous old woman, who threw the stool on which she sat, at the Dean of Edinburgh's head, when, in 1637, he attempted to introduce a Scottish Liturgy, and cried as she threw, "Villain, wilt thou say the mass at my lug!" The poet named his mare after this virago.]

Carlisle, June 1., 1787.

Kind, honest-hearted Willie,

I'm sitten down here after seven and forty miles ridin', e'en as forjesket and forniaw'd as a forfoughten cock, to gie you some notion o' my land lowper-like stravaguin sin the sorrowfu' hour that I sheuk hands and parted wi' auld Reekie.

My auld, ga'd gleyde o' a meere has huch-yall'd up hill and down brae, in Scotland and England, as teugh and birnie as a vera devil wi' me. It's true, she's as poor's a sang-maker and as hard's a kirk, and tipper-taipers when she taks the gate, first like a lady's gentlewoman in a minuwae, or a hen on a het girdle; but she's a yauld, poutherie Girran for a' that, and has a stomack like Willie Stalker's meere that wad hae disgeested tumbler-wheels, for she'll whip me aff her five stimparts o' the best aits at a down-sittin and ne'er fash her thumb. When ance her ringbanes and spavies, her crucks and cramps, and fairly soupl'd, she beets to, beets to, and ay the hindmost hour the tightest. I could wager her price to a thretty pennies, that for twa or three wooks ridin at fifty miles a day, the deil-stricket a five gallopers acqueesh Clyde and Whithorn could cast saut on her tail.

I hae dander'd owre a' the kintra frae Dumbar to Selcraig, and hae forgather'd wi' monie a guid fallow, and monie a weelfar'd huzzie. I met wi' twa dink quines in particular, ane o' them a sonsie, fine, fodgel lass, baith braw and bonnie; the tither was clean-shankit, straught, tight, weelfar'd winch, as blythe's a lintwhite on a flowerie thorn, and as sweet and modest's a new-blawn plumrose in a hazle shaw. They were baith bred to mainers by the beuk, and onie ane o' them had as muckle smeddum and rumblegumtion as the half o' some presbytries that you and I baith ken. They play'd me sik a deevil o' a shavie that I daur say if my harigals were turn'd out, ye wad see twa nicks i' the heart o' me like the mark o' a kail-whittle in a castock.

I was gaun to write you a lang pystle, but, Gude forgie me, I gat mysel sae noutouriously bitchify'd the day after kail-time, that I can hardly stoiter but and ben.

My best respecks to the guidwife and a' our common friens, especiall Mr. and Mrs. Cruikshank, and the honest guidman o' Jock's Lodge.

I'll be in Dumfries the morn gif the beast be to the fore, and the branks bide hale.

Gude be wi' you, Willie! Amen!

R. B.

LXIV.

TO MR. JAMES SMITH,

at Miller and Smith's Office, Linlithgow.

[Burns, it seems by this letter, had still a belief that he would be obliged to try his fortune in the West Indies: he soon saw how hollow all the hopes were, which had been formed by his friends of "pension, post or place," in his native land.]

Mauchline, 11th June, 1787.

My ever dear Sir,

I date this from Mauchline, where I arrived on Friday even last. I slept at John Dow's, and called for my daughter. Mr. Hamilton and your family; your mother, sister, and brother; my quondam Eliza, andc., all well. If anything had been wanting to disgust me completely at Armour's family, their mean, servile compliance would have done it.

Give me a spirit like my favourite hero, Milton's Satan:

Hail, horrors! hail, Infernal world! and thou proufoundest hell, Receive thy new possessor! he who brings A mind not be chang'd by place or time!

I cannot settle to my mind.-Farming, the only thing of which I know anything, and heaven above knows but little do I understand of that, I cannot, dare not risk on farms as they are. If I do not fix I will go for Jamaica.[347] Should I stay in an unsettled state at home, I would only dissipate my little fortune, and ruin what I intend shall compensate my little ones, for the stigma I have brought on their names.

I shall write you more at large soon; as this letter costs you no postage, if it be worth reading you cannot complain of your pennyworth.

I am ever, my dear Sir,
Yours,
R. B.
P.S. The cloot has unfortunately broke, but I have provided a fine buffalo-horn, on which I am going to affix the same cipher which you will remember was on the lid of the cloot.

LXV.

TO WILLIAM NICOL, ESQ.
[The charm which Dumfries threw over the poet, seems to have dissolved like a spell, when he sat down in Ellisland: he spoke, for a time, with little respect of either place or people.]
Mauchline, June 18, 1787.
My dear Friend,
I am now arrived safe in my native country, after a very agreeable jaunt, and have the pleasure to find all my friends well. I breakfasted with your gray-headed, reverend friend, Mr. Smith; and was highly pleased both with the cordial welcome he gave me, and his most excellent appearance and sterling good sense.
I have been with Mr. Miller at Dalswinton, and am to meet him again in August. From my view of the lands, and his reception of my bardship, my hopes in that business are rather mended; but still they are but slender.
I am quite charmed with Dumfries folks-Mr. Burnside, the clergyman, in particular, is a man whom I shall ever gratefully remember; and his wife, Gude forgie me! I had almost broke the tenth commandment on her account. Simplicity, elegance, good sense, sweetness of disposition, good humour, kind hospitality are the constituents of her manner and heart; in short-but if I say one word more about her, I shall be directly in love with her.
I never, my friend, thought mankind very capable of anything generous; but the stateliness of the patricians in Edinburgh, and the servility of my plebeian brethren (who perhaps formerly eyed me askance) since I returned home, have nearly put me out of conceit altogether with my species. I have bought a pocket Milton, which I carry perpetually about with me, in order to study the sentiments-the dauntless magnanimity, the intrepid, unyielding independence, the desperate daring, and noble defiance of hardship, in that great personage, Satan. 'Tis true, I have just now a little cash; but I am afraid the star that hitherto has shed its malignant, purpose-blasting rays full in my zenith; that noxious planet so baneful in its influences to the rhyming tribe, I much dread it is not yet beneath my horizon.-Misfortune dodges the path of human life; the poetic mind finds itself miserably deranged in, and unfit for the walks of business; add to all, that thoughtless follies and hare-

brained whims, like so many ignes fatui, eternally diverging from the right line of sober discretion, sparkle with step-bewitching blaze in the idly-gazing eyes of the poor heedless bard, till, pop, "he falls like Lucifer, never to hope again." God grant this may be an unreal picture with respect to me! but should it not, I have very little dependence on mankind. I will close my letter with this tribute my heart bids me pay you-the many ties of acquaintance and friendship which I have, or think I have in life, I have felt along the lines, and, damn them, they are almost all of them of such frail contexture, that I am sure they would not stand the breath of the least adverse breeze of fortune; but from you, my ever dear Sir, I look with confidence for the apostolic love that shall wait on me "through good report and bad report"-the love which Solomon emphatically says "is strong as death." My compliments to Mrs. Nicol, and all the circle of our common friends.

P.S. I shall be in Edinburgh about the latter end of July.

R. B.

LXVI.

TO MR. JAMES CANDLISH.

[Candlish was a classic scholar, but had a love for the songs of Scotland, as well as for the poetry of Greece and Rome.]

Edinburgh, 1787.

My dear Friend,

If once I were gone from this scene of hurry and dissipation, I promise myself the pleasure of that correspondence being renewed which[348] has been so long broken. At present I have time for nothing. Dissipation and business engross every moment. I am engaged in assisting an honest Scotch enthusiast,[174] a friend of mine, who is an engraver, and has taken it into his head to publish a collection of all our songs set to music, of which the words and music are done by Scotsmen. This, you will easily guess, is an undertaking exactly to my taste. I have collected, begged, borrowed, and stolen, all the songs I could meet with. Pompey's Ghost, words and music, I beg from you immediately, to go into his second number: the first is already published. I shall show you the first number when I see you in Glasgow, which will be in a fortnight or less. Do be so kind as to send me the song in a day or two; you cannot imagine how much it will oblige me.

Direct to me at Mr. W. Cruikshank's, St. James's Square, New Town, Edinburgh.

R. B.

FOOTNOTES:

[174] Johnson, the publisher and proprietor of the Musical Museum.

LXVII.

TO ROBERT AINSLIE, ESQ.
["Burns had a memory stored with the finest poetical passages, which he was in the habit of quoting most aptly in his correspondence with his friends: and he delighted also in repeating them in the company of those friends who enjoyed them." These are the words of Ainslie, of Berrywell, to whom this letter in addressed.]
Arracher, 28th June, 1787.
My dear Sir,
I write on my tour through a country where savage streams tumble over savage mountains, thinly overspread with savage flocks, which sparingly support as savage inhabitants. My last stage was Inverary-to-morrow night's stage Dumbarton. I ought sooner to have answered your kind letter, but you know I am a man of many sins.
R. B.

LXVIII.

TO WILLIAM NICOL, ESQ.
[This visit to Auchtertyre produced that sweet lyric, beginning "Blythe, blythe and merry was she;" and the lady who inspired it was at his side, when he wrote this letter.]
Auchtertyre, Monday, June, 1787.
My dear Sir,
I find myself very comfortable here, neither oppressed by ceremony nor mortified by neglect. Lady Augusta is a most engaging woman, and very happy in her family, which makes one's outgoings and incomings very agreeable. I called at Mr. Ramsay's of Auchtertyre as I came up the country, and am so delighted with him that I shall certainly accept of his invitation to spend a day or two with him as I return. I leave this place on Wednesday or Thursday.
Make my kind compliments to Mr. and Mrs. Cruikshank and Mrs. Nicol, if she is returned.
I am ever, dear Sir,
Your deeply indebted,
R. B.

LXIX.

TO WILLIAM CRUIKSHANK, ESQ.

ST. JAMES'S SQUARE, EDINBURGH.
[At the house of William Cruikshank, one of the masters of the High School, in Edinburgh, Burns passed many agreeable hours.]
Auchtertyre, Monday morning.
I have nothing, my dear Sir, to write to you but that I feel myself exceedingly comfortably situated in this good family: just notice enough to make me easy but not to embarrass me. I was storm-staid two days at the foot of the Ochillhills, with Mr. Trait of Herveyston and Mr. Johnston of Alva, but was so well pleased that I shall certainly spend a day on the banks of the Devon as I return. I leave this place I suppose on Wednesday, and shall devote a day to Mr. Ramsay at Auchtertyre, near Stirling: a man to whose worth I cannot do justice. My respectful kind compliments to Mrs. Cruikshank, and my dear little Jeanie, and if you see Mr. Masterton, please remember me to him.
I am ever,
My dear Sir, andc.
R. B.

LXX.

TO MR. JAMES SMITH.
Linlithgow.
[The young lady to whom the poet alludes in this letter, was very beautiful, and very proud: it is said she gave him a specimen of both her temper and her pride, when he touched on the subject of love.]
June 30, 1787.
My dear Friend,
On our return, at a Highland gentleman's hospitable mansion, we fell in with a merry party, and danced till the ladies left us, at three in the morning. Our dancing was none of the French or English insipid formal movements; the ladies sung Scotch songs like angels, at intervals; then we flew at Bab at the Bowster, Tullochgorum, Loch Erroch Side, andc., like midges sporting in the mottie sun, or craws prognosticating a storm in a hairst day.-When the dear lasses left us, we ranged round the bowl till the good-fellow hour of six; except a few minutes that we went out to pay our devotions to the glorious lamp of day peering over the towering top of Benlomond. We all kneeled; our worthy landlord's son held the bowl; each man a full glass in his hand; and I, as priest, repeated some rhyming nonsense, like Thomas-a-Rhymer's prophecies I suppose.-After a small refreshment of the gifts of Somnus, we proceeded to spend the day on Lochlomond, and reach Dumbarton in the evening. We dined at another good fellow's house, and consequently, pushed the bottle; when we went out to mount our horses, we found ourselves "No vera fou but gaylie yet." My two friends and I rode

soberly down the Loch side, till by came a Highlandman at the gallop, on a tolerably good horse, but which had never known the ornaments of iron or leather. We scorned to be out-galloped by a Highlandman, so off we started, whip and spur. My companions, though seemingly gaily mounted, fell sadly astern; but my old mare, Jenny Geddes, one of the Rosinante family, she strained past the Highlandman in spite of all his efforts with the hair halter; just as I was passing him, Donald wheeled his horse, as if to cross before me to mar my progress, when down came his horse, and threw his rider's breekless ae in a clipt hedge; and down came Jenny Geddes over all, and my bardship between her and the Highlandman's horse. Jenny Geddes trode over me with such cautious reverence, that matters were not so bad as might well have been expected; so I came off with a few cuts and bruises, and a thorough resolution to be a pattern of sobriety for the future.

I have yet fixed on nothing with respect to the serious business of life. I am, just as usual, a rhyming, mason-making, raking, aimless, idle fellow. However, I shall somewhere have a farm soon. I was going to say, a wife too; but that must never be my blessed lot. I am but a younger son of the house of Parnassus, and like other younger sons of great families, I may intrigue, if I choose to run all risks, but must not marry.

I am afraid I have almost ruined one source, the principal one, indeed, of my former happiness; that eternal propensity I always had to fall in love. My heart no more glows with feverish rapture. I have no paradisaical evening interviews, stolen from the restless cares and prying inhabitants of this weary world. I have only * * * *. This last is one of your distant acquaintances, has a fine figure, and elegant manners; and in the train of some great folks whom you know, has seen, the politest quarters in Europe. I do like her a good deal; but what piques me is her conduct at the commencement of our acquaintance. I frequently visited her when I was in , and after passing regularly the intermediate degrees between the distant formal bow and the familiar grasp round the waist, I ventured, in my careless way, to talk of friendship in rather ambiguous terms; and after her return to , I wrote to her in the same style. Miss, construing my words farther I suppose than even I intended, flew off in a tangent of female dignity and reserve, like a mounting lark in an April morning; and wrote me an answer which measured me out very completely what an immense way I had to travel before I could reach the climate of her favour. But I am an old hawk at the sport, and wrote her such a cool, deliberate, prudent reply, as brought my bird from her aerial towerings, pop, down at my foot, like Corporal Trim's hat.

As for the rest of my acts, and my wars, and all my wise sayings, and why my mare was called Jenny Geddes, they shall be recorded in a few weeks hence at Linlithgow, in the chronicles of your memory, by

R. B.

LXXI.

TO MR. JOHN RICHMOND.

[Mr. John Richmond, writer, was one of the poet's earliest and firmest friends; he shared his room with him when they met in Edinburgh, and did him many little offices of kindness and regard.]

Mossgiel, 7th July, 1787.

My dear Richmond,

I am all impatience to hear of your fate since the old confounder of right and wrong has turned you out of place, by his journey to answer his indictment at the bar of the other world. He will find the practice of the court so different from the practice in which he has for so many years been thoroughly hackneyed, that his friends, if he had any connexions truly of that kind, which I rather doubt, may well tremble for his sake. His chicane, his left-handed wisdom, which stood so firmly by him, to such good purpose, here, like other accomplices in robbery and plunder, will, now the piratical business is blown, in all probability turn the king's evidences, and then the devil's bagpiper will touch him off "Bundle and go!"

If he has left you any legacy, I beg your pardon for all this; if not, I know you will swear to every word I said about him.

I have lately been rambling over by Dumbarton and Inverary, and running a drunken race on the side of Loch Lomond with a wild Highlandman; his horse, which had never known the ornaments of iron or leather, zigzagged across before my old spavin'd hunter, whose name is Jenny Geddes, and down came the Highlandman, horse and all, and down came Jenny and my bardship; so I have got such a skinful of bruises and wounds, that I shall be at least four weeks before I dare venture on my journey to Edinburgh.

Not one new thing under the sun has happened in Mauchline since you left it. I hope this will find you as comfortably situated as formerly, or, if heaven pleases, more so; but, at all events, I trust you will let me know of course how matters stand with you, well or ill. 'Tis but poor consolation to tell the world when matters go wrong; but you know very well your connexion and mine stands on a different footing.

I am ever, my dear friend, yours,

R. B.

LXXII.

TO ROBERT AINSLIE, ESQ.

[This letter, were proof wanting, shows the friendly and familiar footing on which Burns stood with the Ainslies, and more particularly with the author of that popular work, the "Reasons for the Hope that is in us."]

Mauchline, 23d July, 1787.

My dear Ainslie,

There is one thing for which I set great store by you as a friend, and it is this, that I have not a friend upon earth, besides yourself, to whom I can talk nonsense without forfeiting some degree of his esteem. Now, to one like me, who never cares for speaking anything else but nonsense, such a friend as you is an invaluable treasure. I was never a rogue, but have been a fool all my life; and, in spite of all my endeavours, I see now plainly that I shall never be wise. Now it rejoices my heart to have met with such a fellow as you, who, though you are not just such a hopeless fool as I, yet I trust you will never listen so much to the temptations of the devil as to grow so very wise that you will in the least disrespect an honest follow because he is a fool. In short, I have set you down as the staff of my old age, when the whole list of my friends will, after a decent share of pity, have forgot me.

Though in the morn comes sturt and strife, Yet joy may come at noon; And I hope to live a merry, merry life When a' thir days are done.

Write me soon, were it but a few lines just to tell me how that good sagacious man your father is-that kind dainty body your mother-that strapping chiel your brother Douglas-and my friend Rachel, who is as far before Rachel of old, as she was before her blear-eyed sister Leah.

R. B.

LXXIII.

TO ROBERT AINSLIE, ESQ.

[The "savage hospitality," of which Burns complains in this letter, was at that time an evil fashion in Scotland: the bottle was made to circulate rapidly, and every glass was drunk "clean caup out."]

Mauchline, July, 1787.

My dear Sir,

My life, since I saw you last, has been one continued hurry; that savage hospitality which[351] knocks a man down with strong liquors, is the devil. I have a sore warfare in this world; the devil, the world, and the flesh are three formidable foes. The first I generally try to fly from; the second, alas! generally flies from me; but the third is my plague, worse than the ten plagues of Egypt.

I have been looking over several farms in this country; one in particular, in Nithsdale, pleased me so well, that if my offer to the proprietor is accepted, I shall commence farmer at Whit-Sunday. If farming do not appear eligible, I shall have recourse to my other shift: but this to a friend.

I set out for Edinburgh on Monday morning; how long I stay there is uncertain, but you will know so soon as I can inform you myself. However I determine, poesy must be laid aside for some time; my mind has been vitiated with idleness, and it will take a good deal of effort to habituate it to the routine of business.

I am, my dear Sir,

Yours sincerely,

R. B.

LXXIV.

TO DR. MOORE.

[Dr. Moore was one of the first to point out the beauty of the lyric compositions of Burns. "'Green grow the Rashes,' and of the two songs," says he, "which follow, beginning 'Again rejoicing nature sees,' and 'The gloomy night is gathering fast;' the latter is exquisite. By the way, I imagine you have a peculiar talent for such compositions which you ought to indulge: no kind of poetry demands more delicacy or higher polishing." On this letter to Moore all the biographies of Burns are founded.]

Mauchline, 2d August, 1787.

Sir,

For some months past I have been rambling over the country, but I am now confined with some lingering complaints, originating, as I take it, in the stomach. To divert my spirits a little in this miserable fog of ennui, I have taken a whim to give you a history of myself. My name has made some little noise in this country; you have done me the honour to interest yourself very warmly in my behalf; and I think a faithful account of what character of a man I am, and how I came by that character, may perhaps amuse you in an idle moment. I will give you an honest narrative, though I know it will be often at my own expense; for I assure you, Sir, I have, like Solomon, whose character, excepting in the trifling affair of wisdom, I sometimes think I resemble,-I have, I say, like him turned my eyes to behold madness and folly, and like him, too, frequently shaken hands with their intoxicating friendship.-After you have perused these pages, should you think them trifling and impertinent, I only beg leave to tell you, that the poor author wrote them under some twitching qualms of conscience, arising from a suspicion that he was doing what he ought not to do; a predicament he has more than once been in before.

I have not the most distant pretensions to assume that character which the pye-coated guardians of escutcheons call a gentleman. When at Edinburgh last winter, I got acquainted in the herald's office; and, looking through that granary of honours, I there found almost every name in the kingdom; but for me,

"My ancient but ignoble blood Has crept thro' scoundrels ever since the flood."

Pope.

Gules, purpure, argent, andc., quite disowned me.

My father was of the north of Scotland, the son of a farmer, and was thrown by early misfortunes on the world at large; where, after many years' wanderings and sojournings, he picked up a pretty large quantity of observation and experience, to which I am indebted for most of my little pretensions to wisdom-I have met with few who understood men, their manners, and their ways, equal to him; but stubborn, ungainly integrity, and headlong, ungovernable irascibility, are disqualifying circumstances; consequently, I was born a very poor man's son. For the first six or seven years of my life, my father was gardener to a worthy gentleman of small estate in the neighbourhood of Ayr. Had he continued in that station I must have marched off to be one of the little underlings about a farm-house; but it was his dearest wish and prayer to have it in his power to keep his children under his own eye, till they could discern between good and evil; so, with the assistance of his generous master, my father ventured on a small farm on his estate. At those years, I was by no means a favourite with anybody. I was a good deal noted for a retentive memory, a stubborn sturdy something in my disposition, and an enthusiastic idiot[175] piety. I say idiot piety, because I was then [352]but a child. Though it cost the schoolmaster some thrashings, I made an excellent English, scholar; and by the time I was ten or eleven years of age, I was a critic in substantives, verbs, and particles. In my infant and boyish days, too, I owed much to an old woman who resided in the family, remarkable for her ignorance, credulity, and superstition. She had, I suppose, the largest collection in the country of tales and songs concerning devils, ghosts, fairies, brownies, witches, warlocks, spunkies, kelpies, elf-candles, dead-lights, wraiths, apparitions, cantraips, giants, enchanted towers, dragons, and other trumpery. This cultivated the latent seeds of poetry; but had so strong an effect on my imagination, that to this hour, in my nocturnal rambles, I sometimes keep a sharp look out in suspicions places; and though nobody can be more sceptical than I am in such matters, yet it often takes an effort of philosophy to shake off these idle terrors. The earliest composition that I recollect taking pleasure in, was The Vision of Mirza, and a hymn of Addison's beginning, "How are thy servants blest, O Lord!" I particularly remember one half-stanza which was music to my boyish ear-

"For though in dreadful whirls we hung High on the broken wave-"

I met with these pieces in Mason's English Collection, one of my school-books. The first two books I ever read in private, and which gave me more pleasure than any two books I ever read since, were The Life of Hannibal, and The History of Sir William Wallace. Hannibal gave my young ideas such a turn, that I used to strut in raptures up and down after the recruiting drum and bag-pipe, and wish myself tall enough to be a soldier; while the story of Wallace poured a Scottish prejudice into my veins, which will boil along there till the flood-gates of life shut in eternal rest.

Polemical divinity about this time was putting the country half mad, and I, ambitious of shining in conversation parties on Sundays, between sermons, at funerals, andc., used a few years afterwards to puzzle Calvinism with so much heat and indiscretion, that I raised a hue and cry of heresy against me, which has not ceased to this hour.

My vicinity to Ayr was of some advantage to me. My social disposition, when not checked by some modifications of spirited pride, was like our catechism definition of infinitude, without bounds or limits. I formed several connexions with other younkers, who possessed superior advantages; the youngling actors who were busy in the rehearsal of parts, in which they were shortly to appear on the stage of life, where, alas! I was destined to drudge behind the scenes. It is not commonly at this green age, that our young gentry have a just sense of the immense distance between them and their ragged playfellows. It takes a few dashes into the world, to give the young great man that proper, decent, unnoticing disregard for the poor, insignificant stupid devils, the mechanics and peasantry around him, who were, perhaps, born in the same village. My young superiors never insulted the clouterly appearance of my plough-boy carcase, the two extremes of which were often exposed to all the inclemencies of all the seasons. They would give me stray volumes of books; among them, even then, I could pick up some observations, and one, whose heart, I am sure, not even the "Munny Begum" scenes have tainted, helped me to a little French. Parting with these my young friends and benefactors, as they occasionally went off for the East or West Indies, was often to me a sore affliction; but I was soon called to more serious evils. My father's generous master died! the farm proved a ruinous bargain; and to clench the misfortune, we fell into the hands of a factor, who sat for the picture I have drawn of one in my tale of "The Twa Dogs." My father was advanced in life when he married; I was the eldest of seven children, and he, worn out by early hardships, was unfit for labour. My father's spirit was soon irritated, but not easily broken. There was a freedom in his lease in two years more, and to weather these two years, we retrenched our expenses. We lived very poorly: I was a dexterous ploughman for my age; and the next eldest to me was a brother (Gilbert), who could drive the plough very well, and help me to thrash the corn. A novel-writer might, perhaps, have viewed these scenes with some satisfaction, but so did not I; my indignation yet boils at the recollection of the scoundrel factor's insolent threatening letters, which used to set us all in tears.

This kind of life-the cheerless gloom of a hermit, with the unceasing moil of a galley-slave, brought me to my sixteenth year; a little before which period I first committed the sin of rhyme. You know our country custom of cou[353]pling a man and woman together as partners in the labours of harvest. In my fifteenth autumn, my partner was a bewitching creature, a year younger than myself. My scarcity of English denies me the power of doing her justice in that language, but you know the Scottish idiom: she was a "bonnie, sweet, sonsie lass." In short, she, altogether unwittingly to herself, initiated me in that delicious passion, which, in spite of acid disappointment, gin-horse prudence, and bookworm philosophy, I hold to be the first of human joys, our dearest blessing here below! How she caught the contagion I cannot tell; you medical people talk much of infection from breathing the same air, the touch, andc.; but I never expressly said I loved her.-Indeed, I did not know myself why I liked so much to loiter behind with her, when returning in the evening from our labours; why the tones of her voice made my heart-strings thrill like an Æolian harp; and particularly why my pulse beat such a furious ratan, when I looked and fingered over her little hand to pick out the cruel nettle-stings and thistles. Among her other love-inspiring qualities, she sung sweetly; and it was her favourite reel to which I attempted giving an embodied vehicle in ryhme. I was not so presumptuous as to imagine that I could make verses like printed ones, composed by men who had Greek and Latin; but my girl sung a song which was said to be composed by a small country laird's son, on one of his father's maids, with whom he was in love; and I saw no reason why I might not rhyme as well as he; for excepting that he could smear sheep, and cast peats, his father living in the moorlands, he had no more scholar-craft than myself.

Thus with me began love and poetry; which at times have been my only, and till within the last twelve months, have been my highest enjoyment. My father struggled on till he reached the freedom in his lease, when he entered on a larger farm, about ten miles farther in the country. The nature of the bargain he made was such as to throw a little ready money into his hands at the commencement of his lease, otherwise the affair would have been impracticable. For four years we lived comfortably here, but a difference commencing between him and his landlord as to terms, after three years tossing and whirling in the vortex of litigation, my father was just saved from the horrors of a jail, by a consumption, which, after two years' promises, kindly stepped in, and carried him away, to where the wicked cease from troubling, and where the weary are at rest!

It is during the time that we lived on this farm that my little story is most eventful. I was, at the beginning of this period, perhaps, the most ungainly awkward boy in the parish-no solitaire was less acquainted with the ways of the world. What I knew of ancient story was gathered from Salmon's and Guthrie's Geographical Grammars; and the ideas I had formed of modern manners, of literature, and criticism, I got from the Spectator. These, with Pope's Works, some Plays of Shakspeare, Tull and Dickson on Agriculture, the Pantheon, Locke's Essay on the Human Understanding, Stackhouse's

History of the Bible, Justice's British Gardener's Directory, Boyle's Lectures, Allan Ramsay's Works, Taylor's Scripture Doctrine of Original Sin, A Select Collection of English Songs, and Hervey's Meditations, had formed the whole of my reading. The collection of Songs was my vade mecum. I pored over them, driving my cart, or walking to labour, song by song, verse by verse; carefully noting the true tender, or sublime, from affectation and fustian. I am convinced I owe to this practice much of my critic craft, such as it is.

In my seventeenth year, to give my manners a brush, I went to a country dancing-school. My father had an unaccountable antipathy against these meetings, and my going was, what to this moment I repent, in opposition to his wishes. My father, as I said before, was subject to strong passions; from that instance of disobedience in me, he took a sort of dislike to me, which, I believe, was one cause of the dissipation which marked my succeeding years. I say dissipation, comparatively with the strictness, and sobriety, and regularity of Presbyterian country life; for though the will-o'-wisp meteors of thoughtless whim were almost the sole lights of my path, yet early ingrained piety and virtue kept me for several years afterwards within the line of innocence. The great misfortune of my life was to want an aim. I had felt early some stirrings of ambition, but they were the blind gropings of Homer's Cyclops round the walls of his cave. I saw my father's situation entailed on me perpetual labour. The only two openings by which I could enter the temple of fortune were the gate of niggardly economy, or the path of little chican[354]ing bargain-making. The first is so contracted an aperture I never could squeeze myself into it-the last I always hated-there was contamination in the very entrance! Thus abandoned of aim or view in life, with a strong appetite for sociability, as well from native hilarity as from a pride of observation and remark; a constitutional melancholy or hypochondriasm that made me fly solitude; add to these incentives to social life, my reputation for bookish knowledge, a certain wild logical talent, and a strength of thought, something like the rudiments of good sense; and it will not seem surprising that I was generally a welcome guest where I visited, or any great wonder that always, where two or three met together, there was I among them. But far beyond all other impulses of my heart, was un penchant à l' adorable moitié du genre humain. My heart was completely tinder, and was eternally lighted up by some goddess or other; and, as in every other warfare in this world, my fortune was various; sometimes I was received with favour, and sometimes I was mortified with a repulse. At the plough, scythe, or reap-hook, I feared no competitor, and thus I set absolute want at defiance; and as I never cared farther for my labours than while I was in actual exercise, I spent the evenings in the way after my own heart. A country lad seldom carries on a love adventure without an assisting confidant. I possessed a curiosity, zeal, and intrepid dexterity that recommended me as a proper second on these occasions; and I dare say, I felt as much pleasure in being in the secret of half the loves of the parish of Tarbolton, as ever did statesman in knowing the intrigues of half the courts of Europe. The very goose feather in my hand seems to know instinctively the well-worn path of my imagination, the favourite theme of my song; and is with difficulty restrained from giving you a couple of paragraphs on the love-adventures of my compeers, the humble inmates of the farm-house and cottage; but the grave sons of science, ambition, or avarice baptize these things by the name of follies. To the sons and daughters of labour and poverty they are matters of the most serious nature: to them the ardent hope, the stolen interview, the tender farewell, are the greatest and most delicious parts of their enjoyments.

Another circumstance in my life which made some alteration in my mind and manners, was, that I spent my nineteenth summer on a smuggling coast, a good distance from home, at a noted school to learn mensuration, surveying, dialling, andc., in which I made a pretty good progress. But I made a greater progress in the knowledge of mankind. The contraband trade was at that time very successful, and it sometimes happened to me to fall in with those who carried it on. Scenes of swaggering riot and roaring dissipation were, till this time, new to me; but I was no enemy to social life. Here, though I learnt to fill my glass, and to mix without fear in a drunken squabble, yet I went on with a high hand with my geometry, till the sun entered Virgo, a month which is always a carnival in my bosom, when a charming fillette, who lived next door to the school, overset my trigonometry, and set me off at a tangent from the spheres of my studies. I, however, struggled on with my sines and co-sines for a few days more; but stepping into the garden one charming noon to take the sun's altitude, there I met my angel,

"Like Proserpine gathering flowers, Herself a fairer flower-"[176]

It was in vain to think of doing any more good at school. The remaining week I stayed I did nothing but craze the faculties of my soul about her, or steal out to meet her; and the two last nights of my stay in the country, had sleep been a mortal sin, the image of this modest and innocent girl had kept me guiltless.

I returned home very considerably improved. My reading was enlarged with the very important addition of Thomson's and Shenstone's works; I had seen human nature in a new phasis; and I engaged several of my school-fellows to keep up a literary correspondence with me. This improved me in composition. I had met with a collection of letters by the wits of Queen Anne's reign, and I pored over them most devoutly. I kept copies of any of my own letters that pleased me, and a comparison between them and the composition of most of my correspondents flattered my vanity. I carried this whim so far, that though I hid not three-farthings' worth of business in the world, yet almost every post brought me as many letters as if I had been a broad plodding son of the day-book and ledger.

My life flowed on much in the same course [355] till my twenty-third year. Vive l'amour, et vive la bagatelle, were my sole principles of action. The addition of two more authors to my library gave me great pleasure; Sterne and Mackenzie-Tristram Shandy and the Man of Feeling were my bosom favourites. Poesy was still a darling walk for my mind, but it was only indulged in according to the humour of the hour. I had usually half a dozen or more pieces on hand; I took up one or other, as it suited the momentary tone of the mind, and dismissed the work as it bordered on fatigue. My passions, when once lighted up, raged like so many devils, till they got vent in rhyme; and then the conning over my verses, like a spell, soothed all into quiet! None of the rhymes of those days are in print, except "Winter, a dirge," the eldest of my printed pieces; "The Death of poor Maillie," "John Barleycorn," and songs first, second, and third. Song second was the ebullition of that passion which ended the forementioned school-business.

My twenty-third year was to me an important æra. Partly through whim, and partly that I wished to set about doing something in life, I joined a flax-dresser in a neighboring town (Irvine) to learn his trade. This was an unlucky affair. My * * * and to finish the whole, as we were giving a welcome carousal to the new year, the shop took fire and burnt to ashes, and I was left, like a true poet, not worth a sixpence.

I was obliged to give up this scheme; the clouds of misfortune were gathering thick round my father's head; and, what was worst of all, he was visibly far gone in a consumption; and to crown my distresses, a belle fille, whom I adored, and who had pledged her soul to meet me in the field of matrimony, jilted me, with peculiar circumstances of mortification. The finishing evil that brought up the rear of this infernal file, was my constitutional melancholy being increased to such a degree, that for three months I was in a state of mind scarcely to be envied by the hopeless wretches who have got their mittimus-depart from me, ye cursed!

From this adventure I learned something of a town life; but the principal thing which gave my mind a turn, was a friendship I formed with a young fellow, a very noble character, but a hapless son of misfortune. He was the son of a simple mechanic; but a great man in the neighbourhood taking him under his patronage, gave him a genteel education, with a view of bettering his situation in life. The patron dying just as he was ready to launch out into the world, the poor fellow in despair went to sea; where, after a variety of good and ill-fortune, a little before I was acquainted with him he had been set on shore by an American privateer, on the wild coast of Connaught, stripped of everything. I cannot quit this poor fellow's story without adding, that he is at this time master of a large West-Indiaman belonging to the Thames.

His mind was fraught with independence, magnanimity, and every manly virtue. I loved and admired him to a degree of enthusiasm, and of course strove to imitate him. In some measure I succeeded; I had pride before, but he taught it to flow in proper channels. His knowledge of the world was vastly superior to mine, and I was all attention to learn. He was the only man I ever saw who was a greater fool than myself where woman was the presiding star; but he spoke of illicit love with the levity of a sailor, which hitherto I had regarded with horror. Here his friendship did me a mischief, and the consequence was, that soon after I resumed the plough, I wrote the "Poet's Welcome."[177] My reading only increased while in this town by two stray volumes of Pamela, and one of Ferdinand Count Fathom, which gave me some idea of novels. Rhyme, except some religious pieces that are in print, I had given up; but meeting with Fergusson's Scottish Poems, I strung anew my wildly-sounding lyre with emulating vigour. When my father died, his all went among the hell-hounds that growl in the kennel of justice; but we made a shift to collect a little money in the family amongst us, with which, to keep us together, my brother and I took a neighbouring farm. My brother wanted my hair-brained imagination, as well as my social and amorous madness; but in good sense, and every sober qualification, he was far my superior.

I entered on this farm with a full resolution, "come, go to, I will be wise!" I read farming books, I calculated crops; I attended markets; and in short, in spite of the devil, and the world, and the flesh, I believe I should have been a wise man; but the first year, from unfortunately buying bad seed, the second from a late harvest, [356] we lost half our crops. This overset all my wisdom, and I returned, "like the dog to his vomit, and the sow that was washed, to her wallowing in the mire."

I now began to be known in the neighbourhood as a maker of rhymes. The first of my poetic offspring that saw the light, was a burlesque lamentation on a quarrel between two reverend Calvinists, both of them dramatis personæ in "Holy Fair." I had a notion myself that the piece had some merit; but, to prevent the worst, I gave a copy of it to a friend, who was very fond of such things, and told him that I could not guess who was the author of it, but that I thought it pretty clever. With a certain description of the clergy, as well as laity, it met with a roar of applause. "Holy Willie's Prayer" next made its appearance, and alarmed the kirk-session so much, that they held several meetings to look over their spiritual artillery, if haply any of it might be pointed against profane rhymers. Unluckily for me, my wanderings led me on another side, within point-blank shot of their heaviest metal. This is the unfortunate story that gave rise to my printed poem, "The Lament." This was a most melancholy affair, which I cannot yet bear to reflect on, and had very nearly given me one or two of the principal qualifications for a place among those who have lost the chart, and mistaken the reckoning of rationality. I gave up my part of the farm to my brother; in truth it was only nominally mine; and made what little preparation was in my power for Jamaica. But, before leaving my native country for ever, I resolved to publish my poems. I weighed my productions as impartially as was in my power; I thought they had merit; and it was a delicious idea that I should be called a clever fellow, even though it should never reach my ears-a poor negro-driver-or perhaps a victim to that inhospitable clime, and gone to the world of spirits! I can truly say, that pauvre inconnu as I then was, I had pretty nearly as high an idea of myself and of my works as I have at this moment, when the public has decided in their favour. It ever was my opinion that the mistakes and blunders, both in a rational and religious point of view, of which we see thousands daily guilty, are owing to their ignorance of themselves.-To know myself had been all along my constant study. I weighed myself alone; I balanced myself with others; I watched every means of information, to see how much ground I occupied as a man and as a poet; I studied assiduously Nature's design in my formation-where the lights and shades in my character were intended. I was pretty confident my poems would meet with some applause; but, at the worst, the roar of the Atlantic would deafen the voice of censure, and the novelty of West Indian scenes make me forget neglect. I threw off six hundred copies, of which I had got subscriptions for about three hundred and fifty.-My vanity was highly gratified by the reception I met with from the public; and besides I pocketed, all expenses deducted, nearly twenty pounds. This sum came very seasonably, as I was thinking of indenting myself, for want of money to procure my passage. As soon as I was master of nine guineas, the price of wafting me to the torrid zone, I took a steerage passage in the first ship that was to sail from the Clyde, for

"Hungry ruin had me in the wind."

I had been for some days skulking from covert to covert, under all the terrors of a jail; as some ill-advised people had uncoupled the merciless pack of the law at my heels. I had taken the last farewell of my few friends; my chest was on the road to Greenock; I had composed the last song I should ever measure in Caledonia-"The gloomy night is gathering fast," when a letter from Dr. Blacklock to a friend of mine, overthrew all my schemes, by opening new prospects to my poetic ambition. The doctor belonged to a set of critics for whose applause I had not dared to hope. His opinion, that I would meet with encouragement in Edinburgh for a second edition, fired me so much, that away I posted for that city, without a single acquaintance, or a single letter of introduction. The baneful star that had so long shed its blasting influence in my zenith, for once made a revolution to the nadir; and a kind Providence placed me under the patronage of one of the noblest of men, the Earl of Glencairn. Oublie-moi, grand Dieu, si

jamais je l'oublie!
I need relate no farther. At Edinburgh I was in a new world; I mingled among many classes of men, but all of them new to me, and I was all attention to "catch" the characters and "the manners living as they rise." Whether I have profited, time will show.
[357]
My most respectful compliments to Miss Williams. Her very elegant and friendly letter I cannot answer at present, as my presence is requisite in Edinburgh, and I set out to-morrow.
R. B.

FOOTNOTES:

[175] Idiot for idiotic.
[176] Paradise Lost, b. iv
[177] "Rob the Rhymer's Welcome to his Bastard Child."-See Poem XXXIII.

LXXV.

TO ROBERT AINSLIE, ESQ.,
BERRYWELL DUNSE.
[This characteristic letter was first published by Sir Harris Nichols; others, still more characteristic, addressed to the same gentleman, are abroad: how they escaped from private keeping is a sort of a riddle.]
Edinburgh, 23d August, 1787.
"As I gaed up to Dunse To warp a pickle yarn, Robin, silly body, He gat me wi' bairn."
From henceforth, my dear Sir, I am determined to set off with my letters like the periodical writers, viz. prefix a kind of text, quoted from some classic of undoubted authority, such as the author of the immortal piece, of which my text is part. What I have to say on my text is exhausted in a letter which I wrote you the other day, before I had the pleasure of receiving yours from Inverkeithing; and sure never was anything more lucky, as I have but the time to write this, that Mr. Nicol, on the opposite side of the table, takes to correct a proof-sheet of a thesis. They are gabbling Latin so loud that I cannot hear what my own soul is saying in my own skull, so I must just give you a matter-of-fact sentence or two, and end, if time permit, with a verse de rei generatione. To-morrow I leave Edinburgh in a chaise; Nicol thinks it more comfortable than horseback, to which I say, Amen; so Jenny Geddes goes home to Ayrshire, to use a phrase of my mother's, wi' her finger in her mouth.
Now for a modest verse of classical authority:

The cats like kitchen; The dogs like broo; The lasses like the lads weel, And th' auld wives too.
CHORUS.
And we're a' noddin, Nid, nid, noddin, We're a' noddin fou at e'en.
If this does not please you, let me hear from you; if you write any time before the 1st of September, direct to Inverness, to be left at the post-office till called for; the next week at Aberdeen, the next at Edinburgh.
The sheet is done, and I shall just conclude with assuring you that
I am, and ever with pride shall be,
My dear Sir, andc.
R. B.
Call your boy what you think proper, only interject Burns. What do you say to a Scripture name? Zimri Burns Ainslie, or Architophel, andc., look your Bible for these two heroes, if you do this, I will repay the compliment.

LXXVI.

TO MR. ROBERT MUIR.
[No Scotsman will ever read, without emotion, the poet's words in this letter, and in "Scots wha hae wi Wallace bled," about Bannnockburn and its glories.]
Stirling, 26th August, 1787.
My Dear Sir,
I intended to have written you from Edinburgh, and now write you from Stirling to make an excuse. Here am I, on my way to Inverness, with a truly original, but very worthy man, a Mr. Nicol, one of the masters of the High-school, in Edinburgh. I left Auld Reekie yesterday morning, and have passed, besides by-excursions, Linlithgow, Borrowstouness, Falkirk, and here am I undoubtedly. This morning I knelt at the tomb of Sir John the Graham, the gallant friend of the immortal Wallace; and two hours ago I said a fervent prayer, for Old Caledonia, over the hole in a blue whinstone, where Robert de Bruce fixed his royal standard on the banks of Bannockburn; and just now, from Stirling Castle, I have seen by the setting sun the glorious prospect of the windings of Forth through the rich carse of Stirling, and skirting the equally rich carse of Falkirk. The crops are very strong, but so very late, that there is no harvest, except a ridge or two perhaps in ten miles, all the way I have travelled from Edinburgh.
I left Andrew Bruce and family all well. I will be at least three weeks in making my tour, as I shall return by the coast, and have many people to call for.[358]
My best compliments to Charles, our dear kinsman and fellow-saint; and Messrs. W. and H. Parkers. I hope Hughoc is going on and prospering with God and Miss M'Causlin.

If I could think on anything sprightly, I should let you hear every other post; but a dull, matter-of-fact business, like this scrawl, the less and seldomer one writes, the better.

Among other matters-of-fact I shall add this, that I am and ever shall be,

My dear Sir,

Your obliged,

R. B.

LXXVII.

TO GAVIN HAMILTON, ESQ.

[It is supposed that the warmth of the lover came in this letter to the aid of the imagination of the poet, in his account of Charlotte Hamilton.]

Stirling, 28th August, 1787.

My dear Sir,

Here am I on my way to Inverness. I have rambled over the rich, fertile carses of Falkirk and Sterling, and am delighted with their appearance: richly waving crops of wheat, barley, andc., but no harvest at all yet, except, in one or two places, an old wife's ridge. Yesterday morning I rode from this town up the meandering Devon's banks, to pay my respects to some Ayrshire folks at Harvieston. After breakfast, we made a party to go and see the famous Caudron-linn, a remarkable cascade in the Devon, about five miles above Harvieston; and after spending one of the most pleasant days I ever had in my life, I returned to Stirling in the evening. They are a family, Sir, though I had not any prior tie; though they had not been the brother and sisters of a certain generous friend of mine, I would never forget them. I am told you have not seen them these several years, so you can have very little idea of what these young folks are now. Your brother is as tall as you are, but slender rather than otherwise; and I have the satisfaction to inform you that he is getting the better of those consumptive symptoms which I suppose you know were threatening him. His make, and particularly his manner, resemble you, but he will still have a finer face. (I put in the word still to please Mrs. Hamilton.) Good sense, modesty, and at the same time a just idea of that respect that man owes to man, and has a right in his turn to exact, are striking features in his character; and, what with me is the Alpha and the Omega, he has a heart that might adorn the breast of a poet! Grace has a good figure, and the look of health and cheerfulness, but nothing else remarkable in her person. I scarcely ever saw so striking a likeness as is between her and your little Beenie; the mouth and chin particularly. She is reserved at first; but as we grew better acquainted, I was delighted with the native frankness of her manner, and the sterling sense of her observation. Of Charlotte I cannot speak in common terms of admiration: she is not only beautiful but lovely. Her form is elegant; her features not regular, but they have the smile of sweetness and the settled complacency of good nature in the highest degree: and her complexion, now that she has happily recovered her wonted health, is equal to Miss Burnet's. After the exercise of our riding to the Falls, Charlotte was exactly Dr. Donne's mistress:-

-"Her pure and eloquent blood Spoke in her cheeks, and so distinctly wrought, That one would almost say her body thought."

Her eyes are fascinating; at once expressive of good sense, tenderness, and a noble mind.

I do not give you all this account, my good Sir, to flatter you. I mean it to reproach you. Such relations the first peer in the realm might own with pride; then why do you not keep up more correspondence with these so amiable young folks? I had a thousand questions to answer about you. I had to describe the little ones with the minuteness of anatomy. They were highly delighted when I told them that John was so good a boy, and so fine a scholar, and that Willie was going on still very pretty; but I have it in commission to tell her from them that beauty is a poor silly bauble without she be good. Miss Chalmers I had left in Edinburgh, but I had the pleasure of meeting Mrs. Chalmers, only Lady Mackenzie being rather a little alarmingly ill of a sore throat somewhat marred our enjoyment.

I shall not be in Ayrshire for four weeks. My most respectful compliments to Mrs. Hamilton, Miss Kennedy, and Doctor Mackenzie. I shall probably write him from some stage or other.

I am ever, Sir,

Yours most gratefully,

R. B

LXXVIII.

TO MR. WALKER,

BLAIR OF ATHOLE.

[Professor Walker was a native of Ayrshire, and an accomplished scholar; he saw Burns often in Edinburgh; he saw him at the Earl of Athol's on the Bruar; he visited him too at Dumfries; and after the copyright of Currie's edition of the poet's works expired, he wrote, with much taste and feeling his life anew, and edited his works-what passed under his own observation he related with truth and ease.]

Inverness, 5th September, 1787.

My dear Sir,

I have just time to write the foregoing,[178] and to tell you that it was (at least most part of it) the effusion of an half-hour I spent at Bruar. I do not mean it was extempore, for I have endeavoured to brush it up as well as Mr. Nicol's chat and the jogging of the chaise would allow. It eases my heart a good deal, as rhyme is the coin with which a poet pays his debts of honour or gratitude. What I owe to the noble family of Athol, of the first kind, I shall ever proudly boast; what I owe of the last, so help me God in my hour of need! I shall never forget.

The "little angel-band!" I declare I prayed for them very sincerely to-day at the Fall of Fyers. I shall never forget the fine family-piece I saw at Blair; the amiable, the truly noble duchess, with her smiling little seraph in her lap, at the head of the table; the lovely "olive plants," as the Hebrew bard finely says, round the happy mother: the beautiful Mrs. G; the lovely sweet Miss C., andc. I wish I had the powers of Guido to do them justice! My Lord Duke's kind hospitality-markedly kind indeed. Mr. Graham of Fintray's charms of conversation-Sir W. Murray's friendship. In short, the recollection of all that polite, agreeable company raises an honest glow in my bosom.

FOOTNOTES:

[178] The Humble Petition of Bruar-water

LXXIX.

TO MR. GILBERT BURNS.

[The letters of Robert to Gilbert are neither many nor important: the latter was a calm, considerate, sensible man, with nothing poetic in his composition: he died lately, much and widely respected.]

Edinburgh, 17th September, 1787.

My dear Brother,

I arrived here safe yesterday evening, after a tour of twenty-two days, and travelling near six hundred miles, windings included. My farthest stretch was about ten miles beyond Inverness. I went through the heart of the Highlands by Crieff, Taymouth, the famous seat of Lord Breadalbane, down the Tay, among cascades and druidical circles of stones, to Dunkeld, a seat of the Duke of Athol; thence across the Tay, and up one of his tributary streams to Blair of Athole, another of the duke's seats, where I had the honour of spending nearly two days with his grace and family; thence many miles through a wild country, among cliffs gray with eternal snows and gloomy savage glens, till I crossed Spey and went down the stream through Strathspey, so famous in Scottish music; Badenoch, andc., till I reached Grant Castle, where I spent half a day with Sir James Grant and family; and then crossed the country for Fort George, but called by the way at Cawdor, the ancient seat of Macbeth; there I saw the identical bed, in which tradition says king Duncan was murdered: lastly, from Fort George to Inverness.

I returned by the coast, through Nairn, Forres, and so on, to Aberdeen,

thence to Stonehive, where James Burness, from Montrose, met me by appointment. I spent two days among our relations, and found our aunts, Jean and Isabel, still alive, and hale old women. John Cairn, though born the same year with our father, walks as vigorously as I can: they have had several letters from his son in New York. William Brand is likewise a stout old fellow; but further particulars I delay till I see you, which will be in two or three weeks. The rest of my stages are not worth rehearsing: warm as I was from Ossian's country, where I had seen his very grave, what cared I for fishing-towns or fertile carses? I slept at the famous Brodie of Brodie's one night, and dined at Gordon Castle next day, with the duke, duchess and family. I am thinking to cause my old mare to meet me, by means of John Ronald, at Glasgow; but you shall hear farther from me before I leave Edinburgh. My duty and many compliments from the north to my mother; and my brotherly compliments to the rest. I have been trying for a berth for William, but am not likely to be successful. Farewell.
R. B

LXXX.

TO MISS MARGARET CHALMERS.
(NOW MRS. HAY.)
[To Margaret Chalmers, the youngest daughter of James Chalmers, Esq., of Fingland, it is said that Burns confided his affection to Charlotte Hamilton: his letters to Miss Chalmers, like those to Mrs. Dunlop, are distinguished for their good sense and delicacy as well as freedom.]
Sept. 26, 1787.
I send Charlotte the first number of the songs; I would not wait for the second number; I hate delays in little marks of friendship, as I hate dissimulation in the language of the heart. I am determined to pay Charlotte a poetic compliment, if I could hit on some glorious old Scotch air, in number second.[179] You will see a small attempt on a shred of paper in the book: but though Dr. Blacklock commended it very highly, I am not just satisfied with it myself. I intend to make it a description of some kind: the whining cant of love, except in real passion, and by a masterly hand, is to me as insufferable as the preaching cant of old Father Smeaton, whig-minister at Kilmaurs. Darts, flames, cupids, loves, graces, and all that farrago, are just a Mauchline * * * * a senseless rabble.
I got an excellent poetic epistle yesternight from the old, venerable author of "Tullochgorum," "John of Badenyon," andc. I suppose you know he is a clergyman. It is by far the finest poetic compliment I ever got. I will send you a copy of it.
I go on Thursday or Friday to Dumfries, to wait on Mr. Miller about his farms.-Do tell that to Lady Mackenzie, that she may give me credit for a

little wisdom. "I Wisdom dwell with Prudence." What a blessed fire-side! How happy should I be to pass a winter evening under their venerable roof! and smoke a pipe of tobacco, or drink water-gruel with them! What solemn, lengthened, laughter-quashing gravity of phiz! What sage remarks on the good-for-nothing sons and daughters of indiscretion and folly! And what frugal lessons, as we straitened the fire-side circle, on the uses of the poker and tongs!

Miss N. is very well, and begs to be remembered in the old way to you. I used all my eloquence, all the persuasive flourishes of the hand, and heart-melting modulation of periods in my power, to urge her out to Harvieston, but all in vain. My rhetoric seems quite to have lost its effect on the lovely half of mankind. I have seen the day-but that is a "tale of other years."-In my conscience I believe that my heart has been so oft on fire that it is absolutely vitrified. I look on the sex with something like the admiration with which I regard the starry sky in a frosty December night. I admire the beauty of the Creator's workmanship; I am charmed with the wild but graceful eccentricity of their motions, and-wish them good night. I mean this with respect to a certain passion dont j'ai eu l'honneur d'être un miserable esclave: as for friendship, you and Charlotte have given me pleasure, permanent pleasure, "which the world cannot give, nor take away," I hope; and which will outlast the heavens and the earth.

R. B.

FOOTNOTES:

[179] Of the Scots Musical Museum

LXXXI.

TO MISS MARGARET CHALMERS.

[That fine song, "The Banks of the Devon," dedicated to the charms of Charlotte Hamilton, was enclosed in the following letter.]

Without date.

I have been at Dumfries, and at one visit more shall be decided about a farm in that country. I am rather hopeless in it; but as my brother is an excellent farmer, and is, besides, an exceedingly prudent, sober man (qualities which are only a younger brother's fortune in our family), I am determined, if my Dumfries business fail me, to return into partnership with him, and at our leisure take another farm in the neighbourhood.

I assure you I look for high compliments from you and Charlotte on this very sage instance of my unfathomable, incomprehensible wisdom. Talking of Charlotte, I must tell her that I have, to the best of my power, paid her a poetic compliment, now completed. The air is admirable: true old Highland.

It was the tune of a Gaelic song, which an Inverness lady sung me when I was there; and I was so charmed with it that I begged her to write me a set of it from her singing; for it had never been set before. I am fixed that it shall go in Johnson's next number; so Charlotte and you need not spend your precious time in contradicting me. I won't say the poetry is first-rate; though I am convinced it is[361] very well; and, what is not always the case with compliments to ladies, it is not only sincere, but just.
R. B.

LXXXII.

TO JAMES HOY, ESQ.
GORDON CASTLE
[James Hoy, librarian of Gordon Castle, was, it is said, the gentleman whom his grace of Gordon sent with a message inviting in vain that "obstinate son of Latin prose," Nicol, to stop and enjoy himself.]
Edinburgh, 20th October, 1787.
Sir,
I will defend my conduct in giving you this trouble, on the best of Christian principles-"Whatsoever ye would that men should do unto you, do ye even so unto them."-I shall certainly, among my legacies, leave my latest curse to that unlucky predicament which hurried-tore me away from Castle Gordon. May that obstinate son of Latin prosebe curst to Scotch mile periods, and damned to seven league paragraphs; while Declension and Conjugation, Gender, Number, and Time, under the ragged banners of Dissonance and Disarrangement, eternally rank against him in hostile array.
Allow me, Sir, to strengthen the small claim I have to your acquaintance, by the following request. An engraver, James Johnson, in Edinburgh, has, not from mercenary views, but from an honest, Scotch enthusiasm, set about collecting all our native songs and setting them to music; particularly those that have never been set before. Clarke, the well known musician, presides over the musical arrangement, and Drs. Beattie and Blacklock, Mr. Tytler, of Woodhouselee, and your humble servant to the utmost of his small power, assist in collecting the old poetry, or sometimes for a fine air make a stanza, when it has no words. The brats, too tedious to mention, claim a parental pang from my bardship. I suppose it will appear in Johnson's second number-the first was published before my acquaintance with him. My request is-"Cauld Kail in Aberdeen," is one intended for this number, and I beg a copy of his Grace of Gordon's words to it, which you were so kind as to repeat to me. You may be sure we won't prefix the author's name, except you like, though I look on it as no small merit to this work that the names of many of the authors of our old Scotch songs, names almost forgotten, will be inserted.

I do not well know where to write to you-I rather write at you; but if you will be so obliging, immediately on receipt of this, as to write me a few lines, I shall perhaps pay you in kind, though not in quality. Johnson's terms are:-each number a handsome pocket volume, to consist at least of a hundred Scotch songs, with basses for the harpsichord, andc. The price to subscribers 5s.; to non-subscribers 6s. He will have three numbers I conjecture.

My direction for two or three weeks will be at Mr. William Cruikshank's, St. James's-square, New-town, Edinburgh.

I am,

Sir,

Your's to command,

R. B.

LXXXIII.

TO REV. JOHN SKINNER.

[The songs of "Tullochgorum," and "John of Badenyon," have made the name of Skinner dear to all lovers of Scottish verse: he was a man cheerful and pious, nor did the family talent expire with him: his son became Bishop of Aberdeen.]

Edinburgh, October 25, 1787.

Reverend and Venerable Sir,

Accept, in plain dull prose, my most sincere thanks for the best poetical compliment I ever received. I assure you, Sir, as a poet, you have conjured up an airy demon of vanity in my fancy, which the best abilities in your other capacity would be ill able to lay. I regret, and while I live I shall regret, that when I was in the north, I had not the pleasure of paying a younger brother's dutiful respect to the author of the best Scotch song ever Scotland saw-"Tullochgorum's my delight!" The world may think slightingly of the craft of song-making, if they please, but, as Job says-"Oh! that mine adversary had written a book!"-let them try. There is a certain something in the old Scotch songs, a wild happiness of thought and expression, which peculiarly marks them, not only from English songs, but also from the modern efforts of song-wrights in our native manner and language. The only remains of this enchantment, these spells of the imagination, rests with you. Our true brother, Ross of Lochlee, was likewise "owre cannie"-a "wild warlock"-but now he sings among the "sons of the morning."

I have often wished, and will certainly endea[362]vour to form a kind of common acquaintance among all the genuine sons of Caledonian song. The world, busy in low prosaic pursuits, may overlook most of us; but "reverence thyself." The world is not our peers, so we challenge the jury. We can lash that world, and find ourselves a very great source of

amusement and happiness independent of that world.
There is a work going on in Edinburgh, just now, which claims your best assistance. An engraver in this town has set about collecting and publishing all the Scotch songs, with the music, that can be found. Songs in the English language, if by Scotchmen, are admitted, but the music must all be Scotch. Drs. Beattie and Blacklock are lending a hand, and the first musician in town presides over that department. I have been absolutely crazed about it, collecting old stanzas, and every information respecting their origin, authors, andc. andc. This last is but a very fragment business; but at the end of his second number-the first is already published-a small account will be given of the authors, particularly to preserve those of latter times. Your three songs, "Tullochgorum," "John of Badenyon," and "Ewie wi' the crookit horn," go in this second number. I was determined, before I got your letter, to write you, begging that you would let me know where the editions of these pieces may be found, as you would wish them to continue in future times: and if you would be so kind to this undertaking as send any songs, of your own or others, that you would think proper to publish, your name will be inserted among the other authors,-"Nill ye, will ye." One half of Scotland already give your songs to other authors. Paper is done. I beg to hear from you; the sooner the better, as I leave Edinburgh in a fortnight or three weeks.-
I am,
With the warmest sincerity, Sir,
Your obliged humble servant,-R. B

LXXXIV.

TO JAMES HOY, ESQ.
AT GORDON CASTLE, FOCHABERS.
[In singleness of heart and simplicity of manners James Hoy is said, by one who knew him well, to have rivalled Dominie Sampson: his love of learning and his scorn of wealth are still remembered to his honour.]
Edinburgh, 6th November, 1787.
Dear Sir,
I would have wrote you immediately on receipt of your kind letter, but a mixed impulse of gratitude and esteem whispered me that I ought to send you something by way of return. When a poet owes anything, particularly when he is indebted for good offices, the payment that usually recurs to him-the only coin indeed in which he probably is conversant-is rhyme. Johnson sends the books by the fly, as directed, and begs me to enclose his most grateful thanks: my return I intended should have been one or two poetic bagatelles which the world have not seen, or, perhaps, for obvious reasons, cannot see. These I shall send you before I leave Edinburgh. They

may make you laugh a little, which, on the whole, is no bad way of spending one's precious hours and still more precious breath: at any rate, they will be, though a small, yet a very sincere mark of my respectful esteem for a gentleman whose further acquaintance I should look upon as a peculiar obligation.

The duke's song, independent totally of his dukeship, charms me. There is I know not what of wild happiness of thought and expression peculiarly beautiful in the old Scottish song style, of which his Grace, old venerable Skinner, the author of "Tullochgorum," andc., and the late Ross, at Lochlee, of true Scottish poetic memory, are the only modern instances that I recollect, since Ramsay with his contemporaries, and poor Bob Fergusson, went to the world of deathless existence and truly immortal song. The mob of mankind, that many-headed beast, would laugh at so serious a speech about an old song; but as Job says, "O that mine adversary had written a book!" Those who think that composing a Scotch song is a trifling business-let them try.

I wish my Lord Duke would pay a proper attention to the Christian admonition-"Hide not your candle under a bushel," but "let your light shine before men." I could name half a dozen dukes that I guess are a devilish deal worse employed: nay, I question if there are half a dozen better: perhaps there are not half that scanty number whom Heaven has favoured with the tuneful, happy, and, I will say, glorious gift.

I am, dear Sir,

Your obliged humble servant,

R. B.

LXXXV.

TO MR. ROBERT AINSLIE,

EDINBURGH.

["I set you down," says Burns, elsewhere, to Ainslie, "as the staff of my old age, when all my other friends, after a decent show of pity, will have forgot me."]

Edinburgh, Sunday Morning,

Nov. 23, 1787.

I Beg, my dear Sir, you would not make any appointment to take us to Mr. Ainslie's to-night. On looking over my engagements, constitution, present state of my health, some little vexatious soul concerns, andc., I find I can't sup abroad to-night. I shall be in to-day till one o'clock if you have a leisure hour.

You will think it romantic when I tell you, that I find the idea of your friendship almost necessary to my existence.-You assume a proper length of face in my bitter hours of blue-devilism, and you laugh fully up to my

highest wishes at my good things.-I don't know upon the whole, if you are one of the first fellows in God's world, but you are so to me. I tell you this just now in the conviction that some inequalities in my temper and manner may perhaps sometimes make you suspect that I am not so warmly as I ought to be your friend.
R. B.

LXXXVI.

TO THE EARL OF GLENCAIRN.
[The views of Burns were always humble: he regarded a place in the excise as a thing worthy of paying court for, both in verse and prose.]
Edinburgh, 1787.
My Lord,
I know your lordship will disapprove of my ideas in a request I am going to make to you; but I have weighed, long and seriously weighed, my situation, my hopes and turn of mind, and am fully fixed to my scheme if I can possibly effectuate it. I wish to get into the Excise; I am told that your lordship's interest will easily procure me the grant from the commissioners; and your lordship's patronage and goodness, which have already rescued me from obscurity, wretchedness, and exile, embolden me to ask that interest. You have likewise put it in my power to save the little tie of home that sheltered an aged mother, two brothers, and three sisters from destruction. There, my lord, you have bound me over to the highest gratitude.
My brother's farm is but a wretched lease, but I think he will probably weather out the remaining seven years of it; and after the assistance which I have given and will give him, to keep the family together, I think, by my guess, I shall have rather better than two hundred pounds, and instead of seeking, what is almost impossible at present to find, a farm that I can certainly live by, with so small a stock, I shall lodge this sum in a banking-house, a sacred deposit, expecting only the calls of uncommon distress or necessitous old age.
These, my lord, are my views: I have resolved from the maturest deliberation; and now I am fixed, I shall leave no stone unturned to carry my resolve into execution. Your lordship's patronage is the strength of my hopes; nor have I yet applied to anybody else. Indeed my heart sinks within me at the idea of applying to any other of the great who have honoured me with their countenance. I am ill qualified to dog the heels of greatness with the impertinence of solicitation, and tremble nearly as much at the thought of the cold promise as the cold denial; but to your lordship I have not only the honour, the comfort, but the pleasure of being
Your lordship's much obliged

And deeply indebted humble servant,
R. B.

LXXXVII.

TO JAMES DALRYMPLE, ESQ.
ORANGEFIELD.
[James Dalrymple, Esq., of Orangefield, was a gentleman of birth and poetic tastes-he interested himself in the fortunes of Burns.]
Edinburgh, 1787.
Dear Sir,
I suppose the devil is so elated with his success with you that he is determined by a coup de main to complete his purposes on you all at once, in making you a poet. I broke open the letter you sent me; hummed over the rhymes; and, as I saw they were extempore, said to myself, they were very well; but when I saw at the bottom a name that I shall ever value with grateful respect, "I gapit wide, but naething spak." I was nearly as much struck as the[364] friends of Job, of affliction-bearing memory, when they sat down with him seven days and seven nights, and spake not a word.
I am naturally of a superstitious cast, and as soon as my wonder-scared imagination regained its consciousness, and resumed its functions, I cast about what this mania of yours might portend. My foreboding ideas had the wide stretch of possibility; and several events, great in their magnitude, and important in their consequences, occurred to my fancy. The downfall of the conclave, or the crushing of the Cork rumps; a ducal coronet to Lord George Gordon and the Protestant interest; or St. Peter's keys to * * * * * *.
You want to know how I come on. I am just in statu quo, or, not to insult a gentleman with my Latin, in "auld use and wont." The noble Earl of Glencairn took me by the hand to-day, and interested himself in my concerns, with a goodness like that benevolent Being, whose image he so richly bears. He is a stronger proof of the immortality of the soul, than any that philosophy ever produced. A mind like his can never die. Let the worshipful squire H. L., or the reverend Mass J. M. go into their primitive nothing. At best, they are but ill-digested lumps of chaos, only one of them strongly tinged with bituminous particles and sulphureous effluvia. But my noble patron, eternal as the heroic swell of magnanimity, and the generous throb of benevolence, shall look on with princely eye at "the war of elements, the wreck of matter, and the crush of worlds."
R. B.

LXXXVIII.

TO CHARLES HAY. ESQ.,

ADVOCATE.

[The verses enclosed were written on the death of the Lord President Dundas, at the suggestion of Charles Hay, Esq., advocate, afterwards a judge, under the title of Lord Newton.]

Sir,

The enclosed poem was written in consequence of your suggestion, last time I had the pleasure of seeing you. It cost me an hour or two of next morning's sleep, but did not please me; so it lay by, an ill-digested effort, till the other day that I gave it a critic brush. These kind of subjects are much hackneyed; and, besides, the wailings of the rhyming tribe over the ashes of the great are cursedly suspicious, and out of all character for sincerity. These ideas damped my muse's fire; however, I have done the best I could, and, at all events, it gives me an opportunity of declaring that I have the honour to be, Sir, your obliged humble servant,

R. B.

LXXXIX.

TO MISS MN.

[This letter appeared for the first time in the "Letters to Clarinda," a little work which was speedily suppressed-it is, on the whole, a sort of Corydon and Phillis affair, with here and there expressions too graphic, and passages over-warm. Who the lady was is not known-or known only to one.]

Saturday Noon, No. 2, St. James's Square,

New Town, Edinburgh

Here have I sat, my 'dear Madam, in the stony altitude of perplexed study for fifteen vexatious minutes, my head askew, bending over the intended card; my fixed eye insensible to the very light of day poured around; my pendulous goose-feather, loaded with ink, hanging over the future letter, all for the important purpose of writing a complimentary card to accompany your trinket.

Compliment is such a miserable Greenland expression, lies at such a chilly polar distance from the torrid zone of my constitution, that I cannot, for the very soul of me, use it to any person for whom I have the twentieth part of the esteem every one must have for you who knows you.

As I leave town in three or four days, I can give myself the pleasure of calling on you only for a minute. Tuesday evening, some time about seven or after, I shall wait on you for your farewell commands.

The hinge of your box I put into the hands of the proper connoisseur. The broken glass, likewise, went under review; but deliberative wisdom thought it would too much endanger the whole fabric.

I am, dear Madam,

With all sincerity of enthusiasm,

Your very obedient servant,
R. B.

XC.

TO MISS CHALMERS.
[Some dozen or so, it is said, of the most beautiful letters that Burns ever wrote, and dedicated to the beauty of Charlotte Hamilton, were destroyed by that lady, in a moment when anger was too strong for reflection.]
Edinburgh, Nov. 21, 1787.
I have one vexatious fault to the kindly-welcome, well-filled sheet which I owe to your and Charlotte's goodness,-it contains too much sense, sentiment, and good-spelling. It is impossible that even you two, whom I declare to my God I will give credit for any degree of excellence the sex are capable of attaining, it is impossible you can go on to correspond at that rate; so like those who, Shenstone says, retire because they make a good speech, I shall, after a few letters, hear no more of you. I insist that you shall write whatever comes first: what you see, what you read, what you hear, what you admire, what you dislike, trifles, bagatelles, nonsense; or to fill up a corner, e'en put down a laugh at full length. Now none of your polite hints about flattery; I leave that to your lovers, if you have or shall have any; though, thank heaven, I have found at last two girls who can be luxuriantly happy in their own minds and with one another, without that commonly necessary appendage to female bliss-A LOVER.
Charlotte and you are just two favourite resting-places for my soul in her wanderings through the weary, thorny wilderness of this world. God knows I am ill-fitted for the struggle: I glory in being a Poet, and I want to be thought a wise man-I would fondly be generous, and I wish to be rich. After all, I am afraid I am a lost subject. "Some folk hae a hantle o' fauts, an' I'm but a ne'er-do-weel."
Afternoon-To close the melancholy reflections at the end of last sheet, I shall just add a piece of devotion commonly known in Carrick by the title of the "Wabster's grace:"-
"Some say we're thieves, and e'en sae are we, Some say we lie, and e'en sae do we! Gude forgie us, and I hope sae will he! Up and to your looms, lads."
R. B.

XCI.

TO MISS CHALMERS.
[The "Ochel-Hills," which the poet promises in this letter, is a song, beginning,
"Where braving angry winter's storms The lofty Ochels rise,"

written in honour of Margaret Chalmers, and published along with the "Banks of the Devon," in Johnson's Musical Museum.]

Edinburgh, Dec. 12, 1787.

I am here under the care of a surgeon, with a bruised limb extended on a cushion; and the tints of my mind vying with the livid horror preceding a midnight thunder-storm. A drunken coachman was the cause of the first, and incomparably the lightest evil; misfortune, bodily constitution, hell, and myself have formed a "quadruple alliance" to guaranty the other. I got my fall on Saturday, and am getting slowly better.

I have taken tooth and nail to the Bible, and am got through the five books of Moses, and half way in Joshua. It is really a glorious book. I sent for my bookbinder to-day, and ordered him to get me an octavo Bible in sheets, the best paper and print in town; and bind it with all the elegance of his craft.

I would give my best song to my worst enemy, I mean the merit of making it, to have you and Charlotte by me. You are angelic creatures, and would pour oil and wine into my wounded spirit.

I enclose you a proof copy of the "Banks of the Devon," which present with my best wishes to Charlotte. The "Ochel-hills" you shall probably have next week for yourself. None of your fine speeches!

R. B.

XCII.

TO MISS CHALMERS.

[The eloquent hypochondriasm of the concluding paragraph of this letter, called forth the commendation of Lord Jeffrey, when he criticised Cromek's Reliques of Burns, in the Edinburgh Review.]

Edinburgh, Dec. 19, 1787.

I begin this letter in answer to yours of the 17th current, which is not yet cold since I read it. The atmosphere of my soul is vastly clearer than when I wrote you last. For the first time, yesterday I crossed the room on crutches. It would do your heart good to see my hardship, not on my poetic, but on my oaken stilts; throwing my best leg with an air! and with as much hilarity in my gait and countenance, as a May frog leaping across the newly harrowed[366] ridge, enjoying the fragrance of the refreshed earth, after the long-expected shower!

I can't say I am altogether at my ease when I see anywhere in my path that meagre, squalid, famine-faced spectre, Poverty; attended as he always is, by iron-fisted oppression, and leering contempt; but I have sturdily withstood his buffetings many a hard-laboured day already, and still my motto is-I Dare! My worst enemy is moi-même. I lie so miserably open to the inroads and incursions of a mischievous, light-armed, well-mounted banditti, under the banners of imagination, whim, caprice, and passion: and the heavy-armed veteran regulars of wisdom, prudence, and forethought move so very, very slow, that I am almost in a state of perpetual warfare, and, alas! frequent defeat. There are just two creatures I would envy, a horse in his wild state traversing the forests of Asia, or an oyster on some of the desert shores of Europe. The one has not a wish without enjoyment, the other has neither wish nor fear.

R. B.

XCIII.

TO SIR JOHN WHITEFOORD.

[The Whitefoords of Whitefoord, interested themselves in all matters connected with literature: the power of the family, unluckily for Burns, was not equal to their taste.]

Edinburgh, December, 1787.

Sir,

Mr. Mackenzie, in Mauchline, my very warm and worthy friend, has informed me how much you are pleased to interest yourself in my fate as a man, and (what to me is incomparably dearer) my fame as a poet. I have, Sir, in one or two instances, been patronized by those of your character in life, when I was introduced to their notice by * * * * * friends to them and honoured acquaintances to me! but you are the first gentleman in the country whose benevolence and goodness of heart has interested himself for me, unsolicited and unknown. I am not master enough of the etiquette of these matters to know, nor did I stay to inquire, whether formal duty bade, or cold propriety disallowed, my thanking you in this manner, as I am convinced, from the light in which you kindly view me, that you will do me the justice to believe this letter is not the manœuvre of the needy, sharping author, fastening on those in upper life, who honour him with a little notice of him or his works. Indeed, the situation of poets is generally such, to a proverb, as may, in some measure, palliate that prostitution of heart and talents, they have at times been guilty of. I do not think prodigality is, by any means, a necessary concomitant of a poetic turn, but I believe a careless indolent attention to economy, is almost inseparable from it; then there must be in the heart of every bard of Nature's making, a certain modest sensibility, mixed with a kind of pride, that will ever keep him out of the way of those windfalls of fortune which frequently light on hardy impudence and foot-licking servility. It is not easy to imagine a more helpless state than his whose poetic fancy unfits him for the world, and whose character as a scholar gives him some pretensions to the politesse of life-yet is as poor as I am.

For my part, I thank Heaven my star has been kinder; learning never elevated my ideas above the peasant's shed, and I have an independent fortune at the plough-tail.

I was surprised to hear that any one who pretended in the least to the manners of the gentleman, should be so foolish, or worse, as to stoop to traduce the morals of such a one as I am, and so inhumanly cruel, too, as to meddle with that late most unfortunate, unhappy part of my story. With a tear of gratitude, I thank you, Sir, for the warmth with which you interposed in behalf of my conduct. I am, I acknowledge, too frequently the sport of whim, caprice, and passion, but reverence to God, and integrity to my fellow-creatures, I hope I shall ever preserve. I have no return, Sir, to make you for your goodness but one-a return which, I am persuaded, will not be unacceptable-the honest, warm wishes of a grateful heart for your happiness, and every one of that lovely flock, who stand to you in a filial relation. If ever calumny aim the poisoned shaft at them, may friendship be by to ward the blow!

R. B.

XCIV.

TO MISS WILLIAMS,
ON READING HER POEM OF THE SLAVE-TRADE.

[The name and merits of Miss Williams are widely known; nor is it a small honour to her muse that her tender song of "Evan Banks" was imputed to Burns by[367] Cromek: other editors since have continued to include it in his works, though Sir Walter Scott named the true author.]

Edinburgh, Dec. 1787.

I know very little of scientific criticism, so all I can pretend to in that intricate art is merely to note, as I read along, what passages strike me as being uncommonly beautiful, and where the expression seems to be perplexed or faulty.

The poem opens finely. There are none of these idle prefatory lines which one may skip over before one comes to the subject. Verses 9th and 10th in particular,

"Where ocean's unseen bound Leaves a drear world of waters round,"

are truly beautiful. The simile of the hurricane is likewise fine; and, indeed, beautiful as the poem is, almost all the similes rise decidedly above it. From verse 31st to verse 50th is a pretty eulogy on Britain. Verse 36th, "That foul drama deep with wrong," is nobly expressive. Verse 46th, I am afraid, is rather unworthy of the rest; "to dare to feel" is an idea that I do not altogether like. The contrast of valour and mercy, from the 36th verse to the 50th, is admirable.

Either my apprehension is dull, or there is something a little confused in the apostrophe to Mr. Pitt. Verse 55th is the antecedent to verses 57th and

58th, but in verse 58th the connexion seems ungrammatical:-
"Powers . . . .
With no gradation mark'd their flight, But rose at once to glory's height."
Ris'n should be the word instead of rose. Try it in prose. Powers,-their flight marked by no gradations, but [the same powers] risen at once to the height of glory. Likewise, verse 53d, "For this," is evidently meant to lead on the sense of the verses 59th, 60th, 61st, and 62d: but let us try how the thread of connexion runs,-
"For this . . . . The deeds of mercy, that embrace A distant sphere, an alien race, Shall virtue's lips record and claim The fairest honours of thy name."
I beg pardon if I misapprehended the matter, but this appears to me the only imperfect passage in the poem. The comparison of the sunbeam is fine.
The compliment to the Duke of Richmond is, I hope, as just as it is certainly elegant The thought,
"Virtue . . . . Sends from her unsullied source, The gems of thought their purest force,"
is exceeding beautiful. The idea, from verse 81st to the 85th, that the "blest decree" is like the beams of morning ushering in the glorious day of liberty, ought not to pass unnoticed or unapplauded. From verse 85th to verse 108th, is an animated contrast between the unfeeling selfishness of the oppressor on the one hand, and the misery of the captive on the other. Verse 88th might perhaps be amended thus: "Nor ever quit her narrow maze." We are said to pass a bound, but we quit, a maze. Verse 100th is exquisitely beautiful:-
"They, whom wasted blessings tire."
Verse 110th is I doubt a clashing of metaphors: "to load a span" is, I am afraid, an unwarrantable expression. In verse 114th, "Cast the universe in shade," is a fine idea. From the 115th verse to the 142d is a striking description of the wrongs of the poor African. Verse 120th, "The load of unremitted pain," is a remarkable, strong expression. The address to the advocates for abolishing the slave-trade, from verse 143d to verse 208th, is animated with the true life of genius. The picture of oppression:-
"While she links her impious chain, And calculates the price of pain; Weighs agony in sordid scales, And marks if death or life prevails,"-
is nobly executed.
What a tender idea is in verse 108th! Indeed, that whole description of home may vie with Thomson's description of home, somewhere in the beginning of his Autumn. I do not remember to have seen a stronger expression of misery than is contained in these verses:-
"Condemned, severe extreme, to live When all is fled that life can give"
The comparison of our distant joys to distant objects is equally original and

striking.

The character and manners of the dealer in the infernal traffic is a well done though a horrid picture. I am not sure how far introducing the sailor was right; for though the sailor's common characteristic is generosity, yet, in this case, he is certainly not only an unconcerned witness, but, in some degree, an efficient[368] agent in the business. Verse 224th is a nervous .... expressive-"The heart convulsive anguish breaks." The description of the captive wretch when he arrives in the West Indies, is carried on with equal spirit. The thought that the oppressor's sorrow on seeing the slave pine, is like the butcher's regret when his destined lamb dies a natural death, is exceedingly fine.

I am got so much into the cant of criticism, that I begin to be afraid lest I have nothing except the cant of it; and instead of elucidating my author, am only benighting myself. For this reason, I will not pretend to go through the whole poem. Some few remaining beautiful lines, however, I cannot pass over. Verse 280th is the strongest description of selfishness I ever saw. The comparison of verses 285th and 286th is new and fine; and the line, "Your arms to penury you lend," is excellent. In verse 317th, "like" should certainly be "as" or "so;" for instance-

"His sway the hardened bosom leads To cruelty's remorseless deeds: As (or, so) the blue lightning when it springs With fury on its livid wings, Darts on the goal with rapid force, Nor heeds that ruin marks its course."

If you insert the word "like" where I have placed "as," you must alter "darts" to "darting," and "heeds" to "heeding" in order to make it grammar. A tempest is a favourite subject with the poets, but I do not remember anything even in Thomson's Winter superior to your verses from the 347th to the 351st. Indeed, the last simile, beginning with "Fancy may dress," andc., and ending with the 350th verse, is, in my opinion, the most beautiful passage in the poem; it would do honour to the greatest names that ever graced our profession.

I will not beg your pardon, Madam, for these strictures, as my conscience tells me, that for once in my life I have acted up to the duties of a Christian, in doing as I would be done by.

R. B.

XCV.

TO MR. RICHARD BROWN,
IRVINE.

[Richard Brown was the "hapless son of misfortune," alluded to by Burns in his biographical letter to Dr. Moore: by fortitude and prudence he retrieved his fortunes, and lived much respected in Greenock, to a good old age. He said Burns had little to learn in matters of levity, when he became

acquainted with him.]
Edinburgh, 30th Dec. 1787.
My dear Sir,
I have met with few things in life which have given me more pleasure than Fortune's kindness to you since those days in which we met in the vale of misery; as I can honestly say, that I never knew a man who more truly deserved it, or to whom my heart more truly wished it. I have been much indebted since that time to your story and sentiments for steeling my mind against evils, of which I have had a pretty decent share. My will-o'wisp fate you know: do you recollect a Sunday we spent together in Eglinton woods! You told me, on my repeating some verses to you, that you wondered I could resist the temptation of sending verses of such merit to a magazine. It was from this remark I derived that idea of my own pieces, which encouraged me to endeavour at the character of a poet. I am happy to hear that you will be two or three months at home. As soon as a bruised limb will permit me, I shall return to Ayrshire, and we shall meet; "and faith, I hope we'll not sit dumb, nor yet cast out!"
I have much to tell you "of men, their manners, and their ways," perhaps a little of the other sex. Apropos, I beg to be remembered to Mrs. Brown. There I doubt not, my dear friend, but you have found substantial happiness. I expect to find you something of an altered but not a different man; the wild, bold, generous young fellow composed into the steady affectionate husband, and the fond careful parent. For me, I am just the same will-o'-wisp being I used to be. About the first and fourth quarters of the moon, I generally set in for the trade wind of wisdom: but about the full and change, I am the luckless victim of mad tornadoes, which blow me into chaos. Almighty love still reigns and revels in my bosom; and I am at this moment ready to hang myself for a young Edinburgh widow, who has wit and wisdom more murderously fatal than the assassinating stiletto of the Sicilian banditti, or the poisoned arrow of the savage African. My highland dirk, that used to hang beside my crutches, I have gravely removed into a neighbouring closet, the key of which I cannot command in case of spring-tide paroxysms. You may guess of her wit by [369] the following verses, which she sent me the other day:-
Talk not of love, it gives me pain, For love has been my foe; He bound me with an iron chain, And plunged me deep in woe!
But friendship's pure and lasting joys. My heart was formed to prove,- There, welcome, win, and wear the prize, But never talk of love!
Your friendship much can make me blest- O why that bliss destroy? Why urge the odious one request, You know I must deny?[180]
My best compliments to our friend Allan.
Adieu!
R. B.

FOOTNOTES:

[180] See song 186, in Johnson's Musical Museum. Burns altered the two last lines, and added a stanza:
Why urge the only one request You know I will deny! Your thought if love must harbour there, Conceal it in that thought; Nor cause me from my bosom tear The very friend I sought.

XCVI.

TO GAVIN HAMILTON.
[The Hamiltons of the West continue to love the memory of Burns: the old arm-chair in which the bard sat, when he visited Nanse Tinnocks, was lately presented to the mason Lodge of Mauchline, by Dr. Hamilton, the "wee curly Johnie" of the Dedication.]
[Edinburgh, Dec. 1787.]
My dear Sir,
It is indeed with the highest pleasure that I congratulate you on the return of days of ease and nights of pleasure, after the horrid hours of misery in which I saw you suffering existence when last in Ayrshire; I seldom pray for any body, "I'm baith dead-sweer and wretched ill o't;" but most fervently do I beseech the Power that directs the world, that you may live long and be happy, but live no longer than you are happy. It is needless for me to advise you to have a reverend care of your health. I know you will make it a point never at one time to drink more than a pint of wine (I mean an English pint), and that you will never be witness to more than one bowl of punch at a time, and that cold drams you will never more taste; and, above all things, I am convinced, that after drinking perhaps boiling punch, you will never mount your horse and gallop home in a chill late hour. Above all things, as I understand you are in habits of intimacy with that Boanerges of gospel powers, Father Auld, be earnest with him that he will wrestle in prayer for you, that you may see the vanity of vanities in trusting to, or even practising the casual moral works of charity, humanity, generosity, and forgiveness of things, which you practised so flagrantly that it was evident you delighted in them, neglecting, or perhaps profanely despising, the wholesome doctrine of faith without works, the only anchor of salvation. A hymn of thanksgiving would, in my opinion, be highly becoming from you at present, and in my zeal for your well-being, I earnestly press on you to be diligent in chanting over the two enclosed pieces of sacred poesy. My best compliments to Mrs. Hamilton and Miss Kennedy.
Yours in the L-d,
R. B.

XCVII.

TO MISS CHALMERS.

[The blank which takes the place of the name of the "Gentleman in mind and manners," of this letter, cannot now be filled up, nor is it much matter: the acquaintance of such a man as the poet describes few or none would desire.]

Edinburgh, Dec. 1787.

My dear Madam,

I just now have read yours. The poetic compliments I pay cannot be misunderstood. They are neither of them so particular as to point you out to the world at large; and the circle of your acquaintances will allow all I have said. Besides, I have complimented you chiefly, almost solely, on your mental charms. Shall I be plain with you? I will; so look to it. Personal attractions, Madam, you have much above par; wit, understanding, and worth, you possess in the first class. This is a cursed flat way of telling you these truths, but let me hear no more of your sheepish timidity. I know the world a little. I know what they will say of my poems; by second sight I suppose; for I am seldom out in my conjectures; and you may believe me, my dear Madam, I would not run any risk of hurting you by any ill-judged compliment. I wish to show to the world, the odds between a poet's friends and those of simple prosemen. More for your information, both the pieces go in. One of them, "Where braving [370] angry winter's storms," is already set-the tune is Neil Gow's Lamentation for Abercarny; the other is to be set to an old Highland air in Daniel Dow's collection of ancient Scots music; the name is "Ha a Chaillich air mo Dheith." My treacherous memory has forgot every circumstance about Les Incas, only I think you mentioned them as being in Creech's possession. I shall ask him about it. I am afraid the song of "Somebody" will come too late-as I shall, for certain, leave town in a week for Ayrshire, and from that to Dumfries, but there my hopes are slender. I leave my direction in town, so anything, wherever I am, will reach me.

I saw yours to ; it is not too severe, nor did he take it amiss. On the contrary, like a whipt spaniel, he talks of being with you in the Christmas days. Mr.has given him the invitation, and he is determined to accept of it. O selfishness! he owns, in his sober moments, that from his own volatility of inclination, the circumstances in which he is situated, and his knowledge of his father's disposition;-the whole affair is chimerical-yet he will gratify an idle penchant at the enormous, cruel expense, of perhaps ruining the peace of the very woman for whom he professes the generous passion of love! He is a gentleman in his mind and manners-tant pis! He is a volatile school-boy-the heir of a man's fortune who well knows the value of two times two!

Perdition seize them and their fortunes, before they should make the amiable, the lovely , the derided object of their purse-proud contempt!

I am doubly happy to hear of Mrs. 'srecovery, because I really thought all was over with her. There are days of pleasure yet awaiting her:

"As I came in by Glenap, I met with an aged woman: She bad me cheer up my heart, For the best o' my days was comin'."

This day will decide my affairs with Creech. Things are, like myself, not what they ought to be; yet better than what they appear to be.

"Heaven's sovereign saves all beings but himself- That hideous sight-a naked human heart."

Farewell! remember me to Charlotte.

R. B.

XCVIII.

TO MRS. DUNLOP.

[The poet alludes in this letter, as in some before, to a hurt which he got in one of his excursions in the neighbourhood of Edinburgh.]

Edinburgh, January 21, 1788.

After six weeks' confinement, I am beginning to walk across the room. They have been six horrible weeks; anguish and low spirits made me unfit to read, write, or think.

I have a hundred times wished that one could resign life as an officer resigns a commission: for I would not take in any poor, ignorant wretch, by selling out. Lately I was a sixpenny private; and, God knows, a miserable soldier enough; now I march to the campaign, a starving cadet: a little more conspicuously wretched.

I am ashamed of all this; for though I do want bravery for the warfare of life, I could wish, like some other soldiers, to have as much fortitude or cunning as to dissemble or conceal my cowardice.

As soon as I can bear the journey, which will be, I suppose, about the middle of next week, I leave Edinburgh: and soon after I shall pay my grateful duty at Dunlop-House.

R. B.

XCIX.

TO MRS. DUNLOP.

[The levity with which Burns sometimes spoke of things sacred, had been obliquely touched upon by his good and anxious friend Mrs. Dunlop: he pleads guilty of folly, but not of irreligion.]

Edinburgh, February 12, 1788.

Some things in your late letters hurt me: not that you say them, but that you mistake me. Religion, my honoured Madam, has not only been all my life my chief dependence, but my dearest enjoyment. I have, indeed, been the luckless victim of wayward follies; but, alas! I have ever been "more fool than knave." A mathematician without religion is a probable character; an irreligious poet is a monster.

R. B.

C.

TO THE REV. JOHN SKINNER.

[When Burns undertook to supply Johnson with songs for the Musical Museum, he laid all the bards of Scotland[371] under contribution, and Skinner among the number, of whose talents, as well as those of Ross, author of Helenore, he was a great admirer.]

Edinburgh, 14th February, 1788.

Reverend and dear Sir,

I have been a cripple now near three months, though I am getting vastly better, and have been very much hurried beside, or else I would have wrote you sooner. I must beg your pardon for the epistle you sent me appearing in the Magazine. I had given a copy or two to some of my intimate friends, but did not know of the printing of it till the publication of the Magazine. However, as it does great honour to us both, you will forgive it.

The second volume of the songs I mentioned to you in my last is published to-day. I send you a copy which I beg you will accept as a mark of the veneration I have long had, and shall ever have, for your character, and of the claim I make to your continued acquaintance. Your songs appear in the third volume, with your name in the index; as, I assure you, Sir, I have heard your "Tullochgorum," particularly among our west-country folks, given to many different names, and most commonly to the immortal author of "The Minstrel," who, indeed, never wrote anything superior to "Gie's a sang, Montgomery cried." Your brother has promised me your verses to the Marquis of Huntley's reel, which certainly deserve a place in the collection. My kind host, Mr. Cruikshank, of the High-school here, and said to be one of the best Latins in this age, begs me to make you his grateful acknowledgments for the entertainment he has got in a Latin publication of yours, that I borrowed for him from your acquaintance and much respected friend in this place, the Reverend Dr. Webster. Mr. Cruikshank maintains that you write the best Latin since Buchanan. I leave Edinburgh to-morrow, but shall return in three weeks. Your song you mentioned in your last, to the tune of "Dumbarton Drums," and the other, which you say was done by a brother by trade of mine, a ploughman, I shall thank you much for a copy of each. I am ever, Reverend Sir, with the most respectful esteem and

sincere veneration, yours,
R. B.

CI.

TO RICHARD BROWN.

[The letters of Burns to Brown, and Smith, and Richmond, and others of his west-country friends, written when he was in the first flush of fame, show that he did not forget humble men, who anticipated the public in perceiving his merit.]

Edinburgh, February 15th, 1788.

My dear Friend,

I received yours with the greatest pleasure. I shall arrive at Glasgow on Monday evening; and beg, if possible, you will meet me on Tuesday. I shall wait you Tuesday all day. I shall be found at Davies', Black Bull inn. I am hurried, as if hunted by fifty devils, else I should go to Greenock: but if you cannot possibly come, write me, if possible, to Glasgow, on Monday; or direct to me at Mossgiel by Mauchline; and name a day and place in Ayrshire, within a fortnight from this date, where I may meet you. I only stay a fortnight in Ayrshire, and return to Edinburgh. I am ever, my dearest friend, yours,
R. B.

CII.

TO MRS. ROSE, OF KILRAVOCK.

[Mrs. Rose of Kilravock, a lady distinguished by the elegance of her manners, as well as by her talents, was long remembered by Burns: she procured for him snatches of old songs, and copies of northern melodies; to her we owe the preservation of some fine airs as well as the inspiration of some fine lyrics.]

Edinburgh, February 17th, 1788.

Madam,

You are much indebted to some indispensable business I have had on my hands, otherwise my gratitude threatened such a return for your obliging favour as would have tired your patience. It but poorly expresses my feelings to say, that I am sensible of your kindness: it may be said of hearts such as yours is, and such, I hope, mine is, much more justly than Addison applies it,-

"Some souls by instinct to each other turn."

There was something in my reception at Kilravock so different from the cold, obsequious, dancing-school bow of politeness, that it almost got into my head that friendship had occupied[372] her ground without the intermediate march of acquaintance. I wish I could transcribe, or rather transfuse into language, the glow of my heart when I read your letter. My ready fancy, with colours more mellow than life itself, painted the beautifully wild scenery of Kilravock-the venerable grandeur of the castle-the spreading woods-the winding river, gladly leaving his unsightly, heathy source, and lingering with apparent delight as he passes the fairy walk at the bottom of the garden;-your late distressful anxieties-your present enjoyments-your dear little angel, the pride of your hopes;-my aged friend, venerable in worth and years, whose loyalty and other virtues will strongly entitle her to the support of the Almighty Spirit here, and his peculiar favour in a happier state of existence. You cannot imagine, Madam, how much such feelings delight me; they are my dearest proofs of my own immortality. Should I never revisit the north, as probably I never will, nor again see your hospitable mansion, were I, some twenty years hence, to see your little fellow's name making a proper figure in a newspaper paragraph, my heart would bound with pleasure.

I am assisting a friend in a collection of Scottish songs, set to their proper tunes; every air worth preserving is to be included: among others I have given "Morag," and some few Highland airs which pleased me most, a dress which will be more generally known, though far, far inferior in real merit. As a small mark of my grateful esteem, I beg leave to present you with a copy of the work, as far as it is printed; the Man of Feeling, that first of men, has promised to transmit it by the first opportunity.

I beg to be remembered most respectfully to my venerable friend, and to your little Highland chieftain. When you see the "two fair spirits of the hill," at Kildrummie,[181] tell them that I have done myself the honour of setting myself down as one of their admirers for at least twenty years to come, consequently they must look upon me as an acquaintance for the same period; but, as the apostle Paul says, "this I ask of grace, not of debt."

I have the honour to be, Madam, andc.,

R. B.

FOOTNOTES:

[181] Miss Sophia Brodie, of L, and Miss Rose of Kilravock.

CIII.

TO RICHARD BROWN.

[While Burns was confined to his lodgings by his maimed limb, he beguiled the time and eased the pain by composing the Clarinda epistles, writing songs for Johnson, and letters to his companions.]

Mossgiel, 24th February, 1788.

My dear Sir,

I cannot get the proper direction for my friend in Jamaica, but the following will do:-To Mr. Jo. Hutchinson, at Jo. Brownrigg's, Esq., care of Mr. Benjamin Henriquez, merchant, Orange-street, Kingston. I arrived here, at my brother's, only yesterday, after fighting my way through Paisley and Kilmarnock, against those old powerful foes of mine, the devil, the world, and the flesh-so terrible in the fields of dissipation. I have met with few incidents in my life which gave me so much pleasure as meeting you in Glasgow. There is a time of life beyond which we cannot form a tie worth the name of friendship. "O youth! enchanting stage, profusely blest." Life is a fairy scene: almost all that deserves the name of enjoyment or pleasure is only a charming delusion; and in comes repining age in all the gravity of hoary wisdom, and wretchedly chases away the bewitching phantom. When I think of life, I resolve to keep a strict look-out in the course of economy, for the sake of worldly convenience and independence of mind; to cultivate intimacy with a few of the companions of youth, that they may be the friends of age; never to refuse my liquorish humour a handful of the sweetmeats of life, when they come not too dear; and, for futurity,-

"The present moment is our ain, The neist we never saw!"[182]

How like you my philosophy? Give my best compliments to Mrs. B., and believe me to be,

My dear Sir,

Yours most truly,

R. B.

FOOTNOTES:

[182] Mickle.

CIV.

TO MR. WILLIAM CRUIKSHANK.

[The excise and farming alternately occupied the poet's thoughts in Edinburgh: he studied books of husbandry [373]and took lessons in gauging, and in the latter he became expert.]

Mauchline, March 3d, 1788.

My dear Sir,

Apologies for not writing are frequently like apologies for not singing-the apology better than the song. I have fought my way severely through the savage hospitality of this country, to send every guest drunk to bed if they can.

I executed your commission in Glasgow, and I hope the cocoa came safe. 'Twas the same price and the very same kind as your former parcel, for the gentleman recollected your buying there perfectly well.

I should return my thanks for yourhospitality (I leave a blank for the epithet, as I know none can do it justice) to a poor, wayfaring bard, who was spent and utmost overpowered fighting with prosaic wickednesses in high places; but I am afraid lest you should burn the letter whenever you come to the passage, so I pass over it in silence. I am just returned from visiting Mr. Miller's farm. The friend whom I told you I would take with me was highly pleased with the farm; and as he is, without exception, the most intelligent farmer in the country, he has staggered me a good deal. I have the two plans of life before me; I shall balance them to the best of my judgment, and fix on the most eligible. I have written Mr. Miller, and shall wait on him when I come to town, which shall be the beginning or middle of next week; I would be in sooner, but my unlucky knee is rather worse, and I fear for some time will scarcely stand the fatigue of my Excise instructions. I only mention these ideas to you; and, indeed, except Mr. Ainslie, whom I intend writing to to-morrow, I will not write at all to Edinburgh till I return to it. I would send my compliments to Mr. Nicol, but he would be hurt if he knew I wrote to anybody and not to him: so I shall only beg my best, kindest, kindest compliments to my worthy hostess and the sweet little rose-bud.

So soon as I am settled in the routine of life, either as an Excise-officer, or as a farmer, I propose myself great pleasure from a regular correspondence with the only man almost I ever saw who joined the most attentive prudence with the warmest generosity.

I am much interested for that best of men, Mr. Wood; I hope he is in better health and spirits than when I saw him last.

I am ever,

My dearest friend,

Your obliged, humble servant,

R. B.

CV.

TO ROBERT AINSLIE, ESQ.

[The sensible and intelligent farmer on whose judgment Burns depended in the choice of his farm, was Mr. Tait, of Glenconner.]

Mauchline, 3d March, 1788.

My dear Friend,

I am just returned from Mr. Miller's farm. My old friend whom I took with me was highly pleased with the bargain, and advised me to accept of it. He is the most intelligent sensible farmer in the county, and his advice has staggered me a good deal. I have the two plans before me: I shall endeavour to balance them to the best of my judgement, and fix on the most eligible.

On the whole, if I find Mr. Miller in the same favourable disposition as when I saw him last, I shall in all probability turn farmer.

I have been through sore tribulation and under much buffeting of the wicked one since I came to this country. Jean I found banished, forlorn, destitute and friendless: I have reconciled her to her fate, and I have reconciled her to her mother.

I shall be in Edinburgh middle of next week. My farming ideas I shall keep private till I see. I got a letter from Clarinda yesterday, and she tells me she has got no letter of mine but one. Tell her that I wrote to her from Glasgow, from Kilmarnock, from Mauchline, and yesterday from Cumnock as I returned from Dumfries. Indeed she is the only person in Edinburgh I have written to till this day. How are your soul and body putting up?-a little like man and wife, I suppose.

R. B.

[374]

CVI.

TO RICHARD BROWN.

[Richard Brown, it is said, fell off in his liking for Burns when he found that he had made free with his name in his epistle to Moore.]

Mauchline, 7th March, 1788.

I have been out of the country, my dear friend, and have not had an opportunity of writing till now, when I am afraid you will be gone out of the country too. I have been looking at farms, and, after all, perhaps I may settle in the character of a farmer. I have got so vicious a bent to idleness, and have ever been so little a man of business, that it will take no ordinary effort to bring my mind properly into the routine: but you will save a "great effort is worthy of you." I say so myself; and butter up my vanity with all the stimulating compliments I can think of. Men of grave, geometrical minds, the sons of "which was to be demonstrated," may cry up reason as much as they please; but I have always found an honest passion, or native instinct, the truest auxiliary in the warfare of this world. Reason almost always comes to me like an unlucky wife to a poor devil of a husband, just in sufficient time to add her reproaches to his other grievances.

I am gratified with your kind inquiries after Jean; as, after all, I may say with Othello:-

"Excellent wretch! Perdition catch my soul, but I do love thee!"

I go for Edinburgh on Monday.

Yours,-R. B

CVII.

TO MR. MUIR.

[The change which Burns says in this letter took place in his ideas, refers, it is said, to his West India voyage, on which, it appears by one of his letters to Smith, he meditated for some time after his debut in Edinburgh.]

Mossgiel, 7th March, 1788.

Dear Sir,

I have partly changed my ideas, my dear friend, since I saw you. I took old Glenconner with mo to Mr. Miller's farm, and he was so pleased with it, that I have wrote an offer to Mr. Miller, which, if he accepts, I shall sit down a plain farmer, the happiest of lives when a man can live by it. In this case I shall not stay in Edinburgh above a week. I set out on Monday, and would have come by Kilmarnock, but there are several small sums owing me for my first edition about Galston and Newmills, and I shall set off so early as to dispatch my business, and reach Glasgow by night. When I return, I shall devote a forenoon or two to make some kind of acknowledgment for all the kindness I owe your friendship. Now that I hope to settle with some credit and comfort at home, there was not any friendship or friendly correspondence that promised me more pleasure than yours; I hope I will not be disappointed. I trust the spring will renew your shattered frame, and make your friends happy. You and I have often agreed that life is no great blessing on the whole. The close of life, indeed, to a reasoning eye, is,

"Dark as was chaos, ere the infant sun Was roll'd together, or had try'd his beams Athwart their gloom profound."[183]

But an honest man has nothing to fear. If we lie down in the grave, the whole man a piece of broken machinery, to moulder with the clods of the valley, be it so: at least there is an end of pain, care, woes, and wants: if that part of us called mind does survive the apparent destruction of the man-away with old-wife prejudices and tales! Every age and every nation has had a different set of stories; and as the many are always weak, of consequence, they have often, perhaps always, been deceived; a man conscious of having acted an honest part among his fellow-creatures-even granting that he may have been the sport at times of passions and instincts-he goes to a great unknown Being, who could have no other end in giving him existence but to make him happy, who gave him those passions and instincts, and well knows their force.

These, my worthy friend, are my ideas; and I know they are not far different from yours. It becomes a man of sense to think for himself, particularly in a case where all men are equally interested, and where, indeed, all men are equally in the dark.

Adieu, my dear Sir; God send us a cheerful meeting!

R. B.

FOOTNOTES:

[183] Blair's Grave.
[375]

CVIII.

TO MRS. DUNLOP.
[One of the daughters of Mrs. Dunlop painted a sketch of Coila from Burns's poem of the Vision: it is still in existence, and is said to have merit.]
Mossgiel, 17th March, 1788.
Madam,
The last paragraph in yours of the 30th February affected me most, so I shall begin my answer where you ended your letter. That I am often a sinner with any little wit I have, I do confess: but I have taxed my recollection to no purpose, to find out when it was employed against you. I hate an ungenerous sarcasm a great deal worse than I do the devil; at least as Milton described him; and though I may be rascally enough to be sometimes guilty of it myself, I cannot endure it in others. You, my honoured friend, who cannot appear in any light but you are sure of being respectable-you can afford to pass by an occasion to display your wit, because you may depend for fame on your sense; or, if you choose to be silent, you know you can rely on the gratitude of many, and the esteem of all; but, God help us, who are wits or witlings by profession, if we stand for fame there, we sink unsupported!
I am highly flattered by the news you tell me of Coila. I may say to the fair painter who does me so much honour, as Dr. Beattie says to Ross the poet of his muse Scota, from which, by the bye, I took the idea of Coila ('tis a poem of Beattie's in the Scottish dialect, which perhaps you have never seen:)-
Ye shak your heads, but o' my fegs, Ye've sat auld Scota on her legs: Lang had she lien wi' beffs and flegs, Bumbaz'd and dizzie, Her fiddle wanted strings and pegs. Wae's me, poor hizzie."
R. B.

CIX.

TO MISS CHALMERS.
[The uncouth cares of which the poet complains in this letter were the construction of a common farmhouse, with barn, byre, and stable to suit.]
Edinburgh, March 14, 1788.
I know, my ever dear friend, that you will be pleased with the news when I tell you, I have at last taken a lease of a farm. Yesternight I completed a

bargain with Mr. Miller, of Dalswinton for the farm of Ellisland, on the banks of the Nith, between five and six miles above Dumfries. I begin at Whit-Sunday to build a house, drive lime, andc.; and heaven be my help! for it will take a strong effort to bring my mind into the routine of business. I have discharged all the army of my former pursuits, fancies, and pleasures; a motley host! and have literally and strictly retained only the ideas of a few friends, which I have incorporated into a lifeguard. I trust in Dr. Johnson's observation, "Where much is attempted, something is done." Firmness, both in sufferance and exertion, is a character I would wish to be thought to possess: and have always despised the whining yelp of complaint, and the cowardly, feeble resolve.

Poor Miss K. is ailing a good deal this winter, and begged me to remember her to you the first time I wrote to you. Surely woman, amiable woman, is often made in vain. Too delicately formed for the rougher pursuits of ambition; too noble for the dirt of avarice, and even too gentle for the rage of pleasure; formed indeed for, and highly susceptible of enjoyment and rapture; but that enjoyment, alas! almost wholly at the mercy of the caprice, malevolence, stupidity, or wickedness of an animal at all times comparatively unfeeling, and often brutal.

R. B.

CX.

TO RICHARD BROWN.

[The excitement referred to in this letter arose from the dilatory and reluctant movements of Creech, who was so slow in settling his accounts that the poet suspected his solvency.]

Glasgow, 26th March, 1788.

I am monstrously to blame, my dear Sir, in not writing to you, and sending you the Directory. I have been getting my tack extended, as I have taken a farm; and I have been racking shop accounts with Mr. Creech, both of which, together with watching, fatigue, and a load of care almost too heavy for my shoulders, have in some degree actually fevered me. I really forgot the Directory yesterday, which vexed me; but I was convulsed with rage a great part of the day. I have to thank you for the ingenious, friendly, and elegant epistle from[376] your friend Mr. Crawford. I shall certainly write to him, but not now. This is merely a card to you, as I am posting to Dumfries-shire, where many perplexing arrangements await me. I am vexed about the Directory; but, my dear Sir, forgive me: these eight days I have been positively crazed. My compliments to Mrs. B. I shall write to you at Grenada.-I am ever, my dearest friend,

Yours,-R. B.

CXI.

TO MR. ROBERT CLEGHORN.

[Cleghorn was a farmer, a social man, and much of a musician. The poet wrote the Chevalier's Lament to please the jacobitical taste of his friend; and the musician gave him advice in farming which he neglected to follow:- "Farmer Attention," says Cleghorn, "is a good farmer everywhere."]

Mauchline, 31st March, 1788.

Yesterday, my dear Sir, as I was riding through a track of melancholy, joyless muirs, between Galloway and Ayrshire, it being Sunday, I turned my thoughts to psalms, and hymns, and spiritual songs; and your favourite air, "Captain O'Kean," coming at length into my head, I tried these words to it. You will see that the first part of the tune must be repeated.

I am tolerably pleased with these verses, but as I have only a sketch of the tune, I leave it with you to try if they suit the measure of the music.

I am so harassed with care and anxiety, about this farming project of mine, that my muse has degenerated into the veriest prose-wench that ever picked cinders, or followed a tinker. When I am fairly got into the routine of business, I shall trouble you with a longer epistle; perhaps with some queries respecting farming; at present, the world sits such a load on my mind, that it has effaced almost every trace of the poet in me.

My very best compliments and good wishes to Mrs. Cleghorn.

R. B.

CXII.

TO MR. WILLIAM DUNBAR,
EDINBURGH.

[This letter was printed for the first time by Robert Chambers, in his "People's Edition" of Burns.]

Mauchline, 7th April, 1788.

I have not delayed so long to write you, my much respected friend, because I thought no farther of my promise. I have long since give up that kind of formal correspondence, where one sits down irksomely to write a letter, because we think we are in duty bound so to do.

I have been roving over the country, as the farm I have taken is forty miles from this place, hiring servants and preparing matters; but most of all I am earnestly busy to bring about a revolution in my own mind. As, till within these eighteen months, I never was the wealthy master of 10 guineas, my knowledge of business is to learn; add to this my late scenes of idleness and dissipation have enervated my mind to an alarming degree. Skill in the sober science of life is my most serious and hourly study. I have dropt all conversation and all reading (prose reading) but what tends in some way or other to my serious aim. Except one worthy young fellow, I have not one single correspondent in Edinburgh. You have indeed kindly made me an offer of that kind. The world of wits, and gens comme il faut which I lately left, and with whom I never again will intimately mix-from that port, Sir, I expect your Gazette: what Les beaux esprit are saying, what they are doing, and what they are singing. Any sober intelligence from my sequestered walks of life; any droll original; any passing reward, important forsooth, because it is mine; any little poetic effort, however embryoth; these, my dear Sir, are all you have to expect from me. When I talk of poetic efforts, I must have it always understood, that I appeal from your wit and taste to your friendship and good nature. The first would be my favourite tribunal, where I defied censure; but the last, where I declined justice.

I have scarcely made a single distich since I saw you. When I meet with an old Scots air that has any facetious idea in its name, I have a peculiar pleasure in following out that idea for a verse or two.

I trust that this will find you in better health[377] than I did last time I called for you. A few lines from you, directed to me at Mauchline, were it but to let me know how you are, will set my mind a good deal [at rest.] Now, never shun the idea of writing me because perhaps you may be out of humour or spirits. I could give you a hundred good consequences attending a dull letter; one, for example, and the remaining ninety-nine some other time-it will always serve to keep in countenance, my much respected Sir, your obliged friend and humble servant,

R. B.

CXIII.

TO MISS CHALMERS.

[The sacrifice referred to by the poet, was his resolution to unite his fortune with Jean Armour.]

Mauchline, 7th April, 1788.

I am indebted to you and Miss Nimmo for letting me know Miss Kennedy. Strange! how apt we are to indulge prejudices in our judgments of one another! Even I, who pique myself on my skill in marking characters-because I am too proud of my character as a man, to be dazzled in my judgment for glaring wealth; and too proud of my situation as a poor man to be biased against squalid poverty-I was unacquainted with Miss K.'s very uncommon worth.

I am going on a good deal progressive in mon grand bût, the sober science of life. I have lately made some sacrifices, for which, were I vivâ voce with you to paint the situation and recount the circumstances, you should applaud me.

R. B.

CXIV.

TO MISS CHALMERS.

[The hint alluded to, was a whisper of the insolvency of Creech; but the bailie was firm as the Bass.]

No date.

Now for that wayward, unfortunate thing, myself. I have broke measures with Creech, and last week I wrote him a frosty, keen letter. He replied in terms of chastisement, and promised me upon his honour that I should have the account on Monday; but this is Tuesday, and yet I have not heard a word from him. God have mercy on me! a poor d-mned, incautious, duped, unfortunate fool! The sport, the miserable victim of rebellious pride, hypochondriac imagination, agonizing sensibility, and bedlam passions?

"I wish that I were dead, but I'm no like to die!" I had lately "a hair-breadth 'scape in th' imminent deadly breach" of love too. Thank my stars, I got off heart-whole, "waur fleyd than hurt."-Interruption.

I have this moment got a hint: I fear I am something like-undone-but I hope for the best. Come, stubborn pride and unshrinking resolution; accompany me through this, to me, miserable world! You must not desert me! Your friendship I think I can count on, though I should date my letters from a marching regiment. Early in life, and all my life I reckoned on a recruiting drum as my forlorn hope. Seriously though, life at present presents me with but a melancholy path: but-my limb will soon be sound, and I shall struggle on.

R. B.

CXV.

TO MISS CHALMERS.

[Although Burns gladly grasped at a situation in the Excise, he wrote many apologies to his friends, for the acceptance of a place, which, though humble enough, was the only one that offered.]

Edinburgh, Sunday.

To-morrow, my dear madam, I leave Edinburgh. I have altered all my plans of future life. A farm that I could live in, I could not find; and, indeed, after the necessary support my brother and the rest of the family required, I could not venture on farming in that style suitable to my feelings. You will condemn me for the next step I have taken. I have entered into the Excise. I stay in the west about three weeks, and then return to Edinburgh, for six weeks' instructions: afterwards, for I get employ instantly, I go où il plait à Dieu,-et mon Roi. I have chosen this, my dear friend, after mature deliberation. The question is not at what door of fortune's palace shall we

enter in; but what doors does she open to us? I was not likely to get anything to do. I wanted un bût, which is a dangerous, an unhappy situation. I got this without any hanging on, or mortifying solicitation; it is immediate bread, and though poor in comparison of the last eighteen months of my existence, 'tis luxury in com[378]parison of all my preceding life: besides, the commissioners are some of them my acquaintances, and all of them my firm friends.
R. B.

CXVI.

TO MRS. DUNLOP.
[The Tasso, with the perusal of which Mrs. Dunlop indulged the poet, was not the line version of Fairfax, but the translation of Hoole-a far inferior performance.]
Mauchline, 28th April, 1788.
Madam,
Your powers of reprehension must be great indeed, as I assure you they made my heart ache with penitential pangs, even though I was really not guilty. As I commence farmer at Whit-Sunday, you will easily guess I must be pretty busy; but that is not all. As I got the offer of the Excise business without solicitation, and as it costs me only six months' attendance for instructions, to entitle me to a commission-which commission lies by me, and at any future period, on my simple petition, ca be resumed-I thought five-and-thirty pounds a-year was no bad dernier ressort for a poor poet, if fortune in her jade tricks should kick him down from the little eminence to which she has lately helped him up.
For this reason, I am at present attending these instructions, to have them completed before Whit-sunday. Still, Madam, I prepared with the sincerest pleasure to meet you at the Mount, and came to my brother's on Saturday night, to set out on Sunday; but for some nights preceding I had slept in an apartment, where the force of the winds and rains was only mitigated by being sifted through numberless apertures in the windows, walls, andc. In consequence I was on Sunday, Monday, and part of Tuesday, unable to stir out of bed, with all the miserable effects of a violent cold.
You see, Madam, the truth of the French maxim, le vrai n'est pas toujours le vraisemblable; your last was so full of expostulation, and was something so like the language of an offended friend, that I began to tremble for a correspondence, which I had with grateful pleasure set down as one of the greatest enjoyments of my future life.
Your books have delighted me: Virgil, Dryden, and Tasso were all equally strangers to me; but of this more at large in my next.
R. B.

CXVII.

TO MR. JAMES SMITH,
Avon Printfield, Linlithgow.

[James Smith, as this letter intimates, had moved from Mauchline to try to mend his fortunes at Avon Printfield, near Linlithgow.]

Mauchline, April 28, 1788.

Beware of your Strasburgh, my good Sir! Look on this as the opening of a correspondence, like the opening of a twenty-four gun battery!

There is no understanding a man properly, without knowing something of his previous ideas (that is to say, if the man has any ideas; for I know many who, in the animal-muster, pass for men, that are the scanty masters of only one idea on any given subject, and by far the greatest part of your acquaintances and mine can barely boast of ideas, 1.25-1.5-1.75 or some such fractional matter;) so to let you a little into the secrets of my pericranium, there is, you must know, a certain clean-limbed, handsome, bewitching young hussy of your acquaintance, to whom I have lately and privately given a matrimonial title to my corpus.

"Bode a robe and wear it, Bode a pock and bear it,"

says the wise old Scots adage! I hate to presage ill-luck; and as my girl has been doubly kinder to me than even the best of women usually are to their partners of our sex, in similar circumstances, I reckon on twelve times a brace of children against I celebrate my twelfth wedding-day: these twenty-four will give me twenty-four gossipings, twenty-four christenings (I mean one equal to two), and I hope, by the blessing of the God of my fathers, to make them twenty-four dutiful children to their parents, twenty-four useful members of society, and twenty-four approved services of their God! * * *

"Light's heartsome," quo' the wife when she was stealing sheep. You see what a lamp I have hung up to lighten your paths, when you are idle enough to explore the combinations and[379] relations of my ideas. 'Tis now as plain as a pike-staff, why a twenty-four gun battery was a metaphor I could readily employ.

Now for business.-I intend to present Mrs. Burns with a printed shawl, an article of which I dare say you have variety: 'tis my first present to her since I have irrevocably called her mine, and I have a kind of whimsical wish to get her the first said present from an old and much-valued friend of hers and mine, a trusty Trojan, on whose friendship I count myself possessed of as a life-rent lease.

Look on this letter as a "beginning of sorrows;" I will write you till your eyes ache reading nonsense.

Mrs. Burns ('tis only her private designation) begs her best compliments to you.

R. B.

CXVIII.

TO PROFESSOR DUGALD STEWART.

[Dugald Stewart loved the poet, admired his works, and enriched the biography of Currie with some genuine reminiscences of his earlier days.]

Mauchline, 3d May, 1788.

Sir,

I enclose you one or two more of my bagatelles. If the fervent wishes of honest gratitude have any influence with that great unknown being who frames the chain of causes and events, prosperity and happiness will attend your visits to the continent, and return you safe to your native shore.

Wherever I am, allow me, Sir, to claim it as my privilege to acquaint you with my progress in my trade of rhymes; as I am sure I could say it with truth, that next to my little fame, and the having it in my power to make life more comfortable to those whom nature has made dear to me, I shall ever regard your countenance, your patronage, your friendly good offices, as the most valued consequence of my late success in life.

R. B.

CXIX.

TO MRS. DUNLOP.

[A poem, something after the fashion of the Georgics, was long present to the mind of Burns: had fortune been more friendly he might have, in due time, produced it.]

Mauchline, 4th May, 1788.

Madam,

Dryden's Virgil has delighted me. I do not know whether the critics will agree with me, but the Georgics are to me by far the best of Virgil. It is indeed a species of writing entirely new to me; and has filled my head with a thousand fancies of emulation: but, alas! when I read the Georgics, and then survey my own powers, 'tis like the idea of a Shetland pony, drawn up by the side of a thorough-bred hunter to start for the plate. I own I am disappointed in the Æneid. Faultless correctness may please, and does highly please, the lettered critic: but to that awful character I have not the most distant pretensions. I do not know whether I do not hazard my pretensions to be a critic of any kind, when I say that I think Virgil, in many instances, a servile copier of Homer. If I had the Odyssey by me, I could parallel many passages where Virgil has evidently copied, but by no means improved, Homer. Nor can I think there is anything of this owing to the translators; for, from everything I have seen of Dryden, I think him in

genius and fluency of language, Pope's master. I have not perused Tasso enough to form an opinion: in some future letter, you shall have my ideas of him; though I am conscious my criticisms must be very inaccurate and imperfect, as there I have ever felt and lamented my want of learning most.
R. B.

CXX.

TO MR. ROBERT AINSLIE.
[I have heard the gentleman say, to whom this brief letter is addressed, how much he was pleased with the intimation, that the poet had reunited himself with Jean Armour, for he know his heart was with her.]
Mauchline, May 26, 1788.
My dear Friend,
I am two kind letters in your debt, but I have been from home, and horribly busy, buying and preparing for my farming business, over and above the plague of my Excise instructions, which this week will finish.
As I flatter my wishes that I foresee many future years' correspondence between us, 'tis[380] foolish to talk of excusing dull epistles; a dull letter may be a very kind one. I have the pleasure to tell you that I have been extremely fortunate in all my buyings, and bargainings hitherto; Mrs. Burns not excepted; which title I now avow to the world. I am truly pleased with this last affair: it has indeed added to my anxieties for futurity, but it has given a stability to my mind, and resolutions unknown before; and the poor girl has the most sacred enthusiasm of attachment to me, and has not a wish but to gratify my every idea of her deportment. I am interrupted.-Farewell! my dear Sir.
R. B.

CXXI.

TO MRS. DUNLOP.
[This letter, on the hiring season, is well worth the consideration of all masters, and all servants. In England, servants are engaged by the month; in Scotland by the half-year, and therefore less at the mercy of the changeable and capricious.]
27th May, 1788.
Madam,
I have been torturing my philosophy to no purpose, to account for that kind partiality of yours, which has followed me, in my return to the shade of life, with assiduous benevolence. Often did I regret, in the fleeting hours of my late will-o'-wisp appearance, that "here I had no continuing city;" and but for the consolation of a few solid guineas, could almost lament the time

that a momentary acquaintance with wealth and splendour put me so much out of conceit with the sworn companions of my road through life-insignificance and poverty.

There are few circumstances relating to the unequal distribution of the good things of this life that give me more vexation (I mean in what I see around me) than the importance the opulent bestow on their trifling family affairs, compared with the very same things on the contracted scale of a cottage. Last afternoon I had the honour to spend an hour or two at a good woman's fireside, where the planks that composed the floor were decorated with a splendid carpet, and the gay table sparkled with silver and china. 'Tis now about term-day, and there has been a revolution among those creatures, who though in appearance partakers, and equally noble partakers, of the same nature with Madame, are from time to time-their nerves, their sinews, their health, strength, wisdom, experience, genius, time, nay a good part of their very thoughts-sold for months and years, not only to the necessities, the conveniences, but, the caprices of the important few. We talked of the insignificant creatures, nay notwithstanding their general stupidity and rascality, did some of the poor devils the honour to commend them. But light be the turf upon his breast who taught "Reverence thyself!" We looked down on the unpolished wretches, their impertinent wives and clouterly brats, as the lordly bull does on the little dirty ant-hill, whose puny inhabitants he crushes in the carelessness of his ramble, or tosses in the air in the wantonness of his pride.

R. B.

CXXII.

TO MRS. DUNLOP,

At Mr. Dunlop's, Haddington.

[In this, the poet's first letter from Ellisland, he lays down his whole system of in-door and out-door economy: while his wife took care of the household, he was to manage the farm, and "pen a stanza" during his hours of leisure.]

Ellisland, 13th June, 1788.

"Where'er I roam, whatever realms I see, My heart, untravell'd, fondly turns to thee; Still to my friend it turns with ceaseless pain, and drags at each remove a lengthening chain."

Goldsmith.

This is the second day, my honoured friend, that I have been on my farm. A solitary inmate of an old smoky spense; far from every object I love, or by whom I am beloved; nor any acquaintance older than yesterday, except Jenny Geddes, the old mare I ride on; while uncouth cares and novel plans hourly insult my awkward ignorance and bashful inexperience. There is a foggy atmosphere native to my soul in the hour of care; consequently the dreary objects seem larger than life. Extreme sensibility, irritated and prejudiced on the gloomy side by a series of misfortunes and disappointments, at that period of my existence when the soul is laying in her cargo of ideas for the voyage of life, is, I believe, the principal cause of this unhappy frame of mind.[381]

"The valiant, in himself, what can he suffer? Or what need he regard his single woes?" andc.

Your surmise, Madam, is just; I am indeed a husband.

To jealousy or infidelity I am an equal stranger. My preservative from the first is the most thorough consciousness of her sentiments of honour, and her attachment to me: my antidote against the last is my long and deep-rooted affection for her.

In housewife matters, of aptness to learn and activity to execute, she is eminently mistress; and during my absence in Nithsdale, she is regularly and constantly apprentice to my mother and sisters in their dairy and other rural business.

The muses must not be offended when I tell them, the concerns of my wife and family will, in my mind, always take the pas; but I assure them their ladyships will ever come next in place.

You are right that a bachelor state would have insured me more friends; but from a cause you will easily guess, conscious peace in the enjoyment of my own mind, and unmistrusting confidence in approaching my God, would seldom have been of the number.

I found a once much-loved and still much-loved female, literally and truly cast out to the mercy of the naked elements; but I enabled her to purchase a shelter;-there is no sporting with a fellow-creature's happiness or misery.

The most placid good-nature and sweetness of disposition; a warm heart, gratefully devoted with all its powers to love me; vigorous health and sprightly cheerfulness, set off to the best advantage by a more than commonly handsome figure; these, I think, in a woman, may make a good wife, though she should never have read a page but the Scriptures of the Old and New Testament, nor have danced in a brighter assembly than a penny pay-wedding.

R. B.

CXXIII.

TO ROBERT AINSLIE, ESQ.

[Had Burns written his fine song, beginning "Contented wi' little and cantie wi' mair," when he penned this letter, the prose might have followed as a note to the verse; he calls the Excise a luxury.]

Ellisland, June 14th, 1788.

This is now the third day, my dearest Sir, that I have sojourned in these regions; and during these three days you have occupied more of my thoughts than in three weeks preceding: in Ayrshire I have several variations of friendship's compass, here it points invariably to the pole. My farm gives me a good many uncouth cares and anxieties, but I hate the language of complaint. Job, or some one of his friends, says well-"why should a living man complain?"

I have lately been much mortified with contemplating an unlucky imperfection in the very framing and construction of my soul; namely, a blundering inaccuracy of her olfactory organs in hitting the scent of craft or design in my fellow-creatures. I do not mean any compliment to my ingenuousness, or to hint that the defect is in consequence of the unsuspicious simplicity of conscious truth or honour: I take it to be, in some, why or other, an imperfection in the mental sight; or, metaphor apart, some modification of dulness. In two or three small instances lately, I have been most shamefully out.

I have all along hitherto, in the warfare of life, been bred to arms among the light-horse-the piquet-guards of fancy: a kind of hussars and Highlanders of the brain; but I am firmly resolved to sell out of these giddy battalions, who have no ideas of a battle but fighting the foe, or of a siege but storming the town. Cost what it will, I am determined to buy in among the grave squadrons of heavy-armed thought, or the artillery corps of plodding contrivance.

What books are you reading, or what is the subject of your thoughts, besides the great studies of your profession? You said something about religion in your last. I don't exactly remember what it was, as the letter is in Ayrshire; but I thought it not only prettily said, but nobly thought. You will make a noble fellow if once you were married. I make no reservation of your being well-married: you have so much sense, and knowledge of human nature, that though you may not realize perhaps the ideas of romance, yet you will never be ill-married.

Were it not for the terrors of my ticklish situation respecting provision for a family of children, I am decidedly of opinion that the step I have taken is vastly for my happiness. As it is[382] I look to the Excise scheme as a certainty of maintenance!-luxury to what either Mrs. Burns or I were born to.

Adieu.

R. B.

CXXIV.

TO ROBERT AINSLIE, ESQ.

[The kindness of Field, the profilist, has not only indulged me with a look at the original, from which the profile alluded to in the letter was taken, but has put me in possession of a capital copy.]

Mauchline, 23d June, 1788.

This letter, my dear Sir, is only a business scrap. Mr. Miers, profile painter in your town, has executed a profile of Dr. Blacklock for me: do me the favour to call for it, and sit to him yourself for me, which put in the same size as the doctor's. The account of both profiles will be fifteen shillings, which I have given to James Connell, our Mauchline carrier, to pay you when you give him the parcel. You must not, my friend, refuse to sit. The time is short: when I sat to Mr. Miers, I am sure he did not exceed two minutes. I propose hanging Lord Glencairn, the Doctor, and you in trio over my new chimney-piece that is to be.

Adieu.

R. B.

CXXV.

TO ROBERT AINSLIE, ESQ.

["There is a degree of folly," says Burns in this letter, "in talking unnecessarily of one's private affairs." The folly is scarcely less to write about them, and much did the poet and his friend write about their own private affairs as well as those of others.]

Ellisland, June 30th, 1788.

My dear Sir,

I just now received your brief epistle; and, to take vengeance on your laziness, I have, you see, taken a long sheet of writing-paper, and have begun at the top of the page, intending to scribble on to the very last corner.

I am vexed at that affair of the * * *, but dare not enlarge on the subject until you send me your direction, as I suppose that will be altered on your late master and friend's death. I am concerned for the old fellow's exit, only as I fear it may be to your disadvantage in any respect-for an old man's dying, except he has been a very benevolent character, or in some particular situation of life that the welfare of the poor or the helpless depended on him, I think it an event of the most trifling moment in the world. Man is naturally a kind, benevolent animal, but he is dropped into such a needy situation here in this vexatious world, and has such a whoreson hungry, growling, multiplying pack of necessities, appetites, passions, and desires about him, ready to devour him for want of other food; that in fact he must lay aside his cares for others that he may look properly to himself. You have been imposed upon in paying Mr. Miers for the profile of a Mr. H. I did not mention it in my letter to you, nor did I ever give Mr. Miers any such order. I have no objection to lose the money, but I will not have any such profile in my possession.

I desired the carrier to pay you, but as I mentioned only fifteen shillings to him, I would rather enclose you a guinea note. I have it not, indeed, to spare here, as I am only a sojourner in a strange land in this place; but in a day or two I return to Mauchline, and there I have the bank-notes through the house like salt permits.

There is a great degree of folly in talking unnecessarily of one's private affairs. I have just now been interrupted by one of my new neighbours, who has made himself absolutely contemptible in my eyes, by his silly garrulous pruriency. I know it has been a fault of my own, too; but from this moment I abjure it, as I would the service of hell! Your poets, spend-thrifts, and other fools of that kidney, pretend forsooth to crack their jokes on prudence; but 'tis a squalid vagabond glorying in his rags. Still, imprudence respecting money matters is much more pardonable than imprudence respecting character. I have no objection to prefer prodigality to avarice, in some few instances; but I appeal to your observation, if you have not met, and often met, with the same disingenuousness, the same hollow-hearted insincerity, and disintegritive depravity of principle, in the hackneyed victims of profusion, as in the unfeeling children of parsimony. I have every possible reverence for the much-talked-of world beyond the grave, and I wish that which piety believes, and virtue deserves, may be all matter of fact. But in things belonging to, and ter[383]minating in this present scene of existence, man has serious and interesting business on hand. Whether a man shall shake hands with welcome in the distinguished elevation of respect, or shrink from contempt in the abject corner of insignificance; whether he shall wanton under the tropic of plenty, at least enjoy himself in the comfortable latitudes of easy convenience, or starve in the arctic circle of dreary poverty; whether he shall rise in the manly consciousness of a self-approving mind, or sink beneath a galling load of regret and remorse-these are alternatives of the last moment.

You see how I preach. You used occasionally to sermonize too; I wish you would, in charity, favour me with a sheet full in your own way. I admire the close of a letter Lord Bolingbroke writes to Dean Swift:-"Adieu dear Swift! with all thy faults I love thee entirely: make an effort to love me with all mine!" Humble servant, and all that trumpery, is now such a prostituted business, that honest friendship, in her sincere way, must have recourse to her primitive, simple,-farewell!

R. B.

CXXVI.

TO MR. GEORGE LOCKHART,

Merchant, Glasgow.

[Burns, more than any poet of the age, loved to write out copies of his favourite poems, and present them to his friends: he sent "The Falls of Bruar" to Mr. Lockhart.]

Mauchline, 18th July, 1788.

My dear Sir,

I am just going for Nithsdale, else I would certainly have transcribed some of my rhyming things for you. The Miss Baillies I have seen in Edinburgh. "Fair and lovely are thy works, Lord God Almighty! Who would not praise thee for these thy gifts in thy goodness to the sons of men!" It needed not your fine taste to admire them. I declare, one day I had the honour of dining at Mr. Baillie's, I was almost in the predicament of the children of Israel, when they could not look on Moses' face for the glory that shone in it when he descended from Mount Sinai.

I did once write a poetic address from the Falls of Bruar to his Grace of Athole, when I was in the Highlands. When you return to Scotland, let me know, and I will send such of my pieces as please myself best. I return to Mauchline in about ten days.

My compliments to Mr. Purdon. I am in truth, but at present in haste,

Yours,-R. B.

CXXVII.

TO MR. PETER HILL.

[Peter Hill was a bookseller in Edinburgh: David Ramsay, printer of the Evening Courant: William Dunbar, an advocate, and president of a club of Edinburgh wits; and Alexander Cunningham, a jeweller, who loved mirth and wine.]

My dear Hill,

I shall say nothing to your mad present-you have so long and often been of important service to me, and I suppose you mean to go on conferring obligations until I shall not be able to lift up my face before you. In the mean time, as Sir Roger de Coverley, because it happened to be a cold day in which he made his will, ordered his servants great coats for mourning, so, because I have been this week plagued with an indigestion, I have sent you by the carrier a fine old ewe-milk cheese.

Indigestion is the devil: nay, 'tis the devil and all. It besets a man in every one of his senses. I lose my appetite at the sight of successful knavery, and sicken to loathing at the noise and nonsense of self-important folly. When the hollow-hearted wretch takes me by the hand, the feeling spoils my dinner: the proud man's wine so offends my palate that it chokes me in the gullet; and the pulvilised, feathered, pert coxcomb is so disgustful in my nostril that my stomach turns.

If ever you have any of these disagreeable sensations, let me prescribe for you patience; and a bit of my cheese. I know that you are no niggard of your good things among your friends, and some of them are in much need of a slice. There, in my eye is our friend Smellie; a man positively of the first abilities and greatest strength of mind, as well as one of the best hearts and keenest wits that I have ever met with; when you see him, as, alas! he too is smarting at the pinch of distressful circumstances, aggravated by the sneer of contumelious greatness-a bit of my cheese alone will[384] not cure him, but if you add a tankard of brown stout, and superadd a magnum of right Oporto, you will see his sorrows vanish like the morning mist before the summer sun.

Candlish, the earliest friend, except my only brother, that I have on earth, and one of the worthiest fellows that ever any man called by the name of friend, if a luncheon of my cheese would help to rid him of some of his super-abundant modesty, you would do well to give it him.

David,[184] with his Courant, comes, too, across my recollection, and I beg you will help him largely from the said ewe-milk cheese, to enable him to digest those bedaubing paragraphs with which he is eternally larding the lean characters of certain great men in a certain great town. I grant you the periods are very well turned; so, a fresh egg is a very good thing, but when thrown at a man in a pillory, it does not at all improve his figure, not to mention the irreparable loss of the egg.

My facetious friend Dunbar I would wish also to be a partaker: not to digest his spleen, for that he laughs off, but to digest his last night's wine at the last field-day of the Crochallan corps.[185]

Among our common friends I must not forget one of the dearest of them-Cunningham. The brutality, insolence, and selfishness of a world unworthy of having such a fellow as he is in it, I know sticks in his stomach, and if you can help him to anything that will make him a little easier on that score, it will be very obliging.

As to honest J Se, he is such a contented, happy man, that I know not what can annoy him, except, perhaps, he may not have got the better of a parcel of modest anecdotes which a certain poet gave him one night at supper, the last time the said poet was in town.

Though I have mentioned so many men of law, I shall have nothing to do with them professedly-the faculty are beyond my prescription. As to their clients, that is another thing; God knows they have much to digest!

The clergy I pass by; their profundity of erudition, and their liberality of sentiment; their total want of pride, and their detestation of hypocrisy, are so proverbially notorious as to place them far, far above either my praise or censure.

I was going to mention a man of worth whom I have the honour to call friend, the Laird of Craigdarroch; but I have spoken to the landlord of the King's-Arms inn here, to have at the next county meeting a large ewe-milk cheese on the table, for the benefit of the Dumfries-shire Whigs, to enable them to digest the Duke of Queensberry's late political conduct.

I have just this moment an opportunity of a private hand to Edinburgh, as perhaps you would not digest double postage.

R. B.

FOOTNOTES:

[184] Printer of the Edinburgh Evening Courant.

[185] A club of choice spirits.

CXXVIII.

TO ROBERT GRAHAM, ESQ.,

of Fintray.

[The filial and fraternal claims alluded to in this letter were satisfied with about three hundred pounds, two hundred of which went to his brother Gilbert-a sum which made a sad inroad on the money arising from the second edition of his Poems.]

Sir,

When I had the honour of being introduced to you at Athole-house, I did not think so soon of asking a favour of you. When Lear, in Shakspeare, asked Old Kent why he wished to be in his service, he answers, "Because you have that in your face which I would fain call master." For some such reason, Sir, do I now solicit your patronage. You know, I dare say, of an application I lately made to your Board to be admitted an officer of Excise. I have, according to form, been examined by a supervisor, and to-day I gave in his certificate, with a request for an order for instructions. In this affair, if I succeed, I am afraid I shall but too much need a patronizing friend. Propriety of conduct as a man, and fidelity and attention as an officer, I dare engage for; but with anything like business, except manual labour, I am totally unacquainted.

I had intended to have closed my late appearance on the stage of life, in the character of a country farmer; but after discharging some filial and fraternal claims, I find I could only fight for existence in that miserable manner, which I have lived to see throw a venerable parent into the jaws of a jail; whence death, the poor man's last and often best friend, rescued him.[385]

I know, Sir, that to need your goodness, is to have a claim on it; may I, therefore, beg your patronage to forward me in this affair, till I be appointed to a division; where, by the help of rigid economy, I will try to support that independence so dear to my soul, but which has been too often so distant from my situation.

R. B.

CXXIX.

TO WILLIAM CRUIKSHANK.

[The verses which this letter conveyed to Cruikshank were the lines written in Friars-Carse Hermitage: "the first-fruits," says the poet, elsewhere, "of my intercourse with the Nithsdale muse."]

Ellisland, August, 1788.

I have not room, my dear friend, to answer all the particulars of your last kind letter. I shall be in Edinburgh on some business very soon; and as I shall be two days, or perhaps three, in town, we shall discuss matters vivâ voce. My knee, I believe, will never be entirely well; and an unlucky fall this winter has made it still worse. I well remember the circumstance you allude to, respecting Creech's opinion of Mr. Nicol; but, as the first gentleman owes me still about fifty pounds, I dare not meddle in the affair.

It gave me a very heavy heart to read such accounts of the consequence of your quarrel with that puritanic, rotten-hearted, hell-commissioned scoundrel A. If, notwithstanding your unprecedented industry in public, and your irreproachable conduct in private life, he still has you so much in his power, what ruin may he not bring on some others I could name?

Many and happy returns of seasons to you, with your dearest and worthiest friend, and the lovely little pledge of your happy union. May the great Author of life, and of every enjoyment that can render life delightful, make her that comfortable blessing to you both, which you so ardently wish for, and which, allow me to say, you so well deserve! Glance over the foregoing verses, and let me have your blots.

Adieu.

R. B.

CXXX.

TO MRS. DUNLOP.

[The lines on the Hermitage were presented by the poet to several of his friends, and Mrs. Dunlop was among the number.]

Mauchline, August 2, 1788.

Honoured Madam,

Your kind letter welcomed me, yesternight, to Ayrshire. I am, indeed, seriously angry with you at the quantum of your luckpenny; but, vexed and hurt as I was, I could not help laughing very heartily at the noble lord's apology for the missed napkin.

I would write you from Nithsdale, and give you my direction there, but I have scarce an opportunity of calling at a post-office once in a fortnight. I am six miles from Dumfries, am scarcely ever in it myself, and, as yet, have little acquaintance in the neighbourhood. Besides, I am now very busy on my farm, building a dwelling-house; as at present I am almost an evangelical man in Nithsdale, for I have scarce "where to lay my head."

There are some passages in your last that brought tears in my eyes. "The heart knoweth its own sorrows, and a stranger intermeddleth not therewith." The repository of these "sorrows of the heart" is a kind of sanctum sanctorum: and 'tis only a chosen friend, and that, too, at particular sacred times, who dares enter into them:-

"Heaven oft tears the bosom-chords That nature finest strung."

You will excuse this quotation for the sake of the author. Instead of entering on this subject farther, I shall transcribe you a few lines I wrote in a hermitage, belonging to a gentleman in my Nithsdale neighbourhood. They are almost the only favours the muses have conferred on me in that country:-

Thou whom chance may hither lead.[186]

Since I am in the way of transcribing, the following were the production of yesterday as I jogged through the wild hills of New Cumnock. I intend inserting them, or something like them, in an epistle I am going to write to the gentleman on whose friendship my Excise hopes depend, Mr. Graham, of Fintray, one of [386] the worthiest and most accomplished gentlemen not only of this country, but, I will dare to say it, of this age. The following are just the first crude thoughts "unhousel'd, unanointed, unanneal'd:"-

Pity the tuneful muses' helpless train; Weak, timid landsmen on life's stormy main: The world were blest, did bliss on them depend; Ah, that "the friendly e'er should want a friend!" The little fate bestows they share as soon; Unlike sage, proverb'd, wisdom's hard-wrung boon. Let Prudence number o'er each sturdy son, Who life and wisdom at one race begun; Who feel by reason and who give by rule; Instinct's a brute and sentiment a fool! Who make poor will do wait upon I should; We own they're prudent, but who owns they're good?

Ye wise ones, hence! ye hurt the social eye; God's image rudely etch'd on base alloy! But come * * * * * *

Here the muse left me. I am astonished at what yon tell me of Anthony's writing me. I never received it. Poor fellow! you vex me much by telling me that he is unfortunate. I shall be in Ayrshire ten days from this date. I have just room for an old Roman farewell.

R. B.

FOOTNOTES:

[186] See Poems LXXXIX and XC

CXXXI.

TO MRS. DUNLOP.

[This letter has been often cited, and very properly, as a proof of the strong attachment of Burns to one who was, in many respects, worthy.]

Mauchline, August 10, 1788.

My much honoured Friend,

Yours of the 24th June is before me. I found it, as well as another valued friend-my wife, waiting to welcome me to Ayrshire: I met both with the sincerest pleasure.

When I write you, Madam, I do not sit down to answer every paragraph of yours, by echoing every sentiment, like the faithful Commons of Great Britain in Parliament assembled, answering a speech from the best of kings! I express myself in the fulness of my heart, and may, perhaps, be guilty of neglecting some of your kind inquiries; but not from your very old reason, that I do not read your letters. All your epistles for several months have cost me nothing, except a swelling throb of gratitude, or a deep-felt sentiment of veneration.

When Mrs. Burns, Madam, first found herself "as women wish to be who love their lords," as I loved her nearly to distraction, we took steps for a private marriage. Her parents got the hint; and not only forbade me her company and their house, but, on my rumoured West Indian voyage, got a warrant to put me in jail, till I should find security in my about-to-be paternal relation. You know my lucky reverse of fortune. On my éclatant return to Mauchline, I was made very welcome to visit my girl. The usual consequences began to betray her; and, as I was at that time laid up a cripple in Edinburgh, she was turned, literally turned out of doors, and I wrote to a friend to shelter her till my return, when our marriage was declared. Her happiness or misery were in my hands, and who could trifle with such a deposit?

I can easily fancy a more agreeable companion for my journey of life; but, upon my honour, I have never seen the individual instance.

Circumstanced as I am, I could never have got a female partner for life, who could have entered into my favourite studies, relished my favourite authors, andc., without probably entailing on me at the same time expensive living, fantastic caprice, perhaps apish affectation, with all the other blessed boarding-school acquirements, which (pardonnez moi, Madame,) are sometimes to be found among females of the upper ranks, but almost universally pervade the misses of the would-be gentry.

I like your way in your church-yard lucubrations. Thoughts that are the spontaneous result of accidental situations, either respecting health, place, or company, have often a strength, and always an originality, that would in vain be looked for in fancied circumstances and studied paragraphs. For me, I have often thought of keeping a letter, in progression by me, to send you when the sheet was written out. Now I talk of sheets, I must tell you, my reason for writing to you on paper of this kind is my pruriency of writing to you at large. A page of post is on such a dissocial, narrow-minded scale,[387] that I cannot abide it; and double letters, at least in my miscellaneous revery manner, are a monstrous tax in a close correspondence.

R. B.

CXXXII.

TO MRS. DUNLOP.

[Mrs. Miller, of Dalswinton, was a lady of beauty and talent: she wrote verses with skill and taste. Her maiden name was Jean Lindsay.]

Ellisland, 16th August, 1788.

I am in a fine disposition, my honoured friend, to send you an elegiac epistle; and want only genius to make it quite Shenstonian:-

"Why droops my heart with fancied woes forlorn? Why sinks my soul, beneath each wintry sky?"

My increasing cares in this, as yet strange country-gloomy conjectures in the dark vista of futurity-consciousness of my own inability for the struggle of the world-my broadened mark to misfortune in a wife and children;-I could indulge these reflections till my humour should ferment into the most acid chagrin, that would corrode the very thread of life.

To counterwork these baneful feelings, I have sat down to write to you; as I declare upon my soul I always find that the most sovereign balm for my wounded spirit.

I was yesterday at Mr. Miller's to dinner for the first time. My reception was quite to my mind: from the lady of the house quite flattering. She sometimes hits on a couplet or two, impromptu. She repeated one or two to the admiration of all present. My suffrage as a professional man, was expected: I for once went agonizing over the belly of my conscience. Pardon me, ye my adored household gods, independence of spirit, and integrity of soul! In the course of conversation, "Johnson's Musical Museum," a collection of Scottish songs with the music, was talked of. We got a song on the harpsichord, beginning,

"Raving winds around her blowing."[187]

The air was much admired: the lady of the house asked me whose were the words. "Mine, Madam-they are indeed my very best verses;" she took not the smallest notice of them! The old Scottish proverb says well, "king's caff is better than ither folks' corn." I was going to make a New Testament quotation about "casting pearls" but that would be too virulent, for the lady is actually a woman of sense and taste.

After all that has been said on the other side of the question, man is by no means a happy creature. I do not speak of the selected few, favoured by partial heaven, whose souls are tuned to gladness amid riches and honours, and prudence and wisdom. I speak of the neglected many, whose nerves, whose sinews, whose days are sold to the minions of fortune.

If I thought you had never seen it, I would transcribe for you a stanza of an old Scottish ballad, called, "The Life and Age of Man;" beginning thus:

"'Twas in the sixteenth hunder year Of God and fifty-three, Frae Christ was born, that bought us dear, As writings testifie."

I had an old grand-uncle, with whom my mother lived awhile in her girlish years; the good old man, for such he was, was long blind ere he died, during which time his highest enjoyment was to sit down and cry, while my mother would sing the simple old song of "the Life and Age of Man."

It is this way of thinking; it is these melancholy truths, that make religion so precious to the poor, miserable children of men.-If it is a mere phantom, existing only in the heated imagination of enthusiasm,

"What truth on earth so precious as a lie."

My idle reasonings sometimes make me a little sceptical, but the necessities of my heart always give the cold philosophisings the lie. Who looks for the heart weaned from earth; the soul affianced to her God; the correspondent devout thanksgiving, constant as the vicissitudes of even and morn; who thinks to meet with these in the court, the palace, in the glare of public life? No: to find them in their precious importance and divine efficacy, we must search among the obscure recesses of disappointment, affliction, poverty, and distress.

I am sure, dear Madam, you are now more than pleased with the length of my letters. I return to Ayrshire middle of next week: and it quickens my pace to think that there will be a letter from you waiting me there. I must be here again very soon for my harvest.

R. B.

FOOTNOTES:

[187] See Song LII.

CXXXIII.

TO MR. BEUGO,

Engraver, Edinburgh.

[Mr. Beugo was at well-known engraver in Edinburgh: he engraved Nasmyth's portrait of Burns, for Creech's first edition of his Poems; and as he could draw a little, he improved, as he called it, the engraving from sittings of the poet, and made it a little more like, and a little less poetic.]

Ellisland, 9th Sept. 1788.

My dear Sir,

There is not in Edinburgh above the number of the graces whose letters would have given me so much pleasure as yours of the 3d instant, which only reached me yesternight.

I am here on the farm, busy with my harvest; but for all that most pleasurable part of life called social communication, I am here at the very elbow of existence. The only things that are to be found in this country, in any degree of perfection, are stupidity and canting. Prose they only know in graces, prayers, andc., and the value of these they estimate as they do their plaiding webs-by the ell! As for the muses, they have as much an idea of a rhinoceros as of a poet. For my old capricious but good-natured huzzy of a muse-

"By banks of Nith I sat and wept When Coila I thought on, In midst thereof I hung my harp The willow-trees upon."

I am generally about half my time in Ayrshire with my "darling Jean," and then I, at lucid intervals, throw my horny fist across my becob-webbed lyre, much in the same manner as an old wife throws her hand across the spokes of her spinning-wheel.

I will send you the "Fortunate Shepherdess" as soon as I return to Ayrshire, for there I keep it with other precious treasure. I shall send it by a careful hand, as I would not for anything it should be mislaid or lost. I do not wish to serve you from any benevolence, or other grave Christian virtue; 'tis purely a selfish gratification of my own feelings whenever I think of you.

If your better functions would give you leisure to write me, I should be extremely happy; that is to say if you neither keep nor look for a regular correspondence. I hate the idea of being obliged to write a letter. I sometimes write a friend twice a week, at other times once a quarter.

I am exceedingly pleased with your fancy in making the author you mention place a map of Iceland instead of his portrait before his works: 'twas a glorious idea.

Could you conveniently do me one thing?-whenever you finish any head I should like to have a proof copy of it. I might tell you a long story about your fine genius; but as what everybody knows cannot have escaped you, I shall not say one syllable about it.

R. B.

CXXXIV.

TO MISS CHALMERS,

Edinburgh.

[To this fine letter all the biographer of Burns are largely indebted.]

Ellisland, near Dumfries, Sept. 16th, 1788.

Where are you? and how are you? and is Lady Mackenzie recovering her health? for I have had but one solitary letter from you. I will not think you have forgot me, Madam; and for my part-

"When thee, Jerusalem, I forget, Skill part from my right hand!"

"My heart is not of that rock, nor my soul careless as that sea." I do not make my progress among mankind as a bowl does among its fellows-rolling through the crowd without bearing away any mark of impression, except where they hit in hostile collision.

I am here, driven in with my harvest-folks by bad weather; and as you and your sister once did me the honour of interesting yourselves much à l'égard de moi, I sit down to beg the continuation of your goodness. I can truly say that, all the exterior of life apart, I never saw two, whose esteem flattered the nobler feelings of my soul-I will not say more, but so much as Lady Mackenzie and Miss Chalmers. When I think of you-hearts the best, minds the noblest of human kind-unfortunate even in the shades of life-when I think I have met with you, and have lived more of real life with you in eight days than I can do with almost any body I meet with in eight years-when I think on the improbability of meeting you in this world again-I could sit down and cry like a child! If ever you honoured me with a place in your esteem, I trust I can now plead more[389] desert. I am secure against that crushing grip of iron poverty, which, alas! is less or more fatal to the native worth and purity of, I fear, the noblest souls; and a late important step in my life has kindly taken me out of the way of those ungrateful iniquities, which, however overlooked in fashionable license, or varnished in fashionable phrase, are indeed but lighter and deeper shades of villany.

Shortly after my last return to Ayrshire, I married "my Jean." This was not in consequence of the attachment of romance, perhaps; but I had a long and much-loved fellow-creature's happiness or misery in my determination, and I durst not trifle with so important a deposit. Nor have I any cause to repent it. If I have not got polite tattle, modish manners, and fashionable dress, I am not sickened and disgusted with the multiform curse of boarding-school affectation: and I have got the handsomest figure, the sweetest temper, the soundest constitution, and the kindest heart in the county. Mrs. Burns believes, as firmly as her creed, that I am le plus bel esprit, et le plus honnête homme in the universe; although she scarcely ever in her life, except the Scriptures of the Old and New Testament, and the Psalms of David in metre, spent five minutes together either on prose or verse. I must except also from this last a certain late publication of Scots poems, which she has perused very devoutly; and all the ballads in the country, as she has (O the partial lover! you will cry) the finest "wood-note wild" I ever heard. I am the more particular in this lady's character, as I know she will henceforth have the honour of a share in your best wishes. She is still at Mauchline, as I am building my house; for this hovel that I shelter in, while occasionally here, is pervious to every blast that blows, and every shower that falls; and I am only preserved from being chilled to death by being suffocated with smoke. I do not find my farm that pennyworth I was taught to expect, but I believe, in time, it may be a saving bargain. You will be pleased to hear that I have laid aside idle éclat, and bind every day after my reapers.

To save me from that horrid situation of at any time going down in a losing bargain of a farm, to misery, I have taken my Excise instructions, and have my commission in my pocket for any emergency of fortune. If I could set all before your view, whatever disrespect you, in common with the world, have for this business, I know you would approve of my idea.

I will make no apology, dear Madam, for this egotistic detail; I know you and your sister will be interested in every circumstance of it. What signify the silly, idle gewgaws of wealth, or the ideal trumpery of greatness! When fellow-partakers of the same nature fear the same God, have the same benevolence of heart, the same nobleness of soul, the same detestation at everything dishonest, and the same scorn at everything unworthy-if they are not in the dependence of absolute beggary, in the name of common sense are they not equals? And if the bias, the instinctive bias, of their souls run the same way, why may they not be friends?

When I may have an opportunity of sending you this, Heaven only knows. Shenstone says, "When one is confined idle within doors by bad weather, the best antidote against ennui is to read the letters of or write to, one's friends;" in that case then, if the weather continues thus, I may scrawl you half a quire.

I very lately-to wit, since harvest began-wrote a poem, not in imitation, but in the manner, of Pope's Moral Epistles. It is only a short essay, just to try the strength of my muse's pinion in that way. I will send you a copy of it, when once I have heard from you. I have likewise been laying the foundation of some pretty large poetic works: how the superstructure will come on, I leave to that great maker and marrer of projects-time. Johnson's collection of Scots songs is going on in the third volume; and, of consequence, finds me a consumpt for a great deal of idle metre. One of the most tolerable things I have done in that way is two stanzas I made to an air, a musical gentleman of my acquaintance composed for the anniversary of his wedding-day, which happens on the seventh of November. Take it as follows:-

"The day returns-my bosom burns, The blissful day we twa did meet," andc.[188]

I shall give over this letter for shame. If I should be seized with a scribbling fit, before this goes away, I shall make it another letter; and then you may allow your patience a week's respite between the two. I have not room for more than the old, kind, hearty farewell.

To make some amends, mes chères Mesdames, for dragging you on to this second sheet, and to relieve a little the tiresomeness of my unstudied and uncorrectible prose, I shall transcribe you some of my late poetic bagatelles; though I have, these eight or ten months, done very little that way. One day in a hermitage on the banks of Nith, belonging to a gentleman in my neighbourhood, who is so good as give me a key at pleasure, I wrote as follows; supposing myself the sequestered, venerable inhabitant of the lonely mansion.

LINES WRITTEN IN FRIARS-CARSE
HERMITAGE.

"Thou whom chance may hither lead, Be thou clad in russet weed."[189]

R. B.

FOOTNOTES:

[188] Song LXIX.
[189] Poems LXXXIX. and XC.

CXXXV.

TO MR. MORISON,
Mauchline.

[Morison, of Mauchline, made most of the poet's furniture, for Ellisland: from Mauchline, too, came that eight-day clock, which was sold, at the death of the poet's widow, for thirty-eight pounds, to one who would have paid one hundred, sooner than wanted it.]

Ellisland, September 22, 1788.

My dear Sir,

Necessity obliges me to go into my new house even before it be plastered. I will inhabit the one end until the other is finished. About three weeks more, I think, will at farthest be my time, beyond which I cannot stay in this present house. If ever you wished to deserve the blessing of him that was ready to perish; if ever you were in a situation that a little kindness would have rescued you from many evils; if ever you hope to find rest in future states of untried being-get these matters of mine ready. My servant will be out in the beginning of next week for the clock. My compliments to Mrs. Morison.

I am,
After all my tribulation,
Dear Sir, yours,
R. B.

CXXXVI.

TO MRS. DUNLOP,
of Dunlop.
[Burns had no great respect for critics who found blemishes without perceiving beauties: he expresses his contempt for such in this letter.]
Mauchline, 27th Sept. 1788.
I have received twins, dear Madam, more than once; but scarcely ever with more pleasure than when I received yours of the 12th instant. To make myself understood; I had wrote to Mr. Graham, enclosing my poem addressed to him, and the same post which favoured me with yours brought me an answer from him. It was dated the very day he had received mine; and I am quite at a loss to say whether it was most polite or kind.
Your criticisms, my honoured benefactress, are truly the work of a friend. They are not the blasting depredations of a canker-toothed, caterpillar critic; nor are they the fair statement of cold impartiality, balancing with unfeeling exactitude the pro and con of an author's merits; they are the judicious observations of animated friendship, selecting the beauties of the piece. I have just arrived from Nithsdale, and will be here a fortnight. I was on horseback this morning by three o'clock; for between my wife and my farm is just forty-six miles. As I jogged on in the dark, I was taken with a poetic fit as follows:
"Mrs. Ferguson of Craigdarroch's lamentation for the death of her son; an uncommonly promising youth of eighteen or nineteen years of age."
"Fate gave the word-the arrow sped, And pierced my darling's heart."[190]
You will not send me your poetic rambles, but, you see I am no niggard of mine. I am sure your impromptus give me double pleasure; what falls from your pen can neither be unentertaining in itself, nor indifferent to me.
The one fault you found, is just; but I cannot please myself in an emendation.
What a life of solicitude is the life of a parent! You interested me much in your young couple.
I would not take my folio paper for this epistle, and now I repent it. I am so jaded with my dirty long journey that I was afraid to drawl into the essence of dulness with anything [391]larger than a quarto, and so I must leave out another rhyme of this morning's manufacture.
I will pay the sapientipotent George, most cheerfully, to hear from you ere I leave Ayrshire.
R. B.

FOOTNOTES:

[190] Poem XCII.

CXXXVII.

TO MR. PETER HILL.

["The 'Address to Lochlomond,' which this letter criticises," says Currie in 1800, "was written by a gentleman, now one of the masters of the High-school of Edinburgh, and the same who translated the beautiful story of 'The Paria,' published in the Bee of Dr. Anderson."]

Mauchline, 1st October, 1788.

I have been here in this country about three days, and all that time my chief reading has been the "Address to Lochlomond" you were so obliging as to send to me. Were I impannelled one of the author's jury, to determine his criminality respecting the sin of poesy, my verdict should be "guilty! a poet of nature's making!". It is an excellent method for improvement, and what I believe every poet does, to place some favourite classic author in his own walks of study and composition, before him as a model. Though your author had not mentioned the name, I could have, at half a glance, guessed his model to be Thomson. Will my brother-poet forgive me, if I venture to hint that his imitation of that immortal bard is in two or three places rather more servile than such a genius as his required:-e.g.

"To soothe the maddening passions all to peace."

Address.

"To soothe the throbbing passions into peace."

Thomson.

I think the "Address" is in simplicity, harmony, and elegance of versification, fully equal to the "Seasons." Like Thomson, too, he has looked into nature for himself: you meet with no copied description. One particular criticism I made at first reading; in no one instance has he said too much. He never flags in his progress, but, like a true poet of nature's making kindles in his course. His beginning is simple and modest, as if distrustful of the strength of his pinion; only, I do not altogether like-

-"Truth The soul of every song that's nobly great."

Fiction is the soul of many a song that is nobly great. Perhaps I am wrong: this may be but a prose criticism. Is not the phrase in line 7, page 6, "Great lake," too much vulgarized by every-day language for so sublime a poem?

"Great mass of waters, theme for nobler song,"

is perhaps no emendation. His enumeration of a comparison with other lakes is at once harmonious and poetic. Every reader's ideas must sweep the

"Winding margin of an hundred miles."

The perspective that follows mountains blue-the imprisoned billows beating in vain-the wooded isles-the digression on the yew-tree-"Ben-lomond's lofty, cloud-envelop'd head," andc. are beautiful. A thunder-storm is a subject which has been often tried, yet our poet in his grand picture has interjected a circumstance, so far as I know, entirely original:-

"the gloom Deep seam'd with frequent streaks of moving fire."

In his preface to the Storm, "the glens how dark between," is noble highland landscape! The "rain ploughing the red mould," too, is beautifully fancied. "Ben-lomond's lofty, pathless top," is a good expression; and the surrounding view from it is truly great: the
"silver mist, Beneath the beaming sun,"
is well described; and here he has contrived to enliven his poem with a little of that passion which bids fair, I think, to usurp the modern muses altogether. I know not how far this episode is a beauty upon the whole, but the swain's wish to carry "some faint idea of the vision bright," to entertain her "partial listening ear," is a pretty thought. But in my opinion the most beautiful passages in the whole poem are the fowls crowding, in wintry frosts, to Lochlomond's "hospitable flood;" their wheeling round, their lighting, mixing, diving, andc.; and the glorious description of the sportsman. This last is equal to anything in the "Seasons." The idea of "the floating tribe distant seen, far glistering to the moon," provoking his eye as he is obliged to leave them, is a noble ray of poetic genius. "The howling winds," the "hideous roar" of the white cascades, are all in the same style.

I forget that while I am thus holding forth with the heedless warmth of an enthusiast, I am perhaps tiring you with nonsense. I must, however, mention that the last verse of the sixteenth page is one of the most elegant compli[392]ments I have ever seen. I must likewise notice that beautiful paragraph beginning, "The gleaming lake," andc. I dare not go into the particular beauties of the last two paragraphs, but they are admirably fine, and truly Ossianic.

I must beg your pardon for this lengthened scrawl. I had no idea of it when I began-I should like to know who the author is; but, whoever he be, please present him with my grateful thanks for the entertainment he has afforded me.

A friend of mine desired me to commission for him two books, "Letters on the Religion essential to Man," a book you sent me before; and "The World unmasked, or the Philosopher the greatest Cheat." Send me them by the first opportunity. The Bible you sent me is truly elegant; I only wish it had been in two volumes.

R. B.

CXXXVIII.

TO THE EDITOR OF "THE STAR."

[The clergyman who preached the sermon which this letter condemns, was a man equally worthy and stern-a divine of Scotland's elder day: he received "a harmonious call" to a smaller stipend than that of Dunscore-and accepted it.]

November 8th, 1788.

Sir,
Notwithstanding the opprobrious epithets with which some of our philosophers and gloomy sectarians have branded our nature-the principle of universal selfishness, the proneness to all evil, they have given us; still the detestation in which inhumanity to the distressed, or insolence to the fallen, are held by all mankind, shows that they are not natives of the human heart. Even the unhappy partner of our kind, who is undone, the bitter consequence of his follies or his crimes, who but sympathizes with the miseries of this ruined profligate brother? We forget the injuries and feel for the man.

I went, last Wednesday, to my parish church, most cordially to join in grateful acknowledgment to the Author of all Good, for the consequent blessings of the glorious revolution. To that auspicious event we owe no less than our liberties, civil and religious; to it we are likewise indebted for the present Royal Family, the ruling features of whose administration have ever been mildness to the subject, and tenderness of his rights.

Bred and educated in revolution principles, the principles of reason and common sense, it could not be any silly political prejudice which made my heart revolt at the harsh abusive manner in which the reverend gentleman mentioned the House of Stewart, and which, I am afraid, was too much the language of the day. We may rejoice sufficiently in our deliverance from past evils, without cruelly raking up the ashes of those whose misfortune it was, perhaps as much as their crime, to be the authors of those evils; and we may bless God for all his goodness to us as a nation, without at the same time cursing a few ruined, powerless exiles, who only harboured ideas, and made attempts, that most of us would have done, had we been in their situation.

"The bloody and tyrannical House of Stewart" may be said with propriety and justice, when compared with the present royal family, and the sentiments of our days; but is there no allowance to be made for the manners of the times? Were the royal contemporaries of the Stewarts more attentive to their subjects' rights? Might not the epithets of "bloody and tyrannical" be, with at least equal justice, applied to the House of Tudor, of York, or any other of their predecessors?

The simple state of the case, Sir, seems to be this:-At that period, the science of government, the knowledge of the true relation between king and subject, was, like other sciences and other knowledge, just in its infancy, emerging from dark ages of ignorance and barbarity.

The Stewarts only contended for prerogatives which they knew their predecessors enjoyed, and which they saw their contemporaries enjoying; but these prerogatives were inimical to the happiness of a nation and the rights of subjects.

In the contest between prince and people, the consequence of that light of science which had lately dawned over Europe, the monarch of France, for example, was victorious over the struggling liberties of his people: with us, luckily the monarch failed, and his unwarrantable pretensions fell a sacrifice to our rights and happiness. Whether it was owing to the wisdom of leading individuals, or to the justling of parties, I cannot pretend to determine; but likewise happily for us, the kingly power was shifted into another branch of the family, who, as they owed the throne solely to the call[393] of a free people, could claim nothing inconsistent with the covenanted terms which placed them there.

The Stewarts have been condemned and laughed at for the folly and impracticability of their attempts in 1715 and 1745. That they failed, I bless God; but cannot join in the ridicule against them. Who does not know that the abilities or defects of leaders and commanders are often hidden until put to the touchstone of exigency; and that there is a caprice of fortune, an omnipotence in particular accidents and conjunctures of circumstances, which exalt us as heroes, or brand us as madmen, just as they are for or against us?

Man, Mr. Publisher, is a strange, weak, inconsistent being; who would believe, Sir, that in this our Augustan age of liberality and refinement, while we seem so justly sensible and jealous of our rights and liberties, and animated with such indignation against the very memory of those who would have subverted them-that a certain people under our national protection should complain, not against our monarch and a few favorite advisers, but against our whole legislative body, for similar oppression, and almost in the very same terms, as our forefathers did of the house of Stewart! I will not, I cannot enter into the merits of the cause; but I dare say the American Congress, in 1776, will be allowed to be as able and as enlightened as the English Convention was in 1688; and that their posterity will celebrate the centenary of their deliverance from us, as duly and sincerely as we do ours from the oppressive measures of the wrong-headed House of Stewart.

To conclude, Sir; let every man who has a tear for the many miseries incident to humanity feel for a family illustrious as any in Europe, and unfortunate beyond historic precedent; and let every Briton (and particularly every Scotsman) who ever looked with reverential pity on the dotage of a parent, cast a veil over the fatal mistakes of the kings of his forefathers.

R. B.

CXXXIX.

TO MRS. DUNLOP,
At Moreham Mains.

[The heifer presented to the poet by the Dunlops was bought, at the sale of Ellisland stock, by Miller of Dalswinton, and long grazed the pastures in his "policies" by the name of "Burns."]

Mauchline, 13th November, 1788.

Madam,

I had the very great pleasure of dining at Dunlop yesterday. Men are said to flatter women because they are weak; if it is so, poets must be weaker still; for Misses R. and K. and Miss G. M'K., with their flattering attentions, and artful compliments, absolutely turned my head. I own they did not lard me over as many a poet does his patron, but they so intoxicated me with their sly insinuations and delicate inuendos of compliment, that if it had not been for a lucky recollection, how much additional weight and lustre your good opinion and friendship must give me in that circle, I had certainly looked upon myself as a person of no small consequence. I dare not say one word how much I was charmed with the Major's friendly welcome, elegant manner, and acute remark, lest I should be thought to overbalance my orientalisms of applause over-against the finest quey[191] in Ayrshire, which he made me a present of to help and adorn my farm-stock. As it was on hallow-day, I am determined annually, as that day returns, to decorate her horns with an ode of gratitude to the family of Dunlop.

So soon as I know of your arrival at Dunlop, I will take the first conveniency to dedicate a day, or perhaps two, to you and friendship, under the guarantee of the Major's hospitality. There will soon be threescore and ten miles of permanent distance between us; and now that your friendship and friendly correspondence is entwisted with the heart-strings of my enjoyment of life, I must indulge myself in a happy day of "The feast of reason and the flow of soul."

R. B.

FOOTNOTES:

[191] Heifer.

CXL.

TO MR. JAMES JOHNSON,

Engraver.

[James Johnson, though not an ungenerous man, meanly refused to give a copy of the Musical Museum to Burns, who desired to bestow it on one to whom his family was deeply indebted. This was in the last year of the poet's life, and after the Museum had been brightened by so much of his lyric verse.]

Mauchline, November 15th, 1788.

My dear Sir,
I have sent you two more songs. If you have[394] got any tunes, or anything to correct, please send them by return of the carrier.
I can easily see, my dear friend, that you will very probably have four volumes. Perhaps you may not find your account lucratively in this business; but you are a patriot for the music of your country; and I am certain posterity will look on themselves as highly indebted to your public spirit. Be not in a hurry; let us go on correctly, and your name shall be immortal.
I am preparing a flaming preface for your third volume. I see every day new musical publications advertised; but what are they? Gaudy, hunted butterflies of a day, and then vanish for ever: but your work will outlive the momentary neglects of idle fashion, and defy the teeth of time.
Have you never a fair goddess that leads you a wild-goose chase of amorous devotion? Let me know a few of her qualities, such as whether she be rather black, or fair; plump, or thin; short, or tall, andc.; and choose your air, and I shall task my muse to celebrate her.
R. B.

CXLI.

TO DR. BLACKLOCK.
[Blacklock, though blind, was a cheerful and good man. "There was, perhaps, never one among all mankind," says Heron, "whom you might more truly have called an angel upon earth."]
Mauchline, November 15th, 1788.
Reverend and dear Sir,
As I hear nothing of your motions, but that you are, or were, out of town, I do not know where this may find you, or whether it will find you at all. I wrote you a long letter, dated from the land of matrimony, in June; but either it had not found you, or, what I dread more, it found you or Mrs. Blacklock in too precarious a state of health and spirits to take notice of an idle packet.
I have done many little things for Johnson, since I had the pleasure of seeing you; and I have finished one piece, in the way of Pope's "Moral Epistles;" but, from your silence, I have everything to fear, so I have only sent you two melancholy things, which I tremble lest they should too well suit the tone of your present feelings.
In a fortnight I move, bag and baggage, to Nithsdale; till then, my direction is at this place; after that period, it will be at Ellisland, near Dumfries. It would extremely oblige me, were it but half a line, to let me know how you are, and where you are. Can I be indifferent to the fate of a man to whom I owe so much? A man whom I not only esteem, but venerate.

My warmest good wishes and most respectful compliments to Mrs. Blacklock, and Miss Johnston, if she is with you.

I cannot conclude without telling you that I am more and more pleased with the step I took respecting "my Jean." Two things, from my happy experience, I set down as apothegms in life. A wife's head is immaterial, compared with her heart; and-"Virtue's (for wisdom what poet pretends to it?) ways are ways of pleasantness, and all her paths are peace."

Adieu!

R. B.

[Here follow "The Mother's Lament for the Loss of her Son," and the song beginning "The lazy mist hangs from the brow of the hill."]

CXLII.

TO MRS. DUNLOP.

[The "Auld lang syne," which Burns here introduces to Mrs. Dunlop as a strain of the olden time, is as surely his own as Tam-o-Shanter.]

Ellisland, 17th December, 1788.

My dear honoured Friend,

Yours, dated Edinburgh, which I have just read, makes me very unhappy. "Almost blind and wholly deaf," are melancholy news of human nature; but when told of a much-loved and honoured friend, they carry misery in the sound. Goodness on your part, and gratitude on mine, began a tie which has gradually entwisted itself among the dearest chords of my bosom, and I tremble at the omens of your late and present ailing habit and shattered health. You miscalculate matters widely, when you forbid my waiting on you, lest it should hurt my worldly concerns. My small scale of farming is exceedingly more simple and easy than what you have lately seen at Moreham Mains. But, be that as it may, the heart of the man and the fancy of the poet are the two grand considerations for which I live: if miry ridges and dirty dunghills are to engross the best part of the functions of my soul immortal, I had better been a rook or a magpie at once, and then I should[395] not have been plagued with any ideas superior to breaking of clods and picking up grubs; not to mention barn-door cocks or mallards, creatures with which I could almost exchange lives at any time. If you continue so deaf, I am afraid a visit will be no great pleasure to either of us; but if I hear you are got so well again as to be able to relish conversation, look you to it, Madam, for I will make my threatenings good. I am to be at the New-year-day fair of Ayr; and, by all that is sacred in the world, friend, I will come and see you.

Your meeting, which you so well describe, with your old schoolfellow and friend, was truly interesting. Out upon the ways of the world!-They spoil "these social offsprings of the heart." Two veterans of the "men of the world" would have met with little more heart-workings than two old hacks worn out on the road. Apropos, is not the Scotch phrase, "Auld lang syne," exceedingly expressive? There is an old song and tune which has often thrilled through my soul. You know I am an enthusiast in old Scotch songs. I shall give you the verses on the other sheet, as I suppose Mr. Ker will save you the postage.

"Should auld acquaintance be forgot!"[192]

Light be the turf on the breast of the heaven-inspired poet who composed this glorious fragment. There is more of the fire of native genius in it than in half-a-dozen of modern English Bacchanalians! Now I am on my hobby-horse, I cannot help inserting two other old stanzas, which please me mightily:-

"Go fetch to me a pint of wine."[193]

R. B.

FOOTNOTES:

[192] See Song CCX.

[193] See Song LXXII.

CXLIII.

TO MISS DAVIES.

[The Laird of Glenriddel informed "the charming, lovely Davies" that Burns was composing a song in her praise. The poet acted on this, and sent the song, enclosed in this characteristic letter.]

December, 1788.

Madam,

I understand my very worthy neighbour, Mr. Riddel, has informed you that I have made you the subject of some verses. There is something so provoking in the idea of being the burthen of a ballad, that I do not think Job or Moses, though such patterns of patience and meekness, could have resisted the curiosity to know what that ballad was: so my worthy friend has done me a mischief, which I dare say he never intended; and reduced me to the unfortunate alternative of leaving your curiosity ungratified, or else disgusting you with foolish verses, the unfinished production of a random moment, and never meant to have met your ear. I have heard or read somewhere of a gentleman who had some genius, much eccentricity, and very considerable dexterity with his pencil. In the accidental group of life into which one is thrown, wherever this gentleman met with a character in a more than ordinary degree congenial to his heart, he used to steal a sketch of the face, merely, he said, as a nota bene, to point out the agreeable recollection to his memory. What this gentleman's pencil was to him, my muse is to me; and the verses I do myself the honour to send you are a memento exactly of the same kind that he indulged in.

It may be more owing to the fastidiousness of my caprice than the delicacy of my taste; but I am so often tired, disgusted and hurt with insipidity, affectation, and pride of mankind, that when I meet with a person "after my own heart," I positively feel what an orthodox Protestant would call a species of idolatry, which acts on my fancy like inspiration; and I can no more desist rhyming on the impulse, than an Æolian harp can refuse its tones to the streaming air. A distich or two would be the consequence, though the object which hit my fancy were gray-bearded-age; but where my theme is youth and beauty, a young lady whose personal charms, wit, and sentiment are equally striking and unaffected-by heavens! though I had lived three score years a married man, and three score years before I was a married man, my imagination would hallow the very idea: and I am truly sorry that the inclosed stanzas have done such poor justice to such a subject.

R. B.

CXLIV.

TO MR. JOHN TENNANT.

[The mill of John Currie stood on a small stream which fed the loch of Friar's Carse-near the house of the dame of whom he sang, "Sic a wife as Willie had."]

December 22, 1788.

I yesterday tried my cask of whiskey for the first time, and I assure you it does you great[396] credit. It will bear five waters strong; or six ordinary toddy. The whiskey of this country is a most rascally liquor; and, by consequence, only drank by the most rascally part of the inhabitants. I am persuaded, if you once get a footing here, you might do a great deal of business, in the way of consumpt; and should you commence distiller again, this is the native barley country. I am ignorant if, in your present way of dealing, you would think it worth your while to extend your business so far as this country side. I write you this on the account of an accident, which I must take the merit of having partly designed to. A neighbour of mine, a John Currie, miller in Carsemill-a man who is, in a word, a "very" good man, even for a £500 bargain-he and his wife were in my house the time I broke open the cask. They keep a country public-house and sell a great deal of foreign spirits, but all along thought that whiskey would have degraded this house. They were perfectly astonished at my whiskey, both for its taste and strength; and, by their desire, I write you to know if you could supply them with liquor of an equal quality, and what price. Please write me by first post, and direct to me at Ellisland, near Dumfries. If you could take a jaunt

this way yourself, I have a spare spoon, knife and fork very much at your service. My compliments to Mrs. Tennant, and all the good folks in Glenconnel and Barquharrie.
R. B.

CXLV.

TO MRS. DUNLOP.
[The feeling mood of moral reflection exhibited in the following letter, was common to the house of William Burns: in a letter addressed by Gilbert to Robert of this date, the poet is reminded of the early vicissitudes of their name, and desired to look up, and be thankful.]
Ellisland, New-year-day Morning, 1789.
This, dear Madam, is a morning of wishes, and would to God that I came under the apostle James's description!-the prayer of a righteous man availeth much. In that case, Madam, you should welcome in a year full of blessings: everything that obstructs or disturbs tranquillity and self-enjoyment, should be removed, and every pleasure that frail humanity can taste, should be yours. I own myself so little a Presbyterian, that I approve of set times and seasons of more than ordinary acts of devotion, for breaking in on that habitual routine of life and thought, which is so apt to reduce our existence to a kind of instinct, or even sometimes, and with some minds, to a state very little superior to mere machinery.
This day, the first Sunday of May, a breezy, blue-skyed noon some time about the beginning, and a hoary morning and calm sunny day about the end, of autumn; these, time out of mind, have been with me a kind of holiday.
I believe I owe this to that glorious paper in the Spectator, "The Vision of Mirza," a piece that struck my young fancy before I was capable of fixing an idea to a word of three syllables: "On the 6th day of the moon, which, according to the custom of my forefathers, I always keep holy, after washing myself, and offering up my morning devotions, I ascended the high hill of Bagdat, in order to pass the rest of the day in meditation and prayer."
We know nothing, or next to nothing, of the substance or structure of our souls, so cannot account for those seeming caprices in them, that one should be particularly pleased with this thing, or struck with that, which, on minds of a different cast, makes no extraordinary impression. I have some favourite flowers in spring, among which are the mountain-daisy, the hare-bell, the fox-glove, the wild brier-rose, the budding birch, and the hoary hawthorn, that I view and hang over with particular delight. I never hear the loud solitary whistle of the curlew in a summer noon, or the wild mixing cadence of a troop of grey plovers, in an autumnal morning, without feeling an elevation of soul like the enthusiasm of devotion or poetry. Tell me, my

dear friend, to what can this be owing? Are we a piece of machinery, which, like the Æolian harp, passive, takes the impression of the passing accident? Or do these workings argue something within us above the trodden clod? I own myself partial to such proofs of those awful and important realities-a God that made all things-man's immaterial and immortal nature-and a world of weal or woe beyond death and the grave.
R. B.

CXLVI.

TO DR. MOORE.
[The poet seems, in this letter, to perceive that Ellisland was not the bargain he had reckoned it: he intimated,[397] as the reader will remember, something of the same kind to Margaret Chalmers.]
Ellisland, 4th Jan. 1789.
Sir,
As often as I think of writing to you, which has been three or four times every week these six months, it gives me something so like the idea of an ordinary-sized statue offering at a conversation with the Rhodian colossus, that my mind misgives me, and the affair always miscarries somewhere between purpose and resolve. I have at last got some business with you, and business letters are written by the stylebook. I say my business is with you, Sir, for you never had any with me, except the business that benevolence has in the mansion of poverty.
The character and employment of a poet were formerly my pleasure, but are now my pride. I know that a very great deal of my late eclat was owing to the singularity of my situation, and the honest prejudice of Scotsmen; but still, as I said in the preface to my first edition, I do look upon myself as having some pretensions from Nature to the poetic character. I have not a doubt but the knack, the aptitude, to learn the muses' trade, is a gift bestowed by him "who forms the secret bias of the soul;"-but I as firmly believe, that excellence in the profession is the fruit of industry, labour, attention, and pains. At least I am resolved to try my doctrine by the test of experience. Another appearance from the press I put off to a very distant day, a day that may never arrive-but poesy I am determined to prosecute with all my vigour. Nature has given very few, if any, of the profession, the talents of shining in every species of composition. I shall try (for until trial it is impossible to know) whether she has qualified me to shine in any one. The worst of it is, by the time one has finished a piece, it has been so often viewed and reviewed before the mental eye, that one loses, in a good measure, the powers of critical discrimination. Here the best criterion I know is a friend-not only of abilities to judge, but with good-nature enough, like a prudent teacher with a young learner, to praise perhaps a little more

than is exactly just, lest the thin-skinned animal fall into that most deplorable of all poetic diseases-heart-breaking despondency of himself. Dare I, Sir, already immensely indebted to your goodness, ask the additional obligation of your being that friend to me? I enclose you an essay of mine in a walk of poesy to me entirely new; I mean the epistle addressed to R. G. Esq. or Robert Graham of Fintray, Esq., a gentleman of uncommon worth, to whom I lie under very great obligations. The story of the poem, like most of my poems, is connected with my own story, and to give you the one, I must give you something of the other. I cannot boast of Mr. Creech's ingenuous fair dealing to me. He kept me hanging about Edinburgh from the 7th August, 1787, until the 13th April, 1788, before he would condescend to give me a statement of affairs; nor had I got it even then, but for an angry letter I wrote him, which irritated his pride. "I could" not a "tale" but a detail "unfold," but what am I that should speak against the Lord's anointed Bailie of Edinburgh?

I believe I shall in the whole, 100l. copyright included, clear about 400l. some little odds; and even part of this depends upon what the gentleman has yet to settle with me. I give you this information, because you did me the honour to interest yourself much in my welfare. I give you this information, but I give it to yourself only, for I am still much in the gentleman's mercy. Perhaps I injure the man in the idea I am sometimes tempted to have of him-God forbid I should! A little time will try, for in a month I shall go to town to wind up the business if possible.

To give the rest of my story in brief, I have married "my Jean," and taken a farm: with the first step I have every day more and more reason to be satisfied: with the last, it is rather the reverse. I have a younger brother, who supports my aged mother; another still younger brother, and three sisters, in a farm. On my last return from Edinburgh, it cost me about 180l. to save them from ruin. Not that I have lost so much.-I only interposed between my brother and his impending fate by the loan of so much. I give myself no airs on this, for it was mere selfishness on my part: I was conscious that the wrong scale of the balance was pretty heavily charged, and I thought that throwing a little filial piety and fraternal affection into the scale in my favour, might help to smooth matters at the grand reckoning. There is still one thing would make my circumstances quite easy: I have an excise officer's commission, and I live in the midst of a country division. My request to Mr. Graham, who is one of the commissioners of excise, was, if in his power, to procure me that division. If I were[398] very sanguine, I might hope that some of my great patrons might procure me a Treasury warrant for supervisor, surveyor-general, andc.

Thus, secure of a livelihood, "to thee, sweet poetry, delightful maid," I would consecrate my future days.

R. B.

CXLVII.

TO MR. ROBERT AINSLIE.

[The song which the poet says he brushed up a little is nowhere mentioned: he wrote one hundred, and brushed up more, for the Museum of Johnson.]

Ellisland, Jan. 6, 1789.

Many happy returns of the season to you, my dear Sir! May you be comparatively happy up to your comparative worth among the sons of men; which wish would, I am sure, make you one of the most blest of the human race.

I do not know if passing a "Writer to the signet," be a trial of scientific merit, or a mere business of friends and interest. However it be, let me quote you my two favourite passages, which, though I have repeated them ten thousand times, still they rouse my manhood and steel my resolution like inspiration.

-"On reason build resolve, That column of true majesty in man."

Young. Night Thoughts.

"Hear, Alfred, hero of the state, Thy genius heaven's high will declare; The triumph of the truly great, Is never, never to despair! Is never to despair!"

Thomson. Masque of Alfred.

I grant you enter the lists of life, to struggle for bread, business, notice, and distinction, in common with hundreds.-But who are they? Men, like yourself, and of that aggregate body your compeers, seven-tenths of them come short of your advantages natural and accidental; while two of those that remain, either neglect their parts, as flowers blooming in a desert, or mis-spend their strength, like a bull goring a bramble-bush.

But to change the theme: I am still catering for Johnson's publication; and among others, I have brushed up the following old favourite song a little, with a view to your worship. I have only altered a word here and there; but if you like the humour of it, we shall think of a stanza or two to add to it.

R. B.

CXLVIII.

TO PROFESSOR DUGALD STEWART.

[The iron justice to which the poet alludes, in this letter, was exercised by Dr. Gregory, on the poem of the "Wounded Hare."]

Ellisland, 20th Jan, 1789.

Sir,

The enclosed sealed packet I sent to Edinburgh, a few days after I had the happiness of meeting you in Ayrshire, but you were gone for the Continent. I have now added a few more of my productions, those for which I am indebted to the Nithsdale muses. The piece inscribed to R. G. Esq., is a copy of verses I sent Mr. Graham, of Fintray, accompanying a request for his assistance in a matter to me of very great moment. To that gentleman I am already doubly indebted, for deeds of kindness of serious import to my dearest interests, done in a manner grateful to the delicate feelings of sensibility. This poem is a species of composition new to me, but I do not intend it shall be my last essay of the kind, as you will see by the "Poet's Progress." These fragments, if my design succeed, are but a small part of the intended whole. I propose it shall be the work of my utmost exertions, ripened by years; of course I do not wish it much known. The fragment beginning "A little, upright, pert, tart, andc.," I have not shown to man living, till I now send it you. It forms the postulata, the axioms, the definition of a character, which, if it appear at all, shall be placed in a variety of lights. This particular part I send you merely as a sample of my hand at portrait-sketching, but, lest idle conjecture should pretend to point out the original, please to let it be for your single, sole inspection.

Need I make any apology for this trouble, to a gentleman who has treated me with such marked benevolence and peculiar kindness-who has entered into my interests with so much zeal, and on whose critical decisions I can so fully depend? A poet as I am by trade, these decisions are to me of the last consequence. My late transient acquaintance among some of the mere rank and file of greatness, I resign with ease; but to the distinguished champions of genius and learning, I shall be ever ambitious of being known. The native genius and accurate discernment in Mr. Stewart's critical strictures; the justness (iron justice, for he has no bowels of compassion for a poor poetic sin[399]ner) of Dr. Gregory's remarks, and the delicacy of Professor Dalzel's taste, I shall ever revere.

I shall be in Edinburgh some time next month.

I have the honour to be, Sir,

Your highly obliged, and very

Humble servant,

R. B.

CXLIX.

TO BISHOP GEDDES.

[Alexander Geddes was a controversialist and poet, and a bishop of the broken remnant of the Catholic Church of Scotland: he is known as the author of a very humorous ballad called "The Wee bit Wifickie," and as the translator of one of the books of the Iliad, in opposition to Cowper.]

Ellisland, 3d Feb. 1789.

Venerable Father,

As I am conscious that wherever I am, you do me the honour to interest yourself in my welfare, it gives me pleasure to inform you that I am here at last, stationary in the serious business of life, and have now not only the retired leisure, but the hearty inclination, to attend to those great and important questions-what I am? where I am? and for what I am destined?

In that first concern, the conduct of the man, there was ever but one side on which I was habitually blameable, and there I have secured myself in the way pointed out by Nature and Nature's God. I was sensible that to so helpless a creature as a poor poet, a wife and family were encumbrances, which a species of prudence would bid him shun; but when the alternative was, being at eternal warfare with myself, on account of habitual follies, to give them no worse name, which no general example, no licentious wit, no sophistical infidelity, would, to me, ever justify, I must have been a fool to have hesitated, and a madman to have made another choice. Besides, I had in "my Jean" a long and much-loved fellow-creature's happiness or misery among my hands, and who could trifle with such a deposit?

In the affair of a livelihood, I think myself tolerably secure: I have good hopes of my farm, but should they fail, I have an excise commission, which on my simple petition, will, at any time, procure me bread. There is a certain stigma affixed to the character of an Excise officer, but I do not pretend to borrow honour from my profession; and though the salary be comparatively small, it is luxury to anything that the first twenty-five years of my life taught me to expect.

Thus, with a rational aim and method in life, you may easily guess, my reverend and much-honoured friend, that my characteristical trade is not forgotten. I am, if possible, more than over an enthusiast to the muses. I am determined to study man and nature, and in that view incessantly; and to try if the ripening and corrections of years can enable me to produce something worth preserving.

You will see in your book, which I beg your pardon for detaining so long, that I have been tuning my lyre on the banks of Nith. Some large poetic plans that are floating in my imagination, or partly put in execution, I shall impart to you when I have the pleasure of meeting with you; which, if you are then in Edinburgh, I shall have about the beginning of March.

That acquaintance, worthy Sir, with which you were pleased to honour me, you must still allow me to challenge; for with whatever unconcern I give up my transient connexion with the merely great, those self-important beings whose intrinsic * * * * cealed under the accidental advantages of their * * * * I cannot lose the patronizing notice of the learned and good, without the bitterest regret.

R. B.

CL.

TO MR. JAMES BURNESS.

[Fanny Burns married Adam Armour, brother to bonnie Jean, went with him to Mauchline, and bore him sons and daughters.]

Ellisland, 9th Feb. 1789.

My dear Sir,

Why I did not write to you long ago, is what, even on the rack, I could not answer. If you can in your mind form an idea of indolence, dissipation, hurry, cares, change of country, entering on untried scenes of life, all combined, you will save me the trouble of a blushing apology. It could not be want of regard for a man for whom I had a high esteem before I knew him-an esteem which has much increased since I did know him; and this caveat entered, I shall plead guilty to any other indictment with which you shall please to charge me.[400]

After I had parted from you for many months my life was one continued scene of dissipation. Here at last I am become stationary, and have taken a farm and-a wife.

The farm is beautifully situated on the Nith, a large river that runs by Dumfries, and falls into the Solway frith. I have gotten a lease of my farm as long as I pleased: but how it may turn out is just a guess, it is yet to improve and enclose, andc.; however, I have good hopes of my bargain on the whole.

My wife is my Jean, with whose story you are partly acquainted. I found I had a much-loved fellow creature's happiness or misery among my hands, and I durst not trifle with so sacred a deposit. Indeed I have not any reason to repent the step I have taken, as I have attached myself to a very good wife, and have shaken myself loose of every bad failing.

I have found my book a very profitable business, and with the profits of it I have begun life pretty decently. Should fortune not favour me in farming, as I have no great faith in her fickle ladyship, I have provided myself in another resource, which however some folks may affect to despise it, is still a comfortable shift in the day of misfortune. In the heyday of my fame, a gentleman whose name at least I dare say you know, as his estate lies somewhere near Dundee, Mr. Graham, of Fintray, one of the commissioners of Excise, offered me the commission of an Excise officer. I thought it prudent to accept the offer; and accordingly I took my instructions, and have my commission by me. Whether I may ever do duty, or be a penny the better for it, is what I do not know; but I have the comfortable assurance, that come whatever ill fate will, I can, on my simple petition to the Excise-board, get into employ.

We have lost poor uncle Robert this winter. He has long been very weak, and with very little alteration on him, he expired 3d Jan.

His son William has been with me this winter, and goes in May to be an apprentice to a mason. His other son, the eldest, John, comes to me I expect in summer. They are both remarkably stout young fellows, and promise to do well. His only daughter, Fanny, has been with me ever since her father's death, and I purpose keeping her in my family till she be quite woman grown, and fit for service. She is one of the cleverest girls, and has one of the most amiable dispositions I have ever seen.

All friends in this country and Ayrshire are well. Remember me to all friends in the north. My wife joins me in compliments to Mrs. B. and family.

I am ever, my dear Cousin,

Yours, sincerely,

R. B.

CLI.

TO MRS. DUNLOP.

[The beautiful lines with which this letter concludes, I have reason to believe were the production of the lady to whom the epistle is addressed.]

Ellisland, 4th March, 1789.

Here am I, my honoured friend, returned safe from the capital. To a man, who has a home, however humble or remote-if that home is like mine, the scene of domestic comfort-the bustle of Edinburgh will soon be a business of sickening disgust.

"Vain pomp and glory of this world, I hate you!"

When I must skulk into a corner, lest the rattling equipage of some gaping blockhead should mangle me in the mire, I am tempted to exclaim-"What merits has he had, or what demerit have I had, in some state of pre-existence, that he is ushered into this state of being with the sceptre of rule, and the key of riches in his puny fist, and I am kicked into the world, the sport of folly, or the victim of pride?" I have read somewhere of a monarch (in Spain I think it was), who was so out of humour with the Ptolemean system of astronomy, that he said had he been of the Creator's council, he could have saved him a great deal of labour and absurdity. I will not defend this blasphemous speech; but often, as I have glided with humble stealth through the pomp of Princes' street, it has suggested itself to me, as an improvement on the present human figure, that a man in proportion to his own conceit of his consequence in the world, could have pushed out the longitude of his common size, as a snail pushes out his horns, or, as we draw out a perspective. This trifling alteration, not to mention the prodigious saving it would be in the tear and wear of the neck and limb-sinews of many of his majesty's liege subjects, in the way of tossing the head and tiptoe strutting, would evidently turn out a vast advantage, in enabling us at once to adjust the ceremonials in making a bow, or making way to a great man, and that too within a second of the precise spherical angle of reverence, or[401] an inch of the particular point of respectful distance, which the important creature itself requires; as a measuring-glance at its towering altitude, would determine the affair like instinct.

You are right, Madam, in your idea of poor Mylne's poem, which he has addressed to me. The piece has a good deal of merit, but it has one great fault-it is, by far, too long. Besides, my success has encouraged such a shoal of ill-spawned monsters to crawl into public notice, under the title of Scottish Poets, that the very term Scottish Poetry borders on the burlesque. When I write to Mr. Carfrae, I shall advise him rather to try one of his deceased friend's English pieces. I am prodigiously hurried with my own matters, else I would have requested a perusal of all Mylne's poetic performances; and would have offered his friends my assistance in either selecting or correcting what would be proper for the press. What it is that occupies me so much, and perhaps a little oppresses my present spirits, shall fill up a paragraph in some future letter. In the mean time, allow me to close this epistle with a few lines done by a friend of mine * * * * *. I give you them, that as you have seen the original, you may guess whether one or two alterations I have ventured to make in them, be any real improvement.

"Like the fair plant that from our touch withdraws, Shrink, mildly fearful, even from applause, Be all a mother's fondest hope can dream, And all you are, my charming ..., seem. Straight as the fox-glove, ere her bells disclose, Mild as the maiden-blushing hawthorn blows, Fair as the fairest of each lovely kind, Your form shall be the image of your mind; Your manners shall so true your soul express, That all shall long to know the worth they guess: Congenial hearts shall greet with kindred love, And even sick'ning envy must approve."

R. B.

CLII.

TO THE REV. PETER CARFRAE.

[Mylne was a worthy and a modest man: he died of an inflammatory fever in the prime of life.]

1789.

Rev. Sir,

I do not recollect that I have ever felt a severer pang of shame, than on looking at the date of your obliging letter which accompanied Mr. Mylne's poem.

I am much to blame: the honour Mr. Mylne has done me, greatly enhanced in its value by the endearing, though melancholy circumstance, of its being the last production of his muse, deserved a better return.

I have, as you hint, thought of sending a copy of the poem to some periodical publication; but, on second thoughts, I am afraid, that in the present case, it would be an improper step. My success, perhaps as much accidental as merited, has brought an inundation of nonsense under the name of Scottish poetry. Subscription-bills for Scottish poems have so dunned, and daily do dun the public, that the very name is in danger of contempt. For these reasons, if publishing any of Mr. Mylne's poems in a magazine, andc., be at all prudent, in my opinion it certainly should not be a Scottish poem. The profits of the labours of a man of genius are, I hope, as honourable as any profits whatever; and Mr. Mylne's relations are most justly entitled to that honest harvest, which fate has denied himself to reap. But let the friends of Mr. Mylne's fame (among whom I crave the honour of ranking myself) always keep in eye his respectability as a man and as a poet, and take no measure that, before the world knows anything about him, would risk his name and character being classed with the fools of the times.

I have, Sir, some experience of publishing; and the way in which I would proceed with Mr. Mylne's poem is this:-I would publish, in two or three English and Scottish public papers, any one of his English poems which should, by private judges, be thought the most excellent, and mention it, at the same time, as one of the productions of a Lothian farmer, of respectable character, lately deceased, whose poems his friends had it in idea to publish, soon, by subscription, for the sake of his numerous family:-not in pity to that family, but in justice to what his friends think the poetic merits of the deceased; and to secure, in the most effectual manner, to those tender connexions, whose right it is, the pecuniary reward of those merits.

R. B.

CLIII.

TO DR. MOORE.

[Edward Nielson, whom Burns here introduces to Dr. Moore, was minister of Kirkbean, on the Solway-side.[402] He was a jovial man, and loved good cheer, and merry company.]

Ellisland, 23d March, 1789.

Sir,

The gentleman who will deliver you this is a Mr. Nielson, a worthy clergyman in my neighbourhood, and a very particular acquaintance of mine. As I have troubled him with this packet, I must turn him over to your goodness, to recompense him for it in a way in which he much needs your assistance, and where you can effectually serve him:-Mr. Nielson is on his way for France, to wait on his Grace of Queensberry, on some little business of a good deal of importance to him, and he wishes for your instructions respecting the most eligible mode of travelling, andc., for him, when he has crossed the channel. I should not have dared to take this liberty with you, but that I am told, by those who have the honour of your personal acquaintance, that to be a poor honest Scotchman is a letter of recommendation to you, and that to have it in your power to serve such a character, gives you much pleasure.

The enclosed ode is a compliment to the memory of the late Mrs. Oswald, of Auchencruive. You, probably, knew her personally, an honour of which I cannot boast; but I spent my early years in her neighbourhood, and among her servants and tenants. I know that she was detested with the most heart-felt cordiality. However, in the particular part of her conduct which roused my poetic wrath, she was much less blameable. In January last, on my road to Ayrshire, I had put up at Bailie Wigham's in Sanquhar, the only tolerable inn in the place. The frost was keen, and the grim evening and howling wind were ushering in a night of snow and drift. My horse and I were both much fatigued with the labours of the day, and just as my friend the Bailie and I were bidding defiance to the storm, over a smoking bowl, in wheels the funeral pageantry of the late great Mrs. Oswald, and poor I am forced to brave all the horrors of the tempestuous night, and jade my horse, my young favourite horse, whom I had just christened Pegasus, twelve miles farther on, through the wildest moors and hills of Ayrshire, to New Cumnock, the next inn. The powers of poesy and prose sink under me, when I would describe what I felt. Suffice it to say, that when a good fire at New Cumnock had so far recovered my frozen sinews, I sat down and wrote the enclosed ode.

I was at Edinburgh lately, and settled finally with Mr. Creech; and I must own, that, at last, he has been amicable and fair with me.

R. B.

CLIV.

TO MR. WILLIAM BURNS.

[William Burns was the youngest brother of the poet: he was bred a sadler; went to Longtown, and finally to London, where he died early.]

Isle, March 25th, 1789.

I have stolen from my corn-sowing this minute to write a line to accompany your shirt and hat, for I can no more. Your sister Maria arrived yesternight, and begs to be remembered to you. Write me every opportunity, never mind postage. My head, too, is as addle as an egg, this morning, with dining abroad yesterday. I received yours by the mason. Forgive me this foolish-looking scrawl of an epistle.

I am ever,

My dear William,

Yours,

R. B.
P.S. If you are not then gone from Longtown, I'll write you a long letter, by this day se'ennight. If you should not succeed in your tramps, don't be dejected, or take any rash step-return to us in that case, and we will court fortune's better humour. Remember this, I charge you.
R. B.

CLV.

TO MR. HILL.
[The Monkland Book Club existed only while Robert Riddel, of the Friars-Carse, lived, or Burns had leisure to attend: such institutions, when well conducted, are very beneficial, when not oppressed by divinity and verse, as they sometimes are.]
Ellisland, 2d April, 1789.
I will make no excuse, my dear Bibliopolus (God forgive me for murdering language!) that I have sat down to write you on this vile paper.
It is economy, Sir; it is that cardinal virtue, prudence: so I beg you will sit down, and either compose or borrow a panegyric. If you are going to borrow, apply to * * * * to compose, or rather to compound, something very clever on my remarkable frugality; that I write to one of my most esteemed friends on this wretched paper, which was originally intended for the[403] venal fist of some drunken exciseman, to take dirty notes in a miserable vault of an ale-cellar.
O Frugality! thou mother of ten thousand blessings-thou cook of fat beef and dainty greens!-thou manufacturer of warm Shetland hose, and comfortable surtouts!-thou old housewife darning thy decayed stockings with thy ancient spectacles on thy aged nose!-lead me, hand me in thy clutching palsied fist, up those heights, and through those thickets, hitherto inaccessible, and impervious to my anxious, weary feet:-not those Parnassian crags, bleak and barren, where the hungry worshippers of fame are breathless, clambering, hanging between heaven and hell; but those glittering cliffs of Potosi, where the all-sufficient, all powerful deity, Wealth, holds his immediate court of joys and pleasures; where the sunny exposure of plenty, and the hot walls of profusion, produce those blissful fruits of luxury, exotics in this world, and natives of paradise!-Thou withered sibyl, my sage conductress, usher me into thy refulgent, adored presence!-The power, splendid and potent as he now is, was once the puling nursling of thy faithful care, and tender arms! Call me thy son, thy cousin, thy kinsman, or favourite, and adjure the god by the scenes of his infant years, no longer to repulse me as a stranger, or an alien, but to favour me with his peculiar countenance and protection?-He daily bestows his greatest kindness on the undeserving and the worthless-assure him, that I bring ample documents of

meritorious demerits! Pledge yourself for me, that, for the glorious cause of Lucre, I will do anything, be anything-but the horse-leech of private oppression, or the vulture of public robbery!

But to descend from heroics.

I want a Shakspeare; I want likewise an English dictionary-Johnson's, I suppose, is best. In these and all my prose commissions, the cheapest is always best for me. There is a small debt of honour that I owe Mr. Robert Cleghorn, in Saughton Mills, my worthy friend, and your well-wisher. Please give him, and urge him to take it, the first time you see him, ten shillings worth of anything you have to sell, and place it to my account.

The library scheme that I mentioned to you, is already begun, under the direction of Captain Riddel. There is another in emulation of it going on at Closeburn, under the auspices of Mr. Monteith, of Closeburn, which will be on a greater scale than ours. Capt. Riddel gave his infant society a great many of his old books, else I had written you on that subject; but one of these days, I shall trouble you with a commission for "The Monkland Friendly Society"-a copy of The Spectator, Mirror, and Lounger, Man of Feeling, Man of the World, Guthrie's Geographical Grammar, with some religious pieces, will likely be our first order.

When I grow richer, I will write to you on gilt post, to make amends for this sheet. At present, every guinea has a five guinea errand with,

My dear Sir,

Your faithful, poor, but honest, friend,

R. B.

CLVI.

TO MRS. DUNLOP

[Some lines which extend, but fail to finish the sketch contained in this letter, will be found elsewhere in this publication.]

Ellisland, 4th April, 1789.

I no sooner hit on any poetic plan or fancy, but I wish to send it to you: and if knowing and reading these give half the pleasure to you, that communicating them to you gives to me, I am satisfied.

I have a poetic whim in my head, which I at present dedicate, or rather inscribe to the Right Hon. Charles James Fox; but how long that fancy may hold, I cannot say. A few of the first lines, I have just rough-sketched as follows:

SKETCH.

How wisdom and folly meet, mix, and unite; How virtue and vice blend their black and their white; How genius, the illustrious father of fiction, Confounds rule and law, reconciles contradiction- I sing: If these mortals, the critics, should bustle, I care not, not I, let the critics go whistle.

But now for a patron, whose name and whose glory, At once may illustrate and honour my story.
Thou first of our orators, first of our wits; Yet whose parts and acquirements seem mere lucky hits; [404]With knowledge so vast, and with judgment so strong, No man with the half of 'em e'er went far wrong; With passion so potent, and fancies so bright, No man with the half of 'em ere went quite right; A sorry, poor misbegot son of the muses, For using thy name offers many excuses.
On the 20th current I hope to have the honour of assuring you in person, how sincerely I am-
R. B.

CLVII.

TO MR. WILLIAM BURNS,
SADLER,
CARE OF MR. WRIGHT, CARRIER, LONGTOWN.
["Never to despair" was a favourite saying with Burns: and "firm resolve," he held, with Young, to be "the column of true majesty in man."]
Isle, 15th April, 1789.
My dear William,
I am extremely sorry at the misfortune of your legs; I beg you will never let any worldly concern interfere with the more serious matter, the safety of your life and limbs. I have not time in these hurried days to write you anything other than a mere how d'ye letter. I will only repeat my favourite quotation:-
"What proves the hero truly great Is never, never to despair."
My house shall be your welcome home; and as I know your prudence (would to God you had resolution equal to your prudence!) if anywhere at a distance from friends, you should need money, you know my direction by post.
The enclosed is from Gilbert, brought by your sister Nanny. It was unluckily forgot. Yours to Gilbert goes by post.-I heard from them yesterday, they are all well.
Adieu.
R. B.

CLVIII.

TO MRS. M'MURDO,
DRUMLANRIG.
[Of this accomplished lady, Mrs. M'Murdo, of Drumlanrig, and her daughters, something has been said in the notes on the songs: the poem

alluded to was the song of "Bonnie Jean."]
Ellisland, 2d May, 1789.
Madam,
I have finished the piece which had the happy fortune to be honoured with your approbation; and never did little miss with more sparkling pleasure show her applauded sampler to partial mamma, than I now send my poem to you and Mr. M'Murdo if he is returned to Drumlanrig. You cannot easily imagine what thin-skinned animals-what sensitive plants poor poets are. How do we shrink into the embittered corner of self-abasement, when neglected or condemned by those to whom we look up! and how do we, in erect importance, add another cubit to our stature on being noticed and applauded by those whom we honour and respect! My late visit to Drumlanrig has, I can tell you, Madam, given me a balloon waft up Parnassus, where on my fancied elevation I regard my poetic self with no small degree of complacency. Surely with all their sins, the rhyming tribe are not ungrateful creatures.-I recollect your goodness to your humble guest-I see Mr. M'Murdo adding to the politeness of the gentleman, the kindness of a friend, and my heart swells as it would burst, with warm emotions and ardent wishes! It may be it is not gratitude-it may be a mixed sensation. That strange, shifting, doubling animal man is so generally, at best, but a negative, often a worthless creature, that we cannot see real goodness and native worth without feeling the bosom glow with sympathetic approbation.
With every sentiment of grateful respect,
I have the honour to be,
Madam,
Your obliged and grateful humble servant,
R. B.

CLIX.

TO MR. CUNNINGHAM.
[Honest Jamie Thomson, who shot the hare because she browsed with her companions on his father's "wheat-braird," had no idea he was pulling down such a burst of indignation on his head as this letter with the poem which it enclosed expresses.]
Ellisland, 4th May, 1789.
My dear Sir,
Your duty-free favour of the 26th April I received two days ago; I will not say I perused it with pleasure; that is the cold compliment of[405] ceremony; I perused it, Sir, with delicious satisfaction;-in short, it is such a letter, that not you, nor your friend, but the legislature, by express proviso in their postage laws, should frank.
A letter informed with the soul of friendship is such an honour to human

nature, that they should order it free ingress and egress to and from their bags and mails, as an encouragement and mark of distinction to supereminent virtue.

I have just put the last hand to a little poem which I think will be something to your taste. One morning lately, as I was out pretty early in the fields, sowing some grass seeds, I heard the burst of a shot from a neighbouring plantation, and presently a poor little wounded hare came crippling by me. You will guess my indignation at the inhuman fellow who could shoot a hare at this season, when all of them have young ones. Indeed there is something in that business of destroying for our sport individuals in the animal creation that do not injure us materially, which I could never reconcile to my ideas of virtue.

Inhuman man! curse on thy barb'rous art, And blasted be thy murder-aiming eye! May never pity soothe thee with a sigh, Nor ever pleasure glad thy cruel heart! andc. andc.

Let me know how you like my poem. I am doubtful whether it would not be an improvement to keep out the last stanza but one altogether.

Cruikshank is a glorious production of the author of man. You, he, and the noble Colonel of the Crochallan Fencibles are to me

"Dear as the ruddy drops which warm my heart"

I have a good mind to make verses on you all, to the tune of "Three guid fellows ayont the glen."

R. B.

CLX.

TO MR. SAMUEL BROWN.

[Samuel Brown was brother to the poet's mother: he seems to have been a joyous sort of person, who loved a joke, and understood double meanings.]

Mossgiel, 4th May, 1789.

Dear Uncle,

This, I hope, will find you and your conjugal yoke-fellow in your good old way; I am impatient to know if the Ailsa fowling be commenced for this season yet, as I want three or four stones of feathers, and I hope you will bespeak them for me. It would be a vain attempt for me to enumerate the various transactions I have been engaged in since I saw you last, but this know,-I am engaged in a smuggling trade, and God knows if ever any poor man experienced better returns, two for one, but as freight and delivery have turned out so dear, I am thinking of taking out a license and beginning in fair trade. I have taken a farm on the borders of the Nith, and in imitation of the old Patriarchs, get men-servants and maid-servants, and flocks and herds, and beget sons and daughters.

Your obedient nephew,

R. B.

CLXI.

TO RICHARD BROWN.

[Burns was much attached to Brown; and one regrets that an inconsiderate word should have estranged the haughty sailor.]

Mauchline, 21st May, 1789.

My dear Friend,

I was in the country by accident, and hearing of your safe arrival, I could not resist the temptation of wishing you joy on your return, wishing you would write to me before you sail again, wishing you would always set me down as your bosom friend, wishing you long life and prosperity, and that every good thing may attend you, wishing Mrs. Brown and your little ones as free of the evils of this world, as is consistent with humanity, wishing you and she were to make two at the ensuing lying-in, with which Mrs. B. threatens very soon to favour me, wishing I had longer time to write to you at present; and, finally, wishing that if there is to be another state of existence, Mr. B., Mrs. B., our little ones, and both families, and you and I, in some snug retreat, may make a jovial party to all eternity!

My direction is at Ellisland, near Dumfries

Yours,

R. B.

CLXII.

TO MR. JAMES HAMILTON.

[James Hamilton, grocer, in Glasgow, interested himself early in the fortunes of the poet.]

Ellisland, 26th May, 1789.

Dear Sir,

I send you by John Glover, carrier, the account for Mr. Turnbull, as I suppose you know his address.

I would fain offer, my dear Sir, a word of sympathy with your misfortunes; but it is a tender string, and I know not how to touch it. It is easy to flourish a set of high-flown sentiments on the subjects that would give great satisfaction to-a breast quite at ease; but as one observes, who was very seldom mistaken in the theory of life, "The heart knoweth its own sorrows, and a stranger intermeddleth not therewith."

Among some distressful emergencies that I have experienced in life, I ever laid this down as my foundation of comfort-That he who has lived the life of an honest man, has by no means lived in vain!

With every wish for your welfare and future success,

I am, my dear Sir,
Sincerely yours,
R. B.

CLXIII.

TO WILLIAM CREECH, ESQ.

[The poetic address to the "venomed stang" of the toothache seems to have come into existence about this time.]

Ellisland, 30th May, 1789.

Sir,

I had intended to have troubled you with a long letter, but at present the delightful sensations of an omnipotent toothache so engross all my inner man, as to put it out of my power even to write nonsense. However, as in duty bound, I approach my bookseller with an offering in my hand-a few poetic clinches, and a song:-To expect any other kind of offering from the Rhyming Tribe would be to know them much less than you do. I do not pretend that there is much merit in these morceaux, but I have two reasons for sending them; primo, they are mostly ill-natured, so are in unison with my present feelings, while fifty troops of infernal spirits are driving post from ear to ear along my jaw-bones; and secondly, they are so short, that you cannot leave off in the middle, and so hurt my pride in the idea that you found any work of mine too heavy to get through.

I have a request to beg of you, and I not only beg of you, but conjure you, by all your wishes and by all your hopes, that the muse will spare the satiric wink in the moment of your foibles; that she will warble the song of rapture round your hymeneal couch; and that she will shed on your turf the honest tear of elegiac gratitude! Grant my request as speedily as possible-send me by the very first fly or coach for this place three copies of the last edition of my poems, which place to my account.

Now may the good things of prose, and the good things of verse, come among thy hands, until they be filled with the good things of this life, prayeth

R. B.

CLXIV.

TO MR. M'AULEY.

[The poet made the acquaintance of Mr. M'Auley, of Dumbarton, in one of his northern tours,-he was introduced by his friend Kennedy.]

Ellisland, 4th June, 1789.

Dear Sir,

Though I am not without my fears respecting my fate, at that grand, universal inquest of right and wrong, commonly called The Last Day, yet I trust there is one sin, which that arch-vagabond, Satan, who I understand is to be king's evidence, cannot throw in my teeth, I mean ingratitude. There is a certain pretty large quantum of kindness for which I remain, and from inability, I fear, must still remain, your debtor; but though unable to repay the debt, I assure you, Sir, I shall ever warmly remember the obligation. It gives me the sincerest pleasure to hear by my old acquaintance, Mr. Kennedy, that you are, in immortal Allan's language, "Hale, and weel, and living;" and that your charming family are well, and promising to be an amiable and respectable addition to the company of performers, whom the Great Manager of the Drama of Man is bringing into action for the succeeding age.

With respect to my welfare, a subject in which you once warmly and effectively interested yourself, I am here in my old way, holding my plough, marking the growth of my corn, or the[407] health of my dairy; and at times sauntering by the delightful windings of the Nith, on the margin of which I have built my humble domicile, praying for seasonable weather, or holding an intrigue with the muses; the only gipsies with whom I have now any intercourse. As I am entered into the holy state of matrimony, I trust my face is turned completely Zion-ward; and as it is a rule with all honest fellows to repeat no grievances, I hope that the little poetic licenses of former days will of course fall under the oblivious influence of some good-natured statute of celestial prescription. In my family devotion, which, like a good Presbyterian, I occasionally give to my household folks, I am extremely fond of that psalm, "Let not the errors of my youth," andc., and that other, "Lo, children are God's heritage," andc., in which last Mrs. Burns, who by the bye has a glorious "wood-note wild" at either old song or psalmody, joins me with the pathos of Handel's Messiah.

R. B.

CLXV.

TO MR. ROBERT AINSLIE.

[The following high-minded letter may be regarded as a sermon on domestic morality preached by one of the experienced.]

Ellisland, 8th June, 1789.

My dear Friend,

I am perfectly ashamed of myself when I look at the date of your last. It is not that I forget the friend of my heart and the companion of my peregrinations; but I have been condemned to drudgery beyond sufferance, though not, thank God, beyond redemption. I have had a collection of poems by a lady, put into my hands to prepare them for the press; which horrid task, with sowing corn with my own hand, a parcel of masons, wrights, plasterers, andc., to attend to, roaming on business through Ayrshire-all this was against me, and the very first dreadful article was of itself too much for me.

13th. I have not had a moment to spare from incessant toil since the 8th. Life, my dear Sir, is a serious matter. You know by experience that a man's individual self is a good deal, but believe me, a wife and family of children, whenever you have the honour to be a husband and a father, will show you that your present and most anxious hours of solitude are spent on trifles. The welfare of those who are very dear to us, whose only support, hope and stay we are-this, to a generous mind, is another sort of more important object of care than any concerns whatever which centre merely in the individual. On the other hand, let no young, unmarried, rakehelly dog among you, make a song of his pretended liberty and freedom from care. If the relations we stand in to king, country, kindred, and friends, be anything but the visionary fancies of dreaming metaphysicians; if religion, virtue, magnanimity, generosity, humanity and justice, be aught but empty sounds; then the man who may be said to live only for others, for the beloved, honourable female, whose tender faithful embrace endears life, and for the helpless little innocents who are to be the men and women, the worshippers of his God, the subjects of his king, and the support, nay the vital existence of his country in the ensuing age;-compare such a man with any fellow whatever, who, whether he bustle and push in business among labourers, clerks, statesmen; or whether he roar and rant, and drink and sing in taverns-a fellow over whose grave no one will breathe a single heigh-ho, except from the cobweb-tie of what is called good-fellowship-who has no view nor aim but what terminates in himself-if there be any grovelling earth-born wretch of our species, a renegado to common sense, who would fain believe that the noble creature man, is no better than a sort of fungus, generated out of nothing, nobody knows how, and soon dissipated in nothing, nobody knows where; such a stupid beast, such a crawling reptile, might balance the foregoing unexaggerated comparison, but no one else would have the patience.

Forgive me, my dear Sir, for this long silence. To make you amends, I shall send you soon, and more encouraging still, without any postage, one or two rhymes of my later manufacture.

R. B.

CLXVI.

TO MR. M'MURDO.

[John M'Murdo has been already mentioned as one of Burns's firmest friends: his table at Drumlanrig was always spread at the poet's coming: nor was it uncheered by the presence of the lady of the house and her daughters.]

Ellisland, 19th June, 1789.

Sir,

A poet and a beggar are, in so many points of view, alike, that one might take them for the[408] same individual character under different designations; were it not that though, with a trifling poetic license, most poets may be styled beggars, yet the converse of the proposition does not hold, that every beggar is a poet. In one particular, however, they remarkably agree; if you help either the one or the other to a mug of ale, or the picking of a bone, they will very willingly repay you with a song. This occurs to me at present, as I have just despatched a well-lined rib of John Kirkpatrick's Highlander; a bargain for which I am indebted to you, in the style of our ballad printers, "Five excellent new songs." The enclosed is nearly my newest song, and one that has cost me some pains, though that is but an equivocal mark of its excellence. Two or three others, which I have by me, shall do themselves the honour to wait on your after leisure: petitioners for admittance into favour must not harass the condescension of their benefactor.

You see, Sir, what it is to patronize a poet. 'Tis like being a magistrate in a petty borough; you do them the favour to preside in their council for one year, and your name bears the prefatory stigma of Bailie for life.

With, not the compliments, but the best wishes, the sincerest prayers of the season for you, that you may see many and happy years with Mrs. M'Murdo, and your family; two blessings by the bye, to which your rank does not, by any means, entitle you; a loving wife and fine family being almost the only good things of this life to which the farm-house and cottage have an exclusive right,

I have the honour to be,

Sir,

Your much indebted and very humble servant,

R. B.

CLXVII.

TO MRS. DUNLOP.

[The devil, the pope, and the Pretender darkened the sermons, for more than a century, of many sound divines in the north. As a Jacobite, Burns disliked to hear Prince Charles called the Pretender, and as a man of a tolerant nature, he disliked to hear the Pope treated unlike a gentleman: his notions regarding Satan are recorded in his inimitable address.]

Ellisland, 21st June, 1789.

Dear Madam,

Will you take the effusions, the miserable effusions of low spirits, just as they flow from their bitter spring? I know not of any particular cause for this worst of all my foes besetting me; but for some time my soul has been beclouded with a thickening atmosphere of evil imaginations and gloomy presages.

Monday Evening.

I have just heard Mr. Kirkpatrick preach a sermon. He is a man famous for his benevolence, and I revere him; but from such ideas of my Creator, good Lord deliver me! Religion, my honoured friend, is surely a simple business, as it equally concerns the ignorant and the learned, the poor and the rich. That there is an incomprehensible Great Being, to whom I owe my existence, and that he must be intimately acquainted with the operations and progress of the internal machinery, and consequent outward deportment of this creature which he has made; these are, I think, self-evident propositions. That there is a real and eternal distinction between virtue and vice, and consequently, that I am an accountable creature; that from the seeming nature of the human mind, as well as from the evident imperfection, nay, positive injustice, in the administration of affairs, both in the natural and moral worlds, there must be a retributive scene of existence beyond the grave; must, I think, be allowed by every one who will give himself a moment's reflection. I will go farther, and affirm that from the sublimity, excellence, and purity of his doctrine and precepts, unparalleled by all the aggregated wisdom and learning of many preceding ages, though, to appearance, he himself was the obscurest and most illiterate of our species; therefore Jesus Christ was from God.

Whatever mitigates the woes, or increases the happiness of others, this is my criterion of goodness; and whatever injures society at large, or any individual in it, this is my measure of iniquity.

What think you, madam, of my creed? I trust that I have said nothing that will lessen me in the eye of one, whose good opinion I value almost next to the approbation of my own mind.

R. B.

CLXVIII.

TO MR. .

[The name of the person to whom the following letter is addressed is unknown: he seems, from his letter to Burns to have been intimate with the unfortunate poet,[409] Robert Fergusson, who, in richness of conversation and plenitude of fancy, reminded him, he said, of Robert Burns.]

1789.

My dear Sir,

The hurry of a farmer in this particular season, and the indolence of a poet at all times and seasons, will, I hope, plead my excuse for neglecting so long to answer your obliging letter of the 5th of August.

That you have done well in quitting your laborious concern in * * * *, I do not doubt; the weighty reasons you mention, were, I hope, very, and deservedly indeed, weighty ones, and your health is a matter of the last importance; but whether the remaining proprietors of the paper have also done well, is what I much doubt. The * * * *, so far as I was a reader, exhibited such a brilliancy of point, such an elegance of paragraph, and such a variety of intelligence, that I can hardly conceive it possible to continue a daily paper in the same degree of excellence: but if there was a man who had abilities equal to the task, that man's assistance the proprietors have lost.

When I received your letter I was transcribing for * * * *, my letter to the magistrates of the Canongate, Edinburgh, begging their permission to place a tombstone over poor Fergusson, and their edict in consequence of my petition, but now I shall send them to * * * * * *. Poor Fergusson! If there be a life beyond the grave, which I trust there is; and if there be a good God presiding over all nature, which I am sure there is; thou art now enjoying existence in a glorious world, where worth of the heart alone is distinction in the man; where riches, deprived of all their pleasure-purchasing powers, return to their native sordid matter; where titles and honours are the disregarded reveries of an idle dream; and where that heavy virtue, which is the negative consequence of steady dulness, and those thoughtless, though often destructive follies which are unavoidable aberrations of frail human nature, will be thrown into equal oblivion as if they had never been!

Adieu my dear sir! So soon as your present views and schemes are concentered in an aim, I shall be glad to hear from you; as your welfare and happiness is by no means a subject indifferent to

Yours,

R. B.

CLXIX.

TO MISS WILLIAMS.

[Helen Maria Williams acknowledged this letter, with the critical pencilling, on her poem on the Slave Trade, which it enclosed: she agreed, she said, with all his objections, save one, but considered his praise too high.]

Ellisland, 1789.

Madam,

Of the many problems in the nature of that wonderful creature, man, this is one of the most extraordinary, that he shall go on from day to day, from week to week, from month to month, or perhaps from year to year, suffering a hundred times more in an hour from the impotent consciousness of neglecting what he ought to do, than the very doing of it would cost him. I am deeply indebted to you, first for a most elegant poetic compliment; then for a polite, obliging letter; and, lastly, for your excellent poem on the Slave Trade; and yet, wretch that I am! though the debts were debts of honour, and the creditor a lady, I have put off and put off even the very acknowledgment of the obligation, until you must indeed be the very angel I take you for, if you can forgive me.

Your poem I have read with the highest pleasure. I have a way whenever I read a book, I mean a book in our own trade, Madam, a poetic one, and when it is my own property, that I take a pencil and mark at the ends of verses, or note on margins and odd paper, little criticisms of approbation or disapprobation as I peruse along. I will make no apology for presenting you with a few unconnected thoughts that occurred to me in my repeated perusals of your poem. I want to show you that I have honesty enough to tell you what I take to be truths, even when they are not quite on the side of approbation; and I do it in the firm faith that you have equal greatness of mind to hear them with pleasure.

I had lately the honour of a letter from Dr. Moore, where he tells me that he has sent me some books: they are not yet come to hand, but I hear they are on the way.

Wishing you all success in your progress in the path of fame; and that you may equally escape the danger of stumbling through incautious speed, or losing ground through loitering neglect.

R. B.

CLXX.

TO MR. JOHN LOGAN.

[The Kirk's Alarm, to which this letter alludes, has little of the spirit of malice and drollery, so rife in his earlier controversial compositions.]

Ellisland, near Dumfries, 7th Aug. 1789.

Dear Sir,

I intended to have written you long ere now, and as I told you, I had gotten three stanzas and a half on my way in a poetic epistle to you; but that old enemy of all good works, the devil, threw me into a prosaic mire, and for the soul of me I cannot get out of it. I dare not write you a long letter, as I am going to intrude on your time with a long ballad. I have, as you will shortly see, finished "The Kirk's Alarm;" but now that it is done, and that I have laughed once or twice at the conceits in some of the stanzas, I am determined not to let it get into the public; so I send you this copy, the first that I have sent to Ayrshire, except some few of the stanzas, which I wrote off in embryo for Gavin Hamilton, under the express provision and request that you will only read it to a few of us, and do not on any account give, or permit to be taken, any copy of the ballad. If I could be of any service to

Dr. M'Gill, I would do it, though it should be at a much greater expense than irritating a few bigoted priests, but I am afraid serving him in his present embarras is a task too hard for me. I have enemies enow, God knows, though I do not wantonly add to the number. Still as I think there is some merit in two or three of the thoughts, I send it to you as a small, but sincere testimony how much, and with what respectful esteem,
I am, dear Sir,
Your obliged humble servant,
R. B.

CLXXI.

TO MRS. DUNLOP.
[The poetic epistle of worthy Janet Little was of small account: nor was the advice of Dr. Moore, to abandon the Scottish stanza and dialect, and adopt the measure and language of modern English poetry, better inspired than the strains of the milkmaid, for such was Jenny Little.]
Ellisland, 6th Sept., 1789.
Dear Madam,
I have mentioned in my last my appointment to the Excise, and the birth of little Frank; who, by the bye, I trust will be no discredit to the honourable name of Wallace, as he has a fine manly countenance, and a figure that might do credit to a little fellow two months older; and likewise an excellent good temper, though when he pleases he has a pipe, only not quite so loud as the horn that his immortal namesake blew as a signal to take out the pin of Stirling bridge.
I had some time ago an epistle, part poetic, and part prosaic, from your poetess, Mrs. J. Little, a very ingenious, but modest composition. I should have written her as she requested, but for the hurry of this new business. I have heard of her and her compositions in this country; and I am happy to add, always to the honour of her character. The fact is, I know not well how to write to her: I should sit down to a sheet of paper that I knew not how to stain. I am no dab at fine-drawn letter-writing; and, except when prompted by friendship or gratitude, or, which happens extremely rarely, inspired by the muse (I know not her name) that presides over epistolary writing, I sit down, when necessitated to write, as I would sit down, to beat hemp.
Some parts of your letter of the 20th August, struck me with the most melancholy concern for the state of your mind at present.
Would I could write you a letter of comfort, I would sit down to it with as much pleasure, as I would to write an epic poem of my own composition that should equal the Iliad. Religion, my dear friend, is the true comfort! A strong persuasion in a future state of existence; a proposition so obviously

probable, that, setting revelation aside, every nation and people, so far as investigation has reached, for at least near four thousand years, have, in some mode or other, firmly believed it. In vain would we reason and pretend to doubt. I have myself done so to a very daring pitch; but, when I reflected, that I was opposing the most ardent wishes, and the most darling hopes of good men, and flying in the face of all human belief, in all ages, I was shocked at my own conduct.

I know not whether I have ever sent you the following lines, or if you have ever seen them; but it is one of my favourite quotations, which I keep constantly by me in my progress through life, in the language of the book of Job,

"Against the day of battle and of war"-

spoken of religion:

"'Tis this, my friend, that streaks our morning bright, 'Tis this, that gilds the horror of our night. [411]When wealth forsakes us, and when friends are few, When friends are faithless, or when foes pursue; Tis this that wards the blow, or stills the smart, Disarms affliction, or repels his dart; Within the breast bids purest raptures rise, Bids smiling conscience spread her cloudless skies."

I have been busy with Zeluco. The Doctor is so obliging as to request my opinion of it; and I have been revolving in my mind some kind of criticisms on novel-writing, but it is a depth beyond my research. I shall however digest my thoughts on the subject as well as I can. Zeluco is a most sterling performance.

Farewell! A Dieu, le bon Dieu, je vous commende.

R. B.

CLXXII.

TO CAPTAIN RIDDEL,

Carse.

[The Whistle alluded to in this letter was contended for on the 16th of October, 1790-the successful competitor, Fergusson, of Craigdarroch, was killed by a fall from his horse, some time after the "Jovial contest."]

Ellisland, 16th Oct., 1789.

Sir,

Big with the idea of this important day at Friars-Carse, I have watched the elements and skies in the full persuasion that they would announce it to the astonished world by some phenomena of terrific portent.-Yesternight until a very late hour did I wait with anxious horror, for the appearance of some comet firing half the sky; or aerial armies of sanguinary Scandinavians, darting athwart the startled heavens, rapid as the ragged lightning, and horrid as those convulsions of nature that bury nations.

The elements, however, seem to take the matter very quietly: they did not even usher in this morning with triple suns and a shower of blood, symbolical of the three potent heroes, and the mighty claret-shed of the day.-For me, as Thomson in his Winter says of the storm-I shall "Hear astonished, and astonished sing"

The whistle and the man; I sing The man that won the whistle, andc.

Here are we met, three merry boys, Three merry boys I trow are we; And mony a night we've merry been, And mony mae we hope to be.

Wha first shall rise to gang awa, A cuckold coward loun is he: Wha last beside his chair shall fa', He is the king amang us three.

To leave the heights of Parnassus and come to the humble vale of prose.-I have some misgivings that I take too much upon me, when I request you to get your guest, Sir Robert Lowrie, to frank the two enclosed covers for me, the one of them to Sir William Cunningham, of Robertland, Bart. at Kilmarnock,-the other to Mr. Allan Masterton, Writing-Master, Edinburgh. The first has a kindred claim on Sir Robert, as being a brother Baronet, and likewise a keen Foxite; the other is one of the worthiest men in the world, and a man of real genius; so, allow me to say, he has a fraternal claim on you. I want them franked for to-morrow, as I cannot get them to the post to-night.-I shall send a servant again for them in the evening. Wishing that your head may be crowned with laurels to-night, and free from aches to-morrow,

I have the honour to be, Sir,

Your deeply indebted humble Servant,

R. B.

CLXXIII.

TO CAPTAIN RIDDEL.

[Robert Riddel kept one of those present pests of society-an album-into which Burns copied the Lines on the Hermitage, and the Wounded Hare.]

Ellisland, 1789.

Sir,

I wish from my inmost soul it were in my power to give you a more substantial gratification and return for all the goodness to the poet, than transcribing a few of his idle rhymes.-However, "an old song," though to a proverb an instance of insignificance, is generally the only coin a poet has to pay with.

If my poems which I have transcribed, and mean still to transcribe into your book, were equal to the grateful respect and high esteem I bear for the gentleman to whom I present them, they would be the finest poems in the language.-As they are, they will at least be a testimony with what sincerity I have the honour to be,

Sir,
Your devoted humble Servant,
R. B.

CLXXIV.

TO MR. ROBERT AINSLIE.

[The ignominy of a poet becoming a gauger seems ever to have been present to the mind of Burns-but those moving things ca'd wives and weans have a strong influence on the actions of man.]

Ellisland, 1st Nov. 1789.

My dear Friend,

I had written you long ere now, could I have guessed where to find you, for I am sure you have more good sense than to waste the precious days of vacation time in the dirt of business and Edinburgh.-Wherever you are, God bless you, and lead you not into temptation, but deliver you from evil!

I do not know if I have informed you that I am now appointed to an excise division, in the middle of which my house and farm lie. In this I was extremely lucky. Without ever having been an expectant, as they call their journeymen excisemen, I was directly planted down to all intents and purposes an officer of excise; there to flourish and bring forth fruits-worthy of repentance.

I know not how the word exciseman, or still more opprobrious, gauger, will sound in your ears. I too have seen the day when my auditory nerves would have felt very delicately on this subject; but a wife and children are things which have a wonderful power in blunting these kind of sensations. Fifty pounds a year for life, and a provision for widows and orphans, you will allow is no bad settlement for a poet. For the ignominy of the profession, I have the encouragement which I once heard a recruiting sergeant give to a numerous, if not a respectable audience, in the streets of Kilmarnock.- "Gentlemen, for your further and better encouragement, I can assure you that our regiment is the most blackguard corps under the crown, and consequently with us an honest fellow has the surest chance for preferment."

You need not doubt that I find several very unpleasant and disagreeable circumstances in my business; but I am tired with and disgusted at the language of complaint against the evils of life. Human existence in the most favourable situations does not abound with pleasures, and has its inconveniences and ills; capricious foolish man mistakes these inconveniences and ills as if they were the peculiar property of his particular situation; and hence that eternal fickleness, that love of change, which has ruined, and daily does ruin many a fine fellow, as well as many a blockhead, and is almost, without exception, a constant source of disappointment and

misery.
I long to hear from you how you go on-not so much in business as in life. Are you pretty well satisfied with your own exertions, and tolerably at ease in your internal reflections? 'Tis much to be a great character as a lawyer, but beyond comparison more to be a great character as a man. That you may be both the one and the other is the earnest wish, and that you will be both is the firm persuasion of,
My dear Sir, andc.

CLXXV.

TO MR. RICHARD BROWN.
[With this letter closes the correspondence of Robert Burns and Richard Brown.]
Ellisland, 4th November, 1789.
I have been so hurried, my ever dear friend, that though I got both your letters, I have not been able to command an hour to answer them as I wished; and even now, you are to look on this as merely confessing debt, and craving days. Few things could have given me so much pleasure as the news that you were once more safe and sound on terra firma, and happy in that place where happiness is alone to be found, in the fireside circle. May the benevolent Director of all things peculiarly bless you in all those endearing connexions consequent on the tender and venerable names of husband and father! I have indeed been extremely lucky in getting an additional income of £50 a year, while, at the same time, the appointment will not cost me above £10 or £12 per annum of expenses more than I must have inevitably incurred. The worst circumstance is, that the excise division which I have got is so extensive, no less than ten parishes to ride over; and it abounds besides with so much business, that I can scarcely steal a spare moment. However, labour endears rest, and both together are absolutely necessary for the proper enjoyment of human existence. I cannot meet you anywhere. No less than an order from the Board of Excise, at Edinburgh, is necessary before I can have so much time as to meet you in Ayrshire. But do you come, and see me. We must have a social[413] day, and perhaps lengthen it out with half the half the night before you go again to sea. You are the earliest friend I now have on earth, my brothers excepted; and is not that an endearing circumstance? When you and I first met, we were at the green period of human life. The twig would easily take a bent, but would as easily return to its former state. You and I not only took a mutual bent, but by the melancholy, though strong influence of being both of the family of the unfortunate, we were entwined with one another in our growth towards advanced age; and blasted be the sacrilegious hand that shall attempt to undo the union! You and I must

have one bumper to my favourite toast, "May the companions of our youth be the friends of our old age!" Come and see me one year; I shall see you at Port Glasgow the next, and if we can contrive to have a gossiping between our two bedfellows, it will be so much additional pleasure. Mrs. Burns joins me in kind compliments to you and Mrs. Brown. Adieu!

I am ever, my dear Sir, yours,

R. B.

CLXXVI.

TO R. GRAHAM, ESQ.

[The poet enclosed in this letter to his patron in the Excise the clever verses on Captain Grose, the Kirk's Alarm, and the first ballad on Captain Miller's election.]

9th December, 1789.

Sir,

I have a good while had a wish to trouble you with a letter, and had certainly done it long ere now-but for a humiliating something that throws cold water on the resolution, as if one should say, "You have found Mr. Graham a very powerful and kind friend indeed, and that interest he is so kindly taking in your concerns, you ought by everything in your power to keep alive and cherish." Now though since God has thought proper to make one powerful and another helpless, the connexion of obliger and obliged is all fair; and though my being under your patronage is to me highly honourable, yet, Sir, allow me to flatter myself, that, as a poet and an honest man you first interested yourself in my welfare, and principally as such, still you permit me to approach you.

I have found the excise business go on a great deal smoother with me than I expected; owing a good deal to the generous friendship of Mr. Mitchel, my collector, and the kind assistance of Mr. Findlater, my supervisor. I dare to be honest, and I fear no labour. Nor do I find my hurried life greatly inimical to my correspondence with the muses. Their visits to me, indeed, and I believe to most of their acquaintance, like the visits of good angels, are short and far between: but I meet them now and then as I jog through the hills of Nithsdale, just as I used to do on the banks of Ayr. I take the liberty to enclose you a few bagatelles, all of them the productions of my leisure thoughts in my excise rides.

If you know or have ever seen Captain Grose, the antiquarian, you will enter into any humour that is in the verses on him. Perhaps you have seen them before, as I sent them to a London newspaper. Though I dare say you have none of the solemn-league-and-covenant fire, which shone so conspicuous in Lord George Gordon, and the Kilmarnock weavers, yet I think you must have heard of Dr. M'Gill, one of the clergymen of Ayr, and his heretical book. God help him, poor man! Though he is one of the worthiest, as well as one of the ablest of the whole priesthood of the Kirk of Scotland, in every sense of that ambiguous term, yet the poor Doctor and his numerous family are in imminent danger of being thrown out to the mercy of the winter-winds. The enclosed ballad on that business is, I confess, too local, but I laughed myself at some conceits in it, though I am convinced in my conscience that there are a good many heavy stanzas in it too.

The election ballad, as you will see, alludes to the present canvass in our string of boroughs. I do not believe there will be such a hard-run match in the whole general election.

I am too little a man to have any political attachments; I am deeply indebted to, and have the warmest veneration for, individuals of both parties; but a man who has it in his power to be the father of his country, and who * * * * *, is a character that one cannot speak of with patience.

Sir J. J. does "what man can do," but yet I doubt his fate.

[414]

CLXXVII.

TO MRS. DUNLOP.

[Burns was often a prey to lowness of spirits: at this some dull men have marvelled; but the dull have no misgivings: they go blindly and stupidly on, like a horse in a mill, and have none of the sorrows or joys which genius is heir to.]

Ellisland, 13th December, 1789.

Many thanks, dear Madam, for your sheet-full of rhymes. Though at present I am below the veriest prose, yet from you everything pleases. I am groaning under the miseries of a diseased nervous system; a system, the state of which is most conducive to our happiness-or the most productive of our misery. For now near three weeks I have been so ill with a nervous head-ache, that I have been obliged for a time to give up my excise-books, being scarce able to lift my head, much less to ride once a week over ten muir parishes. What is man?-To-day in the luxuriance of health, exulting in the enjoyment of existence; in a few days, perhaps in a few hours, loaded with conscious painful being, counting the tardy pace of the lingering moments by the repercussions of anguish, and refusing or denied a comforter. Day follows night, and night comes after day, only to curse him with life which gives him no pleasure; and yet the awful, dark termination of that life is something at which he recoils.

"Tell us, ye dead; will none of you in pity Disclose the secret What 'tis you are, and we must shortly be? 'tis no matter: A little time will make us learn'd as you are."[194]

Can it be possible, that when I resign this frail, feverish being, I shall still find myself in conscious existence? When the last gasp of agony has announced that I am no more to those that knew me, and the few who loved me; when the cold, stiffened, unconscious, ghastly corse is resigned into the earth, to be the prey of unsightly reptiles, and to become in time a trodden clod, shall I be yet warm in life, seeing and seen, enjoying and enjoyed? Ye venerable sages and holy flamens, is there probability in your conjectures, truth in your stories, of another world beyond death; or are they all alike, baseless visions, and fabricated fables? If there is another life, it must be only for the just, the benevolent, the amiable, and the humane; what a flattering idea, then, is a world to come! Would to God I as firmly believed it, as I ardently wish it! There I should meet an aged parent, now at rest from the many buffetings of an evil world, against which he so long and so bravely struggled. There should I meet the friend, the disinterested friend of my early life; the man who rejoiced to see me, because he loved me and could serve me.-Muir, thy weaknesses were the aberrations of human nature, but thy heart glowed with everything generous, manly and noble; and if ever emanation from the All-good Being animated a human form, it was thine! There should I, with speechless agony of rapture, again recognise my lost, my ever dear Mary! whose bosom was fraught with truth, honour, constancy, and love.

"My Mary, dear departed shade! Where is thy place of heavenly rest? Seest thou thy lover lowly laid? Hear'st thou the groans that rend his breast?"

Jesus Christ, thou amiablest of characters! I trust thou art no impostor, and that thy revelation of blissful scenes of existence beyond death and the grave, is not one of the many impositions which time after time have been palmed on credulous mankind. I trust that in thee "shall all the families of the earth be blessed," by being yet connected together in a better world, where every tie that bound heart to heart, in this state of existence, shall be, far beyond our present conceptions, more endearing.

I am a good deal inclined to think with those who maintain, that what are called nervous affections are in fact diseases of the mind. I cannot reason, I cannot think; and but to you I would not venture to write anything above an order to a cobbler. You have felt too much of the ills of life not to sympathise with a diseased wretch, who has impaired more than half of any faculties he possessed. Your goodness will excuse this distracted scrawl, which the writer dare scarcely read, and which he would throw into the fire, were he able to write anything better, or indeed anything at all.

Rumour told me something of a son of yours, who was returned from the East or West Indies. If you have gotten news from James or Anthony, it was cruel in you not to let me know; as I promise you on the sincerity of a man, who is weary of one world, and anxious about another, that scarce anything could give me so much pleasure as to hear of any good thing

befalling my honoured friend.[415]
If you have a minute's leisure, take up your pen in pity to le pauvre miserable.
R. B.

FOOTNOTES:

[194] Blair's Grave.

CLXXVIII.

TO LADY W M CONSTABLE.
[The Lady Winifred Maxwell, the last of the old line of Nithsdale, was granddaughter of that Earl who, in 1715, made an almost miraculous escape from death, through the spirit and fortitude of his countess, a lady of the noble family of Powis.]
Ellisland, 16th December, 1789.
My Lady,
In vain have I from day to day expected to hear from Mrs. Young, as she promised me at Dalswinton that she would do me the honour to introduce me at Tinwald; and it was impossible, not from your ladyship's accessibility, but from my own feelings, that I could go alone. Lately indeed, Mr. Maxwell of Carruchen, in his usual goodness, offered to accompany me, when an unlucky indisposition on my part hindered my embracing the opportunity. To court the notice or the tables of the great, except where I sometimes have had a little matter to ask of them, or more often the pleasanter task of witnessing my gratitude to them, is what I never have done, and I trust never shall do. But with your ladyship I have the honour to be connected by one of the strongest and most endearing ties in the whole moral world. Common sufferers, in a cause where even to be unfortunate is glorious, the cause of heroic loyalty! Though my fathers had not illustrious honours and vast properties to hazard in the contest, though they left their humble cottages only to add so many units more to the unnoted crowd that followed their leaders, yet what they could they did, and what they had they lost; with unshaken firmness and unconcealed political attachments, they shook hands with ruin for what they esteemed the cause of their king and their country. The language and the enclosed verses are for your ladyship's eye alone. Poets are not very famous for their prudence; but as I can do nothing for a cause which is now nearly no more, I do not wish to hurt myself.
I have the honour to be,
My lady,
Your ladyship's obliged and obedient

Humble servant,
R. B.

CLXXIX.

TO PROVOST MAXWELL,
OF LOCHMABEN.
[Of Lochmaben, the "Marjory of the mony Lochs" of the election ballads, Maxwell was at this time provost, a post more of honour than of labour.]
Ellisland, 20th December, 1789.
Dear Provost,
As my friend Mr. Graham goes for your good town to-morrow, I cannot resist the temptation to send you a few lines, and as I have nothing to say I have chosen this sheet of foolscap, and begun as you see at the top of the first page, because I have ever observed, that when once people have fairly set out they know not where to stop. Now that my first sentence is concluded, I have nothing to do but to pray heaven to help me on to another. Shall I write you on Politics or Religion, two master subjects for your sayers of nothing. Of the first I dare say by this time you are nearly surfeited: and for the last, whatever they may talk of it, who make it a kind of company concern, I never could endure it beyond a soliloquy. I might write you on farming, on building, or marketing, but my poor distracted mind is so torn, so jaded, so racked and bediveled with the task of the superlative damned to make one guinea do the business of three, that I detest, abhor, and swoon at the very word business, though no less than four letters of my very short sirname are in it.
Well, to make the matter short, I shall betake myself to a subject ever fruitful of themes; a subject the turtle-feast of the sons of Satan, and the delicious secret sugar-plum of the babes of grace-a subject sparkling with all the jewels that wit can find in the mines of genius: and pregnant with all the stores of learning from Moses and Confucius to Franklin and Priestley-in short, may it please your Lordship, I intend to write * * *
[Here the Poet inserted a song which can only be sung at times when the punch-bowl has done its duty and wild wit is set free.]
If at any time you expect a field-day in your town, a day when Dukes, Earls, and Knights pay their court to weavers, tailors, and cobblers, I should like to know of it two or three days beforehand. It is not that I care three skips of a cur dog for the politics, but I should like to see[416] such an exhibition of human nature. If you meet with that worthy old veteran in religion and good-fellowship, Mr. Jeffrey, or any of his amiable family, I beg you will give them my best compliments.
R. B.

CLXXX.

TO SIR JOHN SINCLAIR.

[Of the Monkland Book-Club alluded to in this letter, the clergyman had omitted all mention in his account of the Parish of Dunscore, published in Sir John Sinclair's work: some of the books which the poet introduced were stigmatized as vain and frivolous.]

1790.

Sir,

The following circumstance has, I believe, been committed in the statistical account, transmitted to you of the parish of Dunscore, in Nithsdale. I beg leave to send it to you because it is new, and may be useful. How far it is deserving of a place in your patriotic publication, you are the best judge.

To store the minds of the lower classes with useful knowledge, is certainly of very great importance, both to them as individuals and to society at large. Giving them a turn for reading and reflection, is giving them a source of innocent and laudable amusement: and besides, raises them to a more dignified degree in the scale of rationality. Impressed with this idea, a gentleman in this parish, Robert Riddel, Esq., of Glenriddel, set on foot a species of circulating library, on a plan so simple as to be practicable in any corner of the country; and so useful, as to deserve the notice of every country gentleman, who thinks the improvement of that part of his own species, whom chance has thrown into the humble walks of the peasant and the artisan, a matter worthy of his attention.

Mr. Riddel got a number of his own tenants, and farming neighbors, to form themselves into a society for the purpose of having a library among themselves. They entered into a legal engagement to abide by it for three years; with a saving clause or two in case of a removal to a distance, or death. Each member, at his entry, paid five shillings; and at each of their meetings, which were held every fourth Saturday, sixpence more. With their entry-money, and the credit which they took on the faith of their future funds, they laid in a tolerable stock of books at the commencement. What authors they were to purchase, was always decided by the majority. At every meeting, all the books, under certain fines and forfeitures, by way of penalty, were to be produced; and the members had their choice of the volumes in rotation. He whose name stood for that night first on the list, had his choice of what volume he pleased in the whole collection; the second had his choice after the first; the third after the second, and so on to the last. At next meeting, he who had been first on the list at the preceding meeting, was last at this; he who had been second was first; and so on through the whole three years. At the expiration of the engagement the books were sold by auction, but only among the members themselves; each man had his share of the common stock, in money or in books, as he chose to be a purchaser or not.

At the breaking up of this little society, which was formed under Mr. Riddel's patronage, what with benefactions of books from him, and what with their own purchases, they had collected together upwards of one hundred and fifty volumes. It will easily be guessed, that a good deal of trash would be bought. Among the books, however, of this little library, were, Blair's Sermons, Robertson's History of Scotland, Hume's History of the Stewarts, The Spectator, Idler, Adventurer, Mirror, Lounger, Observer, Man of Feeling, Man of the World, Chrysal, Don Quixote, Joseph Andrews, andc. A peasant who can read, and enjoy such books, is certainly a much superior being to his neighbour, who perhaps stalks besides his team, very little removed, except in shape, from the brutes he drives.

Wishing your patriotic exertions their so much merited success,

I am, Sir,

Your humble servant,

A Peasant.

CLXXXI.

TO CHARLES SHARPE, ESQ.,
OF HODDAM.

[The family of Hoddam is of old standing in Nithsdale. It has mingled blood with some of the noblest Scottish names; nor is it unknown either in history or literature-the fierce knight of Closeburn, who in the scuffle between Bruce and Comyne drew his sword and made[417] "sicker," and my friend Charles Kirkpatrick Sharpe, are not the least distinguished of its members.]

[1790.]

It is true, Sir, you are a gentleman of rank and fortune, and I am a poor devil: you are a feather in the cap of society, and I am a very hobnail in its shoes; yet I have the honour to belong to the same family with you, and on that score I now address you. You will perhaps suspect that I am going to claim affinity with the ancient and honourable house of Kirkpatrick. No, no, Sir: I cannot indeed be properly said to belong to any house, or even any province or kingdom; as my mother, who, for many years was spouse to a marching regiment, gave me into this bad world, aboard the packet-boat, somewhere between Donaghadee and Portpatrick. By our common family, I mean, Sir, the family of the muses. I am a fiddler and a poet; and you, I am told, play an exquisite violin, and have a standard taste in the Belles Lettres. The other day, a brother catgut gave me a charming Scots air of your composition. If I was pleased with the tune, I was in raptures with the title you have given it; and taking up the idea I have spun it into the three stanzas enclosed. Will you allow me, Sir, to present you them, as the dearest offering that a misbegotten son of poverty and rhyme has to give? I have a longing to take you by the hand and unburthen my heart by saying, "Sir, I honour you as a man who supports the dignity of human nature, amid an age when frivolity and avarice have, between them, debased us below the brutes that perish!" But, alas, Sir! to me you are unapproachable. It is true, the muses baptized me in Castalian streams, but the thoughtless gipsies forgot to give me a name. As the sex have served many a good fellow, the Nine have given me a great deal of pleasure, but, bewitching jades! they have beggared me. Would they but spare me a little of their cast-linen! Were it only in my power to say that I have a shirt on my back! but the idle wenches, like Solomon's lilies, "they toil not, neither do they spin;" so I must e'en continue to tie my remnant of a cravat, like the hangman's rope, round my naked throat, and coax my galligaskins to keep together their many-coloured fragments. As to the affair of shoes, I have given that up. My pilgrimages in my ballad-trade, from town to town, and on your stony-hearted turnpikes too, are what not even the hide of Job's Behemoth could bear. The coat on my back is no more: I shall not speak evil of the dead. It would be equally unhandsome and ungrateful to find fault with my old surtout, which so kindly supplies and conceals the want of that coat. My hat indeed is a great favourite; and though I got it literally for an old song, I would not exchange it for the best beaver in Britain. I was, during several years, a kind of factotum servant to a country clergyman, where I pickt up a good many scraps of learning, particularly in some branches of the mathematics. Whenever I feel inclined to rest myself on my way, I take my seat under a hedge, laying my poetic wallet on the one side, and my fiddle-case on the other, and placing my hat between my legs, I can, by means of its brim, or rather brims, go through the whole doctrine of the conic sections.

However, Sir, don't let me mislead you, as if I would interest your pity. Fortune has so much forsaken me, that she has taught me to live without her; and amid all my rags and poverty, I am as independent, and much more happy, than a monarch of the world. According to the hackneyed metaphor, I value the several actors in the great drama of life, simply as they act their parts. I can look on a worthless fellow of a duke with unqualified contempt, and can regard an honest scavenger with sincere respect. As you, Sir, go through your role with such distinguished merit, permit me to make one in the chorus of universal applause, and assure you that with the highest respect,

I have the honour to be, andc.,

Johnny Faa.

CLXXXII.

TO MR. GILBERT BURNS.

[In the few fierce words of this letter the poet bids adieu to all hopes of wealth from Ellisland.]

Ellisland, 11th January, 1790.

Dear Brother,

I mean to take advantage of the frank, though I have not, in my present frame of mind, much appetite for exertion in writing. My nerves are in a cursed state. I feel that horrid hypochondria pervading every atom of both body and soul. This farm has undone my enjoyment of myself. It is a ruinous affair on all hands[418] But let it go to bell! I'll fight it out and be off with it.

We have gotten a set of very decent players here just now. I have seen them an evening or two. David Campbell, in Ayr, wrote to me by the manager of the company, a Mr. Sutherland, who is a man of apparent worth. On New-year-day evening I gave him the following prologue, which he spouted to his audience with applause.

No song nor dance I bring from yon great city, That queens it o'er our taste-the more's the pity: Tho', by the bye, abroad why will you roam? Good sense and taste are natives here at home.

I can no more.-If once I was clear of this cursed farm, I should respire more at ease.

R. B.

CLXXXIII.

TO MR. SUTHERLAND,

PLAYER.

ENCLOSING A PROLOGUE.

[When the farm failed, the poet sought pleasure in the playhouse: he tried to retire from his own harassing reflections, into a world created by other minds.]

Monday Morning.

I was much disappointed, my dear Sir, in wanting your most agreeable company yesterday. However, I heartily pray for good weather next Sunday; and whatever aërial Being has the guidance of the elements, may take any other half-dozen of Sundays he pleases, and clothe them with

"Vapours and clouds, and storms, Until he terrify himself At combustion of his own raising."

I shall see you on Wednesday forenoon. In the greatest hurry,

R. B.

CLXXXIV.

TO WILLIAM DUNBAR, W.S.

[This letter was first published by the Ettrick Shepherd, in his edition of Burns: it is remarkable for this sentence, "I am resolved never to breed up a son of mine to any of the learned professions: I know the value of independence, and since I cannot give my sons an independent fortune, I shall give them an independent line of life." We may look round us and inquire which line of life the poet could possibly mean.]

Ellisland, 14th January, 1790.

Since we are here creatures of a day, since "a few summer days, and a few winter nights, and the life of man is at an end," why, my dear much-esteem Sir, should you and I let negligent indolence, for I know it is nothing worse, step in between us and bar the enjoyment of a mutual correspondence? We are not shapen out of the common, heavy, methodical clod, the elemental stuff of the plodding selfish race, the sons of Arithmetic and Prudence; our feelings and hearts are not benumbed and poisoned by the cursed influence of riches, which, whatever blessing they may be in other respects, are no friends to the nobler qualities of the heart: in the name of random sensibility, then, let never the moon change on our silence any more. I have had a tract of had health most part of this winter, else you had heard from me long ere now. Thank Heaven, I am now got so much better as to be able to partake a little in the enjoyments of life.

Our friend Cunningham will, perhaps, have told you of my going into the Excise. The truth is, I found it a very convenient business to have £50 per annum, nor have I yet felt any of those mortifying circumstances in it that I was led to fear.

Feb. 2.

I have not, for sheer hurry of business, been able to spare five minutes to finish my letter. Besides my farm business, I ride on my Excise matters at least two hundred miles every week. I have not by any means given up the muses. You will see in the 3d vol. of Johnson's Scots songs that I have contributed my mite there.

But, my dear Sir, little ones that look up to you for paternal protection are an important charge. I have already two fine, healthy, stout little fellows, and I wish to throw some light upon them. I have a thousand reveries and schemes about them, and their future destiny. Not that I am a Utopian projector in these things. I am resolved never to breed up a son of mine to any of the learned professions. I know the value of independence; and since I cannot give my sons an independent fortune, I shall give them an independent line of life. What a chaos of hurry, chance, and changes is this world, when one sits soberly down to reflect on it! To a father, who himself knows the world, the thought that he shall have sons to[419] usher into it must fill him with dread; but if he have daughters, the prospect in a thoughtful moment is apt to shock him.

I hope Mrs. Fordyce and the two young ladies are well. Do let me forget that they are nieces of yours, and let me say that I never saw a more interesting, sweeter pair of sisters in my life. I am the fool of my feelings and attachments. I often take up a volume of my Spenser to realize you to my imagination, and think over the social scenes we have had together. God grant that there may be another world more congenial to honest fellows beyond this. A world where these rubs and plagues of absence, distance, misfortunes, ill-health, andc., shall no more damp hilarity and divide friendship. This I know is your throng season, but half a page will much oblige,

My dear Sir,

Yours sincerely,

R. B.

CLXXXV.

TO MRS. DUNLOP.

[Falconer, the poet, whom Burns mentions here, perished in the Aurora, in which he acted as purser: he was a satirist of no mean power, and wrote that useful work, the Marine Dictionary: but his fame depends upon "The Shipwreck," one of the most original and mournful poems in the language.]

Ellisland, 25th January, 1790.

It has been owing to unremitting hurry of business that I have not written to you, Madam, long ere now. My health is greatly better, and I now begin once more to share in satisfaction and enjoyment with the rest of my fellow-creatures.

Many thanks, my much-esteemed friend, for your kind letters; but why will you make me run the risk of being contemptible and mercenary in my own eyes? When I pique myself on my independent spirit, I hope it is neither poetic license, nor poetic rant; and I am so flattered with the honour you have done me, in making me your compeer in friendship and friendly correspondence, that I cannot without pain, and a degree of mortification, be reminded of the real inequality between our situations.

Most sincerely do I rejoice with you, dear Madam, in the good news of Anthony. Not only your anxiety about his fate, but my own esteem for such a noble, warm-hearted, manly young fellow, in the little I had of his acquaintance, has interested me deeply in his fortunes.

Falconer, the unfortunate author of the "Shipwreck," which you so much admire, is no more. After witnessing the dreadful catastrophe he so feelingly describes in his poem, and after weathering many hard gales of fortune, he went to the bottom with the Aurora frigate!

I forget what part of Scotland had the honour of giving him birth; but he was the son of obscurity and misfortune. He was one of those daring adventurous spirits, which Scotland, beyond any other country, is remarkable for producing. Little does the fond mother think, as she hangs delighted over the sweet little leech at her bosom, where the poor fellow may hereafter wander, and what may be his fate. I remember a stanza in an old Scottish ballad, which, notwithstanding its rude simplicity, speaks feelingly to the heart:

"Little did my mother think, That day she cradled me, What land I was to travel in, Or what death I should die!"[195]

Old Scottish song are, you know, a favourite study and pursuit of mine, and now I am on that subject, allow me to give you two stanzas of another old simple ballad, which I am sure will please you. The catastrophe of the piece is a poor ruined female, lamenting her fate. She concludes with this pathetic wish:-

"O that my father had ne'er on me smil'd; O that my mother had ne'er to me sung! O that my cradle had never been rock'd; But that I had died when I was young!

"O that the grave it were my bed; My blankets were my winding sheet; The clocks and the worms my bedfellows a'; And O sae sound as I should sleep!"

I do not remember in all my reading, to have met with anything more truly the language of misery, than the exclamation in the last line. Misery is like love; to speak its language truly, the author must have felt it.

I am every day expecting the doctor to give your little godson[196] the small-pox. They are rife in the country, and I tremble for his fate. By the way, I cannot help congratulating you on his looks and spirit. Every person who sees [420] him, acknowledges him to be the finest, handsomest child he has ever seen. I am myself delighted with the manly swell of his little chest, and a certain miniature dignity in the carriage of his head, and the glance of his fine black eye, which promise the undaunted gallantry of an independent mind.

I thought to have sent you some rhymes, but time forbids. I promise you poetry until you are tired of it, next time I have the honour of assuring you how truly I am, andc.

R. B.

FOOTNOTES:

[195] The ballad is in the Minstrelsy of the Scottish Border, ed. 1833, vol. iii. p. 304.

[196] The bard's second son, Francis.

CLXXXVI.

TO MR. PETER HILL,
BOOKSELLER, EDINBURGH.

[The Mademoiselle Burns whom the poet inquires about, was one of the "ladies of the Canongate," who desired to introduce free trade in her profession into a close borough: this was refused by the magistrates of Edinburgh, though advocated with much eloquence and humour in a letter by her namesake-it is coloured too strongly with her calling to be published.]

Ellisland, 2d Feb., 1790.

No! I will not say one word about apologies or excuses for not writing.-I am a poor, rascally gauger, condemned to gallop at least 200 miles every week to inspect dirty ponds and yeasty barrels, and where can I find time to write to, or importance to interest anybody? The upbraidings of my conscience, nay the upbraidings of my wife, have persecuted me on your account these two or three months past.-I wish to God I was a great man, that my correspondence might throw light upon you, to let the world see what you really are: and then I would make your fortune without putting my hand in my pocket for you, which, like all other great men, I suppose I would avoid as much as possible. What are you doing, and how are you doing? Have you lately seen any of my few friends? What is become of the borough reform, or how is the fate of my poor namesake, Mademoiselle Burns, decided? O man! but for thee and thy selfish appetites, and dishonest artifices, that beauteous form, and that once innocent and still ingenuous mind, might have shone conspicuous and lovely in the faithful wife, and the affectionate mother; and shall the unfortunate sacrifice to thy pleasures have no claim on thy humanity!

I saw lately in a Review, some extracts from a new poem, called the Village Curate; send it me. I want likewise a cheap copy of The World. Mr. Armstrong, the young poet, who does me the honour to mention me so kindly in his works, please give him my best thanks for the copy of his book-I shall write him, my first leisure hour. I like his poetry much, but I think his style in prose quite astonishing.

Your book came safe, and I am going to trouble you with further commissions. I call it troubling you,-because I want only, books; the cheapest way, the best; so you may have to hunt for them in the evening auctions. I want Smollette's works, for the sake of his incomparable humour. I have already Roderick Random, and Humphrey Clinker.-Peregrine Pickle, Launcelot Greaves, and Ferdinand Count Fathom, I still want; but as I said, the veriest ordinary copies will serve me. I am nice only in the appearance of my poets. I forget the price of Cowper's Poems, but, I believe, I must have them. I saw the other day, proposals for a publication, entitled "Banks's new and complete Christian's Family Bible," printed for

C. Cooke, Paternoster-row, London.-He promises at least, to give in the work, I think it is three hundred and odd engravings, to which he has put the names of the first artists in London.-You will know the character of the performance, as some numbers of it are published; and if it is really what it pretends to be, set me down as a subscriber, and send me the published numbers.

Let me hear from you, your first leisure minute, and trust me you shall in future have no reason to complain of my silence. The dazzling perplexity of novelty will dissipate and leave me to pursue my course in the quiet path of methodical routine.

R. B.

CLXXXVII.

TO MR. W. NICOL.

[The poet has recorded this unlooked-for death of the Dominie's mare in some hasty verses, which are not much superior to the subject.]

Ellisland, Feb. 9th, 1790.

My dear Sir,

That d-mned mare of yours is dead. I would[421] freely have given her price to have saved her; she has vexed me beyond description. Indebted as I was to your goodness beyond what I can ever repay, I eagerly grasped at your offer to have the mare with me. That I might at least show my readiness in wishing to be grateful, I took every care of her in my power. She was never crossed for riding above half a score of times by me or in my keeping. I drew her in the plough, one of three, for one poor week. I refused fifty-five shillings for her, which was the highest bode I could squeeze for her. I fed her up and had her in fine order for Dumfries fair; when four or five days before the fair, she was seized with an unaccountable disorder in the sinews, or somewhere in the bones of the neck; with a weakness or total want of power in her fillets, and in short the whole vertebrae of her spine seemed to be diseased and unhinged, and in eight-and-forty hours, in spite of the two best farriers in the country, she died and be d-mned to her! The farriers said that she had been quite strained in the fillets beyond cure before you had bought her; and that the poor devil, though she might keep a little flesh, had been jaded and quite worn out with fatigue and oppression. While she was with me, she was under my own eye, and I assure you, my much valued friend, everything was done for her that could be done; and the accident has vexed me to the heart. In fact I could not pluck up spirits to write to you, on account of the unfortunate business.

There is little new in this country. Our theatrical company, of which you must have heard, leave us this week.-Their merit and character are indeed very great, both on the stage and in private life; not a worthless creature among them; and their encouragement has been accordingly. Their usual run is from eighteen to twenty-five pounds a night: seldom less than the one, and the house will hold no more than the other. There have been repeated instances of sending away six, and eight, and ten pounds a night for want of room. A new theatre is to be built by subscription; the first stone is to be laid on Friday first to come. Three hundred guineas have been raised by thirty subscribers, and thirty more might have been got if wanted. The manager, Mr. Sutherland, was introduced to me by a friend from Ayr; and a worthier or cleverer fellow I have rarely met with. Some of our clergy have slipt in by stealth now and then; but they have got up a farce of their own. You must have heard how the Rev. Mr. Lawson of Kirkmahoe, seconded by the Rev. Mr. Kirkpatrick of Dunscore, and the rest of that faction, have accused in formal process, the unfortunate and Rev. Mr. Heron, of Kirkgunzeon, that in ordaining Mr. Nielson to the cure of souls in Kirkbean, he, the said Heron, feloniously and treasonably bound the said Nielson to the confession of faith, so far as it was agreeable to reason and the word of God!

Mrs. B. begs to be remembered most gratefully to you. Little Bobby and Frank are charmingly well and healthy. I am jaded to death with fatigue. For these two or three months, on an average, I have not ridden less than two hundred miles per week. I have done little in the poetic way. I have given Mr. Sutherland two Prologues; one of which was delivered last week. I have likewise strung four or five barbarous stanzas, to the tune of Chevy Chase, by way of Elegy on your poor unfortunate mare, beginning (the name she got here was Peg Nicholson)

"Peg Nicholson was a good bay mare, As ever trod on airn; But now she's floating down the Nith, And past the mouth o' Cairn."

My best compliments to Mrs. Nicol, and little Neddy, and all the family; I hope Ned is a good scholar, and will come out to gather nuts and apples with me next harvest.

R. B.

CLXXXVIII.

TO MR. CUNNINGHAM.

[Burns looks back with something of regret to the days of rich dinners and flowing wine-cups which he experienced in Edinburgh. Alexander Cunningham and his unhappy loves are recorded in that fine song, "Had I a cave on some wild distant shore."]

Ellisland, 13th February, 1790.

I beg your pardon, my dear and much valued friend, for writing to you on this very unfashionable, unsightly sheet-

"My poverty but not my will consents."

But to make amends, since of modish post I have none, except one poor widowed half-sheet of gilt, which lies in my drawer among my plebeian fool's-cap pages, like the widow of a man[422] of fashion, whom that unpolite scoundrel, Necessity, has driven from Burgundy and Pineapple, to a dish of Bohea, with the scandal-bearing help-mate of a village-priest; or a glass of whisky-toddy, with a ruby-nosed yoke-fellow of a foot-padding exciseman-I make a vow to enclose this sheet-full of epistolary fragments in that my only scrap of gilt paper.

I am indeed your unworthy debtor for three friendly letters. I ought to have written to you long ere now, but it is a literal fact, I have scarcely a spare moment. It is not that I will not write to you; Miss Burnet is not more dear to her guardian angel, nor his grace the Duke of Queensbury to the powers of darkness, than my friend Cunningham to me. It is not that I cannot write to you; should you doubt it, take the following fragment, which was intended for you some time ago, and be convinced that I can antithesize sentiment, and circumvolute periods, as well as any coiner of phrase in the regions of philology.

December, 1789.

My dear Cunningham,

Where are you? And what are you doing? Can you be that son of levity, who takes up a friendship as he takes up a fashion; or are you, like some other of the worthiest fellows in the world, the victim of indolence, laden with fetters of ever-increasing weight?

What strange beings we are! Since we have a portion of conscious existence, equally capable of enjoying pleasure, happiness, and rapture, or of suffering pain, wretchedness, and misery, it is surely worthy of an inquiry, whether there be not such a thing as a science of life; whether method, economy, and fertility of expedients be not applicable to enjoyment, and whether there be not a want of dexterity in pleasure, which renders our little scantling of happiness still less; and a profuseness, an intoxication in bliss, which leads to satiety, disgust, and self-abhorrence. There is not a doubt but that health, talents, character, decent competency, respectable friends, are real substantial blessings; and yet do we not daily see those who enjoy many or all of these good things contrive notwithstanding to be as unhappy as others to whose lot few of them have fallen? I believe one great source of this mistake or misconduct is owing to a certain stimulus, with us called ambition, which goads us up the hill of life, not as we ascend other eminences, for the laudable curiosity of viewing an extended landscape, but rather for the dishonest pride of looking down on others of our fellow-creatures, seemingly diminutive in humbler stations, andc. andc.

Sunday, 14th February, 1790.

God help me! I am now obliged to

"Join night to day, and Sunday to the week."[197]

If there be any truth in the orthodox faith of these churches, I am d-mned past redemption, and what is worse, d-mned to all eternity. I am deeply read in Boston's Four-fold State, Marshal on Sanctification, Guthrie's Trial of a Saving Interest, andc.; but "there is no balm in Gilead, there is no physician there," for me; so I shall e'en turn Arminian, and trust to "sincere though imperfect obedience."

Tuesday, 16th.

Luckily for me, I was prevented from the discussion of the knotty point at which I had just made a full stop. All my fears and care are of this world: if there is another, an honest man has nothing to fear from it. I hate a man that wishes to be a Deist: but I fear, every fair, unprejudiced inquirer must in some degree be a sceptic. It is not that there are any very staggering arguments against the immortality of man; but like electricity, phlogiston, andc., the subject is so involved in darkness, that we want data to go upon. One thing frightens me much: that we are to live for ever, seems too good news to be true. That we are to enter into a new scene of existence, where, exempt from want and pain, we shall enjoy ourselves and our friends without satiety or separation-how much should I be indebted to any one who could fully assure me that this was certain!

My time is once more expired. I will write to Mr. Cleghorn soon. God bless him and all his concerns! And may all the powers that preside over conviviality and friendship, be present with all their kindest influence, when the bearer of this, Mr. Syme, and you meet! I wish I could also make one.

Finally, brethren, farewell! Whatsoever things are lovely, whatsoever things are gentle, whatsoever things are charitable, whatsoever things are kind, think on these things, and think on

R. B.

FOOTNOTES:

[197] Young. Satire on Women.

[423]

CLXXXIX.

TO MR. PETER HILL.

[That Burns turned at this time his thoughts on the drama, this order to his bookseller for dramatic works, as well as his attendances at the Dumfries theatre, afford proof.]

Ellisland, 2d March, 1790.

At a late meeting of the Monkland Friendly Society, it was resolved to augment their library by the following books, which you are to send us as soon as possible:-The Mirror, The Lounger, Man of Feeling, Man of the World, (these, for my own sake, I wish to have by the first carrier), Knox's History of the Reformation; Rae's History of the Rebellion in 1715; any good history of the rebellion in 1745; A Display of the Secession Act and Testimony, by Mr. Gibb; Hervey's Meditations; Beveridge's Thoughts; and another copy of Watson's Body of Divinity.

I wrote to Mr. A. Masterton three or four months ago, to pay some money he owed me into your hands, and lately I wrote to you to the same purpose, but I have heard from neither one or other of you.

In addition to the books I commissioned in my last, I want very much An Index to the Excise Laws, or an Abridgment of all the Statutes now in force relative to the Excise, by Jellinger Symons; I want three copies of this book: if it is now to be had, cheap or dear, get it for me. An honest country neighbour of mine wants too a Family Bible, the larger the better; but second-handed, for he does not choose to give above ten shillings for the book. I want likewise for myself, as you can pick them up, second-handed or cheap, copies of Otway's Dramatic Works, Ben Jonson's, Dryden's, Congreve's, Wycherley's, Vanbrugh's, Cibber's, or any dramatic works of the more modern, Macklin, Garrick, Foote, Colman, or Sheridan. A good copy too of Moliere, in French, I much want. Any other good dramatic authors in that language I want also; but comic authors, chiefly, though I should wish to have Racine, Corneille, and Voltaire too. I am in no hurry for all, or any of these, but if you accidentally meet with them very cheap, get them for me.

And now to quit the dry walk of business, how do you do, my dear friend? and how is Mrs. Hill? I trust, if now and then not so elegantly handsome, at least as amiable, and sings as divinely as ever. My good wife too has a charming "wood-note wild;" now could we four .

I am out of all patience with this vile world, for one thing. Mankind are by nature benevolent creatures, except in a few scoundrelly instances. I do not think that avarice of the good things we chance to have, is born with us; but we are placed here amid so much nakedness, and hunger, and poverty, and want, that we are under a cursed necessity of studying selfishness, in order that we may exist! Still there are, in every age, a few souls, that all the wants and woes of life cannot debase to selfishness, or even to the necessary alloy of caution and prudence. If ever I am in danger of vanity, it is when I contemplate myself on this side of my disposition and character. God knows I am no saint; I have a whole host of follies and sin, to answer for; but if I could, and I believe I do it as far as I can, I would wipe away all tears from all eyes.

Adieu!

R. B.

CXC.

TO MRS. DUNLOP.

[It is not a little singular that Burns says, in this letter, he had just met with the Mirror and Lounger for the first time: it will be remembered that a few years before a generous article was dedicated by Mackenzie, the editor, to the Poems of Burns, and to this the poet often alludes in his correspondence.]

Ellisland, 10th April, 1790.

I have just now, my ever honoured friend, enjoyed a very high luxury, in reading a paper of the Lounger. You know my national prejudices. I had often read and admired the Spectator, Adventurer, Rambler, and World; but still with a certain regret, that they were so thoroughly and entirely English. Alas! have I often said to myself, what are all the boasted advantages which my country reaps from the union, that can counterbalance the annihilation of her independence, and even her very name! I often repeat that couplet of my favourite poet, Goldsmith-

"- States of native liberty possest, Tho' very poor, may yet be very blest."

Nothing can reconcile me to the common terms, "English ambassador, English court," andc. And I am out of all patience to see that[424] equivocal character, Hastings, impeached by "the Commons of England." Tell me, my friend, is this weak prejudice? I believe in my conscience such ideas as "my country; her independence; her honour; the illustrious names that mark the history of my native land;" andc.-I believe these, among your men of the world, men who in fact guide for the most part and govern our world, are looked on as so many modifications of wrongheadedness. They know the use of bawling out such terms, to rouse or lead the rabble; but for their own private use, with almost all the able statesmen that ever existed, or now exist, when they talk of right and wrong, they only mean proper and improper; and their measure of conduct is, not what they ought, but what they dare. For the truth of this I shall not ransack the history of nations, but appeal to one of the ablest judges of men that ever lived-the celebrated Earl of Chesterfield. In fact, a man who could thoroughly control his vices whenever they interfered with his interests, and who could completely put on the appearance of every virtue as often as it suited his purposes, is, on the Stanhopean plan, the perfect man; a man to lead nations. But are great abilities, complete without a flaw, and polished without a blemish, the standard of human excellence? This is certainly the staunch opinion of men of the world; but I call on honour, virtue, and worth, to give the stygian doctrine a loud negative! However, this must be allowed, that, if you abstract from man the idea of an existence beyond the grave, then the true measure of human conduct is, proper and improper: virtue and vice, as dispositions of the heart, are, in that case, of scarcely the same import and value to the world at large, as harmony and discord in the modifications of sound; and a delicate sense of honour, like a nice ear for music, though it may sometimes give the possessor an ecstasy unknown to the coarser organs of the herd, yet, considering the harsh gratings, and inharmonic jars, in this ill-tuned state of being, it is odds but the individual would be as happy, and certainly would be as much respected by the true judges of society as it would then stand, without either a good ear or a good heart.

You must know I have just met with the Mirror and Lounger for the first time, and I am quite in raptures with them; I should be glad to have your opinion of some of the papers. The one I have just read, Lounger, No. 61, has cost me more honest tears than anything I have read of a long time. Mackenzie has been called the Addison of the Scots, and in my opinion, Addison would not be hurt at the comparison. If he has not Addison's exquisite humour, he as certainly outdoes him in the tender and the pathetic. His Man of Feeling (but I am not counsel learned in the laws of criticism) I estimate as the first performance in its kind I ever saw. From what book, moral or even pious, will the susceptible young mind receive impressions more congenial to humanity and kindness, generosity and benevolence; in short, more of all that ennobles the soul to herself, or endears her to others-than from the simple affecting tale of poor Harley?

Still, with all my admiration of Mackenzie's writings, I do not know if they are the fittest reading for a young man who is about to set out, as the phrase is, to make his way into life. Do not you think, Madam, that among the few favoured of heaven in the structure of their minds (for such there certainly are) there may be a purity, a tenderness, a dignity, an elegance of soul, which are of no use, nay, in some degree, absolutely disqualifying for the truly important business of making a man's way into life? If I am not much mistaken, my gallant young friend, A * * * * * *, is very much under these disqualifications; and for the young females of a family I could mention, well may they excite parental solicitude, for I, a common acquaintance, or as my vanity will have it, an humble friend, have often trembled for a turn of mind which may render them eminently happy-or peculiarly miserable!

I have been manufacturing some verses lately; but when I have got the most hurried season of excise business over, I hope to have more leisure to transcribe anything that may show how much I have the honour to be, Madam,

Yours, andc.

R. B.

CXCI.

TO COLLECTOR MITCHELL.

[Collector Mitchell was a kind and considerate gentle man: to his grandson, Mr. John Campbell, surgeon, in Aberdeen, I owe this characteristic letter.]
Ellisland, 1790.
Sir,
I shall not fail to wait on Captain Riddel[425] to-night-I wish and pray that the goddess of justice herself would appear to-morrow among our hon. gentlemen, merely to give them a word in their ear that mercy to the thief is injustice to the honest man. For my part I have galloped over my ten parishes these four days, until this moment that I am just alighted, or rather, that my poor jackass-skeleton of a horse has let me down; for the miserable devil has been on his knees half a score of times within the last twenty miles, telling me in his own way, 'Behold, am not I thy faithful jade of a horse, on which thou hast ridden these many years!'
In short, Sir, I have broke my horse's wind, and almost broke my own neck, besides some injuries in a part that shall be nameless, owing to a hard-hearted stone for a saddle. I find that every offender has so many great men to espouse his cause, that I shall not be surprised if I am committed to the strong hold of the law to-morrow for insolence to the dear friends of the gentlemen of the country.
I have the honour to be, Sir,
Your obliged and obedient humble
R. B.

CXCII.

TO DR. MOORE.
[The sonnets alluded to by Burns were those of Charlotte Smith: the poet's copy is now before me, with a few marks of his pen on the margins.]
Dumfries, Excise-Office, 14th July, 1790.
Sir,
Coming into town this morning, to attend my duty in this office, it being collection-day, I met with a gentleman who tells me he is on his way to London; so I take the opportunity of writing to you, as franking is at present under a temporary death. I shall have some snatches of leisure through the day, amid our horrid business and bustle, and I shall improve them as well as I can; but let my letter be as stupid as * * * * * * * * *, as miscellaneous as a newspaper, as short as a hungry grace-before-meat, or as long as a law-paper in the Douglas cause; as ill-spelt as country John's billet-doux, or as unsightly a scrawl as Betty Byre-Mucker's answer to it; I hope, considering circumstances, you will forgive it; and as it will put you to no expense of postage, I shall have the less reflection about it.
I am sadly ungrateful in not returning you my thanks for your most valuable present, Zeluco. In fact, you are in some degree blameable for my neglect.

You were pleased to express a wish for my opinion of the work, which so flattered me, that nothing less would serve my overweening fancy, than a formal criticism on the book. In fact, I have gravely planned a comparative view of you, Fielding, Richardson, and Smollett, in your different qualities and merits as novel-writers. This, I own, betrays my ridiculous vanity, and I may probably never bring the business to bear; and I am fond of the spirit young Elihu shows in the book of Job-"And I said, I will also declare my opinion," I have quite disfigured my copy of the book with my annotations. I never take it up without at the same time taking my pencil, and marking with asterisms, parentheses, andc., wherever I meet with an original thought, a nervous remark on life and manners, a remarkable well-turned period, or a character sketched with uncommon precision.

Though I should hardly think of fairly writing out my "Comparative View," I shall certainly trouble you with my remarks, such as they are.

I have just received from my gentleman that horrid summons in the book of Revelations-"That time shall be no more!"

The little collection of sonnets have some charming poetry in them. If indeed I am indebted to the fair author for the book, and not, as I rather suspect, to a celebrated author of the other sex, I should certainly have written to the lady, with my grateful acknowledgments, and my own ideas of the comparative excellence of her pieces. I would do this last, not from any vanity of thinking that my remarks could be of much consequence to Mrs. Smith, but merely from my own feelings as an author, doing as I would be done by.

R. B.

CXCIII.

TO MR. MURDOCH,
TEACHER OF FRENCH, LONDON.

[The account of himself, promised to Murdoch by Burns, was never written.]

Ellisland, July 16, 1790.

My dear Sir,

I received a letter from you a long time ago,[426] but unfortunately, as it was in the time of my peregrinations and journeyings through Scotland, I mislaid or lost it, and by consequence your direction along with it. Luckily my good star brought me acquainted with Mr. Kennedy, who, I understand, is an acquaintance of yours: and by his means and mediation I hope to replace that link which my unfortunate negligence had so unluckily broke in the chain of our correspondence. I was the more vexed at the vile accident, as my brother William, a journeyman saddler, has been for some time in London; and wished above all things for your direction, that he might have paid his respects to his father's friend.

His last address he sent me was, "Wm. Burns, at Mr. Barber's, saddler, No. 181, Strand." I writ him by Mr. Kennedy, but neglected to ask him for your address; so, if you find a spare half-minute, please let my brother know by a card where and when he will find you, and the poor fellow will joyfully wait on you, as one of the few surviving friends of the man whose name, and Christian name too, he has the honour to bear.

The next letter I write you shall be a long one. I have much to tell you of "hair-breadth 'scapes in th' imminent deadly breach," with all the eventful history of a life, the early years of which owed so much to your kind tutorage; but this at an hour of leisure. My kindest compliments to Mrs. Murdoch and family.

I am ever, my dear Sir,

Your obliged friend,

R. B.

CXCIV.

TO MR. M'MURDO.

[This hasty note was accompanied by the splendid elegy on Matthew Henderson, and no one could better feel than M'Murdo, to whom it is addressed, the difference between the music of verse and the clangour of politics.]

Ellisland, 2d August, 1790.

Sir,

Now that you are over with the sirens of Flattery, the harpies of Corruption, and the furies of Ambition, these infernal deities, that on all sides, and in all parties, preside over the villanous business of politics, permit a rustic muse of your acquaintance to do her best to soothe you with a song.-

You knew Henderson-I have not flattered his memory.

I have the honour to be, Sir,

Your obliged humble servant,

R. B.

CXCV.

TO MRS. DUNLOP.

[Inquiries have been made in vain after the name of Burns's ci-devant friend, who had so deeply wounded his feelings.]

8th August, 1790.

Dear Madam,

After a long day's toil, plague, and care, I sit down to write to you. Ask me not why I have delayed it so long! It was owing to hurry, indolence, and fifty other things; in short to anything-but forgetfulness of la plus aimable de son sexe. By the bye, you are indebted your best courtesy to me for this last compliment; as I pay it from my sincere conviction of its truth-a quality rather rare in compliments of these grinning, bowing, scraping times.

Well, I hope writing to you will ease a little my troubled soul. Sorely has it been bruised to-day! A ci-devant friend of mine, and an intimate acquaintance of yours, has given my feelings a wound that I perceive will gangrene dangerously ere it cure. He has wounded my pride!

R. B.

CXCVI.

TO MR. CUNNINGHAM.

["The strain of invective," says the judicious Currie, of this letter, "goes on some time longer in the style in which our bard was too apt to indulge, and of which the reader has already seen so much."]

Ellisland, 8th August, 1790.

Forgive me, my once dear, and ever dear friend, my seeming negligence. You cannot sit down and fancy the busy life I lead.

I laid down my goose-feather to beat my brains for an apt simile, and had some thoughts of a country grannum at a family christening; a bride on the market-day before her marriage; or a tavern-keeper at an election-dinner; but the resemblance that hits my fancy best is, that[427] blackguard miscreant, Satan, who roams about like a roaring lion, seeking, searching whom he may devour. However, tossed about as I am, if I choose (and who would not choose) to bind down with the crampets of attention the brazen foundation of integrity, I may rear up the superstructure of Independence, and from its daring turrets bid defiance to the storms of fate. And is not this a "consummation devoutly to be wished?"

"Thy spirit, Independence, let me share; Lord of the lion-heart, and eagle-eye! Thy steps I follow with my bosom bare, Nor heed the storm that howls along the sky!"

Are not these noble verses? They are the introduction of Smollett's Ode to Independence: if you have not seen the poem, I will send it to you.-How wretched is the man that hangs on by the favours of the great! To shrink from every dignity of man, at the approach of a lordly piece of self-consequence, who, amid all his tinsel glitter, and stately hauteur, is but a creature formed as thou art-and perhaps not so well formed as thou art-came into the world a puling infant as thou didst, and must go out of it, as all men must, a naked corse.

R. B.

CXCVII.

TO DR. ANDERSON.

[The gentleman to whom this imperfect note is addressed was Dr. James Anderson, a well-known agricultural and miscellaneous writer, and the editor of a weekly miscellany called the Bee.]

Sir,

I am much indebted to my worthy friend, Dr. Blacklock, for introducing me to a gentleman of Dr. Anderson's celebrity; but when you do me the honour to ask my assistance in your proposed publication, alas, Sir! you might as well think to cheapen a little honesty at the sign of an advocate's wig, or humility under the Geneva band. I am a miserable hurried devil, worn to the marrow in the friction of holding the noses of the poor publicans to the grindstone of the excise! and, like Milton's Satan, for private reasons, am forced

"To do what yet though damn'd I would abhor."

-and, except a couplet or two of honest execration * * * *

R. B.

CXCVIII.

TO WILLIAM TYTLER, ESQ.,
OF WOODHOUSELEE.

[William Tytler was the "revered defender of the beauteous Stuart"-a man of genius and a gentleman.]

Lawn Market, August, 1790.

Sir,

Enclosed I have sent you a sample of the old pieces that are still to be found among our peasantry in the west. I had once a great many of these fragments, and some of these here, entire; but as I had no idea then that anybody cared for them, I have forgotten them. I invariably hold it sacrilege to add anything of my own to help out with the shattered wrecks of these venerable old compositions; but they have many various readings. If you have not seen these before, I know they will flatter your true old-style Caledonian feelings; at any rate I am truly happy to have an opportunity of assuring you how sincerely I am, revered Sir,

Your gratefully indebted humble servant,

R. B.

CXCIX.

TO CRAUFORD TAIT, ESQ.,
EDINBURGH.

[Margaret Chalmers had now, it appears by this letter, become Mrs. Lewis Hay: her friend, Charlotte Hamilton, had been for some time Mrs. Adair, of Scarborough: Miss Nimmo was the lady who introduced Burns to the far-famed Clarinda.]

Ellisland, 15th October, 1790.

Dear Sir,

Allow me to introduce to your acquaintance the bearer, Mr. Wm. Duncan, a friend of mine, whom I have long known and long loved. His father, whose only son he is, has a decent little property in Ayrshire, and has bred the young man to the law, in which department he comes up an adventurer to your good town. I shall give you my friend's character in two words: as to his head, he has talents enough, and more than enough for common life; as to his heart, when nature had kneaded the kindly clay that composes it, she said, "I can no more."

You, my good Sir, were born under kinder stars; but your fraternal sympathy, I well know[428] can enter into the feelings of the young man, who goes into life with the laudable ambition to do something, and to be something among his fellow-creatures; but whom the consciousness of friendless obscurity presses to the earth, and wounds to the soul!

Even the fairest of his virtues are against him. That independent spirit, and that ingenuous modesty, qualities inseparable from a noble mind, are, with the million, circumstances not a little disqualifying. What pleasure is in the power of the fortunate and the happy, by their notice and patronage, to brighten the countenance and glad the heart of such depressed youth! I am not so angry with mankind for their deaf economy of the purse:-the goods of this world cannot be divided without being lessened-but why be a niggard of that which bestows bliss on a fellow-creature, yet takes nothing from our own means of enjoyment? We wrap ourselves up in the cloak of our own better fortune, and turn away our eyes, lest the wants and woes of our brother-mortals should disturb the selfish apathy of our souls!

I am the worst hand in the world at asking a favour. That indirect address, that insinuating implication, which, without any positive request, plainly expresses your wish, is a talent not to be acquired at a plough-tail. Tell me then, for you can, in what periphrasis of language, in what circumvolution of phrase, I shall envelope, yet not conceal this plain story.-"My dear Mr. Tait, my friend Mr. Duncan, whom I have the pleasure of introducing to you, is a young lad of your own profession, and a gentleman of much modesty, and great worth. Perhaps it may be in your power to assist him in the, to him, important consideration of getting a place; but at all events, your notice and acquaintance will be a very great acquisition to him; and I dare pledge myself that he will never disgrace your favour."

You may possibly be surprised, Sir, at such a letter from me; 'tis, I own, in the usual way of calculating these matters, more than our acquaintance entitles me to; but my answer is short:-Of all the men at your time of life, whom I knew in Edinburgh, you are the most accessible on the side on which I have assailed you. You are very much altered indeed from what you were when I knew you, if generosity point the path you will not tread, or humanity call to you in vain.

As to myself, a being to whose interest I believe you are still a well-wisher; I am here, breathing at all times, thinking sometimes, and rhyming now and then. Every situation has its share of the cares and pains of life, and my situation I am persuaded has a full ordinary allowance of its pleasures and enjoyments.

My best compliments to your father and Miss Tait. If you have an opportunity, please remember me in the solemn league and covenant of friendship to Mrs. Lewis Hay. I am a wretch for not writing her; but I am so hackneyed with self-accusation in that way, that my conscience lies in my bosom with scarce the sensibility of an oyster in its shell. Where is Lady M'Kenzie? wherever she is, God bless her! I likewise beg leave to trouble you with compliments to Mr. Wm. Hamilton; Mrs. Hamilton and family; and Mrs. Chalmers, when you are in that country. Should you meet with Miss Nimmo, please remember me kindly to her.

R. B.

CC.

TO .

[This letter contained the Kirk's Alarm, a satire written to help the cause of Dr. M'Gill, who recanted his heresy rather than be removed from his kirk.]

Ellisland, 1790.

Dear Sir,

Whether in the way of my trade I can be of any service to the Rev. Doctor, is I fear very doubtful. Ajax's shield consisted, I think, of seven bull-hides and a plate of brass, which altogether set Hector's utmost force at defiance. Alas! I am not a Hector, and the worthy Doctor's foes are as securely armed as Ajax was. Ignorance, superstition, bigotry, stupidity, malevolence, self-conceit, envy-all strongly bound in a massy frame of brazen impudence. Good God, Sir! to such a shield, humour is the peck of a sparrow, and satire the pop-gun of a school-boy. Creation-disgracing scelerats such as they, God only can mend, and the devil only can punish. In the comprehending way of Caligula, I wish they all had but one neck. I feel impotent as a child to the ardour of my wishes! O for a withering curse to blast the germins of their wicked machinations! O for a poisonous tornado, winged from the torrid zone of Tar[429]tarus, to sweep the spreading crop of their villainous contrivances to the lowest hell!

R. B.

CCI.

TO MRS. DUNLOP.

[The poet wrote out several copies of Tam o' Shanter and sent them to his friends, requesting their criticisms: he wrote few poems so universally applauded.]

Ellisland, November, 1790.

"As cold waters to a thirsty soul, so is good news from a far country."

Fate has long owed me a letter of good news from you, in return for the many tidings of sorrow which I have received. In this instance I most cordially obey the apostle-"Rejoice with them that do rejoice"-for me, to sing for joy, is no new thing; but to preach for joy, as I have done in the commencement of this epistle, is a pitch of extravagant rapture to which I never rose before.

I read your letter-I literally jumped for joy-How could such a mercurial creature as a poet lumpishly keep his seat on the receipt of the best news from his best friend. I seized my gilt-headed Wangee rod, an instrument indispensably necessary in my left hand, in the moment of inspiration and rapture; and stride, stride-quick and quicker-out skipt I among the broomy banks of Nith to muse over my joy by retail. To keep within the bounds of prose was impossible. Mrs. Little's is a more elegant, but not a more sincere compliment to the sweet little fellow, than I, extempore almost, poured out to him in the following verses:-

Sweet flow'ret, pledge o' meikle love And ward o' mony a prayer, What heart o' stane wad thou na move, Sae helpless, sweet, an' fair. November hirples o'er the lea Chill on thy lovely form; But gane, alas! the shelt'ring tree Should shield thee frae the storm.

I am much flattered by your approbation of my Tam o' Shanter, which you express in your former letter; though, by the bye, you load me in that said letter with accusations heavy and many; to all which I plead, not guilty! Your book is, I hear, on the road to reach me. As to printing of poetry, when you prepare it for the press, you have only to spell it right, and place the capital letters properly: as to the punctuation, the printers do that themselves.

I have a copy of Tam o' Shanter ready to send you by the first opportunity: it is too heavy to send by post.

I heard of Mr. Corbet lately. He, in consequence of your recommendation, is most zealous to serve me. Please favour me soon with an account of your good folks; if Mrs. H. is recovering, and the young gentleman doing well.

R. B.

CCII.

TO LADY W. M. CONSTABLE.
[The present alluded to was a gold snuff-box, with a portrait of Queen Mary on the lid.]
Ellisland, 11th January, 1791.
My Lady,
Nothing less than the unlucky accident of having lately broken my right arm, could have prevented me, the moment I received your ladyship's elegant present by Mrs. Miller, from returning you my warmest and most grateful acknowledgments. I assure your ladyship, I shall set it apart-the symbols of religion shall only be more sacred. In the moment of poetic composition, the box shall be my inspiring genius. When I would breathe the comprehensive wish of benevolence for the happiness of others, I shall recollect your ladyship; when I would interest my fancy in the distresses incident to humanity, I shall remember the unfortunate Mary.
R. B.

CCIII.

TO WILLIAM DUNBAR, W.S.
[This letter was in answer to one from Dunbar, in which the witty colonel of the Crochallan Fencibles supposed the poet had been translated to Elysium to sing to the immortals, as his voice had not been beard of late on earth.]
Ellisland, 17th January, 1791.
I am not gone to Elysium, most noble colonel, but am still here in this sublunary world, serving my God, by propagating his image, and[430] honouring my king by begetting him loyal subjects.
Many happy returns of the season await my friend. May the thorns of care never beset his path! May peace be an inmate of his bosom, and rapture a frequent visitor of his soul! May the blood-hounds of misfortune never track his steps, nor the screech-owl of sorrow alarm his dwelling! May enjoyment tell thy hours, and pleasure number thy days, thou friend of the bard! "Blessed be he that blesseth thee, and cursed be he that curseth thee!!!"
As a further proof that I am still in the land of existence, I send you a poem, the latest I have composed. I have a particular reason for wishing you only to show it to select friends, should you think it worthy a friend's perusal; but if, at your first leisure hour, you will favour me with your opinion of, and strictures on the performance, it will be an additional obligation on, dear Sir, your deeply indebted humble servant,
R. B.

CCIV.

TO MR. PETER HILL.

[The poet's eloquent apostrophe to poverty has no little feeling in it: he beheld the money which his poems brought melt silently away, and he looked to the future with more fear than hope.]

Ellisland, 17th January, 1791.

Take these two guineas, and place them over against that d-mned account of yours! which has gagged my mouth these five or six months! I can as little write good things as apologies to the man I owe money to. O the supreme curse of making three guineas do the business of five! Not all the labours of Hercules; not all the Hebrews' three centuries of Egyptian bondage, were such an insuperable business, such an infernal task!! Poverty! thou half-sister of death, thou cousin-german of hell: where shall I find force of execration equal to the amplitude of thy demerits? Oppressed by thee, the venerable ancient, grown hoary in the practice of every virtue, laden with years and wretchedness, implores a little-little aid to support his existence, from a stony-hearted son of Mammon, whose sun of prosperity never knew a cloud; and is by him denied and insulted. Oppressed by thee, the man of sentiment, whose heart glows with independence, and melts with sensibility, inly pines under the neglect, or writhes in bitterness of soul, under the contumely of arrogant, unfeeling wealth. Oppressed by thee, the son of genius, whose ill-starred ambition plants him at the tables of the fashionable and polite, must see in suffering silence, his remark neglected, and his person despised, while shallow greatness in his idiot attempts at wit, shall meet with countenance and applause. Nor is it only the family of worth that have reason to complain of thee: the children of folly and vice, though in common with thee the offspring of evil, smart equally under thy rod. Owing to thee, the man of unfortunate disposition and neglected education, is condemned as a fool for his dissipation, despised and shunned as a needy wretch, when his follies as usual bring him to want; and when his unprincipled necessities drive him to dishonest practices, he is abhorred as a miscreant, and perishes by the justice of his country. But far otherwise is the lot of the man of family and fortune. His early follies and extravagance, are spirit and fire; his consequent wants are the embarrassments of an honest fellow; and when, to remedy the matter, he has gained a legal commission to plunder distant provinces, or massacre peaceful nations, he returns, perhaps, laden with the spoils of rapine and murder; lives wicked and respected, and dies a scoundrel and a lord.-Nay, worst of all, alas for helpless woman! the needy prostitute, who has shivered at the corner of the street, waiting to earn the wages of casual prostitution, is left neglected and insulted, ridden down by the chariot wheels of the coroneted Rip, hurrying on to the guilty assignation; she who without the same necessities to plead,

riots nightly in the same guilty trade.
Well! divines may say of it what they please; but execration is to the mind what phlebotomy is to the body: the vital sluices of both are wonderfully relieved by their respective evacuations.
R. B.

CCV.

TO MR. CUNNINGHAM.
[To Alexander Cunningham the poet generally communicated his favourite compositions.]
Ellisland, 23d January, 1791.
Many happy returns of the season to you, my dear friend! As many of the good things[431] of this life, as is consistent with the usual mixture of good and evil in the cup of being!
I have just finished a poem (Tam o' Shanter) which you will receive enclosed. It is my first essay in the way of tales.
I have these several months been hammering at an elegy on the amiable and accomplished Miss Burnet. I have got, and can get, no farther than the following fragment, on which please give me your strictures. In all kinds of poetic composition, I set great store by your opinion; but in sentimental verses, in the poetry of the heart, no Roman Catholic ever set more value on the infallibility of the Holy Father than I do on yours.
I mean the introductory couplets as text verses.
ELEGY
ON THE LATE MISS BURNET, OF MONBODDO.
Life ne'er exulted in so rich a prize As Burnet lovely from her native skies; Nor envious death so triumph'd in a blow, As that which laid th' accomplish'd Burnet low.
Let me hear from you soon.
Adieu!
R. B.

CCVI.

TO A.F. TYTLER, ESQ.
["I have seldom in my life," says Lord Woodhouselee, "tasted a higher enjoyment from any work of genius than I received from Tam o' Shanter."]
Ellisland, February, 1791.
Sir,
Nothing less than the unfortunate accident I have met with, could have prevented my grateful acknowledgments for your letter. His own favourite poem, and that an essay in the walk of the muses entirely new to him,

where consequently his hopes and fears were on the most anxious alarm for his success in the attempt; to have that poem so much applauded by one of the first judges, was the most delicious vibration that ever thrilled along the heart-strings of a poor poet. However, Providence, to keep up the proper proportion of evil with the good, which it seems is necessary in this sublunary state, thought proper to check my exultation by a very serious misfortune. A day or two after I received your letter, my horse came down with me and broke my right arm. As this is the first service my arm has done me since its disaster, I find myself unable to do more than just in general terms thank you for this additional instance of your patronage and friendship. As to the faults you detected in the piece, they are truly there: one of them, the hit at the lawyer and priest, I shall cut out; as to the falling off in the catastrophe, for the reason you justly adduce, it cannot easily be remedied. Your approbation, Sir, has given me such additional spirits to persevere in this species of poetic composition, that I am already revolving two or three stories in my fancy. If I can bring these floating ideas to bear any kind of embodied form, it will give me additional opportunity of assuring you how much I have the honour to be, andc.
R. B.

CCVII.

TO MRS. DUNLOP.
[The elegy on the beautiful Miss Burnet, of Monboddo, was laboured zealously by Burns, but it never reached the excellence of some of his other compositions.]
Ellisland, 7th Feb. 1791.
When I tell you, Madam, that by a fall, not from my horse, but with my horse, I have been a cripple some time, and that this is the first day my arm and hand have been able to serve me in writing; you will allow that it is too good an apology for my seemingly ungrateful silence. I am now getting better, and am able to rhyme a little, which implies some tolerable ease, as I cannot think that the most poetic genius is able to compose on the rack.
I do not remember if ever I mentioned to you my having an idea of composing an elegy on the late Miss Burnet, of Monboddo. I had the honour of being pretty well acquainted with her, and have seldom felt so much at the loss of an acquaintance, as when I heard that so amiable and accomplished a piece of God's work was no more. I have, as yet, gone no farther than the following fragment, of which please let me have your opinion. You know that elegy is a subject so much exhausted, that any new idea on the business is not to be expected: 'tis well if we can place an old idea in a new light. How far I have succeeded as to this last, you[432] will judge from what follows. I have proceeded no further.

Your kind letter, with your kind remembrance of your godson, came safe. This last, Madam, is scarcely what my pride can bear. As to the little fellow, he is, partiality apart, the finest boy I have for a long time seen. He is now seventeen months old, has the small-pox and measles over, has cut several teeth, and never had a grain of doctor's drugs in his bowels.

I am truly happy to hear that the "little floweret" is blooming so fresh and fair, and that the "mother plant" is rather recovering her drooping head. Soon and well may her "cruel wounds" be healed. I have written thus far with a good deal of difficulty. When I get a little abler you shall hear farther from,

Madam, yours,

R. B.

CCVIII.

TO THE REV. ARCH. ALISON.

[Alison was much gratified it is said, with this recognition of the principles laid down in his ingenious and popular work.]

Ellisland, near Dumfries, 14th Feb. 1791.

Sir,

You must by this time have set me down as one of the most ungrateful of men. You did me the honour to present me with a book, which does honour to science and the intellectual powers of man, and I have not even so much as acknowledged the receipt of it. The fact is, you yourself are to blame for it. Flattered as I was by your telling me that you wished to have my opinion of the work, the old spiritual enemy of mankind, who knows well that vanity is one of the sins that most easily beset me, put it into my head to ponder over the performance with the look-out of a critic, and to draw up forsooth a deep learned digest of strictures on a composition, of which, in fact, until I read the book, I did not even know the first principles. I own, Sir, that at first glance, several of your propositions startled me as paradoxical. That the martial clangour of a trumpet had something in it vastly more grand, heroic, and sublime, than the twingle twangle of a jew's-harp: that the delicate flexure of a rose-twig, when the half-blown flower is heavy with the tears of the dawn, was infinitely more beautiful and elegant than the upright stub of a burdock; and that from something innate and independent of all associations of ideas;-these I had set down as irrefragable, orthodox truths, until perusing your book shook my faith.-In short, Sir, except Euclid's Elements of Geometry, which I made a shift to unravel by my father's fire-side, in the winter evening of the first season I held the plough, I never read a book which gave me such a quantum of information, and added so much to my stock of ideas, as your "Essays on the Principles of Taste." One thing, Sir, you must forgive my

mentioning as an uncommon merit in the work, I mean the language. To clothe abstract philosophy in elegance of style, sounds something like a contradiction in terms; but you have convinced me that they are quite compatible.
I enclose you some poetic bagatelles of my late composition. The one in print[198] is my first essay in the way of telling a tale.
I am, Sir, andc.
R. B.

FOOTNOTES:

[198] Tam o' Shanter

CCIX.

TO DR. MOORE.
[Moore admired but moderately the beautiful ballad on Queen Mary, and the Elegy on Captain Matthew Henderson: Tam o' Shanter he thought full of poetical beauties.-He again regrets that he writes in the language of Scotland.]
Ellisland, 20th February, 1791.
I do not know, Sir, whether you are a subscriber to Grose's Antiquities of Scotland. If you are, the enclosed poem will not be altogether new to you. Captain Grose did me the favour to send me a dozen copies of the proof sheet, of which this is one. Should you have read the piece before, still this will answer the principal end I have in view: it will give me another opportunity of thanking you for all your goodness to the rustic bard; and also of showing you, that the abilities you have been pleased to commend and patronize are still employed in the way you wish.
The Elegy on Captain Henderson, is a tribute to the memory of a man I loved much. Poets [433] have in this the same advantage as Roman Catholics; they can be of service to their friends after they have passed that bourne where all other kindness ceases to be of avail. Whether, after all, either the one or the other be of any real service to the dead, is, I fear, very problematical; but I am sure they are highly gratifying to the living: and as a very orthodox text, I forget where in scripture, says, "whatsoever is not of faith is sin;" so say I, whatsoever is not detrimental to society, and is of positive enjoyment, is of God, the giver of all good things, and ought to be received and enjoyed by his creatures with thankful delight. As almost all my religious tenets originate from my heart, I am wonderfully pleased with the idea, that I can still keep up a tender intercourse with the dearly beloved friend, or still more dearly beloved mistress, who is gone to the world of spirits.

The ballad on Queen Mary was begun while I was busy with Percy's Reliques of English Poetry. By the way, how much is every honest heart, which has a tincture of Caledonian prejudice, obliged to you for your glorious story of Buchanan and Targe! 'Twas an unequivocal proof of your loyal gallantry of soul, giving Targe the victory. I should have been mortified to the ground if you had not.

I have just read over, once more of many times, your Zeluco. I marked with my pencil, as I went along, every passage that pleased me particularly above the rest; and one or two, I think, which with humble deference, I am disposed to think unequal to the merits of the book. I have sometimes thought to transcribe these marked passages, or at least so much of them as to point where they are, and send them to you. Original strokes that strongly depict the human heart, is your and Fielding's province beyond any other novelist I have ever perused. Richardson indeed might perhaps be excepted; but unhappily, dramatis personæ are beings of another world; and however they may captivate the unexperienced, romantic fancy of a boy or a girl, they will ever, in proportion as we have made human nature our study, dissatisfy our riper years.

As to my private concerns, I am going on, a mighty tax-gatherer before the Lord, and have lately had the interest to get myself ranked on the list of excise as a supervisor. I am not yet employed as such, but in a few years I shall fall into the file of supervisorship by seniority. I have had an immense loss in the death of the Earl of Glencairn; the patron from whom all my fame and fortune took its rise. Independent of my grateful attachment to him, which was indeed so strong that it pervaded my very soul, and was entwined with the thread of my existence: so soon as the prince's friends had got in (and every dog you know has his day), my getting forward in the excise would have been an easier business than otherwise it will be. Though this was a consummation devoutly to be wished, yet, thank Heaven, I can live and rhyme as I am: and as to my boys, poor little fellows! if I cannot place them on as high an elevation in life, as I could wish, I shall, if I am favoured so much of the Disposer of events as to see that period, fix them on as broad and independent a basis as possible. Among the many wise adages which have been treasured up by our Scottish ancestors, this is one of the best, Better be the head o' the commonalty, than the tail o' the gentry.

But I am got on a subject, which however interesting to me, is of no manner of consequence to you; so I shall give you a short poem on the other page, and close this with assuring you how sincerely I have the honour to be,

Yours, andc.

R. B.

Written on the blank leaf of a book, which I presented to a very young lady, whom I had formerly characterized under the denomination of The Rose Bud. * * *

CCX.

TO MR. CUNNINGHAM.

[Cunningham could tell a merry story, and sing a humorous song; nor was he without a feeling for the deep sensibilities of his friend's verse.]

Ellisland, 12th March, 1791.

If the foregoing piece be worth your strictures, let me have them. For my own part, a thing that I have just composed always appears through a double portion of that partial medium in which an author will ever view his own works. I believe in general, novelty has something in it that inebriates the fancy, and not unfrequently dissipates and fumes away like other intoxication, and leaves the poor patient, as usual, with[434] an aching heart. A striking instance of this might be adduced, in the revolution of many a hymeneal honeymoon. But lest I sink into stupid prose, and so sacrilegiously intrude on the office of my parish-priest, I shall fill up the page in my own way, and give you another song of my late composition, which will appear perhaps in Johnson's work, as well as the former.

You must know a beautiful Jacobite air, There'll never be peace 'till Jamie comes hame. When political combustion ceases to be the object of princes and patriots, it then you know becomes the lawful prey of historians and poets.

By yon castle wa' at the close of the day, I heard a man sing, tho' his head it was grey; And as he was singing, the tears fast down came- There'll never be peace till Jamie comes hame.

If you like the air, and if the stanzas hit your fancy, you cannot imagine, my dear friend, how much you would oblige me, if by the charms of your delightful voice, you would give my honest effusion to "the memory of joys that are past," to the few friends whom you indulge in that pleasure. But I have scribbled on 'till I hear the clock has intimated the near approach of

That hour, o' night's black arch the key-stane.-

So good night to you! Sound be your sleep, and delectable your dreams! Apropos, how do you like this thought in a ballad, I have just now on the tapis?

I look to the west when I gae to rest, That happy my dreams and my slumbers may be; Far, far in the west is he I lo'e best, The lad that is dear to my babie and me!

Good night, once more, and God bless you!

R. B.

CCXI.

TO MR. ALEXANDER DALZEL,
FACTOR, FINDLAYSTON.
[Cromek says that Alexander Dalzel introduced the poetry of Burns to the notice of the Earl of Glencairn, who carried the Kilmarnock edition with him to Edinburgh, and begged that the poet would let him know what his views in the world were, that he might further them.]
Ellisland, 19th March, 1791.
My dear Sir,
I have taken the liberty to frank this letter to you, as it encloses an idle poem of mine, which I send you; and God knows you may perhaps pay dear enough for it if you read it through. Not that this is my own opinion; but the author, by the time he has composed and corrected his work, has quite pored away all his powers of critical discrimination.
I can easily guess from my own heart, what you have felt on a late most melancholy event. God knows what I have suffered, at the loss of my best friend, my first and dearest patron and benefactor; the man to whom I owe all that I am and have! I am gone into mourning for him, and with more sincerity of grief than I fear some will, who by nature's ties ought to feel on the occasion.
I will be exceedingly obliged to you, indeed, to let me know the news of the noble family, how the poor mother and the two sisters support their loss. I had a packet of poetic bagatelles ready to send to Lady Betty, when I saw the fatal tidings in the newspaper. I see by the same channel that the honoured REMAINS of my noble patron, are designed to be brought to the family burial-place. Dare I trouble you to let me know privately before the day of interment, that I may cross the country, and steal among the crowd, to pay a tear to the last sight of my ever revered benefactor? It will oblige me beyond expression.
R. B.

CCXII.

TO MRS. GRAHAM,
OF FINTRAY.
[Mrs. Graham, of Fintray, felt both as a lady and a Scottish one, the tender Lament of the fair and unfortunate princess, which this letter contained.]
Ellisland, 1791.
Madam,
Whether it is that the story of our Mary Queen of Scots has a peculiar effect on the feelings of a poet, or whether I have, in the enclosed ballad, succeeded beyond my usual poetic success, I know not; but it has pleased me beyond any effort of my muse for a good while[435] past; on that

account I enclose it particularly to you. It is true, the purity of my motives may be suspected. I am already deeply indebted to Mr. Graham's goodness; and what, in the usual ways of men, is of infinitely greater importance, Mr. G. can do me service of the utmost importance in time to come. I was born a poor dog; and however I may occasionally pick a better bone than I used to do, I know I must live and die poor: but I will indulge the flattering faith that my poetry will considerably outlive my poverty; and without any fustian affectation of spirit, I can promise and affirm, that it must be no ordinary craving of the latter shall ever make me do anything injurious to the honest fame of the former. Whatever may be my failings, for failings are a part of human nature, may they ever be those of a generous heart, and an independent mind! It is no fault of mine that I was born to dependence; nor is it Mr. Graham's chiefest praise that he can command influence; but it is his merit to bestow, not only with the kindness of a brother, but with the politeness of a gentleman; and I trust it shall be mine, to receive with thankfulness, and remember with undiminished gratitude.
R. B.

CCXIII.

TO MRS. GRAHAM,
OF FINTRAY.
[The following letter was written on the blank leaf of a new edition of his poems, presented by the poet, to one whom he regarded, and justly, as a patroness.]
It is probable, Madam, that this page may be read, when the hand that now writes it shall be mouldering in the dust: may it then bear witness, that I present you these volumes as a tribute of gratitude, on my part ardent and sincere, as your and Mr. Graham's goodness to me has been generous and noble! May every child of yours, in the hour of need, find such a friend as I shall teach every child of mine, that their father found in you.
R. B.

CCXIV.

TO THE REV. G. BAIRD.
[It was proposed to publish a new edition of the poems of Michael Bruce, by subscription, and give the profits to his mother, a woman eighty years old, and poor and helpless, and Burns was asked for a poem to give a new impulse to the publication.]
Ellisland, 1791.
Reverend Sir,
Why did you, my dear Sir, write to me in such a hesitating style on the

business of poor Bruce? Don't I know, and have I not felt, the many ills, the peculiar ills that poetic flesh is heir to? You shall have your choice of all the unpublished poems I have; and had your letter had my direction, so as to have reached me sooner (it only came to my hand this moment), I should have directly put you out of suspense on the subject. I only ask, that some prefatory advertisement in the book, as well as the subscription bills, may bear, that the publication is solely for the benefit of Bruce's mother. I would not put it in the power of ignorance to surmise, or malice to insinuate, that I clubbed a share in the work from mercenary motives. Nor need you give me credit for any remarkable generosity in my part of the business. I have such a host of peccadilloes, failings, follies, and backslidings (anybody but myself might perhaps give some of them a worse appellation), that by way of some balance, however trifling, in the account, I am fain to do any good that occurs in my very limited power to a fellow-creature, just for the selfish purpose of clearing a little the vista of retrospection.

R. B.

CCXV.

TO MRS. DUNLOP.

[Francis Wallace Burns, the godson of Mrs. Dunlop, to whom this letter refers, died at the age of fourteen-he was a fine and a promising youth.]

Ellisland, 11th April, 1791.

I am once more able, my honoured friend, to return you, with my own hand, thanks for the many instances of your friendship, and particularly for your kind anxiety in this last disaster, that my evil genius had in store for me. However, life is chequered-joy and sorrow-for on Saturday morning last, Mrs. Burns made me a present of a fine boy; rather stouter, but not so handsome as your godson was at his time of life. Indeed I look on your little namesake to be my chef d'œuvre in that species of manufacture, as I look on Tam o' Shanter to be my standard performance in the poetical line. 'Tis[436] true, both the one and the other discover a spice of roguish waggery, that might perhaps be as well spared; but then they also show, in my opinion, a force of genius and a finishing polish that I despair of ever excelling. Mrs. Burns is getting stout again, and laid as lustily about her to-day at breakfast, as a reaper from the corn-ridge. That is the peculiar privilege and blessing of our hale, sprightly damsels, that are bred among the hay and heather. We cannot hope for that highly polished mind, that charming delicacy of soul, which is found among the female world in the more elevated stations of life, and which is certainly by far the most bewitching charm in the famous cestus of Venus. It is indeed such an inestimable treasure, that where it can be had in its native heavenly purity, unstained by some one or other of the many shades of affectation, and unalloyed by some one or other of the many species of caprice, I declare to Heaven, I should think it cheaply purchased at the expense of every other earthly good! But as this angelic creature is, I am afraid, extremely rare in any station and rank of life, and totally denied to such a humble one as mine, we meaner mortals must put up with the next rank of female excellence-as fine a figure and face we can produce as any rank of life whatever; rustic, native grace; unaffected modesty, and unsullied purity; nature's mother-wit, and the rudiments of taste; a simplicity of soul, unsuspicious of, because unacquainted with, the crooked ways of a selfish, interested, disingenuous world; and the dearest charm of all the rest, a yielding sweetness of disposition, and a generous warmth of heart, grateful for love on our part, and ardently glowing with a more than equal return; these, with a healthy frame, a sound, vigorous constitution, which your higher ranks can scarcely ever hope to enjoy, are the charms of lovely woman in my humble walk of life.

This is the greatest effort my broken arm has yet made. Do let me hear, by first post, how cher petit Monsieur comes on with his small-pox. May almighty goodness preserve and restore him!

R. B.

CCXVI.

TO .

[That his works found their way to the newspapers, need have occasioned no surprise: the poet gave copies of his favorite pieces freely to his friends, as soon as they were written: who, in their turn, spread their fame among their acquaintances.]

Ellisland, 1791.

Dear Sir,

I am exceedingly to blame in not writing you long ago; but the truth is, that I am the most indolent of all human beings; and when I matriculate in the herald's office, I intend that my supporters shall be two sloths, my crest a slow-worm, and the motto, "Deil tak the foremost." So much by way of apology for not thanking you sooner for your kind execution of my commission.

I would have sent you the poem; but somehow or other it found its way into the public papers, where you must have seen it.

I am ever, dear Sir,

Yours sincerely,

R. B.

CCXVII.

TO .

[This singular letter was sent by Burns, it is believed, to a critic, who had taken him to task about obscure language, and imperfect grammar.]

Ellisland, 1791.

Thou eunuch of language: thou Englishman, who never was south the Tweed: thou servile echo of fashionable barbarisms: thou quack, vending the nostrums of empirical elocution: thou marriage-maker between vowels and consonants, on the Gretna-green of caprice: thou cobler, botching the flimsy socks of bombast oratory: thou blacksmith, hammering the rivets of absurdity: thou butcher, imbruing thy hands in the bowels of orthography: thou arch-heretic in pronunciation: thou pitch-pipe of affected emphasis: thou carpenter, mortising the awkward joints of jarring sentences: thou squeaking dissonance of cadence: thou pimp of gender: thou Lion Herald to silly etymology: thou antipode of grammar: thou executioner of construction: thou brood of the speech-distracting builders of the Tower of Babel; thou lingual confusion worse confounded: thou scape-gallows from the land of syntax: thou scavenger of mood and tense: thou murderous accoucheur of infant learning; thou ignis fatuus, misleading the steps of benighted ignorance: thou pickle-herring in the puppet-show of nonsense: thou faithful recorder of barbarous idiom: thou[437] persecutor of syllabication: thou baleful meteor, foretelling and facilitating the rapid approach of Nox and Erebus.

R. B.

CCXVIII.

TO MR. CUNNINGHAM.

[To Clarke, the Schoolmaster, Burns, it is said, addressed several letters, which on his death were put into the fire by his widow, because of their license of language.]

11th June, 1791.

Let me interest you, my dear Cunningham, in behalf of the gentleman who waits on you with this. He is a Mr. Clarke, of Moffat, principal schoolmaster there, and is at present suffering severely under the persecution of one or two powerful individuals of his employers. He is accused of harshness to boys that were placed under his care. God help the teacher, if a man of sensibility and genius, and such is my friend Clarke, when a booby father presents him with his booby son, and insists on lighting up the rays of science, in a fellow's head whose skull is impervious and inaccessible by any other way than a positive fracture with a cudgel: a fellow whom in fact it savours of impiety to attempt making a scholar of, as he has been marked a blockhead in the book of fate, at the almighty fiat of his Creator.

The patrons of Moffat-school are, the ministers, magistrates, and town-council of Edinburgh, and as the business comes now before them, let me beg my dearest friend to do everything in his power to serve the interests of a man of genius and worth, and a man whom I particularly respect and esteem. You know some good fellows among the magistracy and council, but particularly you have much to say with a reverend gentleman to whom you have the honour of being very nearly related, and whom this country and age have had the honour to produce. I need not name the historian of Charles V. I tell him through the medium of his nephew's influence, that Mr. Clarke is a gentleman who will not disgrace even his patronage. I know the merits of the cause thoroughly, and say it, that my friend is falling a sacrifice to prejudiced ignorance.

God help the children of dependence! Hated and persecuted by their enemies, and too often, alas! almost unexceptionably, received by their friends with disrespect and reproach, under the thin disguise of cold civility and humiliating advice. O! to be a sturdy savage, stalking in the pride of his independence, amid the solitary wilds of his deserts; rather than in civilized life, helplessly to tremble for a subsistence, precarious as the caprice of a fellow-creature! Every man has his virtues, and no man is without his failings; and curse on that privileged plain-dealing of friendship, which, in the hour of my calamity, cannot reach forth the helping hand without at the same time pointing out those failings, and apportioning them their share in procuring my present distress. My friends, for such the world calls ye, and such ye think yourselves to be, pass by my virtues if you please, but do, also, spare my follies: the first will witness in my breast for themselves, and the last will give pain enough to the ingenuous mind without you. And since deviating more or less from the paths of propriety and rectitude, must be incident to human nature, do thou, Fortune, put it in my power, always from myself, and of myself, to bear the consequence of those errors! I do not want to be independent that I may sin, but I want to be independent in my sinning.

To return in this rambling letter to the subject I set out with, let me recommend my friend, Mr. Clarke, to your acquaintance and good offices; his worth entitles him to the one, and his gratitude will merit the other. I long much to hear from you.

Adieu!

R. B.

CCXIX.

TO THE EARL OF BUCHAN.

[Lord Buchan printed this letter in his Essay on the Life of Thomson, in

1792. His lordship invited Burns to leave his corn unreaped, walk from Ellisland to Dryburgh, and help him to crown Thomson's bust with bays, on Ednam Hill, on the 22d of September.]

Ellisland, August 29th, 1791.

My Lord,

Language sinks under the ardour of my feelings when I would thank your lordship for the honour you have done me in inviting me to make one at the coronation of the bust of Thomson. In my first enthusiasm in reading the card you did me the honour to write me, I overlooked[438] every obstacle, and determined to go; but I fear it will not be in my power. A week or two's absence, in the very middle of my harvest, is what I much doubt I dare not venture on. I once already made a pilgrimage up the whole course of the Tweed, and fondly would I take the same delightful journey down the windings of that delightful stream.

Your lordship hints at an ode for the occasion: but who would write after Collins? I read over his verses to the memory of Thomson, and despaired.-I got indeed to the length of three or four stanzas, in the way of address to the shade of the bard, on crowning his bust. I shall trouble your lordship with the subjoined copy of them, which, I am afraid, will be but too convincing a proof how unequal I am to the task. However, it affords me an opportunity of approaching your lordship, and declaring how sincerely and gratefully I have the honour to be, andc.,

R. B.

CCXX.

TO MR. THOMAS SLOAN.

[Thomas Sloan was a west of Scotland man, and seems, though not much in correspondence, to have been on intimate terms with Burns.]

Ellisland, Sept. 1, 1791.

My dear Sloan,

Suspense is worse than disappointment, for that reason I hurry to tell you that I just now learn that Mr. Ballantyne does not choose to interfere more in the business. I am truly sorry for it, but cannot help it.

You blame me for not writing you sooner, but you will please to recollect that you omitted one little necessary piece of information;-your address.

However, you know equally well, my hurried life, indolent temper, and strength of attachment. It must be a longer period than the longest life "in the world's hale and undegenerate days," that will make me forget so dear a friend as Mr. Sloan. I am prodigal enough at times, but I will not part with such a treasure as that.

I can easily enter into the embarras of your present situation. You know my favourite quotation from Young-

-"On reason build Resolve! That column of true majesty in man;"
and that other favourite one from Thomson's Alfred-
"What proves the hero truly great, Is never, never to despair."
Or shall I quote you an author of your acquaintance?
"Whether doing, suffering, or forbearing, You may do miracles by-persevering."
I have nothing new to tell you. The few friends we have are going on in the old way. I sold my crop on this day se'ennight, and sold it very well. A guinea an acre, on an average, above value. But such a scene of drunkenness was hardly ever seen in this country. After the roup was over, about thirty people engaged in a battle, every man for his own hand, and fought it out for three hours. Nor was the scene much better in the house. No fighting, indeed, but folks lying drunk on the floor, and decanting, until both my dogs got so drunk by attending them, that they could not stand. You will easily guess how I enjoyed the scene; as I was no farther over than you used to see me.
Mrs. B. and family have been in Ayrshire these many weeks.
Farewell; and God bless you, my dear friend!
R. B.

CCXXI.

TO LADY E. CUNNINGHAM.
[The poem enclosed was the Lament for James, Earl of Glencairn: it is probable that the Earl's sister liked the verses, for they were printed soon afterwards.]
My Lady,
I would, as usual, have availed myself of the privilege your goodness has allowed me, of sending you anything I compose in my poetical way; but as I had resolved, so soon as the shock of my irreparable loss would allow me, to pay a tribute to my late benefactor, I determined to make that the first piece I should do myself the honour of sending you. Had the wing of my fancy been equal to the ardour of my heart, the enclosed had been much more worthy your perusal: as it is, I beg leave to lay it at your ladyship's feet. As all the world knows my obligations to the late Earl of Glencairn, I would wish to show as openly that my heart glows, and will ever glow, with the most grateful sense and remembrance of his lordship's goodness. The[439] sables I did myself the honour to wear to his lordship's memory, were not the "mockery of woe." Nor shall my gratitude perish with me!-if among my children I shall have a son that has a heart, he shall hand it down to his child as a family honour, and a family debt, that my dearest existence I owe to the noble house of Glencairn!
I was about to say, my lady, that if you think the poem may venture to see

the light, I would, in some way or other, give it to the world.
R. B.

CCXXII.

TO MR. AINSLIE.
[It has been said that the poet loved to aggravate his follies to his friends: but that this tone of aggravation was often ironical, this letter, as well as others, might be cited.]
Ellisland, 1791.
My dear Ainslie,
Can you minister to a mind diseased? can you, amid the horrors of penitence, remorse, head-ache, nausea, and all the rest of the dd hounds of hell, that beset a poor wretch, who has been guilty of the sin of drunkenness-can you speak peace to a troubled soul?
Miserable perdu that I am, I have tried everything that used to amuse me, but in vain: here must I sit, a monument of the vengeance laid up in store for the wicked, slowly counting every chick of the clock as it slowly, slowly, numbers over these lazy scoundrels of hours, who, dn them, are ranked up before me, every one at his neighbour's backside, and every one with a burthen of anguish on his back, to pour on my devoted head-and there is none to pity me. My wife scolds me! my business torments me, and my sins come staring me in the face, every one telling a more bitter tale than his fellow.-When I tell you even * * * has lost its power to please, you will guess something of my hell within, and all around me-I begun Elibanks and Elibraes, but the stanzas fell unenjoyed, and unfinished from my listless tongue: at last I luckily thought of reading over an old letter of yours, that lay by me in my book-case, and I felt something for the first time since I opened my eyes, of pleasurable existence.Well-I begin to breathe a little, since I began to write to you. How are you, and what are you doing? How goes Law? Apropos, for connexion's sake, do not address to me supervisor, for that is an honour I cannot pretend to-I am on the list, as we call it, for a supervisor, and will be called out by and bye to act as one; but at present, I am a simple gauger, tho' t'other day I got an appointment to an excise division of 25l. per annum better than the rest. My present income, down money, is 70l. per annum.
I have one or two good fellows here whom you would be glad to know.
R. B.

CCXXIII.

TO COL. FULLARTON.
OF FULLARTON.

[This letter was first published in the Edinburgh Chronicle.]
Ellisland, 1791.
Sir,
I have just this minute got the frank, and next minute must send it to post, else I purposed to have sent you two or three other bagatelles, that might have amused a vacant hour about as well as "Six excellent new songs," or, the Aberdeen 'Prognostication for the year to come.' I shall probably trouble you soon with another packet. About the gloomy month of November, when 'the people of England hang and drown themselves,' anything generally is better than one's own thought.
Fond as I may be of my own productions, it is not for their sake that I am so anxious to send you them. I am ambitious, covetously ambitious of being known to a gentleman whom I am proud to call my countryman; a gentleman who was a foreign ambassador as soon as he was a man, and a leader of armies as soon as he was a soldier, and that with an eclat unknown to the usual minions of a court, men who, with all the adventitious advantages of princely connexions and princely fortune, must yet, like the caterpillar, labour a whole lifetime before they reach the wished height, there to roost a stupid chrysalis, and doze out the remaining glimmering existence of old age.
If the gentleman who accompanied you when you did me the honour of calling on me, is with you, I beg to be respectfully remembered to him.
I have the honour to be,
Sir,
Your highly obliged, and most devoted
Humble servant,
R. B.
[440]

CCXXIV.

TO MISS DAVIES.
[This accomplished lady was the youngest daughter of Dr. Davies, of Tenby, in Pembrokeshire: she was related to the Riddels of Friar's Carse, and one of her sisters married Captain Adam Gordon, of the noble family of Kenmure. She had both taste and skill in verse.]
It is impossible, Madam, that the generous warmth and angelic purity of your youthful mind, can have any idea of that moral disease under which I unhappily must rank us the chief of sinners; I mean a torpitude of the moral powers, that may be called, a lethargy of conscience. In vain Remorse rears her horrent crest, and rouses all her snakes; beneath the deadly fixed eye and leaden hand of Indolence, their wildest ire is charmed into the torpor of the bat, slumbering out the rigours of winter, in the chink of a ruined

wall. Nothing less, Madam, could have made me so long neglect your obliging commands. Indeed I had one apology-the bagatelle was not worth presenting. Besides, so strongly am I interested in Miss Davies's fate and welfare in the serious business of life, amid its chances and changes, that to make her the subject of a silly ballad is downright mockery of these ardent feelings; 'tis like an impertinent jest to a dying friend.

Gracious Heaven! why this disparity between our wishes and our powers? Why is the most generous wish to make others blest, impotent and ineffectual-as the idle breeze that crosses the pathless desert! In my walks of life I have met with a few people to whom how gladly would I have said-"Go, be happy! I know that your hearts have been wounded by the scorn of the proud, whom accident has placed above you-or worse still, in whose hands are, perhaps, placed many of the comforts of your life. But there! ascend that rock, Independence, and look justly down on their littleness of soul. Make the worthless tremble under your indignation, and the foolish sink before your contempt; and largely impart that happiness to others, which, I am certain, will give yourselves so much pleasure to bestow."

Why, dear Madam, must I wake from this delightful revery, and find it all a dream? Why, amid my generous enthusiasm, must I, find myself poor and powerless, incapable of wiping one tear from the eye of pity, or of adding one comfort to the friend I love!-Out upon the world, say I, that its affairs are administered so ill! They talk of reform;-good Heaven! what a reform would I make among the sons and even the daughters of men!-Down, immediately, should go fools from the high places, where misbegotten chance has perked them up, and through life should they skulk, ever haunted by their native insignificance, as the body marches accompanied by its shadow.-As for a much more formidable class, the knaves, I am at a loss what to do with them: had I a world, there should not be a knave in it.

But the hand that could give, I would liberally fill: and I would pour delight on the heart that could kindly forgive, and generously love.

Still the inequalities of life are, among men, comparatively tolerable-but there is a delicacy, a tenderness, accompanying every view in which we can place lovely Woman, that are grated and shocked at the rude, capricious distinctions of fortune. Woman is the blood-royal of life: let there be slight degrees of precedency among them-but let them be ALL sacred.-Whether this last sentiment be right or wrong, I am not accountable; it is an original component feature of my mind.

R. B.

CCXXV.

TO MRS. DUNLOP.

[Burns, says Cromek, acknowledged that a refined and accomplished woman was a being all but new to him till he went to Edinburgh, and received letters from Mrs. Dunlop.]

Ellisland, 17th December, 1791.

Many thanks to you, Madam, for your good news respecting the little floweret and the mother-plant. I hope my poetic prayers have been heard, and will be answered up to the warmest sincerity of their fullest extent; and then Mrs. Henri will find her little darling the representative of his late parent, in everything but his abridged existence.

I have just finished the following song, which to a lady the descendant of Wallace-and many heroes of his true illustrious line-and herself the mother of several soldiers, needs neither preface nor apology.[441]

Scene-a field of battle-time of the day, evening; the wounded and dying of the victorious army are supposed to join in the following

SONG OF DEATH.

Farewell, thou fair day, thou green earth, and ye skies Now gay with the bright setting sun; Farewell, loves and friendships, ye dear tender ties- Our race of existence is run!

The circumstance that gave rise to the foregoing verses was, looking over with a musical friend M'Donald's collection of Highland airs, I was struck with one, an Isle of Skye tune, entitled "Oran and Aoig, or, The Song of Death," to the measure of which I have adapted my stanzas. I have of late composed two or three other little pieces, which, ere yon full-orbed moon, whose broad impudent face now stares at old mother earth all night, shall have shrunk into a modest crescent, just peeping forth at dewy dawn, I shall find an hour to transcribe for you. A Dieu je vous commende.

R. B.

CCXXVI.

TO MRS. DUNLOP.

[That the poet spoke mildly concerning the rebuke which he received from the Excise, on what he calls his political delinquencies, his letter to Erskine of Mar sufficiently proves.]

5th January, 1792.

You see my hurried life, Madam: I can only command starts of time; however, I am glad of one thing; since I finished the other sheet, the political blast that threatened my welfare is overblown. I have corresponded with Commissioner Graham, for the board had made me the subject of their animadversions; and now I have the pleasure of informing you, that all is set to rights in that quarter. Now as to these informers, may the devil be let loose tobut, hold! I was praying most fervently in my last sheet, and I must not so soon fall a swearing in this.

Alas! how little do the wantonly or idly officious think what mischief they do by their malicious insinuations, indirect impertinence, or thoughtless blabbings. What a difference there is in intrinsic worth, candour, benevolence, generosity, kindness,-in all the charities and all the virtues, between one class of human beings and another! For instance, the amiable circle I so lately mixed with in the hospitable hall of Dunlop, their generous hearts-their uncontaminated dignified minds-their informed and polished understandings-what a contrast, when compared-if such comparing were not downright sacrilege-with the soul of the miscreant who can deliberately plot the destruction of an honest man that never offended him, and with a grin of satisfaction see the unfortunate being, his faithful wife, and prattling innocents, turned over to beggary and ruin!

Your cup, my dear Madam, arrived safe. I had two worthy fellows dining with me the other day, when I, with great formality, produced my whigmeeleerie cup, and told them that it had been a family-piece among the descendants of William Wallace. This roused such an enthusiasm, that they insisted on bumpering the punch round in it; and by and by, never did your great ancestor lay a Suthron more completely to rest, than for a time did your cup my two friends. Apropos, this is the season of wishing. My God bless you, my dear friend, and bless me, the humblest and sincerest of your friends, by granting you yet many returns of the season! May all good things attend you and yours wherever they are scattered over the earth!

R. B.

CCXXVII.

TO MR. WILLIAM SMELLIE,

PRINTER.

[When Burns sends his warmest wishes to Smellie, and prays that fortune may never place his subsistence at the mercy of a knave, or set his character on the judgment of a fool, he had his political enemies probably in his mind.]

Dumfries, 22d January, 1792.

I sit down, my dear Sir, to introduce a young lady to you, and a lady in the first ranks of fashion too. What a task! to you-who care no more for the herd of animals called young ladies, than you do for the herd of animals called young gentlemen. To you-who despise and detest the groupings and combinations of fashion,[442] as an idiot painter that seems industrious to place staring fools and unprincipled knaves in the foreground of his picture, while men of sense and honesty are too often thrown in the dimmest shades. Mrs. Riddel, who will take this letter to town with her, and send it to you, is a character that, even in your own way, as a naturalist and a philosopher, would be an acquisition to your acquaintance. The lady, too, is a votary to the muses; and as I think myself somewhat of a judge in my own trade, I assure you that her verses, always correct, and often elegant, are much beyond the common run of the lady-poetesses of the day. She is a great admirer of your book; and, hearing me say that I was acquainted with you, she begged to be known to you, as she is just going to pay her first visit to our Caledonian capital. I told her that her best way was, to desire her near relation, and your intimate friend, Craigdarroch, to have you at his house while she was there; and lest you might think of a lively West Indian girl, of eighteen, as girls of eighteen too often deserve to be thought of, I should take care to remove that prejudice. To be impartial, however, in appreciating the lady's merits, she has one unlucky failing: a failing which you will easily discover, as she seems rather pleased with indulging in it; and a failing that you will easily pardon, as it is a sin which very much besets yourself;-where she dislikes, or despises, she is apt to make no more a secret of it, than where she esteems and respects.

I will not present you with the unmeaning compliments of the season, but I will send you my warmest wishes and most ardent prayers, that Fortune may never throw your subsistence to the mercy of a Knave, or set your character on the judgment of a Fool; but that, upright and erect, you may walk to an honest grave, where men of letters shall say, here lies a man who did honour to science, and men of worth shall say, here lies a man who did honour to human nature.

R. B.

CCXXVIII.

TO MR. W. NICOL.

[This ironical letter was in answer to one from Nicol, containing counsel and reproof.]

20th February, 1792.

O thou, wisest among the wise, meridian blaze of prudence, full-moon of discretion, and chief of many counsellors! How infinitely is thy puddle-headed, rattle-headed, wrong-headed, round-headed slave indebted to thy supereminent goodness, that from the luminous path of thy own right-lined rectitude, thou lookest benignly down on an erring wretch, of whom the zig-zag wanderings defy all the powers of calculation, from the simple copulation of units, up to the hidden mysteries of fluxions! May one feeble ray of that light of wisdom which darts from thy sensorium, straight as the arrow of heaven, and bright as the meteor of inspiration, may it be my portion, so that I may be less unworthy of the face and favour of that father of proverbs and master of maxims, that antipode of folly, and magnet among the sages, the wise and witty Willie Nicol! Amen! Amen! Yea, so be it!

For me! I am a beast, a reptile, and know nothing! From the cave of my ignorance, amid the fogs of my dulness, and pestilential fumes of my political heresies, I look up to thee, as doth a toad through the iron-barred lucerne of a pestiferous dungeon, to the cloudless glory of a summer sun! Sorely sighing in bitterness of soul, I say, when shall my name be the quotation of the wise, and my countenance be the delight of the godly, like the illustrious lord of Laggan's many hills? As for him, his works are perfect: never did the pen of calumny blur the fair page of his reputation, nor the bolt of hatred fly at his dwelling.

Thou mirror of purity, when shall the elfine lamp of my glimmerous understanding, purged from sensual appetites and gross desires, shine like the constellation of thy intellectual powers!-As for thee, thy thoughts are pure, and thy lips are holy. Never did the unhallowed breath of the powers of darkness, and the pleasures of darkness, pollute the sacred flame of thy sky-descended and heaven-bound desires: never did the vapours of impurity stain the unclouded serene of thy cerulean imagination. O that like thine were the tenor of my life, like thine the tenor of my conversation! then should no friend fear for my strength, no enemy rejoice in my weakness! Then should I lie down and rise up, and none to make me afraid.-May thy pity and thy prayer be exercised for, O thou lamp of wisdom and mirror of morality! thy devoted slave.

R. B.

[443]

CCXXIX.

TO FRANCIS GROSE, ESQ., F.S.A.

[Captain Grose was introduced to Burns, by his brother Antiquary, of Friar's Carse: he was collecting materials for his work on the Antiquities of Scotland.]

Dumfries, 1792.

Sir,

I believe among all our Scots Literati you have not met with Professor Dugald Stewart, who fills the moral philosophy chair in the University of Edinburgh. To say that he is a man of the first parts, and what is more, a man of the first worth, to a gentleman of your general acquaintance, and who so much enjoys the luxury of unencumbered freedom and undisturbed privacy, is not perhaps recommendation enough:-but when I inform you that Mr. Stewart's principal characteristic is your favourite feature; that sterling independence of mind, which, though every man's right, so few men have the courage to claim, and fewer still, the magnanimity to support:-when I tell you that, unseduced by splendour, and undisgusted by wretchedness, he appreciates the merits of the various actors in the great drama of life, merely as they perform their parts-in short, he is a man after your own heart, and I comply with his earnest request in letting you know that he wishes above all things to meet with you. His house, Catrine, is within less than a mile of Sorn Castle, which you proposed visiting; or if you could transmit him the enclosed, he would with the greatest pleasure meet you anywhere in the neighbourhood. I write to Ayrshire to inform Mr. Stewart that I have acquitted myself of my promise. Should your time and spirits permit your meeting with Mr. Stewart, 'tis well; if not, I hope you will forgive this liberty, and I have at least an opportunity of assuring you with what truth and respect,

I am, Sir,
Your great admirer,
And very humble servant,
R. B.

CCXXX.

TO FRANCIS GROSE, ESQ., F.S.A.

[This letter, interesting to all who desire to see how a poet works beauty and regularity out of a vulgar tradition, was first printed by Sir Egerton Brydges, in the "Censura Literaria."]

Dumfries, 1792.

Among the many witch stories I have heard, relating to Alloway kirk, I distinctly remember only two or three.

Upon a stormy night, amid whistling squalls of wind, and bitter blasts of hail; in short, on such a night as the devil would choose to take the air in; a farmer or farmer's servant was plodding and plashing homeward with his plough-irons on his shoulder, having been getting some repairs on them at a neighbouring smithy. His way lay by the kirk of Alloway, and being rather on the anxious look-out in approaching a place so well known to be a favourite haunt of the devil and the devil's friends and emissaries, he was struck aghast by discovering through the horrors of the storm and stormy night, a light, which on his nearer approach plainly showed itself to proceed from the haunted edifice. Whether he had been fortified from above, on his devout supplication, as is customary with people when they suspect the immediate presence of Satan; or whether, according to another custom, he had got courageously drunk at the smithy, I will not pretend to determine; but so it was that he ventured to go up to, nay, into, the very kirk. As luck would have it, his temerity came off unpunished.

The members of the infernal junto were all out on some midnight business or other, and he saw nothing but a kind of kettle or caldron, depending from the roof, over the fire, simmering some heads of unchristened children, limbs of executed malefactors, andc., for the business of the night.-It was in for a penny in for a pound, with the honest ploughman: so without ceremony he unhooked the caldron from off the fire, and pouring out the damnable ingredients, inverted it on his head, and carried it fairly home, where it remained long in the family, a living evidence of the truth of the story.

Another story, which I can prove to be equally authentic, was as follows:

On a market day in the town of Ayr, a farmer from Carrick, and consequently whose way lay by the very gate of Alloway kirk-yard, in order to cross the river Doon at the old bridge, which is about two or three hundred yards farther on than the said gate, had been detained by his business, till by the time he reached Alloway it was the wizard hour, between night and morning.

Though he was terrified with a blaze stream[444]ing from the kirk, yet it is a well-known fact that to turn back on these occasions is running by far the greatest risk of mischief, he prudently advanced on his road. When he had reached the gate of the kirk-yard, he was surprised and entertained, through the ribs and arches of an old gothic window, which still faces the highway, to see a dance of witches merrily footing it round their old sooty blackguard master, who was keeping them all alive with the power of his bag-pipe. The farmer stopping his horse to observe them a little, could plainly descry the faces of many old women of his acquaintance and neighbourhood. How the gentleman was dressed tradition does not say; but that the ladies were all in their smocks: and one of them happening unluckily to have a smock which was considerably too short to answer all the purpose of that piece of dress, our farmer was so tickled, that he involuntarily burst out, with a loud laugh, "Weel luppen, Maggy wi' the short sark!" and recollecting himself, instantly spurred his horse to the top of his speed. I need not mention the universally known fact, that no diabolical power can pursue you beyond the middle of a running stream. Lucky it was for the poor farmer that the river Doon was so near, for notwithstanding the speed of his horse, which was a good one, against he reached the middle of the arch of the bridge, and consequently the middle of the stream, the pursuing, vengeful hags, were so close at big heels, that one of them actually sprung to seize him; but it was too late, nothing was on her side of the stream, but the horse's tail, which immediately gave way at her infernal grip, as if blasted by a stroke of lightning; but the farmer was beyond her reach. However, the unsightly, tailless condition of the vigorous steed was, to the last hour of the noble creature's life, an awful warning to the Carrick farmers, not to stay too late in Ayr markets.

The last relation I shall give, though equally true, is not so well identified as the two former, with regard to the scene; but as the best authorities give it for Alloway, I shall relate it.

On a summer's evening, about the time that nature puts on her sables to mourn the expiry of the cheerful day, a shepherd boy, belonging to a farmer in the immediate neighbourhood of Alloway kirk, had just folded his charge, and was returning home. As he passed the kirk, in the adjoining field, he fell in with a crew of men and women, who were busy pulling stems of the plant Ragwort. He observed that as each person pulled a Ragwort, he or she got astride of it, and called out, "Up horsie!" on which the Ragwort flew off, like Pegasus, through the air with its rider. The foolish boy likewise pulled his Ragwort, and cried with the rest, "Up horsie!" and, strange to tell, away he flew with the company. The first stage at which the cavalcade stopt, was a merchant's wine-cellar in Bordeaux, where, without saying by your leave, they quaffed away at the best the cellar could afford, until the morning, foe to the imps and works of darkness, threatened to throw light on the matter, and frightened them from their carousals.

The poor shepherd lad, being equally a stranger to the scene and the liquor, heedlessly got himself drunk; and when the rest took horse, he fell asleep, and was found so next day by some of the people belonging to the merchant. Somebody that understood Scotch, asking him what he was, he said such-a-one's herd in Alloway, and by some means or other getting home again, he lived long to tell the world the wondrous tale.

I am, andc.,

R. B.

CCXXXI.

TO MR. S. CLARKE,

EDINBURGH.

[This introduction of Clarke, the musician, to the M'Murdo's of Drumlanrig, brought to two of the ladies the choicest honours of the muse.]

July 1, 1792.

Mr. Burns begs leave to present his most respectful compliments to Mr. Clarke.-Mr. B. some time ago did himself the honour of writing to Mr. C. respecting coming out to the country, to give a little musical instruction in a highly respectable family, where Mr. C. may have his own terms, and may be as happy as indolence, the devil, and the gout will permit him. Mr. B. knows well how Mr. C. is engaged with another family; but cannot Mr. C. find two or three weeks to spare to each of them? Mr. B. is deeply impressed with, and awfully conscious of, the high importance of Mr. C.'s time, whether in the winged moments of symphonious exhibition, at the keys of harmony, while listening seraphs cease their own less de[445]lightful strains; or in the drowsy arms of slumb'rous repose, in the arms of his dearly beloved elbowchair, where the frowsy, but potent power of indolence, circumfuses her vapours round, and sheds her dews on the head of her darling son. But half a line conveying half a meaning from Mr. C. would make Mr. B. the happiest of mortals.

CCXXXII.

TO MRS. DUNLOP.

[To enthusiastic fits of admiration for the young and the beautiful, such as Burns has expressed in this letter, he loved to give way:-we owe some of his best songs to these sallies.]

Annan Water Foot, 22d August, 1792.

Do not blame me for it, Madam;-my own conscience, hackneyed and weather-beaten as it is in watching and reproving my vagaries, follies, indolence, andc., has continued to punish me sufficiently.

Do you think it possible, my dear and honoured friend, that I could be so lost to gratitude for many favours; to esteem for much worth, and to the honest, kind, pleasurably tie of, now old acquaintance, and I hope and am sure of progressive, increasing friendship-as for a single day, not to think of you-to ask the Fates what they are doing and about to do with my much-loved friend and her wide-scattered connexions, and to beg of them to be as kind to you and yours as they possibly can?

Apropos! (though how it is apropos, I have not leisure to explain,) do you not know that I am almost in love with an acquaintance of yours?-Almost! said I-I am in love, souse! over head and ears, deep as the most unfathomable abyss of the boundless ocean; but the word Love, owing to the intermingledoms of the good and the bad, the pure and the impure, in this world, being rather an equivocal term for expressing one's sentiments and sensations, I must do justice to the sacred purity of my attachment. Know, then, that the heart-struck awe; the distant humble approach; the delight we should have in gazing upon and listening to a messenger of heaven, appearing in all the unspotted purity of his celestial home, among the coarse, polluted, far inferior sons of men, to deliver to them tidings that make their hearts swim in joy, and their imaginations soar in transport-such, so delighting and so pure, were the emotions of my soul on meeting the other day with Miss Lesley Baillie, your neighbour, at M. Mr. B. with his two daughters, accompanied by Mr. H. of G. passing through Dumfries a few days ago, on their way to England, did me the honour of calling on me; on which I took my horse (though God knows I could ill spare the time), and accompanied them fourteen or fifteen miles, and dined and spent the day with them. 'Twas about nine, I think, when I left them, and riding home, I composed the following ballad, of which you will probably think you have a dear bargain, as it will cost you another groat of postage. You must know that there is an old ballad beginning with-

"My bonnie Lizzie Baillie I'll rowe thee in my plaidie, andc."

So I parodied it as follows, which is literally the first copy, "unanointed, unanneal'd;" as Hamlet says.-

O saw ye bonny Lesley As she gaed o'er the border? She's gane like Alexander, To spread her conquests farther.

So much for ballads. I regret that you are gone to the east country, as I am to be in Ayrshire in about a fortnight. This world of ours, notwithstanding it has many good things in it, yet it has ever had this curse, that two or three people, who would be the happier the oftener they met together, are, almost without exception, always so placed as never to meet but once or twice a-year, which, considering the few years of a man's life, is a very great "evil under the sun," which I do not recollect that Solomon has mentioned in his catalogue of the miseries of man. I hope and believe that there is a state of existence beyond the grave, where the worthy of this life will renew their former intimacies, with this endearing addition, that, "we meet to part no more!"

. . . . "Tell us, ye dead, Will none of you in pity disclose the secret, What 'tis you are, and we must shortly be?"

Blair

A thousand times have I made this apostrophe to the departed sons of men, but not one of them has ever thought fit to answer the question. "O that some courteous ghost would blab it out!" but it cannot be; you and I, my friend,[446] must make the experiment by ourselves and for ourselves. However, I am so convinced that an unshaken faith in the doctrines of religion is not only necessary, by making us better men, but also by making us happier men, that I should take every care that your little godson, and every little creature that shall call me father, shall be taught them.

So ends this heterogeneous letter, written at this wild place of the world, in the intervals of my labour of discharging a vessel of rum from Antigua.

R. B.

CCXXXIII.

TO MR. CUNNINGHAM.

[There is both bitterness and humour in this letter: the poet discourses on many matters, and woman is among them-but he places the bottle at his elbow as an antidote against the discourtesy of scandal.]

Dumfries, 10th September, 1792.

No! I will not attempt an apology.-Amid all my hurry of business, grinding the faces of the publican and the sinner on the merciless wheels of the Excise; making ballads, and then drinking, and singing them! and, over and above all, the correcting the press-work of two different publications; still, still I might have stolen five minutes to dedicate to one of the first of my friends and fellow-creatures. I might have done as I do at present, snatched an hour near "witching time of night," and scrawled a page or two. I might have congratulated my friend on his marriage; or I might have thanked the Caledonian archers for the honour they have done me (though, to do myself justice, I intended to have done both in rhyme, else I had done both long ere now). Well, then, here's to your good health! for you must know, I have set a nipperkin of toddy by me, just by way of spell, to keep away the meikle horned deil, or any of his subaltern imps who may be on their nightly rounds.

But what shall I write to you?-"The voice said cry," and I said, "what shall I cry?"-O, thou spirit! whatever thou art, or wherever thou makest thyself visible! be thou a bogle by the eerie side of an auld thorn, in the dreary glen through which the herd-callan maun bicker in his gloamin route frae the faulde!-Be thou a brownie, set, at dead of night, to thy task by the blazing ingle, or in the solitary barn, where the repercussions of thy iron flail half affright thyself as thou performest the work of twenty of the sons of men, ere the cock-crowing summon thee to thy ample cog of substantial brose-Be thou a kelpie, haunting the ford or ferry, in the starless night, mixing thy laughing yell with the howling of the storm and the roaring of the flood, as thou viewest the perils and miseries of man on the foundering horse, or in the tumbling boat!-or, lastly, be thou a ghost, paying thy nocturnal visits to the hoary ruins of decayed grandeur; or performing thy mystic rites in the shadow of the time-worn church, while the moon looks, without a cloud, on the silent ghastly dwellings of the dead around thee! or taking thy stand by the bedside of the villain, or the murderer, pourtraying on his dreaming fancy, pictures, dreadful as the horrors of unveiled hell, and terrible as the wrath of incensed Deity!-Come, thou spirit, but not in these horrid forms; come with the milder, gentle, easy inspirations, which thou breathest round the wig of a prating advocate, or the tête of a tea-sipping gossip, while their tongues run at the light-horse gallop of clishmaclaver for ever and ever-come and assist a poor devil who is quite jaded in the attempt to share half an idea among half a hundred words; to fill up four quarto pages, while he has not got one single sentence of recollection, information, or remark worth putting pen to paper for.

I feel, I feel the presence of supernatural assistance! circled in the embrace of my elbowchair, my breast labours, like the bloated Sybil on her three-footed stool, and like her, too, labours with Nonsense.-Nonsense, suspicious name! Tutor, friend, and finger-post in the mystic mazes of law; the cadaverous paths of physic; and particularly in the sightless soarings of school divinity, who, leaving Common Sense confounded at his strength of pinion, Reason, delirious with eyeing his giddy flight; and Truth creeping back into the bottom of her well, cursing the hour that ever she offered her scorned alliance to the wizard power of Theologic Vision-raves abroad on all the winds. "On earth Discord! a gloomy Heaven above, opening her jealous gates to the nineteenth thousandth part of the tithe of mankind; and below, an inescapable and inexorable hell, expanding its leviathan jaws for the vast residue of mortals!!!"-O doctrine! comfortable and[447] healing to the weary, wounded soul of man! Ye sons and daughters of affliction, ye pauvres miserables, to whom day brings no pleasure, and night yields no rest, be comforted! "'Tis but one to nineteen hundred thousand that your situation will mend in this world;" so, alas, the experience of the poor and the needy too often affirms; and 'tis nineteen hundred thousand sand to one, by the dogmas of * * * * * * * * that you will be damned eternally in the world to come!

But of all nonsense, religious nonsense is the most nonsensical; so enough, and more than enough of it. Only, by the by, will you or can you tell me, my dear Cunningham, why a sectarian turn of mind has always a tendency to narrow and illiberalize the heart? They are orderly; they may be just; nay, I have known them merciful: but still your children of sanctity move among their fellow-creatures with a nostril-snuffing putrescence, and a foot-spurning filth, in short, with a conceited dignity that your titled * * * * * * * * or any other of your Scottish lordlings of seven centuries standing, display when they accidentally mix among the many-aproned sons of mechanical life. I remember, in my plough-boy days, I could not conceive it possible that a noble lord could be a fool, or a godly man could be a knave-How ignorant are plough-boys!-Nay, I have since discovered that a godly woman may be a *****!-But hold-Here's t'ye again-this rum is generous Antigua, so a very unfit menstruum for scandal.

Apropos, how do you like, I mean really like, the married life? Ah, my friend! matrimony is quite a different thing from what your love-sick youths and sighing girls take it to be! But marriage, we are told, is appointed by God, and I shall never quarrel with any of his institutions. I am a husband of older standing than you, and shall give you my ideas of the conjugal state, (en passant; you know I am no Latinist, is not conjugal derived from jugum, a yoke?) Well, then, the scale of good wifeship I divide into ten parts:-good-nature, four; good sense, two; wit, one; personal charms, viz. a sweet face, eloquent eyes, fine limbs, graceful carriage (I would add a fine waist too, but that is so soon spoilt you know), all these, one; as for the other qualities belonging to, or attending on, a wife, such as fortune, connexions, education (I mean education extraordinary) family, blood, andc., divide the two remaining degrees among them as you please; only, remember that all these minor properties must be expressed by fractions, for there is not any one of them, in the aforesaid scale, entitled to the dignity of an integer.

As for the rest of my fancies and reveries-how I lately met with Miss Lesley Baillie, the most beautiful, elegant woman in the world-how I accompanied her and her father's family fifteen miles on their journey, out of pure devotion, to admire the loveliness of the works of God, in such an unequalled display of them-how, in galloping home at night, I made a ballad on her, of which these two stanzas make a part-

Thou, bonny Lesley, art a queen, Thy subjects we before thee; Thou, bonny Lesley, art divine, The hearts o' men adore thee.

The very deil he could na scathe Whatever wad belang thee! He'd look into thy bonnie face And say, "I canna wrang thee."

-behold all these things are written in the chronicles of my imaginations, and shall be read by thee, my dear friend, and by thy beloved spouse, my other dear friend, at a more convenient season.

Now, to thee, and to thy before-designed bosom-companion, be given the precious things brought forth by the sun, and the precious things brought forth by the moon, and the benignest influences of the stars, and the living streams which flow from the fountains of life, and by the tree of life, for ever and ever! Amen!

CCXXXIV.

TO MR. THOMSON.

[George Thomson, of Edinburgh, principal clerk to the trustees for the encouraging the manufactures of Scotland, projected a work, entitled, "A select Collection of Original Scottish Airs, for the Voice, to which are added introductory and concluding Symphonies and Accompaniments for the Pianoforte and Violin, by Pleyel and Kozeluch, with select and characteristic Verses, by the most admired Scottish Poets." To Burns he applied for help in the verse: he could not find a truer poet, nor one to whom such a work was more congenial.][448]

Dumfries, 16th Sept. 1792.

Sir,

I have just this moment got your letter. As the request you make to me will positively add to my enjoyments in complying with it, I shall enter into your undertaking with all the small portion of abilities I have, strained to their utmost exertion by the impulse of enthusiasm. Only, don't hurry me-"Deil tak the hindmost" is by no means the cri de guerre of my muse. Will you, as I am inferior to none of you in enthusiastic attachment to the poetry and music of old Caledonia, and, since you request it, have cheerfully promised my mite of assistance-will you let me have a list of your airs with the first line of the printed verses you intend for them, that I may have an opportunity of suggesting any alteration that may occur to me? You know 'tis in the way of my trade; still leaving you, gentlemen, the undoubted right of publishers to approve or reject, at your pleasure, for your own publication. Apropos, if you are for English verses, there is, on my part, an end of the matter. Whether in the simplicity of the Ballad, or the pathos of the song, I can only hope to please myself in being allowed at least a sprinkling of our native tongue. English verses, particularly the works of Scotsmen, that have merit, are certainly very eligible. "Tweedside"' "Ah! the poor shepherd's mournful fate!" "Ah! Chloris, could I now but sit," andc., you cannot mend;[199] but such insipid stuff as "To Fanny fair could I impart," andc., usually set to "The Mill, Mill, O!" is a disgrace to the collections in which it has already appeared, and would doubly disgrace a collection that will have the very superior merit of yours. But more of this in the further prosecution of the business, if I am called on for my strictures and amendments-I say amendments, for I will not alter except where I myself, at least, think that I amend.

As to any remuneration, you may think my songs either above or below price; for they should absolutely be the one or the other. In the honest enthusiasm with which I embark in your undertaking, to talk of money, wages, fee, hire, andc., would be downright prostitution of soul! a proof of each of the song that I compose or amend, I shall receive as a favour. In the rustic phrase of the season, "Gude speed the wark!"

I am, Sir,

Your very humble servant,

R. B.

FOOTNOTES:

[199] "Tweedside" is by Crawfurd; "Ah, the poor shepherd," andc., by Hamilton, of Bangour; "Ah! Chloris," andc., by Sir Charles Sedley-Burns has attributed it to Sir Peter Halket, of Pitferran.

CCXXXV.

TO MRS. DUNLOP.

[One of the daughters of Mrs. Dunlop was married to M. Henri, a French gentleman, who died in 1790, at Loudon Castle, in Ayrshire. The widow went with her orphan son to France, and lived for awhile amid the dangers of the revolution.]

Dumfries, 24th September, 1792.

I have this moment, my dear Madam, yours of the twenty-third. All your other kind reproaches, your news, andc., are out of my head when I read and think on Mrs. H'ssituation. Good God! a heart-wounded helpless young woman-in a strange, foreign land, and that land convulsed with every horror that can harrow the human feelings-sick-looking, longing for a comforter, but finding none-a mother's feelings, too:-but it is too much: he who wounded (he only can) may He heal!

I wish the farmer great joy of his new acquisition to his family. * * * * * I cannot say that I give him joy of his life as a farmer. 'Tis, as a farmer paying a dear, unconscionable rent, a cursed life! As to a laird farming his own property; sowing his own corn in hope; and reaping it, in spite of brittle weather, in gladness; knowing that none can say unto him, 'what dost thou?'-fattening his herds; shearing his flocks; rejoicing at Christmas; and begetting sons and daughters, until he be the venerated, gray-haired leader of a little tribe-'tis a heavenly life! but devil take the life of reaping the fruits that another must eat.

Well, your kind wishes will be gratified, as to seeing me when I make my Ayrshire visit. I cannot leave Mrs. B, until her nine months' race is run, which may perhaps be in three or four weeks. She, too, seems determined to make me the patriarchal leader of a band. However, if Heaven will be so obliging as to let me have them in the proportion of three boys to one girl, I shall be so much the more pleased. I hope, if I am spared with them, to show a[449] set of boys that will do honour to my cares and name; but I am not equal to the task of rearing girls. Besides, I am too poor; a girl should always have a fortune. Apropos, your little godson is thriving charmingly, but is a very devil. He, though two years younger, has completely mastered his brother. Robert is indeed the mildest, gentlest creature I ever saw. He has a most surprising memory, and is quite the pride of his schoolmaster.

You know how readily we get into prattle upon a subject dear to our heart: you can excuse it. God bless you and yours!

R. B.

CCXXXVI.

TO MRS. DUNLOP.

[This letter has no date: it is supposed to have been written on the death of her daughter, Mrs. Henri, whose orphan son, deprived of the protection of all his relations, was preserved by the affectionate kindness of Mademoiselle Susette, one of the family domestics, and after the Revolution obtained the estate of his blood and name.]

I had been from home, and did not receive your letter until my return the other day. What shall I say to comfort you, my much-valued, much-afflicted friend! I can but grieve with you; consolation I have none to offer, except that which religion holds out to the children of affliction-children of affliction!-how just the expression! and like every other family they have matters among them which they hear, see, and feel in a serious, all-important manner, of which the world has not, nor cares to have, any idea. The world looks indifferently on, makes the passing remark, and proceeds to the next novel occurrence.

Alas, Madam! who would wish for many years? What is it but to drag existence until our joys gradually expire, and leave us in a night of misery: like the gloom which blots out the stars one by one, from the face of night,

and leaves us, without a ray of comfort, in the howling waste!
I am interrupted, and must leave off. You shall soon hear from me again.
R. B.

CCXXXVII.

TO MR. THOMSON.
[Thomson had delivered judgment on some old Scottish songs, but the poet murmured against George's decree.]
My Dear Sir,
Let me tell you, that you are too fastidious in your ideas of songs and ballads. I own that your criticisms are just; the songs you specify in your list have, all but one, the faults you remark in them; but who shall mend the matter? Who shall rise up and say, "Go to! I will make a better?" For instance, on reading over "The Lea-rig," I immediately set about trying my hand on it, and, after all, I could make nothing more of it than the following, which, Heaven knows, is poor enough.
When o'er the hill the eastern star, andc.[200]
Your observation as to the aptitude of Dr. Percy's ballad to the air, "Nannie, O!" is just. It is, besides, perhaps, the most beautiful ballad in the English language. But let me remark to you, that in the sentiment and style of our Scottish airs, there is a pastoral simplicity, a something that one may call the Doric style and dialect of vocal music, to which a dash of our native tongue and manners is particularly, nay peculiarly, apposite. For this reason, and upon my honour, for this reason alone, I am of opinion (but, as I told you before, my opinion is yours, freely yours, to approve or reject, as you please) that my ballad of "Nannie, O!" might perhaps do for one set of verses to the tune. Now don't let it enter into your head, that you are under any necessity of taking my verses. I have long ago made up my mind as to my own reputation in the business of authorship, and have nothing to be pleased or offended at, in your adoption or rejection of my verses. Though you should reject one half of what I give you, I shall be pleased with your adopting the other half, and shall continue to serve you with the same assiduity.
In the printed copy of my "Nannie, O!" the name of the river is horribly prosaic.[201] I will alter it:
Behind yon hills where Lugar flows.
Girvan is the name of the river that suits the idea of the stanza best, but Lugar is the most agreeable modulation of syllables.
[450]
I will soon give you a great many more remarks on this business; but I have just now an opportunity of conveying you this scrawl, free of postage, an expense that it is ill able to pay: so, with my best compliments to honest

Allan, Gude be wi' ye, andc.

Friday Night.

Saturday Morning.

As I find I have still an hour to spare this morning before my conveyance goes away, I will give you "Nannie, O!" at length.

Your remarks on "Ewe-bughts, Marion," are just; still it has obtained a place among our more classical Scottish songs; and what with many beauties in its composition, and more prejudices in its favour, you will not find it easy to supplant it.

In my very early years, when I was thinking of going to the West Indies, I took the following farewell of a dear girl. It is quite trifling, and has nothing of the merits of "Ewe-bughts;" but it will fill up this page. You must know that all my earlier love-songs were the breathings of ardent passion, and though it might have been easy in aftertimes to have given them a polish, yet that polish, to me, whose they were, and who perhaps alone cared for them, would have defaced the legend of my heart, which was so faithfully inscribed on them. Their uncouth simplicity was, as they say of wines, their race.

Will ye go to the Indies, my Mary? andc.[202]

"Gala Water" and "Auld Rob Morris" I think, will most probably be the next subject of my musings. However, even on my verses, speak out your criticisms with equal frankness. My wish is not to stand aloof, the uncomplying bigot of opiniâtreté, but cordially to join issue with you in the furtherance of the work.

R. B.

FOOTNOTES:

[200] Song CLXXVII

[201] It is something worse in the Edinburgh edition-"Behind yon hills where Stinchar flows."-Poems, p 322.

[202] Song CLXXIX.

CCXXXVIII.

TO MR. THOMSON.

[The poet loved to describe the influence which the charms of Miss Lesley Baillie exercised over his imagination.]

November 8th, 1792.

If you mean, my dear Sir, that all the songs in your collection shall be poetry of the first merit, I am afraid you will find more difficulty in the undertaking than you are aware of. There is a peculiar rhythmus in many of our airs, and a necessity of adapting syllables to the emphasis, or what I would call the feature-notes of the tune, that cramp the poet, and lay him under almost insuperable difficulties. For instance, in the air, "My wife's a wanton wee thing," if a few lines smooth and pretty can be adapted to it, it is all you can expect. The following were made extempore to it; and though on further study I might give you something more profound, yet it might not suit the light-horse gallop of the air so well as this random clink:-

My wife's a winsome wee thing, andc.[203]

I have just been looking over the "Collier's bonny dochter;" and if the following rhapsody, which I composed the other day, on a charming Ayrshire girl, Miss Lesley Baillie, as she passed through this place to England, will suit your taste better than the "Collier Lassie," fall on and welcome:-

O, saw ye bonny Lesley? andc.[204]

I have hitherto deferred the sublimer, more pathetic airs, until more leisure, as they will take, and deserve, a greater effort. However, they are all put into your hands, as clay into the hands of the potter, to make one vessel to honour, and another to dishonour. Farewell, andc.

R. B.

FOOTNOTES:

[203] Song CLXXX.
[204] Song CLXXXI.

CCXXXIX.

TO MR. THOMSON.

[The story of Mary Campbell's love is related in the notes on the songs which the poet wrote in her honour. Thomson says, in his answer, "I have heard the sad story of your Mary; you always seem inspired when you write of her."]

14th November, 1792.

My Dear Sir,

I agree with you that the song, "Katherine Ogie," is very poor stuff, and unworthy, altogether unworthy of so beautiful an air. I tried to mend it; but the awkward sound, Ogie, recurring so often in the rhyme, spoils every attempt at introducing sentiment into the piece. The foregoing song[205] pleases myself; I think it [451] as in my happiest manner: you will see at first glance that it suits the air. The subject of the song is one of the most interesting passages of my youthful days, and I own that I should be much flattered to see the verses set to an air which would ensure celebrity. Perhaps, after all, 'tis the still glowing prejudice of my heart that throws a borrowed lustre over the merits of the composition.

I have partly taken your idea of "Auld Rob Morris." I have adopted the two first verses, and am going on with the song on a new plan, which promises pretty well. I take up one or another, just as the bee of the moment buzzes in my bonnet-lug; and do you, sans ceremonie, make what use you choose of the productions.

Adieu, andc.

R. B.

FOOTNOTES:

[205]

Ye banks and braes and streams around The castle o' Montgomery.

Song CLXXXII

CCXL.

TO MR. THOMSON.

[The poet approved of several emendations proposed by Thomson, whose wish was to make the words flow more readily with the music: he refused, however, to adopt others, where he thought too much of the sense was sacrificed.]

Dumfries, 1st December, 1792.

Your alterations of my "Nannie, O!" are perfectly right. So are those of "My wife's a winsome wee thing." Your alteration of the second stanza is a positive improvement. Now, my dear Sir, with the freedom which characterizes our correspondence, I must not, cannot alter "Bonnie Lesley." You are right; the word "Alexander" makes the line a little uncouth, but I think the thought is pretty. Of Alexander, beyond all other heroes, it may be said, in the sublime language of Scripture, that "he went forth conquering and to conquer."

For nature made her what she is, And never made anither. (Such a person as she is.)

This is, in my opinion, more poetical than "Ne'er made sic anither." However, it is immaterial: make it either way. "Caledonie," I agree with you, is not so good a word as could be wished, though it is sanctioned in three or four instances by Allan Ramsay; but I cannot help it. In short, that species of stanza is the most difficult that I have ever tried.

R. B.

CCXLI.

TO MR. THOMSON.

[Duncan Gray, which this letter contained, became a favourite as soon as it

was published, and the same may be said of Auld Rob Morris.]
4th December, 1792.
The foregoing ["Auld Rob Morris," and "Duncan Gray,"[206]] I submit, my dear Sir, to your better judgment. Acquit them or condemn them, as seemeth good in your sight. "Duncan Gray" is that kind of light-horse gallop of an air, which precludes sentiment. The ludicrous is its ruling feature.
R. B.

FOOTNOTES:

[206] Songs CLXXXIII. and CLXXXIV.
CCXLII.
TO MRS. DUNLOP.
[Burns often discourses with Mrs. Dunlop on poetry and poets: the dramas of Thomson, to which he alludes, are stiff, cold compositions.]
Dumfries, 6th December, 1792.
I shall be in Ayrshire, I think, next week; and, if at all possible, I shall certainly, my much-esteemed friend, have the pleasure of visiting at Dunlop-house.
Alas, Madam! how seldom do we meet in this world, that we have reason to congratulate ourselves on accessions of happiness! I have not passed half the ordinary term of an old man's life, and yet I scarcely look over the obituary of a newspaper, that I do not see some names that I have known, and which I, and other acquaintances, little thought to meet with there so soon. Every other instance of the mortality of our kind, makes us cast an anxious look into the dreadful abyss of uncertainty, and shudder with apprehension for our own fate. But of how different an importance are the lives of different individuals? Nay, of what importance is one period of the same life, more than another? A few years ago, I could have laid down in the dust, "careless of the voice of the morning;" and now not a few, and these most helpless individuals, would, on losing me and my exertions, lose both their "staff and shield." By the way, these helpless ones have lately got an addition; Mrs. B having given me a fine girl since I wrote you. There is a charm[452]ing passage in Thomson's "Edward and Eleonora:"
"The valiant in himself, what can he suffer? Or what need he regard his single woes?" andc.
As I am got in the way of quotations, I shall give you another from the same piece, peculiarly, alas! too peculiarly apposite, my dear Madam, to your present frame of mind:
"Who so unworthy but may proudly deck him With his fair-weather virtue, that exults Glad o'er the summer main! the tempest comes, The rough winds rage aloud; when from the helm, This virtue shrinks, and in a corner

lies Lamenting-Heavens! if privileged from trial, How cheap a thing were virtue?"

I do not remember to have heard you mention Thomson's dramas. I pick up favourite quotations, and store them in my mind as ready armour, offensive or defensive, amid the struggle of this turbulent existence. Of these is one, a very favourite one, from his "Alfred:"

"Attach thee firmly to the virtuous deeds And offices of life; to life itself, With all its vain and transient joys, sit loose."

Probably I have quoted some of these to you formerly, as indeed when I write from the heart, I am apt to be guilty of such repetitions. The compass of the heart, in the musical style of expression, is much more bounded than that of the imagination; so the notes of the former are extremely apt to run into one another; but in return for the paucity of its compass, its few notes are much more sweet. I must still give you another quotation, which I am almost sure I have given you before, but I cannot resist the temptation. The subject is religion-speaking of its importance to mankind, the author says,

"'Tis this, my friend, that streaks our morning bright."

I see you are in for double postage, so I shall e'en scribble out t'other sheet. We, in this country here, have many alarms of the reforming, or rather the republican spirit, of your part of the kingdom. Indeed we are a good deal in commotion ourselves. For me, I am a placeman, you know; a very humble one indeed, Heaven knows, but still so much as to gag me. What my private sentiments are, you will find out without an interpreter.

I have taken up the subject, and the other day, for a pretty actress's benefit night, I wrote an address, which I will give on the other page, called "The rights of woman:"

"While Europe's eye is fixed on mighty things."

I shall have the honour of receiving your criticisms in person at Dunlop.

R. B.

CCXLIII.

TO R. GRAHAM, ESQ.,

FINTRAY.

[Graham stood by the bard in the hour of peril recorded in this letter: and the Board of Excise had the generosity to permit him to eat its "bitter bread" for the remainder of his life.]

December, 1792.

Sir,

I have been surprised, confounded, and distracted by Mr. Mitchell, the collector, telling me that he has received an order from your Board to inquire into my political conduct, and blaming me as a person disaffected to government.

Sir, you are a husband-and a father.-You know what you would feel, to see the much-loved wife of your bosom, and your helpless, prattling little ones, turned adrift into the world, degraded and disgraced from a situation in which they had been respectable and respected, and left almost without the necessary support of a miserable existence. Alas, Sir! must I think that such, soon, will be my lot! and from the d-mned, dark insinuations of hellish, groundless envy too! I believe, Sir, I may aver it, and in the sight of Omniscience, that I would not tell a deliberate falsehood, no, not though even worse horrors, if worse can be, than those I have mentioned, hung over my head; and I say, that the allegation, whatever villain has made it, is a lie! To the British constitution on Revolution principles, next after my God, I am most devoutly attached; you, Sir, have been much and generously my friend.-Heaven knows how warmly I have felt the obligation, and how gratefully I have thanked you.-Fortune, Sir, has made you powerful, and me impotent; has given you patronage, and me dependence.-I would not for my single self, call on your humanity; were such my insular, unconnected situation, I would despise the tear that now swells in my eye-I could brave misfortune, I could face ruin; for at the worst, "Death's thousand doors stand open;" but, good God! the tender concerns that I have mentioned, the claims and ties that I see at this moment, and feel around me, how they unnerve courage, and wither resolution[453]! To your patronage, as a man of some genius, you have allowed me a claim; and your esteem, as an honest man, I know is my due: to these, Sir, permit me to appeal; by these may I adjure you to save me from that misery which threatens to overwhelm me, and which, with my latest breath I will say it, I have not deserved.

R. B.

CCXLIV.

TO MRS. DUNLOP.

[Burns was ordered, he says, to mind his duties in the Excise, and to hold his tongue about politics-the latter part of the injunction was hard to obey, for at that time politics were in every mouth.]

Dumfries, 31st December, 1792.

Dear Madam,

A hurry of business, thrown in heaps by my absence, has until now prevented my returning my grateful acknowledgments to the good family of Dunlop, and you in particular, for that hospitable kindness which rendered the four days I spent under that genial roof, four of the pleasantest I ever enjoyed.-Alas, my dearest friend! how few and fleeting are those things we call pleasures! on my road to Ayrshire, I spent a night with a friend whom I much valued; a man whose days promised to be many; and on Saturday last we laid him in the dust!

Jan. 2, 1793.

I have just received yours of the 30th, and feel much for your situation. However, I heartily rejoice in your prospect of recovery from that vile jaundice. As to myself, I am better, though not quite free of my complaint.-You must not think, as you seem to insinuate, that in my way of life I want exercise. Of that I have enough; but occasional hard drinking is the devil to me. Against this I have again and again bent my resolution, and have greatly succeeded. Taverns I have totally abandoned: it is the private parties in the family way, among the hard-drinking gentlemen of this country, that do me the mischief-but even this I have more than half given over.

Mr. Corbet can be of little service to me at present; at least I should be shy of applying. I cannot possibly be settled as a supervisor, for several years. I must wait the rotation of the list, and there are twenty names before mine. I might indeed get a job of officiating, where a settled supervisor was ill, or aged; but that hauls me from my family, as I could not remove them on such an uncertainty. Besides, some envious, malicious devil, has raised a little demur on my political principles, and I wish to let that matter settle before I offer myself too much in the eye of my supervisors. I have set, henceforth, a seal on my lips, as to these unlucky politics; but to you I must breathe my sentiments. In this, as in everything else, I shall show the undisguised emotions of my soul. War I deprecate: misery and ruin to thousands are in the blast that announces the destructive demon.

R. B.

CCXLV.

TO MR. THOMSON.

[The songs to which the poet alludes were "Poortith Cauld," and "Galla Water."]

Jan. 1793.

Many returns of the season to you, my dear Sir. How comes on your publication?-will these two foregoing [Songs clxxxv. and clxxxvi. be of any service to you? I should like to know what songs you print to each tune, besides the verses to which it is set. In short, I would wish to give you my opinion on all the poetry you publish. You know it is my trade, and a man in the way of his trade may suggest useful hints that escape men of much superior parts and endowments in other things.

If you meet with my dear and much-valued Cunningham, greet him, in my name, with the compliments of the season.

Yours, andc.,

R. B.

CCXLVI.

TO MR. THOMSON.

[Thomson explained more fully than at first the plan of his publication, and stated that Dr. Beattie had promised an essay on Scottish music, by way of an introduction to the work.]

26th January, 1793.

I approve greatly, my dear Sir, of your plans. Dr. Beattie's essay will, of itself, be a treasure. On my part I mean to draw up an appendix to the Doctor's essay, containing my stock of anecdotes, andc., of our Scots songs. All the late Mr.[454] Tytler's anecdotes I have by me, taken down in the course of my acquaintance with him, from his own mouth. I am such an enthusiast, that in the course of my several peregrinations through Scotland, I made a pilgrimage to the individual spot from which every song took its rise, "Lochaber" and the "Braes of Ballenden" excepted. So far as the locality, either from the title of the air, or the tenor of the song, could be ascertained, I have paid my devotions at the particular shrine of every Scots muse.

I do not doubt but you might make a very valuable collection of Jacobite songs; but would it give no offence? In the meantime, do not you think that some of them, particularly "The sow's tail to Geordie," as an air, with other words, might be well worth a place in your collection of lively songs?

If it were possible to procure songs of merit, it would be proper to have one set of Scots words to every air, and that the set of words to which the notes ought to be set. There is a navïeté, a pastoral simplicity, in a slight intermixture of Scots words and phraseology, which is more in unison (at least to my taste, and, I will add, to every genuine Caledonian taste) with the simple pathos, or rustic sprightliness of our native music, than any English verses whatever.

The very name of Peter Pindar is an acquisition to your work. His "Gregory" is beautiful. I have tried to give you a set of stanzas in Scots, on the same subject, which are at your service. Not that I intend to enter the lists with Peter-that would be presumption indeed. My song, though much inferior in poetic merit, has, I think, more of the ballad simplicity in it.

[Here follows "Lord Gregory." Song clxxxvii.]

My most respectful compliments to the honourable gentleman who favoured me with a postscript in your last. He shall hear from me and receive his MSS. soon.

Yours,

R. B.

CCXLVII.

TO MR. CUNNINGHAM.

[The seal, with the coat-of-arms which the poet invented, is still in the family, and regarded as a relique.]

3d March, 1793.

Since I wrote to you the last lugubrious sheet, I have not had time to write you further. When I say that I had not time, that as usual means, that the three demons, indolence, business, and ennui, have so completely shared my hours among them, as not to leave me a five minutes' fragment to take up a pen in.

Thank heaven, I feel my spirits buoying upwards with the renovating year. Now I shall in good earnest take up Thomson's songs. I dare say he thinks I have used him unkindly, and I must own with too much appearance of truth. Apropos, do you know the much admired old Highland air called "The Sutor's Dochter?" It is a first-rate favourite of mine, and I have written what I reckon one of my best songs to it. I will send it to you as it was sung with great applause in some fashionable circles by Major Roberston, of Lude, who was here with his corps.

There is one commission that I must trouble you with. I lately lost a valuable seal, a present from a departed friend which vexes me much.

I have gotten one of your Highland pebbles, which I fancy would make a very decent one; and I want to cut my armorial bearing on it; will you be so obliging as inquire what will be the expense of such a business? I do not know that my name is matriculated, as the heralds call it, at all; but I have invented arms for myself, so you know I shall be chief of the name; and, by courtesy of Scotland, will likewise be entitled to supporters. These, however, I do not intend having on my seal. I am a bit of a herald, and shall give you, secundum artem, my arms. On a field, azure, a holly-bush, seeded, proper, in base; a shepherd's pipe and crook, saltier-wise, also proper in chief. On a wreath of the colours, a wood lark perching on a sprig of bay-tree, proper, for crest. Two mottos; round the top of the crest, Wood-notes wild: at the bottom of the shield, in the usual place, Better a wee bush than nae bield. By the shepherd's pipe and crook I do not mean the nonsense of painters of Arcadia, but a stock and horn, and a club, such as you see at the head of Allan Ramsay, in Allan's quarto edition of the Gentle Shepherd. By the bye, do you know Allan? He must be a man of very great genius-Why is he not more known?-Has he no patrons? or do "Poverty's cold wind and crushing rain beat keen and heavy" on him! I once, and but once, got a glance of that noble edition of the noblest pastoral in the world; and dear as it was, I mean[455] dear as to my pocket, I would have bought it; but I was told that it was printed and engraved for subscribers only. He is the only artist who has hit genuine pastoral costume. What, my dear Cunningham, is there in riches, that they narrow and harden the heart so? I think, that were I as rich as the sun, I should be as generous as the day; but as I have no

reason to imagine my soul a nobler one than any other man's, I must conclude that wealth imparts a bird-lime quality to the possessor, at which the man, in his native poverty, would have revolted. What has led me to this, is the idea, of such merit as Mr. Allan possesses, and such riches us a nabob or government contractor possesses, and why they do not form a mutual league. Let wealth shelter and cherish unprotected merit, and the gratitude and celebrity of that merit will richly repay it.
R. B.

CCXLVIII.

TO MR. THOMSON.
[Burns in these careless words makes us acquainted with one of his sweetest songs.]
20th March, 1793.
My dear Sir,
The song prefixed ["Mary Morison"[207]] is one of my juvenile works. I leave it in your hands. I do not think it very remarkable, either for its merits or demerits. It is impossible (at least I feel it so in my stinted powers) to be always original, entertaining, and witty.
What is become of the list, andc., of your songs? I shall be out of all temper with you, by and bye. I have always looked on myself as the prince of indolent correspondence, and valued myself accordingly; and I will not, cannot, bear rivalship from you, nor anybody else.
R. B.

FOOTNOTES:

[207] Song CLXXXVIII.

CCXLIX.

TO MR. THOMSON.
[For the "Wandering Willie" of this communication Thomson offered several corrections.]
March, 1793.
Here awa, there awa, wandering Willie, Now tired with wandering, haud awa hame; Come to my bosom, my ae only dearie, And tell me thou bring'st me my Willie the same.
Loud blew the cauld winter winds at our parting; It was na the blast brought the tear in my e'e; Now welcome the simmer, and welcome my Willie, The simmer to nature, my Willie to me.
Ye hurricanes, rest in the cave o' your slumbers! Oh how your wild horrors

a lover alarms! Awaken, ye breezes! blow gently, ye billows! And waft my dear laddie ance mair to my arms.
But if he's forgotten his faithfulest Nannie, O still flow between us, thou wide, roaring main; May I never see it, may I never trow it, But, dying, believe that my Willie's my ain!
I leave it to you, my dear Sir, to determine whether the above, or the old "Thro' the lang muir I have followed my Willie," be the best.
R. B.

CCL.

TO MISS BENSON.
[Miss Benson, when this letter was written, was on a visit to Arbigland, the beautiful seat of Captain Craik; she is now Mrs. Basil Montagu.]
Dumfries, 21st March, 1793.
Madam,
Among many things for which I envy those hale, long-lived old fellows before the flood, is this in particular, that when they met with anybody after their own heart, they had a charming long prospect of many, many happy meetings with them in after-life.
Now in this short, stormy, winter day of our fleeting existence, when you now and then, in the Chapter of Accidents, meet an individual whose acquaintance is a real acquisition, there are all the probabilities against you, that you shall never meet with that valued character more. On the other hand, brief as this miserable being is, it is none of the least of the miseries belonging to it, that if there is any miscreant whom you hate, or creature whom you despise, the ill-run of the chances shall be so against you, that in the overtakings, turnings, and jostlings of life, pop, at some unlucky corner, eternally comes the wretch upon you, and[456] will not allow your indignation or contempt a moment's repose. As I am a sturdy believer in the powers of darkness, I take these to be the doings of that old author of mischief, the devil. It is well-known that he has some kind of short-hand way of taking down our thoughts, and I make no doubt he is perfectly acquainted with my sentiments respecting Miss Benson: how much I admired her abilities and valued her worth, and how very fortunate I thought myself in her acquaintance. For this last reason, my dear Madam, I must entertain no hopes of the very great pleasure of meeting with you again.
Miss Hamilton tells me that she is sending a packet to you, and I beg leave to send you the enclosed sonnet, though, to tell you the real truth, the sonnet is a mere pretence, that I may have the opportunity of declaring with how much respectful esteem I have the honour to be, andc.
R. B.

CCLI.

TO PATRICK MILLER, ESQ.,
OF DALSWINTON.
[The time to which Burns alludes was the period of his occupation of Ellisland.]
Dumfries, April, 1793.
Sir,
My poems having just come out in another edition, will you do me the honour to accept of a copy? A mark of my gratitude to you, as a gentleman to whose goodness I have been much indebted; of my respect for you, as a patriot who, in a venal, sliding age, stands forth the champion of the liberties of my country; and of my veneration for you, as a man, whose benevolence of heart does honour to human nature.
There was a time, Sir, when I was your dependent: this language then would have been like the vile incense of flattery-I could not have used it. Now that connexion is at an end, do me the honour to accept this honest tribute of respect from, Sir,
Your much indebted humble servant,
R. B.

CCLII.

TO MR. THOMSON.
[This review of our Scottish lyrics is well worth the attention of all who write songs, read songs, or sing songs.]
7th April, 1793.
Thank you, my dear Sir, for your packet. You cannot imagine how much this business of composing for your publication has added to my enjoyments. What with my early attachment to ballads, your book, andc., ballad-making is now as completely my hobby-horse as ever fortification was Uncle Toby's; so I'll e'en canter it away till I come to the limit of my race-God grant that I may take the right side of the winning post!-and then cheerfully looking back on the honest folks with whom I have been happy, I shall say or sing, "Sae merry as we a' hae been!" and, raising my last looks to the whole human race, the last words of the voice of "Coila"[208] shall be, "Good night, and joy be wi' you a'!" So much for my last words: now for a few present remarks, as they have occurred at random, on looking over your list.
The first lines of "The last time I came o'er the moor," and several other lines in it, are beautiful; but, in my opinion-pardon me, revered shade of Ramsay!-the song is unworthy of the divine air. I shall try to make or mend.

"For ever, Fortune, wilt thou prove,"[209] is a charming song; but "Logan burn and Logan braes" is sweetly susceptible of rural imagery; I'll try that likewise, and, if I succeed, the other song may class among the English ones. I remember the two last lines of a verse in some of the old songs of "Logan Water" (for I know a good many different ones) which I think pretty:-

"Now my dear lad maun faces his faes, Far, far frae me and Logan braes."[210]

"My Patie is a lover gay," is unequal. "His mind is never muddy," is a muddy expression indeed.

"Then I'll resign and marry Pate, And syne my cockernony-"

This is surely far unworthy of Ramsay or your book. My song, "Rigs of barley," to the same tune, does not altogether please me; but if I can mend it, and thrash a few loose sentiments

.[457] out of it, I will submit it to your consideration. "The lass o' Patie's mill" is one of Ramsay's best songs; but there is one loose sentiment in it, which my much-valued friend Mr. Erskine will take into his critical consideration. In Sir John Sinclair's statistical volumes, are two claims-one, I think from Aberdeenshire, and the other from Ayrshire-for the honour of this song. The following anecdote, which I had from the present Sir William Cunningham of Robertland, who had it of the late John, Earl of Loudon, I can, on such authorities, believe:

Allan Ramsay was residing at Loudon-castle with the then Earl, father to Earl John; and one forenoon, riding or walking, out together, his lordship and Allan passed a sweet romantic spot on Irvine water, still called "Patie's mill," where a bonnie lass was "tedding hay, bare-headed on the green." My lord observed to Allan, that it would be a fine theme for a song. Ramsay took the hint, and, lingering behind, he composed the first sketch of it, which he produced at dinner.

"One day I heard Mary say,"[211] is a fine song; but, for consistency's sake, alter the name "Adonis." Were there ever such banns published, as a purpose of marriage between Adonis and Mary! I agree with you that my song, "There's nought but care on every hand," is much superior to "Poortith cauld." The original song, "The mill, mill, O!"[212] though excellent, is, on account of delicacy, inadmissible; still I like the title, and think a Scottish song would suit the notes best; and let your chosen song, which is very pretty, follow as an English set. "The Banks of the Dee" is, you know, literally "Langolee," to slow time. The song is well enough, but has some false imagery in it: for instance,

"And sweetly the nightingale sang from the tree."

In the first place, the nightingale sings in a low bush, but never from a tree; and in the second place, there never was a nightingale seen or heard on the banks of the Dee, or on the banks of any other river in Scotland. Exotic rural imagery is always comparatively flat.[213] If I could hit on another stanza, equal to "The small birds rejoice," andc., I do myself honestly avow, that I think it a superior song.[214] "John Anderson, my jo"-the song to this tune in Johnson's Museum, is my composition, and I think it not my worst:[215] if it suit you, take it, and welcome. Your collection of sentimental and pathetic songs, is, in my opinion, very complete; but not so your comic ones. Where are "Tullochgorum," "Lumps o' puddin," "Tibbie Fowler," and several others, which, in my humble judgment, are well worthy of preservation? There is also one sentimental song of mine in the Museum, which never was known out of the immediate neighbourhood, until I got it taken down from a country girl's singing. It is called "Craigieburn wood," and, in the opinion of Mr. Clarke, is one of the sweetest Scottish songs. He is quite an enthusiast about it; and I would take his taste in Scottish music against the taste of most connoisseurs.

You are quite right in inserting the last five in your list, though they are certainly Irish. "Shepherds, I have lost my love!" is to me a heavenly air-what would you think of a set of Scottish verses to it? I have made one to it a good while ago, which I think * * *, but in its original state it is not quite a lady's song. I enclose an altered, not amended copy for you,[216] if you choose to set the tune to it, and let the Irish verses follow.

Mr. Erskine's songs are all pretty, but his "Lone-vale"[217] is divine.

Yours, andc.

R. B.

Let me know just how you like these random hints.

FOOTNOTES:

[208] Burns here calls himself the "Voice of Coila," in imitation of Ossian, who denominates himself the "Voice of Cona."-Currie.

[209] By Thomson, not the musician, but the poet.

[210] This song is not old; its author, the late John Mayne, long outlived Burns

[211] By Crawfurd.

[212] By Ramsay.

[213] The author, John Tait, a writer to the Signet and some time Judge of the police-court in Edinburgh, assented to this, and altered the line to,

"And sweetly the wood-pigeon cooed from the tree."

[214] Song CXXXIX.

[215] Song LXXX.

[216] Song CLXXVII.

[217]

"How sweet this lone vale, and how soothing to feeling, Yon nightingale's notes which in melody meet."

The song has found its way into several collections.

CCLIII.

TO MR. THOMSON.

[The letter to which this is in part an answer, Currie says, contains many observations on Scottish songs, and on the manner of adapting the words to the music, which at Mr. Thomson's desire are suppressed.]

April, 1793.

I have yours, my dear Sir, this moment. I shall answer it and your former letter, in my desultory way of saying whatever comes uppermost.[458]

The business of many of our tunes wanting, at the beginning, what fiddlers call a starting-note, is often a rub to us poor rhymers.

"There's braw, braw lads on Yarrow braes, That wander through the blooming heather,"

you may alter to

"Braw, braw lads on Yarrow braes, Ye wander," andc.

My song, "Here awa, there awa," as amended by Mr. Erskine, I entirely approve of, and return you.

Give me leave to criticise your taste in the only thing in which it is, in my opinion, reprehensible. You know I ought to know something of my own trade. Of pathos, sentiment, and point, you are a complete judge; but there is a quality more necessary than either in a song, and which is the very essence of a ballad-I mean simplicity: now, if I mistake not, this last feature you are a little apt to sacrifice to the foregoing.

Ramsay, as every other poet, has not been always equally happy in his pieces; still I cannot approve of taking such liberties with an author as Mr. Walker proposes doing with "The last time I came o'er the moor." Let a poet, if he choose, take up the idea of another, and work it into a piece of his own; but to mangle the works of the poor bard, whose tuneful tongue is now mute for ever, in the dark and narrow house-by Heaven, 'twould be sacrilege! I grant that Mr. W.'s version is an improvement; but I know Mr. W. well, and esteem him much; let him mend the song, as the Highlander mended his gun-he gave it a new stock, a new lock, and a new barrel.

I do not, by this, object to leaving out improper stanzas, where that can be done without spoiling the whole. One stanza in "The lass o' Patie's mill" must be left out: the song will be nothing worse for it. I am not sure if we can take the same liberty with "Corn rigs are bonnie." Perhaps it might want the last stanza, and be the better for it. "Cauld kail in Aberdeen," you must leave with me yet awhile. I have vowed to have a song to that air, on the lady whom I attempted to celebrate in the verses, "Poortith cauld and restless love." At any rate, my other song, "Green grow the rashes," will never suit. That song is current in Scotland under the old title, and to the merry old tune of that name, which, of course, would mar the progress of your song to celebrity. Your book will be the standard of Scots songs for the future: let this idea ever keep your judgment on the alarm.

I send a song on a celebrated toast in this country, to suit "Bonnie Dundee." I send you also a ballad to the "Mill, mill, O!"[218]

"The last time I came o'er the moor," I would fain attempt to make a Scots song for, and let Ramsay's be the English set. You shall hear from me soon. When you go to London on this business, can you come by Dumfries? I have still several MS. Scots airs by me, which I have picked up, mostly from the singing of country lasses. They please me vastly; but your learned lugs would perhaps be displeased with the very feature for which I like them. I call them simple; you would pronounce them silly. Do you know a fine air called "Jackie Hume's Lament?" I have a song of considerable merit to that air. I'll enclose you both the song and tune, as I had them ready to send to Johnson's Museum.[219] I send you likewise, to me, a beautiful little air, which I had taken down from viva voce.[220]

Adieu.

R. B.

FOOTNOTES:

[218] Songs CXCII. and CXCIII.
[219] Song CXCIV.
[220] Song CXCVIII.

CCLIV.

TO MR. THOMSON.

[Thomson, it would appear by his answer to this letter, was at issue with Burns on the subject-matter of simplicity: the former seems to have desired a sort of diplomatic and varnished style: the latter felt that elegance and simplicity were "sisters twin."]

April, 1793.

My dear Sir,

I had scarcely put my last letter into the post-office, when I took up the subject of "The last time I came o'er the moor," and ere I slept drew the outlines of the foregoing.[221] How I have succeeded, I leave on this, as on every other occasion, to you to decide. I own my vanity is flattered, when you give my songs a place in your elegant and superb work; but to be of service to the work is my first wish. As I have [459] often told you, I do not in a single instance wish you, out of compliment to me, to insert anything of mine. One hint let me give you-whatever Mr. Pleyel does, let him not alter one iota of the original Scottish airs, I mean in the song department,

but let our national music preserve its native features. They are, I own, frequently wild and irreducible to the more modern rules; but on that very eccentricity, perhaps, depends a great part of their effect.
R. B.

FOOTNOTES:

[221] Song CCXXXIV.

CCLV.

TO JOHN FRANCIS ERSKINE, ESQ.,
OF M A R.

[This remarkable letter has been of late the subject of some controversy: Mr. Findlater, who happened then to be in the Excise, is vehement in defence of the "honourable board," and is certain that Burns has misrepresented the conduct of his very generous masters. In answer to this it has been urged that the word of the poet has in no other thing been questioned: that in the last moments of his life, he solemnly wrote this letter into his memorandum-book, and that the reproof of Mr. Corbet, is given by him either as a quotation from a paper or an exact recollection of the words used: the expressions, "not to think" and be "silent and obedient" are underlined.]

Dumfries, 13th April, 1793.

Sir,

Degenerate as human nature is said to be, and in many instances, worthless and unprincipled it is, still there are bright examples to the contrary; examples that even in the eyes of superior beings, must shed a lustre on the name of man.

Such an example have I now before me, when you, Sir, came forward to patronize and befriend a distant, obscure stranger, merely because poverty had made him helpless, and his British hardihood of mind had provoked the arbitrary wantonness of power. My much esteemed friend, Mr. Riddel of Glenriddel, has just read me a paragraph of a letter he had from you. Accept, Sir, of the silent throb of gratitude; for words would but mock the emotions of my soul.

You have been misinformed as to my final dismission from the Excise; I am still in the service.-Indeed, but for the exertions of a gentleman who must be known to you, Mr. Graham of Fintray, a gentleman who has ever been my warm and generous friend, I had, without so much us a hearing, or the slightest previous intimation, been turned adrift, with my helpless family, to all the horrors of want. Had I had any other resource, probably I might have saved them the trouble of a dismission; but the little money I gained by my publication, is almost every guinea embarked, to save from ruin an only brother, who, though one of the worthiest, is by no means one of the most fortunate of men.

In my defence to their accusations, I said, that whatever might be my sentiments of republics, ancient or modern, as to Britain, I abjured the idea!-That a constitution, which, in its original principles, experience had proved to be every way fitted for our happiness in society, it would be insanity to sacrifice to an untried visionary theory:-that, in consideration of my being situated in a department, however humble, immediately in the hands of people in power, I had forborne taking any active part, either personally, or as an author, in the present business of Reform. But, that, where I must declare my sentiments, I would say there existed a system of corruption between the executive power and the representative part of the legislature, which boded no good to our glorious constitution; and which every patriotic Briton must wish to see amended.-Some such sentiments as these, I stated in a letter to my generous patron, Mr. Graham, which he laid before the Board at large; where, it seems, my last remark gave great offence; and one of our supervisors-general, a Mr. Corbet, was instructed to inquire on the spot, and to document me-"that my business was to act, not to think; and that whatever might be men or measures, it was for me to be silent and obedient."

Mr. Corbet was likewise my steady friend; so between Mr. Graham and him, I have been partly forgiven; only I understand that all hopes of my getting officially forward, are blasted.

Now, Sir, to the business in which I would more immediately interest you. The partiality of my countrymen has brought me forward as a man of genius, and has given me a character to support. In the Poet I have avowed manly and independent sentiments, which I trust will be found in the man. Reasons of no less weight than the support of a wife and family, have pointed out as the eligible, and, situated as I was, the only eligible line of life for me, my present occupation. Still my honest fame is my[460] dearest concern; and a thousand times have I trembled at the idea of those degrading epithets that malice or misrepresentation may affix to my name. I have often, in blasting anticipation, listened to some future hackney scribbler, with the heavy malice of savage stupidity, exulting in his hireling paragraphs-"Burns, notwithstanding the fanfaronade of independence to be found in his works, and after having been held forth to public view and to public estimation as a man of some genius, yet quite destitute of resources within himself to support his borrowed dignity, he dwindled into a paltry exciseman, and slunk out the rest of his insignificant existence in the meanest of pursuits, and among the vilest of mankind."

In your illustrious hands, Sir, permit me to lodge my disavowal and defiance of these slanderous falsehoods. Burns was a poor man from birth, and an exciseman by necessity: but I will say it! the sterling of his honest worth, no poverty could debase, and his independent British mind, oppression might bend, but could not subdue. Have not I, to me, a more precious stake in my country's welfare than the richest dukedom in it?-I have a large family of children, and the prospect of many more. I have three sons, who, I see already, have brought into the world souls ill qualified to inhabit the bodies of slaves.-Can I look tamely on, and see any machination to wrest from them the birthright of my boys,-the little independent Britons, in whose veins runs my own blood?-No! I will not! should my heart's blood stream around my attempt to defend it!

Does any man tell me, that my full efforts can be of no service; and that it does not belong to my humble station to meddle with the concern of a nation?

I can tell him, that it is on such individuals as I, that a nation has to rest, both for the hand of support, and the eye of intelligence. The uninformed mob may swell a nation's bulk; and the titled, tinsel, courtly throng, may be its feathered ornament; but the number of those who are elevated enough in life to reason and to reflect; yet low enough to keep clear of the venal contagion of a court!-these are a nation's strength.

I know not how to apologize for the impertinent length of this epistle; but one small request I must ask of you further-when you have honoured this letter with a perusal, please to commit it to the flames. Burns, in whose behalf you have so generously interested yourself, I have here in his native colours drawn as he is, but should any of the people in whose hands is the very bread he eats, get the least knowledge of the picture, it would ruin the poor bard for ever!

My poems having just come out in another edition, I beg leave to present you with a copy, as a small mark of that high esteem and ardent gratitude, with which I have the honour to be,

Sir,

Your deeply indebted,

And ever devoted humble servant,

R. B.

CCLVI.

TO ROBERT AINSLIE, ESQ.

["Up tails a', by the light o' the moon," was the name of a Scottish air, to which the devil danced with the witches of Fife, on Magus Moor, as reported by a warlock, in that credible work, "Satan's Invisible World discovered."]

April 26, 1793.

I am d-mnably out of humour, my dear Ainslie, and that is the reason, why

I take up the pen to you: 'tis the nearest way (probatum est) to recover my spirits again.

I received your last, and was much entertained with it; but I will not at this time, nor at any other time, answer it.-Answer a letter? I never could answer a letter in my life!-I have written many a letter in return for letters I have received; but then-they were original matter-spurt-away! zig here, zag there; as if the devil that, my Grannie (an old woman indeed) often told me, rode on will-o'-wisp, or, in her more classic phrase, Spunkie, were looking over my elbow.-Happy thought that idea has engendered in my head! Spunkie-thou shalt henceforth be my symbol signature, and tutelary genius! Like thee, hap-step-and-lowp, here-awa-there-awa, higglety-pigglety, pell-mell, hither-and-yon, ram-stam, happy-go-lucky, up-tails-a'-by-the-light-o'-the-moon,-has been, is, and shall be, my progress through the mosses and moors of this vile, bleak, barren wilderness of a life of ours.

Come then, my guardian spirit, like thee may I skip away, amusing myself by and at my own light: and if any opaque-souled lubber of mankind complain that my elfine, lambent, glim[461] merous wanderings have misled his stupid steps over precipices, or into bogs, let the thickheaded blunderbuss recollect, that he is not Spunkie:-that

"Spunkie's wanderings could not copied be: Amid these perils none durst walk but he."-

I have no doubt but scholar-craft may be caught, as a Scotchman catches the itch,-by friction. How else can you account for it, that born blockheads, by mere dint of handling books, grow so wise that even they themselves are equally convinced of and surprised at their own parts? I once carried this philosophy to that degree that in a knot of country folks who had a library amongst them, and who, to the honour of their good sense, made me factotum in the business; one of our members, a little, wise-looking, squat, upright, jabbering body of a tailor, I advised him, instead of turning over the leaves, to bind the book on his back.-Johnnie took the hint; and as our meetings were every fourth Saturday, and Pricklouse having a good Scots mile to walk in coming, and, of course, another in returning, Bodkin was sure to lay his hand on some heavy quarto, or ponderous folio, with, and under which, wrapt up in his gray plaid, he grew wise, as he grew weary, all the way home. He carried this so far, that an old musty Hebrew concordance, which we had in a present from a neighbouring priest, by mere dint of applying it, as doctors do a blistering plaster, between his shoulders, Stitch, in a dozen pilgrimages, acquired as much rational theology as the said priest had done by forty years perusal of the pages.

Tell me, and tell me truly, what you think of this theory.

Yours,

Spunkie.

CCLVII.

TO MISS KENNEDY.

[Miss Kennedy was one of that numerous band of ladies who patronized the poet in Edinburgh; she was related to the Hamiltons of Mossgiel.]

Madam,

Permit me to present you with the enclosed song as a small though grateful tribute for the honour of your acquaintance. I have, in these verses, attempted some faint sketches of your portrait in the unembellished simple manner of descriptive truth.-Flattery, I leave to your lovers, whose exaggerating fancies may make them imagine you still nearer perfection than you really are.

Poets, Madam, of all mankind, feel most forcibly the powers of beauty; as, if they are really poets of nature's making, their feelings must be finer, and their taste more delicate than most of the world. In the cheerful bloom of spring, or the pensive mildness of autumn; the grandeur of summer, or the hoary majesty of winter, the poet feels a charm unknown to the rest of his species. Even the sight of a fine flower, or the company of a fine woman (by far the finest part of God's works below), have sensations for the poetic heart that the herd of man are strangers to.-On this last account, Madam, I am, as in many other things, indebted to Mr. Hamilton's kindness in introducing me to you. Your lovers may view you with a wish, I look on you with pleasure; their hearts, in your presence, may glow with desire, mine rises with admiration.

That the arrows of misfortune, however they should, as incident to humanity, glance a slight wound, may never reach your heart-that the snares of villany may never beset you in the road of life-that innocence may hand you by the path of honour to the dwelling of peace, is the sincere wish of him who has the honour to be, andc.

R. B.

CCLVIII.

TO MR. THOMSON.

[The name of the friend who fell a sacrifice to those changeable times, has not been mentioned: it is believed he was of the west country.]

June, 1793.

When I tell you, my dear Sir, that a friend of mine in whom I am much interested, has fallen a sacrifice to these accursed times, you will easily allow that it might unhinge me for doing any good among ballads. My own loss as to pecuniary matters is trifling; but the total ruin of a much-loved friend is a loss indeed. Pardon my seeming inattention to your last commands.

I cannot alter the disputed lines in the "Mill[462] Mill, O!"[222] What you think a defect, I esteem as a positive beauty; so you see how doctors differ. I shall now, with as much alacrity as I can muster, go on with your commands.

You know Frazer, the hautboy-player in Edinburgh-he is here, instructing a band of music for a fencible corps quartered in this county. Among many of his airs that please me, there is one, well known as a reel, by the name of "The Quaker's Wife;" and which, I remember, a grand-aunt of mine used to sing, by the name of "Liggeram Cosh, my bonnie wee lass." Mr. Frazer plays it slow, and with an expression that quite charms me. I became such an enthusiast about it, that I made a song for it, which I here subjoin, and enclose Frazer's set of the tune. If they hit your fancy, they are at your service; if not, return me the tune, and I will put it in Johnson's Museum. I think the song is not in my worst manner.

Blythe hae I been on yon hill.[223]

I should wish to hear how this pleases you.

R. B.

FOOTNOTES:

[222] "The lines were the third and fourth:

'Wi' mony a sweet babe fatherless, And mony a widow mourning.'

As our poet had maintained a long silence, and the first number of Mr. Thomson's musical work was in the press, this gentleman ventured, by Mr. Erskine's advice, to substitute for them, in that publication.

'And eyes again with pleasure beam'd That had been blear'd with mourning.'

Though better suited to the music, these lines are inferior to the original."-Currie.

[223] Song CXV.

CCLIX.

TO MR. THOMSON.

[Against the mighty oppressors of the earth the poet was ever ready to set the sharpest shafts of his wrath: the times in which he wrote were sadly out of sorts.]

June 25th, 1793.

Have you ever, my dear Sir, felt your bosom ready to burst with indignation, on reading of those mighty villains who divide kingdoms, desolate provinces, and lay nations waste, out of the wantonness of ambition, or often from still more ignoble passions? In a mood of this kind to-day I recollected the air of "Logan Water," and it occurred to me that its querulous melody probably had its origin from the plaintive indignation of some swelling, suffering heart, fired at the tyrannic strides of some public destroyer, and overwhelmed with private distress, the consequence of a country's ruin. If I have done anything at all like justice to my feelings, the following song, composed in three-quarters of an hour's meditation in my elbow-chair, ought to have some merit:-

O Logan, sweetly didst thou glide.[224]

Do you know the following beautiful little fragment, in Wotherspoon's collection of Scots songs?[225]

Air-"Hughie Graham."

"Oh gin my love were yon red rose, That grows upon the castle wa'; And I mysel' a drap o' dew, Into her bonnie breast to fa'!

"Oh there, beyond expression blest, I'd feast on beauty a' the night, Seal'd on her silk-saft faulds to rest, Till fley'd awa by Phœbus light!"

This thought is inexpressibly beautiful; and quite, so far as I know, original. It is too short for a song, else I would forswear you altogether unless you gave it a place. I have often tried to eke a stanza to it, but in vain. After balancing myself for a musing five minutes, on the hind legs of my elbow-chair, I produced the following.

The verses are far inferior to the foregoing, I frankly confess: but if worthy of insertion at all, they might be first in place; as every poet who knows anything of his trade, will husband his best thoughts for a concluding stroke.

Oh were my love yon lilac fair, Wi' purple blossoms to the spring; And I a bird to shelter there, When wearied on my little wing!

How I wad mourn, when it was torn By autumn wild and winter rude! But I wad sing on wanton wing, When youthfu' May its bloom renewed.[226]

R. B.

FOOTNOTES:

[224] Song CXCVI.

[225] Better known as Herd's. Wotherspoon was one of the publishers.

[226] See Song CXCVII.

[463]

CCLX.

TO MR. THOMSON.

[Thomson, in his reply to the preceding letter, laments that anything should untune the feelings of the poet, and begs his acceptance of five pounds, as a small mark of his gratitude for his beautiful songs.]

July 2d, 1793.

My dear Sir,

I have just finished the following ballad, and, as I do think it in my best style, I send it you. Mr. Clarke, who wrote down the air from Mrs. Burns's wood-note wild, is very fond of it, and has given it a celebrity by teaching it to some young ladies of the first fashion here. If you do not like the air enough to give it a place in your collection, please return it. The song you may keep, as I remember it.

There was a lass, and she was fair.[227]

I have some thoughts of inserting in your index, or in my notes, the names of the fair ones, the themes of my songs. I do not mean the name at full; but dashes or asterisms, so as ingenuity may find them out.

The heroine of the foregoing is Miss M'Murdo, daughter to Mr. M'Murdo, of Drumlanrig, one of your subscribers. I have not painted her in the rank which she holds in life, but in the dress and character of a cottager.

R. B.

FOOTNOTES:

[227] Song CXCVIII.

CCLXI.

TO MR. THOMSON.

[Burns in this letter speaks of the pecuniary present which Thomson sent him, in a lofty and angry mood: he who published poems by subscription might surely have accepted, without any impropriety, payment for his songs.]

July, 1793.

I assure you, my dear Sir, that you truly hurt me with your pecuniary parcel. It degrades me in my own eyes. However, to return it would savour of affectation; but, as to any more traffic of that debtor and creditor kind, I swear by that honour which crowns the upright statue of Robert Burns's Integrity-on the least motion of it, I will indignantly spurn the by-past transaction, and from that moment commence entire stranger to you! Burns's character for generosity of sentiment and independence of mind, will, I trust, long outlive any of his wants which the cold unfeeling ore can supply; at least, I will take care that such a character he shall deserve.

Thank you for my copy of your publication. Never did my eyes behold in any musical work such elegance and correctness. Your preface, too, is admirably written, only your partiality to me has made you say too much: however, it will bind me down to double every effort in the future progress of the work. The following are a few remarks on the songs in the list you sent me. I never copy what I write to you, so I may be often tautological, or perhaps contradictory.

"The Flowers o' the Forest," is charming as a poem, and should be, and must be, set to the notes; but, though out of your rule, the three stanzas beginning,

"I've seen the smiling of fortune beguiling,"

are worthy of a place, were it but to immortalize the author of them, who is an old lady of my acquaintance, and at this moment living in Edinburgh. She is a Mrs. Cockburn, I forget of what place, but from Roxburghshire.[228] What a charming apostrophe is

"O fickle fortune, why this cruel sporting, Why thus perplex us, poor sons of a day?"

The old ballad, "I wish I were where Helen lies," is silly to contemptibility. My alteration of it, in Johnson's, is not much better. Mr. Pinkerton, in his, what he calls, ancient ballads (many of them notorious, though beautiful enough, forgeries), has the best set. It is full of his own interpolations-but no matter.

In my next I will suggest to your consideration a few songs which may have escaped your hurried notice. In the meantime allow me to congratulate you now, as a brother of the quill. You have committed your character and fame, which will now be tried, for ages to come, by the illustrious jury of the Sons and Daughters of Taste-all whom poesy can please or music charm.

Being a bard of nature, I have some pretensions to second sight; and I am warranted by the spirit to foretell and affirm, that your great-grand-child will hold up your volumes, and say, with honest pride, "This so much admired selection was the work of my ancestor!"

R. B.

FOOTNOTES:

[228] Miss Rutherford, of Fernilee in Selkirkshire, by marriage Mrs. Patrick Cockburn, of Ormiston. She died in 1794, at an advanced age.

CCLXII.

TO MR. THOMSON.

[Stephen Clarke, whose name is at this strange note, was a musician and composer; he was a clever man, and had a high opinion of his own powers.]

August, 1793.

My dear Thomson,

I hold the pen for our friend Clarke, who at present is studying the music of the spheres at my elbow. The Georgium Sidus he thinks is rather out of tune; so, until he rectify that matter, he cannot stoop to terrestrial affairs.

He sends you six of the rondeau subjects, and if more are wanted, he says

you shall have them.
Confound your long stairs!
S. Clarke.

CCLXIII.

TO MR. THOMSON.

["Phillis the Fair" endured much at the hands of both Burns and Clarke. The young lady had reason to complain, when the poet volunteered to sing the imaginary love of that fantastic fiddler.]

August, 1793.

Your objection, my dear Sir, to the passages in my song of "Logan Water," is right in one instance; but it is difficult to mend it: if I can, I will. The other passage you object to does not appear in the same light to me.

I have tried my hand on "Robin Adair," and, you will probably think, with little success; but it is such a cursed, cramp, out-of-the-way measure, that I despair of doing anything better to it.

While larks with little wing.[229]

So much for namby-pamby. I may, after all, try my hand on it in Scots verse. There I always find myself most at home.

I have just put the last hand to the song I meant for "Cauld kail in Aberdeen." If it suits you to insert it, I shall be pleased, as the heroine is a favourite of mine; if not, I shall also be pleased; because I wish, and will be glad, to see you act decidedly on the business. 'Tis a tribute as a man of taste, and as an editor, which you owe yourself.

R. B.

FOOTNOTES:

[229] Song CXCIX.

CCLXIV.

TO MR. THOMSON.

[The infusion of Highland airs and north country subjects into the music and songs of Scotland, has invigorated both: Burns, who had a fine ear as well as a fine taste, was familiar with all, either Highland or Lowland.]

August, 1793.

That crinkum-crankum tune, "Robin Adair," has run so in my head, and I succeeded so ill in my last attempt, that I have ventured, in this morning's walk, one essay more. You, my dear Sir, will remember an unfortunate part of our worthy friend Cunningham's story, which happened about three years ago. That struck my fancy, and I endeavoured to do the idea justice as follows:

Had I a cave on some wild distant shore.[230]

By the way, I have met with a musical Highlander in Breadalbane's Fencibles, which are quartered here, who assures me that he well remembers his mother singing Gaelic songs to both "Robin Adair," and "Grammachree." They certainly have more of the Scotch than Irish taste in them.

This man comes from the vicinity of Inverness: so it could not be any intercourse with Ireland that could bring them; except, what I shrewdly suspect to be the case, the wandering minstrels, harpers, and pipers, used to go frequently errant through the wilds both of Scotland and Ireland, and so some favourite airs might be common to both. A case in point-they have lately, in Ireland, published an Irish air, as they say, called "Caun du delish." The fact is, in a publication of Corri's, a great while ago, you will find the same air, called a Highland one, with a Gaelic song set to it. Its name there, I think, is "Oran Gaoil," and a fine air it is. Do ask honest Allan or the Rev. Gaelic parson, about these matters.

R. B.

FOOTNOTES:

[230] Song CC.

CCLXV.

TO MR. THOMSON.

[While Burns composed songs, Thomson got some of the happiest embodied by David Allan, the painter, whose illustrations of the Gentle Shepherd had been favourably received. But save when an old man was admitted to the scene, his designs may be regarded as failures: his maidens were coarse and his old wives rigwiddie carlins.]

[465]

August, 1793.

My dear Sir,

"Let me in this ae night" I will reconsider. I am glad that you are pleased with my song, "Had I a cave," andc., as I liked it myself.

I walked out yesterday evening with a volume of the Museum in my hand, when turning up "Allan Water," "What numbers shall the muse repeat," andc., as the words appeared to me rather unworthy of so fine an air, and recollecting that it is on your list, I sat and raved under the shade of an old thorn, till I wrote one to suit the measure. I may be wrong; but I think it not in my worst style. You must know, that in Ramsay's Tea-table, where the modern song first appeared, the ancient name of the tune, Allan says, is

"Allan Water," or "My love Annie's very bonnie." This last has certainly been a line of the original song; so I took up the idea, and, as you will see, have introduced the line in its place, which I presume it formerly occupied; though I likewise give you a choosing line, if it should not hit the cut of your fancy:

By Allan stream I chanced to rove.[231]

Bravo! say I; it is a good song. Should you think so too (not else) you can set the music to it, and let the other follow as English verses.

Autumn is my propitious season. I make more verses in it than all the year else. God bless you!

R. B.

FOOTNOTES:

[231] Song CCI.

CCLXVI.

TO MR. THOMSON.

[Phillis, or Philadelphia M'Murdo, in whose honour Burns composed the song beginning "Adown winding Nith I did wander," and several others, died September 5th, 1825.]

August, 1793.

Is "Whistle, and I'll come to you, my lad," one of your airs? I admire it much; and yesterday I set the following verses to it. Urbani, whom I have met with here, begged them of me, as he admires the air much; but as I understand that he looks with rather an evil eye on your work, I did not choose to comply. However, if the song does not suit your taste I may possibly send it him. The set of the air which I had in my eye, is in Johnson's Museum.

O whistle, and I'll come to you, my lad.[232]

Another favourite air of mine is, "The muckin' o' Geordie's byre." When sung slow, with expression, I have wished that it had had better poetry; that I have endeavoured to supply as follows:

Adown winding Nith I did wander.[233]

Mr. Clarke begs you to give Miss Phillis a corner in your book, as she is a particular flame of his, and out of compliment to him I have made the song. She is a Miss Phillis M'Murdo, sister to "Bonnie Jean." They are both pupils of his. You shall hear from me, the very first grist I get from my rhyming-mill.

R. B.

FOOTNOTES:

[232] Song CCII.
[233] Song CCIII.

CCLXVII.

TO MR. THOMSON.
[Burns was fond of expressive words: "Gloaming, the twilight," says Currie, "is a beautiful poetic word, which ought to be adopted in England." Burns and Scott have made the Scottish language popular over the world.]
August, 1793.
That tune, "Cauld kail," is such a favourite of yours, that I once more roved out yesterday for a gloamin-shot at the muses; when the muse that presides o'er the shores of Nith, or rather my old inspiring dearest nymph, Coila, whispered me the following. I have two reasons for thinking that it was my early, sweet simple inspirer that was by my elbow, "smooth gliding without step," and pouring the song on my glowing fancy. In the first place, since I left Coila's native haunts, not a fragment of a poet has arisen to cheer her solitary musings, by catching inspiration from her, so I more than suspect that she has followed me hither, or, at least, makes me occasional visits; secondly, the last stanza of this song I send you, is the very words that Coila taught me many years ago, and which I set to an old Scots reel in Johnson's Museum.
Come, let me take thee to my breast.[234]
If you think the above will suit your idea of [466]your favourite air, I shall be highly pleased. "The last time I came o'er the moor" I cannot meddle with, as to mending it; and the musical world have been so long accustomed to Ramsay's words, that a different song, though positively superior, would not be so well received. I am not fond of choruses to songs, so I have not made one for the foregoing.
R. B.

FOOTNOTES:

[234] Song CCIV.

CCLXVIII.

TO MR. THOMSON.
["Cauld kail in Aberdeen, and castocks in Strabogie," are words which have no connexion with the sentiment of the song which Burns wrote for the air.]
August, 1793.

Song.
Now rosy May comes in wi' flowers.[235]
So much for Davie. The chorus, you know, is to the low part of the tune. See Clarke's set of it in the Museum.
N.B. In the Museum they have drawled out the tune to twelve lines of poetry, which isnonsense. Four lines of song, and four of chorus, is the way.[236]

FOOTNOTES:

[235] Song CCV.
[236] See Song LXVII.

CCLXIX.

TO MISS CRAIK.
[Miss Helen Craik of Arbigland, had merit both as a poetess and novelist: her ballads may be compared with those of Hector M'Neil: her novels had a seasoning of satire in them.]
Dumfries, August, 1793.
Madam,
Some rather unlooked-for accidents have prevented my doing myself the honour of a second visit to Arbigland, as I was so hospitably invited, and so positively meant to have done.-However, I still hope to have that pleasure before the busy months of harvest begin.
I enclose you two of my late pieces, as some kind of return for the pleasure I have received in perusing a certain MS. volume of poems in the possession of Captain Riddel. To repay one with an old song, is a proverb, whose force, you, Madam, I know, will not allow. What is said of illustrious descent is, I believe, equally true of a talent for poetry, none ever despised it who had pretensions to it. The fates and characters of the rhyming tribe often employ my thoughts when I am disposed to be melancholy. There is not, among all the martyrologies that ever were penned, so rueful a narrative as the lives of the poets.-In the comparative view of wretches, the criterion is not what they are doomed to suffer, but how they are formed to bear. Take a being of our kind, give him a stronger imagination and a more delicate sensibility, which between them will ever engender a more ungovernable set of passions than are the usual lot of man; implant in him an irresistible impulse to some idle vagary, such as arranging wild flowers in fantastical nosegays, tracing the grasshopper to his haunt by his chirping song, watching the frisks of the little minnows in the sunny pool, or hunting after the intrigues of butterflies-in short, send him adrift after some pursuit which shall eternally mislead him from the paths of lucre, and yet curse him

with a keener relish than any man living for the pleasures that lucre can purchase; lastly, fill up the measure of his woes by bestowing on him a spurning sense of his own dignity, and you have created a wight nearly as miserable as a poet. To you, Madam, I need not recount the fairy pleasures the muse bestows to counterbalance this catalogue of evils. Bewitching poetry is like bewitching woman; she has in all ages been accused of misleading mankind from the councils of wisdom and the paths of prudence, involving them in difficulties, baiting them with poverty, branding them with infamy, and plunging them in the whirling vortex of ruin; yet, where is the man but must own that all our happiness on earth is not worthy the name-that even the holy hermit's solitary prospect of paradisiacal bliss is but the glitter of a northern sun rising over a frozen region, compared with the many pleasures, the nameless raptures that we owe to the lovely queen of the heart of man!
R. B.

CCLXX.

TO LADY GLENCAIRN.
[Burns, as the concluding paragraph of this letter proves, continued to the last years of his life to think of the composition of a Scottish drama, which Sir Walter[467] Scott laments he did not write, instead of pouring out multitudes of lyrics for Johnson and Thomson.]
My Lady,
The honour you have done your poor poet, in writing him so very obliging a letter, and the pleasure the enclosed beautiful verses have given him, came very seasonably to his aid, amid the cheerless gloom and sinking despondency of diseased nerves and December weather. As to forgetting the family of Glencairn, Heaven is my witness with what sincerity I could use those old verses which please me more in their rude simplicity than the most elegant lines I ever saw.
"If thee, Jerusalem, I forget, Skill part from my right hand.
My tongue to my mouth's roof let cleave, If I do thee forget, Jerusalem, and thee above My chief joy do not set."-
When I am tempted to do anything improper, I dare not, because I look on myself as accountable to your ladyship and family. Now and then, when I have the honour to be called to the tables of the great, if I happen to meet with any mortification from the stately stupidity of self-sufficient squires, or the luxurious insolence of upstart nabobs, I get above the creatures by calling to remembrance that I am patronized by the noble house of Glencairn; and at gala-times, such as new-year's day, a christening, or the kirn-night, when my punch-bowl is brought from its dusty corner and filled up in honour of the occasion, I begin with,-The Countess of Glencairn! My

good woman with the enthusiasm of a grateful heart, next cries, My Lord! and so the toast goes on until I end with Lady Harriet's little angel! whose epithalamium I have pledged myself to write.

When I received your ladyship's letter, I was just in the act of transcribing for you some verses I have lately composed; and meant to have sent them my first leisure hour, and acquainted you with my late change of life. I mentioned to my lord my fears concerning my farm. Those fears were indeed too true; it is a bargain would have ruined me, but for the lucky circumstance of my having an excise commission.

People may talk as they please, of the ignominy of the excise; 50l. a year will support my wife and children, and keep me independent of the world; and I would much rather have it said that my profession borrowed credit from me, than that I borrowed credit from my profession. Another advantage I have in this business, is the knowledge it gives me of the various shades of human character, consequently assisting me vastly in my poetic pursuits. I had the most ardent enthusiasm for the muses when nobody knew me, but myself, and that ardour is by no means cooled now that my lord Glencairn's goodness has introduced me to all the world. Not that I am in haste for the press. I have no idea of publishing, else I certainly had consulted my noble generous patron; but after acting the part of an honest man, and supporting my family, my whole wishes and views are directed to poetic pursuits. I am aware that though I were to give performances to the world superior to my former works, still if they were of the same kind with those, the comparative reception they would meet with would mortify me. I have turned my thoughts on the drama. I do not mean the stately buskin of the tragic muse.

Does not your ladyship think that an Edinburgh theatre would be more amused with affectation, folly, and whim of true Scottish growth, than manners which by far the greatest part of the audience can only know at second hand?

I have the honour to be,
Your ladyship's ever devoted
And grateful humble servant,
R. B.

CCLXXI.

TO MR. THOMSON.

[Peter Pindar, the name under which it was the pleasure of that bitter but vulgar satirist, Dr. Wolcot, to write, was a man of little lyrical talent. He purchased a good annuity for the remainder of his life, by the copyright of his works, and survived his popularity many year.]

Sept. 1793.

You may readily trust, my dear Sir, that any exertion in my power is heartily at your service. But one thing I must hint to you; the very name of Peter Pindar is of great service to your publication, so get a verse from him now and then; though I have no objection, as well as I can, to bear the burden of the business.

You know that my pretensions to musical taste are merely a few of nature's instincts, untaught and untutored by art. For this reason, many musical compositions, particularly[468] where much of the merit lies in counterpoint, however they may transport and ravish the ears of your connoisseurs, affect my simple lug no otherwise than merely as melodious din. On the other hand, by way of amends, I am delighted with many little melodies, which the learned musician despises as silly and insipid. I do not know whether the old air "Hey tuttie taitie," may rank among this number; but well I know that, with Frazer's haut-boy, it has often filled my eyes with tears. There is a tradition, which I have met with in many places in Scotland, that it was Robert Bruce's march at the battle of Bannockburn. This thought, in yesternight's evening walk, warmed me to a pitch of enthusiasm on the theme of liberty and independence, which I threw into a kind of Scottish ode, fitted to the air, that one might suppose to be the gallant Royal Scot's address to his heroic followers on the eventful morning.

Scots, wha hae wi' Wallace bled.[237]

So may God ever defend the cause of truth and liberty, as he did that day! Amen.

P.S. I showed the air to Urbani, who was highly pleased with it, and begged me to make soft verses for it; but I had no idea of giving myself any trouble on the subject, till the accidental recollection of that glorious struggle for freedom, associated with the glowing ideas of some other struggles of the same nature, not quite so ancient, roused my rhyming mania. Clarke's set of the tune, with his bass, you will find in the Museum, though I am afraid that the air is not what will entitle it to a place in your elegant selection.[238]

R. B.

FOOTNOTES:

[237] Song CCVII.
[238] Song CCVIII.

CCLXXII.

TO MR. THOMSON.

[This letter contains further proof of the love of Burns for the airs of the Highlands.]

Sept. 1793.

I dare say, my dear Sir, that you will begin to think my correspondence is persecution. No matter, I can't help it; a ballad is my hobby-horse, which, though otherwise a simple sort of harmless idiotical beast enough, has yet this blessed headstrong property, that when once it has fairly made off with a hapless wight, it gets so enamoured with the tinkle-gingle, tinkle-gingle of its own bells, that it is sure to run poor pilgarlick, the bedlam jockey, quite beyond any useful point or post in the common race of men.

The following song I have composed for "Oran-gaoil," the Highland air that, you tell me in your last, you have resolved to give a place to in your book. I have this moment finished the song, so you have it glowing from the mint. If it suit you, well!-If not, 'tis also well!

Behold the hour, the boat arrive!

R. B.

CCLXXIII.

TO MR. THOMSON.

[This is another of the sagacious letters on Scottish song, which poets and musicians would do well to read and consider.]

Sept. 1793.

I have received your list, my dear Sir, and here go my observations on it.[239]

"Down the burn, Davie." I have this moment tried an alteration, leaving out the last half of the third stanza, and the first half of the last stanza, thus: As down the burn they took their way, And thro' the flowery dale; His cheek to hers he aft did lay, And love was aye the tale. With "Mary, when shall we return, Sic pleasure to renew?" Quoth Mary, "Love, I like the burn, And aye shall follow you."[240]

"Thro' the wood, laddie"-I am decidedly of opinion that both in this, and "There'll never be peace till Jamie comes hame," the second or high part of the tune being a repetition of the first part an octave higher, is only for instrumental music, and would be much better omitted in singing.

"Cowden-knowes." Remember in your index that the song in pure English to this tune, beginning,

"When summer comes, the swains on Tweed,"

[469]

is the production of Crawfurd. Robert was his Christian name.[241]

"Laddie, lie near me," must lie by me for some time. I do not know the air; and until I am complete master of a tune, in my own singing (such as it is), I can never compose for it. My way is: I consider the poetic sentiment correspondent to my idea of the musical expression; then choose my theme; begin one stanza: when that is composed, which is generally the most difficult part of the business, I walk out, sit down now and then, look out for objects of nature around me that are in unison and harmony with the cogitations of my fancy, and workings of my bosom; humming every now and then the air with the verses I have framed. When I feel my muse beginning to jade, I retire to the solitary fire-side of my study, and there commit my effusions to paper; swinging at intervals on the hind-legs of my elbow-chair, by way of calling forth my own critical strictures as my pen goes on. Seriously, this, at home, is almost invariably my way.

What cursed egotism!

"Gil Morice" I am for leaving out. It is a plaguy length; the air itself is never sung; and its place can well be supplied by one or two songs for fine airs that are not in your list-for instance "Craigieburn-wood" and "Roy's wife." The first, beside its intrinsic merit, has novelty, and the last has high merit as well as great celebrity. I have the original words of a song for the last air, in the handwriting of the lady who composed it; and they are superior to any edition of the song which the public has yet seen.

"Highland laddie." The old set will please a mere Scotch ear best; and the new an Italianised one. There is a third, and what Oswald calls the old "Highland laddie," which pleases me more than either of them. It is sometimes called "Ginglin Johnnie;" it being the air of an old humorous tawdry song of that name. You will find it in the Museum, "I hae been at Crookieden," andc. I would advise you, in the musical quandary, to offer up your prayers to the muses for inspiring direction; and in the meantime, waiting for this direction, bestow a libation to Bacchus; and there is not a doubt but you will hit on a judicious choice. Probatum est.

"Auld Sir Simon" I must beg you to leave out, and put in its place "The Quaker's wife."

"Blythe hae I been on yon hill,"[242] is one of the finest songs ever I made in my life, and, besides, is composed on a young lady, positively the most beautiful, lovely woman in the world. As I purpose giving you the names and designations of all my heroines, to appear in some future edition of your work, perhaps half a century hence, you must certainly include "The bonniest lass in a' the warld," in your collection.

"Dainty Davie" I have heard sung nineteen thousand nine hundred and ninety-nine times, and always with the chorus to the low part of the tune; and nothing has surprised me so much as your opinion on this subject. If it will not suit as I proposed, we will lay two of the stanzas together, and then make the chorus follow, exactly as Lucky Nancy in the Museum.

"Fee him, father:" I enclose you Frazer's set of this tune when he plays it slow: in fact he makes it the language of despair. I shall here give you two stanzas, in that style, merely to try if it will be any improvement. Were it possible, in singing, to give it half the pathos which Frazer gives it in playing, it would make an admirably pathetic song. I do not give these verses for any merit they have. I composed them at the time in which "Patie

Allan's mither died-that was about the back o' midnight;" and by the lee-side of a bowl of punch, which had overset every mortal in company except the hautbois and the muse.

Thou hast left me ever, Jamie.[243]

"Jockie and Jenny" I would discard, and in its place would put "There's nae luck about the house,"[244] which has a very pleasant air, and which is positively the finest love-ballad in that style in the Scottish, or perhaps in any other language. "When she came ben she bobbit," as an air is more beautiful than either, and in the andante way would unite with a charming sentimental ballad.

"Saw ye my father?" is one of my greatest favourites. The evening before last, I wandered out, and began a tender song, in what I think is its native style. I must premise that the old way, and the way to give most effect, is to have no starting note, as the fiddlers call it, but to [470] burst at once into the pathos. Every country girl sings "Saw ye my father?" andc.

My song is but just begun; and I should like, before I proceed, to know your opinion of it. I have sprinkled it with the Scottish dialect, but it may be easily turned into correct English.[245]

"Todlin hame." Urbani mentioned an idea of his, which has long been mine, that this air is highly susceptible of pathos: accordingly, you will soon hear him at your concert try it to a song of mine in the Museum, "Ye banks and braes o' bonnie Doon." One song more and I have done; "Auld lang syne." The air is but mediocre; but the following song, the old song of the olden times, and which has never been in print, nor even in manuscript, until I took it down from an old man's singing, is enough to recommend any air.[246]

Now, I suppose, I have tried your patience fairly. You must, after all is over, have a number of ballads, properly so called. "Gil Morice," "Tranent Muir," "Macpherson's farewell," "Battle of Sherriff-muir," or, "We ran, and they ran," (I know the author of this charming ballad, and his history,) "Hardiknute," "Barbara Allan" (I can furnish a finer set of this tune than any that has yet appeared;) and besides do you know that I really have the old tune to which "The cherry and the slae" was sung, and which is mentioned as a well-known air in "Scotland's Complaint," a book published before poor Mary's days?[247] It was then called "The banks of Helicon;" an old poem which Pinkerton has brought to light. You will see all this in Tytler's history of Scottish music. The tune, to a learned ear, may have no great merit; but it is a great curiosity. I have a good many original things of this kind.

R. B.

FOOTNOTES:

[239] Mr. Thomson's list of songs for his publication.
[240] This is an alteration of one of Crawford's songs.
[241] His Christian name was William.
[242] Song CXCV.
[243] Song CCIX.
[244] By William Julius Mickle.
[245] The song here alluded to is one which the poet afterwards sent in an entire form:-
"Where are the joys I hae met in the morning."
[246] Song CCX.
[247] A curious and rare book, which Leyden afterwards edited.

CCLXXIV.

TO MR. THOMSON.

[Burns listened too readily to the suggestion of Thomson, to alter "Bruce's Address to his troops at Bannockburn:" whatever may be the merits of the air of "Louis Gordon," the sublime simplicity of the words was injured by the alteration: it is now sung as originally written, by all singers of taste.]

September, 1793.

I am happy, my dear Sir, that my ode pleases you so much. Your idea, "honour's bed," is, though a beautiful, a hackneyed idea; so, if you please, we will let the line stand as it is. I have altered the song as follows:-[248]

N. B. I have borrowed the last stanza from the common stall edition of Wallace-

"A false usurper sinks in every foe, And liberty returns with every blow."

A couplet worthy of Homer. Yesterday you had enough of my correspondence. The post goes, and my head aches miserably. One comfort! I suffer so much, just now, in this world, for last night's joviality, that I shall escape scot-free for it in the world to come. Amen.

R. B.

FOOTNOTES:

[248] Song CCVII.

CCLXXV.

TO MR. THOMSON.

[The poet's good sense rose at last in arms against the criticisms of the musician, and he refused to lessen the dignity of his war-ode by any more alterations.]

September, 1793.

"Who shall decide when doctors disagree?" My ode pleases me so much that I cannot alter it. Your proposed alterations would, in my opinion, make it tame. I am exceedingly obliged to you for putting me on reconsidering it, as I think I have much improved it. Instead of "sodger! hero!" I will have it "Caledonian, on wi' me!"

I have scrutinized it over and over; and to the world, some way or other, it shall go as it is. At the same time it will not in the least hurt me, should you leave it out altogether, and adhere to your first intention of adopting Logan's verses.

I have finished my song to "Saw ye my father?" and in English, as you will see. That there is a syllable too much for the expression of the air, is true; but, allow me to say, that the mere dividing of a dotted crotchet into a crotchet and a quaver, is not a great matter: however, in that I have no pretensions to cope in judgment with you. Of the poetry I speak [471] with confidence; but the music is a business where I hint my ideas with the utmost diffidence.

The old verses have merit, though unequal, and are popular: my advice is to set the air to the old words, and let mine follow as English verses. Here they are:-

Where are the joys I have met in the morning?[249]

Adieu, my dear Sir! the post goes, so I shall defer some other remarks until more leisure.

R. B.

FOOTNOTES:

[249] Song CCXI.

CCLXXVI.

TO MR. THOMSON.

[For "Fy! let us a' to the bridal," and "Fy! gie me my coggie, Sirs," and "There's nae luck about the house," Burns puts in a word of praise, from a feeling that Thomson's taste would induce him to exclude the first-one of our most original songs-from his collection.]

September, 1793.

I have been turning over some volumes of songs, to find verses whose measures would suit the airs for which you have allotted me to find English songs.

For "Muirland Willie," you have, in Ramsay's Tea-Table, an excellent song beginning, "Ah, why those tears in Nelly's eyes?" As for "The Collier's Dochter," take the following old bacchanal:-

"Deluded swain, the pleasure, andc."[250]

The faulty line in Logan-Water, I mend thus:
How can your flinty hearts enjoy The widow's tears, the orphan's cry?
The song otherwise will pass. As to "M'Gregoira Rua-Ruth," you will see a song of mine to it, with a set of the air superior to yours, in the Museum, vol. ii. p. 181. The song begins,
Raving winds around her blowing.[251]
Your Irish airs are pretty, but they are rank Irish. If they were like the "Banks of Banna," for instance, though really Irish, yet in the Scottish taste, you might adopt them. Since you are so fond of Irish music, what say you to twenty-five of them in an additional number? We could easily find this quantity of charming airs; I will take care that you shall not want songs; and I assure you that you would find it the most saleable of the whole. If you do not approve of "Roy's wife," for the music's sake, we shall not insert it. "Deil tak the wars" is a charming song; so is, "Saw ye my Peggy?" "There's nae luck about the house" well deserves a place. I cannot say that "O'er the hills and far awa" strikes me as equal to your selection. "This is no my ain house," is a great favourite air of mine; and if you will send me your set of it, I will task my muse to her highest effort. What is your opinion of "I hae laid a herrin' in saut?" I like it much. Your jacobite airs are pretty, and there are many others of the same kind pretty; but you have not room for them. You cannot, I think, insert "Fy! let's a' to the bridal," to any other words than its own.
What pleases me, as simple and naive, disgusts you as ludicrous and low. For this reason, "Fy! gie me my coggie, Sirs," "Fy let's a' to the bridal," with several others of that cast, are to me highly pleasing; while "Saw ye my father, or saw ye my mother?" delights me with its descriptive simple pathos. Thus my song, "Ken ye what Meg o' the mill has gotten?" pleases myself so much, that I cannot try my hand at another song to the air, so I shall not attempt it. I know you will laugh at all this: but "ilka man wears his belt his ain gait."
R. B.

FOOTNOTES:

[250] Song CCXII.
[251] Song LII.

CCLXXVII.

TO MR. THOMSON.
[Of the Hon. Andrew Erskine an account was communicated in a letter to Burns by Thomson, which the writer has withheld. He was a gentleman of talent, and joint projector of Thomson's now celebrated work.]

October, 1793.

Your last letter, my dear Thomson, was indeed laden with heavy news. Alas, poor Erskine![252] The recollection that he was a co-adjutator in your publication, has till now scared me from writing to you, or turning my thoughts on composing for you.

[472]

I am pleased that you are reconciled to the air of the "Quaker's wife;" though, by the bye, an old Highland gentleman, and a deep antiquarian, tells me it is a Gaelic air, and known by the name of "Leiger m' choss." The following verses, I hope, will please you, as an English song to the air.

Thine am I, my faithful fair:[253]

Your objection to the English song I proposed for "John Anderson my jo," is certainly just. The following is by an old acquaintance of mine, and I think has merit. The song was never in print, which I think is so much in your favour. The more original good poetry your collection contains, it certainly has so much the more merit.

SONG.-BY GAVIN TURNBULL.[254]

Oh, condescend, dear charming maid, My wretched state to view; A tender swain, to love betray'd, And sad despair, by you.

While here, all melancholy, My passion I deplore, Yet, urg'd by stern, resistless fate, I love thee more and more.

I heard of love, and with disdain The urchin's power denied. I laugh'd at every lover's pain, And mock'd them when they sigh'd.

But how my state is alter'd! Those happy days are o'er; For all thy unrelenting hate, I love thee more and more.

Oh, yield, illustrious beauty, yield! No longer let me mourn; And though victorious in the field, Thy captive do not scorn.

Let generous pity warm thee, My wonted peace restore; And grateful I shall bless thee still, And love thee more and more.

The following address of Turnbull's to the Nightingale will suit as an English song to the air "There was a lass, and she was fair." By the bye, Turnbull has a great many songs in MS., which I can command, if you like his manner. Possibly, as he is an old friend of mine, I may be prejudiced in his favour; but I like some of his pieces very much.

THE NIGHTINGALE.

Thou sweetest minstrel of the grove, That ever tried the plaintive strain, Awake thy tender tale of love, And soothe a poor forsaken swain.

For though the muses deign to aid And teach him smoothly to complain, Yet Delia, charming, cruel maid, Is deaf to her forsaken swain.

All day, with fashion's gaudy sons, In sport she wanders o'er the plain: Their tales approves, and still she shuns The notes of her forsaken swain.

When evening shades obscure the sky, And bring the solemn hours again, Begin, sweet bird, thy melody, And soothe a poor forsaken swain.

I shall just transcribe another of Turnbull's, which would go charmingly to "Lewie Gordon."

LAURA.

Let me wander where I will, By shady wood, or winding rill; Where the sweetest May-born flowers Paint the meadows, deck the bowers; Where the linnet's early song Echoes sweet the woods among: Let me wander where I will, Laura haunts my fancy still.

If at rosy dawn I choose To indulge the smiling muse; If I court some cool retreat, To avoid the noontide heat; If beneath the moon's pale ray, Thro' unfrequented wilds I stray; Let me wander where I will, Laura haunts my fancy still.

When at night the drowsy god Waves his sleep-compelling rod, And to fancy's wakeful eyes Bids celestial visions rise, While with boundless joy I rove Thro' the fairy land of love; Let me wander where I will, Laura haunts my fancy still.

The rest of your letter I shall answer at some other opportunity.

R. B.

FOOTNOTES:

[252] "The honorable Andrew Erskine, whose melancholy death Mr. Thomson had communicated in an excellent letter, which he has suppressed."-Currie.

[253] Song CCXIII.

[254] Gavin Turnbull was author of a now forgotten volume, published at Glasgow, in 1788, under the title of "Poetical Essays."

CCLXXVIII.

TO JOHN M'MURDO, ESQ.,
WITH A PARCEL.

[The collection of songs alluded to in this letter, are only known to the curious in loose lore: they were[473] printed by an obscure bookseller, but not before death had secured him from the indignation of Burns.]

Dumfries, [December, 1793.]

Sir,

'Tis said that we take the greatest liberties with our greatest friends, and I pay myself a very high compliment in the manner in which I am going to apply the remark. I have owed you money longer than ever I owed it to any man. Here is Kerr's account, and here are the six guineas; and now I don't owe a shilling to man-or woman either. But for these dd dirty, dog's-ear'd little pages,[255] I had done myself the honour to have waited on you long ago. Independent of the obligations your hospitality has laid me under, the consciousness of your superiority in the rank of man and gentleman, of itself was fully as much as I could ever make head against; but to owe you money too, was more than I could face.

I think I once mentioned something to you of a collection of Scots songs I have for some years been making: I send you a perusal of what I have got together. I could not conveniently spare them above five or six days, and five or six glances of them will probably more than suffice you. When you are tired of them, please leave them with Mr. Clint, of the King's Arms. There is not another copy of the collection in the world; and I should be sorry that any unfortunate negligence should deprive me of what has cost me a good deal of pains.

I have the honour to be, andc.

R. B.

FOOTNOTES:

[255] Scottish Bank notes.

CCLXXIX.

TO JOHN M'MURDO, ESQ.,

DRUMLANRIG.

[These words, thrown into the form of a note, are copied from a blank leaf of the poet's works, published in two volumes, small octavo, in 1793.]

Dumfries, 1793.

Will Mr. M'Murdo do me the favour to accept of these volumes; a trifling but sincere mark of the very high respect I bear for his worth as a man, his manners as a gentleman, and his kindness as a friend. However inferior now, or afterwards, I may rank as a poet; one honest virtue to which few poets can pretend, I trust I shall ever claim as mine:-to no man, whatever his station in life, or his power to serve me, have I ever paid a compliment at the expense of truth.

The Author.

CCLXXX.

TO CAPTAIN .

[This excellent letter, obtained from Stewart of Dalguise, is copied from my kind friend Chambers's collection of Scottish songs.]

Dumfries, 5th December, 1793.

Sir,

Heated as I was with wine yesternight, I was perhaps rather seemingly impertinent in my anxious wish to be honoured with your acquaintance.

You will forgive it: it was the impulse of heart-felt respect. "He is the father of the Scottish county reform, and is a man who does honour to the business, at the same time that the business does honour to him," said my worthy friend Glenriddel to somebody by me who was talking of your coming to this county with your corps. "Then," I said, "I have a woman's longing to take him by the hand, and say to him, 'Sir, I honour you as a man to whom the interests of humanity are dear, and as a patriot to whom the rights of your country are sacred.'"

In times like these, Sir, when our commoners are barely able by the glimmer of their own twilight understandings to scrawl a frank, and when lords are what gentlemen would be ashamed to be, to whom shall a sinking country call for help? To the independent country gentleman. To him who has too deep a stake in his country not to be in earnest for her welfare; and who in the honest pride of a man can view with equal contempt the insolence of office and the allurements of corruption.

I mentioned to you a Scots ode or song I had lately composed, and which I think has some merit. Allow me to enclose it. When I fall in with you at the theatre, I shall be glad to have your opinion of it. Accept it, Sir, as a very humble but most sincere tribute of respect from a man, who, dear as he prizes poetic fame, yet holds dearer an independent mind.

I have the honour to be,

R. B.

CCLXXXI.

TO MRS. RIDDEL,

Who was about to bespeak a Play one evening at the Dumfries Theatre.

[This clever lady, whom Burns so happily applies the words of Thomson, died in the year 1820, at Hampton Court.]

I am thinking to send my "Address" to some periodical publication, but it has not yet got your sanction, so pray look at it.

As to the Tuesday's play, let me beg of you, my dear madam, to give us, "The Wonder, a Woman keeps a Secret!" to which please add, "The Spoilt Child"-you will highly oblige me by so doing.

Ah, what an enviable creature you are! There now, this cursed, gloomy, blue-devil day, you are going to a party of choice spirits-

"To play the shapes Of frolic fancy, and incessant form Those rapid pictures, assembled train Of fleet ideas, never join'd before, Where lively wit excites to gay surprise; Or folly-painting humour, grave himself, Calls laughter forth, deep-shaking every nerve."

Thomson.

But as you rejoice with them that do rejoice, do also remember to weep with them that weep, and pity your melancholy friend.

R. B.

CCLXXXII.

TO A LADY.
IN FAVOUR OF A PLAYER'S BENEFIT.
[The name of the lady to whom this letter is addressed, has not transpired.]
Dumfries, 1794.
Madam,
You were so very good as to promise me to honour my friend with your presence on his benefit night. That night is fixed for Friday first: the play a most interesting one! "The Way to Keep Him." I have the pleasure to know Mr. G. well. His merit as an actor is generally acknowledged. He has genius and worth which would do honour to patronage: he is a poor and modest man; claims which from their very silence have the more forcible power on the generous heart. Alas, for pity! that from the indolence of those who have the good things of this life in their gift, too often does brazen-fronted importunity snatch that boon, the rightful due of retiring, humble want! Of all the qualities we assign to the author and director of nature, by far the most enviable is-to be able "to wipe away all tears from all eyes." O what insignificant, sordid wretches are they, however chance may have loaded them with wealth, who go to their graves, to their magnificent mausoleums, with hardly the consciousness of having made one poor honest heart happy!
But I crave your pardon, Madam; I came to beg, not to preach.
R. B.

CCLXXXIII.

TO THE EARL OF BUCHAN,
With a Copy of Bruce's Address to his Troops at Bannockburn.
[This fantastic Earl of Buchan died a few years ago: when he was put into the family burial-ground, at Dryburgh, his head was laid the wrong way, which Sir Walter Scott said was little matter, as it had never been quite right in his lifetime.]
Dumfries, 12th January, 1794.
My Lord,
Will your lordship allow me to present you with the enclosed little composition of mine, as a small tribute of gratitude for the acquaintance with which you have been pleased to honour me? Independent of my enthusiasm as a Scotsman, I have rarely met with anything in history which interests my feelings as a man, equal with the story of Bannockburn. On the one hand, a cruel, but able usurper, leading on the finest army in Europe to

extinguish the last spark of freedom among a greatly-daring and greatly-injured people; on the other hand, the desperate relics of a gallant nation, devoting themselves to rescue their bleeding country, or perish with her.

Liberty! thou art a prize truly and indeed invaluable! for never canst thou be too dearly bought!

If my little ode has the honour of your lordship's approbation, it will gratify my highest ambition.

I have the honour to be, andc.

R. B.

[475]

CCLXXXIV.

TO CAPTAIN MILLER,

DALSWINTON.

[Captain Miller, of Dalswinton, sat in the House of Commons for the Dumfries district of boroughs. Dalswinton has passed from the family to my friend James M'Alpine Leny, Esq.]

Dear Sir,

The following ode is on a subject which I know you by no means regard with indifference. Oh, Liberty,

"Thou mak'st the gloomy face of nature gay, Giv'st beauty to the sun, and pleasure to the day."

Addison.

It does me so much good to meet with a man whose honest bosom glows with the generous enthusiasm, the heroic daring of liberty, that I could not forbear sending you a composition of my own on the subject, which I really think is in my best manner.

I have the honour to be,

Dear Sir, andc.

R. B.

CCLXXXV.

TO MRS. RIDDEL.

[The dragon guarding the Hesperian fruit, was simply a military officer, who, with the courtesy of those whose trade is arms, paid attention to the lady.]

Dear Madam,

I meant to have called on you yesternight, but as I edged up to your box-door, the first object which greeted my view, was one of those lobster-coated puppies, sitting like another dragon, guarding the Hesperian fruit. On the conditions and capitulations you so obligingly offer, I shall certainly

make my weather-beaten rustic phiz a part of your box-furniture on Tuesday; when we may arrange the business of the visit.
Among the profusion of idle compliments, which insidious craft, or unmeaning folly, incessantly offer at your shrine-a shrine, how far exalted above such adoration-permit me, were it but for rarity's sake, to pay you the honest tribute of a warm heart and an independent mind; and to assure you, that I am, thou most amiable and most accomplished of thy sex, with the most respectful esteem, and fervent regard, thine, andc.
R. B.

CCLXXXVI.

TO MRS. RIDDEL.
[The patient sons of order and prudence seem often to have stirred the poet to such invectives as this letter exhibits.]
I will wait on you, my ever-valued friend, but whether in the morning I am not sure. Sunday closes a period of our curst revenue business, and may probably keep me employed with my pen until noon. Fine employment for a poet's pen! There is a species of the human genus that I call the gin-horse class: what enviable dogs they are! Round, and round, and round they go,-Mundell's ox that drives his cotton-mill is their exact prototype-without an idea or wish beyond their circle; fat, sleek, stupid, patient, quiet, and contented; while here I sit, altogether Novemberish, a d-mn'd melange of fretfulness and melancholy; not enough of the one to rouse me to passion, nor of the other to repose me in torpor, my soul flouncing and fluttering round her tenement, like a wild finch, caught amid the horrors of winter, and newly thrust into a cage. Well, I am persuaded that it was of me the Hebrew sage prophesied, when he foretold-"And behold, on whatsoever this man doth set his heart, it shall not prosper!" If my resentment is awaked, it is sure to be where it dare not squeak: and if- * * * * *
Pray that wisdom and bliss be more frequent visiters of
R. B.

CCLXXXVII.

TO MRS. RIDDEL.
[The bard often offended and often appeased this whimsical but very clever lady.]
I have this moment got the song from Syme, and I am sorry to see that he has spoilt it a good deal. It shall be a lesson to me how I lend him anything again.
I have sent you "Werter," truly happy to have any the smallest opportunity of obliging you.

'Tis true, Madam, I saw you once since I was at Woodlea; and that once froze the very life-blood of my heart. Your reception of me was such, that a wretch meeting the eye of his judge, about to pronounce sentence of death on him[476] could only have envied my feelings and situation. But I hate the theme, and never more shall write or speak on it.

One thing I shall proudly say, that I can pay Mrs. R. a higher tribute of esteem, and appreciate her amiable worth more truly, than any man whom I have seen approach her.

R. B.

CCLXXXVIII.

TO MRS. RIDDEL.

[Burns often complained in company, and sometimes in his letters, of the caprice of Mrs. Riddel.]

I have often told you, my dear friend, that you had a spice of caprice in your composition, and you have as often disavowed it; even perhaps while your opinions were, at the moment, irrefragably proving it. Could anything estrange me from a friend such as you?-No! To-morrow I shall have the honour of waiting on you.

Farewell, thou first of friends, and most accomplished of women; even with all thy little caprices!

R. B.

CCLXXXIX.

TO MRS. RIDDEL.

[The offended lady was soothed by this submissive letter, and the bard was re-established in her good graces.]

Madam,

I return your common-place book. I have perused it with much pleasure, and would have continued my criticisms, but as it seems the critic has forfeited your esteem, his strictures must lose their value.

If it is true that "offences come only from the heart," before you I am guiltless. To admire, esteem, and prize you as the most accomplished of women, and the first of friends-if these are crimes, I am the most offending thing alive.

In a face where I used to meet the kind complacency of friendly confidence, now to find cold neglect, and contemptuous scorn-is a wrench that my heart can ill bear. It is, however, some kind of miserable good luck, and while de haut-en-bas rigour may depress an unoffending wretch to the ground, it has a tendency to rouse a stubborn something in his bosom, which, though it cannot heal the wounds of his soul, is at least an opiate to blunt their poignancy.

With the profoundest respect for your abilities; the most sincere esteem and ardent regard for your gentle heart and amiable manners; and the most fervent wish and prayer for your welfare, peace, and bliss, I have the honour to be,

Madam,

Your most devoted humble servant,

R. B.

CCXC.

TO JOHN SYME, ESQ.

[John Syme, of the stamp-office, was the companion as well as comrade in arms, of Burns: he was a well-informed gentleman, loved witty company, and sinned in rhyme now and then: his epigrams were often happy.]

You know that among other high dignities, you have the honour to be my supreme court of critical judicature, from which there is no appeal. I enclose you a song which I composed since I saw you, and I am going to give you the history of it. Do you know that among much that I admire in the characters and manners of those great folks whom I have now the honour to call my acquaintances, the Oswald family, there is nothing charms me more than Mr. Oswald's unconcealable attachment to that incomparable woman. Did you ever, my dear Syme, meet with a man who owed more to the Divine Giver of all good things than Mr. O.? A fine fortune; a pleasing exterior; self-evident amiable dispositions, and an ingenuous upright mind, and that informed, too, much beyond the usual run of young fellows of his rank and fortune: and to all this, such a woman!-but of her I shall say nothing at all, in despair of saying anything adequate: in my song I have endeavoured to do justice to what would be his feelings, on seeing, in the scene I have drawn, the habitation of his Lucy. As I am a good deal pleased with my performance, I, in my first fervour, thought of sending it to Mrs. Oswald, but on second thoughts, perhaps what I offer as the honest incense of genuine respect, might, from the well-known character of poverty and poetry, be construed into some modification or other of that servility which my soul abhors.

R. B.

[477]

CCXCI.

TO MISS .

[Burns, on other occasions than this, recalled both his letters and verses: it is to be regretted that he did not recall more of both.]

Dumfries, 1794.
Madam,
Nothing short of a kind of absolute necessity could have made me trouble you with this letter. Except my ardent and just esteem for your sense, taste, and worth, every sentiment arising in my breast, as I put pen to paper to you, is painful. The scenes I have passed with the friend of my soul and his amiable connexions! the wrench at my heart to think that he is gone, for ever gone from me, never more to meet in the wanderings of a weary world! and the cutting reflection of all, that I had most unfortunately, though most undeservedly, lost the confidence of that soul of worth, ere it took its flight!
These, Madam, are sensations of no ordinary anguish.-However, you also may be offended with some imputed improprieties of mine; sensibility you know I possess, and sincerity none will deny me.
To oppose those prejudices which have been raised against me, is not the business of this letter. Indeed it is a warfare I know not how to wage. The powers of positive vice I can in some degree calculate, and against direct malevolence I can be on my guard; but who can estimate the fatuity of giddy caprice, or ward off the unthinking mischief of precipitate folly?
I have a favour to request of you, Madam, and of your sister Mrs. , through your means. You know that, at the wish of my late friend, I made a collection of all my trifles in verse which I had ever written. They are many of them local, some of them puerile and silly, and all of them unfit for the public eye. As I have some little fame at stake, a fame that I trust may live when the hate of those who "watch for my halting," and the contumelious sneer of those whom accident has made my superiors, will, with themselves, be gone to the regions of oblivion; I am uneasy now for the fate of those manuscripts-Will Mrs.have the goodness to destroy them, or return them to me? As a pledge of friendship they were bestowed; and that circumstance indeed was all their merit. Most unhappily for me, that merit they no longer possess; and I hope that Mrs.'s goodness, which I well know, and ever will revere, will not refuse this favour to a man whom she once held in some degree of estimation.
With the sincerest esteem,
I have the honour to be,
Madam, andc.
R. B.

CCXCII.

TO MR. CUNNINGHAM.
[The religious feeling of Burns was sometimes blunted, but at times it burst out, as in this letter, with eloquence and fervour, mingled with fear.]

25th February, 1794.
Canst thou minister to a mind diseased? Canst thou speak peace and rest to a soul tost on a sea of troubles, without one friendly star to guide her course, and dreading that the next surge may overwhelm her? Canst thou give to a frame tremblingly alive as the tortures of suspense, the stability and hardihood of the rock that braves the blast? If thou canst not do the least of these, why wouldst thou disturb me in my miseries, with thy inquiries after me?
For these two months I have not been able to lift a pen. My constitution and frame were, ab origine, blasted with a deep incurable taint of hypochondria, which poisons my existence. Of late a number of domestic vexations, and some pecuniary share in the ruin of these cursed times; losses which, though trifling, were yet what I could ill bear, have so irritated me, that my feelings at times could only be envied by a reprobate spirit listening to the sentence that dooms it to perdition.
Are you deep in the language of consolation? I have exhausted in reflection every topic of comfort. A heart at ease would have been charmed with my sentiments and reasonings; but as to myself I was like Judas Iscariot preaching the gospel; he might melt and mould the hearts of those around him, but his own kept its native incorrigibility.
Still there are two great pillars that bear us up, amid the wreck of misfortune and misery. The one is composed of the different modifications of a certain noble stubborn something in man, known by the names of courage, fortitude,[478] magnanimity. The other is made up of those feelings and sentiments, which, however the sceptic may deny them, or the enthusiast disfigure them, are yet, I am convinced, original and component parts of the human soul; those senses of the mind, if I may be allowed the expression, which connect us with, and link us to, those awful, obscure realities-an all-powerful, and equally beneficent God; and a world to come, beyond death and the grave. The first gives the nerve of combat, while a ray of hope beams on the field: the last pours the balm of comfort into the wounds which time can never cure.
I do not remember, my dear Cunningham, that you and I ever talked on the subject of religion at all. I know some who laugh at it, as the trick of the crafty few, to lead the undiscerning many; or at most as an uncertain obscurity, which mankind can never know anything of, and with which they are fools if they give themselves much to do. Nor would I quarrel with a man for his irreligion, any more than I would for his want of a musical ear. I would regret that he was shut out from what, to me and to others, were such superlative sources of enjoyment. It is in this point of view, and for this reason, that I will deeply imbue the mind of every child of mine with religion. If my son should happen to be a man of feeling, sentiment, and taste, I shall thus add largely to his enjoyments. Let me flatter myself that

this sweet little fellow, who is just now running about my desk, will be a man of a melting, ardent, glowing heart; and an imagination, delighted with the painter, and rapt with the poet. Let me figure him wandering out in a sweet evening, to inhale the balmy gales, and enjoy the growing luxuriance of spring; himself the while in the blooming youth of life. He looks abroad on all nature, and through nature up to nature's God. His soul, by swift delighting degrees, is rapt above this sublunary sphere, until he can be silent no longer, and bursts out into the glorious enthusiasm of Thomson,

"These, as they change, Almighty Father, these Are but the varied God.- The rolling year Is full of thee."

And so on, in all the spirit and ardour of that charming hymn. These are no ideal pleasures, they are real delights; and I ask what of the delights among the sons of men are superior, not to say equal to them? And they have this precious, vast addition, that conscious virtue stamps them for her own; and lays hold on them to bring herself into the presence of a witnessing, judging, and approving God.

R. B.

CCXCIII.

TO THE EARL OF GLENCAIRN.

[The original letter is in the possession of the Hon. Mrs. Halland, of Poynings: it is undated, but from a memorandum on the back it appears to have been written in May, 1794.]

May, 1794.

My Lord,

When you cast your eye on the name at the bottom of this letter, and on the title-page of the book I do myself the honour to send your lordship, a more pleasurable feeling than my vanity tells me that it must be a name not entirely unknown to you. The generous patronage of your late illustrious brother found me in the lowest obscurity: he introduced my rustic muse to the partiality of my country; and to him I owe all. My sense of his goodness, and the anguish of my soul at losing my truly noble protector and friend, I have endeavoured to express in a poem to his memory, which I have now published. This edition is just from the press; and in my gratitude to the dead, and my respect for the living (fame belies you, my lord, if you possess not the same dignity of man, which was your noble brother's characteristic feature), I had destined a copy for the Earl of Glencairn. I learnt just now that you are in town:-allow me to present it you.

I know, my lord, such is the vile, venal contagion which pervades the world of letters, that professions of respect from an author, particularly from a poet, to a lord, are more than suspicious. I claim my by-past conduct, and my feelings at this moment, as exceptions to the too just conclusion.

Exalted as are the honours of your lordship's name, and unnoted as is the obscurity of mine; with the uprightness of an honest man, I come before your lordship with an offering, however humble, 'tis all I have to give, of my grateful respect; and to beg of you, my lord,-'tis all I have to ask of you,-that you will do me the honour to accept of it.

I have the honour to be,

R. B.

[479]

CCXCIV.

TO MR. THOMSON.

[The correspondence between the poet and the musician was interrupted in spring, but in summer and autumn the song-strains were renewed.]

May, 1794.

My dear Sir,

I return you the plates, with which I am highly pleased; I would humbly propose, instead of the younker knitting stockings, to put a stock and horn into his hands. A friend of mine, who is positively the ablest judge on the subject I have ever met with, and, though an unknown, is yet a superior artist with the burin, is quite charmed with Allan's manner. I got him a peep of the "Gentle Shepherd;" and he pronounces Allan a most original artist of great excellence.

For my part, I look on Mr. Allan's choosing my favourite poem for his subject, to be one of the highest compliments I have ever received.

I am quite vexed at Pleyel's being cooped up in France, as it will put an entire stop to our work. Now, and for six or seven months, I shall be quite in song, as you shall see by and bye. I got an air, pretty enough, composed by Lady Elizabeth Heron, of Heron, which she calls "The Banks of Cree." Cree is a beautiful romantic stream; and, as her ladyship is a particular friend of mine, I have written the following song to it.

Here is the glen and here the bower.[256]

R. B.

FOOTNOTES:

[256] Song CCXXIII.

CCXCV.

TO DAVID M'CULLOCH, ESQ.

[The endorsement on the back of the original letter shows in what far lands it has travelled:-"Given by David M'Culloch, Penang, 1810. A. Fraser."

"Received 15th December, 1823, in Calcutta, from Captain Frazer's widow, by me, Thomas Rankine." "Transmitted to Archibald Hastie, Esq., London, March 27th, 1824, from Bombay."]

Dumfries, 21st June, 1794.

My dear Sir,

My long-projected journey through your country is at last fixed: and on Wednesday next, if you have nothing of more importance to do, take a saunter down to Gatehouse about two or three o'clock, I shall be happy to take a draught of M'Kune's best with you. Collector Syme will be at Glens about that time, and will meet us about dish-of-tea hour. Syme goes also to Kerroughtree, and let me remind you of your kind promise to accompany me there; I will need all the friends I can muster, for I am indeed ill at ease whenever I approach your honourables and right honourables.

Yours sincerely,

R. B.

CCXCVI.

TO MRS. DUNLOP.

[Castle Douglas is a thriving Galloway village: it was in other days called "The Carlinwark," but accepted its present proud name from an opulent family of mercantile Douglasses, well known in Scotland, England, and America.]

Castle Douglas, 25th June, 1794.

Here, in a solitary inn, in a solitary village, am I set by myself, to amuse my brooding fancy as I may.-Solitary confinement, you know, is Howard's favourite idea of reclaiming sinners; so let me consider by what fatality it happens that I have so long been so exceeding sinful as to neglect the correspondence of the most valued friend I have on earth. To tell you that I have been in poor health will not be excuse enough, though it is true. I am afraid that I am about to suffer for the follies of my youth. My medical friends threaten me with a flying gout; but I trust they are mistaken.

I am just going to trouble your critical patience with the first sketch of a stanza I have been framing as I passed along the road. The subject is Liberty: you know, my honoured friend, how dear the theme is to me. I design it as an irregular ode for General Washington's birth-day. After having mentioned the degeneracy of other kingdoms, I come to Scotland thus:-

Thee, Caledonia, thy wild heaths among, Thee, famed for martial deed, and sacred song, To thee I turn with swimming eyes; Where is that soul of freedom fled? Immingled with the mighty dead! Beneath the hallowed turf where Wallace lies! Hear it not, Wallace, in thy bed of death! Ye babbling winds in silence sweep, Disturb not ye the hero's sleep. [480]

with additions of
That arm which nerved with thundering fate, Braved usurpation's boldest daring! One quenched in darkness like the sinking star, And one the palsied arm of tottering, powerless age.
You will probably have another scrawl from me in a stage or two.
R. B.

CCXCVII.

TO MR. JAMES JOHNSON.
[The anxiety of Burns about the accuracy of his poetry, while in the press, was great: he found full employment for months in correcting a new edition of his poems.]
Dumfries, 1794.
My dear Friend,
You should have heard from me long ago; but over and above some vexatious share in the pecuniary losses of these accursed times, I have all this winter been plagued with low spirits and blue devils, so that I have almost hung my harp on the willow-trees.
I am just now busy correcting a new edition of my poems, and this, with my ordinary business, finds me in full employment.
I send you by my friend Mr. Wallace forty-one songs for your fifth volume; if we cannot finish it in any other way, what would you think of Scots words to some beautiful Irish airs? In the mean time, at your leisure, give a copy of the Museum to my worthy friend, Sir. Peter Hill, bookseller, to bind for me, interleaved with blank leaves, exactly as he did the Laird of Glenriddel's, that I may insert every anecdote I can learn, together with my own criticisms and remarks on the songs. A copy of this kind I shall leave with you, the editor, to publish at some after period, by way of making the Museum a book famous to the end of time, and you renowned for ever.
I have got an Highland dirk, for which I have great veneration; as it once was the dirk of Lord Balmerino. It fell into bad hands, who stripped it of the silver mounting, as well as the knife and fork. I have some thoughts of sending it to your care, to get it mounted anew.
Thank you for the copies of my Volunteer Ballad.-Our friend Clarke has done indeed well! 'tis chaste and beautiful. I have not met with anything that has pleased me so much. You know I am no connoisseur: but that I am an amateur-will be allowed me.
R. B.

CCXCVIII.

TO MR. THOMSON.

[The blank in this letter could be filled up without writing treason: but nothing has been omitted of an original nature.]

July, 1794.

Is there no news yet of Pleyel? Or is your work to be at a dead stop, until the allies set our modern Orpheus at liberty from the savage thraldom of democrat discords? Alas the day! And woe is me! That auspicious period, pregnant with the happiness of millions. * * * *

I have presented a copy of your songs to the daughter of a much-valued and much-honoured friend of mine, Mr. Graham of Fintray. I wrote on the blank side of the title-page the following address to the young lady:

Here, where the Scottish muse immortal lives, andc.[257]

R. B.

FOOTNOTES:

[257] Song CCXXIX.

CCXCIX.

TO MR. THOMSON.

[Thomson says to Burns, "You have anticipated my opinion of 'O'er the seas and far away.'" Yet some of the verses are original and touching.]

30th August, 1794.

The last evening, as I was straying out, and thinking of "O'er the hills and far away," I spun the following stanza for it; but whether my spinning will deserve to be laid up in store, like the precious thread of the silk-worm, or brushed to the devil, like the vile manufacture of the spider, I leave, my dear Sir, to your usual candid criticism. I was pleased with several lines in it at first, but I own that now it appears rather a flimsy business.

This is just a hasty sketch, until I see whether it be worth a critique. We have many sailor songs, but as far as I at present recollect, they are mostly the effusions of the jovial sailor, not the wailings of his love-lorn mistress. I must here make one sweet exception-"Sweet Annie frae the sea-beach came." Now for the song:-

How can my poor heart be glad.[258]

[481]

I give you leave to abuse this song, but do it in the spirit of Christian meekness.

R. B.

FOOTNOTES:

[258] Song CCXXIV.

CCC.

TO MR. THOMSON.

[The stream on the banks of which this song is supposed to be sung, is known by three names, Cairn, Dalgonar, and Cluden. It rises under the name of Cairn, runs through a wild country, under the name of Dalgonar, affording fine trout-fishing as well as fine scenes, and under that of Cluden it all but washes the walls of Lincluden College, and then unites with the Nith.]

Sept. 1794.

I shall withdraw my "On the seas and far away" altogether: it is unequal, and unworthy the work. Making a poem is like begetting a son: you cannot know whether you have a wise man or a fool, until you produce him to the world to try him.

For that reason I send you the offspring of my brain, abortions and all; and, as such, pray look over them, and forgive them, and burn them. I am flattered at your adopting "Ca' the yowes to the knowes," as it was owing to me that ever it saw the light. About seven years ago I was well acquainted with a worthy little fellow of a clergyman, a Mr. Clunie, who sang it charmingly; and, at my request, Mr. Clarke took it down from his singing. When I gave it to Johnson, I added some stanzas to the song, and mended others, but still it will not do for you. In a solitary stroll which I took to-day, I tried my hand on a few pastoral lines, following up the idea of the chorus, which I would preserve. Here it is, with all its crudities and imperfections on its head.

Ca' the yowes to the knowes, andc.[259]

I shall give you my opinion of your other newly adopted songs my first scribbling fit.

R. B.

FOOTNOTES:

[259] Song CCXXV.

CCCI.

TO MR. THOMSON.

[Dr. Maxwell, whose skill called forth the praises of the poet, had the honour of being named by Burke in the House of Commons: he shared in the French revolution, and narrowly escaped the guillotine, like many other true friends of liberty.]

Sept. 1794.

Do you know a blackguard Irish song called "Onagh's Waterfall?" The air is charming, and I have often regretted the want of decent verses to it. It is too much, at least for my humble rustic muse, to expect that every effort of hers shall have merit; still I think that it is better to have mediocre verses to a favourite air, than none at all. On this principle I have all along proceeded in the Scots Musical Museum; and as that publication is at its last volume, I intend the following song, to the air above mentioned, for that work.

If it does not suit you as an editor, you may be pleased to have verses to it that you can sing in the company of ladies.

Sae flaxen were her ringlets.[260]

Not to compare small things with great, my taste in music is like the mighty Frederick of Prussia's taste in painting: we are told that he frequently admired what the connoisseurs decried, and always without any hypocrisy confessed his admiration. I am sensible that my taste in music must be inelegant and vulgar, because people of undisputed and cultivated taste can find no merit in my favourite tunes. Still, because I am cheaply pleased, is that any reason why I should deny myself that pleasure? Many of our strathspeys, ancient and modern, give me most exquisite enjoyment, where you and other judges would probably be showing disgust. For instance, I am just now making verses for "Rothemurche's rant," an air which puts me in raptures; and, in fact, unless I be pleased with the tune, I never can make verses to it. Here I have Clarke on my side, who is a judge that I will pit against any of you. "Rothemurche," he says, "is an air both original and beautiful;" and, on his recommendation, I have taken the first part of the tune for a chorus, and the fourth or last part for the song. I am but two stanzas deep in the work, and possibly you may think, and justly, that the poetry is as little worth your attention as the music.

[Here follow two stanzas of the song, beginning "Lassie wi' the lint-white locks." Song CCXXXIII.]

I have begun anew, "Let me in this ae night." Do you think that we ought to retain the old chorus? I think we must retain both the old chorus and the first stanza of the old song. I[482] do not altogether like the third line of the first stanza, but cannot alter it to please myself. I am just three stanzas deep in it. Would you have the denouement to be successful or otherwise?-should she "let him in" or not?

Did you not once propose "The sow's tail to Geordie" as an air for your work? I am quite delighted with it; but I acknowledge that is no mark of its real excellence. I once set about verses for it, which I meant to be in the alternate way of a lover and his mistress chanting together. I have not the pleasure of knowing Mrs. Thomson's Christian name, and yours, I am afraid, is rather burlesque for sentiment, else I had meant to have made you the hero and heroine of the little piece.

How do you like the following epigram which I wrote the other day on a

lovely young girl's recovery from a fever? Doctor Maxwell was the physician who seemingly saved her from the grave; and to him I address the following:
TO DR. MAXWELL,
ON MISS JESSIE STAIG'S RECOVERY.
Maxwell, if merit here you crave, That merit I deny: You save fair Jessy from the grave?- An angel could not die!
God grant you patience with this stupid epistle!
R. B.

FOOTNOTES:

[260] Song CCXXVI.

CCCII.

TO MR. THOMSON.
[The poet relates the history of several of his best songs in this letter: the true old strain of "Andro and his cutty gun" is the first of its kind.]
19th October, 1794.
My dear Friend,
By this morning's post I have your list, and, in general, I highly approve of it. I shall, at more leisure, give you a critique on the whole. Clarke goes to your town by to-day's fly, and I wish you would call on him and take his opinion in general: you know his taste is a standard. He will return here again in a week or two, so please do not miss asking for him. One thing I hope he will do-persuade you to adopt my favourite "Craigieburn-wood," in your selection: it is as great a favourite of his as of mine. The lady on whom it was made is one of the finest women in Scotland; and in fact (entre nous) is in a manner to me what Sterne's Eliza was to him-a mistress, or friend, or what you will, in the guileless simplicity of Platonic love. (Now, don't put any of your squinting constructions on this, or have any clishmaclaver about it among our acquaintances.) I assure you that to my lovely friend you are indebted for many of your best songs of mine. Do you think that the sober, gin-horse routine of existence could inspire a man with life, and love, and joy-could fire him with enthusiasm, or melt him with pathos, equal to the genius of your book? No! no! Whenever I want to be more than ordinary in song-to be in some degree equal to your diviner airs-do you imagine I fast and pray for the celestial emanation? Tout au contraire! I have a glorious recipe; the very one that for his own use was invented by the divinity of healing and poetry, when erst he piped to the flocks of Admetus. I put myself in a regimen of admiring a fine woman; and in proportion to the adorability of her charms, in proportion you are

delighted with my verses. The lightning of her eye is the godhead of Parnassus, and the witchery of her smile the divinity of Helicon!

To descend to business: if you like my idea of "When she cam ben she bobbit," the following stanzas of mine, altered a little from what they were formerly, when set to another air, may perhaps do instead of worse stanzas:-

O saw ye my dear, my Phely.[261]

Now for a few miscellaneous remarks. "The Posie" (in the Museum) is my composition; the air was taken down from Mrs. Burns's voice. It is well known in the west country, but the old words are trash. By the bye, take a look at the tune again, and tell me if you do not think it is the original from which "Roslin Castle" is composed. The second part in particular, for the first two or three bars, is exactly the old air. "Strathallan's Lament" is mine; the music is by our right trusty and deservedly well-beloved Allan Masterton. "Donocht-Head" is not mine; I would give ten pounds it were. It appeared first in the Edinburgh Herald, and came to the editor of that paper with the Newcastle post-mark on it "Whistle o'er the lave o't" is mine: the music said to be by a John[483] Bruce, a celebrated violin-player in Dumfries, about the beginning of this century. This I know, Bruce, who was an honest man, though a red-wud Highlandman, constantly claimed it; and by all the old musical people here is believed to be the author of it.

"Andrew and his cutty gun." The song to which this is set in the Museum is mine, and was composed on Miss Euphemia Murray, of Lintrose, commonly and deservedly called the Flower of Strathmore.

"How long and dreary is the night!" I met with some such words in a collection of songs somewhere, which I altered and enlarged; and to please you, and to suit your favourite air, I have taken a stride or two across my room, and have arranged it anew, as you will find on the other page.

How long and dreary is the night, andc.[262]

Tell me how you like this. I differ from your idea of the expression of the tune. There is, to me, a great deal of tenderness in it. You cannot, in my opinion, dispense with a bass to your addenda airs. A lady of my acquaintance, a noted performer, plays and sings at the same time so charmingly, that I shall never bear to see any of her songs sent into the world, as naked as Mr. What-d'ye-call-um has done in his London collection.[263]

These English songs gravel me to death. I have not that command of the language that I have of my native tongue. I have been at "Duncan Gray," to dress it in English, but all I can do is deplorably stupid. For instance:-

Let not woman e'er complain, andc.[264]

Since the above, I have been out in the country, taking a dinner with a friend, where I met with a lady whom I mentioned in the second page in this odds-and-ends of a letter. As usual, I got into song; and returning home

I composed the following:
Sleep'st thou, or wak'st thou, fairest creature andc.[265]
If you honour my verses by setting the air to them, I will vamp up the old song, and make it English enough to be understood.
I enclose you a musical curiosity, an East Indian air, which you would swear was a Scottish one. I know the authenticity of it, as the gentleman who brought it over is a particular acquaintance of mine. Do preserve me the copy I send you, as it is the only one I have. Clarke has set a bass to it, and I intend putting it into the Musical Museum. Here follow the verses I intend for it.
But lately seen in gladsome green, andc.[266]
I would be obliged to you if you would procure me a sight of Ritson's collection of English songs, which you mention in your letter. I will thank you for another information, and that as speedily as you please: whether this miserable drawling hotch-potch epistle has not completely tired you of my correspondence?
Variation.
Now to the streaming fountain, Or up the heathy mountain, The hart, hind, and roe, freely, wildly-wanton stray; In twining hazel bowers, His lay the linnet pours; The lav'rock to the sky Ascends wi' sangs o' joy, While the sun and thou arise to bless the day.
When frae my Chloris parted, Sad, cheerless, broken-hearted, The night's gloomy shades, cloudy, dark, o'ercast my sky. But when she charms my sight, In pride of beauty's light; When through my very heart Her beaming glories dart; 'Tis then, 'tis then I wake to life and joy!
R. B.

FOOTNOTES:

[261] Song CCXXVII.
[262] Song CCXXVIII.
[263] Mr. Ritson, whose collection of Scottish songs was published this year.
[264] Song CCXXIX.
[265] Song CCXXX.
[266] Song CCXVI.

CCCIII.

TO MR. THOMSON.
[The presents made to the poet were far from numerous: the book for which he expresses his thanks, was the work of the waspish Ritson.]
November, 1794.

Many thanks to you, my dear Sir, for your present; it is a book of the utmost importance to me. I have yesterday begun my anecdotes, andc., for your work. I intend drawing them up in the form of a letter to you, which will save[484] me from the tedious dull business of systematic arrangement. Indeed, as all I have to say consists of unconnected remarks, anecdotes, scraps of old songs, andc., it would be impossible to give the work a beginning, a middle, and an end, which the critics insist to be absolutely necessary in a work. In my last, I told you my objections to the song you had selected for "My lodging is on the cold ground." On my visit the other day to my friend Chloris (that is the poetic name of the lovely goddess of my inspiration), she suggested an idea, which I, on my return from the visit, wrought into the following song.

My Chloris, mark how green the groves.[267]

How do you like the simplicity and tenderness of this pastoral? I think it pretty well.

I like you for entering so candidly and so kindly into the story of "ma chere amie." I assure you I was never more in earnest in my life, than in the account of that affair which I sent you in my last. Conjugal love is a passion which I deeply feel, and highly venerate; but, somehow, it does not make such a figure in poesy as that other species of the passion,

"Where love is liberty, and nature law."

Musically speaking, the first is an instrument of which the gamut is scanty and confined, but the tones inexpressibly sweet, while the last has powers equal to all the intellectual modulations of the human soul. Still, I am a very poet in my enthusiasm of the passion. The welfare and happiness of the beloved object is the first and inviolate sentiment that pervades my soul; and whatever pleasures I might wish for, or whatever might be the raptures they would give me, yet, if they interfere with that first principle, it is having these pleasures at a dishonest price; and justice forbids and generosity disdains the purchase.

Despairing of my own powers to give you variety enough in English songs, I have been turning over old collections, to pick out songs, of which the measure is something similar to what I want; and, with a little alteration, so as to suit the rhythm of the air exactly, to give you them for your work. Where the songs have hitherto been but little noticed, nor have ever been set to music, I think the shift a fair one. A song, which, under the same first verse, you will find in Ramsay's Tea-table Miscellany, I have cut down for an English dress to your "Dainty Davie," as follows:-

It was the charming month of May.[268]

You may think meanly of this, but take a look at the bombast original, and you will be surprised that I have made so much of it. I have finished my song to "Rothemurche's rant," and you have Clarke to consult as to the set of the air for singing.

Lassie wi' the lint-white locks, andc.[269]

This piece has at least the merit of being a regular pastoral: the vernal morn, the summer noon, the autumnal evening, and the winter night, are regularly rounded. If you like it, well; if not, I will insert it in the Museum.

R. B.

FOOTNOTES:

[267] Song CCXXXI.

[268] Song CCXXXII.

[269] Song CCXXXIII.

CCCIV.

TO MR. THOMSON.

[Sir Walter Scott remarked, on the lyrics of Burns, "that at last the writing a series of songs for large musical collections degenerated into a slavish labour which no talents could support."]

I am out of temper that you should set so sweet, so tender an air, as "Deil tak the wars," to the foolish old verses. You talk of the silliness of "Saw ye my father?"-By heavens! the odds is gold to brass! Besides, the old song, though now pretty well modernized into the Scottish language, is originally, and in the early editions, a bungling low imitation of the Scottish manner, by that genius Tom D'Urfey, so has no pretensions to be a Scottish production. There is a pretty English song by Sheridan, in the "Duenna," to this air, which is out of sight superior to D'Urfey's. It begins,

"When sable night each drooping plant restoring."

The air, if I understand the expression of it properly, is the very native language of simplicity, tenderness, and love. I have again gone over my song to the tune.

Now for my English song to "Nancy's to the greenwood," andc.

Farewell thou stream that winding flows.[270]

There is an air, "The Caledonian Hunt's Delight," to which I wrote a song that, you will find in Johnson, "Ye banks and braes o' bonnie[485] Doon:" this air I think might find a place among your hundred, as Lear says of his knights. Do you know the history of the air? It is curious enough. A good many years ago, Mr. James Miller, writer in your good town, a gentleman whom possibly you know, was in company with our friend Clarke; and talking of Scottish music, Miller expressed an ardent ambition to be able to compose a Scots air. Mr. Clarke, partly by way of joke, told him to keep to the black keys of the harpsichord, and preserve some kind of rhythm, and he would infallibly compose a Scots air. Certain it is that, in a few days, Mr. Miller produced the rudiments of an air, which Mr. Clarke, with some touches and corrections, fashioned into the tune in question. Ritson, you know, has the same story of the black keys; but this account which I have just given you, Mr. Clarke informed me of several years ago. Now, to show you how difficult it is to trace the origin of our airs, I have heard it repeatedly asserted that this was an Irish air; nay, I met with an Irish gentleman who affirmed he had heard it in Ireland among the old women; while, on the other hand, a countess informed me, that the first person who introduced the air into this country, was a baronet's lady of her acquaintance, who took down the notes from an itinerant piper in the Isle of Man. How difficult, then, to ascertain the truth respecting our poesy and music! I, myself, have lately seen a couple of ballads sung through the streets of Dumfries, with my name at the head of them as the author, though it was the first time I had ever seen them.

I thank you for admitting "Craigieburn-wood;" and I shall take care to furnish you with a new chorus. In fact, the chorus was not my work, but a part of some old verses to the air. If I can catch myself in a more than ordinarily propitious moment, I shall write a new "Craigieburn-wood" altogether. My heart is much in the theme.

I am ashamed, my dear fellow, to make the request; 'tis dunning your generosity; but in a moment when I had forgotten whether I was rich or poor, I promised Chloris a copy of your songs. It wrings my honest pride to write you this; but an ungracious request is doubly so by a tedious apology. To make you some amends, as soon as I have extracted the necessary information out of them, I will return you Ritson's volumes.

The lady is not a little proud that she is to make so distinguished a figure in your collection, and I am not a little proud that I have it in my power to please her so much. Lucky it is for your patience that my paper is done, for when I am in a scribbling humour, I know not when to give over.

R. B.

FOOTNOTES:

[270] Song CCXXXIV.

CCCV.

TO MR. THOMSON.

[Willy and Phely, in one of the lyrics which this letter contained, carry on the pleasant bandying of praise till compliments grow scarce, and the lovers are reduced to silence.]

19th November, 1794.

You see, my dear Sir, what a punctual correspondent I am; though, indeed, you may thank yourself for the tedium of my letters, as you have so flattered me on my horsemanship with my favourite hobby, and have praised the grace of his ambling so much, that I am scarcely ever off his back. For instance, this morning, though a keen blowing frost, in my walk before breakfast, I finished my duet, which you were pleased to praise so much. Whether I have uniformly succeeded, I will not say; but here it is for you, though it is not an hour old.

O Philly, happy be the day.[271]

Tell me honestly how you like it, and point out whatever you think faulty.

I am much pleased with your idea of singing our songs in alternate stanzas, and regret that you did not hint it to me sooner. In those that remain, I shall have it in my eye. I remember your objections to the name Philly, but it is the common abbreviation of Phillis. Sally, the only other name that suits, has to my ear a vulgarity about it, which unfits it, for anything except burlesque. The legion of Scottish poetasters of the day, whom your brother editor, Mr. Ritson, ranks with me as my coevals, have always mistaken vulgarity for simplicity; whereas, simplicity is as much eloignée from vulgarity on the one hand, as from affected point and puerile conceit on the other.

I agree with you as to the air, "Craigieburn-wood," that a chorus would, in some degree, spoil the effect, and shall certainly have none[486] in my projected song to it. It is not, however, a case in point with "Rothemurche;" there, as in "Roy's Wife of Aldivalloch," a chorus goes, to my taste, well enough. As to the chorus going first, that is the case with "Roy's Wife," as well as "Rothemurche." In fact, in the first part of both tunes, the rhythm is so peculiar and irregular, and on that irregularity depends so much of their beauty, that we must e'en take them with all their wildness, and humour the verse accordingly. Leaving out the starting note in both tunes, has, I think, an effect that no regularity could counterbalance the want of.

Try, {Oh Roy's wife of Aldivalloch.
{O lassie wi' the lint-white locks.
and
compare with {Roy's wife of Aldivalloch.
{Lassie wi the lint-white locks.

Does not the lameness of the prefixed syllable strike you? In the last case, with the true furor of genius, you strike at once into the wild originality of the air; whereas, in the first insipid method, it is like the grating screw of the pins before the fiddle is brought into tune. This is my taste; if I am wrong, I beg pardon of the cognoscenti.

"The Caledonian Hunt" is so charming, that it would make any subject in a song go down; but pathos is certainly its native tongue. Scottish bacchanalians we certainly want, though the few we have are excellent. For instance, "Todlin hame," is, for wit and humour, an unparalleled composition; And "Andrew and his cutty gun" is the work of a master. By the way, are you not quite vexed to think that those men of genius, for such they certainly were, who composed our fine Scottish lyrics, should be unknown? It has given me many a heart-ache. Apropos to bacchanalian songs in Scottish, I composed one yesterday, for an air I like much-"Lumps o' pudding."

Contented wi' little and cantie wi' mair.[272]

If you do not relish this air, I will send it to Johnson.

R. B.

FOOTNOTES:

[271] Song CCXXXV.

[272] Song CCXXXVI.

CCCVI.

TO MR. THOMSON.

[The instrument which the poet got from the braes of Athol, seems of an order as rude and incapable of fine sounds as the whistles which school-boys make in spring from the smaller boughs of the plane-tree.]

Since yesterday's penmanship, I have framed a couple of English stanzas, by way of an English song to "Roy's Wife." You will allow me, that in this instance my English corresponds in sentiment with the Scottish.

Canst thou leave me thus, my Katy?[273]

Well! I think this, to be done in two or three turns across my room, and with two or three pinches of Irish blackguard, is not so far amiss. You see I am determined to have my quantum of applause from somebody.

Tell my friend Allan (for I am sure that we only want the trifling circumstance of being known to one another, to be the best friends on earth) that I much suspect he has, in his plates, mistaken the figure of the stock and horn. I have, at last, gotten one, but it is a very rude instrument. It is comprised of three parts; the stock, which is the hinder thigh bone of a sheep, such as you see in a mutton ham; the horn, which is a common Highland cow's horn, cut off at the smaller end, until the aperture be large enough to admit the stock to be pushed up through the horn until it be held by the thicker end of the thigh-bone; and lastly, an oaten reed exactly cut and notched like that which you see every shepherd boy have, when the corn-stems are green and full grown. The reed is not made fast in the bone, but is held by the lips, and plays loose in the smaller end of the stock; while the stock, with the horn hanging on its larger end, is held by the hands in playing. The stock has six or seven ventages on the upper side, and one back-ventage, like the common flute. This of mine was made by a man from the braes of Athole, and is exactly what the shepherds wont to use in that country.

However, either it is not quite properly bored in the holes, or else we have not the art of blowing it rightly; for we can make little of it. If Mr. Allan chooses, I will send him a sight of mine, as I look on myself to be a kind of brother-brush with him. “Pride in poets is nae sin;” and I will say it, that I look on Mr. Allan and Mr. Burns to be the only genuine and real painters of Scottish costume in the world.

R. B.

FOOTNOTES:

[273] Song CCXXXVII.

CCCVII.

TO PETER MILLER, JUN., ESQ.,
OF DALSWINTON.

[In a conversation with James Perry, editor of the Morning Chronicle, Mr. Miller, who was then member for the Dumfries boroughs, kindly represented the poverty of the poet and the increasing number of his family: Perry at once offered fifty pounds a year for any contributions he might choose to make to his newspaper: the reasons for his refusal are stated in this letter.]

Dumfries, Nov. 1794.

Dear Sir,

Your offer is indeed truly generous, and most sincerely do I thank you for it; but in my present situation, I find that I dare not accept it. You well know my political sentiments; and were I an insular individual, unconnected with a wife and a family of children, with the most fervid enthusiasm I would have volunteered my services: I then could and would have despised all consequences that might have ensued.

My prospect in the Excise is something; at least it is, encumbered as I am with the welfare, the very existence, of near half-a-score of helpless individuals, what I dare not sport with.

In the mean time, they are most welcome to my Ode; only, let them insert it as a thing they have met with by accident and unknown to me.-Nay, if Mr. Perry, whose honour, after your character of him, I cannot doubt; if he will give me an address and channel by which anything will come safe from those spies with which he may be certain that his correspondence is beset, I will now and then send him any bagatelle that I may write. In the present hurry of Europe, nothing but news and politics will be regarded; but against the days of peace, which Heaven send soon, my little assistance may perhaps fill up an idle column of a newspaper. I have long had it in my head to try my hand in the way of little prose essays, which I propose sending into the world though the medium of some newspaper; and should these be worth his while, to these Mr. Perry shall be welcome; and all my reward shall be, his treating me with his paper, which, by the bye, to anybody who has the least relish for wit, is a high treat indeed.

With the most grateful esteem I am ever,

Dear Sir,

R. B.

CCCVIII.

TO MR. SAMUEL CLARKE, JUN.,
DUMFRIES.

[Political animosities troubled society during the days of Burns, as much at least as they disturb it now-this letter is an instance of it.]

Sunday Morning.

Dear Sir,

I was, I know, drunk last night, but I am sober this morning. From the expressions Capt.made use of to me, had I had no-body's welfare to care for but my own, we should certainly have come, according to the manners of the world, to the necessity of murdering one another about the business. The words were such as, generally, I believe, end in a brace of pistols; but I am still pleased to think that I did not ruin the peace and welfare of a wife and a family of children in a drunken squabble. Farther, you know that the report of certain political opinions being mine, has already once before brought me to the brink of destruction. I dread lest last night's business may be misrepresented in the same way.-You, I beg, will take care to prevent it. I tax your wish for Mr. Burns' welfare with the task of waiting as soon as possible, on every gentleman who was present, and state this to him, and, as you please, show him this letter. What, after all, was the obnoxious toast? "May our success in the present war be equal to the justice of our cause."-A toast that the most outrageous frenzy of loyalty cannot object to. I request and beg that this morning you will wait on the parties present at the foolish dispute. I shall only add, that I am truly sorry that a man who stood so high in my estimation as Mr. , should use me in the manner in which I conceive he has done.

R. B.

CCCIX.

TO MR. THOMSON.

[Burns allowed for the songs which Wolcot wrote for Thomson a degree of

lyric merit which the world has refused to sanction.]
December, 1794.
It is, I assure you, the pride of my heart to do anything to forward or add to the value of your book; and as I agree with you that the jacobite song in the Museum to "There'll never[488] be peace till Jamie comes hame," would not so well consort with Peter Pindar's excellent love-song to that air, I have just framed for you the following:-
Now in her green mantle, andc.[274]
How does this please you? As to the point of time for the expression, in your proposed print from my "Sodger's Return," it must certainly be at- "She gaz'd." The interesting dubiety and suspense taking possession of her countenance, and the gushing fondness, with a mixture of roguish playfulness, in his, strike me as things of which a master will make a great deal. In great haste, but in great truth, yours,
R. B.

FOOTNOTES:

[274] Song CCXXXVIII.

CCCX.

TO MR. THOMSON.
[In this brief and off-hand way Burns bestows on Thompson one of the finest songs ever dedicated to the cause of human freedom.]
January, 1795.
I fear for my songs; however, a few may please, yet originality is a coy feature in composition, and in a multiplicity of efforts in the same style, disappears altogether. For these three thousand years, we poetic folks have been describing the spring, for instance; and as the spring continues the same, there must soon be a sameness in the imagery, andc., of these said rhyming folks.
A great critic (Aikin) on songs, says that love and wine are the exclusive themes for song-writing. The following is on neither subject, and consequently is no song; but will be allowed, I think, to be two or three pretty good prose thoughts inverted into rhyme.
Is there for honest poverty.[275]
I do not give you the foregoing song for your book, but merely by way of vive la bagatelle; for the piece is not really poetry. How will the following do for "Craigieburn-wood?"-
Sweet fa's the eve on Craigieburn.[276]
Farewell! God bless you!
R. B.

FOOTNOTES:

[275] Song CCLXIV.
[276] Song CCXLV.

CCCXI.

TO MR. THOMSON.

[Of this letter, Dr. Currie writes "the poet must have been tipsy indeed to abuse sweet Ecclefechan at this rate;" it is one of the prettiest of our Annandale villages, and the birth-place of that distinguished biographer.]

Ecclefechan, 7th February, 1795.

My dear Thomson,

You cannot have any idea of the predicament in which I write to you. In the course of my duty as supervisor (in which capacity I have acted of late), I came yesternight to this unfortunate, wicked little village. I have gone forward, but snows of ten feet deep have impeded my progress: I have tried to "gae back the gate I cam again," but the same obstacle has shut me up within insuperable bars. To add to my misfortune, since dinner, a scraper has been torturing catgut, in sounds that would have insulted the dying agonies of a sow under the hands of a butcher, and thinks himself, on that very account, exceeding good company. In fact, I have been in a dilemma, either to get drunk, to forget these miseries; or to hang myself, to get rid of them: like a prudent man (a character congenial to my every thought, word, and deed), I of two evils have chosen the least, and am very drunk, at your service!

I wrote you yesterday from Dumfries. I had not time then to tell you all I wanted to say; and, Heaven knows, at present have not capacity.

Do you know an air-I am sure you must know it-"We'll gang nae mair to yon town?" I think, in slowish time, it would make an excellent song. I am highly delighted with it; and if you should think it worthy of your attention, I have a fair dame in my eye to whom I would consecrate it.

As I am just going to bed, I wish you a good night.

R. B.

CCCXII.

TO MR. THOMSON.

[The song of Caledonia, in honour of Mrs. Burns, was accompanied by two others in honour of the poet's[489] mistress: the muse was high in song, and used few words in the letter which enclosed them.]

May, 1795.

O stay, sweet warbling woodlark, stay![277]
Let me know, your very first leisure, how you like this song.
Long, long the night.[278]
How do you like the foregoing? The Irish air, "Humours of Glen," is a great favourite of mine, and as, except the silly stuff in the "Poor Soldier," there are not any decent verses for it, I have written for it as follows:-
Their groves o' sweet myrtle let foreign lands reckon.[279]
Let me hear from you.
R. B.

FOOTNOTES:

[277] Song CCXLIX.
[278] Song CCL.
[279] Song CCLI.

CCCXIII.

TO MR. THOMSON.
[The poet calls for praise in this letter, a species of coin which is always ready.]
How cruel are the parents.[280]
Mark yonder pomp of costly fashion.[281]
Well, this is not amiss. You see how I answer your orders-your tailor could not be more punctual. I am just now in a high fit for poetizing, provided that the strait-jacket of criticism don't cure me. If you can, in a post or two, administer a little of the intoxicating potion of your applause, it will raise your humble servant's phrensy to any height you want. I am at this moment "holding high converse" with the muses, and have not a word to throw away on such a prosaic dog as you are.
R. B.

FOOTNOTES:

[280] Song CCLIII.
[281] Song CCLIV.

CCCXIV.

TO MR. THOMSON.
[Thomson at this time sent the drawing to Burns in which David Allan sought to embody the "Cotter's Saturday Night:" it displays at once the talent and want of taste of the ingenious artist.]

May, 1795.
Ten thousand thanks for your elegant present-though I am ashamed of the value of it, being bestowed on a man who has not, by any means, merited such an instance of kindness. I have shown it to two or three judges of the first abilities here, and they all agree with me in classing it as a first-rate production. My phiz is sae kenspeckle, that the very joiner's apprentice, whom Mrs. Burns employed to break up the parcel (I was out of town that day) knew it at once. My most grateful compliments to Allan, who has honoured my rustic music so much with his masterly pencil. One strange coincidence is, that the little one who is making the felonious attempt on the cat's tail, is the most striking likeness of an ill-deedie, d-n'd, wee, rumblegairie urchin of mine, whom from that propensity to witty wickedness, and man-fu' mischief, which, even at twa days auld, I foresaw would form the striking features of his disposition, I named Willie Nicol, after a certain friend of mine, who is one of the masters of a grammar-school in a city which shall be nameless.
Give the enclosed epigram to my much-valued friend Cunningham, and tell him, that on Wednesday I go to visit a friend of his, to whom his friendly partiality in speaking of me in a manner introduced me-I mean a well-known military and literary character, Colonel Dirom.
You do not tell me how you liked my two last songs. Are they condemned?
R. B.

CCCXV.

TO MR. THOMSON.
[In allusion to the preceding letter, Thomson says to Burns, "You really make me blush when you tell me you have not merited the drawing from me." The "For a' that and a' that," which went with this letter, was, it is believed, the composition of Mrs. Riddel.]
In "Whistle, and I'll come to ye, my lad," the iteration of that line is tiresome to my ear. Here goes what I think is an improvement:-
Oh whistle, and I'll come to ye, my lad; Oh whistle, and I'll come to ye, my lad; Tho' father and mother and a' should gae mad, Thy Jeanie will venture wi' ye, my lad.
In fact, a fair dame, at whose shrine I, the priest of the Nine, offer up the incense of Parnassus-a dame whom the Graces have attired[490] in witchcraft, and whom the Loves have armed with lightning-a fair one, herself the heroine of the song, insists on the amendment, and dispute her commands if you dare?
This is no my ain lassie,[282] andc.
Do you know that you have roused the torpidity of Clarke at last? He has requested me to write three or four songs for him, which he is to set to

music himself. The enclosed sheet contains two songs for him, which please to present to my valued friend Cunningham.

I enclose the sheet open, both for your inspection, and that you may copy the song "Oh bonnie was yon rosy brier." I do not know whether I am right, but that song pleases me; and as it is extremely probable that Clarke's newly-roused celestial spark will be soon smothered in the fogs of indolence, if you like the song, it may go as Scottish verses to the air of "I wish my love was in a mire;" and poor Erskine's English lines may follow.

I enclose you a "For a' that and a' that," which was never in print: it is a much superior song to mine. I have been told that it was composed by a lady, and some lines written on the blank leaf of a copy of the last edition of my poems, presented to the lady whom, in so many fictitious reveries of passion, but with the most ardent sentiments of real friendship, I have so often sung under the name of Chloris:-

To Chloris.[283]

Une bagatelle de l'amitié.

Coila.

R. B.

FOOTNOTES:

[282] Song CCLV.

[283] Poems, No. CXLVI.

CCCXVI.

TO MR. THOMSON.

[In the double service of poesy and music the poet had to sing of pangs which he never endured, from beauties to whom he had never spoken.]

Forlorn my love, no comfort near, andc.[284]

How do you like the foregoing? I have written it within this hour: so much for the speed of my Pegasus; but what say you to his bottom?

R. B.

FOOTNOTES:

[284] Song CCLVIII.

CCCXVII.

TO MR. THOMSON.

[The unexampled brevity of Burns's letters, and the extraordinary flow and grace of his songs, towards the close of his life, have not now for the first

time been remarked.]
Last May a braw wooer.[285]
Why, why tell thy lover.[286]
Such is the peculiarity of the rhythm of this air, that I find it impossible to make another stanza to suit it.
I am at present quite occupied with the charming sensations of the toothache, so have not a word to spare.
R. B.

FOOTNOTES:

[285] Song CCLIX.
[286] Song CCLX.

CCCXVIII.

TO MRS. RIDDEL.
Supposes himself to be writing from the dead to the living.
[Ill health, poverty, a sense of dependence, with the much he had deserved of his country, and the little he had obtained, were all at this time pressing on the mind of Burns, and inducing him to forget what was due to himself as well as to the courtesies of life.]
Madam,
I dare say that this is the first epistle you ever received from this nether world. I write you from the regions of Hell, amid the horrors of the damned. The time and the manner of my leaving your earth I do not exactly know, as I took my departure in the heat of a fever of intoxication contracted at your too hospitable mansion; but, on my arrival here, I was fairly tried, and sentenced to endure the purgatorial tortures of this infernal confine for the space of ninety-nine years, eleven months, and twenty-nine days, and all on account of the impropriety of my conduct yesternight under your roof. Here am I, laid on a bed of pitiless furze, with my aching head reclined on a pillow of ever-piercing thorn, while an infernal tormentor, wrinkled, and old, and cruel, his name I think is Recollection, with a whip of scorpions, forbids peace or rest to approach me, and keeps anguish eternally awake. Still, Madam, if I could in any measure be reinstated in the good opinion of the fair circle whom my conduct last night[491] so much injured, I think it would be an alleviation to my torments. For this reason I trouble you with this letter. To the men of the company I will make no apology.-Your husband, who insisted on my drinking more than I chose, has no right to blame me; and the other gentlemen were partakers of my guilt. But to you, Madam, I have much to apologize. Your good opinion I valued as one of the greatest acquisitions I

had made on earth, and I was truly a beast to forfeit it. There was a Miss I, too, a woman of fine sense, gentle and unassuming manners-do make on my part, a miserable d-mned wretch's best apology to her. A Mrs. G, a charming woman, did me the honour to be prejudiced in my favour; this makes me hope that I have not outraged her beyond all forgiveness.-To all the other ladies please present my humblest contrition for my conduct, and my petition for their gracious pardon. O all ye powers of decency and decorum! whisper to them that my errors, though great, were involuntary-that an intoxicated man is the vilest of beasts-that it was not in my nature to be brutal to any one-that to be rude to a woman, when in my senses, was impossible with me-but-

Regret! Remorse! Shame! ye three hell-hounds that ever dog my steps and bay at my heels, spare me! spare me!

Forgive the offences, and pity the perdition of, Madam, your humble slave.

R. B.

CCCXIX.

TO MRS. RIDDEL.

[Mrs. Riddel, it is said, possessed many more of the poet's letters than are printed-she sometimes read them to friends who could feel their wit, and, like herself, make allowance for their freedom.]

Dumfries, 1795.

Mr. Burns's compliments to Mrs. Riddel-is much obliged to her for her polite attention in sending him the book. Owing to Mr. B.'s being at present acting as supervisor of excise, a department that occupies his every hour of the day, he has not that time to spare which is necessary for any belle-lettre pursuit; but, as he will, in a week or two, again return to his wonted leisure, he will then pay that attention to Mrs. R.'s beautiful song, "To thee, loved Nith"-which it so well deserves. When "Anacharsis' Travels" come to hand, which Mrs. Riddel mentioned as her gift to the public library, Mr. B. will thank her for a reading of it previous to her sending it to the library, as it is a book Mr. B. has never seen: he wishes to have a longer perusal of them than the regulations of the library allow.

Friday Eve.

P.S. Mr. Burns will be much obliged to Mrs. Riddel if she will favour him with a perusal of any of her poetical pieces which he may not have seen.

R. B.

CCCXX.

TO MISS LOUISA FONTENELLE.

[That Miss Fontenelle, as an actress, did not deserve the high praise which

Burns bestows may be guessed: the lines to which he alludes were recited by the lady on her benefit-night, and are printed among his Poems.]
Dumfries, December, 1795.
Madam,
In such a bad world as ours, those who add to the scanty sum of our pleasures, are positively our benefactors. To you, Madam, on our humble Dumfries boards, I have been more indebted for entertainment than ever I was in prouder theatres. Your charms as a woman would insure applause to the most indifferent actress, and your theatrical talents would insure admiration to the plainest figure. This, Madam, is not the unmeaning or insidious compliment of the frivolous or interested; I pay it from the same honest impulse that the sublime of nature excites my admiration, or her beauties give me delight.
Will the foregoing lines be of any service to you in your approaching benefit-night? If they will I shall be prouder of my muse than ever. They are nearly extempore: I know they have no great merit; but though they should add but little to the entertainment of the evening, they give me the happiness of an opportunity to declare how much I have the honour to be, andc.
R. B.

CCCXXI.

TO MRS. DUNLOP.
[Of the sweet girl to whom Burns alludes in this letter he was deprived during this year: her death pressed sorely on him.]
15th December, 1795.
My dear Friend,
As I am in a complete Decemberish humour, gloomy, sullen, stupid as even the Deity of Dulness herself could wish, I shall not drawl out a heavy letter with a number of heavier apologies for my late silence. Only one I shall mention, because I know you will sympathize in it: these four months, a sweet little girl, my youngest child, has been so ill, that every day, a week or less, threatened to terminate her existence. There had much need be many pleasures annexed to the states of husband and father, for, God knows, they have many peculiar cares. I cannot describe to you the anxious, sleepless hours these ties frequently give me. I see a train of helpless little folks; me and my exertions all their stay: and on what a brittle thread does the life of man hang! If I am nipt off at the command of fate! even in all the vigour of manhood as I am-such things happen every day-gracious God! what would become of my little flock! 'Tis here that I envy your people of fortune.-A father on his death-bed, taking an everlasting leave of his children, has indeed woe enough; but the man of competent fortune leaves

his sons and daughters independency and friends; while I-but I shall run distracted if I think any longer on the subject!

To leave talking of the matter so gravely, I shall sing with the old Scots ballad-

"O that I had ne'er been married, I would never had nae care; Now I've gotten wife and bairns, They cry crowdie! evermair.

Crowdie! ance; crowdie! twice; Crowdie! three times in a day; An ye crowdie! ony mair, Ye'll crowdie! a' my meal away."-

December 24th.

We have had a brilliant theatre here this season; only, as all other business does, it experiences a stagnation of trade from the epidemical complaint of the country, want of cash. I mentioned our theatre merely to lug in an occasional Address which I wrote for the benefit-night of one of the actresses, and which is as follows:-

ADDRESS,

SPOKEN BY MISS FONTENELLE ON HER BENEFIT-NIGHT,

DEC. 4, 1795, AT THE THEATRE, DUMFRIES.

Still anxious to secure your partial favour, andc.

25th, Christmas-Morning.

This, my much-loved friend, is a morning of wishes-accept mine-so heaven hear me as they are sincere! that blessings may attend your steps, and affliction know you not! In the charming words of my favourite author, "The Man of Feeling," "May the Great Spirit bear up the weight of thy gray hairs, and blunt the arrow that brings them rest!"

Now that I talk of authors, how do you like Cowper? Is not the "Task" a glorious poem? The religion of the "Task," bating a few scraps of Calvinistic divinity, is the religion of God and nature; the religion that exalts, that ennobles man. Were not you to send me your "Zeluco," in return for mine? Tell me how you like my marks and notes through the book. I would not give a farthing for a book, unless I were at liberty to blot it with my criticisms.

I have lately collected, for a friend's perusal, all my letters; I mean those which I first sketched, in a rough draught, and afterwards wrote out fair. On looking over some old musty papers, which, from time to time, I had parcelled by, as trash that were scarce worth preserving, and which yet at the same time I did not care to destroy; I discovered many of these rude sketches, and have written, and am writing them out, in a bound MS. for my friend's library. As I wrote always to you the rhapsody of the moment, I cannot find a single scroll to you, except one about the commencement of our acquaintance. If there were any possible conveyance, I would send you a perusal of my book.

R. B.

CCCXXII.

TO MR. ALEXANDER FINDLATER,
SUPERVISOR OF EXCISE, DUMFRIES.

[The person to whom this letter is addressed, is the same who lately denied that Burns was harshly used by the Board of Excise: but those, and they are many, who believe what the poet wrote to Erskine, of Mar, cannot agree with Mr. Findlater.]

Sir,

Enclosed are the two schemes. I would not have troubled you with the collector's one, but[493] for suspicion lest it be not right. Mr. Erskine promised me to make it right, if you will have the goodness to show him how. As I have no copy of the scheme for myself, and the alterations being very considerable from what it was formerly, I hope that I shall have access to this scheme I send you, when I come to face up my new books. So much for schemes.-And that no scheme to betray a friend, or mislead a stranger; to seduce a young girl, or rob a hen-roost; to subvert liberty, or bribe an exciseman; to disturb the general assembly, or annoy a gossipping; to overthrow the credit of orthodoxy, or the authority of old songs; to oppose your wishes, or frustrate my hopes-may prosper-is the sincere wish and prayer of

R. B.

CCCXXIII.

TO THE EDITOR OF THE MORNING CHRONICLE.

[Cromek says, when a neighbour complained that his copy of the Morning Chronicle was not regularly delivered to him from the post-office, the poet wrote the following indignant letter to Perry on a leaf of his excise-book, but before it went to the post he reflected and recalled it.]

Dumfries, 1795.

Sir,

You will see by your subscribers' list, that I have been about nine months of that number.

I am sorry to inform you, that in that time, seven or eight of your papers either have never been sent to me, or else have never reached me. To be deprived of any one number of the first newspaper in Great Britain for information, ability, and independence, is what I can ill brook and bear; but to be deprived of that most admirable oration of the Marquis of Lansdowne, when he made the great though ineffectual attempt (in the language of the poet, I fear too true), "to save a sinking state"-this was a loss that I neither can nor will forgive you.-That paper, Sir, never reached me; but I demand it of you. I am a Briton; and must be interested in the cause of liberty:-I am a man; and the rights of human nature cannot be indifferent to me. However, do not let me mislead you: I am not a man in that situation of life, which, as your subscriber, can be of any consequence to you, in the eyes of those to whom situation of life alone is the criterion of man.-I am but a plain tradesman, in this distant, obscure country town: but that humble domicile in which I shelter my wife and children is the Castellum of a Briton; and that scanty, hard-earned income which supports them is as truly my property, as the most magnificent fortune, of the most puissant member of your house of nobles.

These, Sir, are my sentiments; and to them I subscribe my name: and were I a man of ability and consequence enough to address the PUBLIC, with that name should they appear.

I am, andc.

CCCXXIV.

TO MR. HERON,

OF HERON.

[Of Patrick Heron, of Kerroughtree, something has been said in the notes on the Ballads which bear his name.]

Dumfries, 1794, or 1795.

Sir,

I enclose you some copies of a couple of political ballads; one of which, I believe, you have never seen. Would to Heaven I could make you master of as many votes in the Stewartry-but-

"Who does the utmost that he can, Does well, acts nobly, angels could no more."

In order to bring my humble efforts to bear with more effect on the foe, I have privately printed a good many copies of both ballads, and have sent them among friends all about the country.

To pillory on Parnassus the rank reprobation of character, the utter dereliction of all principle, in a profligate junto which has not only outraged virtue, but violated common decency; which, spurning even hypocrisy as paltry iniquity below their daring;-to unmask their flagitiousness to the broadest day-to deliver such over to their merited fate, is surely not merely innocent, but laudable; is not only propriety, but virtue. You have already, as your auxiliary, the sober detestation of mankind on the heads or your opponents; and I swear by the lyre of Thalia to muster on your side all the votaries of honest laughter, and fair, candid ridicule!

I am extremely obliged to you for your kind mention of my interests in a letter which Mr. Syme showed me. At present my situation in life must be in a great measure stationary, at[494] least for two or three years. The statement is this-I am on the supervisors' list, and as we come on there by

precedency, in two or three years I shall be at the head of that list, and be appointed of course. Then, a friend might be of service to me in getting me into a place of the kingdom which I would like. A supervisor's income varies from about a hundred and twenty to two hundred a year; but the business is an incessant drudgery, and would be nearly a complete bar to every species of literary pursuit. The moment I am appointed supervisor, in the common routine, I may be nominated on the collector's list; and this is always a business purely of political patronage. A collector-ship varies much, from better than two hundred a year to near a thousand. They also come forward by precedency on the list; and have, besides a handsome income, a life of complete leisure. A life of literary leisure with a decent competency, is the summit of my wishes. It would be the prudish affectation of silly pride in me to say that I do not need, or would not be indebted to a political friend; at the same time, Sir, I by no means lay my affairs before you thus, to hook my dependent situation on your benevolence. If, in my progress of life, an opening should occur where the good offices of a gentleman of your public character and political consequence might bring me forward, I shall petition your goodness with the same frankness as I now do myself the honour to subscribe myself
R. B.

CCCXXV.

TO MRS. DUNLOP,
IN LONDON.

[In the correspondence of the poet with Mrs. Dunlop he rarely mentions Thomson's Collection of Songs, though his heart was set much upon it: in the Dunlop library there are many letters from the poet, it is said, which have not been published.]

Dumfries, 20th December, 1795.

I have been prodigiously disappointed in this London journey of yours. In the first place, when your last to me reached Dumfries, I was in the country, and did not return until too late to answer your letter; in the next place, I thought you would certainly take this route; and now I know not what is become of you, or whether this may reach you at all. God grant that it may find you and yours in prospering health and good spirits! Do let me hear from you the soonest possible.

As I hope to get a frank from my friend Captain Miller, I shall every leisure hour, take up the pen, and gossip away whatever comes first, prose or poetry, sermon or song. In this last article I have abounded of late. I have often mentioned to you a superb publication of Scottish songs which is making its appearance in your great metropolis, and where I have the honour to preside over the Scottish verse, as no less a personage than Peter

Pindar does over the English.
December 29th.
Since I began this letter, I have been appointed to act in the capacity of supervisor here, and I assure you, what with the load of business, and what with that business being new to me, I could scarcely have commanded ten minutes to have spoken to you, had you been in town, much less to have written you an epistle. This appointment is only temporary, and during the illness of the present incumbent; but I look forward to an early period when I shall be appointed in full form: a consummation devoutly to be wished! My political sins seem to be forgiven me.
This is the season (New-year's-day is now my date) of wishing; and mine are most fervently offered up for you! May life to you be a positive blessing while it lasts, for your own sake; and that it may yet be greatly prolonged, is my wish for my own sake, and for the sake of the rest of your friends! What a transient business is life! Very lately I was a boy; but t'other day I was a young man; and I already begin to feel the rigid fibre and stiffening joints of old age coming fast o'er my frame. With all my follies of youth, and I fear, a few vices of manhood, still I congratulate myself on having had in early days religion strongly impressed on my mind. I have nothing to say to any one as to which sect he belongs to, or what creed he believes: but I look on the man, who is firmly persuaded of infinite wisdom and goodness, superintending and directing every circumstance that can happen in his lot-I felicitate such a man as having a solid foundation for his mental enjoyment; a firm prop and sure stay, in the hour of difficulty, trouble, and distress; and a never-failing anchor of hope, when he looks beyond the grave.[495]
January 12th.
You will have seen our worthy and ingenious friend, the Doctor, long ere this. I hope he is well, and beg to be remembered to him. I have just been reading over again, I dare say for the hundred and fiftieth time, his View of Society and Manners; and still I read it with delight. His humour is perfectly original-it is neither the humour of Addison, nor Swift, nor Sterne, nor of anybody but Dr. Moore. By the bye, you have deprived me of Zeluco, remember that, when you are disposed to rake up the sins of my neglect from among the ashes of my laziness.
He has paid me a pretty compliment, by quoting me in his last publication.[287]
R. B.

FOOTNOTES:

[287] Edward.

CCCXXVI.

ADDRESS OF THE SCOTCH DISTILLERS TO THE RIGHT HON. WILLIAM PITT.

[This ironical letter to the prime minister was found among the papers of Burns.]

Sir,

While pursy burgesses crowd your gate, sweating under the weight of heavy addresses, permit us, the quondam distillers in that part of Great Britain called Scotland, to approach you, not with venal approbation, but with fraternal condolence; not as what you are just now, or for some time have been; but as what, in all probability, you will shortly be.-We shall have the merit of not deserting our friends in the day of their calamity, and you will have the satisfaction of perusing at least one honest address. You are well acquainted with the dissection of human nature; nor do you need the assistance of a fellow-creature's bosom to inform you, that man is always a selfish, often a perfidious being.-This assertion, however the hasty conclusions of superficial observation may doubt of it, or the raw inexperience of youth may deny it, those who make the fatal experiment we have done, will feel.-You are a statesman, and consequently are not ignorant of the traffic of these corporation compliments-The little great man who drives the borough to market, and the very great man who buys the borough in that market, they two do the whole business; and you well know they, likewise, have their price. With that sullen disdain which you can so well assume, rise, illustrious Sir, and spurn these hireling efforts of venal stupidity. At best they are the compliments of a man's friends on the morning of his execution: they take a decent farewell, resign you to your fate, and hurry away from your approaching hour.

If fame say true, and omens be not very much mistaken, you are about to make your exit from that world where the sun of gladness gilds the paths of prosperous man: permit us, great Sir, with the sympathy of fellow-feeling to hail your passage to the realms of ruin.

Whether the sentiment proceed from the selfishness or cowardice of mankind is immaterial; but to point out to a child of misfortune those who are still more unhappy, is to give him some degree of positive enjoyment. In this light, Sir, our downfall may be again useful to you:-though not exactly in the same way, it is not perhaps the first time it has gratified your feelings. It is true, the triumph of your evil star is exceedingly despiteful.-At an age when others are the votaries of pleasure, or underlings in business, you had attained the highest wish of a British statesman; and with the ordinary date of human life, what a prospect was before you! Deeply rooted in Royal favour, you overshadowed the land. The birds of passage, which follow ministerial sunshine through every clime of political faith and manners, flocked to your branches; and the beasts of the field (the lordly possessors of hills and valleys) crowded under your shade. "But behold a watcher, a holy one, came down from heaven, and cried aloud, and said thus: Hew down the tree, and cut off his branches; shake off his leaves, and scatter his fruit; let the beasts get away from under it, and the fowls from his branches!" A blow from an unthought-of quarter, one of those terrible accidents which peculiarly mark the hand of Omnipotence, overset your career, and laid all your fancied honours in the dust. But turn your eyes, Sir, to the tragic scenes of our fate:-an ancient nation, that for many ages had gallantly maintained the unequal struggle for independence with her much more powerful neighbour, at last agrees to a union which should ever after make them one people. In consideration of certain circumstances, it was covenanted that the former should enjoy a stipulated alleviation in her share of the public[496] burdens, particularly in that branch of the revenue called the Excise. This just privilege has of late given great umbrage to some interested, powerful individuals of the more potent part of the empire, and they have spared no wicked pains, under insidious pretexts, to subvert what they dared not openly to attack, from the dread which they yet entertained of the spirit of their ancient enemies.

In this conspiracy we fell; nor did we alone suffer, our country was deeply wounded. A number of (we will say) respectable individuals, largely engaged in trade, where we were not only useful, but absolutely necessary to our country in her dearest interests; we, with all that was near and dear to us, were sacrificed without remorse, to the infernal deity of political expediency! We fell to gratify the wishes of dark envy, and the views of unprincipled ambition! Your foes, Sir, were avowed; were too brave to take an ungenerous advantage; you fell in the face of day.-On the contrary, our enemies, to complete our overthrow, contrived to make their guilt appear the villany of a nation.-Your downfall only drags with you your private friends and partisans: in our misery are more or less involved the most numerous and most valuable part of the community-all those who immediately depend on the cultivation of the soil, from the landlord of a province, down to his lowest hind.

Allow us, Sir, yet further, just to hint at another rich vein of comfort in the dreary regions of adversity;-the gratulations of an approving conscience. In a certain great assembly, of which you are a distinguished member, panegyrics on your private virtues have so often wounded your delicacy, that we shall not distress you with anything on the subject. There is, however, one part of your public conduct which our feelings will not permit us to pass in silence: our gratitude must trespass on your modesty; we mean, worthy Sir, your whole behaviour to the Scots Distillers.-In evil hours, when obtrusive recollection presses bitterly on the sense, let that, Sir, come like an healing angel, and speak the peace to your soul which the world can neither give nor take away.

We have the honour to be,
Sir,
Your sympathizing fellow-sufferers,
And grateful humble servants,
John Barleycorn-Præses.

CCCXXVII.

TO THE HON. PROVOST, BAILIES, AND
TOWN COUNCIL OF DUMFRIES.

[The Provost and Bailies complied at once with the modest request of the poet: both Jackson and Staig, who were heads of the town by turns, were men of taste and feeling.]

Gentlemen,

The literary taste and liberal spirit of your good town has so ably filled the various departments of your schools, as to make it a very great object for a parent to have his children educated in them. Still, to me, a stranger, with my large family, and very stinted income, to give my young ones that education I wish, at the high fees which a stranger pays, will bear hard upon me.

Some years ago your good town did me the honour of making me an honorary burgess.-Will you allow me to request that this mark of distinction may extend so far, as to put me on a footing of a real freeman of the town, in the schools?

If you are so very kind as to grant my request, it will certainly be a constant incentive to me to strain every nerve where I can officially serve you; and will, if possible, increase that grateful respect with which I have the honour to be,

Gentlemen,
Your devoted humble servant,
R. B.

CCCXXVIII.

TO MRS. RIDDEL.

[Mrs. Riddel was, like Burns, a well-wisher to the great cause of human liberty, and lamented with him the excesses of the French Revolution.]

Dumfries, 20th January, 1796.

I cannot express my gratitude to you, for allowing me a longer perusal of "Anacharsis." In fact, I never met with a book that bewitched me so much; and I, as a member of the library, must warmly feel the obligation you have laid us under. Indeed to me the obligation is stronger than to any other individual of our society; as "Anacharsis" is an indispensable desideratum to a son of the muses.

The health you wished me in your morning's card, is, I think, flown from me for ever. I[497] have not been able to leave my bed to-day till about an hour ago. These wickedly unlucky advertisements I lent (I did wrong) to a friend, and I am ill able to go in quest of him.

The muses have not quite forsaken me. The following detached stanza I intend to interweave in some disastrous tale of a shepherd.

R. B.

CCCXXIX.

TO MRS. DUNLOP.

[It seems that Mrs. Dunlop regarded the conduct of Burns, for some months, with displeasure, and withheld or delayed her usual kind and charming communications.]

Dumfries, 31st January, 1796.

These many months you have been two packets in my debt-what sin of ignorance I have committed against so highly-valued a friend I am utterly at a loss to guess. Alas! Madam, ill can I afford, at this time, to be deprived of any of the small remnant of my pleasures. I have lately drunk deep in the cup of affliction. The autumn robbed me of my only daughter and darling child, and that at a distance too, and so rapidly, as to put it out of my power to pay the last duties to her. I had scarcely begun to recover from that shock, when I became myself the victim of a most severe rheumatic fever, and long the die spun doubtful; until, after many weeks of a sick bed, it seems to have turned up life, and I am beginning to crawl across my room, and once indeed have been before my own door in the street.

"When pleasure fascinates the mental sight, Affliction purifies the visual ray, Religion hails the drear, the untried night, And shuts, for ever shuts! life's doubtful day."

R. B.

CCCXXX.

TO MR. THOMSON.

[Cromek informed me, on the authority of Mrs. Burns, that the "handsome, elegant present" mentioned in this letter, was a common worsted shawl.]

February, 1796.

Many thanks, my dear Sir, for your handsome, elegant present to Mrs. Burns, and for my remaining volume of P. Pindar. Peter is a delightful fellow, and a first favourite of mine. I am much pleased with your idea of publishing a collection of our songs in octavo, with etchings. I am extremely willing to lend every assistance in my power. The Irish airs I shall cheerfully undertake the task of finding verses for.

I have already, you know, equipt three with words, and the other day I strung up a kind of rhapsody to another Hibernian melody, which I admire much.

Awa' wi' your witchcraft o' beauty's alarms.[288]

If this will do, you have now four of my Irish engagement. In my by-past songs I dislike one thing, the name Chloris-I meant it as the fictitious name of a certain lady: but, on second thoughts, it is a high incongruity to have a Greek appellation to a Scottish pastoral ballad. Of this, and some things else, in my next: I have more amendments to propose. What you once mentioned of "flaxen locks" is just: they cannot enter into an elegant description of beauty. Of this also again-God bless you![289]

R. B.

FOOTNOTES:

[288] Song CCLXVI.

[289] Our poet never explained what name he would have substituted for Chloris.-Mr. Thomson.

CCCXXXI.

TO MR. THOMSON.

[It is seldom that painting speaks in the spirit of poetry Burns perceived some of the blemishes of Allan's illustrations: but at that time little nature and less elegance entered into the embellishments of books.]

April, 1796.

Alas! my dear Thomson, I fear it will be some time ere I tune my lyre again! "By Babel streams I have sat and wept" almost ever since I wrote you last; I have only known existence by the pressure of the heavy hand of sickness, and have counted time by the repercussions of pain! Rheumatism, cold, and fever have formed to me a terrible combination. I close my eyes in misery, and open them without hope. I look on the vernal day, and say with poor Fergusson,

"Say, wherefore has an all-indulgent heaven Light to the comfortless and wretched given?"

This will be delivered to you by Mrs. Hyslop, landlady of the Globe Tavern here, which for these many years has been my howff, and where[498] our friend Clarke and I have had many a merry squeeze. I am highly delighted with Mr. Allan's etchings. "Woo'd an' married an' a'," is admirable! The grouping is beyond all praise. The expression of the figures, conformable to the story in the ballad, is absolutely faultless perfection. I next admire "Turnim-spike." What I like least is "Jenny said to Jockey." Besides the

female being in her appearance * * * *, if you take her stooping into the account, she is at least two inches taller than her lover. Poor Cleghorn! I sincerely sympathize with him. Happy I am to think that he yet has a well-grounded hope of health and enjoyment in this world. As for me-but that is a sad subject.
R. B.

CCCXXXII.

TO MR. THOMSON.
[The genius of the poet triumphed over pain and want,-his last songs are as tender and as true as any of his early compositions.]
My dear Sir,
I once mentioned to you an air which I have long admired-"Here's a health to them that's awa, hiney," but I forget if you took any notice of it. I have just been trying to suit it with verses, and I beg leave to recommend the air to your attention once more. I have only begun it.
[Here follow the first three stanzas of the song, beginning,
Here's a health to ane I loe dear;[290]
the fourth was found among the poet's MSS. after his death.]
R. B.

FOOTNOTES:

[290] Song CCLXVII.

CCCXXXIII.

TO MR. THOMSON.
[John Lewars, whom the poet introduces to Thomson, was a brother gauger, and a kind, warm-hearted gentleman; Jessie Lewars was his sister, and at this time but in her teens.]
This will be delivered by Mr. Lewars, a young fellow of uncommon merit. As he will be a day or two in town, you will have leisure, if you choose, to write me by him: and if you have a spare half-hour to spend with him, I shall place your kindness to my account. I have no copies of the songs I have sent you, and I have taken a fancy to review them all, and possibly may mend some of them; so when you have complete leisure, I will thank you for either the originals or copies.[291] I had rather be the author of five well-written songs than of ten otherwise. I have great hopes that the genial influence of the approaching summer will set me to rights, but as yet I cannot boast of returning health. I have now reason to believe that my complaint is a flying gout-a sad business!

Do let me know how Cleghorn is, and remember me to him.
This should have been delivered to you a month ago. I am still very poorly, but should like much to hear from you.
R. B.

FOOTNOTES:

[291] "It is needless to say that this revisal Burns did not live to perform."-Currie.

CCCXXXIV.

TO MRS. RIDDEL,
Who had desired him to go to the Birth-Day Assembly on that day to show his loyalty.
[This is the last letter which the poet wrote to this accomplished lady.]
Dumfries, 4th June, 1796.
I am in such miserable health as to be utterly incapable of showing my loyalty in any way. Rackt as I am with rheumatisms, I meet every face with a greeting like that of Balak to Balaam-"Come, curse me Jacob; and come, defy me Israel!" So say I-Come, curse me that east wind; and come, defy me the north! Would you have me in such circumstances copy you out a love-song?
I may perhaps see you on Saturday, but I will not be at the ball.-Why should I? "man delights not me, nor woman either!" Can you supply me with the song, "Let us all be unhappy together?"-do if you can, and oblige, le pauvre miserable
R. B.

CCCXXXV.

TO MR. CLARKE,
SCHOOLMASTER, FORFAR.
[Who will say, after reading the following distressing letter, lately come to light, that Burns did not die in great poverty.]
Dumfries, 26th June, 1796.
My dear Clarke,
Still, still the victim of affliction! Were you to see the emaciated figure who now holds the pen to you, you would not know your old friend. Whether I shall ever get about again, is only known to Him, the Great Unknown, whose creature I am. Alas, Clarke! I begin to fear the worst.
As to my individual self, I am tranquil, and would despise myself, if I were not; but Burns's poor widow, and half-a-dozen of his dear little ones-

helpless orphans!-there I am weak as a woman's tear. Enough of this! 'Tis half of my disease.

I duly received your last, enclosing the note. It came extremely in time, and I am much obliged by your punctuality. Again I must request you to do me the same kindness. Be so very good, as, by return of post, to enclose me another note. I trust you can do it without inconvenience, and it will seriously oblige me. If I must go, I shall leave a few friends behind me, whom I shall regret while consciousness remains. I know I shall live in their remembrance. Adieu, dear Clarke. That I shall ever see you again, is, I am afraid, highly improbable.

R. B.

CCCXXXVI.

TO MR. JAMES JOHNSON,
EDINBURGH.

["In this humble and delicate manner did poor Burns ask for a copy of a work of which he was principally the founder, and to which he had contributed gratuitously not less than one hundred and eighty-four original, altered, and collected songs! The editor has seen one hundred and eighty transcribed by his own hand, for the 'Museum.'"-Cromek. Will it be believed that this "humble request" of Burns was not complied with! The work was intended as a present to Jessie Lewars.]

Dumfries, 4th July, 1796.

How are you, my dear friend, and how comes on your fifth volume? You may probably think that for some time past I have neglected you and your work; but, alas! the hand of pain, and sorrow, and care, has these many months lain heavy on me! Personal and domestic affliction have almost entirely banished that alacrity and life with which I used to woo the rural muse of Scotia. In the meantime let us finish what we have so well begun.

You are a good, worthy, honest fellow, and have a good right to live in this world-because you deserve it. Many a merry meeting this publication has given us, and possibly it may give us more, though, alas! I fear it. This protracting, slow, consuming illness which hangs over me, will, I doubt much, my ever dear friend, arrest my sun before he has well reached his middle career, and will turn over the poet to other and far more important concerns than studying the brilliancy of wit, or the pathos of sentiment! However, hope is the cordial of the human heart, and I endeavour to cherish it as well as I can.

Let me hear from you as soon as convenient.-Your work is a great one; and now that it is finished, I see, if we were to begin again, two or three things that might be mended; yet I will venture to prophesy, that to future ages your publication will be the text-book and standard of Scottish song and music.

I am ashamed to ask another favour of you, because you have been so very good already; but my wife has a very particular friend of hers, a young lady who sings well, to whom she wishes to present the "Scots Musical Museum." If you have a spare copy, will you be so obliging as to send it by the very first fly, as I am anxious to have it soon.

The gentleman, Mr. Lewars, a particular friend of mine, will bring out any proofs (if they are ready) or any message you may have. I am extremely anxious for your work, as indeed I am for everything concerning you, and your welfare.

Farewell,

R. B.

P. S. You should have had this when Mr. Lewars called on you, but his saddle-bags miscarried.

CCCXXXVII.

TO MR. CUNNINGHAM.

[Few of the last requests of the poet were effectual: Clarke, it is believed, did not send the second note he wrote for: Johnson did not send the copy of the Museum[500] which he requested, and the Commissioners of Excise refused the continuance of his full salary.]

Brow, Sea-bathing quarters, 7th July, 1796.

My dear Cunningham,

I received yours here this moment, and am indeed highly flattered with the approbation of the literary circle you mention; a literary circle inferior to none in the two kingdoms. Alas! my friend, I fear the voice of the bard will soon be heard among you no more! For these eight or ten months I have been ailing, sometimes bedfast and sometimes not; but these last three months I have been tortured with an excruciating rheumatism, which has reduced me to nearly the last stage. You actually would not know me if you saw me-Pale, emaciated, and so feeble, as occasionally to need help from my chair-my spirits fled! fled! but I can no more on the subject-only the medical folks tell me that my last only chance is bathing and country-quarters, and riding.-The deuce of the matter is this; when an exciseman is off duty, his salary is reduced to 35l. instead of 50l.-What way, in the name of thrift, shall I maintain myself, and keep a horse in country quarters-with a wife and five children at home, on 35l.? I mention this, because I had intended to beg your utmost interest, and that of all the friends you can muster, to move our commissioners of excise to grant me the full salary; I dare say you know them all personally. If they do not grant it me, I must lay my account with an exit truly en poëte-if I die not of disease, I must perish with hunger.

I have sent you one of the songs; the other my memory does not serve me with, and I have no copy here; but I shall be at home soon, when I will send it you.-Apropos to being at home, Mrs. Burns threatens, in a week or two, to add one more to my paternal charge, which, if of the right gender, I intend shall be introduced to the world by the respectable designation of Alexander Cunningham Burns. My last was James Glencairn, so you can have no objection to the company of nobility. Farewell.
R. B.

CCCXXXVIII.

TO MR. GILBERT BURNS.
[This letter contained heavy news for Gilbert Burns: the loss of a brother whom he dearly loved and admired, was not all, though the worst.]
10th July, 1796.
Dear Brother,
It will be no very pleasing news to you to be told that I am dangerously ill, and not likely to get better. An inveterate rheumatism has reduced me to such a state of debility, and my appetite is so totally gone, that I can scarcely stand on my legs. I have been a week at sea-bathing, and I will continue there, or in a friend's house in the country, all the summer. God keep my wife and children: if I am taken from their head, they will be poor indeed. I have contracted one or two serious debts, partly from my illness these many months, partly from too much thoughtlessness as to expense, when I came to town, that will cut in too much on the little I leave them in your hands. Remember me to my mother.
Yours,
R. B.

CCCXXXIX.

TO MR. JAMES ARMOUR,
MASON, MAUCHLINE.
[The original letter is now in a safe sanctuary, the hands of the poet's son, Major James Glencairn Burns.]
July 10th [1796.]
For Heaven's sake, and as you value the wefare of your daughter and my wife, do, my dearest Sir, write to Fife, to Mrs. Armour to come if possible. My wife thinks she can yet reckon upon a fortnight. The medical people order me, as I value my existence, to fly to sea-bathing and country-quarters, so it is ten thousand chances to one that I shall not be within a dozen miles of her when her hour comes. What a situation for her, poor girl, without a single friend by her on such a serious moment.

I have now been a week at salt-water, and though I think I have got some good by it, yet I have some secret fears that this business will be dangerous if not fatal.

Your most affectionate son,

R. B.

CCCXL.

TO MRS. BURNS.

[Sea-bathing, I have heard skilful men say, was injudicious: but it was felt that Burns was on his way to the[501] grave, and as he desired to try the influence of sea-water, as well as sea-air, his wishes were not opposed.]

Brow, Thursday.

My dearest Love,

I delayed writing until I could tell you what effect sea-bathing was likely to produce. It would be injustice to deny that it has eased my pains, and I think has strengthened me; but my appetite is still extremely bad. No flesh nor fish can I swallow: porridge and milk are the only things I can taste. I am very happy to hear, by Miss Jess Lewars, that you are all well. My very best and kindest compliments to her, and to all the children. I will see you on Sunday.

Your affectionate husband,

R. B.

CCCXLI.

TO MRS. DUNLOP.

["The poet had the pleasure of receiving a satisfactory explanation of this lady's silence," says Currie, "and an assurance of the continuance of her friendship to his widow and children."]

Brow, Saturday, 12th July, 1796.

Madam,

I have written you so often, without receiving any answer, that I would not trouble you again, but for the circumstances in which I am. An illness which has long hung about me, in all probability will speedily send me beyond that bourn whence no traveller returns. Your friendship, with which for many years you honoured me, was a friendship dearest to my soul. Your conversation, and especially your correspondence, were at once highly entertaining and instructive. With what pleasure did I use to break up the seal! The remembrance yet adds one pulse more to my poor palpitating heart.

Farewell!!!

R. B.

CCCXLII.

TO MR. THOMSON.

[Thomson instantly complied with the dying poet's request, and transmitted the exact sum which he requested, viz. five pounds, by return of post: he was afraid of offending the pride of Burns, otherwise he would, he says, have sent a larger sum. He has not, however, told us how much he sent to the all but desolate widow and children, when death had released him from all dread of the poet's indignation.]

Brow, on the Solway-firth, 12th July, 1796.

After all my boasted independence, curst necessity compels me to implore you for five pounds. A cruel wretch of a haberdasher, to whom I owe an account, taking it into his head that I am dying, has commenced a process, and will infallibly put me into jail. Do, for God's sake, send me that sum, and that by return of post. Forgive me this earnestness, but the horrors of a jail have made me half distracted. I do not ask all this gratuitously; for, upon returning health, I hereby promise and engage to furnish you with five pounds' worth of the neatest song-genius you have seen. I tried my hand on "Rothemurche" this morning. The measure is so difficult that it is impossible to infuse much genius into the lines; they are on the other side. Forgive, forgive me!

Fairest maid on Devon's banks.[292]

R. B.

FOOTNOTES:

[292] Song CCLXVIII.

CCCXLIII.

TO MR. JAMES BURNESS,
WRITER, MONTROSE.

[The good, the warm-hearted James Burness sent his cousin ten pounds on the 29th of July-he sent five pounds afterwards to the family, and offered to take one of the boys, and educate him in his own profession of a writer. All this was unknown to the world till lately.]

Brow, 12th July.

My dear Cousin,

When you offered me money assistance, little did I think I should want it so soon. A rascal of a haberdasher, to whom I owe a considerable bill, taking it into his head that I am dying, has commenced process against me, and will infallibly put my emaciated body into jail. Will you be so good as to accommodate me, and that by return of post, with ten pounds? O James! did you know the pride of my heart, you would feel doubly for me! Alas! I am not used to beg! The worst of it is, my health was coming about finely; you know, and my physician assured me, that melancholy and low spirits are half my disease; guess then my horrors since this business began. If I had it settled, I would be, I think, quite well in a manner. How shall I use the[502] language to you, O do not disappoint me! but strong necessity's curst command.

I have been thinking over and over my brother's affairs, and I fear I must cut him up; but on this I will correspond at another time, particularly as I shallyour advice.

Forgive me for once more mentioning by return of post;-save me from the horrors of a jail!

My compliments to my friend James, and to all the rest. I do not know what I have written. The subject is so horrible I dare not look it over again.

Farewell.

R. B.

CCCXLIV.

TO JAMES GRACIE, ESQ.

[James Gracie was, for some time, a banker in Dumfries: his eldest son, a fine, high-spirited youth, fell by a rifle-ball in America, when leading the troops to the attack on Washington.]

Brow, Wednesday Morning, 16th July, 1796.

My dear Sir,

It woulddoing high injustice to this place not to acknowledge that my rheumatisms have derived great benefits from it already; but alas! my loss of appetite still continues. I shall not need your kind offer this week, and I return to town the beginning of next week, it not being a tide-week. I am detaining a man in a burning hurry.

So God bless you.

R. B.

PART V. REMARKS ONSCOTTISH SONGS AND BALLADS

[The following Strictures on Scottish Song exist in the handwriting of Burns, in the interleaved copy of Johnson's Musical Museum, which the poet presented to Captain Riddel, of Friars Carse; on the death of Mrs. Riddel, these precious volumes passed into the hands of her niece, Eliza Bayley, of Manchester, who kindly permitted Mr. Cromek to transcribe and publish them in the Reliques.]

THE HIGHLAND QUEEN.

This Highland Queen, music and poetry, was composed by Mr. M'Vicar, purser of the Solebay man-of-war.-This I had from Dr. Blacklock.

BESS THE GAWKIE.

This song shows that the Scottish muses did not all leave us when we lost Ramsay and Oswald, as I have good reason to believe that the verses and music are both posterior to the days of these two gentlemen. It is a beautiful song, and in the genuine Scots taste. We have few pastoral compositions, I mean the pastoral of nature, that are equal to this.

OH, OPEN THE DOOR, LORD GREGORY.

It is somewhat singular, that in Lanark, Renfrew, Ayr, Wigton, Kirkudbright, and Dumfries-shires, there is scarcely an old song or tune which, from the title, andc., can be guessed to belong to, or be the production of these countries. This, I conjecture, is one of these very few; as the ballad, which is a long one, is called, both by tradition and in printed collections, "The Lass of Lochroyan," which I take to be Lochroyan, in Galloway.

THE BANKS OF THE TWEED.

This song is one of the many attempts that English composers have made to imitate the Scottish manner, and which I shall, in these strictures, beg leave to distinguish by the ap[503]pellation of Anglo-Scottish productions. The music is pretty good, but the verses are just above contempt.

THE BEDS OF SWEET ROSES.

This song, as far as I know, for the first time appears here in print.-When I was a boy, it was a very popular song in Ayrshire. I remember to have heard those fanatics, the Buchanites, sing some of their nonsensical rhymes, which they dignify with the name of hymns, to this air.

ROSLIN CASTLE.

These beautiful verses were the production of a Richard Hewit, a young man that Dr. Blacklock, to whom I am indebted for the anecdote, kept for some years as amanuensis. I do not know who is the author of the second song to the tune. Tytler, in his amusing history of Scots music, gives the air to Oswald; but in Oswald's own collection of Scots tunes, where he affixes an asterisk to those he himself composed, he does not make the least claim to the tune.

SAW YE JOHNNIE CUMMIN? QUO' SHE.

This song, for genuine humour in the verses, and lively originality in the air, is unparalleled. I take it to be very old.

CLOUT THE CALDRON.

A tradition is mentioned in the "Bee," that the second Bishop Chisholm, of Dunblane, used to say, that if he were going to be hanged, nothing would soothe his mind so much by the way as to hear "Clout the Caldron" played. I have met with another tradition, that the old song to this tune,

"Hae ye onie pots or pans, Or onie broken chanlers,"

was composed on one of the Kenmure family, in the cavalier times; and alluded to an amour he had, while under hiding, in the disguise of an itinerant tinker. The air is also known by the name of

"The blacksmith and his apron,"

which from the rhythm, seems to have been a line of some old song to the tune.

SAW YE MY PEGGY.

This charming song is much older, and indeed superior to Ramsay's verses, "The Toast," as he calls them. There is another set of the words, much older still, and which I take to be the original one, but though it has a very great deal of merit, it is not quite ladies' reading.

The original words, for they can scarcely be called verses, seem to be as follows; a song familiar from the cradle to every Scottish ear.

"Saw ye my Maggie, Saw ye my Maggie, Saw ye my Maggie Linkin o'er the lea?

High kilted was she, High kilted was she, High kilted was she, Her coat aboon her knee.

What mark has your Maggie, What mark has your Maggie, What mark has your Maggie, That ane may ken her be?"

Though it by no means follows that the silliest verses to an air must, for that reason, be the original song; yet I take this ballad, of which I have quoted part, to be old verses. The two songs in Ramsay, one of them evidently his own, are never to be met with in the fire-side circle of our peasantry; while that which I take to be the old song, is in every shepherd's mouth. Ramsay, I suppose, had thought the old verses unworthy of a place in his collection.

THE FLOWERS OF EDINBURGH.

This song is one of the many effusions of Scots Jacobitism.-The title "Flowers of Edinburgh," has no manner of connexion with the present verses, so I suspect there has been an older set of words, of which the title is all that remains.

By the bye, it is singular enough that the Scottish muses were all Jacobites.-I have paid more attention to every description of Scots songs than perhaps anybody living has done, and I do not recollect one single stanza, or even the title of the most trifling Scots air, which has the least panegyrical reference to the families of Nassau or Brunswick; while there are hundreds satirizing them.-This may be thought no panegyric on the Scots Poets, but I mean it as such. For myself, I would always take it as a compliment to have it said, that my heart ran before my head,-and surely the gallant though[504] unfortunate house of Stewart, the kings of our fathers for so many heroic ages, is a theme * * * * * *

JAMIE GAY.

Jamie Gay is another and a tolerable Anglo-Scottish piece.

MY DEAR JOCKIE.

Another Anglo-Scottish production.

FYE, GAE RUB HER O'ER WI' STRAE.

It is self-evident that the first four lines of this song are part of a song more ancient than Ramsay's beautiful verses which are annexed to them. As music is the language of nature; and poetry, particularly songs, are always less or more localized (if I may be allowed the verb) by some of the modifications of time and place, this is the reason why so many of our Scots airs have outlived their original, and perhaps many subsequent sets of verses; except a single name or phrase, or sometimes one or two lines, simply to distinguish the tunes by.

To this day among people who know nothing of Ramsay's verses, the following is the song, and all the song that ever I heard:

"Gin ye meet a bonnie lassie, Gie her a kiss and let her gae; But gin ye meet a dirty hizzie, Fye, gae rub her o'er wi' strae.

Fye, gae rub her, rub her, rub her, Fye, gae rub her o'er wi' strae: An' gin ye meet dirty hizzie, Fye, gae rub her o'er wi' strae."

THE LASS O' LIVISTON.

The old song, in three eight-line stanzas, is well known, and has merit as to wit and humour; but it is rather unfit for insertion.-It begins,

"The Bonnie lass o' Liviston, Her name ye ken, her name ye ken, And she has written in her contract To lie her lane, to lie her lane." andc. andc.

THE LAST TIME I CAME O'ER THE MOOR.

Ramsay found the first line of this song, which had been preserved as the title of the charming air, and then composed the rest of the verses to suit that line. This has always a finer effect than composing English words, or words with an idea foreign to the spirit of the old title. Where old titles of songs convey any idea at all, it will generally be found to be quite in the spirit of the air.

JOCKIE'S GRAY BREEKS.

Though this has certainly every evidence of being a Scottish air, yet there is a well-known tune and song in the north of Ireland, called "The Weaver and his Shuttle O," which, though sung much quicker, is every note the very tune.

THE HAPPY MARRIAGE.

Another, but very pretty Anglo-Scottish piece.

THE LASS OF PATIE'S MILL.

In Sinclair's Statistical Account of Scotland, this song is localized (a verb I must use for want of another to express my idea) somewhere in the north of Scotland, and likewise is claimed by Ayrshire.-The following anecdote I had from the present Sir William Cunningham, of Robertland, who had it from the last John, Earl of Loudon. The then Earl of Loudon, and father to Earl John before mentioned, had Ramsay at Loudon, and one day walking together by the banks of Irvine water, near New-Mills, at a place called Patie's Mill, they were struck with the appearance of a beautiful country girl. His lordship observed that she would be a fine theme for a song.-Allan lagged behind in returning to Loudon Castle, and at dinner produced this identical song.

THE TURNIMSPIKE.

There is a stanza of this excellent song for local humour, omitted in this set.-Where I have placed the asterisms.

"They tak the horse then by te head, And tere tey mak her stan', man; Me tell tem, me hae seen te day, Tey no had sic comman', man."

HIGHLAND LADDIE.

As this was a favourite theme with our later Scottish muses, there are several airs and songs[505] of that name. That which I take to be the oldest, is to be found in the "Musical Museum," beginning, "I hae been at Crookieden." One reason for my thinking so is, that Oswald has it in his collection, by the name of "The Auld Highland Laddie." It is also known by the name of "Jinglan Johnie," which is a well-known song of four or five stanzas, and seems to be an earlier song than Jacobite times. As a proof of this, it is little known to the peasantry by the name of "Highland Laddie;" while everybody knows "Jinglan Johnie." The song begins

"Jinglan John, the meickle man, He met wi' a lass was blythe and bonie."

Another "Highland Laddie" is also in the "Museum," vol. v., which I take to be Ramsay's original, as he has borrowed the chorus-"O my bonie Highland lad," andc. It consists of three stanzas, besides the chorus; and has humour in its composition-it is an excellent, but somewhat licentious song.-It begins

"As I cam o'er Cairney mount, And down among the blooming heather."

This air, and the common "Highland Laddie," seem only to be different sets.

Another "Highland Laddie," also in the "Museum," vol. v., is the tune of several Jacobite fragments. One of these old songs to it, only exists, as far as I know, in these four lines-

"Where hae ye been a' day, Bonie laddie, Highland laddie? Down the back o' Bell's brae, Courtin Maggie, courtin Maggie."

Another of this name is Dr. Arne's beautiful air, called the new "Highland Laddie."

THE GENTLE SWAIN.

To sing such a beautiful air to such execrable verses, is downright prostitution of common sense! The Scots verses indeed are tolerable.

HE STOLE MY TENDER HEART AWAY.

This is an Anglo-Scottish production, but by no means a bad one.

FAIREST OF THE FAIR.

It is too barefaced to take Dr. Percy's charming song, and by means of transposing a few English words into Scots, to offer to pass it for a Scots song.-I was not acquainted with the editor until the first volume was nearly finished, else, had I known in time, I would have prevented such an impudent absurdity.

THE BLAITHRIE O'T.

The following is a set of this song, which was the earliest song I remember to have got by heart. When a child, an old woman sung it to me, and I picked it up, every word, at first hearing.

"O Willy, weel I mind, I lent you my hand To sing you a song which you did me command; But my memory's so bad I had almost forgot That you called it the gear and the blaithrie o't.-

I'll not sing about confusion, delusion or pride, I'll sing about a laddie was for a virtuous bride; For virtue is an ornament that time will never rot, And preferable to gear and the blaithrie o't.-

Tho' my lassie hae nae scarlets or silks to put on, We envy not the greatest that sits upon the throne; I wad rather hae my lassie, tho' she cam in her smock, Than a princess wi' the gear and the blaithrie o't.-

Tho' we hae nae horses or menzies at command, We will toil on our foot,

and we'll work wi' our hand; And when wearied without rest, we'll find it sweet in any spot, And we'll value not the gear and the blaithrie o't.-
If we hae ony babies, we'll count them as lent; Hae we less, hae we mair, we will ay be content; For they say they hae mair pleasure that wins bu groat, Than the miser wi' his gear and the blaithrie o't-
I'll not meddle wi' th' affairs of the kirk or the queen; They're nae matters for a sang, let them sink, let them swim; On your kirk I'll ne'er encroach, but I'll hold it stil remote, Sae tak this for the gear and the blaithrie o't."
MAY EVE, OR KATE OF ABERDEEN.
"Kate of Aberdeen" is, I believe, the work of poor Cunningham the player; of whom the following anecdote, though told before, deserves a recital. A fat dignitary of the church coming past Cunningham one Sunday, as the poor poet was busy plying a fishing-rod in some stream near Durham, his native country, his reverence reprimanded Cunningham very se[506]verely for such an occupation on such a day. The poor poet, with that inoffensive gentleness of manners which was his peculiar characteristic, replied, that he hoped God and his reverence would forgive his seeming profanity of that sacred day, "as he had no dinner to eat, but what lay at the bottom of that pool!" This, Mr. Woods, the player, who knew Cunningham well, and esteemed him much, assured me was true.
TWEED SIDE.
In Ramsay's Tea-table Miscellany, he tells us that about thirty of the songs in that publication were the works of some young gentlemen of his acquaintance; which songs are marked with the letters D. C. andc.-Old Mr. Tytler of Woodhouselee, the worthy and able defender of the beauteous Queen of Scots, told me that the songs marked C, in the Tea-table, were the composition of a Mr. Crawfurd, of the house of Achnames, who was afterwards unfortunately drowned coming from France.-As Tytler was most intimately acquainted with Allan Ramsay, I think the anecdote may be depended on. Of consequence, the beautiful song of Tweed Side is Mr. Crawfurd's, and indeed does great honour to his poetical talents. He was a Robert Crawfurd; the Mary he celebrates was a Mary Stewart, of the Castle-Milk family, afterwards married to a Mr. John Ritchie.
I have seen a song, calling itself the original Tweed Side, and said to have been composed by a Lord Yester. It consisted of two stanzas, of which I still recollect the first-
"When Maggy and I was acquaint, I carried my noddle fu' hie; Nae lintwhite on a' the green plain, Nor gowdspink sae happy as me: But I saw her sae fair and I lo'ed: I woo'd, but I came nae great speed; So now I maun wander abroad, And lay my banes far frae the Tweed."-
THE POSY.
It appears evident to me that Oswald composed his Roslin Castle on the modulation of this air.-In the second part of Oswald's, in the three first

bars, he has either hit on a wonderful similarity to, or else he has entirely borrowed the three first bars of the old air; and the close of both tunes is almost exactly the same. The old verses to which it was sung, when I took down the notes from a country girl's voice, had no great merit.-The following is a specimen:

"There was a pretty May, and a milkin she went; Wi' her red rosy cheeks, and her coal black hair; And she has met a young man a comin o'er the bent, With a double and adieu to thee, fair May.

O where are ye goin, my ain pretty May, Wi' thy red rosy cheeks, and thy coal black hair? Unto the yowes a milkin, kind sir, she says, With a double and adieu to thee, fair May.

What if I gang alang with thee, my ain pretty May, Wi' thy red rosy cheeks, any thy coal-black hair; Wad I be aught the warse o' that, kind sir, she says, With a double and adieu to thee, fair May."

MARY'S DREAM.

The Mary here alluded to is generally supposed to be Miss Mary Macghie, daughter to the Laird of Airds, in Galloway. The poet was a Mr. John Lowe, who likewise wrote another beautiful song, called Pompey's Ghost.-I have seen a poetic epistle from him in North America, where he now is, or lately was, to a lady in Scotland.-By the strain of the verses, it appeared that they allude to some love affair.

THE MAID THAT TENDS THE GOATS.

BY MR. DUDGEON.

This Dudgeon is a respectable farmer's son in Berwickshire.

I WISH MY LOVE WERE IN A MIRE.

I never heard more of the words of this old song than the title.

ALLAN WATER.

This Allan Water, which the composer of the music has honoured with the name of the air, I have been told is Allan Water, in Strathallan.

THERE'S NAE LUCK ABOUT THE HOUSE.

This is one of the most beautiful songs in the Scots, or any other language.-The two lines,

"And will I see his face again! And will I hear him speak!"

as well as the two preceding ones, are unequalled almost by anything I ever heard or read: and the lines,

"The present moment is our ain, The neist we never saw,"-

are worthy of the first poet. It is long posterior to Ramsay's days. About the year 1771, or 72, it came first on the streets as a ballad; and I suppose the composition of the song was not much anterior to that period.

TARRY WOO.

This is a very pretty song; but I fancy that the first half stanza, as well as the tune itself, are much older than the rest of the words.

GRAMACHREE.

The song of Gramachree was composed by a Mr. Poe, a counsellor at law in Dublin. This anecdote I had from a gentleman who knew the lady, the "Molly," who is the subject of the song, and to whom Mr. Poe sent the first manuscript of his most beautiful verses. I do not remember any single line that has more true pathos than

"How can she break that honest heart that wears her in its core!"

But as the song is Irish, it had nothing to do in this collection.

THE COLLIER'S BONNIE LASSIE.

The first half stanza is much older than the days of Ramsay.-The old words began thus:

"The collier has a dochter, and, O, she's wonder bonnie! A laird he was that sought her, rich baith in lands and money. She wad na hae a laird, nor wad she be a lady, But she wad hae a collier, the colour o' her daddie."

MY AIN KIND DEARIE-O.

The old words of this song are omitted here, though much more beautiful than these inserted; which were mostly composed by poor Fergusson, in one of his merry humours. The old words began thus:

"I'll rowe thee o'er the lea-rig, My ain kind dearie, O, I'll rowe thee o'er the lea-rig, My ain kind dearie, O, Altho' the night were ne'er sae wat, And I were ne'er sae weary, O; I'll rowe thee o'er the lea-rig, My ain kind dearie, O."-

MARY SCOTT, THE FLOWER OF YARROW.

Mr. Robertson, in his statistical account of the parish of Selkirk, says, that Mary Scott, the Flower of Yarrow, was descended from the Dryhope, and married into the Harden family. Her daughter was married to a predecessor of the present Sir Francis Elliot, of Stobbs, and of the late Lord Heathfield.

There is a circumstance in their contract of marriage that merits attention, and it strongly marks the predatory spirit of the times. The father-in-law agrees to keep his daughter for some time after the marriage; for which the son-in-law binds himself to give him the profits of the first Michaelmas moon!

DOWN THE BURN, DAVIE.

I have been informed, that the tune of "Down the burn, Davie," was the composition of David Maigh, keeper of the blood slough hounds, belonging to the Laird of Riddel, in Tweeddale.

BLINK O'ER THE BURN, SWEET BETTIE.

The old words, all that I remember, are,-

"Blink over the burn, sweet Betty, It is a cauld winter night: It rains, it hails, it thunders, The moon, she gies nae light: It's a' for the sake o' sweet Betty, That ever I tint my way; Sweet, let me lie beyond thee Until it be break o' day.-

O, Betty will bake my bread, And Betty will brew my ale, And Betty will be my love, When I come over the dale: Blink over the burn, sweet Betty,

Blink over the burn to me, And while I hae life, dear lassie, My ain sweet Betty thou's be."

THE BLITHSOME BRIDAL.

I find the "Blithsome Bridal" in James Watson's collection of Scots poems, printed at Edinburgh, in 1706. This collection, the publisher says, is the first of its nature which has been published in our own native Scots dialect-it is now extremely scarce.

JOHN HAY'S BONNIE LASSIE.

John Hay's "Bonnie Lassie" was daughter of John Hay, Earl or Marquis of Tweeddale, and late Countess Dowager of Roxburgh.-She died at Broomlands, near Kelso, some time between the years 1720 and 1740.

THE BONIE BRUCKET LASSIE.

The two first lines of this song are all of it that is old. The rest of the song, as well as those songs in the Museum marked T., are the works of an obscure, tippling, but extraordinary body of the name of Tytler, commonly known by the name of Balloon Tytler, from his having projected a balloon; a mortal, who, though he drudges about Edinburgh as a common printer, with leaky shoes, a sky-lighted hat, and knee-buckles as unlike as George-by-the-grace-of-God, and Solomon-the-son-of-David; yet that same unknown drunken mortal is author and compiler of three-fourths of Elliot's pompous Encyclopedia Britannica, which he composed at half a guinea a week!

SAE MERRY AS WE TWA HA'E BEEN.

This song is beautiful.-The chorus in particular is truly pathetic. I never could learn anything of its author.

Chorus.

"Sae merry as we twa ha'e been, Sae merry as we twa ha'e been; My heart is like for to break, When I think on the days we ha'e seen."

THE BANKS OF FORTH.

This air is Oswald's.

THE BUSH ABOON TRAQUAIR.

This is another beautiful song of Mr. Crawfurd's composition. In the neighbourhood of Traquair, tradition still shows the old "Bush;" which, when I saw it, in the year 1787, was composed of eight or nine ragged birches. The Earl of Traquair has planted a clump of trees near by, which he calls "The New Bush."

CROMLET'S LILT.

The following interesting account of this plaintive dirge was communicated to Mr. Riddel by Alexander Fraser Tytler, Esq., of Woodhouselee.

"In the latter end of the sixteenth century, the Chisolms were proprietors of the estate of Cromlecks (now possessed by the Drummonds). The eldest son of that family was very much attached to a daughter of Sterling of Ardoch, commonly known by the name of Fair Helen of Ardoch.

"At that time the opportunities of meeting betwixt the sexes were more rare, consequently more sought after than now; and the Scottish ladies, far from priding themselves on extensive literature, were thought sufficiently book-learned if they could make out the Scriptures in their mother-tongue. Writing was entirely out of the line of female education. At that period the most of our young men of family sought a fortune, or found a grave, in France. Cromlus, when he went abroad to the war, was obliged to leave the management of his correspondence with his mistress to a lay-brother of the monastery of Dumblain, in the immediate neighbourhood of Cromleck, and near Ardoch. This man, unfortunately, was deeply sensible of Helen's charms. He artfully prepossessed her with stories to the disadvantage of Cromlus; and, by misinterpreting or keeping up the letters and messages intrusted to his care, he entirely irritated both. All connexion was broken off betwixt them; Helen was inconsolable, and Cromlus has left behind him, in the ballad called 'Cromlet's Lilt,' a proof of the elegance of his genius, as well as the steadiness of his love.

"When the artful monk thought time had sufficiently softened Helen's sorrow, he proposed himself as a lover: Helen was obdurate: but at last, overcome by the persuasions of her brother, with whom she lived, and who, having a family of thirty-one children, was probably very well pleased to get her off his hands-she submitted, rather than consented to the ceremony; but there her compliance ended; and, when forcibly put into bed, she started quite frantic from it, screaming out, that after three gentle taps on the wainscot, at the bed-head, she heard Cromlus's voice, crying, 'Helen, Helen, mind me!' Cromlus soon after coming home, the treachery of the confidant was dis[509]covered,-her marriage disannulled,-and Helen became Lady Cromlecks."

N. B. Marg. Murray, mother to these thirty-one children, was daughter to Murray of Strewn, one of the seventeen sons of Tullybardine, and whose youngest son, commonly called the Tutor of Ardoch, died in the year 1715, aged 111 years.

MY DEARIE, IF THOU DIE.

Another beautiful song of Crawfurd's.

SHE ROSE AND LOOT ME IN.

The old set of this song, which is still to be found in printed collections, is much prettier than this; but somebody, I believe it was Ramsay, took it into his head to clear it of some seeming indelicacies, and made it at once more chaste and more dull.

GO TO THE EWE-BUGHTS, MARION.

I am not sure if this old and charming air be of the South, as is commonly said, or of the North of Scotland. There is a song, apparently as ancient us "Ewe-bughts, Marion," which sings to the same tune, and is evidently of the North.-It begins thus:

"The Lord o' Gordon had three dochters, Mary, Marget, and Jean, They wad na stay at bonie Castle Gordon, But awa to Aberdeen."

LEWIS GORDON.

This air is a proof how one of our Scots tunes comes to be composed out of another. I have one of the earliest copies of the song, and it has prefixed, "Tune of Tarry Woo."-

Of which tune a different set has insensibly varied into a different air.-To a Scots critic, the pathos of the line,

""Tho' his back be at the wa',"

-must be very striking. It needs not a Jacobite prejudice to be affected with this song.

The supposed author of "Lewis Gordon" was a Mr. Geddes, priest, at Shenval, in the Ainzie.

O HONE A RIE.

Dr. Blacklock informed me that this song was composed on the infamous massacre of Glencoe.

I'LL NEVER LEAVE THEE.

This is another of Crawfurd's songs, but I do not think in his happiest manner.-What an absurdity, to join such names as Adonis and Mary together!

CORN RIGS ARE BONIE.

All the old words that ever I could meet to this air were the following, which seem to have been an old chorus:

"O corn rigs and rye rigs, O corn rigs are bonie; And where'er you meet a bonie lass, Preen up her cockernony."

THE MUCKING OF GEORDIE'S BYRE.

The chorus of this song is old; the rest is the work of Balloon Tytler.

BIDE YE YET.

There is a beautiful song to this tune, beginning,

"Alas, my son, you little know,"-

which is the composition of Miss Jenny Graham, of Dumfries.

WAUKIN O' THE FAULD.

There are two stanzas still sung to this tune, which I take to be the original song whence Ramsay composed his beautiful song of that name in the Gentle Shepherd.-It begins

"O will ye speak at our town, As ye come frae the fauld."

I regret that, as in many of our old songs, the delicacy of this old fragment is not equal to its wit and humour.

TRANENT-MUIR.

"Tranent-Muir," was composed by a Mr. Skirving, a very worthy respectable farmer near Haddington. I have heard the anecdote often, that Lieut. Smith, whom he mentions in the ninth stanza, came to Haddington after the[510] publication of the song, and sent a challenge to Skirving to meet him at Haddington, and answer for the unworthy manner in which he had noticed him in his song. "Gang away back," said the honest farmer, "and tell Mr. Smith that I hae nae leisure to come to Haddington; but tell him to come here, and I'll tak a look o' him, and if I think I'm fit to fecht him, I'll fecht him; and if no, I'll do as he did-I'll rin awa."-

TO THE WEAVERS GIN YE GO.

The chorus of this song is old, the rest of it is mine. Here, once for all, let me apologize for many silly compositions of mine in this work. Many beautiful airs wanted words; in the hurry of other avocations, if I could string a parcel of rhymes together anything near tolerable, I was fain to let them pass. He must be an excellent poet indeed whose every performance is excellent.

POLWARTH ON THE GREEN.

The author of "Polwarth on the Green" is Capt. John Drummond M'Gregor, of the family of Bochaldie.

STREPHON AND LYDIA.

The following account of this song I had from Dr. Blacklock.

The Strephon and Lydia mentioned in the song were perhaps the loveliest couple of their time. The gentleman was commonly known by the name of Beau Gibson. The lady was the "Gentle Jean," celebrated somewhere in Hamilton of Bangour's poems.-Having frequently met at public places, they had formed a reciprocal attachment, which their friends thought dangerous, as their resources were by no means adequate to their tastes and habits of life. To elude the bad consequences of such a connexion, Strephon was sent abroad with a commission, and perished in Admiral Vernon's expedition to Carthagena.

The author of this song was William Wallace, Esq. of Cairnhill, in Ayrshire.

I'M O'ER YOUNG TO MARRY YET.

The chorus of this song is old. The rest of it, such as it is, is mine.

M'PHERSON'S FAREWELL.

M'Pherson, a daring robber, in the beginning of this century, was condemned to be hanged at the assizes of Inverness. He is said, when under sentence of death, to have composed this tune, which he called his own lament or farewell.

Gow has published a variation of this fine tune as his own composition, which he calls "The Princess Augusta."

MY JO, JANET.

Johnson, the publisher, with a foolish delicacy, refused to insert the last stanza of this humorous ballad.

THE SHEPHERD'S COMPLAINT.

The words by a Mr. R. Scott, from the town or neighbourhood of Biggar.

THE BIRKS OF ABERFELDY.

I composed these stanzas standing under the falls of Aberfeldy, at or near

Moness.

THE HIGHLAND LASSIE O.

This was a composition of mine in very early life, before I was known at all in the world. My Highland lassie was a warm-hearted, charming young creature as ever blessed a man with generous love. After a pretty long tract of the most ardent reciprocal attachment, we met by appointment on the second Sunday of May, in a sequestered spot by the banks of Ayr, where we spent the day in taking a farewell before she should embark for the West Highlands, to arrange matters among her friends for our projected change of life. At the close of autumn following she crossed the sea to meet me at Greenock, where she had scarce landed when she was seized with a malignant fever, which hurried my dear girl to the grave in a few days, before I could even hear of her last illness.

FIFE, AND A' THE LANDS ABOUT IT.

This song is Dr. Blacklock's. He, as well as I, often gave Johnson verses, trifling enough[511] perhaps, but they served as a vehicle to the music.

WERE NA MY HEART LIGHT I WAD DIE.

Lord Hailes, in the notes to his collection of ancient Scots poems, says that this song was the composition of a Lady Grissel Baillie, daughter of the first Earl of Marchmont, and wife of George Baillie, of Jerviswood.

THE YOUNG MAN'S DREAM.

This song is the composition of Balloon Tytler.

STRATHALLAN'S LAMENT.

This air in the composition of one of the worthiest and best-hearted men living-Allan Masterton, schoolmaster in Edinburgh. As he and I were both sprouts of Jacobitism we agreed to dedicate the words and air to that cause. To tell the matter-of-fact, except when my passions were heated by some accidental cause, my Jacobitism was merely by way of vive la bagatelle.

UP IN THE MORNING EARLY.

The chorus of this is old; the two stanzas are mine.

THE TEARS OF SCOTLAND.

Dr. Blacklock told me that Smollet, who was at the bottom a great Jacobite, composed these beautiful and pathetic verses on the infamous depredations of the Duke of Cumberland after the battle of Culloden.

WHAT WILL I DO GIN MY HOGGIE DIE.

Dr. Walker, who was minister at Moffat in 1772, and is now (1791) Professor of Natural History in the University of Edinburgh, told the following anecdote concerning this air.-He said, that some gentlemen, riding a few years ago through Liddesdale, stopped at a hamlet consisting of a few houses, called Moss Platt, when they were struck with this tune, which an old woman, spinning on a rock at her door, was singing. All she could tell concerning it was, that she was taught it when a child, and it was called "What will I do gin my Hoggie die?" No person, except a few females at Moss Platt, knew this fine old tune, which in all probability would have been lost had not one of the gentlemen, who happened to have a flute with him, taken it down.

I DREAM'D I LAY WHERE FLOWERS WERE SPRINGING.

These two stanzas I composed when I was seventeen, and are among the oldest of my printed pieces.

AH! THE POOR SHEPHERD'S MOURNFUL FATE.

Tune-"Gallashiels."

The old title, "Sour Plums o' Gallashiels," probably was the beginning of a song to this air, which is now lost.

The tune of Gallashiels was composed about the beginning of the present century by the Laird of Gallashiel's piper.

THE BANKS OF THE DEVON.

These verses were composed on a charming girl, a Miss Charlotte Hamilton, who is now married to James M'Kitrick Adair, Esq., physician. She is sister to my worthy friend Gavin Hamilton, of Mauchline, and was born on the banks of the Ayr, but was, at the time I wrote these lines, residing at Herveyston, in Clackmannanshire, on the romantic banks of the little river Devon. I first heard the air from a lady in Inverness, and got the notes taken down for this work.

MILL, MILL O.

The original, or at least a song evidently prior to Ramsay's is still extant.-It runs thus,

Chorus.

"The mill, mill O, and the kill, kill O, And the coggin o' Peggy's wheel, O, The sack and the sieve, and a' she did leave, And danc'd the miller's reel O.- As I came down yon waterside, And by yon shellin-hill O, There I spied a bonie bonie lass, And a lass that I lov'd right well O."

WE RAN AND THEY RAN.

The author of "We ran and they ran"-was a Rev. Mr. Murdoch M'Lennan, minister at Crathie, Dee-side.

WALY, WALY.

In the west country I have heard a different edition of the second stanza.- Instead of the four lines, beginning with, "When cockle-shells, andc.," the other way ran thus:-

"O wherefore need I busk my head, Or wherefore need I kame my hair, Sin my fause luve has me forsook, And sys, he'll never luve me mair."

DUNCAN GRAY.

Dr. Blacklock informed me that he had often heard the tradition, that this air was composed by a carman in Glasgow.

DUMBARTON DRUMS.

This is the last of the West-Highland airs; and from it over the whole tract of country to the confines of Tweedside, there is hardly a tune or song that one can say has taken its origin from any place or transaction in that part of Scotland.-The oldest Ayrshire reel, is Stewarton Lasses, which was made by the father of the present Sir Walter Montgomery Cunningham, alias Lord Lysle; since which period there has indeed been local music in that country in great plenty.-Johnie Faa is the only old song which I could ever trace as belonging to the extensive county of Ayr.

CAULD KAIL IN ABERDEEN.

This song is by the Duke of Gordon.-The old verses are,

"There's cauld kail in Aberdeen, And castocks in Strathbogie; When ilka lad maun hae his lass, Then fye, gie me my coggie.

Chorus.

My coggie, Sirs, my coggie, Sirs, I cannot want my coggie; I wadna gie my three-girr'd cap For e'er a quene on Bogie.-

There's Johnie Smith has got a wife, That scrimps him o' his coggie, If she were mine, upon my life I wad douk her in a bogie."

FOR LAKE OF GOLD.

The country girls in Ayrshire, instead of the line-

"She me forsook for a great duke,"

say

"For Athole's duke she me forsook;"

which I take to be the original reading.

These were composed by the late Dr. Austin, physician at Edinburgh.-He had courted a lady, to whom he was shortly to have been married; but the Duke of Athole having seen her, became so much in love with her, that he made proposals of marriage, which were accepted of, and she jilted the doctor.

HERE'S A HEALTH TO MY TRUE LOVE, andc.

This song is Dr. Blacklock's. He told me that tradition gives the air to our James IV. of Scotland.

HEY TUTTI TAITI.

I Have met the tradition universally over Scotland, and particularly about Stirling, in the neighbourhood of the scene, that this air was Robert Bruce's march at the battle of Bannockburn.

RAVING WINDS AROUND HER BLOWING.

I Composed these verses on Miss Isabella M'Leod, of Raza, alluding to her feelings on the death of her sister, and the still more melancholy death of her sister's husband, the late Earl of Loudon; who shot himself out of sheer heart-break at some mortifications he suffered, owing to the deranged state of his finances.

TAK YOUR AULD CLOAK ABOUT YE.

A part of this old song, according to the English set of it, is quoted in Shakspeare.

YE GODS, WAS STREPHON'S PICTURE BLEST?

Tune-"Fourteenth of October."

The title of this air shows that it alludes to the famous king Crispian, the patron of the honourable corporation of shoemakers.-St. Crispian's day falls on the fourteenth of October old style, as the old proverb tells:

"On the fourteenth of October Was ne'er a sutor sober."

SINCE ROBB'D OF ALL THAT CHARM'D MY VIEWS.

The old name of this air is, "the Blossom o' the Raspberry." The song is Dr. Blacklock's.

YOUNG DAMON.

This air is by Oswald.

KIRK WAD LET ME BE.

Tradition in the western parts of Scotland tells that this old song, of which there are still three stanzas extant, once saved a covenanting clergyman out of a scrape. It was a little prior to the revolution, a period when being a Scots covenanter was being a felon, that one of their clergy, who was at that very time hunted by the merciless soldiery, fell in, by accident, with a party of the military. The soldiers were not exactly acquainted with the person of the reverend gentleman of whom they were in search; but from suspicious circumstances, they fancied that they had got one of that cloth and opprobrious persuasion among them in the person of this stranger. "Mass John" to extricate himself, assumed a freedom of manners, very unlike the gloomy strictness of his sect; and among other convivial exhibitions, sung (and some traditions say, composed on the spur of the occasion) "Kirk wad let me be," with such effect, that the soldiers swore he was a dd honest fellow, and that it was impossible he could belong to those hellish conventicles; and so gave him his liberty.

The first stanza of this song, a little altered, is a favourite kind of dramatic interlude acted at country weddings, in the south-west parts of the kingdom. A young fellow is dressed up like an old beggar; a peruke, commonly made of carded tow, represents hoary locks; an old bonnet; a ragged plaid, or surtout, bound with a straw rope for a girdle; a pair of old shoes, with straw ropes twisted round his ankles, as is done by shepherds in snowy weather: his face they disguise as like wretched old age as they can: in this plight he is brought into the wedding-house, frequently to the astonishment of strangers, who are not in the secret, and begins to sing-

"O, I am a silly auld man, My name it is auld Glenae," andc.

He is asked to drink, and by and bye to dance, which after some uncouth excuses he is prevailed on to do, the fiddler playing the tune, which here is commonly called "Auld Glenae;" in short he is all the time so plied with liquor that he is understood to get intoxicated, and with all the ridiculous gesticulations of an old drunken beggar, he dances and staggers until he falls on the floor; yet still in all his riot, nay, in his rolling and tumbling on the floor, with some or other drunken motion of his body, he beats time to the music, till at last he is supposed to be carried out dead drunk.

MUSING ON THE ROARING OCEAN.

I composed these verses out of compliment to a Mrs. M'Lachlan, whose husband is an officer in the East Indies.

BLYTHE WAS SHE.

I composed these verses while I stayed at Ochtertyre with Sir William Murray.-The lady, who was also at Ochtertyre at the same time, was the well-known toast, Miss Euphemia Murray, of Lentrose; she was called, and very justly, "The Flower of Strathmore."

JOHNNIE FAA, OR THE GYPSIE LADDIE.

The people in Ayrshire begin this song-

"The gypsies cam to my Lord Cassilis' yett."-

They have a great many more stanzas in this song than I ever yet saw in any printed copy.-The castle is still remaining at Maybole, where his lordship shut up his wayward spouse, and kept her for life.

TO DAUNTON ME.

The two following old stanzas to this tune have some merit:

"To daunton me, to daunton me, O ken ye what it is that'll daunton me?- There's eighty-eight and eighty-nine, And a' that I hae borne sinsyne, There's cess and press and Presbytrie, I think it will do meikle for to daunton me.

But to wanton me, to wanton me, O ken ye what it is that wad wanton me- To see gude corn upon the rigs, And banishment amang the Whigs, And right restor'd where right sud be, I think it would do meikle for to wanton me."

THE BONNIE LASS MADE THE BED TO ME.

"The Bonnie Lass made the Bed to me," was composed on an amour of Charles II. when skulking in the North, about Aberdeen, in the time of the usurpation. He formed une petite affaire with a daughter of the house of Portletham, who was the "lass that made the bed to him:"-two verses of it are,

"I kiss'd her lips sae rosy red, While the tear stood blinkin in her e'e; I said, My lassie, dinna cry, For ye ay shall make the bed to me.

She took her mither's holland sheets, And made them a' in sarks to me; Blythe and merry may she be, The lass that made the bed to me."

ABSENCE.

A song in the manner of Shenstone.

This song and air are both by Dr. Blacklock.

I HAD A HORSE AND I HAD NAE MAIR.

This story is founded on fact. A John Hunter, ancestor to a very respectable farming family, who live in a place in the parish, I think, of Galston, called Bar-mill, was the luckless hero that "had a horse and had nae mair."-For some little youthful follies he found it necessary to make a retreat to the

West-Highlands, where "he feed himself to a Highland Laird," for that is the expression of all the oral editions of the song I ever heard.-The present Mr. Hunter, who told me the anecdote, is the great-grandchild of our hero.

UP AND WARN A' WILLIE.

This edition of the song I got from Tom Niel, of facetious fame, in Edinburgh. The expression "Up and warn a' Willie," alludes to the Crantara, or warning of a Highland clan to arms. Not understanding this, the Lowlanders in the west and south say, "Up and waur them a'," andc.

A ROSE-BUD BY MY EARLY WALK.

This song I composed on Miss Jenny Cruikshank, only child of my worthy friend Mr. William Cruikshank, of the High-School, Edinburgh. This air is by a David Sillar, quondam merchant, and now schoolmaster in Irvine. He is the Davie to whom I address my printed poetical epistle in the measure of the Cherry and the Slae.

AULD ROB MORRIS.

It is remark-worthy that the song of "Holy and Fairly," in all the old editions of it, is called "The Drunken Wife o' Galloway," which localizes it to that country.

RATTLIN, ROARIN WILLIE.

The last stanza of this song is mine; it was composed out of compliment to one of the worthiest fellows in the world, William Dunbar, Esq., writer to the signet, Edinburgh, and Colonel of the Crochallan Corps, a club of wits who took that title at the time of raising the fencible regiments.

WHERE BRAVING ANGRY WINTER STORMS.

This song I composed on one of the most accomplished of women, Miss Peggy Chalmers, that was, now Mrs. Lewis Hay, of Forbes and Co.'s bank, Edinburgh.

TIBBIE, I HAE SEEN THE DAY.

This song I composed about the age of seventeen.

NANCY'S GHOST.

This song is by Dr. Blacklock.

TUNE YOUR FIDDLES, ETC.

This song was composed by the Rev. John Skinner, nonjuror clergyman at Linshart, near Peterhead. He is likewise author of "Tullochgorum," "Ewie wi' the crooked Horn," "John o' Badenyond," andc., and what is of still more consequence, he is one of the worthiest of mankind. He is the author of an ecclesiastical history of Scotland. The air is by Mr. Marshall, butler to the Duke of Gordon; the first composer of strathspeys of the age. I have been told by somebody, who had it of Marshall himself, that he took the idea of his three most celebrated pieces, "The Marquis of Huntley's[515] Reel," his "Farewell," and "Miss Admiral Gordon's Reel," from the old air, "The German Lairdie."

GILL MORICE.

This plaintive ballad ought to have been called Child Maurice, and not Gil Maurice. In its present dress, it has gained immortal honour from Mr. Home's taking from it the ground-work of his fine tragedy of Douglas. But I am of opinion that the present ballad is a modern composition; perhaps not much above the age of the middle of the last century; at least I should be glad to see or hear of a copy of the present words prior to 1650. That it was taken from an old ballad, called "Child Maurice," now lost, I am inclined to believe; but the present one may be classed with "Hardyknute," "Kenneth," "Duncan, the Laird of Woodhouselie," "Lord Livingston," "Binnorie," "The Death of Monteith," and many other modern productions, which have been swallowed by many readers as ancient fragments of old poems. This beautiful plaintive tune was composed by Mr. M'Gibbon, the selector of a collection of Scots tunes. R. B.

In addition to the observations on Gil Morice, I add, that of the songs which Captain Riddel mentions, "Kenneth" and "Duncan" are juvenile compositions of Mr. M'Kenzie, "The Man of Feeling."-M'Kenzie's father showed them in MS. to Dr. Blacklock, as the productions of his son, from which the Doctor rightly prognosticated that the young poet would make, in his more advanced years, a respectable figure in the world of letters.

This I had from Blacklock.

TIBBIE DUNBAR.

This tune is said to be the composition of John M'Gill, fiddler, in Girvan. He called it after his own name.

WHEN I UPON THY BOSOM LEAN.

This song was the work of a very worthy facetious old fellow, John Lapraik, late of Dalfram, near Muirkirk; which little property he was obliged to sell in consequence of some connexion as security for some persons concerned in that villanous bubble the ayr bank. He has often told me that he composed this song one day when his wife had been fretting o'er their misfortunes.

MY HARRY WAS A GALLANT GAY.

Tune-"Highlander's Lament."

The oldest title I ever heard to this air, was, "The Highland Watch's Farewell to Ireland." The chorus I picked up from an old woman in Dumblane; the rest of the song is mine.

THE HIGHLAND CHARACTER.

This tune was the composition of Gen. Reid, and called by him "The Highland, or 42d Regiment's March." The words are by Sir Harry Erskine.

LEADER-HAUGHS AND YARROW.

There is in several collections, the old song of "Leader-Haughs and Yarrow." It seems to have been the work of one of our itinerant minstrels, as he calls himself, at the conclusion of his song, "Minstrel Burn."

THE TAILOR FELL THRO' THE BED, THIMBLE AN' A'.

This air is the march of the corporation of tailors. The second and fourth stanzas are mine.

BEWARE O' BONNIE ANN.

I composed this song out of compliment to Miss Ann Masterton, the daughter of my friend Allan Masterton, the author of the air of Strathallan's Lament, and two or three others in this work.

THIS IS NO MINE AIN HOUSE.

The first half stanza is old, the rest is Ramsay's. The old words are-

"This is no mine ain house, My ain house, my ain house; This is no mine ain house, I ken by the biggin o't.

Bread and cheese are my door-cheeks, My door-cheeks, my door-cheeks; Bread and cheese are my door-cheeks, And pancakes the riggin o't. [516]

This is no my ain wean; My ain wean, my ain wean; This is no my ain wean, I ken by the greetie o't.

I'll tak the curchie aff my head, Aff my head, aff my head; I'll tak the curchie aff my head, And row't about the feetie o't."

The tune is an old Highland air, called "Shuan truish willighan."

LADDIE, LIE NEAR ME.

This song is by Blacklock.

THE GARDENER AND HIS PAIDLE.

This air is the "Gardener's March." The title of the song only is old; the rest is mine.

THE DAY RETURNS, MY BOSOM BURNS.

Tune.-"Seventh of November."

I composed this song out of compliment to one of the happiest and worthiest married couples in the world, Robert Riddel, Esq., of Glenriddel, and his lady. At their fire-side I have enjoyed more pleasant evenings than at all the houses of fashionable people in this country put together; and to their kindness and hospitality I am indebted for many of the happiest hours of my life.

THE GABERLUNZIE MAN.

The "Gaberlunzie Man" is supposed to commemorate an intrigue of James the Fifth. Mr. Callander, of Craigforth, published some years ago an edition of "Christ's Kirk on the Green," and the "Gaberlunzie Man," with notes critical and historical. James the Fifth is said to have been fond of Gosford, in Aberlady parish, and that it was suspected by his contemporaries, that in his frequent excursions to that part of the country, he had other purposes in view besides golfing and archery. Three favourite ladies, Sandilands, Weir, and Oliphant (one of them resided at Gosford, and the others in the neighbourhood), were occasionally visited by their royal and gallant admirer, which gave rise to the following advice to his majesty, from Sir David Lindsay, of the Mount, Lord Lyon.

"Sow not your seed on Sandylands, spend not your strength in Weir, And ride not on an Elephant, For gawing o' your gear."

MY BONNIE MARY.

This air is Oswald's; the first half stanza of the song is old, the rest mine.

THE BLACK EAGLE.

This song is by Dr. Fordyce, whose merits as a prose writer are well known.

JAMIE, COME TRY ME.

This air is Oswald's; the song mine.

THE LAZY MIST.

This song is mine.

JOHNIE COPE.

This satirical song was composed to commemorate General Cope's defeat at Preston Pans, in 1745, when he marched against the Clans.

The air was the tune of an old song, of which I have heard some verses, but now only remember the title, which was,

"Will ye go the coals in the morning."

I LOVE MY JEAN.

This air is by Marshall; the song I composed out of compliment to Mrs. Burns.

N.B. It was during the honeymoon.

CEASE, CEASE, MY DEAR FRIEND, TO EXPLORE.

The song is by Dr. Blacklock; I believe, but am not quite certain, that the air is his too.

AULD ROBIN GRAY.

This air was formerly called, "The bridegroom greets when the sun gangs down." The words are by Lady Ann Lindsay, of the Balcarras family.

DONALD AND FLORA.

This is one of those fine Gaelic tunes, preserved from time immemorial in the Hebrides; they seem to be the ground-work of many of our finest Scots pastoral tunes. The words of this song were written to commemorate the unfortunate expedition of General Burgoyne in America, in 1777.

O WERE I ON PARNASSUS' HILL.

This air is Oswald's; the song I made out of compliment to Mrs. Burns.

THE CAPTIVE ROBIN.

This air is called "Robie donna Gorach."

THERE'S A YOUTH IN THIS CITY.

This air is claimed by Neil Gow, who calls it his lament for his brother. The first half-stanza of the song is old; the rest mine.

MY HEART'S IN THE HIGHLANDS.

The first half-stanza of this song is old; the rest is mine.

CA' THE EWES AND THE KNOWES.

This beautiful song is in true old Scotch taste, yet I do not know that either air or words were in print before.

THE BRIDAL O'T.

This song is the work of a Mr. Alexander Ross, late schoolmaster at Lochlee; and author of a beautiful Scots poem, called "The Fortunate Shepherdess."

"They say that Jockey 'll speed weel o't, They say that Jockey 'll speed weel o't, For he grows brawer ilka day, I hope we'll hae a bridal o't: For yesternight nae farder gane, The backhouse at the side wa' o't, He there wi' Meg was mirden seen, I hope we'll hae a bridal o't.

An' we had but a bridal o't, An' we had but a bridal o't, We'd leave the rest unto gude luck, Altho' there should betide ill o't: For bridal days are merry times, And young folks like the coming o't, And scribblers they bang up their rhymes, And pipers they the bumming o't.

The lasses like a bridal o't, The lasses like a bridal o't, Their braws maun be in rank and file, Altho' that they should guide ill o't: The boddom o' the kist is then Turn'd up into the inmost o't, The end that held the kecks sae clean, Is now become the teemest o't.

The bangster at the threshing o't. The bangster at the threshing o't, Afore it comes is fidgin-fain, And ilka day's a clashing o't: He'll sell his jerkin for a groat, His linder for anither o't, And e'er he want to clear his shot, His sark'll pay the tither o't

The pipers and the fiddlers o't, The pipers and the fiddlers o't, Can smell a bridal unco' far, And like to be the middlers o't; Fan[293] thick and threefold they convene, Ilk ane envies the tither o't, And wishes nane but him alane May ever see anither o't.

Fan they hae done wi' eating o't, Fan they hae done wi' eating o't, For dancing they gae to the green, And aiblins to the beating o't: He dances best that dances fast, And loups at ilka reesing o't, And claps his hands frae hough to hough, And furls about the feezings o't."

TODLEN HAME.

This is perhaps the first bottle song that ever was composed.

THE BRAES O' BALLOCHMYLE.

This air is the composition of my friend Allan Masterton, in Edinburgh. I composed the verses on the amiable and excellent family of Whitefoords leaving Ballochmyle, when Sir John's misfortunes had obliged him to sell the estate.

THE RANTIN' DOG, THE DADDIE O'T.

I composed this song pretty early in life, and sent it to a young girl, a very particular acquaintance of mine, who was at that time under a cloud.

THE SHEPHERD'S PREFERENCE.

This song is Dr. Blacklock's.-I don't know how it came by the name, but the oldest appellation of the air was, "Whistle and I'll come to you, my lad." It has little affinity to the tune commonly known by that name.

THE BONIE BANKS OF AYR.

I composed this song as I conveyed my chest so far on the road to

Greenock, where I was to embark in a few days for Jamaica.
I meant it as my farewell dirge to my native land.
JOHN O' BADENYON.
This excellent song is the composition of my worthy friend, old Skinner, at Linshart.
"When first I cam to be a man Of twenty years or so, I thought myself a handsome youth, And fain the world would know; In best attire I stept abroad, With spirits brisk and gay, And here and there and everywhere, Was like a morn in May; No care had I nor fear of want, But rambled up and down, And for a beau I might have pass'd In country or in town; I still was pleas'd where'er I went, And when I was alone, I tun'd my pipe and pleas'd myself Wi' John o' Badenyon.
Now in the days of youthful prime A mistress I must find, For love, I heard, gave one an air And ev'n improved the mind: On Phillis fair above the rest Kind fortune fixt my eyes, Her piercing beauty struck my heart, And she became my choice; To Cupid now with hearty prayer I offer'd many a vow; And danc'd, and sung, and sigh'd, and swore, As other lovers do; But, when at last I breath'd my flame, I found her cold as stone; I left the jilt, and tun'd my pipe To John o' Badenyon.
When love had thus my heart beguil'd With foolish hopes and vain, To friendship's port I steer'd my course, And laugh'd at lover's pain A friend I got by lucky chance 'Twas something like divine, An honest friend's a precious gift, And such a gift was mine: And now, whatever might betide, A happy man was I, In any strait I knew to whom I freely might apply; A strait soon came: my friend I try'd; He heard, and spurn'd my moan; I hy'd me home, and tun'd my pipe To John o' Badenyon.
Methought I should be wiser next, And would a patriot turn, Began to doat on Johnny Wilks, And cry up Parson Horne. Their manly spirit I admir'd, And prais'd their noble zeal, Who had with flaming tongue and pen Maintain'd the public weal; But e'er a month or two had past, I found myself betray'd, 'Twas self and party after all, For a' the stir they made; At last I saw the factious knaves Insult the very throne, I curs'd them a', and tun'd my pipe To John o' Badenyon."
A WAUKRIFE MINNIE.
I picked up this old song and tune from a country girl in Nithsdale.-I never met with it elsewhere in Scotland.
"Whare are you gaun, my bonie lass, Whare are you gaun, my hinnie, She answer'd me right saucilie, An errand for my minnie.
O whare live ye, my bonnie lass, O whare live ye, my hinnie, By yon burn-side, gin ye maun ken, In a wee house wi' my minnie.
But I foor up the glen at e'en, To see my bonie lassie; And lang before the gray morn cam, She was na hauf sa sacie.
O weary fa' the waukrife cock, And the foumart lay his crawin! He

wauken'd the auld wife frae her sleep, A wee blink or the dawin.
An angry wife I wat she raise, And o'er the bed she brought her; And wi' a mickle hazle rung She made her a weel pay'd dochter.
O fare thee weel, my bonie lass! O fare thee weel, my hinnie! Thou art a gay and a bonie lass, But thou hast a waukrife minnie."
TULLOCHGORUM.
This first of songs, is the master-piece of my old friend Skinner. He was passing the day,[519] at the town of Cullen, I think it was, in a friend's house whose name was Montgomery. Mrs. Montgomery observing, en passant, that the beautiful reel of Tullochgorum wanted words, she begged them of Mr. Skinner, who gratified her wishes, and the wishes of every Scottish song, in this most excellent ballad.
These particulars I had from the author's son, Bishop Skinner, at Aberdeen.
FOR A' THAT AND A' THAT.
This song is mine, all except the chorus.
AULD LANG SYNE.
Ramsay here, as usual with him, has taken the idea of the song, and the first line, from the old fragment which may be seen in the "Museum," vol. v.
WILLIE BREW'D A PECK O' MAUT.
This air is Masterton's; the song mine.-The occasion of it was this:-Mr. W. Nicol, of the High-School, Edinburgh, during the autumn vacation being at Moffat, honest Allan, who was at that time on a visit to Dalswinton, and I, went to pay Nicol a visit.-We had such a joyous meeting that Mr. Masterton and I agreed, each in our own way, that we should celebrate the business.
KILLIECRANKIE.
The battle of Killiecrankie was the last stand made by the clans for James, after his abdication. Here the gallant Lord Dundee fell in the moment of victory, and with him fell the hopes of the party. General Mackay, when he found the Highlanders did not pursue his flying army, said, "Dundee must be killed, or he never would have overlooked this advantage." A great stone marks the spot where Dundee fell.
THE EWIE WI' THE CROOKED HORN.
Another excellent song of old Skinner's.
CRAIGIE-BURN WOOD.
It is remarkable of this air that it is the confine of that country where the greatest part of our Lowland music (so far as from the title, words, andc., we can localize it) has been composed. From Craigie-burn, near Moffat, until one reaches the West Highlands, we have scarcely one slow air of any antiquity.
The song was composed on a passion which a Mr. Gillespie, a particular friend of mine, had for a Miss Lorimer, afterwards a Mrs. Whelpdale. This young lady was born at Craigie-burn Wood.-The chorus is part of an old foolish ballad.

FRAE THE FRIENDS AND LAND I LOVE.

I added the four last lines, by way of giving a turn to the theme of the poem, such as it is.

HUGHIE GRAHAM

There are several editions of this ballad.-This, here inserted, is from oral tradition in Ayrshire, where, when I was a boy, it was a popular song.-It originally had a simple old tune, which I have forgotten.

"Our lords are to the mountains gane, A hunting o' the fallow deer, And they have gripet Hughie Graham, For stealing o' the bishop's mare.

And they have tied him hand and foot, And led him up, thro' Stirling town; The lads and lasses met him there, Cried, Hughie Graham, thou art a loun.

O lowse my right hand free, he says, And put my braid sword in the same; He's no in Stirling town this day, Dare tell the tale to Hughie Graham.

Up then bespake the brave Whitefoord, As he sat by the bishop's knee, Five hundred white stots I'll gie you, If ye'll let Hughie Graham gae free.

O haud your tongue, the bishop says, And wi' your pleading let me be; For tho' ten Grahams were in his coat, Hughie Graham this day shall die.

Up then bespake the fair Whitefoord, As she sat by the bishop's knee; Five hundred white pence I'll gie you, If ye'll gie Hughie Graham to me.

O haud your tongue now, lady fair, And wi' your pleading let it be; Altho' ten Grahams were in his coat, It's for my honour he maun die.

They've ta'en him to the gallows knowe, He looked to the gallows tree, Yet never colour left his cheek, Nor ever did he blink his e'e [520]

At length he looked around about, To see whatever he could spy: And there he saw his auld father, And he was weeping bitterly.

O haud your tongue, my father dear, And wi' your weeping let it be; Thy weeping's sairer on my heart, Than a' that they can do to me.

And ye may gie my brother John My sword that's bent in the middle clear; And let him come at twelve o'clock, And see me pay the bishop's mare.

And ye may gie my brother James My sword that's bent in the middle brown; And bid him come at four o'clock, And see his brother Hugh cut down.

Remember me to Maggy my wife, The neist time ye gang o'er the moor, Tell her she staw the bishop's mare, Tell her she was the bishop's whore.

And ye may tell my kith and kin, I never did disgrace their blood; And when they meet the bishop's cloak, To mak it shorter by the hood."

A SOUTHLAND JENNY.

This is a popular Ayrshire song, though the notes were never taken down before. It, as well as many of the ballad tunes in this collection, was written from Mrs. Burns's voice.

MY TOCHER'S THE JEWEL.

This tune is claimed by Nathaniel Gow.-It is notoriously taken from "The muckin o' Gordie's byre."-It is also to be found long prior to Nathaniel

Gow's era, in Aird's Selection of Airs and Marches, the first edition under the name of "The Highway to Edinburgh."

THEN, GUID WIFE, COUNT THE LAWIN'.

The chorus of this is part of an old song, no stanza of which I recollect.

THERE'LL NEVER BE PEACE TILL JAMIE COMES HAME.

This tune is sometimes called "There's few gude fellows when Willie's awa."-But I never have been able to meet with anything else of the song than the title.

I DO CONFESS THOU ART SAE FAIR.

This song is altered from a poem by Sir Robert Ayton, private secretary to Mary and Ann, Queens of Scotland.-The poem is to be found in James Watson's Collection of Scots Poems, the earliest collection printed in Scotland. I think that I have improved the simplicity of the sentiments, by giving them a Scots dress.

THE SODGER LADDIE.

The first verse of this is old; the rest is by Ramsay. The tune seems to be the same with a slow air, called "Jackey Hume's Lament"-or, "The Hollin Buss"-or "Ken ye what Meg o' the Mill has gotten?"

WHERE WAD BONNIE ANNIE LIE.

The old name of this tune is,-

"Whare'll our gudeman lie."

A silly old stanza of it runs thus-

"O whare'll our gudeman lie, Gudeman lie, gudeman lie, O whare'll our gudeman lie, Till he shute o'er the simmer?

Up amang the hen-bawks, The hen-bawks, the hen-bawks, Up amang the hen-bawks, Amang the rotten timmer."

GALLOWAY TAM.

I have seen an interlude (acted at a wedding) to this tune, called "The Wooing of the Maiden." These entertainments are now much worn out in this part of Scotland. Two are still retained in Nithsdale, viz. "Silly Pure Auld Glenae," and this one, "The Wooing of the Maiden."

AS I CAM DOWN BY YON CASTLE WA.

This is a very popular Ayrshire song.

LORD RONALD MY SON.

This air, a very favourite one in Ayrshire, is evidently the original of Lochaber. In this manner most of our finest more modern airs have had their origin. Some early minstrel, or musical shepherd, composed the simple, artless original air; which being picked up by the[521] more learned musician, took the improved form it bears.

O'ER THE MOOR AMANG THE HEATHER.

This song is the composition of a Jean Glover, a girl who was not only a whore, but also a thief; and in one or other character has visited most of the Correction Houses in the West. She was born I believe in Kilmarnock,-I took the song down from her singing, as she was strolling through the country, with a sleight-of-hand blackguard.

TO THE ROSE-BUD.

This song is the composition of aJohnson, a joiner in the neighbourhood of Belfast. The tune is by Oswald, altered, evidently, from "Jockie's Gray Breeks."

YON WILD MOSSY MOUNTAINS.

This tune is by Oswald. The song alludes to a part of my private history, which it is of no consequence to the world to know.

IT IS NA, JEAN, THY BONNIE FACE.

These were originally English verses:-I gave them the Scots dress.

EPPIE M'NAB.

The old song with this title has more wit than decency.

WHA IS THAT AT MY BOWER DOOR.

This tune is also known by the name of "Lass an I come near thee." The words are mine.

THOU ART GANE AWA.

This time is the same with "Haud awa frae me, Donald."

THE TEARS I SHED MUST EVER FALL.

This song of genius was composed by a Miss Cranston. It wanted four lines, to make all the stanzas suit the music, which I added, and are the four first of the last stanza.

"No cold approach, no alter'd mien, Just what would make suspicion start; No pause the dire extremes between, He made me blest-and broke my heart!"

THE BONIE WEE THING.

Composed on my little idol "the charming, lovely Davies."

THE TITHER MORN.

This tune is originally from the Highlands. I have heard a Gaelic song to it, which I was told was very clever, but not by any means a lady's song.

A MOTHER'S LAMENT FOR THE DEATH OF HER SON.

This most beautiful tune is, I think, the happiest composition of that bard-born genius, John Riddel, of the family of Glencarnock, at Ayr. The words were composed to commemorate the much-lamented and premature death of James Ferguson, Esq., jun. of Craigdarroch.

DAINTIE DAVIE.

This song, tradition says, and the composition itself confirms it, was composed on the Rev. David Williamson's begetting the daughter of Lady Cherrytrees with child, while a party of dragoons were searching her house to apprehend him for being an adherent to the solemn league and covenant. The pious woman had put a lady's night-cap on him, and had laid him a-bed with her own daughter, and passed him to the soldiery as a lady, her daughter's bed-fellow. A mutilated stanza or two are to be found in Herd's collection, but the original song consists of five or six stanzas, and were their delicacy equal to their wit and humour, they would merit a place in any collection. The first stanza is

"Being pursued by the dragoons, Within my bed he was laid down; And weel I wat he was worth his room, For he was my Daintie Davie."

Ramsay's song, "Luckie Nansy," though he calls it an old song with additions, seems to be all his own except the chorus:

"I was a telling you, Luckie Nansy, Luckie Nansy [522]Auld springs wad ding the new, But ye wad never trow me."

Which I should conjecture to be part of a song prior to the affair of Williamson.

BOB O' DUMBLANE.

Ramsay, as usual, has modernized this song. The original, which I learned on the spot, from my old hostess in the principal inn there, is-

"Lassie, lend me your braw hemp heckle, And I'll lend you my thripplin-kame; My heckle is broken, it canna be gotten, And we'll gae dance the bob o' Dumblane.

Twa gaed to the wood, to the wood, to the wood. Twa gaed to the wood-three came hame; An' it be na weel bobbit, weel bobbit, weel bobbit An' it be na weel bobbit, we'll bob it again."

I insert this song to introduce the following anecdote, which I have heard well authenticated. In the evening of the day of the battle of Dumblane, (Sheriff Muir,) when the action was over, a Scots officer in Argyll's army, observed to His Grace, that he was afraid the rebels would give out to the world that they had gotten the victory.-"Weel, weel," returned his Grace, alluding to the foregoing ballad, "if they think it be nae weel bobbit, we'll bob it again."

FOOTNOTES:

[293] Fan, when-the dialect of Angus.

THE BORDER TOUR

Left Edinburgh (May 6, 1787)-Lammermuir-hills miserably dreary, but at times very picturesque. Lanton-edge, a glorious view of the Merse-Reach Berrywell-old Mr. Ainslie an uncommon character;-his hobbies, agriculture, natural philosophy, and politics.-In the first he is unexceptionably the clearest-headed, best-informed man I ever met with; in the other two, very intelligent:-As a man of business he has uncommon merit, and by fairly deserving it has made a very decent independence. Mrs. Ainslie, an excellent, sensible, cheerful, amiable old woman-Miss Ainslie-her person a little embonpoint, but handsome; her face, particularly her eyes, full of sweetness and good humour-she unites three qualities rarely to be found together; keen, solid penetration; sly, witty observation and remark; and the gentlest, most unaffected female modesty-Douglas, a clever, fine, promising young fellow.-The family-meeting with their brother; my compagnon de voyage, very charming; particularly the sister. The whole family remarkably attached to their menials-Mrs. A. full of stories of the sagacity and sense of the little girl in the kitchen.-Mr. A. high in the praises of an African, his house-servant-all his people old in his service-Douglas's old nurse came to Berrywell yesterday to remind them of its being his birthday.

A Mr. Dudgeon, a poet at times,[294] a worthy remarkable character-natural penetration, a great deal of information, some genius, and extreme modesty.

Sunday.-Went to church at Dunse[295]-Dr. Howmaker a man of strong lungs and pretty judicious remark; but ill skilled in propriety, and altogether unconscious of his want of it.

Monday.-Coldstream-went over to England-Cornhill-glorious river Tweed-clear and majestic-fine bridge. Dine at Coldstream with [523]Mr. Ainslie and Mr. Foreman-beat Mr. F in a dispute about Voltaire. Tea at Lenel House with Mr. Brydone-Mr. Brydone a most excellent heart, kind, joyous, and benevolent; but a good deal of the French indiscriminate complaisance-from his situation past and present, an admirer of everything that bears a splendid title, or that possesses a large estate-Mrs. Brydone a most elegant woman in her person and manners; the tones of her voice remarkably sweet-my reception extremely flattering-sleep at Coldstream.

Tuesday.-Breakfast at Kelso-charming situation of Kelso-fine bridge over the Tweed-enchanting views and prospects on both sides of the river, particularly the Scotch side; introduced to Mr. Scott of the Royal Bank-an excellent, modest fellow-fine situation of it-ruins of Roxburgh Castle-a holly-bush, growing where James II. of Scotland was accidentally killed by the bursting of a cannon. A small old religious ruin, and a fine old garden planted by the religious, rooted out and destroyed by an English hottentot, a maitre d'hotel of the duke's, a Mr. Cole-climate and soil of Berwickshire, and even Roxburghshire, superior to Ayrshire-bad roads. Turnip and sheep husbandry, their great improvements-Mr. M'Dowal, at Caverton Mill, a friend of Mr. Ainslie's, with whom I dined to-day, sold his sheep, ewe and lamb together, at two guineas a piece-wash their sheep before shearing-seven or eight pounds of washen wool in a fleece-low markets, consequently low rents-fine lands not above sixteen shillings a Scotch acre-magnificence of farmers and farm-houses-come up Teviot and up Jed to Jedburgh to lie, and so wish myself a good night.

Wednesday.-Breakfast with Mr.in Jedburgh-a squabble between Mrs. , a crazed, talkative slattern, and a sister of hers, an old maid, respecting a relief minister-Miss gives Madam the lie; and Madam, by way of revenge, upbraids her that she laid snares to entangle the said minister, then a widower, in the net of matrimony-go about two miles out of Jedburgh to a roup of parks-meet a polite, soldier-like gentleman, a Captain Rutherford, who had been many years through the wilds of America, a prisoner among the Indians-charming, romantic situation of Jedburgh, with gardens, orchards, andc., intermingled among the houses-fine old ruins-a once magnificent cathedral, and strong castle. All the towns here have the appearance of old, rude grandeur, but the people extremely idle-Jed a fine romantic little river.

Dine with Capt. Rutherford-the Captain a polite fellow, fond of money in his farming way; showed a particular respect to my bardship-his lady exactly a proper matrimonial second part for him. Miss Rutherford a beautiful girl, but too far gone woman to expose so much of a fine swelling bosom-her face very fine.

Return to Jedburgh-walk up Jed with some ladies to be shown Love-lane and Blackburn, two fairy scenes. Introduced to Mr. Potts, writer, a very clever fellow; and Mr. Somerville, the clergyman of the place, a man and a gentleman, but sadly addicted to punning.-The walking party of ladies, Mrs.and Misshre sister, before mentioned.-N.B. These two appear still more comfortably ugly and stupid, and bore me most shockingly. Two Miss , tolerably agreeable. Miss Hope, a tolerably pretty girl, fond of laughing and fun. Miss Lindsay, a good-humoured, amiable girl; rather short et embonpoint, but handsome, and extremely graceful-beautiful hazel eyes, full of spirit, and sparkling with delicious moisture-an engaging face-un tout ensemble that speaks her of the first order of female minds-her sister, a bonnie, strappan, rosy, sonsie lass. Shake myself loose, after several unsuccessful efforts, of Mrs.and Miss , and somehow or other, get hold of Miss Lindsay's arm. My heart is thawed into melting pleasure after being so long frozen up in the Greenland bay of indifference, amid the noise and nonsense of Edinburgh. Miss seems very well pleased with my bardship's distinguishing her, and after some slight qualms, which I could easily mark, she sets the titter round at defiance, and kindly allows me to keep my hold; and when parted by the ceremony of my introduction to Mr. Somerville, she met me half, to resume my situation.-Nota Bene-The poet within a point and a half of being d-mnably in love-I am afraid my bosom is still nearly as much tinder as ever.

The old cross-grained, whiggish, ugly, slanderous Miss , with all the poisonous spleen of a disappointed, ancient maid, stops me very unseasonably to ease her bursting breast, by[524] falling abusively foul on the Miss Lindsays, particularly on my Dulcinea;-I hardly refrain from cursing her to her face for daring to mouth her calumnious slander on one of the finest pieces of the workmanship of Almighty Excellence! Sup at Mr. 's; vexed that the Miss Lindsays are not of the supper-party, as they only are wanting. Mrs.and Miss still improve infernally on my hands.

Set out next morning for Wauchope, the seat of my correspondent, Mrs. Scott-breakfast by the way with Dr. Elliot, an agreeable, good-hearted, climate-beaten old veteran, in the medical line; now retired to a romantic, but rather moorish place, on the banks of the Roole-he accompanies us almost to Wauchope-we traverse the country to the top of Bochester, the scene of an old encampment, and Woolee Hill.

Wauchope-Mr. Scott exactly the figure and face commonly given to Sancho Panca-very shrewd in his farming matters, and not unfrequently stumbles on what may be called a strong thing rather than a good thing. Mrs. Scott all the sense, taste, intrepidity of face, and bold, critical decision, which usually distinguish female authors.-Sup with Mr. Potts-agreeable party.-Breakfast next morning with Mr. Somerville-the bruit of Miss Lindsay and my bardship, by means of the invention and malice of Miss . Mr. Somerville sends to Dr. Lindsay, begging him and family to breakfast if convenient, but at all events to send Miss Lindsay; accordingly Miss Lindsay only comes.-I find Miss Lindsay would soon play the devil with me-I met with some little flattering attentions from her. Mrs. Somerville an excellent, motherly, agreeable woman, and a fine family.-Mr. Ainslie, and Mrs. S, junrs., with Mr. , Miss Lindsay, and myself, go to see Esther, a very remarkable woman for reciting poetry of all kinds, and sometimes making Scotch doggerel herself-she can repeat by heart almost everything she has ever read, particularly Pope's Homer from end to end-has studied Euclid by herself, and in short, is a woman of very extraordinary abilities.-On conversing with her I find her fully equal to the character given of her.[296]-She is very much flattered that I send for her, and that she sees a poet who has put out a book, as she says.-She is, among other things, a great florist-and is rather past the meridian of once celebrated beauty.

I walk in Esther's garden with Miss Lindsay, and after some little chit-chat of the tender kind, I presented her with a proof print of my Nob, which she accepted with something more tinder than gratitude. She told me many little stories which Misshad retailed concerning her and me, with prolonging pleasure-God bless her! Was waited on by the magistrates, and presented with the freedom of the burgh.

Took farewell of Jedburgh, with some melancholy, disagreeable sensations.-Jed, pure be thy crystal streams, and hallowed thy sylvan banks! Sweet Isabella Lindsay, may peace dwell in thy bosom, uninterrupted, except by the tumultuous throbbings of rapturous love! That love-kindling eye must beam on another, not on me; that graceful form must bless another's arms; not mine!

Kelso. Dine with the farmers' club-all gentlemen, talking of high matters-each of them keeps a hunter from thirty to fifty pounds value, and attends the fox-huntings in the country-go out with Mr. Ker, one of the club, and a friend of Mr. Ainslie's, to lie-Mr. Ker a most gentlemanly, clever, handsome fellow, a widower with some fine children-his mind and manner astonishingly like my dear old friend Robert Muir, in Kilmarnock-everything in Mr. Ker's most elegant-he offers to accompany me in my English tour. Dine with Sir Alexander Don-a pretty clever fellow, but far from being a match for his divine lady.-A very wet day * * *-Sleep at Stodrig again; and set out for Melrose-visit Dryburgh, a fine old ruined abbey-still bad weather-cross Leader, and come up Tweed to Melrose-dine there, and visit that far-famed, glorious ruin-come to Selkirk, up Ettrick; the whole country hereabout, both on Tweed and Ettrick, remarkably stony.

Monday.-Come to Inverleithing, a famous shaw, and in the vicinity of the palace of Traquair, where having dined, and drank some Galloway-whey, I hero remain till to-morrow[525]-saw Elibanks and Elibraes, on the other side of the Tweed.

Tuesday.-Drank tea yesternight at Pirn, with Mr. Horseburgh.-Breakfasted to-day with Mr. Ballantyne of Hollowlee-Proposal for a four-horse team to consist of Mr. Scott of Wauchope, Fittieland: Logan of Logan, Fittiefurr: Ballantyne of Hollowlee, Forewynd: Horsburgh of Horsburgh.-Dine at a country inn, kept by a miller, in Earlston, the birth-place and residence of the celebrated Thomas a Rhymer-saw the ruins of his castle-come to Berrywell.

Wednesday.-Dine at Dunse with the farmers' club-company-impossible to do them justice-Rev. Mr. Smith a famous punster, and Mr. Meikle a celebrated mechanic, and inventor of the threshing-mills.

Thursday, breakfast at Berrywell, and walk into Dunse to see a famous knife made by a cutler there, and to be presented to an Italian prince.-A pleasant ride with my friend Mr. Robert Ainslie, and his sister, to Mr. Thomson's, a man who has newly commenced farmer, and has married a Miss Patty Grieve, formerly a flame of Mr. Robert Ainslie's.-Company-Miss Jacky Grieve, an amiable sister of Mrs. Thomson's, and Mr. Hood, an honest, worthy, facetious farmer, in the neighbourhood.

Friday.-Ride to Berwick-An idle town, rudely picturesque.-Meet Lord Errol in walking round the walls.-His lordship's flattering notice of me.-Dine with Mr. Clunzie, merchant-nothing particular in company or conversation-Come up a bold shore, and over a wild country to Eyemouth-sup and sleep at Mr. Grieve's.

Saturday.-Spend the day at Mr. Grieve's-made a royal arch mason of St. Abb's Lodge,[297]-Mr. William Grieve, the oldest brother, a joyous, warm-hearted, jolly, clever fellow-takes a hearty glass, and sings a good song.-Mr. Robert, his brother, and partner in trade, a good fellow, but says little. Take a sail after dinner. Fishing of all kinds pays tithes at Eyemouth.

Sunday.-A Mr. Robinson, brewer at Ednam, sets out with us to Dunbar.

The Miss Grieves very good girls.-My bardship's heart got a brush from Miss Betsey.

Mr. William Grieve's attachment to the family-circle, so fond, that when he is out, which by the bye is often the case, he cannot go to bed till he see if all his sisters are sleeping wellPass the famous Abbey of Coldingham, and Pease-bridge.-Call at Mr. Sheriff's where Mr. A. and I dine.-Mr. S. talkative and conceited. I talk of love to Nancy the whole evening, while her brother escorts home some companions like himself.-Sir James Hall of Dunglass, having heard of my being in the neighbourhood, comes to Mr. Sheriff's to breakfast-takes me to see his fine scenery on the stream of Dunglass-Dunglass the most romantic, sweet place I over saw-Sir James and his lady a pleasant happy couple.-He points out a walk for which he has an uncommon respect, as it was made by an aunt of his, to whom he owes much.

Misswill accompany me to Dunbar, by way of making a parade of me as a sweetheart of hers, among her relations. She mounts an old cart-horse, as huge and as lean as a house; a rusty old side-saddle without girth, or stirrup, but fastened on with an old pillion-girth-herself as fine as hands could make her, in cream-coloured riding clothes, hat and feather, andc.-I, ashamed of my situation, ride like the devil, and almost shake her to pieces on old Jolly-get rid of her by refusing to call at her uncle's with her.

Past through the most glorious corn-country I ever saw, till I reach Dunbar, a neat little town.-Dine with Provost Fall, an eminent merchant, and most respectable character, but undescribable, as he exhibits no marked traits. Mrs. Fall, a genius in painting; fully more clever in the fine arts and sciences than my friend Lady Wauchope, without her consummate [526] assurance of her own abilities.-Call with Mr. Robinson (who, by the bye, I find to be a worthy, much respected man, very modest; warm, social heart, which with less good sense than his would be perhaps with the children of prim precision and pride, rather inimical to that respect which is man's due from man) with him I call on Miss Clarke, a maiden in the Scotch phrase, "Guid enough, but no brent new:" a clever woman, with tolerable pretensions to remark and wit; while time had blown the blushing bud of bashful modesty into the flower of easy confidence. She wanted to see what sort of raree show an author was; and to let him know, that though Dunbar was but a little town, yet it was not destitute of people of parts.

Breakfast next morning at Skateraw, at Mr. Lee's, a farmer of great note.-Mr. Lee, an excellent, hospitable, social fellow, rather oldish; warm-hearted and chatty-a most judicious, sensible farmer. Mr. Lee detains me till next morning.-Company at dinner.-My Rev. acquaintance Dr. Bowmaker, a reverend, rattling old fellow.-Two sea lieutenants; a cousin of the landlord's, a fellow whose looks are of that kind which deceived me in a gentleman at Kelso, and has often deceived me: a goodly handsome figure and face, which incline one to give them credit for parts which they have not. Mr. Clarke, a much cleverer fellow, but whose looks a little cloudy, and his appearance rather ungainly, with an every-day observer may prejudice the opinion against him.-Dr. Brown, a medical young gentleman from Dunbar, a fellow whose face and manners are open and engaging.-Leave Skateraw for Dunse next day, along with collector , a lad of slender abilities and bashfully diffident to an extreme.

Found Miss Ainslie, the amiable, the sensible, the good-humoured, the sweet Miss Ainslie, all alone at Berrywell.-Heavenly powers, who know the weakness of human hearts, support mine! What happiness must I see only to remind me that I cannot enjoy it!

Lammer-muir Hills, from East Lothian to Dunse, very wild.-Dine with the farmer's club at Kelso. Sir John Hume and Mr. Lumsden there, but nothing worth remembrance when the following circumstance is considered-I walk into Dunse before dinner, and out to Berrywell in the evening with Miss Ainslie-how well-bred, how frank, how good she is! Charming Rachael! may thy bosom never be wrung by the evils of this life of sorrows, or by the villany of this world's sons!

Thursday.-Mr. Ker and I set out to dine at Mr. Hood's on our way to England.

I am taken extremely ill with strong feverish symptoms, and take a servant of Mr. Hood's to watch me all night-embittering remorse scares my fancy at the gloomy forebodings of death.-I am determined to live for the future in such a manner as not to be scared at the approach of death-I am sure I could meet him with indifference, but for "The something beyond the grave."-Mr. Hood agrees to accompany us to England if we will wait till Sunday.

Friday.-I go with Mr. Hood to see a roup of an unfortunate farmer's stock-rigid economy, and decent industry, do you preserve me from being the principal dramatis persona in such a scene of horror.

Meet my good old friend Mr. Ainslie, who calls on Mr. Hood in the evening to take farewell of my bardship. This day I feel myself warm with sentiments of gratitude to the Great Preserver of men, who has kindly restored me to health and strength once more.

A pleasant walk with my young friend Douglas Ainslie, a sweet, modest, clever young fellow.

Sunday, 27th May.-Cross Tweed, and traverse the moors through a wild country till I reach Alnwick-Alnwick Castle a seat of the Duke of Northumberland, furnished in a most princely manner.-A Mr. Wilkin, agent of His Grace's, shows us the house and policies. Mr. Wilkin, a discreet, sensible, ingenious man.

Monday.-Come, still through by-ways, to Warkworth, where we dine.-Hermitage and old castle. Warkworth situated very picturesque, with Coquet Island, a small rocky spot, the seat of an old monastery, facing it a little in the sea; and the small but romantic river Coquet, running through it.-Sleep at Morpeth, a pleasant enough little town, and on next day to Newcastle.-Meet with a very agreeable, sensible fellow, a Mr. Chattox, who shows us a great many civilities, and who dines and sups with us.

Wednesday.-Left Newcastle early in the morning, and rode over a fine country to Hexham to breakfast-from Hexham to Wardrue, the celebrated Spa, where we slept.

Thursday-Reach[527] Longtown to dine, and part there with my good friends Messrs. Hood and Ker-A hiring day in Longtown-I am uncommonly happy to see so many young folks enjoying life.-I come to Carlisle.-(Meet a strange enough romantic adventure by the way, in falling in with a girl and her married sister-the girl, after some overtures of gallantry on my side, sees me a little cut with the bottle, and offers to take me in for a Gretna-Green affair.-I, not being such a gull, as she imagines, make an appointment with her, by way of vive la bagatelle, to hold a conference on it when we reach town.-I meet her in town and give her a brush of caressing, and a bottle of cider; but finding herself un peu trompé in her man she sheers off.) Next day I meet my good friend, Mr. Mitchell, and walk with him round the town and its environs, and through his printing-works,

andc.-four or five hundred people employed, many of them women and children.-Dine with Mr. Mitchell, and leave Carlisle.-Come by the coast to Annan.-Overtaken on the way by a curious old fish of a shoemaker, and miner, from Cumberland mines.
[Here the manuscript abruptly terminates.]

FOOTNOTES:

[294] The author of that fine song, "The Maid that tends the Goats."
[295] "During the discourse Burns produced a neat impromptu, conveying an elegant compliment to Miss Ainslie. Dr. B. had selected a text of Scripture that contained a heavy denunciation against obstinate sinners. In the course of the sermon Burns observed the young lady turning over the leaves of her Bible, with much earnestness, in search of the text. He took out a slip of paper, and with a pencil wrote the following lines on it, which he immediately presented to her.
"Fair maid, you need not take the hint, Nor idle texts pursue:- 'Twas guilty sinners that he meant,- Not angels such as you."
Cromek.
[296] "This extraordinary woman then moved in a very humble walk of life:-the wife of a common working gardener. She is still living, and, if I am rightly informed, her time is principally occupied in her attentions to a little day-school, which not being sufficient for her subsistence, she is obliged to solicit the charily of her benevolent neighbours. 'Ah, who would love the lyre!"'-Cromek.
[297] The entry made on this occasion in the Lodge-books of St Abb's is honorable to
"The brethren of the mystic level."
"Eyemouth, 19th May, 1787.
"At a general encampment held this day, the following brethren were made royal arch masons, viz. Robert Burns, from the Lodge of St. James's, Tarbolton, Ayrshire, and Robert Ainslie, from the Lodge of St. Luke's, Edinburgh by James Carmichael, Wm. Grieve, Daniel Dow, John Clay, Robert Grieve, andc. andc. Robert Ainslie paid one guinea admission dues; but on account of R. Burns's remarkable poetical genius, the encampment unanimously agreed to admit him gratis, and considered themselves honoured by having a man of such shining abilities for one of their companions."
Extracted from the Minute Book of the Lodge by Thomas Bowbill

THE HIGHLAND TOUR

25th August, 1787.

I leave Edinburgh for a northern tour, in company with my good friend Mr. Nicol, whose originality of humour promises me much entertainment.-Linlithgow-a fertile improved country-West Lothian. The more elegance and luxury among the farmers, I always observe in equal proportion, the rudeness and stupidity of the peasantry. This remark I have made all over the Lothians, Merse, Roxburgh, andc. For this, among other reasons, I think that a man of romantic taste, a "Man of Feeling," will be better pleased with the poverty, but intelligent minds of the peasantry in Ayrshire (peasantry they are all below the justice of peace) than the opulence of a club of Merse farmers, when at the same time, he considers the vandalism of their plough-folks, andc. I carry this idea so far, that an unenclosed, half improven country is to me actually more agreeable, and gives me more pleasure as a prospect, than a country cultivated like a garden.-Soil about Linlithgow light and thin.-The town carries the appearance of rude, decayed grandeur-charmingly rural, retired situation. The old royal palace a tolerably fine, but melancholy ruin-sweetly situated on a small elevation, by the brink of a loch. Shown the room where the beautiful, injured Mary Queen of Scots was born-a pretty good old Gothic church. The infamous stool of repentance standing, in the old Romish way, on a lofty situation.

What a poor pimping business is a Presbyterian place of worship; dirty, narrow, and squalid; stuck in a corner of old popish grandeur such as Linlithgow, and much more, Melrose! Ceremony and show, if judiciously thrown in, absolutely necessary for the bulk of mankind, both in religious and civil matters.-Dine.-Go to my friend Smith's at Avon printfield-find nobody but Mrs. Miller, an agreeable, sensible, modest, good body; as useful, but not so ornamental as Fielding's Miss Western-not rigidly polite à la Français, but easy, hospitable, and housewifely.

An old lady from Paisley, a Mrs. Lawson, whom I promised to call for in Paisley-like old lady W, and still more like Mrs. C, her conversation is pregnant with strong sense and just remark, but like them, a certain air of self-importance and a duresse in the eye, seem to indicate, as the Ayrshire wife observed of her cow, that "she had a mind o' her ain."

Pleasant view of Dunfermline and the rest of the fertile coast of Fife, as we go down to that dirty, ugly place, Borrowstones-see a horse-race and call on a friend of Mr. Nicol's, a Bailie Cowan, of whom I know too little to attempt his portrait-Come through the rich carse of Falkirk to pass the night. Falkirk nothing[528] remarkable except the tomb of Sir John the Graham, over which, in the succession of time, four stones have been placed.-Camelon, the ancient metropolis of the Picts, now a small village in the neighbourhood of Falkirk.-Cross the grand canal to Carron.-Come past Larbert and admire a fine monument of cast-iron erected by Mr. Bruce, the African traveller, to his wife.

Pass Dunipace, a place laid out with fine taste-a charming amphitheatre bounded by Denny village, and pleasant seats down the way to Dunnipace.-The Carron running down the bosom of the whole makes it one of the most charming little prospects I have seen.

Dine at Auchinbowie-Mr. Monro an excellent, worthy old man-Miss Monro an amiable, sensible, sweet young woman, much resembling Mrs. Grierson. Come to Bannockburn-Shown the old house where James III. finished so tragically his unfortunate life. The field of Bannockburn-the hole where glorious Bruce set his standard. Here no Scot can pass uninterested.-I fancy to myself that I see my gallant, heroic countrymen coming o'er the hill and down upon the plunderers of their country, the murderers of their fathers; noble revenge, and just hate, glowing in every vein, striding more and more eagerly as they approach the oppressive, insulting, blood-thirsty foe! I see them meet in gloriously triumphant congratulation on the victorious field, exulting in their heroic royal leader, and rescued liberty and independence! Come to Stirling.-Monday go to Harvieston. Go to see Caudron linn, and Rumbling brig, and Diel's mill. Return in the evening. Supper-Messrs. Doig, the schoolmaster; Bell; and Captain Forrester of the castle-Doig a queerish figure, and something of a pedant-Bell a joyous fellow, who sings a good song.-Forrester a merry, swearing kind of man, with a dash of the sodger.

Tuesday Morning.-Breakfast with Captain Forrester-Ochel Hills-Devon River-Forth and Tieth-Allan River-Strathallan, a fine country, but little improved-Cross Earn to Crieff-Dine and go to Arbruchil-cold reception at Arbruchil-a most romantically pleasant ride up Earn, by Auchtertyre and Comrie to Arbruchil-Sup at Crieff.

Wednesday Morning.-Leave Crieff-Glen Amond-Amond river-Ossian's grave-Loch Fruoch-Glenquaich-Landlord and landlady remarkable characters-Taymouth described in rhyme-Meet the Hon. Charles Townshend.

Thursday.-Come down Tay to Dunkeld-Glenlyon House-Lyon River-Druid's Temple-three circles of stones-the outer-most sunk-the second has thirteen stones remaining-the innermost has eight-two large detached ones like a gate, to the south-east-Say prayers in it-Pass Taybridge-Aberfeldy-described in rhyme-Castle Menzies-Inver-Dr. Stewart-sup.

Friday.-Walk with Mrs. Stewart and Beard to Birnam top-fine prospect down Tay-Craigieburn hills-Hermitage on the Branwater, with a picture of Ossian-Breakfast with Dr. Stewart-Neil Gow[298] plays-a short, stout-built, honest Highland figure, with his grayish hair shed on his honest social brow-an interesting face, marking strong sense, kind openheartedness, mixed with unmistrusting simplicity-visit his house-Marget Gow.

Ride up Tummel River to Blair-Fascally a beautiful romantic nest-wild grandeur of the pass of Gilliecrankie-visit the gallant Lord Dundee's stone.

Blair-Sup with the Duchess-easy and happy from the manners of the family-confirmed in my good opinion of my friend Walker.

Saturday.-Visit the scenes round Blair-fine, but spoiled with bad taste-Tilt and Gairie rivers-Falls on the Tilt-Heather seat-Ride in company with Sir William Murray and Mr. Walker, to Loch Tummel-meanderings of the [529] Rannach, which runs through quondam Struan Robertson's estate from Loch Rannach to Loch Tummel-Dine at Blair-Company-General Murray-Captain Murray, an honest tar-Sir William Murray, an honest, worthy man, but tormented with the hypochondria-Mrs. Graham, belle et aimable-Miss Catchcart-Mrs. Murray, a painter-Mrs. King-Duchess and fine family, the Marquis, Lords James, Edward, and Robert-Ladies Charlotte, Emilia, and children dance-Sup-Mr. Graham of Fintray.

Come up the Garrie-Falls of Bruar-Daldecairoch-Dalwhinnie-Dine-Snow on the hills 17 feet deep-No corn from Loch-Gairie to Dalwhinnie-Cross the Spey, and come down the stream to Pitnin-Straths rich-les environs picturesque-Craigow hill-Ruthven of Badenoch-Barracks-wild and magnificent-Rothemurche on the other side, and Glenmore-Grant of Rothemurche's poetry-told me by the Duke of Gordon-Strathspey, rich and romantic-Breakfast at Aviemore, a wild spot-dine at Sir James Grant's-Lady Grant, a sweet, pleasant body-come through mist and darkness to Dulsie, to lie.

Tuesday.-Findhorn river-rocky banks-come on to Castle Cawdor, where Macbeth murdered King Duncan-saw the bed in which King Duncan was stabbed-dine at Kilravock-Mrs. Rose, sen., a true chieftain's wife-Fort George-Inverness.

Wednesday.-Loch Ness-Braes of Ness-General's hut-Falls of Fyers-Urquhart Castle and Strath.

Thursday.-Come over Culloden Muir-reflections on the field of battle-breakfast at Kilravock-old Mrs. Rose, sterling sense, warm heart, strong passions, and honest pride, all in an uncommon degree-Mrs. Rose, jun., a little milder than the mother-this perhaps owing to her being younger-Mr. Grant, minister at Calder, resembles Mr. Scott at Inverleithing-Mrs. Rose and Mrs. Grant accompany us to Kildrummie-two young ladies-Miss Rose, who sung two Gaelic songs, beautiful and lovely-Miss Sophia Brodie, most agreeable and amiable-both of them gentle, mild; the sweetest creatures on earth, and happiness be with them!-Dine at Nairn-fall in with a pleasant enough gentleman, Dr. Stewart, who had been long abroad with his father in the forty-five; and Mr. Falconer, a spare, irascible, warm-hearted Norland, and a nonjuror-Brodie-house to lie.

Friday-Forres-famous stone at Forres-Mr. Brodie tells me that the muir where Shakspeare lays Macbeth's witch-meeting is still haunted-that the country folks won't pass it by night.

Venerable ruins of Elgin Abbey-A grander effect at first glance than Melrose, but not near so beautiful-Cross Spey to Fochabers-fine palace, worthy of the generous proprietor-Dine-company, Duke and Duchess, Ladies Charlotte and Magdeline, Col. Abercrombie, and Lady, Mr. Gordon and Mr., a clergyman, a venerable, aged figure-the Duke makes me happier than ever great man did-noble, princely; yet mild, condescending, and affable; gay and kind-the Duchess witty and sensible-God bless them!

Come to Cullen to lie-hitherto the country is sadly poor and unimproven.

Come to Aberdeen-meet with Mr. Chalmers, printer, a facetious fellow-Mr. Ross a fine fellow, like Professor Tytler,-Mr. Marshal one of the poetæ minores-Mr. Sheriffs, author of "Jamie and Bess," a little decrepid body with some abilities-Bishop Skinner, a nonjuror, son of the author of "Tullochgorum," a man whose mild, venerable manner is the most marked of any in so young a man-Professor Gordon, a good-natured, jolly-looking professor-Aberdeen, a lazy town-near Stonhive, the coast a good deal romantic-meet my relations-Robert Burns, writer, in Stonhive, one of those who love fun, a gill, and a punning joke, and have not a bad heart-his wife a sweet hospitable body, without any affectation of what is called town-breeding.

Tuesday.-Breakfast with Mr. Burns-lie at Lawrence Kirk-Album library-Mrs.a jolly, frank, sensible, love-inspiring widow-Howe of the Mearns, a rich, cultivated, but still unenclosed country.

Wednesday.-Cross North Esk river and a rich country to Craigow.

Go to Montrose, that finely-situated handsome town-breakfast at Muthie, and sail along that wild rocky coast, and see the famous caverns, particularly the Gariepot-land and dine at Arbroath-stately ruins of Arbroath Abbey-come to Dundee through a fertile country-Dundee a low-lying, but pleasant town-old Steeple-Tayfrith-Broughty Castle, a finely situated ruin, jutting

into the Tay.[530]
Friday.-Breakfast with the Miss Scotts-Miss Bess Scott like Mrs. Greenfield-my bardship almost in love with her-come through the rich harvests and fine hedge-rows of the Carse of Gowrie, along the romantic margin of the Grampian hills, to Perth-fine, fruitful, hilly, woody country round Perth.
Saturday Morning.-Leave Perth-come up Strathearn to Endermay-fine, fruitful, cultivated Strath-the scene of "Bessy Bell, and Mary Gray," near Perth-fine scenery on the banks of the May-Mrs. Belcher, gawcie, frank, affable, fond of rural sports, hunting, andc.-Lie at Kinross-reflections in a fit of the colic.
Sunday.-Pass through a cold, barren country to Queensferry-dine-cross the ferry and on to Edinburgh.

FOOTNOTES:

[298] Another northern bard has sketched this eminent musician-
"The blythe Strathspey springs up, reminding some Of nights when Gow's old arm, (nor old the tale,) Unceasing, save when reeking cans went round, Made heart and heel leap light as bounding roe. Alas! no more shall we behold that look So venerable, yet so blent with mirth, And festive joy sedate; that ancient garb Unvaried,-tartan hose, and bonnet blue! No more shall Beauty's partial eye draw forth The full intoxication of his strain. Mellifluous, strong, exuberantly rich! No more, amid the pauses of the dance, Shall he repeat those measures, that in days Of other years, could soothe a falling prince, And light his visage with a transient smile Of melancholy joy,-like autumn sun Gilding a sear tree with a passing beam! Or play to sportive children on the green Dancing at gloamin hour; or willing cheer With strains unbought, the shepherd's bridal day."
British Georgics, p. 81

THE POET'S ASSIGNMENT OF HIS WORKS

Know all men by these presents that I Robert Burns of Mossgiel: whereas I intend to leave Scotland and go abroad, and having acknowledged myself the father of a child named Elizabeth, begot upon Elizabeth Paton in Largieside: and whereas Gilbert Burns in Mossgiel, my brother, has become bound, and hereby binds and obliges himself to aliment, clothe, and educate my said natural child in a suitable manner as if she was his own, in case her mother chuse to part with her, and that until she arrive at the age of fifteen years. Therefore, and to enable the said Gilbert Burns to make good his said engagement, wit ye me to have assigned, disponed, conveyed and made over to, and in favours of, the said Gilbert Burns, his heirs, executors, and assignees, who are always to be bound in like manner, with, himself, all and sundry goods, gear, corns, cattle, horses, nolt, sheep, household furniture, and all other moveable effects of whatever kind that I shall leave behind me on my departure from this Kingdom, after allowing for my part of the conjunct debts due by the said Gilbert Burns and me as joint tacksmen of the farm of Mossgiel. And particularly without prejudice of the foresaid generality, the profits that may arise from the publication of my poems presently in the press. And also, I hereby dispone and convey to him in trust for behoof of my said natural daughter, the copyright of said poems in so far as I can dispose of the same by law, after she arrives at the above age of fifteen years complete. Surrogating and substituting the said Gilbert Burns my brother and his foresaids in my full right, title, room and place of the whole premises, with power to him to intromit with, and dispose upon the same at pleasure, and in general to do every other thing in the premises that I could have done myself before granting hereof, but always with and under the conditions before expressed. And I oblige myself to warrant this disposition and assignation from my own proper fact and deed allenarly.

Consenting to the registration hereof in the books of Council and Session, or any other Judges books competent, therein to remain for preservation and constitute.
Proculars, andc. In witness whereof I have wrote and signed these presents, consisting of this and the preceding page, on stamped paper, with my own hand, at the Mossgiel, the twenty-second day of July, one thousand seven hundred and eighty-six years.
(Signed)
ROBERT BURNS.

Upon the twenty-fourth day of July, one thousand seven hundred and eighty-six years, I, William Chalmer, Notary Publick, past to the Mercat Cross of Ayr head Burgh of the Sheriffdome thereof, and thereat I made due and lawful intimation of the foregoing disposition and assignation to his Majesties lieges, that they might not pretend ignorance thereof by reading the same over in presence of a number of people assembled. Whereupon William Crooks, writer, in Ayr, as attorney for the before designed Gilbert Burns, protested that the same was lawfully intimated, and asked and took instruments in my hands. These things were done betwixt the hours of ten and eleven forenoon, before and in presence of William M'Cubbin, and William Eaton, apprentices to the Sheriff Clerk of Ayr, witnesses to the premises.
(Signed)
William Chalmer, N.P.
William M'Cubbin, Witness.
William Eaton, Witness.

www.ingramcontent.com/pod-product-compliance
Lightning Source LLC
Chambersburg PA
CBHW082221150125
20470CB00030B/674

* 9 7 8 1 5 1 1 7 5 9 3 2 8 *